DESTINY

DESTINY
SALLY BEAUMAN

BANTAM BOOKS

TORONTO · NEW YORK · LONDON · SYDNEY · AUCKLAND

This is a work of fiction. Names, characters, places, and incidents either are the product of the author's imagination or are used fictitiously. Any resemblance to actual events or locales or persons, living or dead, is entirely coincidental.

DESTINY
A Bantam Book / April 1987

Library of Congress Cataloging-in-Publication Data

Beauman, Sally.
  Destiny

  I. Title.
PR6052.E223D4   1987   823'.914   86-47598
ISBN 0-553-05183-0

Published simultaneously in the United States and Canada

PRINTED IN THE UNITED STATES OF AMERICA

0 9 8 7 6 5 4 3 2 1

FOR JAMES,
THE KINDEST OF MILITARY PHILOSOPHERS,
AND FOR ALAN,
WITH MY LOVE

Whether we fall by ambition, blood, or lust,
Like diamonds, we are cut with our own dust. . . .

WEBSTER: THE DUCHESS OF MALFI

PROLOGUE

PARIS, 1959

The authorization was for two million dollars. It was the last letter of the day.

He read through the paragraphs carefully, checking each line, and taking his time. Across the desk from him his senior secretary waited patiently, nothing in her manner betraying the fact that she was newly engaged, very much in love, and very anxious to go home. He glanced up at her and smiled. Outside the plate-glass windows the sun still shone, and from the street below, insulated and muffled by the glass, came the hum of the Paris traffic. It was six o'clock.

Paris in the summer; the Seine on a warm evening. He had known once, he thought, how the end of the day felt, when the evening was full of promise. Not now. He bent his head to the papers once more, picked up his platinum pen, and signed. *Edouard de Chavigny*.

He slid the white paper across the black desk, and then taking pity on her, said, "You may go now."

Her head lifted at once; she looked startled. Then the color rushed into her cheeks, and her eyes lit.

"It's only six o'clock."

"I know that. I suggest you go now. Before one of the telephones rings." His voice became dry. "Before I change my mind."

"Thank you."

She needed no more prompting. As she gathered the papers, Edouard rose. He moved across the room, and stood with his back to her, looking out the windows. The commercial sector of Paris. Below him, in the street, the traffic was heavy; he saw it move forward, stop, move forward again. He rested his forehead for a moment against the glass. Across the street, a long way below, the wind caught the leaves of a plane tree;

they were the dull heavy green of midsummer, but just for a second, as the air lifted them, and the light caught them, they danced.

"I'm leaving soon, in any case."

She had reached the door, but when he spoke, she stopped. He could feel the curiosity in her gaze, a curiosity that was understandable, since he rarely left the de Chavigny building before eight.

"So early?" She could not keep the surprise out of her voice, and Edouard turned back with a lazy smile.

"Why not?" he said. "It's a fine evening."

He knew then, even as he spoke, even as he smiled, that the need was coming back, as strongly and as abruptly as it always did, just as if the past three weeks of uneasy celibacy had never happened.

The door closed, and with a sense of despair he turned back to the window and this time pressed his forehead hard against the glass. The need possessed him; it infiltrated, blackly, every corner of his mind, clouding his vision, smothering any ability to think. The need, and the despair in the need; they came always together. He turned angrily away from the glass.

He wanted a woman. Women, for a time, always made him forget.

There were other palliatives, he had learned that. Music. Speed, for he liked to drive fast. Alcohol, sometimes.

Work, often. But none of them was as swift, and none of them was as certain as sex; sex freed him for a while—until the next time the pain came back.

He despised the need, and he had come to hate the remedy, and so—as he always did—he tried to fight it. Leaving his offices, dismissing his driver, he took his own car, the black Aston-Martin that Grégoire had so loved. It was powerful, and fast; he edged it through the crowded streets, holding the great engine in check, and then made his way out of the city, where he could accelerate. He switched on the radio and turned up the volume. Music and speed; the combination sometimes worked.

He felt as if the Beethoven fueled the car, as if he traveled on sound—and for a time, he grew calmer. He knew why this had happened, knew precisely what had provoked the need now. Memories, of course—which he could never keep entirely at bay, no matter how hard he contrived to fill every second of every day. Memories which came at him when he least expected them, out of the calm of a summer evening, out of the expectation seen in a woman's face: images of his past, the recollection of happiness which could never be recaptured.

The music reached a small angry crescendo, then tumbled away. He thought, resigning himself: *very well; a woman then*—and at the next intersection, he turned off.

The Right Bank, past expensive houses and expensive shops. He passed the showrooms of the de Chavigny jewelry division, the celebrated windows. From the corner of his eye, he glimpsed black velvet and the bright ice of diamonds. He, so notorious for his gifts to women, had never given diamonds. Sapphires, rubies, emeralds—yes, but never diamonds. He had never even been tempted; something made him hold them back.

"A perfect stone, Edouard." His father's voice. Holding the diamond to the light. "Do you see? Perfect coloration. Without flaws."

He spun the wheel, heading toward the Pont Neuf. He was not seeking perfection now, he told himself. Nor absolutes. Life was without absolutes, and without certainties. Except, of course, death—and he glanced down at the Seine, which sparkled.

The Left Bank. He took the Quai des Augustins, then swung right into the Boulevard St. Michel. There he slowed, and began to look for a woman.

The streets were crowded. People milled and pushed outside the shops, the métro, the corner *tabac*. The evening air was still and balmy. From the cafés, as he passed, came the sound of the breathy love song he had heard played everywhere, all summer.

He could feel the impulsion mounting now, and the despair gathering force, and he slowed the car, letting it cruise past the cafés. A great many tourists, and—in this quarter—students; he caught the sound of their voices in the hot still air: English, American, Italian, Swedish. He saw heads turn as he passed, saw women's faces. They glanced at the powerful car, they glanced at the driver, then leaned forward again over their little cups of *café noir*, fumbling for a Gauloise, glancing back more lingeringly, giggling . . .

No one I know, or need know, he thought; a stranger, a foreigner, a woman here in Paris today and elsewhere tomorrow. Two girls caught his eye as he slowed at an intersection. They were sitting out on the *terrasse*. One, a redhead; as he glanced in her direction, he saw her throw back her head and laugh. A beautiful, slender neck, full breasts, the milk-white skin of redheads. Her companion could have been French: a Juliette Greco lookalike, of whom there were many. Wearing black, of course, with long mournful black hair, a dead-white face, eyes ringed with heavy black liner. She looked nervous, not quite at ease in her coffee-bar existentialist uniform; she fiddled with her coffee spoon.

He hesitated for a second, then touched the accelerator.

He always avoided women with red hair because they reminded him of a part of his past he preferred to forget, and the girl's boldness alienated him. The other looked like the kind of woman who went through life getting hurt; if that was her fate, he did not want to contribute to it.

He turned down a narrow side street, past the dark walls and jutting gargoyles of the Église St. Severin. Past a Moroccan restaurant, and the scents of cumin and meat roasting on an open grill; past huge jagged graffiti: *Algérie Française.* He averted his eyes from the words, and turned the wheel abruptly.

Two more streets, narrow, winding: a tramp, out cold, lying across the vents of the métro; two lovers, arm in arm, laughing together as they came out of a cinema. A tight bend, and then right, into the Rue St. Julien le Pauvre.

Ahead of him, on the left-hand side, there was a small park, and beyond it the tiny church of St. Julien, one of the most ancient in Paris. In the park, children were playing; he caught for an instant the sound of their voices above the murmur of the traffic on the quai beyond. He caught a flash of color from their clothes: navy, white, scarlet—French children's colors, liberation colors. And then he saw the woman.

Afterward—eight, ten, twelve years later—that moment would come back to him with absolute precision. Just as it was then: the cries of the children; the sound of the cars; the rustle of the gravel as the children ran; the sensation of color in the corner of the eye; the mounting urgency and simultaneous despair in his own body; and then—the woman. The girl.

When he saw her, there was suddenly nothing but her. All sound was silenced; space narrowed to the space she occupied. He saw only the woman, bright space, and her face, lifted.

She was standing outside the small church, and looking up at it, her face raised and outlined against the light, her back to the street. She had hair of an extraordinary pale gold, reaching just to her shoulders, the ends cropped bluntly, as if she had taken the scissors to it herself. As he looked, the breeze lifted the hair away from her face, creating a halo of light around her profile.

She turned then, for an instant, with a half-frown, as if she had felt his gaze, or someone had called to her. But he had not called; he had not moved; the powerful car stood stationary, twenty feet away. She drew her brows together, looking down the street in the direction of the quai, and he was close enough to see that her brows were dark and straight above wide-spaced gray-blue eyes of exceptional beauty.

She did not appear to see him, and she turned back again to inspect the church. Edouard stared at her. His pulse had slowed; the insistent hammering of the senses had stopped; he was conscious, dimly, of a dreamlike sense of power, a hallucinatory clarity, as if he moved toward her while he remained still.

She was perhaps nineteen, maybe a little older. Tall. Very slender.

Wearing the international uniform of the young: blue Levi jeans; flat canvas shoes; the plainest white T-shirt, which clung to the contours of her high rounded breasts. There were a thousand other girls in St. Germain wearing clothes almost exactly similar. There had been dozens in the cafés he had just passed. But this girl resembled none of them; he looked at her and saw physical perfection, beauty as undeniable, as assertive, as perfection in any other form. He saw it in the girl as he would have seen it in the heart of a diamond. So he hesitated only a fraction, and then—as he had known he would—eased the car forward, pulled into the curb, and stopped.

He had meant to get out of the car to approach her, but she forestalled him. As he reached for the door handle, she turned and looked at him: a long straight quantifying look, without flirtatiousness, without coyness. She looked at him as if she were memorizing his face for an identity line-up, and Edouard looked back at her. Then, before he could move, she walked over to the car.

She stood there, at the end of the long black hood, and looked at him gravely, still with that slight frown knitting her brows, almost as if she half-recognized him and was trying to place him in her memory. Her stance was calm and graceful, and he could see the quality in her face now, as well as the beauty: the intelligence in her eyes, the character in the set of her lips.

Her face silenced him; the need and the despair left him, leaving his mind washed clear and extraordinarily calm.

He looked at her, and felt a shock of recognition: a woman who was at once familiar to him; a woman he had never seen before.

Her eyes met his levelly, and then, quite suddenly she smiled. There was a certain mockery in the smile, a teasing quality, as if she had just decided to make something easy for him.

"I'm sorry. I thought I recognized you."

She spoke in French, the accent correct, but not quite perfect. English, he thought, or American.

"I thought the same."

"Then we're both mistaken."

"Or both right."

He smiled at her then, and then stopped smiling abruptly because he realized he must do something and say something quickly—and he had no idea in the world what it might be. His mind was locked into a cadence of such calm that it was very difficult to think of words at all. Especially words that could so easily be misinterpreted; he was suddenly appalled by the possibility that she might misunderstand.

To give himself time, as much as anything else, he opened his door, got out of the car, and walked around to stand at her side. As he did so, he felt a certain amusement. He knew his own reputation; he knew people spoke of his charm, and claimed that he turned it on and off at will. He knew he was judged cold, and unresponsive, and that people who did not know how much it cost him spoke enviously of his self-possession.

He felt no self-possession now, and he certainly did not feel cold or unresponsive; he felt disarmed—a man of thirty-four, and at the same time, a vulnerable boy.

She was tall for a woman, but he was taller still. She lifted her face, and looked up into his eyes. There was a silence, which seemed to him to go on for several hours, or possibly several lifetimes. Then he said— something had to be said—"I think you ought to have dinner with me." He supposed he said it with charm, he certainly tried to, but to say anything at all seemed so absurd that he instantly wished he had said nothing. He felt a moment's dissociation, in which he saw them both with a third person's eyes: a tall, dark-haired man in a beautifully cut, very formal black suit which resembled in every respect all the other suits he wore, and a slender fair-haired young woman. It was instantly obvious to him that she would refuse. Probably indignantly.

"Ought?" She frowned very slightly again, and then her face cleared. "I think so too," she said firmly, and without waiting for him to open the door of the car, opened it herself and climbed in.

Edouard returned to the driver's seat. He started the engine. He released the brake, pushed in the clutch, engaged the gears—he sup- posed he did all these things, though he was not conscious of any of them. The car moved forward. As they passed the arched doorway of St. Julien, she glanced at him. "It's such a beautiful church. And it was locked. Can one ever go in?"

She spoke as if she had known him all her life. Edouard instantly felt the wildest elation.

"You can. I shall take you," he answered, accelerating.

It was *then*, he thought later—then that the obsession began. He was wrong, of course, and he came to realize that eventually.

It had begun before, long before—many years before he met her. A great gap of time, and all of it speeding forward to one place: that street, that church, that woman, and that still summer evening.

Pure chance. Sometimes he found that fact calming; at other times he found it frightening.

PART ONE

EDOUARD

LONDON, 1940

The house in Eaton Square was in the center of Thomas Cubitt's celebrated terrace, built on the south side, and more elaborate in design than its neighbors. Tall Corinthian pilasters framed the windows of the first floor drawing room, and a graceful balcony ran the width of the building.

Edouard liked the balcony; it was an excellent position from which to snipe at the heads of the Nazis at present occupying the air raid warden's sheds in the square gardens. However, the balcony was now out of bounds. It had been damaged, his mother decreed, in the last raid. He looked at it scornfully. It did not look damaged to him.

Eaton Square was the jewel of the Duke of Westminster's London estates, and Hugh Westminster was an old friend of his mother's. The instant he had heard she was leaving Paris, he had put this house at her disposal. For this, Edouard was grateful. He would have preferred, naturally, to stay in France, with Papa, at St. Cloud, at the château in the Loire, or at the summer house at Deauville. But since that was impossible, and England it had to be, then it was better to be right in the middle of London. Here, he had a truly excellent view of the war. The daily fighter attacks of the late summer had given way now to night bombing raids, but in August there had been a spectacular dogfight between a Spitfire and a Messerschmitt ME 110, of which he had had, from the balcony, a grandstand view.

He had feared, when Papa had announced they must leave, that his mother would bury them deep in the country somewhere, for safety's sake. But luckily she seemed not to have considered that possibility. His brother, Jean-Paul, had to be in London, of course, because he had a very important job. He was on General de Gaulle's personal staff, organizing the activities of the Free French Army which would, one day soon, with a little assistance from the Allies, liberate France. His mother had always bowed to the needs and demands of her elder son—Edouard wished the same were true of *his* demands—and besides, she loved London. Sometimes, Edouard thought, as she swept in in her beautiful furs and jewels, as she left for another party, sometimes he thought his mother was enjoying the war almost as much as he was.

He leaned against the tall windows now, and breathed against the glass. The square panes were crisscrossed with tape to safeguard against bomb blast. In one of the misted triangles, he wrote his name, idly. Edouard Alexandre Julien de Chavigny. It was such a long name—in the end it took two triangles. He paused, then added: *Age—Quatorze ans.*

He frowned, and looked out across the square. On the far side he could see the house that had received a direct hit a few nights before. Its remains gaped blackly: tilting side walls and a pile of burned timbers and rubble. His valet said no one had been killed, that the house had been empty, but Edouard suspected he had been instructed to say that. He himself was not so sure. He wished he were not fourteen. He wished he were ten years older, like Jean-Paul. Or eighteen. Eighteen would be enough. You could enlist then. You could do something useful. You could fight the Boches. Not sit around at home like a stupid girl, and do lessons, lessons, lessons.

One of the air raid wardens came into view, and Edouard aimed at his tin helmet, squinting down the length of his arm. Pe-ow! Got him in one!

He felt a moment's satisfaction, then a quick annoyance. With an angry gesture, he turned away from the window. He was too old for such games, he knew that really. He was fourteen, almost fifteen. His voice had broken, or started to break. There was soft down on his cheeks now; quite soon he was going to need a razor. There were other signs too: his body stirred, and hardened, when he looked at some of the maids. He had dreams at night, long glorious frenetic dreams, which left his sheets damp in the morning—sheets that his valet, not the maids, removed with a knowing smile. Oh yes, his body was altering; he wasn't a child anymore; he was almost—almost—a man.

Edouard de Chavigny had been born in 1925, when his mother, Louise, was thirty. Several miscarriages had punctuated the years between the birth of Jean-Paul and this son, her second and last child. During her final pregnancy Louise had been very ill, nearly losing the baby on several occasions. After the birth, a hysterectomy was performed, and slowly—first at the Château de Chavigny in the Loire, and then at her parents' home in Newport—she recovered. To those who knew her only slightly, who encountered her only at parties, or balls, or receptions, Louise then seemed exactly as she had always been. A celebrated beauty, famed for her elegance and exquisite taste; only daughter of a steel baron, one of the richest men in America; brought up like a princess, her every whim catered to by an adoring father, Louise was—had always been—lovely, demanding, and irresistible. Irresistible even to Xavier, Baron de Chavigny—and he had long been regarded as one of the most elusive bachelors in Europe.

When he first went to America, in 1912, to open the Fifth Avenue showrooms of the de Chavigny jewelry empire, Xavier instantly became the toast of the East Coast. Society matrons vied for his attendance at their parties. They paraded their daughters before the handsome young man without subtlety or shame, and Xavier de Chavigny was charming, and attentive, and infuriatingly noncommittal.

To East Coast mothers he embodied the advantages of Europe: he was electrifyingly handsome, highly intelligent; he had perfect manners, a fortune, and an ancient title.

To East Coast fathers, he had the additional advantage of a superb business head. This was no idle French aristocrat content to let his fortune dwindle away while he had a good time. Like most Frenchmen of his class, he understood the importance of land; he held on to, and built up, his already vast estates in France. Unlike most Frenchmen of his class, he had a thoroughly American taste for commerce. He built up the de Chavigny jewelry empire, founded by his grandfather in the nineteenth century, into the largest and most renowned enterprise of its kind, rivaled internationally only by Cartier. He enlarged, and improved, his vineyards in the Loire. He extended his investments into banking, steel production, and the diamond mines in South Africa, which provided the raw materials for de Chavigny jewelry—jewelry that had bedecked the crowned heads of Europe, and now bedecked the uncrowned heads of rich and discerning Americans.

Oh yes, the East Coast fathers remarked in their clubs, de Chavigny was smart. He had American virtues as well as European ones. Sure, he called his racehorse trainer every morning, but he called his stockbrokers first.

Xavier met Louise in London, when she was nineteen and he twenty-nine and she was being introduced to English society. It was late in 1914. Xavier had been wounded in the early months of the war, and—to his fury and disgust—released from active service. They met at one of the last great coming-out balls of the war years: she wearing a Worth dress of the palest pink silk; he wearing the uniform of a French officer. His leg wound had healed sufficiently to permit him to dance with her three times; he sat out three more dances with her. Next morning he presented himself to her father in their suite at Claridges with a proposal of marriage. It was accepted a decorous three weeks later.

They were married in London, spent their honeymoon on the Sutherland estates in Scotland, and returned to Paris with their two-year-old son, Jean-Paul, at the end of the war. In Europe, Louise quickly became as celebrated for her charm, her taste, and her beauty as she had been in America. Their hospitality, their generosity, and their style became a byword on two continents. And the Baron de Chavigny proved to have one quality no one had expected in a Frenchman: he was a devoted, and entirely faithful, husband.

So, seven years later, when Louise de Chavigny recovered from the difficult birth of her second son, and began to appear in society once more—to look, to charm, to dress just as she had always done—those who did not know her well assumed the charmed life continued. There had been a sad episode, a difficult period, but it was over. When, in 1927, the Baronne de Chavigny celebrated her return to Paris from Newport by purchasing Coco Chanel's entire spring collection, her female acquaintances smiled: *Plus ça change, plus c'est la même chose. . . .*

Those who knew her better—her aging parents, her husband, Jean-Paul, and the little boy whom she never nursed and infrequently saw—found another Louise. They found a woman whose capriciousness increased year by year, a woman given to swift and sometimes violent changes of mood, to sudden elation, and to equally sudden depression.

This was not discussed. A series of physicians was hired and fired. The Baron de Chavigny did everything in his power to please her. He gave her new jewels: a set of perfectly matched sapphires; a magnificent necklace of rubies made by de Chavigny for the last Czarina, which had found its way back to the Baron in the wake of the revolution. Louise said the rubies made her think of blood; they made her think of a cellar in Ekaterinberg. She refused flatly to wear them. The Baron bought her furs: sables of such quality, each pelt could be drawn through the circumference of a wedding ring. He bought her racehorses; a superb Irish hunter, for she liked to ride to hounds. He bought her cars: a Delage, a Hispano-Suiza, a Rolls-Royce Silver Ghost; a sports car built to order in Bugatti's factory. And when these bagatelles failed to please her, he took her traveling. To England; to the West Coast of America, where they were guests at Pickfair, and her spirits revived, briefly. To India, where they stayed in the Viceroy's palace, and shot tiger with the Maharaja of Jaipur. To Italy, where they had an audience with the Pope. Back to England. Back to France.

Each night he would escort her to the door of her bedroom:
Ça va mieux, ma chérie?
Pas mal. Mais je m'ennuie, Xavi, je m'ennuie. . . .
Then she would turn away from his kiss, and close the door.

In 1930, when his wife was thirty-four and the Baron was forty-four, he finally took the advice his male friends had been giving him for some years, and took a mistress. He made sure Louise found out, and to his delight, jealousy revived her. It also excited her, he observed with a sinking heart, when, in bed together once more, she questioned him feverishly, obsessively, about his *affaire.*

Did she do this, Xavi? Or this?

She leaned back on the lace pillows, her thick black hair tumbling around her perfect face, her dark eyes glittering, her full lips rouged. The Baron had torn the lace of her negligee in his impatience, and that had pleased her. She had high rounded childish breasts, which he had always loved, and her slender creamy body was still as lithe as a young girl's. She lifted her breasts in her hands now, and offered them up to his seeking mouth.

Calme-toi, sois tranquille, je t'aime, tu sais, je t'adore. . . .

He took the small pointed nipples between his lips and kissed them gently. He would be slow, this time, he promiséd himself. Very slow. He could hold back, and he would, bringing her to climax once, twice, three times before he came—and she would tremble, and cling to him, the way she used to. The memory made him hard, and she felt his body stir against her belly. She pushed him, feverishly, quickly, lifting his head.

"Not like that. I don't want that."

She spoke in English now when they made love; before it had always been in French.

"Put it in my mouth, Xavi. Go on. I know you like it. Put it there—let me suck you. . . ."

She pulled him up in the bed, maneuvered him so his stiff shaft was poised above her lips. She smiled at him, touched the tip of him once, twice, with a little snakelike flick of the tongue.

"Your cock tastes of me. It tastes salty. I like that. . . ."

Her eyes shone up at him darkly. She opened the full red lips, and he shuddered as he felt the warmth of her mouth, the steady sucking. He shut his eyes. She was good at this, she always had been. She knew how to tease, to draw her tongue softly around the line of his retracted foreskin. She knew how to quicken his response, sucking him just hard enough, so he thrust against the roof of her mouth, sucking him sweetly, moistly, rhythmically. Now she drew her hands slowly down over his buttocks, slipped them between his legs, massaged him there where the skin was loose and damp from their lovemaking. She cupped his balls in her delicate hands, and tilted her head back, so he felt as if he were driving at the back of her throat. He felt the surge begin, start to build.

Then suddenly she stopped sucking. She let the full penis slip from between her lips and looked up at him.

"Did she do this for you, Xavi? Did she? Can she suck you like I can? Tell me, Xavi—say it into my ear while you do it—I want to know. What else did you do with her, Xavi? Did you just fuck her, or more than that? Does she like it up the ass? Xavi—tell me, *tell me. . . .*"

Her coarseness both repelled and excited him. He felt his erection start to fade as he looked down into those dark eyes, that rapacious mouth. He shut his eyes, and pushed her back on the pillows. Then he shifted position, parted her legs, thrust up inside her desperately. She arched her back and cried out. Xavier began to thrust: deep, then shallow, deep once more. The hardness was coming back into his penis. He drove it into her, pulled out, then thrust again. To his own surprise the image of his mistress came into his mind. He saw her plump accommodating body, her large breasts with their dark nipples, heard her panting breath. That image brought him to climax. He groaned, and spilled himself into his wife's still body, hating himself, hating her. When he withdrew, she pulled her nails sharply down his back.

"You bastard. You were thinking of her then, weren't you? Weren't you?"

Xavier looked down at her.

"I thought that was what you wanted," he said coldly. Then he left her, and went to sleep in his own room.

In the years after that he made love to his wife on occasion, and to a succession of other women with greater frequency, and with growing desperation. With a sense of despair he realized that, more and more, he was drawn to young women, women who resembled his wife as she had looked when he first saw her, and first fell in love with her. Sometimes, when the resemblance was too slight, and he had difficulty maintaining his erection, he would close his eyes and conjure up the image of his wife when she was young. Her rose-scented flesh; her mixture of shyness and ardor; the certainty of her love for him. This image never failed him. It brought him to orgasm even in the arms of a Les Halles whore.

In private he drew back into himself, cutting himself off deliberately from his oldest male friends, immersing himself, when the women were insufficiently diverting, in the complexities of his business and his estates. In public, he and his beautiful wife remained as they had always been: devoted, extravagant, generous, everywhere seen, everywhere envied, everywhere admired. If tongues wagged occasionally—even the most perfect marriage needed certain *divertissements* eventually, and both the Baron and the Baronne were so commendably discreet—he ignored them. His wife had taught him one thing at least, he told himself. She had taught him the true meaning of *ennui,* shown him what it meant to live out your days in a prison of grayness. It was one of the few gifts he wished had never been bestowed on him.

He foresaw the coming war quite clearly, several years before most

of his friends and business acquaintances. In 1933, when Adolf Hitler
became Reich Chancellor, he warned his friends that it would mean war,
and they laughed at him. He sold his interests in the German steel
industry in 1936 at a profit, and bought into the British and American
industries instead. After the occupation of the Rhineland the same year,
he transferred all his holdings, and a substantial part of his capital, from
France to Switzerland and New York. Ownership of the de Chavigny
company was transferred from his private hands to those of a holding
company registered in Lucerne, in which he held ninety percent of the
shares, and his son Jean-Paul, ten percent. His personal collection of
jewels, his paintings, his silver, the most valuable and least replaceable
of the furniture from three houses in France was packed up and sent
likewise to Switzerland, where it was stored. In 1937 he began planning
the arrangements necessary for his family to leave France, should the
invasion he feared take place. By the time of the annexation of Czecho-
slovakia and Austria in 1938, these plans were complete. Their efficiency was proven eighteen months later. Louise and her two sons left
France in May 1940, shortly before British troops were evacuated from
Dunkirk. By June 14 the same year, when the Germans reached Paris,
the de Chavigny showrooms were still open, but Xavier de Chavigny
had apparently stripped himself of almost all assets.

When called upon to do so, he made himself and his showrooms
accessible to the officers of the German High Command, and through
this polite compliance, often provided information of considerable assistance to his fellow members of the Sixth Cadre, Paris Resistance. He
gave up women, and tried not to think of his wife.

To his surprise he discovered that he missed neither Louise nor his
mistresses, and that the *ennui* which had dogged him for so long had
gone. He had a purpose in life again, a *raison d'être*, all the more intense
because he knew his life was in constant danger.

He was not fearful for himself, but he was fearful—still—for Louise
and for his children. He would have felt safer, much safer, if they had
agreed to his original plans, and gone to America. England, he knew, as
he watched the progress of war, was not far enough.

The reason for this was simple: his wife, Louise, was half-Jewish.
Her mother, Frances, had been born a Schiff, and had grown up within
the confines of German-Jewish New York society, in which the distinction of being, originally, from Frankfurt—like the Rothschilds and the
Warburgs—counted for a great deal. Frances grew up within the charmed
circle of the "One Hundred," and she numbered among her uncles,
aunts, and innumerable cousins, a formidable roster of Warburgs, Loebs,
Lehmans, and Seligmans. She was expected to make a dynastic marriage;
when, at the age of nineteen, she eloped with John McAllister, her

family cut her off, and the reverberations of shock from that mixed marriage continued for decades.

Frances turned her back on her childhood, on that world of Fifth Avenue mansions, and worship at Temple Emanu-El. John McAllister was rich when she married him, for he had inherited an empire in steel from his Scots emigré father. He invested in the Northern Pacific Railroad, and became richer still. Frances McAllister concentrated her energies on being assimilated, and—since she was beautiful, clever, and charming, as well as very rich—she succeeded to a very large extent. Frances graced the McAllister box in the Diamond Horseshoe at the Metropolitan Opera, boxes from which her Jewish relations were excluded; she built a house at Newport, not, of course, at Elberon, where her uncles and aunts maintained their mansions. She brought up Louise very carefully; her own Jewish origins were not hidden, but reference to them was not encouraged. Louise, aware as she grew older that her mother's background marked her out from the rest of her contemporaries, became extremely careful never to refer to them at all. Like the newness of her father's wealth, it became a subject that was, quite simply, barred. She converted to Catholicism and, once she married Xavier, she bent her considerable energies to a new role, that of being the Baronne, and more French than the French themselves.

So fierce were her efforts in this respect that Xavier de Chavigny, who was without racial prejudice, almost forgot the question of his wife's ancestors. Since their race was a matter of indifference to him, he assumed, negligently and slightly grandly, that they were also a matter of indifference to everyone else. Until 1938: then, he knew, they could no longer be ignored. For if Louise was half-Jewish, his children were therefore one quarter Jewish. With an enemy prepared patiently to trace heredity back through eight, nine generations in their search for Jewish blood, a half-Jewish mother, a Jewish grandmother, was a terrible threat. So the plans had been thorough, and the Baron was in no doubt of their necessity. But still he worried: had they been thorough enough?

Edouard lay back on the silk brocade-covered sofa, propped a cushion under his feet, opened the book on his lap, and stared into the fire. He felt extremely comfortable, and slightly somnolent, as he often did after finishing an English tea.

Tea, he decided, was one of the meals the English understood. The other was breakfast. He disapproved of porridge—that was too disgusting even to consider—but grilled bacon, coddled eggs, devilled kidneys, or kedgeree—these were splendid, a great improvement on a simple croissant and café au lait. Edouard was already tall; he had inherited his father's looks, and closely resembled him, with his almost jet black hair, and startlingly deep blue eyes. Like his father, he had the build of a natural athlete: wide shoulders, long legs, and narrow hips. He was growing fast—five feet eleven already—and he was always, always hungry.

Now he had just consumed an excellent tea brought in on silver trays by the butler, Parsons, and by the senior parlor maid, and solemnly laid out for him before the fire on several small tables. Hot buttered crumpets with English honey, tiny cucumber sandwiches, three different kinds of cake, his favorite tea, Lapsang Souchong, with its delicate smoky taste.

Edouard read *The Times* each morning; on sorties around the city he had glimpsed the long lines of shoppers outside food shops, and the limited stock on sale. He was perfectly well aware that the kind of meals his mother took for granted would be served in her household were now, in wartime, exceptional—possibly even unpatriotic. But he knew the household had been carefully stocked before the war, and besides, he was always so hungry. Was it really going to help the war effort if he refused a second slice of *filet de boeuf en croûte*, or a second spoonful of Sevruga? He thought not. It would only offend the cook.

He glanced down guiltily at the book on his lap. His Latin assignments. He was supposed to have translated at least five pages of Virgil before tomorrow morning; so far he had completed only two. In France he was taught Latin by an elderly Jesuit who was given to dozing off most conveniently as Edouard stumbled through *The Aeneid*. But his English tutor was another matter.

He had been hired by Edouard's mother on the recommendation of a friend, and Edouard was perfectly sure that his papa would have disapproved of him deeply. Hugo Glendinning was a man of uncertain age, too old to be drafted, and probably in his mid-forties, though he could look older. He was very tall, very thin, and very elegant in a raffish kind of way. He had graying hair, worn slightly too long in Edouard's conservative opinion, and he would run his hands through it before uttering the melodramatic groan that signified Edouard had just committed another appalling solecism. He was an old Etonian, an Oxford classics scholar, his eyes were habitually vague, and he had a mind like a razor. On the day of his arrival he had confounded Edouard by chain-smoking Black Russian cigarettes throughout their tutorial.

Of his family background and his academic qualifications Papa would have approved—Edouard had no doubts about that. But of his politics? Edouard was more doubtful. Hugo Glendinning had fought in the Spanish Civil War; it had become rapidly obvious to Edouard that he was a political radical—something Edouard had never encountered before; more than that, he was probably a Socialist.

His tutorials were unconventional, to say the least. The first day he had tossed two books at Edouard: the first was *The Iliad*, the other the dreaded *Aeneid*.

"Right." He put his feet up on the table in front of him and stretched. "The first page of each. Read them. Then translate."

Edouard groped his way through the texts while Hugo Glendinning leaned back with closed eyes and a pained expression around the mouth. When Edouard fumbled to a halt, he sat up abruptly.

"Well. You're not a total dunce, which is something, I suppose." He looked at Edouard keenly. "There might be some glimmerings of intelligence there. Deeply buried, of course, but latent. I could do a great deal better than that when I was nine. I wonder . . . are you lazy?"

Edouard considered this possibility, which had never been put to him before.

"I do hope not." Hugo extinguished one cigarette, and lit another. "It's *extremely* boring, laziness. I detest it above all things. *Now* . . ." He leaned forward, suddenly, and fixed Edouard with his gaze. "What is *The Iliad* about?"

Edouard hesitated. "It's about—er—well, the Greeks and the Trojans . . ."

"And?"

"The Trojan War."

"Precisely so." Hugo smiled. "War. You have possibly observed that there is a war going on at present?"

Edouard rallied. "A very different war."

"You think so? Well, literally, yes, you are right. Homer is not going to describe the activities of tanks and aeroplanes. However. War is war. Killing is killing. *The Iliad* is perhaps not the remote and irrelevant document you seem to consider it. I suggest you compare—let me see—Book Sixteen, 'The Death of Patroclus,' with this morning's account in *The Times* of yesterday's aerial battles over the south coast. The one is bellicose propaganda of the most unimaginative kind, and the other is—the other is art." He paused. "Possibly, if you heard it read with slightly more correct pronunciation, and a genuine attempt to honor the rhythms of Homer's verse structure. . . . Let us see. . . ."

He leaned back in his chair again and shut his eyes. Not once looking at the book before him, he began to recite in Greek. Edouard sat silently.

At first, he resisted. Hugo Glendinning seemed to him dreadfully arrogant and extremely rude: none of his French tutors would have dared to speak to him in this way. He had no intention of being impressed or interested. Then, gradually, in spite of himself, he began to listen. And it was extraordinary—that liquid, fluid, impassioned lan-

guage, so very different from the dry halting way it sounded when his
Jesuit tutor read it, stopping every two lines to construe them.

He began to listen more closely, looked down at his own book, and
the words—already familiar to him—began to take new shape and life of
their own: he saw the battlefield, saw the light glint on the weapons,
heard the cries of the dying men. From that moment he was hooked.
For the first time in his life, Edouard looked forward to lessons, and
worked. One day, one day he was going to force Hugo Glendinning to
pay him a compliment; if it killed him he'd do it.

When they came to Latin, Hugo tossed Caesar's *Gallic Wars* aside.
"Good clear pedestrian stuff." He sniffed. "Ditches and ramparts. We'll
stick to Homer for war, I think. Now . . . what about love? Sexual
attraction? Passion? You're interested in that, I presume? I was, at your
age. . . ."

"Aren't you now?" Edouard put in slyly, and Hugo smiled.

"Possibly. That is beside the point. We shall read *The Aeneid*,
naturally. But also Catullus, I think. You've read Catullus?"

"No." Edouard felt a pulse of excitement. As far as his Jesuit
teacher was concerned, Catullus was most definitely not on the curricu-
lum for fourteen-year-old boys.

"Then let us begin." Hugo paused. "Catullus is a wit and a cynic.
He mocks his own passion, but at the same time acknowledges his
enslavement. We may usefully compare some of these poems with
certain of Shakespeare's sonnets. In both cases the emotions described
may be a little difficult for a boy to understand. Are you able to imagine
how a man feels when he is obsessed, physically and spiritually, with a
woman? A woman whose character and moral worth he despises?"

Edouard hesitated. He thought of his mother and father, and of
certain scenes, certain conversations overheard.

"Possibly," he said cautiously.

Hugo's eyes turned dreamily to the window.

"Sexual infatuation—and that is what we are talking about, of
course—sexual infatuation seems to me a very interesting condition. A
great deal more interesting than romantic love, with which it is often
confused. It is powerful, and it is deadly. It is also, alas, commonplace.
As commonplace for us as it was in Rome in 60 B.C. or in Elizabethan
London." He smiled dryly. "I have no doubt you will experience it
yourself at some time. Then you will no doubt assume, as we all do, that
your experience is unique. Of course it is not. Let us begin then. By the
way, did you know Catullus was thirty when he died?"

And so it went on. No matter how hard he tried, Edouard could
never predict the course of the next day's lessons. Sometimes they
would dart about in history—not carefully working their way through the
French kings and learning their dates as he had always done before, but

leaping centuries and continents. The French Revolution, the Russian Revolution, the American Civil War. Suddenly, Hugo would pounce.

"Why was that war fought, do you think, Edouard?"

"Well—to free the slaves in the South."

"Nonsense. Yankee propaganda. It was no such thing. It was fought primarily for commercial reasons, because the northern states regarded the wealth of the South with acquisitive eyes. It improved the lot of the Negro slave only marginally. You are aware, I take it, that a black man in the southern states of America still does not possess the vote?" He paused. "Not that the English have any cause for smugness in that respect, of course. Next week we will look at the lamentably slow extension of suffrage in this country, the abolition of property requirements, which previously protected the interests of the ruling classes, and the extension of voting rights to women." He stopped. "You find that amusing?"

Edouard shrugged. "I've read about Suffragettes. I can't see that women need to vote. Papa says he never met a woman who was remotely interested in politics. Maman never bothers to vote."

Hugo frowned. "Do women have minds?"

"Of course."

"Then do you not think that they should exercise them? As you should yours. It is the mark of a lazy mind, Edouard, to rely on *idées reçues*. Question. Always question. And *think*. . . ."

Edouard tried. He could see the logic of Hugo's arguments, but it was often very difficult to apply those arguments to life. It was all very well to talk about suffragettes, and women's minds, but Edouard found it exceedingly difficult to consider their minds at all. How could you think about that when, he found, his eyes were always drawn to their slim ankles, to the whisper of their petticoats, to that sweet line between the soft curve of their breasts?

He shut the Virgil midway through Dido's impassioned pleas to Aeneas. Damn, damn—he could not concentrate. He could feel that stirring, that tension between the legs; his head was filled with rapturous and confused images: breasts, and thighs, pillows and tumbled hair, moistness and mounting pleasure. He knew what he wanted to do; he wanted to go up to his bedroom, and lock his door, and shut himself up with those images, touch himself, slowly, rhythmically bring his body to shuddering and guilty release. Guilty, because the priests' lectures about the evils of self-abuse, the temptations of the devil made flesh, had begun years ago, when he was eight or nine, and had continued ever since. Jean-Paul said that was all rubbish, that all adolescent boys masturbated—it was a stage you went through, that was all. Once you started having women, you needed it less and less. Edouard was sure he was right; he hoped he was right; he thought that if he dared to ask

Hugo, Hugo would certainly agree. But still, he couldn't quite shake off the warnings of the priests.

Father Clément said it made hair grow on the palms of your hands even if you only did it once. "It will be there, my child, like the mark of Cain, for all to see. Remember that."

Edouard surreptitiously looked down at his palms. There was no hair there yet, and if Father Clément was right, there certainly ought to be. Surely it couldn't be true? But Father Clément also said masturbation was a sin; it had to be acknowledged in the confessional, and Edouard had acknowledged it. The conversation had been hideously embarrassing.

"Were you alone when you did this thing, my son?"

"Yes, Father."

"You are sure of that, my son?"

"Yes, Father."

That confused Edouard. Who else would he have been with? he wanted to ask. But he didn't dare. Each time resulted in thirty Hail Marys and an admonition never to commit the sin again. Yet he was hardly out of the confessional before he felt the need more strongly than ever. He sighed. What he had really wanted to ask the priest was why the fact that it was forbidden seemed to make him want to do it more. But he didn't dare to ask that, either.

He stood up, and looked at the clock. Then opened *The Aeneid* again, because distraction was the best remedy, he knew that. When fifteen lines of Latin translation had taken effect, and the stubborn erection had finally faded, he felt the satisfaction of virtue triumphant. He looked at the clock again. Nearly six. At six, Jean-Paul was due back, and with luck, if Jean-Paul hadn't forgotten all about it, he might have news for him. Important news—the most important there could possibly be. If he had been in Paris, Papa would have arranged it, as he had for Jean-Paul. But since he wasn't, Jean-Paul had promised him, *sworn*, that he would take on the responsibility. Jean-Paul, this very day, was going to arrange Edouard's first woman.

From Edouard's earliest childhood, Jean-Paul had been the most important figure in his life. He loved his papa, and admired him greatly, but his father, though always kind, was remote. As a small child, Edouard saw him, as he saw his mother, at appointed times. He would be brought down to the drawing room from the nursery wing at St. Cloud at precisely four each day, accompanied by his elderly English nanny. There he would sit, trying not to squirm about or make too much noise, while his parents either questioned him politely about his day and the progress of his lessons, or occasionally, seemed to forget he was there at all and simply talked to each other.

At four-thirty he was returned to the nursery, and made to eat a horrible English nursery supper, because his nanny had made it quite clear from her arrival that her word was law, and her charge would be brought up in the proper English manner. So Edouard would eat loathsome overboiled eggs from an egg cup, or—even more horrible—bread and milk from a bowl, and all the while the most delicious smells would drift up the back staircase from the kitchens below: roast partridge in autumn, grilled salmon in summer. Oh, the delights of that kitchen! The huge bowls of thick cream; the mountains of freshly picked raspberries and wild strawberries. The tiny shrimps, the dark blue lobsters that turned clear pink when the cook boiled them. The freshly baked bread, the pale butter, the rows of cheeses laid out on little straw mats in the larder. Occasionally, on Nanny's one afternoon off a week, he would creep down to the kitchen, and Francine, the cook, would seat him at the long deal table and gaily feed him little tidbits—tastes of the glories destined for the Baron's dining room, of whose secrets she was fiercely proud.

But those were the special days. Ordinarily, he had his nursery supper, presided over unsmilingly by Nanny, then he was bathed, and then he was put to bed. Once or twice a week his father or mother would make the journey to the nursery wing to kiss him good night. His mother would sparkle with jewels, the silk of her dress would rustle, she would smell of roses, and he would hear her laughter on the stairs before she came into the room. She came up to him only when she was happy, so she always seemed to be laughing. She had a high brittle laugh; when Edouard was young, it used to frighten him a little: she sounded as she looked—frail, as if she might break.

His papa smelled of cologne, and sometimes of cigars, and it was more fun when he came, because he stayed longer than Maman, and could sometimes be persuaded to do imitations, or to talk. Edouard liked to talk to his father. He was interested in what Papa did. His father explained to him about grapes and vines and vintages; about diamonds and the secrets of their cutting. Sometimes, at the four o'clock visits when his mother was out, Papa would dismiss Nanny and take Edouard into his study. Then, if he was in a good mood, he would unlock his safe and show Edouard jewels, teaching him about settings, about design, about quality. By the time he was seven Edouard could see at once if a diamond was flawless, even without a glass, just by holding it against the light. But those were rare days, hedged in by rules and formalities. It was to Jean-Paul that he was close, to Jean-Paul that he could talk.

One of his first memories of his brother was of his glorious return for the holidays from his *école militaire*. He must have been about four or five, his brother about fourteen. He wore the uniform of the college, a uniform that was plain, but to Edouard magnificent. He ran to his elder brother, and Jean-Paul gave a whoop of welcome, and lifted him up in the air and perched him on his shoulders. It had seemed to Edouard then, and ever since, that his brother was a model of everything a French gentleman and a soldier ought to be.

He was handsome, but in a very different way from Edouard himself, being shorter and more heavily built. He took after his American grandfather—with his Scots ancestry—being fair-skinned, with thick reddish-blond hair and eyes of a paler blue than his brother's. His beard was red, or would have been had he ever allowed it to grow, which he did not; but he had to shave twice a day, and that seemed to Edouard the epitome of manliness.

He was always, unfailingly, good-tempered. Edouard never had to worry with him, as he did with his mother, that his mood might suddenly change, or that his temper would spark. Edouard had hardly ever seen him angry, unless his horse had gone unexpectedly lame in mid-hunt, or he had had a poor day's shooting. Even then, his anger was brief and soon forgotten. He was easygoing, lazily, irrepressibly so: it was the great source of his charm, to men as well as to women.

Nothing could persuade him to do anything that bored him: as a boy, he disliked lessons, rarely read a book, never attended a serious play, though he became fond of chorus girls. He liked popular music—easy tunes, which he could whistle or hum; the only paintings he liked in his father's collection were those by Toulouse-Lautrec. The Cézannes, the magnificent Matisse, the Gauguins, the Monets—these interested Jean-Paul not at all. The Lautrecs, Edouard suspected, found favor only because of their subject matter. Jean-Paul preferred champagne or beer to the complexities of clarets, horses to art, certainties to questions. The de Chavigny jewelry empire, which he would one day inherit, frankly bored him. It was useful to have expert family advice when he wanted some pleasing trifle for a woman, but that was all. Apart from the difference in price, Jean-Paul couldn't tell garnets from rubies, and he had no intention of learning.

He was so *certain* of everything, that was what he most admired and envied in his brother, Edouard sometimes thought. Perhaps it was because he was the elder, the heir. Jean-Paul had grown up safe in the knowledge that without lifting one finger or exercising one muscle of his brain, he would one day be one of the richest men in Europe. He would be the Baron. He was born to a role, a position in life, and it would never have occurred to him to question it.

Edouard, too, would be rich, that went without saying. But he would not inherit the title, and if he was not to fritter away his life, he would have to find some function, some purpose—and he had no idea what it might be. He felt himself, in contrast to his brother, to Jean-Paul's massive sureness on every matter from politics to the bedroom, to be insubstantial, shot through with uncertainties and doubts. He knew he was more intelligent than Jean-Paul. He knew he saw things and understood things more quickly and more acutely—but that ability seemed to him useless. Jean-Paul simply didn't bother, and Jean-Paul was happy. That was the other source of his charm—his capacity to enjoy life, to revel in the moment, and never once to worry about the past or the morrow.

Also, Jean-Paul was not stupid. Anything that interested him, he mastered; he had always wanted to go into the army, and his military record was exemplary. He was without physical fear, Edouard knew that, whether he was on horseback or battleground. He was one of the finest shots in France; he was unexpectedly graceful on a dance floor. He could drink his fellow officers under the table, and had never been known to experience a hangover. And he was irresistible to women.

According to Jean-Paul, he had his first woman when he was thirteen—it was one of the maids at the château in the Loire—and had not looked back since. When he was fifteen, his father, as was customary in their class, had arranged for him to be initiated into the pleasures of the act of love by a Frenchwoman renowned in Paris for her tact in such matters.

Jean-Paul had not admitted to his father his previous experiences, and the woman in question had, according to Jean-Paul, been pleasantly surprised by his accomplished performance. Jean-Paul had from the first been only too delighted to explain to his eager younger brother exactly what a man's requirements were, what he did, and what he could expect the woman to do in return. His descriptions were couched in the language of the barrack room, and were marvelously exact.

He needed a fuck a day, he said negligently, as Edouard's eyes rounded. Sometimes more, but on average, one a day. The time of day didn't matter, though he himself favored the afternoon—that way the evening could be given over to drinking, and after drinking a man performed less well. All kinds of women were delightful to fuck: experienced women, inexperienced women, young ones, old ones, beautiful ones, plain ones, thin ones, fat ones.

"Plain ones?" Edouard looked at him anxiously. The women of his dreams were always beautiful.

Jean-Paul winked. "It's nice to kiss a pretty face. I admit that. But for a good fuck, it's not the face that counts. You're not looking at their faces then, I can assure you, little brother."

What constituted a good fuck? That was what Edouard wanted to know. Did that mean there could be bad ones also? Here Jean-Paul was annoyingly less exact. The question seemed to puzzle him.

Virgins were a bad fuck in general, he conceded eventually. He would advise Edouard to steer clear of virgins, until it came to his own wife, naturally. With a virgin, sex could be messy and unpleasant, and they were nervous, and didn't know what to do, and frightened of getting pregnant, which was absurd. Virgins were a responsibility, and best avoided.

Married women—now they were a much better bet. Half of them—especially here in England, where the men were so undersexed—were desperate for it. They knew what to do and when, and with the correct tutelage from the man could become highly imaginative. Jean-Paul then described some of their more inventive methods, and some of his tried and proven techniques, and Edouard listened in astonishment. Jean-Paul assured him that women's mouths could be as pleasurable as their cunts, in some cases, more so, because certain women could be a little unresponsive at the crucial moment of a conventional fuck.

"Some of them can't come," Jean-Paul explained obligingly. "God knows why, but they can't, and frankly, you've got other things to worry about without fretting too much about that. If they do come, all well and good. It feels wonderful—you remember in the Loire, watching the cows being milked when you were small? Well, it feels like that. Like being milked. Their muscles retract—inside, you see. But if that shows no sign of happening, forget it, press on. That's the answer, little brother. And if you want, try their mouths. They all pretend to be shocked to begin with, say they can't, turn up their eyes, and so on. Doesn't mean a thing. They love it."

"Do they . . . I mean if you do that . . ." Edouard hesitated. "I mean, what do they do, when it comes out? Do they spit it out?"

Jean-Paul gave a shout of hearty laughter.

"Sometimes. The prissy ones. The good ones swallow it."

"*Swallow* it?" Edouard stared. "Do they like the taste?"

"God knows." Jean-Paul shrugged. "I'm not worrying about that then, I can assure you. . . ."

And so it went on, an endless narrative. This position versus that one; the advantages of a slow fuck, and the occasional pleasures of a quick one. Lying down; standing up; dressed; undressed; from the front—the missionary position, Jean-Paul said—or from behind, curved together like spoons, the way animals did it. Contraception; the disadvantages of the sheath; the *capote anglaise;* how to time the moment of withdrawal for coitus interruptus; how, at certain times in a woman's monthly cycle, you could fuck quite safely with no danger of pregnancy at all.

Edouard's head spun with it all. Jean-Paul assured him it was all terribly simple, and that when the moment came, he would know just what to do—men just did, that was all. But it didn't sound simple to Edouard. It sounded terribly, terribly complicated. He was not at all sure that he'd manage it; he was certain he'd get it all wrong, and make a mess of it. And there was one other thing that bothered and perplexed him very much. Finally, plucking up his courage, he raised the matter.

"What about love, Jean-Paul?" he asked. "I mean—do you love them, when you're making love? Is that why it's called that? It seems as though it would be a little difficult. With so many. Is it possible to love them all?"

Jean-Paul threw back his head with laughter.

Love? Love didn't come into it—he should have explained. That was lesson number one, the first essential. He put his arms around Edouard's shoulders, and his face became serious.

"We're talking about pleasure, little brother. About sex. Not love—put love out of your mind, it will only confuse you. You have to be quite clear about what you want. You take pleasure from the woman—with luck you give her pleasure. That's all. Sometimes you *like* them—some women can be very good company, very charming, even intelligent. I've had good talks with women as well as good fucks. Some you don't like—and that's rather different. But love is not involved. Take my advice. A hint of the first symptom, and move on. Another woman will quickly cure you of all that nonsense."

"But wouldn't it be better—" Edouard persisted. "Wouldn't it *feel* better if you loved them? When you did it?"

"I really couldn't say. I've never been in love."

"*Never?* But people do fall in love, don't they? In books. In poems. Papa fell in love with Maman at first sight. He told me once."

"Did he?" Jean-Paul's face clouded. "Well, obviously the condition exists. I distrust it, that's all. It's a snare. A trap. You'll find women talk about it a good deal—far more than men. And why do they talk about it? Because they want you to marry them. It's part of the game they play. Admit you love them—never do it, believe me, Edouard—and they start expecting a proposal. Any man will tell you the same." He paused. "Did Papa really say that about Maman? You're not inventing it?"

Edouard shook his head. Jean-Paul frowned. It was one of the few times Edouard ever saw him look uncertain. It was also one of the few times he chose to disregard his brother's advice. Naturally, Jean-Paul ought to know, but Edouard nonetheless refused to believe him. He did not tell his brother, but he continued to think about love. He continued to believe, as he had always believed in his romantic and innocent heart, that to love and to make love must be one of the great human experiences, one that would change a man's life forever. He was impatient to have a woman, yes; but he was also impatient to love one. Soon, he would say to himself. Let it be soon.

The conversation about love, as opposed to sex, had taken place in France some three years before. It had not been repeated. Now, as Edouard heard steps outside, the sound of Parsons opening the front door, Jean-Paul's deep voice and the clear light ring of a woman's, Edouard smiled to himself.

Things had changed in those three years. Now, Jean-Paul was engaged to be married. His fiancée was English, young, and extremely beautiful. Jean-Paul must know by now that he had been wrong, Edouard thought a little smugly. He was engaged. He had fallen for the snare after all. And so, even Jean-Paul must be in love at last.

Lady Isobel Herbert, eldest daughter of the Earl of Conway, was eighteen, dazzling, and imperiously aware of it. She came into the Eaton Square drawing room now as she always entered a room—quickly, gracefully, restlessly, tossing aside a silver fox cape before Jean-Paul could assist her, and throwing it negligently over a chair. Before she was halfway across the room, she was already reaching for her cigarette case and holder, and turning to Jean-Paul impatiently.

"Darling, light this for me. And make me a cocktail, would you? I'm exhausted. I'm dying for a drink. Make me something wicked, and *extremely* intoxicating. I'm quite worn out with decision-making—how I hate decisions, too beastly." She flung herself down onto the sofa and stretched out decoratively, full-length. "Edouard. Darling. How are you?"

Edouard gave her a half bow, and retreated to the window seat from which he could stare at her unobserved.

All his life he had been used to beautiful women. His mother was famed for her looks; many of her friends were equally lovely. But Isobel Herbert was unlike any woman Edouard had ever known. She had been debutante of her year, and it was rumored, though unconfirmed, that she had turned down one prince, a duke, two sons of lesser peers, and one importunate Italian count before accepting the proposal of the Baron de Chavigny's heir. Edouard knew that she had a reputation for what the English called being "fast," and if that was so, he admired it. She was quite unlike the demure Catholic daughters of the French aristocracy whom Jean-Paul had occasionally, unwillingly, escorted. She had bright red hair, which flamed like red gold in sunlight, and deepened to chestnut in shadow. It was shingled shorter than a man's at the back, falling forward over her lovely capricious face in the front. She painted her face blatantly—tonight her lips were bright scarlet; even her nails were painted, which Edouard's mother would never have countenanced. She was tall, and slender as a boy, and tonight she was wearing a short-skirted black sheath of silk which was superbly and insolently understated. It was Schiaparelli; Edouard, who had an expert eye in such matters, knew that at once. Both slender bare arms were weighted with heavy ivory bracelets from wrist to elbow. The celebrated Conway pearls were slung around her neck, and she fiddled with them negligently, as if they were Woolworth beads, while she waited for her cocktail. She was never still: that was one of the things that most fascinated Edouard. She reminded him of something exotic, and swift: a hummingbird, or an exquisitely figured butterfly.

Now she swung around to Edouard, stretching out her hand for inspection.

"We've got it. I chose it this afternoon. Goodness, it was difficult! It gave me quite a headache. It's rather sweet, I think. Tell me, Edouard. You're the expert, Jean says. Do you approve?"

Silently Edouard crossed the room. He took the hand she proferred him, and looked down at her fingers. The "sweet" ring was very simple. A square-cut emerald almost an inch across. It was dark green, mounted in twenty-four-carat gold. Since Edouard recognized it at once, he knew also that it was flawless and unique. It had been mined in South America, cut in the de Chavigny workrooms by his grandfather's greatest gem cutter, and had belonged to Kaiser Wilhelm, whose family had sold it back to his father between the wars. It was exquisite, and it was widely regarded as unlucky. He stared at it for a moment in silence, then he released Isobel's hand.

"I approve. It's very beautiful. It matches your eyes."

Isobel gave a delighted laugh. "How charming you are, Edouard! Jean—you hear? Edouard is charming—not like you at all." She glanced up at Edouard from under her lashes. "And for such a young man, he's very cunning. He says exactly what he knows a woman will like to hear. Not like you at all, Jean . . ."

"Ah, but I make very good cocktails." Jean smiled and placed a glass in her hand. "Edouard hasn't learned to do that. Not yet."

"Cocktails! Cocktails!" Isobel tossed her head. "What kind of an accomplishment is that? The barman at the Four Hundred can make cocktails—and I don't intend to marry him."

"I have other accomplishments as well, my darling." Jean-Paul held on to her hand, and kissed her fingers lightly.

"You do? I shall make you list them for me at once, and then I shall learn them by heart. Now, quickly—paper, Edouard, and a pen . . ." She was on her feet again. Edouard silently found her some writing paper and a fountain pen, and Isobel sat down again, frowning in a show of concentration.

"Now, this is very serious! No mocking. I need to know this. In fact, I realize now I should have done it weeks ago. If the list is too short, I warn you, Jean—I shall leave you. Break off the engagement, just like that . . ." She snapped her fingers and Jean-Paul groaned good-naturedly. He stretched back in his chair and attempted to concentrate.

"I'm very rich," he began slowly.

"Rich? Rich?" Isobel frowned. "That's an exceedingly bad beginning. It's very vulgar of you to think I would be interested in such a thing. And besides—lots of men are rich. Try again."

"I shall be Baron de Chavigny . . ."

"Worse and worse. Papa says French titles are at best suspect and at worst absurd. Again."

Jean-Paul smiled. "I shall give my wife everything her heart desires. . . ."

"I have most of it already."

Jean-Paul frowned, and Edouard leaned forward eagerly. "He's very good-natured," he prompted. "Very. He almost never loses his temper. And he never sulks."

"Never sulks? That's good. I'll write that down." She paused. "I'm not sure about the temper though—that might be a little dull. I find men charming when they are in a rage." She tapped the paper with the pen. "Go on."

"He's handsome," Edouard put in again. "You can't expect him to say that, but I can."

"Oh, very well. Handsome." The emerald eyes flicked up at Edouard. "I think you will be more handsome one day, but that's beside the point. So—what do we have, Jean? Good looks and a refusal to sulk. It's not a great deal."

Jean-Paul stretched and put his hands behind his head. To Edouard's surprise he looked slightly irritated.

"I am a jealous and demanding lover," he said firmly. "Or so I'm told."

Isobel ignored the slight edge in his voice. She scribbled on the paper.

"Jealous is good. Demanding sounds good. Are you romantic, though?"

She wrote the word, and then crossed it out.

"No, I don't think you are, not at all." She glanced up at the clock. "We've been engaged just three days, and it's at least an hour since you last kissed me. I don't think you're romantic at all."

"Then I shall have to change your mind."

Jean-Paul stood up, crossed the room, leaned over her chair, and kissed her. Edouard watched for a second uncomfortably, then turned away to the window. He had the oddest feeling that this kiss had been provoked, and for his benefit, not his brother's. He turned around as Jean-Paul drew back, and the emerald eyes flashed up at him for a second, as if Isobel were amused, as if she shared a secret with him from which his brother was excluded. To his horror and distress he felt his body begin to respond, to stir. He turned away miserably.

"I've got lessons to do. Latin. I'd better go and get started. . . ." He began to move to the door, but Isobel sprang up.

"No—don't do that. We're going to stop this silly game now. It's too boring. If we go on, I shall end up with five words on a piece of paper, and then I'll have to give Jean back this emerald. And I don't want to do that. I'm attached to it. And to you, Jean darling—now, don't frown. You know I love to tease you. I shall go up to see your mother— she won't mind, will she, Jean? I want to show her this. And we're going to start making marvelous *lists*. Women adore list-making, did you know that, darling? We can't have a proper wedding without lots of them, which will be sheer heaven. Now. There! I'm going. . . ." She glanced over her shoulder. "I shall leave you two to *talk*. . . ."

When the door closed behind her, there was a little silence. Edouard had gone bright red. He stared at his brother accusingly.

"Oh God. She *knows*. Isobel knows. You didn't tell her? You can't have told her?"

"I might have mentioned it." Jean-Paul shrugged. "Why shouldn't she know? She thought it was a fine idea. She said it was sweet."

Edouard glanced at his brother doubtfully. He inflected the word *sweet* with a sarcasm he did not trouble to hide.

"I'm embarrassed, that's all. I'd just rather she didn't know. I—I thought it was something private. A secret. Just between you and me."

"So it is. So it is. Now, come on. Cheer up." Jean-Paul smiled. "I've good news. I've arranged it."

"Arranged it? You have?"

Jean-Paul pulled a small pasteboard card from his uniform pocket and slipped it into Edouard's hand.

"Tomorrow afternoon, at three. Maman will be out all day. I checked. Glendinning takes you only in the mornings on Saturday, yes? So— you've plenty of time to get there. The address is on the card." He paused. "She's perfect, Edouard. Perfect in every respect. Not too young, not too old. Very experienced. A delightful woman. French—I thought that might help. Not a tart—nothing like that. Very clean. She has—well, she's kept, if you understand me. But the gentleman in question is elderly and often away, and she likes younger men." He shrugged. "She's a good fuck, Edouard. I can recommend her personally."

"You can?"

"But of course. You don't think I'm going to send my little brother off without checking the services provided?" Jean smiled. "I had her the other afternoon."

"The other afternoon? But—Jean, you're engaged now."

Jean-Paul grinned. He glanced at the door, then back at Edouard.

"Oh, little brother," he said slowly. "You didn't seriously imagine that would make any difference? Did you?"

Célestine Bianchon had first come to England in 1910, at the age of sixteen, to appear as a dancer and singer in Henry Pelissier's Alhambra Follies. She was very pretty, with just the degree of plumpness then considered essential for beauty, she danced gracefully, and—untaught— sang with a naturally sweet high clear voice. She rapidly acquired her quota of followers, stage-door johnnies who would fill her dressing room with flowers, and who competed furiously for the privilege of wining and dining her after the show at the Café de l'Europe in Leicester Square. They would eat and drink champagne until three in the morning, surrounded by the writers, actresses, and young men of good family who made up this *demi-monde,* and then Célestine would return in a hansom to the less glamorous environs of Finsbury Park: sometimes alone, more often not. She still looked back on those years of her life, which continued until the outbreak of the Great War, as the high point of her existence.

But Célestine, of French peasant stock, was also a realist. Unlike some of her friends at the Alhambra, she accepted bouquets and presents, but did not expect proposals of marriage; such elevations, it was true, did occasionally occur, but they were rarities. Célestine was happy with a series of protectors; she had no wish to return to France. As the years passed, and the first bloom of her beauty faded, the protectors became less distinguished and less young, but Célestine accepted this. It was natural, inevitable, it did nothing to affect her spirits. As a girl she had numbered English peers among her admirers. Now, in 1940, she was forty-six, and her gentleman was a retired businessman living in Hove, who had invested his meager capital in a series of lodging houses in different parts of London and the Home Counties. This suited Célestine, because it meant he visited her only once or twice a week. And besides, he rarely questioned her as to how she spent the rest of her time. He was sixty-four, and Célestine was fond of him. He was less virile, but much kinder, than many of her past lovers; he paid for her small flat in Maida Vale; he bestowed on her a small allowance from which she was able to save a little each week against her old age; and he bothered to talk to her—she appreciated that.

It had never occurred to Célestine that she was deceiving him. She regarded her afternoons with other gentlemen as something quite apart from this central arrangement, occasions which could cause no harm because they would never be discovered. Célestine had realized early that the less men knew, the better it was. They came to her for one purpose, and she fulfilled it to the best of her considerable abilities. It was good fortune for her that the war had brought so many Frenchmen to London, and that an afternoon with one French officer had since brought her a steady stream of satisfied military customers.

Her small pasteboard card was now in the wallets of a number of General de Gaulle's staff, and that pleased Célestine. It brought her a little extra money; a certain spirit of patriotism was involved; and besides, after all these years, it was pleasant to speak French again in the boudoir. When she passed the headquarters of the Free French, Célestine never failed to blow a kiss in its direction, and to wish the young men there a silent *bonne chance.*

She had been honored to accommodate the dashing young heir to the Baron de Chavigny. She had been flattered when, at the end of some rampant lovemaking, he had explained to her as only a Frenchman could, the predicament of his younger brother. It was by no means the first time that she had performed such a role, and she agreed to it at once. She was curious to meet this young Edouard, and with a smile to herself, she wondered if, with her assistance, he could not become a far more accomplished lover than his energetic but unsubtle brother.

She prepared for him carefully, knowing from experience that the kind of clothing—tight-waisted corselets in black lace that lifted her full breasts and left them exposed, garter belt, fine stockings, thin negligee— which appealed strongly to her older clients, was likely to terrify a boy. When she had finished preparing herself, she was pleased with the costume: it was erotic without being blatant, white rather than black, adorned with pretty ribbons and lace, the whole ensemble discreetly hidden beneath a dressing gown of pale blue crêpe de chine. She arranged her hair carefully, and slipped her tiny pretty feet into blue high-heeled slippers decorated with maribou feathers. Jean-Paul had thoughtfully provided a bottle of champagne for the occasion, and it was ready on ice. She also set the kettle to boil: some young men preferred tea the first time. Then she sat down to wait.

Edouard had taken a taxi to the unfamiliar area of Maida Vale. He arrived there at two-fifteen and spent forty-five minutes pacing the streets in an agony of indecision. Several times he almost called another cab and returned home, but he knew that would have been cowardice, and he couldn't have faced Jean-Paul. So, in the end, he presented himself at the door at precisely three o'clock and pressed the bell nervously.

Jean-Paul had said five pounds. That seemed to Edouard not just mean, but graceless. So he had removed from the stores in Eaton Square a large box of French hand-dipped chocolates—impossible to obtain such things in London now—and had placed a ten-pound note inside it, then carefully rearranged ribbons and wrappings. He had also purchased a small bunch of roses from a flower seller, and he juggled roses and chocolates as he waited.

He had never felt so uncertain and inadequate in his life, never so little inclined even to look at a woman. That feeling disappeared at once when Célestine opened the door, tripped up the stairs before him in her maribou slippers, and led him into her sitting room. Chattering gaily in French, she put him at ease at once. She poured him a glass of champagne, which he drank in one gulp, and then, to his great relief she simply sat down, as if they were old friends, and began to talk.

Edouard looked at her, and he thought that she might not be young, but she was enchanting. She reminded him of certain Renoir paintings in his father's collection, with her reddish-blond hair piled on top of her head, and the wisps that curled around her ears, and her soft throat. She had clear blue eyes, and the tiny wrinkles around them only increased the warmth of her smile. She needed, and wore, very little makeup, and her complexion still had the clarity and the delicate coloring of a much younger woman.

He stared, riveted, as she gently swung one smooth leg, and twisted her ankle as if to admire her blue slippers. When she leaned forward to offer him a second glass of champagne, and he politely refused, her dressing gown fell open a little, and he glimpsed the luscious curve of her full breasts. That was enough; to his delight he felt his body start to respond. And Célestine seemed to know, because she stood up and gently led him into her bedroom, where, to his increasing delight, she first undressed him, and then allowed him to remove her robe. With sudden rash confidence he pushed her back onto the clean white sheets and began to kiss her passionately. Less than five minutes later, to his shame and mortification, he burst into tears.

Célestine lay back on the pillows and held the boy close in her arms. He wept angrily against her breasts, and gently Célestine stroked his hair as a mother would, until the first spasm of anger and grief left him, and he lay more quietly in her arms. She looked down at the dark bent head, and her warm heart was filled with compassion. If only he knew, this handsome young boy, that it was almost always like this, the first time; that he was neither the first nor the last man to weep like an angry child at what he believed was his unique failure. Very gently, stroking his thick hair all the while, she began to talk.

"*Vas-y, mon petit.* There's no need for tears now. The first time it's always like this, believe me. You are excited, you are impatient, it is only natural—don't worry. So you come quickly—too quickly, you think. You imagine I will be offended, maybe? I can assure you that is not the case. I take it as a compliment, *mon chéri*, a compliment—you hear me? It is good to know, when you are my age, that you can still please a young man so much. And besides, we have plenty of time, as much time as you want. And you will find, *mon chéri*, that at your age such an event is a trifle, over and forgotten the next minute. The next time, and there will be so many next times, it will be better, and then better and better—until eventually, you will teach *me*, it is you who will dictate, you who will—how do they say it here?—call the shots?"

She smiled, and continued the soft stroking. "Do you imagine, *chéri*, that to make love is a skill we are all born with? That we know, men and women both, exactly what to do, and the best, the most pleasurable way of doing it, the very first time? I assure you that is not the case. One must learn, *chéri*. Gradually. It is a little like a lesson in school, *hein*? Only in this case, it is a pleasurable lesson. One everyone enjoys. . . ."

She smiled against his hair as she felt his strong young body grow less tense. Soon, she thought, in a minute, much more quickly than he realizes, he will be hard again, and ready to make love a second time. But meanwhile, she must not rush him. He was like a young animal, she thought, a shy young animal; anything too sudden, too direct, and she would startle and frighten him. No, she must be gentle and slow, very slow. And he was so beautiful! So beautiful. She had almost forgotten how beautiful a very young man's body could be: the smoothness of the skin, like a girl's, the tautness of the muscles. The tight curve of the buttocks, the flatness of the stomach, the strength of the thighs. She felt a slow pleasurable ripple of desire. Such eyes—that extraordinary deep blue; and that black, black hair . . . She stroked the wide shoulders. He was more relaxed now.

Carefully she drew them both up to a sitting position. A certain practicality now, she thought. Yes, that might be the thing. "*Chéri* . . ." She lifted his hands, making her request quite casual and matter-of-fact. "It seems a little unfair. You look so comfortable, so beautiful, and I—I am still in this stupid thing. And besides . . ." She teasingly caught his eye. "It is a little damp, *hein*? Would you help me to undo it? At the back there, that's right, all those little hooks and eyes, so difficult to reach. And my stockings! Really, I think I have no need of my stockings. . . ."

He slipped the stockings off first. Then, with fumbling fingers, he undid the white lace corselet. Célestine was naked. She smiled at him, and Edouard gazed, enraptured. He had seen pictures, of course—Jean-Paul had shown him some—but he had never seen a woman naked before. He could never have imagined such opulence of flesh, such loveliness. Célestine had full heavy breasts with wide rosy-pink nipples. Her hips curved out from a still-small waist; between her legs there was a triangle of reddish-gold hair, curly, springy to the touch, startling against the creamy curve of her thighs. Almost without thinking, he touched her there, very lightly, feeling the crisp hairs, and to his astonishment and delight, Célestine gave a little moan of response.

He looked up at her, startled, and her lips curved, the blue eyes sparkled.

"But yes—that surprises you? It shouldn't. It feels nice when you touch me there. It might feel nice, too, I think, if you kissed me. Just a little kiss, *chéri*. . . ."

Somewhat awkwardly, Edouard put his arms around her, and bent his face to hers. He gave her a chaste kiss on her closed lips, very gently, and Célestine gave a deep sigh.

"Oh, so good. I like your kiss. A little more, I beg you. . . ."

This time, as his lips touched the soft warmth of hers, she parted them. Edouard touched them softly with his tongue, and she sighed again, and moved closer to him.

"*Comme ça, chéri. Ah, oui, comme ça* . . ."

She drew his tongue into her mouth, gently, persuasively, holding him in her arms so that he did not press too hard or too close, and just their mouths were joined. Edouard felt a shudder of delight pass through his body; she began to caress his neck and shoulders and back, and at once, immediately, he felt his penis leap and harden. He felt Célestine's lips curve into a smile of triumph. She gave a low laugh, and drew back from him just a little, looking down.

"Ah, but you see what has happened? So quickly? An instant and you are big again. So big and hard and strong. You are quite a man, *chéri*, you know that? With this, you can give a woman such pleasure, *chéri*, such pleasure. . . ."

She was careful not to touch him, and when he tried to push her back against the pillows again, she gently stopped him. She shook her head reprovingly, and to her delight she saw a teasing light come into his eyes. He could be amused—good! Then his confidence was growing.

"Wait?" He smiled. "Not too fast?"

Célestine took his hand.

"For my sake," she said softly. "You know that for a woman to make love is a wonderful thing. She wants it to last, to be slow. She cannot always be as quick as a man. She cannot always be as quickly aroused as a man. He has to help her."

She lifted his palm, and pressed it against her breast. "Touch me there, *chéri*. Oh, how I want you to stroke me, there, you see? Like that. Yes, like that . . ."

Edouard slipped his hands under her breasts and felt their full weight. Then, almost before he knew what he was doing, he did the thing he had been longing to do, had dreamed of doing. He lowered his mouth, kissed the smooth flesh. Then he buried his head between the mounds of her breasts, lifted them, caressed them, took the soft pink nipples in turn between his lips. He teased them with his tongue, and felt their points grow hard. A tremor ran through his body, and Célestine held him.

"*Doucement, doucement, mon chéri. Pas trop vite . . . doucement.*" He steadied, paused, felt the tremor subside. Then he looked up at her.

"*Comme ça? Tu aimes comme ça?*" He took the nipple between his lips once more, and sucked. This time it was Célestine who trembled.

"*Mais oui. Tu sais bien. Comme ça, Edouard, comme ça . . .*"

Célestine could feel her own body responding, the pulse beating up through her blood, as if an invisible chain of nerves connected her breasts and her womb, and every one of those nerves sang out with pleasure. She felt herself grow moist, and it was harder for her to keep still. She wanted to part her legs, to let him touch her there. He was learning fast, she thought, very fast. . . .

He lifted his mouth from her breasts, and kissed her. "*Mais, que tu es belle, si belle. . . .*"

He muttered against her mouth, his breath coming fast, and Célestine fought with her own instincts, fought to make the kiss slow and gentle. Not too passionate, not too deep, not too long, not yet, not yet. His penis was hard against her stomach, and she moved slightly to free him, frightened that the pressure might make him come.

"*Doucement, Edouard.*" She let her hands stroke the fine hard curve of his buttocks, and moved a little so their bodies lay side by side. When she judged he was a little calmer once more, she took his hand, and raised it to her lips.

"You are so good. It feels so good when you touch me. You know that? You can feel, I think, that I like it, yes? You see—it makes my nipples go so hard when you touch me, when you kiss me there. That is the first sign, Edouard, but there are others. . . ." Very slowly she drew his hand down, over the curve of her stomach to the triangle of gold hair. She let it rest there awhile, then she parted her legs.

"You see? A woman's secret place, the part of her only her lover knows. You see, *chéri*—how soft, how moist? That is because you make me want you, Edouard, want you very much. . . ."

Edouard let his hand be drawn down to the softness, the moistness. He parted the two soft lips, and felt a place of mystery, of folds and crevices, felt one tight hard bud. He touched it delicately with his forefinger, and to his wonderment, Célestine arched back with a little cry. He leaned forward and kissed her, a long slow sweet kiss, and all the time his hand gently stroked, gently explored. Célestine moved beneath him; she lifted her knees and parted her thighs wider, and she seemed to Edouard infinitely soft, infinitely pliant, infinitely and wondrously open. He withdrew his hand, and Célestine took it and kissed it, and for the first time in his life Edouard smelled the honied scent of a woman ready to make love, musky, slightly salt, like a sea creature.

He slipped his hand down once more, Célestine moved slightly, and his finger slipped easily, gently, inside her. He groaned then, and Célestine knew she must be quick.

With the deftness of experience, she moved so he was between her thighs. She withdrew his hand gently, and guided the full head of his penis to the soft entrance. One tiny lift of her hips, and he was inside her. She knew better than to move then; she kept still and quiet, though she was very aroused by his beauty and his gentleness, and she longed to move, to draw him down deep inside her. But she stayed still, and let him thrust; three, four, five times. Then he came inside her with a shuddering cry, and Célestine wrapped her arms tenderly and protectively around him.

L ess than an hour later, he was hard again, much more relaxed, clearly proud of himself. Célestine felt proud too. And she liked him, she thought, as she looked fondly down at him while he sucked at her full breasts. She liked the absence of bravado, the instinctive care and delicacy of his touch. Oh, he would make a fine lover, this man, she thought—perhaps even a great one, an extraordinary one, and there were very few of those. He would not be like some of them, such greedy animals, so coarse, so quick, and afterward so furtive. No, he would be sure, giving pleasure as well as taking it—open, responsive . . .

"*Tu seras—exceptionnel, tu sais* . . ." she murmured, and the boy lifted his head. The compliment pleased him, but it also amused him, and she liked that. She liked his quick intelligence, his capacity for amusement. After all, lovemaking was not always a serious affair, that was very dull. Passion, yes, women wanted that, but also a little teasing. "Teach me—show me . . ." He hesitated. "I want to give you pleasure in return. . . ."

Célestine sighed, and stroked his hair. Like many women of her kind, she found it difficult to reach orgasm with a man. She had long ago accepted this. She enjoyed lovemaking, and the absence of climax never worried her greatly. She found fulfillment enough in embraces and caresses, and if she did not, then it was easy enough to relieve the tension in her body after the man had gone. To give pleasure was her pleasure; when she had been younger, with her first lover, her second, it had been different. They had been able to bring her to a peak of excitement, quite easily. But they had left, and it had become harder; she thought sometimes that her own mind held her back, refused to let her give everything to men who were—more and more often—strangers.

But she was touched by the boy's request, so she smiled up at him. "Watch—let me show you."

Gently she slipped her hand between her legs, one finger between the lips; she moved.

"You see? Where you touched me before, *chéri*. If you touch me there—not too hard, quite softly, there's no need to be quick. . . ."

She withdrew her hand, its fingers glistening. Edouard touched her as she had touched herself, felt the small hard swelling of her clitoris between the soft lips, and then, on impulse, knelt, and bent his head, and kissed her. That heady moist salt scent; he touched the little swollen bud gently with his tongue, and the effect was instantaneous. Again she arched, her hands came down to cradle his head as he lapped. His hand reached for the swell of her breasts, and Célestine moaned.

"Like that?" He paused for an instant, and she quickly drew him back.

"Oh, yes—Edouard, yes. There. Like that . . ."

Célestine trembled. It was not that he was perfectly expert, but someone more expert could have left her unmoved. It was him, she realized with surprise, as she felt the waves of heat start to build in her groin. It was something about him, a little magic, the fact that he wanted to please her, the way he looked at her body, lustfully, of course, but also tenderly, shyly. It reminded her of the past, and it felt good, so good . . . and yes, it was going to happen after all, she knew it would happen now: she felt her body poise, wait for the sudden rush of sensation, and as if he sensed that, he stopped the soft rhythmic motion of his tongue, the pressure of his lips, so she cried out in an agony of sudden want. Then he touched her again, his mouth moist, his hands clasping her hips and lifting her up to him, and she cried out as the tide of heat took her. Edouard felt the fierce sudden pulse against his lips. He moved, thrust hard up inside her, and felt to his great joy the soft contraction and relaxing of her body against his flesh.

This time there were more than four or five thrusts. He discovered, triumphantly, how fine, how extraordinary, how tantalizing it felt to withdraw almost out of her body, and then to push so deep he felt he touched the neck of her womb; to alter his rhythm from slow to fast and back to slow. And he discovered how it felt when Célestine, too, moved, slowly at first, and then more insistently, circling as he pulled back from her, circling again as he thrust. He came with a sharp agonizing sweetness, and afterward she lay along the curve of his arm, and they both slept a little, their bodies entwined.

When he woke, Célestine lifted his chin in her hand, and looked down with amusement and understanding into his eyes.

"You learn fast. So fast. Soon, I shall have nothing to teach you. . . ."

Edouard laughed, and slipped his arms around her. He was covered in silken sweat, his body heavy with a sweet languor.

"I want to see you again. Soon. And then again and again. Célestine. Célestine. . . ."

"I should like that," Célestine answered simply.

That night, Edouard dined at home with his mother and Jean-Paul, the only guest being Isobel. Such occasions, when they were *en famille*, were rarely a success. Jean-Paul chafed at them, and itched to be off to a nightclub. Louise, perhaps because she sensed this, perhaps simply because she, too, wished for more brilliant company, was often irritable. Usually, Edouard would try hard to cheer them both, and to supply some of the spirit and gaiety there was at family meals in France, when his father was present.

But tonight, seated at the long table, wearing evening dress, he was dreamy and abstracted. Try as he would, he could not concentrate on what was being said, or who was saying it. His mind was miles across London, in a little room in Maida Vale.

These dinners were never brief affairs, for Louise insisted on rigorous standards. They were served by Parsons and two immaculate footmen; there were never less than six courses; the wine was always exceptionally fine. Tonight, the evening seemed to Edouard interminable. The foie gras was without taste; the grilled sole was cardboard; the pheasant he pushed away scarcely touched.

This unusual loss of appetite did not go unremarked. Once or twice Edouard looked up to find Isobel, who was seated opposite him, regarding him mischievously, her emerald eyes glinting, a little smile curving her bright scarlet lips. She, too, said very little. The conversation dragged, and Louise became peevish. When peevish, she complained, and tonight she grew quite eloquent—nothing suited her. She found London dull, she told Isobel; it was quite amusing at first, but now, more and more she missed Paris. The same faces, again and again—and really, though Englishmen could be charming, Englishwomen were so *odd*, so dowdy most of them, and so lacking in chic—here she gave Isobel a sharp glance. And then there was their passion for animals, their obsession with dogs; it was charming to stay the weekend in the country, yes, but then to be leaped upon by labradors . . . to be expected to go for long walks, even when it was raining . . . truly the English were a curious race, quite unlike the French, quite unlike Americans. And then—well, of course, she missed dearest Xavi so terribly. So little news got through, and she worried constantly.

"He should have known how much I would worry." Her voice rose slightly. "To have packed us off here, and left us to fend for ourselves . . . I know you won't agree with this, Jean-Paul, but really, on reflection, it seems to me a little selfish. Dearest Xavi can be so terribly obstinate. I'm perfectly sure he could have come with us if he wished. He can have no idea how difficult life is. One can't buy petrol—which seems to me perfectly absurd—how on earth is one supposed to motor out of London? I live in dread that one of the servants will give notice, because—well, you will know this, Isobel—it's quite impossible to find replacements. The men are all in the army, and the women are all making ball bearings in factories—what can they be *doing* with all those ball bearings? And these wretched sirens. *Just* when one is about to go out, they always sound, and then the streets are cleared. I don't think Xavi understands how *wearing* it all is. . . ."

"There is a war on, Maman." Jean-Paul looked up. He winked at Isobel, and Louise, who saw the wink, flushed.

"Jean-Paul, please, there is no need to take that attitude. I know that. I've just been *explaining* that I know that. I must say that neither you nor Edouard help, you know. Both of you—tied up with your own affairs, you never seem to give a thought to *my* feelings. . . ." She broke off. At the word *affairs*, Jean-Paul had given a snort of laughter. Louise's face grew tight; her dark eyes glared down the length of the table.

"Have I said something to amuse you, Jean-Paul? Please explain. We should all like to share the joke."

"Forgive me, Maman." Jean-Paul gave her his most winning smile. Edouard glanced up, waiting to see how he would extricate himself. He always could: Louise could never be angry with him for long—she always succumbed to his charm—and sometimes Edouard thought Jean-Paul was contemptuous of her for that.

"It's just that you know what you say isn't true. Edouard and I are devoted to you. You know that. . . ."

"You might make it a little more obvious, occasionally." Louise gave him a reproving glance, but she was mollified.

Jean-Paul rose to his feet with a masterful air, and the discreetest glance at his watch.

"Dearest Maman." He came to her side and lifted her hand in his.

"You're tired. You should rest more, you know. Come—why don't you let me show you to your room? I'll have your coffee brought up to you there. I'll send your maid to you—no arguments now. I promised Papa to look after you. You shall have a really good night's sleep. . . ."

It worked like a charm. Louise rose, and leaned on his arm. She left them without protest. At the door, Jean-Paul looked back and gave Edouard and Isobel another wink. Isobel rose restlessly to her feet the moment the door was shut. She tossed her napkin on the table. Edouard, returning with difficulty from the room in Maida Vale, looked at her uncertainly.

"Does he always manage your mother like that?" The green eyes met his for a second, curiously. Edouard rose.

"Usually." He shrugged. "She adores Jean-Paul. She always has. He can do anything with her. . . ." He paused. "She doesn't mean everything she says, you know," he added defensively, for his mother often made him ashamed. "It's just her way of speaking. And she gets very strung-up. . . ."

"Oh, never mind, anyway." Isobel moved off impatiently. "Let's play some music. I want to dance. . . ."

She reached for Edouard's hand and dragged him out of the dining room into another room which they sometimes used in the evenings. It had a smooth parquet floor, and sometimes Edouard would patiently wind the gramophone and play records while Jean-Paul and Isobel danced together dreamily in the center of the room. He had never danced with Isobel himself, but tonight she selected a record, she wound the gramophone, she pushed aside the rug.

"Come on. . . ." She stood in the center of the floor, and lifted her arms to him, scarlet lips smiling, emerald eyes glinting with amusement and challenge. "You can dance, I suppose? If you can't, I'll teach you. . . ."

"I can dance." Edouard stepped forward and took her in his arms. In fact, he danced rather well, and felt eager to demonstrate that, but when he attempted to waltz, Isobel pulled him closer.

"Not like that. Don't let's be ambitious. Let's just shuffle, it's more peaceful. . . ."

They shuffled. The music was soft and low, the record pleasantly scratchy; Isobel felt light in his arms, and after a while, Edouard relaxed. They stepped and turned, turned and stepped; his mind drifted away again to the afternoon, and to Célestine. He began to feel extraordinarily happy.

Once or twice, Isobel lifted her face and looked at him. The record ran down, she replaced it, rewound the handle, and drifted back into his arms with a little smile on her lips.

"You're laughing at me. . . ." Edouard looked down at her.

"No, I'm not. I'm laughing at myself. It's a long time since I've felt so invisible. It's good for my vanity."

"Invisible? You?"

"Oh, Edouard. So gallant. There's no need to pretend. You're miles away. That's all right. I don't mind. I quite like it. It's restful."

She sighed, and after a while, as they continued to circle, she rested her face gently against his shoulder. Edouard was a little surprised at this, but he said nothing; they were still dancing in this way when Jean-Paul returned to them. He stood and watched them for a while, leaning against a chair and smoking a cigarette. Isobel ignored him. When, finally, the record ran down again, Jean-Paul rewound it, and then he cut in.

"My turn, I think. My fiancée."

He danced with Isobel for the remainder of the evening, and it was only after she left, and they were alone together, that Edouard noticed his brother was not in a very good temper. Jean-Paul removed the record from the gramophone irritably, scratching it as he did so. Then he paced up and down the room, as if he found it confining.

"Was Maman all right?" Edouard looked up at him.

"What? Oh, yes. She was fine. She just wanted some attention paid her. Like all women." Jean-Paul slumped in a chair; one foot tapped the carpet.

"I expect she does miss Papa," Edouard began hesitantly. "It can't be easy for her. . . ."

"You think so?" Jean-Paul gave a bark of laughter. "Well, you may be right, but I doubt it. I'd say it was simpler than that—she wants everyone at her beck and call, running round her in small circles, paying court to her. Isobel's precisely the same. I tell you, little brother, it wears me out sometimes. Women." He frowned. His face had taken on a sullen expression, and Edouard was puzzled. He felt a little embarrassed that Jean-Paul should speak in this way—it seemed to him disloyal. As if sensing that, Jean-Paul looked up. He stretched, and then grinned.

"Still. They have their uses, eh? We wouldn't be without them. So—tell me, let's get down to something more important. How did you get on this afternoon? Good, was she?"

Edouard was aware he was blushing. He looked at the carpet. Jean-Paul was adopting a man-to-man tone that he usually found flattering; now, for the first time, something in him resisted it.

"It was fine," he said stiffly, after a pause. "Thank you, Jean-Paul, for arranging it."

Jean-Paul threw back his head and gave a bellow of laughter.

"He's embarrassed. I do believe my own little brother is embarrassed. Fine? What kind of a report is that? Don't I get a few more details? I went to a lot of trouble, you know, Edouard, to fix this . . ."

Edouard stood up. He looked at his brother, and he thought of Célestine, and for the first time in his life two loyalties conflicted. He knew, quite suddenly, that he couldn't bear to tell Jean-Paul what had happened. He couldn't bear to tell anyone; it belonged to himself and Célestine.

"Oh, you know." He shrugged, hesitated. "I don't really want to talk about it."

"I see." There was a pause. "That bad, was it? Oh, well . . ."

Jean-Paul yawned and stretched once more. The smile on his face broadened, as if the supposition of Edouard's failure pleased him. Edouard looked at him in confusion: Why should that be?

Jean-Paul stood up and put his arm around Edouard's shoulders.

"Well, well, happens to everyone. Better luck next time. Don't worry about it, eh?" He chuckled to himself. "You won't be seeing her again, then? Well, there's plenty of others—just let me know when you want another address. Maybe she just didn't suit you. I shouldn't worry. Not yet, anyway, little brother. . . ."

He went off to bed then, humming the dance tune to himself, obviously in a high good humor. Edouard watched him go with a sense of puzzled dismay. Beneath the bonhomie he had detected resentment, even rivalry—had it not been Jean-Paul, he might even have thought jealousy. The idea perturbed him, then he pushed it out of his mind. It was a ridiculous idea, and a disloyal one: Jean-Paul was his brother, he was the most generous of men.

Still, a certain caution remained, a slight wariness. The next afternoon he returned to Célestine and spent a rapturous two hours with her.

When he returned to Eaton Square, Jean-Paul was there, and quizzed him on his absence.

"I—was walking in the park," Edouard replied before he could stop himself.

He *had* walked through the park on the way to Célestine's flat, but nonetheless it was a lie, designed to mislead, and Edouard knew it.

He felt guilty afterward, and ashamed. It was the first time in his life that he had ever lied to his brother.

HÉLÈNE

ALABAMA, 1950

O ut back behind the trailer, there was a tree. She didn't know what kind of tree, and Mother didn't know either: it was an American tree, she said, they didn't have trees like that in England. It was real big—very big, she corrected herself carefully, and its branches hung down low. If she took a chair out and balanced on it carefully, she could pull off long strands of the stuff that grew on it. Spanish moss, Mother said it was called; it looked spooky when the light was fading. But not now. Now it was the middle of the August afternoon, and very hot, and she had made a little pile of it in the dirt in front of the trailer.

Lovely soft crinkly gray moss. And some little rocks that Mother called pebbles, and some daisies. She was making a garden, an English garden, for when Mother came home.

The window of the trailer was open, and she could see the big round face of the clock that stood on top of the icebox. She could see the little red stickers Mother put on it by the four and the twelve. She couldn't read the time yet, not quite, but when the hands were pointing at those two stickers, Mother would be home. They were nearly there; not long now. The garden was all finished, and she had three crackers left. Maybe she'd eat them now.

She broke a corner off, and handed it to Doll politely, the way Mother had shown her. But Doll just stared up with her painted eyes, so Hélène ate it for her. Then she ate the other crackers, and carefully brushed the crumbs off her dress. She looked down at her skirt anxiously. The dust was a horrible red-brown. It left marks everywhere, and Mother said to stay put, and not to get into trouble, not to move from right there in front of the trailer. Not to get dirty.

You didn't get dirty in English gardens. The grass grew the way it should there, and there were gardeners to keep it watered in summer, and the ladies sat in wicker chairs and the servants brought them iced lemonade in long cool glasses. Not nasty lemonade that came in bottles like Coke, but fresh lemonade, made with fruit and water and sugar, with a long silver spoon to stir it.

She glanced over her shoulder guiltily. She'd like some lemonade. Making the garden had made her throat all dry and tickly. She'd even like some Coke, or that funny green tea Mississippi Mary made, that tasted of mint like toothpaste. But she wasn't allowed to talk to Mary. And if the Tanner children came by, Mother said not to talk to them either, but just to go and sit inside in the trailer and wait for her to come home.

She pushed a long fair lock of hair back from her sticky forehead. The Tanner children wouldn't come by anyway. She knew where they were, she could hear them shouting. They were down by the river, in the waterhole there, and they were skinny-dipping. She'd never done that, of course, but she'd crept up on them once and watched them. It looked nice. It looked like fun. The boys and the girls, no clothes, and jumping in and out of the brown water and splashing. It looked so cool, that brown water, so cool and lovely. And besides, it was interesting. All the Tanner girls looked like she did, but the Tanner boys were different. They had this funny thing between their legs, like a little pouch, and then, just when she was craning her head to get a better look, one of the Tanner boys spread his legs, and held this thing, and a big arc of water came out, right down in the pool, and all the other children laughed. She told Mother about that, and Mother got very cross. She slapped her, hard, on the arm, so there was a big red mark. She said the Tanners were common. "White trash or black trash," Mother said, "either way, you stay away from them."

"But why do they have that thing, Mother?" she asked when she'd stopped crying.

"Because boys are different from girls."

"Do all boys have one? Did Daddy?"

"Yes. All boys have them." Her mother sighed.

"But what do they *do* with them? Why haven't I got one?"

"Because girls don't need them. They're dirty. Now, come and have tea."

Hélène stood up. She felt guilty. She shouldn't be remembering that—Mother would be cross. Mother thought she'd forgotten all about it. But she hadn't. She remembered, even though it was a very long time ago, last summer maybe. And she often thought about what she'd seen, when she was in bed at night, and Mother was sewing, and it was so hot she couldn't sleep. Thinking about it made her feel good, and made her feel bad—and kind of funny, warm in between her thighs.

Sometimes she'd put her hand there, in between her legs, and that felt nice too. Then she went to sleep.

But it was better not to think about that now. Now the hands of the clock were nearly touching the two stickers. She'd go and sit on the trailer steps. That way she'd see Mother the moment she reached the dirt track. She picked up Doll, and brushed down her frock, and seated her on the hot step beside her.

From here, you could see the layout of the trailer park quite well, and Hélène liked that. Over behind her was the creek, and the creek led down to the river, and the river went on a bit and then it joined the Alabama River, which was really very big, though not beautiful like the rivers in England.

In England there was the Thames, and that went through London, where the king and queen lived in a palace, and where Mother had lived too.

And then there was the Avon, and the Avon went through another town whose name she forgot, which was where Shakespeare had lived. Shakespeare was English, and he was the best writer in the whole world, Mother said. Mother had acted in one of his plays once, in a lovely dress. And when Hélène was bigger, Mother was going to teach her some of his poems to say, and that was why she had to be careful now, and talk properly, like Mother, and not do that horrible droopy drawl like the Tanner children, so when she said the poems she would say them right, like an English lady. A E I O U—lovely and open and soft; she should have practiced her vowels this afternoon. She'd promised Mother, and then she'd forgotten.

She swung her legs back and forth now, mouthing the sounds, looking around the trailer park. Their trailer was one of the oldest, painted dark green, with the rust coming through. It had two rooms, a bedroom where she and Mother slept in little narrow beds, and the room where they ate their meals and she did her lessons, and where they listened to the wireless in the evenings. Then there were the steps she sat on now, and the little yard where she'd made her garden. 'Round back by the tree there was a pump, and what Mother called the outhouse, which smelled nasty and was full of flies in the summer. There was a white picket fence 'round the yard, and a little gate, and a path. Then there were more trees—thank God, Mother said, because it meant they didn't have to see the other trailers. There were eight of them, two of them occupied by the Tanners, who had seven children and another on the way, Mother said. Mr. Tanner drank, and he beat Mrs. Tanner up sometimes—they could hear her screaming—but Mother said to take no notice, there was nothing they could do. Men were like that, she said, and Mrs. Tanner was an ignorant fool to put up with it.

"Did Daddy hit you, Mother?"

"Once. He hit me once. That was enough."

Then her lips went in a hard straight line, and she looked unhappy, so Hélène didn't ask her anymore. Daddy must have been a bad man, she thought sometimes, and anyway, she didn't remember him at all. He lived in Louisiana; she and Mother had lived there, too, for a little while, before they came here. She didn't remember Louisiana either. Daddy was a soldier, and Mother met him when he was fighting in the war. And now he was in Korea, which was a long way away, farther than Louisiana: a good thing, Mother said, and she didn't care if he never came back. Daddy didn't know where she and Mother lived; if he looked for them—which he wouldn't, Mother said with a sniff—he'd never find them, and that was good, too, because they were safe and happy just the way they were, and one day—one day soon—they would both go back to England together, which was where they belonged.

Beyond the other trailers there was a field. It had been a cotton field once, Mother said, part of the Calverts' plantation, but they let it go during the war, when Major Calvert was away fighting the Germans. Now only a few colored people lived there, in tarpaper shacks, and she was on no account to go down there, not even to see Mississippi Mary. Then there was the road, and down the road, Orangeburg, where there was a gas station, and the market and the bank and the hotel and Cassie Wyatt's, where Mother did the ladies' hair three mornings a week. Beyond Orangeburg, there was Selma, and Montgomery, which was the state capital, and then Birmingham—but she'd never been there.

Mother said not to worry, why should she care about Birmingham? When she was older, they'd go to New York, and walk down Fifth Avenue, and go into all the lovely shops. And then they'd take a boat, or maybe even an airplane, and they'd go to London, and Paris, and Rome. London had been bombed by the Germans, of course, and Mother hadn't seen it for nearly five years, but she said it would still be beautiful. There were parks there—big parks, not like the trailer park at all—with lots of green grass, and trees and flowers; and there were bandstands, where soldiers played marches and waltzes.

When they had the money, Mother said, then they would go. And they wouldn't be stopping off to see Birmingham, Alabama—not them, no sir!

She turned her head. The hands on the clock were on the red stickers right now. Mother would be coming; she was never late. "Punctuality is the courtesy of princes," she said. And she'd be coming the other way, down the track that led from the plantation and the big house, because today was Saturday, and Saturday she did Mrs. Calvert's hair. Not at Cassie Wyatt's beauty parlor—Mrs. Calvert would never go *there*, Mother said—but right in her own bedroom.

Hélène had gone there with Mother once, just once—to help hold the pins, Mother said to Mrs. Calvert, but Hélène knew that wasn't the reason. Mother wanted her to see the house: a proper house, tall and white, with pillars and a veranda. Mrs. Calvert had a colored butler, and proper servants, the way a lady should, and she fretted a lot, and said the sun made her head ache, so the blinds had to be kept down. It was cool and dark in her room, and very quiet, and there was just the smell of the hair tongs, and of scent, and freshly ironed linen and flowers.

It was lovely, Hélène thought. All those glittery crystal bottles beneath the looking glass on her dressing table, and big heavy silver brushes. Mrs. Calvert herself was a disappointment though. She was thin and scrawny, and when Hélène stood up close, she could see where the powder had caked on Mrs. Calvert's sallow skin, and how her mouth turned down in little lines at the corners. She was a Yankee, Mother said, which meant she came from the North, New York, maybe, or Boston. A lady, Mother said, and a good few years older than her husband, she added with a little smile.

She had gray hairs. Mother had to touch them up with some special stuff from a bottle that smelled horrid. They always called it "touching-up," but when Mother was home, she'd laugh and wink, and say, "Better take along the dye bottle."

When they left the big house that time, they met Major Calvert on the veranda. He was wearing a white suit. Hélène had never seen a man in a white suit before. He looked very tall and very suntanned and very handsome, and when he saw her, he'd gotten to his feet and come over. He'd just stood there, looking her up and down, until Mother had introduced her. And then Hélène had known just what to do, of course; Mother had taught her. She held out her hand, and looked him in the eye, and said "How do you do?" just the way Mother had shown her. And Major Calvert had stared, and then he had laughed, a great burst of laughter. And then he had shaken her hand very solemnly, and said something to her mother that Hélène couldn't hear.

"What did he say, Mother?" she had asked as soon as they were out of earshot. And Mother had smiled.

"He asked how old you were, and I said five, and he said you were going to be a beauty."

Hélène had stopped in her tracks.

"A beauty? You mean, beautiful? Like a lady?"

"But of course." Her mother patted her fondly on the shoulder. "Haven't I always told you?"

And she had. Always. For as long as Hélène could remember. And that was nice, she thought as, looking up, she saw her mother's figure come into view beyond the trees.

Very nice. But not as nice as when Major Calvert said it, because Major Calvert was a man and a gentleman. He smelled of cologne, and the skin of his hands felt smooth, and when he took her hand, he'd done something very unexpected, something Mother had never mentioned, never done when they practiced shaking hands together. He'd pressed the tip of one finger into the damp curve of her palm; lightly at first, then a little more, and then he'd just scratched the surface of her skin, secretly, with one perfectly manicured nail.

She hadn't told Mother. She might have been cross, and then Hélène wouldn't be allowed back to the big house, not ever. And she wanted to go again very much. She wanted to see the big silver brushes, and smell the clean linen, and see Major Calvert again. Because when he touched her palm like that, it felt nice. It made her feel warm and soft and breathless. The way she felt when she'd watched the Tanner boys in the waterhole.

And that was odd. Because although Major Calvert was a man, he looked very handsome and very clean. So why did he make her feel the same way the dirty things did, the things she was never to mention?

She rose quickly to her feet. Better not to think of it; it was naughty, and Mother might notice something was wrong. She waved, suddenly happy to have a secret and happy to see her mother.

"Look," she said. "I've made you an English garden."

After supper were the best times: Hélène loved them. Then the light grew soft, and the air was cooler; the little cotton curtains flapped in the breeze at the open window, and outside, the grasshoppers sang. Then she had her mother to herself, and she had her special lessons, which weren't like lessons at all—more like a game she was very very good at.

And tonight was special. For her mother had come back with a surprise, a brown paper parcel that she'd hidden away at once in the bedroom, though Hélène had seen the excitement in her eyes. She would be allowed to look later, Mother said. If she did her lessons well.

So they had what Mother called "nursery supper." She was very specific on this point. The meal in the middle of the day was luncheon, never dinner, which was what the Tanner children called it, because they didn't know any better. Then there was afternoon tea, not taken at the table, Mother explained, but in the drawing room, assuming you had one, and since they didn't, they imagined it. Then there was supper, and when she was grown-up, there would be dinner instead, served at eight.

For supper they had boiled eggs and white bread and butter, sliced very thin, with the crusts cut off. Never anything fried. Mother said fried foods were vulgar, and gave you a bad complexion. Then there was a little cheese, and then there was fruit, and the fruit was complicated, because you had to eat it with a knife and a fork, and an orange had to be peeled one way, and an apple another, and sometimes Hélène got them muddled up, and then Mother would frown.

After that, Mother switched on the wireless, and they listened to the news broadcast, which was very boring, Hélène thought, and all about wars in places she'd never heard of except Korea. And then, when the dishes were washed, then came the best part. The lessons.

Tonight she had to lay a place at the oilcloth-covered table, with all the knives and forks and spoons in the right places. It didn't look very good, even Mother admitted, because all the cutlery was the same size, instead of different sizes, the way it should have been—but still, the placing could be correct. When she had finished, she perched on a cushion on the chair and waited. Back straight. Arms tucked in by her sides because when you went to a banquet or a big dinner you couldn't stick your elbows out—it took up too much room.

Mother smiled. "Good. Now tonight, you will be having a little soup. A clear soup, I think—consommé, you remember? And then fish—sole, perhaps, or a little poached turbot. Then the main course, which might be chicken, or meat, or game, and there will be vegetables, of course, which will be brought 'round to you. On which side will the servant stand?"

"On my left, Mother."

"Good. And the knives and forks—in which order do you use them?"

"From the outside in, Mother."

"Good. And if there are little rolls, bread of some kind?"

"Broken off, piece by piece, Mother. With the fingers. Never cut with the knife. That is for the butter."

"Excellent. And the wineglasses?"

Hélène looked down at the line of three thick glass beakers.

"The same as the knives and forks. From the outside in. Even if the glass is refilled, never drink more than three altogether, and sip them slowly. . . ." She grinned. "Fingers 'round the stems, none sticking out."

"Good." Her mother sighed. "Three glasses is not a rule, you understand, but it is prudent. Now . . . after the main course, what might you have then?"

"Pudding, Mother."

"Pudding, precisely. *Not* dessert—that is the term for the fruit and the nuts which are brought in at the end of the meal. And certainly not 'sweet.' There may be a savory—do you remember what a savory is?"

"Devils in harness?"

"On horseback." A faint smile. "There are others, of course. Now

. . ." She gestured to the glass pepper pot and salt shaker in the center of the wooden table. "Those are?"

"The salt and the pepper, Mother. And sometimes there might be mustard." She lifted her face proudly, pleased to be doing so well. "We don't say 'cruet,' but if someone did, we'd pass them just the same and not smile."

"Excellent. And that?" She gestured to the piece of paper towel that lay beside Hélène's plate.

"Is a napkin."

"And since we've already reached the savory, it should have been where, for some time?"

Hélène's hand flew to her lips.

"Oh! I forgot. On my lap, Mother."

"With your hands, if I'm not mistaken."

The reproof was mild. Hélène's hands quickly darted under the table.

"Very good. One last thing. You have eaten your fruit—perfectly, of course, *not* dropping orange peel under the table, but we'll forget about that. What happens next?"

"Well . . ." Hélène hesitated. "We will talk for a bit, and I must make sure to talk to the person on my right and on my left, and not allow myself to be . . . to be . . ."

"Monopolized. Very good. Go on."

"And then I wait for the hostess to look up. She might catch my eye, or lay down her napkin, but I must be ready. Then she stands up and all the other women stand up, and we follow her out of the room. And the men stay behind and drink port. And tell funny stories . . ."

"Yes. Yes." Her mother stood up. "What they do is of no concern to you. And anyway . . ." She hesitated, looking a little lost for a moment. "That practice may be dying out now. I'm not quite sure. Since the war, you know. Things are more informal now, and of course I've been away a long time. . . ." Her voice trailed away. "But it's best to know."

"Yes, Mother." She hesitated, raising her eyes to her mother's face. "Did I do well?"

"Very well, my darling. You may get down now."

Hélène clambered down, and ran to her mother.

Her mother had seated herself in the one comfortable armchair they possessed. It was ugly, Hélène thought, with yellow wooden legs and a greasy red cover. But her mother had draped it with a beautiful old paisley shawl she had brought from England. Now, as Hélène climbed onto her lap and nestled her head against her shoulder, her mother let her head fall back against the shawl and closed her eyes. Tilting her head, Hélène looked at her carefully.

Her mother was beautiful, she thought. She was very thin, but then they often didn't have much to eat, especially if Cassie Wyatt was late paying her mother her wages, as she was sometimes. But she always smelled clean and flowery, and she always made up her face, and set her hair in pins every evening. No one else around here looked like her mother, no one. She had soft brown hair, which she cut herself, and marcel waves, so her hair rippled. She was pale, and never sat out in the sun because it burned her skin. Her eyebrows were plucked into two thin arches and her eyes were large and widely spaced, like Hélène's own. They were violet, that was how she came to be given her name, she said. She was Violet Jennifer Fortescue—or she had been when she acted on the stage in England. Here, she was Craig, Mrs. Craig, because that was Daddy's name, and Hélène was Hélène Craig. Hélène didn't like the name Craig so much; it would be nicer, she thought, to be Hélène Fortescue, and when she was grown-up, she would be. She would act on the stage, like Mother, and then she could use any name she liked. Or maybe in the movies—the films, Mother said. There was a movie theater in Selma, and her mother took her there sometimes for a treat. Hélène loved the movies. She sat there as still as a mouse. She thought her mother looked like Carole Lombard—only better, because Carole Lombard's hair was dyed silver-blond, and Mother's was its natural color.

Mother had a sister called Elizabeth; she sent her a card every Christmas and some years Elizabeth sent one back. Their mother and father were dead, which was why it was especially difficult for Hélène and her mother to go back to England, because where would they live?

"Couldn't we live with Elizabeth, just to begin with?" Hélène asked. But Mother shook her head. She and Elizabeth did not get on very well, she said. Elizabeth was older, and she had always resented her, because their daddy made a favorite of her. Once he had taken Violet to Paris, just the two of them, and they had had the most wonderful time, because Paris was the most beautiful city in the world, even more beautiful than London. When they returned, Elizabeth had been horrid, and sulked. She still lived in the house in Devon where they grew up, although she wasn't married, and lived alone, and it was much too big for her. They couldn't go back there, Mother said; Elizabeth wouldn't want them, and it would make Mother too sad, remembering.

"Elizabeth is jealous of me," Mother said. "I married, and she ended up on the shelf."

Hélène sighed. She knew what that meant. It meant Elizabeth was an old maid, and that was a terrible fate, the worst thing that could happen to a woman. It meant men didn't like you; it meant you were plain and dull, and had to spend the rest of your life stuck up on a shelf like an old jam jar. It made her very anxious sometimes, thinking about that. What if it happened to her?

On the other hand, marriage didn't seem too good either. Mrs. Calvert had married, and she looked sour and miserable. Mrs. Tanner had married, and her husband got drunk and beat her up. Mother had married, and when she talked about that, which she hardly ever did, it made her cry.

Hélène wanted to know if she had been in love with Daddy, because that was the way it went, she knew that much. First you fell in love, and then the man asked you to marry him, and then he loved you and looked after you for always. Only sometimes it wasn't like that, and she wanted to know why. Mother wouldn't tell her. She just said it was wartime, and she had been very young, she had been a G.I. bride; then she changed the subject. She hadn't worn a white dress or a veil— Hélène had discovered that. Because of the war again, Mother said. Hélène thought that might be the reason it had all gone wrong: Mother hadn't done it the proper way; she'd worn a suit, not a special dress, and she'd gone to some office place, not a church. It couldn't have been a very good beginning, Hélène thought. When she got married, she wouldn't make that mistake.

She often wanted to ask Mother more about getting married, and about Daddy, because she would have liked to know more about him. But it made Mother restless when she asked those questions, and tonight she looked tired, and a little bit on edge, as if she had something on her mind. So Hélène curled up on her lap, and asked her the questions she knew Mother liked. About the life Mother led when she was a little girl, and the house she lived in, and the dresses she wore, and the parties she went to, and how, when she was nineteen years old, she ran away from home to be an actress. Hélène had heard all the answers a hundred times before, but she still loved to hear them. Her mother would begin slowly at first, and she would have to coax the stories from her. Then, gradually, her violet eyes would light up, and two bright hectic spots of color would appear in her cheeks, and then she would talk quickly, all the words spilling over one another.

White satin and fox furs, and champagne for breakfast, and a place called the Café Royal, which had nearly been bombed one night when Mother was there dancing. Parties that began in dressing rooms backstage, and went on all night. Men who wore dinner jackets, and sometimes tails. A clever man who wore a silk dressing gown, and played the piano and sang witty songs. Makeup by Leichner and Max Factor, which came in little greasy tubes with numbers on them—Mother had some still. Flowers. Mother always wore a rose pinned to her dress when she went out to supper. She had a lot of admirers, and her favorite dress, which she didn't have anymore, was made of mauve silk that emphasized the color of her eyes. Cars—Daimler cars, with leather seats. And songs—lots of songs. Mother sang them to her sometimes, standing in the middle of the little room, her eyes bright, her cheeks flushed, the lamplight shining on her hair. Her favorite song was about lilacs.

She sang it beautifully, in her high clear voice, and when she had finished, Hélène clapped, and Mother curtsied and laughed, and Hélène said: "What are lilacs, Mother?" And Mother said they were white flowers, or purple, and they smelled of springtime and England, and Major Calvert's gardener grew them at the big house.

Then she stopped suddenly, and she cried. She said it could be a very hard life, sometimes, being an actress. People didn't take you seriously.

Tonight, Mother didn't sing, and she answered Hélène's careful questions too quickly, as if she were worried about something. Money probably. So, after a little silence, Hélène pressed her mother's hand, and reminded her. The surprise.

"Ah, yes! The surprise. . . ."

Slowly, her mother stood up, and then she took Hélène's hand and led her into the bedroom. In the middle of Mother's bed was the brown cardboard box.

Very carefully her mother undid the string around it, and lifted the lid. Hélène clasped her hands together in excitement, and watched.

Very carefully, running her hands over the material, smoothing out the creases, her mother lifted out a dress. She held it against herself for a moment, and sighed. Then, very gently, she laid it out on the bed. Hélène stared at it. She could see the happiness on her mother's face, and she didn't dare say anything.

The dress was made of some silky stuff. It was gray and white, with a smudgy sort of pattern on it that Hélène didn't like. It had a big collar, and pads in the shoulders and a little belt of the same material that fastened around the waist. On the edge of the collar there was a small round black stain.

They both gazed at the dress for a while in silence, and then, quickly, suddenly, her mother bent forward and touched the material. She smoothed back the collar.

"You see, Hélène? Look! Bergdorf Goodman. On the label, right there. It's a beautiful shop, Hélène. On Fifth Avenue. Very exclusive. Terribly expensive. This is pure silk—look. Feel. Isn't that beautiful?" For a second she buried her head against the folds of the skirt.

"Pure silk. I haven't touched a silk dress—haven't worn one for—" She broke off, and laughed nervously. "For a long time."

Hélène stared at the dress. She swallowed.

"It's got a mark on it, Mother, look. Right there—on the collar. It's dirty! It's not new. . . ."

Her mother swung around, and the violet eyes flared.

"Of course it's not new. Do you think I could afford to buy a dress like this? I couldn't buy it—not on a *year* of Cassie Wyatt's wages. . . ." Her voice had risen. Then something made her change her tone. She met Hélène's eyes, and her own dropped for a second, then looked up again, full of pleading.

"It's *beautiful*, Hélène. Can't you see that? Oh, I know it's plain, but beautiful things often are—you have to learn that. And it's been worn, of course. There's the mark—but that's nothing. I can get that out, you'll see. And it's too big—look. Mrs. Calvert is taller than I am, so I'll have to take it up. And she's bigger in the hips—so, you see? I'll take it in here, just a pinch, and what with that and the hem, there'll be some material left over—just a bit. We can make Doll a new dress, I thought. A proper dress, for parties, and . . ."

"That's Mrs. Calvert's dress?" Hélène stared at her mother. She watched as the color washed up over the pale cheeks. "She gave it to you? You mean it's a hand-me-down—like the Tanners?"

"Not at all like the Tanners." Her mother's mouth snapped into a hard line, and she stood up. Her hands were shaking. "It's a dress, that's all. A beautiful dress. It's hardly been worn. Mrs. Calvert was throwing it out, and . . ."

"Did Mrs. Calvert give it to you?" Something made her ask the question again—she couldn't stop herself. Her heart suddenly felt tight and hurtful, and somehow she knew, just *knew*, before her mother's eyes fell, before she looked away, before she answered.

"No." She turned her back, and bent over and began to fold the dress up again. "As a matter of fact, she didn't. Major Calvert did. It was going out, with a whole lot of other things, and he saw it, and he rescued it. For me. Because he thought I'd like it. Because he thought it would suit me. And it will." She slammed the box lid shut. "You don't understand. You've never seen good dresses. Wait till I wear it—then you'll see. . . ."

Mother was angry. Hélène could feel it. She was angry and she was upset. It was like there was a horrible current of wind swirling round the room, and her mother was caught up in it—slamming things away, banging drawers, telling Hélène to hurry up now and fetch water and get into bed, she was only a little girl, not seven yet, and it was way past her bedtime. . . .

Silently Hélène washed and undressed and climbed into her narrow bed. Then Mother came over and sat down, and took her hand, and Hélène knew she was sorry, and they just stayed there, not speaking.

Finally, Mother stood up. She backed away from the bed a little bit, and Hélène thought she was going to go out and close the door behind her, but she didn't; she stayed.

"Hélène . . ." she said at last. "You're not asleep? You know it's Sunday tomorrow?"

Hélène yawned, and snuggled down farther under the thin scratchy sheets. Tomorrow was Sunday; yes, she knew that. Sundays, Mother did the washing, then they went walking together, down by the creek.

"I . . . I have to go out, Hélène. Just for a bit. Not for long. In the afternoon."

Hélène sat up. "But we go walking in the afternoon!"

Her mother sighed. "I know we do, darling. But not tomorrow—all right? Mother has to go out. She has to—to see a friend tomorrow."

Hélène stared, round-eyed. "A friend? Can't I come? What friend? Is it someone I know?"

"No. No." Her mother made soothing noises. "And you can't come tomorrow. Another time, maybe. If you're a good girl. And we'll go walking just as soon as Mother gets back—the way we always do. All right?"

Hélène began to cry. She didn't know why, and she couldn't stop. All she knew was that suddenly everything was going wrong. First, there was the surprise, which wasn't a nice surprise at all, but a horrid one. And now this. The tears welled up in her eyes and plopped down her face and onto the sheets.

"Oh, Hélène . . ." Her mother crossed quickly to the little bed and put her arms around her tight. Too tight. Hélène's face was pressed up against Mother's thin shoulders, and she could feel Mother was tense, all stiff and wiry—just like she wanted to cry too.

"My darling. Don't cry. Don't be silly now. You're tired—that's all. And you're still a little girl, and—" Mother broke off. She pulled back suddenly, with a kind of desperate lurch. And her voice was all funny, not soft and calm the way it usually was, but thin and choked.

"I'm thirty-one, Hélène. Thirty-one. That's not old. It's young. I'm still young. And . . . Mother needs friends, darling. Everyone does. You wouldn't want Mother to be lonely—to have no friends—would you?"

Hélène looked at her carefully. Her own tears had stopped as suddenly as they started. But Mother hadn't noticed; she had turned her face away.

"No," she said at last, and Mother sighed.

She bent and kissed Hélène on the forehead and settled her back down under the sheets. Then she turned out the lamp and moved to the door.

"Mother?"

"Yes, darling?"

"Will you wear your new dress to meet your friend?"

There was a little silence, then her mother gave a soft laugh.

"I might do," she said. "I might do."

She sounded almost gay. Then she shut the door.

She did wear the new dress. She must have been up half the night sewing it, and cleaning it and pressing it, because when she tried it on, it fit and the stain had gone.

She looked at herself carefully in the cracked old glass in the bedroom. Then she laughed, and clapped her hands, and twirled around.

"You see? Darling? It looks pretty, doesn't it? Just the way Mother said?"

Hélène stuck out her lip and stared at her silently. Mother had washed her hair, too, so it shone in the sunlight, and she'd painted her face extra carefully. Her eyebrows were a bit more marked than usual, and her mouth was a scarlet cupid's bow. Her mother stopped her twirl and came over and gave her a hug.

"Now, don't sulk, darling—don't. It makes you look ugly. Mother won't be long—she told you. And look—I tell you what—why don't we dress you up too? In your special frock. And let Mother do your hair. Then we'll both be fine ladies, and when Mother gets back, we'll go walking, yes? Down by the creek in our pretty frocks, and we'll hold hands, and sing a bit, and pretend we're in Regents Park in London, and we're going to listen to the band. Shall we do that? Shall we?"

Hélène said nothing, but Mother hardly noticed. She seemed very excited, and flurried. She pushed and pulled Hélène into her best dress. It was a pretty dress, and normally Hélène liked it. Mother had made it, and done the smocking on the front, and made a little lacy collar from an old petticoat. She wore it when they went to the movie theater in Selma. But today it felt uncomfortable. Too tight and too hot and scratchy under the arms. She could feel herself sweating, and the trailer felt airless, as if there were going to be a storm.

Little beads of sweat stood out on Mother's forehead and along her upper lip.

Mother brushed Hélène's long fair hair till it shone too. Then she got out the curling tongs, and heated them up, and twisted the long fair locks into ringlets. Hélène could see she was trying to please her, and the more Mother tried, the hotter and stiffer she felt.

Finally, Mother looked at her watch, and then she said, "And now—something very special. You shall have some too. Just this once."

Then she went and pulled out the little drawer in the cheap yellow chest by her bed, and rummaged around in the back, and drew out the box. The special box.

It was plain white, with gold writing on it, and inside, in a little carved bed lined with yellowing white satin, was a bottle with a glass stopper. It was a very small bottle, and right down in the bottom of it there was a tiny bit of orangy-brown oily liquid. Very very carefully Mother tipped up the bottle so some of the liquid went on the inside of the glass stopper, then she took the stopper out. She rubbed the stuff behind her ears, and on the pale blue veins on the insides of her wrists, and then she did the same to Hélène.

Hélène wrinkled her nose.

"It smells funny."

"It's the most expensive scent in the world." Her mother was staring at the bottle. "You remember? I told you. It's called *Joy*, and it smells like springtime." Suddenly her face went sad. "I've had that bottle seven years. And now it's all gone."

Hélène thought she might throw the bottle away then, but she didn't. She put the stopper back, put the bottle in its box, and placed it back in the drawer. She sighed.

"Never let scent stand in the light, Hélène. It goes off. Remember that. And now . . ." She looked at her watch again, and gave a little gasp. "I must go. I'm late. You'll be a good girl now, won't you? Stay right by the trailer now, the way you always do. And remember the stickers on the clock. When the hands reach the stickers, Mother will be home. . . ."

She kissed Hélène, and hugged her very tight, and then she went. Hélène watched her. She walked down the steps and across the yard. When she was beyond the fence, she broke into a little run.

Hélène went into the kitchen and stood by the icebox and looked at the clock. She frowned. The stickers had been moved. One was by the twelve, the way it always was. The other was by the six.

She stared at the clock uncertainly. Did that mean Mother would be home sooner than usual—or later? She tried to figure it out for a while, but it was hot and stuffy in the trailer, so in the end she gave up and went outside. She examined her garden. It looked horrid. All the flowers were shriveled up in the sun, and the rocks were in the wrong place. She gave them a little kick with her shoe. Rocks, *not* pebbles. Maybe, if she got some water from the pump, and put it on the flowers, they'd pick up again. Doubtfully, she fetched a bottle, filled it, and then, growing interested in her task, knelt down, and carefully poured the water. It was difficult. It all ran about in the dust and didn't soak in where she wanted it to. The moss shifted, and the shriveled dandelions fell over.

"What you doin' that for? They're dead."

Slowly Hélène lifted her head. It was one of the Tanners—Billy Tanner, she thought. She squinted up into the sun: yes, it was Billy Tanner all right. He was leaning on the little picket fence and watching her. She looked at him silently. He was very brown, and he had that ugly haircut all the Tanners had, a crew cut, Mother said it was called, so short that his scalp gleamed in the sun through the brown spikes. My, but he was ugly! He had no shirt on, and no shoes—but then the

Tanners never wore shoes except to school—and he was wearing blue jeans cut off at the knees. They were so old they were almost white. She stared at him for a while, but she didn't answer him. Maybe if she kept quiet he'd just go away. She poured some more water into the dust. Billy Tanner gave a quick squint up at the trailer, then opened the gate, and came right into the yard. He stopped a few feet away, and began to scuff at the dirt. His feet were filthy; there was red dust all the way up around the ankle.

"They're dead. It won't do no good waterin' 'em. Not when they're dead." He paused. "You want me to get you some fresh ones? I know where there's plenty. Better'n that. Real big ones. Down by the creek."

Hélène sat back on her heels and looked at him cautiously. He made the offer casually, but it was a nice offer. Most of the Tanners would have jeered, or kicked the rocks all over. But Billy was nicer than the other Tanners, she remembered that. Once, when Mississippi Mary used to look after her, she fell over in the trailer park, and Billy Tanner picked her up and washed the cut under the pump. She hesitated.

"It's an English garden," she said finally. "It looked pretty yesterday."

Billy grinned. He squatted down beside her in the dirt. "An English garden? You ever see an English garden?"

"No. But my mother has. She told me all about them. They're all green and they have lots and lots of flowers. Like the gardens up at the Calverts', only better."

"Uh-huh." He bent forward and deftly rearranged the rocks. "You want to do it like that—make a dam, see? Then the water won't run out. You want to try it again now?"

Hélène tried. She poured the water cautiously. It formed a pool right in front of the rocks, just the way she wanted. Gradually it drained away, and she smiled.

"Thank you."

" 'S all right." He shrugged. He was looking at her sideways, Hélène saw, looking at her hair, and the best dress, and her bare legs and sandals. It made her feel odd at first, to be looked at like that, but he didn't touch her or anything, and after a while she began to like it.

"Your hair looks real pretty, you know that?" He spoke suddenly, and to Hélène's surprise she saw that he colored up as he spoke. His face went beet-red, and he wasn't smiling.

"I saw a girl looked like you, once. In a picture book. In the schoolhouse."

Hélène looked at him uncertainly, wondering if this were a compliment. But before she could answer, Billy wrinkled up his nose and laughed.

"You smell real funny though. Yuk—what a stink!"

"What do you know? It's scent. French scent. My mother gave me some. It's the most expensive scent in the world, so there, Billy Tanner!"

"It is?"

"Yes, it is. It's called *Joy*." She gave him a dignified glance, then held out her wrist. "Smell properly, there—see? It's nice."

Billy hesitated, then bent awkwardly over her wrist. He sniffed.

"You mean perfume? That's some kind of perfume?" His eyes were round with disbelief. "It smells like an old tomcat."

"It does *not*!" Hélène snatched her wrist away angrily.

"Suit yourself." He shrugged and stood up. He moved off a few paces, looked up at the sky, then down at the dirt, then back at her.

"Your mama out? You want to come swimming?" He hesitated. "I know a good place. 'Round back of the old cotton field. No kids, no niggers. It's great." He paused. "I ain't even taken my brothers 'n' sisters 'round by there."

"I'm not allowed. I have to stay here. Till my mother gets back. When the hands on the clock reach those red stickers—see, there, in the kitchen." Hélène paused importantly. "She's gone out to see a friend."

Billy strode over to the trailer and stared in the window. Then he laughed.

"Six! She ain't comin' back till six. That's more'n three hours from now. What you goin' do for three hours? Stick around in the dirt? You must be crazy. Come swimming. Your mama'll never even know."

Hélène stared at him. She wanted to go. Suddenly she wanted to go very much. He was right. It was horrid just sitting here waiting, horrid and hot and lonesome. She bit her lip.

"I—I can't swim," she said eventually.

"I'll teach you. No problem." He began to whistle, then stopped. "How old are you, anyways?"

"Seven."

This seemed to surprise him, because he looked at her again, slowly, up and down, the way he had before.

"I thought you was older than that. You look older." He paused. "You're just a kid."

"I am not." Hélène stood up indignantly. "I can read and write, and . . ."

"Letters? You mean you can read letters? Since when?"

"Since I was five. My mother taught me. Before I started school." She paused, looking at him appraisingly. "Can you read letters?"

"Sure. Sure I can. I read a book. Two maybe. With pictures, you know—like I said. My mama was real proud when she heared me spellin' it out. It's more 'n my daddy can do, and he's a grown man."

Hélène listened to this carefully. He didn't seem to be ashamed of the fact that his father couldn't read. She hesitated.

"How old are you?"

"Eleven. Twelve come Thanksgiving." He scuffed the dust. "You comin' swimming—yes or no?"

Hélène took a deep breath.

"All right." She looked back anxiously at the clock. "But just for a little while."

"Sure." Billy laughed. He looked pleased, and vaulted the little gate. "Come on, then. You talk real funny, anyone ever tell you that?"

The pool was in a little hollow, surrounded by cottonwood trees. To reach it, they took the dirt track that led up to the Calverts' plantation, and then cut off along a ditch that ran through the fields. Far over to their left Hélène could see the roofs of the tarpaper shacks where Mississippi Mary lived and a curl of smoke drifting up into the lead blue of the sky. Away to their right were the cotton fields Major Calvert still worked, then a great line of swamp cypress that shielded the house and gardens from the fields.

She followed Billy with difficulty, stumbling along over rutted mud, sharp grass and brambles catching at her dress. She felt hot and out of breath and filled with excitement and alarm all at once. Her skin was clammy, and her best dress clung to her body and itched her under the arms. After a while Billy came to a halt. He rolled some saliva around in his mouth and then spat in the dust. He grinned at her, and she noticed for the first time how blue his eyes were against the tan of his skin. He held out his hand and gave a jerk of the head.

"Through there. See?"

Hélène stared, wide-eyed. He was pointing to the cottonwood trees which grew down the sides of a small gully. They were right in behind the swamp cypress.

"In there? But that's so near the big house. It's right by the gardens, isn't it?"

Billy winked. "Sure is. But we ain't goin' in the front way."

He pulled her forward, over a ditch, and into some undergrowth. Right there in front of them was a barbed-wire fence. Billy put his fingers to his lips.

"Okay. I'll hold the wire, and you squeeze under it. There's a little bitty gap right there—see? Go on—what you waitin' for? And keep your voice down, okay? We got to sort of creep 'round the edge of the gardens, then we get away to the pool. We'll be just fine then—I told you. Ain't nobody goes near that place . . ."

Hélène hesitated; then, carefully holding her dress away from the wire, she crept underneath. Billy followed her and took her hand again.

She was glad. They were among thick overgrown bushes now, and it was dark and scratchy. Every now and then there was a tiny gap in the branches, and through them she caught a glimpse of green grass, the ends of tall white pillars. Her heart was beating very fast, and she seemed to herself to be making a terrible amount of noise, though Billy could move ahead of her quite soundlessly. Once or twice he ducked down and crouched, listening, and Hélène's heart beat even faster. What if someone heard them? What if one of the gardeners found them, or worse, Major Calvert himself? What if he came striding through the shrubbery in his white suit, and . . . she tugged desperately at Billy's hand. He stopped.

Hélène felt herself go crimson with embarrassment. She stood there, stock still, clutching her skirts.

"Billy. Billy. I want to . . . I have to . . ."

Billy's face split apart in a wide grin. "It's okay. I felt like that the first time I come through here. It's the keeping quiet that does it. You can piss behind the bush right there. It's okay. I won't look."

Hélène stared at him in astonishment. He didn't look embarrassed at all, and she'd just learned a new word. Not a word Mother would like, she was certain of it.

She gave a little giggle. Billy raised his eyes to the sky.

"Girls! Hurry . . ."

So Hélène went behind the bush, and when she came out she felt a whole lot better. She took Billy's hand again, and they went on, Indian file. Hélène stepped where he stepped; that way she made hardly any noise, and she felt pleased with herself. Piss, she said softly to herself under her breath. Piss. It was a nice word. She liked it. She was learning.

Just on the edge of the gully and the cottonwood trees, there was a little clearing. You couldn't see the big house now, it was hidden by shrubs, and Hélène guessed they must be in back of it. In front of them there was some scrubby ill-kept grass, as yellow and brown as the grass in the trailer park. On their right she could just see a funny little wooden shack, surrounded by bushes. Billy paused. He looked to the right and left. Hélène tugged his hand.

"Billy, Billy—what's that place there? That little shack?"

Billy grinned. "That? That's some kind of summerhouse, they call it. Nice and private, you know?"

"Private?" Hélène stared at him. He seemed to be amused by something, and she couldn't imagine what. She knew what summer-houses were: they had them in English gardens.

"Sure." Billy hesitated. "My mama says old man Calvert had it put up. Used to go there with the nigger ladies—you know? But I guess I don't believe that. Just an old story, I guess . . ."

Hélène's eyes grew round.

"Old man Calvert? You mean Major Calvert?"

Billy laughed. "Not him! His old daddy, I mean. Died a long ways back—a real mean sonuvabitch, my mama says . . ." He pulled her hand. "Come on now—over here."

He pulled her quickly across the grass, into the gully and out of sight. Then down through the trees, a sharp steep drop, and there was the pool.

They stopped, and Hélène looked at it silently. It was cooler in here under the trees, and the water was still and brown. On its surface two dragonflies darted and lit; their wings were iridescent. She frowned. "Nigger ladies?" She'd never said that word before, and she knew her mother wouldn't like it. "I don't understand. Why would a white man take a nigger lady to a summerhouse?"

"Well now, it's a mystery, I guess. . . ." Billy drawled, and Hélène felt cross for a minute because she realized there was something he knew and he wasn't going to tell her. Then the next minute she forgot all about it, because Billy let go her hand, and dived clean into the water, jeans and all.

He surfaced, spluttering. Diamonds of water ran down his face.

"You comin' in?"

Hélène hesitated. The etiquette of this situation was beyond her. She didn't know what she ought to do, and she didn't much care. All she knew was that she was hot, and she wanted to be in that water.

"I shall take my dress off," she said at last, with dignity. "I shall swim in my knickers."

"Suits me. Anyways you like." Billy ducked casually back under the water.

Carefully and methodically, Hélène undressed. She took off her sandals and folded her dress neatly on top of them. Then she tiptoed down to the edge of the water. Billy swam over and stood up. He held out his hand to her.

"Come on." He looked at her again, and again she saw that queer look in his eyes. They went very serious, and they seemed to turn darker. He looked at her like he wanted to go on looking for a long time, and couldn't quite believe what he saw.

"Come on," he said again, more softly this time. Then he reached up, very gently took her hand, and helped her down into the water.

Hélène gave a little cry. She could feel soft cool mud between her toes, and the water was so cold it almost took her breath away. She moved a step forward, and the ground wasn't there. Water was washing up over her hair and chin. She floundered and cried out.

Billy caught her. She felt his arms come around her and lift her up, and then before she knew it, she was floating.

"Isn't it just great?" Billy smiled at her, and she noticed he had a chip in his front tooth. "Isn't that just the greatest feeling in the whole wide world?"

"Oh, it is, Billy," she said. "It is."

A fterward they sat on the muddy bank in a patch of sunlight to get dry. From time to time, Billy picked up little bits of rock and tossed them into the pool, and they watched the ripples widen. He'd become very quiet, Hélène thought.

"I wasn't very good," she said at last in a small voice. "It's harder than it looks."

"You done good." Billy sounded definite. "You swum three strokes. Four maybe. Near on four."

There was a little silence. Billy threw another stone.

"You want to come here again?" he said at last, his voice very casual. "I'll bring you, if you want to. Your mama works some mornings over at Cassie Wyatt's place, right? I'll bring you then, maybe."

"Would you?" Hélène turned to him with an eager smile. "I'd like that very much." She stopped and frowned.

"I shouldn't though. My mother would be very cross if she knew."

"Don't tell her. Why let on? Folks need a secret—everybody does. I remember my daddy sayin' that." He paused. "This place is my secret. I like it here. It's quiet and it's pretty, real pretty. I come here sometimes—in winter even. Just to be by myself. When I get sick of the other kids—you know."

He hesitated, and she knew he was looking at her again in that way he did, though she didn't turn her head.

"It can be your secret, too, if you want." With a funny stealthy movement he took her hand, and then let it go again.

"You're pretty, too, real pretty. So it kind of makes sense, bringin' you here. You know . . ." He hesitated again, as if unsure whether to go on, and Hélène turned to look at him. "You know, the other kids, they don't want to have nothin' to do with you. Say you're stuck up, that kind of thing. But I don't think so. You talk funny, that's for sure." He grinned. "But that ain't your fault. And they say your mama has fancy ways, and she give you a stupid fancy name. But I think it's a real pretty name, and I never even said it. Not to you."

Hélène looked at him uncertainly.

"It's French," she said at last, still not sure if he might not burst out laughing the way some of the other Tanner kids did once when she told them.

"It's really an English name, but you're supposed to say it the way the French do. My mother likes it like that. She says it's softer. Like—you know—sort of like a sigh.''

"I like that. You've got a funny English voice and a funny French name, and they suit you. And your hair—you know, when the sun shines on your hair, it's the same color as corn when it's ripe. I've seen corn that color—all gold. I saw it up in Iowa once. Fields of it. I've got an uncle, up in Iowa—'' He broke off, and stood up. He tossed one last little rock into the pool and watched the ripples. "So—you goin' to come with me here again? Let me teach you to swim real good? Let it be our secret—just you and me?''

Hélène got to her feet. She put on her sandals slowly, then pulled her dress on over her shoulders. Billy pulled up the zipper for her. All the time she did that she was trying to think—knowing she ought to say no, and knowing she didn't want to. She felt queer inside, all excited and happy somehow, like she wanted to dance.

She looked up into Billy's eyes, which were as blue as a kingfisher's wing.

"All right, Billy," she said.

Billy leaned forward. He planted a dry quick kiss on her cheek.

"That's our secret too," he said. His face had gone beet-red again. "And don't tell no one I did it, see?''

"No, Billy."

"I don't want no one saying I'm stuck on some kid, all right? We're friends, okay? Now—let's go home.''

He helped her back up the steep gully and through the cottonwood out into the clearing. Then he stopped, and she saw his head go up, like an animal's, as he listened. She didn't know why at first, then she heard it too. A man's voice, muffled; then a woman's laugh; then a funny noise, a bit like a sigh, a bit like a groan. It was coming from the little wood shack, the summerhouse. She saw Billy glance at the shack, then back at her, then he grabbed her hand and started to run. He didn't stop running, not even in the bushes, not till they were under the wire and out on the edge of the fields again. Then he stopped. They were both panting.

"What was that, Billy, in the shack? What was it?''

"Some folks. Nothin' . . .''

"Could you see them? I couldn't see them. What were they doing?''

"Just a little. Lovemakin'—courtin'—you know.''

"I don't—I don't . . .'' He had moved off again, and she had to run to keep up with him. "Who was it? Could you see? Was it a colored lady?''

"No way. She was white." He stopped for a second, frowned, then shook his head. "None of our business, anyways. Come on home now—look." He gestured up to the sky. "It's going to rain real soon. Hurry."

But the rain held off. Billy got her back to the yard and left her there, and she sat outside in the heavy sun until her knickers and her hair were quite dry. That was a relief: no questions from Mother now, and if there were, she'd just say she got wet over by the pump, getting the water.

Her mother came into sight just as the first large drops of rain began to fall. Hélène saw her look up at the sky, and down at her dress, and then start to run. She ran awkwardly in her best high-heeled shoes, and her hair was mussed up from the wind, and she couldn't have touched up her face because her lipstick was all gone. She ran in through the little gate and scooped Hélène up, and ran into the trailer with her, laughing.

"Just in time! It's going to pour. And I'm late. . . ." She glanced at the clock and then at Hélène. "A little late. But I had such a nice time, and . . ." She came to a stop.

"Did you look after yourself, my darling? I missed you, you know, and now we can't go for our walk—not in this downpour. . . ." She hesitated, and turned round, and Hélène thought she had never seen her mother's eyes look so bright, or her face so pale.

Hélène sat down on one of the wooden chairs. She kept her back very straight.

"It doesn't matter about the walk," she said carefully. She paused. "Will you be going out to see your friend again?"

Her mother was pleating the silk of her dress between her fingers, her head bent, but now she looked up.

"Maybe. I might. Just sometimes—you know. Not often."

"Can I come too?"

"No, darling." She looked away. "Not for the moment. This is Mummy's friend, you see. But one day, maybe . . . We'll have to see. This is a special friend, you see. A sort of secret friend, can you understand that? You know how Mother hates gossip, and how she's told you about the people 'round here, the Tanners and Cassie Wyatt. . . ." She gave a sudden angry gesture with her fingers. "Talk, talk, talk, all day long. Nothing better to do. Well, I don't want them to talk about me, do I? So . . ." She paused, and then knelt down and put her arm around Hélène.

"So—don't mention this to anyone, will you, darling?—you know, if you come in to Cassie Wyatt's with me, the way you do sometimes. Or if anyone came to the trailer while I was away. Don't mention Mother has a friend, will you, Hélène? It'll be more fun that way. It can be our secret, do you see?"

Hélène looked at her steadily. Her mother's face was smiling, but her eyes were wide and anxious. Hélène knew, just the way she'd known with Billy, that her mother was leaving something out, that there was something she wasn't saying. She felt that tight hurt feeling around her heart again. When her mother bent to kiss her, she turned her face away, so the kiss just brushed her hair. "All right," she said at last. "May I have a cookie now? I'm hungry."

Her mother jumped to her feet quickly. Too quickly. And she didn't correct the word "cookie" to biscuit, either. Hélène couldn't understand it at all. It was like the times Mother lost her temper, and was sorry afterward, and tried to make amends.

She watched her mother coldly as she reached into the kitchen cupboard, and she was glad she'd gone to the swimming hole, glad she'd been with Billy Tanner, glad she hadn't told her mother.

Let her have her secrets, she thought. She didn't care. She hugged her arms around herself, and smiled. She had two secrets now. Going swimming with Billy, and the way Major Calvert shook her hand. That was a start.

It might be nice to have some more.

EDOUARD

LONDON—PARIS, 1941—1944

"Edouard. Edouard. I have the impression—misguided no doubt—that you are not concentrating. That you are in some secret world of your own, to which I, alas, do not have access."

Hugo Glendinning looked up suddenly from the book he had been reading aloud, and fixed Edouard with his blue eyes. Edouard jumped.

"Edouard." Hugo sighed. "Have you heard a word of this? One word?" He pushed the book away from him impatiently, and lit another cigarette. Edouard looked down at the account of the Napoleonic campaigns, and hastily tried to find the place where Hugo had left off. It could have been pages before. He had no idea.

"Edouard." Hugo was attempting patience. "Two months ago now, on June twenty-second to be precise, the armies of the Reich attacked Russia. It is possible, just possible, that this may be the turning point in this never-ending war. It thus seems a good moment, a reasonable moment, to examine the fate of Napoleon Bonaparte and his armies when he attempted a similar enterprise. We shall look—we are looking, or I was—at the historical accounts of that campaign. We may then go on and compare them with the fictional account in Tolstoy's *War and Peace*. This seems to me a timely, indeed imaginative choice. Certain of your own ancestors fought in those campaigns. Unless I am mistaken, the eighth Baron de Chavigny, who seems to have ingratiated himself with the upstart Corsican very successfully, was killed at the Battle of Borodino. You therefore have a personal reason for finding this subject as interesting and instructive as I do. You will shortly be celebrating your sixteenth birthday. It is not a particularly taxing subject for a young man of your age and ability. And yet I sense your interest is less than total. Would you like to tell me why?"

Edouard did not look up. Why? he wanted to say. Why, Hugo?

Because I don't give a toss for Napoleon or Russia or even the Germans very much. Tolstoy can go hang, and take his interminable novel with him. All I want is to be left in peace and allowed to think about Célestine—Célestine, the most beautiful, the most adorable, the most heavenly woman who ever lived. He knew perfectly well, of course, that he would say, could say, no such thing; though he had a nasty suspicion, once he looked up and saw Hugo's expression, that his tutor had a keen idea of what he thought. His voice had been sarcastic, but there was a slightly tolerant smile on Hugo's lips.

"Oh, I don't know. . . ." Edouard shut his book with a bang. "I just can't seem to concentrate, Hugo. Do we have to do history today? Couldn't we do something else?"

"Why not?" said the unpredictable Hugo, taking Edouard totally by surprise. "What do you propose instead? Geography? Mathematics?"

"Christ—no." Edouard groaned.

"You're very good at mathematics. Rather better than I. I find it quite difficult to keep up with you. But then, it's not my favorite subject, and never was. So. What else? Is there any subject of a remotely academic kind that you feel could engage your intelligence this morning?"

"Poetry." Edouard shrugged. "I wouldn't mind reading some poetry."

"Very well then. Poetry it shall be."

With every appearance of good humor Hugo turned to the high bookshelves of the schoolroom. He replaced the accounts of Napoleon's campaigns and drew out a slim volume.

"We shall continue with the metaphysicals. John Donne." He slapped the volume down on Edouard's desk. "I shall speak, you will follow, then we shall discuss. Page sixteen. *The Anniversarie.*"

Edouard dutifully opened the book; the words on the page danced before his eyes; then Hugo quietly began to speak, from memory, as he always did:

All Kings and all their favourites,
All glory of honours, beauties, wits,
The Sun itself, which makes times, as they pass,
Is elder by a year, now, than it was
When thou and I first one another saw:
All other things, to their destruction draw,
Only our love hath no decay,
This, no tomorrow hath, nor yesterday . . .

Edouard shut his eyes. He thought, for a second—*oh, God, he knows, somehow he knows*—because it was almost a year since he first went to Célestine's. Then that suspicion left him—what did he care what Hugo knew, or anyone, for that matter? He let the words flow into his mind. And he thought, *Yes! That's right. Donne is right. He says it more beautifully than I could ever say it, but that is what I feel. I love her. I've loved her from almost the first moment I saw her, and I shall always love her.* He bent over the book. *Only our love has no decay* . . . Wasn't that just what he had tried to say to Célestine, yesterday, when he lay in her arms? Oh, probably he had made a mess of it, and not said it very well, because it had mattered so much, and he had been longing to tell her for such a long time—but that was what he had *meant*. That he loved her now and would always love her. That he simply couldn't stop thinking about her. That she was in his thoughts every second he was apart from her. That during lessons, at night, alone in his room, her image tortured him. He dreamed feverishly of her lips, and her soft thighs, of her breasts and her kisses; her body seemed entwined in his thoughts as it was entwined in his when they made love. He wanted her all the time. It was driving him insane, he felt possessed with whispers and caresses, the scent of her skin, the feel of her hair in his hands, glancing touches, bodies slipping together like silk—ah, Célestine! And it was torturing him, the uncertainty, never knowing what she felt, whether she cared for him at all. . . .

Célestine, Célestine, dis-moi que tu m'aimes. . . .

Ne t'inquiéte pas, sois tranquille, bien sûr que, je t'aime, mon petit garçon, mon chéri. . . .

But she turned her face away when she said it. And yesterday, when he had made his great declaration, she had looked so sad. So terribly sad. She had taken his face between her hands and looked down into his eyes.

"Edouard, listen to me. It's not right for you to say such things. Even to think them. I know you mean them, I know you believe them, but it's not right. Be serious now, *hein?* Think. I am not young anymore, and you are young—very young. You have your whole life ahead of you, Edouard, and—listen to me—there will be lots of women for you. Lots. Oh, you don't believe me now, maybe, but when you are older, then you will see I was right. There will be lots of women—and then, one day, there will be a special woman, the woman you want to have your children, and you will know, when the moment comes. And then, Edouard, *then* you should say these things. Save them, *chéri,* never squander them. Save them for the woman you want to be your wife. . . ."

Edouard had wanted to cry with anger and frustration; he had wanted to cry out that he wanted her for his wife, Célestine, his goddess, his love—no one else. And damn what anyone else thought of them.

But Célestine had stopped him from saying a word. She put her hand over his lips and shook her head.

"No," she said. "No. I won't let you say these things. You are not even to think them. What we have here is simple and good and it is enough. If you say any more, I shall be angry."

Edouard clenched his fist under the desk. He would not be quiet! he resolved. He would not! The next time he saw Célestine, he would tell her, no matter how angry it made her.

Hugo's voice came to a halt. There was a silence. Then the door shut quietly, and both Hugo and Edouard looked up at once. Edouard's mother was standing there, quite still, in the doorway. As they looked up, she smiled.

"What a beautiful poem, Mr. Glendinning. I've never heard it before. Forgive me—but I couldn't bear to interrupt."

There was a second's pause, then Edouard quickly rose to his feet. Hugo also rose, but more slowly, staring at Louise across the room.

She looked very lovely, Edouard thought. She was wearing a pale pink dress of soft chiffon, with a loose jacket that seemed to drift on the air as she moved. Her slender neck was wound with pearls, and a faint flush of color stained her cheeks. Edouard was thrown by her appearance: she had never visited the schoolroom before. Hugo, too, appeared, for once, nonplussed. He stood behind his desk as if transfixed.

Louise lifted her lovely head, her eyes alight with mischief. She sniffed.

"Why, Mr. Glendinning, I believe you've been smoking! Do you always smoke during Edouard's tutorials?"

"I—well—yes. Sometimes." Hugo looked down at the brimming ashtray and blushed.

"Oh, well—I'm sure Edouard doesn't mind." Louise did not look at her son; she kept her eyes on Hugo. "You find it helps you concentrate, perhaps?"

"Yes," said Hugo, more strongly. "I do."

"I wonder . . ." Louise's brows drew together in a little frown. "Would it be very inconvenient, Mr. Glendinning, if you let Edouard go now?" She looked at the tiny de Chavigny watch on her wrist, gold, fastened in a way she had made fashionable, with a velvet ribbon. "I've been meaning to have a talk with you—ask you about Edouard's progress—so many things. I feel I should try to plan ahead for him, for his further education, you know, but everything is so uncertain—this terrible war! I should be so very grateful for your advice. . . ."

"But of course." Hugo made what seemed to Edouard a ridiculous attempt at a half bow. "I should be delighted. We had almost finished our work for today, in any case, and . . ."

"Oh, *good*." Louise gave him an enchanting smile, as if she had expected him to refuse her request, even though all three were well aware that that was an impossibility.

"Edouard, darling, run along now. I'm sure you have things to occupy you. . . ."

"I imagine so," Hugo put in dryly, and for a moment, as Edouard moved quickly to the door, their eyes met. Edouard saw the mockery and the understanding in Hugo's face. Then it was gone, and he simply stood there, looking donnish, elegantly rumpled, and totally trapped. Edouard shut the door.

He had observed this mesmeric effect his mother had on men since his earliest childhood. It amused him, yet it also slightly irritated him that Hugo should not be exempt. It did not occur to him for one moment that his mother's arrival in mid-tutorial had been other than an accident of whim. She had evinced no interest whatsoever in his academic progress before; she never asked about Hugo. Edouard had assumed that, in her usual way, she had more or less forgotten his existence.

Some forty minutes later, he discovered he must have been wrong. He returned to the schoolroom to find the copy of Donne's poems. He would copy the one Hugo had read and take it to Célestine. There was no sound from the room, and he opened the door quietly.

Hugo and his mother were locked in a fierce embrace. His mother had removed the filmy jacket. Hugo's head was buried against her breast. Her back was to the door. Neither was aware he saw them.

Edouard shut the door as silently as he had opened it, and returned to his room. He had, in some part of his mind, always suspected that his parents were not faithful to each other; he had half-known, but refused to contemplate, the fact that his mother took lovers.

But this. How long? he thought. How long?

There was a bottle of mineral water beside his bed, and a glass. He picked up the glass, and threw it with great savagery at the nearest mirror.

The next morning, he waited until they were midway through their tutorial and there was a pause in the lesson.

He picked up a pencil, and held it balanced between his fingers. "Tell me," he said as Hugo looked up. "Tell me. Are you fucking my mother?"

There was a brief silence. Edouard had chosen his term carefully, for maximum effect, but Hugo's face betrayed no reaction. He opened the book in front of him.

"Yes. As a matter of fact, I am."

"Has it been going on for a long time?"

"Since I was first employed. More or less." Hugo passed his hand over his brow. "Does it make any difference?"

"I just wondered. I thought I ought to know." Edouard paused; he felt astonishingly calm. "Are you in love with her?"

"No." Hugo hesitated. "Not in the sense you mean."

"But you can't stop?"

"No." Hugo looked away. "I should find that very difficult—to stop."

"Does it make you feel guilty? Knowing my father is in France. That he could be killed at any moment."

There was a long silence. Eventually Hugo closed the book on his desk.

"It makes me hate myself. If that's any consolation to you."

"But you still do it?"

"Yes. I still do it."

"I see." The pencil snapped between Edouard's fingers. Carefully he aligned the two halves on the desk. "Well. Thank you for answering my questions. You did say once that questions should always be answered. Never evaded. As I recall."

"Did I say that?" Hugo gave a slight smile. "Then I'm sure I was correct." He paused. "Would you like to continue with the lesson, or would you prefer me to leave?"

"I should like to continue with the lesson."

"Poetry?"

"Perhaps not."

"Very well." He glanced out the window, across the square. There were now two blackened gaps on the north side.

"Then let us turn to *War and Peace*, shall we?"

"I'd prefer mathematics."

"As you like." Hugo flicked open his textbook. He looked up. "You're quite right, of course," he said. "It is reassuring, isn't it, even when you are not gifted at a subject, for it to be so precise? No paradoxes. No mess. Everything exact. Not like literature at all."

"Or life," said Edouard, and they smiled at each other.

In the small study off his bedroom, Edouard had, when he first arrived in London, erected a series of maps and charts and calendars, on which he marked the progress of the war with pins and small flags. To begin with, he had noted advances and withdrawals, significant raids and battles, with great care. After his first meeting with Célestine, he had continued the practice, but less energetically. He also marked, on the same calendar, and using carefully coded references only he could understand, the glorious progress of his first affair. So, the references to Célestine—always in red—were from the first side by side with the references to war—always in blue. Unconsciously at first, then with a sense of amused pleasure in the parallel, he began to associate the fate of Célestine with the fate of his own country.

He hated to see the outline of France dominated by the German flag; he hated to think of Célestine imprisoned in that little flat in Maida Vale, dependent on the patronage of an elderly Englishman. He dreamed that one day soon they would both be free of tyranny. The armies of the Free French would one day liberate France; he himself would free Célestine. Once the war was over, he would take Célestine back to France, where she rightly belonged, and he would care for her. He would marry her one day, but the thought of confronting Papa with that proposition was chilling, and so he happily put it aside for the moment. Time enough to think of that; meanwhile, he dreamed of the apartment he would buy her—overlooking the Jardins du Luxembourg, he thought— and the long long afternoons they would spend there, and the presents, the wonderful presents that would be hers. This plan was now secret. He had not quite dared to tell Célestine of it, in case he made her angry, or sad. And he could not tell Jean-Paul, who was the only other person he might have taken into his confidence.

The problem was he could no longer talk to Jean-Paul, not with that easy and happy frankness he had always taken for granted. He could not quite have said why, except it was something to do with Célestine, but a certain shadow had come between himself and his brother over the past year. It was partly, Edouard thought, that Jean-Paul was under a strain. He worked hard, long hours at the Free French Headquarters; the moment he could get away, he drank and caroused with equally desperate energy. Nightly bombing raids and lack of sleep, living daily with the arbitrariness of injury or death—these affected everyone's nerves, Edouard's included, for he lived in fear that of all the bombs that fell on London, one might fall on that little flat in Maida Vale. So perhaps it was just that they were both suffering from tension; but if he was honest with himself, Edouard knew that was not the whole truth.

The truth was that Jean-Paul resented Edouard's seeing Célestine, and never lost an opportunity to tease his brother about it. At first, the teasing had been quite casual: coarsely put questions as to Edouard's progress, which Edouard had carefully avoided answering. Then Jean-Paul had started plying him with other addresses and telephone numbers, and had been noticeably irritated when he discovered Edouard had used none of them.

"You're not *still* seeing her?" he had said about two months after Edouard's first visit. "Little brother—I'm beginning to think you didn't listen to all those things I said. . . ."

So, to protect himself and Célestine, Edouard would lie. When the lies made him uneasy, he tried simply to be evasive. He didn't deny he was seeing Célestine, but he didn't volunteer the information either. It made no difference. Somehow, Jean-Paul *knew*. His latest tactic was to refer to Edouard's involvement in public, at every opportunity.

"My little brother's in love," he had said the previous night, when he and Edouard and Isobel were alone. "Head over heels. *Bouleversé*. What do you think, Isobel—sweet, isn't it?"

The emerald eyes flashed across the room at Edouard. Isobel smiled a slow secretive smile.

"Charming. Edouard has a heart."

"And with a tart too. The original tart with a heart of gold. Forty-six, forty-seven maybe. And very experienced . . . So they say."

Edouard clenched his fists; the desire to hit his brother was almost overwhelming. He moved quickly to the door, aware, even through his anger, that he was being used. Jean-Paul seemed to want to hurt him, but his remarks were also being directed at Isobel in some way. Hostility was sharp in the air. Isobel stood up.

"What do you understand of experience?" Her voice was icy.

"More than you, evidently." Jean-Paul shrugged.

"Fumblings in taxis. Gropings. Darling, you really are a terrible peasant sometimes. I think I'll go home."

She reached for her furs. Jean-Paul's face took on a mulish look. He sat down and put his feet up with conscious rudeness.

"As you wish. I have plans for this evening. They don't depend upon you."

Isobel swept out. On the stairs she clasped Edouard's arm.

"Darling Edouard. My car's outside, but I don't want to drive. Be an angel. Take me home, will you?"

The car was a Derby Bentley. They drove through the silence of the blacked-out streets, past shelters and roadblocks, past the great darkness of the park, to the gray bulk of Conway House at the foot of Park Lane. Isobel lit a cigarette; she said nothing until Edouard pulled up. Then she flicked the glowing stub of the cigarette carelessly out the window.

"When the war ends. If it ever ends—" She paused. "That's what we're waiting for. The end of the war. Then we'll get married." She glanced down at the emerald on her finger and twisted it. Then she looked up at Edouard over the collar of her furs and smiled.

"I won't sleep with him. That's the thing, you see. It wounds his vanity terribly. He says I'm cold. Heartless." She gave a low laugh. "I don't think I am. Do you, Edouard?"

Edouard had no chance to answer her. She leaned across and kissed him on the lips. A slow kiss. He smelled her expensive scent, tasted her lipstick, felt the furs brush his cheek. Then she drew back.

"Darling Edouard. I'm so glad you're in love. I hope you're terribly happy."

Edouard walked back. He skirted the closed park and walked north to Maida Vale. He stood in the street and stared up at the window of Célestine's bedroom. It was one of the nights when the gentleman from Hove visited London. According to Célestine, the old man wasn't capable of making love anymore. He liked to talk, very occasionally to kiss a little. It was nothing. It meant nothing. Edouard stared at the blacked-out window in an agony of doubt. Then he slowly walked home to Eaton Square. That had been a few weeks before. The incident had not been referred to again, and since then Edouard had avoided his brother. So he had not talked to him about Célestine, or Jean-Paul's engagement, or the infidelities of their mother.

Once he would have done so. Not now.

Sunday, December 7, 1941, was the day the course of the war changed decisively. It was the day before Edouard's sixteenth birthday. He knew that on the actual day of his *anniversaire* there would be no escape from his family. There would be a luncheon at Eaton Square, and in the evening Jean-Paul and some of his cronies were taking him out. Jean-Paul had planned the expedition, with many accompanying winks and nudges, for months. Edouard knew he could not refuse.

So he intended to spend the day before his birthday with Célestine: he would celebrate it then, in the way he wanted, with the one person in London who mattered to him.

He wanted to take Célestine out to dinner, but she firmly refused. They might be seen; it would not be prudent; no, no. So, in the end, they agreed to spend the afternoon together. They would not stay in her flat, Edouard insisted; they would go out; they would go to Hampstead Heath. To Edouard, who dreamed of walking with Célestine through the parks of Paris, or—better still—through the chestnut woods and water meadows of his father's estates in the Loire, this expedition, long planned, took on the prospect of an idyll. When he woke that morning and saw the sun shone, he was not surprised. On such a day, what else could it do?

He met Célestine at her flat, and in her small sitting room she pirouetted for him shyly.

"You like it? You like my new costume? It took so many coupons—say you like it, Edouard! I chose it for you."

Edouard looked at her. It was one of the very few occasions on which he had seen Célestine dressed, and with a lurchingly painful sense of guilt and betrayal, he knew he was disappointed. Célestine's body was made for undress; in lingerie, half-revealed, half-hidden with wisps of silk and ribbons and lace, she looked entrancing. Dressed, her mysteries were dulled.

The new suit was bright blue—too blue, and of a cheap shiny utility material. It was a little too tight over her full breasts and wonderful hips; the seams of her black market stockings were not straight; the blouse was fussy and ill cut, and her hat, perched jauntily on the pile of reddish-gold curls, was too young for her. In the same second Edouard felt disappointment—and self-hatred for his own disloyalty. Quickly he kissed her, and at the touch of her lips he felt instantly reassured.

"Célestine—my darling. It's lovely. You are lovely. . . ."

He shut his eyes and buried his face against her neck. When he took her back to Paris it would be different. It was just that she was poor, that was all, which made his disloyalty all the worse. When she was in France with him, she would dress like a queen. He would take her to the collections, teach her; she would quickly learn.

On the heath it was windy, and Edouard's spirits soared. It was like being in the country—almost like being in the country. There was a slight mist, and from here the desolation wrought by the bombing was almost invisible; they climbed the hill beyond the lakes and stood looking out over the city; they could see through the mist the clusters of barrage balloons and the dome of St. Paul's. Edouard wanted to run and jump and shout and make the rooks rise from the bare branches, but Célestine's shoes had heels that sank into the mud, and so they had to keep to the paths. By the time they reached the top of the slope, she was out of breath.

"*Mon dieu*." She pressed her little hand to her heart. "Edouard, do you always walk so fast?"

"Never. Only today. Because today I'm so happy." He put his arms around her and kissed her. Célestine smiled.

"Then in future I shall walk with you only when you are sad . . . Edouard. Stop that. Someone may see us. . . ."

"I don't care. Let them. I want the world to see us, so there." He kissed her again.

"*Sois tranquille. Tu es méchant, tu sais?*" She reproved him, but she smiled. Eventually Edouard took off his cashmere overcoat and persuaded her to sit on it with him on the grass. They sat quietly, looking out over London. After a little while Célestine opened her handbag and took out a small parcel. It was tied with pink ribbon.

"For you." She pressed it into his hands, blushing. "For your birthday. I hope you like it. It was very difficult—I wanted to find you something you would like, and . . . well, it is the color of your eyes. Not quite perhaps, but nearly."

Edouard unwrapped the parcel. Inside was a tie of very bright blue imitation silk. Quickly he pressed her to him.

"Darling—it's beautiful. How clever you are. You shouldn't have . . . look. I shall put it on at once."

He quickly pulled off the hand-stitched foulard silk bought by the dozen from Jermyn Street, and stuffed it into his pocket.

Célestine helped him fasten the new tie around his neck. Then she looked at it doubtfully; against the pale gray of his Prince of Wales check suit, the blue looked brighter than ever.

"Oh, Edouard. I'm not sure. In the shop the color looked very pretty. But now . . ."

"It's beautiful. Whenever I wear it I shall think of you. Thank you, Célestine."

Célestine smiled. She rested her head happily against his shoulder.

"It's nice here," she said at last. "I'm glad we came, Edouard."

"We'll come here again. Lots of times." He pressed her hand tight. "And to other places too. Oh, Célestine, when the war ends . . . think, just think, of all the places I can take you then. . . ."

He paused, wondering if now was the moment, wondering whether he dared tell her about Paris, the little flat, the furniture he planned to buy. But Célestine sat up.

"Don't. Please, Edouard, don't. Don't talk about the future, not now. I just want to think about today, and being here, and feeling so happy. . . ."

"Why? Why, Célestine?" He turned to her impulsively. "Can't you see I want to talk about the future, and you always stop me? It makes me happy to think ahead, to plan, to . . ."

"To dream." Very slowly she turned to him, and to his dismay he saw the contentment had left her face, and her eyes were full of tears.

"Célestine—don't. Please don't. I can't bear to see you cry—my darling, don't." He tried to kiss the tears away, tried to kiss her lips, but Célestine stopped him gently.

"Dearest Edouard." Her voice was very soft. "You know it can't go on. Not like this. It just can't. If you think about it, you'll know I am right."

Edouard stared at her, then quickly bent and buried his face against her breasts.

"Don't say that. Don't. I love you. You know I love you. If you left me, if it ended, I'd die. . . ."

His voice shook with passion, and Célestine sighed. She put her arms around him and held him tight. She thought that she loved him, yes, she, a woman of her experience, forty-seven years old, loved a boy of sixteen, and she had known it for months, months. Last love and first love: both equally painful. She dried her eyes. It was important, she thought, that Edouard never know.

"People don't die of love." She lifted his face to hers and smiled, her voice growing brisker. "You think so now—but they don't. Old age, sickness, rifle shots—but not broken hearts. You'll see one day. Look! I shall make you a prediction!" Her voice became almost gay. "One day—some years from now maybe—you'll have to think quite hard to remember my name. And then it will come to you, and you'll say, 'Ah, yes, Célestine, that was it. I was fond of her once. I wonder what's become of her now?' And by the time you do that . . ." Her lips curved. "By that time I shall be a very old lady, *extremely* respectable—a little ill-tempered perhaps, especially first thing in the morning. With gray hair. And some memories—memories I shall discuss with no one, naturally, of when I was perhaps a little less respectable, a little less straight-laced." She stood up, took his hand, and drew him to his feet. Edouard looked at her sulkily, and Célestine laughed and tucked his arm through hers.

"Now. Stop looking so sad. I am happy again—you see? This is our special afternoon, and already you are cross with me. Come, Edouard. I have had enough of your fresh air. Take me home. . . ."

In her flat, in bed, Edouard made love to her feverishly, as if he could force the memory of her words away with every thrust into her flesh. When they both lay back, exhausted, he turned to her fiercely. He looked down into her flushed face; he looked at the red-gold hair tumbled across the pillow; he thought of his mother in Hugo Glendinning's arms. He gripped Célestine's shoulders very tightly.

"Tell me. *Tell* me, Célestine. Tell me there is no one else."

Célestine looked up into his blazing eyes, into that fierce young face. The visits from other gentlemen she had terminated some months previously; her protector did not count. It was not a state of affairs she could allow to continue; she knew that in her heart.

She pressed her lips gently against his throat. "There is no one else now."

"For how long? How long, Célestine?"

"I don't know. *Chéri*, I don't know. . . ."

He started to pull away from her angrily, and she clasped his wrist. "Edouard, please, don't be angry. Don't you see? I don't want to lie to you."

He got up from the bed and stood for a moment looking down at her, his brows drawn together in an angry scowl. "I wish you would then, at least sometimes. It might be easier." Then he pulled on his clothes and flung out of the flat. It was their first serious quarrel.

Edouard caught a cab home, slammed the front door savagely before the startled Parsons could reach it, and stormed up the stairs to the drawing room. He flung open the door and found a crowd of people: his mother; Lady Isobel; Hugo; the French ambassador and his wife; a group of French officers; Jean-Paul. Jean-Paul advanced on him, his face flushed, a champagne bottle held aloft.

"He's back just in time. Little brother, come and join us. We're celebrating . . . you haven't heard the news? The Japanese attacked Pearl Harbor this morning. They bombed the American fleet. . . ."

Edouard stared at him in confusion. Jean-Paul put his arm around his shoulders and laughed.

"Don't you understand, little brother? Don't you see? It's terrible news, of course, but America will come in now. It's only a matter of time! We shall win the war after all. . . ."

Across the room, the French ambassador, in white tie and tails, rose with a flourish. "Madame . . ." He bowed to Louise. "With your permission? I shall propose a toast." He lifted his glass, and everyone in the room stood up. "The Americans. Our new allies!"

"The Americans . . ."

"The Yanks. God bless them." Isobel drained her glass.

"Such a relief, after all this time. Really, I feel quite proud. . . ." Louise smiled at the English banker who stood by her side. She rested one hand lightly and absentmindedly on his sleeve. Hugo Glendinning, watching this exchange, turned away to the window.

Jean-Paul ruffled Edouard's hair affectionately. "Little brother . . ." He grinned. "Where the devil did you get that appalling tie?"

T he following evening, Jean-Paul set about celebrating Edouard's birthday in the manner he considered appropriate. He organized a motley party of British and French officers, prevailed upon Isobel to rally a group of her prettier debutante friends, and booked seats for the new and undemanding hit at His Majesty's Theatre—*Lady Behave.*

"If there's a bloody raid, we'll just damn well ignore it," he announced to Edouard before he left. "On to the Café Royal for supper afterward, and then—on to a few other places I have in mind. Minus the ladies."

He gestured around the group of men who were knocking back whiskies in the Eaton Square drawing room. "Have to get a few in before the women join us. You know everyone? Pierre. François. Binky. Sandy. Chog."

Edouard looked around the group of young men. He was the only one in evening dress, the only one not in uniform. Jean-Paul moved away to supervise Parsons' dispensing of the drinks, which he considered slow, and the man addressed as Chog came across, gazed at Edouard fixedly, then lifted his glass.

"Tally-ho. Down the hatch. Your birthday, Jean says. Jolly good show."

He swallowed the remaining whisky in one gulp, went red in the face, and moved off smartly in the direction of Parsons. It was at that point that the women came in. Edouard looked from them to the assembled men with a sinking heart.

As if to spite Jean-Paul, Isobel, who had many decorative friends, had, this evening, selected the plainest. They stood bunched in a group by the door, living evidence that all Louise's remarks about the dowdiness of London society women had merit. Five plump girls in unflattering frocks; one tall thin one, with a narrow clever face, her angular figure encased in a hideous brocade. Isobel, who was looking radiant and rebellious, had clearly chosen them with great care. They looked as dismayed by the men as the men clearly were by them: the two groups met with hostile stares. Jean-Paul flushed with anger.

"Darling—I'll do the introductions, leave it to me." Isobel sailed forward with a dazzling smile. "Harriet, this is Binky. Binky, this is Anne, and Charlotte, and Elizabeth—goodness, this is complicated, I'm sure you all know one another already. Chog, how simply *lovely* to see you. It's been too long. . . ."

She held out her hand to Chog, alias Lord Vvyan Knollys, but Chog to his friends since preparatory school. Her smile grew even more radiant, and Edouard suppressed a groan. Chog was one of Isobel's pet hates; she could discourse on his failings—and often did—for hours.

Across the room, Jean-Paul, his face set, was bowing over the hand of the tall thin girl, Lady Anne Kneale; both he and Edouard had met her before, for she was one of Isobel's oldest friends. Jean-Paul disliked her, if that were possible, almost as much as Isobel disliked Chog. He was now making a steely and determined effort not to let that dislike show. Edouard turned away, suppressing a smile. The atmosphere, he felt, did not augur well for the evening.

By the time they all reached the theater in a fleet of cars and taxis, Isobel's face had set in that fixed and glittering smile, and Edouard knew it meant trouble. He suspected Jean-Paul did, too, for he was more than usually assertive. They arrived late, and the show had already started. Jean-Paul interpreted this as an especial rudeness on the part of the management.

"I've seen this show four times," he announced loudly as they all gathered in the foyer. "They know me backstage. You'd think they'd have the courtesy to hold the curtain for five minutes, damn it. . . ."

"Twenty minutes, darling." Isobel put her arm through Edouard's. "And I can't see that it matters in the least. It's the silliest show in London, isn't it, Anne?"

"It has quite a lot of competition, but actually, you might be right. . . ."

Anne Kneale drawled the words in a way clearly designed to provoke. She and Isobel exchanged glances. Jean-Paul flushed.

"Well, I like it. Edouard will enjoy it. Now, let's get a move on, shall we?"

"I wonder why Jean likes it so much?" Isobel's cheek brushed Edouard's shoulder; the emerald eyes flashed up at him mockingly. "I can't imagine, can you, Anne? Can you, little brother?"

During the first half of the show the men in their party were loudly responsive and the women muted. Isobel hardly bothered to look at the stage. She sat next to Edouard, and fluttered her program, and stared around the house, and all the time she rested her thigh against his. At one point there were nudgings and muffled whisperings from the men as one young actress made her first entrance, and Jean-Paul lifted his opera glasses and focused them on the stage ostentatiously. Chog laughed, and Isobel put her hand with its emerald ring on Edouard's thigh. She turned her head.

"Do you know, Edouard, I really don't think I can bear this," she said in a low distinct voice.

To his own surprise Edouard took her hand in his and pressed it. He held it until the intermission came, and they all withdrew to the bar for champagne.

"Jolly little piece, what?" Chog propped himself against the bar and smiled at Edouard with the kindliness derived from considerable quantities of alcohol. "Not too demanding, you know? I like that. Nothing too serious. Serious theater makes my balls ache."

François and Pierre started a complicated argument in French as to whether or not such a play could be performed in Paris, and, if so, whether or not it might appeal to a *boulevardier* audience. Isobel set down her glass of champagne untasted, and disappeared to the ladies' room. After some hesitation her friends accompanied her. The minute the women had gone, the men relaxed.

"You saw her?" Jean-Paul turned to the man called Sandy, who was wearing the uniform of the Brigade of Guards. "The little one in the last scene—the one with the lovely eyes? She's new. She wasn't in it last time I came."

"I told you. I know her. Not worth the bother." Sandy sighed.

"How do you know?"

"Tried it. No dice. Rather a prissy girl. Gets on her high horse at the drop of a hat. Frightfully boring."

"You'd like to bet on that?"

Jean-Paul's face had its mulish look. Sandy shrugged.

"My dear fellow. By all means try. Maybe your Gallic charm will win the day. It has been known."

"Awfully thin." Chog outlined a more impressive female form with his hands. "I wouldn't bother, old chap."

"I like her eyes." Jean-Paul was not to be swayed. "She has beautiful eyes. Violet eyes."

"She's called Violet." Sandy yawned. "Not enormously original, is it?"

"Violet eyes make my balls ache," said Chog in the manner of one settling the matter.

"Send your card 'round," said the one called Binky helpfully. "Never know your luck."

"My friend . . ." Jean-Paul put his arm around him. "That is exactly, but exactly, what I plan to do."

He drew his card out of his uniform pocket and was still in the process of writing something on it when François gave a cough, and Pierre nudged him. Isobel had returned.

She stood looking at them all for a moment, her friends hovering in the background. Then she gave them her most ravishing smile.

"The most extraordinary thing has happened," she said brightly. "Do you know, I've developed an *allergy* to this play? I really don't think I could possibly sit through the second half. In fact, by the oddest coincidence, we all feel the same way." She gestured to the group of young women behind her. Anne Kneale laughed, and Isobel glanced at her reprovingly.

"So, we've all decided to leave you, and just *jump* in the cars and go home. No! Don't say a single word. This is Edouard's birthday, and I wouldn't have that spoiled for anything. So you just go back in and forget us altogether. Darling Edouard . . ." She stood on tiptoe and kissed his cheek. "Happy Birthday. I hope you have a lovely evening. . . ."

She turned, disappeared through the throng at the bar, and was gone. There was a moment's silence. The men looked at one another. Edouard looked at the floor.

"Tant pis." Jean-Paul, unruffled, finished writing on his card. He

beckoned to the barman; the card and a five-pound note exchanged hands. Jean-Paul turned around. He smiled.

"And now, now, *mes amis*, we start to enjoy ourselves. Yes?"

Jean-Paul was an habitué of numerous fashionable restaurants and clubs in the West End of London. Since he was who he was, and had a reputation as a big spender and lavish tipper, he was welcomed fulsomely in spite of the fact that his parties often became a little wild. The places he favored all had a clientele that was chic, rich, and slightly *louche*. A mixture of officers, London society, black marketeers, actresses, and chorus girls—that was the sort of companionship Jean-Paul favored. He haunted the Caprice, the Ivy, and the Café Royal, and, if the evening went on, and promised well, the notorious Four Hundred. He was an easily satisfied customer. A good table, assiduous service, plenty to drink, beautiful women within view, tinkling piano music, if possible a small dance floor: this was enough; Jean-Paul was content. He liked the Café Royal, he said, because he always had a good time there. With its elaborate mirrors and scurrying waiters, it reminded him of the Dôme or the Coupole—it reminded him of Paris.

Tonight, as his party were obsequiously ushered to their table, he was in high good humor. He had won the first part, at least, of his bet. Trooping along with him were five fellow officers, Edouard, and two women. The prettier, who had three lines in *Lady Behave*, must be Violet, Edouard thought, for she had violet eyes. The plainer seemed to be there to give Violet moral support. She was, she confided to Edouard, in the theatrical profession herself, but just beginning. In *Lady Behave* she was a walking understudy. The war had hit the theatrical profession very badly, she told him, very badly indeed. The best you could hope for, really, was a tour entertaining troops.

Jean-Paul was noisily determined that Edouard was going to have a good time. He insisted Edouard sit between the two young women, Violet on his left and Irene—a name he pronounced in the French manner, very gallantly—on Edouard's right. Jean-Paul himself sat opposite them, and the other young men arranged themselves as they pleased.

Irene giggled. "Oh, doesn't it sound lovely the way he says it, Vi? Much more romantic. There's a Frenchman for you."

"How do you say it?" Edouard said gallantly, his spirits sinking.

"I. Re. Ne." She giggled again. "Horrible, isn't it? I never liked it myself, but there you are, you're stuck with the name God gave you, aren't you? Some's lucky, some's not. Take Violet now. I think that's a lovely name, don't you? Especially when you've got eyes to match. I said to the other girls, I said—you shouldn't call her Vi, you really shouldn't. It's a crying shame. But what can you do? Vi she was, and Vi she stuck. . . ."

Edouard turned to look at Violet curiously. She had said nothing since she had joined them at the stage door, and she was now sitting silently. One thin hand was clutching the stem of her champagne glass; the other was crumbling a bread roll. She was very pretty, he thought, though not the type Jean-Paul usually favored. She was terribly thin, with small delicate bones, wrists he could easily have circled with finger and thumb. She had a tiny heart-shaped face, softly waved brown hair. She was pretty enough, but not startlingly so, until she looked up and you saw the eyes that had attracted Jean-Paul's notice. They were huge, thickly fringed with dark lashes, and the color of pansies; they looked slightly dreamy, and also slightly afraid. Edouard looked at the eyes, the thin wrists, the slightly shabby frock of pale mauve silk, the wilting rose she had pinned to her neckline, and he felt pity rise. She looked a born victim; he hoped desperately that Jean-Paul would leave her alone.

"I say, Miss Fortescue. Violet, isn't it? May I call you Violet?" On her other side Chog leaned forward. "That was a frightfully good show, you know. We all thought so. Frightfully good."

"Did you think so?" The violet eyes lifted slowly to Chog's face. Her voice was soft, well-educated, quite different from Irene's raucous tones.

"I'll say. And you, too, of course. Frightfully good." Chog's fund of compliments exhausted, he cast around wildly for another topic of conversation. "Must be jolly good fun, being an actress. Frightfully hard. Never know how you manage it. Learning all those lines."

"Three lines isn't terribly taxing."

"What? Oh, gosh. Yes. Well. Was it only three? Thought it was far more than that."

"How kind. I must have said them especially well."

Edouard glanced at her with renewed interest. There was not a hint of a smile; she appeared completely serious. Chog, unsure if he was being teased, hesitated, and then laughed. The champagne arrived, Irene claimed Edouard's attention once more, and he heard no more of the fragments of conversation from his right.

Francois, Pierre, and Jean-Paul began a heated conversation about the progress of the war: exactly when the Americans could be expected to come in; whether the Boches would ever take Moscow; whether Rommel would take Tobruk; whether any of them would see France free again. Edouard joined in the conversation briefly, when Irene went off to dance with Binky, but no one was listening to anything he said, so after a while he gave up. He leaned back in his chair and drank champagne, although he knew he had already had more than enough, and wished he were old enough to do something useful, wished the evening would end, wished he hadn't quarreled with Célestine. The quarrel had left him miserable all day; now the drink, and the stuffy air, the cigar smoke, the piano music, the flushed faces and loud voices, all made him long to be back with her, to lie in her arms, to be at peace in the quiet of her room.

"Is he really the Baron de Chavigny?" Suddenly the girl called Violet turned to him, her question taking him by surprise. She nodded across the table at Jean-Paul, who was predicting the Boches would be driven out of France by the end of '42. "Your friend. Is he?"

"He's my brother." Edouard returned to the room with difficulty. He was aware that his own voice was slightly slurred. "And no, he's not the Baron de Chavigny. Not yet. He will be. Our father is—at present."

Violet's delicate plucked brows drew together in a little frown. "Oh, I see. I just wondered. He wrote that on his card, you see. The one he sent round. And—well, I wondered if it was a joke. Men do play jokes like that sometimes, you know."

"They do?"

"Oh, yes!" She clasped her thin hands together. "If they want to persuade you to come out—that sort of thing. I usually say no, you see. But tonight I felt a little low. Tired. And I was intrigued. So I said yes."

"Women are always intrigued by my brother."

He was aware the moment the words were out that it was hardly the most polite thing to say. A slight flush rose over her cheekbones, but she seemed not greatly to mind.

"Are you giving me a warning?"

She arched her brows as she said it, and widened her eyes, her manner coquettish, but slightly amateurishly so. Edouard felt impatient. He had been wrong earlier; she was just like all the other women Jean-Paul picked up and discarded—silly, he thought.

"Who knows?" He shrugged. "Do you need one?"

Her blush deepened then, so he felt boorish and instantly repenant.

"Oh, I don't know. I haven't been in London long. I was brought up in Devon."

Edouard knew that was a cue of some kind, that he ought to ask her about Devon or something, because she seemed quite eager he should do so. But he had never been there, knew nothing about it, and—just then—his mind felt as if it couldn't grapple with the problem of that county at all. There was an awkward silence, at the end of which the girl called Violet nervously lifted her champagne glass.

"Oh, well," she said. "It's your birthday, isn't it? Happy Birthday."

It was the last thing she said to him. Shortly afterward, Jean-Paul showed signs of impatience, and kept looking at his watch. Pierre had become lachrymose; the fate of *la belle France* was too much for him.

Jean-Paul ushered them all out into a pitch-black Piccadilly Circus, and announced the night was still young.

There were some dissenters. Pierre and François announced they were leaving. A brother officer had given them a bottle of Marc, and they intended to return home and drink it and continue their argument. Binky had to report for a briefing next morning, and thought he'd better call it a day. Edouard privately felt that the night was not young but hideously old, and the sooner it was terminated the better. But he could see the scowl of disappointment beginning on Jean-Paul's face, and so he kept silent. Sandy announced that he was game; he felt like a bit of a spree. And at that, Jean-Paul revived.

Three men, one boy, and two women piled into Chog's Daimler, and set about the business of escorting the ladies home. This took longer than anyone had anticipated, because the ladies lived in digs in Islington, which Chog had never heard of and insisted was near Basingstoke. They drove around in the blackout for what seemed to Edouard hours, with Chog announcing at intervals that they must almost be there now, and if the M.P.'s got him this time, he was done for. Sandy had thoughtfully brought along a bottle of brandy; the women sat on the men's laps, and everyone except Violet and Edouard sang, untunefully, but with gusto.

"You silly boys! You're mad—you are." Irene gave an ear-splitting screech. "We're there! I told you so. Look, up there's the Angel. Go right, and right again . . . that's it! Anyone for a nightcap?"

"Irene—it's late. I don't think that would be a good idea."

The girl called Violet had scrambled out of the car first; Irene fell out after her, with many gigglings and pinchings and shrieks. "Someone pinched my bum! They did! I swear I felt a pinch, Vi, right there. Oh, you're naughty boys, you are. I told you, Vi. I said, never trust a Frenchman. . . ."

"Mesdames." Jean-Paul had also extricated himself from the car. He bowed over their hands with a gallantry Edouard knew was designed to get rid of them quickly with a minimum of fuss. He held on to Violet's hand appreciably longer than he did Irene's.

"I was honored you could join us. . . . À votre service. . . . Au revoir. . . ."

He escorted them to their door, saw them inside, then weaved his way back to the Daimler and heaved himself inside.

"Christ, Jean, you lay it on thick. . . ." Sandy yawned as Chog shifted the gears with a crunch, and the car swerved around in a circle, narrowly missing a lamppost. "I told you she was a prissy piece. Why bother?"

"Why not?" Jean shrugged; he winked at Edouard. "I like her eyes. Anyway, who cares? We've got rid of them now. Let's go on to the Four Hundred. . . ."

They went on to the Four Hundred, but Jean-Paul grew restive and said he found it boring. Then they went to a place called Vic's, where a young man wearing makeup sat at the piano and played songs. They had a brandy there, then Sandy said he couldn't stand being in the same room with such frightful nancy-boys. They barreled out onto the sidewalk, and Edouard looked at the street, which was rising and falling in the most peculiar way, like waves. He suggested they might go home.

"Go home? Go home?" Chog appeared incensed at this suggestion. He staggered about the sidewalk and made punching motions in the air. "This is London! This is wartime! We can't go home! Who suggested that? Go on—which one of you fellows said it? Say it again, damn it, and I'll knock him down. . . ."

"Nobody said it. Nobody said a thing. . . ." Sandy made pacifying noises. He paused. "The thing is. The problem is. Where can we go? I mean—where can a fellow have a good time? That's what we want. That's what we deserve, eh? A proper English good time."

Chog loomed up out of the darkness, his round face pale and incandescent with inspiration. He waved his arms like a windmill. "I know! Of course. I know! We'll go to Pauline's. Pauline's is just the place."

Jean-Paul and Sandy exchanged glances.

"Pauline's? Can we get in, do you think, Chog?"

"Get in? Get in? Of course we can get in." Chog moved purposefully back to the Daimler, which was parked with one wheel on the sidewalk. "You're with me," he said grandly. "There isn't a place in London won't welcome me. And my friends. My special friends."

"Are you sure it's all right?" Sandy hung back. He nudged Jean-Paul. "What about Edouard?"

"Edouard's all right. Edouard's my friend." Chog put a plump arm around Edouard's shoulder. He lurched. " 'S Edouard's birthday, isn't it? He's a man now. You are a man, aren't you, Edouard? You want to come to Pauline's, don't you?"

"Of course he does." Jean-Paul decided the matter. He opened the Daimler's doors and pushed Edouard inside. Edouard slumped onto the leather seat. Jean-Paul clambered in beside him and patted his thigh. "Not a word to Maman about this, eh? She might think you were a bit young. Women never understand these things. . . ."

"Women? Who mentioned women?" Chog was in the driver's seat attempting to locate the steering wheel. "I'll sing you a song about women. This song is a wonderful song, and it says it all. I shall sing it to you now."

And he did.

Like a bird scenting carrion, Pauline Simonescu had arrived in London in 1939 with the advent of war. No one knew her exact origins, but rumors proliferated: she was Romanian; she had been brought up in Paris; she had been the mistress of King Carol of Romania; she had Gypsy blood, or Jewish, or Arab; she had previously run the most luxurious brothel in Paris, but, like the Baron de Chavigny, had foreseen the arrival of the Germans; she had left just in time. She had money, but her Mayfair establishment was also bankrolled: by a famous and distinguished city financier; by the American wife of an English peer with whom she had a lesbian alliance; by a German steel magnate attempting to corrupt the morale of the Allied officer classes. She was discreet; she was a spy; she took drugs; she never touched alcohol. Her world was the twilit zone where the pleasures money and connections bought shaded from excess into vice; no one liked her, but many found her useful. As far as Chog was concerned, she was a madam, and her premises were just off Berkeley Square.

But where exactly? They drove three times around the square, squinting through the darkness at the side streets; then the Daimler ran out of petrol.

"Not to worry," Chog cried cheerfully as they all piled out onto the sidewalk. "Easier on foot. My nose will lead me to it."

He turned right into a dark street of expensive houses, felt the stubs of eighteenth-century railings that had gone to be melted down for bomb casings, and began to count. Three houses along, he stopped, just as the air-raid siren began to wail and searchlights suddenly knifed the sky.

"*Merde. . . .*"

"It's all right, for God's sake. We're *there.* I told you my nose would find it. . . ." He lifted his nose into the air, sniffed loudly, and began to yowl like a dog. Sandy and Jean-Paul doubled up with laughter.

"I can smell it. I can smell it. I can smell— Ah, good evening." The door opened; very dim light spilled out over the impressive portico steps. A very large black man in a white suit with a gold bracelet stood in the doorway.

Chog looked at him, and he looked at Chog.

"Lord Vvyan Knollys." He waved at Sandy. "The Earl of Newhaven. Two very old friends of mine who are . . . who are—French."

The black man did not move.

"Oh, for God's sake. I was here last Tuesday." He began fumbling for his wallet.

Jean-Paul stepped forward superbly.

"The Baron de Chavigny presents his compliments to Madame Simonescu."

A folded twenty-pound note exchanged hands with scarcely a rustle. The black man stepped back, the four entered, and the door shut.

"Jean-Paul . . ."

"Edouard. Shut up."

They were ushered out of the narrow passageway into a magnificent and brilliantly lit hall. The floor was marble; a huge crystal chandelier scintillated, throwing diamond light on the wide, branched staircase, on two superb Fragonards and one Titian. Flesh tints eddied before Edouard's eyes. At the foot of the staircase a tiny woman held out her hand with the air of a grand duchess.

Pauline Simonescu was perhaps five feet tall, certainly no more. She made stature seem unimportant. Jet black hair was combed straight back from a handsome, slightly vulpine face dominated by the strength of the nose and the glitter of the black eyes. She was dressed in a full-length scarlet dress with a neckline that made no attempt to disguise angular masculine shoulders. From her ears, pendant rubies the size of pigeon eggs hung like gouts of blood. The hand she held out to them was weighted with a matching ring. Edouard, as he bent over it, recognized de Chavigny workmanship.

She greeted each of them in turn, pausing a little to look more closely at Jean-Paul.

"Monsieur le Baron." A fractional pause. "But of course. I am acquainted with your father. He is well, I hope?"

Her voice was deep, heavily accented. Jean-Paul, for once discomfitted, stammered some reply to which she scarcely listened. She twisted her head a little to one side, and Edouard was reminded of a bird. There was the sound of a distant explosion, well muffled.

"The bombs." She shrugged the wide shoulders. "In a moment we shall hear the lorries. I dislike them more. They make me think of tumbrels—but of course, that is only fancy. Come with me. What will you drink? What will you smoke? We have some fine cognac. There is a case left of the 'thirty-seven Krug, which is excellent. Perhaps you prefer malt whisky?"

She was leading them toward a magnificent drawing room. Through its half-open doors, Edouard could hear the sounds of conversation and laughter, the clink of glasses, the rustle of dresses. He glimpsed young men in uniform, older men in evening dress, beautiful women, none of them old. He heard the click of a roulette wheel; an Aubusson carpet rippled; the tall carved mahogany doors bent on their hinges. He leaned up against the wall. Sandy and Chog were having a whispered conversation. Pauline Simonescu turned.

"But of course, you are correct. Tonight is the special night—you are fortunate. Carlotta is here." She paused. "Also Sylvie—you remember her, perhaps, Lord Vvyan? And Leila, our little Egyptian. Mary—

she came to me from Ireland, a true Celt, such beautiful red hair. Christine. Pamela. Patricia. Joanne—you like Americans? I am looking ahead, you see, to when the brave American boys join forces with the Allies. Juliet. Adeline. Beatrice. But no. Tonight you would like to see Carlotta. You have taste. Carlotta is not for every day, but then, this is not every day. It is a mad time, this war, a hectic time for the nerves of you brave young men. And Carlotta is so soothing."

She stepped to one side.

"Downstairs. Pascal will show you the way. The Krug, I think. And perhaps some coffee for our young friend? He looks a little tired, and it would be such a pity if he couldn't . . ."

"Participate?" Sandy put in with a chuckle of laughter. Madame Simonescu's black eyes flashed.

"Exactly so." She lifted her hand; the ruby struck the light.

"Pascal."

The black man materialized. He bowed.

"*Suivez-moi.*"

Once it had been a cellar, Edouard thought, or perhaps a dark half-basement, the domain of servants. But there was no trace of that now, except that the room was only dimly lit by the flicker of candles, and there were no windows. The floor was thickly carpeted; the walls and ceiling were tented in dark red velvet, on which a series of pictures in severe black frames hung at intervals. Set in a U-shape around a square of bare polished wood were three couches also upholstered in red velvet. At their corners were low tables, on one of which stood two silver ice buckets containing the bottles of Krug, and on the other a silver tray with black coffee. The four men sat down. Pascal opened the champagne, poured it, poured the coffee, and left. The door closed softly behind him. Music began to play. In the distance Edouard heard the soft explosions of bombs. He drank the coffee.

"We're in luck. Just us."

"We must be in that old bitch's good books for some reason. Maybe she likes you, Jean-Paul. Or perhaps Edouard struck a chord. . . ."

"Have you seen her before, this Carlotta?"

"No. But I've heard."

"Is it true that she . . . ?"

"And more. So I've heard."

"One after another?"

"She likes it like that."

"And the others watch, while she . . . ?"

"But of course."

"Jesus. Who goes first?"

"Over the top, men! Who got us in here, I'd like to know?"

"We'll all pull together . . ."

"No, we bloody well won't. Me first. Then Jean. Then you."

"What about Edouard?"

"Edouard after Jean."

"Sod off. Why should I have to wait?"

"Patience, *mes amis.* We shall conduct ourselves like gentlemen. . . ."

"Ballocks."

"Each in turn. And then . . ."

"Then what, for God's sake?"

"Then the men among us give the lady a repeat performance. . . ."

"Roll me *over . . .*"

"In the *clover . . .*"

"Roll me *over . . .*"

"And do it again!"

They finished in unison. Hearty male laughter was followed by silence.

"God. This place is a bit creepy. Don't you think, chaps? Reminds me of chapel at school."

"Holy."

"As the actress said to the bishop."

"That wasn't what the actress said to the bishop."

"What say we open the other bottle of champers? Jean-Paul?"

A cork popped softly.

"Down the hatch!"

"Dutch courage . . ."

Edouard had fallen asleep. He opened his eyes and found his head was much clearer. For a moment he didn't know where he was, then he saw the candles and the red velvet, and the pictures. The pictures. His eyes focused on them in disbelief. Hands and apertures; great breasts and thighs; open mouths; spread buttocks; women open and softly pink like ripe fruit; men proudly staggering under the weight of gigantic phalluses. For a moment the room seemed to him as red as hell. The candles flared; shadows flickered on the red walls, and words and images swooped through his mind like a dark tide: the confessional box; Father Clément; his beautiful Célestine.

Célestine. He stood up.

"Jean-Paul. I'm not staying."

One of them pushed him, so he fell back onto the couch. Jean-Paul's arm came around his shoulders like a vise.

"Not now. Look."

Carlotta—it had to be she—and two other women had come into the room.

She remained in front of the door; they moved to the wooden square between the couches. One girl was white, the other black; the white girl carried a silk cushion. She set it on the floor, then lowered herself gracefully and leaned back on it. The black girl knelt beside her. Both were wearing thin loose dresses of transparent gauze. They looked at each other. Carlotta looked at the four men.

She was tall, and exceptionally beautiful. Long jet black hair tumbled around her face and over the red silk shawl she wore draped across her breasts and shoulders. Her head was tilted back haughtily, the eyes were dark and arrogant, the painted carmine mouth wide and full. She wore a tightly waisted full-skirted dress of black silk that reached to the floor, and she stood as a flamenco dancer stands before the dance begins: poised, and still.

Jean-Paul sighed; she began to sing. The two girls on the floor lifted their arms and embraced each other.

Carlotta's low throaty contralto voice was without sweetness, but had a gutter edge to it that gave it power. She sang first in Spanish, a rasping lingering night-club song, and Edouard understood not one word of it. Then she switched to German, a song of wicked allure, shot through with Berlin melancholy. Cheap music, and Edouard was mesmerized; he felt as if his limbs had turned to stone.

On the floor in front of them, the two women were now naked. Their slender full-breasted bodies were oiled, and their pubic hair had been shaved, which Edouard thought ugly. He found their graceful pantomime unarousing.

Slowly, to the rhythms of the music, they began to move; three beats, four of the song. Their limbs entwined and relaxed; their hands moved and then were still. Dark skin and pale: Edouard looked up, Carlotta's eyes met his, he felt his penis leap and harden. Carlotta took off her shawl.

Under it, her breasts were bare, the nipples rouged, exposed above the black silk like those of a Cretan priestess. Very slowly she lifted her hands as she sang, and caressed the dark aureole. Edouard saw her nipples stiffen; beside him Jean-Paul groaned. The song came to an end, but the hypnotic beat of the music continued.

Carlotta's feet were bare. Silently she came across the room to the four men. Edouard felt her silk skirt brush his trousers. She paused, looking from face to face. None of them spoke; they just stared at her. Then Chog made an attempt; he leaned forward, grasping for the black silk skirt. "Me first . . ." he said thickly.

Carlotta flicked the skirt away from his hand. She looked down at him contemptuously, then, as if making an elaborate curtsy, she knelt, the black skirt belling out in a circle, and parted his thighs. Behind her, the two women lay entwined, writhed, but no one was watching them.

Carlotta leaned forward. Her bare uplifted breasts rested against the thick wool of Chog's Guards' trousers. His mouth was parted slackly; he was sweating, his breath coming fast. He reached up a small pink hand to the luscious breasts, and Carlotta knocked it aside. He leaned back with a sigh, and her jeweled fingers stroked upward from knee to groin, touched the swollen bulge beneath the thick wool, once, twice, very lightly. Then, button by button, she undid his fly, and drew out a thick stubby penis. She held it a moment in her hands appraisingly, bent forward so her dark nipples brushed fleetingly over the taut stretched skin; Chog's body shuddered convulsively. She parted his thighs farther, and reached in to cup his balls in her hands.

Edouard tried to wrench his eyes away, but he couldn't. His penis was rock hard, pressing to be released, pulsing with the need to touch, to come. Beside him Jean-Paul shifted on the couch, muttered something thickly under his breath, reached down, and touched the bulge of his own erection.

Carlotta had eased Chog's trousers lower. He lay sprawled back, legs apart, the angry red shaft jutting up between Carlotta's heavy breasts. Slowly she took the knob into her red mouth, and began to suck.

Her prowess was legendary; it was clear she took pride in her skill. Her hands and her lips never stopped moving, and the rhythms she used constantly changed. Her magnificent breasts heaved; the expression of contempt in her eyes never lessened. She bent her throat, holding back her own hair so the other men should have a clearer view, and, using only her lips, she took the whole of the swollen member into her mouth. On the red sofa Chog's hands jerked and clenched; he bent his head so he could see as well as feel what she was doing to him. Both Jean-Paul and Sandy were touching themselves now, holding their crotches as if terrified that merely watching would bring them to climax.

Chog began to grunt; he heaved his plump body up to thrust into her mouth. And he began to swear, his voice just audible over the beat of the music.

"Yes. Oh yes. You bitch. You fucking bitch. More. Yes." His voice was hoarse. His hands clenched. "Whore. Fucking whore. Cunt."

A spasm shook his body. Carlotta quickly drew back, lips parted. The other men saw the first spurts of semen travel from tip to mouth—it was one of the things they had paid to see. Then her mouth closed over the throbbing shaft once more, until the frantic pumping stopped. Then she lifted her head, and swallowed. Jean-Paul's hands were already fumbling with his fly as she turned to him. Carlotta smiled for the first time, widely, tauntingly, removed Jean-Paul's fingers from his fly, and parted his trousers quickly, expertly. Edouard looked down. His brother's penis was large, longer than Chog's and thicker, engorged with blood; Carlotta looked down at it for a second as if it were a particular prize. She darted out her tongue and touched the tiny hole at its tip. Jean-Paul shuddered. He reached his hands down frantically, trying to grasp her breasts.

"Vite, chérie, vite. . . ."

Edouard looked away. The spell had been unbroken up until the moment Chog began to swear. Then, abruptly, it had shattered. His erection was gone; he felt violently sick. Carlotta's seeking mouth, the slumped form of Chog, his uniform still in obscene disarray, the clingings and twinings of the girls on the floor, the panting of his brother next to him, his glazed eyes—all this was suddenly so obscene to him, so repellent, he knew he could not stay in that room one second longer.

As Carlotta took the full length of Jean-Paul's penis into her mouth, Edouard stood up and pushed past her blindly. No one tried to stop him, they were all too far gone for that. They hardly even looked up. He pushed out through the door, stopped on the stairs, heard, less muffled this time, the crash and thunder of another explosion, thought of Célestine, ran up the last flight into the marbled hall.

The doors to the drawing room were shut now. The hall was empty, except for Pauline Simonescu. She was standing by the entrance door, head tilted, listening. She showed no surprise when Edouard burst from the stairwell; it was as if she had been expecting him.

He walked quickly to the door, and she stopped him, resting one hand on his arm.

"Wait. The all clear hasn't sounded yet. It will go in a minute."

Edouard almost brushed her aside, then he hesitated. A peculiar energy, like an electric current, seemed to flow from her thin hand, from the clawlike fingers. He looked down at her uncertainly; then he heard the wail of the siren start up. "There. It is over. You see?" She unfastened the door and held it back just enough for Edouard to slip through.

"Au revoir, Monsieur le Baron. . . ." Her voice was soft and its intonation mocking.

Edouard looked at her in confusion, paused, then ran down the steps and into the dark.

On the night of December 5, Xavier de Chavigny was sitting in a basement room beneath a small café in the working-class suburb of La Villette. Five men and one woman sat with him. In the center of the room was a small billiard table, though no one was playing billiards; if necessary, however, the game could apparently be resumed at any instant.

The café bore the name Unic, which amused the Baron, for there was nothing unique about it; it resembled exactly the other small restaurants in this area which had somehow managed to stay open during the Occupation. It served cheap meals to French workers employed by the Germans on the nearby railroad, and it smelled of boiled cabbage.

Like the other men in the room, the Baron wore the anonymous blue overalls, boots, and béret of the *ouvrier*; like them, he smoked hand-rolled cigarettes made of pungent cheap tobacco, making each one last as long as possible, smoking it right down to the tip of the butt. He had come here this evening, as he always did, on a bicycle, and he would return the same way, changing his clothes where he left his vehicle, in a small shed in the warren of streets and alleyways of Les Halles. He was certain that the care he had taken had been repaid. He had not been followed. He had never been followed.

And yet—there was something wrong.

He looked carefully around the faces in the room. Three of the men were his age, two younger; they were all workers, originally of peasant stock; their faces were coarse, their accents and language coarser, and the Baron regarded them as his brothers. He was grateful to them for accepting him; he admired their innate restraint, their dour refusal at first to do more than simply work with him. He had had to prove himself to earn their friendship, and now that he knew it was won, he valued it more highly than any other friendship he had ever had. All the men in the room, and the one woman, were under sentence of death. Each put his life in the hands of the others; if any turned informer, they were all dead. That knowledge bound them, the Baron knew—but not because of fear, because of trust.

It was due to these men and their work together over the past one and a half years that the Baron knew he had changed forever. He was harder, more ruthless—they had taught him to kill. He was also more angry, and angry with himself.

When he looked back now on his past life, on the ease and luxury he had never questioned, he saw a stranger. How had it been possible for him to live like that, to think like that, to have been so blind? To have worried about his wife's neurotic whims, to have placated her with gifts, one of which cost more than men like this earned in a lifetime of labor? To have fretted over the design of pieces of rock, to have enjoyed the intricacies of the stock market, to have worried whether a horse won a race. If he survived this war, the Baron sometimes thought he would abandon all that. He had no clear idea of what his new life would be; he just knew that it would be, had to be, different.

Meanwhile, though he kept up the outward appearance of his former life, retained his house at St. Cloud, retained his servants, continued to frequent his workshops and the de Chavigny showrooms, on the Rue du Faubourg St. Honoré, in private he lived very differently. No black market goods. Bad food—the same kind of food most Parisians had to eat. The men here were not aware of that, but to the Baron it was important. It was his private gesture of brotherhood.

The mood of the meeting had been good, more optimistic than it had been for months. Paris was full of rumors, and the chief rumor now was that the Boches were taking a hammering on the Eastern Front, that they were being driven back, that the troops of the Third Reich would not take Moscow after all. Two fellow members of his cadre were Communists; this rumor especially pleased them. They were equally pleased by the other rumor: that America must enter the war soon.

Meanwhile there was the day-to-day reality of their work, the small gestures that could do no more than nibble away at the hold of the occupying forces, but which meant so much to the cadre: the blowing-up of a section of railroad; the bombing of a small power plant; the passing of information across France through the network, across the Channel.

At best they halted trains for a couple of days, threw German communications into chaos for a few hours in one small region, killed a few, a very few, men. It was better than nothing—better than sitting scratching your ass while the jackboots marched over you, as Jacques said; but it was not enough. Every man in the room, the Baron included, hungered for something more, for something big, something that would really bust a hole in the smooth, relentlessly efficient German war machine. And some months ago, thanks to Jacques, thanks to Jacques's young mistress, they had found it.

Efficiency could be a weakness as well as a strength. Regimens, routines, punctuality, plans made well in advance, confirmed by a superb bureaucratic machine, and then rigorously adhered to—these, the tenets of the German High Command, made for precision and also, sometimes, predictability. That efficiency, the Baron hoped, was not only the High Command's great asset, but also its Achilles heel.

Once a month, always on the second Thursday, at precisely eleven A.M. a briefing was held at Paris Headquarters. It was attended by the overall commander of the German forces in France; his senior officers and aides; those men directly responsible to the commander-in chief of the German Army; and those on the French staff of the chief of OKW, overall head of all three branches of the armed forces of the Third Reich.

The senior officers concerned were taken at high speed, with armed escort, in three Mercedes. They were collected from their different departments between ten-fifteen and ten forty-five A.M., and then driven to their headquarters by a variety of routes. The Baron smiled to himself. Not an infinite variety. Six in total. That was the weakness. That and the fact that one of the drivers was susceptible to young women, and Bernadette, Jacques's mistress, was a very attractive young woman.

The six routes were, quite simply, rotated. This coming Thursday, unless there was a change in plan, for which the cadre had contingency arrangements, the route would be the same route taken six months ago. Route "C": south down the Boulevard Haussmann; left into the Boulevard Malesherbes; left again into the narrower Rue Surène, and—*there was the weakness!* Jacques had cried, stabbing the map with one nicotine-stained finger—left into the very narrow Rue d'Aguesseau. There the cavalcade slowed, had to slow, and there, *there* was the place for the bomb.

There was a small *épicerie* on the corner. For the last six months the van that made its weekly deliveries had called on a Thursday. After making his delivery, the driver took a *café noir* in a room behind the shop with its owner, Monsieur Planchon. The van remained outside for forty-five minutes, minimum. If it went up at precisely the right second, it would take the first Mercedes, and its occupants with it. The most senior officers always traveled in the first car.

Planchon would be interrogated, there was no question of that. He was prepared for it, and he knew nothing. He would tell the interrogators the truth: that the van driver was a new man that day, a man he had never met before, that he had disappeared into thin air in the general fracas after the bomb went off. The van driver would not be found. The Baron profoundly hoped he would not be found, because the van driver was sitting across the table from him now, and the Baron had no illusions: if the Gestapo got him, he would talk, sooner or later. And then they were all dead.

The Baron felt infinitely weary. They had gone over this again and again, for over six months; every person in the room knew the details by heart, but tonight, as they went over them again, the atmosphere was different: it was charged with excitement, the smoky air vibrated with it. The Baron looked at the faces bent over the map: Jacques, with his broken nose, the physique of a former fighter, tracing the streets on the map for the hundredth time; Leon, lighting another cigarette; Henri; Didier; young Gérard, Jacques's cousin, who was only nineteen, and the most eager of the men; and Jeannette.

The Baron's eyes lingered on her longer than the others. She was twenty-one, small and dark, with a thin nervous face that lit up when she smiled, which she did rarely. A woman, in fact, without nerves, a woman of courage, fueled by hate. Her younger sister had been raped by a group of drunken German soldiers in the week Paris fell; her hatred of the occupying forces was personal and intense. Too intense, probably, the Baron thought—it was better to be without emotion as far as possible—but this woman was able to curb the passion of her hatred when she needed. She had been with them for over a year now, broken in gradually, slowly given work of greater responsibility, just as they all had been. In another world, another life, the Baron knew he would have been attracted to her. Now he accepted her, as the others did, as a comrade, a member of a team. He looked away.

He didn't want her to die. He didn't want any of them to die. They had been over these plans again and again, and they seemed perfect. He could not fault them. None of them could fault them.

And yet every instinct in his body told him there was something wrong.

Why? Because it was too perfect? Was that it?

He shut his eyes tiredly. He was under strain, as they all were; he was physically exhausted, that was all. If he had had one good reason for his unease, one item of justification, he would have called this off. But he had none.

He leaned back in his chair, betraying nothing of what he felt. They would find out, he thought. Tomorrow morning, at eleven.

When he reached the house at St. Cloud later that night, he sat in his room for a long while, smoking and thinking. He knew he would not sleep. And he knew quite well when it was that this feeling had started, when he had felt the first sensation of alarm.

Two days ago. He shut his eyes, drew on the cheap cigarette, stubbed it out in the Baccarat ashtray.

The afternoon General Ludvig von Schmidt visited the de Chavigny showrooms in the Rue du Faubourg St. Honoré.

The general was thirty-five, tall, fair, blue-eyed, the perfect Aryan. He came of an old German military family, and, like his father and grandfather before him, had risen rapidly through the officer ranks. He had attended Heidelberg University; he was an educated, intelligent, cultured man, who had reached senior rank before Hitler became Reichsführer, and who had joined the Nazi party unusually late in life. In another existence, the Baron thought, he might have liked this man. He liked him now, if he was honest.

The general was interested in jewelry and knowledgeable about the history of its design. He had good and educated taste for music and for painting, and occasionally, when he came to the showrooms, he and the Baron would talk. First, it had been in the showroom itself. Then, one day, the Baron had invited him for a drink in the beautiful apartment he kept on the upper floors. It was something he often did with high-ranking German officers. Tiny items imparted over a cognac had often proved useful to him, and to his cadre, in the past.

He obtained no information from General von Schmidt, and something prevented the Baron from seeking it. The two men would sit side by side and discuss Matisse, or Mozart, the works of Flaubert, the designs of Fabergé.

The Baron sensed that General von Schmidt loathed the Nazis; he sensed his disillusion with the conduct of the war and its spiraling follies, sensed his disgust with the anti-Semitic policies that, for the first time in France, began operating in 1941. He sensed all this, though none of it was ever discussed, and occasionally he pitied this proud, reticent man. If he had been a professional soldier in 1939, he thought, if he had been German, not French, what would he have done? Might he not have ended up like General von Schmidt, the unwilling but efficient servant of a régime he realized too late he detested?

Two days ago, in that elegant salon, General von Schmidt had set down his glass of cognac. There had been a restlessness, a tension in him that the Baron had not seen before. He had risen and turned away to the windows.

"You must miss your family. Your wife. Your sons—very much."

"Naturally."

"They left Paris at the right time." He paused. Still he did not turn around. "Did it never occur to you to go with them?"

The Baron tensed. "No," he answered carefully. "No. It would not have been possible. I had too many responsibilities here."

"But of course. I understand that perfectly." Again he paused. Then he turned around and looked the Baron in the eye. "Have you thought of it since? Recently, for instance?"

The Baron wondered if he was being warned. He stood up with a smile. "It would be a little difficult now, don't you think? There is the Channel to consider. I was never a very good swimmer."

General von Schmidt smiled politely at the little joke. "Of course. It was just a thought."

"Another cognac?"

"Thank you. It is excellent as always, but no, I must leave you."

At the door, and this was not their custom, they shook hands.

"Monsieur." A half bow. The heels clicked together with military precision. "I am pleased to have known you."

"And I you, General." The Baron paused. "You are leaving Paris?"

"It is possible my regiment may be seconded elsewhere."

"Of course."

The Baron thought of the Eastern Front. He hesitated, then said the thing he had never expected to say to a German. *"Au revoir, mon ami."*

General von Schmidt did not smile.

"Good-bye, my friend," he said. Then quickly left the room.

Two days ago. It could mean nothing. It could mean the end. The Baron lit another cigarette. Sometimes he felt so tired now that he was beyond caring what happened to him. But he still cared about the others.

He stood up and put a record, much played, on the gramophone. *The Magic Flute.*

If he could not sleep, he could at least think. He could go over the plans again. And again. And listen to Mozart, which always reminded him that it was good to be alive.

On the morning of December 6, the motorcade containing the senior officers of the German High Command, France, drove down the Boulevard Haussmann at 10:50 A.M. It turned left into the Boulevard Malesherbes at 10:56. Left into the Rue Surène at 10:58. Exactly on schedule.

From the window of the small *atelier* down the street, the Baron and Jacques watched. Jacques leaned forward.

"Come on, you bastards, *come on. . . .*"

At 10:59 the motorcade stopped, some one hundred and fifty yards short of the corner of the Rue d'Aguesseau. There was silence. Then the bomb went off. It blew in the front of the *épicerie;* it obliterated the delivery van; not so much as the tires of the first Mercedes were touched.

The minute the sound of the explosion died away, there was the sound of running feet, the shouts of German commands. The Baron and Jacques were already on the stairs. They separated without a word being spoken. Jacques was sighted by a German foot patrol ten minutes later as he wove his way through the nearby back streets. He died in the fire of their Schermeisser machine guns as he reached for his pistol.

The Baron was arrested at St. Cloud an hour later. He was interrogated and tortured by the Gestapo for longer than the others—for no reason he could understand, since they knew everything already. Jeannette died under interrogation; her questioners had particularly imaginative techniques when dealing with women. Leon cut his own throat in his cell, and the officer responsible for his safety was demoted. Henri, Didier, and Gérard were hanged. Jacques's mistress, Bernadette, who had betrayed them, died slowly at the hands of the Resistance a few months later. And the Baron, as befitted his rank, was executed by a German firing squad on the night of his younger son's birthday.

E douard was told of his father's death when, in the first light of day, he finally reached the house in Eaton Square after the long walk from Madame Simonescu's. Hugo Glendinning broke the news to him. It had come through that night to the information service at Free French Headquarters by radio transmitter. General de Gaulle's senior aide had brought the news to Louise personally at eleven P.M., when she returned from a party at the house of an English banker. The general had sent his personal condolences for an old friend and a brave Frenchman. *La lutte continue*, the message had ended.

It was some hours later that Jean-Paul learned that his father was dead, and that, on the two occasions the previous evening when he had claimed to be the Baron de Chavigny, he had spoken the exact truth. He discovered it when, after searching across London with Hugo, Edouard finally found him.

He was not at Madame Simonescu's. He was not at any one of the succession of clubs and drinking holes he had visited that night. He was not at Conway House, and Isobel had not seen him. He was not at headquarters. He was asleep in the bedroom of a small flat in Maida Vale, and he received the news from Edouard in Célestine Bianchon's sitting room.

Célestine looked at the two brothers, one very pale and one very flushed, and said nothing. She knew it was the end. She knew he would never come back to her, her beautiful Edouard. She could see it in the way he stood, proud, upright, never looking at her once. She could see it in his eyes, whose anger frightened her, and whose pain cut her to the heart.

She would have liked to explain, she thought sadly. Not now, naturally, but later. She would have liked to tell him the truth: that she loved him, and that because she loved him, she knew a sudden end was easier for her than a slow one. Jean-Paul, arriving on her doorstep very drunk at three in the morning, ready to make love after a brief sleep, had provided the means.

That Jean-Paul hated her for her hold on his brother she had quickly sensed as she lay under him; that this quick violent thrusting into her body was his way of breaking that hold she also knew. She made no attempt to stop him, or to assist him, and it didn't take long. Six or seven angry jabs, and he came, swearing. Her last love affair was over. *Cochon*, Célestine thought as Jean-Paul rolled off her, grunting. She was just getting up from the bed when the doorbell rang.

Now she looked at Edouard, and she knew she had done the right thing. He was free of her, and even the pain of this was better than the inevitable alternative. To have watched Edouard tire of her, fall out of love, grow up; to have seen him guiltily trying to hide what he felt—no, she thought, she would not have wanted that.

She looked at him, and felt one last temptation, one last hope. She could tell him; she could explain. And if she did . . . She pushed the temptation aside. It would still be over; she knew it as she looked at his face. She had been part of his youth, part of that short sweet time between boyhood and manhood, and that time was over. A man, not a boy, turned back to look at her as his brother left the room. His features were stiff with repressed emotion.

"I apologize for asking this. But does my brother owe you anything?"

"No," she answered quietly.

"I owe you—a great deal." His control almost broke.

"Nothing, Edouard."

He inclined his head, looked at her once more, and left the room.

A month later, Célestine received a short formal note from him, asking her to contact him if she were ever in need. She kept the note but did not answer it.

A month after that, her elderly English protector suffered a stroke and, after a brief illness, died. Some weeks later, when Célestine was daily expecting notice to leave her flat, she received a small parcel from solicitors acting on behalf of Edouard de Chavigny. Inside it was the deed to the house in Maida Vale, made out in her name, and details of an annuity to be paid to her monthly for the duration of her life. She thought of sending both back, of writing to Edouard; but she knew he meant well, and besides, she was nearly forty-eight and more than ever a realist.

So she acknowledged the gifts in a letter of formal thanks to the solicitors. It was eventually passed on to Edouard; Célestine did not hear from him again.

After a few months, cutting her losses and closing her heart, she took a new lover, and began once more to entertain the brave young men from Free French Headquarters. Occasionally, they gossiped idly about their friends, and the name de Chavigny would be mentioned.

So she learned that the Baronne de Chavigny had been quick to find consolation for the loss of her husband in the arms of an English banker; that—to no one's surprise—the engagement of Jean-Paul to Lady Isobel Herbert was broken off at Lady Isobel's request a respectful two months after the death of his father. And she heard that the younger brother, Edouard, was proving a firebrand, cutting a swath through the women of London society. He and his brother were very close, her informants said with a wink. They were notorious, they hunted in pairs.

Célestine was surprised to hear this. She felt a certain sad pride that her lessons in lovemaking were being put to good use, but the closeness of the two brothers disturbed her slightly. She knew how much Edouard admired his brother, and sometimes, thinking of that, she worried for him. Such fierce loyalty! He would be disillusioned, she thought, before long.

W hat Célestine could not know was the degree to which grief first drew the two brothers together. They had both loved their father; he had seemed to them indestructible. In the horror and confusion and pain of the days immediately succeeding the news of his death, days in which Louise took to her bed and refused to see anyone, the two turned to each other, and all the barriers between them fell away.

Jean-Paul found it impossible to contain his grief; he wept openly; he turned to Edouard, who could not weep, and sought consolation from him like a bewildered child.

Night after night, they stayed up late, talking and talking, going over the past. Jean-Paul drank a good deal on these occasions—it helped him, he said—and as it grew late, so he grew lachrymose and self-pitying.

"I feel such *guilt*," he said one night, clutching Edouard's arm. "Using his title—that very night. How could I have done that? God, I hate myself, Edouard."

"It made no difference. Not then. And anyway—as it happened— you had the right."

"I know. I *know*. But it doesn't make me feel any better. And to have gone to that bitch Simonescu's—to have been there, when . . . God in heaven, I can't bear to think of it." He bent his flushed face, and wiped his eyes, and gripped Edouard's arm more tightly.

"I hate myself, Edouard—yes, I do, I mean it. I'm ashamed of the way I've behaved. Drinking—women—I'm going to give it all up, you know. Reform. I feel I owe it to Papa—I have to do it for him. I don't know why I do it in any case—women, what do they mean to me? Nothing. You can't talk to them—I'd rather talk to a man any day. You can't trust them. Look at Célestine—I feel terrible about that, Edouard, but perhaps it's done some good. If it's opened your eyes, it will have been worth it. She didn't hesitate, you know. Straight into bed. Couldn't wait to get it. They're all the same, women. Bitches. Liars. Every one of them. . . ."

"Jean-Paul . . ."

"Say you'll never let that happen again, Edouard. Tell me. Never let a woman come between us again. . . ." He lifted his face to Edouard's, his eyes watering. "They do that, you know. They try it every time. And I can't stand it. I need you, little brother. I need you now, more than ever. This terrible grief, this pain—thinking about all the responsibilities Papa has left me. It makes me afraid, Edouard. I can't cope with it, not without you. . . ."

He bent his head and sobbed. Edouard knew that the tears came from brandy as well as from grief, but he was touched. He thought of Célestine, and felt only a cold anger; she had betrayed him, she had perhaps lied to him all along. What did such a woman matter compared to the love he felt for his brother?

"Jean-Paul." He put his arm around his brother's shaking shoulders, and attempted to calm him. "Don't say those things. Don't think them. I'm your brother. We have to think about the future now. We have to think about Papa, and all the things he worked for. When the war is over, we can go back to France. We can begin again. Papa laid the foundations. We can build on them, you and I. It's what he would have wanted."

"I suppose so." Jean-Paul wiped his tears away with the back of his hand. He straightened up and blew his nose.

"Think of it, Jean-Paul. All those companies. They're our legacy. We can build them up—it will be a memorial to Papa."

"Yes. Yes." Jean-Paul sounded irritable. "But I can't talk about that now. I can't think about it. I'm a soldier—I have other responsibilities. There's a war on. Edouard—be a little realistic. . . ."

Edouard sighed. Each time they returned to this topic, Jean-Paul's reaction was the same. So, come to that, was the response of Louise. When, one afternoon, thinking it might console her to speak of Xavier and his work, Edouard asked her what she thought his father would have wanted to happen in the future, Louise turned pettishly away.

"With his companies? Edouard, how should I know? What extraordinary questions you do ask."

"I just thought . . ."

"Well, don't. You *will* meddle. Jean-Paul is the Baron, not you. When the war is over, he will take care of these things. There's no need for you to concern yourself at all. And it's most unfeeling of you to ask me at such a time! Really, you can be so insensitive. How can you discuss his business affairs at a time like this?"

"His *work*, Maman." Edouard's mouth set obstinately. "It mattered to him very much. I want to feel we're carrying it on—that we're doing what he would have wished. . . ."

"What you want to feel is entirely irrelevant. And you have no right to bother me at such a time. I never concerned myself with Xavi's business affairs. In fact, I always thought that he paid far too much attention to them himself. It was an eccentricity—all his friends said so. He could perfectly well have devoted himself to his estates, just as they did. This obsession with finance, with commerce—I never understood it at all. . . ."

She gave a little haughty toss of the head; Edouard felt suddenly very angry. He stood up.

"Really, Maman?" He looked at her coldly. "You surprise me. After all, you grew up with commerce, I thought. It was steel—not estates—that provided your father with a fortune."

Louise's lovely face flushed crimson. All references to the source of her own family's money had long been forbidden.

"You may leave me," Louise said. "And send Jean-Paul up," she added as he reached the door.

It was from the day of that conversation that Edouard found his attitude to his mother changing. Before, she had dazzled and perplexed him; her coldness to him, which he had never understood, had made him all the more eager to win her affection. But now, and he knew this, he began to draw back a little, and to judge her. The grief he felt for his father sharpened his vision; he looked at his mother in a new cooler dispassionate way; he no longer made so many excuses for her. When, some months after his father's death, he realized that she had begun a new affair, something in his heart closed to her forever.

That, he knew, he would never forgive.

He began to feel as if, with Xavier's death, all the certainties in his world had disappeared, and he lived in a state of flux and change, in which there were no longer any sureties. His loyalties, to his mother and his mistress, had been misplaced; the patterns he had seen in the world were all broken.

"That happens," Hugo said to him kindly, when Edouard tried to explain his feelings. "It passes. Don't clutch at beliefs. Wait, and let them come to you."

"Wait?" Edouard looked up. "For what? What do you believe in, Hugo?"

"I?" Hugo smiled dryly. "Well now. I believe in good claret. And Sobranie cigarettes . . ."

"Don't joke. The English always joke."

"Very well." Hugo smiled at his earnestness. "I believe in some of the things we have read together. I believe in hard work." He hesitated. "I believe in certain people. Sometimes."

"Not God?"

"Not really, I'm afraid, no."

"Politics?"

"Ah, politics. Well, I believe in certain creeds—as you may have gathered. I don't have a great deal of faith that they will substantially alter the world. I did once perhaps. Less now."

"What about love?" Edouard fixed him with his gaze, and Hugo, after a pause, let his eyes drop.

"Edouard." He sighed. "We should have read less poetry."

"But you said you believed in the things we read. How can you believe the words if you don't believe the things the words are about?"

"I believe in them while I read."

"And afterward?"

"Ah, afterward—I waver."

Edouard pushed his books across his desk. "It's not a great deal," he said at last in a bleak voice, and Hugo, paying him the compliment he felt was his due, spoke seriously.

"No, it isn't."

"But don't you *mind*, Hugo?" He turned to him passionately. "Don't you want things to believe in? Don't you want to feel a sense of purpose?"

"Certainly not. A terrible heresy. A delusion and a snare. Much better see the world as it is." Hugo turned away. "Very little endures. Much of life is random. We invent ideals and beliefs to give shape to the shapeless. Love. Honor. Faith. Truth. They're *words*, Edouard. . . ."

"I don't think you really believe that."

Edouard lifted his face stubbornly, and Hugo turned back. He looked at the boy's face and gave a little shrug.

"Maybe not. You could be right." He paused. "If I sound bitter and cynical, and I probably do, there are reasons for it just now."

"My mother?"

"Partly that. Yes. I told you I should find it difficult to stop. However, that's something we ought not to discuss. Shall we return to the Virgil now? If you intend to sit Oxford entrance, you have a considerable amount of work to do."

"Hugo . . ."

"What?"

"I like you."

"Excellent. I find that reassuring. Now, turn to page fourteen."

Edouard bent his head; he applied his mind to the words, and he found they calmed him.

Afterward, he was grateful to Hugo. Dryness and irony helped; they gave him a new detachment, a different perspective on life. Time passed; he discovered that he was able to compartmentalize his feelings and his thoughts in a way he had not done before.

It was, after all, perfectly possible to contain the grief he felt for his father. He locked it away in the part of his mind that made plans for the future; it did not need, anymore, to affect his behavior every moment of each day. He could grieve and get drunk with Jean-Paul, he discovered; he could grieve, and still work with Hugo.

When, one night, after weeks of melancholy abstinence, Jean-Paul turned to him with a groan and said, "The hell with it, little brother. What we need is a woman," he made another discovery. He could make love, too, perfectly pleasurably, without feeling any emotion at all, without any desire ever to see the woman again. When he confided this discovery to Jean-Paul, his brother seemed pleased.

"You're growing up. You're a man, at last," he said, as if welcoming him, belatedly, to the club.

At the time, this remark pleased Edouard. He was then much swayed by Jean-Paul, and was later to see that it was at this point in their lives that they were closest to each other. Jean-Paul absorbed a love and a loyalty which had once been directed to his father, to his mother, and to Célestine: for a while, Edouard's devotion to him was unquestioning. Sometimes, it was true, he had doubts. He would remember Jean-Paul's promises of reform and see how quickly they had been forgotten. He would observe that his brother could be coarse and occasionally cruel. But his loyalty overrode these criticisms, and Jean-Paul's approbation warmed him.

When he heard of Célestine's financial predicament from one of Jean-Paul's fellow officers, it was to his brother that he turned. Haltingly, he explained that despite everything that had happened, he wanted to make some provision for Célestine.

Jean-Paul found the idea vastly amusing. The house would cost—what? Six hundred pounds? And an annuity as well? He shrugged. The sum of money was minimal. If Edouard wanted to be indulgent, why not?

"As a gift?" He frowned slightly, and took another swallow of brandy. "Out of your trust fund?"

"I feel I owe her something, Jean-Paul. . . ."

"Very well—I'll authorize it. Go and see Smith-Kemp, our solicitor here. He'll fix it. A very discreet man. He understands these matters. . . ."

He paused, his brows still drawn together, as if he were calculating something. Then, with another shrug and a sigh, he downed the last of his drink.

"Why not, after all?" He stood up. "Pay her off. Always a sound policy with women, eh, little brother?"

Again Edouard felt that sense of doubt and distaste. Was that what he was doing—paying Célestine off? He had not seen it in that way, and Jean-Paul's interpretation seemed to him brutal.

But this feeling passed, and the matter was not discussed again. Jean-Paul seemed to forget about it. Edouard saw the solicitor, the arrangements were made, and once that embarrassment was over, Edouard felt as if he had passed through some baptism of fire. He had taken the proper course; he was indeed a man of the world now. He felt quite proud of his new identity.

"You've changed, Edouard," Isobel said to him on the day after she had broken her engagement, when Edouard had called on her.

She had been looking at him for a long time before she said this, watching him across the vast space of the Conway House drawing room. Then she stood up and crossed to him. She looked down into his eyes.

"You have. You're harder. I liked you better before. Oh, Edouard, why do things change? Why do people?"

Her candor touched him. His faith in his new detached and cynical persona suddenly wavered. He had been proud of it a moment before, and probably had been flaunting it. Now he stood up.

"I haven't changed," he said quickly. "Not in that way. I still—" He broke off, uncertain quite what he had meant to say next.

Isobel continued to look at him closely, and then, slowly, she began to smile. "Maybe not." Her eyes danced at him. "Maybe there's hope for you still. I think there is—I see it, there in your eyes. When I look very closely. Just a little trace of a soul. Dear Edouard. I shall look for it next time I meet you. Tell Jean he's a bad influence on you—will you do that? Tell him tonight. Tell him from me. . . ."

Edouard did so, thinking Jean-Paul would be amused. His brother's response was truculent.

"Typical," he said. "A typical woman. She knows how close you and I are, and she can't stand it. Bad influence? What the hell does she mean by that? You're my brother. I open my heart to you. Really, Edouard, I feel that." He gave a gusty sigh. "I have no secrets from you."

When he said this, Jean-Paul meant it most sincerely. He was aware that it was not strictly true, but his interpretation of truth was comfortable and elastic. He shared with Edouard everything that mattered, he told himself. The few things he chose to leave out were unimportant.

One of the things he neglected to mention concerned the little actress, Violet Fortescue. During the period immediately after his father's death, when Jean-Paul's mind had been filled with muddled intentions of reform, he did—just as he said—make an effort to avoid the easy sophisticated women he had sought out before. He found to his own surprise that he needed comfort from a quite different type; he renewed his acquaintance with Violet on an impulse, and found her astonishingly soothing. She was shy, sensitive, and undemanding. She was touched by the story of his father's death; she was not without snobbery, and was flattered that the new Baron should confide in her; she was grateful to sit and listen to him talk. Jean-Paul found her quietness soothed him, her silences calmed him, her obvious sympathy touched him. She fell in love with him very easily, and when he realized that, it seemed natural to him to make love to her—something that had not occurred to him before, for though he liked her eyes, he found her physical type unappealing. She proved to be a virgin, and the Baron found her lovemaking too shy and too passive; they did not make love very often, the Baron finding he preferred just to look down into those wide violet eyes and talk.

When she became pregnant, he was very angry. He felt he had been cheated, trapped. To have made love—what?—four or five times, not very enjoyably at that, and then to find himself in this situation. At once the appeal of the violet eyes faded; the expression of unquestioning love and trust began to annoy him. Suddenly she seemed to him clinging—a quality he had always detested in women—and vulnerable. When he could not disguise the irritation he felt, and he saw her face become pinched and fearful, he became angrier still. She seemed to invite rejection even before he offered it; the more overt he was, the more brutally frank, the more she wept and clung. He loathed such masochism.

She refused absolutely to consider an abortion. The Baron was obliged to make himself clear: marriage was out of the question. There was the war; he hoped shortly to be returning to France. He regretted it, but for a man in his position, marriage could not be undertaken lightly; his wife would be the Baronne de Chavigny. Only a woman from a certain kind of background could undertake a position such as that. . . . There he floundered.

Violet folded her hands in a way he had come to hate.

"You think I am not good enough for you."

"Please, my dear. It's not a question of that."

"My father came from an old Devon family." Her voice shook. "I was brought up to be a lady. . . ."

The Baron decided to lie. He said he knew that, of course he knew that; he had been aware of it the first time he met her. But unhappily his family fortunes had been adversely affected by the war. To save the family companies, the family estates, he himself had no choice: he must make a dynastic marriage; it must be an heiress or nothing.

She listened to all this very quietly, and accepted it. The Baron never knew whether she believed him or not. But from that point she seemed to give up the fight. She became utterly passive, as if she no longer had any mind of her own. Physically she was not strong, and her pregnancy weakened her; for the first two months she was frequently sick and could keep down very little food. The Baron hoped she would lose the baby, have a miscarriage. He knew it was brutal, and was half-ashamed, but really it seemed the best solution for everyone involved.

By the end of 1942, when she was four months pregnant and had not suffered a miscarriage, the Baron came to a decision. He could make arrangements for her and the child to be kept, of course, but he foresaw an eternal saga of pleading demands if he did that, and besides, the thing that seemed to appall her most was the stigma of bearing an illegitimate child. So the Baron decided to find her a husband. He found the perfect candidate in an American G.I., Corporal Gary Craig of Baton Rouge, Louisiana, at present serving with the U.S. Army, 4th Infantry Division, to whom he was introduced by his commanding officer, a friend and drinking companion in London of the Baron's.

Craig was a giant of a man, a heavy drinker, not overly bright, but not a man to pass up an opportunity to earn himself a few bucks. The Baron had to meet him only once, and that was on the occasion when the money changed hands. The preliminary work was all kindly undertaken by the Baron's buddy, who also ensured that all the paperwork involved when a G.I. married a British national went through with the minimum of fuss. It cost the Baron five thousand dollars, and Gary Craig, who had never seen so much money in his life, thought it was a gas.

"She's a real pretty girl, I'm told?" He grinned. "Sounds like y'all got yourself a deal, gentlemen."

Violet agreed to the proposition without argument or emotion. Her eyes looked to the Baron now like a sleepwalker's; she neither abused him nor thanked him, she just said yes. To the Baron's great relief Gary Craig avoided getting killed the next year at the D-Day landings. Both men, the one with the 4th Infantry, the other as an officer in General Jacques Leclerc's French 2nd Armored Division, were among the victorious troops who liberated Paris on August 25, 1944. By this time the baby, a girl whom neither man had seen, had been born in a private London clinic, the costs being met by the Baron as previously agreed, and was fourteen months old.

Sergeant Gary Craig was discharged from the U.S. Army late in 1944, after the death of his father, and returned to his parents' small farm in Louisiana to await his bride and child.

Violet and the little girl joined him in late 1945, sailing from Southampton on the *Argentina* along with many other G.I. brides. The Baron, who was not without feelings, arranged for a glorious bouquet of white roses and violets to be delivered to the ship, and then instructed his London solicitors to close their files on Mrs. Craig, formerly Fortescue. That done, Jean-Paul heaved a sigh of relief. It was an unsavory episode and a close shave; he was profoundly glad Edouard did not know of it, as he would almost certainly have been censorious.

Jean-Paul felt relief. Louisiana was a long way away.

Edouard, still in London, heard of the scenes of the liberation of Paris at second hand in his brother's letters. But together with his mother and French friends, he watched the newsreels and saw General de Gaulle lead his victorious troops down the Champs-Élysées.

He watched for Jean-Paul proudly, and when he saw him marching, not so very far behind the General himself, he cheered wildly and wept, just as everyone else was cheering and weeping.

He was eighteen years old; France was free; and his brother, the Baron de Chavigny, had never looked more like a hero.

HÉLÈNE

ALABAMA, 1955—1958

"Y ou ever done it with a boy?"

Priscilla-Anne had her hair in a new ponytail. It was scraped right back off her face and tied with a pink ribbon. It wasn't too big a ponytail, because Priscilla-Anne was waiting for her hair to grow, but Hélène looked at it enviously. She'd like to wear her hair like that, and wear a skirt like Priscilla-Anne's, that flared right out in a circle and had stiff crinkly petticoats underneath. Priscilla-Anne was chewing gum. When Hélène didn't answer, she took the gum out, inspected the pink globule carefully, then stuck it back in her cheek. She lay back on the dried-out grass, and put her hands underneath her head, and sighed. Her breasts stuck up provocatively in their new Maidenform bra. Hélène looked away miserably. She wanted a bra; her mother was resisting the idea. Priscilla-Anne swore blind that hers was now 34C.

"You gone deaf, or what?" Priscilla-Anne poked her with her toe. She raised herself back on one elbow and looked at Hélène thoughtfully. "I *said*—have you ever done it with a boy?"

They were up on the bank behind the ballpark, waiting for the school bus to take them back to Orangeburg. Down below, the senior boys of Selma High were working out. Hélène could just make out the figure of Billy Tanner. He was taller and more muscular than anyone else. She broke off a short stem of grass and chewed on it, keeping her eyes on the ballpark, avoiding Priscilla-Anne's curious stare. She hesitated. The question was a difficult one: she knew it, and Priscilla-Anne knew it.

She didn't want to admit the truth, not even to Priscilla-Anne, who was her best friend, and she didn't want to lie either. Most of the girls lied—or exaggerated, anyway. At least, she suspected they did, but she couldn't be sure. And if they weren't lying when they boasted in the locker room, what did that make her? Hélène sighed. She was beginning to think there must be something wrong with her. Sometimes she was positive she was the only girl in Selma Junior High who'd never even been kissed. She turned around to Priscilla-Anne reluctantly. Her one hope was that Priscilla-Anne's question was a fairly idle one, just a cue, maybe. Priscilla-Anne was looking dreamy again, the way she often did these past months. Hélène cleared her throat.

"Not exactly," she said carefully. "No." She waited a beat. "Have you?"

"Well now . . ." Priscilla-Anne's eyes took on a cunning look, and her wide, pink-lipsticked lips spread apart in a conspiratorial smile. Hélène relaxed. It was all right. It was just a prompt. Priscilla-Anne wanted to talk.

She lay there for a moment, just staring up at the sky. Then, quite suddenly, she stopped smiling and sat up abruptly. Her breasts jounced. Hélène looked jealously away.

"I haven't been all the way—okay?"

"Sure. Sure. Of course."

"I mean, there's petting and there's petting—you know?"

"Sure."

"But . . ." She hesitated, and her voice fell. "You remember Eddie Haines—lives out Maybury way? His daddy owns that big gas station on the highway there. Tall. Big." She giggled. "Some jock. You remember him at the Maybury game last fall?"

"You know I remember." Hélène smiled. "I also remember how you looked when he first asked you out on a date. Sort of weak at the knees, and misty-eyed, and—"

Priscilla-Anne gave her a push.

"Will you shut up? This is serious, Hélène. Truly." She stopped, then sighed. "I love him."

Hélène's eyes widened. She stared at Priscilla-Anne with new respect.

"You do? You're sure? Oh, Priscilla-Anne . . ." They looked at each other for a moment, wide-eyed. "Is it nice? I mean—does it feel good?"

"Good?" Priscilla-Anne laughed. "It feels great."

"And does he love you?"

Hélène leaned forward impulsively, reaching for Priscilla-Anne's hand. Priscilla-Anne's eyes dropped.

"Well, I guess so. I think so. I mean, obviously he hasn't said so yet—we've only had four dates. What boy is going to say that after four dates? But . . . when he looks at me, you know—he looks like he does, and—" She broke off suddenly, and her grip on Hélène's hand tightened.

"If I tell you the God's honest truth, Hélène, do you swear, just swear, you won't breathe a word to one living soul?"

"Oh, I swear. Priscilla-Anne, I swear."

"You do?" Priscilla-Anne looked at her doubtfully for a moment, then she sighed. "Well, I shouldn't probably be telling you this—and I wouldn't, maybe, if I wasn't so worried. Well, not worried, exactly, but I've been thinking about it and thinking about it, till I thought I was just going to go crazy, and . . . Hélène, you know what I think the problem is? I think folks lie, that's what I think. I think they just don't come out with the simple plain truth."

"The truth?" Hélène stared at her. "How do you mean?"

"Well . . ." Priscilla-Anne sat up and settled herself comfortably on her haunches. She leaned forward earnestly. "The thing is, they don't *warn* you—not the way they ought to. They all say a girl ought to do this, and she'd better not do that, and they just go and leave out the most important part—that you're enjoying it yourself! I mean, it feels real nice, and I don't know, but I don't think your mind is working too clear. So just when you *know*, back of your mind, that you ought to be giving him the red light, what happens? You go give him the green one before you've even noticed. . . ."

She paused dramatically to let this piece of information sink in, and Hélène listened respectfully. She just knew that everything Priscilla-Anne said would be useful to her one day—she hoped one day very soon. Meantime, she didn't want to interrupt the flow. Priscilla-Anne was a year older; she'd be fourteen next month. And Priscilla-Anne had breasts: real breasts, like a woman. Maybe when Hélène grew some—if she ever did—she'd have to face the same problem. Green light or red: she couldn't wait.

"You want me to tell you what he did?" Hélène nodded energetically, and Priscilla-Anne drew closer. She held up one finger.

"First date—okay? He kisses me. And just as I'm beginning to get used to it, and enjoying it and all, you know what he does? He goes and kind of pushes with his tongue, and he puts it *inside*. Right inside my mouth! You remember, like Susie told us that time? She called it French kissing? And when she told us, I just thought that was the most *disgusting* thing I ever heard, and everybody knows she's not much better than a slut anyway. . . . But you know, he did it, and Hélène, I swear to God, it felt great. Just great."

"Oh, Priscilla-Anne." Hélène stared at her round-eyed. She gave a nervous little giggle. "On the first date? He did that on the *first* date?"

"Wait, there's more." Priscilla-Anne raised a second finger.

"On the *second* date—he puts his hand right there." She indicated the extreme tip of her breast.

"Right there?"

"Right *there*. Well, then I pushed his hand off, and he waited awhile, then he moved it right back again. It was kind of funny, you know? And he laughed, and I laughed, and then . . . *then*, he started moving his finger back and forth, back and forth, real slow, right on the tip there, where a baby would suck. . . ." Priscilla-Anne blushed. "And Hélène, it just felt so good I thought I was going crazy. I knew I ought to stop him, but he was moving about so fast, kind of squirming, and then, before I knew it—his hand was inside."

"Inside?" Hélène swallowed. "You mean under your sweater?"

"Under my sweater to begin with." Priscilla-Anne looked over her shoulder and lowered her voice. "And then, right under my bra. I was so surprised! I do not *know* how he did it. One minute it was all tight and done up, in fact I was getting so warmed up and so hot I felt I was goin' to bust right out of the thing any minute, and then—it's undone. And he's touching me. *Really* touching me."

There was a silence, and the two girls stared at each other. Hélène's mind was working frantically, trying to remember the things she'd heard the other girls say. It was all so complicated. Above the waist was all right, she was pretty sure about that, but not right away. Not on the second date. On the fifth, or the sixth, maybe, or even later, but that quick! Priscilla was watching her reaction anxiously. Now she leaned forward.

"You think that was wrong? On the second date? You think he'll think I'm easy? You think he'll tell the other guys?"

"No, no, of course not." Hélène tried not to sound dubious. "I mean, if you love him. If he loves you . . ."

"Well, I don't know." Priscilla-Anne shook her head. "It's real hard. You see, the thing is, we've had four dates. Number five is tonight. He's borrowing his daddy's car, and he's taking me to the new movie at the drive-in. And I just *know* that he's going to want to sit in the backseat, and—"

She broke off, and glanced back down the road beyond the ballpark. In the distance the orange shape of the school bus could just be made out, approaching slowly in a cloud of dust. Priscilla-Anne stood up. She brushed down her skirt and picked up her books. She eyed Hélène as she got slowly to her feet.

"You want to stop off at my place on the way back? Come in the store? The new fountain's arrived. I'll get my daddy to fix us a soda if you like."

Hélène hesitated, and suddenly Priscilla-Anne laughed. She linked her arm through Hélène's.

"Oh, come on. Why not? You never will. What you worrying about—your mother? She can wait awhile, can't she?"

Hélène hesitated. Down below, she saw Billy Tanner look up. He stared in their direction for a second, lifted his hand in a quick salute, then let it fall. She shrugged.

"Okay," she said lightly. "Why not for once?"

Priscilla-Anne grinned. "I'll tell you what happened on dates three and four if you do." She paused, and Hélène saw her eyes fall to Hélène's neat white shirt, then back to her face.

"In fact, if you like, I'll do more than that. You know what you told me—about your mother, and how she wouldn't buy you a bra yet and all? Well, come back with me, and you can have one of my old ones." She nudged Hélène in the ribs.

"I hardly wore it. It's almost new. But then I've been growing real fast. . . ."

Hélène stopped in her tracks. Her face went scarlet.

"Priscilla-Anne! Would you? You think I need it?"

"Sure do . . . now, come *on*. That dumb nigger drives the bus is new. It's late—and my throat is just parched. . . ."

B y the time they ran down the slope and skirted the ballpark there was a whole crowd of kids scrambling to get on the bus. Priscilla-Anne and Hélène had to stand at the back of the line, and by the time they climbed aboard, there was only one seat left. Priscilla-Anne grinned; she snapped her gum, and her eyes roved the bus—checking out the talent, she called it.

"You take it," she said, pushing Hélène into the last seat. "It's okay. I prefer to stand."

The bus started to move off, then it stopped. The driver was looking back over his shoulder. Hélène saw him haul on the brake. He *was* new; a man of about fifty, very thin. He was wearing a shiny gray suit frayed at the cuffs, and a white nylon shirt. The bones on his wrists stuck out. She saw him turn, and she saw him hesitate. Priscilla-Anne did, too, because she gave him a long cool stare, then turned her head and began to hum a tune.

"Miss. Miss. You gonna sit down, or what?"

He was trying to make a joke of it. There was a flash of white teeth. The conversation in the bus fell away. Suddenly, there was dead silence. Priscilla didn't even turn her head. "Miss. Miss. You gotta sit down. It's against the regulations to stand. . . ."

Very slowly, Priscilla-Anne turned her head. She had an audience now, and she knew it. She was enjoying herself, Hélène could see it. Very slowly she brushed an imaginary fleck of dust off her sleeve. She turned her head, just a fraction.

"You talking to me, boy?"

The heat in the bus was intense. The silence seemed to shimmer. In back, someone laughed. The driver raised his eyes. He just looked at Priscilla-Anne awhile, not moving, not speaking. Then, very slowly, he turned back and released the brake. The bus moved off. Conversation started up again, Priscilla-Anne began to hum once more and swing her hips to the tune, and Hélène felt sick.

"Why'd you do that?" she said when they'd gotten off the bus in Orangeburg. "Priscilla-Anne—why'd you call him 'boy' like that? He didn't mean any harm. He was only doing his job."

"Who cares?" Priscilla-Anne gave a toss of the head. "He's just a dumb nigger drivin' a bus. He'd be picking cotton if the machines didn't do it better. No nigger talks to me like that. And don't say a word to Daddy, for God's sake, or he'll go *wild*. For months now, it's been 'nigras, nigras, nigras'—ever since that Supreme Court decision, you know."

Hélène sighed. She read the newspapers like anyone else; of course she knew. The case of *Brown* vs. *Board of Education*, and the new Supreme Court ruling, stating that segregated education was unconstitutional. Oh, yes, she knew. Priscilla-Anne's father wasn't the only one who had talked of nothing else for months. "My daddy says there's just one good thing. If it ever happens—and my daddy says it won't, he says the South won't stand for it—I'll be out of school before they start bussing them in. Can you imagine, Hélène—sitting next to one of them in class?" Priscilla laughed. "They smell, you know. It's true. They smell real funny. And my daddy says that guy—what's his name—Earl Warren—he says he'd better just not set foot in Alabama or the lynching parties'll be out. . . ."

"Mississippi Mary didn't smell." Hélène frowned. "Or if she did, she smelled nice. You remember, I told you, Mississippi Mary? I never did know why they called her that. She was my nurse. For a bit. When I was little . . ."

"What, her? That fat one? Lived over by the old cotton fields? Yeah—I remember. She died a while back, didn't she?"

"That's right."

"And all the other niggers got drunk at the funeral. Je*sus*! Who cares? You goin' to come get that soda?"

Hélène nodded. They crossed the street, went by Cassie Wyatt's beauty parlor, past the old hotel, which was closed up now. They were building a motel now, a brand-new one, with bungalows on the outskirts of town. Rumor had it Priscilla-Anne's father had bought the hotel site. He was going to knock the old place down and extend his store.

The store had changed, too, over the last few years. Merv Peters had installed new shelves and fridges; you served yourself now: no waiting, except at the checkout. And now there was the soda fountain too: a long white counter, shiny-topped high stools, rows of syrup bottles, and a radio set tuned to WQXA. Nonstop country and western: Priscilla-Anne thought it was square.

Hélène shook hands shyly with Priscilla-Anne's father and perched on top of the stool. She was thinking about Mississippi Mary. Surely she was right? She hadn't smelled funny, and she'd been kind. She used to lift Hélène up and rock her against those mountainous breasts, and sing those lovely slow songs till Hélène fell asleep. That was when she was little, of course, before she was big enough to stay on her own. Then Mississippi Mary had left, and Hélène didn't see her again till that time she went by her tarpaper shack, and Mississippi Mary gave her the cool sweet green tea. And Mother had been so angry when she found out. . . . She frowned.

She hadn't cried or anything, but she was sorry Mississippi Mary was dead, and she was sorry for the bus driver. She wished Priscilla hadn't spoken to him like that. . . .

When they'd finished the soda, Merv told them to cut along, and they went up to Priscilla-Anne's bedroom. Hélène stared at it wide-eyed. She'd never imagined a girl her own age could have a room so pretty! Everything was sugar-pink. There were sugar-pink flounces on the bed, and sugar-pink frills on the draperies. There was proper wallpaper with roses on it, and a row of walkie-talkie dolls, all in pink dresses.

Priscilla-Anne gestured around it negligently.

"Nice, huh? My daddy just did it up for me. He'll do anything for me now, since my mama walked out. He's lonesome, I guess." She shrugged. "And he's doing all right now, what with the new soda fountain and all. Going places, you know? Says there's no reason Orangeburg has to stay a one-horse town." She sighed. "I don't know, though. It'd be nice to leave, I think. Go someplace bigger. Montgomery, maybe. That's great." She turned her head. "You ever think of leaving?"

"Maybe. Yes. Sometimes."

Priscilla frowned. "You don't talk about it so much now, though. You used to—remember? How your mother was going to take you back to England and all. London." She shrugged. "I didn't like you so much then. London. And you talked funny. You were a little fancy, you know? Stuck-up. Everybody said so—except for Billy Tanner, of course."

Hélène went red. She turned away and pretended to look at the dolls.

"We're saving up." She hesitated. "Mother is, you know. But it's expensive—to go back to England. It's a long way away." She turned to look at Priscilla-Anne. "There's a box," she added finally. "Mother has an old tin box. And when we have some extra money we put it in there, and when there's enough—one day—we'll go, I guess."

"A box? Your mother keeps her money in a *box*?" Priscilla-Anne seemed to find that funny because she started to laugh, and then stopped and shrugged. "Well, why not, I guess. A bank, a box, who cares? Except . . ." She hesitated. "It's going to take a while, isn't it? I mean, working for Cassie Wyatt, your mama can't make that much. . . ."

"She makes more now," Hélène interrupted eagerly. "She works more hours, now that I'm in school. Five afternoons a week, and . . ."

"She works afternoons?" Priscilla-Anne frowned. "She does? That's funny."

"What's funny?"

"Well, I went by Cassie Wyatt's the other week." Priscilla-Anne tossed the ponytail and looked at herself in the mirror.

"Right after school. My daddy said I could get my hair done—I wanted it the way Susie has it, you know, with those kind of wispy little curls in front—and I wanted your mother to do it, because everyone says she's real good. She does your hair, yes? And that always looks real nice. . . ."

"And?"

"She wasn't there. Your mama. Cassie Wyatt said I'd have to wait for the vacation, 'cause your mother worked only mornings."

"Mornings? That can't be right. She must have made a mistake." There was a little silence. Priscilla-Anne looked at her, then back at her own reflection, and there was something in her eyes Hélène didn't understand. A bit as if she were laughing at her, a bit as if she felt sorry for her. Then she shrugged. " 'Spose so. I probably got it wrong. You want to try that bra now?"

Priscilla-Anne helped her. Hélène took her blouse off, and Priscilla-Anne did the bra up, because Hélène's hands were shaking. Then she came around the front and looked at Hélène critically.

"You see? I was right. It fits. You fill it just fine. . . ." She rolled her eyes comically, so they both began to giggle.

"Hélène Craig, you is all woman. . . ." she said in an exaggerated drawl.

"I am not. Look . . ." Hélène pulled at the front of the bra.

"There's a bit there, but all the rest is empty, you can feel it."

"Just so long as no one else does," Priscilla-Anne said in a throaty voice, and they both began to giggle again. Then Priscilla-Anne found a tissue and showed her how to stuff it down in front.

"There you are," she said at last. "It's fine, see? You just do that for a few weeks, until you grow a bit more. You'll fill out in no time. Billy Tanner'll go just *wild*. . . ."

"Will you shut up about Billy Tanner?" Hélène gave her an affectionate push.

"Okay, okay, I'll shut up about Billy Tanner. Who wants to talk about him anyway? He is *so* dumb. You know, when he reads, he runs his finger along the lines, just like a kid, and kind of mouths the words, just to make sure he's getting them out all neat. . . ."

"That's not true!"

"It is so! And his daddy's on welfare. Eddie Haines told me. Just like a nigger. He drinks so much he hasn't had work in ten years, and—"

"Priscilla-Anne, you just shut up now! That's not Billy's fault. Billy works so hard. He cooks evenings after school, over in that place in Maybury. . . ."

"You ever been there? Greasy burgers and collard greens on the side. Yuk!"

"And weekends at the garage. He's going to be a mechanic, he told me. He's clever with cars, engines, that kind of thing. . . ."

"Doesn't own one, though, does he?" Priscilla-Anne tossed her head. "Doesn't own one and never will. Billy Tanner's going no place fast. You must be crazy to go with a boy like him."

"I don't go with him." Hélène hesitated. "I just see him sometimes. 'Round the trailer park. That's all. And I like him. He may be slow, but he's kind, and . . ."

"Look." Priscilla-Anne waved her hand irritably. "We didn't come here to talk about Billy Tanner. We came to talk about Eddie. Now—you want to hear what happened—yes or no?"

Hélène hesitated. She was hurt by what Priscilla-Anne had said, and she wanted to leave, but she didn't like to. After all, Priscilla-Anne had been generous. She had given her the bra. And besides, deep down, even though she didn't want to admit it to herself, she did want to hear, yes.

"Okay," she said at last, with a sigh. "I want to hear. What happened?"

She sat down on the bed, and after a brief pause Priscilla-Anne sat down next to her.

"You swear you won't tell? Remember? Okay . . ." She sighed deeply. "Well, I don't know if you are going to believe this. I hardly did myself. Date three, pretty much the same as date two, only more so if you get my meaning. Date *four*—he gets it out."

Hélène's jaw dropped. "What—just like that?"

"No, stupid. Not right away, of course not." Priscilla-Anne looked scornful. "This is a *long* session we're talking about now. I think he kind of lost control a little, because he respects me, I know he does, he said so. But we were kissing a lot, and his hands were in there—you know, where they were before, only both of them this time. And it was driving me wild, and him wild, and then—well, he sort of made me touch him, through his pants. And Hélène, I swear to you, he felt so hard and big, I got scared. I mean, I could *not* believe it. You remember those diagrams they did in biology? Well, it looked real small, you know? But this wasn't small, I could feel it, and then . . ."

"Then he got it out?"

"He did."

"Wow!" Hélène gave a nervous shiver.

"And you know where we were at the time?" Priscilla-Anne began to laugh. "We were in my daddy's den."

"In your daddy's den? You're joking."

"I am not. We were in his den. Right there on that imitation-leather couch he has, the one he's so proud of. And you know what I thought? It just suddenly popped right into my head out of nowhere. I thought, what if anything happens—I mean . . ." She lowered her voice. "What if he *comes*, right? And then I thought: oh, well, that's okay. If he does, it's only imitation leather, thank God, and we can wipe it right off with a tissue. My daddy'll never know. And then I laughed."

"You laughed? Then? When he had it out? Did Eddie mind?"

"Mind? He went crazy. Well, he put it away first, of course, just sort of stuffed it back in his pants and zipped them up real quick. And *then* he went crazy. Hélène, I tell you, I just cried and cried. I thought, this is it. He's going to walk right out that door, and I'll never see him again. But I guess Eddie felt sorry for me, because when I cried, he came right back, and he put his arms around me, and I kissed him, and then—after a while, you know—he got it out again."

"Priscilla-Anne Peters, you are lying! He didn't."

"Sure did." A small dimple appeared in Priscilla-Anne's cheek. "I told him I wanted a second look, so there!"

"You never dared!"

"I did. And anyway . . ." Priscilla stretched. "It was the truth. I did. I mean, I've seen the boys in the gym, who hasn't? I know what a hard-on looks like, sticking out of a pair of gym shorts. But not like that. Close up, you might say. In living Technicolor."

There was a long silence. Hélène's mind whirled with images, all of them cloudy and imprecise.

"Did it . . . was it . . ." She hesitated. "Was it nice?"

Priscilla-Anne frowned; she considered.

"Well, it was funny-looking, I guess," she said finally. "Real big, the way I said. And it doesn't keep still the way I thought it would. It sort of waves up and down, like a wand. And it was a weird sort of color. Reddish—reddish-purple almost." She swallowed. "Do you think they're all like that, or just his?"

"I don't know. All of them, I guess. Did . . ." Hélène looked up. She knew she was going to start laughing again in a minute, and that Priscilla-Anne wanted to laugh too. "Did you touch it?"

"I did not! What do you take me for?" Priscilla-Anne gave her an indignant push. "He wanted me to, and I wouldn't. But you know what

I thought? I thought, Jesus, it is *so* big, I just don't see how it ever fits up inside—you know."

"Oh, my God!" Hélène clapped her hand over her mouth. Then she started to laugh, and Priscilla-Anne started to laugh, and they clung to each other, shaking, till the tears ran down their faces. Priscilla-Anne stopped first.

"Stop," she said. "This is serious." She gave Hélène a shake, and Hélène gurgled. "It is. I told you. I've got to decide, I've just got to make up my mind right now, and you've got to help me. What do I do tonight? At the drive-in."

"You mean you think he'll try . . ."

"Sure." Priscilla set her lips. "They're all the same. A little more each time."

"There isn't a lot more he could do. I'd have thought."

"Shows how much you know!" Priscilla's eyes flashed scorn. "I can think of at least three things, right off. I know! Susie Marshall told me, for sure. Said she wouldn't do it, *which* I don't believe. Listen . . ." She glanced at the door, then leaned forward and spoke rapidly, directly into Hélène's ear. Hélène's eyes grew larger and larger.

"In a handkerchief! He didn't!"

"He did so! And then . . ." Priscilla leaned forward and spoke some more. Then she drew back, and they stared at each other.

"It's true! I didn't believe it either. Not to begin with. I mean, isn't that just the dirtiest thing you ever heard?"

"And they like it?"

Priscilla-Anne nodded knowledgeably. "More'n going all the way. Some of them. That's what Susie Marshall said."

"But the girls—the girls can't like it. Ugh!" Hélène pulled a face. "I bet it tastes just horrible."

"Susie Marshall said it doesn't. *And* you don't get pregnant. She said." Priscilla sighed. "So what do I do?"

Hélène shook her head worriedly. "I don't know. You just say no, I suppose. If you were very firm . . ."

"I'm not so good at that." Priscilla-Anne made a wry face. "I don't look the part—you know what I mean? It's all right for you. You're younger than me, but you can look real stern when you want, you know that? You know, when you're angry? Your eyes look just like blue ice. And your voice helps—sounding different, all cool and English. Lots of the kids are scared of you, you know. Not me, because you're my best friend. But some of the others. But I don't know . . . I'm different. When I say no, it comes out sounding just like the opposite."

Hélène stood up. She frowned, trying to remember. "You could say—I know. That if he respected you, he wouldn't do it. . . ."

"Wow!" Priscilla's eyes lit up. "That's good."

"My mother said that . . ." Hélène shrugged. "It might work. I don't know."

"I like it! I'll try it. It's a winner!" She began to parade up and down the room, then struck an attitude in front of the mirror. *"If you respected me, Eddie, you just wouldn't do that."* She swung around. "How'd it sound?"

"Not bad." Hélène grinned. "You could try it a bit cooler. More earnest—as if you were deeply hurt, and—what's the word?—affronted. That's it. Try it again."

Priscilla tried it again. This time she sounded as if she had something stuck in her throat, so Hélène coached her a bit more. Eventually Priscilla sighed.

"That's it," she said. "That's as good as I'm ever going to get it. It's not as good as you, but still—" She broke off and looked at Hélène for a moment in the mirror.

"You could be an actress," she said. "You know—the way you told me once you wanted to be? Well, I reckon you could. You're smart. You can do anything with your voice. And your face—well, even I never know what you're really thinking, 'cause you can be real secretive when you want to be. And then you say something like that, just a line, nothing you really mean, and *I* believe you, so I just *know* Eddie would. I tell you—I wish I could do that."

Hélène laughed. "Why?" she said. "Why would you want to?"

"I don't know." Priscilla shrugged. "It would make me feel powerful, I guess. I don't know—you spook me sometimes. You don't bother much, but I bet if you wanted to, well, you could make boys do anything you like. You could drive them just wild. . . ."

"Do you think so?" Hélène stared at her.

"Yeah." Priscilla hesitated. "Men too," she added. "Maybe."

Hélène walked home slowly. It was a mile from Orangeburg to the trailer park, down the main street, along the highway a bit through the Calverts' cotton fields, then off along a dusty dirt road. It was hot; another few weeks and it'd be hotter still, and humid, so your skin felt itchy and clammy all the time, and even at nights the trailer felt airless. The new bra was uncomfortable; the shoulder straps were too tight, and the clips on the back cut her skin. The schoolbooks felt heavier by the minute. She scuffed her shoes in the dust and glanced at herself in the store-front glass as she went past. She'd have to make some excuse to her mother for coming back late. Her mother didn't like her stopping off; her mother didn't want her to visit friends; her mother didn't approve of Priscilla-Anne Peters. Hélène knew that from the way her mother's mouth tightened up when Priscilla-Anne's name was mentioned. But she didn't say so. All she said was, "It's not polite to accept invitations you can't return, Hélène. Remember that."

"Why can't I return it?" Hélène stuck her lip out obstinately. "I could bring Priscilla-Anne back here sometime."

"Here? Here?" Two hectic spots of color flared in her mother's cheeks. "You want your friend to see how we have to live? And have half of Orangeburg talk about it?"

"She knows I live in the trailer park."

"Knowing and seeing are two different things. Now, let's change the subject, shall we? I don't intend to argue about it. When I say no, I mean no."

That had been a while back, when she was in fifth grade. Then, Hélène had been sulky. She thought her mother was being stupid. Now, as she dragged up the dirt path and the trailer park came into view, she wondered.

Two of the old trailers were empty now. They'd been empty for years. No one else had moved in, and the trailers had just been left to rot. One had a great gaping hole in the roof. Their windows had been smashed by the younger Tanner kids. Old May still lived in one of the others, but her husband was dead now, and everyone said old May was crazy. She was fat and dirty, and she never set foot outside the trailer, or if she did, Hélène never saw her. There was a young couple in the next, and they'd made an effort when they first moved in. They'd put in boxes full of plastic flowers round the window, and the husband had painted the trailer sunshine yellow. But they had two kids now, and a third on the way, the yellow paint was all peeling off, and the sun had bleached the color from the flowers. The wife was sitting on the step, the way she always seemed to do, her hair in curlers, two half-naked little kids playing in the dirt with a couple of the Tanner children. She lifted her head lazily as Hélène trudged past.

"Hi, Hélène. Hot, ain't it?"

"Yes. Very." Hélène gave her a polite little smile, and then looked the other way. The woman took a last drag on the cigarette in her mouth, then tossed the butt end in among the plastic flowers. Hélène felt as if she suddenly wanted to scream: *Don't do that—don't do it. It's dirty and ugly and horrible—horrible.*

Her mother wasn't home, but that was nothing unusual these days. She'd come back with a couple of packages around six, and say she'd been to the market, that she'd just realized they'd run out of bread, or sugar, or tea. Hélène used to mind, once. Not now. Now she wouldn't have to account for being late, which was a relief.

The trailer felt like an oven. She opened all the windows and the door, but it hardly made any difference. There was no breeze, and all the flies came in, that was all. She dumped the bag of books down on the table and poured herself a tall glass of cold milk. She was just so hot. And dirty. What she'd like right now was just to stand under a shower, a proper shower, and let the cold water run and run and run. Or go down to the pool, maybe, with Billy, and swim. But she hardly ever did that anymore. All the hours God made, it seemed, Billy worked. And when he wasn't working, it seemed to her that he avoided her. She couldn't understand it. She thought he liked her still. He seemed to like her, but every time she mentioned swimming, or even just going for a walk, Billy's gaze slid away, and he turned red, and made an excuse. She could go on her own, of course—nothing to stop her. But she was a little afraid. It was so quiet down by the pool. She'd done it once, and she hadn't enjoyed it—not the way she did with Billy. All the time she swam she felt as if someone were watching her, in behind the cotton-wood trees. And in the end she'd just clambered out fast, and run through the bushes all the way home.

She kicked off her shoes, went into the bedroom, and flung herself down on her bed. Her mother's bed wasn't made, and the room smelled slightly sour, like unwashed linen. Hélène closed her eyes. Sometimes she thought her mother didn't care so much—not anymore.

She thought of Priscilla-Anne's bedroom, with its pink frills. She thought of the new bathroom Merv Peters had had installed, which Priscilla-Anne had showed her on the way out: all gleaming tiles, and the bathroom suite pink, not white. She'd never even seen a pink one before, didn't know they made them.

"Don't you just love pink?" Priscilla-Anne had sighed. "I guess it's just about my favorite color."

Hélène opened her eyes again. A fat bluebottle buzzed. The walls were stained with rust; it came through the paint no matter what you did. There was practically no color left in the thin little cotton draperies: they hung at the window like rags. One of the legs on her bed was half broken, and the screw her mother had put in was coming out, so the bed tilted crazily to one side every time you moved. The old yellow chest seemed to Hélène to get yellower and yellower and uglier and uglier by the day.

She didn't go to church, never had, though her mother wrote "Episcopalian" with a flourish on the school forms, in the section headed religion. Nationality: English. Age: twelve. Religion: Episcopalian. Hélène shut her eyes again. She didn't even know what it meant, not really. But she did pray sometimes; lately, she did. Always the same prayer. She said it now, silently, screwing up her eyes. *God. Jesus. Dear God. Sweet Jesus. Get me out of here.*

After a bit, feeling better, she added, *And Mother.* Then she swung her long legs off the bed. She rummaged around under her mother's bed. There was a real litter of stuff there—her mother was a real magpie, a hoarder. Hélène pulled some of the stuff out and looked at it in disgust. Why did she keep all this junk?

Bits of cheap lace off petticoats long thrown away.. A box of old buttons and glass beads. A pair of dirty white cotton gloves gone yellow now, and with holes in the fingers. Her mother used to wear white gloves—when? Centuries ago. *A lady always wears gloves. Leather, not fabric* . . . had her mother said that? Well, these were fabric all right, dime-store stuff. Horrible. Hélène tossed them aside.

There was a great stack of magazines too. Years old, some of them. Her mother brought them back from Cassie Wyatt's. They were thumbed and stained, and smelled acrid from hair lacquer. Hélène flicked the pages. Smart bright women: bright red smiles, and crisp hair, shiny shoes with high heels and neat, tailored suits. These women didn't live in dirty old trailers. You only had to look at them to know: they lived in smart new houses, with a car in the driveway, and dinner in the oven. They had husbands, and the husbands wore suits, and came home at six every day. They had a barbecue in the backyard, and they all went to the beach for vacations. They had TVs and electric ovens, and big iceboxes. They had showers, too, just like Priscilla-Anne's, so they could wash anytime they felt like it. She flicked a page.

They used something called Tampax, too, because they were women who led an active life, and there were photographs of them doing so—on a beach, or horseback riding even. She knew what Tampax was, but you couldn't use it if you were a girl—Susie Marshall said so. It wouldn't go up; you weren't big enough. She thought they sounded dangerous— what if they got stuck? But they had to be better than what she had to wear: that horrible pink elastic belt, and those thick napkins. Napkins! Her mother called them "towels": napkins were what you put on your lap at dinner. But whatever you called them, they were horrible. If you were stupid enough to wear pants then, they stuck out, and all the boys nudged one another and smirked. They made her feel dirty; they made her feel ashamed. But maybe that was just her mother. Once she'd really wanted to start. The older girls made such a drama of it: clutching their stomachs and saying the pain was real bad, and bringing in notes from their mothers saying they couldn't do gym or go swimming. She didn't care then how painful it was, she just wanted to *start*. And then when she did, her mother wouldn't talk about it, not at all. She made it quite clear that what had happened was something that was never, ever discussed. She went out and bought the belt and a blue packet of the things and hid them in back of one of the drawers. "They're in there," she said. "When you need them."

So she talked to Priscilla-Anne about it, and then she felt a whole lot better. She could talk to Priscilla-Anne, and she couldn't talk to her mother. Not the way they used to talk. Not often, anyhow. Sometimes it was like her mother didn't want her to grow up, didn't want her to become a woman. All that stuff about not needing a bra, for instance. Sometimes she thought it made her mother angry, angry in a funny hopeless kind of way, her growing-up. Other times she thought it was just that her mother was too tired, or too busy. She often looked tired now. In the mornings, she was puffy under the eyes, and there were thin little lines now around her mouth that weren't there before. Evenings, sometimes, she looked really exhausted and worried. She'd fall asleep sometimes right there in the chair.

She was still beautiful, Hélène thought. But not quite as beautiful as she used to be. And sometimes when Hélène met her in town, she felt embarrassed. Her mother was so old-fashioned! She still wore her hair the same way, all those careful waves and a side part. She didn't have a perm like most of the mothers, or bangs over the forehead. Out in the sunlight, her makeup could look funny too. That pale powder she wore, and the way she still painted her lips in that bow: no one else did that anymore. And then, the way she talked! So English, still. Using fifteen words when she could have used three. *"Do you think I could possibly have . . . How do you do . . ."* when everybody else just said "Hi!" and had done with it. Helene had seen people stare; seen the sideways glances, the smirks. In Cassie Wyatt's; in the market.

She frowned. Her mother didn't belong. And Hélène felt as if she didn't belong either. She wasn't English, and she wasn't American. She could talk like the other girls when she wanted. She had a quick ear; she knew it. Oh, she could mimic them all right. She did it now, quietly, to herself, listening carefully. Just like Priscilla-Anne, that slow, lazy drawl. But still, she didn't do it. Not unless she was alone. Because she wasn't sure in her own mind if she did want to be like the other girls. She didn't. Not altogether. They'd jeered when she first went to school; she used to cry about it every night. And she'd never forgiven them—never. *Take no notice, darling,* her mother had said then. *They're rude and ignorant. They don't know any better. . . .*

She'd believed her mother then. Her mother did know better. Her mother knew about England, and big houses and green lawns and balls and ladies and wearing gloves and not cutting bread with a knife at the dinner table.

But sometimes, now, she wasn't so sure. Sometimes that whole world—the world her mother had once talked about all the time, and now mentioned more and more rarely—sometimes that whole world seemed unreal. It existed, she supposed, but maybe not quite the way her mother described. And even if it did—did she care for it? Why should she, when she was stuck here in the trailer park? And if God didn't do something soon, she'd be stuck here forever.

Hélène Craig, she whispered to herself quietly. *Hélène Fortescue*. But even that didn't help anymore, not the way it used to. The names sounded hollow. Sometimes she felt as if she didn't exist at all, as if she were nobody.

And sometimes she wondered if colored people felt like that, belonging and not belonging, all at once. She pushed the pile of magazines away angrily. That was stupid. Better not say that. Not ever. Not to anyone.

The tin box was right at the back of the bed, all covered in dust and fluff. When had *that* last been opened? Hélène opened it now, and looked inside. There were the two dark blue English passports, her mother's and her own, because she had been born in England. And there was the money—quite a lot of it. Crumpled dollar bills, a few fives, lots and lots of quarters and dimes. Once upon a time she and Mother used to do the arithmetic. If they saved so much, every week— not that much really, no more than the price of a packet of soap powder, or a box of cornflakes—if they did that every week without fail, and never raided the box, not even at Christmas, then in so many weeks, and so many years . . . Hélène sighed. How much did it cost for two people to go to Europe, to England?

Five hundred dollars, her mother had said once, and then laughed. It was a nice round figure anyway, she said. But that had been a few years back. Would five hundred still be enough?

Hélène wasn't sure. There wasn't five hundred in here, anyway, nowhere near. She frowned, trying to concentrate. The last time they had counted it, yes, she was pretty sure, had been her eleventh birthday. She remembered, because it was not long after she'd first started her period, and the birthday had begun all right, but ended badly. Her mother had started crying—for no reason Hélène could see. But she'd cried a lot, and said Hélène was growing up so fast, and then she'd gotten the box out and counted the money, and there had been . . . two hundred and thirty dollars. Yes, she was sure, because it sounded like so much. A few odd nickels and dimes as well, but basically, two hundred and thirty dollars.

Slowly and carefully, she reached into the box and began to count the money. She put it in neat stacks, fives in one pile, ones in another. After a while she sat back on her heels. Then recounted, to make sure.

But she was right. It had gone down, not up. There was a little over a hundred and fifty dollars in the box. No way would a hundred and fifty dollars get two people to England.

She stared at the money for a while, till her head felt tight and hot, and she knew if she looked at it any longer, she would start to cry. Then she gathered it all up, stuffed it back into the box, and stuffed the box under the bed again. Where had it gone? She couldn't imagine. On schoolbooks? Clothes? It might be clothes. Her mother did have new dresses sometimes, and she never said where they came from, except that she had got them cheaply, they were a bargain. And she was growing so fast; her mother bought material and made her new clothes. It might be that.

Hélène stood up and stared out the window. God, she thought. Please God. If I don't stop growing out of things, then we're just never going to get to England.

Her mother came back around six. She was wearing a pink dress Hélène hadn't seen before, and it suited her. Hélène could see right away that she was in a good mood. She sang to herself while she made supper, and she asked Hélène a lot of questions, about school, about homework, the way she tried to do the nights she wasn't tired. Hélène thought she didn't listen to the answers too carefully, because her eyes had a dreamy half-focused look. But she didn't mind. She felt guilty now for all those things she'd thought about her mother earlier. It wasn't her fault she talked the way she did. And she *was* pretty. Tonight her eyes were shining, and she looked almost beautiful again, the way she used to do.

Hélène was wondering if she should ask her about Cassie Wyatt's and that mixup over her mother working afternoons, but even though she seemed in a good mood, Hélène didn't quite dare. Her mother hated being questioned about her movements, Hélène had learned that now: she called it prying. So instead, she decided to risk telling her about Priscilla-Anne, about stopping at the Peters' house on the way home. And it was all right: her mother just nodded and smiled, and never said a thing.

Encouraged, Hélène went on. She told her about the soda fountain and the walkie-talkie dolls, and the frilly pink bedroom. Her mother's eyebrows arched; a little smile played about her lips.

"It was lovely, Mother. So pretty. Oh, and they have a new bathroom too—and you know, that's pink as well? A proper shower, with a glass door. And shiny pink tiles. And the bathtub is pink and so is the wash basin—just imagine! Even the . . ."

"Pink?" The eyebrows arched a little higher. "Darling. Rather vulgar."

Hélène lowered her eyes. "I thought it was nice," she said slowly, and again that awful uncertainty came back. She was wrong again, it seemed. She'd thought it was pretty, and it wasn't. Her mother said it was vulgar. Just like that. She raised her eyes again, slowly, to her mother's face. How could her mother be so certain?

There was a little silence. Her mother leaned back in her chair, "And after that?" she said at last. "What did you do after that? You weren't waiting for me too long, I hope?"

She asked the question out of habit, Hélène thought. Once, it had truly worried her if she was late. Hélène wasn't sure if it did so much now. She hesitated, drawing lines on the oilcloth with her fingernail, plucking up courage.

"I just mooched about. For a bit." She shrugged. "And then— then, I started thinking. . . ."

She swallowed. She still didn't dare come right out with it. If her mother knew she'd counted the money in the box, she'd be angry. And when she was angry, she frightened Hélène. Those spots of color came into her cheeks, and the veins stood out in her temples, and the violet eyes flashed, or filled with tears, and her voice would rise, and she would start to shake.

"I was just wondering, you know. If we were still saving up to go to England."

Her mother sat up then, at once. Her eyes grew intent, and she seemed about to say something, and then checked herself. Her face had gone hard and tight. Then, all at once, it softened again, and she smiled. A long slow odd smile, slightly secretive.

"Of course, my darling," she said. "Of course we are. I've always told you that, haven't I? I wouldn't forget." She paused. Hélène's eyes never left her face. "It's just that . . . well, we've been here a long time now, and you're settled in school, and sometimes I think it might be nicer to stay."

"Stay?" Hélène felt herself go very red. "Here? In the trailer park?"

Her mother laughed. "No, darling, of course not. Stay—in this place—a moment longer than we had to? No, darling, I don't mean that at all. It's just that . . . if our circumstances changed. Changed quite considerably. Then it might be very pleasant to stay in America, even in Alabama, don't you think?"

"Changed? Changed how?" Her voice rose uncontrollably, but her mother only smiled.

"For the better, of course, darling. If we had more money, for instance, quite a lot of money. And a nice place to live. If we had a car—all the new clothes we wanted. If we could forget about budgeting forever, and just buy almost anything we wanted . . ." She waved her hands a little vaguely in the air. "If that happened, then I don't think I would mind staying here." She looked at Hélène's hot skeptical face. "Darling, don't look so stubborn, it's very unattractive. After all, parts of Alabama are very beautiful. There are some beautiful houses—lovely gardens, almost like English ones." She smiled coaxingly. "There are lawns, and flowers, camellias in the spring. There are gardeners, and you can still get servants here—why, some people in Alabama live in a way scarcely anyone in England can afford these days, and . . ."

Hélène stood up. She couldn't bear to listen anymore. Her mother must be going crazy. It was all a dream, a fantasy—just like going back to England.

"Where?" she cried. She made a wild waving gesture at the window. "Where? Gardens? Servants? Camellias? You see any of those outside in that trailer park?"

"Not there. Of course not there." Her mother's voice had risen now too. "I wasn't talking about out there. You know I wasn't. . . ."

"Then where?"

"Lots of places. You've seen them." She hesitated. "The Calverts' for instance. They have beautiful camellias up at the Calverts'. . . ."

"They do? They do?" Hélène knew she was almost shouting now, and she couldn't stop. She pushed away from the table and made for the open door. She knew she had to run out, go away, go someplace. She just couldn't bear to be in that hot stuffy little room a second longer. She couldn't bear to see that expression on her mother's face, half-crumpled, half-hopeful, and the violet eyes suddenly afraid. At the door she spun round, her throat so tight with pain and love and anger all mixed up that she could hardly speak.

"Who cares about the Calverts?" she said. "Who cares? What are you planning now, Mother? Buying the Calverts' house with a hundred and fifty dollars?"

She just ran, to begin with, not thinking where she was going, just wanting to be alone. She ran, and the tears streamed down her face, and then after a while she stopped. She was over on the edge of the old cotton fields, and she knew where she wanted to go. Down by the pool. Into that cool brown water. Without pausing, she jumped the ditch, ducked under the wire, began to run through the shrubbery. She didn't slow to look at the house, or the lawn, or even the little summerhouse. If someone saw her, she couldn't have cared less. In minutes she was in the shade of the cottonwood trees, and half-sliding, half-falling down the slopes to the water.

She stood there on the edge for a moment, feeling the sudden coolness of the air dry the tears on her face. Then she pulled off all her clothes, throwing them down carelessly. She stood for a moment, naked under the trees, sunlight and shadows patterning her skin. Then she dived into the water.

Billy had taught her well, and she swam strongly, but the pool was not nearly as large as it had seemed to her when she was little, so she just went back and forth, back and forth, compulsively, unthinkingly, until she was breathless, and all the anger and shame and confusion were gone.

Then she stopped, and stood up in the shallows, and tilted her head back, so the long wet skein of her fair hair, darkened by the water, laced and rippled down her back. She looked down at her own body, at the long narrow flanks; she was the tallest girl in her class by two inches. Skin, pale in this light, gold in the sun. A tiny triangle of hairs between her thighs now. Her breasts were soft and small, lifting from her rib cage. Her nipples were hard and pointed from the cold of the water; their aureoles looked wide and dark. That was how they went when boys touched you, Priscilla-Anne said. Boys liked that; they liked to touch them, and then kiss them, and touch the nipples with their tongue, and suck on them. And when they did that, Priscilla-Anne said, it felt amazing, incredible, just magical . . . like you never wanted them to stop.

Slowly she lifted her wet hands and ran them up over her body. Up over the curve of hips and waist, up over her rib cage, and under her breasts. She cupped them delicately in her palms—she could do that now—and then, very carefully, she caressed the hard nipples with her fingers. She felt a wave of sudden pleasure, a shiver of delight.

Quickly, guiltily, she dropped her hands and looked over her shoulder. There was no one there, of course—who would there be? Billy would be working over at the café; no one else ever came here.

Yet now the anger had gone, she felt suddenly a little afraid once more, the way she had the last time. As if someone were watching her, someone who saw what she had just done. She stared, wide-eyed, into the shadows. Dappled light; the grayish trunks of the cottonwoods; nobody.

Still, she wanted to leave, wanted to get back to the trailer park—now, quickly, before the light started to go, and the shadows darkened. She pulled herself out of the water, and, shivering now, began to pull on her clothes, dragging them on over her wet skin as quickly as she could. She wouldn't bother with the bra, not now, it was too difficult to fix. Just the white blouse, which stuck to her damp skin, and the cotton pants, and the skirt which was too short for her already. She wrung out her hair as best she could, but it still hung in damp tendrils around her face and shoulders. Then, flushed, nervous, she stuffed the bra into her pocket, slipped her bare feet into her shoes, and clambered up the bank as fast as she could. Head bent, she ducked under the branches and came out onto the patch of scrubby grass, into the sunshine.

A man in a white suit was standing there. He was standing right in the center of the grass, near the summerhouse, and he was looking straight at her. For one moment she had the sensation that he knew where she'd been and that he was waiting for her, but she dismissed that thought. She stopped dead.

He had his hands in his pockets, and the sun was behind him, so he looked very tall, and very dark, and very cool and very elegant. Just the way he'd looked on his veranda all those years before. He spoke first.

"Well now, ma'am," he said, smiling, and kind of drawling out the words. Then he took a step forward, and another step, and held out his hand. The smile grew wider. "Do you still say how do you do the way you used to? And shake hands?"

Hélène bit her lip. She looked up at him uncertainly.

"Sometimes," she said.

Then she took his hand, and he solemnly shook it. She stared at him, half-expecting him to do as he had all those years before, to press a little, and scratch with his nail, there in the damp circle of her palm. But he didn't. He simply shook her hand quite formally, and then he let it go, and then he looked at her.

He looked at her for what seemed an eternity, though it couldn't have been more than a couple of seconds. He looked at her long wet hair and her flushed face. He looked at the wet blouse that clung to the outline of her breasts. He looked at the short schoolgirl skirt and the long bare tanned legs. He looked at her the way Billy Tanner looked, as if he couldn't quite believe what he saw. And quite suddenly, Hélène relaxed.

It was all right, she thought. It was all right. He wasn't angry, and even if he were, she had the oddest feeling that she could stop him if she wanted.

He smiled again, a beautiful warm smile, displaying even white perfect teeth.

"You've grown up," he said at last in a perfectly matter-of-fact voice. "You remember me? You're Hélène, aren't you? Hélène Craig." He paused. "Well, since you're on my land, Hélène Craig, can I offer you something to drink?"

"I . . . thank you very much. But—well, I ought to be getting home now, and . . ."

"Don't be absurd." He smiled, and then, to her astonishment, he took her arm, firmly but lightly, resting it through his, the way her mother had shown her, for all the world as if he were taking her in to dinner. He moved off, and Hélène went with him.

"So. What will it be? Mint julep? Whiskey sour? Coke? Bourbon on the rocks?"

Hélène laughed nervously. "I don't drink. Not alcohol. I'm—well, I'm twelve. My mother says that's too young."

"You astonish me. Twelve? I took you for a grown-up young woman."

Hélène flushed with pleasure. "A limeade would be nice."

"Then a limeade it shall be."

They *processed*, that was the word, Hélène thought. Not walked: walked was much too ordinary a word. Across the grass, past the old summerhouse, and over the lawns in full view of the tall windows of the big house. Along past the tall white portico, along past the magnolia tree that reached almost up to the roof. Arm in arm, right up the veranda steps, in through the huge entrance hall, across a cool stone floor, and into the most beautiful room she had ever seen in her whole life.

It was so big, she couldn't believe it. Why, it must have been forty feet long, fifty maybe. And the ceiling was very high, and there were four huge windows. Their blinds were lowered against the evening sun.

He showed her to a chair, and Hélène sat down in it. It was the softest, most comfortable, most luxurious-feeling she'd ever known. Silk, against her bare legs, and cushions that were plump with finest goose down. She leaned back, slightly dazed, her heart beating very fast. Major Calvert went over to a cabinet on the far side of the room, and at first she thought he was going to ring for the butler, but he didn't do that. He mixed the drinks himself, from a silver tray: whiskey for him, she saw, on rocks of ice which he took with tongs from a silver bucket. And limeade for her, *eau-de-nil* green, in a long thin glass. He turned back with the drinks in his hand, and looked at her again. Then he went over, as if it were an afterthought, and shut the tall mahogany doors. And then he brought her her drink and sat down on a chair opposite her.

Hélène clutched the glass in her hand. There was a tiny table of polished wood right next to her, with flowers on it, and a little silver tray which looked as if it might be meant to stand a glass on. But she couldn't be sure. Her eyes turned to the room, but it was too immense, too extraordinary to take in all at once. She just had a confused impression that everything shone: the tables, the silver ashtrays and photograph frames, the grand piano at the far end, the gilt frames of the paintings on the wall. And there were flowers everywhere: hothouse flowers and palms. The scent of the flowers came to her on the still cool air, and her eyes dazzled. She looked back at Major Calvert.

He was sitting there, apparently perfectly relaxed, his legs crossed at the knee, one perfectly polished shoe tapping idly on the carpet.

His skin was deeply tanned, his hair and moustache just as dark as she remembered. As she looked at him, he reached into his pocket and drew out a gold cigarette case and a lighter.

"You don't smoke, either, I take it?" The corners of his lips lifted. "Would you mind if I did?"

"Oh. No. No. Of course not."

He lit the cigarette and inhaled slowly. He didn't seem to feel the need to say anything, but Hélène did. The silence was terrifying.

"I shouldn't have been there," she burst out suddenly. "I do realize that. In the pond, I mean. I'm sorry."

"Please." He made an amused, courteous gesture of the hands. "It's very hot. If that's where you were, feel free to go there anytime you like." He paused. "Is it a good place to swim? Do you go there often?"

Hélène looked at him uncertainly, for he put the question slightly oddly. Then she shook her head.

"No. Not often. Not now."

"But you did once?"

"For a while. Years ago."

He sighed. The answer seemed to please him.

"To tell you the truth, it's a little scary." She paused. "It's shadowy in there. You feel like you're being watched."

He didn't answer this, but drew on the cigarette. There was silence again; in a corner, a clock chimed.

"It certainly is very hot," Hélène said at last. Her mind was whirling. She knew there ought to be lots of things she could say, but right then she couldn't think of one of them. "Is Mrs. Calvert at home?"

Out it came, just like that, sounding idiotic. But Major Calvert didn't seem to mind. He just looked up, absently, as if he were thinking of something else.

"What? Oh, no. She's visiting. Her family, you know. Up in Philadelphia."

Hélène considered this information. Major Calvert said nothing more, but he was looking at her again. He put his cigarette out and slipped his hand back into his pocket. She didn't know why, perhaps it was the way he was looking at her, so quietly like that, but Hélène felt more and more self-conscious. She could feel the color mounting in her cheeks, and she felt peculiar, excited and nervous all at once. She drained the glass of limeade quickly.

"You'd like another?"

"Oh, no. Thank you." She twisted her hands nervously in her skirt.

"You still sound English. Not American at all. Remarkable." He spoke so suddenly he made her jump. She smiled.

"Do I? I can sound American too. When I want to."

"Can you now?" He leaned forward. "Say something to me, then, in American. . . ."

Hélène drew in her breath. She let her lashes fall, then looked up again at him.

"I'm sorry I was trespassin' on your land, Major Calvert. . . ." It came out perfectly, a slow southern drawl, demure, with just a little provocative edge. Major Calvert looked at her for a second intently, then he threw back his head and laughed. Just the way she remembered.

"Well now—who'd have believed it?" He stopped laughing. "You're a clever young woman. As well as a pretty one." He leaned forward suddenly, his dark teasing eyes meeting hers. "Do they tell you that, all the boys 'round here? I'm sure they do. That you're pretty? More than that. That you're beautiful?"

Hélène's heart seemed to miss a beat. A quick shiver of excitement went through her, like an electric pulse and just as quick, there and then gone. She lowered her eyes again and stood up.

"I'd better be getting home now. Thank you for the drink, Major Calvert."

"It's been a pleasure, ma'am."

He stood up in the same moment, and his voice sounded as if he were teasing her. But she looked up, and he didn't seem to be. His eyes were dark brown and quite serious. He was standing close to her suddenly, and Hélène could see that his breath was coming a little fast.

"Your hair's still wet, Hélène Craig. You know that?" he said, and his voice sounded odd and kind of thick. Then he lifted his hand and he touched her hair. He lifted one long strand very slowly, and let it run through his fingers. Hélène didn't move. "And your blouse. It's wet almost right through." She saw his tongue pass over his lips, saw his chest rise and fall under the elegant white jacket. And then he touched her. Her sleeve first, and then, slowly and deliberately, looking right down into her wide, shocked eyes, her breast. A light touch, so she knew he could feel the swell of her breast through the wet material, but a movement that could just as easily be passed off.

She knew she ought to do something. Tell him to stop, knock his hand away, run out of the room, something; but somehow she couldn't do any of those things. She just stood there, looking at him.

"Wet through. Right down to the skin."

His voice was deep and thick now, and kind of whispery. For a moment he stayed still just like that, then his hand tightened over her breast suddenly. Still his eyes never left hers, and Hélène thought confusedly that it was as if he were looking for something there, something he could read, and she didn't know what it was. Then he slipped his hand in under the blouse, easily, gently, and cupped her naked breast in the dry palm of his hand. Again, he stayed like that, quite still. Then he moved his fingers, once, twice, over her nipple, with a feather-light touch that was piercingly exquisite.

Then he removed his hand, and it was as if nothing had happened at all. He simply took her arm, the way he had before, and led her courteously to the door.

In the entrance hall he looked down into her face. He looked quite composed again now, quite relaxed, and that odd intentness had gone from his eyes.

"Would you like to come here again someday, Hélène Craig?" He paused. "See 'round the plantation maybe?"

Hélène hung her head. "I don't know. Perhaps."

Her answer seemed to please him once more, for he smiled.

"Fine," he said. "Fine. Anytime you feel ready, you just let me know. Doesn't matter when."

"It doesn't?" Hélène lifted her head, her blue eyes flaring with doubt.

He shook his head.

"No, ma'am." He touched her arm. "I can wait."

It was her fifteenth birthday, and Billy Tanner said that was something special, something to celebrate. Billy had graduated from Selma High now; he was working in the garage over Maybury way, working full-time, earning good money, he said.

"We could go out. Have dinner someplace," Billy said. "Celebrate in style . . ."

Hélène looked at him uncertainly. Billy seemed to avoid her less these days; he'd even promised he might take her swimming again sometime. But he'd never asked her out on a date.

"Just you and me, Billy?"

Billy's face went a dull brick red. "You'd rather we made it a double date maybe?"

Hélène hung her head. She thought she might prefer to be alone with Billy, but she didn't like to say so. She didn't want to sound pushy.

"I could ask Priscilla-Anne, I s'pose," she muttered.

"Okay. Sure. Why not?"

So she had asked Priscilla-Anne, and Priscilla-Anne's eyebrows had disappeared right up under her carefully groomed bangs.

"Billy Tanner? Billy *Tanner*? You must be kidding. In a restaurant? *He's* paying?"

"I guess so."

"Okay." Priscilla-Anne sighed. "Some celebration. I'll check it out with Dale, okay? Because then we can go in his car. I'm not going on some bus. No way . . ."

And so here they all were, crammed into Dale Garrett's Buick. She and Billy in the back, Priscilla-Anne and Dale in front; Dale driving, one hand on the wheel only, and Priscilla-Anne laughing, and opening up a six-pack. She tossed two cans into the back, and opened one for herself; Budweiser squirted all over the dash. Then one for Dale. She tilted her head back; one hand rested on Dale's thigh, and he said something Hélène couldn't catch, and Priscilla-Anne laughed. Hélène leaned back

in her seat. Dale was Priscilla's latest beau. She'd lost count how many
there had been between Eddie Haines and him. Six at least; seven
maybe. And she herself was fifteen—fifteen years, two and a half days.
When was her life going to start?

Next to her, Billy carefully opened a can of beer and handed it to
her. He left his own unopened. Billy didn't drink, and Hélène thought
she knew why—because of his father.

She stole a glance at him, and her heart contracted. She could just
see how hard he'd tried. The crew cut had gone, some years back. Now
Billy wore his dark hair combed straight back; it was shiny with grease.
He had his good suit on; the one he wore to weddings and funerals. It
didn't fit too well, and there were threadbare patches on the elbows. He
was wearing a shirt and a tie, too, and you could see they made him
uncomfortable, because every so often he'd reach up a finger and slip it
under the collar, as if it were choking him. He'd cut himself shaving,
and there was a little nick just below where he was trying to grow his
sideburns. He smelled too strongly of aftershave, and he was sitting bolt
upright, both hands on his knees. He hadn't said one word since they'd
gotten into the car.

Hélène felt embarrassed, and hated herself for it. She tried not to
look at Dale Garrett up front. He was loaded, or so Priscilla-Anne said.
His daddy owned a fertilizer plant over Montgomery way. He had a
college degree, a Buick, and a reputation as long as your arm. Priscilla-
Anne loved him. *He's the one, Hélène,* she'd say. *This time I just know. He's
the one.* Dale Garrett was wearing a sport jacket and a button-down
Brooks Brothers shirt. No grease on *his* hair; it flopped over his forehead
when he laughed—which he did often. A red and gold fraternity ring
gleamed on his finger. Hélène looked away: she didn't even like Dale
Garrett that much. He was a snob, she thought, and a boaster; clean-cut
good looks, sure enough, but not nearly as good-looking as Billy, with
his kingfisher-blue eyes. Not nearly as nice, either. So how come, when
she looked at him and then looked at Billy, she felt pity, and then
shame?

"You made a reservation, Tanner?" Dale turned and grinned over
his shoulder. He tossed the Budweiser can out the window.

"No." Billy's voice was quiet. "Didn't need to. It won't be full."

"Hope you're right, Tanner . . ." Hélène saw him glance across at
Priscilla-Anne, and wink. "I mean, these fancy places, they can be
funny about that. Turning up without a reservation, you know?"

"It'll be all right."

"Hope so. Because I worked up quite an appetite today, thinking
about tonight and all. In more ways 'n one . . ." His hand came down
over Priscilla-Anne's and adjusted it slightly. "Yes sir! I fancy myself a

good steak, and plenty of fries, salad on the side. A little French wine, maybe. They have French wine in this place of yours, Tanner?"

"Sure." Billy's face looked pale and tight. "I mean, I guess they do."

"*French* wine, I said, Tanner." Dale laughed. "I mean, this is a celebration, right?" He grinned at Hélène in the rearview mirror. "French name, French wine. Makes sense, don't you think?"

Hélène said nothing. Her eyes locked with Dale's for a second, then slid away. He was trying to rile Billy, she knew that. And her, too, maybe. She made him feel uncomfortable, with her funny name and her funny voice, she could tell that. Dale liked to place people, she thought, and he couldn't quite place her. It was the nervousness that was making him so rude. Quietly she reached across the backseat and found Billy's hand. She gave it a hard squeeze.

The restaurant was on the outskirts of Montgomery someplace.

"Not downtown?" Dale said as Billy leaned forward and started to give him directions.

"No. Not downtown. Make a left here. . . ."

Past the turning to the airport, under a bridge, and onto the main highway into town. They passed a parking lot, a garage, two gas stations, traffic lights. Billy was beginning to look excited, and proud. He gestured with his hand.

"Over there. There. Make a right now. . . ."

Dale Garrett spun the wheel. They came to a stop. There was a silence, broken by a stifled giggle from Priscilla.

"Here?" Dale's voice sounded disbelieving. "Howard *Johnson's?*"

"That's it." Billy was already getting out of the car. He came around to Hélène's side, opened her door, and carefully helped her out.

"The restaurant," he said to her softly, and she could feel the nervousness in his body. "What did he think I meant—the coffee shop?"

"It's lovely, Billy," Hélène said quickly. "Just lovely. Thank you."

Priscilla-Anne and Dale were necking, so she and Billy walked on ahead of them, in through the lobby and into the restaurant itself. It was very large, and half empty. A line of white businessmen on stools by the bar; acres of shiny red banquettes. The captain was wearing red too; he was Billy's age, no more, and his face was spotted with pimples. He looked Billy up and down, and Hélène could see the sneer start way back in his eyes. Then he looked at her, and his eyes widened.

"We'd like a table," Billy said firmly. "Over there in the window."

The man came as near to giving a shrug as he could, then he turned back to Hélène and gave her a long stare.

"Sure thing. This way. Ma'am."

Hélène felt the color flood up over her face. She followed him to the table and sat down. Two menus were tossed down on the table.

"We need two more. There'll be four of us," Billy said, but the man had already gone.

Hélène looked up to find Billy staring at her. She wondered if he'd noticed the man's rudeness, because if he had, he didn't seem to care. His face looked soft, and gentle, and intent, and the blue eyes blazed like the sky on a summer's day.

"You look beautiful," Billy said simply. "You look—well, I guess you're just about the most beautiful thing I ever saw in my life."

"Billy?"

"So I don't give a damn, okay?" He gave a quick smile, and the blue eyes crinkled around the corners. "Not about Dale Garrett, or that guy over there, either. Not about anything. Just so long as I can go right on looking at you. That's all."

"Billy, I . . ." She hesitated, not quite sure what to say, because what he said surprised her and pleased her, and also made her feel a little afraid. Something in her was holding back, and all she knew was that she didn't want Billy to be hurt, not ever. And especially not by her. "I . . . you like my dress?"

It was a white dress, cotton, and it showed off the tan of her skin. When her mother had showed it to her, she'd danced around the room for joy. It was the prettiest dress she'd ever worn.

"I like your dress."

"My mother made it. For my birthday. She got the material cheap, she said, and . . ."

"Does she know? Where you are tonight?" Billy's face had clouded slightly. "I mean, did you tell her you were going out with me?"

"No, Billy." She raised her eyes pleadingly to his face.

"She thinks I'm not good enough to take you out?"

"No, Billy, of course not. It's not that. It's just that she doesn't like me to go out on dates. Not with anyone. She says I'm still too young, and so I said I was going over to Priscilla-Anne's. . . ."

"Too young?" Billy frowned. "You're almost a woman." He hesitated. "Seems to me."

There was a little silence, and she saw him glance up. On the far side of the restaurant Dale and Priscilla-Anne were just coming in.

"My daddy got married when he was eighteen." Billy fiddled with his knife. "My mama wasn't more'n sixteen, seventeen, when I was born. Still . . ." He sighed. "Maybe yours sees things differently, being from England and all. . . . You want to look at the menu now?"

Hélène picked up the card and raised it in front of her face. The prices danced before her eyes, and she felt a little sick. Everything seemed so expensive, and for all he said, she knew Billy didn't earn that much. Half of what he earned, more maybe, went to his mother. Maybe, if she said she wasn't very hungry, if she just ordered a salad?

But Billy would be disappointed if she did that, she knew. He'd been planning this for weeks, months maybe.

And her mother—what would her mother say if she knew where she was? Hélène wasn't sure anymore. She'd lied, to be safe, because if she'd told her the truth, her mother might have lost her temper and refused to let her go. But on the other hand, she might have just accepted it, said nothing at all.

Hélène didn't understand her mother these days, she was so unpredictable, so strange. Sometimes she was up, high as a kite, filled with the weird tense excitement that Hélène had come to recognize and to dread. Dread, because it meant it wouldn't last long. The next day she'd suddenly be down. She'd drag herself around like she hardly had the energy to move anymore. She'd listen and nod while Hélène talked, but her wide violet eyes would have this blank look in them, as if she were locked away in some world of her own, as if she didn't hear a word that was being said. She took less care of herself now. She was terribly thin, and never seemed to want to eat, and there were gray streaks in her hair, and she didn't set it in pins, not the way she used to.

Sometimes Hélène thought she drank. She'd found a vodka bottle once, wrapped up in paper, empty, hidden away in the garbage can, and after that she'd watched her mother carefully. But she never saw her drink, never found another bottle. She slept a lot, too, especially these last weeks; Hélène had noticed it. Sometimes she'd come home from school, and her mother would be in bed. She'd just stayed there, she said. It was simpler; her head ached so. It didn't matter; Cassie Wyatt had two new assistants. She could cope now. She'd have to.

And the money. The prices on the menu swam before her eyes. She didn't want to think about the money or the old tin box. Last time she'd looked it'd been down to forty-three dollars. . . .

She'd wanted to tell *someone*, talk to *someone*, but loyalty held her back. Once, just once, she'd tried. Half-tried. *Sometimes I think I'll never go to England,* she had said to Priscilla-Anne. But Priscilla-Anne had just laughed. "Honey, did you ever really believe you would? Quit dreaming. Orangeburg isn't so bad. . . ." She'd made a face, gestured down Main Street. "Stay here! You could always marry Billy Tanner. . . ."

Hélène shut her eyes. She wouldn't think about it, she wouldn't. It was her birthday! She ought to feel happy. If she got to thinking too much, the cage closed in, and then she felt sick and mean and scared; she felt like an animal in a trap.

Billy was reading the menu now; one finger was moving down the long lines of print. His lips moved. Priscilla-Anne nudged Dale in the ribs, and it was all Hélène could do not to reach across and grab the menu. *Don't do that, Billy,* she wanted to cry. *I know you're worth a hundred of them, but can't you see they're laughing at you? Oh, Billy, can't you?*

Then the waiter came over, and Billy tried to give him everyone's order, and got all tangled up and blushed scarlet.

"I'll settle for a steak. And fries."

The waiter smirked.

"And how would you like the steak cooked, sir?"

Billy stared at him blankly.

"Why, just the way you always cook them, I guess," he said finally.

"He means how d'you want it, Billy?" Priscilla-Anne took pity on him. "You know—rare, medium, well-done?"

"Oh. Well-done. . . ."

"I'll have the same," Hélène said quickly.

Priscilla-Anne gave her order. Then the waiter turned to Dale. The smirk disappeared.

"Sir?"

"Well now . . ." Dale leaned back on the banquette. He had seated himself next to Hélène; now he stretched his arms along the back of the seat above her shoulders.

"I'll have the *filet*. Rare. Fries. Onions on the side. A large salad. Roquefort dressing. I guess you don't have a wine list in this place?"

"No, sir."

"Then I'll take a bourbon on the rocks. And a beer. How about you, Tanner?"

"Nothing for me."

"That'll be it then." Dale grinned. "These lovely ladies are under age. . . ."

When the waiter brought the bourbon, ice tinkling, Dale lifted his glass.

"To Hélène." He swung around to face her, eyes glittering, mouth moist. "You know, I can't believe you're just fifteen years old? You look so grown-up now. . . ." His eyes fell to her breasts, then back up to her face. "Priscilla-Anne, honey," he drawled, "how come you never told me you had such a cute little friend?"

He began as he meant to go on, never losing a chance to put Billy down, never missing a chance to flirt with Hélène. Billy hardly spoke; once she realized what was happening, Priscilla-Anne's face set in hard lines. Whenever Hélène tried to catch her eye, she turned her face away. Hélène sat there while he systematically destroyed the evening. Dale alone seemed to be enjoying himself. He ate with relish. He swilled back several glasses of beer, and the more he drank, and his color rose, the more flagrant he became.

When Hélène pushed half her steak and most of her french fries aside, uneaten, Dale laughed. His hand circled her shoulders, his fingers briefly caressed her bare arm.

"That how you keep that figure of yours, Hélène? She's just so slender! Why, I bet my two hands'd go right around her waist—what do you think, Priscilla-Anne?"

Priscilla-Anne drained her glass of ice water in one gulp. She was wearing a pink knit top, very tight. Her face was pink, too, and her eyes were round with indignation.

"And they wouldn't fit 'round mine?" She glared around the table. "That what you're saying, Dale?"

Dale laughed. "Course I'm not, honey. I can think of better places to put them when I'm with you, you know that. . . ."

Priscilla-Anne's face softened; she gave a nervous laugh.

Hélène quickly shifted so she was out of Dale's grasp. Billy, who had stopped eating, picked up his knife and fork again, and went on patiently trying to saw the steak. When the waiter finally took the plates away, no one wanted anything else—except Dale. Dale ordered cheesecake, and another highball, and coffee. When the coffee came, he poured the cream carefully over the back of the spoon, so it floated in a pale circle on the coffee below. He sipped it, then turned to Hélène. He had a thin line of cream along his upper lip.

"Just the way I like it. Smooth and creamy on top, hot and dark underneath . . ." He smiled, regarding her with lowered lids, then leaned back expansively on the seat.

"Well now. That was good. Thank you, Tanner. A real fine meal." He half-suppressed a belch. "Where d'you work, Tanner, by the way? I don't think you said—"

"Over Maybury way. At Haines's garage."

"You don't say! You know Eddie Haines? Used to be at Selma High? He's an old boyfriend of Priscilla-Anne's—you know him?"

"I've come across him." Billy glanced at Priscilla-Anne. "He's married now."

"Don't I know it!" Priscilla-Anne tossed her head. "Married Susie Marshall, used to be a grade ahead of us. Married her just in time, I heard. . . ."

"Strange . . ." Dale wasn't listening. "Didn't know Haines hired white boys. I thought, the wages he pays, he could get only niggers. . . ."

"You thought wrong then." Slowly Billy replaced his cup on his saucer.

"Dale's starting law school in the fall," Priscilla-Anne interjected quickly into the ugly silence that followed. Hélène saw her glance nervously at Dale. "He plans to start his own law practice here in Montgomery—don't you, Dale? And his daddy made a real big contribution to George Wallace's campaign, and Dale's been working on his campaign staff. Speech-writing and research and all . . ."

"Is that so?" Billy looked at him across the table, and Dale shrugged. He threw Priscilla-Anne a little smile.

"Certainly is." He made a deprecating gesture. "Don't actually write any of the speeches, you understand. Spend a lot of time making coffee as a matter of fact. But it's a real privilege, you know? An honor. He's a fine man, Wallace. Smart. Knows we're going to need all the smart lawyers down here we can get, the way things are going in Washington right now. Federal government sticking its finger into every little pie. Goddamn Yankees trying to tell us what we should and shouldn't do. I tell you—it just makes my blood boil. And that Lyndon Johnson, selling us all down the river the way he did, voting for a civil rights bill. Getting it through the Senate like that. He'd sell his old grandmama for a bucket of shit, and he calls himself a southerner. . . ." He broke off with a smile. "Sorry, ladies. I guess I get carried away. But my daddy says, every time he hears the words *civil rights*, he goes reachin' for his gun. And I feel the same way. Niggers voting? Sitting in the same schools with white girls and white boys? That's commie talk. Jews and commies. But I tell you one thing. It'll never happen. No way. Not here in Alabama . . ."

He came to a stop, then winked across the table at Billy. "Still, mustn't talk politics, eh, Tanner? Don't want to bore the little ladies, now, do we? Ain't met a lady yet didn't turn her eyes up and start to yawn the minute politics was mentioned. . . ."

"Will you excuse me?" Hélène stood up quickly. Billy's face had gone hard and tight; he was staring at Dale across the table. But Dale didn't seem to notice. He made an elaborate show of rising to his feet to let Hélène pass. Priscilla-Anne rose, too, and Dale laughed.

"Don't you keep us waiting too long now. . . ."

The minute the door of the ladies' room closed behind them, Priscilla-Anne rounded on her. "Hélène Craig, you two-timin' cat—what d'you think you're doing? Call yourself my friend . . ."

Her cheeks were flushed; Hélène could see that she was close to tears.

"Doing? I'm not doing anything. It's him. It's Dale. I can't help the way he behaves. I'm not encouraging him. . . ."

"Oh, you're not? Well, it doesn't look that way to me—not where I'm sitting. Oh, you keep quiet and you don't say much, I give you that. But you don't need to. You just look at him with those blue eyes of yours, and it's the biggest come-on I've ever seen. Why, Susie Marshall had nothing on you. . . ."

"That's not true!" Hélène caught her arm, and Priscilla-Anne brushed her angrily aside. "I wouldn't do that—you know I wouldn't. You're my friend, Priscilla-Anne."

"Was. I was your friend." She gave a toss of the head. "I was so dumb. Listening to you. I should have known. All the other kids, they warned me. 'Stay away from Hélène Craig,' they said. 'Why would you want to be friends with a girl like her?' But I liked you. I trusted you. I must have been crazy."

"Priscilla-Anne . . ."

"I broke up with Eddie Haines because of you!" Priscilla-Anne's voice rose in a wail. "Listening to you, going along with all those dumb things you told me to say! *If you respected me, Eddie, you just wouldn't do that*—remember that? Remember how we practiced it up in my room? And then I said it, and you know what? That was my last date with Eddie. He took up with Susie Marshall then, and—"

"You can't blame me for that!" Hélène stared at her in disbelief. Priscilla-Anne's tears had started to fall. "I didn't know that was going to happen. I was just trying to help. . . ."

"You were?" Priscilla-Anne gave her an angry push. She turned to the mirror and began to fumble in her purse. "Well, I thought that *then*. But I don't think that *now*. Now I know better. I think you did it on purpose. You wanted me to break up. Because you were jealous, Hélène Craig, that's all. Just mean and jealous . . ."

"Jealous? Of Eddie Haines? You've got to be joking."

"Oh, I have?" In the mirror Priscilla-Anne's eyes narrowed. Their gaze met. "And I suppose you're going to say you're not jealous of Dale either? That you wouldn't rather have him drive you home tonight than that creep Billy Tanner?" She rubbed angrily at her swollen eyes with a tissue, then unscrewed her mascara wand, and began poking it jerkily at her lashes. Hélène watched her.

"I would say that," she answered at last, slowly. "Yes, I would say that. I'm not jealous of you and Dale, Priscilla-Anne. Truly. I wish you'd believe me." She shrugged. "If you want to know the truth, I don't even like him very much. I think he's rude. He drinks too much. He has no manners worth mentioning, and . . ."

It was the wrong tack. In the mirror Priscilla-Anne's eyes hardened, and she turned around slowly.

"Oh, you think so? You'd know, for sure. I mean, they teach you real fancy manners back there in the trailer park, huh? In that crummy dump you're so ashamed of that you never even asked me back there. Jesus, Hélène Craig, you're something, you know that? Why, a man like Dale wouldn't bother giving you the time of day if it wasn't for me. He knows white trash. He can smell it—same as I can. . . ."

Priscilla-Anne was shaking. She still had the mascara wand in her hand. Now she screwed it in place and put it back into her purse. She pulled the zipper shut. She turned to the mirror. Hélène stood absolutely still; her skin felt very hot, and then ice-cold. The tiled floor beneath her feet seemed to ripple like a wave. In the glass Priscilla-Anne stared fixedly at her crisp blond bangs. She lifted them with one finger, let her hand fall.

"How many times you do it with Billy Tanner to get to come to a place like this?" Her voice was very deliberate. "Five times? Six? Ten? D'you go down on him, Hélène, the way Susie Marshall told us that time? That what you did? I mean, Billy makes what? Fifty-five dollars a week? Sixty? It's a big deal for a guy like Billy to come to a hick place like this. You must have done somethin' special to fix it. Or maybe I'm wrong. Maybe you give it away easy. Like your mama. I mean, every man in Orangeburg knows your mama'll shake her tail for a new dress. And for a bottle of liquor—well, I hear she gets very original then. Must be kind of weird, I always thought, wearing a dress like that—" she flicked her wrist at Hélène's white dress—"and countin' up on your fingers how many screws it took your mama to pay for it. . . ."

"Shut your dirty lying mouth!" Hélène sprang forward, but Priscilla-Anne was too quick for her. She ducked away out of reach of Hélène's upraised hand. Into the cubicle. The door slammed; the bolt was rammed into place. From inside, Priscilla-Anne laughed a horrible nervous excited laugh.

"Oh, come *on*, Hélène, don't get mad at me. Don't try telling me you didn't *know*. I mean, didn't you ever *ask* yourself why you never had a date? You must have known. Billy Tanner, okay. But what decent boy wants to go with the daughter of a slut?"

There was a silence. Hélène stared at the locked door. She knew if she didn't get out fast, she'd cry, and if she didn't cry, she'd vomit. She got back to the table somehow; the room was a blur. Dale had another beer in front of him now; his handsome face was flushed, and he was laughing.

"Oh, come on, Tanner. You can tell me. I mean, we all know. When a man wants a good time—and I mean a *good* time—there's nothin', but nothin', warms him up like black—"

"Billy. Get me out of here." She spoke softly, but Billy had already seen her face and was on his feet. There was a little plastic tray on the table, and on the tray was the check. Billy fumbled with his billfold. Note after note; he hesitated, then added one more. The billfold was empty. Dale was leaning back, watching, a broad smile on his face. "You-all leaving us now? That's a shame. A real shame . . ."

Billy leaned across the table. He was taller than Dale, and bigger. The smile froze on Dale's face.

"One word," Billy said softly. "You just say one more word, college boy, and I'll knock your teeth right down your throat. You got that?" Then he took Hélène's arm, and they walked out.

They got a ride as far as Orangeburg, then they walked. Just before they reached the trailer park, Billy stopped. There was a moon, on the wane but still quite full. It lit the dirt road, and the trees, and the pallor of Billy's face. His eyes were glittering blue, as if he were angry. He didn't look at Hélène, he just stared straight past her at the trees.

"It's going to change." He jerked out suddenly. "It's going to change. Someday soon. He can't see it. Most of them can't see it. But it will." He lifted his hand and let it fall. "He's been to college. He probably reads more books in a week than I get through in a year, and he can't see it. No more'n my daddy can, and most of the folks 'round here. But it will change—it's wrong, so it's got to, that's all. I didn't always think that way. Not when I was a kid. And if I said what I thought now, my daddy'd smash me in the face. But I think it just the same. I look around here—and all I see is hate. All I've ever seen is hate. Hate and fear. Everybody scratching, scratching, just to keep their little place on the heap, just to keep from slipping a little bit lower. I'm way down near the bottom, so I can see, I can see what it does to people. My daddy now. My daddy hasn't worked in thirteen years, and he drinks more liquor than is good for him, but you know what? My daddy thinks he's okay. Because he knows, whatever happens, he's a white man, so no matter what, he can't go down to the bottom of the heap. That's for colored folks. My daddy thinks he hates them, but he doesn't, not really. He needs them, do you see? He needs them, because they're the only thing my daddy has left, the only thing he can look down on. . . ." His voice died away, and he turned back and looked down into her face.

"I wanted so much. . . ." He frowned. "I wanted so much for you to have a good time tonight. I wanted, and I planned, and it got all messed up. And . . ."

"Oh, Billy. Hold me. Just hold me tight. . . ." Hélène stepped forward blindly, and his arms came around her hard. She bent her head against his chest and the hammer of his heart, and she cried. It seemed to her she cried for a long time; cried for herself and her mother and Billy and his daddy; cried for Alabama, and for being fifteen years old; cried because the moon shone on, and the trees moved in the breeze. All the time she cried Billy never said a word. He just held her steadily, and rested his face against her hair. When, finally, she stopped, he lifted her face gently up to his, and looked down into her eyes.

"I wish you were for me," he said, his voice very gentle and very sad. "I wish I could believe you would be—ever. I've wished for it, and even prayed for it, for just as long as I can remember. And tonight—I'd planned on telling you. How I felt. I thought . . . I hoped. But I was kidding myself all along. I knew it all the time, maybe." He frowned, and the kingfisher-blue eyes were like stars. "I wished I could see into the future sometimes. See what will happen—to you. Because I don't know where you're going, but it's going to be a long way from here. That I know. And I'd like for you to be safe, and happy, wherever it is. And I'd like to think you'd remember. Remember me. The things we did . . ."

"Billy?"

"I care for you." He took her hand, and held it, just for a moment. "Ever since you first came here. Ever since you were a little kid. You're beautiful. And you're special. There's no one else like you. When I look at you, it's like the sun and the moon were shining up there in the same sky. That's all. I just wanted you to know. It won't change nothing. I don't expect you to feel the same way. But I wanted you to know."

Hélène bent her head. She felt the tears start up behind her eyes.

"You know what Priscilla-Anne said tonight?" She couldn't look at him. "She said . . . she said my mother was a whore." She forced the word out, and Billy's head went up, quick, like an animal scenting danger. He took a step forward, and Hélène held up her hand. "She did. That's what she said. She said everyone in Orangeburg knew it except maybe me. All the men. She said . . ."

Billy's arms came around her. "Never mind what she said. Put it out of your mind. She's jealous."

"I can't put it out of my mind. I'll never forget it. Not as long as I live. And I want you to tell me. Please, Billy. I can't ask anyone else. I want to know. Is that the truth? Is that what they say?"

"Folks say a lot of things." He sounded awkward and embarrassed. "Your mother's different, like you, and they don't like that, they can't bear that. . . ."

"Is it *true?*"

Billy's eyes dropped for a second, and Hélène felt her heart grow cold and still within her. After a while, Billy looked up. Then he stepped forward and gripped her arms tight. "You just listen to me," he said. "Listen. People do things—all kinds of things—if they have no money. If they're lonely. If they're running out of hope. You going to condemn them for that? I wouldn't. Because who knows what you'd do if you found yourself in their shoes? If you got desperate." He broke off. "She loves you, Hélène. She's looked after you, the best she could. And no matter what she did—"

"But what does that make *me?*"

"It doesn't make you anything. You're you. You're the most beautiful thing I ever saw in all my life. You're Hélène. And I think . . . I think you could be just about anything you wanted. You understand? Anything." He gave her a little shake, then let her go.

"Come on now. It's late. I don't want you to cry no more. I'll walk you home."

They walked in silence through the trees, across the thin grass, past the other trailers, all dark. Then Hélène gave a little cry, and started to run. The green trailer's door was open; light spilled out in a yellow patch onto the grass; the radio was playing, very low, and right from the little picket gate they could see her mother's body lying in a heap on the floor.

Billy was up the steps and into the trailer ahead of her. Hélène stepped in after him, her eyes blinking after the dark. She stared around her stupidly, confusedly, then knelt. The trailer smelled of vomit. She lifted her mother's head gently, and the violet eyes opened, then closed. Her mother groaned. Billy was standing stock still in the middle of the tiny room.

"Billy—what's happened? What is it?"

"Liquor." His voice was matter-of-fact. He lifted a bottle from the floor. It was empty. "She take all this—tonight?"

"Tonight? I don't know. She doesn't drink. I thought she didn't drink. That is . . ."

"Here. I'll lift her." Billy bent down. His blue eyes met hers, and he gave a grim little smile. "It's all right. She'll be okay. I know just what to do."

Afterward, Hélène couldn't bear to think of the scene that followed, it was so degrading. Her mother's legs wouldn't hold her up, and Billy had to support her and hold her head. Somehow he got her outside, into the air. There were horrible retching sounds, and Hélène covered her ears with her hands.

"You clean up in there meanwhile," Billy called in through the door. He sounded almost amused, quite cheerful. "She'll be okay soon. Let her get it up. Then she can sleep."

When he finally brought her mother back inside, Hélène stared at her in horror. Her face was chalk-white. There were black shadows under her eyes. She smelled horrible. Her eyes were open now, but it was as if she couldn't see. They fixed on Hélène for a moment, then on Billy, then on clear air. She moaned.

"I've fixed the bed." Hélène looked at Billy uncertainly.

"Fine." He lifted her mother and carried her like a rag doll into the bedroom. Then he laid her tenderly down on the bed as if she were a child. He turned her on her side and removed the pillow. Then he drew the sheet over her and tucked her in.

"Should I give her anything?"

"Nothing. It'll only make her throw up. She'll have a headache in the morning. You can give her some seltzer then." The grin faded from his features. He took her arm and drew Hélène gently into the next room.

"She never done that before?"

"No. Never."

"Something happen to upset her, or what?"

"Nothing. She was fine when I left. I thought she was fine. She seemed very happy—oh, Billy!"

"Don't fret. It's probably a one-time thing. Maybe she just felt down about something, and you were out. She took a drink to cheer herself up, then didn't know when to stop. . . ." He was trying to comfort her, Hélène could see that. She could also see the doubt and the unease way back in his eyes.

"You want me to stay?"

"No, Billy. It's all right. You've got to go to work in the morning. I'll stay with her. Don't worry about me."

Billy smiled, an odd, crooked smile.

"But I do," he said. 'I guess I'll always worry about you."

In the doorway, Hélène reached awkwardly for his hand. She squeezed it tight.

"Thank you, Billy," she whispered. "For everything."

He didn't touch her. He didn't kiss her. He just went down the steps and out into the little yard. Hélène watched him in the moonlight, his tall lithe figure.

"I will remember, Billy," she called suddenly after him. "I will. . . . Everything you said. Always . . ."

But Billy didn't turn, or look back, and so she never knew if he heard her.

When he was out of sight, Hélène shut the door. Slowly she went back into the bedroom and sat down on her bed. She looked at her mother's thin shoulders, at the graying hair against the sheet, the pale face. Her mother was breathing heavily.

After a little while, her mother suddenly opened her eyes. She stared straight at Hélène, though Hélène thought she didn't see her.

"Oh, God," she said quite distinctly. "Sweet Jesus. What have I done with my life?"

Then she closed her eyes again, and slept.

T wo days later, Hélène was walking home from school along the Orangeburg road, when a big, black open-topped Cadillac came alongside. A man in a white shirt was driving; a white linen jacket was tossed on the backseat. The Cadillac came to a halt; Hélène stopped. She glimpsed a flashing smile, a tanned hand extended.

"Hélène Craig. Well now. How do you do?"

"Hi." Hélène took the hand, and let it go again quickly. "Major Calvert?"

"Ned. Call me Ned." Again the smile. "It's a long while since I was in uniform." He swung back the passenger door. "It's hot. You want a ride?"

Hélène hesitated. Deep within her she felt something stir, a forbidden excitement, like a note struck against a glass, there and then gone. She had never been in a Cadillac. She walked around the car and got in.

He looked at his watch, a gold Rolex on a leather strap, then back at Hélène.

"It's early yet. You'd like to see the plantation now? It's a fine evening."

He spoke as if there had been no time gap, as if the past three years had telescoped, and the previous invitation had been made no more than a few days ago. He spoke as if quite certain she would remember it.

"All right." She folded her hands on her lap.

He gunned the accelerator; the Cadillac pulled away fast and smooth, and cool air gusted through her hair. She gave an involuntary cry of pleasure, and Ned Calvert smiled. Hélène looked at him sideways. A handsome man, a real southern gentleman—that was what they said about Ned Calvert. When she was younger, she'd thought he looked like Clark Gable in *Gone With the Wind*, and she hadn't been so wrong, either. That very dark hair, drawn back from the broad, tanned face; the dark clipped moustache; wide shoulders; powerful tanned arms; a thickset muscular frame; one gold signet ring on his left hand. The nearest thing to an English gentleman in Orangeburg County. Only she didn't believe so much in English gentlemen anymore.

"I'm forty-three years old." He was still smiling, eyes on the road ahead. "You're fifteen now. My, but it's a fine evening. Just drivin' along feels fine. Don't you think, Hélène Craig?"

"It feels cool."

He turned his head for a second; one quick glance of the dark brown eyes. His foot came down hard on the pedal, and the car surged. Straight past the dirt track that led up to the trailer park. "It does. Cool and fast and free. I like drivin'."

He cut off the highway a few miles farther on, around the north side of the plantation, through the flat hot cotton fields. At intervals there were trees, clumps of southern pine or cottonwood that provided the only shade in the flat landscape. The pickers used to take their morning breaks there, he said, in the days when the crop was all picked by hand. "Hard work, pickin' cotton." He grinned. "I did it once, when I was a little boy. Wheedled away at my old daddy, said I wanted to know how it felt. So in the end he let me. Lasted twenty minutes maybe, no more. Never wanted to try it since . . . cotton's a mean plant. Scratches your hands to pieces. Cuts you apart. Breaks your back, bending. Gets up your nose so you think you'll never breathe clear again." He shrugged. "Machines do it better. Quicker, cleaner. Expensive to begin with, but cheaper in the long run. I started the switchover a few years back. Another couple of years, and none of it'll be picked by hand. . . ." He stopped the car. "My great-great-granddaddy started this place. Slave labor then, back in the bad old days. He had five hundred pickin' cotton. I won't need more than forty, forty-five maybe, a year or two on." He sighed. "Things are changing. Times are changing. The South isn't the way it was—not when I was a boy. . . ."

Hélène glanced at him sideways. It was impossible to tell if he welcomed change or regretted it. She said nothing, and after a while he started up the engine again, and they drove on. She had thought of him as a silent man, his silences perturbing and unnerving her. But now he talked and talked, hardly even looking at her, bombarding her with information—yield, acreage, boll weevils, insecticides, commodity crops; her head spun. It seemed to her he was talking to himself, or carrying on some argument with someone else who wasn't there. Eventually he stopped the car again. Two hundred yards away there was a group of tarpaper shacks, a curl of wood-smoke, two or three dark figures. Suddenly, he slammed his hand down on the steering wheel.

"A hundred and fifty years! That's what they don't understand, those goddamn Yankees up in Washington. History—that's what you're looking at. History. A way of life that works, that's gone on working . . . I grew up with it. I know." He lifted his hand and pointed to the shacks. "You see those? My daddy had those put up. I own them. Maintain them. Keep the roofs fixed. Put in the pumps, the water supply. Pay them more wages, and they just drink it away. So I do the same thing my daddy did, and his daddy before him. They need a doctor, I fix it for them to see one. They run short of food, I take care of it. They're *happy*, that's what they can't understand up north. . . ." He broke off, then pointed. In the distance Hélène could just see the steep roof of the big house beyond the trees. From the roof a patch of color drooped in the still air. Ned Calvert turned back to her.

"You American enough to recognize that flag?"

"Of course." Hélène gave him a scornful glance. "It's the Confederate flag."

Ned Calvert grinned. "Sure is. My granddaddy flew it. My daddy flew it. And sure as hell I'm not planning on taking it down. . . ."

"You don't have a son," Hélène said quietly.

"What?" He looked at her intently suddenly, then his face crinkled up and he threw back his head and laughed.

"You're straight. I like that. No—I don't have a son. But then, I'm not planning on dying just yet, either." He leaned across and pushed open her door. Just for a second she felt the heat of his skin.

"Come on out. Have a look around." He got out beside her, gave her a quick glance. "One thing though. You don't shake hands with the nigras—you know that? They wouldn't understand."

"Y̶our mother all right, is she?"

He was driving her back as the shadows lengthened, taking a roundabout route, Hélène thought, that skirted the fields and wound over toward the house. He put the question suddenly, out of a long, abstracted silence, startling her. Her hands tightened in her lap.

"Yes. Fine." She paused. "Tired maybe. She hates it when it's very hot like this."

"Good. I just got thinking . . . Mrs. Calvert was expecting her Saturday, to fix her hair, you know, the way she always does. And she didn't come. Didn't send word, either, which is unusual. So I just thought I would check. That she wasn't sick. That you all were all right, you know?"

He seemed tense, Hélène thought as he put the question. But then she saw his hands relax on the wheel, and at once she, too, relaxed. For a moment she thought he might have heard something, some gossip. But then she dismissed that thought. Not about the drinking the other night anyway: only she and Billy knew about that, and Billy would never talk.

"You like a little drink, Hélène Craig?"

Hélène jumped. Again she felt that queer little prickle of nervous excitement.

"Up at your house, you mean?"

"No." He slowed, and swiveled around to look at her. A long slow smile. "No. Not there. You're not a little girl now. My wife might not understand." He paused. "But then there's a lot of things Mrs. Calvert doesn't understand. About me." He leaned across and flicked open the glove compartment, drew out a silver flask.

"Bourbon." He grinned. "I come ready equipped. Nothing like a good long swig of neat bourbon at the end of a long hot day. You ever try it?"

"No."

"Then try it now."

He unscrewed the cap, handed her the flask. Hélène hesitated, then tipped it back. It felt like liquid fire in her throat. She swallowed and half-choked. Ned Calvert laughed.

"You like it?"

Hélène made a wry face.

"What doesn't Mrs. Calvert understand about you?"

"Lots of things." He took the flask back from her and tilted his head. She watched his tanned throat move as he drank. "I'll tell you someday."

He stopped the car, pulled on the brake, lowered the flask. "You know where we are right now? See the swamp cypress right there? We're in behind the creek—where you went swimming once upon a time." He leaned across and pushed open her door. "Let's stretch our legs. Be nice, don't you think, just to sit down awhile in the shade? And I know just the place." He'd slipped the flask into his hip pocket. As Hélène got out, he took her hand in his, casually, swinging their arms as they walked. Hot sun on their heads and then cool shade. A yellowhammer moved in the branches above them, then darted out into the light. They went through the trees, and she knew the swimming hole was down to their right. Her heart was beating very fast. Then they came out onto dry scrubby grass, and the little dark summerhouse was right in front of them. He looked over his shoulder, quickly, once, then drew her inside. There were three rough benches, built in around the sides; an open doorway, half obscured by flamecreeper. He sat down and patted the bench beside him.

"See? It's so quiet and cool in here. No one ever comes by. I like it here. Always did. Have some more bourbon."

Hélène sat down cautiously. She took the flask, tilted it, and swallowed. Ned Calvert watched her, and she saw his face through the shadows, just as she remembered it in the drawing room: still intent, watching, watching.

"I've been hearing things about you, Hélène Craig." He took the flask back from her, and slipped it between his lips, a long swallow.

"About me?" Hélène gave a nervous laugh. "There's not much to hear."

"There isn't?" He lowered the flask again, and just looked at her. His voice was very quiet. "You're going with that Tanner boy, works over Haines's garage. That's what I heard."

"Billy?" She turned around, startled. "Who told you that?"

"I hear things. Never mind where. Folks talk." He paused. "So I thought I'd give you a word of warning, that's all. You want to stay away from that boy."

"From Billy?" Her blue eyes flashed. "Why so?"

"He's not for you. Not for any decent white girl. That's what I've heard. Not for a girl who wants to keep her self-respect."

"I respect Billy! I like him."

"Sure you do. Sure you do." He sighed. "But you're just a little girl still. In some ways. And living the way you do, your mother being English and all, it's maybe not so easy for you to understand. I just want for you to be careful, not to get hurt, that's all."

"Hurt? By Billy?" Her chin rose. "Billy would never do anything to hurt me."

"Not directly, maybe. I'm sure he's a fine boy at heart. Just misguided, that's all. Maybe not too sharp, so he gets drawn in when he ought to draw back, means no harm—maybe you're right. But Billy's got some strange friends—he tell you about them? He tell you how close he's getting with some of the other men work over Haines's garage? Nigras?" There was a little silence. Hélène stared at him.

"Negroes? No, Billy never told me that."

"You see? And why? Because he's ashamed, that's why. Deep down inside himself he knows it's not right, knows there's some roads no white man ought to cross. Folks 'round here, they won't stand for it. They got a nasty name for a boy like Billy. Nigger-lover, they say. You ever heard that term?"

"Of course I have!"

"Well then, you don't want folks saying that about Billy. Or about you because you go with Billy. Do you?" He flicked a speck of dust off the white trousers, raised his head to look out the doorway.

"Billy's been seen. Talkin' with them. Eatin' with them. Went over to a nigra eating house with them just the other day. Sitting there, putting back chitlings and black-eyed peas and sweet potatoes, just like he couldn't see the color of his own skin." His voice had risen. "Folks don't like it. Things are quiet enough now, but they never stay quiet, not anymore. There's trouble coming. I can scent it, because I lived here all my life, and I know the smell."

He turned back to her, and his gaze was opaque, slightly abstracted. Hélène stared at him. She felt afraid. "You wouldn't want Billy to get hurt, now, would you?"

"No. I wouldn't want that."

"Then you ought to warn him maybe. Tell him about the talk. Tell him to remember who he is before it gets too late." He paused. "And then stay clear. 'Round here your mama doesn't have too many friends—you know that?"

"Yes, I know that." Priscilla-Anne's voice rang in her ears; she felt the blood begin to surge up in her cheeks. He looked at her steadily.

"People 'round here talk about her. Mrs. Calvert and I—we pay no heed to that kind of talk. But you're a sweet girl. You don't want folks talking about you. Do you?"

Hélène's face was flushed. She hung her head. "No. I don't want that," she said in a small voice.

"Here." He held the flask out to her. "Don't go upsetting yourself now. Have some bourbon."

Hélène took the flask with shaky hands. She took a long swallow. The bourbon hit the back of her throat, then flared in her stomach. She shut her eyes, and then opened them again. Her head didn't feel too clear, and it seemed very hot in the little summerhouse, but she did feel better. And he was being very kind. It was confusing, her mother and Billy all at once, but yes, she was sure he was being kind.

"Your lips are wet. You've gotten bourbon all around your mouth. Hélène Craig, I'll have to teach you. How to drink from a flask . . ." As he spoke, he moved closer to her and leaned forward. His arm came around her shoulders. He lowered his face and his mouth was suddenly very close.

"Wet," he said. "You remember?"

And his voice was suddenly thick, the way it had been once before. And then, very deliberately, very slowly, he put his mouth over hers. His lips were wet and firm; she felt his tongue against her lips, felt his mouth curve into a smile. He licked the bourbon from her lips, then his arm around her shoulders tightened, and he parted her lips with his tongue. Her body went rigid. She felt his tongue lap hers, gently, playfully, then more forcefully; then he began to suck, first her lips, then her tongue.

"Open your lips—more. Yes . . ."

He was sucking her tongue into his mouth, between the moist firm lips. Hélène's head spun. Images, words, fragments; things Susie Marshall had whispered and Priscilla-Anne had confirmed. She felt her body shiver, and his hand moved up and closed over the swell of her breast. He smelled of cologne and mint and bourbon, and a little muskily of sweat; she saw his tanned skin, so close before her eyes, then she shut her eyes and gave herself up to that dark warm space in which there was nothing except his mouth and hers. He drew back. One hand continued to fondle her breast.

"You do that with Billy Tanner? You do that with any of the boys?"

His voice was husky, mesmeric. Hélène shook her head.

"I thought so. You know how long I've wanted to do that? A long long time. You could never guess how long. And I knew it would be worth the wait." He cradled both breasts in his hands, leaned her back so she looked up into his eyes. "You knew, didn't you?" he said. "Right back when you were a little girl. Even then you knew. I could see it in your eyes."

Then he lowered his mouth to hers again, hard and strong and long, until he felt Hélène start to shake.

"Undo your shirt, honey. Let me look."

He was lifting his hands to the buttons of her blouse as he spoke. Hélène tried to push them away.

"No, please. You mustn't. It isn't right."

"I've seen you." He pushed her hands aside. "Three years ago. I saw you then. Saw you in the pool. Saw you touch yourself, and then look over your shoulder like you were scared. You wanted it then, didn't you? When you were twelve years old. You were wanting it, and thinking about it, and . . . sweet Jesus, let me look."

He pulled at the last buttons and one of them popped. Then he was wrenching the shirt off her shoulders and reaching behind for the fastening of her bra.

"No, please. Let me go. You mustn't. . . ."

He had it undone. Then his fingers were under the shoulder straps, easing it forward and off. Her breasts were full now, full and rounded and heavy, the aureole wide and dark, the skin pale. She heard him expel his breath in a long sigh. She tried to lift her hands and cover herself, but her head felt muzzy, full of shadows shot through with light, and her hands couldn't move very fast. He caught them easily and pushed them aside, leaning forward, his lips parted and moist.

"You're big. Such a little slender thing, and you're *big*. . . . You're beautiful. So beautiful. It's been driving me crazy, thinking about you. Did you know that—how crazy you could make a man? Let me—gently— look. See how soft you are, right there?" He lifted one finger and brushed it across her nipple. Hélène cried out. "You see? It feels good. It feels nice. You don't need to be afraid. Watch. So soft, and I can make it go all hard. Like this."

He bent his head. She felt his mouth, warm and wet, against her skin. He drew his tongue across her nipples, first one, then the other, his breath coming fast against her skin.

"Feel it? You feel it . . . yes?" His lips circled the aureole; he sucked the hardening nipple between his lips, and Hélène felt herself arch back involuntarily as the pleasure shot through her body like a flame. He sucked harder, greedily, first one breast, then the other, the way all the other girls had told her men did, and years of dreams and images and shadowy imaginings spun and whirled in her brain. She could feel heat building up inside her like she felt when she was a little girl and she couldn't sleep at night. And she knew it was wrong, knew she shouldn't feel it, that she felt it more, maybe, because it was wrong.

"You see?" He lifted his face from her breasts, his hands closing over them tight. His mouth was slack, wet with saliva from his sucking.

"You like it? It feels good? Tell me, honey. Tell me how good it feels. You know what it does to me? Can you feel that? Look—come closer. Sit across my lap. Straddle me. . . ." His arms tightened around her, lifted her awkwardly, slid her up and across so her legs were on either side of his thighs. His glazed eyes looked up at her; he was panting, his voice so thick he could hardly speak. "You feel it now. There . . ." He gave a sharp thrust with his groin. "Feel how hard I am, how big? You did that. You made me like that. Because you're beautiful, so beautiful. You know I get hard just looking at you, not even touching? Just looking and I'm so hard I could burst my pants? Touch me. Give me your hand. Just on the outside now. There—see? There's nothing to be afraid of. It feels good. Doesn't it feel good?"

He pressed her hand down, onto his groin, onto the bulge of his penis under the white linen trousers. Hélène's head swayed against his neck; everything was black now, black and hot, and . . .

"You all right, honey?" She felt his body stiffen suddenly, heard, dimly, that his voice had changed. He gripped her upper arms and shook her head. "You okay? You going to pass out or what? Jesus. Shit. Hélène . . . look at me now. . . ."

"I'm going to be sick." Her own voice seemed to come from a long way away. Her body felt terribly cold, and her neck had gone all weak, so her head wouldn't stay up.

"Here. Quick. Get off of me. . . ." He was pushing her, half-lifting her, thrusting her outside the little hut. She fell on her knees by the bushes. Then she vomited all the bourbon she'd drunk.

He didn't watch her, that was the only good thing. The minute it started happening, he turned and went back into the hut. When it was over, she just crouched there for a moment, shaking, her mind clear as crystal now, filled with words and images, and her body sick with shame. Eventually, a little unsteadily, she got back to her feet. He had come back now, and was standing in the door watching her, her bra and shirt in his hand. She couldn't look at him. She let him take charge.

"Better?" He sounded almost amused, his voice back to normal, and all the alarm she had heard in it gone. "Okay, now come back inside here and put these on. Then I'll drive you home." Inside the hut he helped her into the bra, did it up, fastened her shirt. Then he unscrewed the silver flask again. "Okay. Now, rinse your mouth out with this. Then spit. You'll feel a whole lot better."

Hélène did as she was told. Then she looked up at him for the first time, and he grinned.

"You took a swallow too much, that's all. On an empty stomach maybe. It's easy enough done. You feel better now?" Hélène nodded. "Now, sit down. I want you to listen. I'm not going to touch you, honey. It's all right. There. That's the way. . . ." Shakily, she sat down. He stood in the shadows, looking down at her. "I didn't know . . . I didn't figure on the bourbon affecting you like that. I'd forgotten, I guess, how it can be with hard liquor the first time. . . ."

Slowly Hélène raised her head and looked at him. She knew he didn't want to talk about the liquor. He lifted his hand and wiped it across his forehead, and she saw he was sweating hard.

"I guess . . . I guess I got a bit carried away back there. Frightened you, maybe. I'm sorry if I did that, honey. . . ." He moved then, as if encouraged by the fact that she said nothing. He sat down, near her but not too close, then after a while, he took her hand. "You angry with me, Hélène? I don't ever want you to be angry—not with me." He paused. "You see—I guess it's hard for you to understand. But a girl like you—a woman like you. Well, a man finds himself alone with her, when he's admired her a long time, thought how beautiful she was and—and then it's not too easy for him to behave maybe the way he ought to behave. You understand that?"

"I—I suppose so."

"Well, I'm telling you, honey, that's the way it is." A note of irritation came into his voice. "You just listen now, and you'll understand. I'm a man, Hélène, just an ordinary man, and I have needs and wants, the same as all men do. Not all women feel the same way. Sometimes they don't want a man to be touching them, kissing them, and when that happens it's hard on the man, Hélène, real hard. He kind of shuts himself up inside; he gets to feeling dead—half-alive at best. Now, no disrespect to Mrs. Calvert, but she and I have been married a long time now, and for years, honey, *years* . . . well, it's God's truth, I've been a very unhappy man."

"You? Unhappy?" Hélène lifted her head.

"That's right."

"You mean you don't love Mrs. Calvert anymore?"

"Well, not exactly, honey. My wife is a fine woman, and I admire her, and I wouldn't ever want to hurt her. But—put it like this—I don't feel about her the way I do about you."

"About me?" Hélène's eyes widened, and he moved quickly, crouching before her and clasping her hands in his, so she looked down into his face.

"Well, you must know *that* . . ." He smiled at her. "You think I would bring you here, and kiss you—do all those things—if I didn't admire you? If you hadn't just driven me so wild that I hardly knew what I was doing anymore? Maybe . . ." He frowned. "Maybe, if I hadn't heard about your seeing Billy Tanner, I might have managed to hold it in. But when I heard that, I swear to you, Hélène, I felt so angry, so jealous, I could hardly think anymore. . . ."

"You were jealous? Of Billy Tanner?" She stared at him in disbelief, and he shook his head.

"I most certainly was. What man wouldn't be, thinking of a girl with another boy—a girl he knows he wants to love."

Hélène stood up slowly.

"That can't be true. It can't be."

Quickly, he was by her side, pressing her against him. Then he released her, and looked down into her eyes.

"Would I lie to you? Honey, would I?" His hand snaked about her waist, and he gave her a little half-playful squeeze. "Hélène, I'm not a man who lies about things like that. Don't you think that now, or you'll make me mad. Now, listen to me . . . I know I did wrong. I know I let things get out of hand. But I want you to say you'll see me again. Just sometimes. Just so's I can look at you, and we can walk and talk and go for a drive maybe, the way we did today. Nothing more. There's no harm in that, is there?"

"I—I suppose not. If we just did that." Hélène hesitated. Whispery doubts crowded in at the back of her mind, but he was looking her straight in the eye now, and he was almost pleading.

"Thursday," he said. "I could pick you up right after school, on the Orangeburg road. We could go for a little drive, then I'd drop you off home. No one needs to know—just us. It could be our little secret." He hesitated. "You wouldn't want to tell anyone. Your mother—you wouldn't want to tell her." Hélène sighed and plucked at her skirt.

"No. I don't talk to her so much these days. Not the way I used to."

He sighed. What she said seemed to ease his mind. "Thursday then. Promise me. Make me happy."

"All right. Maybe." She swallowed. "But you promise—what you said? Just a drive?"

"I promise. I swear it to you, Hélène." He pressed his mouth quickly and lightly against her hair.

"You're the most beautiful thing I ever saw—you know that? Now, come on—I'll drive you home. I'll drop you off just before the trailer park. That okay with you?"

EDOUARD

OXFORD—ALGERIA—FRANCE, 1949–1958

"Tell him I shall be there at once."

"At once, milady?"

"*Almost* at once. I'm in London at the moment. In the bath, actually. But in a minute I shall just *jump* in the car, and then I'll be in Oxford before you can blink."

"Yes, milady."

"He is *there*, I suppose?"

"Yes, milady. He has finals next week."

This was said meaningfully; there was a sigh at the other end of the line.

"How perfectly horrible. In that case I shall certainly hurry."

The receiver was replaced. Mr. Bullins, porter at Magdalen College for forty years, and senior porter for the last ten, put on his bowler hat and the bland expression he always assumed on such occasions and walked to staircase 111 in New Buildings, overlooking the Deer Park, where E.A.J. de Chavigny had some of the most desirable rooms in college. Below him was H.J.E. Dudley, Lord Sayle; above him were the rooms of his closest friend, the Honorable C.V.T. Glendinning. The gentlemen's titles did not appear on the hand-painted signs at the foot of the staircase; in certain other Oxford colleges such practices were countenanced: not, Mr. Bullins thought proudly, in Magdalen, which, in his opinion, was not only the most beautiful college in Oxford, but also the only one of any consequence.

He puffed his way up to the first floor, and finding the outer door open, knocked on the inner one.

He entered to find Edouard de Chavigny stretched out in an armchair, wearing cricket flannels, with a copy of John Maynard Keynes's *Treatise on Money* open on his lap. He did not appear to be reading it.

Mr. Bullins regarded him with approval. It was well known in college that, barring some accident, Mr. de Chavigny would take a First in his politics, philosophy, and economics finals. This was good; what was even better—and the more remarkable, given that the gentleman was French—was that he would do so in the proper manner: with little apparent effort on his part, with a negligent modesty, as befitted an English gentleman.

In Mr. Bullins's opinion, the war had had a regrettable effect upon Oxford, and even upon Magdalen. A number of undergraduates were men in their mid-twenties who had served in the war and whose university education had therefore been deferred. These young men, taciturn, hard-working, serious, did not conduct themselves in what Mr. Bullins considered the correct manner. Edouard de Chavigny did: he was a fine athlete, with a blue for cricket, and had taken so well to rowing that even though a late starter, he had narrowly missed selection for the Oxford eight. He spoke successfully at Union debates; he had acted with the Oxford University Dramatic Society; he knew how to enjoy himself. He gave parties at which a great deal of champagne was consumed; he attended other parties; he entertained young women to luncheon parties in his rooms—women whose fashionable faces Mr. Bullins recognized from society magazines such as the *Tatler*, which formed his own favorite bedtime reading. He dressed superbly while looking as if clothes were unimportant to him. He was extemely good-looking, and extremely charming, generous to his scout, and to Mr. Bullins on numerous occasions. In short, Mr. Bullins admired him, and—this was rarer still—liked him. He would go far, this young man, Mr. Bullins considered, and he looked forward to reading of his progress once he left Oxford.

He cleared his throat as the young man looked up.

"Lady Isobel Herbert, Mr. de Chavigny," he announced. "She has just telephoned. She says that she is in the bath now, sir, but that she will be with you shortly."

He conveyed the message at ten-thirty in the morning. Lady Isobel's idea of time was exceedingly flexible. She arrived at Magdalen in her Derby Bentley at three-fifteen. Edouard, who had had plenty of time to speculate, was still surprised by her arrival. He could think of no reason to account for it. Over the past few years, since she had broken off her engagement to Jean-Paul, he had seen her on various occasions—at balls in London, or at country-house weekends, once at Christian Glendinning's parents' house, but they had spoken only briefly. That was all. She had never visited him in Oxford before; he had not been alone with her for years—not since the war, not since London. He assumed the visit must be one of Isobel's whims, and there had been many of those. A brief flirtation with the Communist Party, done mainly to shock, he supposed. A narrowly avoided divorce scandal involving a prominent Member of Parliament. At least two further broken engagements that he could remember: one to a Battle of Britain flying ace, the other to an Italian count internationally celebrated as a racing driver. Isobel seemed to like danger at second hand, he thought, and wondered again why she was coming.

She walked into his rooms without knocking, wearing an emerald-green silk dress, no hat, and the Conway pearls. The sun caught her dazzling hair, and as Edouard sprang to his feet, she smiled at him.

"Tell me, darling Edouard," she said, "have you learned to make cocktails yet?"

And then he knew why she had come.

She drank two dry martinis, and said she wasn't hungry and didn't want to eat. Then she lit a cigarette and curled up on the window seat. Edouard waited.

"Shall you get your first? I hear you're going to."

"Perhaps."

"Hugo said you would. I ran into him the other day."

"How is he?"

"All right." She paused. "No—probably not very all right. Unhappy, I think. A bit lost. Feeling he hasn't done things he ought to have done—hasn't fulfilled his promise. I don't know. Jagged. The way lots of people are. I saw his cousin Christian in the quad as I came in. Wearing a pink silk shirt and a yellow tie. He hasn't changed." She smiled. "Is he still your best friend?"

"My closest friend, yes."

"I'm glad. I like him." She hesitated. "He's madly queer, of course."

"Even so."

Isobel flicked ash out of the window carelessly and frowned.

"How's Jean-Paul? Still fighting?"

"He's still in the army. A desk job, mainly. He might be posted to Indochina, I suppose. It's in the cards. He spends most of his leaves in Algeria—at our vineyards, you know. He likes it there."

"Who minds the shop when he's away?"

Edouard shrugged. "I shall. When I go down from Oxford."

"Do you want to do that?"

"I do, yes. Jean hasn't much time—and I think I might do it quite well." He hesitated. "Everything's stood still, you see, since my father died. There's a lot of room for development. Expansion."

"I miss Jean sometimes." She stood up restlessly. "He made me

smile. He could be so predictable. I'm afraid I behaved rather badly."
She paused. "Of course, I miss the emerald too. You know, I was
disproportionately fond of that emerald." The green eyes met his, and
the lips widened into a smile.

Edouard hesitated. "It's an unlucky stone. I didn't want to say
that when you chose it. But it is supposed to be unlucky."

"Is it?" She was looking at him very intently. "Well, that would
explain an awful lot of things." She turned and looked at the door across
the room. "Is your bedroom in there?"

"Yes. It is."

"Oh, good."

She crossed in front of him and went into the bedroom. There was
a silence, then she called to him. He walked slowly over to the door and
stood looking down at her. The emerald dress was in a heap on the
floor, and Isobel's slender pale boyish body was stretched out naked on
his narrow college bed. Her hair flared across the pillow; there was a
triangle of red-gold between her narrow thighs; the Conway pearls lay
between her small white breasts.

"Darling Edouard. You don't mind, do you? You see, I wanted to
do this ages ago. . . ." She paused, and her wide greenish cat's eyes
shone up at him. "I'm going to be married, Edouard, did I tell you? The
racing driver one, after all. Next week, I think, after some Grand Prix
thing he's racing in. If he isn't killed first, of course. And so I knew I
must do this now. I couldn't bear to be married if I hadn't. . . ."

Edouard crossed to the bed, sat down beside her, and took her
slender hand in his.

"You don't have to worry about anything." She smiled. "I have one
of those beastly Dutch cap things. I put it on before I left London.
They tell me you'd never know it was there. . . ."

He bent his head and gently kissed her lips, then he drew back and
touched her cheek with his finger.

"You're crying."

"Only a little bit. I'll stop in a moment. It's probably all that
waiting. Tell me, darling Edouard—you did know, didn't you?"

He looked at her steadily.

"I suppose I did. Yes."

"Oh, I'm so *glad*. That makes it much simpler. Dear Edouard,
would you mind if I just watched—while you undressed?" Edouard
smiled. He took off his clothes, and Isobel curled up on the bed
watching him, like a little cat. Then she drew him onto the covers and
pushed him gently back. "Darling Edouard. Don't kiss me. Not yet.
You don't need to do anything. I'm quite ready. I'm wet. I was quite
wet when I was drinking the first martini. You have the most wonderful

. . . the most beautiful . . . I've ever seen. And I just want to do—*this*. . . ."

With great grace she straddled his body and paused for a moment, upright above him, her body as pale and slender as a wand. Then she touched his full penis with one slender hand, and guided its head between her legs. He felt the moistness, felt the narrow aperture, then slowly, her eyes never leaving his, she lowered herself down as if she were impaling herself on his flesh.

"Darling Edouard. I shall come almost at once if you move just the tiniest bit. Oh, yes . . ."

He moved, and she did. Then she kissed him. They made love all afternoon, and sometimes she was creamy and calm and slow as a cat being stroked, and sometimes the cat arched her back, and revealed claws. Edouard came into her body with a feeling of shuddering release, and the afternoon seemed to pass in a dream he had had, or she had had long before.

As dusk fell, he kissed her damp thighs, and then her mouth, and Isobel held his head and looked into his eyes. Her own glittered like emeralds, but without tears this time. "Darling Edouard," she said. "I love you in a very special way and I knew you would understand. I did do the right thing, didn't I?"

"Most certainly." He smiled.

"Do you like me? I've always liked you."

"Yes, I do." He kissed her gently. "I've always liked you very much."

"I thought so. I'm glad. I'd much rather be liked than loved. On the whole. And now I must go home." She sprang up from the bed with that quick restless grace which had always delighted him, and pulled on her green dress.

"I shall send you a piece of my wedding cake." Her lips curved mischievously. "It will be encrusted with that terrible white icing pastry cooks are always so proud of, and far too sweet. But I love those little box things with the lacy paper that they pack it in. So I'll send it. You can eat it before your finals, and wedding cake is terribly lucky—everyone says—so then you'll be certain to get your First, and . . ."

"Isobel . . ."

"If I stay one more minute, I shall cry again," she said. "And that would be in very poor taste. Good-bye, darling Edouard. And take care of yourself."

The following week he sent a telegram: *Thank you for the cake, Edouard.* Three months later, after his First was announced with the other Oxford and Cambridge examination results in *The Times*, he received a telegram at the house in St. Cloud. It read: *I see you ate it. Isobel.* He did not hear from her again for another eight years.

When Edouard left Oxford and returned to France to begin work on the administration of the de Chavigny companies and estates, he was appalled by what he found. During his years at Oxford, he had spent part of his vacations in France, but those relatively short periods had given him no idea of the chaos that had prevailed since his father's death.

With Jean-Paul's casual agreement—"Of course, go ahead, little brother. You'll find it's a terrible bore"—he began a systematic investigation of the de Chavigny empire: the jewelry company, its workshops and showrooms in Europe and America; the estates and vineyards in the Loire and in Algeria; the stockholdings; the capital assets; the property the Baron had retained in France and abroad. Everywhere he found the same thing: elderly employees attempting to run things as they thought the old Baron would have wanted, out of touch with new ideas, fearful of making any decision on their own, and consequently stalling, allowing problems to build up. No new blood had come into the affairs of de Chavigny for years: everywhere Edouard found stagnation and apathy. It was as if a great machine had been left running so long that no one had noticed, or cared, that it was running down.

After the execution of Xavier de Chavigny, the German High Command had taken over the house and gardens at St. Cloud, and had used the beautiful late-seventeenth-century mansion to quarter troops. This Edouard knew: what he could not understand was that in the years since the end of the war, Jean-Paul had made no attempt to restore the house. He had carved out a small apartment for himself in one of the wings, kept on the remnants of an elderly staff of servants, and left the rest of the place as it was.

Knowing what he would find when he went there, and knowing that it would pain him, Edouard delayed the moment when he would make a formal inspection of the house. He went, finally, on a beautiful September day in 1949, some three months after he came down from Oxford.

From the distance, as he drove toward it, the great house appeared unchanged. The sun struck the steep blue slates of the roof, and the glass of the tall ranked windows of the main façade.

The elderly servants greeted him nervously; silently, Edouard went on a tour of the house. There was little furniture, for most of that was stored in Switzerland, and the few pieces that remained had been damaged beyond repair. The walls were bare of the famous Brussels tapestries; his footsteps echoed on uncarpeted floors. Edouard stared around him in mounting disbelief and anger. The paneling was scarred with initials and obscenities; greenish damp from blocked gutterings seeped through walls hung with silk that was torn and ripped. On the great curving staircase that was one of the most celebrated features of the house, half the banisters had been ripped out and used for firewood.

In the ballroom, the Venetian mirrors that lined the walls had been smashed; doors hung on broken hinges; the place stank of mice and damp.

The servants had done their best: they had tried to clean the house for his arrival, but their efforts only heightened the destruction Edouard found. Slowly he went upstairs: his father's bedroom, his dressing room, his bathroom, where the mahogany paneling had been axed and the old fittings of brass and copper had been wrenched from their sockets and looted. His mother's bedroom, once hung with hand-painted eighteenth-century Chinese wallpaper, now ripped and defaced and stained with urine. The library, where the bookcases had been smashed. Room after room, twenty bedrooms in all, and then the attics, where the roof had leaked, and where ceilings had caved in. Edouard went back down the stairs; he stood in the huge marble-floored foyer and closed his eyes. He saw the house as it had once been, in his childhood—still, ordered, each thing in it the finest and most beautiful example of its kind. He thought of the dinners, for eighteen, twenty, thirty people; he thought of the dances, and the whisper of music from the ballroom; of the quiet afternoons he had sometimes spent in his father's study. He opened his eyes again; the old butler looked at him anxiously.

"We tried, Monsieur Edouard . . ." The old man gave a helpless gesture. "You see. We have washed all the floors."

Edouard wanted to weep with anger and frustration, but he hid his feelings out of consideration for the old man. The next day, he returned to the house with Louise. His mother, who had taken one look at the place when she first returned to France, had been firm. She was beyond coping with it; she had no intention of living there; she had moved, instead, to an early eighteenth-century town house in the Faubourg Saint-Germain, a quarter of Paris still preferred by the pre-Napoleonic French aristocracy. She returned to St. Cloud with obvious reluctance. Paris was more convenient in any case; the memories of St. Cloud were too painful. When Edouard pressed her, she shrugged irritably. "Edouard. The place is too far gone. It belongs to the past. I think Jean-Paul should sell it. . . ."

She left, half an hour after she arrived, in her stately dark blue Bentley. Edouard stood for a while, alone in the gardens. He watched her car depart; he stood on the terrace and looked across toward the city, then back toward the house. The gardens were overgrown and neglected, the gravel paths a wilderness of weeds, the formal hedges unclipped for years. A few late roses struggled through the encroaching tangles of nettles and bindweed. Edouard stood looking around him, his mouth set, his hands clenched. His mother was not interested; Jean-Paul was not concerned: very well, then, he would do what had to be done, and he would do it alone.

It was the same in the Loire, at the Château de Chavigny, where the famous mirrored salon, built for the seventh Baron de Chavigny, had been used as a shooting gallery. It was the same in the vineyards there: production of wine had almost ceased during the war years; acres had been decimated by disease; attempts at postwar wine production had been sporadic and ill-organized. Edouard tasted some of these thin sour wines with disgust, and gave orders that the entire cellar stock be jettisoned forthwith.

"But Monsieur de Chavigny, what shall we do with it?" The elderly *régisseur* looked around the vast cellars in despair.

"It's of no consequence. Pour it down the drains if necessary. I will not have such wine sold under the de Chavigny label." He paused, feeling a momentary pity for the old man. "Would you drink this?"

The *régisseur* hesitated, then smiled a slow gap-toothed smile. "No, Monsieur de Chavigny. I should prefer not to."

"I also." Edouard pressed his arm, not unkindly. "Scrap it. We shall begin again."

This grand tour of Edouard's took over six months. At the end of that time, by working ceaselessly, he had been through every file in every office. He had seen every room in every house, and had personally interviewed every one of the old Baron's servants, and all his senior employees. He had been to his father's lawyers; to his father's banking partners and advisors; to his stockbrokers at the Bourse; to his accountants. He had visited Switzerland, London, Rome, and New York. In that time, he had despaired. It had seemed to him, about halfway through his investigation, that in the past five years Jean-Paul had done one thing and one thing only. He had, with Edouard's assistance, erected a memorial to their father in the chapel at the Château de Chavigny where he and his ancestors were buried. But the true memorial to his father, the empire Xavier de Chavigny had so painstakingly and brilliantly built up during his lifetime—that he had simply allowed to decay.

By the end of the six months, Edouard's old resolve grew fiercer: he would restore that empire to its former glory, and then he would develop it, increase it, expand it. It could be done. Gradually, in the second half of the six months, he grew in confidence. He began to see ways, to make plans. Thanks to his father's prewar prudence, a fortune was there; it simply had to be deployed. And it should be deployed: it would be his tribute to his father, his memorial to the reticent man he had scarcely known but deeply loved, and who had died so courageously. His and Jean-Paul's tribute. He did not doubt for an instant that once he explained things to his brother, once he made him see what assets were available and how they could be used, Jean-Paul would rise from his lethargy and be as engaged, as excited, and as determined as Edouard.

Armed with papers, his head filled with lists of stockholdings, production figures, statistics of pre- and postwar profits and losses, with preliminary architectural plans for the restoration, first, of the three houses in France, and ideas for those property holdings abroad, Edouard arranged to meet his brother for a week-long series of discussions. Jean-Paul was at first resistant; eventually, when Edouard pressed him, and after changing their proposed schedule three times, he agreed to a week in the autumn of 1950, when he would be on leave. They would meet in Algeria, at the Maison Alletti, the large low-built white house which the old Baron had had built in the late 1920s and which formed the base for his Algerian vineyards and timber plantations. It was built among gardens on the slope of a hill, overlooking the city and the breathtaking bay of Algiers.

Edouard demurred, but Jean-Paul was adamant. It was there or nowhere. He spent all his leaves there now; he liked Algeria; besides, Edouard should see for himself the vineyards and plantations there. They were doing well, Jean-Paul said proudly. He had taken a personal interest in them; there, he said a little pettishly, Edouard would find room for no complaints.

E douard had never been to North Africa; he was unprepared for the beauty of Algiers itself and the magnificence of the surrounding country, with its rugged sun-burned hills, its narrow winding roads which would suddenly open up on views of a vivid blue Mediterranean Sea. From the start it fascinated him: a country and a city at once so French and so Arab, in which two cultures very different from each other seemed to him at first to blend triumphantly. He could sit on a terrace in the French quarter, sipping wine, and feel he was in France. The wide formal boulevards of Algiers, the plane trees with their trunks painted white, the tall graceful white-painted houses with their balconies and shutters, the shade of the squares reserved for Europeans—all these reminded him of the France he had loved so much as a child: the towns of the South—Arles, or Nîmes or Avignon; some of the small towns of the Loire. Here was a city relatively unscarred by war, with signs of growing prosperity. He could drink good wine; eat French food superlatively cooked and apparently available in abundance; be waited upon as he had been waited upon in the old days before the war, by a succession of polite, quiet, efficient, well-trained servants, all of whom were Arab, all of whom spoke perfect French.

But there was another Algiers, of which he caught, in the first couple of days, heady glimpses. There was the Algiers of the Arabs themselves: the old Casbah, the Arab quarter of the city, was built on a

hill. A fascinating warren of steep narrow alleyways, of flat-roofed tene-
ment housing, it was visible from the French quarter, visible almost
throughout the city; that teeming place filled with barefooted children,
with women shrouded from head to foot in black, who clasped their
headdresses across their faces and between their teeth, and never raised
their eyes.   ·

In that zone of the city that lay between the French quarter and the
Casbah, Edouard caught glimpses of the Arabic world. The scents of
North African cooking, of couscous, of saffron and cumin and turmeric;
street markets, where they sold powdered dyes and spices, sticks of
sandalwood for burning, little piles of henna powder and ground indigo.
He smelled the scents eagerly, gazed, fascinated, at the henna-stained
feet and palms of the women and children, listened to the cries of the
muezzin and the harsh guttural shouts in a language he could not
understand—and he saw, he thought, why Jean-Paul was so drawn to
Algeria.

He announced his intention of visiting the Casbah. Jean-Paul yawned.
If he wanted. It could be arranged. He must take a servant with him,
naturally—they knew how to get rid of the beggars. And besides, it was
not entirely safe to go alone.

"Go if you must." He shrugged. "But watch your wallet. And stay
well clear of the women."

So, for the first few days of his visit, Edouard explored the city
alone, except for the servant. In the evenings Jean-Paul made an effort
to entertain him, and held a number of elaborate dinner parties. They
ate outdoors, under a vine pergola on a wide terrace overlooking the sea.
The elaborate French dishes were cooked to perfection by the Arab
cook and served gracefully by Arab boys in white uniforms, the eldest of
whom seemed about fifteen years old. All the guests were French. The
majority owned vineyards. Several, like Jean-Paul, had military experience or backgrounds. Their wives were chic, exquisitely dressed—far
better than the majority of women in postwar Paris. Their jewels sparkled, and their talk palled. Edouard found them stiflingly boring, and
curiously closed.

The women could discuss with animation the latest novel to take
Paris by storm, the politics of the Comédie Française, the reputations of
actors, writers, musicians, politicians, painters. They regarded them
from afar, with a delicate patronage. The consensus was clear: France
was finished; Europe was finished; they were better off here. Edouard
listened to them and disliked what he heard. He had been naive, he saw
that now. He returned to the Arab quarter, and saw the poverty, no
longer as picturesque, but as a by-product of French colonial prosperity.
It made him angry; Jean-Paul's smugness, and that of his friends, made
him angrier still. He said nothing; it would be useless to discuss the

politics of the country with Jean-Paul. Instead, when a week had passed, during which time he and Jean-Paul had made one cursory visit to the Baron's vineyards and had inspected perhaps one eighth of that vast acreage, Edouard decided to return to the purpose of his visit. He bearded Jean-Paul when his brother finally got up at about eleven in the morning.

"Jean-Paul—please. Could we not look at these company figures? Discuss my plans?"

Jean-Paul sighed and stretched back in his wicker armchair. "Oh, very well, little brother. But I'll think better over a *pastis*."

So, for the next two hours, they sat on the terrace, and Edouard talked. He produced sheafs of paper; he rounded off figures to make his calculations simpler; he kept them all in francs, because Jean-Paul became hopelessly confused by rates of exchange. Jean-Paul drank three *pastis* and smoked *kif*.

"You're sure you wouldn't like some?" He passed Edouard a silver box in which cigarettes of *kif* mixed with tobacco were ready rolled.

"No, thank you."

"It's very relaxing."

"Jean-Paul . . ."

"Oh, all right, all right. I follow you so far, I think. Go on."

Edouard continued his dissertation over lunch. He could see that the *pastis*, the wine, and the *kif* had taken effect. Jean-Paul's eyes were pinkish and glazed; his color had risen; his immaculate white clothes already looked crumpled. Edouard knew he was wasting his time, but he couldn't stop. This was so important, he had done so much work—he had to make Jean-Paul understand.

After lunch they took coffee, thick Arabic coffee. Jean-Paul lay back on the silken divan and closed his eyes.

"Jean-Paul." Edouard's voice was hoarse with desperation. "Surely—can't you see? For our father's sake. He built all this up. Oh, it was big before he started, but he made it great. There are so many possibilities. We could build on what he did—Jean-Paul. It was his life's *work*. We can't just let it disintegrate into the dust."

Jean-Paul opened his eyes, and Edouard looked up. While he had been talking an Arab serving woman had silently entered the room. She stood now, head bowed, just inside the door.

"Time for my siesta." Jean-Paul heaved himself to his feet. They looked at each other, Jean-Paul focusing his eyes with difficulty, and Edouard saw the coarsening in his brother which he had been trying to ignore for days. He was overweight, thickening around the waist; his face was perpetually flushed; he was still handsome, but his features were heavy now, and the once strong jawline was jowled. Edouard looked at him and felt a sickening dismay.

"I have to rest in the afternoons." Jean-Paul's voice was defiant. "It's the climate here. It's so damn hot. I'll be able to think more clearly this evening. When it's cooler . . ."

He glanced across the room to the silent figure of the Arab woman, who still stood waiting, head bowed. He grinned at Edouard, winked.

"A sleep and a fuck." He spoke in English, presumably so the woman would not understand, and Edouard suddenly felt furiously angry. "Then I'll be all right. We'll talk again. This evening. Really. I'm grateful to you, Edouard. I can see how much work you've done. . . ."

They did talk again that evening. Edouard forced his brother. He pushed him into an upright chair.

"No *pastis*. No wine. No *kif*." He slammed a pile of papers down on the table. "You listen, Jean-Paul, and you listen properly. I've sweated over all this for six months, and I'm not going to see that work wasted. So you listen, damn it, or I'll get the next plane out and leave you to cope with the whole damn lot."

"All right. All right." Jean-Paul lifted his hands amiably. "There's no need to get so hot under the collar. You were always hot-tempered, impatient. I'm just slower than you, that's all. Now explain again, and explain slowly."

Edouard explained. At the end of his impassioned arguments, Jean-Paul stood up. "All right. Fine. Okay."

"What do you mean, all right, okay?"

"I mean, do it." Jean-Paul put his hand on his shoulder. "I can't—you must know that. I wouldn't know where to begin. You do it. All the things you said. I trust your judgment. I'm sure you're right. You were always the clever one. Just let me know what I have to sign—make as much of it as possible over to yourself, and get on with it. All right, little brother? *Now* can I have that *pastis*?"

Edouard looked at his brother. At the eyes which slid away from his own in embarrassment. His mouth tightened, and he stood up. "Very well, I'll do as you say. And by all means ring for your *pastis*."

And so it was, in 1950, that Edouard effectively became the Baron de Chavigny. Jean-Paul signed over power of attorney to his brother in all the financial affairs of his companies, and Edouard, Baron in all but name, returned to Paris and began work.

Initially both brothers found they were delighted with the arrangement.

Edouard defined his work to himself in two stages: first he would restore, then he would build and expand.

All the furniture, silver, paintings, and the private jewelry collection stored in Switzerland by his father were returned to France. The huge house at Deauville, with its gardens and private beach, was sold to one of the newly oil-rich Americans beginning to invest in European property. It had, in any case, rarely been used. Edouard used the capital to buy a smaller house near the Normandy coast, telling himself that—one day—his children, or Jean-Paul's, might like to stay there. The rest of the capital was used to defray the very great costs of restoring the house at St. Cloud and the Château de Chavigny in the Loire. When the structural work on the houses was completed, the furniture, tapestries, paintings, carpets, and hangings were restored and replaced. This, and the restoration of the celebrated gardens of both houses, took two years. Even Louise de Chavigny, whom he took to St. Cloud for a triumphant tour when the work was finished, was impressed.

"It's quite lovely, Edouard. As lovely as it ever was. And you've made some additions. . . ." Her eyes flicked over the Louis XIV furniture of the formal salon. "You have my eye. You've chosen well."

"You can return here now, Maman. Your rooms are ready for you. Just as they were. Only the curtains aren't yet complete; the identical silk could not be found. But they're being rewoven now, in England. They'll be ready very soon. The same design, the same dye even—I've had them copied exactly. . . ."

"No, Edouard. I shall stay in Paris. I'm used to it now." She gave a little gesture out toward the windows, to the formal *parterre* which had taken twenty men as many months to relay and replant. "Too many memories, Edouard. I told you."

Edouard moved into the house at St. Cloud alone.

With his father's employees he was generous but firm. The elderly among the servants were asked to retrain the new staff to their old exacting standards; they were then retired, with pensions of a size that made Edouard's Parisian friends complain. Word gets around, they said; for God's sake stop—or they'll all be demanding de Chavigny–style settlements. Edouard shrugged.

"They stayed with my father right through the war. They deserve that and more."

The vineyards in the Loire were plowed up and replanted, using vine stock free from disease. A new *régisseur*, trained on the estates of Baron Philippe de Rothschild, was brought in. Edouard toyed with the idea of having the de Chavigny wine labels redesigned, and ornamented, with each vintage, by a leading artist, as Rothschild had. But he abandoned the plan: to learn from Baron Philippe's expertise was sensible, to copy him too flagrantly was not. It was what was in the bottle that finally counted. Within five years, wine production had doubled prewar levels, and the quality was consistently improving. The first year that they obtained a vintage of acceptable quality, he sent a dozen cases to his old *régisseur* to lay down, and invited him for a tasting. He watched the old man as he carefully sniffed the wine, sipped it, rolled it around his palate. He waited.

"It's not perfect. . . ." The old man frowned.

"Is any wine perfect?"

"Four years from now, yes, by then . . ." The old man's face broke into a grin. "But I could drink this, Monsieur de Chavigny. Oh, yes. Without difficulty."

Edouard embraced him. *"Et voilà. Je suis content."*

With the central part of his father's empire, Edouard moved cautiously. De Chavigny still had an unrivaled reputation for the quality of stones used in its jewelry designs and for the perfection and artistry with which they were cut and set.

He had inherited four major outlets: in New York, Paris, London, and Rome, all of which had come through the war intact, all of which were in prime locations, and all of which had suffered from neglect. Proceeding much as he had done with his houses, Edouard first refurbished them. He brought in a new interior designer, Ghislaine Belmont-Laon; her work on these showrooms made her name. Cleverly, Mme. Belmont-Laon retained the formality of the nineteenth-century rooms, with their mahogany showcases and cabinets, and yet, by her use of color and light, contrived to give them a modern elegance. She introduced soft blues, and a color that came to be known as de Chavigny gray: the rooms, understated and severe, were the perfect backdrop for the jewelry and the silver. At the sumptuous party held to celebrate the reopening of the showrooms in the Rue du Faubourg St. Honoré, Edouard looked around him with pride, but he knew his work had scarcely begun. He had provided one essential, a glittering showcase for the de Chavigny merchandise. Now he was eager to expand, to diversify into other luxury products, as his rivals Cartier and Asprey were already doing very successfully. The world had changed: de Chavigny could no longer cater just to the needs of those who had arrived; it had to make provision for those on the way up. Leather goods, desk accessories, smoking accessories, tableware, the little playthings of the conspicuously affluent—Edouard knew that these, adorned with the de Chavigny name and crest, could be marketed for high prices and to a much wider market than that which could afford the most superlative jewelry in the world.

Edouard began to commission feasibility studies for new de Chavigny showrooms in Geneva, Milan, Rio de Janeiro, and—in the longer term—for Wilshire Boulevard in Los Angeles. But he knew that for his expansion plans to work, he needed two things: further capital investment, and a designer of genius.

The investment, he knew, would be no problem. His French and Swiss bankers had already indicated their eagerness to participate in any expansion of the company. His chief financial advisor, Simon Scher, a young Englishman who, after Cambridge, had trained at the Harvard Business School, was urging him to go public.

"If we floated shares in de Chavigny on the open market tomorrow," he told Edouard, "you would be oversubscribed four times. The money is there, the confidence is there. . . . It's the fifties now—the recovery has started."

But Edouard had no intention of going public; he wanted de Chavigny to remain a private company, as it had always been, with the reins of power firmly in one pair of hands: his hands. And he thought he could do without the high-interest assistance of French or Swiss bankers. John McAllister, his American grandfather, had sold out his interest in his family steel and railroad holdings shortly before the Wall Street crash; he had died toward the end of the war, a few months after his wife. His fortune, conservatively estimated in excess of one hundred million dollars, had come intact to his beloved daughter, Louise. It was handled by a prominent Wall Street firm, with the utmost caution, the bulk of it invested in government bonds, gilt-edged securities, and land from Oregon to Texas.

Louise took no interest in her fortune. Her investments provided her with an annual income of well over a million dollars, in addition to the trusts and investments left to her directly by her husband. Provided she could buy anything she wanted, when she wanted—and it never occurred to her to do otherwise—Louise was happy.

Edouard had already begun his campaign to persuade his mother to divert some of her capital holdings into an expansion program for de Chavigny, but he knew he had to proceed slowly. Louise had gone so far as to allow him access to her papers and portfolio: he and Simon Scher were working on them now. But he knew it would be useless to press his mother too hard for any major decision. She balked at commitments over money as well as over men. Edouard knew that the more rational his arguments were, the more likely she was to resist them. She had an iron whim.

But if he could not persuade her when the time came to move, Jean-Paul could. Anything her beloved son asked of her, Louise gave. It caused Edouard to feel bitter sometimes, but he accepted facts. After all, it made little difference: he would persuade Jean-Paul, Jean-Paul would persuade Louise: the route was more circuitous, that was all. In his business dealings Edouard had discovered he had a talent for the circuitous approach: he was beginning to derive great pleasure from deploying it.

But the designer of genius: ah, now, that was more difficult. The last great designer de Chavigny had employed, Vlacek, a Hungarian Jew trained in Russia in the Fabergé workrooms, had been discovered by

Edouard's father and brought to de Chavigny to design the collection that launched his first American showrooms in 1912. Vlacek had been a prize, and he had been loyal: all attempts to woo him away from de Chavigny—and there had been many—had failed. He had remained with the company until his eyesight began to fail in the early 1930s; he had died during the war.

Like all great jewelry companies, de Chavigny had a huge and jealously guarded archive of designs, dating back, in this case, to the mid-nineteenth century. Those designs could be, and were, constantly reused, either in their original form or adapted to accord with changing fashion and taste. They were the company's lifeline. But the last great de Chavigny collections had been designed by Vlacek in the late 1920s. Edouard longed for a new collection, for revolutionary designs that would set competitors like Cartier by the ears; designs that would reflect the postwar world, and which would use to the full the latest technology.

Truly great jewelry designers are as rare as any other great artist. Edouard knew what he was looking for, a Picasso, a Matisse, whose medium was not paint but rare stones and precious metals; the genius who would be the linchpin of his whole enterprise. Wherever he was—in America, in the Middle East, one side or the other of a newly divided Europe—and whether he was still unknown or already being trained by one of de Chavigny's rivals, Edouard intended to find him. He had a handpicked team whose sole function was to do just that. They infiltrated the workshops of his rivals; they viewed all the new designs of every major jewelry company in the world, they attended the graduating shows of every major training college; they consulted, circumspectly, with discerning collectors such as Florence Gould. They would find the man, sooner or later. Then Edouard would go to him.

And make him an offer he couldn't refuse.

For four years, Edouard lived for his work. He found it addictive, stimulating, endlessly absorbing, and he allowed nothing—certainly no personal involvements—to distract him. He played equally hard, and with the same restless energy, quickly discovering that the two worlds—his days of board meetings and company maneuvers, his evenings and weekends of parties—overlapped, and fed one another. He was in constant demand.

Parisian hostesses fought for his presence at their dinner parties, opera galas, and charity balls. He attended private views, and with the help of his Oxford friend Christian Glendinning, cousin to his former tutor Hugo, he began to buy paintings, and to add to his father's unrivaled collection of twentieth-century European art.

Christian, who came from a long line of English country gentlemen whose only aesthetic investment was in bloodstock, was a maverick, and the despair of his family when Edouard first met him. He was outrageously affected, flamboyantly homosexual, and extremely clever. When his father realized that Christian had no intention of returning to the family estate in Oxfordshire and breeding prime Herefordshire cattle for the rest of his life, he gave him a modest amount of capital and washed his hands of him. Christian used it to open a small gallery as soon as he left Oxford. He put on the first English show of American Abstract Expressionists, and the British critics sniffed. He sold two Rothkos and one superb Jackson Pollock to his friend Edouard de Chavigny, and after that he never looked back. By 1954 he had one of the most successful modern art galleries in Cork Street, London, a branch in Paris, and another planned for Madison Avenue. Edouard de Chavigny, his most loyal and discerning client, had the basis for a collection that one day would be rivaled only by Paul Mellon and the New York Museum of Modern Art.

To Christian's distress and incomprehension, Edouard bought horses as well as paintings. He reinvested in his father's stud farm in Ireland, and brought in Jack Dwyer, the best trainer in the country, poaching him from the stables of his mother's old friend Hugh Westminster without a qualm. Christian accompanied him once to Ireland to watch a new filly run, took one look through the field glasses, announced he was already dying of boredom, and departed to look at paintings. He returned to England on Edouard's new plane with fifteen excellent Jack Yeats oils; Edouard returned secure in the knowledge that he had a winner for the Prix de l'Arc de Triomphe, the prime meeting in the French racing calendar and the one he had set his heart on winning.

But then, as Christian acidly remarked, his friend Edouard was a man of many parts—not just one, as he had suspected when he had first met Edouard in London. Edouard de Chavigny passed from opera box to grouse moor with equal elegance and aplomb. In the autumn he fished and shot in Scotland; in the winter he skied in Gstaad or St. Moritz, where he invested heavily in hotels. In the summer he might be a guest at a Mediterranean villa or at his house on the Costa Smeralda. He might be staying at Southampton, Long Island, with an American newspaper tycoon, or visiting distant American cousins at Newport. Wherever he was there would be a woman, but never the same woman for very long.

The gossip columnists of Europe and the East Coast fought to keep up with him. Who was his latest mistress? Which of the many candidates would he finally marry? The Italian diva, whose operatic performances he faithfully attended from La Scala to the Met—for four months? The English marchioness, widowed during the war, who was the most beautiful of the legendary Cavendish sisters? The daughter of Old Money from Massachusetts, or the daughter of New Money from Texas? Would he marry Clara Delluc, the least celebrated of his mistresses, and the one to whom he always returned after forays elsewhere?

It would be a Frenchwoman, naturally, said the hopeful mothers of ancient lineage and impeccable Catholic upbringing, when they discussed the matter in their Paris drawing rooms. And not a Frenchwoman like Clara Delluc either, but one of his own class, and a virgin. A man like Edouard de Chavigny liked to play the field, so much was understood, but when it came to choosing a *wife*, well, then the qualifications required were somewhat different.

Meanwhile, there was the question of his *presents*, to which much time and many column inches were devoted. Edouard de Chavigny was a Frenchman; he understood that women, when abandoned, liked some small remembrance to soften the blow and to recall tender memories. Edouard de Chavigny always gave jewels. That alone was not remarkable. It was the *choice* of jewels that attracted attention; that, and the manner of their delivery.

The jewels were carefully, some said mockingly, chosen to reflect the woman. Emeralds, if their eyes were green. Exquisitely matched sapphires if their eyes were blue. If their complexion was their most celebrated feature, then perhaps a long necklace of perfect pearls. Gold bracelets, each as thick as a child's wrist, if their hair was blond; amber, ebony, ivory, white gold, amethysts. . . . The gifts were beautiful, almost priceless, and, of course, from de Chavigny. They were delivered to the woman concerned by Edouard de Chavigny's English manservant, without any accompanying message. None was needed; the jewels signified dismissal, announced the relationship was at an end. This was accepted, this was known; it was a rule from which Edouard never relented, never deviated.

One other thing was also known. He never gave diamonds.

The columnists delighted in that. It gave them the pin for endless stories; it gave them a myth. He would give diamonds when he loved, they said. It was simple; poetic. He was saving the diamonds until then; with that gesture the world would know that Edouard de Chavigny, now one of the five most eligible bachelors in Europe, had finally chosen the woman he wanted as his wife.

It was a story that Edouard was often questioned about, by women as well as journalists. It was one on which he always refused to comment, as he did on all questions about his personal life. Nothing could persuade him to confirm or deny. He would smile, and change the subject.

It took four years for Edouard to discover the one aspect of his life the columnists had never suspected: he was lonely.

He returned to the house in St. Cloud late one night in 1954, hollow with fatigue. He had returned that day from an exhausting round of deals and meetings in New York. The rubies rumored to have belonged once to Marie Antoinette had been dispatched to the diva, who always wore scarlet. His senior secretary had been instructed to cancel his engagements for that evening to give him a few hours peace before a six-month period in which his diary was entirely filled.

It was summer, and he walked around the beautiful gardens alone, admiring the beds of shrub roses which had been laid out here as they had been in Josephine Bonaparte's gardens at Malmaison. The scholarship, the skill, the work, and the love which had gone into this section of his gardens struck him forcibly. He smelled the scent of the roses, and realized it was the first time he had walked here, the first time he had looked at them, in four years.

He longed then, suddenly, and with a passion that had been suppressed so long that it took him by surprise, for someone to share all this with. Someone to talk to. Someone to love. Not his mother, with whom his relations remained cool and formal. Not his brother, who had now left the army and spent most of the year in Algiers. None of his friends. Certainly none of his women. Someone else.

Someone he trusted, he thought, returning to his study, and sitting up alone late into the night—and he trusted so few people. Someone who was with him for himself, not because he was a man of influence and power and wealth. Someone with whom he could be free.

He let himself think, as he had not done for many years, of Célestine, of their year together in London, and as he had known it would, the memory made him deeply unhappy. He finally went to bed, cursing himself for his own sentimentality, certain the feeling was due to tiredness and jet lag, no more. It would have disappeared in the morning.

Next day he fulfilled all his engagements as usual. The feeling was still there. As if he had everything, and nothing. Months passed; the feeling did not go away.

Then, that autumn, and quite by chance, something happened that was to alter his life. On a visit to the Château de Chavigny to inspect that year's vintage, he caught sight of a small boy playing in the gardens of one of the estate cottages. Edouard was on horseback; he stopped to look at the child, who was about eight or nine years old, and exceptionally beautiful. The child looked back at him. Then a girl, too young to be his mother, rushed out of the cottage, clasped the child by the hand, and pulled him, protesting, indoors.

Edouard made inquiries; the servants were embarrassed. He persisted, and discovered that the little boy was called Grégoire. His mother was now the wife of one of the estate carpenters, and the boy was Jean-Paul's son, fathered after a drinking bout during his first visit to the Loire after the war. Jean-Paul confirmed the story negligently. Yes, it was true, he accepted paternity. He had seen the boy once or twice since, and he seemed a nice enough lad—a little backward perhaps, but his mother was ashamed of him, and refused to send him to school, perhaps fearing the other children would tease him. Jean-Paul shrugged. He would be all right. When he grew up, there would always be work for him on the estate.

This meeting took place in Paris, where Jean-Paul was visiting Louise briefly before returning to Algeria. Edouard sat and watched his brother as he spoke, his own face growing hard and still. Jean-Paul was sprawled in a chair, his complexion flushed; he was drinking brandy though it was the middle of the day. He seemed annoyed at Edouard's questions, but apart from that, sublimely unconcerned.

"You feel no responsibility for him, then?" Edouard leaned forward.

"Responsibility? Edouard—if a man had to be responsible for every little by-blow, where would it end? The boy is perfectly happy. I imagine he's in good health. I fail to see why I should concern myself with him any further."

"I see. And his mother—have you made any provision for her?"

"Good God no." Jean-Paul stood up angrily. "She's married now, isn't she? I give her husband employment. These people are peasants, Edouard, and proud of it—they accept these things. Their way isn't our way. And besides, give her money, and people would talk. Half the pregnant women on the estate would be swearing I fathered their children. Mind your own business for once, can't you, Edouard? Really—it's not your affair."

Edouard looked at him, red in the face with indignation, reaching for the brandy bottle, glancing toward his brother uneasily, as if he feared more self-justification would be needed. In that moment the last of Edouard's illusions about his brother fell away. He stopped making excuses for him; he let his loyalty and his trust slip aside, and he saw Jean-Paul clearly. Perhaps Jean-Paul read the disgust and the anger in his face; Edouard thought that he did, for he started, in a stubborn voice, on a whole new series of excuses. He was still in mid-speech when Edouard turned and walked out of the room.

Edouard went back to the Loire. He went back to the small house in which Grégoire lived and attempted to interview his mother. The attempt was not a success. The woman refused to sit in his presence; she kept looking over her shoulder as if she feared her husband would come in. Edouard saw that she had bruises on her wrists and that one side of her face, which she tried to turn away from him, was swollen. He looked around the cottage with a sense of despair. It was poorly and sparsely furnished; a brave effort had been made to keep it tidy and clean. The woman had four other children by her marriage; they crept into the room, peeped at Edouard, and crept away.

"I manage," the woman kept saying in response to his questions. "I manage. I get by."

"But five children . . ." He hesitated. The cottage was without heat, except from a stove; there was no running water.

"My sister helps me." Her face grew set. "I told you. We manage."

Finally, Edouard left her. He returned to the château, furious with himself that he could have allowed people to live in this way. He called in his estate manager, rebuked him, and angrily ordered that there should be a complete overhaul of the property of every de Chavigny tenant. The houses should be repaired and modernized; proper plumbing should be installed, and more adequate heating. . . . The manager listened to this; he frowned.

"It will be expensive. The question arose, immediately after the war. I discussed it with the Baron then. He said—"

"I don't give a damn what he said," Edouard roared, unable to contain his anger. "I want this done, do you understand? And I want it done now."

Later that day, when he left the garden to walk by the river alone, a small figure appeared from the bushes beside the path. It attached itself to him, and Edouard, looking down, recognized the young girl he had seen with Grégoire, pulling him back into the cottage. He stopped. The girl looked up at him. She had a square, intense face, and very dark hair. The mother's sister, Edouard thought, and was correct. Her name was Madeleine.

"I heard this morning. I was listening." She looked up at him, clearly terrified to be speaking to him, and yet determined to go on.

"She won't tell you—my sister. She's too frightened. He drinks. He beats her up. He hates Grégoire. He resents him—he always has. He's not a bad man, but he has a violent temper. He always blames Grégoire. He takes his belt to him—I try and hide him sometimes, but he always finds him in the end. I wish—I wish someone would do something. . . ."

The words had all tumbled out, one upon another. Now she stopped, biting her lip. Edouard, moved by her words, lifted his hand gently to touch her arm, and to his horror, she flinched as if she expected him to hit her.

"Please." Edouard looked at her in consternation. "I mean you no harm. I'm not angry. I'm glad you came after me. I wanted to help— that's why I came to see your sister. Here"—he held out his hand to her—"come back to the house with me. Then we can sit down and you can explain properly."

Madeleine was reluctant, but finally agreed. She shrank from entering the château, and had to be cajoled inside. Once there, she sat nervously on the edge of a Louis XIV chair, her bare legs drawn together, her hands in her lap. Edouard ordered her a *citron pressé,* and then quietly listened as—slowly at first, then with gathering confidence— she told him the whole story. It was predictable enough, and Edouard's face grew taut as he listened. When she had finished, he suggested gently that perhaps he might meet Grégoire.

Her face lifted. She flushed, and pressed her hands together. "You would do that?" She paused. "But not here. It would frighten him. I'll bring him—to the stables. May I do that? He won't be so shy there. He loves horses. . . ."

Edouard smiled, and agreed. Madeleine stood up. She looked about the room, and then back at him.

"So many *things,*" she said in a puzzled voice as she left. "What do you do with them?"

"I look at them, I suppose." Edouard shrugged. He was aware that, half the time, he hardly saw them.

Madeleine frowned. "They must make a lot of dusting." She left then, and Edouard, amused by her words, which had touched some chord in him, looked at the room with new eyes. Things indeed; priceless things—which gathered dust just as cheap ones did. The room suddenly seemed to him both overcrowded and empty.

The next day he went to the stables as arranged, and the meeting with Grégoire took place. Madeleine left them alone after a while, and at first Grégoire was shy and hardly spoke.

Edouard took him on a tour of the stables; he showed him the tack room; he introduced him to the horses, and gave the little boy lumps of sugar to offer them. Gradually Grégoire seemed to relax: he explained that he was allowed to help the stable boys sometimes; he would have liked to ride, too, but of course he was not allowed to do that.

"You are allowed now. Here." Edouard lifted the little boy into the saddle of one of the older horses. He was very light, and his bones felt as delicate as a bird's. He looked down at Edouard from the horse's back, and Edouard looked up at him. The boy's mother was from the Landes region, and Grégoire took after her rather than Jean-Paul: he was very thin, very tanned, with a narrow solemn face, and thick black hair. He looked down, and for the first time, smiled.

Edouard felt something snap inside him. In that instant it was as if some dam erected long ago around his heart had been breached. He took Grégoire riding. He canceled his appointments for a week, and stayed in the Loire, spending each day with the boy. At the end of that week, Grégoire was allowed to canter. He executed the run well, without mishap; Edouard's heart was in his mouth as he watched him. When the boy drew his horse in triumphantly beside him, he felt more pride, more sense of achievement than he had felt in four years of high-powered business dealings.

He talked to Grégoire. He talked to the boy's mother. He talked to Madeleine. With their glad acceptance, it was agreed: Grégoire should return to Paris with Edouard and live at St. Cloud. Edouard would arrange for his education; he would take care of the boy personally. Madeleine would accompany Grégoire to Paris for a while, to help him adjust, and then—when she felt ready, when Grégoire felt ready—Edouard would help her find training and work. He outlined these plans stiffly, fearing a proud rejection. When he finished, Grégoire's mother fell to her knees, all control gone. She kissed his hand and wept; Edouard, helping her back to her feet, felt rebuked by that gratitude. He had been blind to need, he thought, ashamed. He would never be so blind again.

Edouard was worried that it might be difficult for Grégoire to adjust to St. Cloud, and that he might be homesick. But his worries proved groundless. The little boy loved the place. He was made a great pet of by Edouard's manservant, George, and by his cook. If other servants resented him, these two carefully shielded him. Edouard set aside a part of each day to be with him.

That winter, he took him skiing. In the spring he took him to the house in Normandy. He spent hours on the beach with Grégoire, quite alone, just swimming and talking and playing. It was after that holiday, when they returned to Paris, that Madeleine said one day: "You don't need me anymore. Grégoire doesn't need me. I have never known him so happy."

She was then eighteen, serious, intense, and very single-minded. She loved children, she said. She would like to be a children's nurse. Yes, she would like to train to do that.

Edouard made inquiries, and finally arranged that she should go to the place of her choice, Norland College in England, which had trained generations of nannies.

"You're sure? You're certain, Madeleine? You don't have to leave—there is always a home for you here."

"I'm certain. I want to learn. I want to work." She stopped abruptly. "I wish to thank you, and I don't know how. You have changed my life."

"Ah, but you changed mine," Edouard said.

After Madeleine left, Edouard spent more and more time with the little boy—every free moment. Grégoire called him "uncle," at his request, which caused great gossip in Paris, but Edouard did not care.

He felt like the boy's father; he loved and cared for Grégoire as if he were his son. And at the back of his mind, knowing that Jean-Paul had never married and seemed unlikely to, knowing that he himself had met no woman he wished to make his wife, he thought: Grégoire could be my heir. Everything I have done could be for him. He will carry on from me, perhaps, as I have carried on from my father.

He consulted his lawyers and altered his will. Then, slowly at first, he began to prepare the little boy for this possible destiny. He never spoke of this inheritance, but he tried, gently, to introduce Grégoire to some aspects of his business empire. As his father had shown him jewels, so he showed them to Grégoire. He took him to all the different workshops de Chavigny maintained in different parts of Paris: he let him watch these highly skilled men at work, the specialists in metal work, the specialists in inlay work and enamels, the gem cutters, the gem setters, the team of highly skilled men who made the mechanisms for clocks and watches.

These, Grégoire especially loved. He had, Edouard saw, a technical mind, and loved to see how working parts fitted together. He would sit for hours, quite silent, watching the assembling of minute coils and springs; he seemed to find the exactitude satisfying.

He loved cars, Edouard quickly discovered that, and—since Edouard loved them too—this became a shared pleasure. But whereas Edouard loved cars for their design and their beauty, and collected them on that basis, Grégoire loved them for the engines under their gleaming hoods.

Some of their happiest hours together were spent driving, or look-ing at cars, or simply in the huge garages at St. Cloud, where Grégoire would contentedly remove wheels, and then replace them, and Edouard would contentedly watch him. His mechanic gave Grégoire lessons, and the little boy learned very quickly. After a few months he could strip down the simpler engines, service and reassemble them. When he had finished such a task, he would lift his face, streaked with oil and grease, beaming with contentment.

"I can do it," he would say to Edouard. "Look. Everything in the right place."

Edouard smiled at him gently; at such times his own life seemed to him equally simple; the components were there—they had been assembled.

The weeks passed happily. They went to the Loire and toured the vineyards together. They returned to the house in Normandy and, one weekend, just for the excitement of it, camped outside, making a fire on the beach, cooking their own supper, and burning it. Neither of them minded the burned taste in the least; they sat side by side on the sand, the tall dark man, and the small dark boy; at peace together.

"I'd like to stay here forever, just like this," Grégoire said.

"So should I," Edouard answered.

Later, in sleeping bags, with Grégoire quiet and breathing peacefully, Edouard lay on his back and looked up at the stars. It was the first time in his life that he had slept out of doors; as a boy, he and Jean-Paul had often pleaded to do this, and it had always been forbidden. Now, breathing the cool night air, listening to the soft sucking of the sea against the sand, Edouard experienced great happiness. He glanced toward Grégoire, knowing that happiness sprang from him; he had brought Edouard love; he had also given back to him a sense of purpose.

The next day they went riding, the boy in riding clothes made for him by Edouard's English tailors, a miniature copy of Edouard's own. As they were returning, Grégoire grew quiet and thoughtful.

"What are you thinking about, Grégoire?"

"Of you. And of me." The child hesitated. "I call you 'uncle,' but I wish sometimes . . ."

"Wish what? Tell me."

"I wish I could call you Papa." Grégoire raised his dark eyes to Edouard's face. "Just when we are alone. I understand that."

Edouard drew in his horse. He dismounted and lifted Grégoire down beside him. He put his arms around him.

"I wish you were my son," he said very gently. "I wish it very much. And I feel as if you were. That's the most important thing, don't you think, Grégoire? Names don't really matter. Not between us."

"Je vous aime." Grégoire slipped one small hand around Edouard's neck and planted a loud kiss on his brow.

"Et je t'aime aussi, tu sais. . . ."

"Beaucoup?"

"Bien sûr. Beaucoup."

It was the first time they had ever spoken of the affection they felt. It made Edouard alive with happiness.

When they returned to Paris, however, he discovered that his relationship with Grégoire, so simple to him, was less simple to others. His mother summoned him; she made it clear that she wished to see him alone.

She gave him tea; she chatted of this and that. Edouard waited. He had been aware from the first that Louise disapproved of Grégoire, and disapproved of this informal adoption. She had previously limited her expression of that disapproval to hints, and to glancing remarks; now, clearly, she had decided the time had come to be more open. She was cautious though, and Edouard, watching her, realized that his relationship with his mother was changing yet again—that it had, perhaps, been altering over a period of time.

Louise had still not agreed to divert any of her capital into the de Chavigny companies, and Edouard, biding his time, had not pressed her. But she no longer treated him with the old irritable dismissiveness; she knew of Edouard's reputation as a businessman, and obviously had heard his abilities praised, for she now regarded him warily, as if trying to decide whether, after all, she might have been wrong, and her younger son might be of use to her. There was a certain speculativeness in her glance now when she looked at him; she listened when he advised her on her investment portfolio, and—increasingly—she took his advice. She spoke of some of those investments now, in particular some of her land investments in Texas, which her American advisors were counseling her to sell.

What she said was of interest to Edouard, but he could see that it was by way of a preamble. His mother wanted his help; she, also, he felt more and more certain, wanted to attack him on the question of Grégoire. In the past she would have done so at once; not now. Now she was cautious, and Edouard—to his surprise—realized she was weighing the risk of offending him.

"Dearest Edouard," she said at last, finally coming to the point. "I did just want to raise the question of that boy. . . ."

"Grégoire?"

"Yes. Grégoire." Her mouth tightened a little. "People do talk, you know, Edouard. They say such wicked and wounding things. . . ."

"It's of no concern to me. Let them say what they like."

"Of course. Of course." Louise attempted to sound soothing. "I realize you're in a very difficult position. Really, it is Jean-Paul's responsibility. And you will step in, Edouard . . ."

"Someone had to."

"I fail to see why. And to take things this far . . ." Louise gave a small toss of her head. "Having the boy live with you. Treating him as if he were your own son, your legitimate son. It's unfair to *him*, Edouard, to take him out of his station in that way. He'll never be totally accepted, you know that. And he won't be able to return home. He'll fit in nowhere—he'll be neither fish nor fowl. . . ."

Edouard turned away. He was angered, and for a moment was tempted to reply that Louise herself had managed to fit in to French society despite her origins and her antecedents, but he curbed himself.

"He fits in with me," he answered stubbornly. "At the moment that is all that concerns me."

"But Edouard, how can he?" Louise was now quivering with indignation. "Obviously, you're fond of him, but surely you can see? His *accent*, Edouard. You'll never eliminate it altogether, you know. And he looks so surly, so shifty—he won't meet my eyes. . . ."

"That's because you make him shy and self-conscious, that's all." Edouard sighed. "Look, why don't you make an effort? Let me bring him here. Try to talk to him. You'll see then—when he relaxes, he's delightful. *Maman*, he's your *grandchild*, surely you can overcome your prejudices for once. . . ."

There was a small silence. Louise looked at him, a long speculative glance. He could see her deciding whether to agree or disagree; he could see her weigh the advantages and the possible disadvantages. The moment when he knew his mother finally acknowledged that she needed him was then, when she lowered her eyes, and gave a small resigned sigh of agreement.

Edouard looked at her bitterly. When, as a child, he had been desperate for her love, and had offered his own, she had always turned away from him. Now, because she needed something from him, she was prepared to give in. Not that she wanted his love even now; she did not—just his advice, just his financial acumen. Well, it was a bargain of sorts, he thought coldly.

"Very well, Edouard. Bring him here for tea next week. I'll try, for your sake."

So she signaled her capitulation, recognized the alteration in the balance of power between them. Edouard, watching her, wondered if she had any idea that it was too late.

Grégoire did not want to visit Louise. He opposed the expedition to the Faubourg Saint-Germain with an obstinacy and a truculence that surprised Edouard.

"She doesn't like me," he said in a small flat voice. "I know she doesn't. I don't want to go."

Nothing Edouard said could overcome this opposition. When the day came, Grégoire was carefully prepared: he was given a new haircut; George himself supervised his washing procedure, which was inclined to be haphazard. The boy was arrayed in a neat gray flannel suit, with a tie, a white shirt, and beautifully polished shoes. In the back of the car taking them in to Paris, he sat with his hands clasped on his bare knees, and a tight, closed expression on his face. Edouard tried very hard to persuade him to talk, and to relax; Grégoire would not say one word.

When they arrived at Louise's house, Grégoire raised a small pinched face to Edouard's, and Edouard took his hand and pressed it.

"Half an hour, Grégoire. That's all. There's nothing to be afraid of."

Grégoire marched into the house like a small marionette. In the drawing room he took a great deal of persuading to sit down, and then, when Louise finally joined them, drifting in in her rose silk dress, Grégoire seemed so overcome that he forgot to rise. He remembered, but too late, and then stumbled to his feet too quickly, almost knocking over the tiny wine table that stood by his side.

"Grégoire—how lovely that you could come. Do sit down again. . . ."

Louise straightened the table a little too ostentatiously. Grégoire crimsoned, and slowly sat down.

"Now, Grégoire. I'm so longing to hear. You must tell me *everything* you've been doing. Do you like it at St. Cloud? How are your lessons coming along? Do you work hard at them? Edouard always did—but then, darling Edouard was such a clever little boy. . . ."

So she began, and so she went on. Edouard sat to one side, helplessly, while Louise bombarded Grégoire with questions, and Grégoire stammered increasingly brief replies.

The tea was brought in by two of Louise's housemaids. Grégoire sat on the extreme edge of his chair. Louise poured tea from a silver pot into cups of Sèvres porcelain.

"Edouard, if you'd pass that to Grégoire—on the little table there— yes, that's right. And then—I thought—perhaps one of these?" She indicated a silver dish on which were cucumber sandwiches one inch square. "Or those?" Another dish, with exquisitely decorated little biscuits. A third, with elegant little mouthfuls of *patisserie*. "An English tea. Edouard always adored that when we stayed in London. And little boys are always so *hungry*, aren't they? Now, Grégoire, which would you like? I chose them specially for you. . . ."

"None, thank you, Madame. . . ."

Grégoire raised his small face; his lips were set.

"None?" Louise's eyes rounded. "You're sure? Well, of course, perhaps you're not used . . . Edouard, won't you have one of these?"

Edouard took one of the tiny sandwiches, and sat down again grimly. Grégoire was now hemmed in by the tiny precarious wine table. Balanced upon it were a Sèvres plate, a Sèvres cup and saucer. Grégoire was sitting with his legs tucked firmly back, his elbows pressed against his sides.

"So, tell me Grégoire," Louise went on brightly after a pause. "If you don't like Latin, and you don't like arithmetic, what do you like? There must be something, I suppose?"

"Grégoire is very clever with his hands," Edouard put in quickly. "He can take a clock apart and put it back together again. And a car engine too—François has been helping him, hasn't he, Grégoire?"

"Sometimes." Grégoire looked sullenly down at the floor.

"I don't need him now. I can do it on my own." He raised his eyes to Louise's face. "I worked on a Porsche last week, all on my own. And one day Uncle Edouard said he might let me work on the Aston-Martin. It's my favorite car."

This was the longest speech he had made. Edouard could see the pleading expression come into his eyes, and the desperation for approval. Perhaps Louise saw it, too, for she gave a little laugh.

"Grégoire, how charming! But that wasn't quite what I meant. I'm sure Edouard doesn't need another mechanic. . . . Oh! You've finished your tea—how quickly you drink! Here, let me pour you another cup. . . ."

This was so overtly rude that Edouard was about to intervene; but before he could speak, Grégoire rose to his feet. He lifted the Sèvres cup and saucer from the table in front of him, and advanced toward Louise, who was sitting there smiling at him, silver teapot poised.

When he was perhaps one foot away from her, Grégoire dropped the cup. It fell to the floor and instantly smashed. Louise gave an exclamation of displeasure, and Edouard rose to his feet; Grégoire remained absolutely still, looking down at the smashed cup. Had it been deliberate? Edouard hesitated, unsure; it had happened so quickly that it was difficult to know.

Grégoire raised his eyes from the floor to Louise's face: "I'm sorry," he said in a flat voice. "It's broken. That was clumsy of me."

The defiance in his tone was masked, but it was there. Louise heard it and flushed. Edouard heard it, too, and it was then that he became almost certain that the dropping of the cup had been no accident.

The episode was passed over; shortly afterward Edouard and Grégoire left. In the car, returning home, Grégoire was very quiet. As they reached St. Cloud, he turned to Edouard with a sudden anxiousness in his face.

"I don't think I'll be asked to go there again. Not after breaking that cup, do you think?"

The hope that this might indeed be the case was transparent in his face—so transparent that Edouard suppressed a smile.

"I'm sure my mother will not mind—it was only a cup. But perhaps we might not go there again—for a while anyway." He paused. "Grégoire, did you mean to do it? Tell me truthfully now."

A small frown appeared on Grégoire's face. Edouard saw a brief struggle take place.

"She doesn't like me," Grégoire said at last in a small stubborn voice. "I told you she didn't. I told you I didn't want to go there."

It was no answer, and it was a complete answer; Edouard, recognizing something of Jean-Paul in the implacability of the reply, hearing in it, too, that note of bland stubbornness with which some of his workmen in the Loire would resist argument and change with an age-old peasant resilience, sighed and decided it might be wiser to leave the subject there.

The episode was better forgotten, he thought; he would not risk exposing Grégoire to Louise's unkindness again. Days passed; weeks passed. Once Grégoire was certain that he was reprieved from all further visits to the Faubourg Saint-Germain, his nature became open and sunny once again.

I n the spring of that year, 1955, not long after this meeting, the tutor Edouard had hired for Grégoire left to take up an appointment elsewhere. Edouard, searching around for a replacement, hit on the idea of Hugo Glendinning.

He had seen Hugo from time to time in the intervening years; he knew from Hugo's cousin Christian that his former tutor had fallen on hard times. A prestigious teaching post at Winchester had been terminated abruptly some years before, and Hugo had failed to hold another since. The regimen of the major public schools did not suit him, Christian explained. He was too individualistic, too eccentric. Christian was sure he would be delighted to go to France and work for Edouard. Private tutors in England were less in demand these days, Christian said with a smile; times were changing.

Edouard was a little uncertain about the decision. He would have preferred Grégoire to go to school and mix with other children. But the little boy, having missed so many years of schooling, was backward in his lessons, and Edouard feared that he would be teased. He would wait another couple of years, he told himself, until Grégoire had had a chance to catch up, and was more confident. He thought of Hugo, who had revolutionized his own thinking, who had made him challenge and question for the first time. He thought of Hugo's ability to excite interest, to stimulate thought. He reminded himself of Hugo's dedication, his wisdom, his kindness, and his wit. He heard Hugo's voice saying lines of poetry to him that remained with him still: he came to a decision, and wrote to him. It was his first major mistake.

Hugo had never suffered fools gladly. Edouard, not a fool, and possessed of a quick and nimble mind, had forgotten that side of his nature, which he, in any case, had rarely seen. Also, time had passed, and Hugo had changed. A youthful tendency to impatience had, over the years, modulated into a marked irascibility. Hugo looked at his contemporaries, less clever than himself, and saw them outstrip him. He blamed political bias, but when he had stood as a Labor candidate in the 1945 elections in which the Socialists swept to postwar victory, Hugo had not won his seat. He was in his fifties, unmarried, and out of touch with postwar educational methods. He had never taught boys who were less than well grounded in traditional academic subjects. He and Grégoire met, and it was almost instant dislike.

Grégoire's ability to take a clock to pieces and put it together again, to strip down a car engine, to harness a horse and ride it well, to know and to cherish the names and characteristics of plants and animals—all these abilities meant nothing to Hugo at all.

At first, Hugo tried to be patient. He understood that the boy had had little formal education until Edouard took him under his wing. He could now read and write in French, and had learned a little English from Edouard, but that was the extent of his achievements. Enthusiastically, curbing the dislike he felt, Hugo embarked on a plan that would give Grégoire a solid foundation in all the subjects he considered of importance. These did not include anything remotely mechanical, certainly not the workings of the internal combustion engine. Education, to Hugo, was literature, history, and languages first, everything else a very poor second.

Their tutorials did not go well. Grégoire could be stubborn. It did not take Hugo long to decide that the boy was willful: he could learn, he just did not want to. He was lazy; he refused to concentrate. To his own horror, Hugo, the lifelong Socialist, found himself blaming the boy's peasant stock. Hating himself for that snobbery, he drove the boy harder, refusing to admit to himself that he was failing.

He knew he had failed at so many things, but never as a teacher, never as that. Now here was a boy who listened stolidly while Hugo read to him some of the greatest literature in the world; who yawned over Villon; who stared out the window longingly while Hugo read de Maupassant or Flaubert.

Hugo would not, could not, lower his standards; the boy would not, could not, raise his. They reached an impasse very soon—but neither told Edouard, Hugo out of pride, Grégoire because he could not bear to disappoint him.

L ate in the summer of 1955, when the weather was very hot, Edouard left for America on business. He had decided to investigate for himself the question of his mother's land investments in Texas, the holdings her Wall Street advisors seemed so eager she should sell, so eager that Edouard was a little suspicious. He would be away two weeks: when he returned, he told Grégoire, they would go away on holiday, to the sea perhaps, as they had the year before.

Grégoire missed Edouard; his concentration did not improve. The schoolroom at St. Cloud was stiflingly hot day after day; Hugo's temper did not improve either. Once, to his own dismay, he almost hit the child out of frustration, and only just curbed himself in time. Furious, he decided to abandon Latin for the moment and concentrate on French. If the boy would not listen to poetry, then he should be forced at least to understand some grammar.

He set Grégoire pages of text to learn, sequence after sequence of rules. Then he tested him on them.

One afternoon, about a week after Edouard's departure, he noticed the boy was quieter than usual, and slightly flushed. He asked him sarcastically if he felt all right. Grégoire looked down.

"I have a headache," he said eventually.

"I also have a headache." Hugo slapped his textbook down on his desk. "I would have less of a headache if you concentrated. Now. The conjugations of these irregular verbs. We will go over them again. Perhaps if you remember them, you will forget your maladies."

The boy bent his head over the book with a docility unlike him. The next day it was the same. He volunteered nothing. He sat in sullen silence. He refused to eat his lunch. At two they returned to the schoolroom.

"You are sulking, Grégoire. Would you like to tell me why?"

The boy raised his flushed face. "I don't feel very well."

"You would feel better if you worked. Laziness is enough to make anyone feel ill."

"Truly. My head aches. I would like to lie down."

The little boy lowered his head on his arms, and Hugo gave a sigh of exasperation. He got up, crossed to the boy, and felt his forehead. He felt a little hot, but the schoolroom was stifling, so it was hardly surprising.

"Grégoire—these devices may have worked with your previous tutor, they will not work with me." Hugo returned to his desk. "If I told you lessons were over for the day and you could go swimming, no doubt a miraculous recovery would take place. I have no intention of doing that. Now, sit up, please, and make an attempt to concentrate. Open your grammar to page fourteen."

Slowly the boy did as he was told.

By half-past three, when their lessons were normally over, Hugo felt he was getting into his stride. The boy was quiet; he appeared to be listening; certainly he wasn't staring out the window for once. Hugo glanced at his watch and decided to press on for another half hour.

At five minutes to four, Grégoire went into convulsions. It happened very suddenly, and without warning. Suddenly Hugo heard a harsh sibilant inhalation of breath. He looked up in alarm. The boy's head had arched back; his eyes had rolled up; one arm and one leg jerked, then his whole body. He fell off his chair and onto the floor. Hugo had no idea what to do. Frantically he rang for the servants. He fetched water and splashed it over the twitching boy. He loosened his collar, attempted to put a ruler between his teeth, and failed. Just after four, the convulsion stopped.

An ambulance was called. Grégoire had a second convulsion on the way to the hospital. The top pediatrician in Paris was summoned from his home in the suburbs. He informed a white-faced Hugo that the boy almost certainly had meningitis. They would perform a lumbar puncture to make sure. And after that . . .

"Then what? Then what?" Hugo was distraught.

"Then you pray, Monsieur. I will do the best I can, naturally. If he had been admitted sooner, I should have been more optimistic. That is all I can say."

Hugo first telephoned the de Chavigny offices, and told them to contact Edouard immediately; then, for the first time in many years, he prayed. Edouard was contacted in the middle of a meeting at six-fifteen Eastern Standard Time. He left immediately for the airport and chartered a jet. Grégoire died the next day, in the early morning, two hours before Edouard reached the hospital.

He took the boy's small still limp body in his arms, and wept with a passion of which his business associates would not have believed him capable.

Three months later, Hugo was drowned in a boating accident; there were rumors of suicide, which were hushed up. He left Edouard his library, and when Edouard heard this, he angrily sent the whole collection to auction. Grégoire was buried in the de Chavigny chapel, to the fury of Louise and the indifference of Jean-Paul, and Edouard tried to begin to rebuild his life.

It was from that time, his friends judged, that he became a changed man. They had always respected Edouard de Chavigny. Now they began to fear him.

I n the early fifties, Edouard had commissioned Émil Lassalle, pupil of Le Corbusier, and the leading Modernist architect in France, to design the new administrative headquarters for the de Chavigny parent company in Paris. By late 1955, the tall black glass tower Lassalle designed was completed; it was the first building of its kind in Paris, the subject of much controversy and subsequent imitation, to become a landmark in the commercial sector.

In the winter of that year, Edouard arrived there punctually at nine, as he always did. As always, he was driven from St. Cloud in his black Rolls-Royce Phantom; as always, when his driver held back the door, and he climbed out, he looked up at Lassalle's building, that tall dark tower, and then passed inside. He was not looking forward to the events that he knew lay ahead of him that morning, but he dismissed all such thoughts from his mind: pleasant and unpleasant, most tasks were equal to him now: he viewed them with the same cold dispassion—so many tasks in each day, so many days in each week, so many weeks in each year. He stepped into his private elevator and pressed the button for the eighteenth floor.

In his office on the twelfth floor of the same building, Gérard Gravellier, head of the archive department of de Chavigny, was standing at the window. He had watched the Rolls-Royce pull up, as he did most mornings. He had watched the tall black-suited figure pass quickly inside. Once Edouard was out of sight, he turned away from the window thoughtfully, brushing a few flecks of dandruff absentmindedly from the shoulders of his suit. The suit had been tailored for him in London at a cost of some one hundred and fifty guineas—not by Edouard de Chavigny's own tailors, Gieves of Savile Row, but by another man who could do a cheaper, and passable, imitation.

Gravellier felt nervous, so nervous he'd been unable to eat breakfast. But now he tried to calm himself: there was no reason for nerves, he told himself. He knew the reason for this meeting. It was to discuss the new storage and filing systems to be used for the archive of de Chavigny designs, which had been replanned from scratch at Edouard de Chavigny's insistence, and which would become fully operational that week, when the archive was finally moved to its new headquarters. The new system involved some staffing reductions, voluntary retirements; it was probably that which Edouard de Chavigny wanted to discuss, or some details of the system. Edouard de Chavigny's eye for detail was well known; no aspect, however small, connected with the running of his companies escaped his notice. The remembrance of that brought the nervousness back. Gérard Gravellier was beginning to sweat.

When the buzzer went off on his new chrome and ash desk, he jumped. *Calm down*, he said to himself. He began to recite a litany of his own successes to himself as he passed down the quiet, thickly carpeted corridors to the executive elevator that went up to the eighteenth floor: a new apartment in the smart suburb of Beauséjour; a smaller apartment, in Montparnasse, with a most accommodating young mistress; two cars, one of the largest and latest registration Citroën Familiale; a generous expense account, which was not queried too closely—he hoped was not queried too closely. He had a degree in fine arts from the Sorbonne; he had further training from the Victoria and Albert Museum in London, and the Beaux Arts in Paris; he knew more about the history of the design of jewelry in general, and of the de Chavigny company in particular, than anyone else except the man he was going to see now. He sighed and mopped his brow. He was indispensable. He hoped.

It was his first visit to Edouard de Chavigny's offices in the penthouse suite on the eighteenth floor. When he stepped out of the high-speed elevator, his eyes widened. The break with tradition was complete. The outer reception area was vast, an ocean of pale beige and white, glass and chrome. Three huge natural leather couches surrounded a Corbusier table; two extremely beautiful receptionists sat at Corbusier desks. They both wore plain silk blouses, pearls, and Hermès scarves knotted loosely around their throats. Gérard Gravellier looked at them sideways. Both were highly desirable, the one on the left especially; both looked as if they wouldn't get on their backs for anyone less than Edouard de Chavigny himself; both had the kind of accent that made his toes curl, and wish he'd opted for the more costly tailor. *Bon genre.* It was a type he detested.

"You'll have to wait just a little while, Monsieur Gravellier," one had said. No apology; no explanation; no offer of coffee; nothing. He sat there sweating for forty-five minutes.

Then the inner office, even more discreetly sumptuous, and two more smooth bitches, secretaries this time, both looking as if they had starch in their well-bred pants. Jesus! Then the inner sanctum; precisely one hour after he'd first been called; he was sure it was deliberate.

He went in through the plain mahogany door, and stopped. The office was very large and startlingly austere. He had expected antiques, flowers, the portraits of past Barons de Chavigny, which had always hung in the old Baron's offices. There were none. The walls were hung with abstracts; his jaw dropped slightly as he took them in: one Picasso, from his Cubist period; two superb Braques; an early Kandinsky; a Mondrian; one of Rothko's red series; a vast and tormented Jackson Pollock. On the black bookcase behind the desk were three exquisite bronzes: a Brancusi, a Henry Moore, a Giacometti. He swallowed. It was a long walk to the chair in front of the desk.

He made it hesitantly. Edouard de Chavigny looked up. Gravellier looked at him curiously. He was thirty now, he knew, but he looked slightly older. Tall, well over six feet, with wide shoulders, and the same magnetic good looks as his father. Tanned skin, strong features; that striking combination of very black hair and dark blue eyes. Gravellier felt as if the eyes looked straight into his head and out the other side. He glanced enviously at the suit: plain black, with a vest, four buttons at the cuff, whereas his had only three. He swore silently to himself. The difference between a two-hundred-guinea suit and a five-hundred-guinea one was only too obvious at close hand. A white shirt; a black knitted silk tie. The man looked as if he were in mourning.

"Do sit down."

Gravellier sat. The huge black desk was flanked by a complicated system of telephones and intercoms; on the top of it was one platinum de Chavigny pen and one plain white folder. Nothing else—and this man knew what was happening in Rome, Tokyo, or Johannesburg about two months before the men on the spot found out about it. How did he do it? He eased his collar away from his neck. There was silence. He knew these silences, they were famous. They were designed to unnerve you, to make you start jabbering indiscreetly. He swallowed, and started jabbering.

"I am filled with admiration for the new headquarters, Monsieur de Chavigny. I just wanted to say that. It will make a great difference to our—er—corporate image, I feel sure. To have the privilege of working in such modern, such advanced offices. Already I hear that—"

"I did not call you here to discuss the offices."

Gravellier coughed. The voice was incisive, and cold, and he knew he ought to relax, to keep calm, above all to shut up, but somehow he couldn't.

"No, of course, Monsieur de Chavigny. If you are concerned about the transfer of the archive, I just wanted to assure you that it is right on schedule. I brought some papers with me in case you . . . I have the details here. Layout. The new staffing arrangements . . ."

"Monsieur Gravellier. How long have you worked for de Chavigny?"

"Twenty-one years, Monsieur de Chavigny."

"Twenty-one years, two months and three weeks." He flicked open the white file in front of him. Gravellier tried desperately to read it upside down.

"I have here the report of the head of our security division."

There was another of those silences. Gravellier went white.

"I don't think we need to itemize the details, do you? You began passing details of archive designs fourteen months ago. Comparatively trivial details to begin with, which was why you were allowed to continue. I wanted to see how far you would go." Another silence.

"Last month you were given access to highly confidential details regarding our plans for designs for 1956 and 1957. You recall them, I am sure. They were coded 'white ice,' and involved the extensive use of platinum, white gold, and diamonds. It makes no difference, in fact, whether you recall them or not, since they were invented for your benefit, and the benefit of the rival company to whom you passed those confidential details yesterday afternoon." He gave a wintry smile. "Our actual details for 1956 and 1957 designs are, needless to say, quite different, and you will not be receiving them. You are fired."

Gravellier stood up, blood washing over his face, sickness rising in his stomach. *You bastard*, he thought incoherently. *You cold-blooded bastard. Eighteen months. You gave me enough rope for eighteen months, and now* . . . He gripped the back of the chair in front of him.

Edouard de Chavigny looked up. His face betrayed no emotion.

"Your company mortgage is canceled. Unless you can make private arrangements, the company will foreclose. Your company car was impounded this morning. The company has informed your two banks, where you have substantial overdrafts, I understand, that your employment with us has ceased, and we cannot be regarded as guarantors. Your pension plan with this company is void. Our solicitors filed action for breach of trust, fraud, and embezzlement this morning. Is there anything else?"

"Monsieur de Chavigny. Please . . ." Gravellier clasped his sweating palms together. "I'm a married man. I have four children. They're still in school. The eldest is only eleven, and . . ."

There was another silence. For one moment, the most glorious moment in the world, Gravellier thought he had got through to him. At the mention of his children, the eyes of the man behind the desk flickered. Then he closed the white file in front of him with a snap.

"There are two officers outside. One is from the Inspecteurs des Finances. The other is from the Préfecture Île de la Cité. You will find you are under arrest. Good morning."

Gravellier made it as far as the door. Then he looked back, anger and fear and loathing rising in him like bile. He looked at that perfect suit, that perfectly inexpressive face, those cold eyes.

"Goddamn you." His voice choked. "Twenty-two years. I hope you rot in hell."

When the door closed on him, Edouard de Chavigny sat very still. He looked into the turbulence, the red and the black at the heart of the Jackson Pollock painting. He smiled a small bitter smile and pushed the white folder aside. He was already in hell. It didn't take the curse of a man like Gerard Gravellier to take him there.

He had always had a capacity for ruthlessness. Before, he had curbed it; now he gave it rein. Disloyalty, subterfuge, inefficiency: these he had once rectified; now he punished. What he wanted done, he wanted done exactly, and by yesterday. Those who could stand the pace flourished; those who could not went to the wall. Those who crossed him, and there were fewer and fewer of those, quickly had cause to regret it.

A small jeweler in Switzerland who for years had made good profits by flagrantly copying de Chavigny designs, using inferior stones, low-carat metals, and cheap workmanship, and then passing them off as de Chavigny originals through an impenetrable network of shady dealers and retailers, found its bank was suddenly very glad to extend credit for new workshops and an expansion program. The jeweler was overjoyed; he began spending heavily. When he was at his most extended, his bank, a subsidiary of a larger group headed by Crédit Suisse, one of the de

Chavigny company's Swiss bankers, suddenly called in his loans. He was unable to repay, and asked for an extension. The extension was refused at the head office; the jeweler went bankrupt.

The advertising company in London handling the de Chavigny accounts, and responsible for the image of de Chavigny jewelry and wine in Great Britain, was twelve hours late with its new presentation, not an uncommon occurrence. They lost the account the same day. Within six weeks their most aggressive rivals had a new de Chavigny campaign under way—and not on the drawing boards, on the pages of every major magazine in the country.

"How did he do it? How did that sonuvabitch do it so quickly?" The art director stared at the glossy double-page spread in *Harper's Bazaar* enviously; he knew, just knew, that it was going to sweep every goddamn award.

"I don't know," said the marketing director. "But you better get your arse on the deck. We've just had another six major cancellations."

Six months later, the advertising agency was taken over by its successful rivals; two months after that they were both incorporated into de Chavigny (advertising) a new company with offices in London, Paris, Zurich, Milan, and New York, registered in the Balearic Islands, and with sole responsibility for the marketing of all de Chavigny products and investments, from steel through hotels and property, worldwide. The president of the company, its executive director, and the man holding the controlling interest in its shares was Edouard de Chavigny.

Both his mother and brother found that this new ruthlessness in Edouard's character did not spare members of his own family. In January 1956, Jean-Paul made one of his rare visits to Paris. His object was to persuade Edouard—not persuade, he kept reminding himself, *tell!* who was the Baron de Chavigny after all?—to invest in further acreage of vineyards in Algeria, as well as timber and olive plantations there. Jean-Paul was in no doubt that he was on to a good deal.

"That cretin Olivier de Courseulles is selling up. Lock, stock, and barrel. He's nervous. Got the wind up. The first sign of unrest and he's running for his life. Edouard: there're twenty-five thousand hectares of olives. They produce some of the best oil in the region. Thirty thousand of timber. Just under a thousand of vines—but it's some of the best land there is. And he's letting it go for a song. Because he's in a hurry. And we're friends. I told him there'd be no problem."

"You shouldn't have done that." His brother tapped the surface of his black desk with his platinum pen.

"Why not?" Jean-Paul stared at him blankly. "You mean there's some difficulty? There can't be. I looked at those last reports you sent me, the financial returns. Well, I know I'm no financial expert, but even I can see the money's there."

"It's not a question of that. Why do you think he is selling? At such a remarkably charitable price?"

"Well, as I say, he's nervous. Obviously, the political situation being what it is out there at the moment, things are a bit unstable."

"Highly unstable."

"But that won't *last*, for God's sake. The French government won't stand for it, we won't stand for it, damn it. Any more trouble, and they'll send in troops. Clean it up in no time. I know the Arabs, you don't. They couldn't organize a strike, let alone a revolution. All that talk is just alarmist rubbish."

"If you were wrong, and they did somehow manage to organize a revolution . . ." Edouard's voice was coldly sarcastic. "Have you any idea what would happen to French-owned land afterward?"

"Well, it would be repossessed, I suppose." Jean-Paul's voice took on a belligerent note. "But that's irrelevant. I'm telling you, it can't happen, and it won't happen. Algeria is a French colony, for God's sake. Perhaps you've forgotten that."

"Have you observed recent events in Indochina?"

"Of course I damn well have. It's totally different."

"The answer is no."

Jean-Paul, his face flushed and perplexed, stared at his brother. He hardly knew him, he realized suddenly. This cool, dark-suited man was a stranger.

"Look, little brother"—he leaned across the desk—"I didn't expect this. I don't understand it. You sit there, looking like God. You just say no—you don't deign to give me any reasons."

"I can give you plenty of reasons. Most of them are contained in the report I had drawn up which is in front of you now." Edouard looked at his watch. "It's a high-risk investment, on which, if the political situation worsens, we stand to make a total loss. I am not always against high-risk investments. I am against this one."

Jean-Paul's mouth set. "Perhaps you're forgetting something. I am the Baron de Chavigny. Not you. In the final analysis, what I say goes. I can overrule you on this."

"Fine. You can have my resignation in the morning." Edouard stood up; his eyes were dark with anger. Jean-Paul began to feel seriously alarmed.

"Wait a minute, now. Don't get on your high horse with me. God—your temper, Edouard. You know I don't want that. You know I always let myself be advised by you, and of course I'll bow to your judgment on this if I have to. . . ." He hesitated, a cunning look suddenly coming into his eyes. "The thing is, just occasionally, you might listen to me. In this case I know what I'm talking about. And after all—you scratch my back, I'll scratch yours. That's what business is about, they tell me. You wanted me to talk to Mother about her investments, about making money over to de Chavigny. Well, I'm happy to do that; in fact, I'm seeing her this afternoon, and I'll mention it. But I don't see why I should when you're being so mulish about this. Can't you see, Edouard? I practically promised Olivier de Courseulles. I shall look like an absolute fool if I change my mind now."

Edouard sat down again with a tight smile.

"By all means discuss that with *Maman*. Whether you do or not, I am not going to change my mind."

Jean-Paul flung out. The same afternoon he took tea with Louise de Chavigny in the pale gray and rose-pink salon of her house in the Faubourg St. Germain. He sipped China tea from eighteenth-century Limoges cups, and his plump bottom squirmed on the silk-upholstered bergère armchair—made for beauty, not comfort. Louise, as beautiful as ever, the lines of her face almost invisible since her most recent face-lift, wearing the latest sheath from Dior, its narrow shape flattering her slender figure, sat opposite him, calmly and charmingly talking about nothing at all. Jean-Paul eyed the Limoges plate of *patisserie*, provided for his benefit. Perhaps just one more eclair—they were minute enough in all conscience. He reached out a large pink hand and conveyed the marvelous confection of light pastry, chocolate, and cream to his mouth. Louise watched him fastidiously.

"Jean-Paul, you have put on a lot of weight since I last saw you. You should go on a diet. Exercise more. Edouard rides every morning, you know, in the Bois de Boulogne."

Jean-Paul frowned. He decided to come to the point. Not very subtly, he raised the question of Louise's investment portfolio. Louise's eyebrows rose.

"Oh, but darling, I thought you saw Edouard this morning? Then surely you know, it's all taken care of—though it's very sweet of you to ask." She paused to light a cigarette with her platinum de Chavigny lighter. "Really, it's all so complicated, but it seems I was being rather badly advised. And by such a reputable firm too. Papa always trusted them implicitly. I trusted them too. So, of course, I'm all the more grateful to Edouard." Her eyes narrowed slightly. "He really is very clever, you know. Far cleverer than I realized." Jean-Paul glowered. This was not a song he had heard her sing before.

"You see, there were all these land holdings." Louise waved her cigarette vaguely. "They were advising me to sell, and it seemed they had a taker who was offering a very generous price. Some of it was ranch land; most of it was semi-desert, I believe. And I'd seen a most delightful villa. . . . Have you heard of St. Tropez, Jean? The most charming place—so peaceful—just a tiny fishing village really. The house was perfect—well, it would have been perfect, it needed a complete overhaul, of course, redecorating from top to bottom, and then I'd thought of building some guest houses, and it seemed a little silly to have a villa with perfect anchorage unless I used it, so I'd thought of a yacht. . . ." Her voice trailed away. "So, all in all, last year I was quite ready to liquidate some of my American assets, and I would have done so, had it not been for Edouard."

"He advised against it?"

"Darling, it turned out there was oil there. A greal deal, simply waiting to be pumped to the surface. So, of course, it was worth considerably more than I'd been offered, and there were the most unpleasant suggestions flying around. That my advisors had been bribed . . . Well, I transferred my portfolio, naturally, as soon as Edouard explained. They've gone out of business anyway now. The most dreadful scandal. It was on the front page of *The New York Times*—surely you must recall, Jean-Paul?"

"I don't read *The New York Times* in Algiers."

"Darling, you should." Louise's dark eyes warmed. "I never did, or not the financial pages anyway. But I do now. And *The Wall Street Journal* and the *Financial Times* and—"

"So what happened about the land?" Jean-Paul interrupted her quickly.

"I sold it, of course. To the oil consortium." Louise gave a little smile. "For rather a lot of money. And substantial shareholdings in the consortium itself. Edouard has a fifteen percent share, I believe, and I have the same, which makes up thirty percent. Not a controlling interest then, but a powerful one. Do you see?"

Jean-Paul saw. He took another choux pastry to console himself.

"So Edouard has the investment capital he needs for his expansion program?"

He knew it was hardly worth putting the question. Louise gave a light laugh.

"Darling, really, you must try to keep up more. He had that six months ago, at least."

"You sold other stock?"

"Well, Edouard advised it, darling. And I was going to consult you, but really, Algeria is a long way away, and you never seem to be in Paris . . . so, yes, I sold some rather boring stock that was as safe as Fort Knox and about as immobile, and invested in de Chavigny. It was a wise decision, Jean-Paul. Very wise. The company is diversifying, growing so fast it's almost unbelievable. I shouldn't think Edouard wants any further investment just now—but if he did, darling, if you have, you know, a little pin money, then you couldn't be better advised than to—"

"It's *my* company." Jean-Paul stood up, his face red with anger.

"It's my company; Edouard is employed by me. I just wish sometimes that someone, somewhere, would remember that."

He looked down at his mother, who appeared quite unflustered by his rage. She had always known which way the wind was blowing, he thought savagely. Always. His mother—whose preference for himself, devotion to himself, he had always taken for granted. Well, he wasn't the favorite anymore, that much was obvious. Edouard had sneaked in behind his back. He hesitated, his anger subsiding quickly, as it always did, and leaving him feeling exhausted. He couldn't fight Edouard, he knew that. He didn't have the ability, and he didn't have the strength. So he'd just damn well have to do what Edouard said, and go back to Algeria with his tail between his legs. His little brother.

"Tell me something, Maman." He spoke suddenly, the question rising up out of the confusion and indignation in his mind. "Tell me. Does Edouard frighten you sometimes?"

"Frighten me?" Louise's eyes widened.

"Well, he's so changed. I find him changed. So cold. Humorless. He doesn't feel like my brother anymore. It's like talking to a machine."

"A useful machine. A highly efficient one."

"Yes, but he's my brother, damn it. We were always so close."

"Edouard is close to no one these days."

"Why not? What the hell's wrong with him?"

"Darling, how should I know? He prefers it that way. And I must confess, it makes things easier. He and I get along very well now. We talk about business, and he inquires after my health and remembers my birthday and so on. . . ." She shrugged. "I always used to feel such *demands* from Edouard. Even when he was a very little boy. It was as if he always *needed* something—it was terribly exhausting. Now he makes no demands at all. No emotional demands. Really, it's much better that way."

Jean-Paul hesitated; he had never reciprocated his mother's old affection for him, and he now felt actual dislike. But he wanted to understand.

"What about women?"

"Ah, women." Louise smiled a slow smile, and smoothed down the skirt of her dress. "Well, there are a lot of those, or so I hear. Edouard never discusses them with me."

"Is he going to get married?" He blurted out the question, and Louise shrugged.

"Possibly. Someday. He'd like an heir. He has dynastic leanings, I think, just as your father did. And you've never married, Jean-Paul."

"Well—I never found the right woman. It doesn't mean I won't." He shifted about anxiously from foot to foot. To his own surprise, all his anger against Edouard had evaporated. He was beginning to feel unhappy for his brother. Louise frowned, and stood up. "Of course, it is terribly important whom Edouard marries," she began thoughtfully. "Terribly important. I think about it often."

"Why, Maman?"

"Oh, darling, it's obvious. Edouard is an obsessive—surely you can see that? He's obsessed about his work—obsessed with building some kind of memorial to your father. He was totally obsessed with that dreadful little boy Grégoire—he even brought him to tea here, you know, and the child had no manners at all, he broke one of the Sèvres cups—Edouard said he was nervous. . . . And so, if Edouard were to fall in love, to marry, he'd be equally obsessive then. His wife would be able to influence him, Jean-Paul, and—"

"Influence him? Some woman?" Jean-Paul laughed. "You must be joking. No one influences Edouard."

"Not yet." Louise turned away. "But that may change. You don't understand your brother, Jean-Paul. He's not a machine, you see. Underneath, underneath he's a very passionate man."

Jean-Paul thought of what their mother had said when he had his farewell interview with his brother. He had given in about the purchase of the land, of course. Edouard had made no acknowledgment of his capitulation. Jean-Paul looked at the man behind the desk. The eyes were like flint. He felt a terrible impotent welling-up of affection. "My plane doesn't leave till nine. We've got time to go out. Get a drink. Have dinner even. What d'you say, Edouard? I hate talking in offices. Can't relax in them. Never could."

"I'm sorry." Edouard glanced down at his thin gold de Chavigny watch. "I have appointments all evening. I can't break them."

"Damn it—you can cancel. Come on, Edouard—I've hardly seen you in years. I could do with a drink."

"I'm sorry. I'm behind schedule as it is."

Jean-Paul rose awkwardly to his feet. "Oh, all right then. It's a pity. Maybe you'll be coming out to Algeria soon? Yes? I'd like that. . . ."

"It's possible." Edouard paused. "If the political situation were to worsen."

"Yes. Fine. Well, let me know. You call me, though—not some goddamn secretary. Is that a deal?"

Edouard looked up, and smiled for the first time. "It's a deal."

They shook hands. At the door Edouard pressed a small file into Jean-Paul's hands.

"Something that might interest you," he said shortly. "Read it on the plane. Or when you get back . . ."

Jean-Paul was traveling first class. He started on the martinis before takeoff. Halfway across the Mediterranean, when the stewardess seemed oddly unresponsive to his overtures, he idly opened the file.

It contained the details of the funding of a new pediatric clinic outside Paris, to be built with a donation from the de Chavigny company and funded annually from the company's charity portfolio. Jean-Paul flicked the pages; he couldn't see why Edouard had given him this. De Chavigny now had a number of such projects—as tax deductions, he imagined.

Then he turned the page. The infectious diseases wing was being personally funded by his brother. Jean-Paul stared at the figure. Ten million dollars down the drain sounded like rather a lot. Then he understood. The wing was to be named in memory of his son, Grégoire.

I n the spring of the following year, 1957, Marie-Aude Roussain, Edouard de Chavigny's senior secretary, a young woman of considerable ability and renowned for the fact that she never became flustered, called Edouard in his office. She was very flustered indeed.

"I'm extremely sorry, Monsieur de Chavigny, but I have someone on the line who wants to speak to you personally. She—er—she won't go away. I told her you were unavailable, but . . ."

"Who is it?"

"She says she is the Contessa Sforza-Bellini, sir."

"Get rid of her. I've never heard of her in my life."

Edouard moved to flick the switch on his intercom. Then he stopped. "Wait a minute. Does she sound English?"

"Yes, Monsieur de Chavigny. Very."

"Put her on at once. And cancel all my appointments for this evening."

There was a startled silence from the outer office.

"Cancel them, Monsieur de Chavigny? But you have a reception at the Saudi-Arabian ambassador's at seven, a meeting with the U.S. Undersecretary of the Interior about the Little Big Inch Pipeline at eight; Simon Scher is meeting with you at St. Cloud at nine, and you are due at the Duchesse de Quinsac-Plessan's reception at ten. . . ."

"I said cancel them. And put me through."

"Yes, Monsieur de Chavigny."

Marie-Aude stared at her telephone with dislike. Who the hell was this woman?

"I'm putting you through now, Contessa."

In his office, Edouard picked up the telephone. "Isobel! Where are you? The Ritz? I'm on my way now."

Among the grand Paris hotels, the Ritz has one incomparable advantage: it is located in the Place Vendôme, and the Place Vendôme is adjacent to one of the most tempting shopping streets in the world, the Rue du Faubourg St.-Honoré.

Isobel had taken advantage of this proximity. She had already visited the de Chavigny showrooms there, and because she was feeling nervous, she had been more than usually extravagant. She sat waiting for Edouard at a table in the beautiful *jardin intérieur*. She was wearing her favorite Dior, a narrow dress of *violette de Parme* silk crêpe, and a de Chavigny collar of amethysts and diamonds. Her thin leather elbow-length gloves had been dyed to match the dress, and she had intended to wear her most devastating hat, with a black lace veil. She had put it on and taken it off three times; it now lay on the the chair beside her. Her thick hair was consequently a little disarranged; it flamed against the light. She was extremely pleased to note that every man in the room was staring at her. It was her thirty-sixth birthday, and on such a day the stares were reassuring.

She saw Edouard first—she had positioned herself so that she would be able to. A tall dark man in a very dark suit, striding across the room.

Then he was beside her, and looking down at her, and Isobel for a second was taken aback. She knew he had changed, that he was a man of thirty-two now, a successful man, a powerful man—probably quite different from the young man she had known. She had read about him in the newspapers, seen him once or twice on television, seen photographs of him in magazines. Still, she was unprepared.

The gentleness had gone from his face. That vulnerability which she remembered—there was no trace. The man who looked down at her was startlingly good-looking—the moment his tall lithe figure entered the room every woman in the place had looked up—but he was also a little frightening. There were lines now from nose to mouth; the lips were stern; she had seen him take in the room, who was there, with whom, in one cold appraising glance as he entered. She thought: *Oh, God, I've done the wrong thing.* And then, slowly, he smiled, and the smile lit the dark blue eyes and transformed the face, and she knew it was all right; she hadn't done the wrong thing after all.

"Darling Edouard," she said. He took her hand and raised it to his lips, his eyes never leaving her face. She felt a moment's self-consciousness and doubt, because she knew she had changed, too, that there were lines around the emerald eyes that hadn't been there the last time he saw her.

"It's eight years. Almost eight." She hesitated, and Edouard thought, she's changed; she never hesitated before; she's more beautiful than ever.

"They just vanished," he said, and, still holding her hand, sat down beside her.

"Two martinis." The hovering waiter sped away. Edouard never turned his head. He looked at Isobel. She knew he was remembering the last time they had drunk martinis together, and what she had said to him then. She saw the amusement in his eyes, the question which he was delicately careful not to put.

"Actually, yes," she said. "And this time they haven't even arrived."

They talked, easily at first, then a little less spontaneously. Isobel, watching him, watching the mobile, expressive features, the charm for which he was celebrated, thought: *He has changed; there is a guard there that he cannot drop.* She wondered if he ever dropped it; she could sense that however fluently he talked, however intently he listened—and he listened very intently—his mind was at the same time pursuing some other parallel track. Eventually, refusing another drink, she rested her hand on his arm.

"Darling Edouard. This is very selfish of me. I'm sure I'm keeping you from a million other appointments."

He looked genuinely surprised. "No. Of course not. I'm taking you out to dinner." He paused. "That is, of course, if I'm not keeping you from a million other engagements."

"No. None."

They smiled at each other, and he stood up and drew back her chair. "Good. Shall we go? Where would you like? We could go to Maxim's. The Grand Vefour. You choose. . . ."

"Nowhere grand." Isobel tossed back the red-gold hair and picked up her hat. "Somewhere different. Somewhere simple. Where we won't meet anyone we know. Take me somewhere I've never been before. Surprise me. . . ."

"Very well." She saw the corners of his mouth lift. He led her out into the huge marble-floored foyer. Just as they approached the doors, he stopped as if he had suddenly come to a decision.

"After dinner I want you to come back to St. Cloud. I'd like you to see the house."

"Darling Edouard—I should love that."

"Perhaps . . ." He hesitated. "Perhaps you ought to inform your maid?"

Isobel stared at him, then laughed, drew her arm through his, and pulled him toward the door.

"Darling Edouard, you are a sweet idiot. I haven't traveled with a maid for years. You are looking at a woman who has survived Europe, South America, and East Africa—entirely without a maid. Now, aren't you impressed?"

"Deeply." He helped her into the seat of the Bentley Continental he was driving. As he pulled away, he turned to her with a smile.

"East Africa? What were you doing there?"

Isobel stretched luxuriously, and tossed her devastating black hat onto the jump seat behind her.

"Buying lions," she said negligently.

He took her to a tiny café in the industrial suburbs, an area of Paris that Isobel had never visited before. She assumed he had chosen the place, the Café Unic, arbitrarily. But to her surprise, the patron and his very large, round-faced wife greeted him like a long-lost son. They kissed Edouard on both cheeks, they patted him on the back, they looked at Isobel hard and long, and they seemed to approve of what they saw.

The café was empty. They were seated at a small table with a red-checked cloth surmounted by a clean one of starched white linen, with two glass beakers, two knives, and two forks, and a basket of the most delicious freshly baked bread. The wine, which arrived in a carafe, was a strong excellent *vin ordinaire*. The meal that accompanied it was a feast, cooked and served by the *patron* with justifiable pride: tiny *moules marinière* that tasted as if they had been cut from the rocks that morning; *bifteck*, brown and crisp on the outside, perfectly rare within; a platter of thin crisp sizzling-hot *pommes frites;* an excellent salad served in a plain white bowl. The best Camembert that Isobel had ever tasted, which the *patron* said proudly had come from his brother's farm in the Auge region of Normandy—the only Camemberts worth buying, he assured them, came from there.

They both ate hungrily, and when they had finished, and were sipping their *cafés noirs* and the tiny glasses of wonderful rough *marc de bourgogne*, Isobel leaned back with a smile.

"That was the most wonderful meal I have ever had. Much better than Maxim's. Thank you, Edouard."

"I thought you would like it. Now—tell me about the lions."

Isobel hesitated. "Well," she began carefully, "I was widowed two years ago—you know that. You wrote to me."

"Yes." The dark blue eyes looked up, met hers.

"And then—I was rather at a loss, I suppose. I'd been leading such a rackety life—Edouard, you can't imagine. Rushing about from one racetrack to another, always on planes or trains. Then, very suddenly, it was over. All that time, all those years. I'd been so busy, I'd had no time to think. Just the next ticket, the next hotel. I preferred not to think, perhaps. I don't know. Anyway, suddenly it was over, and I thought—"

She broke off and reached for his hand. "Darling Edouard. I know you'll understand. I thought I wanted to do something useful. Be useful. To someone. Something." She looked away. "And that was difficult. I wasn't brought up to be useful. I had a stupid girls' education. No training of any sort. Even in the war—now I look back—when lots of other women were doing sensible things . . . driving ambulances, joining the army, being land-girls . . . I never did anything like that." She shrugged. "I suppose I felt guilty—ten years too late."

"So—what did you do—to be useful?" He put the question gently, and Isobel sighed.

"I went home. To England. To Papa. Oh, Edouard—I can't tell you how sad it was. I'd hardly been back for years—only briefly, when Mama died. This time . . . well, they'd sold the London place years before. It's been pulled down—now it's a hotel. That kept the wolf from the door for a little while, I think. But not long enough. So— anyway—I went to the country. And there Papa was, all alone in that great place, hundreds of rooms, not enough servants, missing Mama— terribly lonely. William is always in London—he's in the City now—do you remember Will, my eldest brother? So there he was, in a merchant bank, desperately trying to restore the family fortunes. And there was Papa in this great mausoleum, worrying about bills." She shrugged. "It really is the most impossible place. No matter what you do, it's never enough. There are one hundred and seventy-five rooms, two acres of roof—can you imagine? Well, of course you can. But in this case most of it hadn't been touched since 1934, and part of it had been requisitioned for troops during the war. So, in short, it was a total mess. Papa didn't know what to do, and then he got talking to some of his cronies, and he decided on a 'grand scheme.' Open the house. Paying visitors. They could troop round and look at the Rubenses and the Gainsboroughs— the ones that are left. Papa had to sell some of the best ones. They could go into the chapel, and the Adam library, and the red drawing room, and with a bit of luck they'd be so busy looking at the Chippendale and the Hepplewhite, they wouldn't notice the holes in the rugs." She sighed. "It was a good idea. But it didn't really work. It costs five shillings and sixpence to go round, and you need an awful lot of those to mend two acres of roof. So. Papa decided to have a game park."

"A game park?" Edouard's eyebrows rose, and Isobel nodded solemnly.

"Absolutely. A game park. Lions and giraffes and wildebeest. Roaming over the parkland. And as a matter of fact, mad as it sounds, it was rather a good idea." She smiled impishly. "They look rather sweet.

Capability Brown would have approved, I'm sure. And they don't seem to mind the rain—which surprised me. And Papa adores them. He goes out and talks to the lions every morning from the back of a Land-Rover, and they all have names, just the way the dairy herd had when we were children. Only not Daisy and Posy and Rose, of course, but African names—Ngumbe, Banda, things like that. Papa spent weeks researching it."

"And do the people come to see the lions?"

"In droves. Absolute droves. Much more fun than the Rubenses, and I must say I rather agree. So. There you are. I went off to Kenya to buy lions. It turned out to be the most useful thing I could do." The green eyes flicked up at him teasingly, but also a little apprehensively, as if she were afraid he might mock her. Edouard, who knew she was most vulnerable when she seemed most frivolous, pressed her hand. She snatched it away with a sudden quick anger.

"Oh, Edouard, don't. Don't be kind. I know it's ridiculous. I despise myself. I wish sometimes—oh, God, I don't know . . . I just wish I had been a man, that's all. Then—"

He took her hand back and raised it gently to his lips. "You are the most beautiful woman I know. Also one of the cleverest, however much you pretend not to be. I'm very very glad you are not a man. Now." He stood up. "Come back to St. Cloud with me."

I t was late when they reached the great house, but the moon was full, and the night air was warm and still. Edouard, at Isobel's suggestion, took her on a grand tour. They walked through the wild informal gardens, then through the *allées* of clipped hornbeam, then yew, to the rose garden, and on to the *parterre*, which had been planted with herbs and—for the spring—wallflowers. Isobel sighed.

"Gilly flowers—that's the old English name. I love them. I love their scent." She picked one, and held it to her face, and in the lights which shone from the long windows of the house, Edouard saw that the color of the flower, that rich deep red shot through with gold, was the color of her hair. There was a little silence between them, then they moved on.

He showed her the stables, and one of the old mares nuzzled Isobel's hand with a mouth as soft as velvet. Then he took her into a long flat-roofed building like a small aircraft hangar. He flicked the light switch, and Isobel gave a cry of delight. There were twenty cars—no, more, thirty at least—each one of them perfect, each the finest example of its *marque*. She moved along the rows in delight: a Bugatti, a Jensen, a

Bristol, one of the great Mulliner Bentleys, the legendary Porsche 356, a Rolls-Royce Silver Ghost with running boards.

Isobel ran from one to another, touching the gleaming coach work, the shining chrome. Edouard stood back by the doors, watching her, his face oddly closed. Isobel turned back to him.

"Edouard—they're beautiful. Absolutely beautiful. The Bugatti must be unique—only seven were built, weren't they? I thought there was none left. . . ." She mused. "I didn't know you liked cars so much."

He shrugged. "I like driving fast. Alone. I do that sometimes at night, when I need to think."

"But so many . . ."

"Yes." He shrugged. "I bought them really for someone else. Someone I knew who was interested in cars." He turned to the door. "I suppose it's a little absurd to keep them all now."

He switched off the light and began to walk away. Isobel looked after him. She had heard about the little boy Grégoire, Jean-Paul's son, so people said. She had heard about Edouard's attachment to him. She felt a stab of pity: was that what the cars were for? A priceless collection, for a little boy?

She ran after Edouard, and put her arm through his. Later, after looking at the rest of the house, they returned to Edouard's study on the first floor. A quietly efficient English manservant brought them coffee and Armagnac, and then withdrew. Isobel moved restlessly around the room. It was like Edouard, she thought, a room that contrived to be both French—with its delicate painted paneling—and also English in the severity of the furnishings. A room that was restrained, masculine, and formal. Bookcases of leather-bound volumes; some exceptionally fine eighteenth-century watercolors; a Chippendale writing desk; chairs covered in exquisitely faded Spitalfields silk. Each object in the room was perfect of its kind; each spoke of taste and discernment, and unlimited means, and also of loneliness. Like the rest of the house, the room felt cared-for and curiously empty.

She looked down at Edouard. He was sitting before the log fire, his Armagnac untouched, his face in repose, somber. As she looked at him, he suddenly turned and held out his hand to her.

Isobel took it, and he drew her down so she sat on the silk rug at his feet, on a pattern of birds and flowers, of blues and scarlets and browns. She rested her head against his knee, and he rested his hand against her hair.

"Now," he said softly. "Tell me, Isobel."

She turned her head to look up at him. With that intuitive understanding she had always had with him, she knew exactly what he meant.

"I was happy, Edouard. I did love him, you see. And I think he loved me, in his way. But he loved danger more." She paused, surprised that her own voice should be steady. She had spoken of her marriage to no one, not during it, not since her husband's death. "I knew what would happen all along. I'm sure he did. I think he almost wanted it. He wouldn't have liked old age, even middle age. He wouldn't have liked losing. So I think it ended the way he would have wanted it to end. Very quickly. One skid. The car exploded. I was watching."

There was a silence. Then Edouard said, "You never had children."

"No." The green eyes clouded momentarily. "I wanted them, to begin with, wanted them very much. And then I realized it would be impossible. He couldn't have attachments—not really. It would have made him unable to race."

"Weren't you an attachment?"

"Oh, no." Isobel smiled. "I'm much too good an actress for that. He thought I liked the danger as much as he did. In fact, every race, I used to be sick. Before it, and after. And I used to pray, of course. All the time. On every single bend. But he never knew that."

There was a little silence. Edouard stared into the fire, and eventually Isobel lifted her head once more. "And you?" she said gently. "Darling Edouard, tell me."

"There is nothing to tell."

"In eight years?" She smiled up at him, wishing she could will the tension out of his body, wishing she could make him relax that guard. "I've read about you," she went on after a pause in which he did not answer her. "Lots of things. You're very famous now, Edouard."

"Anything you've read is sure to be lies."

"That's a shame. Some of it was rather poetic." She smiled up at him wickedly. "Those presents. For your mistresses. Jewels to match the color of their eyes, or their hair, or their skin. Black pearls. Sapphires. Rubies. Never diamonds." She paused. "I read all that, and I cheered. I thought: that's my Edouard. It had style." She reached for his hand. "Was it true?"

"Some of it." He paused. "None of it mattered in the least."

"Really?" Her eyes met his, and she began to smile.

"Really."

They held each other's gaze for a moment, a look of understanding and amusement, and then, both at once, they began to laugh. Isobel felt the tension leave his body, saw the amusement, and then the sudden seriousness in his eyes.

They stopped laughing; Edouard leaned forward, gathered her in his arms and kissed her. Then he drew back, looked down into her face, and said: "Will you marry me, Isobel?"

And Isobel rested her face against his arm, and sighed.

"Darling Edouard," she said. "Of course I will. You know quite well that's why I came back to see you."

Then Edouard took her into his bedroom, and they remained there for three days and three nights. On the fourth day, they drove out into the country, and were married by an extremely flustered official in a small *mairie*, some fifty kilometers outside Paris. No guests. No reporters.

Isobel had her wedding ring first. She chose her engagement ring belatedly in the de Chavigny Paris showrooms. She passed over the trays of sapphires, and rubies, and diamonds; she chose an emerald. When Edouard slipped it onto her finger, she looked up at him and smiled.

"This one has no superstitions attached to it, I hope." Edouard put his arms around her.

"My darling, none. It's very very lucky, I promise you."

They had six months of unclouded happiness. They made love a disproportionate amount, Isobel told him, in the certain knowledge that Edouard would then make love to her again. He was the best lover she had ever had: the most skillful, the most understanding, the most gentle, the most fierce. He took her body, and he made it come alive. They were inseparable. In six months that included many business trips, they were never apart for one night. Other women ceased to exist for Edouard; he gently terminated his affair with Clara Delluc, and Isobel, knowing this woman had meant more to him than any of the others, asked if she might meet her; she did, and the two women became friends.

Isobel found herself fascinated by the diversity and challenge of Edouard's work; she also quickly found that she could be of help to him. Not simply as a hostess—"the only task I was ever trained for," she said to him wryly—but also as an advisor. Like her husband, she had sharp and brilliantly intuitive instincts for people; she knew at once whom Edouard could trust. But she was more patient and more sympathetic than he, and so colleagues and advisors Edouard might have overlooked, Isobel drew out, and nurtured. Being English, she knew little about wine—that had been her father's province. There, she was content to let Edouard educate her. Being a woman, and coming from the background she did, she knew a great deal about jewelry. There, Edouard discovered, she could educate him. Her taste, which had never been for understatement, influenced his, which had always been a little austere.

"I adore these." She held up a heavy necklace of cabochon rubies intertwined with emeralds and pearls.

"Thank you. They're Bulgari."

"Don't sulk. They're wonderful. Pagan. A little barbaric. Jewelry ought to be like that. It ought to be flamboyantly seductive. To show off a little. Diamonds seem to me totally pointless if they're discreet."

It was Isobel who found Edouard his designer of genius, succeeding by chance where his headhunters, in years of patient searching, had failed.

She had a friend from finishing school, Maria, who came from a rich Hungarian family, and who had fled her country for Paris in 1956, at the time of the Russian invasion. Maria had brought out no money, but she had smuggled out some of her jewels. Isobel helped her friend to settle in Paris and find work; one day Maria asked her if de Chavigny might be interested in buying her jewelry.

"It seems pointless to me now." She smiled at Isobel. "I can't think how I ever cared for the things. But the money would be useful." She laid the jewels out on the bed in the small atelier she was renting. Isobel took one look at them, and telephoned Edouard.

They had been made for Maria by a Polish emigré, Floryan Wyspianski, a man in his early thirties who had settled in Budapest after the war. He was skillful, Maria said—she and his mother had always loved his work—but he was not very successful. He had only a small shop; it was difficult, in Budapest, for a Pole.

Edouard examined the jewelry carefully, standing in the north light of the atelier's large window. He looked at the pieces with the naked eye, then with his glass, while behind him Isobel held her breath.

What he saw was incredible to him: imperfect stones, yes, flawed, sometimes of poor coloration, but cut and set with such skill and ingenuity that their imperfections were disguised. Dazzlingly accomplished workmanship. Some of the most original and beautiful designs he had seen in thirty years.

He could trace the influences, he thought; this man had used scholarship as well as talent. One of the necklaces—a collar of Byzantine magnificence—had clearly been influenced by the classical revivalist designs of Fortunato Castellani, and his pupil Giuliano, whom Edouard's great-grandfather had once tried to woo into working for him in London. The use of enamel, the brilliant understanding of color, yes, that piece reminded him of Giuliano, though the design was more subtle, less heavy. That necklace was one of Wyspianski's early pieces, Maria said. Later, he had moved away from these classic designs; he had become interested in Arab jewelry, she said, and in their techniques of wiring jewels so delicately and invisibly that they moved with their wearer. This necklace, she said, picking up another, this was the last piece she had bought from him. It showed the Arab influence, she thought.

Edouard held the necklace reverently. It was the finest of the pieces Maria had bought: the work of a master. A delicate circlet of gold wired with pearls and diamonds, the diamonds shaped like flowers, the pearls suspended like dew from their petals. Alexander Reza, at the turn of the century, had done work resembling this, but never anything so fragile.

Edouard looked back at the collection. What excited him most of all was that these pieces, each so different, each showing a restless determination to experiment, all had the signature of Wyspianski. They bore the unmistakable stamp of one man's genius: to anyone who knew anything about jewelry, that was immediately obvious. Looking at them, he knew at once that his long search was over. He turned around slowly.

"Yes?" Isobel was trembling with excitement.

"Yes. Oh, yes."

There was a silence. Isobel and Maria exchanged glances.

"There is a problem," Isobel admitted finally, with reluctance. "Wyspianski is still in Hungary. With his family. He would like to leave, but he cannot."

"That is no problem. I shall get him out."

Maria sighed. She did not know Edouard very well. "Alas—it is impossible. Two years ago—yes. A year ago—maybe. Now the Russian hold is very tight. It cannot be done."

"I shall do it."

He flew, with Isobel, to Moscow the following week. One month later, the young wife of a senior member of the Politburo was astonishing her friends with a necklace, earrings, and bracelets of positively Czarist splendor. The Pole, Floryan Wyspianski, and his wife and young daughter had exit visas from Hungary.

"Bribery and corruption," Isobel said tartly as she drew her sables more tightly around her, and they mounted the steps to Edouard's plane for the flight back to Paris. Edouard looked injured.

"I tried pleas first. Rational arguments. Commercial incentives. Bribery and corruption were a last resort."

"Have you tried them before?" Isobel looked up at him curiously.

"Of course. When I had to." Edouard scowled suddenly. "It was one of the things I hated most. Discovering there was no one—almost no one—who could not be bought."

That had been one month before. Wyspianski and his family were due in Paris the next week. Isobel, thinking of that as she walked in the gardens at St. Cloud in the autumn sunshine, hugged herself with secret joy. That afternoon she had been to see her doctor in Paris. He had finally been able to confirm what she had believed and prayed for these past six weeks. She was going to have a baby. A baby—and the designer Edouard had been searching for so long. Both at once. Isobel danced for sheer happiness.

Now, she thought, now Edouard will have what I know he wants so desperately, what I want for him. A child. An heir. A family. And that darkness, that sadness she still sometimes glimpsed in his eyes, will be banished forever.

She lifted her arms up to the warmth of the sun, filled with a sudden wild joy. It shone on the falling leaves, on the burnished red-gold of her hair. She turned her face to the light, and silently, incoherently, not knowing which deity she addressed, she thanked the gods, who had been so kind to her, and to the husband she loved so much. *Tonight*, she thought; *this evening, as soon as he comes home, I shall run to meet him, and I shall tell him.*

A day later, Edouard still did not know about the baby.

Isobel had heard the wheels of his car on the gravel. She ran quickly around to the front of the house, just as she had planned. The driver was already pulling away in the Rolls, and Edouard already striding toward the house. Isobel took one look at his face, and kept silent. They went into the small drawing room they always used when they were alone in the house. Edouard kissed her, but absentmindedly. He began pacing up and down the room. He poured himself a drink. Isobel refused one, and watched him, knowing something was wrong, longing to speak, to burst out with her news, and knowing she must make herself wait. Eventually he sat down, and passed his hand tiredly across his brow.

"My darling, I'm sorry. I thought you would have seen the newspapers. Heard the news. You obviously haven't?"

"No. I went into Paris—for some fittings." Isobel hesitated, then sat down. "Then I was in the gardens. . ."

"I warned him." He put down his glass angrily. "I told Jean-Paul this would happen—nearly two years ago now. I knew this was inevitable." He paused. "The Front de Libération Nationale blew up the second largest *gendarmerie* in Algiers this morning. Thirteen men died. Two others were shot by snipers. Fifteen men—in one day. And of course, nine French policemen have already been killed during the past month. Reprisals, they say, for those raids that were made on the Casbah." He shrugged wearily. "I spoke to Mendès-France briefly, this evening. It's going to get worse, Isobel, much worse."

"But there are French troops there, Edouard. . . ." She hesitated. "They will stop it, won't they? Stop the terrorism?"

"My darling, it's not terrorism. It's a revolution. If you'd been there, if you'd seen the country, you'd understand. The FLN won't rest until the French are out—every last *colon*."

"But it's a French colony. . . ."

"It's an Arab country." He stood up angrily. "The days of colonialism are *over*. Finished. Jean-Paul can't see that, and never will. As far as Jean-Paul is concerned, the French haven't put a foot wrong. They've built roads and bridges and rail systems. Houses. Hotels. Factories. They've created a civil service, and trained Arabs to work like French bureaucrats. Jean-Paul thinks the French brought prosperity to a poor country, and he goes on believing it because he takes care never to set foot outside the European quarter. So he never sees the poverty. Never smells the squalor. Do you know why it is that Jean-Paul's Algerian estates are so prosperous? Why they make the profits of which he's so proud? Because he pays his Algerian workers a pittance, that's why. They earn in a year what he'd pay a French worker in a month. But they're still better off than the other Arabs, the ones that don't work for the French. And so he can make his profits, and feel like a philanthropist at the same time. Isobel, I loved Algeria when I first saw it; but the poverty—the attitudes, the intolerance. I came to hate it. I've hated it more every time I've been back. When I saw Jean-Paul there, I was *ashamed*. Ashamed of my own brother."

Isobel looked at him silently. She had rarely heard him speak with such vehemence, never seen him so angry.

"Eighteen months ago"—he swung around to her again—"in 1956, when there were clear signs of what was going to happen, Jean-Paul came to me, and asked that the company invest in more estates out there. Vineyards. Olive plantations. They belonged to a friend of his who'd decided to get off the sinking ship quickly. I turned him down—and do you know that to this day, Jean-Paul has no idea why?" He paused, his voice growing calmer. "I gave him financial reasons. Business reasons. Of which there were many. And in the end he accepted it. Profit and loss, that's what we talked about. But it wasn't the true reason I refused him. The true reason was that I want nothing to do with that country while it remains as it is, and if it hadn't been for Jean-Paul, I'd have ceased all our operations out there years ago."

Isobel smiled. "And Jean-Paul can be as stubborn as a mule, and you knew perfectly well that if you told him what you felt, he would have dug in his heels and insisted." She sighed. "You can be terribly devious, Edouard."

"Possibly." Edouard looked down at her. "Do you think I did the wrong thing?"

"I don't know," Isobel said quietly, and looked away.

There was silence, a moment of tension between them. Edouard thought of Isobel's family, of her grandfathers, uncles, cousins, who had propped up and maintained an empire, who had fought, and ruled, in India, in Africa. He thought it unlikely she would understand his arguments, and he felt a sense of distance, a moment's regret, there and then gone.

Isobel, bending her head, thought: *I can't tell him about the baby; not now.* She sensed his withdrawal from her, and slowly looked up.

"You're going out there, aren't you, Edouard?"

Her quickness and her resignation touched him. The regret instantly passed, and he crouched down to her, and took her hands gently in his. "My darling, I have to. I've tried speaking to Jean-Paul on the telephone, and it's hopeless. I shall have to go out. I want to persuade him to come back to France."

"Leave Algeria?" Isobel's eyes widened. She felt a moment's scorn. In her family, the men had never walked out on their colonial responsibilities. She thought of her father's many remarks on that subject, his outrage when India was finally granted independence. But her mind shied away from politics, and she had no wish to cross Edouard on that front. She sighed, and chose her words carefully.

"Surely he'll never agree to that, Edouard? He loves it there, you told me. It's obviously meant so much to him, since he left the army. He'll never agree to leave the vineyards, his land. . . ."

"It won't be his land much longer whether he goes or stays." Edouard's tone was dismissive. He stood up and moved away. "He might as well realize that now. Two years from now—maybe more, maybe as much as five, though I doubt it—the French will pull out. You're probably right about Jean-Paul. But I have to try. Algiers isn't a safe place for any Frenchman—particularly one like Jean-Paul—"

He broke off abruptly, an expression of distaste on his features. Then he swallowed the last of his drink, shrugged, turned back. "So— I have to try to persuade him. That's all. He is my brother."

Isobel watched him closely. She wondered what he meant by that last remark about his brother, so quickly bitten off, but she knew better than to ask.

"When are you going?" she said quietly.

"Tomorrow."

"I shall come with you."

"My darling, no." He swung around again, his face softening. "Not this time. I'd rather you stayed here."

Isobel stood up. "If you go, I go," she said firmly. "And if it's too dangerous for me, then it's too dangerous for you. And you don't think that, do you?"

"No, of course not, but—"

"Then I'm coming with you." She gave him her most disarming smile. "You know perfectly well that I can persuade you, so you might just as well give in now with good grace. . . ."

"Oh, really?" She saw his lips curve at her challenge, and before he could protest, she crossed quickly to him.

"Darling Edouard. I'm coming. No ridiculous arguments. Kiss me. If you like, we can argue later."

She put her arms around his neck, and Edouard managed to resist her for about thirty seconds. Then he groaned, and then he kissed her.

They did argue about it, later, but Isobel got her way. When Edouard left for the airport the next morning, Isobel was with him. And she still hadn't told him.

Jean-Paul leaned back, and watched the naked boy who was oiling his body. He had long, supple fingers, slender hands with surprising strength. They worked their way down over Jean-Paul's flesh, expertly kneading the muscles, smoothing the lax skin, seeking the most sensitive folds and crevices. Down over the stomach to the groin, then back to the chest, feeling for each rib under its layer of flabby muscle and fat.

He parted Jean-Paul's thighs, and began on his legs. Slowly up from the ankle and then down again. The knee, then the still strong muscles of the thighs. Slowly up to the groin once more. Then, at last, between his legs, under his balls, feeling the loose pouchy skin of the scrotum, carefully under and back, tracing the crevice of the buttocks with one delicate forefinger. Then back to the ankles again. Jean-Paul closed his eyes. Jesus, the little bastard knew how to tease.

Jean-Paul's body was pale but flushed red on the face, neck, and arms, where he had been burned by the sun. He was fresh from the shower; his body smelled of the oil, which was scented with jasmine. The boy smelled, faintly, of sweat, and also of something else—of poverty, of cheap food, overcrowded lodgings, oil applied to hair that was not quite clean, Arab buses, dust. Jean-Paul liked the smell. It was part of the ritual, part of the game, part of the reality: servant and master.

The boy was very beautiful. He was half-Arab, with a pale olive skin that now gleamed golden in the thin ribbons of light from the half-closed shutters. He could pass for a European, an Italian or a Frenchman from one of the southern regions, like Provence. He had been a student in France—or so he said. Jean-Paul wasn't sure if he believed him. But he spoke good French with scarcely a trace of an Algerian accent, so it might be true. He said he was nineteen years old; he also said he was an orphan, but they all said that, they thought it made people pay more. He worked as an elevator boy in one of the smaller French hotels, moonlighting occasionally by serving drinks in a café in the evenings. That was where Jean-Paul had first met him. Three months ago.

Up again from knee to groin, that delicate forefinger tracing, tracing. Jean-Paul could feel himself getting hard at last. He opened his eyes, his consciousness hazed and slowed by the *kif* he had smoked, and focused with difficulty on the watch on the bedside table. Nearly four; Jesus, they didn't have long. Edouard and Isobel would be back at five. Not that they were likely to walk into his bedroom, but still . . . The need for secrecy, the need for haste, excited him. He reached down and grabbed the boy's wrist.

"Come on. Come on. Get on with it. . . ."

The boy's black eyes flicked up at his face impassively, with just the slightest suggestion of contempt. He knelt between Jean-Paul's legs, bent his head, and began to lick. Jean-Paul grunted, cupped the boy's head in his hands. He liked that contempt, that resentment; the first time he saw it in the boy's face he knew it reminded him of something, but it was weeks before it came to him what it was. Then, suddenly, he remembered. That night in the war, the night his father died, the night at that bitch Simonescu's, with Carlotta. She had looked just the way the boy did, and Jean-Paul liked it because it made him feel . . . what did it make him feel? His mind drifted away on the tides of the *kif*, and then floated back. It made him feel powerful, that was it, because he paid, he bought, and even if they hated him, they sold. That felt good; simple and good. It made him feel big. He felt his penis strain and press to the back of the boy's throat. He almost gagged, and Jean-Paul's hand tightened around the nape of his neck, pulling him down, so he was fully in the boy's mouth.

The first time he'd done it with a boy, he'd been ashamed. He knew it was commonplace here, taken for granted almost. Other men talked openly about it in the club, when they'd had a few drinks. *Tighter, sweeter, better than a woman any day*—that was what they said. The boys were more skilled, less inhibited than the Arab women, ready to do anything, anything, for money.

Jean-Paul had felt slightly disgusted; also oddly threatened, and beneath it all, excited. It wasn't for him: he was no pansy; he liked women, not boys with made-up eyes and sly insinuating glances. But still, he liked to hear about it from the others.

Then, the first time—well, he'd been drunk, so drunk he hardly knew what was happening, so it didn't matter. Then, the next time he went with a woman: nothing—nothing that counted. Plenty of excitement, plenty of anxiety, and no hard-on; just a limp cock hanging between his legs. Not a twitch out of it, no matter what she did, and she'd tried everything. So he went back to a boy—one of the best, came highly recommended. He'd been fearing the worst, but no, the boy undressed him, and there it was, standing up proudly, his machinery in full working order once again. The boy had been impressed, and he'd seen plenty. He'd said it was very big, too big, even with oil, even with

Vaseline. He'd cried out when Jean-Paul pushed up him. But that was just another trick they had, like being an orphan. It didn't mean anything, not really.

There had been a lot of boys after that, and some women, but he found them less exciting than he used to. Especially the French ones. He'd had a good line going with a number of the wives out here—what man hadn't? They were all bored out of their minds, had nothing else to think about except bed. But after the boys they seemed tiresome: too demanding, wanting love as well as sex; too many ideas about how it should be done, and which position they liked best, and whether they came or not. *I don't give a shit*, he'd wanted to say. *Just shut up and let me get the fuck on with it.* But he hadn't, of course. He'd just stopped going back for more. He got it from the boys instead. The boys who did exactly what he said, when he told them. . . .

Mother of God!

He'd never done that before, and it felt good. Very good. No doubt about it, this boy was a find. The best.

"That's enough. Lie down. . . ."

He pushed the boy back, and pulled his cock out of his mouth. The boy never said a word. He just moved to the other side of the bed, and lay on his back. He didn't have an erection—but then he hardly ever did. Jean-Paul had stopped worrying about that weeks ago.

"*Imbecile.* Turn over. . . ."

The *kif* was beginning to wear off, and Jean-Paul could feel irritation, incipient anger, somewhere at the edge of his mind. It often took you like that, when the *kif* was wearing off, but it didn't matter: anger helped.

"Lift your ass."

The boy raised himself a little from the bed. Jean-Paul looked down at his own oiled body, then spat onto his palm for added lubrication.

He held himself poised for a moment, then he thrust hard into the boy's body. The boy cried out, once. Then he bit his lip, and was silent. Jean-Paul heaved and thrust, panting now, holding the boy's beautiful narrow pelvis tight between his hands. Heat and rage built in his body, such rage, swirling through the clouds of *kif*, that it was blinding, fiercer than desire for an instant, so he lost his rhythm, misjudged his pace. Like war, he thought confusedly, like war, like battle, fucking is like that, it's . . .

Then the thought eddied away again out of the grasp of his mind; he looked down at the subservient curve of the boy's back, found his rhythm again, pumped, and came. He slumped across him, breathing heavily, feeling a little sick. Too much *kif*. He must lay off the *kif*. It played tricks on your mind when you least expected it. He'd nearly blown the whole thing then.

The boy waited five minutes. He always waited five minutes. Then he got up, and went into the bathroom. There was the sound of running water. He came out dressed. Jean-Paul had lit a cigarette. He smiled at the boy. "There's a present for you. Over on the chest."

The boy didn't even glance at the folded franc notes. He pouted, and hung his head.

"I don't want presents. I told you."

Jean-Paul sighed. This was a new tack—it had started about two weeks ago.

"What do you want then? You must want something. I'm only trying to show you how grateful I am. I like you—you know that."

He lifted his hand to the boy, but the boy ignored him.

He looked at Jean-Paul sulkily. "I told you." His voice was hardly audible. "I want us to be friends."

"We are friends. Good friends. You know that." Jean-Paul gave a sigh of exasperation.

"No, we're not. You just want me here for this." The boy gestured sullenly at the bed. "We never meet anywhere else. Just here. Just for this."

"Well, where should we meet, for God's sake? What do you want me to do—take you down to the club? An hotel? You know that's impossible."

"You could meet me for a drink sometimes." The boy stuck his lip out obstinately. "That's what friends do. They meet for drinks—in a café, or a restaurant. They go out for a meal. We could do that. I can pass—you know I can. You said so. I'm half-French. I studied in France. . . ."

His voice was rising petulantly. Jean-Paul looked anxiously at his watch. It was nearly five.

"All right, all right. We'll do that sometime. We'll meet in a café—have a drink. Go to a cinema maybe. Will that make you happy?"

"It might. When?"

"I don't know when." Jean-Paul heaved himself upright and reached for his dressing gown. "Look, we can't argue about it now. I haven't got time. I told you. I've got friends here. My brother. His wife. They'll be back soon. Now, be a good boy and run along. . . ."

"I won't come again." The boy raised his face, and to Jean-Paul's horror, the black eyes were welling with tears. "Not unless we can be friends. I don't like it."

"All right. All right." Jean-Paul hurriedly crossed the room and picked up the francs from the chest. He pushed them into the boy's top pocket. He could hear a car drawing up on the drive outside. Quickly he added one more note: thirty francs, that ought to do it. In the boy's terms, it was a fortune. The boy didn't move. Jean-Paul gave him an exasperated push.

"Look, go on now. I'll meet you. We'll arrange it next time, I promise. . . ."

"Not next time. Now."

"All right. Very well. I'll meet you tomorrow. The Café de la Paix—you know it, off the Place de la Révolution. . . ."

Instantly the boy's face lit up. "You will? You promise? What time?"

"About six. I'll meet you at six. I might not be able to stay long." He frowned. "I might have to bring my friends—and if they're there—well, you'll be careful, won't you? Pretend it's a casual meeting—something like that?" Already he regretted giving in, but it was too late now, the boy's face was alight with excitement.

"Your brother? You mean I'll meet your brother? You will introduce me? I will be very proud—and very careful. I promise you. I don't want you to be ashamed of me. You'll see—I know how to behave. Truly."

He looked so eager that Jean-Paul was quite touched. He gave him an affectionate pat on the bottom.

"Very well. Don't let me down now—all right?" He hesitated, then squeezed the boy's arm. "You've been good today, very good."

"I hope so. I want you to have pleasure." He spoke a little stiffly, and again Jean-Paul thought he saw that flash of resentment in the eyes, there and then gone. The boy was proud, that was all. He glanced at the window, and the boy nodded.

"It's all right. I'll go out the back way. Through the kitchen."

Just after five the next day, Edouard and Jean-Paul left the offices of the governor general. They were escorted down long corridors—cooled by fans, for the weather was still very warm—by a senior aide, who was French, and by his aide, an Algerian. Flanked by the two men, they walked down a wide marble staircase and out into the brilliant sunshine. The senior aide stopped, and made a polite half bow.

"*Monsieur le Baron*. Monsieur de Chavigny. I hope we have been of assistance to you." He paused, then turned to Edouard. "You are returning to France tomorrow, I think you said, Monsieur de Chavigny?"

"Yes."

"If in the meantime, we can be of any further assistance, I shall be honored—"

"Of course." Edouard cut him off. "Thank you. Thank you both."

He glanced at both men. The Frenchman smiled suavely; the

Algerian, a small dark man in heavy hornrimmed spectacles, did not smile. He had not uttered one word during their entire briefing. The two aides turned back toward the offices, and Edouard and Jean-Paul walked slowly down the wide steps to the street.

Jean-Paul paused at a kiosk to buy a pack of Gauloises. They were handed to him by a tiny nut-brown man in a red fez who also sold little packets of sugared almonds and pistachios. And newspapers. *Figaro; Le Monde;* the *Herald-Tribune; The Wall Street Journal; El Moudjahid,* the main Algerian daily, which was in French. Edouard glanced at the large photograph on the front page and looked away. He moved to the shade of a palm tree as Jean-Paul counted out his change. A military vehicle passed, filled with French paratroopers. The offices were closing; the wide elegant boulevard was busy with traffic. He looked down it, past the beautiful white shuttered houses to the bay in the distance, and the blue glitter of the sea.

"Come on." Jean-Paul put an arm around his shoulders. "Let's get a drink. I'm parched. It's so bloody hot. I told Isobel we'd wait for her at the Café de la Paix. . . ."

"Isobel? I thought she was staying up at the villa to rest?"

"Oh, she changed her mind at the last moment. Wanted to look at some shop or other—you know what women are like. She's got the car—we can all drive back together."

"Oh, very well. But I don't want to stay long. I've some calls to make. . . ." Edouard shrugged, and allowed himself to be drawn along the street toward the Place de la Révolution. They crossed the square and went into the café. It was already beginning to fill up with French businessmen, and Jean-Paul made purposefully for a table in the window. He sat down.

"Two *pastis.*" He leaned back in his chair. "We'll see Isobel from here. And it's cooler inside with the fans. . . ." He paused to light his Gauloise, and drew on it deeply, looking appraisingly at his brother. It was a mystery to him how Edouard managed it, he thought. There he was, at the end of a solid day of meetings with French officials, looking exactly the way he had when they set out. His white linen suit was unmarked, and uncrumpled. He wasn't sweating. He didn't look hot. Jean-Paul glanced down at his own suit, which was too tight for him, and damned uncomfortable. There was wine on the sleeve, and it was a mass of sweaty creases. However, he didn't care; he was feeling smug. Maybe now Edouard would see—he didn't know it all.

"Well. *Salut.*" He lifted the glass of *pastis,* and took a large swallow. "Feeling better are you now, little brother?"

"Should I?" Edouard regarded him coolly.

"I would have thought so, yes. All right, all right—I know you wouldn't listen to me, but maybe you'll listen to them. They've got their finger on the pulse. If there was going to be trouble, serious trouble, they'd know about it. And what did they tell you—every single one of them? Exactly the same as I told you. It'll all blow over. It's under control."

"That was what they said, yes."

"And you don't believe them, I suppose? Jesus, Edouard, you can be bloody arrogant, you know. The governor general lays it on the line, no 'ifs' or 'buts,' and you—you don't believe him."

"I wasn't impressed by the governor general." Edouard paused. "I was interested in that junior aide—"

"What—the Algerian fellow? Never said a word. Looked scared shitless if you ask me."

"That's precisely what I thought was interesting." Edouard's voice was cold. He turned his head and looked around the café. Its clientele was almost entirely male, with just a few women—secretaries being bought a drink by their bosses, presumably. The café was closed to Algerians; everyone in it was French.

"Oh, I give up." Jean-Paul finished his drink, and called to the waiter for another. "What the hell—let's not argue anymore, Edouard. I'm sick of it. You've had your say, and I'm not going to change my mind. Now—let's forget it. It's your last evening here, for God's sake. Loosen up a bit, can't you? Let's have a good time."

Edouard's face had suddenly cleared. He stood up. "There's Isobel. She's looking for us. Excuse me a moment. . . ." He walked out onto the *terrasse*, and Jean-Paul saw Isobel spot him, turn, smile, move quickly into his embrace. He sighed, and lit another cigarette. They were very happy, that much was obvious, and he was glad of that. He hadn't felt jealous—why should he? The thing between himself and Isobel had been so long ago, he had difficulty remembering it, and it had been a mistake from the first. And she seemed to suit Edouard, to understand him. He was different with her than with everyone else—gentler, softer, more like the old Edouard. It was clear she knew how to get through to him, and that was a good thing. He'd been beginning to think no one could anymore. Well, she was very beautiful, and they'd have a child soon, he imagined, and that ought to make Edouard happy. . . . He heaved himself to his feet as they approached the table. Isobel was laughing at something Edouard had just said; she was wearing a white linen suit, and her green eyes sparkled. She reached up now to kiss him on both cheeks.

"Jean-Paul—that car of yours is a monster. And the traffic! I've had to park miles away. And then I got lost. Look—I've brought you both a present. . . ."

She handed them two little tissue paper parcels, tied with string and sealed with wax. They slowly unwrapped them, while Isobel watched them eagerly.

"It's sandalwood—sticks of sandalwood. You know, Jean-Paul. Don't they smell heavenly? You put them in a little brazier thing, like a tiny cup, and they smolder—the man said they'll scent the whole room. Oh . . ." She leaned back. "I wanted to get so many things—just because the colors were so lovely. Powdered indigo—that wonderful blue, like lapis. And henna. And spices, of course—cumin and turmeric—oh, and they had saffron, piles of it, freshly dried, and . . ."

The two men looked at each other. Edouard sighed. "Darling—have you been in the Algerian quarter?"

Isobel looked vague. "I might have been. I'm not sure where I was. . . ."

"Don't lie. . . ."

"Oh, all right. I nearly was. I didn't go too far, truly. Just to the part in between—the no-man's land." Her eyes shone mischievously. "And then I found the market, and then I came back here. Now, don't look so stern. Say thank you."

"Thank you," they said in chorus. Then Edouard smiled. "Oh, all right, forget it. You're safely here anyway. I might have known we couldn't keep you within bounds. . . ." He gestured to the waiter. "What will you have to drink, my darling?"

"Oh, just some Perrier and ice," Isobel said casually. Edouard looked at her in surprise.

"You're sure? You wouldn't like a glass of wine? An *apéritif?*"

"No, darling, really. I'm too thirsty. Perrier would be lovely." She hesitated. "And actually—I'm starving. Walking must have made me hungry. Maybe I'll have a sandwich. No, I won't. I'll have a glass of cold milk."

"A glass of Perrier and a glass of cold milk?"

Edouard stared at her. She nodded unconcernedly.

"That's it. Thank you, darling."

The waiter's eyebrows rose as he took the order, but he made no comment. He returned shortly with the two drinks, and Isobel calmly sat and sipped the milk, a secretive smile on her beautiful face. Tomorrow, she thought. I shall be able to tell him tomorrow. The second we leave.

Oh, hurry up, tomorrow! She looked around the café as Edouard and Jean-Paul talked. She thought it was beautiful. She thought every single person in it, all the graying businessmen, all the young secretaries, were beautiful. The world was beautiful. She glanced up at Edouard as he leaned forward across the table to make some point: the thick black hair, the sharply etched features, the incisiveness with which he always spoke. She wondered if the baby would look like him; she hoped it would—babies with red hair looked horrible. No, she could have a red-haired baby later. But this baby, boy or girl, she wanted this baby to look like Edouard, who had made her happy, truly happy, for the first time in her life. Surreptitiously, she slipped her hands beneath the table and rested them against her stomach. She wished she were not still so flat, wished the baby would grow quickly. She wanted to feel its body, see her stomach swell, have Edouard rest his hand there, over the curve, and feel their baby stir beneath his fingers. Four months: they began to move at four months, that was what the doctor had said. Her face had fallen.

"So long! Another two months!"

He had smiled patiently. "A lot of other things have to happen first. And they're happening now—even though you're unaware of it. At two months, you can see the head of the fetus quite clearly, and the curve of the spine. By three months, the arms are discernible, and the legs, and the features. By four months, Madame de Chavigny, when you'll start to feel it stir—and then maybe give you a hefty kick—the fetus is—"

Oh, not fetus! she had wanted to say. The baby. My baby. Edouard's baby. Our miracle—for that was how it felt, how she hoped it felt for all women. A miracle: new life. She looked up, then touched Jean-Paul's arm.

A boy was standing next to the table, looking at Jean-Paul shyly. He was very young, and handsome in a slightly effeminate way: about eighteen or nineteen, Isobel thought. A southerner, perhaps, with very dark hair and an olive skin. He was wearing a nylon drip-dry shirt, open at the neck, freshly pressed trousers; he had a leather satchel of books under his arm. A student, perhaps.

"*Monsieur le Baron* . . ." The boy spoke hesitantly, and Jean-Paul looked up. To Isobel's surprise he went beet-red, flushing from the collar of his shirt to the roots of his now receding hair. He stood up and held out his hand with slightly excessive cordiality.

"Why, François! How nice to run into you. How are you? Were you just passing? Maybe you'd like a drink . . . Join us, join us."

Edouard looked up in surprise, and the boy eagerly drew forward a chair. He put the satchel of books on the floor and sat down. Jean-Paul made vague informal introductions.

"This is Edouard, my brother. Isobel, his wife. Edouard, Isobel, this is François. . . . Did I mention him to you? He's a student, working over here for a few months. I've been helping him to find his feet a bit in Algiers."

The boy gave a nervous smile. Jean-Paul gestured to the waiter.

"François, what will you have? Just coffee? You're sure? Fine. Nothing for you, Edouard? Another Perrier, Isobel, yes? And I'll have a *pastis.* . . ."

The waiter disappeared. There was an awkward silence. Then the boy said, very formally, "I am honored to meet you." He nodded at

Isobel. At Edouard. Isobel glanced at her husband, and saw that his face had hardened and his eyes were angry. He looked across the table at Jean-Paul, and Jean-Paul's eyes slid away. He lit another cigarette, and Isobel noticed his hands were shaking slightly. He offered one to the boy, and the boy politely refused. He sat there, looking from face to face expectantly. Isobel leaned forward, feeling sorry for him.

"A student? Where are you studying?"

"At Lyons, Madame." He paused, then added, with a slight swagger. *La philosophe. Et les sciences politiques.*"

"Goodness." Isobel cast around in her mind for some comment to make. There didn't seem to be one. She couldn't imagine why Jean-Paul had issued the invitation to join them.

"I read the same subjects. . . ." Edouard was now making an effort. He hesitated. "You are enjoying your stay in Algiers?"

"Oh, very much." The boy's eyes went from face to face. He smiled. "I find I am learning a great deal."

"You're late returning to your course," Edouard said pleasantly. "The university term began at the beginning of the month." There was a little silence. The boy's color rose. He lowered his eyes. "Well, yes," he muttered. "I needed to work here just a little longer. To raise the tuition, you know. I had permission—from my professor."

"François is a clever boy," Jean-Paul cut in quickly. "In the top five percent of his class, so he tells me." He took a large swallow of *pastis,* and looked at his watch pointedly. If the hint was directed at the boy, he seemed not to take it. He took another small sip of his coffee. Edouard was tapping the table idly with one finger, which Isobel knew was a sign of irritation. Jean-Paul seemed to have exhausted his conversational overtures. She leaned forward quickly.

"And your work here? Are you enjoying that?"

"It's not bad." The boy shrugged indifferently "I work in one of the hotels—the Marine. It overlooks the bay." He paused, and Isobel saw him glance at Jean-Paul slyly. "I work the elevators," he went on more expansively. "The pay's bad, of course, but the tips are good. The French always tip very generously. If they're pleased with you."

Edouard turned his head; he gave the boy a cold stare. Isobel looked around the table in confusion. She could sense some undercurrent of tension which she was at a loss to explain. Jean-Paul was looking flustered and embarrassed; she knew that Edouard was coldly furious. Only the boy seemed quite at ease. He turned now and glanced up at the clock above the bar. Then drained his coffee.

"It's getting late. I'm on the evening shift tonight."

"Please. Don't let us detain you." Edouard's voice was icy. Isobel stared: it was so unlike him—she couldn't think why he was being so rude.

"Maybe Francois would like some more coffee," she began, and then stopped. The boy was getting to his feet. His color had risen, and Isobel felt very embarrassed for him.

"No. Thank you, Madame." He bowed to each of them in turn. "I must go. I shall be late. I am honored to have met you."

His eyes met those of Jean-Paul for an instant. The boy fumbled in the pocket of his shirt and drew out a couple of crumpled notes. "Please . . ." He tossed them down onto the small saucer on the table. "I must pay for my coffee. Messieurs. Madame."

"François—please, there's no need for that. I . . ." Jean-Paul half-rose from his seat, but the boy had gone, weaving his way through the throng of people behind the bar. Jean-Paul shrugged and sank back into his chair. He looked very flushed, almost guilty, Isobel thought curiously.

Edouard stood up. "We should go," he said curtly. "I'll fetch the car and bring it around. Where did you leave it, Isobel?"

"In the Rue Pascal. Just around the corner to the right and then first right and—"

"I'll find it. I know it."

Edouard walked out, his face stiff with anger. There was another awkward silence, broken by the laughter from the bar. Isobel frowned.

"I'm sorry, Jean-Paul. What was that all about? Edouard's not usually so rude."

"Oh, God knows. He's been in a foul temper all day. He has these moods. You must be used to them by now. . . ."

"I suppose so." Isobel shrugged. "Oh, well, it doesn't matter. I hope your friend wasn't offended, that's all." She stopped, suddenly catching sight of the notes in the saucer. She reached across, and unfolded them. "Oh, look, Jean-Paul. Your friend's made a mistake. You'd better keep this for him. There's thirty francs here. . . ." She stopped. Jean-Paul's color had suddenly faded; he sat very still.

"His satchel," he said. "His satchel of books. Did he take it?" Isobel bent down. She straightened up with a smile.

"No—he's left that too. What a forgetful young man! Jean-Paul, you'll have to take it with us, and—"

She stopped. Jean-Paul was clasping her wrist. She saw his eyes grow round, bewilderment and disbelief on his face. Then the bomb in the satchel went off.

Edouard was in the car, on the far side of the square, when he heard the explosion. It was deafeningly loud; he felt hot air burn his face; the car veered across the road. In the equally deafening silence that followed, he looked up, and saw the dust, glass, debris, settle in slow motion. Then he was out of the car and running. He ran toward the remains of the café as everyone else ran away.

Suddenly the square was filled with fleeing people. He pushed past them frantically, his eyes smarting from the dust. Then he stopped. The bomb had taken out the café, and the two floors above it. Girders gaped. Half the wall of the next house had been blown out, and he could see into the room beyond. An iron bedstead, skewed across a smashed floor; a torn curtain—I have seen this before, he thought, still with his mind in that crazed slow motion. Where? In the blitz.

The curtain flapped in a glassless window. In front of him was a mound of concrete blocks, dust, jagged glass, and twisted metal. It was fifteen feet, twenty feet high. Yellow dust was settling, choking his throat. The mound of masonry was still, and silent. No moans; no sighs; no cries; nothing. He stared at it in frozen incomprehension. Trapped under one of the huge concrete blocks was part of a man's leg, severed at the knee. The black trouser material was ripped to ribbons; the shoe, intact, was still on. Farther up, like part of a discarded doll, was the top half of a woman's torso, blood billowing from where the head should have been, the remnants of a flowered dress settling under the dust.

Not Isobel, he thought. Not Isobel. Isobel was wearing white. He heard someone cry out, a terrible cry, and then realized it was himself.

He was not alone now. A woman was standing near him, an old woman, plump, with gray hair, wearing a black dress. She, too, was staring at the debris. He saw her lift her arms in a slow gesture of horror, or perhaps rage, to the clear sky above. He saw her mouth open, but he did not hear her scream.

Then both the woman and Edouard fell to their knees. They began frantically to scrabble in the stone and dust. Behind them, in the city, Edouard heard the sirens begin to wail.

Forty-three people died in the explosion, among them Isobel and Jean-Paul, who, so close to the bomb, were killed instantly. The majority of the bodies could not be identified from their remains; a few were confirmed by dental records, or by jewelry and belongings that survived the blast intact.

The boy François, also known as Abdel Saran, and a member of the FLN since the age of sixteen, was picked up within twenty-four hours. His elder brother had been shot by a French *gendarme* in a street incident two years before. François, alias Abdel, died—according to the army reports—in his cell, of self-inflicted injuries. Four years after his death, much as Edouard had predicted, Charles de Gaulle ended the strife in Algeria, the majority of the French left, and Algeria became a free state.

Edouard never returned there to see the accuracy of his own prophecies. When the immediate formalities were over, he left Algeria for the last time, and flew back to Paris, where he shut himself away in the house at St. Cloud, seeing no one.

It was there, about two weeks later, when he forced himself to look at Isobel's correspondence, that he found the letter from her gynecologist with the recommendations she had requested regarding maternity clinics. It had been mailed the day they left for Algeria. He understood at once why she had not told him; he remembered the glass of milk in the café, and for the first time in weeks he was able to weep.

Once a Catholic, always a Catholic. He did not blame the boy, or Jean-Paul, or Algeria, or colonialism, or even himself: he blamed God, the deity of his childhood, whom he had not worshipped since his sixteenth birthday.

Once, Jean-Paul had accused him of acting like God, and that accusation had stayed with him, paining him. Yet if he, just a man, could not find it in his heart to condemn his brother or the boy who had used his brother's weaknesses to lure him to his death—how could this God of love of his childhood destroy so savagely and so arbitrarily? Not just his brother, not just his murderer, but a woman of Isobel's innocence and courage, the life of a child not yet born? And—more than that—do it day after day, month after month, year after year, throughout this miserable planet he was supposed to have created? For the past weeks Edouard had had to force himself to look at newspapers: all he saw there when he opened them was confirmation and repetition: accident, sickness, violence, and sudden death, handed out evenly to the guilty and the innocent. It was that which made his anger so violent: the knowledge that it was not his alone; that it was shared and felt by thousands upon thousands of others, rich and poor, strong and weak, man and woman, parent and child, all around the world. A God that created a world that should logically hate and revile its creator? No, he could not believe in such a God. But if he did encounter that God, he thought, his dearest wish would be to spit in his face.

Some three months after the bombing, at the very end of the old year and on the eve of the next one, choosing the date with a certain bitter amusement, Edouard left the house at St. Cloud in the late evening, and drove, alone, into the center of Paris.

He took the car which had been Grégoire's favorite, and also, by chance, Isobel's. Its long black hood gleamed in the light of the passing streetlamps, and its powerful engine echoed through empty streets. He avoided those parts of Paris where revelers had gathered to celebrate the New Year out of doors with drink and dancing. He drove through the back streets, and the quieter residential boulevards, where people had either ignored the date and retired to sleep, or were celebrating it in the privacy of their homes.

He drove past the Café Unic, where his father, and Jacques, and other members of their cadre had held their last meeting, and where he had dined with Isobel the night he asked her to marry him. He drove past the parks and gardens where he had played as a child; past the houses of some of his past mistresses; past the apartment where Clara Delluc lived. He drove past the house of his mother, who, he knew, was holding a party that night for her new lover, a celebrated patron of the arts. He drove past the École Militaire, where his brother had begun his career as a soldier, in that uniform he still remembered so clearly. He drove past the dark oiled surface of the Seine; he saw a *bateau-mouche* pass, brilliant with lights, saw two lovers, entwined in each other's arms in the shadows; saw a *clochard* out cold, slumped over the warmth of the vents from the métro, a brown paper bag and a puddle of alcohol by his side. He drove through the poorest streets of Paris, and some of the richest ones, and at length, shortly before midnight, stopped the car in a wide and gracious street of tall and beautiful houses.

He had not visited the place he was seeking before, but he knew it was there, and had heard tales of it from numerous acquaintances. Pauline Simonescu, finding the austerities of postwar London bad for business, had moved back to Paris at about the same time he, too, had returned—from Oxford. That coincidence pleased him. It was as if she had been waiting for him for all these years.

Some of his acquaintances favored her premises by night; like Jean-Paul, they felt the dark hours were the ones in which to drink and go hunting. Others favored the day, the long pleasures of an afternoon. *It makes little difference in any case*, one of them had said to him once. *In that house the shutters are always closed, the lamps lit. In that house it is always night.*

He thought of that remark now as he paused outside the house. It was dark, and silent, from the outside no different from the respectable family mansions that flanked it. Ah, but when you entered it . . .

He knocked once on the door, and it was instantly opened, not by the black man whom he had been expecting, but by Pauline Simonescu herself. Perhaps she heard his steps before he knocked—she opened the door very quickly—and he wondered for a moment if she had been standing exactly as she had when he last saw her—just inside the door, her head on one side, listening, as she had listened to the bombs, and to the all-clear siren which she heard before it was sounded.

She did not greet him, but drew him quickly inside into another marble-floored hall, so similar in form to the previous one, with its glittering crystal lights and its wide forked staircase, that for a moment he felt only confusion, a sense of time warped, speeding him at once back and forward.

He looked around him. The Fragonards. The Titian. From the adjoining room the sound of conversation and laughter. Madame Simonescu drew him forward, into the light, her hand, again wearing the heavy ruby, resting with a light tension on his arm. Again he felt that sense of an unseen force, an intense will. She said nothing; her head was slightly tilted, listening.

He listened, too, and for a moment the noises from the next room ceased, and he heard only a great and total silence, a silence that extended beyond the city, beyond the planet, a silence as empty and bleak and beautiful as space, as the universe itself; the endless harmonious silence of the spheres.

Then, through the silence, he heard the advent of the year: the ringing of the church bells, the rattles, the hoots of the ships on the Seine, the clatter and concatenation of men and women.

He looked at Pauline Simonescu, and felt a great and total relief, as if a burden of enormous weight had been lifted from his shoulders. He knew he needed to say nothing; she needed no fumbled accounts of the past, no pleas, no explanations. She knew him, and he recognized her; they had both heard the silence.

"*Monsieur le Baron*," she said as she had said to him once before.

Then, not even glancing at the room beyond, or at a woman who had come out onto the stairs, she led him away to a small room of perfect luxury at the back of the house, which was clearly her own. She seated him before the blaze of a bright fire; she brought him, unasked, a glass of the Armagnac he preferred. Then she seated herself opposite him, and drew forward a small table on which were two packs of cards.

An ordinary pack, a tarot pack; she spread them out on the polished mahogany. The Baron looked down at their butterfly colors, and saw they were very old and much used. He saw images: a ruined tower—and he thought of those black gaps behind the Eaton Square terrace; death by drowning—and he thought of Hugo Glendinning; a hanged man—and he thought of his father's cadre; two lovers—he thought of himself and Isobel; a king of cups, a queen of diamonds—he thought of nothing.

Pauline Simonescu looked up, her thin hands moving over the cards, her black eyes holding his. Her fingers hovered over *La Morte, Les Amoureaux,* over the king of cups: the jester.

"*Monsieur le Baron*," she said. "It is the beginning of the new year. First, I shall read the cards for you. Then, if you still wish, you can do whatever it was you came here to do." She smiled.

"The cards first. Then you can begin your future."

HÉLÈNE

ALABAMA, 1959

"How d'you figure on wearing it, honey? You want it up, down? In a ponytail, maybe?"

Cassie Wyatt's capable hands cradled her head. Looking into the mirror, she turned Hélène's head first one way, then the other. "You've got beautiful hair, you know that, honey? Just like silk, and thick! Why, you could do just about anything with hair like this."

Hélène's eyes met Cassie's in the mirror. Cassie winked.

"This a special date, or what?"

"Sort of. I want to look nice."

"No problem." Cassie's plain features split apart in a grin. "Nice which way, that's what I'm askin'."

"Not up. And not a ponytail." Hélène hesitated. "I thought if you could just trim it a bit, and make it wave a bit more maybe . . ."

"You leave it to me, honey."

She picked up her scissors, then rested her hands on Hélène's shoulders, still staring at her reflection in the glass.

"You've grown up real fast," she said suddenly. "Real fast—you know that? Sixteen, and a real head-turner, honey." She paused. "You ever catch any of those Grace Kelly movies at the drive-in? *Rear Window? High Society?* That come 'round again the other week. I reckon you remind me a bit of her. We could try something like that—back off of your face. You willin' to let me try?"

"Sure."

"Fine. Here we go."

She began to lift the long honey-colored hair on her comb, and to snip at it. To begin with, Hélène watched her, then gradually her attention drifted away. She was excited. It *was* a special date, though she couldn't explain to Cassie just how special. She was going out to dinner with Ned Calvert. His wife was away, and he was taking Hélène out to a restaurant, somewhere fancy, he said, just the two of them.

And she had a new dress—not an altered dress, not a homemade dress, a new one from a store! Last time she'd seen him, Ned had slipped a twenty-dollar bill into her hand.

"A little present for my girl," he said. "Don't you argue now. I want you to go over to Montgomery, and go right in a store, and buy yourself just the prettiest dress you can find. And then wear it for me. . . ."

She had felt faint with excitement, walking around the store, but she'd found the dress, and it was perfect. It was pink and white checked cotton, with a low sweetheart neckline, and puff sleeves that left most of her arms bare. It had a paper nylon petticoat which was stiff and scratchy, and made the skirt stick out in a big circle, just the way Priscilla-Anne's dresses did. She'd had enough money left over to buy some underwear too: little frilly panties, and a lacy bra, with wire built in under the cups so it lifted her breasts. And now she was having her hair done. She just wished it didn't take so long, because she couldn't wait to get home and put it all on and look in the mirror.

"You been over to Montgomery today?" Cassie was looking at her reflection. "Saw you gettin' off the bus, so I figured you had."

"Oh, yes. I was just looking in the stores—you know."

"Any trouble on the bus?" Cassie frowned.

"No. No trouble."

"Was the other day. You hear about that? Over Maybury way? The coloreds been boycottin' the buses there weeks now, of course. And I don't know but I didn't sympathize with them, just a little, you know? Must feel bad, always havin' to ride way back in the bus. Ought to have their own buses, the way I see it."

She paused, then started snipping again. "But there was a big protest over Maybury last week. Fightin'. Some colored boy got himself cut up real bad, I heard." She let a lock of hair fall. "You want to be careful now, Hélène. It's gettin' so it's not safe to take a bus no more. . . ."

"It was fine. No trouble."

"How's your mama doin'?" Cassie obviously decided to change the subject. She paused, and her kind face clouded. "I miss her, you know, Hélène. I mean, I knew she wasn't feelin' too good, but I never figured on her leavin', not like that."

Hélène's eyes dropped. Her mother had left Cassie Wyatt's a month ago.

"She's fine," she answered in a small voice. "Okay—you know?"

"I sure hope so, honey." Cassie sighed. "Your mama and me, we go a long ways back. . . ."

Hélène could hear the pity in her voice. She knew Cassie knew her mother didn't have another job; everyone in Orangeburg must know that. She tilted her chin.

"We might go back to England soon," she said proudly. "When I finish school next year. My mother's busy—making plans. That sort of thing."

"Sure, honey."

Cassie's face took on a closed expression. She said no more. She shook out the towel around Hélène's neck, and a cascade of honey-colored hair fell to the floor.

"Let's get that washed and set now. Then I'll put you under the dryer, okay?"

It took hours under the dryer. Hélène thought. It was baking hot under the hood, and the metal rollers and pins Cassie had used got hotter and hotter by the minute. Hélène flicked the pages of *Redbook*, glanced at a tattered copy of *Time* magazine. It was nearly two years out of date. She closed the magazine. There was a whole world out there, waiting: Hollywood, New York, England, Europe.

Ned Calvert had been to Europe—in the war first, but on vacations as well. He and Mrs. Calvert had been to London, Paris, and Rome. They stayed at the finest hotels, he said; they went to the theaters and museums and art galleries. In London they went to the races; in Paris they took a trip on a *bateau-mouche* down the Seine; in Rome, Mrs. Calvert said, the men had no manners.

She pushed the magazines aside. Across the salon Susie Marshall's mother was having her hair done. She had bright red hair, dyed and permed into a frizz; Cassie was touching up the roots. Hélène caught Mrs. Marshall's eyes in the mirror, and Mrs. Marshall looked right through her.

Small-town blues. That was what Priscilla-Anne used to call it, afternoons when school was through, up behind the ball park. Feeling trapped. Feeling mean. Feeling impatient.

Priscilla-Anne was engaged to Dale Garrett now, and the rumor was, she was pregnant. They were going to marry in the fall and move into a large house on a brand-new estate outside Montgomery, an estate Merv Peters was developing. Merv Peters was rising fast now; the house was their wedding present. Priscilla-Anne was jubilant. At least, that's what Hélène had heard. Priscilla-Anne didn't talk to her anymore, not since the night at Howard Johnson's. She didn't sit next to her in class either, and the others had followed her example.

Hélène Craig: social leper.

She set her lips. She didn't care. Let them gossip; let the boys smirk. Did you get small-town blues in Montgomery too? She didn't know, but she hoped you did. She hoped Priscilla-Ann got them real *bad*. One thing for sure—it was not going to happen to her, to Hélène.

She was leaving. Soon, one day soon, she was going to get out of Orangeburg for good and all, and take her mother with her. Then she'd go to England, and Europe, Paris maybe. And she'd become rich and famous, so famous they heard about her even back in Orangeburg. And then maybe one day she'd come back, come into town in a big Cadillac car, and a couture dress and jewels, and when she did that, she'd look right through them all, all the boys at Selma High, all Priscilla-Anne's friends, look through them like they were invisible. The way they looked at her now.

The hair dryer was giving her a headache. She shut her eyes and tried to hold on to the dream, which wasn't a dream, she told herself firmly: it was something that was going to happen. Something she was going to make happen. You could do that, she believed it, if you were certain enough, determined enough.

The best part of the dream was that her mother would be happy then too. Hélène would find her somewhere wonderful to live, and her mother would have all the clothes she wanted, and not have to worry about money ever again. And she would get well. She wasn't well now, Hélène could see it. She seemed so tired all the time, dragging herself around the trailer as if she had no energy at all. She was very thin, and hardly ever ate anything; her skin was sallow and dull, like crêpe. She was doing dressmaking since leaving Cassie's—sewing things, altering things, and that brought in a little, but it couldn't be enough, Hélène knew.

Hélène had wanted to leave school, and get a job, but when she'd suggested it, her mother had been terribly upset. Those two bright spots of color flared up in her cheeks, and she'd started to shake. Hélène had to finish her education, she said. She must. You needed an education to get on in the world.

Hélène didn't agree. She looked at the newspapers and magazines, and she listened to the radio, and she thought there were lots of ways you could get on in the world, education or no education. Sportsmen got on, and singers, and dancers and writers and movie stars and fashion models, and people like Merv Peters, who started off with a little business and built it into a big one. Beautiful women got on in the world. And she was beautiful. She knew that now, she'd finally realized it was true. She didn't see it so much when she looked in the mirror; she saw it in the boys' eyes, in men's eyes. She saw it in Billy's; she saw it in Ned's, that fixity, that intentness, that fascination. It made her feel powerful when she saw that response; it made her feel happy; it made her feel safe.

Because she knew, just knew, that no matter what happened, no matter if she flunked school, or had no talent, couldn't act, she still had that. The one certain weapon in her armory: her beauty. If all else failed, her beauty could be relied on. Her beauty was going to be her ticket out.

She gave Susie Marshall's mother a radiant smile as she left the beauty parlor. *You old bitch*, she thought. *Some day I'll show you. . . .*

When she got back to the trailer, her mother was out, and Hélène was relieved. She didn't want her to see the shopping bags. She'd have to explain the dress somehow, and she was working on a story, but if her mother saw the bags, it would be harder.

She stood still in the hot little bedroom, thinking. She hated to tell her mother lies, and it seemed to her sometimes that the lies got bigger every day, until sometimes she felt as if she were drowning in them, and she got mixed-up and frightened, so she hardly knew what was lies and what was truth anymore. But she had to tell lies. The lies enabled her to meet Ned Calvert; they'd enabled her to meet him, more and more often, for nearly a year. It was the beginning of July now; the first time he'd taken her for a ride in the Cadillac it had been early September—so it was ten months. Ten months!

It didn't feel that long; it wasn't that long really, because two months of that time he'd been away, up in Philadelphia, visiting with Mrs. Calvert's family.

It was while he was away she had begun to think that maybe she was in love with him. She had missed him. Until they stopped, she hadn't realized how much she had come to look forward to those evenings, to the times when he took her for walks and drives, the times they talked. But when he was away, she felt lonely. There was nothing to look forward to anymore.

He had felt just the same way; he told her when he came back from Philadelphia. That was when he said that he couldn't go on like this anymore, that he had to tell her. They were friends, yes, of course they were friends; but she must know, she must have realized—he loved her. He was crazy for her. All the time in Philadelphia he thought about her and thought about her. It was driving him insane. . . .

Quickly Hélène bent and hid the shopping bags under the bed. Then she heated some water on the stove, and carried a big pail of it into the bedroom. She wrenched shut the horrible faded little curtains over the windows, and began to wash, soaping bits of her body at a time. She hated it, she thought, scrubbing viciously at her skin. Hated having to wash like this. Hated having no bathroom. Hated being poor. Someone like Ned couldn't understand that. He'd been born rich. He took it all for granted.

She threw the washcloth into the water and sat back on her haunches, letting the air dry her skin.

When Ned wasn't there, she remembered only the good things about him, she thought. The lovely clean scent of his skin; the cologne he always wore; the soft fabrics of his beautiful clothes; his voice, with its rich educated southern drawl; the strength when he put his arms around her; the comforting sense of his age, his experience, his knowledge. He had taste; she liked the fact that he knew about things like wine, and food, and houses and paintings and gardens and cars. He was rich, and his richness fascinated her, because it seemed to her to make him certain about everything, from the cut of a suit to a question of politics. He had influence—he was on first-name terms with all the famous politicians and leading businessmen in Alabama; when Ned Calvert heard the news, he didn't get it from a paper, he got it direct, from a friend, over dinner or lunch. He didn't boast about that; he took it for granted that the only watch was a Rolex, the only car a Cadillac or a Lincoln, that when you took a vacation, you went to Europe.

And he didn't mind when she asked questions; he seemed to like it, as if it amused him and flattered him to teach her. So a lot of the time when they met, especially to begin with, he used to talk, and Hélène used to listen. He might be explaining how to tell the difference between claret and burgundy; he might be explaining why the civil rights movement would never get a hold in the South, because it was against the nature of things; either way, he talked on, in that slow, sure voice, and—since Hélène had quickly discovered that only one thing irritated him, and that was the possibility that she thought differently—she learned to keep quiet, to question, but rarely to voice an opinion, and then only on something uncontroversial.

He had begun to call her "little girl" quite early on, and to Hélène's own surprise, she had discovered she responded to the term almost instinctively. At once a thousand tiny memories came back, of other women she had watched, Priscilla-Anne, trying to placate Dale Garrett, her mother even, trying to charm some man behind a store counter. Then, there it was, ready-made, the role. She could slip into it at once: innocent, kittenish, naïve, trusting, nonargumentative, using her feminine wiles to get her way. Being coy, being teasing, being flattering— being hypocritical.

Yes, hypocritical. Hypocrisy was involved, if she admitted the truth. Because all the time he talked and she listened, there was one part of her mind that kept up its own cool independent commentary, which sifted what he said, weighed it, and, quite often, rejected it—though he never knew.

She didn't agree with what he said about colored people. She didn't agree with his comments on poor whites, like the Tanners. She didn't like the way he ostentatiously referred to blacks always as "nigras," never using the cruder term like other whites in Orangeburg, even though she could tell he felt the same way about them. She didn't like it the time he made jokes about Jews and liberals in Washington. She thought his ideas about women were wrong. A man liked to put a woman up on a pedestal, he said. He liked to care for her, and look up to her. It was important for a man to respect a woman, the way he respected her.

"And Mrs. Calvert?" she had said, unable to stifle the thought.

"Of course Mrs. Calvert," he had said solemnly, but she could see he was annoyed.

Women were made for marriage, he said another time. They were made for motherhood. There was nothing finer than the sight of a mother and her child. He couldn't understand all these working women. What did it do for them? What did it do for their husbands? What man wanted to think he couldn't provide for his wife and family, that what he brought home wasn't enough?

"Men have their pride, Hélène," he said once. "They don't talk about it maybe, but it's there. It's a fierce thing, a fine thing. Like pride in your country, pride in being an American."

Don't women have pride? Hélène wanted to ask, but she kept silent.

Sometimes she thought she must be some kind of a freak, thinking these things the way she did, knowing that cool voice was there all the time in her own mind, and it wouldn't go away.

Did the other girls at Selma High think like that too? Did Priscilla-Anne, when she was with that oaf, Dale Garrett?

Hélène had no way of knowing. If they did, they never said so, even in the days when she still had friends in school, before they started ostracizing her. So, maybe she was a freak, maybe there was something wrong with her. Because all her life there it had been, that old refrain: love and marriage—a woman's true purpose in life, the source of her status, the source of her identity.

That was what all the girls at Selma High seemed to want, so why didn't she want it? Why, whenever she thought about it, did she start to feel trapped?

And guilty. She turned and looked at herself in the mirror.

Guilty, because she *must* love Ned Calvert. If she didn't love him, why did she go on seeing him, a married man? Why did she let him kiss her, and sometimes touch her, and why did she like it when he did that? Slowly, she ran her hand up over her naked body, feeling a shiver of excitement, of anticipation as she did so. It was quite clear, she thought. Everything the other girls had ever said, everything her mother had said, everything she had ever read, had been united on one point. Men and women were different. Men could feel physical desire for a woman they did not love. But women felt it only when they loved a man: their emotions and their physical feelings went hand in hand. So, kissing was all right, petting was permissible, because they were privileges the woman offered up in the name of love. On that altar she could, eventually, safely sacrifice her virginity. Not otherwise. Otherwise you were cheap, an easy lay. Men talked about you in the locker room, and they despised you even if they slept with you. And if men despised you, that was the end, because where was your identity then?

She must love Ned Calvert, she thought. She must. Loving was quite different from liking; it certainly didn't mean that you had to agree with everything a person said. You just had to stop those disagreements from getting in the way.

She felt a flurry, then, of doubt and indecision. Uncertainty washed through her mind in gray panicking waves.

She had let Ned give her the money for this dress. She had let him kiss her. She liked it when he kissed her. She loved him—when she thought about it like that, she was almost certain she did.

Shut up, she said to that still small voice in her head; *shut up, go away, go someplace else.*

She reached for the new underclothes, reached for the new dress.

I am dressing to go and meet my lover, she said to herself. *A fine man.*

She felt a quickening excitement as she let herself slip into the role. The still small voice grew quieter. By the time she had the dress on, and looked at herself again in the mirror, she had managed to silence it completely.

"Would you like a cup of tea, Mother? Shall I boil some water?" Her mother had just gotten back. She was sitting at the kitchen table, staring down at the oilcloth. Hélène waited for her to look up, waited for the questions about the dress, but none came.

"What? Oh, yes. Thank you. It's so very hot. I'm thirsty. Whenever did it last rain?"

Her mother never even turned her head. Quietly Hélène fetched the water, lit the butane gas.

"Hélène . . ."

"Yes, Mother?"

"What's the date?"

Hélène glanced at the calendar that hung by the stove.

"It's the fifteenth, Mother. July fifteenth."

"I thought so." Her mother bent her head.

Hélène made the tea, put the milk in a pitcher, the way her mother preferred, and put the cup and saucer and milk on the table in front of her. Her mother didn't seem to see them, so Hélène added the milk herself.

"Hélène. Would you go into the bedroom and get the box out? I'd like you to tell me . . . to count the money in there."

Hélène hesitated, but something in her mother's manner frightened her, so she fetched the box, and opened it, and counted the money inside. There was a silence.

"Well?"

"Twenty dollars, Mother. Nearly twenty dollars. There're two fives, and some singles, and a lot of quarters and dimes. Nineteen dollars and eighty-five cents."

Her mother bent her head and started to cry.

Hélène got up quickly and went across and put her arms around her. But her mother didn't touch her or clasp her or anything. She just went on crying, terrible gasping sobs that shook her thin shoulders. Then, just as suddenly as she had begun, she stopped.

"Fetch me a handkerchief, would you, Hélène? I'm sorry. I'm just tired, that's all. There's no point in crying. None at all."

Hélène fetched her the handkerchief, and her mother wiped her eyes and blew her nose. Hélène sat down and took her hand. She wanted to cry too; she always did when she saw her mother like this; it made her whole heart ache with a terrible impotent pain and pity.

"Mother, please . . ." she said gently. "Don't be sad. Don't cry. I can't bear to see you like this. If you're worried—if there's something wrong—can't you tell me? I could help, I know I could."

"I need some money." Her mother interrupted her suddenly, as if she hadn't heard a word Hélène said. "I need seventy-five dollars. I have to have it. I have to."

Hélène stared at her; she felt alarm tighten around her heart. She opened her mouth, and before she could speak, her mother stood up. She was twisting the wet handkerchief between her fingers.

"I have to see a doctor. I'm not well, Hélène. I've known it for a while now—you said yourself. And you were right. I realize that now. I have to see a doctor and I need the money. Seventy-five dollars. I must have it. I must."

"Mother, what's *wrong?* How aren't you well? You've been coughing a lot at night. Is that it, Mother? Are you worried about the coughing?"

"Yes, the coughing and . . . and other things. I'm not well, that's all." Her mother sounded almost angry. "I haven't felt well for a long time now, and I must see a doctor. I can't let it go on. I have to see a doctor and I have to pay him, and then there might be medication, drugs—drugs are expensive, Hélène, they don't come free, you know. I need seventy-five dollars. There's twenty there. So I need fifty-five more. Sixty maybe. Where am I going to get sixty dollars, just like that?"

Hélène stared down at the dress she was wearing. She felt sick and afraid. That very afternoon she'd had a twenty-dollar bill in her hand. Not as much as her mother said she needed, but twenty dollars all the same.

She swallowed. Ned's voice swam in her mind. *Take it, Hélène. I want you to, honey. I like to give my little girl presents.*

She stood up, the heat mounting in her cheeks.

"I might be able to help, Mother. I might. I think I might be able to get hold of sixty dollars."

Her mother had been pacing up and down the room. Now she stopped and turned to Hélène, her eyes wide with hope. Almost at once the hope died; the violet eyes went blank.

"I need it now, Hélène. You can't get sixty dollars. Not just like that . . ."

"I could, Mother. I know I could . . ." Hélène moved impulsively around the table. The lie was on her lips almost before she had time to think. "Merv Peters would let me have it, I know he would. You know I helped out there sometimes—at the soda fountain, after school? Well, he wants me to do it more often, on a regular basis, he said so. Saturday mornings as well. They get busy then. He said . . . he said he'd pay me five dollars every Saturday, and five dollars for the evenings after school. That's ten dollars a week, Mother, think of that—and he'd advance me some money, I know he would if I asked him. If I said I needed it . . ."

She came to a stop. None of it was true. She'd never worked the soda fountain. Merv Peters had mentioned it once, ages ago, but it had never come to anything, and he'd hardly give her a job now—Priscilla-Anne would see to that. But the soda-fountain story had explained her absences after school these past months, and her mother had never questioned it. She looked at her mother's tense white face, and for a second she longed to throw herself into her mother's arms and tell her the truth, everything. And she might have done it if she hadn't seen her mother's face change.

Hope lit up in the violet eyes; her hands stopped twisting the handkerchief. She drew in her breath.

"You could do that, Hélène? You really think he'd agree?"

"I know he would, Mother."

"Oh, Hélène." Her mother's face crumpled, and she held out her arms to her. Hélène ran into them, and held her mother close. She was the taller of the two now; her mother's body felt very frail in her arms. After a while, her mother drew back. She made an attempt at a smile, gestured at the pink gingham.

"Such a pretty dress. You're going over to the soda fountain tonight? You said something—I can't quite remember . . . Could you ask him, Hélène? Ask him tonight?"

"I'll bring the money back with me." Hélène helped her mother back into the chair. "I'll bring it back with me, I promise. And then you can see the doctor, and get well again, and then—" She hesitated, looking down at her mother's bent head. "Then we ought to talk more, Mother. You remember—the way we used to do? We ought to—plan. Think. I could leave school. I could . . ." Her mother looked up.

"It's gone six, Hélène. Oughtn't you to be leaving? I'll be all right. I'll be fine. I feel better now. I don't want to hold you up."

She reached for the teacup, picked it up, and sipped the half-cold tea. Hélène moved uncertainly to the door.

"I might be a little late getting back, Mother. . . ."

"That's all right, darling. I know where you are. I shan't be worried. Run along now."

Ned was waiting for her outside the old summerhouse. They had often met there this past month, on the evenings Ned didn't pick her up on the Orangeburg road. Tonight he was waiting as usual, pacing up and down the grass outside, smoking a cigarette. Hélène saw him before he saw her, and her heart leapt. He looked so impatient for her to arrive. She had been running, and now she increased her pace, across the grass, cannoning into his arms. She clung to him then, her shoulders heaving, her breath coming fast, fighting back the tears, and Ned laughed with surprise and pleasure, and then held her tight, rocking her back and forth.

"Whoa there, whoa there," he said softly against her hair. "You seem in a mighty fine hurry to get here. . . . What's this now?" He tilted her face up to his. "Something happen to upset you, honey?"

Hélène shook her head and buried her face again against his chest. She couldn't tell him, not yet. She'd have to ask him and try to explain, but later, she thought—later.

"I'm all right." She pressed her lips against his fine lawn shirt. She could feel the thud of his heart. "I was just running, that's all. I wanted to see you."

"And I wanted to see you, honey. I've been counting the minutes. . . ." He took her arms and held her away from him so he could look her up and down. Hélène stepped back shyly, smoothing back her tumbled hair. His eyes rested on her flushed face, her anxious eyes. Slowly they fell to the neckline of the pink gingham, then down, then up. He gave a long sigh.

"You look beautiful, Hélène." His voice was soft, and his eyes had taken on that intent look they did sometimes, so Hélène knew he meant what he said. "You look just beautiful. And your hair. You've had your hair fixed." He lifted his hand and touched her hair, then slipped his fingers down a little way, and caressed her throat. "It makes me so happy, you know that? Just to see you look the way you do. To know you went right out, and chose that, for me. . . . Give me a kiss, honey, just a little kiss. Doesn't my little girl want to tell me she's pleased to see me now?"

He kissed her parted lips as he spoke, drawing her close against him, and holding her carefully, protectively, in the circle of his arms.

"Oh, honey. If you knew what you did to me." He looked down into her upturned face and smiled. Then he took her arm and rested it through his.

"I've got a little surprise for you. You come along with me now, and you'll see. . . ."

He set off toward the house. Hélène trotted beside him, quickening her steps to keep up with his long strides. He took her around the shrubbery and out onto the lawns, in full view of the windows. Hélène stopped.

"Where are we going? I thought—I thought we were going to a restaurant?"

"Change of plan. I thought of something nicer. You'll see. Come on now."

He led her right up and into the house, holding her hand now. Across the cool hall, into that vast living room. Hélène shivered as the cool air of the house hit her skin. The blinds were down, and the lamps were lit, though it was broad daylight outside. Ned saw her glance at the windows, and he smiled.

"More private that way. And I've sent the servants out. We won't be disturbed. Look, Hélène. . . ."

At the far side of the drawing room he threw back the tall double doors with a flourish. The room beyond was the dining room, which Hélène had never seen before. It was a huge room, cooled by fans that rotated slowly overhead. At one end was a heavy antique sideboard laden with ornate silver dishes. The blinds were down here, too, and the room was lit by candles ranged in tall candelabra down the center of the long mahogany table. Their flickering light shone on porcelain and crystal, on gardenias from the estate, on fruit from its hothouses. The table would have seated twenty people with ease. At one end of it, two places had been laid.

She stopped, and Ned gave a low laugh.

"Look."

He moved to the sideboard and began lifting silver covers.

"Lobster. Cold chicken. A special sauce our cook makes, with grapes—it's delicious, you ever had that, Hélène? Melons. Fresh raspberries and peaches. Cream." He moved on to an ice bucket. "Champagne, getting nice and cold now. French champagne—Krug, you ever heard of that, Hélène? All just waiting for us to serve ourselves. Better than any restaurant hereabouts, don't you think, honey?" He glanced at her face, saw the doubt there, and moved back quickly to her side.

"Hélène, say you're pleased. I wanted you to be pleased. I wanted you here tonight, don't you see? Just this once—eating by my side, at my table, in my house. My little girl. My lovely little girl. Eating here like the lady she is. Drinking champagne. We're celebrating, Hélène, don't you know that?"

"What are we celebrating?" She looked at him uncertainly.

"Why, I guess we'll have to see." He grinned. "You and I, we've got plenty to celebrate, I'd say."

He took her hand and led her back into the drawing room.

"Now you just sit tight there, and I'll bring you some champagne. Sip it nice and slow now . . . remember the bourbon."

Hélène remembered the bourbon only too clearly, so she was careful. One glass of champagne. One glass of wine with dinner. Even so, she knew the alcohol was affecting her. It made her head feel light, and her spirits rose, and she was glad of that. Ned was being attentive, and amusing, telling her some story about a congressman he knew; he seemed relaxed, perfectly at ease, sitting underneath a rather ugly portrait of his father, just as if this dinner were the most normal thing in the world.

He did not seem bothered by how much he drank, she noticed. Three glasses of champagne to her one; at least four glasses of wine; after dinner, when they returned to the drawing room, he poured a bourbon on the rocks.

He was sitting opposite her, his legs stretched out comfortably, smoking a cigar. The pungent smoke drifted across the space between them. Hélène thought; *The next time he puts his glass down, then I shall ask him about the money. I'll have to. I can't put it off any longer.*

He put the glass down, and she did. There was a silence. He looked across the room at her as if what she said surprised him. Then he smiled slowly and took a long pull on the cigar.

"Sixty dollars?"

"It would be a loan, of course. I'd pay you back, every cent. It's just that I need it now. I . . . I need it for a friend."

"Sure you do. Anyone I know?"

"No. No—you don't know them."

"Well now—let's see."

He reached inside his white jacket and drew out a fat billfold made of crocodile skin. There was a thick wad of notes inside it. He looked at the notes, then at her, then he closed the billfold and put it away.

"Come here, honey."

He patted the seat beside him, and Hélène got up slowly and moved across. As she sat down, he took her hand.

"You going to be nice to me tonight, Hélène? You going to make me feel happy? You do that, and I'll be honored to help you out. I told you. I like to give my little girl presents, you know that. . . ." He took another long swig of the bourbon. His hand felt sweaty though the room was cool. Gently but insistently he lowered her hand and pressed it against the thick muscles of his thigh.

"Give me a kiss, Hélène. Just one little kiss . . ."

Hélène leaned forward. His lips looked full and red; and he had that glazed look in his eyes again. Carefully she pressed her mouth against his.

"Not like that, honey . . ." He shifted a little in his seat. "Open your mouth, you know the way I like to kiss you. More. Yes. Oh, honey, like that . . ."

She could taste the bourbon on his lips. His moustache was rubbing her skin. He tilted her back, leaning against her with his full weight, his hand moving up over her dress. His tongue moved in her mouth, deep and warm.

"Honey, what are you wearing under that dress?" He squeezed her breast playfully, so the wire cups of the bra bit into her skin. "I think you bought something else besides the dress, something else to please me. Did you do that, Hélène? Did you?"

Hélène lowered her eyes. Her heart was beating very fast, and her throat felt tight and dry.

"Maybe . . ."

Her voice came out low and husky, and she saw the answering response in his eyes as she looked up. It excited her, and confused her, the quickness of that reaction, the ease with which she could evoke it.

"You're a little fox, you know that? A cute, wicked little fox. You know just how to drive a man wild. Where'd you learn that, Hélène? A little girl like you." He lowered his mouth to her neck and nuzzled wetly at the skin beneath her ear. "You like it, don't you?" he whispered thickly. "You pretend not to sometimes, but I know. Tell me, Hélène, tell me you like it when I kiss my own little girl. . . ."

"I do like that. I like it when you kiss me."

"And when I touch you? You like that too, honey?"

"Sometimes." She looked away. "Maybe I shouldn't."

"Now, don't you say that; don't you think it, you hear?" He lifted his hand and began to stroke her throat. "If it feels good, it feels good. No sense in denying what you feel, honey. You know I'm just crazy about you. You know I'd never hurt you. And besides, you trust me, honey. I know you do. You wouldn't come to me for help if you didn't trust me, I know that."

His voice had been soft; now it took on a slightly hard edge. For the first time, Hélène felt a dart of alarm, a sense that things were slipping out of her control. He began to kiss her again, and to stroke the full curve of her breasts under the thin cotton dress. Then, abruptly, adjusting his trousers, he stood up, just at the moment when Hélène had decided she must tell him to stop. He took her hand.

"It's hot in here, don't you think? Let's go someplace cooler, more comfortable. . . ."

He half-led, half-pulled her out of the room, across the hall, and up the wide stairs. If he heard her protests, he gave no sign of it. On the wide galleried landing, he pulled her against him tightly, his breath coming fast, one hand fumbling for the handle of a door. He pushed it back and drew her inside.

They were in his wife's bedroom. Hélène recognized it at once, even after all these years. The blinds were up, and moonlight striped the floor. It gleamed on the triple looking-glass, the heavy silver brushes, the cut-glass bottles. There were white linen dust sheets over the upholstered chairs. Ned moved away from her and roughly pulled off one of them. He turned, and tossed it across his wife's bed, over the embroidered silk cover. He adjusted it fussily, smoothing out the folds, so there was a square of white linen right in the middle of the silk. Then he started to undo his belt.

Hélène stood very still. For a moment, she could feel the clutch of bobby pins in her hand, could smell the hair tongs, could see the sallow skin, the powder caking in the heat. She lifted her hands.

"I can't. What are you doing? Ned—please . . ."

"Look, honey, let's not play games anymore, all right?" He lurched slightly, his mouth smiling, his voice filled with a sudden impatience.

"You want a present, you just be nice to me, all right? Real nice, the way I know you can be."

His fingers were on his fly; she heard the zipper as he moved toward her. He laughed and reached for her hand.

"Come on now, Hélène. Give me your hand. Don't tease now. Don't you know? Men don't like women who tease. That's it. Now touch me, honey. Go on, slip your hand right inside my pants. Nice and slow." He gave a grunt of pleasure.

"That's it. That's it, honey. That feel good? Feel big? You see what you do to me now. . . ."

He had her hand trapped between his palm and the thrust of his flesh. The heat of his skin, the size of his erection, terrified her. She couldn't move, and he seemed to interpret her silent stillness as acquiescence. He drew her over to the bed, lifted her in his arms, pushed her back onto the white square of sheeting. Then he began to take off his clothes, taking his time, as if he enjoyed stripping in front of her.

Hélène sat absolutely still on the sheet and watched him. Her mind stopped all its darting and flurrying, and became hard and cold and clear. She understood, completely, and with a sense of calm detachment, as if this were happening to someone else.

He had been leading up to this for months, waiting perhaps for the moment when his wife was away. Asking him to lend her the money had given him an additional excuse, that was all. Now, she saw, he felt perfectly justified in what he was doing. It was a bargain, an exchange. She had accepted a present; now she wanted money, and he wanted this. Love was not involved, of course not—how stupid she had been. Just sex and commerce. Sixty dollars worth of a good time.

He kept his boxer shorts on. Hélène looked at him. Undressed, his body was powerful and square, thickening around the waist, with the beginnings of a paunch. There was a mat of thick black hair across his chest, narrowing to a line that disappeared beneath the waistband of the shorts. Compared to the tan on his face and neck and arms, the rest of his body was startlingly white. His erection made the shorts pucker and bulge. He had his hands on his hips, and a smile of absolute confidence on his mouth. Hélène looked at him and knew she hated him with all her heart.

"You ever seen a man like this before?"

"No."

He grinned. "Let's make you feel a little more comfortable, okay, honey?"

His fingers reached for the zipper of her frock, tangled in her hair. As he undid it, his hands shook a little. He eased it off over her head and tossed it onto the floor. Then he kneeled back on the bed and just looked at her.

"Jesus. Sweet Jesus."

He didn't bother to undo the bra. He just lifted her breasts higher in the lacy cups so the nipples were exposed. Then he pushed her back and began to suck. Half-kneeling, half-crouching, he burrowed his head against her flesh. Hélène lay quite still; she watched him and felt him from a long way away, a million miles away, the other side of the moon. With a part of her mind she had not known she possessed, she was calculating where she'd make him stop. At first he was too busy to notice how quietly she lay. He was too busy licking and sucking and probing. His fingers moved down, flickered across her smooth stomach, hesitated, then moved on down. They glanced across the sheer nylon, felt for the pubic mound, tweaked the nylon aside, gripped her painfully by the pubic hair the way a man might grab a dog by the scruff of the neck.

"Part your legs, honey. Just a little bit now. I won't hurt you. I want to give my little girl a good time. Let me feel, let me touch. Is that nice, honey? That feel good when I touch you there?"

One finger inserted between the lips, searching, pressing too hard. He jiggled the finger about.

"You're still dry, honey. Wait awhile now." He gave a low laugh. "A woman's just like a car, you know that? Have to give them time to warm up."

He jiggled the finger about some more, and Hélène winced.

"Come on now, honey, you're not tryin', you know that? Here." He withdrew his hand abruptly, and reached for hers. "You feel me now, get to know me. Feel how warmed up I am, how hot . . ."

He pulled her hand in through the slit in the boxer shorts, guiding it roughly over the smooth hard skin of the shaft, down to the loose skin, the swing of his balls. They felt damp and crumpled, round and hard inside, like little rocks. The shaft of his penis dipped and lifted as she touched. Hélène shut her eyes.

"You want to take a closer look, honey? See the goods?" She could tell from his voice he was smiling, could feel him easing the boxer shorts down over his hips.

"Open your eyes now, honey. Take a good long look."

Hélène looked. His flesh looked red and swollen. The tip of his penis was like an eye, she thought. A small unwinking eye; at its center, one moist wet pearl of white.

"You can kiss me down there, honey. It feels real nice." His hand closed around himself, as if to display himself the better. A tremor ran through his body.

"Honey . . . I can't hold back much longer. You know what I want." His voice was thick and indistinct; he was trying to straddle her, two thick thighs either side of her waist. Hélène raised her clear blue eyes and looked him directly in the face.

"I'm not going all the way."

The words came out quite distinctly. She saw his eyes widen for a second in surprise. But it was only for an instant; his face was flushed, his lips slack, his eyes purposeful again. It was as though he didn't see her, she thought detachedly.

"Sure, sure. Lie back . . ." He was panting. He pushed her back roughly, his hands fumbling for her breasts, cupping them up and together so they made a narrow channel of flesh for the shaft of his penis. Then he began to rub himself, back and forth, back and forth, with an angry erratic motion. Above her, his face contorted and swayed.

"Like that. Like that. That feels good. So good. Jesus—don't move now. You're so big. Just a little girl and so . . ."

For a second the friction increased frantically, furtively. Then it stopped; his body went rigid, and his breath was expelled in a groan. Hélène had shut her eyes; it was all very very quick. Now she opened them in sudden alarm; he sounded as if he were dying. Then she felt wetness spurt across her breasts and throat. Then he slumped on top of her, breathing hard.

After a few minutes, she pushed him a little, and he rolled off her. Carefully she sat up and swung her legs over the edge of the bed. She looked back at the square of white sheeting. It had been accurately placed; no mess on the silk of his wife's bed. How many times had he done that before—and why there? She didn't care, but she felt coldly curious.

"I should go home now."

He sat up, pulling up the boxer shorts. "Sure. But we better clean you up a bit first."

It was he who fetched the tissues and rubbed at her skin and hair. Quite without embarrassment, she noted. "Best skin lotion in the world." He grinned. "That's what they say, honey."

Hélène put on her dress and zipped it up. She waited silently while he got into his shirt and pants. "Could I have the money now?"

Not "present"—money. She said it quite clearly. She wanted him to know she understood, that she wasn't deceived. Above all, she wanted him to know that she had felt nothing. He had bought himself a good time, that was all.

He frowned. She could see he was offended, but he tried to pass it off.

"You've got kind of a blunt way of putting things." He hesitated, his hand on his jacket. "That all it meant to you? Come on now, honey?"

"I thought you said you liked to give me presents?"

This time she couldn't keep the scorn out of her voice, and he heard it. His face darkened. Very deliberately he took out his billfold. He counted the notes out, tens, onto his wife's dressing table. Thirty. Forty. Fifty. Fifty-five. He gave her a cunning smile and put the billfold back into his pocket.

"I need sixty."

"Five on account. You get that next time you're nice to me."

Hélène looked at him. Then she walked stiffly across the room and picked up the money. He caught her hand.

"Jesus—you're something, you know that? I don't believe this. I've seen more tact in a New Orleans cat house. . . ." His fingers tightened around her wrist. "Come on now, honey—why are you acting this way? I did something to upset you, or what? Hélène, talk to me, say something. You enjoyed yourself, didn't you? I gave you a good time. . . ."

"I have to go now." She freed her wrist and turned. She was starting to shake, and she wanted to get out of the room before he noticed.

"Hélène . . ."

There was a note of pleading in his voice. He lifted his hand to her, and she looked back at him for a moment.

"Hélène, honey, please. Wait a minute. . . ."

"I won't!" Suddenly the anger and the hurt overflowed. She stamped her foot. "I hate you. I hate myself. You shouldn't have done that. You shouldn't."

Her voice rose, and choked. She knew she sounded like a child. She also knew she would never be a child again. She turned quickly and ran from the room.

That night there was a riot in Orangeburg. There were several different versions as to how it started.

Some people said it began when three white men and a white woman came out of a bar, and a Negro man made a remark about the woman as she passed him on Main Street.

Others said it began when three white men in a Chevy tried to pick up a Negro girl, and her boyfriend fought them off when they tried to pull her into the car.

Some people blamed liquor; some blamed local Negro activists, the same ones responsible for the protests about segregation on buses. Some blamed the heat—the humidity was high, and the temperature hadn't dropped below ninety degrees for over a week. Some blamed the state police, others the federal government. But whatever the causes, and however the riot began, its results were clear.

Leroy Smith, aged seventeen, Negro, employed as a mechanic at Haines's garage, Route 48, was pronounced dead on arrival at Montgomery County Hospital, of stab wounds to the heart.

Three other boys, all black, were detained in custody, awaiting trial. Two white boys were held for questioning, and later released. Two store fronts were smashed in; one car was set ablaze. There were no civilian witnesses.

Hélène heard the sirens. They woke her at one in the morning as she lay in her narrow bed, sleeping fitfully. Her mother turned her head, and stirred, but did not wake. The sirens screamed through the dark, and eventually Hélène got up, and went out, and sat on the step outside.

The air was heavy with heat. In the darkness the branches of the trees hardly moved. Thin moonlight shone on the Spanish moss, so the trees seemed to crawl with silver snakes. Thick furry white moths blundered into the light, then back into the shadows. A firefly shone red, then disappeared.

Across the trailer park, she could hear voices, the opening and shutting of doors; and beyond, where the road was, headlights brightened the sky as the sirens screamed past. She sat there for an hour, maybe more, not knowing what had happened, but able to imagine, because it had happened before; she knew what the sirens meant—hatred and death.

After two, the sirens stopped. No more headlights lit the sky. The voices in the trailer park ceased; doors shut. Over in the distance, beyond the cotton fields, she heard the freight train go through, the rattle of its wheels carrying on the still air: hatred and death, hatred and death, hatred and death . . . Its whistle wailed as it went through the Orangeburg crossing; then there was silence.

She sat there still, until—her eyes accustomed to the dark now—she saw a shadow move over beyond the trees. She stood up; the shadow moved again. Then she ran down the steps, across the yard, out through the picket gate.

"Billy?"

He was standing under the trees, his face very pale in the moonlight. Even from where she stood she could see that he was hurt. There was blood on his shirtfront, a long jagged red cut down his cheek.

"Billy! You're hurt. Are you all right? What did they do to you? What happened?"

He took her hands as she reached out to him and held them loosely in his own.

"Leroy's dead. He was getting married next week. I went to the hospital. I knew he must be dead, but I kept thinking. I kept hoping. There were cops everywhere, in the lobby, in the corridors . . . it was swarming with them. They wouldn't let me in. They wouldn't tell me if he was dead or not. A nurse told me finally. His girl was there by then, and when she heard it, she started screaming." He covered his ears with his hands. "I can still hear her. She couldn't believe it—it all happened so quick. I was with them. I saw it. I saw the whole thing. Leroy did nothing—*nothing*, hardly spoke even. And when the knife went in, he didn't even holler. He just doubled up like he was winded. Then his eyes rolled back, and he kicked—just a little bit, with one leg. I knew then. He was my friend. I worked with him three years. I promised him I'd be there—at the wedding."

Quite suddenly, his legs crumpled. He went down into the dirt, in a crouching position, his arms around his body, his head bent. Hélène stood still for a moment, looking down at him, then quickly she crouched beside him, her arms around him. She felt terribly cold, and suddenly very afraid.

"Billy . . ." Her lips had gone so dry, she had to force the words out. "Billy. You saw it? You saw who did it? You recognized them?"

"Yes." He didn't lift his head.

"Billy. Billy. Look at me. Did you tell the police?"

He looked up then, slowly.

"Not yet." He gave a sudden grimace. "Tried to. Seemed to me they had a hearing problem suddenly."

"But you're going to tell them? Make a statement?"

"The station'll be quieter come morning." He shrugged. "I guess I'll go down there then."

He looked up at her then, and lifted his hand to her face. "You're crying." He sounded surprised. "Hélène—why're you crying?"

"You know why. Oh, Billy, you know."

He looked into her eyes steadily for a while. Then, very gently, he wiped the tears away. His face looked quite altered. It had set in hard lines, and Hélène thought he looked older than she had ever seen him. He looked tired, and though his eyes rested on her face, they looked as far away as the summer sky.

"I don't want you to get hurt, Billy."

"I'm not hurt." His mouth twisted into a smile, and she knew he was misunderstanding her deliberately. "Look. It's just a scratch. . . ."

"Billy . . ."

"It's simple. There's no choice. Not if I want to go on living with myself. That's all." He stood up then and drew Hélène to her feet. "One day . . ." He stopped, put his arms around her loosely, started again. "One day—you'll go away from here. I just wish I could go with you, that's all. . . ."

"You could!" Impulsively, Hélène reached out to him. "You could, Billy! We could go together. We don't have to stay here. We could pack up and leave, we could find work somewhere else. Somewhere different! Somewhere that wasn't like this. We could do it, Billy—we could!"

"I wish I thought that. I wish I believed it."

"But you don't."

"No," he said gently. "I don't. But you'll go—I'm certain of that. And it makes me glad. Whatever you do, whatever happens, I'll feel a part of it too. I'll be happy that way. And proud."

Hélène stared at him; then she turned her head away.

"You don't know me, Billy," she said. "You don't. If you knew me, really knew me, you wouldn't say that."

"I know you. Better than you think. And I do say it." Gently he touched her face, turning her back so he could look into her eyes, though Hélène felt he looked into her heart.

"Go back to bed now." He pushed her away gently. "It's late."

"I want to stay. I want to be with you, Billy."

"Not now. I need to be alone. I need to think."

Hélène got up at six. Although the sun was low, it was already very hot, the damp heavy oppressive heat that could only be broken by a storm. Next to her mother's bed, on the little yellow chest, was the neat pile of green dollars she had given her mother the previous night. She would see it again, first thing, on waking.

Hélène cleaned up the little kitchen: no dishes from the night before; once again, her mother hadn't eaten. She straightened the now threadbare paisley shawl over the chair. She swept the floor and wiped down the oilcloth, and then carefully arranged the breakfast dishes for her mother and herself. She drew water from the pump and heated it, and then, when she heard her mother stirring, she took it in to her so she could wash.

"Clean things," her mother said when she sat up. "I need clean things, Hélène."

It took her a long while to get ready. When she finally came out into the kitchen, Hélène could see the effort she had made. Her hair was carefully combed; she had made up her face, so her mouth looked startlingly red against the pallor of her skin. She had put on mascara, and it had smudged a little. She was wearing her best dress, and her best shoes, with high thin heels. They needed mending. She glanced down at them regretfully as she sat down, then adjusted the seams of her stockings.

"My last new pair." She smiled at Hélène vaguely. "I've been keeping them back."

Hélène quietly made her tea, but her mother took only a few sips, without milk. She wouldn't eat anything. Hélène sat down and leaned across the table.

"Mother. Mother. I want you to listen to me."

Her mother looked up. The violet eyes met Hélène's, and then slid away.

"Mother, please. It's important. I've been thinking. We have to leave here, Mother. We have to."

"Of course, darling. I know that." Again the violet eyes turned to Hélène's face, and again Hélène knew her mother hardly saw her, let alone listened to her. Helplessly, she reached across and took her mother's hand.

"Listen, Mother, oh, please listen. I know we always talked about it before, when I was little, and we planned, and we tried to save, and then we forgot it for a while, and then we talked about it again. But I don't mean it like that, Mother. Not now. I mean it seriously. We have to go—right away from here. It's . . . it's a bad place. A horrible place. It gets into your bones and your mind. It . . . it takes all your energy away and all your willpower." She broke off. Her mother was not listening.

"Mother." She set her mouth. "I'm going to write Elizabeth. Your sister Elizabeth. I'm going to write to her today."

That got through to her. Hélène saw the comprehension come back into her mother's eyes. She pressed her hand more tightly.

"I'm going to write to her, Mother, and explain. I'm going to tell her how ill you've been, and how we need help." She drew in her breath. "I'm going to ask her to send us the fare back to England. I'm sure she'll help us, Mother. She's your sister. You've never asked her for anything else. And if she won't help . . . then I'm going to leave school. Not in two years, now. I'm going to leave school, and get a job and earn the money. It might take a bit longer, but I can do it, Mother, I know I can. I can take two jobs, the way Billy Tanner used to. Work evenings as well as days. I'm young, Mother! I could do it easily. A year from now, we'd have enough. Think of it, Mother. Just one more year, that's all! Maybe not that long. If Elizabeth helped us, it could be a couple of months, a few weeks. . . ."

Her mother moved, a quick jerky movement back from the table. Her ankle caught the leg of the chair as she moved, and her stocking snagged against the rough wood. There was a little silence. Slowly her mother extended her leg and looked down. As she stretched her leg, the white run made its way up the stocking from ankle to knee. She looked up at Hélène. She said, "I'm pregnant."

It was not a word Hélène had ever heard her mother use. She said it in a small flat voice, without emotion. Then she gave a little cough and cleared her throat.

"Two months. Eight weeks. They'll do it up to three months, but the longer you leave it, the more dangerous it is. At two months it should be quite safe. I have the money now—thank you for that, Hélène. I shall go over to Montgomery today and get it seen to."

She spoke as if she were having a tooth out that had been troubling her.

"Mother . . ."

"It's perfectly all right, darling. I know it's against the law, but it's a very silly unrealistic law, and, thank goodness, there always have been doctors who recognize that and are prepared to help you. Doctors—and other people of course. They used to say that Mississippi Mary did something of that kind occasionally, but I don't know about that. I wouldn't go anywhere like that, so you needn't worry. The man in

Montgomery is a proper doctor. He has qualifications. Medical qualifications. I shall be perfectly all right." Her mother paused. Carefully she removed her hand from Hélène's. She raised her eyes and looked out the window. Her face was composed, her voice level.

"He'll do it today. I believe it's very quick and quite simple. I shall be home this evening, at about six, because you have to rest for a little while after the operation. And when I get back, we'll talk about all your plans, darling. Tonight. Or tomorrow. But you do see, don't you, Hélène, that I can't really think about them now?" She paused, and gave a little frown, as if she were trying to remember something that had slipped her mind, something very minor—an item on a shopping list maybe.

"I hadn't intended to tell you this, of course. It's not something one discusses really, is it?" She gave a faint smile. "But I think, on the whole, that you ought to know. You see, I've been very stupid, I understand that now. And I'd like to believe you wouldn't make the same mistakes. You should never trust a man, Hélène. Never rely on them, ever." She lifted her hand in a vague waving gesture. "It's very difficult, of course. One thinks one's in love—women do think that. And then one is so terribly vulnerable. I sometimes think, if women didn't fall in love so foolishly, their lives would be much simpler and much happier. They wouldn't believe the lies, then, you see. I believed your father's lies, Hélène. And he lied about everything. He said . . . he said he had a farm to return to when he got out of the army. He said we'd live in a lovely house, and when I arrived here, I found I had to live in a quite horrible little bungalow place, with his mother and father and brothers and sisters. He said he worshipped the ground I walked on, Hélène. . . ." She hesitated fractionally. "And I don't know why, but it was wartime, and Americans seemed so glamorous then, and he was quite unlike anyone I'd ever met before. And so I married him, and I came over here, with you, a tiny baby. And then I found out that none of it was true. None of it. Then I left, of course. I had my pride." She stopped, and her eyes returned to Hélène's face. "You were born in England, darling. I always thought that was very important to remember. You will always remember it, won't you?"

"Mother. Please. Stop. Don't go on." Hélène bent her head, and her mother sighed.

"Yes, well, I suppose you're right. There's absolutely no point in thinking about the past. I do realize that now. I've thought about the past far too much. And there's really no point, because one learns nothing from it at all. History repeats itself. One simply goes on making the same mistakes, and listening to the same lies—exactly the same ones, just said by a different voice—and one believes them." She pushed the cup and saucer away from her, flicked the teaspoon idly with her finger.

"Well, I shall never do it again. Not after today. And I hope you've been listening to me, Hélène, because it's very important to me that you understand what I've said. You're a woman now, darling, and your life is just beginning, and —"

She stopped quite suddenly, so Hélène looked up. She was looking at the clock on the wall. The old red stickers were still there, in the old positions, now grubby and faded, but still there.

"Do you remember how you used to wait for me, darling, when Mother went out? You were such a good child." She smiled fondly at a space somewhere above Hélène's head. "There was a gray and white dress, from Bergdorf Goodman's. Such a lovely dress! Pure silk. I hadn't seen silk for years. Not since before the war. That was when it began, with that dress. Oh, it had started before that, in a mild way. I used to see him looking at me sometimes, when I went up to the house to do his wife's hair. But that was the first time I ever agreed to meet him. The day after he gave me that dress . . ."

Hélène felt her body go rigid in the chair. Sickness crawled in her stomach. Dreamily, her mother's voice went on.

"It was so lovely, Hélène. He used to take me for drives around the plantation. And there was an old summerhouse in the garden, where we used to meet. It was a little tumbledown, of course, but it reminded me of my childhood. We had a summerhouse quite like that, in the house where I grew up. I remember telling him. He was very interested. He can be such a charming man: so good-looking, and such perfect manners. . . ."

She trailed off momentarily, as if something in her memory did not quite tally with her words, and Hélène clenched her fingernails into the palms of her hands.

"It was very romantic, Hélène. It's important you understand that. I wouldn't like you to think I was involved in anything—well, sordid, or unpleasant. Oh, I knew he was married, of course, but he was unhappily married, and somehow that seemed to make a difference. I thought . . . well, there was a time when I thought that he would get a divorce and marry me. He said he wanted to, you see, and there were no children, so it could have been quite simple. Except the money is all hers. It's her money that keeps the plantation going. So, of course, it would have been difficult for him, I understood that. I never pressured him, Hélène—I think it's so vulgar somehow, when women do that. I was prepared to wait. He talked about marriage quite often. We used to plan—oh, you know, silly things. What we would do with the house when we lived there. How we would decorate it. How we should entertain. Mrs.

Calvert never entertained much, which seemed to me very wrong, considering who she is, and her position here. I would have behaved very differently. . . ."

"Mother—please!"

"Well, I did believe him, Hélène." Her mother's voice contained a mild rebuke. "Do you remember that evening—when you had counted the money, and you talked about going back to England, and we quarreled? I did try to tell you then—how it might have been. He'd promised me then, you see, that he'd talk to his wife." She paused. "He never did, needless to say. I don't think he meant to lie, not exactly. Men never do. They tell lies, and they half-believe them at the time. That's why you have to be so careful, Hélène. It's why it's so terribly easy to believe them."

"Mother." Hélène leaned forward. All she could think was that somehow she had to get her mother to stop, stop this terrible calm mad conversation. The urgency in her voice had some effect. The dreamy violet eyes turned back to her.

"Yes, darling?"

"Mother—does he know?"

"About this, darling?" Her mother smiled. "No. Of course not." She hesitated. "You see, darling, he has someone else."

"Someone else?" Hélène's face went white.

"I don't know who, naturally. It's not my concern. I think, to be honest, that there were probably always . . . others. Now and again. Colored women. His father was like that—or so I've heard. He's a southerner. It's in his blood. It's just a thing he has—I didn't want to know about it, and if it happened, it happened. It was quite a different thing between him and me—I knew that. In our case, it went on for a long time. A very long time. Sometimes we would quarrel, of course, and there were periods—sometimes quite long periods—when we didn't meet. But in the end he would always come back to me. I think he did love me, Hélène. For a time. Until quite recently, we still met fairly often. Not as often as before, but he still needed me. Sometimes. Then this happened, which was very stupid of me, very careless, but he'd been away in Philadelphia for two months, and I was so glad to see him when he got back. . . ." She stopped for a moment, her face softening, then took a small sip of her tea.

"You know, I'm quite proud of myself, Hélène, for saying nothing. I could have told him, I suppose. It would have been so easy to plead and weep, but really, I couldn't bear to do that. So I just shan't see him again, that's all. He need never know, Hélène. The thing is"—she paused—"he reminded me of your father, I think. I'm sure that was it. That was why it all began. The first time I met your father, I was wearing a silk frock—such a lovely frock, Hélène, pale mauve, and I used to pin a rose on the shoulder. We went to the Café Royal, I remember, a large party of us—it was such a brilliant evening, so gay, and everyone so charming. I knew then that your father admired me. I could see it—"

She broke off abruptly. She bent her head, then shook it slightly, as if to clear her mind. Her eyes, which had begun to sparkle, went dull again.

"Seventeen years ago. And now this. How stupid."

Hélène stood up. When he got back from Philadelphia. Two months ago. She pressed her hands down flat on the table to stop herself shaking.

"I'd like to kill him," she said. "Oh, God, I'd like to kill him."

Her mother looked up abstractedly, as if she hadn't spoken. Then she turned her face to the clock on the icebox; the hands were on nine. She stood up. "Would you fetch my bag, Hélène? I've packed up some things I might need. It's in the bedroom."

I t was impossible to move in Orangeburg without being watched. It was one of the things Hélène most hated about the place.

"Spit in Main Street at two," Billy used to say when they were kids. "Go over to Maybury at three, they'll tell you where the spit landed."

Sometimes Hélène could see the watchers. There were plenty of people in Orangeburg with nothing better to do than lounge against the store fronts and gossip, especially when the weather was mean and hot, the way it was now. Sometimes it was just a curtain, moving at a window, or a shadow on the screen; still, she could feel the eyes.

Today it was bad, worse than usual. Two storefronts were boarded up; there was broken plate glass on the sidewalk. Not a colored person in sight—just groups of white men and white women, huddled conversations that broke off as she and her mother went past, and started up again the moment they went by.

The wreck of the burned-out car had been shifted. At the end of Main Street, a squad car was pulled up in a patch of shade; on its roof a blue light revolved and revolved. Dust in the air; tension you could smell. Hélène and her mother stood by the bus stop, and the air shimmered.

The bus stop was right outside Cassie Wyatt's beauty parlor. Right in the sun; there was no shade. Her mother seemed not to notice the heat. She just stood there, clutching the small carryall, staring down the street the way the bus would come. Hélène was not to go into Montgomery with her; her mother wouldn't let her.

After a while, Cassie Wyatt came out, still wearing the smock she wore to cut hair. It was Saturday morning, and she must have been busy. Through the glass, Hélène could see all four dryers going full blast. One of the new assistants was cutting hair, another was washing hair at the new basins Cassie had just installed. Basins with a scoop for the neck, so you bent backwards, not forward, to have your hair washed. Cassie was proud of the new basins: they were the latest thing.

Hélène saw her come toward her mother, and then, as she looked at her, saw Cassie's face change. She stopped, her eyes shocked, then she stepped forward and put her hand on Hélène's mother's arm.

"Violet? Violet—you okay?" She drew back, and Hélène saw her glance down at the small carryall.

"I'm fine, thank you, Cassie. I'm just waiting for the Montgomery bus." Her mother hardly turned her head.

"You want to come in and sit down for a bit? It's so hot, and that darned bus—well, you never know when that'll turn up. Could be another half hour. Come in and rest your feet. I've got the fans on. . . ."

"Thank you, Cassie, but I think I see the bus coming now." Her mother turned her face then, slightly. One tear slowly rolled down her cheek, and she brushed it away.

Cassie's plain features softened; she looked genuinely distressed. "Come on, Violet," she said gently. "You don't look well. Come in and rest awhile. You can go in back if you prefer. It's quiet there. There's plenty more buses. Go in later, why don't you?"

"I have to go in now. I have an *appointment*, Cassie."

Her mother made it sound like something grand, a business meeting, an important lunch. She lifted her hand and waved at the bus. She was wearing white fabric gloves with a small darn on one of the fingers.

"It's all right, Cassie," Hélène muttered. People were starting to stare. Inside the salon, one of the assistants stopped cutting to watch.

Along the street the dust rose as the bus approached.

Cassie turned to Hélène. "You going with your mother, Hélène?"

"No. She's not going with me." Her mother answered. Hélène dragged her shoe in the dirt.

"I'm waiting for her, Cassie," she said awkwardly. "I'll be meeting the bus when she gets back."

The bus pulled up; the doors hissed open. Her mother hesitated. "Do I have my purse? Oh, yes. Here it is." She turned quickly to Hélène and placed a dry kiss on her cheek. "Good-bye, darling. I'll see you tonight. Around six . . ."

Then she climbed aboard. The doors hissed shut. There was a blue belch of diesel, and the bus pulled off. Hélène lifted her hand to wave, and then dropped it again. She looked at her watch, her sixteenth birthday present; she shook it, because sometimes it stopped. But it was ticking okay. It was ten o'clock.

She wanted to do a lot of things. She wanted to go back to the trailer and just lie down on the little bed and cry. She wanted to go up to the plantation and shoot Ned Calvert in the heart. She wanted to write to Elizabeth and mail the letter right away. She wanted to talk to Billy. She wanted to get the next bus into Montgomery, and find her mother, and take her home. She wanted to set the clock back a month, a year, as far back as she could, till before all this happened, all this began. She wanted not to hear her mother's voice anymore, calm, self-deluding, telling her all those things and ripping a torn world further apart.

In the end she just walked up Main Street and turned off past the gas station, around back of the parking lot. There was some vacant land there, and real estate signs announcing a new building development.

No one went there. There was a falling-down tin shack that gave some shade, and Hélène sat down, staring in front of her, willing the time to pass. She looked at the clumps of nettles and old strip of concrete path, a wall covered in poison ivy. There had been a house here once; where she sat had been part of its garden. She shut her eyes against the heat, and her mind said: *England, Europe, England.* After a while, she got up again and began to walk back toward the gas station. Then she stopped.

A long black open-topped Cadillac was parked by the pumps. Ned Calvert was leaning up against the trunk. He had his back to her, and he was busy talking. There was a whole group of them, five white men. Merv Peters was there, and a younger man—Eddie Haines, she thought. Then two others she didn't recognize. One of them had a hunting rifle slung over his shoulder.

She watched them for a while, crouching back against the wall. Then she turned and crept away, going around the back way to Main Street. Down an alleyway, past garbage cans, and backyards strung with washing. Past a wall on which someone had painted the letters *KKK* in red paint. She looked at the letters and spat. Then she walked on.

She hung around on Main Street for a while, pretending to look in store windows, waiting for the next bus back from Montgomery. For some crazy reason, she thought her mother might be on it. But only two white men got off. The bus pulled away. *Please God*, Hélène thought. *Let her be safe. Let her be okay.*

She knew what kind of a place her mother would be going, in spite of what she said. Rich people didn't go to Montgomery to get abortions, even she knew that much. They went out of state. They took a plane to Puerto Rico or Mexico, where there were private clinics that did that kind of thing. Susie Marshall had known someone who had known someone who had done it once. Either that, or they paid a smart doctor, a really expensive doctor, to say they needed the operation for medical reasons. What kind of doctor did abortions for seventy dollars? And how did they do it? *I don't know*, Susie Marshall had said that time. *I guess they sort of scrape it out. I mean, it's not a real baby, is it? It's just sort of Jell-O. I guess . . .*

Hélène shivered. She felt sick. Her throat was so dry she could hardly swallow. She desperately wanted a drink of water, and she wondered if she dared go into Merv Peters's and order a soda. He wasn't there, she knew that. . . . She walked along the street and peered inside. Priscilla-Anne wasn't there either; it was all right. There was a girl she didn't know serving at the counter.

Hélène pushed open the door and went in. Cold air hit her. Merv Peters had had air conditioners installed the previous year, and a jukebox. It was playing now.

She seated herself on a tall stool by the window, from where she could see Main Street and the bus stop. There were some girls from Selma High over in a corner by the jukebox, giggling and talking in hushed tones. If they saw her come in, they carefully took no notice.

"A soda, please." She counted out a little bundle of nickels. The girl slid the cold glass across the counter.

"Thank you."

"You're welcome."

An Elvis Presley record came to an end; one of the girls in the corner slid a quarter into the slot, punched some buttons. A rich Negro voice singing *Blue Moon* filled the room, deep, husky, lingering, sad. The white girls leaned back in their chairs, quieter now, their eyes dreamy.

They played it three times in succession. Hélène made the soda last that long. Then she slid off the stool and walked out. She liked that record. And she knew she never wanted to hear it again. Not as long as she lived. Never.

"Billy Tanner . . ."

One of the girls by the jukebox spoke the name; the door closed on her words. Hélène looked down the street and saw what they had seen.

Billy was walking down the sidewalk on Main Street. He was alone, and walking slowly. As he walked, he was watched. Cassie Wyatt came to the door of her salon; one of her assistants craned her head to look out the window. Outside the hardware store, a man was sweeping the sidewalk; he stopped sweeping and leaned on his broom. He was in

Billy's way, blocking the sidewalk, but he didn't move aside. Billy had to step off into the street to go past.

He passed the patrol car, still with its blue light revolving, and one of the policemen got out. He leaned against its door, just watching, one hand on the roof, one hand on his holster. Quite suddenly, the street was silent. No one called out; no one moved. A woman coming out of Merv Peters's grocery store hesitated, a big bag of shopping in her arms. She had a child with her. She looked down the street, then down at the child, then she pushed open the grocery store door and dragged the child back inside. Hélène glanced behind her. The girls from Selma High had left the jukebox; they were all crowding around the window, their faces pale, their eyes round with expectation. One of them had her hair in curlers. Hélène looked back at the street; light glinted on glass and hot metal. Billy kept on walking. Down by the gas station, a powerful engine revved, and then gunned.

Hélène stood still for a moment, under the canopy, in the shade. Then she ran out into the heat of the street, across the road, onto the far sidewalk. She took Billy's arm.

"Billy," she said. "Billy. Let's go home. Let's go swimming." Her clear English voice carried way down the street. Billy looked down at her; he shook his head, tried to release his arm, but Hélène took no notice. She clasped it more tightly. Billy sighed, then smiled, and they walked on.

Neither of them spoke. They walked side by side, down Main Street, past the stores, past the confusion of houses, used-car lots, and liquor shops that marked the outskirts of town. They came out past the first cotton fields, crossed the tracks by the Orangeburg crossing, passed the old decaying frame houses built for whites, where Negroes now lived; passed the square brick Southern Baptist chapel, and the big sign that said JESUS SAVES! All the way a black Cadillac kept ten yards behind them.

Halfway between the town and the trailer park, Hélène stopped. Billy tried to make her go on alone, but she held on tight to his arm, and wouldn't move. The Cadillac slowed, approached, came alongside. Ned Calvert couldn't look at her—he kept his eyes on the road ahead—but the others did. Five grinning white faces, two up front, three in back, sun glinting on chrome tail fins and the barrel of a hunting rifle. Hélène stared at them: Ned Calvert, Merv Peters, Eddie Haines, the two others she didn't recognize.

"You looking for something?" Suddenly she screamed the words at them. "You want to say what it is you're looking for?" Her words bounced off the chrome, were swallowed up into the hot silent air. One of the men laughed.

Eddie Haines took the gum out of his mouth and flicked it into the road.

"You just lost yourself a job, boy. . . ." he called, and touched Ned Calvert's shoulder.

The Cadillac swerved in close, dust rising. Then it pulled away fast. Hélène watched it disappear. Then she looked at her watch. Past noon, almost one. The sun was almost vertical over their heads as they turned off the highway and began slowly to walk toward the trailer park.

"You shouldn't go gettin' yourself involved." Billy's blue eyes looked down into hers. "You know where I'd been?"

"To the police station? Of course I knew."

"You shouldn't have done it." He shook his head. "I don't want trouble for you."

"Billy." She pressed his arm. "It's hot. Let's swim." They were standing under the cotton trees, in the still, shaded air. The shadows of branches striped their skin. There was no sound except their breathing.

"Hélène?"

"I want to swim, Billy."

She stepped back from him; light and shadow glanced in her mind. The heat of the morning, and the cool of the cottonwoods. She knew exactly what she meant to do. Not why—but the "why" didn't matter; it was very unimportant, very small.

Billy was watching her, his body tense and wary, as if he could sense something hectic and wild in her behind the calm of her voice.

Hélène lifted her hands, which did not shake at all, and began to unbutton her blouse. She took off the blouse, her wristwatch, the blue jeans, the sandals, the underclothes. Billy never moved. When she was naked, she stood still for a moment; Billy sighed. Then she turned, and slipped like a fish into the cold brown water. She surfaced, and tossed back her wet hair from her face, rivulets of water glittering like diamonds on her arms.

"Please, Billy. . . ."

For a moment she thought he was going to refuse, though she knew he understood. Then, slowly, he pulled off his shirt, eased off his sneakers. He kept his jeans on, and came into the water slowly, the water inching up over his body, as if he were going to a baptism. When the water was up to his chest, he paused; then he smiled at her, a slow crooked smile. Suddenly he ducked his head down and under the water, and came up in a shower of spray. He laughed, a loud sudden shout of pure elation that echoed through the trees; then he swam in the water beside her.

They swam for a long while, side by side, back and forth, never touching. Hélène climbed out first. She stood on a part of the bank that sloped gently, a hollow of ferns and shadows. She waited. She knew he would come to her; she knew time had stopped; she knew Orangeburg didn't exist, nor Montgomery, nor the past, nor the future. There was just—this: one right thing in a world gone crazy.

Finally Billy came out of the water. He climbed up the bank and stood beside her, looking down into her face. A kingfisher flash of blue; eyes that were sad and troubled.

"I can't," he said at last. "Not now. Not like this. I can't do the wrong thing by you—you know that."

"The right thing! The *right* thing!" She lifted her hands and rested them against his chest. "It's very important. I know you understand."

"I understand." He covered her hands lightly with his, pressed them.

"That doesn't make it right. Now. Here . . ."

"*Especially* here." She lowered her head. "I want you to be the *first*, Billy."

She felt his hands tighten over hers, and his body give a little jerk. She glanced up quickly.

"You knew? You knew I was seeing Ned Calvert?"

"I saw you together one time." Billy shrugged. "I knew better than to say anything. Knew you'd find out soon enough—what he is. It was better that way."

"Don't talk about him! I don't want to think about him! Billy, please—I'll never ask you for anything else ever again. Just this."

"I loved you a long time. So long. Long as I can remember." He shook his head; a tremor ran through his body. "If I'd thought you loved me back . . . if I'd ever thought that . . ."

He paused, and as Hélène opened her mouth to speak, he lifted one finger gently to her lips. "Don't you go telling lies now. No lies, you hear? There's no need for lies. Not between you and me . . ."

Hélène looked up at him. His face looked gentle, and his eyes immeasurably sad. Slowly she lifted her arms and wound them around his neck, her breasts brushing against his bare chest. She pressed her lips to his cheek, then softly against his mouth. Then she drew back.

"I know I'm right. I know I was never more right in my whole life." Her blue eyes blazed up at him. "I know I could make you, Billy . . ."

"I know it too." Billy smiled. "I understand. There's no need for that."

Gently he put his arms around her, then he drew her down onto the ground beside him. He looked into her eyes then, as if there were something he wanted her to understand, something he couldn't say.

"First and last." He frowned slightly. "You were always that, Hélène. Where I begin and where I end. That's all. Tell me you know that."

"I know." Her voice broke.

"That's all right then," Billy said.

As he bent his head, and kissed her lips, she heard a bird stir among the branches.

W hen they lay beside the pool, Billy had three hours left to live. They killed him just around five, where the track from the trailer park met the Orangeburg road.

Hélène heard the shot when she was halfway down the track, starting the walk back to Orangeburg to meet her mother. She stopped; the noise was very loud; a flock of ring doves rose clattering from the trees, wheeled over her head, then settled again in the silence. Then she heard running feet, the tearing of undergrowth, the slam of a car door, the screech of wheels on dusty tarmac. When she reached the place where they had left him, the air still smelled of scorched rubber. Billy was lying on his back in the grass by the side of the highway. His hands were relaxed; he lay in an attitude of sleep except that his eyes were open.

She fell to her knees by his side, panting. There was a film of sweat across his forehead; the freckles across his cheekbones were each distinct; his hand was warm to the touch. She thought: *He's all right; they didn't do it; they missed; they meant to scare him is all; he's all right.* Then she saw the red and the grayish-white on the grass, seeping out of the back of his head. She gave a cry and put her hands down to cradle his head, to heal the wound, to hold him together, to piece him back, to hide him—she didn't know what. Then his head lolled and she saw what they had done with their shotgun; the back of his head had gone; Billy had gone. She lifted her head like an animal and started to scream.

T here were so many people, suddenly so many. She couldn't imagine where they came from so quickly, or why, when there was nothing they could do—it was too late. Children, dragged hastily to one side; the young couple from the trailer park; a man passing in his car, who stopped, and then turned into the bushes and threw up; the doctor from Orangeburg—who had called *him*? Couldn't they see Billy didn't need a doctor, not now? They were all looking, looking, and she hated them for it. She crouched over Billy, because she didn't want them to see him, not the way he was, and they didn't understand, they kept pulling at her, and saying things, and trying to get her to move.

Then there was a ripple, a sound like a sigh; she saw feet moving back. She looked up, and Mrs. Tanner came through the crowd. She had the latest baby on her hip, its fat legs hooked around her flowered pinafore. She stopped, and put the baby down.

Then she knelt down next to Hélène. She didn't cry out; she didn't speak; she just looked. She lifted Billy's hand and held it in hers. One of Billy's shirt buttons was undone; gently she laid his hand down and did up the button. As she did so the rain began, quite suddenly, the way it did after the hot days. Heavy drops splashed onto her head, onto Billy's shirt. She put her hands out, fingers splayed, as if she could keep the rain off him.

"His new shirt. His clean shirt. I just laundered this shirt." She lifted her head and her eyes met Hélène's with the same blue gaze as her son's. "My oldest. My firstborn son. Billy . . ." Her voice rose. She reached forward and shook him suddenly, as if she could wake him from this deep sleep. "Billy. What they done to you? What they done to my boy?"

Then she bent down and cradled him in her arms. She stayed that way until the police came. When they tried to move her, she hit out at them with her arms, wildly, then stopped, her eyes focusing on Hélène's face as if she saw her for the first time. She pushed her violently, her hands wet with rain and blood, her face suddenly contorted with hate.

"You get away from him, you hear? Just get away. What you want with my son? I warned him about you. I told him. Stay clear of that girl. I said, that girl is trouble, Billy, you look at her and you'll get hurt. Way back when he was a little kid I told him. . . ."

The hate went out of her body then; one moment she was rigid with it, the next it was gone. She went limp, and they moved her away. The baby began to cry; the air flashed white and blue; the ambulance siren screamed; the people were being moved back.

Hélène stood up and groped her way to the side of the road. She crouched there, while behind her, people moved, and shouted instructions, and the baby's cry grew to a howl. She was still crouching there when Cassie Wyatt pulled up in her old beaten-up Ford. She went over to the patrol car; she said something; she came back to Hélène. She bent down to her, her face furrowed and gray with tiredness, and lifted her to her feet.

"Get in the car, honey. Just get in. That's right. You're doin' fine. You got to come with me now, honey. Your mama needs you. She's askin' for you. Hélène—you hear what I'm saying to you?" She turned on the ignition. "Your mama needs you, honey, needs you real bad. . . ."

Her mother had come back on the four o'clock bus, two hours early. She had collapsed on the sidewalk outside Cassie's beauty parlor, and Cassie closed up shop and took her inside. When she saw the bleeding, she got her into the Ford and drove to the Catholic hospital in Maybury. There was a bigger hospital nearer Orangeburg, but you had to have medical insurance to go there. "No Blue Cross card, they let you die on the sidewalk," Cassie said.

The nuns knew what had happened. When they realized, Cassie said, their faces went pale and shut, but they took Violet in just the same. The first transfusion seemed to work. When Hélène and Cassie got there that evening, her mother was conscious. There was a crucifix above her bed, and an IV in her arm, and a woman at the end of the ward who kept groaning. Hélène looked down into her mother's face. Her skin looked white and papery, stretched very tight across the bones. Her hands rested on cool white starched sheets; air-conditioning whispered; outside, the rain fell.

"This is a very nice place, Cassie," she said. "They have a garden. One of the nuns told me. They let you sit out there, you know. When you're better."

It was the last thing Hélène heard her say. They gave her a second transfusion during the night. She died fifteen minutes before Cassie and Hélène got there the next morning. The sister who told them had a soft calm voice. She sounded as if she were praying. After a while, she stood up; the beads of her rosary glittered against the black of her skirt. Her mother was ready now, she said. Hélène could see her.

They drew the cotton curtains around the bed, and the sister stood back, but did not leave her. Hélène looked down at her mother. The IV had been removed, the bed tidied. Her mother's hands were crossed on her chest, and her eyes were closed. Her features looked sharp and peaked. She didn't look like her mother at all, Hélène thought. When she bent, finally, and rested her lips against her mother's forehead, her skin was dry and cold. She didn't know what to do after that. There seemed nothing to stay for—her mother was not here—but she didn't like to leave either.

After a while, the sister sighed, and took her by the arm, and led her away. She gave her a neatly labeled shopping bag with her mother's clothes, and the zip-up carryall she had taken with her into Montgomery. Hélène opened it when she got back to Cassie's. Inside there was a freshly laundered handkerchief, some clean underclothes, a comb, and a small notebook with nothing written in it. The underclothes were neatly folded around something hard and square. When Hélène opened them up, she found the old box of Joy, which her mother used to perfume her things, since, in Alabama, even the notions departments had never heard of lavender sachets.

Her mother died on the Sunday morning; the funeral was the following Wednesday, and Cassie and Hélène were the only mourners. Cassie paid for two big wreaths, fashioned from mauve *immortelles*, one in the shape of a circle, the other a heart. Hélène knew her mother would have hated them. All the way back from the Orangeburg cemetery, Cassie fretted.

"They should've been violets," she said over and over. "I know she would have liked that. I had to settle for the color, that's all. They last well—that's a comfort. But they should have been violets. I just wished they'd had some of those."

That evening she tried to make Hélène eat, and Hélène tried, too, because she knew Cassie was being kind, and she didn't want to hurt her feelings. She managed a little of Cassie's fried chicken, but every mouthful choked her. At last Cassie quietly took the plates away. When she came back into the room her face was flushed, and she had a manila envelope in her hand. She put it down on the table, then she sat down opposite Hélène. She looked awkward, and fidgety.

"We got to talk this through, honey," she said at last. "We got to. You ain't cried. You ain't said one single solitary thing nearly. We got to talk it through."

She hesitated, and when Hélène said nothing, she burst out, "Honey, you can't stay in Orangeburg, not now. You got to go someplace else, some place real far from here. Your mother, she had a sister in England. She used to tell me about her, and the house where they grew up and all. I figure you ought to go to her. She's your own flesh and blood. I figure—when she knows about your mother—she'll be glad to take you in. Your daddy now—" she stopped—"I thought about him too. But Violet never wanted nothing from him. Told me once she didn't know if he was alive or dead and didn't care either. And I know for sure he never lifted one finger to find you all, or help you, and Violet wouldn't go to him, no matter when things were hard. But her sister . . . I think Violet would have wanted that. She talked about England so much. Not so much of late, it's true. But in the old days. When she first came to work with me. If she could speak now, Hélène, I reckon that's what she'd say."

She paused, the color rising in her cheeks. Then she pushed the manila envelope across the table.

"Five hundred dollars. Take it, honey. It's yours."

Hélène stared at the envelope; slowly she raised her head. Cassie nodded and smiled.

"I kept it by me. Kept it for a rainy day, as the saying goes." She shrugged. "Then I thought—what the hell am I keepin' it for? I ain't as young as I was; I got no kids of my own; the business is doing fine now. I don't need it. You do." She leaned across the table. "Honey, I checked. You got enough there to get a train and a plane. A ticket out, and a bit left over to help you get started in England. I wish it was more, that's all. I was real fond of your mama, Hélène. I reckon I owed her a lot, helpin' me get started with the business the way she did. And it hurts my heart to think of all the things went wrong for her. So you take it now, you hear me? You take it, or I'll start gettin' mad. . . ."

Hélène rested her hand on the envelope. She kept it there a moment, then slowly she slid it back across the table.

"Cassie," she began slowly. "Cassie—I can't. I'm grateful to you— more grateful than I could ever say. But I can't take this. It wouldn't be right. And anyway . . . you must know, Cassie. You saw. I can't go. Not now."

Cassie's mouth tightened. "You mean that Tanner business—that what you mean?"

"I know who did it." Hélène's voice was steady. "I know why they killed Billy. And I know who. I'm not going. Not until I've said what I know."

There was a silence. Cassie suddenly looked terribly tired. She leaned her face on her hands, and when she straightened up, her voice was sharp with anger.

"Don't folks *ever* learn? I took you for a lot of things, Hélène Craig, but I never took you for a fool until now. You got a head on your shoulders, girl—you use it." She leaned back in her chair and folded her arms. "Okay, you got something to tell. You tell me. You saw them, did you? Saw their faces? Saw the gun in their hands? Saw the gun go off?"

"No—not exactly . . ." Hélène looked at her in confusion. "But they did it to stop Billy talking, to stop him giving evidence about the other night. I know that! You know it—everyone in Orangeburg knows it! You saw Billy when he came out of the police station—you must have seen the car following him."

"I saw the Calvert Cadillac. Saw the folks in the car. Saw it drive off down Main Street." Cassie's mouth snapped shut. "Couldn't say if it was following you and Billy or not. It was just drivin'—that's all I saw."

"Well, it's not all *I* saw. . . ." Hélène's voice rose in indignation. "I saw them all talking—up by the gas station. Ned Calvert. Merv Peters. Eddie Haines. Two others. One of them had a hunting rifle. They followed us down the road, nearly to the trailer park. Then Eddie Haines shouted out that Billy just lost himself his job. Then they drove off. . . ."

"It ain't a crime firing a man. Not as I know of. Not in this state. Shooting's a crime. Sometimes . . ." She sighed, and her voice softened. "Hélène, honey, can't you see what I'm sayin' to you? You go down to the station, they'll laugh in your face. You got no evidence, honey. None at all."

"I haven't?" Hélène looked at her uncertainly.

"Honey, if you'd seen them do it, you know what'd happen? The same thing happened to Billy, that's all." She gave a bitter smile. "You'd find the whole machinery of justice just run out of gas. Its wheels'd turn so slow you wouldn't believe it. And then you'd end up the way Billy did. Dead. Hit by an automobile. Drowned swimming in the river. How long you lived in this place, honey? How come you don't know things like that?" She stopped, her fingers resting on the manila envelope. Slowly she pushed it back across the table.

"You think Billy Tanner'd want you to get hurt any more than your mama would? When it'll do no good. When it won't change one thing? When you didn't see enough, and if you had, you'd never make it to a court to say so? Billy was no fool, 'spite of what folks said 'round here. When he went down to that station he knew—knew he was puttin' a noose right around his neck. That was his *choice*, honey, don't you see? You ain't got a choice, not unless you're figurin' on dyin' along with Billy. So you take that money and you go. First thing. Soon as you can. There's a train in the morning. . . ." She pushed the envelope under Hélène's hand.

"Think of it as a loan, honey. Think of it any ways you like. But take it. Take it for me, okay? I've seen enough hate and enough killin'." Hélène slowly picked up the envelope. She raised her eyes to Cassie's face.

"It was Ned Calvert," she said slowly. "Maybe he didn't hold the gun himself, but he was involved. He killed Billy. And he killed my mother."

She saw Cassie's eyes widen as she took in Hélène's words. Then slowly her face composed itself again. She rested her hands on the table and levered herself tiredly to her feet. She turned away.

"I hear a lot of talk when I'm workin'," she said quietly. "Women's talk. I heard a lot of talk about Ned Calvert. I heard talk about your mama. I even heard talk about you—and sometimes it was all three together. I don't want to hear no more. It makes me so weary, my bones start to ache. I thought Ned Calvert was one smart sonuvabitch the first time I laid eyes on him, and if ever a man had it comin' to him, he's that man. But nothin's going to touch him, honey, you got to understand that—leastways, not in Orangeburg, it ain't. Forget him. Put him right out of your mind. Take the money. . . ." She turned around and looked at Hélène's face, her eyes apprehensive, as if what she saw there alarmed her.

"He'll *die*, honey," she said. "One of these days, he'll just up and die. Then he'll face his Maker. There's justice in the next world if there ain't in this. Sooner or later—it comes to us all. You'll see. . . ."

There was a silence. The girl didn't believe her, Cassie could see that; at the mention of divine justice, her lips curled. She sat looking down at the manila envelope. Then, after a few minutes, her fingers closed over it. She picked it up off the table, and with a sudden odd passionate gesture, pressed it against her heart.

"I'll take it. Thank you, Cassie. I'll do as you say."

She looked away, and then quickly, with an awkward grace, she got up and hugged Cassie tightly. She pressed her face into Cassie's bony shoulders.

"You've been so kind," she said. "So kind. I'll never forget that, Cassie. I'll pay this back one day. I promise."

Cassie patted her shoulder; she dropped a quick kiss on Hélène's hair. Then she tilted Hélène's chin up, and looked down into her face with a troubled frown. The beautiful blue-gray eyes met hers, then slid away.

Cassie stepped back. What she saw in Hélène's face frightened her. She saw affection for herself, gratitude—sure. But she also saw something else, something the girl was trying to hide.

Hate.

Such a beautiful face. Such a young girl. And such hate.

Cassie went into the kitchen to fix some coffee, and Hélène sat alone in the shabby sitting room. She shut her eyes and let the loathing loose. It swept up through her body, a current of astonishing power.

He'll pay, she thought. *He'll pay.*

She slipped her finger under the flap of the envelope, lifted it exultantly above her head, and shook it. All Cassie's carefully saved dollar bills cascaded over her head and fluttered to the ground.

Not in the next world, she thought. *In this.*

When Cassie came back with the coffee, Hélène was sitting at the table quietly. The fat manila envelope was on the table in front of her. She smiled at Cassie, that astonishing smile she had always had, which could light up a whole room. Cassie sighed, and sat down.

Such a beautiful kid, she thought. That queer intense look had gone now; the blue eyes that met hers were no longer cold, they were open and frank. Cassie relaxed. She'd been upset, that was all, and that was natural enough after what she'd been through. But she was young, she'd get over it. Why, she looked better already. Extraordinary—the kid looked almost happy now.

"We'll send your aunt a wire in the morning," she said. "Tell her what happened. Tell her you're comin' home."

"Home?" She looked puzzled for a moment, then she nodded quickly. "Oh, yes. Of course. Fine, Cassie."

No more argument. That was a relief. The girl was going to be practical, and that always helped.

Cassie sighed, and began to pour the coffee. It was going to be all right, she thought. It was going to be all right.

That night, Hélène went to bed on the fold-out couch in Cassie's small living room. She lay there quietly, listening to the sounds of Cassie moving about in her bedroom next door; the creak of floorboards, then the sigh of springs as she climbed into bed.

The band of light beneath the door disappeared, and Hélène lay in the dark. Her face felt stiff with the tears she had not cried, and her body ached. She could feel the grief, not just in her mind, which was where she expected it to be, but in her body too—a dull sick ache lodged in her stomach and around her heart. She had never seen death before, and now its images flared in her mind: the quickness of it, the finality of it. She saw Billy, lying in the grass by the roadside; she saw her mother, hands neatly folded across her breast. She'd read once that people who had died looked tranquil, as if they slept. It wasn't true, she thought. They looked dead; you looked at them, and you knew—they'd gone; they were never coming back.

The images made the pain tighten in her chest, and she tried to force them away, but she couldn't control her mind that way. Back they came, vivid as lightning, and after a while, quite suddenly, she began to cry.

She didn't want Cassie to hear her and come in, so she turned and buried her face in the pillow until the awful hot choking grief stopped, and she was calmer.

She pushed the covers back then, and sat on the edge of the bed, holding the manila envelope with Cassie's money in it clasped tight in her hand. She sat and stared into the dark, listening to the night noises. The occasional car; voices; later—much later—the whistle of the freight train as it went through the Orangeburg crossing. Billy was dead; her mother was dead, and the trains still ran on time. Death, so large to her, was a tiny thing, and she hated the rest of the world then for its calm and its callousness.

After a while, she tried to pray. She knelt beside the bed and folded her hands, the way her mother had showed her when she was little. But no words would come; she could envisage no God. She stood up again, picked up the envelope, and pressed it tight against her heart. Then, because there was no point in talking to some God she didn't believe in, she talked to Billy and her mother, silently, the words burned into her mind.

"Mother. Billy. I won't forget you. I promise I won't forget you."

She said the words over and over again, and as she did so, her breathing grew steadier, and her mind calmer, and she began to think about the future. She could not see it clearly, and it mixed with words from the past—Billy's prophecies, all the things her mother had dreamed of achieving—but just to think of it buoyed her up. She felt as if her mother and Billy came to her then, and urged her on: whatever she did, it would be for them, all their ambitions and all their dreams were hers now, that was their legacy.

"I promise," she said out loud in a small quiet voice.

Down the street a cat yowled. Hélène climbed back into the small narrow bed. She did not sleep; she began to make plans.

Next day, she and Cassie went back to the trailer in the early morning. Cassie looked at the oilcloth on the table, and the red chair and the paisley shawl, and she started to cry.

"It just don't seem real," she kept saying. "So quick. I can't credit it."

Hélène sat her down at the table and made her some tea. Then she pulled out an old cardboard suitcase and began to pack. After a while, Cassie dried her tears, and watched her silently. The girl's face was tight and set; she packed quickly and methodically. A few clothes, some books. She reached under the bed and pulled out an old black tin box, and knelt back on her heels, looking at it.

"We used to keep our money in here." Her voice was flat.

"Our savings. To go back to England. It's all gone now."

"Hélène . . ."

Cassie rose awkwardly to her feet, and Hélène swung around. She lifted her pale face, and the blue eyes blazed.

"I'm going to be someone, Cassie. You'll hear of me. Everyone in Orangeburg will—you wait and see. You'll read about me in magazines. I'm going away, and I'll never come back to this place—not until—" She broke off, biting her lip, as if angry with herself for this outburst. Cassie was taken aback, and then touched. She shook her head sadly; she knew that feeling—everyone did. She'd had it herself, years ago, when she was a kid, when she still believed fairy tales came true. She walked over and rested her hand gently on Hélène's shoulder.

"Sure you will, honey," she said. "Sure you will." The girl looked up at her; Cassie could tell from her face that she knew Cassie didn't believe her, but Hélène said nothing. She just turned back to the suitcase and pushed a few more things into it: a bundle of old photographs and papers; two dark blue passports with a gold crest on them—her mother's and her own. Cassie bent forward and picked up the one that had belonged to Violet. A small faded photograph; under "Profession," Violet had written "Actress." Cassie sighed and handed the passport back. She turned away.

"What about all these, honey?" She pulled back a thin cotton curtain and gestured hopelessly at Violet's dresses. "These. Your mother did so love clothes. And she was so clever with her needle—you can't leave these. . . ."

Hélène got up. She looked at the dresses, pushed the hangers back and forth. A pink dress; a navy one; they were all a little shabby, all carefully pressed, protected from the wooden hangers with paddings of tissue paper. At the end of the row was a gray dress, a smudgy pattern, silky material. Cassie could see the label, and it said "Bergdorf Goodman." Hélène pushed the dresses to one side.

"I don't want them. I'm not taking them. I'm starting from scratch."

She turned away and fastened the small cardboard suitcase. "Shall we go now, Cassie? I don't want to miss the train."

Cassie shrugged, and sighed, and led the way back to the car. She knew better than to argue. Grief affected people oddly, she knew that: some folks wanted to hang on to everything, others just wanted to get rid of it all. She'd come back later, she thought, and pack up all those things. Hélène might change her mind later, and then she'd be glad Cassie had kept them.

The girl's composure alarmed Cassie a little. All the way into Montgomery, she kept glancing across at her. But there was no sign of tears; Hélène just sat there, with that tight set look on her face; she hardly said one single word. In Montgomery, they sent a telegram to Violet's sister, Elizabeth, and made the plane reservations; then Cassie drove Hélène to the station.

It was very hot again, and they waited for the train in the shade. Hélène was swinging her cardboard suitcase and staring down the line.

"You made your plans, honey?" Cassie said at last, a little anxiously.

"Oh, yes. Lots of plans."

"I mean—you've thought what you're going to do, when you get to England and all?"

"I don't know exactly, I'll begin somewhere. Find a job. Learn to type, perhaps. Or train for the stage . . ." Hélène turned her head slightly.

"What—like Violet?" Cassie was surprised, and also touched.

Her question seemed to disconcert Hélène slightly; she glanced away again.

"I suppose so."

Cassie frowned. "It's a hard life, I reckon. Getting work. Starting out. Looks aren't everything. I mean, for something like that, you'd have to know the right people maybe. I don't know. Violet always said—"

"The train's coming." Hélène interrupted her, and pointed. Looking down the line, Cassie saw the signal change to green. She sighed. Better not say any more. There wasn't time, and anyway, Hélène probably wouldn't listen. It was a comfort to her, maybe, spinning daydreams like that—something to cling to, something to keep her going. She smiled, and gave Hélène a quick affectionate squeeze.

"Well, you be sure and write to me now. Let me know how things are. How you're getting on in England . . ."

She helped Hélène on to the train with the suitcase, and found her a seat. At the last moment, just before Cassie climbed down again onto the platform, Hélène turned back to her, put her arms around her, and hugged her tight. Cassie caught the glint of tears in her eyes then, before she buried her face in Cassie's breast. But she said nothing, and Cassie climbed down and slammed the door.

The whistle blew, the train jerked, and gathered speed. Cassie stood and watched it pull out of the station; she could see Hélène's face at the window, and she looked so defiant and so brave that Cassie was touched. She had always been easily moved, and now tears came to her eyes.

She waved until the train rounded a curve and went out of sight; then she turned to go. She smiled to herself, and shook her head. Hélène was a good girl, but she was just a child still, and kids were all the same. How easy they thought life was, how simple. You wanted something, and you got it: how many girls left small towns, thinking they were going to be famous, thinking they were going to be rich? Hélène was a dreamer, she decided, looking back down the track. A dreamer, like her mother. *Poor Violet*, she thought, and decided to go back by way of the cemetery.

On the train it was hot and airless; the coach she was in was almost empty. Hélène pulled down the shade as far as it would go and closed her eyes. The rhythm of the train, and the sound of its wheels, lulled her. She listened to the wheels, and it seemed to her they whispered a new message: *famous and rich*, they said, and—sometimes—*powerful and free*. The heat in the coach was making her sleepy, so she was no longer quite certain whether the images in her mind came to her awake, or sleeping. She saw herself doing *some*thing impossibly well, so well that Billy and her mother were proud of her, and her mother kissed her, and pressed her lips against her ear, and said in her soft low voice: *You have done it, Hélène, all the things I dreamed of doing.*

She saw herself wrapped in furs, holding a bouquet of white roses; she saw herself slipping into the back of a long black limousine; she saw herself coming into a room, and Ned Calvert rising to his feet, afraid of her and afraid of the things she had the power to do to him.

When she opened her eyes again, the air was cooler, and it was growing dark. Some of the images seemed foolish then—white roses, limousines!—and she blushed, remembering then what she had said to Cassie, and wishing she had kept silent. Cassie hadn't believed her, she had seen that; she'd thought it was a daydream, a fantasy; she had looked the way Priscilla-Anne used to look when Hélène talked about going back to England. She wouldn't make that mistake again, she thought. It was the way people had looked at her mother; it was hateful to be pitied; she wanted to be invulnerable.

She discovered a way the next day, on the last leg of the train journey. The coaches were fuller now, as they went farther north. The landscape outside the window was different; the people were different; their voices were quicker, and their accents sharper. She knew no one, she thought, as at each station more people joined the train; and none of them knew her. She found that idea extraordinarily freeing. Suddenly, she saw, she could leave it all behind: Orangeburg and the trailer park; being poor; being ashamed. No one on this train knew about her mother, they hadn't listened to gossip about how she came by her dresses; no one on the train knew about Ned Calvert, and how Hélène had deceived herself into believing she loved him; no one even knew she was Hélène Craig, unless she chose to tell them.

During the morning, she fell into conversation with a plump middle-aged woman who was traveling to New York City to see her grandchildren. She produced photographs; she told Hélène her life story, and that of half her family. Then, clearly intrigued by Hélène's accent, she settled back to hear Hélène's in return.

She was knitting; as Hélène spoke, her needles never stopped moving. Hélène told her that she was English, and visiting America for the first time; she had been staying with distant cousins in the South, and was now returning home to London. Hélène spoke, she waited for the needles to stop moving, and for the woman to look up, and stare, and accuse her of lying. But nothing happened. The woman nodded and smiled, and said it must be exciting, traveling such a long way, and she surely hoped Hélène had enjoyed seeing America.

It was so simple! Hélène felt exhilarated . . . free. She was no longer Hélène Craig, trapped in Orangeburg; she was a new person, a new woman—and that woman could be anything she chose to make her.

When the train pulled into Pennsylvania Station and her companion said good-bye to her, Hélène felt a moment of compunction. The woman had been kind, and she had lied to her. . . . The next moment, the guilt had gone. It had not felt like a lie after all; it had felt like a rehearsal.

Before she went out to the airport, there was one thing she had to do, and she did it, clutching the cardboard suitcase tighty, pushing through the throng of people. She walked up Fifth Avenue, for Violet's sake, and looked carefully in all the store windows.

It was very hot, and the air eddied. She lifted her face and looked at the buildings towering into the sky. She looked down, and the mica in the sidewalks glittered like diamonds. People—so many people; the smell of pretzels being sold on a cross street; cars, nose to tail, right along the length of the avenue. The air smelled of bustle and purpose, so she felt she wanted to run, to shout. She looked at St. Patrick's Cathedral, and stared at the entrance to the Plaza hotel, and watched the people come and go.

She could feel the heart of the city beating through the soles of her feet, and pounding in the air she breathed, and she longed to ride the buses, ride the subway, explore the city, and make it her own.

But she did not have enough time, or enough money, so, in the end she crossed the street, and stood for Violet's sake outside the windows of Bergdorf Goodman.

On the sidewalk the temperature was well into the eighties. Bergdorf's windows were full of winter furs.

HÉLÈNE
AND EDOUARD

FRANCE, 1959

"I designed this one for your wife. For your late wife . . ." Floryan Wyspianski, a great bear of a man, spoke awkwardly, unable to disguise his emotion. He gestured to a brooch at the far end of the long table on which the collection of his work was displayed. Edouard looked at it. A cabochon emerald, mounted in gold, and surrounded by rubies—a splendid thing, something a czarina might have worn, or a maharaja—or a woman who disliked reticent jewelry.

Edouard smiled. "Isobel would have loved that. It's her taste exactly."

"I'm glad. I hoped I was right. People spoke of her, and I listened. . . ."

"Thank you, Floryan." Edouard pressed his arm.

He walked back down the table, looking at the pieces which had been laid out for his inspection, and which he had watched over at every stage from the earliest drawings. The collection was almost finished; there were just a few pieces still to be completed. They would be launched, and exhibited, first in Paris, then in London, then in New York, that November. Months of planning, and the jewelry was everything he had hoped for, and more. He would have liked Isobel to see this—she, after all, had made it possible. Edouard looked at the necklaces, and the tiaras and the bracelets, moonstones and lapis, black pearls and rose-cut diamonds, opals and rubies; he closed his eyes to their beauty and saw Isobel, in the drawing room at Eaton Square, holding out her hand, showing off her emerald, mocking and celebrating her "sweet" ring.

He left Floryan Wyspianski shortly after that, and spent the night with a woman at Pauline Simonescu's.

Usually, when he went there, he stayed only a few hours. But that night the need was very great, and the despair was very strong, and he remained with the woman, burying the past in her flesh, until the morning. She was, like all the women there, young, beautiful, skilled, and obliging. She had long black hair, which she drew silkily across his skin, and—perhaps because she sensed his need, she attempted to fake her orgasm.

Edouard pressed his hand against her throat. "Don't pretend. . . ."

She grew still, and her dark eyes flew open. He moved within her strongly, slowly, moving toward the black place he sought, and the brief extinction in the beat of sensation. And, perhaps because of the way he held her, perhaps because of what he said, perhaps because of something in him, an urgency which communicated itself, he felt her begin to respond truly. Her eyelids fluttered and closed; her neck arched back; her breath came in quick short pants, and she turned her head from side to side, moaning.

He waited, pushed again, waited once more—sure in these last moments as he pushed them both closer to the edge. His hands gripped her more tightly; he was aware of no emotion. When he felt the pulsing of her climax begin, it was easy to push deeper and harder this time, because it meant nothing, it was merely a question of timing. She cried out; Edouard pressed his hand across her mouth, and came.

Afterward, she was shaken, and she cried. She clung to him, and told him this had never happened to her before. She begged him to come to her again.

Edouard drew away from her instantly. His mind settled into a cold hard pattern: distaste and self-disgust. He caught her wrist and raised her face to him.

"An hour after I leave here tomorrow, half an hour, sooner—I shall have forgotten your face. I won't remember your name. I won't remember anything that happened tonight. I never do. You should know that."

She knelt back on her heels, looking at him, her dark hair falling in deep wings on either side of her face. She had stopped crying.

"I'll make you remember," she said. "I will. I'll make it so you never forget."

Then she drew the palm of her hand steadily across his thigh.

"You're beautiful," she said, and bent her head. "There," she said gently. "There, like that, you see? Oh, yes."

Edouard lay back and closed his eyes. Her ministrations happened to someone else. Later, in the early hours of the morning, at first light, that other person, that other man, pushed into the shadows of her body again, fucking toward oblivion, and it was only when the brief oblivion came that he knew the man was himself.

He left shortly after six, walking out into a deserted street. A cat yowled, leapt down from a wall, and pressed itself lovingly against his ankles. Edouard looked down at it, then up at Pauline Simonescu's shuttered house. He had an image of two dark wings of hair, a pale face—but it was already fading. He hated himself at that moment, as he had hated himself all night.

Two years, and it was over. He would not go back. Not to Pauline Simonescu herself, who on occasion still read the cards for him, and made up a fictitious future. Not to the women. None of it.

He would stay away from women altogether, he told himself. He was sickened by the sequence, by a sexual respite which never lasted, but which must always, sooner or later, be repeated: emptiness after emptiness. And besides, he did harm, he had seen that tonight, though the details were already receding.

He turned away, and with a mew, the cat left him.

No more women, no matter how strong the need. It was a resolution he kept for three weeks.

T hree weeks, and a warm summer evening. Signing papers in a silent office, while a secretary waited, disguising the impatience she felt to join her lover.

Three weeks, and the vacancy of his life appalled him. He looked out the window and watched the leaves dance. He turned away and tried to think of his work. He summoned up the image of the Wyspianski jewels, and they glittered coldly. He thought of Partex Petrochemicals, in which he and his mother held such a powerful slice of voting stock. He thought of the new chairman of Partex, the flamboyant Texan, Drew Johnson, his friend, his appointee; the *putsch* against the ineffective outgoing chairman had been perfectly planned and perfectly executed, the idea Edouard's, the organization of it Johnson's. He had enjoyed the plotting well enough, while it lasted—it had a point, it made a strong company stronger. But as soon as it was over, he felt the emptiness settle over him again.

Johnson was full of plans. Partex was now the fourth largest oil-producing company in America. He wanted it to be the largest, quickly. Edouard admired that drive, that dedication, and that sense of purpose. He could even participate in it for a while. But then, increasingly, he would draw back. The fourth largest, the second largest, the largest of all: in the end, how much did it matter?

He turned away and looked at the ranked cupboards that contained file upon file. He looked at the telephones. He could work. He could find himself a woman. The pursuit of profit, the pursuit of pleasure. He turned away from them both, angrily.

Leaving his offices, he dismissed his driver for the night and climbed into the black Aston-Martin. He left the city so he could drive at speed, to Mozart.

When he knew they were failing him also, he turned back toward Paris at the first opportunity. A woman then.

Not *the* woman; he no longer believed in her existence. Just *a* woman, any woman. A foreigner. A stranger. Someone here today and elsewhere tomorrow—random sex in a random life.

He drove through expensive streets on the Right Bank, glimpsed the bright ice of diamonds in the de Chavigny showrooms, and headed onto the Pont Neuf, along the Quai des Augustins.

The past was beating its insistent pulse in his head; beside him the Seine sparkled. And a few streets away, a few minutes away, a tall slender girl came to a halt outside a small church.

She had been walking the streets at random, also listening to the past. Now she stopped, and lifting her face to the sunlight, looked at the building in front of her. The Église St. Julien le Pauvre. She was poor. She had precisely ten francs in her purse. She smiled.

Just past the church, there was a small park. There were children there, playing. She heard their shouts. She saw, in the corner of her eye, the colors of their clothes. Red, white, and blue. American colors. Independence colors.

Ｓhe had been in Paris almost a week, and before that in England: three days in Devon, three days with Elizabeth, her mother's sister.

She did not want to think of those three days. She had gone there so expectantly, bouncing along the narrow roads in a country bus, craning her head for her first view of the house, the first view of her mother's garden. That place her mother had conjured up over the years, until, with repetition of the stories, Hélène believed she knew it: knew the green lawns, and the summerhouse; knew each tree; knew the place where the white-painted benches were drawn up in the shade; saw, quite clearly, the figures gathered there for the ritual of tea.

It had not been like that. It had been ugly, and in Elizabeth—she had sensed it at once—there had been no welcome, only an old spite and an old hate.

She looked now at the church, at the rounded archway, and she forced the memory out of her mind. She forced it back with the other memories, of Billy lying dead, of her mother, and the click of the nun's rosary, of Ned Calvert, and a man with a gun, and a black Cadillac. She could not get rid of any of these memories, not altogether; at night they came to life in her dreams but during the day there was a certain place in her mind where they were bearable. There the images still replayed, but they were distanced, like a film she had once seen, like things that had happened to someone else. She would not let them into the forefront of her mind. She would not. She had come to Paris—*the most beautiful city in the world, Hélène, even more beautiful than London*—and it *was* beautiful. She walked around it each day, on her own, a series of pilgrimages. As long as she kept walking, and kept looking, she felt all right. She didn't start to shake then, or to cry. That happened only if she stayed too long in one place, and let the memories start to snake back.

Her new life was beginning, the one she'd planned and dreamed of so long. She was just thinking that; she remembered it, later, because it was at exactly that moment that she heard the car.

It was a large black car of a kind she could not identify, and she was never quite sure which she saw first, the car, or the man who was driving it. For a moment she thought he had called out to her, then she realized her mistake. It must have been one of the children in the park. She turned away, heard the car come closer, and turned back.

This time she looked directly at the man, and saw he was looking at her with a slightly puzzled expression on his face, as if he thought he recognized her. That was odd, because she felt the same, although the next instant she knew that was ridiculous—she had never seen him before in her life.

Ever since she left Orangeburg, she had seen the world and her surroundings with a heightened clarity, as if she were still in shock. Colors, gestures, faces, movements, nuances of speech, they were all now startlingly vivid and clear to her, and she saw this man, too, in this way, as if he came at her slowly, out of a dream.

The car he drove was black, his suit was black, his hair was black. As she looked at him, he bent forward slightly to turn off the engine of the car, and as he straightened up, and looked at her again, she saw in a silence that was thunderous, that his eyes were a very dark blue, like the sea in shadow.

She walked toward him then, and stopped at the end of the car's hood. She knew quite suddenly what was going to happen next; the knowledge of it flashed through her mind. She thought perhaps he knew, too, because his face grew still for a moment, and very intent, and his eyes looked puzzled, as if he felt some blow, some unexpected stab—the knife had struck, and he had not seen it coming.

She said something, and he said something in reply—it didn't matter what the words were, she could see he knew that as well as she did. The words were just a transition, a necessary corridor between two rooms.

Then he got out of the car and walked around to her. Hélène looked at him. At once she knew that she was going to love him; she felt the brightness of it in her mind; felt something within her shift, realign, and settle.

She climbed into the car, and they drove through the streets of Paris on a summer's evening, and she wanted the streets, and the driving, and the evening light to go on forever.

He stopped the car outside the Dôme in Montparnasse, and turned to look at her. It was a direct look, and it instantly made her want to hide, to run away. But there were other ways of hiding from people, more effective ways; she had learned that since leaving Orangeburg. She thought of the woman on the train; she thought of other people since then, and other stories told to them. No decision was involved; all she knew was that she didn't want him to know who she was; she didn't want anyone to know who she was. She wanted them to know her only as the woman she meant to become, the woman she was going to invent. Not Hélène Craig: she had left Hélène Craig behind forever.

"You know, you haven't told me your name," he said as he steered her gently into the crowded restaurant.

"Helen Hartland," she answered.

And after that, nothing was simple.

Her name was Helen Hartland, she said. She was eighteen years old, and English. Her family bore the same name as the village near which they lived in Devon. It was near the coast; their house overlooked the sea, and it had a very beautiful garden. Did he like gardens?

Her father had been a hero, an RAF pilot, killed in the last months of the war. Her mother, Violet Hartland, had been an author—quite well known in England, though the romances she wrote were out of fashion now. She had lived alone with her mother, who had died when she was sixteen. Since then she had lived with her mother's sister. She had left England a week ago and come to Paris on impulse. At present she was working in a café on the Boule Miche; she shared a room nearby with a French girl who also worked in the café. No, she hadn't yet decided how long she would stay.

She told him all this over dinner at the Dôme, in a quiet even voice, answering each question he put with careful consideration, apparently oblivious to the swirl of the famous and the fashionable around their table.

They were speaking in English by then, and her voice fascinated Edouard. He had always had a precise ear for accents; his years in England during the war and his visits there since had given him the ability to place an English man or woman as precisely as he could someone French. He knew his own voice, speaking English, hardly betrayed the fact that he was a foreigner. It still had lingering traces of Oxford and of Hugo Glendinning's prewar upper-class drawl. This girl's voice he could not place at all. It had an unusual clarity and perfection of enunciation—a perfection usually encountered only in those for whom English was a second language. It betrayed no regional influence; it was educated, harmonious, slightly old-fashioned, and curiously classless. He could not place the voice, by accent, phraseology, or slang, and he could not place her.

For someone so young she was remarkably self-possessed. Yet there was no attempt to make an impression, or even to try to please. She did not flirt; she did not pretend interest unless she felt it. She simply sat there, calmly cocooned in the perfection of her beauty, either unaware of, or indifferent to, the fact that every man in the restaurant between the ages of twenty and sixty had been staring in her direction from the moment she entered the room.

She drank two glasses of wine, and refused a third. When the waiter addressed Edouard by his title, she glanced up at him with that level blue-gray gaze, but registered nothing more. She might have heard of him, she might not; he had no way of telling.

When they had finished their meal and were drinking their coffee, she put down her cup and looked up at him.

"This place is very famous, isn't it?"

"Very." Edouard smiled. "In the twenties and the early thirties it was the great haunt of writers and painters. Picasso, Gertrude Stein, Hemingway, Scott Fitzgerald, Ford Madox Ford. . . . Here and at the Coupole—there's great rivalry between them still. Only now—"

He paused, glancing across at a noisy group in the corner. "Now they vie more for the attention of film stars and singers and fashion models. The writers go elsewhere—the cafés on the Boulevard St. Germain, for instance. Deux Magots—Sartre goes there, and Simone de Beauvoir. . . ."

"I'm glad you brought me here. Thank you."

She leaned back in her chair and looked carefully around the huge mirrored interior, at the waiters in their long white aprons, at the dazzle of people. A man at a nearby table raised his glass to her with a smile, and she gave him a cold stare. Edouard leaned forward.

"You've not been here before?"

"Oh, no. But I want to learn about places like this."

She spoke with complete seriousness. Edouard's eyebrows rose.

"You want to *learn* about them?"

"But of course. And other places too. And things. So many things."

She lifted her hand and began to count items on her slender fingers, a little smile hovering about her lips.

"About cafés and restaurants. About food. About wine. About

clothes—beautiful clothes, like that woman over there is wearing. About paintings, buildings, books. About cars. Houses. Furniture. Jewelry. All those things." She raised her clear eyes candidly to his face. "I expect you would find that hard to understand. . . ." She paused. "Have you ever been hungry—really hungry?"

"Very hungry, I suppose—yes, once or twice."

"I feel hungry for that. For all those things. To know about them. To understand them. I—well, I grew up in a very small place."

"Is that why you came to Paris?"

Edouard looked at her curiously, for a note of emotion had crept into her voice for the first time.

As if she were aware of that, too, and regretted it, she smiled quickly. "One of the reasons. And I've been working hard. Do you know what I do every morning before I start work, and every evening when I've finished?"

"Tell me."

"I walk around Paris, and I look at things. Markets. Galleries. Houses. Churches. And shops, of course. It's rather difficult to go into the very grand ones, because I don't have the right clothes, but I look in their windows. I look at dresses, and hats, and gloves, and shoes, and stockings. I look at handbags and silk underwear. I've been to Vuitton, and Hermès, and Gucci, and yesterday I stood outside Chanel and Givenchy and Dior—I'd been saving those. You can't see any clothes there of course, unless you go inside, so I made do with the name-plates." She gave a wry smile.

"I see." Edouard, touched and amused, hesitated. "And of all the things you have seen, which did you like the best?"

"That's difficult." She frowned. "At first everything seemed perfect. Then I began to know what I *didn't* like—things covered in initials, things with too much gold, things that . . . that proclaimed themselves too much. But best of all—yes—best of all, I liked a pair of gloves."

"A pair of gloves?"

"They were very beautiful gloves." Her color rose a little. "At Hermès. They were very plain, the softest gray kid. Just to the wrist. They had three tucks *there*." She indicated the place on the back of her hand. "And they had a small flat stitched bow, just there at the top of the wrist. And they were beautiful. I love beautiful gloves. So did my mother. She must have had dozens. . . ."

"I see." Edouard looked at her solemnly. The gray-blue eyes met his defiantly, as if she dared him to mock her. He glanced down at the white linen cloth.

"And jewelry," he said carefully. "Do you want to learn about that too? Do you look in jewelers' windows?"

"Sometimes." She lowered her eyes. "I have looked in yours. It is yours, isn't it, in the Rue du Faubourg St. Honoré?"

"It is indeed."

"I went there two days ago. And then Cartier's." A mischievous glint came into her eyes.

"And which display did you prefer? Mine, or my rival's?"

"To be truthful, Cartier. But I'm so ignorant. I know nothing about stones, nothing about settings. . . ."

"Do you know which stone you prefer?"

"Oh, yes! I know that. Of course. I like diamonds."

"They're not necessarily the most valuable. . . ." He watched her closely. "A perfect emerald—a dark green emerald, which is very rare now, can be worth more."

"Oh, it's not a question of *value*." A little scorn crept into her voice. "I like diamonds because they are clear. Without color. Because they are cold and hot at the same time. Like fire and ice. The diamonds I looked at—" She hesitated. "It was like looking at light. Into the heart of light. You probably think that is stupid."

"Not at all. I think precisely the same. Do you know that the diamond has one very curious property—something that makes it unique among stones?"

"No."

"Do you know how a diamond feels when you hold it in your hand? It feels cold. Ice cold. So cold it burns your skin."

"Fire and ice?"

"As you said. Precisely."

Their eyes met for a moment, and held. Edouard felt his mind loosen and spin, had the sensation for a second that he was falling from a great height, a long fearsome free fall, heady, exhilarating, and also terrifying. *King of cups; queen of diamonds* . . . the memory of Pauline Simonescu's card readings flickered into his mind and then was gone.

She also experienced something; he could see that. Her eyes widened, her lips parted, she drew in a little quick breath, as if in surprise. For an instant she looked startled, then wary. Slowly, Edouard reached across the table and rested his hand lightly over hers. It was the first time he had touched her, and it unleashed in him a violent perturbation of feeling, more intense than anything he had experienced since he was a boy. He had wanted her from the moment he saw her; now he felt his body surge with a desire so intense he trembled.

He had a good instinct for self-preservation, honed to perfection over the years. Now, quickly, he withdrew his hand and stood up.

"It's late. I must take you home."

She looked up, apparently unmoved by his abruptness, and then slowly rose to her feet. Calm in the corolla of her beauty, she followed him from the restaurant, and climbed into the soft leather seat of the Aston-Martin. During the drive back, she did not speak once, but sat there quietly, apparently relaxed, gazing out at the streets and boulevards. Edouard, a powerful man used to recognizing power in others, usually in men, sensed it now in her. He could feel its emanations: these were as discernible to him as a perfume in the air. He glanced toward her and felt his flesh harden and leap; the wide lips, the high full breasts, the long slender line of hips and thighs. Her slightest movement spoke of sexual promise, infinite delight. And yet her eyes seemed to him both mocking and disdainful, as if she knew the power of her own beauty, and half-despised the immediate response it awoke.

He slowed as they approached the brightly lit café where she had said she worked, and she straightened.

"Would you drop me off here?"

"Let me take you back to your house."

"No, here would be better. I have a very bad-tempered concierge." She smiled. "It's only a couple of streets. I'll walk it later. I need to see the owner anyway—to check my schedule tomorrow."

She turned to him, and held out a long slender hand. "Thank you. It was a lovely dinner. I enjoyed myself very much."

She shook his hand solemnly, and Edouard cursed the heavens and his own apparent inability to say one coherent word. He felt as if he wanted to ask her to marry him. Or go home with him. Or go away with him. Or something. Anything.

"Do you work here every day?" he finally managed as he helped her from the car.

She looked at him with a slow smile. "Oh, yes. I finish work around six. Good-bye."

She turned without another glance, threaded her way through the tables outside, and disappeared into the café.

Edouard stared after her, wondering if he had the strength to drive away from that place and never go back, and knowing he had not. He turned back toward his car. He was aware, dimly, of faces and voices and laughter from the crowded tables on the *terrasse*, of an ordinary world going on somewhere else. A pretty girl glanced in his direction, but Edouard did not see her. On the far side of the *terrasse* a small plump and ugly man, sitting alone, also looked up, and watched him attentively. Edouard did not see him either. He was thinking that this woman was eighteen years old. Where had she learned that absolute assurance, that apparently calm knowledge of her own sexual sovereignty? Had some man taught it to her—and if so, what man, where, and under what circumstances?

He groaned aloud, climbed back into the Aston-Martin, drove at high speed back to St. Cloud, and there attempted to drown her memory in a bottle of Armagnac, and a night without sleep.

In the morning he sent to Hermès, and bought the pair of gray kid gloves. Around the finger of one of them, he slipped a solitaire diamond ring. The diamond was a fifteen-carat stone, graded "D," the highest classification, for purity of color, and "IF," internally flawless, for clarity. It had been cut by a master; it burned with a blue-white fire; it was the perfect marriage between nature and art.

He put gloves and ring back in their box and closed the lid. Then he waited, in feverish anxiety, for six o'clock to come.

The second night, he took her to dinner at the Coupole. Her manner was unchanged. She accepted his arrival outside the crowded café without question. She was calm and polite. As before, she answered his questions, but volunteered little. She asked only the most neutral questions in return. None of the usual woman's subterfuge, to which he was accustomed: no questions subtly designed to elicit information about his private life; no attempt to discover whether he was married, or whether any other woman held sway. She spoke to him about his work and his professional life; she asked him questions about Paris, about France and the French. She gave no sign that she was aware of the sexual magnetism Edouard felt, and he—reeling from the waves of it—desperately tried to make himself as calm and detached as she was.

He forced himself to look at her coolly, as he might have a potential employee. She was wearing a plain cotton shift that evening, of a gray-blue color close to that of her eyes. No jewelry, just a very ordinary cheap watch, which she shook occasionally, because, she said, it sometimes stopped. She had very lovely hands, with long slender fingers, the oval nails cut short and unpolished, like a schoolgirl's. She sat very straight, and there was an exceptional stillness about her, an absence of vivacity that could have been dull, but which in her case was powerfully mesmeric.

Once or twice, looking at her closely, Edouard wondered if she had lied about her age. She could sometimes look much younger than eighteen, like a solemn child unaware of her own eroticism, a child in a Victorian photograph. At other times, she looked older than she said, like a woman in her twenties, in the prime of her beauty. Often, especially when she looked at him directly, the two impressions—of innocence and of sensuality—overlapped. Then, he found himself looking into the grave and lovely face of a well-brought-up young woman, a young woman who might have attended a convent school, who had led a sheltered life, and whose pure and steady gaze aroused in him sensations and thoughts and imaginings that were anything but pure.

Then, the immediate response of his own body and mind shocked him deeply; the strain of puritanism in his nature battled with his own strong sensuality; he imagined making love to her, and hated himself for the seduction of the images that ricocheted through his mind. To his own dismay, he found the male and female roles to which he was accustomed were reversing themselves. It was he, despising himself as he did so, who heard himself asking questions designed to prompt personal revelations. It was she who gracefully but firmly turned all those probing questions aside.

It was impossible to look at her dispassionately, he thought. His mind attempted to make judgments, but the judgments of his mind were drowned out by the clamor of his senses. She was not even wearing scent—she smelled of soap, of freshly washed skin and hair, of herself. To Edouard it was the most intoxicating perfume he had ever known.

Eventually, when he was in a state of turmoil that those who knew him or worked with him would have imagined impossible, he abruptly suggested they should leave.

"Very well."

Their eyes met; neither of them moved; Edouard's mind blurred.

"I could take you home. Or—if you preferred—we could go back to my house at St. Cloud. It's just outside Paris."

His voice trailed away. The gray-blue eyes regarded him levelly. Edouard felt a whole series of idiotic and embarrassing disclaimers surge through his mind. He wanted her to understand—this was not a calculated lead-up, not a routine move in a routine seduction, he had no ulterior motives: quite simply he could not bear to think of another evening without her presence.

"Thank you. I would like that."

He drove them back very fast, with music playing, and as he did so, he felt a rising exhilaration. The speed and the triumphant music of the Mozart quartet seemed to him to bridge the silence between them, so he felt a sense of perfect communion. *She knows; she understands*, he thought incoherently and triumphantly.

He never brought women back to St. Cloud. The only exception to that rule had been his wife. Now, just as he had done with Isobel, he walked first through the gardens, fragrant with lilies, and stood at the edge of the *parterre*, looking across the silver sky to the red glow of the city in the distance. He did so deliberately, in a frantic last-ditch attempt to save himself, thinking that comparisons and memories would then come to him, and sever the fine strong thread with which this magical woman bound him.

No comparisons occurred to him; no memories came back. He, who had always felt he could never escape from the past, now found that the past had relinquished its hold; it had gone; he was free of it. Standing there in the garden, he was aware of nothing but the woman beside him. Without speaking a word—and she was totally silent—she obliterated everything but the present.

After a while, Edouard took her hand, and held it in his. Then, slowly, they walked back to the house together. He took her up to the study in which, in another life, another man had proposed to Isobel. Hardly aware of what he was doing, he poured drinks. She moved slowly around the room as he did so. She lightly touched the needlepoint cover of one of the chairs; the Spitalfields silk of another; she looked at the Turner watercolors. Edouard put down the drinks, forgetting their existence, and moved to her side. She turned to look up at him, and quite suddenly he found it easy to speak.

"Do you know what is happening? Do you understand?" he said gently.

"I don't know. I'm not sure." She hesitated. "It frightens me a little."

"It frightens me too." Edouard smiled.

"I could leave . . ." She glanced toward the door, then back at him. "Perhaps, if I left now . . ."

"Do you want to do that?"

"No." Two wings of color mounted in her cheeks.

"It's just that—I hadn't expected . . . I hadn't planned—"

She broke off, and Edouard reached across and took her hand in his. He let it rest there gently, and looked down into her face. He was touched, and a little amused, that a woman so young should speak so earnestly of plans, and perhaps she sensed that, because she frowned slightly, as if even the gentlest mockery made her unsure.

"You think that's foolish?"

"No, I don't." Edouard's face grew serious. "I live my whole life by plans. Everything ordered and scheduled and precise. I have lived that way for years, ever since—" He hesitated. "For a long time."

"And now?"

"I know they don't matter in the least. I always knew that, anyway." He gave a shrug, half-turned away. "Plans. Schedules. Strategies. They pass time. They order it—they enable one to forget how empty it is."

He still held her hand lightly, but his face was averted. Hélène stood very still, looking at him. Light danced in her mind; she felt a dreamlike calm, and through the calm, a hectic certainty. It had been there from the moment she first saw him, and all evening she had been trying to argue it away. All evening, while she sat there opposite him in the Coupole, pretending to be calm, her mind had been filled with argument. This is not happening, it said at first; then—it is happening, but it is not too late, it can still be stopped.

Then, when they first reached St. Cloud, and she saw this house in all its magnificence, other ugly voices began, with other ugly refrains. They spoke with her mother's voice; they spoke with Priscilla-Anne's; they reminded her that men lied to women, especially when they wanted them; they lied the way Ned Calvert had lied.

Those warnings had been whispering away in her head until she came into this room, and until Edouard began to speak. Now they were still chattering away somewhere at the back of her mind, but their messages seemed not just mean, but also absurd. It occurred to her, as she looked carefully at Edouard, that even a man like this could be vulnerable.

"Edouard." It was the first time she had used his name, and he swung around to her at once. "Do you think you know—do you think one knows, when something is so right that there aren't any choices anymore?"

"Yes. I do."

"So do I." She looked at him solemnly, and then, before Edouard could speak again, she drew in her breath as if to steady herself, and took a small step forward.

"I want to stay," she said. "I don't want to go at all. I never did, really. There—I've said it." She hesitated then, her chin lifted, and her face took on a slightly defiant expression.

"Women aren't supposed to say things like that, are they? But it seems stupid to lie about that. I don't see the point. I do want to stay. I would have stayed with you last night if you had asked me. Probably when I first met you. We could have gotten into your car and driven straight back here, and I would have—stayed. Just like that. Not knowing you at all. Except I do feel as if I know you. I like you. Do you think that's wrong? Are you shocked?"

Edouard was amused, and also touched. The quaint and serious way in which she spoke, the odd combination of directness and shyness, the innocent assumption that what she was saying was somehow forward, when he was used to women who expressed their desires casually— all these things affected him deeply. He felt curiously rebuked by that innocence, and he knew that if he let her see the amusement he felt, she would be deeply mortified. He stepped forward and took her hand gently.

"No," he said seriously. "I'm not shocked. And I certainly don't think it's wrong. I want you to stay. I want it more than anything in the world. Now—do you find that shocking?" Her lips curved in a slow smile. "No."

"When I left my office the night we met—" Edouard hesitated. He wondered if he should go on, and almost broke off. She lifted her eyes to his face, and he felt suddenly that he owed it to her to be truthful. "That night—I was looking for a woman. Any woman. There were reasons for that—there's no point in saying what they were, not now, they'd sound like excuses, and I don't want that. I was looking for a woman—which is something I've done often in the past, and I met *the* woman. That was what I felt. You have to know that. I want you to know that. I'm aware of how that must sound. There's no reason why you should believe me—but I swear to you, it's the truth."

He stopped abruptly, and let his hand fall. Deep color had washed up over her face. Edouard turned away, furious with himself for having spoken. She was too young to understand; he had no right to introduce complexities of that kind. . . . He must have sounded like the most hackneyed of seducers.

"I'm sorry." His voice was very formal. "I should not have said that. You'll want to go now. . . ."

He started to move away from her, his face averted. Hélène looked at him, frowning slightly. She knew how it felt, to invite rejection, to anticipate pain and thus prevent others from inflicting it: she had learned that technique in Orangeburg, year by year. She had assumed, naïvely, that it was one peculiar to herself, and yet now she recognized it in someone else.

She stepped forward, and he turned. "Edouard, that makes no difference. I'm glad you said it. I still want to stay."

The light came back into his eyes then. She reached out, took his hand, and pressed it against the swell of her breast.

They looked at each other. Beneath his fingertips, Edouard felt the beating of her heart.

I n his bedroom, she stood at a little distance from him, and unfastened her dress. When she was naked, she stood perfectly still, her hands by her sides, only the rapidity of her breathing, the rise and fall of her breasts, revealing her emotion.

Her breasts were the color of ivory, their aureoles wide, the nipples already hard. Edouard looked at the long perfect curve from thighs to hips to narrow waist, at the grave child's face and the woman's voluptuousness. Hélène bit her lip; she stood quite still, watching him as he undressed.

When he was naked, she stepped forward and sank to her knees. She pressed her face against his stomach, and then, with a quick animal directness, she gently kissed the dark hair that ran in a line from chest to navel, and then down.

Across his bed there was a length of embroidered Chinese silk, cream silk embroidered with butterflies and birds of paradise, and flowers. She looked at the silk and, just for an instant, she saw Mrs. Calvert's room again. She saw Ned drape the silk cover with that square of white sheeting; she saw that confident smile spread across his face. The image was there; she shivered, and it was gone. Edouard lifted his arms and drew her down onto the cover beside him. She felt the warmth of his skin; his body brushed against hers, and she heard herself give one small startled sigh; then she lay still.

They lay quietly side by side for a long while, hardly moving. Then, very gently, Edouard turned her face to his; he looked into her eyes, and she looked back at him.

She felt his breath brush her skin, then the touch of his lips, then his hands. She closed her eyes; there was no sound, only a touching that washed her mind clear. He entered her very gently, and she felt a little pain, then a great peace. She felt, as she moved under him, as if he took her down under the sea, fathom upon fathom, into the emerald dark, a place where the tides moved and shifted in her blood.

"Wait," Edouard said once, when her climax was very close, and he could sense that because she was inexperienced she was struggling too frantically to reach it.

"Hélène. Wait. With me, not against me."

He said her name in the French manner, instinctively; she opened her eyes, and was still for a moment. Then her eyes fluttered shut, and she began to move with a new rhythm, so attuned to his, so powerful and so sweet that he almost lost control.

She came suddenly, arching beneath him; Edouard felt the control, the expertise acquired in years of meaningless lovemaking begin to slip, to desert him, and with relief he let it go. There was a hot dark star in his mind, a source he must reach; Hélène said his name at the moment he possessed it, and he felt his body shudder in the violence of the release.

Afterward they lay still, and neither spoke. When his mind grew calmer, and he eased himself from her body, Edouard felt a certain fear. He waited, tensing, for the self-hatred to come back, for the countersurge of disgust that always followed desire. It did not come; he felt only a great quietude, and—after a while—the tension left his body and dissolved.

Hélène spoke first. She reached for his hand and pressed it. Her voice was a little broken still.

"Edouard. You took the past away. . . ."

He could hear the wonder in her voice, and—since he felt it, too, and how many years since that had happened?—he smiled from pure delight.

"The past, yes," he said.

They fell asleep together.

The next day, much later the next day, he suddenly remembered the present from Hermès. Carefully wrapped, tied with the distinctive Hermès ribbon, it was still in his study, forgotten from the night before. He fetched it, and brought it back to her. Hélène was sitting up in bed, leaning against a pile of lace pillows. He rested it carefully in her hands.

"It's a present. For you. I meant to give it to you yesterday but . . ."

"A present? For me?" For a moment she looked touchingly young, like a child at Christmas; then her eyes dropped, and he saw a strange hesitancy, a wariness, come into her face.

She looked down at the box, afraid to open it. For an instant, she heard Ned Calvert's voice, that slow seductive southern drawl. *You're my sweet little girl; I like to give my little girl presents. . . .*

Then she looked up and saw Edouard's face. On it there was an expression of such gentleness, of such excitement—masked by an attempt to appear nonchalant—that she felt instantly ashamed of the memory, of connecting those two events and those two men. The image of Ned Calvert disappeared, and for an instant new images came, of the long night and the long morning, pulsing in her body; then, eagerly, she pulled at the ribbon and opened the box.

A pair of gloves—*the* gloves. Her heart lifted that he should have remembered. A diamond ring; a most beautiful ring. She stared down into the blue-white fire of the stone, and then looked up at Edouard uncertainly.

He moved to the bed and sat down beside her, taking her hand in his.

"When I was a boy . . ." he spoke awkwardly, as if he had rehearsed this speech in his mind, and now that he came to say it, the words eluded him. "When I was a boy—fifteen, sixteen years of age—a little younger than you are now, I fell in love with a much older woman. It was during the war. I was living in London—she was my first love affair, my first mistress, if you like. My brother introduced us. . . ." He paused. "It was an infatuation, I suppose. My brother thought so then—but I've never been able to think of it like that, even now. It was perfectly real to me. I was very young, and very obsessed, and after a while—a year, a little longer, it ended. Her name was Célestine."

He broke off, and Hélène watched him silently.

"She was a kind woman, I see that now. She was always very patient with me, and very generous. There were things she said to me that I will always remember—but one in particular . . ." He hesitated. "I hadn't learned to be wary of words then, I was too young and too inexperienced. I was given to making the most passionate declarations—I had convinced myself we had a future, you see. When I did that, whenever I did that, she would always stop me. She said I shouldn't squander words; that one day I would meet the woman I loved, and I should save the words until then. Use, careless use, devalued them; they became common currency. . . . When she said that, I was very angry. But I came to realize that she was right. Since then, whatever else I've done, and whatever else I've been, I've never lied to a woman. I've never pretended an emotion I did not feel." He gave a quick impatient shrug. "I'm aware that's not much of an achievement."

He stopped then. Hélène looked at him quietly.

"Why are you telling me this?"

"Because you will hear things about me, if you haven't heard them already, and I want you to know the truth. I have given women presents, you see, in the past—there was a time when I was quite famous for it. Jewelry from my company—rubies, pearls, you can imagine the sort of thing. When an affair ended."

He spoke quite casually, almost impatiently, and Hélène felt a cold dull ache settle around her heart.

"When it ended?" She looked down at the ring. "Oh, I see."

"No, you don't." He reached forward and gripped her hand more tightly. "I have never given any woman diamonds, until now. Never. They are the stone I think the most beautiful, the stone my father loved the best. I kept them back, just as I kept the words back. I wanted to have something, something that was not tainted, something I could give with a free heart, with my love. When the moment came."

There was a silence. He spoke calmly, but Hélène could see the struggle in his face. She looked from him to the ring, and then back to his eyes. She felt a little light-headed, caught up in a sudden and unreasoning sweep of joy; her mind sang with it. For a moment she stood again outside a small church, heard a child's cry, saw a flash of color in the air, and then his face. Was that how it felt, to see the future?

"I knew," she said.

"I knew too."

His hand tightened around hers, then released it. Carefully, Hélène disengaged the ring from the Hermès glove. She slipped it on her finger; cold, hard, bright. She lifted her hand, and the diamond struck the light.

Later, Edouard said, "You must stay. You must. We shall fetch your things."

"I have a suitcase." Hélène smiled. "That's all. One suitcase. Everything I own in the world."

"Then we must fetch it. We'll go together."

"No." She shook her head. "It won't take long. I must do it myself."

Edouard argued, and when he failed to persuade her to change her mind, gave in.

She took a taxi into Paris, left it on the Right Bank, crossed the Seine, and then ran all the way to the roominghouse where she had been staying. To her relief, she met no one; even the old dragon of a concièrge was not at her usual place by the door.

Hélène ran up the stairs, and half-fell into the little room in which she had been sleeping. It took a moment to find her suitcase, a moment to unlock it and thrust into it the few clothes she had brought with her.

She went to shut it, and then paused. Kneeling back on her heels, pushing aside a crumpled skirt and a blouse, she looked at the bundle of papers and photographs; she looked at Orangeburg and her mother and the past.

She stared at them silently, feeling time fracture. Orangeburg, Billy, her mother, Ned Calvert, Cassie Wyatt, Priscilla-Anne; lying in a narrow bed at night, with the thin curtains flapping in the breeze, and the smell of the mud drifting up from the river. It felt unreal, remote, a sequence from a film once seen. Three days had obscured sixteen years.

She picked up one of the photographs of Violet, and hugged it tight against her heart. She closed her eyes, and fragments of the past moved jerkily through her mind, like flotsam carried by a river. Her mother, and Billy's mother, blaming her for Billy's death. She saw Mrs. Tanner bend over Billy and fasten the button on his shirt; she saw her spread her fingers, and the rain begin to fall.

She had dreamed that image night after night, in the weeks since she had left Orangeburg. It made her afraid to sleep, and when it came, she would jerk herself awake and sit up in bed, the sweat cooling on her forehead, her eyes staring into the dark, telling Mrs. Tanner and telling herself that it was not her fault Billy died the way he did.

She opened her eyes again. Violet gazed back at her sweetly from the photograph, her lips curved in a cupid's bow. She was wearing a frivolous little hat.

Hélène gave a shiver. She pushed the photograph back in the suitcase and closed it. She felt, obscurely, that she owed them something— all of them, Violet and Billy and Mrs. Tanner—and that she did not have the right to be happy yet. She had no sooner framed the thought in her own mind than she rebelled against it. Billy would have understood; her mother would have understood. Her mother would have done precisely the same thing. All for love. . . .

Yet that idea, too, was chilling. Was she turning into her mother after all? She stood up and lifted the suitcase onto the narrow single bed. She did not have to return to Edouard, she told herself. She could send the ring back. She need not see him again. She could begin to do all the things she had planned to do. She could. Surely she could?

She stood, frowning obstinately at the suitcase. Then, quickly, clumsily, she grabbed it, pushed open the door, and ran down the stairs and into the street. She ran all the way from the lodginghouse to the Seine, and there, by the Pont Notre Dame, she stopped. The water glinted, flowing fast; the pinnacles of Notre Dame soared against the light; beside the river, in the sunshine, lovers strolled, their arms around each other. She hailed a taxi.

When she reached St. Cloud, Edouard was waiting for her outside. He was pacing the gravel in front of the house, and when he saw the cab, and saw her start to run toward him, he held out his arms.

"I was afraid," he said as he held her. "I don't know why, but I thought you might not come back. . . ." Hélène dropped the suitcase she was holding, and buried her face against his chest.

"I had to come back," she said—to Edouard, to her mother, to Billy, to all of them. "I had to."

"What made you come to Paris?"

It was a question Edouard had not asked her before, and he asked it suddenly, out of a long contented silence. It was early evening, a perfect warm Paris evening, and they were sitting on the *terrasse*, outside the Deux Magots, two glasses of Pernod on the small round table in front of them. Edouard had added water to the clear liquid, and Hélène watched it turn milky; she liked the cool taste of anise, the lulling warmth when the drink hit the stomach. She felt like a cat curled in the sun, at peace with the world.

"Be careful," Edouard had said with a smile, "It's quite strong, Hélène."

Hélène had smiled. She liked to hear him use her name. She liked to hear him pronounce it in the French manner, just as her mother had always done. It made her guilty sometimes, for Edouard still thought that her real name was Helen Hartland; but it was curiously comforting—as if he knew her truly, despite her lies.

Now she felt as if she wanted just to stay here in this spot forever, watching the constant procession of people, trying to understand the bursts of conversation from the neighboring tables. His question made her jump.

"My mother loved Paris. She often spoke of it. I'd never been here. . . ." She hoped he would ask her nothing more, because she hated to evade his questions now. Now she regretted that odd secretive instinct which had made her lie to him the day they first met. Every morning she would wake in his arms and tell herself that today would be different, today she would tell him the truth. *I didn't grow up in England, Edouard. I lied to you. I grew up in America. In the South. In Alabama.*

She rehearsed the words often enough. But when she came to speak them, she always lost courage and held back. Her lies had trapped her: Edouard would be hurt by them, or angered. She would have to explain *why* she lied, and once she began, she would have to tell him everything: about her mother and the abortion, and Billy and Ned Calvert. . . . Shame at the memory made her blush; she felt the heat sweep up over her neck and burn in her cheeks. Would he change toward her if he knew? She looked away; it seemed to her then that he might.

Edouard saw the blush and misinterpreted it; he smiled, and leaned back in his chair.

"If you hadn't stopped to look at the church, just then . . . if I had driven a different route . . . if my work schedule had been different . . . if your mother hadn't talked to you about Paris . . ." He gave a shrug. "So many 'ifs.' I like that. It reminds me the gods are kind—occasionally."

Hélène looked up at him. His dark blue eyes met hers, slightly mockingly; then his gaze grew steady and intent. The clamor around them stilled; Hélène felt the world tilt and perspective alter. No café, no Paris, no Alabama, no past: just the two of them. Such pure delight, from one glance! She felt so elated, suddenly so insane with happiness, that she wanted to do something mad—sing, dance, shout—turn around to the people at the next table and tell them that she was in love, and she understood it now—all the stories, all the poems, all the songs. Her mind sang, it felt so alive, and so sure. She leaned across the table and held out her hand, palm upward.

Edouard reached across and laid his hand in hers. As soon as he touched her, she wanted him; expectation arced through her body; her mind clouded over with a now familiar lassitude.

She had read about desire in books, and the girls at school had talked about it, but none of the things she had read, or they had said, had prepared her for this feeling, for the urgency of it, and its peculiar blinding quality. It was sharp and sweet, pleasurable and painful—and Edouard felt it too. She had learned to recognize it in his eyes, and he in hers, and that secret bond intoxicated her. It filled her with exhilarating recklessness; it made her feel both drugged and excited at once. She looked at Edouard, who was gesturing with sudden impatience to the waiter; she knew that he felt the same thing, exactly the same thing—but no one else would have known. To the waiter, to the other people in the café, he must have appeared unmoved, formal, impassive. None of them could hear these secret communications between them, none of them could see Edouard as she saw him now. They saw only a man; she saw a lover—her lover—and the urgency and the secrecy made her exultant.

Edouard looked up. "Yes?"

She nodded, and he stood up, his face set. He took her arm, hesitated only a moment, and just when Hélène was thinking—oh, quickly, somewhere, it doesn't matter where—he began to lead her swiftly away from the café into the maze of narrow streets that lay behind the church of St. Germain-des-Prés. He walked fast, and Hélène stumbled to keep up with him.

A small street; a little square shaded by a tree; a cluster of modest hotels, with tall narrow façades, and shutters closed against the evening sun. Notes tossed across the surface of an old polished mahogany counter; a signature scrawled; a heavy iron key, and a proprietor, a fat man smoking a cigar. He hardly bothered to look up.

The room was on the first floor, and Edouard was reaching for her before he opened the door. He pushed her back against it and leaned against her, so she could feel his weight and the hardness of his penis pressing against her belly and her thighs. She moaned, and Edouard unbuttoned her blouse, his hands fumbling a little in his impatience. She felt his mouth against her throat, his tongue against the sharp points of her nipples. She began to tug impatiently at his belt: no time to undress, no time, no time, no time.

The small lace panties she wore were wet. Edouard slipped them down over her thighs; he parted the lips of her sex, and she cried out, pressing herself down against his palm and fingers, rubbing against him like a little animal. She wanted to hold his penis in her hand, and fumbled to free it from his clothes. But the moment she touched him, it was not enough. She wanted him inside her; she wanted to feel him fill her. Edouard grasped her hips, pulling her down on him as he thrust up; mouth to mouth, sex to sex.

"Open your eyes," Edouard said, drawing back from her a little. She opened her eyes and looked down. She watched it, this magical, infinitely pleasurable joining. It was very arousing to her, to watch and to feel; it was wonderful and unbearable, the suspense when he withdrew a little, and she saw him glistening and strong before he pushed again.

He always knew exactly when she was about to come. Today their arousal was very violent, and it was very quick. She pressed against him feverishly, was suddenly still for one moment, as she always was the second before climax. He loved her as she always looked then, for she looked as blind as he felt. One last long push. They shuddered against each other. It was less than ten minutes since they had left Deux Magots.

Afterward, Edouard said untruthfully, "We could have waited, I suppose, until we got back to St. Cloud."

"Could we?" Hélène smiled.

She moved away from him then, and looked at the room for the first time. It had one tall shuttered window, an enormous and magisterial bed covered in crimson satin, and a huge battered armoire. There was one small rug, and a bidet in the corner, with a curtain.

"What is this place?"

"An hotel. Of a kind. Not respectable in the least. It rents rooms by the hour to people in need. I most certainly shouldn't have brought you here."

"I'm glad you did. I like it." Hélène turned to him defiantly. "I like the ridiculous cupboard and the ridiculous bed. I like everything. It has no secrets. It's made for lovers, and it's proud of it."

"The wallpaper could perhaps be improved," Edouard murmured.

"You're not to criticize it." Hélène rounded on him. "It's perfect, and I love it."

"We could always stay . . ." Edouard began to smile. "I imagine it is possible to rent a room an entire night as well as an hour." He moved in a purposeful way toward the bed. "Since you like the decor so much. . ." he murmured, drawing Hélène down onto the crimson satin.

They made love more slowly this time, to the companionable creaking of bedsprings. When it was dark, they went out and had dinner in a small local restaurant filled with solemn Frenchmen eating dinner alone, their napkins tucked under their chins as they ate with great seriousness. No one recognized Edouard; the elderly waiters in their long white aprons served them with solicitude, with sidelong glances and occasional smiles, as if it pleased them, on a summer's night, to serve two people who were so splendidly oblivious to everything except each other. Then they walked back through the quiet streets, and back to the room with its crimson bed. In the morning, quite early, they took croissants and café au lait in thick china bowls; it was brought to them in their room, and they ate at a small table with the shutters thrown back, and a view across the square with its central tree.

Outside, a large cat, a stately tabby, uncurled from a window ledge, stretched, and then ambled across the square, her tail a waving plume. Hélène watched her; she watched the light catch the leaves of the tree, listened to the sounds of a city coming to life in the early morning. She turned to Edouard impulsively, unaware that he had been watching her gravely.

"I used to think so much about what I would be—about what I would become. Oh, Edouard—I used to make so many plans!" She gave a little shake of her head. "When I'm with you—I don't think of that at all. It doesn't seem to matter. I don't have to become anything. I just am. . . ." She raised her eyes anxiously to his face. "Do you understand that? Do you think it's wrong?"

"I feel the same," Edouard said quietly, "so I can't judge."

"It's beautiful here. Paris is beautiful. I love you, Edouard," she said, and then—with one of the quick shy gestures he loved, she turned her face and buried it against his shoulder. Edouard held her gently, and pressed his lips against her hair.

"My darling," he said gently. "My darling."

They left the hotel hand in hand, talking and laughing, just after nine. As they stepped into the square, Edouard halted, paused for an instant, and then, taking Hélène's arm in his, walked on. Looking up, she saw a tall, extremely elegant woman, her eyes obscured by dark glasses. The woman stared in their direction, then turned away down a side street.

When they were out of earshot, Edouard sighed. "Ghislaine Belmont-Laon," he said. "The greatest gossip in Paris. She decorated a number of our showrooms some years back. She haunts the shops off the Rue Jacob. She also haunts my mother. . . ."

Hélène stopped; she looked up at him. "Did she recognize you?"

"Oh, certainly, I imagine. Ghislaine misses nothing."

"You mean, she'll tell your mother, your friends. . . ." Hélène asked; Edouard had begun to smile.

"That she saw me coming out of an extremely insalubrious hotel at nine in the morning with a beautiful young woman? Oh, without a doubt. My mother, by lunchtime, and the rest of Paris by this evening . . ."

"And do you mind?" Hélène looked at him curiously; she felt a little afraid.

"Mind? I don't give a damn. They'll find out sooner or later, anyway. That's inevitable. I don't intend to hide you away. It's just that—" He paused, and his face grew serious. "I'm used to their gossip and their lies, and you're not. I don't want you to be hurt by it, and I had hoped we might avoid it for a few more weeks."

He said nothing more, indeed seemed to forget the incident, but it left Hélène with a small nagging sense of unease. She wished they had not been seen; she wished Edouard had mentioned no time span; it was as if she and Edouard had been locked away in a special place, until suddenly the cold world had intruded. She saw herself for a moment, then, as an outsider might see her: a young girl, without money or friends; an older man, both powerful and rich.

That afternoon, Edouard took her to Chanel, and then to Hermès, where he had arranged that she be fitted for riding clothes.

"Why should I need riding clothes? Edouard, that's crazy. . . ." she had said, but Edouard had only smiled and said, "Wait and see." He had bought her dresses before, in the two weeks they had been in Paris. Then, she had accepted the presents with a free heart, gladly and excitedly. But that afternoon, everything was sullied. The assistants at Hermès were courteous, but Hélène prickled with shame under their careful expert eyes. A rich man's mistress; a gold digger: she felt as if she saw contempt in their gaze. She said nothing to Edouard. That night, his mother, Louise de Chavigny, telephoned him at St. Cloud.

The conversation was brief, and on Edouard's side, uninformative. He took the call in his bedroom, and when it was over, Hélène saw that his face was clouded. She watched him fearfully.

He sat still for a moment, staring at the floor. When he looked up and held out his hand to her, his face cleared. "Shall we leave Paris for a while?" he said abruptly, taking her by surprise. "Shall we? I want to show you the Loire . . . I want to take you riding there." He had been planning this, then: she instantly felt giddy with happiness. It was only later, when Edouard had offered no further explanation of the phone call, that the former unease returned.

Was he taking her to the Loire, in spite of what he said, because an unsuitable mistress was less visible there than in Paris? She hated the thought; she argued with it; it left her, and then returned. She thought of Edouard's friends, she thought of his mother, and felt a flurry of panic. If they met her—worse, if they knew who she really was—what would their reaction be then? She imagined their cold and hostile stares: *the latest girl Edouard's picked up*—she could almost hear their drawling voices. It was like Orangeburg, only much worse than Orangeburg: they would look down on her; they would see her for the sham she was—and if they did that, they might influence Edouard. Edouard might come to see her with their eyes.

They traveled to the Loire in Edouard's private plane. And for the first week, in that fairy-tale house, she oscillated between intense happiness and dragging despair. The more she longed to tell Edouard the truth, the more urgent and imperative it became to do so, the more frightening and impossible it seemed.

He loves me; he cannot love me: the two phrases beat a constant tattoo in her mind. Days passed; a week passed, and sometimes Hélène felt as if she were going mad: one moment on the mountaintop, the next deep in the valley; in the sun one instant, the next in shadow.

Edouard taught her to ride; she learned quickly. It was late August, then September, day after day of strong clear sunshine with no hint of autumn, but Hélène felt as if April inhabited her mind and her heart and made them volatile. She would go to bed at night feeling rapturously happy; then, some nights, she would dream of Billy. She would hear his mother's accusing voice, and it would stay with her when she woke, so that the next morning would be sullied. She would withdraw a little into herself, and she could see that Edouard sensed that withdrawal, and that it pained him. If only she could explain to him, she felt then, if only she could tell him the whole truth . . . she would even turn to him sometimes, impatiently, all the necessary sentences framed in her mind and crying out to be spoken. And then, at the very last moment, she would find herself unable to say them; she would say something else instead.

"I feel so uncertain one moment, and so sure the next. Edouard, is it like that when you love someone?" she asked him one night, kneeling beside him, tightening her arms around his neck, and looking anxiously into his eyes.

"In the beginning, perhaps. I feel it too." He bent his head and pressed his lips against her hand; he was afraid, sometimes, to let her see how much her innocence and her candor touched him. When he looked up and saw that her face was troubled, he pulled her close to him and held her tightly in his arms.

"Never doubt," he said fiercely. "Doubt anything else, but not this. You can't. I won't let you."

A t the end of the second week of September, Edouard was forced, reluctantly, to return to Paris for business reasons. The first Wyspianski collection was due to be launched, first in Europe, then in America, later that year, and although the collection itself was all he had hoped for, and the arrangements for the launch had been proceeding smoothly, there were certain elements within de Chavigny that had been opposed to the collection, and the scale of it, for some time. Two of his directors in particular had been fighting a patient rearguard action; since he had left Paris, they had been dragging their feet.

"But why should they do that?" Hélène asked. Edouard had shown her some of the Wyspianski designs, and even she, without expert knowledge, could see that they were exquisite.

"A thousand reasons, my darling." Edouard gave a dismissive gesture of the hand. "Sometimes I think it's because they just like to oppose me for the sake of it. Sometimes I think they're empire-building. Sometimes they have arguments which seem cogent enough to them— commercial arguments. I don't always blame them. They're interested in balance sheets, in boosting profits. They're not interested in producing art—particularly art they think won't sell. Wyspianski's designs are unusual and expensive. They're aimed at a tiny clientele. There have always been people at de Chavigny who think that market is dying, that we should concentrate our energies on our other divisions—property, hotels, that kind of thing. They'd be quite happy to run down the jewelry division—even sell it off. They can't do that now, not while I'm here, so they content themselves with being uncooperative. That's all. There used to be someone in the company who took care of this sort of thing for me—he'd see a minor revolt brewing, and deal with it quickly. But he's working for me in America now—and I haven't found another trouble-shooter. Don't worry." He smiled. "I can sort it out very quickly. I'll fly there and be back the same day."

He left early the next morning, carefully making sure that word of his impending arrival was spread at his Paris headquarters. Once there, he was equally careful to behave as if there were no particular urgency about his visit. He spent the morning going over routine matters; he had a brief luncheon with his old friend Christian Glendinning, who was in Paris to supervise the new exhibition just transferred from his Cork Street gallery in London to his Left Bank gallery. Christian remarked, with a certain glint in his eye, that Edouard seemed in excellent spirits. He returned to work, and then and only then did he summon the two executives in question to his offices.

He watched them with interest as they came in. Monsieur Brichot, the elder of the two, was pale and voluble, clearly nervous. He was a man in his early sixties, a thorough, hardworking, unimaginative man who had long ago risen as high as he ever would. He perhaps resented the fact that his promotions had ceased; certainly, he liked to meddle, interfering here, probing there, firing off long memoranda concerning the affairs of other departments. Perhaps he thought such meddling was proof of his energy and devotion; perhaps he was merely fussy. It was the first time that he had, however, gone as far as blocking a directive from Edouard himself, and Edouard felt fairly certain that he had been put up to it by de Belfort, the man who came into the room with him now.

Philippe de Belfort was also pale, but not from nerves, Edouard was sure of that. While Brichot made a little rush across the room, approached a chair, and was then not quite sure whether to sit in it, de Belfort came in at a leisurely, unhurried pace. He was a tall thick-set man a few years younger than Edouard. He was stately in all his movements, and always spoke with a slow, ponderous weight. He had pale fair hair above his heavy pale face, and eyes of an indeterminate color, heavily lidded. They gave his face an expression of arrogance, almost of sneering. He reminded Edouard, then and always, of some fish, large and pallid, which flourished in the deepest regions of the sea, where light could not reach. Edouard did not like him, but he admired him. He could appear pompous, and he was certainly lacking in charm, but he was smart, astute, and determined, the ablest recruit to the company since the days of Simon Scher.

He had come to de Chavigny some five years previously, armed with impressive credentials: a father, now dead, who had been a distinguished and famous stockbroker; first class degrees from the Sorbonne and the London School of Economics; a period with the Rothschilds, where he had been recognized from the first as a high flyer. A man who spoke French, English, German, and Spanish with equal fluency; a man who was not afraid of responsibility or decision-making, who weighed matters with a quickness and deftness of mind that was at odds with the ponderousness of his speech; a man who, Edouard knew, pursued social connections in Paris and in London with the same energy and resourcefulness which he applied to his work; a man who would go far, and who behaved, always, as if he were not on the way to some future eminence, but had already arrived there, perhaps at birth.

Now, while Brichot hesitated awkwardly, gazing at Edouard across his desk, de Belfort moved to a chair and sat down, in one heavy assertive movement, as if to say, I will sit here for the meantime; my proper place is the other side of the desk.

He and Edouard looked at each other; then de Belfort turned his head; his gaze slowly took in the entire room. He did this each time he came into this office, as if it amused him to enumerate its contents. Edouard looked at him with a slight frown. It was a source of constant irritation to him that de Belfort, a man who had already galvanized the accessories section, where he was responsible for the manufacturing and selling of a highly profitable new kind of merchandise for de Chavigny, should be a man to whom he felt an instinctive antipathy. De Belfort had drive; he had a kind of commercial imagination and daring which Edouard knew he himself also possessed; they were, in some ways, alike—and yet Edouard could never feel at ease with him. Between them, always, and he had sensed it from the first, there was a barrier of will, an unspoken antagonism.

Brichot, who finally sat now, had already given up; that much was obvious. Edouard had hardly begun his questions, when, with a small nervous fluttering of the hands, Brichot burst out, "I did feel . . . I'm afraid that . . . de Belfort said . . . it seemed wise . . ." He dried up.

"*We* felt," de Belfort cut in with a cold glance at his colleague, "we felt that although the promotion budget for the Wyspianski Collection had been discussed and approved, there were numerous signs of an escalation in costs."

"That's right. Escalation. That's what we thought. . . ."

"And so," de Belfort continued firmly, "it seemed advisable to delay final authorization while we ran some rechecks."

There was a silence. Brichot looked up at the ceiling—one of those famous de Chavigny silences! De Belfort continued to look straight in front of him, his pale eyes fixed on a point somewhere to the side of Edouard's head.

"And have those rechecks been completed?" Edouard asked finally in a polite voice which made Brichot quake.

"Oh, yes." De Belfort's tone was almost casual. "They were completed this morning. All the problems have been ironed out. I gave the final authorization myself. An hour ago, actually. I would have informed you. But unfortunately you were out at lunch."

The pale eyes shifted for a second to Edouard's face. The reference to lunch had sounded reproachful. Brichot, detecting the criticism, gave a nervous sniff. He took his handkerchief out of his pocket, then put it back again.

"Good." Edouard stood up. "Then I need keep you no longer. Perhaps, Philippe"—he turned to de Belfort—"on another occasion, if you have doubts of this kind, you would come to me direct?"

"But of course. It was just that I was reluctant to interrupt your vacation. . . ."

He made his way to the door at a dignified pace. Brichot hung back, and then scuttled after him.

Edouard watched them go thoughtfully. Brichot was harmless. A timid man, close to retirement, who would be rewarded for a lifetime's work with a seat on the board—a backseat. But de Belfort was a different matter. Edouard was certain that de Belfort disliked him as much as he disliked de Belfort. A man who was an asset, and a man who was also, possibly, a threat. Edouard frowned and returned to his work.

Later, when he was just congratulating himself that everything had been tied up, and he could leave, he received a telephone call from his mother. He picked up the receiver resignedly. Louise launched straight into the attack.

Did she always have to hear from chance acquaintances that Edouard was in Paris? Did he never consider that weeks had gone by, and she had not seen him? That she was no longer young? That her doctors were quite concerned?

She went on in this vein for some while. Eventually, Edouard interrupted her: "Very well, Maman. I'll be with you shortly. But I can't stay long."

Louise's voice at once purred with pleasure. Edouard hung up. He knew the real reason for the summons, and he wondered how long Louise would take to come to the point.

She took half an hour. In that time, reclining on a chaise longue, pressing her hand to her brow but looking otherwise radiant, she told him about the failings of her servants, and of her previous doctor. She discussed her symptoms, real and imaginary, with zest. Most of her ailments were pure invention, and their quickest cure was usually a new lover. But she had fewer lovers now, and longer gaps between them. She must be enduring such a gap now, Edouard thought, shocked a little by his own detachment.

His mind drifted away to the Loire and to Hélène. Louise gave him a gallant smile.

"But enough of my problems, my darling. I must say you're looking marvelously well. It must be all the fresh air, and the riding. . . . You should take a holiday more often. It obviously agrees with you."

"Thank you, Maman," Edouard said, and waited.

"Of course, I've been thinking about you a great deal, Edouard." She leaned forward elegantly, her dress falling in soft folds. "Shall I tell you what I thought? You won't be cross? I thought, darling Edouard, that it's really time you considered marrying again."

She let the sentence float away in the air. Edouard regarded her equably.

"Have you, Maman? How curious. I was thinking just the same thing myself."

"Were you, darling?" Louise's perfectly plucked eyebrows rose slightly. She smiled ingenuously. Edouard wondered how accurate the gossip was, and precisely how much of it Louise had heard. "I'm *so* glad. After all, one can't mourn forever—even I realized that eventually, after poor Xavi died. One must look to the future. One has a life to live, after all. One has responsibilities. . . ."

She gave a suitably vague gesture of the hand, and then stood up. "Of course, in your case, it's not a simple matter. I do understand that. You deserve someone so very special—and I just wondered, I had been thinking, when you return from the Loire, darling Edouard . . . perhaps if I held a little party. It seems such an age since I had a party. Nothing too large—but there were several charming people I thought I might invite. The youngest Cavendish girl, you remember her, Edouard? And Sylvie de Castallane. Or Monique . . . no perhaps not Monique. Plenty of money, of course, but not quite . . . No. And then there're some charming Americans. Gloria Stanhope—you remember? I stayed at their place on Long Island last year? The loveliest girl, and—"

"Maman. Forgive me." Edouard stood up. "I should hate for you to waste your time."

"Waste my time?" Louise's eyes widened. "Edouard, how can you think such a thing?" She gave a little smile. "All right, I'm matchmaking, just a bit. But mothers do that, darling, they enjoy it. You mustn't mind. And I do so want to be sure you will be happy, darling, that you find someone suitable, because I'd hate for you to be hurt. You can be so *unpredictable*, Edouard—even rash, occasionally. Now, don't frown, you know it's true. . . ."

"Maman." Edouard cut her short. He looked at Louise, and Louise's gaze dropped. "Shall we stop this charade? You've been listening to Paris gossip. You've been listening to Ghislaine Belmont-Laon, who—God knows—has no idea what she's talking about. And now you're curious. It's why you invited me here. Might it not be easier just to say so?"

Louise glanced up at him and smiled. She was not in the least discomposed; he should have remembered, Edouard thought grimly, that she had a ruthless conviction in the power of her own charm. Now she gave him a rueful, almost flirtatious look.

"Very well. How clever you are, Edouard. I admit it. People have been talking a bit. And I was a little concerned. Well, a diamond was mentioned—she was wearing it when you took her to Givenchy. And Hermès. And then I heard she was with you in the Loire—you never take anyone there. So, naturally, I did begin to wonder. She's very young, I hear, and English, and no one seems to have the least idea who she is, and of course, Edouard, I know you have affairs, it would hardly be natural if you didn't, so perhaps it's just *that*, because it did *not* sound as if she were quite—"

"Her name is Helen Hartland." Edouard moved to the door. "And it isn't simply an affair, brief or otherwise. Beyond that, I think my private life is no concern of yours. . . ."

His face was stony. Louise took a step after him and called his name, but the door had already closed.

I n the Loire, the day was hot, and the hours without Edouard seemed to take an eternity to pass.

In the morning, after Edouard left, Hélène walked for a while through the formal gardens of the château, and across the park to the water meadows. She had ridden this way often with Edouard these past weeks; they had stopped their horses just here, on this bluff of land.

She sat there for a while, in the cool blue shade of the chestnut trees, looking out across the wide expanse of the Loire. It curved away into the distance, a calm silver, without ripples, so still it seemed not to move. A dragonfly hovered over the water, and she watched the sun catch the rainbow of its wings: she thought of the pool under the cottonwoods, and, picking up a small handful of stones, and tossing them into the water, she watched their circles widen, and thought of Billy.

She had tried to think of him these past weeks—when she was in Paris, when she first came here with Edouard. She had an odd superstitious sense that she *ought* to think of him, that she ought not to let one day pass without remembering him, and the things he had done, and the things he had said. If she did not think of him, it made his death so very final, as if his whole existence had been erased.

But she did not always think of him. Sometimes, she was aware, a day would go past—two days, sometimes three, and in her happiness, in her absorption with Edouard, Billy would be forgotten.

Now, without any conscious prompting on her part, he came back to her very vividly: she saw him as a child; she saw him as a young man. She could see the resignation in his eyes, the sad acceptance that no matter what she had done, she did not love him as he loved her.

She stood up quickly. She ought to have mourned him better, she thought with a sudden sense of shame; she owed him that, at the very least. If she had cared for him, if his death had really mattered to her, should she have come here at all?

It's wrong to be so happy, she told herself, as she had that day alone in Paris. She turned back toward the château, and at once, by some perverse mechanism of the mind, all the happiness she had felt began to drain away; she looked around her with new eyes.

She had walked farther than she intended, in any case; crossing the park there was very little shade, and the sun, now almost vertical above her, made her head ache. She stopped once or twice, shading her eyes and feeling an unusual lethargy come over her.

In the distance, the château shimmered in the heat. Light made its pale stone gleam; it glinted from the steep slate roofs; it reflected back at her from the turrets, from the great banks of windows. Alone, without Edouard, to whom it was simply one of several childhood homes, the house seemed curiously unreal, a mirage, or an illustration on a picture postcard: not a place where she could really be living, or had any right to live; not a place where a girl who grew up on the wrong side of the tracks could ever really belong. She had come to love this house, and yet today, the closer she walked to it, the more distant it seemed.

Once indoors, she was served luncheon, formally, exactly as they were served it when Edouard was there. One place at one end of a long shining table. Ranked silver knives and forks; ranked Baccarat glasses. *The servant will stand on my left, Mother, and the napkin will be on my lap. . . . And if there is a finger bowl, the tips of the fingers only, darling, remember—you're not washing your hands!*

She bent her head, shut her eyes, and then opened them again. The room was cool, and quiet, but she felt hot, and without any appetite for the delicious food. She pushed it to one side; its taste was cloying. She felt a sudden quick rush of nausea, and stood up. For a second, the room blurred, then steadied. She saw the servant look at her, his face concerned; he took a step forward, and Hélène looked at him in embarrassment.

She didn't know how to dismiss him; she didn't know what to say in English, let alone French; she stared at him for a moment in an agony of uncertainty, trying frantically to remember how Edouard behaved. She couldn't think; she couldn't recall; when she was with him, he blinded her to all else.

The servant saved her. Seeing the color come back into her face, he gave a half bow, and opened the door for her. Hélène walked past, stiffly and self-consciously: did he despise her, this polite efficient well-trained man? Did they all despise her, did they gossip about her in the servants' hall, did they see her as an intruder? That was how she felt, she realized, as, thankfully, she reached the privacy of her rooms: an intruder, a stranger, a woman who had no place here.

The rooms Edouard had given her adjoined his, and looked out across the park. They had once belonged to, and had been furnished for, one of his ancestors, Adeline de Chavigny, a great beauty of the court at Versailles. Both she and her husband had gone to the guillotine a few days after their king.

Hélène wandered from the boudoir to the bedroom, gently touching the things that had once belonged to Adeline. The soft gray silk curtains on the four-poster; the chair covered in needlework—petitpoint, sewed by Adeline herself; the fan she had once held; the Aubusson carpet woven to her choice of design; the backgammon table whose ivory scorecard still bore her name, and beneath it the words *Le Roi*.

She had died bravely, Edouard said. Hélène stopped in front of the gray marble chimney piece, and looked at the portrait of Adeline that hung above it. Coolly beautiful, she stood in the park of the château, flanked on one side by the bitch setter given her by Louis XVI, and on the other by her eldest son, who escaped the guillotine and grew up to become one of Napoleon's great generals. The old order and the new: Adeline stood between the two, gazing out of the frame, an image of serenity. She was smiling, beautifully and frostily. The smile made Hélène feel like a usurper; she turned away.

She closed the shutters and adjusted the louvres so the afternoon light slanted into the room and striped the walls and floor. Then she lay down on the bed and stared at the portrait. Adeline and her pet dog; Adeline and her son. Perhaps it was easier to die bravely, she thought sleepily, if you knew your son would survive you, if you had sent him away to safety, as Adeline had done in sending her son to England.

She closed her eyes. The room felt airless and hot, and her head ached. Edouard's father had died bravely too, Edouard had told her. In front of a German firing squad, because of his work with the Resistance. He had looked so like Edouard in the photograph Edouard had shown her, and it was because of his father that Edouard cared so much about his work. Xavier de Chavigny and his son; Adeline de Chavigny and her son. The names moved dreamily through her mind; she felt herself grasp them, and then felt them eddy away. Generation after generation; Edouard's family had lived in this part of the Loire for centuries, and it was only now, she thought, that she was beginning to understand what that must mean for someone like Edouard. Such continuity: it made death quite a small thing, like a baton-change in a relay race. *My father is dead*, Edouard had said, *but in his work here he lives on.* . . . He had gestured up at the house across the gardens and the park, toward the Loire in the distance. . . .

She had not wanted to sleep, but sleep stole upon her, peacefully at first, so she felt as if she floated on water. Past the river bank, under the branches of the chestnut trees, drifting toward the cottonwoods, where she had expected to find Edouard, and then saw that it was Billy who was waiting for her. Billy smiled and helped her climb the bank; she lay down beside him, and because she knew he was going to die very soon it was terribly important that this be right. It was her last present to Billy, the last present anyone would ever give him. She let her hands rest in the cool hollow beneath his shoulder-blades, and she told him that it was the right time, and the right place and the right thing, and Billy seemed to understand; she could see the comprehension clear in his eyes, and it was only when she began to stroke his back that she realized something was wrong. His skin felt so very cold, and when she looked down at his arm, she could see the color seeping out of it, and the skin growing pale.

She shook him a little; he felt heavy and inert in her arms. A moment before he had been touching her, but now he was so very still, not moving at all. She felt something cool and wet against her face, and thought it was Billy's tears, but when she looked up, there were no tears, just blood. She could feel it in her hair and on her breasts and on her face and in her eyes. It was sticky and it smelled sweet and sour, and then Ned Calvert was there, telling her it was the best skin lotion in the world, and she opened her mouth and started screaming, very loudly and quite silently.

She woke, and jerked herself upright, shaking. She was bathed in sweat; her head was pounding. She looked around the still room, with its stripes of light, and for a moment she did not know where she was. She was still trapped in the dream, which was the worst dream she had ever had.

She sat very still; the colors of the dream were vivid in her mind.

She drew in her breath, tried to steady herself, and waited, her heart beating very fast, until the dream began to fade. It was only a nightmare, she told herself; it was entirely normal that she should dream like this. It would go away in a while. It would leave her.

But there was something she had seen in that dream, there had been an item of truth in its distortions. There, somewhere there, was something she should look at, something she should confront with her waking mind. *I must think*, she told herself; and she tried to make the dream come back, sequence after sequence. On the river, drifting toward the cottonwoods, and then . . . but the dream would not come back. Obstinately it evaded her, even as she reached for it, and now the room was reasserting itself, and the afternoon was reasserting itself, and the dream had gone. She stood up, and went into the bathroom, and splashed cold water against her hot face. She dried her skin on the soft white towels and felt calmer. Only a dream. Only a dream.

She went back into her bedroom and opened the shutters. The sun was lower in the sky, and the air was cooler. She walked back and forth in the room, one part of her mind still intent on pursuing the dream, and another part already beginning to calculate the number of hours left before Edouard would return. Time seemed very slow; it was inching forward.

Against one wall of the room there was a small inlaid bureau which had been made for Adeline de Chavigny. It was supplied with writing paper and pens, and after a while, Hélène sat down and idly drew out a sheet of paper. She picked up a pen. She toyed with the idea of writing to Cassie.

There was no one else to write to; she uncapped the pen, and looked down at the paper in front of her. Then, hurriedly, she wrote the date, and, under it: *Dear Cassie.* Then she stopped, and laid down the pen. Just the action of writing Cassie's name brought the past back. There it was, sharply, all around her: the trailer park, the hot air, her mother leaning back listlessly in the old red chair. She saw Cassie's kind, careworn face: *Take this, honey, I won't be needing it . . .*

She lifted her head and looked at the room in which she sat. So many beautiful things; so many valuable things. All the people she had grown up with, all the people she had loved—they had all been so poor. They'd worked and scratched and saved, and at the end of it, they couldn't have afforded to buy one thing in this room, not one single exquisite item. Could Edouard understand that? she wondered. Could a man like Edouard ever understand what it meant to be poor? No, she told herself, he could not, and in that moment, she felt a little distanced from him. In her world, she thought, people died and left no trace. They did not leave houses and gardens and portraits and traditions behind them; they had little, and they left nothing—in Billy's case, not even so much as a photograph.

She looked down at the paper in front of her, unsure if she were angry with herself, or with Edouard, or with life itself. She would not write to Cassie now, she decided. If she wrote, what would she say? That she was so much in love that the past no longer seemed real, and that when she was with Edouard, she was so happy she was content to let the future take care of itself? Cassie would not even be surprised if she wrote that. She'd expect it. That was what people did: they made all sorts of solemn resolves and promises, and then they didn't keep to them, and people who were kind, like Cassie, were careful never to remind them of that fact.

She stared down at the paper, and her eyes blurred with tears. Irritably, she brushed them away. She could not go on telling lies, she decided. Tonight, when Edouard returned from Paris, she would tell him the truth. Who she was and what she had been. She would tell him about her mother and about Ned Calvert. She would tell him about Billy. She would tell him about being poor. She would leave out nothing.

It was wrong to go on lying like this, as if she were ashamed, and it was terrible to have kept Billy a secret; it was like killing him twice. Perhaps that was why she had those horrible dreams, she thought, because she went on telling lies. She picked up the writing paper impatiently, and was about to crumple it up into a ball and throw it away when something stopped her. Perhaps it was thinking of the dream again, which made her mind uneasy; perhaps the idea had been there in her mind before, and she had resolutely pushed it away until then—but whatever the reason, she hesitated, and then smoothed out the paper again and looked at it, and her skin grew chill.

She looked at the words; she looked at the date she had written. The letters and the numbers seemed to grow very large and then very small. They danced before her eyes, and, as she stared at them, their significance altered, re-formed, and took on a new and implacable shape.

Her mouth felt dry; her body tensed. She continued to stare at the date for a long while, her mind frantically calculating. Then, with a little cry, she ripped the paper into fragments and threw them away.

The date she had written was September 15th. It was two months almost to the day since her mother had taken that last bus trip into Montgomery; two months since Hélène had waited for her in Orangeburg; two months since she had gone down to the pool with Billy. *It's the right thing, Billy, the right thing. . . .*

September 15th. It was the day she realized nothing would be right ever again. It was also the day Edouard asked her to marry him.

He asked the question in a way very typical of him—without preamble, tacked on at the end of other sentences, other pieces of information, so that he startled her. He had not noticed that anything was wrong. A moment before, he had been talking about his mother.

"She had heard about us. I was summoned for an interrogation. Like all my mother's interrogations, it was oblique—but she has a certain instinct, I admit that. She has never once questioned me about my private life before, so she had perhaps guessed . . . I don't know. It doesn't matter, in any case. Except that I was delayed, and I wanted very much to be here." He paused. "I wanted to be here, and to be with you. I wanted to ask you to marry me."

His voice was level, almost matter-of-fact. Only one small gesture, a quick lifting of the hand, betrayed any emotion. They were standing in his bedroom; it faced out across the park of the château, and beyond the window, the light was beginning to fade. Early evening, and a day which seemed to Hélène to have gone on forever. She looked at Edouard; she would always remember him, she thought, as he looked then, his hair slightly disheveled, his face intent, his dark eyes watchful, a smile—because he was happy; she could feel the happiness radiating from him—beginning on his lips.

He said the words, and she went on hearing them, echoing through her mind. She couldn't move, she couldn't speak; she couldn't think or even feel anymore; all her faculties seemed numb. The silence that followed seemed intensely loud, and to last a very long time. In the silence, she saw his face change, and when she could bear it no longer, she turned her face away miserably. Still he waited, and then, very slowly, he crossed to her, lifted his hand, and turned her face to his, so that she was forced to look into his eyes.

He looked at her for a long time, his face grave and still, then he said, very deliberately, although his voice caught on the words, "If I am wrong about this, then I am wrong about everything. *Everything.* Do you understand? If this is a lie, there is no truth left. Is that what you are saying? Is that what you mean, when you turn away your face like that?"

Hélène could hardly bear to meet his eyes, the pain and the anger in them were so intense. She felt burned by that look; the word *no* was clamoring in her mind, so loud and so insistent that she felt certain Edouard must hear it too. But her lips remained stiff; the word would not be spoken. Edouard continued to look at her, and all vitality left his face; it became hard, and set, and terrifyingly cold. Then, without another word, he let his hand fall and turned away.

He had almost reached the door when she said his name. She cried it out, hardly conscious of doing so, and Edouard swung round. She saw the hope come back into his eyes, although the uncertainty and the anger remained. Then he crossed back to her swiftly and took her in his arms. He pressed his lips against her hair; he tilted back her face and began feverishly to kiss her eyes, her mouth, her throat. Neither of them spoke, and because the closeness of anger and sexuality was not something which she had ever experienced before, what happened next shocked Hélène very much.

He undid her dress, his hands rough and hasty. He began to draw her toward the bed, and when she hung back, he pulled her down onto the floor beside him. Usually, she would have reached for him, she would have helped him, eagerly, to remove his clothes, and when she did not, she saw his face darken. He stood up then, his eyes never leaving her face, and began to undress. She watched him loosen his tie; she watched him undo his belt; she could not watch him do that without wanting him, but now the fact that she wanted him made her curiously and suddenly angry, as if wanting him were a weakness in herself.

When he was naked he knelt beside her and lifted her into his arms. He buried his face against her throat, and as Hélène felt the warmth of his bare skin against hers, she arched back with a little cry. At once, his eyes became intent; he looked almost triumphant then, as if he were determined that what she would not say, he would make her show. He touched her then, in a certain place, and in a certain way to which they both knew she responded, and she did respond, but this time some part of her mind remained locked away, shut up tight in some blind and female obstinacy. He was forcing her, he was using his knowledge of her and their past lovemaking, and for a moment she almost hated him for that. She drew her nails sharply down his arm, and the blood welled.

After that, it was not like making love at all, it was like a battle between them. Edouard was her enemy and her lover, and when he did not draw back, but forced her down under his weight, she knew that in some strange way he was closer to her now when he fought her, than he had ever been when he was gentle. She struggled against him, glad that the anger had come so suddenly, and had wiped out all the unhappiness and despair she had felt.

This, at least, was very quick, and very simple. Edouard meant to prove something to her, and she was determined not to let him. He was stronger than she was, though, a great deal stronger. It needed very little force on his part to hold her still, and very little force to enter her. He pushed once, and then, just when that dark blind part of her mind had resolved that she would lie motionless, and that she would defeat him with cold passivity, he gently turned her face to his, and looked down into her eyes.

He remained quite still, and Hélène, looking up at him, saw the love and the desperation naked in his face. There was no more contest then; it was over as suddenly as it had begun—there never had been a contest between them, she thought, except perhaps in her own mind.

"Oh, Edouard," she said sadly, and, reaching for his hand, she lifted it and pressed it against her lips. There was blood on his wrist, where she had scratched him. She pressed her mouth against it, and as she tasted the sharp iron taste of his blood, he began to move, gently at first, then more strongly.

"No, wait," she said then, and pushed him back gently, so he slipped out of her body with a soft sucking sound. He knelt back, and she bent her head and took him in her mouth. Edouard groaned, and cradled her head. He felt hard and alive against her lips; she loved the taste of him, she thought, with a sudden wild and yet gentle happiness; she loved the taste of him, which was also the taste of sex, tangy and salt.

She sucked him gently, drawing him deeper into her mouth, and when she felt him shudder, she felt also an extraordinary sense of power, the same power he had over her, quite equal. It filled her with great gentleness, that realization. When he began to lose control, she trembled also. He held her tightly, cupping her head in his hands; she touched him with her tongue, one particular place, and he came, spasm after spasm, life spurting into her mouth.

She cried then, and they stayed, clinging to one another, both shaking, their bodies wet with sweat, for a long time. Finally, Edouard drew back a little.

"You see," he said quietly. "Ah, Hélène, do you see?" She nodded silently. She did see, she thought. She saw just how much she loved him, and how much he loved her. In anger and in gentleness, there it was between them, this bond. As if he read her mind, Edouard lifted her hand, and pressed it between his own. "You can say one of two things," he said in a low voice. "You can say 'yes,' or you can say 'no.' But whatever you say, I am bound to you, and you are bound to me. We are as much married now as we could ever be—all the rest is just ceremony. Hélène—tell me you believe that."

"I believe that."

"Then *why*—earlier? Hélène, why did you turn away like that? Why?"

She hesitated. Then, because she could not bear to hurt him anymore, when she loved him so much, she bent her head.

"I don't know. I was afraid," she said finally. It was an evasion, and she waited for him to sense it, she waited for him to question her, but he did not. He gave a sigh of relief.

"My darling. Never be afraid. Not now. What can we fear now?" he said tenderly, and wrapped his arms around her.

Later, when they were in bed and Edouard slept, Hélène lay, tense and wakeful, and thought about the fear. She calculated its precise nature. She counted the weeks and months of it. She told herself she might be wrong. In the end she slept, and when she woke in the morning, there the fear was, waiting for her.

She rested her hands loosely across her stomach, and tried to will it away. Edouard still slept. Restlessly, she slipped out of bed, and went into the bathroom. As soon as she was on her feet, she felt the nausea. Cold sweat on the back of her neck, a sensation of weightlessness. She retched, leaning against the cool marble basin, and shaking. She splashed water on her face, and the nausea passed.

She turned the faucet off, on again, and then off once more. She looked at her own pale face in the glass, and saw the strain in it, the shadows beneath her eyes. *Billy's child,* said a small flat voice in her mind; *Billy's baby.* She had known at once, when she looked at the date on the letter to Cassie.

Billy was not dead; he lived on in her, he would live on in his child. That was the gift she had given him when they went down to the pool the day he died; that was the reason for the dreams she had and the guilt she felt. She turned away from the mirror and looked through into the bedroom where Edouard lay, still sleeping. She ought to feel glad, she told herself, for Billy's sake. It was wrong of her not to feel glad. Billy had loved her and Billy was dead: she *owed* Billy this child.

She knew, she thought dully, what she would have to do. She could see the course of action quite clearly; she stood there, turning it back and forth in her mind, and for a moment it seemed quite simple. Then she went back into the bedroom and looked at Edouard's sleeping face, and knew immediately that it was not simple at all.

Edouard's face was still, his features composed. He looked, as sleepers do, both peaceful and vulnerable. Her heart twisted with love for him; the pain of it ached in her mind, and her resolve immediately weakened.

She bent and pressed her lips gently against his forehead. She felt his breath warm against her cheek. After all, she told herself, it might not be true, there could be other explanations. It would be wrong and foolhardy to act before she was absolutely certain.

Edouard's eyes flickered open, and the flurry of ideas in her mind resolved themselves into one phrase. She thought: *Perhaps—but not yet.*

Edouard knew that something was wrong, and the knowledge tormented him. It was an instinctual knowledge, and when he tried to confront it rationally, reasonably—when had it begun, how had it begun, why had it begun?—he could find no answers. There had been some shift, some very delicate change, he sensed it with every part of his being. He thought, sometimes, that he could date it: it had begun on the day he went to Paris; sometimes he felt quite certain of that. But on other occasions even that certainty slipped away from him. Had it begun then, or was that merely the first time he had been aware of it?

And what, precisely, was it that he sensed? Hélène's behavior had not changed; they had not quarreled; there was no physical estrangement between them; *nothing was wrong.*

So he argued—but it was not what he felt. What he felt in her was slight, almost imperceptible, and difficult for him to name. A tension, perhaps; a reticence, which had always been there, but was now a little more marked; a withdrawal from him, delicate, sad, reluctant maybe, but a withdrawal just the same, step by step.

There was one thing in particular which she did—she had always done it, but now he noticed it more and more. She would be sitting quietly, listening to him, even talking, and then, quite suddenly, her eyes would change. He had the impression, then, that she saw something, or heard something, or remembered something very real to her; from that—whatever it was—he was totally excluded.

He had always found that quality in her mysterious, and because mysterious, arousing. It was like a challenge, a barrier he determined to break down. When he made love to her, he would have the illusion, while the act lasted, that the barrier had gone and he had reached her at last. Then the illusion would founder; it was as if he lurched, constantly, between a sensation of union and a sensation of loss.

He was used, he told himself cynically, to women who gave themselves easily in every sense; their eagerness to do so bored him very quickly. Hélène always eluded him. She was more candid, more direct, more forthright, than almost any other woman he had known. Her love was there; she spoke of it; it illumined her face and her eyes; she attached no conditions to it, seeming either unaware, or uncaring, that this affection she gave him so openly made her vulnerable to him. It might have occurred to her that he could hurt her—Edouard was not sure; she might have concealed that awareness out of pride, rather as he did. But he thought not. He thought the quality she possessed was simpler, and rarer: she had courage, and he loved her for it.

Yet still, in some way he could not define, he knew she was not open with him. She gave absolutely: she also withheld absolutely. The paradox disturbed him; it obsessed him; it was like a riddle which he had to solve.

Sometimes he thought the answer was quite simple: she had lied. Not about the important things between them, not about the love she felt—he never felt that—but about other things, yes, he felt she had not always told him the truth. She disliked being questioned about the past—he had discovered that almost immediately. Now, occasionally, he noticed slight inconsistencies, and vaguenesses. Tiny details, dates, places—they did not always quite square with things she had told him before. He felt that she was deliberately hiding something from him. Yet she was so young, what could she want to hide? What was the point of it? Some fact about her parentage? The circumstances which had made her leave England? A former love affair? His suspicions made him jealous, and he despised jealousy. So, when his instinct was to cross-examine her, to make her tell him whatever the truth was, he always held back. She would tell him eventually, that was what he told himself, and it was important that she should do so freely, of her own will. So he waited, and she volunteered nothing; she would not talk about the past, and she would not, he realized with growing despair, she would not talk about the future.

This, again, was unusual in a woman, in his experience. Most of the women he had known had been only too eager to tie the future down. *When will you call me, Edouard? When shall I see you again?* He had always loathed that kind of insistence, and resisted it. Now, positions were reversed, now when it was he who longed to make plans, and pledges, it was Hélène who stubbornly resisted all attempts to look further than tomorrow.

That refusal—or, rather, that gentle but firm evasion—tormented him most of all. Eternity, a lifetime: he felt like a gambler so convinced of the outcome of the game, that he had to stake all.

"I shall always love you," he said to her once, and then held his breath.

"I shall always love you, Edouard," she answered quite calmly, meeting and holding his gaze. He felt instantly, immoderately happy, and a little shamed by the simplicity and certainty with which she spoke. Assurances? He and Hélène did not need assurances—they were vulgar and trivial things. The next day, he saw again that distant look in her eyes, and he knew he would have given his soul for an assurance then, trivial or not.

Two days after he returned from Paris, sensing that barrier between them which he could not understand, he had made a conscious decision. Thinking that the barrier was perhaps of his own making, he had told her fully and for the first time, first about Grégoire, then about his marriage, the death of his brother, of Isobel and their child.

It was something he had spoken of to no one, and he found the words almost impossible to say. If she had attempted to comfort him then, if she had said any of the awkward consolatory things people said on such occasions, he knew he would find it unbearable, that, even though he loved her, he would wish he had remained silent. But she did neither of those things; she listened to him quietly, and when he had finished, she wept, fiercely, as if his grief were her own.

He loved her for those tears; he felt more bound to her then than he ever had before. But this sense of union did not last. By the very next day he once again despaired. He had shown his trust in her; yet still she held back: she could not, or would not, trust him.

A week passed. The end of September was approaching, and Edouard knew that he must soon return to Paris. Hélène must return with him; anything else was impossible. But in Paris, in the autumn, they could not be alone together as they had been here. He would have to begin a public life once more, and Hélène—of necessity—would have to be part of it.

Edouard wondered sometimes if that prospect frightened her, or if she disliked it, and if it was that feeling which she attempted to hide from him. It could be that simple, after all, he told himself, wanting to believe it. Perhaps, in bringing her here to the Loire, in giving them these weeks alone together, he had done the wrong thing. Perhaps he should have let her see, right from the beginning, the kind of life he had to lead. If he could just show her, he thought, that he wanted her there with him, that his public life need not be daunting, despite the gossip. . . .

It was then that Edouard conceived the idea of holding a dinner party at the château before they returned to Paris. Hélène did not oppose the idea, though she tried to persuade him to postpone it, and Edouard, seeing her reluctance, became more and more certain that she was needlessly afraid of the transition from a private to a public alliance. He teased her gently for her objections, and went ahead with his plans.

The dinner was arranged for September 24. It was an occasion which Edouard never forgot. Afterward, whenever he looked back, trying to understand the past, he saw that evening as a point of division in his life.

The guest list was formidable. The Duc and Duchesse de Varenges, both elderly—they had been close friends of Edouard's father. Jean-Jacques Belmont-Laon and his wife, Ghislaine, the interior decorator—their invitation an act of pure defiance on Edouard's part. *People will talk*, he had said with a smile. *Let them. If we invite Ghislaine, we will give them all a head start*. . . . Christian Glendinning, the art dealer, and one of Edouard's oldest friends. Clara Delluc, who worked with Ghislaine as a textile designer, and who had been Edouard's mistress for many years. *It has been over between us for a long time, my darling. There is no ill feeling. You will like Clara. She and Isobel were friends. I want you to meet some people you can trust*. . . . A quartet of American business associates, other couples, most of them French, the women very elegant, every single person at the table much older than she was, and apparently perfectly assured. People who were part of the framework of Edouard's life; people who had known him for years, some of them since before she was born. The Duc de Varenges on her right; Christian Glendinning on her left. The Duc, a kindly man who spoke excellent English, was discoursing on the subject of fishing. He had been doing so for some time.

Hélène's head was turned toward him; she listened with seeming interest; she hoped she did so, for in reality she heard not one word.

Twenty people; Edouard and herself. She glanced up and met Edouard's eyes. He was smiling at her gently, down the length of the table, as if to encourage her. The occasion itself frightened her; but the enormity of what she had decided she must do made her mind freeze with fear. Edouard would be hurt, and if she had had any choice, she felt as if she would rather have died than hurt him.

But there was no choice, not anymore. The certainty had grown, all week. She wished, passionately, that she could have persuaded Edouard not to hold this terrible dinner. She wished none of these people had met her. It might have been easier for Edouard then.

"Trout." The Duc de Varenges shook his head. "I particularly like trout. Wily creatures. Full of guile. Better sport even than salmon, though most people wouldn't agree with me. I don't suppose you like fishing? Very few women do, in my experience." He sounded regretful, quite sad. Hélène looked at him blankly; for a moment she had been quite unaware of his existence.

"I've never fished, I'm afraid," she said quickly.

"Ah, well. Ah, well." He smiled at her kindly. "You must persuade Edouard to teach you."

"I would like that."

The words were spoken before she could stop herself. It was the truth, and it was also a lie, because it would never happen. The Duc was benignly assuming a future which did not exist; so were most of the other people at the table, she could tell it from their curious glances. So was Edouard. She knew that, she had let it happen, and she should have stopped it.

Oh, God, she thought. *Oh, God. What have I done?*

From his vantage point, at the head of the table, Edouard looked at Hélène. She was wearing the white dress he had bought her at Givenchy, and he thought she looked more beautiful than he had ever seen her. Givenchy was a genius, and these dresses of his, famous for their pure lines, were made for Hélène. He had known that, and Givenchy himself had sensed it immediately. Plain white silk satin, cut with a narrow boned bodice, the long skirt a slender bell. It left her throat and her shoulders quite bare: absolute severity and absolute sensuality: Givenchy had seen at once the paradox that was at the heart of Hélène's beauty.

Her pale gold hair was drawn back from her forehead, and fastened simply at the nape of her neck, emphasizing the oval of her face, the calm and dazzling perfection of her features. She was pale—she was afraid of this dinner, he knew that—but now, he saw with relief, a little color had come back into her face. It stained her cheeks, and made her eyes glow; the Duc had been talking to her, and she had just answered . . . perhaps she was beginning to relax, to see that there was nothing to fear. Edouard felt a surge of optimism. His instinct in arranging this evening had been right, he thought.

He glanced to his left. Ghislaine Belmont-Laon was looking at Hélène coldly. She had accepted the invitation with a transparent eagerness for which Edouard felt contempt. His mistress, being put on trial for his friends: Ghislaine had come as insolently near to hinting at that as she dared, but then, Ghislaine was a fundamentally stupid woman, he thought impatiently. If they but knew it, it was his guests, not Hélène, who were on trial. . . .

He looked down the table, which was covered in an embroidered muslin cloth; it covered, in the country manner, another cloth of a richer color—a fashion begun in his grandmother's day and adhered to ever since.

The lights of the candles softened the rich yellows and blues and pinks of the Limoges porcelain. They deepened the colors of the pyramids of fruit. The center of the table was decorated as it had been in his childhood, with wildflowers and vine leaves. He loved the simplicity and the charm of the arrangement—one Louise de Chavigny, with her sharp sophisticated taste, had never understood, and always hated.

He felt a momentary sadness, a powerful nostalgia then, for the past, for all those lost summers between the wars. The tennis parties at which Papa always allowed Louise to win; the games of Racing Demon and Bezique with his grandmother in the evenings; the adventures with Jean-Paul . . . He had tasted his first glass of wine in this room, at this table, his father carefully adding a little water, in case, for a three-year-old, it should prove too strong. A Chinon; it had tasted of raspberries. . . .

He looked once more at Hélène. She was talking to Christian now. He thought: *We could come here with our children. Every summer. For so many years* . . .

Around the table, Edouard's tendency to abstraction, to an uncharacteristic lack of attentiveness, did not go unremarked. The Duchesse de Varenges, among others, noted it, and smiled indulgently. She was devoted to Edouard, and it was time he remarried; the girl—she knew nothing about her of course, but still—the girl seemed charming. She had been very patient with poor dear Alphonse, who could be a little tedious on the subject of fishing. *Bon genre*, the Duchesse decided, and felt pleased. She was not in sympathy with modern manners; it was a pleasure to meet a young woman so beautiful and so modest, though it was perhaps a pity she was not French. At one time she had entertained hopes that Edouard might come to appreciate the virtues of her niece, her favorite niece, who would in many ways have made him a most excellent wife. But there: her niece was plain, and this young woman was exquisite; Edouard was as susceptible to looks as any other man. . . .

Her eyes turned from face to face at the table, giving each person there a magisterial stare. She looked at Ghislaine Belmont-Laon and her husband with frank dislike, and at one of the Americans with fascination. The man was wearing a white jacket, which his wife referred to as a tux. Extraordinary. Her eyebrows rose. Could such a thing be *de rigueur* in America? Really, Edouard had the most colorful friends. . . .

Opposite the Duchesse, seated close to Edouard, though not as close as she would have liked, Ghislaine Belmont-Laon glanced across at Jacqueline de Varenges, and noted, to her own satisfaction, that the appalling woman was looking even more of a fright than usual. Her tiara, for which Ghislaine might cheerfully have bartered her soul, was perched on top of her head like a cozy on an egg. And her dress! Where could she have found one that particular shade of bilious green?

Ghislaine looked down at her own dress, which was Balenciaga, and at the diamonds around her wrists, which were borrowed. She gave a small smile of satisfaction. She felt less satisfied when she looked up again, and saw again the Givenchy this new woman of Edouard's was wearing. Givenchy was inimitable, of course, and she had to admit that those sculpted dresses of his were very hard to wear. To look good in them, a woman must be tall and slender; it also helped to be beautiful. The girl was carrying it off well, she had to admit that. Quite well. Though she looked no more than a child . . . She glanced across at Edouard again. It was a pity. Men of Edouard's type were always the first to be attracted by apparent innocence, by the lack of guile that accompanied youth. It made her extremely impatient: men could be so very stupid. Such qualities never lasted, and besides, a man like Edouard would find them boring before long. Edouard was a sensualist, for all his apparent asceticism, and he was after all notoriously fickle. A girl like that had been lucky to hold him for a month, two months, or however long it was. She certainly could not hope to hold him much longer. What Edouard needed, Ghislaine told herself, was a woman of sophistication and understanding; a woman of resources; a woman who understood the kind of games and ploys necessary to maintain the interest of a clever, and dangerous, man. A woman such as herself . . .

This thought, one she had had before, on many occasions, made her body stir with a quick secret pleasure. She looked at Edouard, and tried to imagine how he would be in bed.

Across the table from Ghislaine, her husband Jean-Jacques, who had been watching her with a certain amusement, saw her glance, and knew at once what his wife was thinking. Well, she could try, he thought, and no doubt would in due course; he had no objections— when Ghislaine had a new lover, she left him wonderfully free to pursue his own inclinations. But she would have to wait until this girl had disappeared from the scene, as, presumably, she would: all Edouard's women did, sooner or later. Right now, Ghislaine was wasting her time. Edouard's face bore an expression no man could misinterpret; he looked as if he had been in bed with this girl all afternoon, and couldn't wait for his guests to leave, so he could go back to bed with her.

Jean-Jacques turned his head. He regarded Helen Hartland with a practiced and expert eye. Well, he didn't blame Edouard for that. He would have liked the chance himself; just looking at her, just imagining, made him hard. Was she good? He felt instinctively that she would be; there was something about the mouth, something about the way she moved—and she looked so pure. The untouchable ones, the ones who looked like ice—they were invariably the hottest ones, when it came to it. He stared resentfully at the dress she was wearing. Givenchy; and Edouard had chosen it, he'd have laid a bet on that. It was typical of Edouard's taste. Who but Edouard would take a woman with a body like that, and put it in a fifty-thousand-franc straitjacket, so you couldn't see a damn thing. . . .

Next to Hélène, Christian Glendinning was making an attempt to be charming. He was aware that it did not seem to be getting him very far, which was surprising. Christian had no compunction about using his well-known charm: it had moved mountains in the past—so why not now? He was a little suspicious of this young woman, and she was astute. Perhaps she sensed his wariness, and it was that which under-mined his efforts?

He sighed, and tried harder. He had, after all, promised Edouard to be on his best behavior—this dinner would be an ordeal for anyone in her position, and she seemed so very young. Younger than she claimed, he would have said, though why should she lie? And certainly very tense. He had tried to talk about England, thinking that might put her at her ease, but it seemed to make her even more tense, which was curious. . . .

Christian looked at her carefully: he had heard rumors about her in Paris, and he had been longing to meet her, because he adored dramas of any kind, and the arrival of this woman was clearly a drama of the most splendid kind. For a start, Edouard was quite clearly wildly in love: *bouleversé*. Christian had never seen him so stricken, and he was enjoying the spectacle tremendously. He himself fell in and out of love with monotonous regularity—and always, alas, with such wildly unsuitable young men—but Edouard, well, he had begun to think that Edouard was immune from the condition.

It was easy to see how it had happened, of course: she was astonishingly lovely, just as everyone had said. He liked her voice, which was distinctly unusual, low, and slightly halting in its rhythms, so that he had to lean quite close to her sometimes to catch what she said. And her face: Christian, who was not attracted by female beauty, was nonetheless interested in it. He regarded it with a critical eye, just as he might have a face in a painting. So grave, and so still: a face from another era, he thought; she reminded him, in that stiff, sculpted dress, of certain Spanish portraits he had always loved. A young infanta, yes, that was it; and there was just a suggestion, as there was in certain of those portraits, that the beautiful child was trapped. . . .

He sighed. He was getting fanciful, and had probably drunk too much of Edouard's excellent wines. Now the Sauternes had been brought, a Château d'Yquem. He lifted his glass.

"Nectar and ambrosia," he said in his extremely affected clipped voice. "Really, dining with Edouard is a little like dining with the gods. . . ."

Hélène laughed; it was the first time she had laughed all evening. Across the table, Clara Delluc, who had been watching her gently and sadly, suddenly straightened up. *How extraordinary*, she thought. She had not noticed the resemblance before, but when she smiled, this Hélène was so very like Jean-Paul. . . .

The guests were leaving: Alphonse and Jacqueline de Varenges first, then the group of Americans to whom, Hélène realized, she had hardly spoken all evening, then several other French couples, then Jean-Jacques Belmont-Laon and his wife, who said, "My dear! In Paris—we must meet again. I shall arrange a luncheon—no, not you, Jean-Jacques, just Hélène and I. *À deux.* I shall so look forward to it. . . ." A glance down at the diamond ring Hélène wore on her finger; a smile on her taut beautiful face that was like honey and vinegar, and then she was gone. Hélène watched her sweep across the room, her husband in her wake. At the doorway, she stopped, the skirt of her Balenciaga swirled. She reached up to kiss Edouard on both cheeks.

"Hélène?"

She felt a touch on her arm, and, turning, found Clara Delluc by her side. She was smiling.

"I have to leave now, and we've hardly had a chance to speak. I'm so sorry. I do hope we shall meet again, in Paris. . . ."

This time the sentiment was sincere. Hélène looked at Clara, and knew that she liked her, just as Edouard had said she would. She had short unruly hair, and wide-spaced dark brown eyes; they were regarding Hélène kindly, a little uncertainly, as if there were something which she wanted, and hesitated, to say.

"I felt—I wanted you to know. . . ." She pressed Hélène's arm impulsively. "I'm so happy. For you, and also for Edouard. You're very young, and you perhaps don't realize—how changed he is. How much happier he looks. I'm grateful to you for that—all his friends will be. I just wanted you to know, we, all the people who care for him, we wish you both well. . . ."

She spoke rapidly, frowning a little as she did so, as if it cost her some effort to say this. Hélène looked into her face, and the sympathy she saw there was so genuine that for one insane moment she longed to take Clara's arm and confide in her, ask her advice, anything. . . . But the moment passed, and then Clara was gone.

Hélène watched her leave, sadly. She would not be meeting Ghislaine for luncheon. She would not be meeting Clara. She would never see any of these people, ever again, and yet none of them seemed to sense it. None of them seemed to realize there was anything wrong.

Perhaps she was a natural actress, after all, just as Priscilla-Anne once said, she thought with a sudden sense of derision. Perhaps, without being aware of it, all those years of childish deceptions and secrecies had paid off, and she had just given a performance she had been rehearsing for years.

But it was one thing to keep up a pretense to strangers; it was quite another to do so to Edouard. He was standing talking to Christian, the last of the remaining guests, and Christian, who was staying at the château, was insisting volubly, and with elephantine discretion, that yes, he really was most frightfully tired, and that if they would both forgive him, he would leave them.

She looked at Edouard as he talked to his old friend. His face was relaxed, animated, as he spoke; she could see the happiness in it. He glanced at her, amusement in his eyes, as if to say—*we shall be alone soon.*

She realized then that her choice was a very simple one. Either way, hurt was involved, but one way the hurt was less—for Edouard, if not for herself. Christian was leaving, and as Edouard turned back to her, she thought that she had to act—just a little while longer. She had to act very very well, so that Edouard did not suspect, and then it would all be over.

When they went to bed later that night, Edouard left the shutters open, and the curtains undrawn; he liked to look at her body in the moonlight, which shadowed its curves and crevices, and lit her skin with silver. That night, the moon filled the room with a strong unfaltering radiance, and Edouard said, "The moon is full. Look at it, Hélène. So bright. And no stars."

She turned her face to the window, and then turned back to him, drawing him to her with a kind of desperate urgency.

Later, when they lay quietly together, she suddenly twisted up, pulling him with her, so they knelt in front of each other. She lifted her hands and pressed them on either side of his face, and Edouard saw, to his consternation, that her face was very pale, and her eyes glittered with tears.

"Edouard. You do believe that I love you? Tell me you do. *Promise* me you do. Promise me you will."

In answer, he bent to kiss her, but she stopped his lips with her hand.

"No. You must say it. I want to hear you say it. Just once." She was trembling, and her voice had risen slightly, as if it mattered to her very much that he should say this thing which he had always assumed to be obvious.

"I believe it. You know I believe it. My darling—what's wrong?"

"Nothing. I wanted to be sure. I don't know why," she said. Then she lay back down against the pillows and closed her eyes. Edouard lay down beside her, puzzled, but touched, by this curious plea. It was the first time she had ever asked anything of him, he realized, and that thought made him suddenly very happy. He kissed her face, and tasted the salt of her tears on her cheeks. He wiped them away gently with his hand; her eyes opened, and she smiled at him.

Edouard clasped her in his arms, and they lay still. Nothing else was said, and after a while, Hélène's breathing grew soft and regular, and Edouard was sure she slept.

He closed his own eyes, and let his mind slip into the dark. In the past, sleep had often eluded him. That night he rested as peacefully as a child.

When he woke in the morning, the space beside him was empty, and Hélène, who had made her decision, was gone.

PART TWO

THE SEARCH

1959

"S he will come back," Christian said.

It was late at night. Helen Hartland had now been missing for forty-eight hours, and Christian and Edouard were alone in his study at the Château de Chavigny. Edouard had been speaking for some time, and Christian had listened to his story quietly. He injected his remark into the long silence that followed, trying to bring conviction to his voice. Usually, he was adept at the social lie, the accommodating untruth. Now, perhaps because it mattered, and he wanted very much to be of comfort, he knew his words sounded hollow. Edouard looked up at him, his eyes watchful and dark in the pallor of his face. Their gazes met.

"You think so?" Edouard said coolly, and he attempted a smile, one Christian recognized from their undergraduate days: the English smile, the Oxford smile, the smile that said, Anything is bearable if you treat it with irony. The attempt was a failure; Christian averted his eyes.

Edouard bent his head once more to his desk. On it was a photo-graph of Hélène, taken by one of his stable boys and brought to him with some embarrassment, but an obvious desire to help, by his groom that morning. It had been taken the previous week, as he and Hélène returned from their ride. It was the only photograph of her which he possessed; she had just reined in her horse, and she was smiling—at him, Edouard thought, but he was outside the frame.

He stared at it now, frowning, as if the image in front of him held some secret, as if it could somehow answer all the questions that thronged and ached in his mind, all of which resolved themselves into one question, one ache of pain: *Why?* Also, of course, *where?* But, his mind numbed with shock and incomprehension, the question of where she might have gone, which he knew to be the most practical one, kept slipping away from him. As he tried to get a grip on his thoughts, they constantly veered back to the "why," and the great void that opened up in his heart. If he only understood why, he felt, then the answer to all the other questions, including the "where," would somehow follow.

Yet the question why, to which his obstinate mind was drawn irresistibly, also terrified him, because he knew that it had a simple and a logical answer. She had left because she did not love him. There. He let himself think the words, at last, which he had been fighting to keep at a distance for two days, and to his own surprise the pain he felt immediately lessened, because he knew the words were false. They were reasonable, yes. They were logical, yes. To have left when she did, and as she did, without word, leaving everything he had ever given her behind, the pair of gray gloves from Hermès, and the square diamond ring laid neatly on top of them by her bedside, the Givenchy dress, with all the other dresses and the riding clothes, neatly hung away in the closets in her dressing room—to have done that, to have left so finally, as if the previous seven weeks had never happened—yes, he could see that looked like a rejection, a negation of everything that had taken place and everything that had been said.

Yet, instantly, his mind refused to accept that explanation. He saw her face as she had looked at him that last night, and he heard her voice telling him that she loved him, and he knew that he believed in that still, and that he would go on believing in it—that if it was not true, there was no truth, and he was back in a life that was a wasteland.

He glanced at Christian, who was sitting by the fire, and was tempted for a moment to tell him what he felt. But Christian, a man who believed in nothing except possibly the truthfulness of great art, and who certainly placed little reliance on the ability of any love to endure, would not understand, he thought. Besides, he had already said more than enough to Christian that night. He sighed and bent his head again to the photograph.

Across the room, Christian watched him with a pity he was careful to hide beneath his customary detachment. He looked at his friend, and he knew that he was already regretting the things he had spoken of earlier. Poor Edouard, he thought. How hellish it must be to be so proud. Why was it so important to him, never to show that he was hurt? Was he different with women? Had he been different with Helen? Did he allow himself to show his vulnerability then? Christian looked at his friend's bent head, and frowned. He supposed that he must. The realization hurt him a little. That Edouard, whom he deeply loved, could be closer to a woman than he was to his oldest friend was something Christian found incomprehensible. It was a barrier between them, he supposed, a barrier of understanding between a heterosexual and a homosexual man, and even the greatest friendship could not cross it. Christian felt a second's jealousy, a dislike of Helen Hartland intensified by a lifetime's distrust of women; then he pushed it aside. He leaned forward.

"I should like to help, Edouard," he said awkwardly, expecting rebuff. To his surprise, Edouard looked up at once, and met his eyes.

"I need your help," he said simply.

Christian stared at him in astonishment. Edouard had never, in all the years of their friendship, made such an admission. Christian instantly felt a most undignified and idiotic delight. His face lit up.

"What do you want me to do? I'll do anything, Edouard, you know that. I—"

"I want you to help me look for her." Edouard paused. He looked down. "I feel I have to stay here—for another day or so at least—just in case she—" He broke off, looked up again. "Would you go to Paris for me, Christian? I've instigated other inquiries, in England, but I thought, perhaps, if someone went to Paris . . . She could have gone back there. The café I told you about, where she was working before . . ."

Christian had begun to smile at Edouard's stiff, almost legal phraseology. Now he sprang to his feet excitedly.

"Of course! The café! And she said she had a room nearby, didn't she? We can get that photograph copied. I can take that. I'll ask at that café. I'll ask at all the cafés. Someone's bound to remember her. Someone will know where she was staying. She could have gone back there. Even if she's moved on since—"

He broke off. Edouard's face wore a dry expression, and Christian gave a shrug, a half-ashamed smile. He loved action, and he was above all things impetuous.

"I'm sorry. I'm running ahead. But I'll do it, Edouard—of course I will. I'll go tomorrow. I'll be fantastically thorough. I . . . well, actually, I've always rather wanted to play private detective. . . ."

The words were out before he had time to curb himself, and for one awful moment Christian thought he had gone too far. He knew he sounded whimsical, and he knew he sounded frivolous—he very often did when he was, above all, serious. There was a moment's silence. Their gazes met.

"How fortunate for me," Edouard said in that dry tone he had used before. Then he smiled again. The Oxford smile. This time the attempt was more successful, and Christian felt reassured. It was not until he left the room some while later, and—pausing outside the closed door—heard, from inside, the sudden giving-in to anguish suppressed, the peculiarly painful sound of a man's tears, that he realized exactly how iron was his friend's self-control, how well he could act when he wanted to.

He listened for a moment, and then turned quietly away. His determination to help Edouard redoubled. The hell with her, he thought angrily. She was a young, inexperienced girl, not worth the tears of a man like Edouard. But if Edouard wanted her back—well, at least it should be fairly easy to find her.

Paris, he thought, not without a certain arrogance; she probably had gone back to Paris. She probably had returned to exactly the place where she knew she would certainly be sought. He smiled to himself confidently: a typical woman's contrivance, he thought, designed to disturb and provoke. A piece of melodrama, signifying nothing.

By the end of tomorrow, he thought as he drifted off to sleep, she will either have come back, or we'll have found her.

Christian found the café easily enough. He spent the morning with Edouard, assisting him with the inquiries his aides were making in England. He left the Loire after lunch, and had a long and exhausting drive back to Paris. By the time he reached the café, it was late, and already dark.

It was called the Café Strasbourg, and it stood near the corner where the Boulevard St. Michel debouched into the square of the same name. An unpromising place, Christian thought, with none of the gaiety of some of its rivals farther south on the boulevard. Six tables outside on the *terrasse;* six booths inside, partitioned off from one another by ugly high-backed seats of fumed oak. Smeary mirrors advertising Pernod; a waiter and waitress on duty, both looking bored; and the *patron* inside behind the small bar—a short dark man with an Adolf Hitler moustache, polishing glasses lugubriously. Easing himself into the situation, Christian stationed himself inside, at one of the booths, and, planting his elbow a few inches from a drooping rubber plant, ordered an omelette and a glass of wine. He would have a picnic of *foie gras*, he consoled himself, when he returned to his apartment later. Meanwhile he noted with interest as he chewed his way through the leathery meal that the Café Strasbourg obviously did employ casual staff. The waitress was French, a student from the look of her; but the waiter, a tall good-looking boy, had an American accent. His spirits rose. He ordered a *fine à l'eau* with his coffee, lit one of his Black Russian cigarettes, and leaned thoughtfully back in his seat. In a minute he would beard the proprietor. He was beginning to feel quietly confident that he was on the right track.

Some half an hour later, his confidence had been shattered. At first, the *patron* would hardly speak to him, hardly glance at the photograph Christian slid across the bar. Christian, who spoke perfect French, had to be most persuasive to get him to talk at all. The man warmed slightly when he realized Christian was not from the police; he warmed slightly more when Christian slid a thousand-franc note across with the photograph, and he became positively expansive once he grasped the essentials of Christian's hastily improvised story, which was that he was looking for his younger sister, who had run away from home and was nearly breaking her father's heart.

At this, the small man's dark eyes became moist. He, too, it seemed, had a daughter, his only child, and she, too, had done nothing but cause her poor father trouble. They moved to a booth, and Christian bought the *patron* a drink. Clasping a schnapps, the small man gave the photograph his full attention, and with transparent honesty dashed Christian's hopes one by one.

No, he would swear it in any court in the land, he had never laid eyes on this young woman: who could forget such a face? Yes, he employed foreigners quite often—they did not have work permits, and so did not require the exorbitant wages French waiters now demanded— here he winked. But this girl, no. And she had told a friend she worked here? Really, girls were without shame—his own daughter, yes, he had to confess it, was precisely the same.

"You're sure? This would have been about seven weeks ago. The first week of August?"

The *patron* sighed: "Monsieur, I have told you. Not in August— never."

He hesitated, and then, clearly eager to help, gestured outside to the *terrasse*, where the waiter was serving some new arrivals. That boy might be able to help, he suggested. He was a good boy, bright, a cut above the rest, American, hard-working, good-looking, and with an eye for the girls. He'd been at the Strasbourg nearly three months now, working shifts. He had a room nearby, knew the neighborhood; it would be worth asking him—he might recognize the girl from her picture.

At the mention of the room nearby, Christian looked up with interest. The *patron* stood up and gestured through the window. After a pause, the waiter came back inside; there was a brief conversation with his employer. Then the boy turned. Christian felt himself examined by a pair of clear and astute hazel eyes. The boy hesitated, then shrugged and slid into the seat opposite him. Christian looked at him, and the boy gave a frank, open smile.

"Lewis Sinclair, hi." He held out his hand. "Monsieur Schreiber tells me you're looking for someone. How can I help?"

Silently, Christian slid the photograph across the table. Lewis Sinclair bent his head, and Christian looked at him appraisingly. Ivy League, he thought: even in a waiter's uniform it stuck out a mile. The feet that were negligently crossed under the table were wearing hand-stitched loafers. Thick blond hair, bleached by New England summers, expertly cut in the conventional prep school style, falling forward slightly over the clean-cut handsome face. Tall, athletically built, with shoulders wide enough and powerful enough to have made him an asset to a football team. A golden boy, Christian thought, and then—no, not a boy, a man, twenty-four, possibly even twenty-five, but with the typically boyish good looks of his class and type, the kind who would still look boyish when he was pushing forty. A firm handshake, a direct gaze, a hint of arrogance in the manner, and an accent that was twenty-four-carat Harvard Yard.

Christian had encountered many such young men in America; he was a little wary of them, just as he was wary of their equivalents in England. Unconventional himself, it had taken him some years to learn not to underestimate the apparently conventional, to realize that under that civilized veneer, they could be tough. He looked at Lewis Sinclair now with interest, and some surprise. The watch he wore was Tiffany's, and while Christian could imagine it might amuse such a boy to slum it for a while on the Left Bank, three months on shifts at the Strasbourg seemed to be overdoing it. He waited. Lewis Sinclair gave the photograph his full attention for about thirty seconds. Then he looked up, with that same frank look Christian instinctively distrusted, and shook his head.

"Sorry. I can't help. She's a beautiful girl, and I wouldn't mind meeting her. But I've never seen her around here."

"I know she didn't work here . . ." Christian paused. "But she might have visited the café—hung around the neighborhood maybe."

"If she came in here, I wasn't waiting tables, that's for sure. I'd remember."

"She would have been rather differently dressed. . . ."

"Well, yes. I guess not too many women hang round the Boule Miche in jodhpurs and hacking jacket."

He gave a disarming smile to soften the sharpness of his comeback, and when he received no answering smile from Christian, he did what his class and type always did, Christian thought: he went on the attack.

"She's your—sister—I think Monsieur Schreiber said?" Just an insolent hint of a pause before the word *sister*, and a dismissive glance at Christian's elegant but raffish clothes.

"My sister, yes."

"And she's run away from home?"

"That's right."

"Too bad." He sighed, and glanced down at the Tiffany watch. "Well, I'd like to help, but I'm sorry, I can't. You could ask around the other cafés. Except there are quite a few of them, and the staff turnover is high. It could be a wild goose chase. . . ."

"I realize that."

Lewis Sinclair gave a slight smile, as if the very impossibility of Christian's task gave him a certain smug satisfaction. Christian, watching him, registered that fact with interest. He also observed that, when he thanked M. Schreiber for his help, and remarked that he would continue his search the next day, he had one or two other leads he could follow up, the boy reacted. Very slightly, it was true: just a brief tensing of the body, a quick appraising glance. But the reaction was there.

Christian left the café and strolled across the street. In spite of having drawn a blank, he was beginning to enjoy himself; the night was warm and balmy, and he didn't feel like giving up yet.

He bought some cigarettes at the corner *tabac*—only Gauloises, but they would have to do—and strolled on around the corner and into a side street. Then he doubled back, so he had a clear view of the café, and waited.

He did not have to wait long. He saw Monsieur Schreiber come out and fasten the shutters. Lewis Sinclair piled the last of the chairs on the tables. Then he went back inside, came back out with a Burberry trenchcoat over his arm, and wished Monsieur Schreiber good night. He looked quickly up and down the boulevard, and then, with long easy strides, crossed, and turned into a side street. Christian waited five seconds, and then, feeling more and more like Humphrey Bogart, set off after him.

The pursuit was easy. Lewis Sinclair never once looked back, and besides, even at this time of night there were still plenty of people on the streets. Sinclair turned right into the Rue St. Jacques, then left again into the maze of narrow streets and old houses that lay between the Sorbonne to the south, and the Seine to the north. Christian, who knew this area well, felt a quickening excitement: they were now less than five minutes' walk from the place where Edouard had first seen Helen Hartland.

Halfway down a dimly-lit street, outside a tall, narrow house, Lewis Sinclair stopped abruptly. At the far end of the street, Christian also stopped. He felt he should shrink back into a doorway: there was no doorway. He shrank back against the wall as best he could, and held his breath. The precaution was unnecessary: clearly Sinclair had something on his mind, and it was not the possibility of his being followed.

He felt in his trouser pockets. He swore. He lifted the Burberry, and shook it out. He felt in his trouser pockets again. Christian smiled to himself maliciously. Oh, dear: no keys.

Sinclair hesitated some time, looking up at the dark house in front of him, and then, seeming to brace himself, stepped forward and hammered on the door. The reason for his reluctance rapidly became obvious. He had to thump hard on the knocker several times before anything happened. Then a light went on at a ground floor window, and a shutter was thrown back. Lewis Sinclair retreated, and clear on the still air came a sound familiar to any Parisian: the shrill-voiced complaint, the outraged indignation, of an elderly female concierge roused from her respectable sleep by the inconsiderate near-imbecility of one of her tenants.

This one was a mistress of the art, Christian thought to himself with a smile, as the tide of invective carried down the street. It went on, imaginatively, for a good two minutes; finally, the door opened, and Sinclair was admitted.

When the bar of light at the ground floor window had been snapped off, and there was silence once more, Christian padded softly down the street and looked up at the house. It was still in darkness, so Sinclair must have a room at the back. He waited a short while, but there were no signs of further activity, and the thought of his Paris flat grew increasingly tempting.

Shortly after midnight, Christian left. He walked back to his very beautiful apartment, converted from a seventeenth-century merchant's house in the Rue des Grand Augustins, made himself some toast, opened a tin of *foie gras* and a fine bottle of Montrachet, and enjoyed his midnight feast. He telephoned Edouard, who, he knew, would not be asleep, and hoped he sounded cautiously optimistic.

Then he went to bed. He would return to Sinclair's lodginghouse the next morning, he thought sleepily, as he lay back. It was not much of a lead, but it was better than nothing.

At six, he woke suddenly, surfacing from a tangle of dreams, totally alert. He sat bolt upright in bed, staring across the room to the photograph of Helen Hartland which he had propped against the brushes on his dressing chest the night before. Quite suddenly, something Edouard had said, just a tiny detail, leapt back into his mind with a hideous new clarity. *"I left her at the café. She said she lived in a room nearby, and would walk back later. She said she had a very bad-tempered concierge. . . .*

"Oh, hell and damnation," Christian cried, and, wrenching at his silk pajamas, began to pull on his clothes.

He was back at the house by six forty-five, and it was too late.

The concierge launched into a superb tirade, and Christian, whose command of vitriolic insult and veiled obscenity was accomplished in four languages, gave as good as he got. But it was hopeless: Lewis

Sinclair and his friend had a room in the house, yes, but they had left, paid up and gone, at five that morning.

"Friend? Friend?" By this time Christian had the old woman backed into a corner, and she was getting nervous. "Was this the friend?"

He produced the photograph and waved it under her nose. The old woman peered at it, and then began to laugh. She twisted her face up at him in malignant triumph.

This the friend? No, it wasn't. *Cochon. Imbecile*—he had it all wrong. Sinclair shared the room with another man, an American also. No, she didn't even know his name, it was Sinclair who paid the rent. The friend was Sinclair's age: fat, ugly, hardly spoke French, slunk in and out at all times, and never so much as a word of greeting—bearded, dark—*un espèce d'animal*. . . . The concierge spat energetically onto the pavement.

Christian backed off from her in confusion. He had been so *certain*, for a moment, so *certain*. He hesitated, and then proffered the photograph again. Had this young woman perhaps visited Sinclair or his friend? Could she have been with them when they left? The old woman showed signs of becoming tearful. Her voice rose in a high-pitched whine.

She didn't know. How could she tell? Hundreds of young women came to the house—filthy types mostly, in trousers so tight you could see their bottoms. Not women like *that*. She flicked the photograph. Not ladies.

Christian changed tack. He produced a hundred-franc note, which disappeared into her clawlike hand with speed. The note had the required effect. It stopped her whining, and it got him up to the room Sinclair had rented. The old woman gave him the key, and Christian bounded up to the fourth floor, the top floor of the house, and let himself in.

The room was long and narrow, and—as he had suspected—at the back of the house; it had a certain bohemian charm: old threadbare rugs; two narrow beds; one or two pieces of old furniture that were quite attractive; a view of rooftops; white-painted walls, adorned with posters, most of them for films by the young directors of the *nouvelle vague*. It had been carefully cleared. Even the wastepaper basket was empty.

Christian peered around the room. He was beginning to feel extremely stupid. It was odd that Sinclair and his friend should have departed so suddenly. It was odd to leave at five in the morning. Beyond that fact, which could have a thousand explanations, there was absolutely nothing to connect this room or its former occupants with Helen Hartland—other than an overexcited imagination and, Christian thought ruefully, a diet of too many B movies. He was about to leave, when he heard a girl's voice on the landing outside.

"Lewis? Lewis? Is that you? I thought I heard something. . . ."
Christian froze, and then relaxed when he realized the voice was American. A second later the door was pushed back, and a small plump fluffy-haired brunette came into the room. She was wearing flat ballet slippers, tight trousers, and an oversized sweater; Christian quickly learned, once she had recovered from her surprise at seeing him, that her name was Sharon, and she came from Duluth. It was Sharon who changed everything.

Christian proceeded to become extremely charming then. Within five minutes Sharon was smoking one of his cigarettes, and sitting beside him on the overstuffed red sofa, chattering away as if she had known him all her life. She seemed surprised to find Lewis gone, and perhaps a little disappointed, but she recovered quickly.

"Oh, well, he just took off, I guess. Thad too. What do you know?"

"Thad?"

She gave a little giggle.

"His friend. Thad. I don't know his other name. Thad the weirdo, I called him." She pulled a face. "Like, hunchback of Notre Dame time, you know? Squat. Kind of gross-looking. Glasses. Frizzy black beard. If you're a friend of Lewis's, you must have seen him—they were inseparable—and, you know, once seen, never forgotten, huh?"

"I'm not a friend of Lewis's." Christian took the plunge. "Well, not exactly. I'm looking for someone I thought Lewis knew. This girl. She's my sister."

He produced the photograph, with no great optimism. To his eternal surprise, Sharon bent over it, and the instant she saw it, her face lit up.

"Hey! It's Helen! What do you know? Doesn't she look great? I mean, I guess she *always* looked great, you know—but I never saw her look like that. . . ."

"You know her?" Christian stared at Sharon's excited face. He suddenly felt extremely faint.

"Know her? I sure do. She was here a week—the first week of August. Slept in my room—I work nights in a bar over in the Pigalle district, so I sleep days—I just got off duty now. I did it as a favor to Lewis—like she had no money, no place to stay, you know? Wow! And she's your sister? How about that? I wondered what had happened to her . . . you know, she just took off. Madame Mystery. Even Lewis had no idea where she'd gone. . . ."

Christian stood up: he held out his arm.

"Sharon," he said gallantly, "this calls for a drink. You must tell me more. . . ."

"A drink?" Sharon blushed and giggled. "It's not even seven-thirty in the morning."

"In Paris one can get a drink at any hour of the day or night. It is one of the most civilized aspects of the city. . . ."

"It sure beats Duluth." She giggled again.

"We shall go to a bar I know, and we shall have champagne." He took Sharon's arm and propelled her to the door. "And then you will tell me everything. . . ."

"I'll try. . . . Say—do all Englishmen talk like you?"

"Very few now, alas." Christian gave her his most dazzling smile. "You are looking, Sharon, at a vanishing breed. . . ."

"Too bad," Sharon said, and trotted happily after him.

"Okay, this is the way it was." Sharon took a sip from her glass of champagne, rested her elbows on the table, and leaned forward. "I've been in Paris since May. I first met Lewis in July sometime, at the Café Strasbourg. He was waiting tables, and he got me a job there— I didn't stay long though. That creep Schreiber!" She pulled a face. "Like, starvation wages, you know?"

"I can imagine." Christian smiled encouragingly. "Lewis didn't mind the wages, presumably?"

"Lewis? You've got to be kidding! Lewis is loaded. That job is just a gas to him—a way of passing the time. Thad made him take it. To keep him out of trouble, he said. That's all. You do know who Lewis is, I guess?"

"I met him only briefly . . . Ivy League, I thought."

Sharon giggled. "Right. With that accent he could chip glass, huh?" She paused. "Lewis is Old Money. Lots of it. Daddy's the Sinclair in Sinclair Lowell Watson—and they're the biggest investment bank on the East Coast. Lewis is the only son and heir."

"Oh, I see."

Christian leaned back thoughtfully while a quiet and efficient waiter served them their food: lightly scrambled eggs decorated with shavings of black truffle. Warm brioches. It looked delicious, and Sharon began to eat with relish, but Christian suddenly found he had no appetite. Helen Hartland seemed to have a gift for attracting rich men, he thought. He did not look forward to telling Edouard that fact. "So—" Sharon forked up some eggs, and smiled. "So—Lewis did me a favor, and I did him one. I got him the room back there, just across the hall from me. He and Thad moved in sometime in July."

"This Thad seems an odd kind of friend for a man like Lewis Sinclair." Christian frowned. "Did he work at the Café Strasbourg as well?"

"Thad? No way." She gave him a scornful glance. "I told you, Thad's weird. He never had a job—all Thad did was go to the movies."

"The movies?"

"Sure. He's crazy about them. Spends all day watching them. Starts right in after breakfast, and goes on from movie theater to movie theater, all day. You can do that in Paris, you know. Imagine—being in a city like this, and spending day after day in the dark in some flea pit—"

"And Thad's American too?"

"Oh, sure. From L.A., I think. I don't know—I don't know much about him one way or another. Just that he was always around. Whenever I went into their room—there he'd be. Sitting in the corner, never saying a word. . . ." She gave a little shiver. "I tell you, Thad gave me the creeps. . . ."

"But Lewis liked him, presumably?"

"Oh, he and Lewis were like *that*. . . ." She held up her hand, with two fingers crossed. Christian looked at her and raised his eyebrows. Sharon giggled, and blushed.

"Okay. I'll say it. I really liked Lewis, you know—like, I saw him, and I flipped. He's a really good-looking guy, right? But he never asked me out on a date—nothing. And after a while I did begin to wonder about him and Thad—whether they might be, well, fairies, you know. . . ."

Not Sinclair, Christian thought, knowing his instinct in such matters was near infallible. Sinclair had struck him as aggressively heterosexual. He smiled obligingly: Sharon, whose instincts in this respect were clearly less developed than his own, was looking at him slightly flirtatiously.

"But you decided you were wrong?" he prompted her.

"Yeah. When Helen—when your sister turned up." Sharon paused, and Christian sat very still. Sharon sighed.

"I can't blame him," she went on. "I mean, she's just so incredible-looking. And Lewis was crazy about her—that stuck out a mile. Thad, too, maybe. With him it was difficult to tell. All I know is, I went in their room one evening, and they couldn't take their eyes off her. Like, she hardly said a word, and they both kept staring at her. I felt jealous at first. Who wouldn't?"

"Do you know how they met?"

"I'm not sure. It was more or less a straight pickup, I guess. Like, she was just off the boat from England, and one of them ran into her in the street—Lewis, I think. And she had hardly any money and no place to go, as I said, so they took her back to their place, and fixed it for her to stay in my room. It wasn't for long. Seven days—eight maybe. Then she went out one evening, and never came back." She frowned, and her wide blue eyes took on an anxious expression. "So—I don't know where she is now, or where she's been since. I just hope she's all right. I liked her, you know?"

"Did you talk to her much? You can't remember anything she said that might give me an idea where she is now?"

"No. I talked to her a little, once or twice. But she seemed very withdrawn, you know? Sad, maybe. Kind of lost. I caught her crying one time, just sitting in my room, and I tried to cheer her up. But she just went out. She went out a lot, Lewis said. All day. On her own . . ."

"Not with Thad? Or Lewis?"

"No. She kept them at arm's length, the same way she did me."

"So . . ." Christian paused. "You wouldn't have said she was— involved with either of them. Having an affair, anything like that?"

"No way." Sharon pushed her empty plate aside and leaned forward again on her elbows. "She was grateful to them, I could see that. And she must have been lonely, but nothing more than that. I mean, she wouldn't have looked at Thad—what woman would? And if Lewis had got lucky, I'd have known—he boasts, you know—and besides, he's not too good at hiding his feelings. That's what drove him so crazy, I thought. I mean, Lewis is the kind of guy most girls fall over for, right? And she used to look at him like he wasn't there. He's not used to it. It drove him *wild* . . . I tell you, your sister has some technique. I could really learn from her. . . ."

"You thought that's what it was, technique?" Christian was beginning to feel much better. He even managed to eat a little of his food.

"Not really. No. It just seemed to come natural to her. Like, the original ice princess, you know? If you're worried on that score, I don't think you need be. . . ." She paused. "Lewis was really broken up when she left."

"You don't think she could have come back? In the last couple of days . . ."

"She could have." Sharon blushed a little. "I haven't been back to my room that much—not for a week or so. I met this really terrific guy—you know how it is. . . ." She hesitated, as if expecting him to be censorious, and when Christian patted her hand, and assured her that indeed, he did know, only too well, she grinned.

"So. She could have been there. I think Lewis still has the key I gave Helen before. And that old witch of a concièrge is half blind— she'd never know. She doesn't know half of what goes on around there. Maybe she did come back. Maybe that's why they took off. I mean, that surprised me. Lewis hadn't mentioned a thing. But then, Lewis gets around anyway. He's got the bread, and he likes to party. I was surprised he stayed in Paris as long as he did. I used to tease him. Say I'd look him up when we both got back to the States, invite myself up to Boston . . ."

"And would you?"

Sharon gave him a scornful glance. "Give me a break. You think I'm stupid? Paris is one thing. Back home, a guy like Lewis wouldn't give me the time of day. Your sister, yes. But then, your sister's got class. . . ." She sighed, and Christian found himself liking her. Her acceptance of the social division between herself and a man like Sinclair was wry and realistic—but not bitter. He gestured to the waiter, and then turned back to her.

"I want to thank you," he said simply. "You've been a great help. And it's very important to me—my sister, well, you could say she's causing a lot of heartache. . . ."

"Oh, I'll bet." Sharon looked at him speculatively. "She'll cause a lot more before she's through." She paused. "She's not your sister, is she? Am I right?"

Christian sighed. "No. All right. She's not."

"I guessed as much." Sharon patted his hand, then drew her own away quickly. "Well. I wish you luck. You've been nice. I just wish I could help you more."

Christian signed the bill, and then glanced up. He could see that she was thinking, hesitating.

"Is there something else?" He leaned forward. "You can tell me. Whatever it is, I need to know. . . ."

Sharon frowned. She leaned back in her chair. "Well, it's nothing, I guess. Just an impression I got—I could be wrong. But it did strike me as odd. . . ."

"Tell me."

"Well, I was thinking—when you were asking those questions earlier, about Lewis and Thad. You see, if I'd had to say Helen was interested in one or the other, the answer would have been yes, up to a point. But it would have been Thad."

"Thad?" Christian stared at her, and Sharon gave a quick gesture of the hand.

"Oh, not romantically. I don't mean she was attracted to him or anything like that, don't get me wrong. Just that he *interested* her. He was different when she was around. Like, normally, he's as silent as the grave, right? Never talks. And when she was there—he did. Droned on and on for hours. It bored the pants off me. I think it got on Lewis's nerves too. But Helen, she just sat there as still as a mouse, taking it all in. . . ."

"She did?" Christian regarded her with interest. "Can you remember what he was talking about?"

Sharon grinned. "Sure. I told you. The movies—what else?"

"I have the rundown on Sinclair Lowell Watson. It came through by Telex an hour ago. Together with some subsidiary information on Lewis Sinclair. There's more to come. I know the bank, in any case. We've had dealings of a minor nature with them in the past. . . ."

Edouard passed some Telex sheets across the plain black surface of the desk in his Paris office. He sounded dismissive—but then, to Edouard, Sinclair Lowell Watson was small. Christian sighed, and glanced down at the papers in his hand. He had telephoned Edouard that morning, the moment he left Sharon; Edouard had left the Château de Chavigny immediately, in his private plane. It was now two o'clock on the same day.

Christian looked up at his friend. Of the man so close to the breaking point the previous day, there was now no trace. There were still the shadows beneath the eyes, betraying the lack of sleep, but he was elegantly and immaculately dressed in a three-piece black suit, freshly barbered, freshly shaved. He radiated a cold purposive energy. Christian felt very strongly, at that moment, he would not have liked to be Lewis Sinclair.

"We don't know for certain that she went back to that house, Edouard," he began mildly. "Or that she left with Sinclair and his friend . . ."

"Sinclair left abruptly at five in the morning, shortly after you had gone to the Café Strasbourg and asked questions. I think the conclusion is obvious." Edouard cut him off coldly. He tapped the surface of his desk with his platinum pen.

"They seem just to have been friends, Edouard. Hardly that—casual acquaintances. Really, all it amounts to is that they helped her find a room. . . ."

"We know of no other friends. I think it is possible that Hélène returned there, and that when Sinclair realized someone was looking for her, he and his friend spirited her away. At five o'clock in the morning. Until I come up with a better possibility, I intend to pursue this one. That's all."

Christian shrugged. He knew better than to argue with Edouard when he was in this mood. He bent his head to the Telex sheets and began to read. As he read, his admiration for Edouard, and his nervousness, increased. The papers gave him a brief and extremely thorough rundown on Sinclair Lowell Watson itself—its past history and current standing, most of which, he suspected, Edouard would already have known. It also gave him a brief, but telling, biographical sketch of Lewis Sinclair.

Aged twenty-five, as he had thought. The only son, with four elder sisters. The recipient of a trust fund from his Sinclair grandfather, which brought him an income of around one hundred thousand dollars a year. Educated at Groton and Harvard: an undistinguished university career from an academic point of view. A suggestion that a place had been obtained with some difficulty, probably on the strength of the family's long connection with the university, though possibly on the strength of Lewis's athletic ability. Lewis Sinclair had been the Harvard University football team's star running back. Christian smiled to himself, and congratulated himself on his own instincts. The golden boy. The footballer. The—what was the American term? Oh, yes—the jock. He looked up.

"Edouard . . ." He gave his friend a teasing reproachful smile. "You're slipping. This is three years out of date. Lewis Sinclair left Harvard in 1956. What's he been doing since?" Edouard allowed himself a small tight smile.

"I'll tell you later this afternoon."

"It's a good Bostonian background. . . ."

"A predictable Bostonian background," Edouard said curtly. "Four generations of irreproachable, high-minded business dealings on his father's side. A mother who is a New York heiress in her own right, and can trace her family back to the early Dutch settlers and beyond. A record of civic service and charitable good works. And a not too intelligent son—the fifth child, you note, after four girls—who grows up, or perhaps does not grow up, both rich and spoiled. . . ."

"You can't know that, Edouard, not from this."

"I've also spoken to a close friend in New York. A Wall Street man who knows the Sinclairs well. Lewis Sinclair is, I hear, something of a playboy. . . ." Edouard's lip curled with distaste, and Christian suppressed a smile. "He has a taste for what my friend calls 'partying.' I gather that's mostly what he's been doing for the last three years. As I say, I shall know more this afternoon."

Christian looked at Edouard apprehensively. For years he had heard much gossip about the ruthlessness of Edouard de Chavigny. Since he had never encountered it, he had discounted the stories, and attributed them to envy. Obviously, Edouard was not a saint in his business dealings—what man as successful as he could be? But Machiavellian, devious, with a killer instinct for the jugular of his opponents and rivals? No, Christian had always thought such claims exaggerated. Suddenly he was not so sure, and his new doubts made him fearful.

"Edouard—I've heard of your vendettas," he began lightly. "I hope you're not going to allow this to become one. Lewis Sinclair has done nothing wrong. . . ."

"A vendetta?" Edouard looked at him coldly. "A vendetta implies passionate emotion, surely? I feel nothing for Lewis Sinclair. Sinclair is purely and simply a means to an end."

Christian looked at him doubtfully. He felt sure Edouard thought he was speaking the truth, but he wondered if that was entirely the case. If Edouard were jealous—and Christian could imagine his being intensely and frighteningly so—then his attitude to Lewis Sinclair could hardly be as coldly logical as he claimed. Edouard, of course, would never admit to himself that he was jealous: he despised all petty emotions, and Christian felt sure that Edouard would classify jealousy as petty. Christian, who knew very well what it was to be eaten alive by that emotion, to feel, day by day, its corrosive effect on the mind and soul, did not share that valuation.

"It is possible, Edouard"—he leaned forward—"it is possible that Lewis Sinclair might be trying to help Helen—isn't it worth remembering that? If there is a connection between them now, she may be grateful to him. . . ." It was the wrong thing to have said: he realized that the moment the words were out. Edouard's eyes became even more stony in their regard. He looked at Christian, and then away.

"Yes, well, as you say. That could be the case. I will bear it in mind." He paused, and Christian saw some struggle take place within him. When he looked back, the mask of cold efficiency had slipped just a little, and the emotion beneath it showed through.

"I have to do this, Christian. I have nothing else to go on. The reports from London are complete, and . . ."

"No Helen Hartland?" Christian said gently.

"No birth record for anyone of that name who is conceivably of the correct age." He paused. "No record of any books by an author called Violet Hartland in the British Library. No pilot by the name of Hartland flew with the RAF during the war." He aligned the pen on his desk with the folder in front of him.

Christian looked away. Edouard had admitted before that Hélène might have lied—but not about anything important, he had felt. Christian sighed: was a name not important, or her parentage?

Edouard cleared his throat. "You remember—she said she had been brought up in Devon. In a village also called Hartland. She continued to live there, after her mother died, with an aunt. . . ."

"I remember, yes. She mentioned it to me, too, at dinner."

"There is a village called Hartland in Devon. A small place, quite remote, on the north coast. My aides . . ." He paused. "I'm having checks made now. I expect it will come to nothing, but—if I did decide to go there myself, I wondered, Christian, would you come with me?"

The appeal in his eyes was naked. Christian felt a rush of affection for him.

"Of course I will," he answered quietly. "You know that. And meanwhile?"

"Meanwhile, I shall trace Lewis Sinclair. I shall find out where he's gone."

Christian looked at him in bewilderment. Edouard sounded so very certain.

"Can you do that, Edouard? I'd have thought that if a person wanted to disappear for a while, it would be quite easy. After all, Sinclair could be practically anywhere in Europe by now. For all we know he could have gone straight to the airport, and taken a plane to New York, or Boston, or . . ."

"He didn't do that. My aides have checks on all the transatlantic flights out of Paris. The minute Lewis Sinclair gets his passport stamped, or makes a plane reservation, I shall know about it."

"And if he doesn't? If he takes a train? Or a car? If he hitchhikes? If he just holes up in Paris? Edouard—it's impossible. How do you trace him then?"

Edouard stood up. "It's very simple." He shrugged. "In the modern world there is one almost infallible way of tracing anyone. . . ."

"And that is?"

"My dear Christian. *Money*."

When Christian had left him, Edouard picked up his private-line telephone and put a call through the operator to a number in New York. His friend on Wall Street, a man of power and influence whose investment bank was a household name, came directly on the line. Edouard went straight to the point.

"You've spoken to your contact in the Internal Revenue Service?"

"Yes, I have. And he's come through. Well, he owes me a favor. He can start monitoring the details of all Lewis Sinclair's accounts by tomorrow. Possibly later today. But you have to realize, Edouard, this is against just about every state and federal regulation there is. It's highly irregular. I had to lean on him hard, and I didn't like doing it. . . ."

"I appreciate that. Thank you. However, we both know that this can be done, and is done—whatever the laws. . . ."

"Yes, but Jesus, Edouard. I just hope there's a really good reason for this. I mean, Robert Sinclair is an old friend of mine. We were at college together. God, when I go up to Boston, I stay at his place. We play golf together. Emily Sinclair and my wife are like *that*. They've been friends since Chapin. . . ."

"There is a good reason. I can't say more than that. I give you my absolute assurance, my word, that any information I receive will not fall into the wrong hands, or be used to the detriment of Lewis Sinclair or his family in any way. . . ."

The banker sighed. "All right. Consider it done. Now, tell me what you'll want to know."

"Everything. I am interested in his checking accounts, you understand. I want every withdrawal monitored. I want all details of moneys taken out: when, how much, and where. I am particularly interested in any moneys transferred abroad, to Europe for instance, no matter how small the amount. Transfers to foreign banks. Checks drawn at shops or hotels. Do you have the details of any credit cards?"

"I have the numbers in front of me now."

"Excellent. Then I should like those accounts monitored also. Plus any addresses with which the card companies or his bank correspond. If Lewis Sinclair writes a check to a drugstore for a bottle of aspirin, I want to know about it." He paused. "Is that enough for you to go with?" There was a chuckle at the other end of the line; the grudging admiration of one ruthlessly thorough man for another.

"I guess it gets us started. And you want this information when?"

Edouard smiled. "We know each other," he said. "By yesterday." And he hung up.

In the silence that followed, Edouard felt, as he always felt at moments of great stress, very calm. He looked around his office, at the cool understated room, the austere furnishings, the paintings. He looked at the turmoil of paint in the Pollock, and quite suddenly, as the pain came back, the pain and confusion of her leaving, he bent his head and buried it in his hands.

Why? A voice cried in his mind as the images flashed across the dark retina of his closed eyes: his father, Grégoire, Jean-Paul, Isobel, their baby, Hélène: the people he had loved, the people he had lost, one after another. Why, why, *why?*

I n 1959 the district of Trastevere in Rome had yet to become fashionable. Trastevere was then much as it had been for centuries—a poor area of the city, its narrow streets and beautiful piazzas, its ancient churches and its palaces penetrated by very few tourists. Located on the left bank of the Tiber, well away from the expensive shops, smart hotels, and most visited sites, Trastevere was raucous, crowded, cheap, and very beautiful.

Thaddeus Angelini, whose ancestors came from this part of Rome, looked at the narrow shaded passageways, at the balconies hung with cages of songbirds, and at the wash strung across the streets like flags, and thought it was the perfect place in which to film. Lewis Sinclair looked at the crowded street markets, the inexpensive cafés and restaurants which hummed with life day and night, and thought it was a perfect place in which to disappear. Hélène's opinion was unheard: it occurred neither to Thad nor to Lewis to consult her.

They had arrived there the previous night, after a long and circuitous train journey. Now, it was mid-afternoon, the sun was warm, and Lewis Sinclair had left in search, he explained to the others, of a headquarters for them. A luxurious headquarters, he had added with a smile. Trastevere was picturesque, but he did not intend to spend the next two months sleeping in that flea pit of a *pensione*.

Hélène sat alone with Thad at a café in the Piazza di Santa Maria, opposite the church that was said to be the oldest in Rome. In front of her was a small cup of espresso, untouched. Thad was talking, a low monologue which had already continued for some half an hour, and Hélène, hardly hearing him, was looking at the beautiful mosaic that ornamented the façade of Santa Maria, and which depicted, on either side of the Madonna, five wise virgins, and five foolish ones.

Thad was describing, in detail, a dolly shot used by Hitchcock in *Vertigo*. Hélène's head ached; she still felt sick, and the procession of virgins on the church façade seemed to mist, and then to clarify alarmingly, partly because she was finding it difficult to blink back the tears.

What she had done was irrevocable: so she told herself again and again. She had decided to do it, and she had done it—and there could be no going back.

It had been hard to leave. She had planned it all so very carefully and precisely, sure that it was the best way, because any other way would have involved explanations. She had packed her suitcase, and folded the Hermès gloves, and laid the ring on top of them, and then—when it was time to leave and to run away—she had stopped; it seemed so terrible to leave without saying anything. She wanted to leave him a note, a letter—something. But if she began writing, she might never find the strength to go.

So she slipped out of the huge house, feeling like a thief, and after that it was simple: one lift, all the way to Paris. In Paris, she'd gone back to Lewis and Thad, and slept in Sharon's old room, because she couldn't think, once she got there, where else to go, or what to do next. Lewis had wanted to ask her questions, but Thad had made him be quiet. He shoved Lewis out of the room, and looked at her for a long time, chewing on his beard thoughtfully. Then he said, "I knew you'd come back. You had to. We've got the money. We're going to make the movie. You can be in it, if you like. You know, the way I told you."

And it was true, he had talked about making a film, when she stayed there before. Then, Hélène had believed him; you did, somehow, when Thad talked. Later, when she was in the Loire, everything Thad had said had seemed unreal—boasting, maybe. Things like that didn't happen, not in real life. And anyway, Thad wasn't real to her anymore, and neither was Lewis. Only Edouard was real.

Now, when he talked about the film, and explained that Lewis was helping to back it, Hélène listened, and felt she did not care very much. Thad and Lewis, however, were both very excited about the project, and they talked about it a lot.

"It's a small part," Lewis said.

"It was a small part." Thad corrected him. "It's getting bigger."

"And it's low budget. Experimental," Lewis added.

Thad sucked his teeth. He said. "Oh, Jesus. Just shut up, will you, Lewis?"

Hélène sat and listened to them. Her head felt tight and hot, and all she could think about was whether Edouard would come after her, whether he would look for her.

She thought he must, and the second day, she slipped out of the house and sat near the Café Strasbourg. Every time a black car passed, her heart seemed to stop beating. But none of them was Edouard's car, and by the end of the afternoon, she realized he was not going to come. That was what she had intended, but the realization hurt her very much.

She went back to the roominghouse and tried to make plans. They were going to make the film in Rome; Thad was vague as to how long it would take. They would pay her some money, of course. Not very much, but as much as they could, and her expenses while she was in Rome.

"Don't worry," Lewis said. "You'll be with us. We'll look after you."

Hélène wondered if she could do it; she wondered if there was time. Her body was still unchanged now, but what if the baby suddenly started to grow? What if she began to swell up like a melon when they were halfway through? What would she do then?

But no, she was almost sure that you could hide it, until the fourth month anyway, and by then they should be finished.

She said "yes" in the end, and Lewis was thrilled. Thad just shrugged; the possibility of her saying "no" had apparently never occurred to him. Hélène shut herself in Sharon's room and told herself this was the best thing that could have happened. She would be earning some money; she would have somewhere to stay; she would be beginning her career. She began to cry.

That was the third day. Late that night, or rather, very early the next morning, Lewis came into her room and woke her up.

"We have to go," he said a little evasively. "Split. You know."

Hélène struggled up in bed, and stared at him uncertainly.

"Go? Go where? Why? What time is it?"

"Nearly five." Lewis smiled. "We're going to Rome. Thad's decided to get started—and we have to go anyway. Problems."

"Problems? What kind of problems?"

"Money. Rent. The usual kind. It's better if we leave now—can you get dressed quickly?"

Somehow, she hadn't quite believed him. Lewis, with money problems? It didn't make sense. But she couldn't stay here without Lewis and Thad; all her money was used up. She got out of bed tiredly, waited for the waves of nausea to recede, and then packed her suitcase.

The long circuitous and exhausting train journey, and now they were here. It was so very hot, and Thad was still talking, talking. She had been sick twice on the train, and felt as if she might be sick again, any minute.

She shut her eyes, closed them against the heat and that maddening procession of mosaic virgins. Her mother felt very close now; she had been coming closer and closer, ever since she had left the Loire, and now her voice was all mixed up with Thad's in the craziest way. Thad was telling her about a camera angle, and her mother was telling her that men didn't mean to lie, they probably thought their lies were true when they said them, which was why it was so easy to believe them.

Had Edouard lied to her, then? Had he not loved her? Was that why he had not tried to find her?

Or was he looking for her now? Was he perhaps at the Café Strasbourg at this exact minute, making inquiries, asking the owner, asking the waiters if they knew a woman called Helen Hartland?

Well, if he was, he would discover she had lied. And when he discovered that, he would stop looking. She felt quite certain of that. He would feel angry and betrayed, and that would be the end of it.

She opened her eyes again. It was better that way, in the end. She stared at the procession of virgins on the church façade. They advanced; they receded: five of them foolish, five of them wise.

What made them wise, exactly? She became aware of the fact that Thad had stopped speaking, and that he had been silent for some time.

Finally, he reached across and patted her hand awkwardly, like someone patting a dog. He always wore tinted glasses, which made it difficult to see his eyes, or read his expression. Now he appeared to be looking at her with a kind of doglike concern.

"You all right, Helen? You feel sick again?"

"No. I'm all right." She swallowed. "I was just—I don't know—thinking about the past, I suppose."

"Tell me about the past," Thad said. It was something he had said to her before. He seemed very anxious, Hélène thought, to hear her life story.

She turned to look at him. Thad was very very ugly. She suspected, she was not sure, that he was also very clever. Thad made her a little afraid. She felt sometimes as if he could look into her mind and see all the pictures there.

She was determined not to let him do that. She had let Edouard come close to her, and she intended never to do that again. It was simpler when people were distant. When they were distant, she felt safe.

She drew in her breath and began to tell Thad a lie. It was very like the time on the train, with the woman who was knitting. At first she expected him to interrupt every moment, and say, "Come on now, that's not true." But he never interrupted once.

Hélène invented. She made up an English family. All sorts of details and twists came to her as she spoke. The family's name was Craig—Thad and Lewis had seen her passport, so it had to be. This family usually called her "Helen," though she was christened "Hélène."

There was a stepfather who was a little like Ned Calvert, and a mother, now dead, who was very like Violet. From this family, in particular the stepfather, she had run away. He might look for her, she told Thad earnestly, but he wouldn't look very hard, and even if he found her, she would never go back.

Thad never uttered a word. He just listened; his small dark eyes never left her face.

When, finally, she finished, Hélène looked at him anxiously. Somehow it was important Thad should believe her: the story was like an audition, or a test.

Thad made no comment at all. When she stopped speaking, he sat silent for a while, and then shook his head. He looked at her solemnly.

"Wow," he said. "Some story."

Hélène despised him a little at that moment. He had been so easy to take in.

It was a long time before she realized her mistake.

There was only one painting in the Principessa's bedroom, and it hung directly above the bed. It was a Dali.

Kneeling on the black silk sheets, while the Principessa went through a repertoire that had made her celebrated on two continents, Lewis Sinclair found that, unless he closed his eyes, he could not avoid looking at it.

For what seemed to him an eternity, he stared at a putrefying desert landscape in which detumescent flesh, propped on crutches, merged with the sand. A deliquescent watch face, without hands, mocked the minutes: Lewis measured them in the soft interminable lappings of the Principessa's practiced tongue.

It was hardly a turn-on. Lewis, always a pragmatist, and aware it was important to please the Principessa, took the coward's way out.

Feigning a pleasure he did not feel, he shut his eyes. When the Principessa stopped her ministrations, she did so abruptly, and not, Lewis thought, at the most logical or the most tactful moment. His eyes snapped open to see the wide lips draw back from the little nibbling pearly teeth in a sweet smile. "Your turn, Lewis, *mi amore*. . . ."

Fuck you, Lewis thought, and did so, roughly.

When it was over the Principessa yawned, and stretched her tawny limbs. She stroked the marks on her arms where Lewis had left scratches, and favored him with a long slow satisfied smile.

"Lewis. Lewis. What a very wicked boy you are. Surely you didn't learn such things at Harvard?"

"Baltimore."

Lewis reached across for the cigarettes, lit two, and passed one to the Principessa. She levered herself up on the black silk pillows, and inhaled deeply.

"Baltimore. Baltimore?" She frowned. "Where is this Baltimore?"

"It's a port, Principessa." Lewis gave her his best boyish, slightly crooked grin.

"Near Boston?"

"Near Washington. But worth a detour. . . ."

The Principessa laughed. "Lewis, Lewis . . . and I thought you were a good American boy. I can see I underestimated you. . . ."

Her eyes clouded speculatively, and Lewis shifted in the bed. It looked as if a further demonstration of his own virtuosity might be needed to clinch the deal he had in mind, and—just then—he didn't have the energy. Fortunately, the Principessa appeared at least temporarily sated. She coiled one magnificent leg around his hips and rubbed up against him in a serpentine fashion, but then she drew back thoughtfully. She lay there, smoking her cigarette—recharging, no doubt, Lewis thought. She reminded him at that moment of a great python enjoyably digesting a substantial supper, resting awhile, appetite only temporarily in abeyance. Lewis was unsure whether to broach his deal now, or wait.

"So—you are going to make a film, you and your friends, Lewis. Mmmm, my clever little godchild . . ." She laughed, and flicked her tongue across the tips of Lewis's nipples. Lewis wriggled.

"You should have told me before." Her large dark eyes looked up at him reproachfully. "I could have introduced you to so many useful people. Federico now—you know Federico? He would adore you, Lewis. . . ."

"He would?"

"But certainly. So blond. So golden. So . . . well, perhaps not. It is no matter." She paused thoughtfully, stroking his thigh with one long pink opalescent nail. "What kind of film, Lewis? You didn't tell me."

"The cheap kind," Lewis said firmly. "We haven't got a lot of money."

"And your friend, the ugly one, he will direct it? Oh, Lewis, is he any good?"

"He's good." Lewis shrugged. He knew what she was leading up to. "Better than good, maybe."

"And the girl, Lewis—is she going to be in it?"

"She might be. It's up to Thad really. If he wants to use her. Something small, you know. I couldn't care less. If it keeps him happy . . ."

"Is he screwing her?"

"Who knows?" Lewis looked away.

"Are you screwing her, Lewis?"

Lewis knew the answer had to be quick, and convincing. If the Principessa suspected his interest in Helen, her vanity would be wounded. Then she wouldn't help them.

"Me? That kid?" He smiled. "You've got to be joking."

The opalescent nail dug a little more deeply into the muscles of his thigh.

"But you'd like to?"

"No way." Lewis lowered his mouth to her arched throat. "Not my type at all, Principessa."

He did not lie well, but, luckily, this lie seemed to convince her—the lie, and what he did next, which was almost one hundred percent guaranteed to distract her. The Principessa sighed.

After a brief pause, in which the appetite of the python showed signs of reawakening with alarming rapidity, Lewis lifted his head, and, keeping her pinioned beneath him, said, "So—how about it? Can we stay here? Can we film some scenes here? Yes or no?"

"Evil boy."

She pouted, an expression that made the wrinkles in the lovely face more noticeable. Tough, Lewis thought, looking at her with that expression of lazy lust that had always come naturally, and which years of practice had perfected; tough—how even the best plastic surgeons couldn't keep the ravages of time at bay forever.

"I suppose you could. . . ." She paused teasingly. "I shall be away three months. You can stay here that long. Maybe . . . If you promise to behave. No scandals, Lewis. Raphael wouldn't like it."

Lewis smiled. Prince Raphael, descendant of the Sforzas and Medicis, was as famous for his complaisance as was his wife for her erotic inventiveness. Since he preferred the company of adolescent boys, such complaisance was understandable. Lewis bent his head, and nuzzled the Principessa's nipples; they were rouged.

"No scandals, Principessa. Promise."

"No parties, Lewis. You swear to me?"

Lewis thought of the Principessa's own party, the previous evening, which he had attended alone—fortunately. In the course of it, two dwarves had proved that all the inflammatory rumors about the size of their sexual organs were well-founded, and a man dressed in cardinal's robes—and, it proved later, little else—had propositioned him flagrantly amid the resplendent, and recherché, volumes in Prince Raphael's ancestral library. Lewis sighed, and raised his clear hazel eyes.

"Principessa—would I?"

"You might, Lewis, you might. I've heard rumors. . . ."

"All lies. I'll be the perfect house guest. I'll keep an eye on the servants, and the guards. . . ."

"You will?"

"I'll look after the dogs. You know I love dogs, Principessa. . . ."

The beautiful face clouded. "Oh, my poor babies. I shall miss them so much. They'll pine, Lewis, they always do. . . ."

Lewis suppressed a groan. He hated dogs, and the Principessa had twenty-seven, not counting the Dobermans that guarded the estate grounds.

"Prime steak twice a day. Proper exercise. They'll live like kings."

"You *swear*, Lewis?"

"I swear, Principessa."

"All right. You've persuaded me. You evil boy."

Big deal, Lewis thought. The Principessa had three houses in Italy, one in Monte Carlo, one in Tangier—though that was primarily for her husband's benefit—one on the beach in Jamaica, and one just off Fifth Avenue in the East Sixties. Most of them, at one time or another, were occupied by a sequence of spongers whom the Principessa found diverting—which was why he had come to her in the first place. That, and the fact that this *palazzo*, in the hills some ten kilometers outside Rome, was like a fortress. There were the Dobermans; there were hired hoods on the gates; there was twenty-four-hour security. No one could get in, and—more to the point—no one could get out. Helen would make no further unscheduled disappearances: of that, Lewis was determined.

"You're using me, you wicked boy. Don't think I don't know that. . . ." The Principessa gave his arm a painful pinch.

"I love you too. Turn over."

Lewis gave her a slap, a playful slap, quite hard. The Principessa moaned; she turned over onto her stomach obligingly. Lewis, averting his eyes from the Dali once more, prepared to give her full recompense for her generosity.

The Principessa arched her back, still unsuspecting. Her hands on the black sheets flexed and unflexed in pleasurable anticipation. Lewis maneuvered himself into position; slapping her had made him hard.

"Oh, Lewis . . ." She gave a little sigh. "'You've grown up so fast. To think—I held you in my arms when you were a little little baby. . . . I was very young myself then, naturally. . . ." Lewis held himself poised above her. The Principessa had no children of her own, and she was the same age, exactly the same age, as his mother. Did she think he didn't know that, the vain stupid bitch?

"Oh, yes?"

He moved suddenly, taking her completely by surprise. Her cry of pain encouraged him.

Face set, eyes shut, Lewis thrust. With a force he enjoyed, he showed her a few other things he'd learned in Baltimore.

An hour later, Lewis returned to the café in Trastevere where Thad and Helen were waiting for him. He saw them before they saw him. From a distance, it looked as if she was speaking; then Thad looked up, peered nearsightedly across the square, and turned back to her. As Lewis came closer, it was the drone of Thad's voice he picked up.

"So—he did it by process. He must have." Thad placed his plump elbows on the table. "It's the only way he could have gotten the effect. First he must have done the separate dolly shot down the stairs. Then he must have filmed the actor, in front of a transparency screen, and—"

As Lewis reached their table, he stopped in mid-sentence. Helen looked up, but made no other acknowledgment of Lewis's presence. Beauty and the beast, Lewis thought. He smiled as Thad raised his face inquiringly.

"Hi, Lewis. Fixed?"

"Absolutely."

"How long have we got?"

Thad didn't attempt congratulations or thanks, and Lewis felt a second's passing irritation.

"Three months. She's away three months. That long enough?"

"Yeah. More than."

"How long do you need then?"

"Six weeks." Thad looked bored. "Six weeks two days maybe."

"Jesus, Thad, you're such a bullshitter." Lewis slid easily into a chair beside them. "You can't know that exactly. . . ."

"Yes, I can. I have a shooting script. Everything."

"It's news to me."

Lewis gestured to the waiter to bring him some coffee. It was unlike Thad to show off, he thought. Perhaps it was for Hélène's benefit. He turned back and leaned across the table.

"Well, if you have it, Thad, can I see it?"

"No."

"Why not? Where is it, for God's sake?"

"In here." Thad tapped his own forehead, and giggled.

Lewis shrugged. He turned away to Helen, took her hand, and lightly pressed it.

"How are you feeling now—okay?"

"Fine. I'm fine." She withdrew her hand.

"You'll like the Principessa's place." He tried to sound encouraging. "It's huge. The perfect base. And for the filming—well, there are rooms there that just blow your mind. Also . . ." He hesitated. He had not told Helen about the man who had come to the Strasbourg asking for her, but she might have guessed. "Also—it's very private. Quiet. So—"

"It sounds perfect." She cut him off with that cool English voice, with a glance of those remote gray-blue eyes. "Was it very difficult to persuade her, the Principessa?"

Something in that cool appraising glance made Lewis blush; he hoped she did not notice.

"Easy," he answered quickly. "She's very generous. An old friend of my mother's, you know. . . ."

Thad giggled. Lewis gave him a hard stare. Sometimes Thad's tactlessness and general uncouthness got on his nerves.

"She knows *everyone*," he went on reprovingly. "Artists. Actors. Writers. Directors. She would have introduced us to Fellini, she said so. . . ."

"Tell her not to bother."

Thad took off his glasses, panted on them, then polished them on his greasy sleeve. Lewis watched him with distaste.

"You don't want to meet Fellini? Why not?"

"Fellini's films suck," Thad pronounced, and replaced his glasses.

An English garden.

The black Rolls-Royce Phantom had met Edouard's plane at Plymouth airport. It was now driving through the increasingly narrow Devon roads, going northward. It was a cold gray day in early November—early afternoon, and the light was already failing. Christian glanced at Edouard, who had not spoken since they climbed into the car; his friend's face was averted. He was staring out at the high banks and hedges that lined the roads, his face pale and expressionless.

The thin light, the low scudding clouds, the high banks, all gave Christian a sense of claustrophobia, of driving down a tunnel. When, occasionally, there was a gate, a gap in the banks and hedges, he looked out across the landscape with a sense of relief. Even then, though open and beautiful, the scenery was bleak: few houses; tracts of newly plowed fields with furrows of neatly turned red earth; some clumps of hawthorn bent and twisted by the prevailing winds from the coast. As they crested a rise, Christian glimpsed the sea for the first time; it looked flat, metallic gray, and endless, the horizon invisible behind the banks of low cloud.

"It is near the sea. Just as she said."

Edouard spoke suddenly, making Christian jump. Then he turned his face away again, back to the window. Christian, with a sigh, looked down again at the book that lay in his lap.

Both Christian's parents, but particularly his mother, who was a friend of Vita Sackville-West's, were passionate gardeners: he was therefore familiar with the publication in front of him, *The National Gardens' Scheme*, a guide to gardens opened to the public to raise money for charity. Indeed, his parents' home, Quaires Manor, was listed in the section for Oxfordshire.

It was, Christian thought, a quintessentially English publication; though some small and more modest gardens were included, it was, in the main, a testimony to the obsession of the English upper classes with horticulture: shire by shire, manor by manor, it painstakingly listed the features of the gardens concerned, an herbaceous border here, a bog garden there, topiary work, rose collections, rhododendron collections—and then provided extremely detailed instructions for finding the house and garden concerned, together with the name and title of its owners, and their telephone number. Christian had once annoyed his parents very much by remarking that it ought to be called the Burglars' Bible.

It was not the kind of publication with which Christian would have expected Edouard to be familiar—but then, Edouard's range of interests was wide, and he often surprised Christian with his knowledge of the most esoteric subjects. It was Edouard who had thought of consulting this guide, and who had, in the section devoted to Devon, marked one entry with a thin black line:

Penshayes House (Miss Elizabeth Culverton), Compton, near Stoke-by-Hartland. Two miles south of Milford, right off the B2556, turning sign-posted Home Farm. Seven acres of gardens in a valley within 600 yards of the sea; created by the late Sir Hector Culverton. Historic woodland garden; notable collections of shrub roses and ericaceae. Kitchen garden.

Christian smiled: entrance was a modest one shilling. Hélène's aunt opened her garden every second Wednesday of the month, for three months of the year. The place was remote, and Christian doubted if she raised more than ten pounds a year from her efforts: still, as his mother would have said, that was not the point. The point, as far as Christian could make out—and he was profoundly indifferent to gardens—was that they broke your back and broke your heart, and reverted to a wilderness six months after you died, quick repayment for a lifetime of care. Gardens and women, in Christian's opinion, had much in common with each other: men attempted to tame and train them, and ultimately they failed. It was not an opinion he had expressed to Edouard.

However, it seemed that in one respect at least, Helen had told the truth, partial truth, anyway. The garden overlooking the sea existed. The aunt existed. She had been traced, with the aid of this publication, by an extremely discreet firm of private investigators, retained by an even more discreet firm of City solicitors employed by Edouard.

The investigation had taken some weeks, but it had proved more fruitful than the search for Lewis Sinclair which, Christian knew, had been proceeding simultaneously. Sinclair, of course, moved around, which made it more difficult. The file gradually assembled on him had been a full one; Sinclair's movements in the three years since Harvard were well-documented in a series of gossip-column clippings. A well-heeled hell raiser: parties in New York; parties in Los Angeles and San Francisco. A spell in London, which included a party in Chelsea raided by the police. Gstaad the previous winter. A brief return to Boston, then more partying. All Christian could remember of the files was a series of pictures of Sinclair in disheveled evening dress: in each picture there was a different woman on his arm. So Sinclair moved around, which made the fact that he had now gone to ground so effectively all the more interesting: clearly, Sinclair was being careful.

But Elizabeth Culverton—that was another matter. In this kind of rural area, where families lived for generations, where there were few newcomers and everyone knew everyone else's antecedents and history, it was easy to trace someone. A garden, and a sister called Violet—that had been enough. No one had identified the photograph of Helen Hartland, as Christian still thought of her, but several elderly inhabitants of the villages of Hartland and Stoke-by-Hartland recalled the young Violet Culverton, who lived in the big house and who ran away to go on the stage. It had been a great scandal at the time: the fact that it took place before the war, some twenty-five years earlier, was irrelevant: here, that was yesterday.

Christian flicked the guidebook closed, and gazed out the window. In his experience, there were two kinds of liars: those who invented completely, and those who invented in part, larding their lies with elements of the truth. Helen Hartland came into the second category, he supposed; the existence of Elizabeth Culverton and this house proved it. And that was fortunate from Edouard's point of view—or was it?

Christian glanced across at his friend, and then away. Edouard's obsession disturbed him more and more: naturally he said nothing, but he often wished that the girl had been a more thorough liar. If she had disappeared totally, might that not have been better—for everyone concerned? He sighed, and glanced at a passing signpost, then down at his watch. They were going to be fifteen minutes early.

Edouard pulled the handle of an old-fashioned brass bell, and the bell clanged inside the house. An ugly house: a huge red brick Victorian pile, approached by a long drive through tall and dripping rhododendrons. It looked, and sounded, empty.

Edouard and Christian glanced at each other, stepped back, and looked up at the house. Rows of dark windows, no lights: broken guttering, and walls stained with damp. Even on a summer's day it would not have been attractive; in the cold November light it looked dank and unwelcoming. Edouard pulled the bell again, and as it clanged mournfully, a dog began to bark somewhere in the gardens beyond. Edouard and Christian paused and then, with one accord, set off in the direction of the barking, down a narrow flagged path that ran around the side of the house, past some outbuildings and a decaying stable block, and out into the gardens at the rear. Christian saw a huge expanse of terraced lawns, covered with damp leaves; in the distance, beyond a dripping Wellingtonia and dark yew hedges that needed clipping, he glimpsed the sea.

The dog barked again, and he and Edouard turned. To their right, the path continued. It led past an old summerhouse, its roof caved in and covered with creeper, to a square enclosure which was now bare and mournful, but which was clearly a rose garden.

There, two fat black Labradors cavorted, chasing each other, and a tall woman, secateurs in hand, struggled with an immense rose bush. They saw her before she saw them: a gaunt woman, of about sixty, with short-cropped gray hair. She was wearing a thick corduroy jacket, men's cavalry twill trousers, and mudcaked Wellington boots. Edouard walked forward; the dogs stopped their game, looked up, and growled in warning. The woman disengaged herself from a long thorny branch that tangled in her hair, and stood still, watching them as they approached. Briefly, the sun came out from behind a cloud; it glinted on the blades of her secateurs. Then, with an irritable gesture, she locked them shut, and stepped forward. A weatherbeaten face, sharp blue eyes, angular features: an English fox-hunting face, Christian thought. It wore an extremely unwelcoming expression.

"Oh. You've shown." She stepped forward. "I didn't think you would. Well, since you're here, you'd better come inside, I suppose. I hope this won't take long. It's damned inconvenient. I have seventy-five more of these to prune. . . ."

She drew level with them, gave them both a quick appraising glance, and then strode past them. The dogs started after her, then faltered.

"Come *on*, Livingstone. Stanley, *heel.* . . . Here." She whistled, and the two dogs bounded after her. Edouard and Christian exchanged glances. As they turned to follow her, Christian took Edouard's arm.

"Edouard—you know your reputation for charm. . . ."

"I've heard it mentioned. . . ."

"Well, I rather think this might be the moment to employ it. Don't you?"

They followed Elizabeth Culverton into a cold and cavernous hall. There she yanked off her Wellingtons, tossed her jacket onto a hatstand of antler horns, and stood looking at them, her feet encased in thick wool socks, standing on a tesselated floor of sludge-green and orange tiles.

"You can leave your coats there."

From a welter of riding boots, brogues, and other mudcaked shoes, she selected a pair of men's felt slippers which a dog had chewed, and strode past them, down the dark hall, and into a room beyond. Slowly Christian and Edouard removed their overcoats. Christian looked around him. There was an enormous branching staircase of yellow oak; the Morris-design wallpaper was of dark brown and vaguely predatory flowers; on it were hung, receding into the gloom, an array of bad family portraits. He saw a stuffed fox in a glass cage, more stag heads and antlers, a rack of fishing rods, and a display case of fishing flies. His eyes met Edouard's.

"It's worse inside than out," he said in a low voice. "Which is something of an achievement really . . ."

"Christian, please . . ."

"Oh, all right, all right. I'll behave. . . ."

He trotted after Edouard down the hallway, and followed him into the room beyond. It smelled of wood smoke, and, as they came in, Elizabeth Culverton threw another log onto a dying fire and gave it a hefty kick. Christian looked around him curiously.

The room, clearly once a gentlemen's smoking room, looked as if it hadn't been touched since 1914. It contained many vast and bulging armchairs, some upholstered in worn leather, some in faded chintz. There was a soaring nicotine-brown plaster ceiling, with Gothic spandrels. The walls were paneled in dark oak, and hung with photographs.

Groups of oarsmen; school groups; cricket teams. Men in white flannels, arms crossed, with Kaiser Bill moustaches stared down at him in serried ranks. Over the door there was an oar, inscribed: TRINITY, HEAD OF THE RIVER 1906. Beneath it was another photograph, of six young men surveying them with all the arrogance of privileged youth. It bore the inscription: BEEFSTEAK CLUB, CAMBRIDGE 1910.

Elizabeth Culverton moved to a heavy mahogany side table, picked up a square decanter, and to Christian's relief, poured two inches of whisky into each of three exquisite chipped glasses. She set down the decanter with a bang.

"Can't be bothered to make tea. Kitchen's too bloody cold. I'm bloody cold. You'd like a whisky—yes?" She indicated the two other glasses, picked up her own, and moved back in front of the fire. Behind her was a heavily carved Victorian overmantel some eight feet high, of surpassing ugliness. To her right was an Eton boater on a peg, and to her left, bizarrely, a fan-shaped arrangement of school-prefect canes. They were tied with faded pink bows.

"You might as well sit down. Since you're here," she said gruffly.

Christian, who was feeling weak, grabbed a whisky and sank down into collapsed springs and dog hair. Edouard remained standing. Elizabeth Culverton looked at Christian, and then at Edouard, whose back was to the window, and whose face was in shadow. She paused, and then addressed herself to him.

"Well, I know who you are. Since you've gone to the trouble to find me, I assume it's important. . . ." Her chin lifted combatively. "Before we go any further, perhaps you'd like to explain. Exactly what is your interest in my niece?"

There was a brief silence. Christian's hand, in the act of conveying the whisky to his lips, froze. He felt a nervous and almost irrepressible desire to laugh. For once, he thought, Edouard might have met his match.

Edouard took one step forward. His face came into the light, and he looked directly at Elizabeth Culverton.

"But of course," he said coolly. "I love her, and I wish to marry her. I hope that answers your question."

Elizabeth Culverton was visibly taken aback, not a state with which she was familiar, Christian would have bet on that. She hesitated, blinked, looked down at her glass, and then up again. Then she gave a sudden bark of laughter.

"Well, you're direct, I suppose. That's something." She paused. "If you'll sit down, I'll tell you just why that's a bloody absurd idea. . . ." She gestured at the glass of whisky on the side table, and a slightly malicious glint came into her sharp blue eyes. "And I should have that, if I were you. You might need it."

"Her name is Craig. Hélène Craig—the first name spelled and pronounced in the French manner, which gives you some idea of her mother's taste. She was always a stupid affected woman. Hélène! And the girl is sixteen, seventeen next year."

She said it with virtually no preamble, sitting now, in one of the deep armchairs beside the fire, the glass of whisky in one hand and an unfiltered Senior Service cigarette in the other. She inhaled deeply, coughed, and when Edouard, now also seated, did not answer, she looked a little disappointed. A woman who did not like men, Christian thought; a woman who liked to draw blood.

"What's more . . ." She paused, looking at Edouard speculatively. "You obviously think I can help you—and I can't. I hardly know the girl, and I've no idea at all where she is now. She may contact me again, but I doubt it."

Edouard looked down at his hands, his face set, and Christian, who knew what he must be thinking, felt a dart of pity. He was counting the lies, he thought: name, age, where she grew up; three, so far. Christian leaned forward.

"But she was here—earlier this year? We understood that—"

"Of course she was here." Elizabeth Culverton looked irritable. "And damned thoughtless and inconvenient it was. She had sent a cable, but it was delayed. In the end it arrived about three hours before she did. Damned stupid thing to do. If she'd written, I would have told her not to come. As it was—she had to stay, naturally. What else could I do?"

A note of anxiety had crept into her voice. Edouard looked up, and Elizabeth Culverton drained the whisky in her glass. She levered herself stiffly from her chair, and poured herself another. No soda, no water; her hand shook a little, and the glass clinked against the decanter. She returned to her chair, and Christian watched her with interest. That she felt some emotion was obvious: that she was trying to cover it up was also clear. He glanced across at Edouard, waiting for him to prompt her, but Edouard said nothing. One of his notorious silences. Now Christian saw how effective they could be. To his considerable surprise, Elizabeth Culverton looked at Edouard, looked back into the fire, drew on her cigarette, and then, unprompted, began to speak, her voice now jerky and resentful.

"That probably sounds harsh. I should explain. I never got on with her mother. Violet and I were chalk and cheese. There was no love lost between us. She might have pretended otherwise when it suited her purposes, but I never liked her, even as a child, and when she left, I was heartily glad to see the back of her. She used to write occasionally, and I never answered her letters. I knew she had a child, of course—she angled for an invitation to come back here before it was born—she always did, whenever she was in trouble of any kind. . . ." She paused, drew on her cigarette, and then threw the butt into the smoldering fire. "However. That was a long time ago. Sixteen years ago. I'd had virtually no contact with my sister since then. My half sister. I didn't know she was dead—I didn't even know she'd been ill. Until I received the telegram, and the girl turned up. Then—well, if I'm truthful, I have to say I was surprised. Violet seemed to have brought her up quite well. She was a pleasant enough girl. Well-mannered. Well-spoken. Quite charming, I thought, to begin with. She didn't look well—she was tired out, very pale, obviously distressed at Violet's death. She had nowhere else to go. So, naturally, I had to ask her to stay here." She paused, and two spots of color heightened in her cheeks.

"I intended it to be a temporary arrangement, you understand. And then—well, I quite liked the girl, and I began to consider letting her stay. I live alone, you see, and I have this damned arthritis. There's no help in the house. No help in the garden. We had sixteen gardeners once, in my father's day. Now I have to struggle along on my own. . . ." She gave an angry shrug. "I never mentioned the idea to her. I had no chance. She stayed precisely three days, and then she walked out. I imagine she'd thought I had money, and when she discovered I hadn't— that all went, a long time ago—she left. I washed my hands of her. Which is what I should have done in the first place."

"I see." Edouard looked down at his hands, then stood up. He moved away to the window, so his back was toward them, and looked out over the gardens. The light was fading fast. "It's a fine garden," he said meditatively. "In the summer it must be very beautiful. . . ."

Christian looked up at him in surprise. Edouard sounded perfectly sincere, and Christian couldn't understand why he was wasting time. There were a thousand questions bubbling in his own brain, and he couldn't wait to start asking them. He opened his mouth, and Edouard gave him a quick glance. Christian shut it again, and Elizabeth Culverton, no doubt exactly as Edouard had intended, began speaking again. Her voice, at first defiant and defensive, softened as she spoke.

"It was fine. Very fine. When I was a child. Before the war—when there was staff, when there was money." She gave another bitter bark of laughter. "It would break my father's heart to see it now. He created it, you see. Oh, his father began it, but it was my father's garden. He was a great plantsman in his day. A visionary. Everything I know I learned from him—we were very close. After my mother died, exceptionally so. I was like a son to him. . . ."

Were you now? Christian thought, glancing up at her. Edouard turned back, his face gentle and sympathetic, his eyes holding those of the woman by the fire.

"I begin to understand," he said. "I was very close to my own father." Edouard sat down again and looked into the fire. He appeared to hesitate. "He must have remarried presumably?" His voice was quiet and thoughtful.

"When I was seventeen, yes. A most unfortunate marriage, which he lived to regret. She was called Beryl. Beryl Jenkins. A dreadful, vulgar woman. I loathed her. She might have appealed to a certain type of man, I suppose. The type who likes barmaids. Chorus girls. She had some money—she was the widow of some brewer or something. I never inquired too closely. I imagine the money must have accounted for it. My father had debts. He can hardly have admired her. She was completely unpresentable. None of our friends would receive her. She cut my father off, manipulated him. . . ."

"And Violet was her daughter?"

"Violet was born a year after they married, yes." She snapped the reply, her blue eyes sharp with remembered anger. "Her mother left my father not long afterward. She died a year or two later. Violet remained here." She gestured angrily around the shadowed room. "She grew up here. My father, poor man, doted on her. . . ."

"That must have been very difficult for you," Edouard murmured, and her blue eyes flashed.

"Not really. My father adored me. I knew that. We were as close as ever. But Violet was devious. She played up to him. She was very pretty in an insipid kind of way. She lisped as a child—she was always clinging to my father, climbing up on his lap, wrapping her arms around his neck—that kind of thing. I detest that kind of behavior myself. My father felt protective, I think. She was a very timid child—or she pretended to be. Wouldn't say boo to a goose. No brain, of course. I had no patience with her." She paused.

"She always wanted to be an actress, even when she was little. She used to practice on my father, that's all. She'd preen in front of the looking glass for hours; she used to do recitations for him in the drawing room after dinner—ghastly simpering stuff, Tennyson mostly. She had absolutely no talent whatsoever, but my father was a kind man. He'd encourage her, and then she'd twist him around her little finger. She'd persuade him to give her treats—things we could ill afford by that time. I remember once, he took her to Paris with him. Paris! I told Hélène that. I wanted her to understand—why I disliked her mother so much. It was so unfair. I loved him. I cared for him. He meant nothing to Violet. Two months after he took her to Paris, she ran off. Joined some third-rate touring company somewhere; changed her name. There was a man involved, I imagine. Someone she'd met. Violet wouldn't have had the guts to do it on her own." She paused, and glanced away dismissively. "It killed my father. She never came back, and it broke his heart. The damn stupid doctor said it was pneumonia, but I knew it wasn't. It was grief. I held Violet responsible for his death, and I still do. I wrote then, and told her. I never wanted to see her again."

Edouard was frowning, Christian saw. He shook his head, as if he were reminded of something, but could not quite recall it. In the silence that followed, Elizabeth Culverton lit another cigarette. She seemed to regret her outburst, because when she spoke again, her voice was more measured.

"Nor did I see her," she continued. "She wrote occasionally. She made a foolish marriage—predictably. Some American G.I. The daughter was born here, then they both followed him back to America. It didn't last, I gather. I don't remember the details, and I burnt the letters." She paused. "I have the address where they were living—I did keep that. Somewhere in the South. I can give you that, if you like, but it won't help you. The girl won't have gone back there."

"You think not?"

Elizabeth Culverton had risen stiffly. At Edouard's quiet question, she glanced back over her shoulder.

"I'm sure of it. She hated it. She said so. I believed that—I suppose."

"You didn't believe other things she said?"

"In retrospect, no." She opened the flap of a bureau desk and rummaged inside among an untidy welter of papers. "Ah, here's the address. And here's the cable the girl sent. You can have that too. I don't want it." She paused, looking at Edouard, the two pieces of paper in her hand. Then she handed them to him.

"I told you. The girl was in a disturbed state," she said abruptly. "She was quite calm at first. But there were crying fits. Long silences. Then various garbled stories about her mother and herself. When she left, I decided it was all too highly colored. To be charitable, she was still obviously very shocked by her mother's death, which was sudden. And this place was clearly a disappointment to her. . . ." She paused, the blue eyes growing hard. "And, to be uncharitable, she was a fantasist. Just as her mother always was. Frankly, I'm glad she left." She moved to the door as she spoke, as if to indicate that the interview was over. The men got to their feet, but at the door she suddenly turned back, fixing Edouard with her sharp blue eyes.

"I've heard of you, of course." She made it sound like a concession. "You have horses, don't you? Jack Dwyer's your trainer."

"Yes." Edouard looked slightly puzzled.

Elizabeth Culverton gave a tight malicious smile. "Then perhaps you'll understand when I say that in my experience, whether it's horses, or dogs . . ." She gestured across at the labradors. "Or people. Breeding will out. I know nothing of her father's pedigree, of course. But I would say that Hélène was very much her mother's daughter. It might be as well for you to remember that. Men are exceedingly foolish where women are concerned, so I don't suppose you'll listen. However, you've come a long way, so you may as well have the benefit of my advice, as well as my information."

She turned, and walked out into the hall. Christian, embarrassed by her rudeness, found himself blushing. Edouard appeared quite unmoved. In the hall, he shook hands courteously, and thanked Elizabeth Culverton for her help. Her failure to rile him irritated her, Christian thought.

In the Rolls, Christian leaned back in the seat and sighed. "Dear God. What a ghastly woman. 'Her father's pedigree.' Women like that make me ashamed to be English."

Edouard shrugged. "As a species, they're not confined to England, you know. It is possible to encounter them elsewhere."

"Not if I can avoid it." Christian glanced at him sideways. "You're taking it all very calmly. I was a little disappointed. I was absolutely dying for you to be frightfully rude."

"There was no point. Besides, she was helpful, I thought."

Edouard turned his face to the window and looked out at the dark. Christian watched him curiously.

"Was she? I thought she was no help at all."

"Not of immediate help perhaps. But in the long term . . ." Edouard paused, and then turned back to Christian impulsively. "I feel I need to know her, Christian. That I have to know her to find her. Know who she is. Know what she wants."

Christian looked at him levelly. The eagerness in Edouard's face, the expression in his eyes, reminded Christian of a much younger Edouard, the Edouard he had known as a boy; he was touched, and simultaneously fearful for him.

"You're assuming that what she wants will be you," he said gently, resting his hand on Edouard's arm. "Supposing, when you find her, that isn't the case?"

Edouard hesitated. "Even so," he answered shortly, and turned away once more.

At the airport at Plymouth, an aide was waiting for Edouard. The Rolls drove out to the edge of the runway; across the tarmac Edouard's plane waited, ready to taxi, its engines warming up, a steward hovering in its lighted doorway. Christian remained in the car, which would take him back to London. Edouard got out and stood at the edge of the runway, talking to the aide.

It was raining now, and a strong wind was blowing. Edouard stood there, talking to the man, apparently oblivious to the wind and the rain. Christian saw his face, alert and pale in the flare of the landing lights;

the wind gusted; Edouard appeared to question him, and the man nodded. Just for a moment Edouard lifted his head, and looked up at the sky; then he pressed the man's arm and turned back to the car.

Christian rolled down the window. Even before he saw Edouard's expression he knew what must have happened.

"They traced Sinclair?"

"Yes. This afternoon."

"You're going back to Paris?"

"No. Not Paris. Rome."

"Well, well, well."

Their eyes met for a second, then Edouard stepped back.

"Good luck," Christian called as the car started to move. He wasn't sure if Edouard heard him. He glimpsed his face, pale and set, the rain beating down on his bare head.

The car wheeled. When Christian looked back, Edouard was already in the plane, and its doors were closing.

The movie was called *Night Game,* and it took place entirely during the daylight hours; a fairly typical example of Thad's perversity, Lewis thought. Lewis disliked the title, which suggested to him some pornographic romp, but Thad was adamant. When Lewis argued, Thad simply giggled, and said it sounded better in French.

Beyond that, as Lewis had become irritably aware over the past six weeks, he, who had put up some fifty percent of the backing and had managed to produce free accommodation for the entire crew, had very little idea what the movie was about. On this, the final day of shooting, he was still as much in the dark as he had been on day one. He stood at the top of the stairs in the Principessa's *palazzo,* in his pajamas, clutching a glass of Alka-Seltzer. It was six o'clock in the morning, and he had a bad hangover. In the vast marble-floored foyer below, the production manager, who was French, was supervising the transfer of the last of the equipment into the vans waiting outside. A straggle of crewmen were variously assisting and delaying him; one was French, one was American, and the rest were Italian. It was their polyglot conversation that had wakened him.

Lewis watched them gloomily. Thad and Helen had already left; the final sequences were being shot in Trastevere. Lewis was not needed. He had not been needed for the past six weeks. He drained the last of the Alka-Seltzer. From the kitchen regions, some distance away, he heard the muffled sound of a dog howling. Well, he could always walk some of the damn dogs: that was useful, he supposed.

The trouble was that Thad was by nature extremely secretive,

Lewis decided, as he returned to his room and rang for strong black coffee. When working, as Lewis had discovered, he became almost pathologically so. He had still shown Lewis nothing on paper, certainly nothing resembling the shooting script of which he often spoke. Each morning, Thad would turn up at the shoot with handfuls of crumpled paper covered in spidery notes. He would then go into huddles with the actors, with his lighting cameraman, Victor, or with one of his crew. He would brandish the bits of paper, and pull his beard, and rub his glasses, and mutter. He did not like Lewis around at all, and he became very annoyed if Lewis muscled in on any of these huddled whisperings, as he had at first tried to do.

Lewis himself had no experience of filming, but it seemed to him that Thad worked in a purposely created atmosphere of chaos. He constantly changed his mind. He told one actor one thing about a scene, and another actor something entirely different. He changed lines. He did one take when the scene had seemed to Lewis a hesitant mess, and take after take when the first had been clearly the best. He never sat still. Lewis had some idea that a director sat in a canvas-backed chair and directed. Thad didn't even have a chair, and he was always on his feet, squeezing his fat body around equipment, tripping over cables, peering, poking, adjusting, fiddling. He might spend an hour setting up a shot, another hour moving one of his two leading male actors around like a clockwork toy. His feet had to be here; his head had to be there—exactly in a line with the edge of the window. After Helen's line, he had to count to five, and then turn his head to the camera, so—no, not at that angle, at *this* angle, *yes*. . . .

The actor in question, Lloyd Baker, was a young American Thad had picked up somewhere in Paris. Thad had cast him because of his eyebrows, or so he said; Lewis had agreed because he came cheap. He was not very bright, but he had spent six months at the Actors Studio.

"What's my *motivation* here?" he would whine despairingly as Thad adjusted his elbow by half an inch. "I mean, like, what do you need to see in my face? What am I *thinking* here, Thad?"

"Who gives a fuck? Think about some broad. Think about your mother. Think about Bing Crosby. But get your fucking face in a line with the edge of the window. . . ."

"I can't do it." The actor's handsome face composed itself into a sulk. "If I don't have my motivation, it won't work."

"Listen." Thad took him by the elbow. "You heard of Greta Garbo?"

"Sure I've heard of Garbo. I'm not dumb."

"You know one of the great shots of Garbo? One of the greatest shots in all her movies? The end of *Queen Christina*, right, and it's the last shot of the film, and we get this big, big closeup of her face. . . . And it's, like, mystery, you know, *unfathomable* mystery. You know how Mamoulian got that shot? You know what he said to Greta? He said, 'Think of *nothing*, Greta, nothing,' and she did. . . ."

There was a long silence. Lloyd Baker sighed. "Okay, I've got it. I turn to the camera. I think of nothing. But what's my *motivation?*"

"Jesus Christ. Forget what I said. Forget the moves. Forget the window. Just do it."

They did it. It looked completely undisciplined to Lewis, but Thad simply said, "Print"; afterward, he looked craftily pleased with himself.

On that occasion, Lewis had retired to a nearby bar, and consoled himself with a stiff drink. He had decided there were two alternatives: either Thad was the genius he claimed to be, or he was a total clown. If Lewis had had to take a bet on it at that point, he'd have said the odds were even.

Some years later, of course, when Thad became Hollywood's number one hot property, the wonder boy of the American cinema, Lewis never admitted these early doubts. *I always knew; I never questioned his genius,* he would say sententiously—and who was to argue? Lewis was later profoundly grateful that when he *had* doubted, he had at least kept his mouth shut.

He kept quiet—he thought now as he sipped the black coffee, and put off a little longer the moment when he would have to acknowledge that the day had begun—he kept quiet for two main reasons. One, he was a little afraid of Thad, though he would never admit it. Two, he could see that his doubts were not shared by anyone else: no matter how much Thad seemed to mess them around, Helen and the other actors listened to him reverently.

The crew adored him, to a man. The majority were French, and Thad had met many of them the previous year, when he worked in France assisting the young director François Truffaut on the film that was now causing a European sensation, *The Four Hundred Blows.* Only his cinematographer, Victor, was American—Victor had trained with Thad at the U.C.L.A. Film School, and had worked in America with him on various low-budget shorts. He clearly respected Thad. In the crew's eyes, Thad could deliver the goods, and—since they were all professionals, with growing reputations on the European film circuit—to some extent Lewis bowed to their judgment.

They all seemed to Lewis to be very intense, and very intellectual—not good for too many laughs. They talked about *films noirs,* and *mise en scène;* they discussed the *auteur* theory at length, and read *Cahiers du Cinéma* in their breaks. They had weird taste in movies: one minute they were singing the praises of directors he'd never heard of, like Wajda and Franju and Renoir, and newcomers like Godard and Chabrol and Truffaut; the next they were hymning the American movies Lewis had loved as a boy—westerns and detective movies and comedies. But whereas Lewis never thought beyond the fact that he enjoyed such films, these people discussed them earnestly, take by take, frame by frame, as if they were great art or something. It made Lewis feel out of his depth; if it went on too long, it made him feel embarrassed.

At such times Lewis, who was not an intellectual, and who distrusted intellectuals per se, would wonder how he had gotten himself involved in this crazy circus. He wondered it now, as he drained the last of his coffee and headed for the shower. He knew the answer, of course. He had gotten involved because of Thad. He had stayed involved because of Helen.

He thought about her now, as he got into the shower: the singular delicacy and beauty of her face. He thought about her cool, slightly husky voice. He thought about her unshakable reticence, her quietude, and her physical modesty, which was so inflammatory. He imagined her body, which he had never seen unclothed. The effect was arousing, which was predictable. Less predictably, it was perturbing; it awoke in him all kinds of shadowy emotions, which Lewis was entirely at a loss to explain.

The nearest he could come to summing up his feelings was that Helen made him feel protective. This alarmed him. Protective? There was something badly wrong.

On several occasions during the past week, Lewis had found himself unaccountably unable to sleep. He had padded along the corridors of the *palazzo* to the door of the room where Helen slept. In pajamas and robe, feeling ridiculous, he had then waited outside her door, unable to knock, unable to go in, and equally unable to go back to bed. Once, twice, he thought he had heard the sound of weeping from within. Once, twice, he had tried the handle of the door, and found it locked. Then he had finally crept away.

This lackluster behavior was uncharacteristic, and Lewis could not explain it. Sometimes he tried to imagine what he would have done had he opened the door and gone in. He had expected an arousing fantasy to spring to mind—Lewis thought of himself as a stud—but to his own surprise, he saw himself sitting on the bed beside Helen. Helen needed him, and he held her very gently in his arms.

Lewis stepped out of the shower, and began to towel himself dry. There were innumerable things he should be thinking about. That night's party, to celebrate the end of filming—he had to complete the arrangements for it; he had to pick up the money he'd arranged to have transferred from his bank; he wanted to buy Helen a present; he intended to drop in on the location in Trastevere. But to his dismay, his mind was filled instead with images of Helen. And one image in particular, which dated from a few weeks back, when they were about ten days into the film.

It had been a sequence shot in the *palazzo*, a scene in which Helen was standing at a window, and then turned around. She was turning to look at one of the two lovers she had in the film—Lewis couldn't remember which; it was a simple setup, and there were no words. Thad made her do it twenty-four times. Stand; turn; look. Twenty-four times.

Between takes, Thad would go across to Helen and mutter. Then she would do it again. She never complained once. She showed no sign of irritation, or impatience, or tiredness, though the scene came at the end of a day's shoot. She did not argue, as Lloyd Baker always did; she simply listened to Thad quietly, occasionally said something Lewis could not hear, and then did it again. Until that moment, Lewis thought, his attitude to Helen had been quite simple: he wanted her, period. But that afternoon, something had happened to him. He had been squashed at the back of the room, leaning against the wall, hemmed in by crewmen and equipment, and all he knew was that he didn't care how repetitive it was, or how cramped he felt, he could have stayed there forever, just watching her face, just watching her move. Stand, turn, look. Stand, turn, look. Her image moved in Lewis's mind then, just as it had moved all those weeks before. He could not rid himself of it, nor could he explain its fascination.

Afterward, he had asked Thad to explain the scene, and Thad had smiled, knowingly, secretively. Lewis felt excluded by that smile; it suggested mysteries to which he did not have access.

"So tell me about this character Helen's playing, Thad," he had said aggressively. "She doesn't make much sense to me. I mean—why does she behave that way? Who the hell is she?"

Thad had smiled gently. "She's the missing woman," he'd said. The remark had only irritated Lewis further. But it had stayed with him. Now, as the image of Helen turned and turned again in his mind, he began to see what Thad had meant.

"The missing woman?" Lloyd Baker's brows contracted. "Why missing? I mean, I know where she lives, for God's sake. I'm *screwing* her, Thad. I'm screwing her, and the other guy's screwing her, too, and when I find out about it, it drives me crazy. So how come she's missing?" He shook his head as if to dislodge something stubborn that had lodged in his brain. Then, slowly, his face cleared. "Oh, I *see*. I begin to get you. You mean, like, she's lost, and it's only when she meets me that she—"

"No, Lloyd." Thad sounded very patient. "That's not what I mean."

Lloyd hung his head sulkily. "Well, I think we're going off-track here anyway. I mean, this is one of my major scenes. I was up all night working on this. If we could just concentrate on my character for a second. It seems to me that my motivation here is a little unclear."

"*Everyone's* motivation is unclear, Lloyd. That's life."

"It is?"

"Yeah." Thad yawned. "Let's just do it, okay? I want to move on."

Hélène had been watching this conversation from a seat at one side of the room. It was a small room, dominated by a bed, and crowded with equipment. Now she got up.

This scene, which came early in the film, was the next to the last one they would shoot. After that, there was only the final sequence to do. She walked forward, and as she did so, she thought: *It's almost over. How quick it has all seemed.*

The first week she had begun work, she had been so frightened. It was all so strange, and so complicated, and so unnerving. Every day she'd come in, her hands sweating and shaking with fear. None of it had made any sense. It confused her, shooting out of sequence, going forward in the story, then back. She didn't know what half the equipment was for; she didn't understand the terminology. She couldn't find the spot where she had to stand, and kept missing it. Her arms and legs felt stiff and unnatural, her voice seemed to belong to someone else, and she was waiting, every second, for Thad to start yelling at her, and telling her that she was hopeless, a fraud.

But Thad never yelled at her, though he yelled at most of the others. He never made fun of her or became impatient, as he did with Lloyd. He would just come up to her, and talk to her very quietly in that funny flat voice of his, and when he did that, somehow, it all began to make sense.

"Trust yourself," Thad said.

Trust herself? She had almost wanted to laugh. How could she trust herself? She felt, those first days, as if she no longer knew who she was. Eventually, shyly, expecting some caustic remark, she told Thad this. He smiled his gentle yellow-toothed smile; he seemed pleased.

"That doesn't matter," he said. "In fact, it's good. You aren't Helen, you're Anne."

Anne was the name of her character, and somehow, after Thad said that, she had come to love Anne. Anne freed her. Anne made her able to forget about her arms and her legs and hitting her mark. Anne had a life and an independence of her own, and as the days passed, she became more and more familiar. Now, when Hélène stepped in front of the camera and the lights, she felt no fear at all, only a marvelous freedom and release. It was Anne who spoke, Anne who moved, and Hélène merely embodied her.

Anne grew, and it seemed to Hélène that she herself shrank. She accepted this gladly; she came to look forward to the moment when a take began and the transition took place. During those hours, when she worked, the rest of her life went away. She never thought of Orangeburg, or Edouard; she never thought about the baby; she felt no anxiety and no pain. Anne lived, and she died. She came to crave the moment when that happened, and—after the first month—she realized something that was obvious but which had never occurred to her before. She was doing something, quite on her own, because for all the skill of the crew, for all Thad's expertise, it was she who brought Anne to life. *She* was doing it, and she knew, just knew, that she was doing it well.

She had never felt that before in her life—she saw that now. Never. And it had a profound effect upon her. It made her feel strong.

Not always, it was true. Sometimes the new confidence in herself would waver, sometimes she would feel like the old Hélène, uncertain, unsure. But those moments of uncertainty came only when she was away from the set, and away from Thad. When she was there, working with him, the certainty would always come back.

She felt it now, as the scene with Lloyd Baker began. Anne was waiting for her, and she greeted her like a friend. Two takes; three; four.

Across the room, Thad rose busily to his feet. He said, "Print," and then, looking at Hélène, with the light winking on those glasses of his, he smiled.

"Okay, we'll do the final sequence now. Victor and I will do this on our own with Helen. Clear the set."

He looked oddly excited; he waved his pink hands in the air. It must be because it was nearly over, Hélène thought, and at once felt regret.

Lewis had instructed the Chase Manhattan to transfer some ten thousand dollars to a branch of the Banca Nazionale on the Via Veneto. When he reached the bank, he realized he had set off too soon. It was still too early, and the bank was closed.

Half an hour to kill. Well, the Via Veneto was as pleasant a place as any to do that. He walked up the street a short way and sat down in a sidewalk café close by, opposite the Excelsior Hotel. He ordered an espresso, lit the first cigarette of the day. The sun shone down warmly. Hard to believe it was November; it felt almost like a summer's day. Lewis settled himself comfortably in his chair and prepared to wait. He glanced idly at the other customers sitting outside: Italian businessmen, most of them, men in dark suits and dark glasses, stopping off for coffee on the way to work, reading the morning paper. He glanced away from them, lifted his face to the sun, and began to make plans. One of the dark-suited men was looking at Lewis intently, but Lewis did not notice. Once again, he was thinking about Helen.

If Thad finished on schedule today, as it now seemed certain he would, he would then be tied up editing the picture for six to eight weeks, finishing, he said, around Christmas. He intended to do the editing in Rome, in a friend's cutting room, and he had already suggested that, while he was busy, Lewis should take a vacation. He further suggested, with a kindly smile, that Lewis should take Helen with him. "We don't want to lose her again," Thad said.

Helen, however, had not commented upon the plan. She evaded all Lewis's attempts to elicit a definite promise. Lewis, meanwhile, was full of ideas.

He had several address books, all of them bulging with the names of affluent and generous friends of his parents, and acquaintances of his own, all of whom could be counted on to have Lewis and Helen as their guests for a while.

That, Lewis thought, would look less compromising to her than a hotel. He was sure she would balk at that. But friends—and friends who lived in such marvelous places: Tuscany, for instance, or Venice. Nice. Cannes. The Swiss Alps. Gstaad—no, he had caused a lot of fuss at Gstaad, that might not be a good idea. London, perhaps. London was fun in the pre-Christmas season, and by now everyone would have forgotten that party the police raided.

They could go even farther afield. Mexico—Acapulco, for instance. The Bahamas. The West Indies. He surveyed the possibilities dreamily; it somehow pleased him, the idea of offering Helen her choice of the world. Come to that, they could even go to Boston. He could take Helen home, to the house on Beacon Hill. Home, to his mother and father, who—whenever he spoke to them, which was not often—pressed him to come back. Helen might even like it there, he thought. That superbly understated house, filled with English antiques, organized by discreetly efficient servants who'd been with the family nearly twenty years. He saw an image of Helen sitting by the fireside, taking tea with his mother.

But no; he pushed the idea away quickly. Why should he have thought of taking her there? He hated Boston. He never wanted to go back. He knew what Boston was. He'd been running away from it long enough, after all.

As far back as he could remember, Lewis Sinclair had been trying to escape. As far back as he could remember, his family had had his life all mapped out for him, and were blindly dismissive when Lewis tentatively suggested that there might be alternative routes.

Lewis understood why this had happened; that didn't make it any easier to bear. His parents, Robert and Emily, had had to wait twelve years for the birth of a son. The four daughters who preceded Lewis were much loved, but in certain respects a daughter was of no use. A daughter could not carry on the Sinclair name and tradition; a daughter could not run an investment bank. "I was so happy when you were born that I wept, Lewis," Emily would say. It was a story she repeated often. When he was small it made Lewis feel proud; when he was older, it made him feel trapped.

From the very beginning he was given only the best, and from the beginning, his privileges were accompanied by high-minded lectures. To his parents, to whom the conspicuous consumption of wealth was anathema, privilege and money were acceptable only if they were counterbalanced by a sense of social duty. Lewis's upbringing was simultaneously indulgent and stern. He was given generous presents: beautiful books, serious toys—construction kits, drawing boards, paints. Lewis still remembered the agony of those Christmases and birthdays: how he had longed for guns, skates, comic books, go-carts. How he had had to pretend not to be disappointed when they were smilingly and charmingly withheld.

He was taken to dancing classes. He was taken to the Boston Symphony concerts. He was carefully introduced to art, first in museums and galleries, then in the private collections of his innumerable uncles and cousins and aunts.

When he was older, he was introduced to tennis, swimming, and squash. Lewis had athletic potential, and he enjoyed sports. But he loathed these private coaching sessions as much as he loathed the culture he was force-fed: there was no fun in them; like everything else, they were *lessons*. Life was one long lesson, and as he grew older Lewis learned something terrible: it was a lesson in which he never got top marks.

He had tried, then; he had tried so very hard, his mind swimming with information it obstinately refused to digest. But he never met his parents' standards. He must try harder, they explained—his father directly, his mother more delicately: he was a Sinclair; it was not enough to get by—he must excel.

He loved his mother dearly, and he was in awe of his father; his own mystifying inability ever to please them hurt Lewis very much. "I love you, Mama," he would say when he was small, running to Emily and trying to climb on her lap, trying to hug her. But Robert Sinclair had expressed the opinion that Lewis was too indulged, and so Emily—looking guilty—would ease him away when he did this. "Don't be babyish, Lewis," she would say. "You have to try harder, that's all." And then she would kiss him, also guiltily.

Lewis put down his small cup of espresso; it clattered against the saucer. He looked irritably at his watch. Still another fifteen minutes to wait. Why had he begun to think about Boston, why? He was twenty-five years old, a grown man, and yet whenever his thoughts took this particular tack, the years were immaterial. He felt, then, as confused and as helpless as he had when he was a child; the memories came winging back, they churned in his mind—humiliation after humiliation. They made him feel impotent, and they filled him with a blind, painful anger. Even now, sitting here, he could feel it, the great cry of his childhood welling up again in his heart: *it isn't fair—it isn't fair*.

Quite deliberately—it was a trick he used, and a soothing one—he tried to concentrate on the successes of his life, those occasions—and there were not many of them—when he knew what he was doing, and was sure that he was doing it well.

There had been his achievements on the football field, first at Groton, then at Harvard: they had the power to thrill him still, though his parents had always been dismissive of them. Arrayed in helmet and pads, so much taller than most of his contemporaries, Lewis had felt like a god. There were women: he had always been successful there, right from the beginning. And finally, there was his friendship with Thad.

Lewis smiled to himself, shifting a little in his seat. His parents would not have approved of most of the past women in his life—shocked was more like it. They would not have approved of Thad, either. That fact pleased Lewis very much. To take the opposite course, to flout his parents' wishes—it filled him with a sense of almost vindictive triumph. No more a life always lurching toward the next lecture; no more failures; he had rejected all that, he had abandoned Beacon Hill and all the stuffy values it embodied. He was his own man now, leading his own life, and he wasn't a failure anymore—never had been, really; that was just his parents' interpretation, and he rejected that along with everything else.

He lit another cigarette. A hooker passed, and Lewis winked at her. He could feel the cloak of his new identity settling serenely on his shoulders once more. He was a rebel, he told himself. He had always been a rebel, really, he could see that now. Not a misfit, a rebel. He had become very certain of that fact since meeting Thad.

The bank was opening. Lewis stood up and stretched. He tossed a few lire onto the table, picked up his briefcase, strolled over to the bank, and joined the line at one of the counters. One of the dark-suited men from the café followed Lewis into the bank, and stood not far behind him in the line, but Lewis did not notice him; nor was he aware, when he left the bank some fifteen minutes later, that the man also left, without waiting for his turn at the teller's.

Lewis hailed a cab, and made for his familiar hunting grounds, the beautiful and expensive shops that lined the Piazza di Spagna and the Via Condotti. He ordered the champagne for the party at the *palazzo* that night, and then spent an anxious but pleasurable half hour window-shopping, and deciding on a present for Helen.

He was not familiar with buying gifts for women, other than members of his own family, and it perplexed him a little. His own inclination was for something pretty, frivolous, luxurious—silk lingerie, clothes of some kind, perhaps jewelry. He lingered outside the windows of de Chavigny: there was a very beautiful sapphire pin in the window, and the color of the stones reminded him of Helen's eyes. But some residue of Boston which he could never quite purge made him hesitate. His mother would have considered such a gift quite improper.

Reluctantly, he moved on. His mind fogged. He began to panic. He wanted so much to get her something exciting, but now, everywhere he looked he heard his mother at his elbows saying that no, it was quite unsuitable under the circumstances. Except for his own clothes, Lewis was never very certain in his tastes at the best of times—they had been ridiculed too often in the past. He thought with shame of the presents he had bought his mother as a little boy, things he had saved up for secretly for weeks, and had then purchased in an orgy of excitement. A large dog, made of plaster of Paris and brightly painted; a little clinking bracelet, with gilded charms. "How sweet, Lewis, thank you," his mother had said. The china dog had disappeared into a cupboard; the bracelet had never been worn.

Standing in the Via Condotti, Lewis blushed for a miscalculation sixteen years old. The panic grew worse. A book? No, books were too impersonal. Flowers? He wanted to give her more than that. Perfume? He thought Helen never wore it; perhaps she disliked it.

In the end, compromising, and reminding himself that if Helen did agree to go away with him, this gift would at least be useful, he went into Gucci. There, after further agonizing, he selected a weekend bag. It was extremely expensive, shaped like a Gladstone bag, and made of maroon crocodile skin. It was flamboyant; Lewis was sure his mother wouldn't like it. But he wasn't buying it for his mother, he reminded himself. He was buying it for Helen.

Growing excited, he asked if they could monogram it. They could— but it would take a few hours. Lewis hesitated once more, and then decided to go ahead. The initials were H. C., he told them; he arranged for the bag to be delivered later that day to the Principessa's.

At the mention of that name and that address the stiff assistant unbent considerably; her manner began to approach charm. Lewis left the shop feeling extremely happy. On the way out, he half-collided with a man going in. Lewis looked up at him in annoyance: a tall dark man, wearing a black suit. Someone important, presumably, because two assistants were already bowing and scraping at the door. He brushed past Lewis with a curt apology in Italian; Lewis glanced back, then passed out into the street, and instantly forgot him.

He took another cab across the river to Trastevere, and was stuck for what seemed hours in the hooting, yelling mayhem of a Roman traffic jam. By the time he reached the house where Thad was filming, it was past noon, and Lewis—knowing Thad usually broke for an hour then—was looking forward to joining Thad and Helen for lunch. He let the cab go in the Piazza di Santa Maria, and strolled cheerfully down the narrow side streets, whistling. When he reached the entrance to the house, and went into the hall, he found his way barred. The assistant director, Fabian, a tall languid Frenchman, was lounging at the bottom of the stairs.

Lewis looked up then, past the snaking cables, to a closed door.

"*Salut.*" Fabian gave him a lazy grin, and didn't move.

"Excuse me . . ." Lewis took a purposeful step forward.

"Sorry. It's closed. Thad doesn't want anyone up there."

"That doesn't mean me."

Fabian grinned amiably. "It means everyone. Sorry, Lewis."

Lewis hesitated. He glanced at his watch, then back at Fabian. He felt a sudden nervous dart of alarm. Thad had discouraged him from attending shootings before, but never barred him.

"Aren't they going to break? What the hell's he doing up there?"

Fabian shrugged. "He's on the final sequence. Thad's there—and Victor, and Helen. *C'est tout.* It shouldn't take much longer—then it's a wrap."

Lewis frowned. He knew how this film began—in close-up on Helen's face. He knew how it ended—the same way. It was the bits in between where his knowledge was sketchy. He knew enough, though, to remember that the final sequence took place after the murder, and featured Helen alone; in bed.

He listened carefully. Through the panels of the door above he could just hear the drone of Thad's voice. He pushed Fabian aside and ran up the stairs. The door was locked, and Thad stopped talking the moment he heard Lewis's footsteps. Lewis rattled the door handle furiously. From inside came the familiar high-pitched rasping giggle, then the sound of Thad's footsteps.

"Lewis?" he said through the door. "Fuck off."

Lewis glowered at the door. He considered for a second whether to smash it into matchsticks by barging it with his football player's shoulders, or simply to kick in its panels with his foot. On reflection, he decided either course lacked dignity. Answering Thad lacked dignity. He retreated down the stairs again without another word.

Fabian gave him a fatalistic glance and a very Gallic shrug.

"You would like me to give Thad a message when he comes out?"

"Sure. Tell him I'm going out to get drunk."

"Bien sûr." Fabian yawned.

"And tell him I'm coming back here in an hour."

At this Fabian looked doubtful. "An hour? I think an hour may not be long enough."

"Why not, for chrissake?" Lewis rounded on him belligerently. "The way he described it to me, it's one tiny sequence. One set-up. How long can something like that take?"

"Who knows?" Fabian smiled resignedly.

"Is she naked up there—is that it? Has he got her undressed?"

Fabian slowly lowered one eyelid. "Lewis, *mon ami,* I swear to you, I have no idea. But if he has—he is a lucky man, yes?"

Lewis turned away without another word. He was trembling with an emotion he could not identify. He walked down the street to the edge of the piazza, and went into the first bar he found.

The first *strega* made him feel better; the second, better still. The third was a mistake, and the fourth was a disaster.

It was a small bar, patronized by local workmen. Lewis sat and stared at the bare wooden table, and listened to the clicks of the machine as they played pinball. A television set was on in back somewhere, and dimly he could hear the screams of an Italian football commentator. On another world, another planet, someone, somewhere, was playing Real Madrid.

His head sagged forward. He traced the mark of his wet glass on the tabletop. He wondered, in a fumbling fashion, his brain refusing to work very clearly, whether the feelings he was experiencing were the result of thwarted lust, or jealousy, or betrayal, or love. And who, exactly, had aroused those feelings?

It could have been Helen. It should have been Helen. He was almost certain it *was* Helen.

On the other hand, it could have been Thad.

He had met Thad by accident; it was an accident that changed his life. Sometimes, Lewis felt as if he'd been looking for Thad all his life. He had been in a bad way at the time; the immediate pre-Thad era of his life was one Lewis preferred to forget. He had left Harvard behind, he had escaped from Boston, he had been having a good time—and all at once, he had started to worry. He couldn't remember quite why now—perhaps it was just that he noticed the faces at the parties he attended were getting younger, and he himself older. He wasn't sure.

All he knew was that it suddenly seemed urgent that he should stop drifting, and make a success of his life. In his worst moments, Lewis had always doubted his ability to do that, but at other times he felt a euphoric certainty that somehow, somewhere, he would make the grade. He saw himself, the prodigal son, returning to Boston: a success—but as what precisely?

His mother had always favored politics. She had hinted at her hopes wistfully. She noted the meteoric rise of John F. Kennedy, and hinted more openly. To Emily Sinclair, the Kennedys were Irish-Catholic upstarts. If John Kennedy could achieve so much, what might Lewis, that tall handsome scion of the Sinclairs, do? Lewis's father was more direct. Lewis would go into the family bank, and his refusal to do so immediately after leaving Harvard was wayward and inexplicable.

Lewis meant to have nothing to do with politics, nothing to do with the bank. But when he tried to decide on a profession which would bring him the success he craved, he vacillated. One of the new careers, he felt that instinctively—the kind of thing he read about in newspapers, the kind of thing no Sinclair ever did. Advertising. The music industry. Journalism. Show business. The new make-it-fast professions, where what mattered were your wits and your stamina, not the fact that your parents adorned the Social Register and you had a father to pull strings.

Lewis dabbled with these ideas, pursuing none of them with great vigor, and then, on a whim and a casual invitation from an actress he'd been seeing in New York, he went out to the West Coast. There, quite suddenly, he felt he had found his métier. Not to act—he couldn't act. Not to direct—Lewis was aware of his own limitations. But to *produce* movies, now that attracted him. He liked the fact that it was fluid and unpredictable. It was a little shady, you had to hustle, and he liked that too. The wheeling and dealing, the hype, the gab: he liked all those —he also liked the parties and the girls.

He met a number of young producers while he was out there, and watched them, fascinated. It took quite a while for the obvious to sink in: they were all different from him; they were all Jewish. He confided his ambition to the actress one night, when he was drunk and incautious. She nearly fell out of bed laughing.

Reluctantly, Lewis decided she was right. He grew tired of the actress, tired of Hollywood, tired of the fantasy. He bought a ticket back to the East Coast. It was actually in the back pocket of the jeans he had adopted as California camouflage, when—late one afternoon—the actress announced they were going to a party. His last night in California. Lewis shrugged and agreed.

The party was at a beach house in Venice. It was at that party he felt his life really started, because it was at that party he met Thad.

The actress had introduced him, with a wave of the hand, as "the Toad." She moved quickly away to some guy who was rumored to have a line into MGM casting.

Lewis, hemmed in and unable to escape, learned the Toad's name was Thaddeus Angelini. He was second-generation Italian-American, born and raised in L.A. The Toad provided this brief information, and then lapsed into silence. Lewis squirmed. He still had some residue of Boston manners. He had yet to perfect the Hollywood art of cutting stone-dead someone who had neither reputation, nor influence, nor money, nor hope. So, when his fund of conversation had dried up, and the fat sweating man was still silent, Lewis, growing desperate, asked him what he did.

"I make movies."

The fat man blinked up at him behind shaded glasses.

Lewis, who was naïve, looked at him with marginally more interest. In Hollywood he had met a lot of people with projects, no one with anything under his belt.

"I—er—would I have seen them?"

"It's unlikely. None of them have been made yet."

The fat man giggled—that was the nearest word Lewis could think of to describe the nervous high-pitched rasping sound he made. Lewis swayed on his feet. He thought: Jesus, just my luck; a nut case.

"They're in my head. For the present. At this moment in time." He giggled again, and Lewis decided that he was either nuts, or drunk, or high, or possibly all three. Then he noticed that the man was drinking tea, and didn't seem to smoke. He peered at him more closely through the haze, at which point the fat man gave him a singularly sweet smile, marred only by irregular yellowing teeth.

"Fuck off if you want," he said, in an obliging tone. "I won't mind. Most people do."

It wasn't intended as a challenge, but Lewis interpreted it as such. He had always been contra-suggestible; now, glorying in that, as well as in the cheap white California wine, he pushed past a shrieking group of

Venice fairies and sat down next to the fat man on a cushion on the
floor. The fat man regarded him equably.

"So stay," he said. "Tell me what you're looking for in life."

To his own everlasting surprise, Lewis did.

They talked for an hour—Lewis talked, with occasional interjec-
tions. Then they went back to the fat man's fourth floor walkup downtown, and talked some more. At dawn, Lewis bedded down on the
floor, and when the hangover wore off the next day, they began talking
again. That evening, they went to a Bergman film, *The Seventh Seal*, at a
movie theater near the UCLA campus. Lewis had seen part of it once,
at Harvard. The fat man had seen it thirty-five times. They returned to
his apartment, and this time Thad talked. He talked for four hours
without drawing breath. He talked about that film, and Bergman's other
films.

Lewis understood about fifty percent of what he said, and that fifty
percent seemed to him pure genius. Thad made him see meaning
behind meaning, the way movies related to life; he showed him how it
was possible, technically, to make these meanings mesh, to disguise
them in the form of a story. Lewis listened; art made sense; life made
sense.

The next day he couldn't remember the details as clearly as he had
the night before, but he was still impressed—more than that, he was
hooked. He and Thad became friends. He supposed that was the
word, though he had never experienced friendship like this before.

For a period of two months, the two were rarely apart. They lived
on junk food from takeouts; Lewis continued to sleep on Thad's floor.
They spent most of each day watching movies, and most of each night
talking about them. Thad's benevolent obsession made Lewis relax. For
the first time in his life he felt totally unpressured. Thad expected
nothing from him: if he wanted to come to the movie, he was welcome;
if he didn't, Thad shrugged, and went alone. He was uninterested in
Lewis's background, and never questioned him about it, but when
Lewis felt the need to talk, Thad would listen, like a fat, wise father
confessor. He never passed judgment; he never apportioned blame;
indeed, he seemed to Lewis curiously above all moral questions: for
Thad, such concepts as duty, honor, and truth—the code of the Boston
Brahmin—did not exist. Except in movies.

Lewis, sitting cross-legged on the floor, forking up Chinese takeout,
halfway through a bottle of wine, suddenly realized that he felt free, and
because he felt free, he felt great. By the time he had finished the
bottle of wine, his concept of freedom had grown still wider. The
problem with his parents, he saw it now, was that they were *old*. Most of
his Harvard contemporaries were old—they were born that way. Like his
family, they belonged to the past, Lewis explained, to the gray postwar

Eisenhower world. He and Thad were different. They didn't give a shit about conventions and codes. They didn't need *things* the way Lewis's family did—houses and cars and college degrees and—Lewis cast about wildly—and *money*.

He collapsed exhausted at the end of this emotional speech, and Thad sat quietly nodding. Finally, he spoke.

"Yeah." He paused. "We might need money, though, Lewis. We might need that."

"Money? Money? Who needs it?" Lewis, forgetting about his trust fund in the emotion of the moment, threw his Chinese takeout box high in the air.

"We need it, Lewis. To make movies."

Lewis instantly sobered. He stared at Thad.

"*We* do?"

"Sure. You and I. When we make movies together." Thad yawned, and stood up. "Let's sleep now, yeah?"

"Okay, Thad," Lewis said as meekly as a child.

He bedded down on the floor as usual, and lay awake for hours, staring up at the ceiling. He felt transfigured, remade. Thad wanted to make movies, with *him*. He had announced it casually, as if it were a matter of course, something they both understood. Lewis felt humble, he felt honored, he felt purposeful. When he woke up next morning, he had a hangover, but he still felt the same.

Five words and a yawn, and Thad had given him his *métier*. No one except his football coach had ever shown such simple confidence in him; Lewis felt then as he had felt on the football field, when he caught a perfect pass, feinted, and then ran, winging past the defense, knowing, just knowing, he could make it all the way to the goal line.

Lewis's mind grew foggier; the voice of the television football commentator rose to a screaming pitch. Lewis let his head fall forward on his arms; he slept.

He was still sleeping, some half an hour later, when Thad's cinematographer, Victor—whom Thad had just released—walked past the small bar, whistling, and thinking with some pleasure of the party that night.

In the room in Trastevere, Thad finished loading his camera, and with an odd expression on his face, turned away from Hélène, went to the door, and locked it.

"You do understand?" Thad turned back to her, smiling. "Victor was in the way. It'll go better now. You'll get it."

Hélène looked at him uncertainly. They had been working on this last sequence now for hours, and she knew she wasn't getting it right. He wanted something, a certain look, he said, and she couldn't give it to him.

All afternoon, she'd been unable to understand why. At that moment, when Thad locked the door, and turned around and smiled at her, she knew why, quite suddenly. She didn't feel safe anymore. She felt afraid.

"What are you doing?" she said, hearing her own voice rise. It was a stupid question, and Thad didn't bother to answer it. After all, she could see what he was doing well enough.

He was holding his camera tenderly, and rubbing grease across the lens.

W hen Lewis finally woke, it was late afternoon. He lurched out of the bar. As soon as he was in the fresh air, and vertical, he began to feel violently sick. He weaved his way down an alley, vomited over an earthenware pot of geraniums, and felt slightly better.

He staggered a few more yards to the location house, found Fabian had left, and sank down weakly on the stairs. Above him, the door was still closed. He heard the drone of Thad's voice, and then silence.

He had a vision of Thad, at some point in the past, probably in Los Angeles, explaining that yes, of course, he and Lewis were a team, that was decided, but that as a team, they were not complete. They needed another element, a third factor. They needed, Thad had said, a woman, an actress, only her acting ability was not of primary importance: what they needed, above all, was the right woman, with the right face.

In the three months in Paris, when Lewis had worked at the Café Strasbourg, Thad had spent a lot of time looking for that face. He had interviewed and auditioned about sixty women, as far as Lewis could make out, also behind closed doors. None of them had been right. And then, one night, Thad had turned up at the Strasbourg, sweating, out of breath, gleaming with excitement: he had found her, just met her, in the street, outside the Cinemathèque. And she was perfect. She was waiting back in their room now. Thad had told her he'd find her a place to stay.

They'd left the café and gone straight home. And there, waiting for him, sitting on the sofa in that attic room, was Helen. Her face swam before Lewis's eyes now. He groaned, and slumped back on the stairs, his mind swooping toward a dizzying unconsciousness again. Helen and Thad. Thad and Helen. Helen and Thad and Lewis . . .

He was not sure if he slept, but he felt as if he dreamed. When he surfaced again, Thad was standing over him. For a moment, Lewis couldn't think where he was, and couldn't remember what had happened, he was only aware that his head was throbbing painfully, and that his throat felt parched.

Then something in Thad's manner, something odd, brought his memory rushing back. His head cleared; he looked up at Thad, newly alert.

Thad was shifting about on his feet—always a sign of nervousness in him. The expression on his face was a sickly mixture of suppressed excitement and alarm. He was sweating, though the evening was cool. His hands were in the pockets of his grease-stained jeans, and he jiggled the change and keys that always made his pockets bulge.

"Lewis. It's Helen. She's kind of upset. Can you come up?"

Lewis stood. He gave Thad one long look, and then bounded up the stairs. He came to an abrupt halt in the doorway.

The room was empty, he thought at first. Victor had gone. All the film lights had been switched off, and only one small table lamp was on. Cables snaked all over the floor; equipment was stacked in a corner. By the door was a neat pile of film cans.

The bed that dominated the small room was unmade, and it was a moment before Lewis realized that it must be Helen who was making that horrible noise. He crossed the room in two strides, and pulled the sheet back, his heart hammering fast, an awful sick dread rising in the pit of his stomach.

He didn't know what he expected to see—blood, perhaps, because it sounded as if she were in pain. But there was no blood. Just Helen, crouched in the fetal position in the middle of the bed, making the dry gasping sound people made when they'd been punched in the stomach.

Lewis leaned across and put his arms around her, aware that he was trembling almost as much as she was. Carefully, he lifted her arms away from her face. No bruises, no cuts, no swellings, no apparent injury; wet cheeks. She wouldn't open her eyes. She wouldn't look at him. She just went on making that horrible dry noise. Lewis was so frightened that it was a moment before he realized she was wearing only a thin dressing gown of some silky stuff, and that, under it, she was naked.

He laid her back gently against the pillow, and then drew the sheet up to her shoulders. Then he rounded on Thad, who was shifting from foot to foot in the doorway.

"You bastard. You fucking pervert. Where's Victor? What have you been doing to her?"

He could hardly speak for the choking anger he felt. Thad's gaze slid away from his face. He took his hands out of his pockets and waved them in the air.

"Nothing. Nothing. I didn't touch her."

"Liar. You goddamned liar." Lewis lurched across the room and grabbed Thad by the shirt. He slammed him back against the wall.

"Did you hit her? Did you?"

"Hit her? Of course I didn't fucking well hit her." Thad wriggled his fat body ineffectively. "You think I'd get a kick out of beating up a woman? I never touched her. I didn't do a thing—Lewis, fucking well put me down, will you?"

Slowly Lewis relaxed his grip, letting Thad slide down against the wall. Thad started gabbling nervously.

"I let Victor go. Not long ago. An hour. Maybe two. I lose track when I'm working. I wanted to shoot the very last part myself. I needed to, Lewis. Victor being there, it wasn't right, he was in the way, I could feel it. The vibes were all wrong. It's hand-held, the last bit, and I wanted to do it myself. That's all. That's all we've been doing, Lewis."

"You fat prick. So how come she's in this state now? Look at her—go on, take a really good look. . . ."

He twisted Thad's head around in the direction of the bed. Thad squirmed. "I don't know. I swear to you, Lewis, I don't *know*. I said some things, maybe—I can't remember. It wasn't going right. She wouldn't give me the look, not the look I wanted, and I had to get it, Lewis. Today's the final day. I said six weeks two days, and that's what it is. Lewis, let go of me, for fuck's sake. What are you—drunk or something? You're hurting me, Lewis. Let go. . . ."

"If you've touched her, you asshole—if you've screwed up—I'll hurt you a whole lot more. I'll . . ."

"It's all right, Lewis."

Her voice made him jump. He swung around and saw that she was sitting up in bed, the sheet drawn around her shoulders. She had stopped crying. Later—many years later—Lewis was to realize that that was the first, and the last, occasion on which he saw her cry.

"It's all right, Lewis. Really." She swallowed. Her face was chalk-white under her makeup, and her eyes were enormous and dark against its pallor. Lewis let go of Thad, and crossed slowly back to the bed.

He stood at the edge of it, hesitating, confused, aware that something was happening to him, something in him was changing. Then, awkwardly, he simply held out his hand, and Helen took it.

"It's my fault." Her voice steadied. "Thad was just doing his job. He needed that shot, and I couldn't get it right. He said a few things, that's all. And he—upset me."

She looked up at Thad as she said that. Lewis saw their gazes intersect for a moment, coldly, with a kind of perfect understanding. Then she looked away. Lewis had no doubt she was lying.

Images rose up in his mind, beauteous images and bestial ones. He pushed them away, knowing he feared them, and fearing that, deep down, they also excited him. At that moment, as Thad stood there silently, Lewis sensed for the first time Thad's capacity for domination. He felt a sense of some dark pull, winding him in, winding Helen in. He sensed that he ought to resist in some way, and that nothing in his own nature, nothing in his life had equipped him to do so. He felt he had blundered, brashly, innocently, into something he did not understand, and could not grasp, and that it was desperately important to blunder out again, unscathed. His desire to hit Thad then, to assert his superior physical strength and just to smash Thad into the ground, was very strong. He took a step forward, and then stopped. He pushed his blond hair back from his forehead, and hesitated. He looked from Helen to Thad, from Thad to Helen, and then said, to neither in particular, "Oh, hell. Let's get out of here."

At once, without hesitation, she slid from the bed, pulling the dressing gown around her. She took Lewis's hand.

"Lewis—I want to go with you."

Instantly Lewis felt an obscure sense of triumph, a sudden winging elation, as if he had done battle and won. He looked at Thad, but Thad appeared indifferent. He shrugged.

"The party's started by now, I guess."

"I don't want to go to the party." She turned to Lewis. "I don't want to go back to that house. I want to leave, go somewhere else. *Now.*"

She made the demand with a kind of childish imperiousness, appealing to Lewis as if Thad were not in the room. Lewis found the plea curiously flattering; it was as if she believed that Lewis could deal with anything on her behalf.

"We don't have to go back there. We can go anywhere you like."

"Thank you, Lewis." She pressed his hand. "I'll go and change."

She turned away and went into one of the rooms beyond, which had been used for makeup. She closed the door. As soon as it was closed, Thad let out his breath in a little whistle. He leaned back against the wall, smiling and shaking his head.

"Oh, Lewis. Lewis . . ."

He sounded amused, and infinitely patronizing. Lewis glared at him.

"Can I share the joke?"

"I doubt it, Lewis. I really do."

Lewis looked at him for a moment uncertainly. Then, as his elation evaporated, together with the oddly mystic sense of power he had felt a few moments before, he slumped down on the bed.

His hangover was catching up with him; the confusion was catching up with him. He must still be drunk, he decided. He didn't understand what the hell was going on, just that he felt jealous and angry, involved and excluded, powerful and impotent—all at once. What had just happened felt like a power game, a test of strength, apparently between him and Thad, in fact between Thad and Helen. She had seemed to need him; she had turned to him, not Thad; and yet, somehow, dimly, he had the feeling that he was being used. He buried his face in his hands.

It was at that point that Thad became very gentle. He explained that Helen was very strung up, that making the film had meant a lot to her, that it was the tension of finishing it that had made her snap like that. Women who seemed very calm were always the most hysterical underneath. What she needed now, he suggested, was to go away somewhere and rest, just as he'd been saying for weeks. Obviously, Lewis was the person to go with her. She trusted Lewis, she'd made that obvious.

And someone had to keep an eye on her—they'd agreed on that—otherwise she might just take off again, the way she did in Paris. And neither he nor Lewis wanted that. They wanted to work with her again—when Lewis saw the rushes, he'd understand. She had this incredible quality on film, it was just amazing. Though it was better not to let her know that yet—they didn't want her getting too confident, getting independent. She was very young still, half woman, half child, and when she got these ideas in her head—well, it was like handling a child; it was a good idea to humor her. If she didn't want to go back to the party, back to the *palazzo*, so what, that was no sweat. . . .

He kept on in this vein for some while, until Helen returned. When he saw her then, it seemed to Lewis that what Thad said made sense. She seemed perfectly recovered, still a little pale, but calm, the attack of nerves, if that was what it was, entirely over.

It was decided that Lewis would take her out to dinner, and that over dinner they would plan what to do next, whether to take a break, and if so, when and where. Thad took little part in this exchange. He appeared to have lost all interest. He simply prowled around the room, fiddling with equipment, checking film cans. When Lewis and Helen finally left, he hardly looked up.

"What? Yeah, sure . . . whatever you decide is fine by me. I'll be busy editing. Give me a call. Whenever. Or I'll see you. Fine. . . ."

Lewis took her to dinner at Alfredo's in the Piazza Augusto Imperatore, which was famous for its fettuccine. There, over an excellent meal, and a bottle of Chianti, Lewis felt his spirits revive. In Thad's absence, the scene at the location receded into unreality, and the confusion and alarm Lewis had felt seemed absurd. But it was the first time he had taken

Helen out, the first time he had been alone with her for any length of time, and he found that made him a little awkward.

He looked at Helen covertly. If she had flirted a little, the way women usually did, it might have been easier. But she never flirted, he had observed that over the past six weeks, and he had also observed what happened when a man tried to flirt with her. Several of the crew had tried it. Lloyd Baker had tried it. Lewis had seen Helen's chin lift, and her blue eyes flash and then become cold. Lewis did not intend to risk such a reaction now and—in any case—he found that he did not want to flirt, he did not want to pave the way for a pass. His usual technique with women was brash; it seemed to him shoddy, and quite inappropriate now.

That realization left him out on a limb, however. Lewis was not used to talking to women. To tease, to suggest, to flatter—he was accomplished at all those things. But just to talk—as if to a person of the same sex—no, that was difficult. Neutral ground, he decided, and asked her about the film.

"Are you pleased with it? Are you glad you did it?"

"Thad wouldn't let me see the rushes, so I don't know. But yes—I'm glad I did it. I felt . . ." She hesitated. "I felt *able* to do it. That has never happened to me before."

"Oh, don't worry about the rushes. No one's allowed to look at them. That's just Thad's way. He likes to be secretive." Lewis paused, and looked at her more closely. "Is that true—what you just said? After all, a woman like you . . ." He floundered slightly. "I mean, I'd imagine you were pretty confident about most things. . . ."

"Would you? Well, you're wrong." She smiled, and looked him directly in the eye. Lewis began to feel astonishingly happy.

"I know what you mean, though," he went on in a rush. "You mean you've started to believe in yourself. That's Thad. He has that effect on people—I don't know why. Maybe because his own confidence is so rocklike, I'm not sure. He made me believe—well, he made me feel I could *do* things. You know—you have all sorts of dreams, and you think that's all they are, just dreams, and then someone like Thad comes along, and they aren't dreams anymore. They're reality."

"You felt that?" She looked surprised.

"Yes, I did. I owe Thad a lot." He looked at her, and then away, awkwardly. "This afternoon . . . I'd just like to feel certain. He didn't— Thad didn't hurt you in any way? You're sure?"

"No, he didn't hurt me." A closed look came over her face. "He just—wanted something, and I couldn't give it to him, that's all."

Lewis looked at her carefully. She was choosing her words, and they made him a little uneasy. He sighed.

"Well, Thad's not normal. He wouldn't claim to be. Sometimes I think he's crazy. Crazy like a fox, maybe." He paused, and then burst out with a question he had been wanting to know the answer to for weeks.

"Do you like him? Do you like Thad?"

She took her time answering him; eventually she gave a little shrug. "I don't know. I'm not sure. I just liked working with him, I think. He made me see things."

For some reason, Lewis found this answer pleased him. With a slight sense of guilt he realized that if she had said yes, she liked Thad very much, it would not have been welcome. He began to smile.

"Do you know what Thad's favorite meal is? He has it at least twice every week. Kentucky Fried Chicken, Chinese takeout rice, and Earl Grey tea. Oh, and fortune cookies, if he can get them. Thad loves fortune cookies. . . ."

"He does?"

"Absolutely. I swear it. And he sleeps with his socks on, and never more than four hours a night. . . ."

They both began to laugh. The image of Thad receded; it lost its threat, became a little absurd. This gave Lewis confidence; somehow, it was much easier being with Helen, he decided, when Thad was not there.

"Tell me," he said then, abruptly. "What do you want to do next?" He leaned toward her as he spoke, and for the first time that evening touched her lightly with his hand.

Hélène looked down. Lewis had beautiful hands; she felt the slight pressure on her arm, then, quickly, he drew back. She stared down at the tablecloth. The film was over; she would have to decide; she would have to plan—it was becoming more and more urgent to plan. She looked up at Lewis.

"I don't know," she said simply. "All I was thinking about was finishing the film. I couldn't think beyond that somehow."

"We'll make other movies," Lewis said, with a careless confidence. "Thad wants us to work together again. He must have told you, surely?"

"He mentioned it, yes. I wasn't sure if he meant it, though. I hoped he did."

"Of course he meant it." Lewis was very firm. "We're a team now: you, me, Thad. A triumvirate. A triangle. Thad likes triangles, he thinks they have a magical force."

She smiled, but a little wanly. Lewis leaned forward. "Look," he said. "You remember all those things you told me about your family in England? Well, obviously you can't want to go back to them. And you don't need to. Why should you? Forget them. You're with us now. We're your family now."

Hélène looked away. She had told Lewis some story, weeks ago now; so many weeks, she could no longer remember the details. Was it the same story she had told Thad, or a different one? She wasn't sure. The lies were so confusing, and sometimes they made her feel terribly tired.

"Why don't we take a vacation? We talked about it once, remember? Just a few weeks, just while Thad edits the film. We could have a great time. There're lots of places we could go to. Friends of mine we could stay with . . ." Lewis felt himself begin to blush.

"No strings," he added awkwardly. "I want you to know that." No strings! He heard himself use that awful cliché with amazement. He was even more amazed to realize that he meant it.

Hélène looked at him quietly. If he had not blushed then, if he had not suddenly looked much younger and much more uncertain of himself than he usually did, she might have answered differently. But she was beginning to realize that Lewis Sinclair was not the person she had taken him for at first: he was gentler and kinder. Like her, she saw, he put on an act for the world—and that touched her. If she needed help, she thought suddenly—and she might need help—then she would not be afraid to turn to Lewis. She thought with a sudden longing of going to some quiet place, somewhere she could think, somewhere she could try to come to terms with everything that had happened since she left Orangeburg, and with all the things that were going to happen next.

"I'd like that," she said at last. "I'd like to go somewhere quiet, and restful—we've been working so hard here."

"No problem. Noisy or quiet. We can go anyplace you like." Her sudden acquiescence made his spirits soar. "Paris—we could go back to Paris. . . ."

"No. Not there." She turned her face away.

"I know!" Lewis leaped to his feet. "Let's just get a cab to the airport, and look at all the destinations, and then just decide, shall we? I've always wanted to do that."

Hélène turned back to him. His face was flushed, his eyes bright; slowly she began to smile.

"Just like that? You really mean it?"

"I mean it," Lewis said.

At the airport, she stood in the concourse like a little girl, holding Lewis's hand, and looking at the flight boards. Milan; Athens; Tenerife; New York; Cairo; Algiers; Madrid; Johannesburg; Toronto; Sydney . . .

Lewis gave a shout of laughter.

"Isn't this great? Why did I never do it before? It makes me feel about fifteen years old. . . ."

"Anywhere, Lewis?"

"Absolutely anywhere."

"All right. I'll close my eyes, you read out the flight numbers, and I'll choose one. . . ." Lewis's exhilaration was affecting her. She shut her eyes, and thought for one quick bright second of Edouard. It was right to do it this way, she thought defiantly. It was right for it to be so arbitrary. Edouard's absence made the whole world equal, made each destination an irrelevance.

Lewis began to recite the numbers. She picked one. It was the flight to London. Lewis went straight to the Alitalia desk and bought two first-class tickets. He paid for them by American Express.

Back in Rome, at the house in Trastevere, Thad took his time leaving. He was in no hurry to get back to the party; he disliked parties. For a while he just sat in the room, listening to its silence. Then he got up and began to pack up his camera, his own 16mm camera, of which he was very possessive. No one else was allowed to use it. He wiped the grease from the lens, and then carefully polished it. He dismantled it, piece by piece, and put the components carefully and lovingly into the niches hollowed out for them in the metal carrying case. He shut it and locked it.

He stroked the case as another man might stroke a woman's skin, or a pet animal. Then he laid it in readiness by the door. He checked and rechecked the final cans of film from that day's shoot, then he packed them in their carrying case and zipped it shut. Fussily, he straightened a few lengths of cable, checked a few light fittings. The crew would dismantle the rest of the stuff tomorrow. There was nothing else to do, but he was reluctant to leave. He had come to love this room over the past six weeks. He walked around it. He drew the drapes, then opened them again, and closed the shutters. He prowled around in a circle once more, and finally stopped at the bed. He looked down at it for a long time in silence.

The pillow was crumpled; it still bore the impress of Helen's head. The sheets were creased. The top one, which had covered her, was thrown back in a heap.

After a while, he stepped forward, and climbed onto the bed. He knelt there a moment, facing the pillow, fat thighs apart, his breathing growing more rapid.

Then he bent forward, over the place where her head had lain. He rested like that, squat, crouching, his weight on his elbows and knees. Then, slowly, he lowered his face against the white linen of the pillow-case, and rubbed it back and forth.

He began to pant. He thought of getting out his camera again, and just holding it, even unloaded, but she was not there, so there was no need. With a little jerking movement, he buried his face, hid it in the softness of the pillow, the darkness, and felt the world start to spin. He trembled, then groaned. Some minutes later, he knelt back, and levered his weight off the bed. He had left marks: saliva on the pillowcase, dirt from his shoes on the white sheet.

He brushed at the dirt ineffectively, then straightened the pillow fussily, plumping it out. He drew the sheet back over the bed to hide the shoe marks.

Then he picked up the camera case, the case of film cans, and walked out of the room. He got to the party about the same time that Lewis and Hélène arrived at the airport, and he could tell from the noise as soon as he got to the gates that the party was in full swing.

The goons at the gates had a case of wine and were drunk; one of them seemed to be trying to tell him something, but Thad couldn't be bothered to listen to him. He paid off the taxi there, and started walking up the drive to the house, swinging the heavy cases.

It was cold now, but that didn't seem to matter to the couple he passed, who were lying half-in, half-out of the shrubbery. Thad could see the woman's face, distorted as if in pain, by approaching climax. He passed on without a second glance. The main doors to the *palazzo* were open, light spilled out onto the terrace, and above the music and the sound of voices, he heard a dog howling.

Thad panted up the terrace steps, and paused on the threshold. There seemed to be a lot of people, people he'd never laid eyes on before, people who had presumably invited themselves. The place was one helluva mess already. There were empty champagne bottles rolling around the Principessa's marble-floored hall. Food, squashed-up food, trodden underfoot, was everywhere. And cigarette stubs. One was burning merrily on the top of some carved gilded table thing. Thad sniffed the heavy sweet scent of marijuana. He looked at the burning cigarette, then carefully picked it up and ground it under his heel. It had left a big burn mark on the table.

He looked around him, blinking, a little dazzled by the light. One of his crew was out cold at the bottom of the staircase; one of the extras was feeding caviar from a spoon to the Principessa's tricolored papillon. As Thad hesitated, peering through the throng, he was approached by a six-foot apparition, wearing a low-cut gown, a blond wig that cascaded over its shoulders, and diamonds. It rubbed itself against Thad like an importunate cat, and said a lot of things very fast in husky Italian. When Thad didn't answer, it grabbed his hand, rubbed it against the swell of its alabaster breasts, and then inserted it between its thighs. The apparition had a hard-on.

"Not just now," Thad said amiably, and the apparition tossed its head.

"Well fuck *you*," it said in the accents of pure Brooklyn, and flounced away.

Thad carefully stepped over rolling champagne bottles and advanced a little way into the hall. By the entrance to the crowded drawing room, Fabian greeted him.

"Thad—you're late. Lewis just called from the airport. . . ." Fabian rummaged in his pockets, swaying a little on his feet, and finally drew out a piece of paper on which an address was scrawled. "He and Helen have split. They're going to London. He said to give you this. He'll call you tomorrow. . . ."

"Oh, fine . . ." Thad nodded absentmindedly, and Fabian weaved away. Thad put the piece of paper into his pocket. He looked around him and sighed. If this was an orgy, it was boring. He had just decided to make himself some tea in the kitchen, and then go to bed, when, looking across the huge space of the hall, and past the throng of people, he saw someone he recognized. He paused, and then, shouldering his cases, trotted across the space dividing them.

The man was standing in the doorway of Prince Raphael's library. He was wearing a black three-piece suit of funereal elegance, just as he had been on the two previous occasions when Thad had glimpsed him. His face, as he looked out across the hall, was filled with a cold distaste. The library behind him was empty—a state of affairs that Thad, looking at him appreciatively, could guess was no accident.

Thad puffed to a halt in front of him, and the man, who was very tall, looked down on Thad, who was five feet two, as an eagle might look down at a slug. Thad waited patiently. Gradually, as he had expected, he saw recognition dawn way back in the dark blue eyes. The man had never seen Thad before, of course, but Thad felt reasonably certain that, if he had gotten this far, the man would have been furnished with a description that was all too recognizable.

The man stepped back into the library without a word. Thad silently followed him, shut the door, and—on consideration—locked it.

The library had ceiling frescoes by Benozzo Gozzoli, and, at intervals between the bookcases, a series of bronzes by Benvenuto Cellini which had been in Prince Raphael's family for sixteen generations. The beautiful books, many of them of great antiquity, bound in calf, and tooled with the family arms in gold, were, in the main, of pornography, of which—like his father and grandfather before him—Prince Raphael was an internationally celebrated collector. Thad's eyes flicked up to the frescoes, passed along the Cellini bronzes, along the serried ranks of books, and came to rest on the man who stood now before the carved marble mantelpiece. Thad did not know his name.

Next to him, on the floor, Thad observed something the man had apparently brought with him: a large Gladstone bag, fashioned from maroon crocodile skin. Thad looked from the bag to the man, then back again, slightly puzzled. The one so austere, the other so flamboyant; he would not have expected this man to carry this bag.

Thad, whose smell for power was acute, watched the man, and waited. Since he could tell the man was expecting him to speak, he said nothing. He had a fairly good idea of why the man was here, and he felt a quiet interest in how he would conduct himself. He wouldn't shout, or bluster, or make a scene—Thad was sure of that, and he was right. After waiting a few moments, with no sign of discomposure, the man spoke in a clear even voice, in English, with only the very slightest trace of a French accent.

"Where is she?"

Thad put down his cases.

"Helen Craig?" His voice squeaked a little, as it often did when he was excited. He had wondered if the man knew her by that name, and whether Helen had told him the same lies she had told Thad, or different ones. But he had no way of telling from the man's reaction; not a muscle moved in his face. Thad, who had observed this man twice before—without ever mentioning that fact to Lewis or Helen—examined his face with interest. He had not looked so expressionless those times. Now the man nodded, quickly, curtly.

"She just left," Thad said with a little giggle. He waited a beat to prolong the suspense. "With Lewis."

The man gave him a long cold look. Thad was impressed. Under the force of that stare, lesser men than he would have shriveled. Certainly started talking. Thad did no such thing. He waited, and after a moment, the man turned, with a quick dismissive gesture, and walked toward the door. Thad moved across the room, and sat down, settling his weight on the silk moiré cushions of an elaborately carved gilt couch. He waited until the man had reached the door, and then he said, "I can tell you where they've gone."

He didn't look around, but he knew the man was hesitating, that he wanted to walk out and shut the door on Thad forever. Thad waited philosophically: if he walked out, he walked out. He looked the kind who would, and besides, if he'd traced her this far, he'd probably have no trouble tracing her farther. Lewis was a fool, Thad thought, picking his nose reflectively. After that Englishman had turned up at the Café Strasbourg asking questions, Lewis had been nervous. But sooner or later Lewis would get tired of being careful. So, the guy could leave, no sweat—it was just that Thad hoped he wouldn't. He surreptitiously transferred the substance he had removed from his nose to the underside of the silk cushion. The man turned around, and walked back to him. They looked at each other once more, and this time, Thad thought, the man got his measure more accurately.

Thad smiled. "You're not her father, right? That guy at the Strasbourg, he wasn't her brother?"

"No."

Thad shrugged. "Oh, well. She told me some story, you know, and it seemed to fit. But I didn't really believe it. It was—well—crappy." He paused. "You want to tell me all about it?"

"I don't think I want, or need, to tell you anything at all."

"That's okay." Thad smiled again benignly. "I don't care. I'll tell you where they've gone anyway. But first—let me tell you about the movie. About Helen and the movie."

The man stood very still, and Thad, leaning back on the cushions, began to talk. He talked rapidly for some five minutes, during which the man never interrupted him once. What he had to say seemed simple, for the plot of *Night Game* was simple: two men, one woman, the eternal triangle. The men began as friends and ended as rivals. The woman survived; the two men were less fortunate—one ended up dead, killed by the other. At the beginning of the film, the woman seemed the quarry, the men the hunters. By its end, possibly, these roles were reversed. "It's a comedy," Thad finished helpfully.

"It sounds most amusing."

"It's called *Night Game*. Every scene takes place in daylight—it's the people who are in the dark." Thad paused. "Well, most people are, don't you think? I find that funny."

He had caught the man's attention now. He was looking at Thad thoughtfully.

"Not tragic?"

Thad grinned. "Oh, sure. Tragic *and* funny. Both at the same time. Like life."

The man's mouth tightened. "You're wasting my time. . . ." He started to turn away.

"Oh, I don't think so." Thad's voice was humble. "You see, I got the idea for the movie after I saw you."

The man stopped then, as Thad had known he would, and turned slowly back. He looked at Thad with contempt.

"We've never met, until now."

"Oh, not met, no. But I've seen you twice—it was just that you didn't see *me*." Thad giggled. "I saw you with Helen in Paris. You took her back to the Café Strasbourg one time, and you picked her up there the next evening. She said nothing about it the first time, so I knew it was important. Helen never talks about the things that matter to her—not to me and Lewis anyway. I like that. Her being secretive. It's good.

414 • SALLY BEAUMAN

Lewis doesn't understand it, of course. Isn't even aware of it. But then, Lewis is naïve, you know. Gab gab gab. Lewis gives it all away. . . ."

"Come to the point."

"All right. The point is, when Helen took off for those weeks, I guessed she'd be with you. She was, wasn't she? And that was funny—because Lewis was really broken up, really worried. He thought she wouldn't come back, you see. I didn't say anything. But then I knew she would. So I just, you know, *waited.*" Thad paused. "I never mind waiting. It's a gift I have, being patient."

"My own patience is less extensive. It's beginning to run out. Come to the point."

"The point is . . ." Thad smiled imperturbably. "You've been looking for Helen—I'm right, aren't I? Now you think you've found her. Well, you haven't. I have. Because I understand her. I know her." He looked up, modestly. "If you still want to locate her, I can give you an address in London, and you can go there. But it won't do any good. If you really want to find her—you'll find her in this movie. This one, and the other ones she's going to make. With me."

There was a long silence. Thad, who thrived on tension, eyed Edouard with respect; it was nice to play games with another master. He wondered if the man would make the mistake—the easy mistake—of being dismissive.

Edouard, looking at the fat and slightly ridiculous figure of Thad, was tempted—not to lose his temper, he was not that foolish—but to reject him and what he said, yes, he was tempted by that. A small fat ugly and conceited man; a poseur; a fool. He was tempted to think that, and to say it. But he could feel the force of Thad's will, and that force he never underestimated. He looked at Thad quietly, giving himself time to think ahead as he would in a chess game, looking for his opponent's weakness. The conceit, he thought finally. The fat man had been unable to resist the temptation of making a strong dramatic move, an aggressive move, a bishop moving in a deep diagonal across the board, or the queen, perhaps, brought early into play. Edouard decided on a classic defensive response: the small, apparently irrelevant moving of a pawn. One square.

"I don't understand." He allowed emotion to come into his voice. "It's not possible. I thought I knew her."

"Well, you would, I guess. You think you love her, right?" The fat man sounded both pitying and complacent.

Good, thought Edouard. He loathed to do it, but he nodded.

The fat man seemed pleased. He stood up and shifted about from foot to foot. "You see, you did know her in a way. A bit of her . . ." He jiggled the change in his pockets, then, as he grew more excited, and his voice rose, he took his hands out and waved them, two pudgy pink paws, in the air. "She does that, I've watched her. She gives pieces of herself to people. She doesn't know who she is yet, and she's frightened, so she gives just a bit here, a bit there, testing, you know, waiting for the reaction, and then, when she thinks she's given away too much, she gets afraid. Then she tells a lie. It's all self-protection. She's getting good at it, and she knows it. She told me some really big lies. She told other ones to Lewis. I expect she lied to you. You shouldn't mind. It doesn't matter. She only does it out of fear. Like, she can see she has this incredible effect on people, especially men, and she doesn't understand it. She thinks if they knew her, really knew her, the girl behind the face, they might not want her. They might reject her. She's really insecure, you know? Something happened, I guess, in her childhood. . . ."

Edouard listened to this outburst attentively. Beneath the banality of the speech, he sensed intuition, and sensed it to be sharp. Another little move, he thought. The fat man would now need little prompting. Edouard merely sighed and bent his head; it was enough.

"I've met women like her before. . . ." Thad waved his hands. "Not as beautiful, maybe, but it's the same syndrome. That's why I knew she was right, the moment I saw her. I knew she'd come across on film. It's in the eyes, maybe—like, she hardly moves, and the eyes talk to the camera. My camera. Because I know where to look for it, how to bring it out. She tells my camera the truth. Everything. No lies. She stops being afraid, and she gives herself to it—really. Like sex. I mean it. She'd be good in anybody's movies, but my movies will make her a star. More than a star. A legend."

Edouard looked up. Thad's hands were clasped together, his plump face looked triumphant. Edouard, loathing him at that moment, thought him unbalanced, a little mad, but nonetheless frightening. Then he feared for Hélène.

"You think that's what she wants?"

He put the question coldly, but Thaddeus Angelini was by then beyond caution.

"She doesn't know what she wants, not yet. She'll know when she sees this movie. Or maybe the next one. She'll realize that that's where she *is*—on celluloid." Thad paused, looked back at Edouard pityingly. "You shouldn't mind that she left, you know. I expect it was real for her, in a way. It was just bad timing. She always wanted to act, right back from the time she was a little kid. She told me that, and I believed her. It's just something she knows she's got to do. It's a really heavy thing for her—like, you know, her destiny. If you'd met her later, it might have been different."

"Why?"

Thad looked impatient. "Well, she's a woman. Sooner or later, she'll start thinking about love, and marriage, and having babies. She'll have her career by then, she'll be a star, and then she'll decide she isn't truly *fulfilled*, you know? That she needs something more. It's all bullshit, of course. But women are like that—she'll convince herself, she'll believe it. If you came along then, who knows? You might get lucky." He shrugged. "You'd still get hurt in the end though. She doesn't really need any of that stuff, you see, and eventually she'll realize it. What Helen needs, really needs, only I can give her. . . ."

"And what's that?"

Thad giggled. "Immortality."

Checkmate, Edouard thought—he thinks it's checkmate. He looked at Thad, at the small eyes glinting behind the shaded glasses. He smiled.

"I don't believe you," he said firmly.

Thad looked a little taken aback by the simplicity of the statement, but he rallied quickly.

"You think I'm wrong about the timing?"

"I think you may be right about the timing. I think you're wrong about the result. I think you underestimate women. I think you underestimate Hélène." Edouard paused. "People, too, perhaps. The things you dismiss so easily—love, fulfillment, marriage, children—don't most people, men and women, need them?"

Thad hesitated. He put his hands back into his pockets and jiggled his keys. He looked down at his feet, then up again at Edouard, craftily.

"*I* don't need them."

"You're saying you're less than human."

"Or more than human." Thad smiled.

Edouard looked at him coolly; he was thinking that the fat man probably meant what he said, and that if he did, the deficiency would show up in his films, eventually. He turned away to the door, and Thad, after a moment's pause, hastened after him.

"You want this address or not?" He brandished the slip of paper. Edouard glanced down at it, then away.

"Thank you. I don't need it."

He had reached the door, which he unlocked. Thad put the piece of paper back into his pocket.

"Let me guess—you're going to London, right?"

Edouard turned, and saw that the fat man was still smiling amiably.

"London? After all you've told me? All you've explained? No. I shall return to Paris."

Thad looked at Edouard suspiciously. "You mean you're not going to contact Helen at all?"

"I am not going to contact her, no."

"You want me to give her a message or anything?"

"Hélène and I do not need messengers."

This was said with calculated *hauteur*, and the fat man frowned.

"Why d'you keep calling her Hélène?"

"Because it's her true name," Edouard said. Then he walked out, and closed the door quietly behind him.

T had stared at the door irritably. He disliked others to have the exit line. He savored the prospect of going after the man, achieving the final word, and then rejected the idea. He prowled back into the room and saw that the maroon crocodile bag bore the initials H.C. He gave it a savage kick. After a while, he sat down on the couch again.

The man was probably bluffing, he thought, consoling himself. He was quite a good actor, had a lot of self-control, that was all. And that suit helped: Thad had observed the suit with interest. He himself could learn from that suit, he decided. Not from the man, because he was wrong, misguided, *in the dark*—as most men were where women were concerned.

He took off his spectacles, panted on them, and polished them on his sleeve. Without his glasses, Thad was acutely myopic: the huge room, the frescoes, the books, the bronzes, instantly blurred.

He leaned back on the cushions, aware that he was a little edgy, a little disconcerted, something he rarely felt. And for the second time that day too. First because of Helen; now because of this man. He allowed himself, briefly, to think of the scene that had taken place at the house in Trastevere: the memory filled him with a hot, angry mortification. It had not gone as he intended; the interview with the man had not gone entirely as he intended, either. Both the man and Helen had, in some way, eluded him: he had felt the lasso of his will start to tighten around them, and then—then they had managed to slip free. It was as if they knew something, understood something that Thad himself did not know or understand, and that knowledge gave them a quiet combative power that had thwarted him. It would not always be so, Thad decided.

His gaze flicked up at the volumes of elegantly bound pornography, which he had investigated, in a desultory fashion, some weeks before. Pornography bored him. Its increasingly obscene devices seemed to Thad desperate, pathetic, and always destined to fail. Metaphors for possession, that was all. His face took on a sneering expression. Sexual possession seemed to Thad innately trivial: it was not the possession of which he dreamed; its posturings did not make his pulse beat faster.

Art, now. Art was different. Art was the ultimate possession. He turned his mind back, with pleasure, to the film he had just made. He let it loop through his mind, sequence by sequence, frame by frame: exact, beautiful, potentially perfect; his movie, his creation, his immortal child. He felt immediately calmed, as he always did at such moments; it was an Olympian calm, the calm of potency and absolute control. It made his body stir, and harden.

He rested his hands between his thighs in recognition of that fact, and closed his eyes. The figure of Edouard receded; the figure of Helen advanced. To scan those features, which chance had made perfect for his purposes, made Thad content. He had been given a priceless gift: the perfect instrument, an instrument of flesh and blood: Thad's mind sang with the future harmonies this instrument should play. Composing them, Thad shut his eyes, and let his mind dwell in the sweet negative dark: its blackness and its blankness refreshed him. Soon, as always, it became silvery with images. Thad watched them and assembled them. He listened to them sing.

I n Paris, in his study at St. Cloud, Edouard reached across his desk and drew the telephone toward him.

He was thinking about the conversation with Thaddeus Angelini; he was thinking about Hélène; he was thinking about gifts.

On the desk, next to the telephone, were three things: the photograph of Hélène; the pair of gray gloves from Hermès; the square-cut diamond ring. He looked at them thoughtfully, trying to remain calm. The pain, when he had found those gloves and that ring in her room, had been intense. To have left those—of all things—when he had believed that they were like a sign between them, a talisman of their love.

Now he could look at them more calmly, and the pain was less. It hurt him to think it, but he could see Angelini might be right: the gift of the diamond, like the gift of his love, had been given at the wrong time.

He thought instead now of other, less tangible gifts, gifts Hélène would not even know she had received from him: the gift of time, for instance; the gift of choice; the gift, even, of his absence.

He did not find any of these easy to contemplate. All the way back from Italy he had been thinking, and planning, yet now he almost rebelled. He touched the telephone, and knew that he could go to London, and see her; knew it was more than possible that he could then bring her back.

The temptation was so very strong: he sat, his hand on the telephone, quite still. To have come so far, to have come so close—and then not to follow her to London. For a moment it was unbearable to him: he must go—he had to. Then he thought again of all the things Angelini had said, and again he heard the ring of truth in them.

Hélène was the age now that he had been in London during the war; at her age, he had loved Célestine, worshipped Jean-Paul, learned of the death of his father. A time when the world had changed from second to second; a time when he had grabbed at certainties, and been filled with ambitions, as perhaps Hélène was now. No, he would not go to London.

Instead, as he had planned, he placed a call to Simon Scher, who—two years before—he had transferred to Partex's Texas headquarters. Scher was now Drew Johnson's right-hand man; when he came on the line, Edouard's voice was entirely unemotional.

"Simon? We made a number of acquisitions as part of our diversification policy recently. Correct me if I am wrong. . . ."

In Dallas, Simon Scher smiled at this pleasantry: when was Edouard ever wrong in business matters?

". . . But one of them was a distribution company, I think. A film distribution company."

"That's right. It was called Sphere. It was an asset-stripping exercise on our part. As a company, they were all washed up, but we bought for a good price, and they had some useful real estate."

"What have we done with it?"

"Nothing yet. It was only two months back. We're still investigating the development potential of the property holdings." Scher paused. "You want me to run a check?"

"No." There was a brief pause. "What would it take to relaunch the company?"

"What, as a distribution operation?" Scher's surprise was evident in his voice. "Not a great deal, I suppose. It would depend on the level of commitment we wanted. Two million. You could reactivate for less, but if you were envisaging expansion . . ." He paused. "I can get you some figures, but we ruled out that option. The movie industry is highly volatile at present, and without a production arm, a distribution company is weak. Sphere was in competition with the major studio distribution divisions, and it lost out. It was also weak at the executive level, of course, but that wasn't the only problem by any means. We decided Partex would—"

"I want to reactivate the company."

"What?"

Scher's jaw dropped. He could as soon imagine Edouard's being involved in movies as he could envisage his playing the slot machines at Vegas.

"I want to reactivate it as a distribution company, with a view, shortly, to investment in independent film production."

"Production?" Scher felt as if he were going crazy. He couldn't have heard correctly. "You mean you want us to make movies?"

"Not make them, back them. I'm serious about this, Simon. I'd need to go into it, obviously, but I was thinking in terms of an initial injection of funds in the region of six million. A probable three-year loss period, aiming at turnaround and profit in the fourth year. . . ."

"Edouard. Hang on a minute. This is movies we're talking about. . . ."

"I would be financing the operation personally, and underwriting it, but I do not want my name associated with it in any way. I want Sphere as a fronting operation." He paused. Scher could tell from the tone of his voice that he had begun to make notes. "You'll need a headhunter, a good one, someone who knows the studios inside out. I need Sphere's trading figures for the past ten-year period, and the trading figures of its nonstudio competitors. I need—"

"You need me on a plane," Scher finished for him. He began to smile. It was an insane idea, and all Edouard's insane ideas had a formidable track record.

"I can't make it yesterday," he said dryly. "But I can make it tonight. You want Drew in on this?"

"Of course. He is the chairman."

Scher chuckled. They both knew that as far as Edouard was concerned, that fact need mean nothing.

"Very well then, he's my friend," Edouard corrected himself. "Tell him I need his help."

"If I tell him that, he'll fly over too."

"Then definitely tell him."

There was a brief pause, while Scher spoke to his secretary about flight times, and realized suddenly that it was the first time in ten years' association that Edouard had expressed a need for help. That fact perturbed him slightly. When he came back on the line, his voice was wary.

"You do know the kind of loss we could make on this, Edouard?" he began, feeling foolish. "I'm sure you do, of course, but it would be an entirely new departure for all of us. Distribution is bad enough, but production . . . It's a snakepit, Edouard, it's notoriously unpredictable. We—"

"We have a diversification policy, yes?" Edouard sounded amused.

"Oh, certainly. But with a view to profit. Here, we stand to make— you stand to make—a very heavy loss, and—"

"Oh, I can calculate the loss," Edouard said.

He was looking at the photograph of Hélène as he spoke, and the exact nature of the loss was vivid to him. He saw it for a moment, a future that was a wasteland, a future without Hélène, a future that was a terrible extension of the bleakness of his past.

He hesitated, then he turned the photograph over.

"I can calculate the loss," he said again more firmly.

PART THREE

LEWIS
AND HÉLÈNE

LONDON—PARIS, 1959—1960

"I'm having lunch at that new Italian place I told you about, with some terrific people. Why don't you join us?"

"No, thank you, Lewis."

"I've got some tickets for Covent Garden tomorrow night. They're like gold dust. Callas is singing. Please come."

"No, thank you, Lewis."

"There's a party in the Albany tonight, and we've both been invited. It's one of the most amazing places in London. You must see it."

"Lewis, no. Really."

A hunt ball in Oxfordshire. The opening of a new nightclub in Mayfair. Jazz at the Chester Square home of a newly rich and fashionable Royal Court Theatre playwright. A breakfast party in Brighton. Dancing at the Dorchester . . . after months in Paris and Rome, months of uncustomary social quietude, Lewis had bounced back. He was indefatigable.

"A private viewing at the Glendinning Gallery. Champagne at noon. It's Sorenson's new exhibition. Everyone says it's incredible."

"Lewis, I can't. I'd rather stay here. And besides, I'm sitting for Anne tomorrow."

"So what? Tell her you can't. Anne Kneale is a pain in the neck. You realize she's a dyke, do you?"

"Lewis . . ."

"Well, all right. Maybe she is, maybe she isn't. She certainly looks like one. I don't like her."

"Lewis, we're living in her house. . . ."

"Cottage. You can't swing a cat in here. I hardly know the woman. I can't imagine why she offered to lend it. And I certainly can't imagine why I accepted. . . ."

"I like it here. It's quiet. It's peaceful."

"It's bloody cold. My bed has a mattress made of iron. Last time I ran a bath it took three quarters of an hour to produce three inches of lukewarm water."

"There's a fire. It's pretty. My bed is extremely comfortable."

Lewis's color rose slightly. There was a silence. He was never quite sure, when Helen made remarks like this, whether they sprang from innocence or a desire to tease him. The next day, he began the campaign again.

"We could stay at the Ritz—just move in there to a couple of suites. Why not? We'd be there for Christmas."

"No, Lewis. You move if you like, but I'd rather stay here."

"No. I intend to keep an eye on you. You need looking after. You might disappear again, the way you did in Paris."

"I won't disappear, Lewis. Aren't I always here? You go to your parties, and you come back, and I'm here."

"But I want you to see London. I want London to see you. It must be so dull, staying here all the time. Lunch today—just lunch. Please— join us."

"No, Lewis. I want to be alone. I told you."

"I see. Like Greta Garbo, huh?" He pulled a wry face.

"No, Lewis. Like me."

Lewis gave in. Next day, he returned to the attack, and the day after. Lewis was persistent, and eclectic. The first night of a big new musical. A party on a boat on the Thames. Dinner with the American ambassador. A banquet in the Guildhall. The reception at de Chavigny to launch the new Wyspianski collection of jewelry.

"No, Lewis," she said to each of these invitations in exactly the same tone.

Lewis went anyway, and—sometimes—the next day, she asked him to tell her about his adventures the night before. She asked about the Guildhall banquet. She asked about the de Chavigny reception. Lewis smiled.

"Well, the champagne was incredible, I can tell you that. And everyone was there, of course."

"Was the jewelry beautiful?" she said. She thought of Edouard, showing her the designs.

"I guess so." Lewis shrugged. "I don't know much about jewelry. There were some incredible rubies. And the women there were going crazy over the stuff. Though they were all dripping with jewels already. The Cavendishes—I went with the Cavendishes—had actually gotten all their loot out of the bank. Usually they don't bother. The insurance is hell. They wear paste. Actually—" he gave his Bostonian frown—"I thought it was a bit much. De Chavigny himself was there, of course, and the woman with him—that designer woman, Ghislaine something, I forget her other name, but everybody's using her in New York now—well, she was wearing so many diamonds around her neck she could hardly turn her head. Lucy Cavendish said her mother was miffed. She was wearing their Romanov stuff, and she felt eclipsed. . . ."

"Ghislaine Belmont-Laon," Helen said, surprising him. She frowned slightly, and changed the subject.

The next day she was very quiet, and Lewis thought she looked pale. It worried him, and her refusal to venture out of the little cottage alarmed him slightly. It seemed, increasingly, unnatural and defensive, as if she were frightened of something.

It crossed Lewis's mind that she might be ill in some way—certainly she looked, sometimes, as if she were under strain. But Helen dismissed these worries whenever he voiced them, and after a few days, began to look less pale and washed out. Lewis, after two days' abstinence, began to accept invitations once more. He did so with a certain bravura: it piqued him that Helen seemed indifferent whether he went or stayed.

By late November, when they had been in London for three weeks, a pattern had established itself. Lewis sallied forth, and still tried, sporadically, to persuade Helen to accompany him. He took her continuing refusals with a resigned good grace, an air of bewilderment.

One morning, Lewis was leaving for a lunch appointment, and he was late. Helen was sitting on a couch in front of the window, reading *The Times*. Lewis, putting on his vicuna overcoat, his scarf and his gloves—it was very cold outside—was annoyed to observe that his departure hardly rated a glance. She said good-bye to him absently, though, when he had gone, she did look up to watch him hurry down the street outside.

He had his back to her: she watched him set his face in the direction of the King's Road, where he would pick up a taxi; the wind lifted his fair hair; he thrust his hands into his pockets. He looked elegant; more English than the English.

She watched him until he was out of sight, and then looked down at the newspaper again. It contained a report from New York on the reception held to launch the Wyspianski collection there. There was an erudite and enthusiastic review of Wyspianski's work, and a photograph of the Baron de Chavigny at the reception. Next to him, wearing a dog collar of diamonds, was Ghislaine Belmont-Laon, whose company, it was noted, had just redesigned the interiors of the de Chavigny showrooms off Fifth Avenue.

She put the newspaper down. To have known that Edouard was in London had filled her with a terrible, painful nervous perturbation. Now he was no longer there, she felt glad, she told herself: glad. She looked at the photograph dully. It was only to be expected. Two months—more—had gone by. If it was not Ghislaine Belmont-Laon, it would have been someone else, sooner or later.

After a while, she picked up *The Times* again, and turned to the financial pages. This was something she had begun to do every day, though not if Lewis was there, because he would have laughed at her. Patiently, she made herself read: trusts; equity issues; bonds; commodities. She found it all difficult to understand, yet curiously soothing, and she had an optimistic faith that she could learn, if she tried hard enough. Behind the dry wording of the reports, and the figures which still confused her, she sensed passion and drama, lives, careers, fortunes, made and broken very swiftly—and that interested her. It had occurred to her, reading these reports one day, that money was a means of revenge in ways she had not thought of before. She was thinking of Ned Calvert when the idea came to her: now, if there was a report about the cotton industry, she read that first. Of course, to accumulate money by these means, you first had to have some. She, as yet, did not; she would have to earn some. The necessity to do so was becoming more urgent.

She put down the paper and stared fixedly across the room. The panic was starting to come back, and she fought it down. On one of the chairs, Lewis had tossed a dark green cashmere sweater he had been wearing the previous day. It was an expensive sweater, and she looked at it thoughtfully. She was aware that it would have been very easy to have gone with Lewis to his luncheon. It would have been equally easy to persuade him to stay here. One word. One gesture. She could have made that little, little move at any time since they left Rome.

But she had grown to like Lewis, and so—scrupulously and carefully—she had not made the gesture, nor spoken the word. She did not want to hurt Lewis, and something else, too, held her back—an obstinacy, a stubborn clinging to the memory of Edouard, a reluctance to kill off that quick bright thing that animated her still. But she felt lonely. She also felt afraid. She looked out now at the street, which was wet, and empty. She thought of Lewis, felt relief that she had acted as she had, and then, quite suddenly, an irritable regret.

In the afternoons now, the light faded fast. At half-past four, Hélène would draw the scarlet woolen curtains across the small windows, and light the lamps, and sit in front of the coal fire that burned in the black Victorian grate. Sometimes, she made herself tea. She grew to like these simple rituals. In Alabama, even at the turn of the year, it was never as damp and cold as it was here now.

But she liked this misty weather. She delighted in the russet of the leaves of the London plane trees, the heaps of wet leaves on the sidewalk, the hoarfrost that made grass and branches white in the mornings, and the smell of the London air, which was earthy and acrid, slightly sooty. Best of all, she loved the light, for its softness and grayness, for the haze that sometimes hung over the Thames.

It gave her pleasure to watch time pass so tangibly; to watch the afternoon darken toward evening; to see the streetlamps lit, and the people, heads hunched against the cold, hurrying home from the tube after work. These very ordinary things soothed her. She began to hope that it would snow soon: she had never seen snow except in photographs.

The house had been lent them quite unexpectedly. When they first arrived in London, they had stayed with a friend of Lewis's mother, in a large fashionable apartment in Eaton Square. Their hostess, an American, was in the throes of the pre-Christmas season of parties; a chic woman, she was negligently hospitable. Hélène had shrunk from her, and shrunk from the whirl of activities into which Lewis prepared to plunge with such enthusiasm. Once the work of filming was over, she felt anxious and exhausted; all the events of the previous summer, which had succeeded one another at such speed, pressed in on her; they had begun to enter her dreams at night in chaotic and malign confusion. What she had wanted—she realized, now it had been given her—was a quiet still place, into which she could crawl, and curl up, like an injured animal, and let time pass.

They could not stay at Eaton Square indefinitely, and Lewis had been fretting about this when, quite suddenly, he received the telephone call from the portrait painter, Lady Anne Kneale. He knew her only slightly; she had heard, through a friend of a friend, that he was looking for somewhere to stay, and she offered her cottage.

"It's there. I use the studio behind the house," she said in her gruff way. "But I'm living with a friend at the moment, so you can have it if you want it."

They went around to see it the next day. The inspection did not take long, since it was a tiny terraced house with two bedrooms upstairs, a sitting room and a kitchen downstairs. The bedrooms had brass bedsteads and patchwork quilts, rag rugs and oil lamps. The kitchen had a huge black stove on which to cook, a dresser stacked with a disorderly array of old blue and white Spode china, and a York stone floor which was exceedingly cold. The little sitting room was shabby and pretty, its wooden floor covered with old Turkish kelim rugs, its walls covered with paintings and improvised shelves of books. Two fat red chairs were stationed either side of the fireplace, and on the mantel were two Staffordshire dogs, a blue glass vase filled with brown bird's feathers, an ostrich egg, and a line of smooth gray pebbles. It was not tidy, nor, perhaps, very clean. Lewis's face fell, and Hélène exclaimed with delight.

"Oh, Lewis. I like it so much."

"It's like a doll's house. Christ, it's cold. Why don't the English understand about central heating?"

"Please, Lewis."

"Oh, all right. If you like it."

She discovered then what she had suspected before: Lewis found it difficult to refuse her anything.

They had moved their things there the next day, and they had been here ever since. Lewis used it as a base for his forays to smart parties; Hélène stayed alone. Apart from Anne Kneale, whom Hélène met for the first time, briefly, when they came to look at the house, and who had asked if she might paint her the week after they moved in, she met no one, and she realized then how much she had craved solitude for months, perhaps because she had been used to it as a child, perhaps because solitude was necessary to the healing.

Sometimes she went for walks alone, by the river; once she took the bus north and went to Regents Park, and looked at the lake, and the ducks, and the bandstand where, in the summer months, music would be played.

She stood there, looking at the bright neat wooden structure, and she heard her mother's voice telling her about London, telling her about the parks, the band, the marches they played, and the waltzes. She turned away at last; her mother felt very close.

Then she would return to the little house, and if Lewis was not there, and he rarely was, she would sometimes sit for Anne Kneale, or read, or simply rest in front of the fire, watching the patterns the flames made, or feed Anne Kneale's cat, a huge majestic creature the color of marmalade, who visited periodically, lapped milk, sat on her lap, and watched her with his great amber eyes.

If she had had to explain why she wanted to pass the time like this—and Lewis did sometimes press her, with a kind of mild, good-humored exasperation—she might have said she felt safe.

The little house seemed to her sometimes like a place in a fairy story, a woodcutter's cottage perhaps, in which you were protected from the evils and dangers of the forest beyond. She knew she could not stay there forever, or indeed for very long, but meanwhile she needed to be there, where it was safe and quiet and warm.

Here, she could let the past rest. Here she could plan the future, and this was necessary, more urgent with each passing day, and each passing week. She had to plan; not just for herself, but also for the baby. *Billy's baby*, she said to herself, lacing her hands across the very gentle curve of her stomach. It had not yet begun to move, but her sense of its presence was strong. She could feel it lulling her mind, as it began to alter her body.

Sometimes, sitting in front of the fire, she talked to it.

In Rome, when she had first begun work, the sickness had been very bad. Morning and evening, before work and after it: it had left her weak and drained. That had been the worst time. It was then, in the evenings, when she locked herself in her room at the *palazzo*, that she had written the letters to Edouard.

She wrote compulsively, night after night, telling him on paper all the things she had never told him face to face. She sent none of the letters, and she never reread them when they were finished; she locked them away in a drawer.

Then, as the work continued, there had been a change. "Trust yourself," Thad had said, and those words had seemed to give her strength, not just when she was filming, but also afterward, when she went back to the *palazzo*, and when she was alone.

One night, when they had been filming for about a month, she went up to her room at the *palazzo*, took out that bundle of unsent letters, put them in the empty fireplace, and set light to them. The very next day, as if sensing that something had changed in her, and her mind had set, the sickness stopped. It never returned, and as her confidence in her work grew, she had felt a sense of extraordinary physical well-being, a new abundant energy.

But the turmoil of the past and the anxiety of the future were waiting for her; they began to stake their claim the moment the film was over, the moment she left Rome. Then, the nightmares she had had once or twice in France returned, and they still continued; night after night she had the most horrible dreams.

She held Billy in her arms, then Edouard, and it was Edouard who was dying and bleeding. Her mother danced through her dreams, danced to the song about lilacs, her violet eyes wide and unseeing. Ned Calvert came back, in his white suit, and took her up to his wife's room, and told her she was his wife now, she was trapped, she would be his forever and forever. Hélène looked at him, and at the bright glass bottles that glittered on the dressing table, and she wanted to pick one up and kill him. She picked up the glass bottle, and it turned into a diamond; the diamond was very cold, and it burned her.

These dreams frightened her; she would have liked to tell someone about them, but there was no one to tell except Anne or Lewis, and she could not bring herself to do that.

In the daytime they receded, but still she could not quite shake them off. This frightened her too: she had to be well and strong, she told herself, she had to be—for the baby. She felt she knew this baby: it had become her friend and her confidant. She knew what it would look like, she knew everything about it, even the exact day on which it was conceived: July 16, of course, July 16, because that was the day also on which Billy died. Because of the baby, Billy lived on—they hadn't been able to kill him.

"I have to be well. I have to be strong." She would say it out loud to herself sometimes, rocking backward and forward, her hands clasped tight around her stomach. Strong for the baby's sake, and strong for Billy's. It was important to think about Billy as much as she could, because the baby would never know him. So she tried very hard not to think about Edouard, and when—in spite of her efforts—he crept back into her mind, she always felt guilty.

She hated that almost as much as the dreams. There was no time for guilt now; guilt raised too many questions. It started her mind racing off in all sorts of directions; it hinted at possibilities, choices she might have made, that she refused to face.

Billy's baby. Billy's baby. She said it over and over again, like a litany. She drew the curtains, shut out the world, and retreated to the fire. The litany lulled her mind; it helped her to spin plans for the future.

These plans, she began to realize, had to be specific. They had to be practical.

She had been telling herself this on the afternoon Lewis had allowed to slip by over a protracted lunch. It was evening when he returned to the cottage, and it was raining. He came into the little red room, with its fire, and its pools of amber light, stamping his feet, pulling off his cashmere scarf and his beautiful gloves, brushing the rain from the shoulders of his expensive overcoat, laughing and in mid-complaint about the horrors of the English weather. Quite suddenly, for no apparent reason, he stopped in mid-sentence.

He looked at Helen, who was sitting on a rug in front of the fire. Often, when she looked at him, he felt she did not see him; it was as if she looked beyond him to a quite different face. Now, perhaps because his arrival had startled her, she was looking at him directly and intently, her wide gray eyes thoughtful. Lewis hesitated, then took off his overcoat, pulled off his wet shoes, and sat down.

He was supposed, that evening, to be going on to the theater and to dinner; they both knew this. They looked at each other for a moment; then she looked down, her dark lashes shadowing her cheeks; her color rose slightly. Lewis shifted in his seat; the fire was warming him pleasantly.

"Must you go, Lewis?" she said finally, in a quiet voice. Lewis instantly felt the most extraordinary joy; he felt as if he had been running up an endless succession of escalators and—quite suddenly—he was able to get off.

"I don't have to," he answered quickly. "It's a ghastly night. In fact . . . I don't think I will."

She looked up; the quickness of his capitulation seemed to startle her; then, shyly, she smiled.

She was thinking, in a cool detached and practical way, that she was very young, that she had virtually no money, and that Billy's baby needed a father. She looked at that fact with dispassion, weighing the needs of the baby against the needs of Lewis Sinclair, who, as she had come to understand, was far more vulnerable and uncertain than he had at first seemed to be—Lewis Sinclair, who could be hurt.

Her face did not betray the calculation; Lewis, looking at her, thought his decision to stay home pleased her, but that she was too modest to say so. He felt a startling jolt of pure happiness.

Nothing else was said, but in that small moment the future course of both their lives began to change.

T hree weeks later, as Christmas approached, it snowed heavily. Hélène awoke to find her bedroom unusually light. She slipped out of the high brass bed, and opened the curtains.

It was still early morning, and the snow outside was undisturbed. She looked out on a perfect morning, in which clear and radiant sun shone on a pale new world. Just then, and for the first time, she felt her baby move.

She stood perfectly still, pressing her hands against her stomach, which felt hard under her nightdress. It was a strange sensation, quite unlike any description she had read, and for a moment she thought she had imagined it. Then she felt it again: a slow fluttering, like a bird cupped in the palms of the hands, part of herself and yet separate. That stirring filled her with a sudden and intensely fierce protectiveness; tears stung her eyes. That morning she asked Anne Kneale, as she sat for her in her studio, if she could recommend a London doctor. She paused: a gynecologist.

There was a little silence. Anne looked up, her brush poised. Her clever angular face, with its sharp eyes, rested on Hélène for a moment.

"Yes. I can do that. He's a sanctimonious son of a bitch. Eminent, however."

She paused, and then began to stab at the canvas again, with quick short brushstrokes. Nothing more was said—it was an extremely English moment, Hélène thought. She went to see the eminent man, Mr. Foxworth, at his Harley Street rooms the next afternoon. She did not tell Lewis where she was going.

Mr. Foxworth was tall, and looked distinguished. He wore a pearl-gray three-piece suit, a pearl-gray tie, and a pearl-headed tiepin. In his buttonhole was a pale yellow rosebud, and he sat behind a very large and highly polished desk, writing. On the wall behind him was a neatly arranged row of English landscape paintings, each carefully lit, each small, and each harmonizing gently with the dull but tasteful Regency striped wallpaper. Hélène kept her eyes fixed upon these paintings; Mr. Foxworth kept his eyes fixed upon his desk. He was asking her about her periods, and Hélène could tell that he found her answers unsatisfactory. She had never discussed her periods in front of a man before; she was scarlet with embarrassment.

Eventually he sighed, in a manner that contrived to suggest that not just Hélène but all her sex were a mystery to him, a slightly tiresome mystery. He suggested that she might go next door to his examining room, where a nurse was waiting. He would then examine her. He sounded as if he found the necessity of this regrettable.

The nurse was brisk.

"Remove all your undies," she said, "including the panties. You'll find a gown on the hook."

Hélène did as she said. When she came out in a green linen gown, the nurse assisted her onto a narrow table. It had metal stirrups at the foot, and was protected by a sheet of white paper. Hélène began to feel unclean. The nurse pressed a discreet bell, and after a well-timed pause, Mr. Foxworth joined them.

Staring at a space somewhere above her head, he produced a metal object that resembled a pair of hair tongs. He dangled it from one rubber-gloved hand, while, with the other, he made a few deft preliminary probes.

"This will feel cold at first. Relax your muscles, please," he said. It was the only remark he made during the entire examination.

Hélène instantly tensed. Mr. Foxworth looked mildly irritated. He put Hélène's feet into the stirrups, raising her legs. He inserted the metal object, made some adjustments, and turned a screw. He peered, and felt. Hélène shut her eyes.

When she opened them again, Mr. Foxworth was peeling off the rubber gloves. He snapped them into a ball, and dropped them into a wastebasket. He then pressed her stomach, eased aside the thin gown, and—still gazing at a space somewhere above her head—felt her breasts. Touching her at all seemed to him a distasteful business, and Hélène wondered if this was because she was unmarried, and whether he looked the same way when he examined respectable matrons. When she was dressing again, and the nurse called her Mrs. Craig, she became certain of it.

This discreet unspoken distaste terrified her. She wished that she had put on a ring, pretended to be married—anything rather than face that wall of disapproval.

She went back into Mr. Foxworth's rooms, feeling branded. He was writing; he indicated she should sit; he continued to write. When, finally, he looked up, he was frowning; he began to speak, measuring his words carefully, in the manner of a busy man addressing a small and backward child.

"Miss Craig. The duration of a normal pregnancy is forty weeks. It is now December twenty-second. You are at present around nineteen weeks into pregnancy. It is difficult to be more precise given your incertitude regarding the dates of your menstrual periods." He paused. "I have to tell you, therefore, that if you were to raise the question of termination, I should have to refuse. The requirements of the law are stringent. When the pregnancy has advanced beyond twelve weeks, then the possibility of termination is ruled out. . . . Miss Craig, do you understand what I am saying?"

Hélène's eyes swung back to his face. His words seemed to her completely meaningless, and to come at her across a great divide.

"Termination?" she said finally. "You mean an abortion? But I don't want an abortion. I want to have this baby."

Mr. Foxworth compressed his lips. The term *abortion* was clearly one that pained his sensibilities. He adjusted the calendar on his desk by a few inches.

"Of course. Of course." He sounded suave, soothing, and entirely disbelieving. "Naturally, I understand. You wished to have your pregnancy confirmed. I might have wished you had done so earlier. . . . However. You are in excellent health. We can estimate with a very good degree of accuracy that you will reach full term on or around May fourth—a spring baby. Always so pleasant for the mothers, I think." His face brightened automatically, then sobered, as if he had made this pleasantry many times before, and had only now realized its inaptness. "It is also, of course, still some considerable time away—which is fortunate, as it gives you the opportunity to look ahead, Miss Craig, and to make plans which are in the best interests of yourself and of your child. I wonder . . ." His face became grave. "Had you considered, Miss Craig, the possibilities of adoption?"

He put the question perfectly coolly, as if it were one so obvious as to be hardly worth mentioning. Hélène swallowed; he was looking at her, and at her clothes, his expression blandly dismissive. She was wearing a plain and inexpensive cloth coat, which she had bought some weeks before. She realized that to him it looked like what it was—cheap. And she felt an angry certitude that the way he was speaking to her was somehow related to that coat. To the coat, and the fact that she was not married. She looked at him with a furious loathing, and she thought of her mother. Was that how the little back-street abortionist in Montgomery had looked at her too?

In that second she made herself a promise—which was the old promise really, but given new force: that this would never happen to her again. She would never be patronized again. And, whatever she had to do, her baby was not going to grow up the way she grew up, filled with that painful awful pride that is the by-product of poverty. She stood up.

"I told you. I want this baby. I am not interested in the question of adoption."

Her chin lifted. Mr. Foxworth looked at her narrowly, and then looked back at his notes.

Hélène, staring at his bent head, at the pearl-gray suit, at the two neat wings of gray hair at his temples, thought: He is regretting he ever agreed to see me. If I hadn't used Anne Kneale's name—and title—when I telephoned, he wouldn't have seen me at all. . . .

In this she was quite wrong. Mr. Foxworth was thinking about dates. Given the laws regarding abortion then current in England, he was exceedingly familiar with women who came to him and lied, charmingly and unshakably, about the date of their last period. Rich women; society women; older women; younger women: occasionally they smiled brightly, sometimes they wept. Their object, of course, was to persuade him that they were not as far advanced into pregnancy as they were, and that—therefore—a termination was possible. These women, most of whom were used to getting their way, could become angry, and insulting, when Mr. Foxworth informed them quietly that—as he put it—they must be mistaken.

It was, however, the first time in his professional life that a woman had come to him and attempted to claim that her pregnancy was more advanced than it was: this Miss Craig had attempted to convince him that she was five months pregnant, which would mean that conception had occurred in mid-July. This was out of the question, and he found it curious. He also found it curious that, when he attempted to convey to her the facts, she did not listen. It was as if she quite deliberately blotted out his words, even as he spoke them.

Mr. Foxworth pursed his lips. His professional life was dedicated to the care of women, and yet he did not greatly like or admire the female sex. Women, he felt, had an ability to displace facts that did not suit them, particularly at that nexus where their emotional and sexual lives intersected. This young woman, he assumed, wished, for reasons of her own, to reassure herself that one man was the father of her child rather than another.

Well, that was a phenomenon he *had* encountered before. All men, including married men, were putative fathers in Mr. Foxworth's eyes, and a number of men of his acquaintance were proudly presenting sons and daughters to the world which, Mr. Foxworth knew for certain, were not theirs, the oddity being that the women concerned seemed able to erase this stubborn truth from their minds altogether. After a certain point, they not only claimed their husbands were the fathers of their lovers' children—they actually believed it themselves.

He roused himself from this reverie to look up at his patient. She looked back at him. Her face was flushed, her eyes bright, and her expression was defiant. Mr. Foxworth did not like her; she was extremely young, she was unmarried, and he considered an expression of humility or distress would have been more appropriate.

By way of a reprimand, he eased back his snowy cuff, and looked at his watch. The young woman bit her lip. She unclasped her hands, and thanked him for seeing her. She did so graciously enough, but with a certain irony in her voice to which Mr. Foxworth took exception.

He asked her, pointedly, if she had understood what he said, whereupon she smiled, and asked him how much she owed him. Mr. Foxworth was distressed. He was sure the question was deliberate, and not merely due to ignorance of etiquette. He flushed slightly, rose to his feet, and suggested she leave her address with his receptionist. Notification of his charges—he pronounced this word with some difficulty, since his fees were high and he found it undignified to refer to their existence—would be sent in due course.

Hélène left. Down the wide and elegant staircase, out the heavy front door, down the flight of steps onto the sidewalk of Harley Street. Immediately outside, a taxi had halted: a tall man in middle age descended; holding open the door, he assisted a woman out of the cab—a pretty woman, wearing furs; she leaned upon his arm and looked up at him laughingly. She was roundly, splendidly, obviously pregnant.

Hélène stood for a moment, clutching her thin cloth coat around her, pulling up its collar to shield her face from the cold wind. She looked at them, this man and this woman, oblivious of her existence, and then—as they passed up the steps to the house—she stepped quickly forward and claimed the cab.

May 4—her baby. She could think of nothing else; she was possessed with a sense of urgency. Leaning forward, she gave the driver the Chelsea address. She glanced back at the man and the woman once more, and then—leaning forward again—asked the driver to hurry.

When he heard the front door of the cottage open and shut, Lewis was upstairs, half-dressed and half-undressed, changing to go out. He was not in a good temper. He was annoyed with the room, which was cold. He was annoyed with the ceiling, which sloped, and did not easily accommodate a man six feet three inches tall. He was annoyed with Thad, who telephoned constantly now, badgering him to return to Paris. He was annoyed with Helen, who was anxious about *Night Game*, and who would talk on the phone to Thad at great length. He was annoyed with the girl he had promised to escort that evening to a dinner-dance in Berkeley Square. Above all, he was annoyed with himself. Something was happening to him which he did not understand, and he seemed to have no power to control it.

For a moment, hearing the footsteps downstairs, he hesitated. Then, irritably, he pulled on the starched evening shirt, picked up his black tie, and stared at his handsome reflection in the mirror. He did not have to go to the dance. He could telephone the girl, even this late, and simply cancel. He could stay home. This alternative seemed oddly tempting; he had felt its pull grow stronger and stronger these past weeks, and this burgeoning taste for domesticity alarmed him: he had certainly never experienced it before. However, Helen had suggested he stay home only that one time; the suggestion had not been repeated. Lewis frowned, and decided to go. He began to fashion the tie into a bow.

He was beginning to find it harder and harder to sit in the same room as Helen, a feeling that coexisted unhappily with his intense desire to be there. When he was with her, he wanted to touch her; he wanted to take her hand; he wanted to put his arm around her . . . the need to do these things was beginning to drive him crazy. After all, if he wanted to take her hand, why the hell didn't he? Lewis had been asking himself such questions for months—of which fact he was bitterly aware.

He had no answers. All he knew was that he looked at Helen, and his habitual sexual advances seemed to him shoddy. Some new approach was called for. Lewis had no idea what it was.

He slipped his arms into the sleeves of his black dinner jacket, and pulled it on. A stranger looked back at him from the mirror. He felt he did not know who he was anymore. His whole identity seemed to him in flux, as if it were being forged from minute to minute, and depended, in some mysterious way, upon Helen. Some act of recognition was needed from her, Lewis felt. It was as if Helen alone had the power to free him to be himself.

Lewis disliked introspection. This thought sneaked down the back-stairs from that attic in his mind to which he confined old ideals. Firmly, he thrust it back were it belonged: in the lumber room. He turned away from the mirror and made for the stairs. He needed a cure, a cure he had tried before, and which—this time—he was determined should not fail him.

Helen did not attempt to persuade him to stay in, but she did do one thing which she had never done before. As Lewis opened the door, she solemnly picked up his scarf, and placed it around his neck. Her hand brushed his skin gently as she did so. He caught the clean newly washed scent of her skin and hair. Then she reached up and placed one brief chaste kiss on his cheek. Lewis reeled out into the street. He nearly forgot about his cure there and then; he nearly abandoned both the girl and the dinner-dance. Then he saw a taxi at the end of the street, and he ran after it fast, before he had time to change his mind.

He directed it to Mayfair, and leaned back in the seat, feeling calmer. As the taxi gathered speed up Sloane Street, he began to relax, and to grow more confident.

It would work, he told himself firmly. This time it would damn well work. It was almost seven now. Drinks. Dinner. Dancing. By eleven o'clock at the latest, earlier if possible, Lewis Sinclair was going to get laid.

A t ten, there was a pause in the dancing, and supper was served. The supper room was crowded with braying young Englishmen in tails, and fringed with debutantes and post-debutantes flushed from their exertions on the dance floor. Lewis pushed through the throng to the long tables, where a sumptuous array of food was displayed. Lobster; quails' eggs; *filet de boeuf en gelée;* at the far end, wine jellies as tall as castles, pyramids of fruit, ices and sorbets in silver dishes. The man next to him dropped a quail's egg and promptly trod on it. A bowl of caviar was being rapidly emptied; the lobsters, so beautifully arranged and decorated a moment before, were already in disarray.

Lewis was hot, and sweating, and in a very bad temper. He stuck his elbow into an Englishman's ribs, and maneuvered to the front. He held aloft two plates, one for himself, one for the ex-debutante he had selected for the evening. A harassed waiter put one cracked lobster claw on each, and a ladle of mustard-yellow mayonnaise. Some poached salmon was added and some wilting cucumber; that would damn well have to do, Lewis decided.

He fought his way back to the ex-debutante who, unaware of the fate Lewis intended for her, was talking to a friend. She was wearing a dress of pink chiffon, with a very full skirt. There was a ridge of flesh where her long white kid gloves cut into the plumpness of her upper arms. When she saw Lewis approaching, she unbuttoned the gloves and rolled them back from her wrists.

"Oh, salmon," she said, and made a face. "I rather wanted some of the beef, actually."

"It's all gone," Lewis lied.

"Oh, what a bore. And the caviar?"

Lewis gritted his teeth.

"Hang on a second," he said. "I'll just go and get us some more champagne."

"Hang on to what?" she answered. She clearly considered this a great witticism, because she and her friend dissolved into laughter.

Lewis set his face, and prepared to battle his way to the drinks table. It was barred by lines of Englishmen four deep.

Lewis stood and waited. He hadn't the heart to push; he scarcely had the heart to go on, and it was only obstinacy that prevented his leaving right then. No, he thought, he'd made that bet, and he'd damn well stick to it.

He had already spied out the land, ruled out the possibility of a bedroom, and decided on a bathroom upstairs. The bathroom might be less comfortable, but at least it had a door that locked. All the bedroom keys, Lewis had noted, had been removed: the English were a suspicious bunch.

He leaned against a pillar resignedly, waiting his turn. Once, sex had seemed so marvelously easy. He cast his mind back over some of the women in his past. Their faces and their bodies were shadowy; he couldn't remember most of their names, but then, that was not surprising; none of them had lasted very long.

He liked older women best—or he had once. His longest affair, six weeks, one summer up at Cape Cod, had been with a woman who was his mother's contemporary. She taught literature at a women's college; she taught Lewis the meaning of erogenous, and other things besides. "You will rush so, Lewis. Slow down. You do it as if you hate it. . . ."

Lewis frowned. The remark had stung him, perhaps because there was some truth in it. He had left her not long afterward, anyway.

He didn't like intellectual women, he'd decided. Come to that, he didn't much like women of his own background. All dead from the neck down. No, he much preferred the company of the hookers he picked up off Times Square, or the Baltimore strippers, who cooed over his body, and laughed at his accent, and stung him for a good twenty bucks more than they charged their sailors. So what? It was honest at least, and these girls, with their sharp street language, at least made him laugh. He saw two of them now, quite vividly, one white, one black, one on either side of him in the bed, all three of them bombed out of their skulls on Jack Daniel's.

"C'mon, sugar," the black girl said. "Your mama ever tell you 'bout a chocolate sandwich?"

"Not this kind," Lewis had replied, making a grab at both of them. The words had stimulated him; the two girls had wriggled, and sucked and licked, and all the time, somewhere inside his head, Lewis could see his mother's shocked face. He felt as if he came for a thousand years, pumping and pumping, and afterward the black stripper said, "Hey, big boy, you're sumthin', you know that? You come see me again, and I swear to you, baby, we'll do it for free. . . ."

He never had seen her again. Now he couldn't remember her face either. Just the sweet feeling, fucking that felt like revenge. And what she said, of course.

Lewis shook his head. He had reached the champagne table at last. Two glasses; champagne that was too warm.

How odd, he thought, to forget their faces, and remember their words.

It was ten forty-five, and he had gained the sanctuary of the bathroom upstairs. Lewis had made love in bathrooms before: the ex-debutante, it seemed, had not. She had consumed enough champagne to be persuaded upstairs easily enough. The moment the door was locked, she started having second thoughts. Lewis reached for her. He thought, dully: fifteen minutes to go. It was all right as long as he kissed her. He did that for some while, at the same time furtively exploring the geography of her ball gown, which appeared impenetrable.

It had a lowish neckline, with a tight underbodice. Lewis squeezed experimentally, and felt a handful of whalebone. The full skirt was floor-length. Lewis managed to ease this up to knee level, and then to insinuate his hand underneath. He felt the curve of a thigh, and a nylon stocking. Better still, he felt the metal fastening of a garter. He kissed the girl with slightly more fervor, and shifted his hand an inch higher. She was wearing, he suspected, that ultimate passion-killer, the step-in girdle. Lewis had experience of getting girls out of girdles, and it was not encouraging. He abandoned her skirts, and concentrated his hands, both at once, in the breast area: whalebone and a suggestion of plump flesh—it was like handling a pouter pigeon.

Lewis was aware that he was not all that aroused. There was still a dim sense at the back of his mind that he did not want to be here, and he did not want to be doing this, but he had begun now, and he still felt obstinate. Eleven o'clock. He'd start getting interested in a minute, he told himself. He kissed the girl again, noted that her color had risen, and that her breathing was more rapid; he decided on a bold move—one hand, in a firm scooping movement, straight down her cleavage.

The debutante reacted swiftly. She made a noise of whinnying outrage, and slapped Lewis's hand, hard.

"Beastly American. What do you imagine you're doing?"

She stepped back, and looked down her long English nose at him. Lewis shrugged, and put his hands into his pockets. He gave her a lazy and insolent smile.

"You came up with me. You saw me lock the door. What do you think I'm doing?"

He had drunk a considerable quantity of champagne, enough to make him feel this was irrefutable logic. The ex-debutante clearly disagreed. She gave Lewis a withering look.

"Do you imagine," she said, swaying only very slightly on her feet, "that I intend to lose my virginity to an American, in a bathroom?"

"Which is worse, my nationality, or my choice of location?"

She started to give him another haughty stare, then, redeeming herself slightly, she giggled.

"Honestly, Lewis. You do have the most colossal nerve. . . ."

Lewis hesitated. He estimated that if he tried now, and if he bothered to be persuasive, he could probably make progress of sorts: rebuff, even rude rebuff, was all part of the game. He could woo her. He could kiss her. And the thought of either, he realized, bored him to distraction.

He looked at the ex-debutante, and she looked back at him. She was pretty, and Lewis, who had known her a couple of weeks, liked her. He sighed. The champagne, and also a kind of desperation, made him bold.

"Why not?" he demanded finally. "I mean, in the end, why not? What is it, after all? Why does it have to be such a big goddamned deal?"

To his relief, and also to his surprise, this question did not seem to offend her; Lewis had the distinct impression that it had also, at some point, occurred to her. She frowned, and looked thoughtful.

"*I* don't know." She paused. "I think, I suppose, that you ought to love me."

"Oh, great. Terrific." Lewis suddenly felt very tired. He leaned back against the wall. "We don't have to be married then? Or engaged?"

The girl giggled. "No, Lewis, relax. That's Mummy's generation."

"Well, I suppose that's progress. Of a kind."

"So. If I loved you—it would probably be all right," she went on magnanimously. "Also, if I was sure I wouldn't get pregnant or anything . . ." Here she became a little pink. "But I don't—love you that is—and you don't, and so I won't."

"That's neat." Lewis sighed. "It seems reasonable. Up to a point." He pushed himself off the wall again. "So we couldn't do it just for the hell of it, just because it was fun?"

"No, Lewis, we couldn't." She giggled again.

"It has to be love, huh?"

"That makes it *different*, Lewis." She regarded him earnestly. "It *alters* things."

"Alters things. It does?" Lewis nodded solemnly. He was aware that he was still slightly drunk, but that somewhere, at the back of his mind, a space was clearing. Quite suddenly everything she said was beginning to make sense.

"It would feel different then, would it?" he said slowly. "You know. If we . . . when I . . . when one . . ."

"I think so." The girl looked uncertain. "What do you think?"

"I don't know." Lewis sighed. "I've never been in love." The girl gave him a narrow look. "You said you were twenty-five."

"Even so."

"Lewis, you're a coldhearted seducer," she said cuttingly, and moved to the door.

"I'm not coldhearted," Lewis protested weakly. The space in his mind was still opening and opening, and he was beginning to feel wonderful.

"Yes, you are. The choice of a bathroom was definitely coldhearted."

Lewis suddenly felt stricken. He swung around as she turned the key.

"You're right! You're absolutely right! I apologize!"

"Lewis, you're drunk," she said sternly. Then smiled. "But I forgive you."

She walked out then, in a rustle of chiffon, and Lewis stared into space. From the stairway came the sound of a Viennese waltz. The sweetness of the music, and the sweetness of the new open space in his mind became one.

He looked at his watch. It was eleven, and suddenly, quite clearly, with no more evasions, he understood. He loved Helen! There it was—it was so very simple. There was nothing wrong with him after all; the confusion he had felt these past weeks had one cause and one only. He had been confused because he had refused to acknowledge this central, this wonderful, this all-important fact.

He loved her! So nothing was wrong: on the contrary—everything was right.

Halfway down the staircase, Lewis stopped. From there, he could see through into the ballroom, where, to the strains of the waltz, men and women circled and spun around the dance floor. For a little while, Lewis stood and watched them: the dresses, as bright as jewels and as

delicate as flowers; the men, who seemed to move so surely, the tails of
their black coats spinning out like the full skirts of the women's dresses.
Silver and gold, daffodil yellow, scarlet and black, blue as pale as
moonlight, rose madder. The feet of the dancing couples seemed not to
touch the floor: Lewis thought they circled like planets, they were as
lovely and as stately as stars.

Retrieving his overcoat, he bounded out of the warmth and lights of
the house into the cold glitter of a deserted Berkeley Square. He felt he
had been granted a vision. He felt he could easily walk the few miles
home. And so he did: along Piccadilly, past the shadows of Green Park,
through Knightsbridge, then south toward the river. His feet, in their
thin patent leather evening shoes, were cold, but Lewis was not conscious of that. He was hardly conscious of walking at all. Normally, that
would have meant he was drunk.

Lewis knew he wasn't. He was intoxicated, yes, but by means of
something far more powerful, much headier, than the best Bollinger he
had been drinking that evening. He felt as if the kaleidoscope of his life
had been spun, and all the pieces, all the tiny confusing fragments, had
shifted miraculously into place—the perfect, the enduring, pattern.

He let himself into the little house in Chelsea quietly. It was past
midnight, and the rooms were in darkness. Lewis pulled off his overcoat, and his scarf, and kicked off his wet shoes. In his socks, quietly,
he crept up the narrow stairs. Exultant, and simultaneously terrified, he
tried the door of Helen's room, and found it unlocked.

He opened it, and crept inside.

She was sleeping with the curtains open; the light from the moon
and the reflected light from the snow made the room bright and shadowy, as silvery as a negative of film. Stealthily, Lewis approached the
high wide brass bed, and looked down at her. The long strands of her
hair fanned out across the pillows; her lashes shadowed her cheeks; her
breathing was soft and regular; one arm lay, loose and relaxed, across the
covers. Lewis looked at the milky skin, the soft blue of the veins that
ran up from her wrist. The arm, and the shoulder he could just glimpse,
were bare. She was not wearing a nightgown.

Lewis looked at her and wondered at his own former self—at the
obstinacy, the fear, the callow stupidity he had allowed to blind him so
long. How willful he had been, and how foolish! Now, his hands
trembling, he felt for the sheet, and stealthily, gently, drew the covers
back.

The sheets were of pale pink cotton. In this light, they were the
color of mother-of-pearl. Helen's body, its curves, its peaks and its

valleys, was bleached by the light to the color of pale sand; the shadows under her breasts and between her thighs were mauve, like wisps of smoke. She stirred a little, as if the cold air on her skin were about to wake her; then she lay still again.

Lewis shuddered, from cold less than from some ecstasy of spirit. Feeling a little like a worshipper, a little like an intruder, he pulled off the rest of his clothes.

When he was naked, he climbed into the bed beside her. He lay very still, frightened to let his cold skin brush against hers, but feeling he was not cold, that his body was on fire and that his mind itself burned. He looked at her for a long time; then, very delicately, he allowed his hands to brush over her. They traced the outline of her face, brushed her lashes, brushed the moist slightly parted lips.

He let them move down, slipping his fingers around the curve of her throat, then they stole farther, to the fullness of her breasts. Her body was still, limp, and warm; its passivity, the silence, the sense of secrecy, inflamed Lewis more and more. He bent his head and pressed his lips against hers; he felt the soft warmth of her breath against his cheeks. He hesitated, then, slipping lower under the sheets, he cupped her breasts in his hands, took the rose-colored nipples between his lips, and sucked on them gently, first the one, then the other. Their softness hardened to twin points, and Lewis moaned softly. Helen did not stir, did not move.

Lewis lay on his side, daring to let his thigh press along the length of hers. He was erect, hard; he still felt as if he burned, but also as if he were dreaming. He began to stroke her again, very softly, with just the tips of his fingers, like a blind man. Over the gentle curve of her hips, he tangled his fingers in the shadowed triangle of hair in the cleft of her thighs, then slipped his hand between her thighs, where the skin felt as smooth and as soft as silk.

She stirred then, expelling her breath in a little sigh.

She moved her body slightly, as sleepers do, turning a little toward him, so her breasts brushed against his chest, and his hard penis pressed against her thighs.

Lewis's thoughts spun. He felt as if he were poised somewhere at a great height, ready to dive into deep black water; he touched her once more, his hand shaking, and it seemed he fell, down through the eye of a storm, through the still center of the cyclone of his senses. He felt for her thighs, and parted them.

It was easy to slip inside her, accomplished in one little movement, an adjustment of the hips, virtually no thrust. He was there; he stayed absolutely still, while his mind whirled and beat. It felt like union; it felt also a little like violation; and the sense, then, that the pure and the impure mixed, excited him terribly. Love and lust, the power of that combination, was not something he had ever experienced before. White blinding light, and a black heat, building: he felt his body pulse, knew he need hardly move. He pushed, very gently, once, lay still.

One more little push, wings beating in his mind, and he came. It was like a knife through an artery; as if his blood spurted and drained; a little death.

He felt himself jerk, and tremble; he was wet with sweat. He buried his face between her breasts. He heard a voice, which he supposed was his own. The voice said: *Jesus. Jesus. Jesus.*

When the pulsing stopped, he pulled out of her, and lay still. His mind swooped toward unconsciousness.

Hélène waited until she was certain he was asleep. Then she opened her eyes, and quietly put her arms around him. It had had to happen, she told herself, and she was glad she had made it happen like this.

She touched Lewis's hair. *Not a betrayal,* she thought: *more like a dream.*

I n the morning, Lewis woke first. He slipped out of the bed, crept out of the room and along the landing. In the small icy bathroom, he peed and felt like a god.

He was excited, terrified, exultant all at once. He returned to the landing and paced up and down naked, unaware of the chill. He felt as if he were transfigured, newborn. The man he had been had died a quick brief death, and in his place was a new man. This man felt as if he could do everything and anything; he was infinitely potent; he had grace; he held the world in the palm of his hand.

For this new Lewis, everything was easy—he had superhuman strength. He thought then, with a smile, of the heroes of those stolen comic books of his childhood, the heroes he had loved, the heroes who moved mountains, eliminated wickedness and defied gravity. Today he felt like them, and like them, he flew.

He returned to the little bedroom and climbed back into the bed. When he had drawn the sheets over him, Helen opened her eyes. They looked at each other.

No questions, Lewis thought. What had happened was so strange and so magical he felt questions would spoil it, and make it vanish away. But—*had she slept?* The query sped through his mind, and as if he had spoken the words, she heard his thought. Her lips curved into a slow smile.

"Last night, I dreamed—" she began.

"It wasn't a dream," Lewis interrupted eagerly. "You know it wasn't. . . ."

"No, I suppose not," she said, and though she put her arms around him then, Lewis could hear in her voice a note of regret.

I t *was* all like a dream; the next five days and nights were like a dream, Lewis thought.

It seemed to him that they sped past and yet were slow, with a hallucinatory clarity. He knew those five days would haunt him and stay with him all his life, and he was right. Always, afterward, in spite of everything, he would look back to that time and know that, then, life had been right.

For those five days, with Christmas Day itself falling on the third day, in the center of an arc of happiness, they were totally alone. Lewis took the telephone off the hook, because he did not want Thad's voice interrupting their idyll. They locked the door; no one knocked, but if anyone had, they had agreed not to answer it. They composed the days as they pleased, eating at odd hours, because they suddenly felt hungry, sleeping in the morning or the afternoon, and staying awake at night. There were no outside rhythms, Lewis felt, only the rhythm of loving and lovemaking.

On Christmas Eve, in mid-afternoon, suddenly realizing that it *was* Christmas Eve, they bundled themselves into layers of clothes, and rushed out together, hand in hand, and laughing. Since everything was possible, they went in and out of shops and found everything they needed although it was close to closing time, and Helen had predicted they would find nothing but empty shelves.

They bought a little Christmas tree, and colored baubles, and necklaces of tinsel. They bought dates and apples and grapes, chestnuts, and preserved plums in the most beautiful boxes. A turkey that would have fed twenty, and which would have to be squashed into an oven that was far too small for it. Wrapping paper, candles, a Bethlehem star, a tin of caviar, a box of red and gold crackers with mottos. And presents. Such presents! Lewis took them to Harrods in a taxi, and they found it emptying. They walked through the great halls glittering with decorations, and Lewis wanted to buy her everything in sight. He made her stand by the elevators, and stare at the wall while he rushed from department to department. A flagon of scent, in a bottle like milky rock crystal. An armful of holly and mistletoe, a bouquet of spring flowers. More armfuls of lingerie, boxes of silk and satin and handmade lace. A long necklace of pearls with a diamond clasp. A box of exquisite French soap, shaped like shells. Lewis juggled his parcels, dropped them, laughed, picked them up, and dropped them again. He felt no uncertainty now, none of the inhibition he had experienced in Rome: his taste was sure, unerring, and the cost was immaterial. When he bought a nightgown he had no idea of size, so he described Helen at length, very eloquently, waving his arms, smiling like a man possessed. The woman serving him smiled: Lewis, flushed, tousled, looked particularly handsome; she recognized a young man in the throes of love, and was patient. Black or white—the innocent, or the frankly erotic? Lewis did not care; once sure of the size, he took them both.

When he returned to the elevator area, hardly able to see above the pile of parcels in his arms, Helen was gone. He stopped dead; his heart seemed to stop with pure terror.

Then, the next second, he saw her again, coming toward him, her face also flushed, her arms also full of packages. The relief was so total that he ran to her, and—unable to take her into his arms without dropping everything—just stood there, in the middle of Harrods, while a discreet elevator man averted his gaze, saying, *Oh, my darling. Oh, my darling. . . .*

That night, they decorated the little tree. They tied it with ribbons, strung it with tinsel, hung the pretty baubles from its branches. They had closed the curtains, and lit the fire, turned on only one lamp.

In the soft warm light, the little room looked charming with its red velvet chairs, and its soft worn rugs. Lewis no longer thought of it as shabby—he no longer cared. It was not Anne Kneale's room anymore: it was theirs.

They had forgotten to buy any other food except the turkey, so they feasted on toast and caviar in front of the fire, and looked at the tree, and held hands, and talked.

Lewis knew words were inadequate, but he tried very hard to explain to her how he felt: how, all his life, he had been frightened of failing, and trying to find an alternative route. How he had tried to be what his parents wanted, and then what he wanted, and then what his friends wanted, and finally, what Thad wanted. And now, suddenly, all that was unimportant, because now he could be himself.

"I love you," Lewis said. He buried his face in her lap. "I love you. I love you. I love you."

She bent her head, and kissed his hair. She stroked him gently, like a mother comforting a child. And Lewis felt guilty. He felt he had to confess to her. He poured it all out, the horrible person he had been. The wine, the women, the parties, the confusion. How he had hated it and pretended he liked it, and how he now wished that it had never happened, because he wasn't good enough for her, and he wanted to be.

"That's not true, Lewis," she said. "Please don't believe it. Please don't think it. Lewis—come to bed."

The next day they spent a great many hours cooking that monster of a turkey. Since they had forgotten to buy potatoes, or any other vegetables, they ate it with sweet corn, a can of which they discovered in a cupboard. It tasted delicious. They drank a bottle and a half of a fine Burgundy—Lewis had not forgotten that—and then, feeling a little tipsy, they went for a walk, through deserted streets and along the side of the smooth-flowing river. *Sweet Thames*, Lewis murmured, fragments of that expensive education remaining with him. He caught her hand, and swung it.

She stopped, and looked down at the water. She wondered if what she was doing was wrong, but the thought seemed to her to have no reality. Things happened; you could only control them so much. The wine she had drunk seemed to flow through her mind, lulling it; the slow movement of the river itself was hypnotic. She fixed her eyes on one twig, watched it being carried downriver. The tidal pull was very strong, and she found that comforting.

"I lived near a river once." She pressed Lewis's hand. "It's cold. Let's go home."

They went home. Lit the fire, closed the curtains, locked the door. A make-believe world, Lewis thought, and smiled, liking the idea. They made it, and they believed in it. Nothing else mattered.

They opened their presents in front of the fire. She had bought him a tie, and a scarf, a black leather billfold, a box of linen handkerchiefs, a silk shirt that was the right collar size, and a bottle of Armagnac. She tipped these presents into Lewis's lap, her eyes wide and nervous, as if she were terrified he would scorn them or find them inadequate.

Lewis, who knew she had had no money in Paris, and that the amount she had been paid so far for the film was very little, was deeply touched. He unwrapped each one, slowly and carefully, and she watched him like an anxious child, her hands darting out occasionally to touch a box, to pull at a piece of stubborn wrapping paper. When all the presents had been opened, they knelt, looking at each other. Their laps, and the rug, were strewn with lace and silk and torn paper and shiny ribbons.

"Do you like them? Are they all right? Oh, Lewis. It's hard to buy a man presents. . . ." She glanced at him shyly, stroked the things that lay on her lap. "These are so beautiful, and what I chose is so dull. I would have liked—"

She broke off, and Lewis reached across and took her hand. He wanted to say that only one gift mattered to him then—that if she said she loved him, too, he would have everything he wanted in life. But it seemed wrong, and ungracious, almost unnecessary anyway. He thought, looking into her wide eyes, that she understood.

"My darling." He bent and pressed his lips into the soft palm of her hand. "My darling."

Later, he persuaded her to dress up in some of the things he had chosen. They drank some of the Armagnac, and it became like a marvelous, and for Lewis, arousing game. Palest pink silk shimmering against her skin. Lace that revealed the creamy curves of her breasts. The pearls wound around her throat. A white nightgown of silk through which he could glimpse the darkness of her nipples, the shadowed triangle of her pubic hair. Lewis's body hardened and stirred; he lay back, watching her. She slipped the white nightgown off, and pulled on the black one.

It transformed her; but, he saw, she had also the power to transform herself. She changed, too, with her costumes. The planes of her face seemed to Lewis to alter, so that, a young girl a moment before, she now looked older, a woman. He stared at her, mesmerized: her lips seemed to him fuller, her eyes darker and wider, almost black; she seemed not to move at all, and yet her very stance altered; there was a new erotic jut to her breasts. She looked down at him; Lewis knew the thrust of his erection was obvious; she smiled. She knelt down and began to whisper to him, and as she did so, she changed her voice. Lewis listened in astonishment; her eyes were amused, and he knew she was teasing him, that somewhere, inside, she was the same woman, the same Helen. But just for a moment he could not believe it; she changed herself before his eyes, and he found it almost unbearably erotic, as if he were being tempted, not by one woman, but by many. It aroused him, and it also frightened him a little. He touched her face, held it between his hands, and drew it around so he could look into her eyes.

"Helen? How do you do that? I didn't know you could . . ."

She smiled. "It's a trick I have. I have lots of voices. I have a good ear, that's all." She paused. "I can have an English voice—several English voices. A French one. An Italian one. American ones . . ." She glanced down, her lashes brushing her cheeks. "I can have a southern voice—I can have your voice, I think."

Lewis laughed. "Mine? I don't believe it."

"Listen." She frowned, concentrating. Then she said a few sentences, and Lewis listened, amazed, to Helen speaking his tongue. The clipped Bostonian vowels, a slightly arrogant nasal flatness. Lewis gripped her arms, and gave her a gentle shake. "Stop that. You've convinced me. You're seducing me in my own voice, and I don't like it. It's disturbing."

She stopped instantly. Her color rose, and she looked up at him. When she next spoke, it was with her own voice.

"Is that what I'm doing, Lewis? Seducing you?"

"No, of course not. I didn't mean that. I was just teasing." He went to embrace her, and then something serious and intent in her face stopped him. She lifted her hand and pressed her fingers against his lips.

"I don't want to pretend, Lewis. I don't. I want you to know me as I am. I want to be truthful, Lewis—" She stopped, her eyes wide, her mouth trembling a little, so Lewis suddenly felt an overwhelming protectiveness toward her, an intense and gentle love. He drew her to him, and held her close. He kissed her hair, and her face, and her closed eyes. His Helen. He felt quite certain he knew her, as certain as he was that he loved her. He slipped the black silk over her head, and tossed it to one side. Then he drew her down onto the floor, and in front of the fire, amid the wrappings and the presents, he made love to her. This time, for the first time, she clung to him tightly when he came, and covered his face with shy kisses.

He took her upstairs, lifting her easily in his arms, slid her into the bed, and under the sheets, where it was warm. Then he climbed in beside her, wanting her again, and made love to her again. Before, he had sensed some resistance in her; like a fine strong strand of gossamer, it would not give. This time, to Lewis's wonderment and pride, it snapped. She cried out once, though not his name.

In the morning, the fourth morning, she woke first. Lewis opened his eyes and found her looking down, gently, into his face. He reached for her sleepily, and drew her warm body into his arms, holding her gently and with a sense of happy possession. She waited until she was sure that he was quite awake, then she pressed her slender hands either side of his face, and turned him so he looked at her.

Then, gently, gravely, faltering only a little, but clearly afraid, she told him the truth. She was pregnant.

The baby was due in May. She had seen a doctor, and that was what he had said. She would never, could never, she said, see the baby's father again. It was over, and she never wanted to talk about it. Lewis stared at her in utter stupefaction. He looked down into her face; he looked at the gentle curve of her stomach.

He walked out of the bedroom, leaving her there, went downstairs, looked at the little Christmas tree, wan in the morning light, and wept.

He felt betrayed, of course. He felt also the most raging and acutely painful jealousy. It physically affected him, as if knives were being dug into his flesh, as if something monstrous were tearing him apart. Who? What man? What was his name, and what did he look like? Lewis felt he wanted to see that man, to know him, to confront him face to face, and then fight with him. Had she loved him? Had he loved her? What had he done to her? How, how often, where?

Sexual jealousy is never a dignified emotion. It is ugly and its banality is inescapable. Lewis knew his thoughts were banal and crude, and that fact made the pain worse. Both what he knew and what he did not know tormented him. He looked around the little room, and wanted to cry out, to break things, to howl and to smash blindly.

He leapt to his feet and ran up the stairs. He flung back the door, lifted her in his arms, shook her.

"Tell me you love me. Just tell me that. Tell me that, and I swear, I swear, nothing else matters. . . ."

He could hardly believe it was his voice speaking, this voice which choked on the emotion he felt.

"I care for you, Lewis." She sounded frightened. "I care for you very much."

He wanted to hit her then. *Care* was such a little word. A tiny inadequate pathetic word. He hated her for using it. He lifted his hand, and almost struck her. Then he let it fall, slammed out of the room, slammed back down the stairs, feeling like a fool, feeling like an animal.

He paced up and down the room, back and forth, up and down. He tried to think, to compose his mind, and it went on howling its pain at him. He decided to get drunk, poured out a tumbler of Armagnac, took one swallow, then went into the kitchen and tipped the rest down the sink. He searched for cigarettes, found three empty packets, and one full one, inhaled the nicotine, and felt it calm him, just a little. Then he sat down and stared at the Christmas tree and made himself think.

Anyone familiar with the charity and masochism of intense love— and Lewis was both intensely in love and naturally kind—would be able to predict the course of his thoughts. They were predictable even to Lewis himself. First forgiveness. Then, after a period of further raging, excuses. There his mind became extraordinarily creative. Suddenly he could think of a thousand reasons, a million, why this should have happened, and why Helen had acted as she did. The man had duped her, used her. Maybe she had loved him, but he must have rejected her, because otherwise she would be with him. Maybe she hadn't loved him after all—that lifted his heart for a second. He leapt up from his seat, found a calendar, and began to count weeks like a madman. The time she left them in Paris, those weeks, he decided. Then. And she had come back to them then, of her own accord: he felt his hope soaring. Forgiveness turned to pity. He remembered how ill she had looked sometimes in Rome. He remembered standing outside her bedroom door at the *palazzo*, and hearing her weeping. She must have been so afraid, so lonely. At once she seemed to him brave, to have kept her fears to herself. He felt admiration for such strength, fury with himself for being so obtuse, so unnoticing. In a second, pity had winged into love, love into protectiveness. She had turned to *him*. She had told *him*.

He looked around the little room, and saw it again with yesterday's eyes.

Lewis sat there two hours altogether. At the end of that time, exhausted, cold, unable to force his mind to think anymore, he knew only one thing with any certainty. He loved her. There it was.

Lewis went back up the stairs. She had not moved. Her face was pale and swollen, and he thought she had been crying. Awkwardly and gently, Lewis sat down on the bed and took her hand.

Then, because he didn't know what else to do, he asked her to marry him.

She sat very still. Lewis lifted his face to hers, and clasped her hand.

"Please," he said. "I love you. I wanted to marry you anyway. I've been thinking about it every day since—" He broke off. "The baby doesn't make any difference. Why should it? I'll look after you and I'll look after the baby. I want to, Helen. Please, say you'll marry me. I can't bear this. I'm going mad."

Hélène felt terribly afraid. She could see Lewis had been crying; the expression on his face made him look very young, almost like a boy, and for a moment she saw them both, herself and Lewis, as if from far away: two frightened children, clinging to each other for support.

She was absolutely certain then, for a brief second, that she should refuse. Then she thought of the baby, and how it would be, trying to work, trying to bring up a child on her own. She could see how it would be; the picture was hideously clear in her mind. *I won't let my baby live like that*, she thought, and, taking Lewis's hand, she said "yes."

On the sixth day, Thad arrived from Paris, unannounced. He hammered at the door, and came in, bustling. Thad came—and the world came with him.

Lewis, still in bed, exhausted by his lovemaking, heard Helen open the door to him, heard his voice, and groaned.

"Don't tell me," he said when she came back into the room. "He couldn't get through on the phone, so he's come in person."

"That's right." She was putting on some clothes. She did not look around.

"I'm going to tell him." Lewis threw back the covers and bounced out of bed, suddenly purposeful. He grabbed her from behind, and hugged her.

"Now?"

"Why not? He has to know, sooner or later. Everyone does. And I want them to know. I want the world to know. I feel like shouting it from the rooftops."

"I suppose so. It's just—I'm a little afraid of Thad." Something in her face made Lewis pause. He remembered the scene on location that last day in Trastevere. It had never been explained, never even referred to again. However, now was not the moment to start asking questions about that; it was probably nothing of any importance, and she would explain it to him another time.

In that supposition he was wrong, but, that morning, nothing could shake his confidence, not even Thad. He kissed her, aware that the complicity between them, which excluded Thad, gave him pleasure. He began to look forward with relish to the moment when he broke the news, when he saw the surprise register on Thad's face.

In this ambition he was disappointed. He broke the news to Thad with sly charm, his arm around Helen's waist. Thad blinked once, twice, three times—that was all. He continued to sit still, nursing a mug of tea in his plump lap. Hardly missing a beat, he said amiably, "Hey. That's great. When?"

It was Lewis who blushed, to his own annoyance. He suddenly realized that the way he had said it—Helen is having a baby; we're going to get married—it sounded as if he were the father. His own impetuousity, his perverse desire to score off his friend, had now precipitated them into a very awkward situation indeed. Thad was looking at him imperturbably. Lewis threw him a smile.

"Which? The wedding, or the baby?"

"Both, I guess." Thad took a sip of tea.

"The wedding—as soon as possible. And the baby . . ."

"In the spring," she finished quietly, and Lewis felt a quiet glow of triumph; she had taken her cue from him. The sense of pleasurable complicity intensified.

"Terrific. That's really terrific." Thad put down the tea and stood up. "I'm really glad for you both. Now—about the movie. Or maybe I should say *movies*." He gave a little smile, and his voice took on a wounded note. "There have been *developments*, you know. I've been trying to get you two on the phone for *days*. . . ."

Lewis and Helen exchanged glances. The telephone, Lewis saw, was now back on its cradle. He hoped she had put it there unobtrusively: Thad didn't miss much.

He and Helen sat down, and Thad began to pace up and down, waving his arms. He launched into one of his monologues. The editing on *Night Game* was nearly finished. He had a rough cut; Truffaut had seen it. Various other friends in Paris had seen it. They had all been knocked out. . . .

Thad was never modest; he saw no need to be now. The way he

talked about it, *Night Game* was going to be like *Citizen Kane*: it was going to change people's ideas about cinema overnight. It was going to establish his reputation at a stroke, and—unlike the Welles picture—it was going to be an immediate box-office success. . . .

Lewis listened to this, his attention starting to wander. He had heard Thad hold forth about his own work in this vein before, and had been impressed by it. But that had been in Los Angeles, when they first met. In Rome, he had had his doubts when he watched Thad at work; now, they returned to him. Really, Thad laid it on a bit thick. Did he realize how absurd he sounded? He would reserve judgment, Lewis decided, until he actually saw the film, and saw what happened to it. Meanwhile, Thad sounded boastful, and, as usual, his monomania made him untactful. He had not mentioned Helen's performance once so far, and that oversight irritated Lewis. He glanced at her, and their eyes met. With a sense of satisfaction, Lewis decided she was of the same opinion as himself.

"Now . . ." Thad had turned to the subject of Henri Lebec. Henri Lebec was a rich, homosexual, indolent young Frenchman, heir to the considerable fortune his father had made bottling mineral water. Lebec saw himself as a patron of the arts, and hung around with a lot of film people. Thad had met him through Truffaut, and it was Lebec who, together with Lewis, had put up the money for *Night Game*. Fifty thousand dollars each. Lewis sighed. If *Night Game* died, he would lose that money—but then, he could stand the loss, and so could Lebec. He had been prepared from the first to lose it.

Lewis, who had always had more money than he needed, never thought about it a great deal. He had been prepared to gamble on Thad, and to help him, but if Thad was leading up to a suggestion of further investment in some new project, Lewis knew he intended to refuse. One loss, yes; but he was not profligate and he was not a fool. And from now on, his financial circumstances would be very different. He would have a wife to look after—and the baby.

It became gradually clear, however, that this was not Thad's drift. Thad was now talking about money, quite big money, but it wasn't Lewis's, or Henri Lebec's.

"So the thing is . . ." he was saying, "the word is out. And the distribution deals on *Night Game* are just *falling* into place. Like, suddenly, everyone wants it. We're *hot*. Truffaut thinks I ought to enter it for Cannes. We might even get American release—limited, you know— movie theaters near campuses, a few art houses in New York, that kind of thing. But it's a start. I mean, we could win the fucking Palme d'Or at Cannes and it wouldn't mean a goddamned thing back in L.A., but if we get an American showing, and some good returns, that will mean something. Then we make one more picture in Europe—I'm thinking about London—and then we go back to America with the third. Then we stay there, of course. We won't need to piss around in Europe then. But if we get this backing, the whole process can be speeded up, that's the point. Film Three can be big. And Film *Four* can be—"

"Backing? What backing?" Lewis interrupted testily, and Thad turned around to him, looking injured.

"You haven't been *listening*, Lewis. I just *told* you. . . ."

"Tell me again. I didn't quite grasp it the first time."

"Okay." Thad sighed, sat down again, and adopted a patient tone of voice. "There's this distribution company called Sphere. It's an American distribution company, right? You've got that, Lewis? It was in a bad way, but it's been *bought*. By Partex Petrochemicals."

He produced this name—with which Lewis, a banker's son, was familiar—in the manner of a conjurer producing a rabbit from a hat.

"And?"

"And Partex has big plans for Sphere. They're pouring money into it, Lewis. Oil money. They're expanding the distribution side as of now, and they're going to launch a production financing arm. They want to back independent films. *My* films." Thad gave a smug little smile. "They're smart. They've seen the falling attendance figures in America. They know all about the effect of TV—who doesn't? And they aren't fazed. Because they think, and I *know*, that there's a whole new audience out there, just waiting to to be tapped. The youth audience, Lewis. The ones who are sick to death of watching reruns of *Gunsmoke* every night, the ones who are going to start pouring back into the movie theaters once someone is smart enough to give them the right *product*. Movies that talk to *them*. Not Jane Russell and dancing girls and all that studio crap. Real movies. American movies. The kind of movies I make."

"You've only made one so far."

"Lewis. Lewis. Please. I'm being serious now. . . ."

"Okay. Okay." Lewis shrugged. "And you're saying this company—Sphere—they might want to back you?"

"They want in on the distribution of *Night Game*, and they're talking money about Film Two right now. Not six-figure money, Lewis, seven-figure. We're not talking small time now."

"Uh-huh." Lewis leaned back. Thad's blithe confidence was irritating him more and more. He longed, suddenly, to puncture it. All right, so Thad had always claimed not to understand the complexities of finance—he was just the *director*, he used to say, back in L.A.; that was where Lewis came in; he needed Lewis because Lewis understood figures.

Lewis did, up to a point. He had lived with high finance day in, day out, for the first eighteen years of his life. He could read a balance sheet, sure. He used to read *The Wall Street Journal,* and then face his father's inquisition on its subject matter. He had taken an economics course at Harvard—though that had been mostly theoretical. If he had gone into Sinclair Lowell Watson, he would have been painstakingly trained by his father, and Lewis had always grandly assumed that he would have been more than able to cope. But film finance? That was a minefield. He had listened to the talk in L.A., carefully. In Paris, before it was decided to keep *Night Game* very low budget, and finance it through Lebec and himself, he had briefly, with the aid of Lebec and various contacts of Thad's, tried to raise outside financing, bigger financing, for the picture.

It had been like juggling bubbles. A lot of wheeling, and a lot of dealing. Tax shelter deals. Completion bond deals. Overhead provisions. By the time Lewis felt he was beginning to grasp it, he realized that the people he'd been talking to were not going to deliver. One by one the bubbles had burst.

Rather admiring his own experienced cynicism, he now remarked that the fact that Sphere was talking money meant precisely nothing. When they signed a deal, and, better still, a check—then, he said with a glance at Helen, he might start getting impressed.

Thad looked hurt. "I guess you're right, Lewis," he said in a small humble voice, so Lewis began to feel like a bully. "I don't understand these things too well. I never did. I mean, the guy I met from Sphere— he'd take one look, and he'd know I was a sucker, right?"

"Well, not exactly, Thad." Lewis shifted uneasily. "You could be right. They could be serious. If they made the first move . . ." He hesitated. "How come they heard about us in the first place?"

Thad looked complacent. "They've got their ear to the ground, I guess. There's a lot of interesting work being done in Europe right now, and I'm American. Maybe they picked up on the word about *Night Game.* I don't know. But when this guy Scher saw the rough cut of *Night Game,* he said he liked it a lot. He was just being polite, I guess. Didn't want to hurt my feelings . . ."

"Oh, come on, Thad." Lewis leaned forward. "Are you trying to make me weep, or what? If he said he liked it, he probably did. It's just that that's not the same as writing you a big fat check for the next film, carte blanche, that's all. . . ."

"I know that, Lewis. Now that I think about it. And I never thought it would be carte blanche exactly. . . ." He stole a little look at Helen. A little look at Lewis. Spread his hands.

"Maybe you see, now, Lewis, why I had to come over. I need you back in Paris. I need your help. I can't handle all this without you, Lewis." He gave a gusty sigh. "Still. I suppose I'll have to try. For a while." He gestured at Helen. "Now that all this has happened. Yes?"

Lewis bowed his head. He knew what that meant, and the meekness of Thad's manner did not deceive him for an instant. It meant Thad wouldn't be satisfied until he had Lewis on a plane at the earliest opportunity. Until he did, he would simply sit there and not go away. Lewis looked at Helen; she looked at him. He knew she was thinking the same thing. To Lewis's relief, she spoke first.

"When do you want him, Thad?" she asked.

Thad looked at his fingernails. He said, in a little voice, "How about tomorrow?"

When Thad had gone—he needed to buy some clothes, he said, which had surprised both of them—they discussed this new development. In a way, as she said, it wasn't a new development at all, because they had both known that once Thad finished editing, Lewis would have to re-join him, and throw himself fully into the role that Thad had assigned him. The moment had just arrived a little sooner than expected, that was all.

"You could come with me," Lewis said, putting his arms around her. "If it's not safe for you to fly, we could go over on the boat. Let's do that. Thad can't object, and if he does, I'll tell him to go to hell. I want you with me. I can't bear not to be with you, not now. . . ."

He buried his face against her neck and kissed her. It was she who pointed out the problems of this plan, and who gently dissuaded him. They went into the sitting room, and sat down on the fat red chairs, and talked it all over, back and forth.

The reasonableness of their discussion pleased Lewis: he felt they were both being very adult. Yes, he could see it—he would be tied up with a whole lot of meetings, and Helen wouldn't see him that much anyway. Paris was an hour's flight from London. Whenever there was a gap in the schedule, Lewis could fly back. Helen would be better off staying here, in many ways. It was quiet and calm, and she liked it. She could rest, look after herself and the baby. . . . Here, having felt again that sweet and reassuring sense of complicity, Lewis paused, then broke off. They looked at each other. She took his hand.

"He thinks it's your baby, Lewis," she said finally.

"I know he does." Lewis shrugged. "So what? It's none of Thad's business, either way. It's private. It's you and me and what we decide, what we feel, that matters."

"It's just that it happened so quickly. I didn't know what to say. And we hadn't decided—what we'd tell people."

Lewis could see the uncertainty and the vulnerability in her face. As it always did, it renewed his self-confidence, his sense of protectiveness.

The more vulnerable Helen seemed, the stronger Lewis felt—this seemed to him entirely proper.

"My darling." He bent across, and kissed her. "I love you. We're going to be married. I'll take care of you and the baby. So, in a sense, it *will* be my baby. It *is* my baby. I'll try and be a good father. I like babies. . . ." He smiled. "I'm terrific with my sisters' kids—you ask them, they'll tell you. I'm an uncle six times over already." He tried to lighten his voice, to cheer her up, but in spite of himself, his face grew serious.

"I mean it," he went on awkwardly. "It's not too easy to say. Other people wouldn't understand. Thad wouldn't. So in a way it's better if they don't know. It's just something *we* know. Our secret. I don't want other people poking into our lives, dirtying things. If we understand what we're doing, and if we trust each other . . . if we love each other."

There! He had risked it. Lewis looked at Helen anxiously. Her face softened; her eyes seemed to change from blue to gray, as they did when she was moved or touched. She lifted her hand and pressed it against Lewis's face. "I'm not sure we ought to begin with a lie," she said gently. "That's all."

"It isn't a lie!" Lewis grasped her hands. He felt himself blaze with the most passionate conviction. "It's *our* truth. That's different."

She looked at him. She heard the emotion in his voice, and she could see the intensity in his eyes. She liked Lewis's eyes. They had candor—too much candor sometimes, for it was easy to know what Lewis felt, and that made him vulnerable. Sometimes Lewis reminded her of some medieval figure, a knight riding out to do battle, blissfully unaware that while he was armed with a sword, his enemies were equipped with machine guns. This she perceived as a danger, but briefly. If Lewis girded himself for battle, he did so on her behalf, and she found that flattering. Also, he wanted her to agree with him, wanted it passionately, and she was already used to hiding her doubts and her qualifications from men. Most men, she felt instinctively, were like Ned Calvert: they didn't want to hear them.

She bent her head and agreed.

Lewis leapt to his feet, instantly full of plans. He would telephone from Paris every night. He would fly home at every opportunity. He would handle Thad. All would be well—now and forever. Meanwhile, they would have this evening, this special night. They would be alone. They would go out to dinner at the Caprice, his favorite restaurant. . . . He picked up the telephone and reserved a table for two at eight o'clock.

At seven-thirty that evening, when it became clear to both of them that Thad had not only returned, but that there was no way he was leaving, Lewis made another call and changed the reservation. Still eight o'clock, yes. But for three people.

"He's not staying the goddamn night. That's all. He is not staying."
Helen and Lewis had retreated to the kitchen. Thad was stuck like a limpet to the sofa in the small sitting room. It was now midnight. He had said virtually nothing all through dinner, and had guzzled snails in such a disgusting manner, dripping garlic and butter everywhere, that Lewis had been scarlet with embarrassment. When their taxi had arrived at the Caprice, Thad had climbed in first, before a word had been said. For the past hour he had been sitting by the fire, drinking cups of tea. He was wearing the new clothes he had bought. From the kitchen, Helen and Lewis could see him, squarely in the middle of the room, humming a little tune, and staring into the middle distance. He looked, Lewis thought, completely ludicrous.

First, he had had a haircut, and the beard had been trimmed. Second, the glasses were not bleary as usual, but polished, sparkling and winking against the light. Third, the greasy jeans, the sweaty shirt, the scuffed shoes, the nylon socks that always gave off a perceptible fishy odor, had all disappeared. Thad appeared to have bathed, and he was wearing a suit.

It was not a suit in the sense that Lewis's were. What Thad had on his back in no way resembled those masterpieces of understatement that Lewis possessed, one of which he was wearing now. But a suit it definitely was. A black three-piece suit. The pants just about encased Thad's fat thighs, and the buttons of the vest strained only just percepti-bly across Thad's ample belly. The pants were too short; where they cut off at the ankles it was possible to glimpse short black woolen socks; he wore lace-up black shoes, which twinkled with polish. Lewis, glancing back through the door, groaned aloud.

"Shhh." Helen smiled. "He'll hear you."

"I don't give a damn. He's going. One more cup of tea and that's *it*. He's had three already."

"Shall I tell him, or you?"

"I shall tell him," Lewis said firmly. "I shall do it right now. Watch."

He marched back into the sitting room, Helen behind him, pushed the mug of tea into Thad's pudgy hand—the fingernails were newly clean, Lewis observed—and looked down at him sternly.

"You can have that, Thad, then you have to go."

"Go?" Thad blinked. He looked at the sofa. "Oh, I thought maybe . . ."

"You thought wrong. Tea, and then out. Helen and I want to be alone. This is our last night together."

Lewis felt proud of himself. Thad looked up at him, and his glasses winked and blinked.

"Oh, sure. Right. Okay. No problem. Dumb of me. I should have thought . . ." He paused. "I just wondered, maybe, on the couch, you know . . ."

"No, Thad. Not on the couch. Nowhere. Okay?"

"Okay."

Thad capitulated with good grace. Lewis sat down opposite him, and drew Helen down beside him. He lit a Marlboro, inhaled, and looked at Thad with disbelief. Why a suit? A black suit, of all things.

"I've been thinking . . ." Thad began, and Lewis frowned. That was never a good beginning; it usually heralded a monologue. Lewis felt that if he had to listen to one of them right now, he'd go crazy.

"Fine, Thad, but keep it brief, yes?"

"Sure. Sure." Thad waved a pudgy hand. "But this is important. It concerns you, Lewis. And Helen. Because it's Helen I've been thinking about. The thing is, we need to think about this, and we need to start now. We've got to decide—how we *present* her. Especially when we get back to America. It's key. We need a *strategy*. Did I ever tell you about Grace Kelly—when she went to Hollywood?"

"Not that I recall."

"Well, you know what she did? Every director she went to see, every producer, she wore white gloves. White gloves, for fuck's sake! Like, don't touch *me*, right? Like, I am *class*, you get it? And they went wild. Just *wild*, Lewis. Those white gloves—all the parties—no one could talk about anything else except this incredibly beautiful classy girl who wore white gloves. So—what we need to decide is—what is going to be Helen's white gloves? What is her equivalent, right? Because, of course, something like white gloves, you can't do it twice."

"I could wear black gloves."

Helen's voice held not a trace of sarcasm. It was beautifully judged; Lewis laughed, and it took Thad about forty seconds to realize it was a putdown. He grinned sheepishly, but hardly drew breath.

"The thing is, a lot of it's *right*. The marriage is good. I like the marriage. I mean you, Lewis—old money, Groton, Harvard, for God's sake. All those pricks out there, with their itchy fingers, well, they'll think twice once she's married to you. That's great. That's terrific. Because we want them to get it straight, this woman has class, this woman is beautiful, and this woman is one hundred percent *not* available. That's crucial. I mean, really crucial."

"Well, she isn't available. She'll be married to me. So that's all right, isn't it?"

"Lewis. Lewis. Please." Thad stood up and waved his hands. "We are not talking about facts now. We are talking about *image*. If Helen is going to be in our films, she has to have the right image. . . ."

"If?" Lewis looked up quickly; beside him, he had felt her tense.

"Why the 'if' suddenly? You told me we were a team. You. Me. Helen. It was the perfect combination, or so you said. If you remember, you gave me a long lecture on the subject of triangles."

"Did I?" Thad looked crafty. "I may have said something about that. I said the best films always have a triangular structure. That's true. It's something I've observed."

"So you said. You gave me a long list. It started way back in prehistory, worked its way through *The Third Man* and *Gone With the Wind*, and—"

"Not *Gone With the Wind*. I never said that. *Gone With the Wind* is a bummer. . . ."

"And you went on to say, some hours later—once you had explained that the studio system was finished, dying on its feet, that the independent director, i.e. you, was going to be the savior of the American cinema—you went on to say that he needed a team. He needed an independent producer, and he needed a star. A woman, you said. That was the perfect basic structure. If we got that right, you said, there was nothing we couldn't do—nothing. As I remember."

Thad blinked furiously. He shifted about from one foot to the other, and glared at Lewis. Lewis smiled. He knew the reason for that glare. Thad did not want Helen to know, yet, the extent of his ambitions for her. They should let her realize it gradually. That way they could control her.

Now Helen leaned forward. She frowned, looking at Thad. "A star? Is that what you said? Is that what you thought?"

"Maybe. Maybe. Who knows? Lots of people get to be stars." Thad looked at her dismissively.

"A legend, you said," Lewis threw in, coolly compounding his own treachery.

"Well, legends don't just happen. Legends are *made*," Thad snapped. "Which just happens to be what I'm talking about. Or trying to talk about. The point is, Helen's not right. Not yet. There's a lot of work to do."

He paused, then puffed back to his chair, sat down, and took one very small sip of his brimming tea. Lewis was about to interrupt again. Then he realized that Thad now had Helen's attention. Her eyes were fixed on his face, and she looked, Lewis thought, as if Thad were Moses just down from the mount, and about to start reading out the Ten Commandments.

"There's a lot of work to do." Thad, sensing her interest, gave a little giggle. "Face. Hair. Makeup. Clothes. We've got to have you in the right stuff. Classy stuff. Couture—you know. I want you to look like a woman, not some teenager. I want to look at you and think—money. I want every man who comes to your movies to get a hard-on when he looks at you on screen. I want them to think, God, I'd do anything to have that woman, but I'd never get her, because she's too cool, too classy, and too expensive. . . ."

"Now, wait a minute . . ." Lewis leaned forward angrily. Thad sailed on as if he hadn't spoken.

"I want sex, right? The kind of sex that drives men crazy. So, like, they're in bed with their wives or girlfriends or whatever and they're fantasizing about you. Only all the time they *know* it's a fantasy, because there's no come-on from you at all. And why? Because you look pure. You look so fucking pure it's driving them nuts. It's classic. The ultimate female paradox, right? Artemis and Aphrodite, the virgin and the whore . . ."

"That's it." Lewis stood up. His voice shook with anger. "You can get out of here, Thad, and you can get out right now. I'm not going to listen to that kind of filth, and Helen isn't either."

Thad blinked, and did not move. He looked genuinely astonished. As well he might, Lewis thought guiltily. He had heard much of this before, and never objected.

"I'm sorry, Lewis. Hey—Helen—you're not offended? I'm just tossing ideas around now, explaining the *background*. I'm not talking *literally*. I don't mean you're really a whore, and I know you're not a virgin. . . ."

"*Thad* . . . one more word, just one more word, and I swear . . ."

"Lewis. Lewis. Calm down, will you?" Thad took another swallow of tea. "I'll come to the point, right? Helen, you want me to explain? It won't take long. It's *important* . . . ."

"It's all right, Lewis." She looked at Thad steadily. "Why don't you be more specific?"

"Okay." He held up a pudgy hand, and Lewis sat down. Thad began to itemize on his fingers. "One: the voice. It's good, but it's not good enough. It's too identifiable. Too crisp. Too English. I don't want that. I want something more mysterious. . . . Think Garbo. Think Dietrich. Like, it sounds great—and why? You can't pin them down. They're talking English, and they're not English. . . ."

"Well, obviously they aren't fucking well English," Lewis exploded. "One is Swedish, and the other is German. What's so goddamn mysterious about that?"

"Lewis. Lewis. Trust me, will you? You know they're Swedish. You know they're German. But all those people out there in the dark— they don't know that, and if they do, they're not thinking about it. They're just thinking that she's different, this woman. She's foreign. Exotic. Mysterious . . ."

"If you say that word one more time, I'll throw up. For God's sake, Thad . . ."

"I know what he means." Helen spoke quietly. "He's talking about power. The power you have when you're different. When people can't place you, sum you up . . ."

"That's power?" Lewis looked at her uncertainly.

"Sometimes. I think so. Yes."

Thad watched this exchange with interest. Then he leaned forward. "So—all I'm saying is this. I want Helen to work on the voice. Between now and the next movie. I want it darker, with an edge. A bit less innocent. Keep the purity, but try and blur the accent a little. Mix in a little French or Italian, a suggestion of Europe. Some American . . ."

"It sounds like a bad cocktail." Lewis turned to her. He could hardly believe it, but she seemed to be taking this seriously. "Why don't you try some of your voices on Thad, darling? Show off your accents. He has no idea of your repertoire. . . ."

The minute the words were out, Lewis regretted them. Helen blushed scarlet. Thad hummed, looked up at the ceiling, and then down at the floor.

"He knows already." She spoke in a small flat voice.

"Oh, he does? Since when?"

"Rome, sometime. We talked voices then, briefly."

Thad interrupted. He sounded bored. "Look—I want to move on. Helen knows what I mean, and she knows I'm right. There're more important things to discuss. One, in particular."

"Oh? Only one?" Lewis was now feeling furiously angry. Yet again, as he had in Rome, he felt excluded. He also felt jealous. He stood up. "I mean—why stop at one? I'm sure there're a million helpful little hints Thad could come up with. If we're going to alter Helen's voice, which I happen to think is a beautiful voice just the way it is—why not alter a few other things as well? How about cutting off her hair? Or dying it? How about plastic surgery? How about . . ."

"The name," Thad said with a sudden firmness. "We have to do something about the name. I don't like it."

"Which name?" Lewis rounded on him belligerently. "Helen Craig, or Helen Sinclair? Which is, I might just remind you, Thad, what's she's going to be called very soon."

"Both of them," Thad answered irritatingly. "They both sound English. Ordinary. Dull. I don't like Helen. I don't like Craig. And Sinclair is a bummer."

"Thanks."

"No offense. It's great for a banker. Really, Lewis, just great. But for a movie star, it sucks. Now . . ." He drummed his fingers on his fat thighs. "Let's just go over this. Think. Like—Greta Garbo—two G's right? Marilyn Monroe. Two M's. This new French bimbo, Brigitte Bardot—two B's, and in French it sounds like *bébé*—clever, huh?"

"I'm thinking about them." Lewis returned to his chair and sat down. "I'm also thinking about Carole Lombard. Bette Davis. Katharine Hepburn. Gina Lollobrigida. Marlene Dietrich. They all seem to have gotten by okay without the same initials. . . ."

"I give you that. I'm not laying down the law here. Just making suggestions—you know."

The two men looked at each other. Helen stood up. Her color had risen. She stood there quietly, and both men, suddenly guiltily aware that they had been wrangling over her as if she were not present, fell silent.

"I was christened Hélène. It's on my passport, if you remember, Lewis." She hesitated. "My mother always called me that. She liked it pronounced that way. She said . . . she said that it sounded like a sigh."

There was silence in the room. Lewis saw that her hands trembled slightly, and it seemed to cost her considerable effort to say this. Thad was looking at her intently, his expression unreadable.

"Hélène," he said at last. "That's interesting." The small dark eyes flicked up to her face, and then away. "And it was your mother who called you that?"

"Always."

"Uh-huh." He gave a little secretive smile. Helen glanced at him, as if something in his tone were curious, but Thad said nothing more. He began to hum tunelessly, as he often did when he was thinking. It was some bars before Lewis recognized *The Marseillaise*.

"Also . . ." She went on stiffly. "I grew up in a village called Hartland. I always liked that name. I don't know if . . ."

Lewis looked at her in astonishment. He didn't understand why she was going along with all this, why she didn't protest. She seemed even to like the idea of a new name, a new identity. He was just about to start protesting again, when Thad looked up. The light glinted on his shiny spectacles.

"Hart." He said. "Hartland's too long. Hart. No, Harte with an *e* on the end. Hélène Harte. That's it. That's perfect. Great. What do you think, Lewis?"

Lewis hesitated, looking at Helen. He could see how tense she had become, how pent-up. Color stained her cheeks; her eyes were bright. He felt a moment's anger, an intuition that Thad was playing with her in some way he did not understand, treating in a brusque way something that clearly mattered to her very much. He looked at her eyes, enormous and dark in her delicate face, and the image of a frightened animal at bay came into his mind: hart, heart, Harte . . .

Thad looked away, and, as he did so, Helen, meeting Lewis's eyes, inclined her head. A little nod, a private hint, from which Thad was excluded. At once Lewis's spirits rose.

"I think it might work," he said slowly. "Yes."

"Let's sleep on it." Thad rose. "See you at the airport in the morning, Lewis."

On that note, he left, much to their astonishment—no further delay, no further appeals about the sofa, nothing. He just went. One minute he was there. The next minute he was out the door. The relief was so total, and so unexpected, that Helen and Lewis were left staring at each other in disbelief.

Hélène, Lewis said to her, later, when they made love. *Hélène*.

It *was* like a sigh. It suited her; the softness and the gentleness of the sound pleased him.

Hélène, he said once more, when, after many kisses, long farewells, he left finally for the airport.

Hélène Harte, Hélène said to herself as she looked in the mirror when Lewis had gone. She lifted her hair and turned her face from side to side, learning her own features. Hélène Harte, who would be rich and famous. Hélène Harte, who would be a star, more than a star, a legend. Hélène Harte, who would be the woman she had always imagined, who would go back to Orangeburg, Alabama, in a Cadillac. Hélène Harte, who would show Orangeburg, and Ned Calvert, that she still remembered. It was possible; anything was possible if you wanted it enough, if you willed it enough.

She let her hair fall again around her face, and for an instant, Hélène Craig looked back at her—the girl she had been. She would be her no more. She turned away from the mirror thinking, with a smile, that she would be giving birth twice, to her baby, and her new self.

She did not see the new self with any great precision yet, but that would come. She imagined her, meanwhile, without weakness, immensely strong, remote as a star, but also an avenging angel who came with wings and a sword.

That night she dreamed of Edouard.

The next months passed very swiftly. Lewis felt as if his life were measured by two clocks which kept very different time. One ticked away his progress, and occasional lack of it, with Thad; the other triumphantly recorded the advances of his love.

Lewis threw himself energetically into the wheeling and dealing in Paris. Certainly, he would have preferred to be back with Hélène, but meanwhile he felt that everything he did was on her behalf. He wanted to prove himself to her, he wanted to return to London with triumphs, deals which he could lay before her like the spoils of war. So he worked hard, tried to learn fast, and amazed himself with a toughness and tenacity he had always hoped he possessed but had never before tested to the full.

He took a room overlooking the courtyard in the Plaza-Athénée, his mother's favorite Paris hotel. His first action, on arrival, was to buy himself a fat Mont Blanc fountain pen, and a bottle of black ink. His second was to give the head porter the tip of a lifetime to ensure that the switchboard operator would put his calls through to London without hitch.

He then entered a round of meetings with a fierceness and vivacity that took even Thad by surprise. Sphere, in spite of Thad's claims, was proving elusive, so Lewis chased other contacts. He made endless telephone calls. He pinned people down and refused to allow them to avoid him or palm him off with evasive promises. He haggled, he wheedled, he cajoled, he bullied, he hyped. He employed to the full his patrician manners, his social contacts, and his considerable charm. He took planes around Europe as casually as he took taxis, he had meetings before breakfast, and meetings at midnight. And slowly, painstakingly, he began to make progress: he began to be able to sort the wheat from the chaff—and when it came to raising money for movies, there was a great deal of chaff.

There was Henri Lebec, voluble, eager, who took him to dinner at the Tour d'Argent, and gave Lewis's genitals the most flagrant squeeze under the table at precisely the moment their waiter ignited their crêpes suzette. Lebec had to be discarded: Lewis saw him now for the amateur he was. It reminded him how amateur he himself had been, and he determined to do better. He stopped returning Lebec's calls, and after a while, the Frenchman drifted away to some other project; he appeared more disappointed that Lewis was not homosexual than anything else.

There was the German steel magnate, interested in a tax shelter. There was the production company in Rome, backed by a spaghetti baron, who was interested in Thad's next movie—provided it was made at Cinecittà, and starred the spaghetti baron's girlfriend. There was a Yugoslav group, who seemed under the impression Thad was about to make an epic: they could raise government backing; they could provide an army of three thousand Yugoslavs very cheap—provided, of course, the picture was made in Yugoslavia. There were feelers from an American agent, who passed the word to a producer, who talked to a lawyer, and who then burned up the lines between Hollywood and Paris with thirty-seven phone calls in three days. Then he stopped calling. When Lewis next called back, he had been fired.

Lewis enjoyed all this. He was new to the game, and he refused to be disheartened. Thad, who sometimes gave way to gloom, and who liked to be dramatic, said, "It's a jungle out there, Lewis. A fucking jungle." Lewis supposed it was: it seemed to him also like a fairground—a fairground in which there were a lot of hucksters.

He would outtalk, outhuckster them all, Lewis resolved. And while he was at it, he'd develop his own instinct for the jugular: he might not need it yet, but one day, he was sure, it would be useful.

Meanwhile, no matter how little progress he made, he could always return to the Plaza-Athénée in the evenings. Then he would make his telephone call to Hélène, his private line to reality. When he had hung up, Lewis, who had never written letters in his life if he could avoid it, would pick up his Mont Blanc pen, and cover pages of hotel writing paper in his large rounded schoolboyish hand. Letters to Hélène; love letters: *My darling, my sweet one, my life, my love.* Hélène kept all his letters, and answered them. Her own were simple. Lewis read them and reread them, and then reread them again. He kept them in his pocket; he took them out on planes, in taxis, in bed, in restaurants. They became worn and creased with handling, and to Lewis they were the talismans of love.

T hey were married at Chelsea Town Hall in January. Hélène wore a white woolen dress, a white woolen coat; it was again snowing. The clerk who married them was very solemn; Lewis hardly heard a word he said. The room in which the brief ceremony took place was decorated with plastic chrysanthemums. Lewis dared not look at Hélène until he slipped the ring onto her ice-cold finger, and realized that her hand, too, was shaking.

Outside, they paused on the steps above the snowy street. Hélène looked down at the small bouquet of flowers she was holding. Tiny white roses, white violets, white freesias. She touched their leaves, delicately; the flowers were held in place by thin wires through the calyx.

They had four days together then, before Thad again started calling and sounding plaintive. Then Lewis went back to Paris, began a new set of meetings, and a new set of letters. *My darling, my sweet wife*: that particular term fired him with pride; he used it whenever possible.

H e met Simon Scher, the representative of Sphere Distribution, for the first time the week after his marriage. Before that, when Scher had been mysteriously unavailable, Lewis had begun to think that all Thad's optimism had indeed been misplaced.

The first thing Scher did after shaking hands was to congratulate

Lewis on his recent marriage, which Lewis assumed he must have heard of from Thad. The second thing was to remark that, like Lewis, he had been at Harvard—the business school in his case. The third thing was to open his briefcase. He took out several neat sheaves of paper and laid them on the table between them. Lewis looked at Scher, a small neat man, conservatively dressed: this man did not look like a huckster. They continued to meet, at intervals, throughout February. Lewis continued to seek other sources of finance; he did not intend to make the mistake of putting all his eggs in Scher's basket.

Sphere purchased the distribution rights to *Night Game*, and it began to look as if the film might have a profitable future, on the European art-house circuit, anyway. Thad had been bullied into producing a screenplay for the next film, and a shooting script—though he said in private that he had no intention of adhering to either. They had a detailed budget. There was a detailed schedule. Locations had been chosen, and permission to use them obtained. There was some casting—all of it still provisional apart from Hélène and Lloyd Baker, who was eager to work with Thad again. There was a strong technical and production team. Lewis assembled all this material and information, disseminated it widely, and felt pleased with himself.

Scher took this weighty dossier away with him early in February—he needed to consult, he said. Lewis snatched two days back in London, where Hélène was eager he should meet her gynecologist.

Mr. Foxworth blandly congratulated Lewis on the forthcoming birth of his child; Hélène stared fixedly at the paintings on the wall behind his head. Mr. Foxworth, noting Lewis's Savile Row overcoat, his Tiffany watch, his handmade shoes, was most affable. He noted Lewis's accent, and his unconscious inbred arrogance, and became more affable still. He was sure, he said charmingly, that Mr. Sinclair would prefer his wife to give birth in a private clinic rather than a National Health hospital—excellent though those hospitals indubitably were. His own clinic, in St. John's Wood . . . He allowed his voice to tail away.

Lewis, used to such physicians since childhood, felt reassured. St. John's Wood, he said; naturally. Hélène gave Mr. Foxworth a glance of triumph, which Lewis did not observe.

They went shopping. They went to The White House, in New Bond Street, and bought an exquisite layette, adorned with Brussels lace, embroidered by nuns, and—in the case of the baby's shawl, which was like gossamer—hand knit by elderly craftswomen in Scotland. They discussed the hiring of a nurse for the baby—a nurse was essential in any case, and it would be necessary to leave the baby with her for a few weeks in June, when Hélène and Lewis had to undertake a brief tour to publicize *Night Game* in Europe. Luckily, Anne Kneale's sister could recommend someone very good: Lewis interviewed the young woman, who came with excellent references; he began to feel, day by day, more responsible, more grown-up—though Lewis's own term was *mature*.

One day, coming back to the cottage unexpectedly, he found Hélène reading—of all things—the *Financial Times*. Lewis found this highly amusing, and when she confessed, shyly, that actually she was quite interested in such matters, but she found them hard to understand, Lewis was touched. Here, he felt, he could dazzle—was he not, after all, a Sinclair, his father's son?

The temptation to demonstrate to Hélène some of his own skills—she would, unfortunately, never see him play football—was suddenly strong. Lewis began to explain a few terms, to elucidate certain simple facts, and Hélène listened quietly and attentively and occasionally asked quite intelligent questions. In the end they spent the entire afternoon discussing the stock market, and Lewis enjoyed himself very much. He, who had always been instructed, always lectured, was suddenly the teacher. It was a new role, and his pupil was his wife: Lewis found the experience almost erotic.

"Is it very difficult—to start a portfolio?" Hélène asked him, the next day. Lewis gave a shout of laughter.

"Of course not! Do you want to try? Why not? I'll help you—but later. When the film's launched. When you've had the baby. You've got other things to think about now."

"I know, Lewis," she said, and smiled at him obediently.

B ack in Paris, Sphere procrastinated. At Simon Scher's suggestion, the budget for the new film was revised, and some changes were made to the script. Thad made these swiftly.

"Just tell me what they want, Lewis, and I'll stick it in. It's just *words*, Lewis, whatever they think they want, I can work around it. Just get the money."

This attitude of Thad's caused Lewis some alarm, but he concealed it. He had, by then, seen the master print of *Night Game*—Thad had perversely refused to let him see the rough cut, which, it seemed to Lewis, had been seen by half of Paris.

The moment he saw that print, Lewis's alarms faded. Whenever they reawoke, he reminded himself of its excellence and was reassured. *Night Game* was a wonderful film. It was startling, lucid, and gripping. It was simultaneously very sad, and at moments extremely funny. *Thad knew what he was doing:* forgetting the doubts of Rome, forgetting his current anxieties, Lewis felt proud. He had always had faith in Thad, he told himself; he had never really wavered; and now that faith was vindicated—triumphantly so.

And Hélène—on film, even to Lewis, she was a revelation. He had read that there are some faces the camera loves: now he knew the meaning of that phrase. Seeing her on the screen, Lewis forgot he knew her; it was like meeting her for the first time, and he fell in love with her all over again. Later, having had a few drinks to calm himself, he explained that to the assistant director, the amiable Fabian.

Fabian smiled, and winked. "*Mais, évidemment,*" he said with a shrug. "The film itself—it is like a love letter to her, is it not?"

This annoyed Lewis. He tried to forget the remark immediately.

Scher had also seen the film, in its final version, and had pronounced himself impressed. He went to see it again, with various advisors and aides, at the beginning of April. By the middle of April there was still no final deal for the next movie, and Lewis began to lose patience. At the end of the month Scher suddenly announced that he needed to see it again, this time with the chairman of his parent company Partex, a Texan called Drew Johnson.

Lewis was irritated. He despised Texans. He foresaw this whole saga going on for months more, and then disintegrating, just like all the others. One more bubble burst.

However, he still had no formal commitment from Sphere after months of hard work, so he had no alternative but to agree.

Drew Johnson proved the embodiment of all Lewis's Bostonian prejudices. He attended the private screening, together with his wife, Billy; she wore Givenchy; her husband a shoelace tie, cowboy boots, and a Stetson. Lewis sat beside them in the screening room, bristling with the disdain of his class.

They went on to dinner at the Grand Vefour. The movie was not mentioned once. They went on after that to the Crazy Horse cabaret, renowned throughout Europe for its sauciness and wit. There Drew Johnson had a ball. He whooped. He applauded. He ordered magnums of champagne. Lewis sat in stony silence, and gazed at the beautiful strippers with a new and puritanical distaste. They did nothing for him at all. The biggest breasts, the slenderest thighs, the most salacious gestures, did not stir his body once.

A black Rolls-Royce Phantom collected the Texan and his wife from the club. They were staying outside Paris, with friends; Drew Johnson crushed Lewis's hand in a mighty paw, and invited him out to Orly to his plane the next morning.

Lewis went back to his hotel, wrote to Hélène, and then—for once feeling despondent—decided to get smashed. Next morning, certain the chairman of Partex had loathed *Night Game* and the deal was off, he dragged himself, hung over, out to the airport.

The plane was a Boeing 707. Inside, it had antique linenfold paneling. On the paneling, their frames screwed in, were a Renoir and a Gauguin the Jeu de Paume gallery would have been proud to own. Lewis looked around him sourly, sat down on an eighteenth-century couch that had been converted to hold seat belts, and asked for a glass of tomato juice.

"Tomato juice?" Drew Johnson's bushy white eyebrows rose. "What's going on here? Billy, honey, ring the bell. Our friend Lewis could use a proper drink."

"No, thank you." Lewis gave his cut-glass accent full rein. "It's nine o'clock in the morning, and besides I have nothing to celebrate." He paused, and as the strain told, his temper snapped. "Look. Why not be straight with me, and stop wasting my time? You hated the film. Yes?"

"Hated it?" The Texan smiled. "How d'you figure that? Y'all taking a wrong turn there."

"Hated it. Disliked it. Probably didn't understand it. Either way, I don't know why I'm here, and I might as well leave." He put down his glass, stood up, and moved toward the exit. It was outrage at the linenfold as much as anything that finally did it. He swung back.

"It's a good movie," he said. "Maybe a great one. I can see that, even if you can't. And I'm going to make damn sure Thad gets to make the next one. With or without your help."

There was a silence. Drew Johnson looked at his wife and began to smile. Suddenly he threw back his head in a great shout of laughter.

"You know, I was beginning to think you were some kind of a eunuch? Well, what d'you know? They got balls in Boston after all. . . ."

Six feet five of brawny Texan advanced across the cabin, holding out its hand. Six feet three of elegant Bostonian looked at it with a doubtful disdain.

Drew Johnson's face sobered. His sharp blue eyes met those of Lewis.

"Well, come on now, boy. Even in Boston I guess you get to shake hands on a deal." He paused. "I authorized the financing last night. Your lawyers don't pick too many nits in it, and you'll find y'all just got yourself a backer."

Lewis stared at him. He reached out and grasped Drew Johnson's hand. He smiled.

"You know," he said, "I think I might just change the habits of a lifetime. Right now a drink would be just fine."

"Break out the bourbon, Billy," Johnson roared.

The deal was signed on the first of May. Lewis looked at its fifty pages of closely typed script, and felt a soaring pride. For the deal, he and Thad had formed their own production company. They called it Mirage, because Thad liked that name, and as joint directors, they both signed: Thad in a thin spidery scribble, Lewis with his Mont Blanc pen, in his bold hand.

The day he signed, he called first Hélène, and then his father. This moment, which Lewis had been promising himself for months, was sweet. Item by item Lewis lobbed the information down the line; it felt like a series of perfectly aimed grenades. A budget in seven figures. The possibility of a long-term partnership. Sphere Distribution. Partex Petrochemicals. Drew Johnson.

Impatience at his father's end changed to silence; after the silence came the questions—the exam. Lewis was eloquent; figures flew across the transatlantic cable, and at last he heard the note he'd wanted to hear so long creeping into his father's voice, grudging but there: respect.

Lewis smiled. "Oh, and by the way, I'm married," he added, and hung up.

Lewis had hoped that the deal with Sphere and the birth of Hélène's baby would take place in the same week. But it was not to be. The baby was late: "Nothing to worry about," Mr. Foxworth said. "Very common with first-time mothers." Lewis fretted; finally, late on the evening of May 16, Hélène went into labor. Lewis rushed with her in a taxi to the clinic in St. John's Wood. Mr. Foxworth arrived, smooth in a pearl-gray suit.

Lewis paced the waiting room of the clinic, and smoked two packs of cigarettes. At four o'clock in the morning of May 17, Mr. Foxworth appeared at the door, undoing the strings of a green surgical gown. Lewis looked at him: it was like the movies; it was like the movies—only better, only worse. He stared at the physician in terror; one second stretched to eternity. Through the clouds of cigarette smoke, Mr. Foxworth smiled, indulgently: he congratulated Mr. Sinclair. Mr. Sinclair had a very lovely daughter.

Lewis was ushered into Hélène's room. He was trembling. Discreetly, doctor and nurse withdrew. In her arms Hélène held what seemed to him a tiny bundle, a little, little shape, swathed in a white wool shawl.

She looked up, and Lewis approached the bed. He looked down at the shawl, at the tiny perfect face. He saw smooth pale skin, eyes tightly shut, and a little frown between the brows, as if the baby concentrated hard on sleep. As Lewis bent forward, the baby screwed its face into a tiny fierce grimace. Its lips parted, and it made a small rubbing, seeking movement, pressing its cheek against the shawl. It seemed disgruntled. It wriggled slightly, freeing one hand. The hand was plump-backed, with dimples for knuckles; there was a deep crease where hand met wrist, and Lewis saw, as the tiny fingers clenched and then relaxed, that the fingernails were the color of tiny shells. They needed cutting.

Lewis began to cry. Gently, he reached forward and touched the newborn skin. The baby moved again, snuffled, and the shawl fell back. This seemed to alert her momentarily: she opened her eyes. Lewis stared. A little fuzzy cap of jet-black hair. Eyes that were the strongest, darkest blue he had ever seen.

"Isn't she beautiful?" Hélène said softly, anxiously.

"She's lovely."

Lewis went to touch the soft black hair, and then drew back. The baby looked in his direction with wide unfocused eyes. Lewis wished then, wished passionately and sadly, that the baby's hair had been fair, like Hélène's, like his own. He hated himself for the wish at the instant he felt it. He could hardly fall now at the very first hurdle, when he had been so confident of his ability to stay the course. He turned back to Hélène awkwardly, trying to hide what he felt. He reached for her hand.

"Her eyes are beautiful. And she's so . . . I . . ."

He heard himself failing, heard himself flounder.

Hélène seemed trusting. She lifted her face to his, with a smile of tiredness and serenity.

"Kingfisher blue," she said. "The color of a kingfisher's wing."

Lewis looked down at the baby uncertainly. It was not how he would have described the color. Hélène's grip on his hand suddenly tightened.

"I wonder," Lewis said in a flat voice. "Will they stay that color?"

They decided to call the baby Catharine. Because of her delicate little triangular-shaped face and the wide-spaced blue eyes, which reminded Lewis of a Siamese kitten his mother had owned, this quickly became shortened to Cat.

Like her namesake, Cat was simultaneously aloof, and immensely demanding. When Lewis or Hélène held her, and cooed at her, and stroked her, Cat appeared indifferent. She would screw up her eyes and look away. But the second she was laid in her crib—fed, bathed, changed, ready for her nap—she would start to scream.

She would cry, on a mounting plangent penetrating scale, until she was picked up again. Then she would stop—until they laid her back in the crib. Lewis found it charming at first, then, as the lack of sleep began to tell, irritating. Hélène never complained: she would climb out of bed and go to her at all hours of the night. The days seemed to Lewis to be one long chain of operations: bottles to sterilize, bottles to make up, diapers to change, diapers to soak. Lewis sometimes made up the formula, and sometimes held the baby while she fed—when, briefly, she was quiet—but diapers, he felt, were hardly a man's domain.

After two weeks he suggested that, rather than waiting until they were almost due to leave for Paris, as had been planned, the nurse should join them now. Hélène refused. They had their first quarrel, during the course of which Lewis told her that she cared more for the baby than she did for him, and at the end of which he drank half a bottle of whisky, which at least enabled him, he said snappishly the next day, to get a few hours' sleep.

The day after that, having sulked until he felt better, Lewis repented. If he could then have made love to Hélène, he told himself, he would have felt that the distance between them had been banished. But the doctor had forbidden intercourse for a month, and Hélène seemed not to share Lewis's enthusiasm for alternative methods of release. She climbed into bed each night and fell instantly asleep; Lewis lay beside her, stiff in every muscle with a mixture of sexual frustration and moral indignation, his nerves taut as piano wire. He was waiting for the first wail. Sooner or later—usually sooner—it always came.

By the third week, when the telephone calls from Thad became more frequent, and the packing began, Lewis looked down into Cat's little triangular face with a sense of injured reproach. It seemed to him so unfair. This was not his baby, and yet he had welcomed it into the world. He had set out to love it; he had promised himself he would take care of it—and how did it repay him? Did it seem to sense his concern, his magnanimity? No, it did not.

He decided to say nothing. He would keep the peace. The nurse was arriving that day; three days from now, he and Hélène would be in Paris. Alone.

When, finally, the day came for them to depart, Lewis felt a certain triumph. It was not just that he looked forward to being alone with Hélène, or even to getting a night's uninterrupted sleep, it was also the fact that his will had prevailed. Hélène had not wanted to leave the baby. Right up to the very last minute she had attempted to change Lewis's mind.

But Lewis was obdurate, and he could back up his stand with such sweetly reasonable arguments that, in the end, Hélène had to give in. This, after all, was a publicity tour. It was no place for a newborn infant. Hélène had a tight schedule of interviews, photographic sessions, and public appearances: it was she who was being launched, Lewis argued, not just the film. This, he was aware, was Thad's argument. He used it now without a qualm. He reiterated the fact that they would be away only three weeks, that Hélène could telephone every morning and every evening, that the baby's nurse was highly experienced—far more experienced than Hélène, he added, and that she had the backup of Anne Kneale. Lewis personally thought that Anne Kneale was an interfering dyke, and in his more paranoid moments felt that her kindness to Hélène disguised a sexual attraction. But she was useful to him now as an argument, so Lewis suppressed these feelings. Madeleine and Anne Kneale could cope, he said firmly.

"Now that you're a mother, darling," he said, clinching his argument, "you mustn't forget that you're also my wife. And an actress," he added, but that was an afterthought. Lewis was not really thinking about the premiere of *Night Game*, or the press interest in Hélène, which the publicity man Thad had hired was describing as phenomenal. He was thinking about the suite at the Plaza-Athénée; about its little balcony, where he and Hélène would eat breakfast together in the spring sun; about the wide, wide double bed, in which, uninterrupted by Cat's plaintive cries, Lewis intended to make love to Hélène again and again.

Recaptured joys: Lewis ushered Hélène out to the hired limousine that would drive them to the airport. He felt nothing but optimism. Hélène lingered. Madeleine stood in the doorway of the little cottage holding the baby; Anne Kneale stood behind her, looking up at the sky; Hélène seemed unable to drag herself away. She bent over the baby. She kissed her. She embarked on a whole new series of instructions to Madeleine, all of which she had been over a thousand times before. Lewis, already in the car, tapped his fingers on his knees, looked at his watch. It was nine A.M. He leaned out.

"Hélène. We must hurry. We'll miss the flight at this rate."

Hélène finally tore herself away. She climbed into the back of the car, her cheeks pink. She said nothing.

As the car moved off, Lewis took her hand and pressed it between his own. By the time they were halfway to Heathrow, Lewis felt quite benevolent toward Cat. Left behind, in retrospect, she seemed to him sweet. He pressed Hélène's hand, drew it down against his thigh, and then to his groin. "It will be like a honeymoon," he said.

Back at the cottage, as the car bearing Hélène and Lewis rounded the corner and disappeared from sight, Anne Kneale and the nurse, Madeleine, looked at each other. Anne Kneale looked at her watch, and then down at the baby, who was sleeping. They paused for a moment, then turned and went back inside.

Madeleine fed the baby for a little while, then changed her, and laid her carefully in her crib. She came back downstairs on tiptoe.

Anne was sitting in front of the fire, staring into the flames thoughtfully. She was smoking a cigarette. The two looked at each other, and waited. Five minutes passed. Ten. Fifteen. There was still silence.

Madeleine, born in the Landes region of France, trained at the exclusive Norland College in England, and a fully qualified nursery nurse for the past four years, three of them with Anne Kneale's sister, who had given her the excellent reference, sighed and sat down. She looked at Anne, and gave a little shrug.

"*Incroyable*. It's as if she *knew*."

Anne stubbed out her cigarette, and said nothing. After a while, she got up, went to the studio, and fetched the portrait of Hélène which she had finished some weeks before. She looked at it critically, aware that it was not quite as she had wanted it to be. There were things she had seen in that beautiful face, and which she had wanted to capture; some of them had eluded her. She looked at the picture irritably, and then, carefully and methodically, she began to pack it up. It gave her something to do. It kept her conscience at bay. She liked Hélène, and she was not at all happy with this arrangement.

At ten o'clock, Madeleine, who was also uneasy, went out to the little kitchen to make coffee. At ten-thirty, precisely on schedule, the telephone rang. The two women jumped, and then looked at each other. Slowly, Anne tied the last knot on her packaging, and turned to pick up the receiver.

The voice of her old friend Christian Glendinning, whom she had known since childhood, informed her that Lewis Sinclair and Hélène had boarded their plane ten minutes ago. It had just taken off for Paris.

"Stop panicking," Christian said calmly as Anne began to interrupt. "I'm phoning Eaton Square now. He'll be with you in fifteen minutes. Less, probably."

Ten minutes later, a black Rolls-Royce pulled up outside the door. Anne went to open it; Madeleine looked out the window. She saw the familiar figure, in a dark suit, step out, and cross the sidewalk. She heard Anne's greeting, then the door from the hall opened.

Madeleine blushed crimson. For this man, who had been so good to her, so good to her sister, and so good to her little nephew, Grégoire, Madeleine would have walked through fire. As she saw him, she gave an awkward half bob.

"Madeleine."

"*Monsieur le Baron* . . ."

There was no need for him to ask the question; both women could read it in his eyes, and in the strain of his features. Anne held back the door.

"She's upstairs. The room on the right. She's sleeping." Edouard touched her arm as he passed.

"It's all right, Anne. It won't take long, I promise you." They heard his feet on the stairs, heard him hesitate on the landing. A door opened, there was a brief pause, then it shut.

Madeleine, who had a romantic nature beneath her dark square fierce little face, sighed, and sat down. Anne Kneale, who was not a romantic, but who had been shaken by Edouard's expression, also sat down, bolt upright, counting the minutes, the time it took to sacrifice a new set of loyalties for others that went back a long way. She thought of the first time she had met Edouard, when he was a boy of sixteen—his sixteenth birthday, and that appalling trip Jean-Paul had organized to the theater. She had done this for Isobel, she told herself defensively; for Isobel, whom she had loved, and for Edouard, whom she had always liked, though she was aware she did not understand him. Men were such masochists, she thought. Why seek pain? She shrugged, and lit another cigarette nervously.

Upstairs, Edouard stood very still, looking down at the crib. The baby was awake; she lay there, quite silently, waving her fist before her eyes, and looking up at him. Edouard stared down into a tiny replica of his own face. It owed the delicacy of its features, the golden pallor of its skin, to Hélène, but the hair was as dark as his own, as dark as his father's had been, and the eyes, that remarkable and unusual shade of dark blue, fringed by black lashes, were de Chavigny eyes. The baby blinked, as if to emphasize the point, and Edouard bent forward. He had so little time.

He had rarely held a baby, and to lift one from a crib made him nervous. His hands shook as he disentangled the little body from the covers that swaddled it, and slipped his hand beneath head and neck to support it. He thought the baby might cry out, but she was quite silent, regarding him still with the myopic, slightly drunken gaze of all newborn babies. Edouard lifted her. Her tininess, her lightness, broke his heart.

He looked down into the baby's face, then lifted the tiny body higher, and cradled it against his shoulder. The cap of downy hair brushed his cheek silkily. He could smell the sweet warm milky scent of a very young baby's skin. The baby's head lolled a little; a small burp erupted, which seemed to please her. Edouard patted her back, and the baby swung her little fist, batting it against his lips.

Her mouth made small greedy seeking movements, then opened in a wide pink yawn. A tiny pink tongue, like a kitten's. Edouard lifted his hand, crooked his finger, and let the baby find his knuckle. She sucked on it hard, with an astonishing strength; then, quite suddenly, she wailed. A hiccuping mysterious distress: the tiny face contorted, reddened. Edouard, in response to an instinct he had not known he possessed, pressed her soothingly against his shoulder. The wailing stopped.

When Edouard was quite certain she was calm again, he lowered her gently. He held her in front of him, her body resting easily across the width of his two hands. He looked down into her face, and the baby regarded him with solemnity.

"One day," Edouard said to the baby, to his baby. "One day, I shall come back for you. I promise."

He bent forward and laid her back in her crib, then drew the covers around her warmly.

He stood looking down at her a moment longer, then, knowing that if he lingered he would find it impossible to leave, he turned abruptly, and went down the stairs. The door to the other bedroom was open; the brass rail of its wide double bed was visible. From it, Edouard averted his eyes.

He said good-bye to the two women quickly; Anne Kneale handed him the portrait he had asked her to paint.

He did not open the parcel until later that day, when he was sure he could be alone, and he looked at it, in silence, for a long time.

Later the same day, he had dinner with Christian, who managed to refrain from questions for the duration of the meal, but who, afterward, found it impossible.

"So—what will you do?" he said at last, having fortified himself with a large whisky before he risked the question. Edouard, whose manner throughout the meal had been perfectly normal, looked genuinely surprised at the question.

"Do? I shall wait, of course."

"Wait? But how long?" Christian burst out. Christian loathed waiting.

"For as long as it takes," Edouard replied. Christian sighed. He wanted to plot, to plan, to coerce Edouard into some immediate and dramatic course of action. He knew it was useless. Edouard was well schooled in waiting; his patience always brought results. A thousand wonderfully melodramatic plans surged through Christian's fertile mind in the space of a few seconds. But before he could speak, Edouard—as he had anticipated—discreetly but firmly changed the subject.

EDOUARD

PARIS—ST. TROPEZ, 1962

"Cancer," Philippe de Belfort said. He paused, accepted the glass of whisky Edouard held out to him, and composed his features solemnly. He shook his head.

"A terrible thing. Six months ago—in the best of health. Looking forward to retirement—he'd made some very clever investments, or so I hear. We had luncheon together—he had oysters, I remember it well. Couldn't have looked fitter. On top of the world. I said to him—Brichot, you're a lucky man. Out of the rat race. What are you going to do with all this leisure of yours? And you know what he said? He said—Philippe, I'm going to spend money. All these years I've been accumulating it, and now I'm going to spend it. I'm going to live like there's no tomorrow."

The faintest gleam of malice appeared in de Belfort's even features. It was quickly repressed.

"And of course, he *had* no tomorrow. Well, none to speak of, anyway. Six months later—gone. Terrible. Absolutely terrible. Poor Brichot. Not that I was ever that close to him, you understand—but still, it makes one think, doesn't it? What a very unpredictable world we live in. Oh, yes. *Sunt lacrimae rerum*—I thought of that when I heard the news. *The tears of life*—oh, yes. Not that poor Brichot was particularly interested in poetry."

"The tears of *things*," Edouard murmured.

De Belfort looked up. "What?"

"*Rerum. Things* rather than *life*. Virgil uses a loose term deliberately perhaps. . . ."

An expression of irritation passed across de Belfort's face. He repressed that too.

"Of course. I was forgetting . . . the classics were never my strong point. . . ." There was a short silence. De Belfort gave a weighty sigh.

"It's his wife I feel sorry for. Having to carry on alone. They were very close, I believe. Still, still . . . You went to the funeral, of course?"

"Yes. I was there."

"I would have gone, naturally." De Belfort shifted slightly in his seat. "Unfortunately, circumstances prevented—well, as you know, I was very tied up. The negotiations in London were at a very delicate stage. Very delicate. I didn't like to risk jeopardizing them. . . ."

"But of course," Edouard said politely.

He waited. It was late afternoon, approaching six; they were seated at the far end of Edouard's office, where he held informal meetings, and where a group of austere black leather chairs were grouped around an equally austere glass and chrome table. Beyond them hung the Jackson Pollock; de Belfort looked at it occasionally, his eyes narrowed. He looked as if he might be calculating how much it was worth per square inch.

Edouard, who had a further two hours' work ahead of him, a dinner with Christian, and—after that—a reception at his mother's house to celebrate her birthday, felt impatient. De Belfort had requested this meeting, and he had not come here to lament the loss of Brichot, Edouard was sure of that. There would be another reason, but de Belfort was never direct. He always scuttled toward his main objective sideways, like a crab.

Now he was bending forward over the tabletop, turning his glass back and forth in a ruminative fashion. He was possibly thinking about his erstwhile ally, Brichot; possibly examining his own well-groomed reflection, Edouard was not sure. All he knew was that de Belfort now contrived these informal meetings on every possible occasion. Their pretext was always professional, though de Belfort also clearly hoped to establish a relationship of some kind, and to disarm. But Edouard suspected sometimes that de Belfort sought them for another reason. Not just because he wished advancement, that was too obvious, but because, in some strange way, de Belfort needed them. He needed to be near that which he loathed. . . .

"Our bid for the Rolfson Hotels Group," de Belfort said at last, having let the silence run on longer than he usually dared. "Just one or two points I wanted to bring up. If you can spare me the time . . ."

"Of course."

It was all plausible enough: minor queries and suggestions concerning the forthcoming and long-planned de Chavigny takeover bid for one of the largest and most prestigious of British hotel groups. De Belfort was now the head of the de Chavigny hotel division; it was a powerful position, in which he had proved effective and able, and a position into which Edouard had carefully steered him. Edouard intended him to remain there, prince of that one domain: de Belfort had other ideas.

But he was discreet about his ambitions now. He had come a long way from the days when he was so incautious as to ally himself with a weakling like Brichot. He was now very careful to tread that thin line between suitable executive independence and outright opposition. No more mulish stands over trifling issues. De Belfort was waiting, Edouard knew that, waiting for the day when there might be some major showdown, some epic trial of strength. It would have been prudent—Edouard sometimes thought—to have eased de Belfort out of the company altogether, simply to have gotten rid of him. Yet he had never done it. Now, as he listened carefully while de Belfort fabricated various matters on which, apparently, Edouard's advice was indispensable, he wondered why not.

Because de Belfort amused him, he decided finally, as the man drained the last of his drink. He was the company's Cassius, the one serious threat from within the ranks. Am I so bored, Edouard thought suddenly, so bored with it all, that I need the rivalry of a man like de Belfort to give my work an edge?

"So you think definitely Montague Smythe?" Edouard said as he rose, and de Belfort, taking his cue, also stood up.

"Well, I know we've always dealt through them very successfully in the past. It was just on this occasion, given the particular delicacy of the bid, fears of a counterbid, and so on, whether we might not have thought of one of the younger merchant banks. A more aggressive approach, shall we say—but no. I'm sure you're right. Stick with Montague Smythe . . . absolutely, yes."

He moved to the door, was almost there, and then at the very last minute turned back. It was almost perfectly casual, but it was not very well-timed. Edouard could see de Belfort himself was aware of it, before he spoke.

"Oh, by the way. I almost forgot. Poor Brichot. His seat on the board. You'll be making a replacement, I suppose?"

It was too overt, too naked. De Belfort was fighting hard to appear indifferent, but the tension in his body was visible. The planes of his face were tight with the effort of maintaining that casual smile; his eyes were glittering with panic and ambition suppressed.

For a moment Edouard almost pitied him: poor de Belfort, to want something so much that he made a mistake like that. To put so much energy into hitching himself up the ladder step by step, and all without any clear idea of what he would do when he reached the top.

Their eyes met: de Belfort could not hide the challenge he felt. It was there in his face, naked—all his dislike, all his envy, all his determination to prove himself, one day, the better man. He was not a fool, and he clearly sensed his mistake. He was already starting to turn away with some embarrassed disclaimer, when Edouard spoke.

"Philippe."

"Yes?"

"Pull off this takeover bid, and the seat on the board is yours."

There was a silence. De Belfort flushed crimson. Edouard could see the astonishment, and the suspicion in his eyes, and then—way back—the dawning, slightly contemptuous, triumph. De Belfort recovered quickly; the little speech of thanks, the references to his indebtedness—it was well done, urbanely done, and he had the wit to keep it brief.

As the door closed on him, Edouard turned away. He had been incautious, and he knew it. He paused, considering, then dismissed his doubts impatiently. De Belfort deserved to be on the board; if he went too far it would still be easy to rein him in. . . . Still, his own action puzzled him slightly. It remained with him, perplexing him, that night.

"And so I offered him what he wanted. A seat on the board," he said to Christian over dinner at Vefour.

"And?"

"And nothing. I just wondered afterward why I did it, that's all. I'm still wondering. Why give him what he wants?"

"Why sharpen the knife and then offer him your back, you mean?"

"Well, not exactly. The knife hardly needs sharpening. And I don't intend to turn my back."

"Oh, God, I don't know." Christian shrugged. "Because you're bloody perverse, probably. You like living dangerously. Look at the way you drive."

"I drive very well." Edouard sounded wounded.

"You drive too fast," Christian replied smartly. Then he hesitated; he looked slightly wary for a second. "Also," he went on, more slowly, "also, you have too much energy, so you deliberately foster an enemy, I suppose. If things were different, that wouldn't be the case."

"If things were different?"

Christian heard the coldness enter the voice. He looked away sulkily.

"Oh, damn it, Edouard, you know what I mean."

There was a little silence. Christian cleared his throat. After a while, he said, "I'm sorry."

"Don't be. You're right, of course."

Edouard looked down, and Christian, who knew exactly what he was thinking, sighed. He lit a cigarette, and inhaled deeply. Poor Edouard, he thought. Two and a half years. He hesitated once more, and then, deciding to risk it, said, "I saw her latest film by the way—did I tell you? It hasn't opened here yet, has it? I saw it in London. I thought . . ." Edouard looked up, and the expression in his eyes made Christian waver.

"I thought she was very good," he ended lamely.

"I'm glad you liked it," Edouard answered, and gestured to the waiter to bring them the bill.

Christian subsided. He knew that tone of voice, and he knew that expression.

"Okay, Edouard," he said lightly. "Subject closed."

He wished that it were closed, Edouard thought, shortly afterward, when he left Christian and climbed into the black Aston-Martin. He accelerated in the direction of his mother's house.

He wished it closed, finished, done with forever—sometimes he wished it passionately. He would tell himself then that all that was needed was some action on his part, an action that would somehow sever the tie.

Another woman, perhaps. It was an obvious enough solution: the one Jean-Paul would have recommended. *Love, little brother? Never believe in it. At the first sign of the symptoms, move on—another woman will quickly cure you of all that folly. . . .*

Yes, he had actually considered that course, particularly this last year. He would leave for a party, a dinner, a reception like the one his mother was holding now, and he would tell himself: tonight. Any of the women there who happen to be available, it doesn't matter which, any one of them will do.

The intention would be there. It would still be in his mind when he first walked into the room. He would actually scan the faces one by one. The redhead. The blonde. The brunette—that was the extent of their identity to him. Sometimes he might even reach the point of selecting one, usually the nearest one, and then—whether they were interested or not, inclined or not—the same thing would always happen. The banality of it, the appalling and pointless predictability of it would intrude. He would arrive with a firm intent: he would always leave alone.

His mother, sensing his distaste, and knowing it angered him, now made a great point of introducing him to eligible women. When she observed his annoyance, she redoubled her efforts. Louise now took a perverse and spiteful delight in playing Pandar: at little luncheon parties, at dinners, at receptions such as the one tonight—*Monique, Sylvie, Gwen, Harriet—you haven't met, have you? May I present my darling son, Edouard?*

Edouard watched her now, weaving her way through the crowd of guests to the side of the room where he stood. A word here, a kiss there;

a rose-pink dress of drifting chiffon, ropes of pearls around her throat, her complexion still unimpaired, her figure still slender. It was her sixty-seventh birthday, and Edouard thought, looking at her, of the time he had opened the door of the schoolroom, and seen her in Hugo Glendinning's arms. She had been wearing pink then; at a distance there was no sign that she had aged. Twenty years ago, and the memory was suddenly so acute that it might have been yesterday.

"Darling Edouard. You're so *late*." She reached up to kiss the air beside his cheek. "The evening's almost over."

"It doesn't appear to be." Edouard smiled. There were at least eighty people in the room, and no sign that anyone was leaving. Thank God he hadn't come any earlier.

He pressed a small package into her hand. It contained a brooch of diamonds and pearls commissioned from Vlacek by his father, in the twenties. It had been difficult to acquire it back, and he had thought, foolishly, that its association with Xavier might please her.

"Edouard. How sweet. Thank you."

She put the package down on a side table, unopened, and slipped her arm through his, girlishly.

"Now, Edouard, you're to come with me. And you're not to be disagreeable. . . ."

"I can't stay long, Maman. I'm leaving for New York in the morning . . ." he began, but Louise was not listening. She was propelling him through the room, and it was starting again: the turnings of heads; the whisperings; the sudden alertness in the air; regroupings.

Natalia. Geneviève. Sara. Monique. Consuelo, who was tiny and dark and exotic, like an orchid; Charlotte, another of the ubiquitous Cavendishes, who was tall, and fair and stately, an English Athena.

Edouard adopted his usual role; it fell on his shoulders with the ease of much practice. Polite, considerate, apparently interested, actually withdrawn. Half an hour, he thought, while Charlotte Cavendish told him how much he had been missed in Gstaad that winter. Half an hour, and then, even at the risk of offending Louise, he was leaving.

But Louise had carefully maneuvered him to the far end of the huge reception room, the end away from the doors.

"Tell me, Edouard, is it true you've a Derby winner this year?"

"Oh. Edouard. It's been too long. You're going to New York? When? Well, you must come to dinner. . . ."

"Edouard, I'm madly cross with you. We went to Figaro the other night, yes, that's right, with Jacqueline de Varenges, and I was so certain of seeing you. I wanted to ask you—seriously now. This summer, you did promise . . ."

"This weekend . . ."

"Next month . . ."

It was a long way back to those doors, and the progress was slow. Whenever there was a momentary gap, and Edouard thought he had escaped, there Louise would be at his elbow, simply materializing, with yet another beautiful, rich, and well-connected young woman at her side. Edouard looked at his mother, he looked at face after meaningless face, and again the past came back. He was sixteen years old, standing in the hallway of Pauline Simonescu's house, watching intoxicatedly while the floor rippled, and Pauline Simonescu smiled and listed her girls by name.

He stared at the woman called Consuelo, who had inched her way back for the third time, and was now telling him precisely how long she was staying in Paris, and in which hotel. Edouard felt suffocated by the scent she wore; she seemed quite uncaring that her husband stood a few feet away.

"I do hope you will both enjoy your visit. And now, I'm so sorry. If you will excuse me . . ."

He had almost escaped. The doors were within reach; Louise was temporarily diverted, surrounded by a group of much younger men. Edouard turned, with a sense of relief; he found himself face to face with Ghislaine Belmont-Laon.

"Edouard." She was smiling. "You're wickedly transparent, you know. I never saw a man so obviously eager to get away. . . . Don't worry. I'm not going to detain you. Escape while you can." She made a wry face. "You couldn't give me a light, though, could you, before you run away? I must have misplaced my lighter. . . ."

"Of course . . ." Edouard lit the cigarette for her, feeling almost relieved. He did not especially like Ghislaine, but at least he knew her. They had worked together; with Ghislaine there was only an easy neutrality.

"How's Jean-Jacques?"

Ghislaine had bent forward to light her cigarette; now she straightened and inhaled deeply. She gave him a certain look, one that seemed to imply that the question was better not asked, but since they were old friends, they might as well both be amused by it.

"Edouard. If you want to know the answer to that question, don't ask me. He's around, the way he always is."

"Oh, I see. I'm sorry. And how are you?"

Ghislaine laughed. "Not terribly tactful of you, Edouard. I see your priorities. But I'm fine. Working very hard—you know. Louise wants me to do up that house in St. Tropez for her—did she mention it to you?"

"St. Tropez? No. I thought she'd sold it. She never goes there. . . ."

"Ah, well, she's had a change of heart then, I expect." Ghislaine gave him a sidelong glance, as if she knew something, and he did not.

Then she shrugged. "You know how Louise is. She'll probably cancel it anyway."

She smiled at him; a frank pleasant smile, the smile of an old friend, the easy smile of an independent professional woman who had known Edouard too long, and worked with him too closely to regard him other than as a colleague. She was looking elegant, as she always did, Edouard thought. A narrow black dress that was probably Dior, but which looked like Mainbocher. Ghislaine had found the style that suited her in the late nineteen-thirties; she had had the taste, and the assurance, to stick to it. Fastened on the shoulder was an exquisite brooch: a panther poised to leap, made of gold and onyx.

"Yes, I know you recognize it, Edouard." She had seen his glance. "One of Vlacek's last pieces. De Chavigny, of course. And not mine, I hasten to add. I wish it were, but it's borrowed."

She patted his arm, glanced over her shoulder, and then back at him, with a meaningful smile that Edouard was quite at a loss to understand.

"If you want to make good your escape," she said lightly, "now's your moment, I think. Louise won't even notice—not now."

Edouard wished her good night, and turned away. It was only when he turned that he grasped her meaning.

Across the room, Louise had looked up, her face suddenly alight. She was looking, Edouard saw, at the doorway. And in the doorway stood Philippe de Belfort.

De Belfort was smoothing down the sleeve of an already immaculate dinner jacket. *Impossible,* Edouard thought; then he saw the expression on de Belfort's face, and he knew that it was not impossible. De Belfort was thirty years younger than Louise—but when had that made any difference to his mother?

He left the room; as he passed de Belfort, the two men exchanged the briefest of greetings.

He had intended to drive straight back to St. Cloud when he left his mother's house. But the moment he was in the car, he knew he wouldn't. Instead, he took the opposite direction; he drove, as he had many times before, along the quai, to the place where he had met Hélène.

He drove fast, through the now almost empty streets, the Seine glittering blackly to his left. Near the corner of the Rue St. Julien, he stopped the car; it was past midnight; he walked the rest of the way.

He stood outside the small church where he had first seen her, looking now toward the church, now toward the little park where the children had been playing, now back again toward the quai.

The street was silent, and deserted, the only noise the occasional car passing in the distance. He knew that it was pointless, this compulsion that brought him back here, but he found it comforting all the same. It always calmed him; he could feel the place stilling his mind, so that the noise and the falsehood and the horror of the past hour left him. He felt, almost, at peace. He felt, whenever he was here, and however illogical it might seem, that Hélène was close. Somehow, he could never quite rid himself of the belief that, if he came here, if he stood here, he would—one day—hear footsteps, and look up, and see her.

He stood there for five, perhaps ten minutes. The air was cool and smelled of spring; no cars passed, and for a moment all of Paris was silent.

When the ten minutes had passed, he turned away, reluctantly, and went back to the Aston-Martin. The engine fired, he turned and accelerated away, fast.

It was one o'clock precisely; he was leaving for New York this morning.

"You're crazy, do you know that? It's almost one o'clock in the morning. You can't walk the streets of Paris at this hour."

Lewis lifted his glass, and emptied it. They were in their suite at the Ritz; tonight, Lewis was drinking brandy.

"I know what time it is. And it doesn't matter. I won't be long, Lewis. I just need to go for a walk, that's all. I won't sleep. I need some air. . . ."

She had already edged to the door; Lewis might suggest he come with her; he might even insist. But she thought not; two whiskies, one bottle of claret, three brandies: no, he wouldn't even suggest it, though he might sulk—if he remembered—in the morning.

She looked at Lewis, and thought: I must stop counting the drinks. I have to stop it, it's like spying on him. Lewis was already reaching for the cognac bottle. He lifted his handsome face, then lifted his glass; an ironic salute. He mis-timed it slightly.

"Have it your own way. Don't say I didn't warn you."

Hélène was already opening the door.

There were still people about, and she did not want to be seen or recognized, so she pulled up the collar of her coat and slipped out of the side entrance.

Once she was in the street, she began to hurry. It was quite a long way, but she wasn't aware of the distance; Edouard drew her on.

Twenty-minutes; when she reached the Pont Notre Dame, she was out of breath from running. She stopped on the bridge, and looked down into the water. Across the Seine, a car's engine fired, the noise magnified by the expanse of the river, so it sounded very loud, like a roar.

She ran across the bridge, crossed the quai, and turned into the Rue St. Julien. There she stopped abruptly.

She had been certain she would see him: she realized that, only then, when the street was empty. Somehow, madly, the conviction had been there, and when she found she had been wrong, she felt his absence with such sudden intensity that she could have sunk to her knees on the sidewalk, and wept.

She had never come here before. All the times she had had to be in Paris, and she had never come here, where she had most longed to be. Perhaps that was why she had been so madly convinced, she thought: this place was so firmly rooted in her heart, so occupied by Edouard, that she could not believe that when she came there, he would not be there, too, waiting.

She began to walk up the street, toward the church, toward the place where she had been standing. When she reached it, she stood as she had done that August, looking up at the façade of the church, though she hardly saw it.

She had no idea what would have happened if he had been there. She had not thought once beyond that instant, not of what she would say, nor what she would do—nothing. All she had seen in her mind was that one second, when she would look up and see him, and nothing else would matter because he made the night, the day, and her life bright again.

She stood by the church five minutes, perhaps ten. The blind superstition that she would suddenly hear his footsteps would not leave her. When the ten minutes had passed, she turned away reluctantly, and in the quai, picked up a cab.

It's over. I knew really, she said to herself. She looked at her watch. It was one-thirty; she was promoting her new film; she had three interviews and a photographic session this morning.

Jean-Jacques Belmont-Laon left the private screening room, where he had been watching the new Thaddeus Angelini picture, at seven in the evening. *Short Cut*, it was called, and it starred this new woman, Hélène Harte, about whom, quite suddenly, everyone seemed to be talking.

Well, he could understand that, he thought—and not just because the film was being tipped to win the Palme d'Or at Cannes, and Hélène

Harte the award for best actress. Oh, not just because of that, he thought, settling himself in the backseat of the taxi which would take him home. The film was good, he could see that, though he had not particularly liked it. And *she* was good: the editor of his biggest circulation magazine had been itching to run a feature on her for months, and Jean-Jacques would now certainly give him the go-ahead. . . . But it was not just that; those were purely professional considerations, and fairly minor. Lots of actresses became hot overnight, and his magazines duly featured them.

But this woman was special. Very special. She had produced in Jean-Jacques sensations which he was at a loss to explain, though they were physically obvious enough—he still had an erection. On celluloid, too; in a smoky overcrowded screening room filled with other men. That had never happened to him before. Even Monroe, even Bardot—on film they left him cold. Jean-Jacques was quick to respond to women in the flesh—no doubts on that score, he reminded himself with a smile—but at a distance, on film? No, it was the first time, and it was incredibly strong. He felt almost sick with lust; aching to have a woman.

He slipped his hand down between his thighs, and felt his cock throb. That scene where she undressed—not that you could see a goddamn thing—Angelini could learn, he thought, from Vadim. Then; that was when he'd really felt it, and he couldn't have said why. He wasn't sure if it was she who did it, or Angelini, with the way he filmed her; but there was something about her face, the eyes, the mouth—she had the most incredible mouth—one minute he'd just been watching yet another movie, and the next the images were ricocheting through his mind like bullets. . . .

Mother of God. They were stuck in a traffic jam. Jean-Jacques began to feel he'd go crazy. Unfortunately he'd just had a bust-up with the latest girl, otherwise he'd have gone straight to her apartment. But he was between women at the moment, not that that would last for long. So Ghislaine would just have to do. If she was there, of course, which she usually wasn't. *Be there*, Jean-Jacques thought; *just be there.*

Ghislaine was in, and Jean-Jacques wasted no time with preliminaries—she was his wife, wasn't she? And anyway, Ghislaine understood him; she, too, had her little ways, and one of them, which her oversensitive lovers did not understand, and Jean-Jacques did, was that she liked sex devoid of tenderness.

She knew anyway, as soon as she saw his face; and he knew, as soon as he saw the sudden fixity, the answering avidity in hers. She was in the kitchen when Jean-Jacques came in, and he went straight up to her from behind, pressing up against her buttocks—just in case she was in any doubt about the matter.

True, she wasted a bit of time—she started kissing him, for one thing, and trying to pull him in the direction of the bedroom, and that wasn't what he wanted at all. He wanted to do it right there, in the kitchen, with the door only half closed, and the maid likely to walk in at any moment. . . .

And he didn't want to fuck her, either. That wasn't the image burning a hole in his head. No, he wanted her down on her knees, fully dressed; he wanted her sucking him.

He gave Ghislaine a push, so she half-fell; then he reached for his zipper, fumbling in his haste, and pulled it out—so she could take a good look, so she could see just how big he was.

Sucking was not one of Ghislaine's strong points; she was good enough at it, but he'd known better. Today, however, he didn't care; just the wetness and openess of her mouth was enough for him. He grabbed her by the hair, and tipped her head back; then he began to thrust and pump, back and forth, back and forth. He shut his eyes, and saw Hélène Harte's face, Hélène Harte's mouth; the image was burning; his cock was burning; he felt full of sperm, and it was bursting to get out, into her mouth, into the bitch's throat. . . .

The word *bitch*, or possibly the word *throat*, did it. Jean-Jacques bellowed and shuddered.

It was glorious, just for a second, just for a minute, just until the throbbing and the pumping stopped.

Then he opened his eyes, and felt a profound disgust. A line of copper pans winked; the gas on the stove was still on. And the image had gone: at the very last moment it had slipped away.

He pulled back, and looked at Ghislaine dazedly. The wrong bitch of a woman, the wrong place, the wrong mouth: everything was wrong, somehow.

Ghislaine was still kneeling. She looked up at him, her face white under her makeup, and her eyes murderous.

"Who was it?" she said. "Why don't you tell me? I'd just like to know who it was you were thinking about. . . ." She stopped.

As if it were an afterthought, she added, "Bastard."

Jean-Jacques stared at her. He felt confused. The image had been there in his mind; he'd been sure he was going to possess it, and now he knew—he'd lost it.

"Jesus, Ghislaine . . ." he started to say, reaching down to help her up.

Perhaps something in his wife's face triggered the memory, he wasn't sure. But it was at that moment that the memory came back to him, and he knew where he had seen Hélène Harte before.

It was also the moment in which Ghislaine realized once and for all precisely how much she hated him.

Two days later, Ghislaine had lunch with Louise de Chavigny, in Louise's favorite restaurant, to discuss the redecoration of Louise's house in St. Tropez.

She had not wanted to join Louise, whom she disliked, and her temper was so bad that she had almost cast caution to the wind and canceled, despite the fact that Louise was a catch, an influential client. In the end, she went, and for the first five minutes she hardly heard a word Louise said—not that she said anything worth listening to. Ghislaine's mind had not been able to rid itself of the horrible and humiliating image of that scene in the kitchen with Jean-Jacques: herself on her knees, Jean-Jacques tugging at her hair, his mouth half open, his face flushed crimson. It filled her with rage and loathing—all the more intense because it was impossible to speak of it to anyone. She felt as if she could still taste him in her mouth, that disgusting repellent taste, like the smell of fish. When Louise ordered grilled sole, she felt physically sick.

She swallowed some wine, and forced herself to concentrate. She looked at Louise, who was wearing a new necklace, of opals, and a very chic little hat, with a veil. A veil, even a small one, and at her age, Ghislaine thought scornfully. Louise was waving her hands vaguely and fretfully. The house at St. Tropez was so charming. Such a marvelously romantic setting. But she found it now so very dull-looking, so very démodé. . . . The thing was, she wanted Ghislaine to do it, but could it be done quickly enough?

She lifted her still-lovely face to Ghislaine, and looked at her with that sweet vague hesitancy she used to mask her iron will.

"It must be ready for May," she said. She had previously said the end of the summer. "By mid-May. Edouard said he might come down." She paused and gave a little smile. Ghislaine knew she was not thinking of Edouard when she smiled like that. "And one or two other people, a little later in the summer. A house party. A retreat from Paris. Really, Ghislaine, I find Paris so exhausting these days. . . ."

Philippe de Belfort, Ghislaine thought; she knew it in an instant, and Louise, who knew she knew, and probably wanted her to, looked away with a vague smile.

Ghislaine felt the scorn rise. Really, Louise was incredible. Such vanity. Still to take lovers at her age, and a man virtually the same age as her son. She couldn't imagine, surely, that de Belfort could care for her? De Belfort was interested in only one thing, his own advancement. She looked at Louise for a moment with an appalled curiosity. Did she still go to bed with them? It was possible, she looked in her early fifties, no more, and with Louise, anything was possible. But on the whole,

Ghislaine thought not. What Louise wanted, she suspected—what she had always wanted—was not sex at all, but adoration.

She thought back then to the past, and to Xavier de Chavigny, whom she had met only once or twice, when she was still a young girl. That marvelous man—she had always admired him from afar; when she had still been full of romantic dreams, before she grew up and discovered what most men were like; when she had been young, ah, how she had dreamed of meeting a man like the Baron de Chavigny. And Louise, who had been his wife, whom he had loved madly, everyone said so—she was now reduced to this: to being proud to hint that she had a nothing like Philippe de Belfort as her admirer.

It was then, quite suddenly, when Louise was toying with her food, and describing her house, which was charming, and yet not quite what she wanted, that the fear struck Ghislaine. She looked at Louise, and to her horror saw herself in twenty years' time. Not as stupid as Louise, perhaps; not as self-deluding; but just as disappointed.

She had her work, of course, which made a difference; Louise had never lifted a finger in her life. But still, however hard she tried to avoid it, Ghislaine could see a certain horrible resemblance. Louise had been married only once—Ghislaine three times, all unhappily. For the last ten years she'd been trapped with that peasant Jean-Jacques, loathing him, trying not to mind when her friends smirked because they knew—all Paris knew—about the latest model, the latest typist, the latest calendar girl. Jean-Jacques, who liked best to fuck her when he knew she had just come from her lover's. And the lovers themselves: that procession of unmemorable young men, who invariably failed to give her the most minimal satisfaction . . . was there one of them who loved her, one of them who would ask her to leave Jean-Jacques, and marry him? No, there was not. They liked the fact that she was married: it made them feel safer.

"The *salon* faces out over the sea," Louise was saying with a small discontented pout. "I liked that to begin with, but the light, you know—it reflects, it makes the room so very bright. . . ." Ghislaine hardly heard a word she said. She thought: I'm forty-seven; Louise is sixty-seven. She thought: I could give them up, Jean-Jacques, all the goddamned men. I could concentrate on my work. I could make it on my own. Who needs them—who needs any of them?

Just for a moment she felt courage, she felt confidence: she could see herself doing it. Then the courage deflated like a pricked balloon. She knew it wasn't true; she knew she didn't want it; a woman without a man was nothing, a figure of ridicule—like Louise.

No, she needed a man—and at the same second she acknowledged that fact, she knew with a sudden sharp instinct which man. She saw him quite distinctly—the man who so resembled his father, the man who was the embodiment of all her earliest ideals. How could she have been so stupid? How could she have been so lazy? How could she have known, always, that she was attracted to him, and yet have made no move, have done nothing at all? She set down her fork with a sudden little clatter. She blushed, in a way she had not done since she was a girl, slowly and agonizingly, the heat rushing up over her neck and suffusing her face.

Louise looked at her with a malice which she was at pains to conceal.

Poor Ghislaine, she thought with acid amusement. So she *has* reached the menopause—she always lied about her age, one could never be certain. . . . She would be kind, Louise resolved, and ignore Ghislaine's obvious humiliation.

"So tell me, darling Ghislaine. Will you still do it for me? Can it be done in time?"

Even then, when she could not think for the rush of excitement she felt, Ghislaine managed to keep some of her wits about her. She pretended an impossible schedule of work, she pleaded prior commissions, until Louise—who always wanted something more if she felt she might not get it—was forced to become pressing. Then, and only then, did Ghislaine capitulate.

"For you, my dear," she said with a smile. "Very well."

Louise was an impossible client. She changed her mind a million times a minute, she haggled over prices like an Arab street vendor; Ghislaine did not care. She had the perfect entrée, the perfect opportunity. She could easily manage to remain at the villa until Edouard arrived—she checked the dates and made sure of it. Meanwhile, she threw herself into her work with new energy; it would be beautiful, spectacular, the best thing she had ever done. She was doing it, she felt, for Edouard, not for his fool of a mother—and when he saw it, and admired it, ah, then, what then? She was not sure, except that it might be the beginning.

She worked confidently, surely, for a week. In that time, she lost weight, bought new clothes, had her hair cut, changed the scent she wore. She began to feel like a new woman.

She had little impulses, and she gave in to them: once she rang Edouard's number at St. Cloud, in the hope of hearing his voice, but his manservant answered. Another time, she drove past his offices. She took to lunching at a restaurant he frequented, and one day glimpsed him in the distance. She found she took great delight in speaking of him to her friends: just to say his name gave her pleasure—and of course, there was an additional benefit: her friends all confirmed what she herself had suspected—Edouard was unattached. Edouard—always so sought after, and always so alone.

In seven days she felt she had lived through a year; there had been so many advances in her mind in that time that it was difficult to believe that nothing had actually happened. Ghislaine felt that it had, and that just as she had been transformed, so Edouard could be—once he began to perceive her differently. They were old friends—that was something to build on. He respected her work; he admired her taste; now that she looked back on it, she felt that, yes, there had perhaps always been something special in his manner toward her, an indefinable something. . . . Ah, Edouard!

And then, just when she felt twenty years younger, on the crest of a wonderful wave, it happened. She was walking home from work one beautiful evening, and stopped dead suddenly, in the middle of the sidewalk. Across the street there was a movie theater, and outside the theater was a series of posters. They were photographs of a girl, a very beautiful girl, in a white dress.

Level brows, short dark hair, a wide mouth, a defiant modern stance. The color of the hair, and the shortness of it, confused Ghislaine, just for an instant.

Then she recognized her. The girl from the Loire; the girl in the Givenchy; the girl wearing Edouard's diamond ring. The girl she had first seen coming out of a little disreputable hotel, on Edouard's arm, at nine o'clock in the morning.

Ghislaine stood very still. Then she began to walk again, continuing her walk home, more slowly. Quite suddenly, the evening, the past week, everything, was spoiled.

Halfway down the Boulevard St. Germain, there was a line of the posters, a solid phalanx of them, each eight feet high. From these posters, Edouard averted his eyes. *Short Cut, a Thaddeus Angelini film,* he read, in huge black letters over the entrance of the theater nearby. There was a line of people outside, waiting for the early evening performance; it stretched past the theater and well down the street. Edouard leaned forward, opened the partition, and asked his driver to hurry. He leaned back again on the leather seats and closed his eyes.

He had just been in New York: the city had been plastered with her image. Now it was all over Paris, everywhere he looked. And it would get worse. Once she arrived in Cannes for the film festival, there would be blanket coverage: every newspaper, every magazine; she would be on television, on billboards. . . .

That odd moment had been reached when a name became, almost overnight, and by some curious alchemy, a household word. When it happened, it was always with astonishing rapidity. One moment someone was known only to the few, was being tipped, perhaps, for success and fame, but no more; the next, that person's name was on everyone's lips, familiar to everyone from presidents to fishmongers, public property, part of the common currency of thought.

Edouard had no doubt that Hélène would win the award at Cannes. He thought it would not be very long before she received an Academy Award. He had seen *Short Cut*, of course, long before Christian, long before its release; its almost insolent assurance had filled him with an angry admiration. Annoyingly, Angelini actually possessed some of the genius he had claimed. Hélène, just as Angelini had predicted, possessed, on film, an extraordinary and innocent eroticism. Images from that film, mixed with images from his past, haunted him.

Now there was this new project, *Ellis*, for which Angelini was seeking major backing from Sphere. He planned to make the movie the following year, and a copy of Angelini's screenplay now lay on the desk in Edouard's study at St. Cloud. That evening, Edouard must decide whether to authorize the funding for the film, or not. He had already read the screenplay; tonight, he would read it again.

The black Rolls pulled up outside the de Chavigny showrooms in the Rue du Faubourg St. Honoré. The uniformed doorman advanced, bowing. Edouard entered by his private entrance, and went, as arranged, straight to the vaults.

There, on a special table in a room set apart from the strongrooms, the pieces he had requested be ready for him to inspect had been laid out. A dozen leather jewelcases, exquisitely tooled, their design and decoration redolent of their different periods. Some de Chavigny, some Cartier, one from Wartski's in London, another from Bulgari, one from Van Cleef and Arpels.

Edouard asked to be alone, and then began opening the cases one by one. He was choosing his daughter's birthday present, which, when chosen, would be put back in the special safe in the de Chavigny vaults, until . . . until she was older, Edouard told himself.

Two presents already lay in that safe. One, a necklace of pearls, and superb rose and briolette-cut diamonds, had been the prize of Wyspianski's first collection; it had been placed there to mark Catharine's birth. The second, marking her first birthday, was a tiara designed for the firm of Cartier in 1914: an exquisite circlet of black onyx and circular cut diamonds, surmounted by a ring of pearls. It was—unlike many tiaras—light. He thought Catharine would find it pleasurable to wear it.

Now he moved slowly along the line of boxes, opening them one by one. From Cartier again: a diamond aigrette, commissioned from them by Prince Gortchakov in 1912, a delicate spray plume above a pear-shaped diamond weighing some twenty carats. From de Chavigny: a necklace of sapphire and emerald beads with diamond rondelles, designed by Vlacek for his father in the 1920s. *Not emeralds*, Edouard thought, and turned to the next box.

A serious ring, a very serious ring: a square-cut canary diamond of nearly thirty carats, which Edouard did not greatly like, though the value of the stone was great. A little gold vanity case, enameled and inlaid with lapis lazuli the color of his daughter's eyes. A unique watch, a collector's piece, with works by the celebrated Jean Vergely, mounted on a silk cord, designed in 1925 in the art deco manner, gold and lapis again, with two tiny ruby studs to mark the extremity of the hours. A carved coral necklace, made in China in the eighteenth century, its carved flowers spilling little clusters of onyx, diamonds, and black pearls. A ruby and diamond stomacher brooch, designed for one of the Romanovs; a diamond résille necklace, made by de Chavigny in 1903, copied from a necklace once worn by Marie Antoinette, and bought by the courtesan, la Belle Otéro. . . .

Edouard looked at each piece once. Some of them had a sad history, and these he pushed aside. He hesitated; there was a pair of matching bracelets surmounted with cabochon rubies that had once belonged to the Maharaja of Mysore—Isobel would have adored those, he thought sadly—they, indeed, were superbly pagan. In the end he chose the piece whose value lay in its workmanship, not its stones: the Chinese necklace. It was put in the safe; Edouard left for St. Cloud.

He stared out the windows of the car with blank eyes, seeing nothing of his surroundings. Two and a half years. Sometimes, in his blackest moments, he felt that the certitude and hope he still occasionally experienced were nothing more than a fabrication, a perverse and destructive obsession to which he clung in the midst of the bleakness and pointlessness of his life. At other times, he felt the opposite. He had ceased now to argue with himself. The two opposing possibilities coexisted all the time, like twin poles—the north and south of his mind. The constant oscillation of his spirit between them, he now accepted. If he had had to describe his state of mind he would have said, wryly, that he was resigned.

At St. Cloud he ate a solitary meal, formally served. He then returned to his study, which was unchanged. The same Turner watercolors still hung on the walls; the same rugs lay on the floor, and he thought momentarily of Isobel, sitting there, twisting her face up to him, with that self-mocking emerald glance, telling him about her marriage, about living with a man who wanted to die.

Edouard sat down at his desk. In one of the drawers, which he unlocked, was a plain envelope with an American air mail stamp. It had arrived the previous day, which had been his daughter's birthday.

He opened it once more, and drew out the photograph, and the small sheet of paper attached to it, on which were written a few sentences in Madeleine's handwriting.

The photograph showed a little girl wearing a hand-smocked blue dress; she had bare legs and wore sandals. Her black hair was simply cut, in a straight bob to the shoulders. She was looking directly at the camera, with her dark blue eyes; she was not smiling.

She was standing in a garden, and behind her—just visible—were the walls and windows of a house. Slightly to one side of the child, looking at her proudly, were two women: one was Madeleine, wearing the pale brown Norland College uniform; the other was an older woman, plump, with gray hair.

Madeleine had written, in French:

> Little Cat is two. Cassie and I measured her today. She is two feet and eight inches tall. She is exactly twenty-seven pounds in weight, perhaps a little thin, but she grows very fast. I have lost count of the number of words she knows, because they increase every day. A month ago, Cassie and I thought it was one hundred and ninety-seven, but it is much more now. She knows five words of French: Bonjour; Bonne nuit; Merci beaucoup. For her birthday, I am knitting her a little sweater, in blue, which is her favorite color. It is almost finished, there are just the sleeves to do. Cassie has sewn her a skirt, with a very pretty blue border. She is sleeping much better now, and has a very good appetite. She had a cough, in February, but it cleared up very quickly.

Three words were then crossed out, so they were indecipherable. Underneath, Madeleine had finished:

> This is Cassie and me in the photograph: Cassie is the housekeeper now, and sometimes cooks. Catharine likes her cakes. She came here when we moved to this house, last June. We are good friends, I think. Assuring you, Monsieur le Baron, of my enduring service and respect.

The letter, or note, was then signed. As an afterthought, Madeleine had written: All is well.

Edouard reread the words several times; he looked at the photograph for a long time. Then he slipped it back into the envelope, and put the envelope back in his drawer. Under it was one other, sent by Madeleine on the same date in May the previous year. He had given her strict instructions that this was to be the limit of their correspondence, and Madeleine obeyed him, of course.

Madeleine was not in that household as an informer; that possibility, which seemed to Edouard deeply dishonorable, had been ruled out. It had embarrassed him to spell it out to Madeleine, but he had done so. There was to be no reference, he had said, to other members of the household; no reference to activities that took place, nor to events or conversations that occurred. Madeleine was there for one reason, and one reason only: to ensure that his daughter was safe, and secure, in good hands, and in good health. "Once a year, on her birthday, if you could send me a small photograph," he had said, finding the request very difficult. Madeleine had bent her head; the little notes, which told him everything, and nothing, had been her idea, he assumed, since he had not requested them. Now he did not have the heart to tell her not to write.

He had given the instructions curtly, as he always did when he wished to disguise strong emotion. His mind had blazed with all the things he knew he would want to know. Was Catharine happy? Was her mother happy? What did she do? How did she pass the hours of her day? What did she think? What did she say? What did she feel? Did she love her husband? Did Catharine love him? Did she call Lewis Sinclair Father?

He still wanted to know the answers to those questions, and to a million others, and—proudly—he despised himself for the need, and never spoke of it. He had elected to take this course; insofar as he was able, he would do so without deviating from the iron rails of his personal code.

All is well. He knew why Madeleine had added that postscript. What if she had written the opposite—all is *not* well, everything is wrong, painful, chaotic, Catharine is suffering. . . . What would he have done then? He bent his head wearily in his hands. He was, above all things, thorough and methodical. He had consulted a lawyer, and discussed—as if in the abstract—certain points. The man had looked at him carefully, perhaps pitying him. Then he had folded his hands.

"In the circumstances you describe, *Monsieur le Baron*, the law is perfectly clear." He paused. "The term applicable is *putative father*. The putative father in a case such as the one you describe, is without legal rights. Or claims," he had added gently.

"Entirely?"

"Entirely, *Monsieur le Baron*."

Edouard stood up. He locked the drawer of his desk and put the key in his pocket. He left the room, and the house, took one of his cars—the black Aston-Martin—from the garage, and drove, fast, around the city of Paris for one hour. It was dark, and he drove fast; while he drove he listened to some Beethoven piano pieces—Seven Bagatelles, recorded originally by Schnabel in 1938. It was a recording he particularly liked, and played often at home. The music was sometimes melancholy, abruptly gentle, finally, and assertively, wild. Joyous, too, he supposed.

When he returned to the house, he rang for his servant, George, and asked for Armagnac. It was brought him, George left, and—picking up the screenplay of the film *Ellis*—Edouard began once more to read.

Attached to the script were various reports and memoranda from script consultants and production executives now employed at Sphere: some were for the project, others against. Edouard pushed these aside, and looked only at the words of the screenplay itself. It was long, and would make a film of more than usual duration; it took him nearly two hours to read, for he read it carefully, making occasional notes.

It began on Ellis Island, in 1912; it then traced, and interwove, the stories of three families—one Jewish-Hungarian, one Irish, and one German by origin—as they became American. The birth of a nation: the comparison with D. W. Griffith would probably be made, Edouard thought, and would, no doubt, amuse Thaddeus Angelini.

The film concentrated most closely on the younger generation of the families, and in particular on Lise, a young German orphan, aged fourteen when the film began. This part would be played by Hélène—it had been written for her, of that Edouard had no doubt. It was that part which—he felt certain of it—would win her an Academy Award.

When he had finished reading, he closed the covers of the screenplay, and sat quietly, his hands folded. He knew Angelini's ability as a director. The screenplay moved him; of its stature, he was in no doubt.

If he did not authorize the funding of the film by Sphere, there were other companies only too eager to step into the breach, he knew that. Angelini's reputation was growing fast; Hélène Harte's participation promised commercial success. One studio or another would step in, the film would still be made—though possibly with more interference than if it were funded by Sphere.

He hesitated. He was aware that if he signed this authorization, he was possibly signing away Hélène. The success this would bring her would be absolute; it was not an achievement from which he could envision her walking away. It was, this document, a kind of death warrant for his hopes.

He paused, then picked up his platinum pen and signed his name.

"My dear Louise, I do so see what you mean! Impossible, quite impossible . . ."

They had completed their tour of the house, and had now returned to the *salon* overlooking the sea. Louise was sitting, rather quietly for once, and Ghislaine was standing in the center of the room; as she spoke, she accompanied her words with a suitably extravagant gesture.

"All those little touches of yours, Louise, quite charming. But the rest of it! Such a heavy hand—no, as I thought, we shall have to start from scratch. Everything must go, my dear—absolutely everything."

"Do you think so, Ghislaine? Well, I shall be guided by you, naturally. . . ."

Louise sounded hardly interested. Ghislaine looked at her sharply. Was she losing interest? Was she about to change her mind? Abandon the whole project? It was possible, Ghislaine thought; Louise was capable of changing her mind fifteen times in as many minutes.

She hesitated, looking around her. The villa was exquisite, of course. Magnificently positioned, set high on a hillside some twelve kilometers from St. Tropez itself. Its rooms were large, and light, there was the most glorious terrace, forty hectares of land to ensure total seclusion. . . . And the interior, well, had the house been hers, Ghislaine knew perfectly well that she would have been tempted to keep it exactly as it was. The English designer responsible for it, a flamboyant homosexual, was a man Ghislaine particularly disliked. But his eye was brilliant, she had to admit that. The use of color, the sense of form, the quality of the curtains, the carpets—they alone must have cost a small fortune.

However, it was Louise's house, not hers, and Ghislaine naturally had no intention of telling Louise what she truly thought. But Louise's indifference was worrying her: she had expected opposition, she had expected quibbles. So far there had been none. Ghislaine began to think that there was indeed something seriously wrong.

They were to have lunch on the terrace. Over lunch, Ghislaine returned to the attack; Louise sat there sipping her wine, her eyes on the sea beyond. Ghislaine, feeling her audience slipping away from her, began to feel desperate.

"Simple," she said. "I see it, my dear, as terribly terribly simple. Audaciously simple. In simplicity is elegance—but you know that, you are the very embodiment of it. . . ."

She paused hopefully. Louise acknowledged the flattery with a dreamy smile.

"Cool cool colors," Ghislaine went on, wàrming to her theme. "Those wonderful creams and off-whites darling Syrie used so well, the old monster. Some blue, to remind us of the sea. That delicious gray-green—the color of rosemary."

"Green? I've always rather disliked green. Any shade of green," Louise said ruminatively.

Ghislaine, who was wearing a green dress, drew a deep breath. "Well, perhaps not green," she said hastily. "Dare we use some pink, do you think? I would so love to. That very pale rose pink, shell pink—if we used it terribly carefully. Nothing too obviously feminine. No ghastly frills and furbelows. Everything rather calm and understated. And for the furniture, nothing in the least grand. Wouldn't that be amusing? Louise?"

"Simple things?" Louise smiled vaguely. "Oh, yes. That sounds perfectly charming."

"Some interesting paint treatments," Ghislaine went on doggedly. "All that dreadful wallpaper must come off—it's quite inappropriate in a house like this. And the windows—now we must emphasize those marvelous windows. I wonder—maybe we should bring in Clara Delluc. Let her work on a textile scheme for the whole house—she really is so marvelously original. Dear Clara! I adore her. . . ."

Louise gave a little sigh. She pushed aside her wineglass with just the smallest suggestion of irritation.

"Of course. Of course. I've already told you, Ghislaine—your ideas sound delightful, quite delightful. I'm happy to leave all the details to you. I really don't have the time, and when you get excited, Ghislaine, well, you do rather *bombard* one, you know. . . ."

Ghislaine gave her a glance of pure dislike, which Louise fortunately did not see; she intended, she thought, to charge Louise the earth. . . .

"Very well," she said crisply. "But it's going to be a great rush, you know. The preliminary work's been done, of course, and everyone is standing by. I'll pull out all the stops, my dear—since it's for you. . . ."

Louise did not bother to thank her. Her face was dreamy once more. "It's such a *woman's* house at the moment, don't you think, Ghislaine? That's what's wrong, perhaps. That terrible pansy who did it before, I can't think why I asked him. I was driven to distraction, Ghislaine—he would *nag*. But you've such a wonderfully *masculine* imagination, I've always thought. So I know you'll do it beautifully. I'd like . . ." She paused. "I'd like it to be the kind of house in which a *man* felt comfortable—yes, that's what I want. I see it now."

Ghislaine looked at her narrowly. Of course, she thought: it was perfectly simple. Louise could never manage to think about two things at once. It wasn't that she lacked interest, she was simply too busy thinking about Philippe de Belfort.

W hen they boarded Edouard's plane, which was to fly them back to Paris, Louise's spirits rose. She behaved as if she had been absent several months rather than a few hours. She was being *met* at the airport, she confided to Ghislaine, with a coquettish glance; Ghislaine smiled ingenuously.

"By Edouard? He's just back from New York, isn't he?"

"Edouard? Goodness no, Ghislaine. By Philippe de Belfort . . ."

Louise was, at that point, halfway up the steps to the aircraft. On the top step, she turned, sighed, took a deep breath of carbon monoxide fumes, lifted her face to the sun, and smiled radiantly.

"Isn't it the most wonderful day? You know, Ghislaine, I feel positively young. . . ."

Once they had taken off, Louise asked for champagne. She and Ghislaine both smoked and drank, and the mood between them became quite confidential. Ghislaine was almost enjoying herself, and she knew Louise was too. They talked about dresses, and hats, and the virtues of this *vendeuse* as opposed to that one. They discussed the taste of the many acquaintances and friends they had in common, and agreed it was execrable. Though neither, essentially, liked the other very much, there were links between them, and on such an occasion, warmed by champagne, it was almost possible to feel, if not friendship exactly, then some kind of warm alliance.

"I *adore* Balenciaga." Louise sighed. "Such a genius. But I can't wear his clothes. I simply can't. I'm not tall enough. Now on you, Ghislaine, they are perfect. Absolutely perfect."

"Ah, yes. But you can wear Chanel, my dear, which doesn't suit me at all. Do you know, I remember you in a Chanel dress, in the great days. I can still see it so clearly. It was pink—you were with Xavier, and I remember thinking how exquisite you looked. Goodness, what an age ago. It must have been 1930, somewhere around then. . . ."

Ghislaine had been about to add that she had been fifteen at the time; she just managed to stop herself.

"Ah, yes! I remember it, Ghislaine—quite distinctly!" She gave a sigh. "How young we were!"

On another occasion this bracketing, as if they were the same age, would have annoyed Ghislaine so much that she would have felt bound to make some sharp rebuke. But not now. The champagne was making her benevolent; she did not want the mood spoiled.

They continued to talk, woman-to-woman, and the tone became more confidential still. Ghislaine managed to get in a few questions about Edouard, but Louise was not very informative.

"He's a disappointment to me in some ways, Ghislaine. I shouldn't say it, but it's the truth. We were never close, of course, and now—well,

I never quite find him *sympathetic*. He can be a terrible prude. And of course, with women—quite hopeless, in spite of all those affairs. He doesn't understand us, Ghislaine, and I begin to fear he never will. . . ."

Ghislaine shook her head. "What man does understand women, Louise? When it comes down to it?"

Very few, Louise agreed—though there were occasional exceptions. . . . The two women looked at each other. There was a moment of unspoken but perfect understanding between them. Now was the moment for more intimate revelations, but such revelations had their own code: they must be mutual. This nice balance produced the equivalent of trust.

Ghislaine knew that, and so she began.

"My dear, do you know, I never speak of this, but sometimes . . ."

Louise leaned forward eagerly, wide-eyed. Ghislaine told her certain things about Jean-Jacques, things she was certain Louise knew anyway. To her own surprise, she found it was almost a relief to talk. When she had finished, Louise asked for more champagne, and took her turn.

"No! Louise! Not Xavier—I can't believe it! It can't be true!" Louise nodded solemnly. They were now both enjoying themselves very much. The moment had come to move on from husbands to lovers, and Ghislaine took the plunge. Louise followed suit; certain names were mentioned, and they discovered that—a long time before—there was one young man who had, for a period, entertained them both. This made them laugh.

"Louise, imagine—now you must tell me—I never found him quite . . ."

Louise wiped tears of laughter from her eyes.

"Neither did I. Neither did I! Ghislaine—why ever did we bother? How absurd we were!" She paused, hesitated. "Tell me—the truth now. As a married woman, did it ever make you feel guilty?"

Ghislaine looked at her; a dry look. "Actually no. To tell the truth, quite the reverse."

"Oh, Ghislaine—I do so adore you. You're so wickedly frank. . . ."

The second bottle of champagne was finished; the seal on their newly warm relationship was set. The plane banked, and turned; Ghislaine was aware that she was more than slightly drunk. It was at that moment, when she was quite off her guard, that Louise, also unguarded by this point, made her major, her irreversible, mistake.

It sprang from intimacy and good will, delicately shaded with patronage, and perhaps also from an irrepressible urge just to use Philippe de Belfort's name. She leaned across and pressed Ghislaine's arm.

"My dear—you know you were saying about Jean-Jacques—how mean he is. . . ."

"Mean! He won't part with a sou. If it was up to him, I'd dress at Printemps. I pay for everything, all the couturier's bills, myself. . . ."

Louise's eyes rounded with shock and sympathy.

"Look at this." Ghislaine held out her hand and displayed the ring she was wearing.

"It's lovely, darling. I was admiring it earlier. . . ."

"It's borrowed," Ghislaine said bitterly. "Like most of my jewelry."

"Darling! It's so unfair. Now, listen to me. You're obviously being given all the wrong advice. The money you earn, Ghislaine, you could double it, triple it on the market. And all without doing a thing. Philippe says—"

She broke off, and gave Ghislaine a coy and almost flirtatious glance. "He's terribly clever, you know. Since I began to take his advice—I can't tell you, Ghislaine, what fun it's been. And you could do the same. . . ."

Ghislaine stared at her.

"Philippe's been advising you? Philippe de Belfort? But I thought Edouard . . ."

"Oh, Edouard!" Louise made a little face. "Edouard's so stuffy. So conservative. Clever, of course, but he lacks daring. Now, Philippe . . ."

Ghislaine's mind was growing alert. Louise leaned closer, so her mouth was close to Ghislaine's ear. She lowered her voice to a whisper; she said, "Imagine. One hundred thousand, Ghislaine!"

She drew back again, her eyes sparkling. Ghislaine felt confused.

"Francs?"

"Darling Ghislaine, don't be silly. Sterling. All perfectly aboveboard, arranged through my Swiss bank. In two months."

Ghislaine swallowed.

"Two months?"

"That's what I've cleared, in two months." She gave Ghislaine a little conspiratorial smile. "I was dying to sell and take my profits, but Philippe says no, I should hang on. He thinks it could go up another twenty percent—maybe more. Isn't that delightful? It's that kind of little tip that makes all the difference, Ghislaine. Now do you see what I mean?"

Ghislaine did. One hundred thousand pounds. In two months. She could imagine herself spending it; real jewels, serious jewels, and all of them her own. Resentment rose like bile in her stomach; she knew suddenly that she had never hated Louise so much as she did at that moment, when Louise thought she was being kind. One hundred thousand: chicken feed to Louise, and yet she looked as thrilled as a small girl who had just won a raffle.

"Yes, that's all very well," Ghislaine managed eventually. "You have the capital to do that, Louise. My position, unfortunately—"

"You have to speculate to accumulate, Ghislaine. Never forget that. Then it's just a matter of being on the inside, of getting the right little hints. Now, listen, Ghislaine. Do you have some money at the moment, something that isn't tied up?"

"I suppose so. I've just been paid for the Rothschild designs. And Harriet Smithson's house was finished a month ago, so . . ."

"Darling. I'm going to say one little word to you. Well, three little words actually. But you'll have to act fast. And then you're to forget it was I who mentioned them, you promise?"

"I promise."

"Not a word to anyone. Above all, not a word to Edouard—I can rely on you, Ghislaine? If Edouard knew I hadn't consulted him, he'd be cross, and that would spoil everything. . . ."

"Not a word, my dear, naturally, I swear."

The two women looked at each other, and then Louise smiled. Very carefully and distinctly, she said, "Rolfson Hotels Group."

And in Ghislaine's head, as a thousand alarm bells started to ring, came the most marvelous sense of calm. She saw at once all the advantages that the betrayal of this confidence could bring.

I n his Paris office, the next day, Edouard sat still at his desk. In front of him were pages of figures; opposite him sat Philippe de Belfort. It was the first meeting they had had since Edouard returned from New York the previous morning; it had been called by Edouard, with some urgency. De Belfort, however, seemed quite calm.

Edouard looked at the figures in front of him tiredly. He was blaming himself for the fact that he had lost a day. Yesterday there had been a thousand matters to attend to; he had spent time choosing the present for Catharine; he had spent hours reading the Angelini screenplay at St. Cloud; and all the time there had been this time bomb ticking away. True, he had to delegate; true, this was, strictly speaking, de Belfort's responsibility and de Belfort's domain—but still, it was ultimately his responsibility: Edouard traced and retraced the figures angrily, blaming himself. When he looked up, finally, his voice was very cold.

"We were in touch constantly while I was in New York. Would you tell me why you didn't raise this issue then?"

De Belfort spread his hands. "I knew you'd have been watching the market. I assumed you knew. You did raise the question on one occasion, if I remember correctly. . . ."

His tone was negligent, almost insolent. Edouard's mouth tightened. "I raised the question, and you assured me you'd been keeping a watch on it, and would continue to do so. I was then very tied up with the Partex negotiations, as you know. It was you who were in London, you who were handling this. This is your responsibility. Yesterday—you could have spoken to me yesterday, as soon as I returned. . . ."

"I didn't contact you yesterday, or before that, and for one simple reason. I looked at the situation, and I considered there was no cause for alarm. That is still my view."

"I see."

De Belfort's tone had become slightly aggressive, as it always did whenever his judgment was questioned. Edouard bent his head again to the figures in front of him; after a while, he raised his head, and looked de Belfort straight in the eye.

"The message of these figures is perfectly clear. There's something wrong."

"I fail to see it."

"Then I suggest you look again. It's now May. The price of the Rolfson Hotels Group stock has been rising steadily since February."

"Not that dramatically." De Belfort shrugged. "That happens. Our security has been impeccable. But certain rumors always fly about. The market gets jumpy. . . ."

"Jumpy. Precisely. That's exactly what I would expect. A pattern of rise and fall in the Rolfson stock. It's the classic pre-takeover pattern. And it isn't the pattern we have here. Look. A steady rise, from February onward. Virtually no fallback at all."

"It's unusual, I admit." De Belfort's tone was dismissive. "But these things don't always conform to pattern. There are exceptions to every rule. It was like this for the Mackinnon's bid, in 1959. If it continues, I admit, we may be forced into revising our offer upward a little . . . we'll still be well within our margins. And in any case, I don't think that will be necessary. It won't go on climbing. It'll fall. We've still got over a week to go."

Edouard frowned. There was some sense in what de Belfort said, but he still knew he was uneasy. After a while you developed an instinct for the market; Edouard had been born with that instinct, and use had made it sharp. He looked at the figures once more, and they still said—*wrong*. He looked up again.

"You're sure the security has been absolutely tight?"

"Totally. We've used codes from the first. Not more than four or at the most five people know the name of the company, or the timing of the bid. We start printing the letters to Rolfson shareholders tomorrow, and then it gets more difficult, of course. I personally think that a lot of leaks stem from the printers, and I'd like to have delayed it. But we've been very careful. It's being done by a small firm near Birmingham.

We've used them; Montague Smythe's used them. There's never been trouble in the past. . . ."

"And there's only been this one story in the press? Nothing else?"

Edouard slipped the clipping across the desk. De Belfort hardly gave it a glance.

"That rag? No one pays any attention to that. No one else has picked up on it. The man's a Fleet Street joke. Pure speculation on his part . . ."

"I see he's hinting at the possibility of a counterbid. . . ."

De Belfort sighed. "We've discussed this. Obviously, it's a possibility that you can never absolutely rule out. But in my opinion, given the scale of our offer, and the timing of the bid—just after the Rolfson trading figures have come out, and we know how their shareholders are going to react to *them*—we have nothing to fear. I have to admit—" he eased himself forward in his seat—"I don't quite see the necessity for any alarm on your part—"

"Someone's been buying," Edouard cut him off, his voice like ice. "You're not a fool—you can see that in the figures as well as I can. Someone has been buying, to be precise, for two months, since February, and at regular intervals, in fairly substantial amounts. . . . There can be only one reason for that. There's been a leak about our bid."

"I don't accept that. . . ." De Belfort raised his voice.

Edouard continued, as if he had not spoken at all.

"Someone has been buying. And someone is continuing to buy. There's a seven-point rise in the last three days alone. Which suggests to me that someone not only knows about our offer, they have a strong indication that there's going to be a counterbid." Edouard frowned, and his voice became very quiet. "Someone has already made substantial profits. If there's a counterbid, then, of course, they'll stand to make a great deal more."

"We still have a week to go." De Belfort stood up. His face had flushed with irritation. "These figures are misleading. I'm convinced there'll be a drop in the next few days. We just have to sit this out. . . ."

"I don't intend to do that."

"It doesn't seem to me that we've a lot of choice in the matter."

"Oh, there's always a choice in every matter." Edouard stood up. He looked at de Belfort, a long hard look. Then, still in a quiet voice, he said, "I'm postponing our bid."

"We can't do that. You can't do that."

De Belfort's pale heavy features were suffused with a deep flush, which immediately drained away. He looked at Edouard with his pale, almost colorless eyes, that cold dead-fish stare, which Edouard disliked so much. It took him a second, no more, to regain his control. Then he said heavily, "If we do that, we lose the initiative. The timing will be ruined. If I didn't know better, I would think you were panicking. It's ridiculous to do this. You're undoing everything I've been working on for months. . . ."

Edouard did not reply. He turned, and flicked the intercom switch on his desk. He said: "Get me Montague Smythe on the line. Richard Smythe himself." There was a pause. De Belfort said nothing. He turned away, and began to examine a Rothko painting with great attentiveness. Behind him, in a very calm, a dangerously calm, voice, Edouard said, "Then get him out of the meeting. At once, if you would be so good . . ."

At the window of his suite at the Hotel du Cap d'Antibes, Lewis Sinclair looked out across the beautiful gardens toward the Mediterranean Sea. Hélène was out, being interviewed yet again, and Thad was ensconced in a chair behind him, reading a newspaper. Every so often, a page crackled. Lewis wished, irritably, that Thad would for once go away.

There was a certain prestige attached to staying at the Hotel du Cap during the Cannes Film Festival. Lesser mortals might fight to get the best suites at the Carlton or the Majestic in Cannes itself; the "big brass," as Thad put it, stayed here, some forty minutes' drive away, in this very beautiful—and very expensive—place.

"Sphere is picking up the tab," Thad had said. "It has to be the Cap. I don't care, but it's important for Hélène. She has to be seen in the right place."

And so they were here. They had been here four days, arriving early, before the festival began, so that Thad could cram in as many meetings as possible, so that Bernie Alberg, Hélène's indefatigable press agent, could cram in a few more million interviews, and so that Lewis—now what, exactly, could Lewis do? Swim in the pool; have a drink; swim in the pool again.

Thad rustled a page, and Lewis glared at him over his shoulder. Perhaps Thad saw the glare, or felt it, because—somewhat to Lewis's surprise—he got to his feet shortly afterward.

"Oh, well. A quick shower. Then change. We want to be on time."

Lewis did not bother to answer him. Thad's mania for punctuality irritated him. What if they were late? So what? It was just another dinner, given by just another of the innumerable smooth operators who thrived on the edges of festival itself. Some property developer, in this case, who'd tied up the whole Riviera, as far as Lewis could see. He specialized in selling vast villas to Americans, and during the festival no doubt found rich pickings. He reminded Lewis of a fat well-fed shark.

"Susan Jerome's going to be there."

Thad sounded smug. Susan Jerome was possibly the most influential film critic in America.

"So?" Lewis shrugged.

"And the head of Artists International. It pays to meet these people, Lewis, you know."

"It may pay you. It doesn't pay me. Susan Jerome is a pain in the ass."

"She likes our movies, Lewis. . . ."

"She likes *your* movies. I read that last panegyric, and I don't recall it mentioned me."

Thad made small distressed humming noises. Lewis swung around to glare at him again, and after a moment or two, Thad stopped.

"You ought to talk about it, Lewis," he said. "You really should. After all, I'm right next door, and the walls are thin. I can't help hearing . . . I'm your *friend*, you know, Lewis. Who can you talk to if you can't talk to me?"

There was no answer to that question. Lewis gave a sigh.

"Look, Thad," he said. "Would you mind? Just fuck off, okay?"

Thad did, and Lewis stayed where he was at the window. A long time went by. He could have gone down to the pool; he could have gone for a walk in the gardens; he could have gone down to the bar; he could have read a paper, had a nap. All these possibilities went around and around in Lewis's head, and since none of them tempted him very much, he found it impossible to choose between them. Inertia was preferable.

After a while, he poured himself a gin, to which he added a lot of tonic and a lot of ice. He went back to his station at the window. In the gardens below, a spectacular figure teetered across the lawns on spike-heeled shoes. The figure was clad in a semi-transparent white dress, which appeared to have been sewn on around her luscious curves. Her face was crowned by a blaze of blond hair, and she leaned on the arm of a wizened little man who was a big wheel among Hollywood agents. Stephani Sandrelli, the new Monroe lookalike. Lewis had been introduced to her, too, and the agent, at some point, in some place. He couldn't remember where, and he certainly didn't care. One long blur of faces and names. He poured himself another drink. Hélène was late.

When she came in finally, she stopped in the door, took one look, and said, in that voice he had come to hate, "Oh, Lewis."

The reproach in it was soft, but Lewis could hear it, and it suddenly made him furiously angry—it always did.

He turned, and advanced toward her. Hélène shut the door; then she said, "Lewis, I'm late. I have to change. There isn't time. Lewis—please—don't. Not now . . ."

Lewis did not listen to her. He was suddenly completely certain that this time it was going to be all right. If he was quick, and she was quick; if she didn't goddamn well argue . . .

She gave in, and she did not argue very much. Lewis tried not to look at her face. He kept his head buried against her neck, and it *was* going well, it *was* going to work, this time. . . .

And then, just then, he forgot to look away. He looked down at Hélène, and there it was, the way it always was, the pity in her face. After that, it was hopeless: he knew, and she knew. She tried to put her arms around him, and that made it worse.

He stood up; quite suddenly he was shouting. "It's your goddamn fault. You hear me? Your fault. You can do it on screen, but you can't fucking well do it in bed."

Next door, Thad heard. Lewis was absolutely certain that he heard. He wanted him to hear; it was why he had shouted.

After all, he had to tell someone, and it was true—Thad was his best friend.

Who could he tell, except Thad?

"Susan Jerome. Gregory Gertz—a new director. American. Coming up fast. Joe Stein, head of Artists International. Mrs. Joe Stein—*very* interested in the Maison Jasmine. I told them it had belonged to Colette—well, she spent a weekend there once, I believe. . . ."

The eyes of Gustav Nerval, real estate developer extraordinary, twinkled with delight. They sat on the balcony of his suite at the Hotel du Cap, and Nerval, enjoying himself, was listing his dinner guests that evening for the benefit of the charming Madame Belmont-Laon, and, like the good storyteller that he was, he had saved the best for last.

"Thaddeus Angelini—you've seen *Short Cut?*—it will win the Palme d'Or, that's a certainty. And Hélène Harte. The quite beautiful, the quite gracious. and I think the quite clever, Miss Harte. And her husband, of course."

"Mmmm. Very good." Ghislaine looked at him with amusement. A short stocky dark man, blessed with considerable charm, and—when it came to making money—with prodigious energy. She had heard of him, of course—his name had been a byword on this part of the Riviera for years. And he had heard of her.

She suspected, though she was not sure, that he had arranged their meeting, a few days before, at the house of friends they both shared.

She suspected, though she was not sure, that he had his eye on the villa belonging to the Baronne de Chavigny. She suspected, though she was not sure, that she and Nerval could do business together, and that he knew that as well as she. After all, what could be a better combination than a man like Nerval, who specialized in the sale of beautiful, large, and often sadly dilapidated villas, and Ghislaine Belmont-Laon, who could decorate them so exquisitely?

"You think Joe Stein will buy? Do you always oil your deals this well?"

Nerval laughed. "But of course. If a key will not turn, you must oil it before you can put on the pressure."

"And the others?"

"Decoration. Flattering decoration. Big fish like to meet other big fish. No one of any interest to us. Except Hélène Harte. She won't buy this time, but another year, two years—then I think she might be interested. Here, let me freshen your drink. . . ."

He liked American expressions—perhaps he found they put Americans at their ease. Ghislaine watched him as he crossed from the balcony of his suite to fetch the bottle on ice. They were both drinking Perrier. Ghislaine smiled, and stretched, and tilted her face to the sun.

How well everything was turning out—so well she could hardly believe it. She was ensconced in the guest wing of Louise's villa some sixty kilometers from here; it cost her nothing, she lived and was waited on in luxury. She had innumerable friends in the South of France, and plenty of time to see them while her people got on with the work. She had met Nerval, who might launch her on an entirely new phase of her career. She had, with the profits from her Rothschild commission, put the equivalent of fifteen thousand pounds into stock in the Rolfson Hotels Group, and had watched that stock rise, like a meteor. She had information for which, she felt certain, Edouard would be everlastingly grateful, since he loathed de Belfort, and would be furious to hear he had been advising his mother on her financial affairs; and now, tonight, she was to meet Hélène Harte, about whom she was deeply and jealously curious.

How fortuitously everything had turned out! Most of it unplanned, and yet quite perfect. She would meet Edouard when she next flew back to Paris, ask his advice about her investment in Rolfson, confess to a certain concern about Louise . . . and then time it so that the work in St. Tropez was a little delayed, and she was still there, *in situ*, later in the month, when Louise and Edouard were due to arrive. . . .

Perfect indeed! She had rarely felt happier.

"Tell me," she said, as Nerval returned to his seat—he was such a useful person, she was realizing, because he knew everything about everybody. "Tell me about this Hélène Harte. Who is she? Why is everyone suddenly so carried away by her?"

"Ask Joe Stein what her last movie grossed. He's been trying to get her for A.I. He'll tell you."

"How many films has she made? Until this year, I never heard of her."

"Three. Four maybe, I'm not sure. Yes, four, I think. Two little ones and two big ones." He smiled. "You didn't see her in *Summer*? That was the second, I think. Then there was *A Life of Her Own*—that didn't do so well in Europe, but it was very big in America. And now there's *Short Cut*, and if she's got a percentage of that, well . . ."

"You think she would have a percentage?" Ghislaine gave him a sharp look.

"I think she wouldn't miss a trick. Put it that way." Nerval smiled. "A woman who likes the best hires the best lawyers in town—yes?"

For some reason this irritated Ghislaine. She did not like to think of Hélène Harte as astute; she preferred to think of her as mercenary.

"And the interesting thing . . ." Nerval was continuing to speak, his voice thoughtful. "The interesting thing is—no scandal. Not a breath of it. No nude photographs from the days when she was still struggling. No ex-lovers eager to tell all. No current lovers, come to that. Just the husband." He smiled again. "Maybe they're all just waiting to come out of the woodwork—who knows? Her publicist makes a mystery out of her—and it's worked so far. . . . You know the press. They love that kind of thing."

He broke off; Ghislaine was smiling quietly to herself. It was nice, she thought, to know a little bit of scandal that no one would print—even Jean-Jacques, supposing he had the wit to recognize this Hélène Harte.

No, even he would make sure his magazines didn't take a step out of line—after all, Edouard was a major shareholder.

Nerval stood up. He returned, as always, to the matter at hand. "Anyway," he said, "you don't need to bother with her—not yet. Hélène Harte is just the icing on the cake. . . ."

"And the cake is Joe Stein?" Ghislaine asked innocently. Nerval leaned across; he rested his hand lightly over hers. He clicked his tongue reproachfully.

"Come now, Ghislaine, don't be slow. *Mrs.* Joe Stein." He smiled. "The husbands earn the money. And the wives spend it."

Delightful; fortuitous; perfect, Ghislaine thought.

Twenty-four people in the Nerval party. Twenty-four people divided among four circular tables, six to a table, in the Pavilion Eden Roc, the restaurant of the Hotel du Cap, overlooking the celebrated swimming pool and the sea beyond the rocks.

At Nerval's table, of course, were Joe Stein and his wife; Ghislaine's turn with them would come at the end of the meal. Next to Joe Stein, Hélène Harte. She had arrived late, and was now sitting with her back to Ghislaine. In the press and flurry, Ghislaine had been able to avoid an introduction; she felt fairly certain the actress had not noticed her, and that suited her purposes. She intended to speak to her before the evening was out; meanwhile she was content to bide her time.

At her own table, the up-and-coming American director, Gregory Gertz; a leading Italian actress; Susan Jerome, the American critic; Thad Angelini, a small fat toad of a man, already on his third roll; and best of all—Lewis Sinclair. The husband. Sitting right next to her. Ghislaine had already noticed a certain glassiness in his gaze, a certain care in his gait. She had concluded he was already drunk, and at pains to disguise it.

She allowed her eyes to linger, speculatively, on Hélène Harte's back and neck; she had already inspected her thoroughly, from a safe distance, when she came in.

She would have recognized her immediately, of course. Some faces, unfortunately, you never forgot. Clearly, the short dark hair of *Short Cut* had been a wig; now she wore her hair much as she had that night in the Loire, drawn back from her brow, and fastened in a loose chignon at the nape of her neck with a wide black silk bow. She was wearing a long, narrow, black grosgrain dress, which left her throat and shoulders bare, and hid her breasts completely. Around her throat was a rope of the most exquisite pearls Ghislaine had ever seen. She looked breathtaking, and she still possessed that curious quality of stillness which Ghislaine re-membered from the Loire.

She had changed though. She looked much older, totally a woman, not at all a girl. She was poised, confident, apparently quite assured. Her voice had altered, and—Ghislaine thought—her accent had changed. Now it would have been difficult to have assigned her a nationality: English? American? . . . no, European, a European who had lived outside Europe for a long time.

Her self-possession was now enviable, but there was one thing Ghislaine had noticed, and it had interested her. Hélène Harte kept her eyes on her husband all the time they were having drinks. There had been a little moment, a tiny one, of hesitation, when she realized they were seated at separate tables. A second of dismay, quickly hidden. Lewis Sinclair, realizing the same thing at the same time, had looked pleased.

As soon as they were seated, and before the wine arrived, he discreetly called over a waiter and asked for a dry martini. "Very dry."

He had a clipped expensive Boston accent; the drink disappeared very fast.

He had already greeted Ghislaine formally. Just the quickest glance down at the place cards.

"Please. You must call me Ghislaine." She smiled. "I must have missed you when you arrived."

"Yes. We were a little late. Hélène—my wife—had a number of appointments."

He said this in a flat tone of voice, turning the stem of the martini glass in his fingers. Ghislaine looked at him circumspectly.

A handsome—an extremely handsome—young man, in his mid to late twenties she would have guessed. Well-educated. Well-mannered. Well-dressed. Rich, and used to being so. She made her customary quick little judgments, sniffing him out with all her expertise. She regarded him more closely. He had blond hair, well cut, and worn slightly long in the current English manner. The eyes, which had that odd unfocused look in them that indicated inebriation, were a clear light hazel. Their habitual expression was one of slight anxiety, coupled with defiance. Once or twice he looked up at the fat figure of Thad Angelini, who was seated opposite him, talking busily, and then looked away. He was like a child, Ghislaine thought, checking on parental approval or disapproval. He had looked in the same way at his wife.

Ghislaine bided her time. Sinclair was talking to the Italian actress on his right, in reasonably good French, for she spoke no English. Ghislaine chatted amiably to Gregory Gertz on her left, though she could see he was hardly listening to a word she said, and was longing to engage Angelini. Angelini, meanwhile, was talking to the woman critic, who was questioning him earnestly. The replies Angelini gave her, which Ghislaine could overhear, were not modest. He was going to make two more films this year, very quickly, five weeks each, back to back, working as simply as possible, with the most minimal crew union regulations would allow. The first would be called *Quickstep*, the title of the second was as yet undecided—here he glanced across at Lewis Sinclair with an odd little smile. Susan Jerome interjected a question, and Angelini nodded impatiently. Yes, yes, of course, Hélène Harte would be in both of them; and then, next year, he was moving on to a quite different project. . . .

Ghislaine looked at him with distaste. A monomaniac, a bore, she decided. He emanated a peculiar black negative energy, and she could feel him directing it around the table, sucking them all in, sucking them into some maw of his will.

Ghislaine did not intend to be manipulated in this way. She turned to Lewis Sinclair. She had been careful to see *Short Cut* before she left Paris, and she had disliked it intensely. It seemed to her clever, and cold; it was beyond her understanding that it should be so *à la mode*. Naturally, she kept these opinions to herself. She turned to Lewis, and began praising the film energetically, inserting into her remarks some phrases from the review in *Le Monde*.

Lewis Sinclair, who had produced the picture in question, gave her a muted response. He kept looking out the windows to the rocks, and to the sea, which grew dark.

They had eaten caviar, then quails. They were now eating tiny tender pieces of beef, into which strips of *foie gras* had been cunningly inserted; the Burgundy was exceptionally fine, and Lewis Sinclair, having moved on from champagne, was now on his fourth glass.

"Isn't it rather unusual," Ghislaine asked, unsure whether it was or not, "for three people to have such a *close* association over—what is it now—three films?"

"Four," Sinclair corrected her. "We began in 1959 with a low-budget film, *Night Game*. . . ."

"Oh, but of *course* . . ." said Ghislaine, who had never heard of it.

"So we go a long way back. It's a way of working that's more common in Europe, I suppose. Unusual in Hollywood . . ."

"Hollywood is changing. The American film industry is changing. I've changed it," Angelini cut in, making this pronouncement between mouthfuls of beef. Gregory Gertz gave a small ironic smile. Angelini returned to his conversation with the American critic as if there had been no interruption.

His interjection, and the fact that he had been listening to their conversation, appeared to upset Sinclair. He drained the rest of the Burgundy in his glass.

"As a matter of fact," Lewis went on in a low voice, "I've decided to break away—just for a while. Thad is very tied up right now, and I have a new project I'm developing. To tell you the truth, I don't find producing entirely satisfying. I feel I could bring more to a project, you know. Just recently, I've gotten very interested in writing. I had an idea—it just came to me in a flash—and now I want to do some work on it. Nurse it along . . ." He paused, slightly dolefully. "A change of direction every now and then. I think it's essential, don't you?"

"Absolutely essential. Invigorating," said Ghislaine. She glanced up, saw that Angelini was watching them again, and lowered her eyes. A triumvirate, she thought—and Lewis Sinclair was being eased out of it; interesting.

A waiter removed their plates, and Ghislaine decided to find out a little more. She talked on, while the waiters fussed around them, making quite sure that Sinclair first knew who she was, and what she did. He listened dutifully, politely, without great animation.

"It's fun," she said, having dropped the names of some of her more substantial clients, including that of Louise de Chavigny, to which he did not react at all. "Fun—but not truly creative, of course. Not like your wife's work. Or yours. To make movies now, that must be—"

"You're belittling yourself." He interrupted suddenly, with a sharp glance. "I know your work. I admire it. I've stayed at the Cavendish place in England. You did that, didn't you?" Ghislaine swiftly revised her opinion of him. Not as gullible as she had thought. Not as drunk. And well connected. She proceeded more carefully, spooning up a cold peach which had been laid in a perfect little sea of hot raspberry sauce.

She asked as many questions as she dared. Where they lived—a house in the hills above Los Angeles; built for Ingrid Nilsson, the great star of silent movies, and transported to Hollywood from England, brick by brick.

"It's pretty preposterous, I suppose. But Hélène likes it." No, they had not employed an interior designer; his wife had done it herself; very successfully—it was about to be featured in various magazines. . . . Ghislaine listened carefully. This information irritated her—she disliked talented amateurs above all things. Lewis Sinclair, she noticed, seemed to find it difficult to begin a sentence without the use of his wife's name.

"And are you interested in property here?" Ghislaine asked. She smiled. "I'm sure Gustav will try to tempt you."

"You must ask my wife. It's Hélène who's interested in investing in property. She has a highly developed business sense."

This was said, quite suddenly, with detectable malice. As if he realized that himself, he immediately became contrite. "That is, well, she's very clever in that respect." He had corrected himself quickly, making his tone more gentle; still, for a moment, the resentment had been palpable.

"How clever. How remarkable. And she looks so young. . . ."

"Not so remarkable. She works at it." He gave a small bitter smile. "I help her, of course. Or I used to."

"And tell me—do you have a family, children?" Ghislaine gave him a warm smile.

"We have one daughter. Yes. She's just two."

"How charming! A little girl. And does she take after her mother?"

"I'm sorry?" He was looking at her blankly, as if he hadn't heard what she said. Ghislaine was slightly thrown for a moment.

"I meant . . ."

"Oh, I see. No, not really. No. She doesn't look like Hélène at all. I'm sorry. It's very noisy in here, and . . ."

He was looking around again for a waiter, one hand grasping the stem of his empty wineglass. His need for another drink was suddenly so naked and so obvious that Ghislaine almost felt sorry for him.

To ease the moment, as much as anything else, Ghislaine leaned forward slightly and pressed his arm. "You are a fortunate man. To have a wife who is beautiful, and so accomplished. I can't think how—" She broke off. Lewis Sinclair had turned back to her; he appeared distressed, though whether because of the need for a drink, or the compliment to his wife, Ghislaine could not tell. Across the table, Thad Angelini had lifted his heavy head; he was looking directly at them once more. The light winked and blinked against his spectacles; Lewis glanced at him, glanced back at Ghislaine.

"Oh, Hélène can do anything," he said in a throwaway tone. He tossed his napkin onto the table, pushed aside his coffee cup, and lit a cigarette.

"Almost anything," he added as if it were an afterthought, and across the table Thad Angelini smiled.

Ghislaine waited until it was almost the moment to leave. They had all returned to Nerval's suite for cognac; she had had, as promised, a long conversation with Rebecca Stein, had reassured her on the question of French plumbing, and had overwhelmed her, she devoutly hoped, with her own chic. She would go to inspect the Maison Jasmine with the Steins and Nerval the next day—she might even take them to look at the work being done on Louise's villa, which should impress them, and then she would fly back to Paris for the meeting, the great meeting, with Edouard.

Should she tell him she had met Hélène Harte? No, she thought not. It was better not to remind him. Should she even speak to her as she had planned, or should she just forget the whole thing, and go? After all, what was she? Just one of Edouard's ex-mistresses, and there were many of those.

She had almost decided to go; her mind was very nearly made up; and then Rebecca Stein made her remark.

"Isn't she beautiful?" she said in a wistful voice. She looked across the room to where Hélène Harte stood, her husband, looking bored and morose, on one side of her, Thad Angelini on the other, all smiles.

"*So* lovely." Rebecca Stein shook her head. "Wouldn't you give just anything to look like that? I know I would."

For a moment Ghislaine could hardly believe her ears. She shot Rebecca Stein a venomous glance, but the stupid woman seemed entirely unaware of her lack of tact.

"Of course, she's young." Rebecca Stein smiled. "I guess that helps. After all, neither of us will see forty again, right?"

Forty? Rebecca Stein looked fifty-five if she was a day, and the fact that she had estimated Ghislaine's age with such casual certainty filled

Ghislaine with impotent rage. She wished the woman good night curtly, and crossed the room.

She approached from the side, so Hélène Harte did not see her until they were next to each other, and Ghislaine was shaking hands with Lewis Sinclair. Ghislaine murmured a few pleasantries and then turned to Hélène Harte with what she felt was the perfectly calculated tone of innocent surprise. She spoke half to Sinclair, half to his wife.

"*Quelle bêtise.* I'm so sorry. You must think me very rude—but I've only just this moment realized. Your wife and I have met before. . . ."

Hélène Harte turned her head; their gaze met, and Ghislaine gave her a warm smile.

"You don't remember—well, why should you? It was some years back. Nineteen sixty? No, fifty-nine, I think. At dinner one evening in the Loire. You were staying with Edouard de Chavigny—now do you recall?"

There was a little silence. Hélène Harte frowned, then smiled and shook her head.

"I'm sorry. I think you must be mistaken. We've never met—I would remember, I'm sure."

"Oh, but you must! It's not so long ago—it all comes back to me now. You were wearing the most wonderful white dress, Givenchy, I think. Alphonse de Varenges was sitting next to you, and Edouard had been teaching you to ride, was that it? Yes, I'm sure it was, because I remember, Edouard said—"

"I must have a twin. Or a double." Hélène Harte laughed. "It sounds lovely, but I'm afraid you're mistaken. I've never stayed in the Loire."

It was perfectly done. She spoke so naturally, and with such an air of easy amusement, that for one insane moment Ghislaine herself nearly believed her. She opened her mouth to say something more, and before she could speak, the director, Angelini, took a little step forward.

"Hélène. I'm sorry—I think Joe Stein wants a word . . ."

With that he extricated her; it seemed almost done deliberately. He led the actress away; she looked back with a quick apologetic smile and a lift of the hand; Ghislaine's opportunity had gone.

She and Lewis Sinclair were left alone. They looked at each other. Had he believed his wife? Ghislaine couldn't be certain, but she thought not. He glanced away in her direction, and his face looked crumpled, pinched, like a child's about to cry. Ghislaine almost regretted, then, what she had done.

"How stupid of me," she said quickly. "How could I have made a mistake like that?"

"We all make mistakes," he said dully. He turned back to her, and then, like a child suddenly remembering its manners, offered her his arm.

"You're going now?" he said politely. "Please, let me show you to your car."

"Do you have a twin?"

"Lewis . . ."

"Or a double?"

"This is silly, Lewis. . . ."

"Of course you don't. You're unique. We all know that. Hélène Harte—the most beautiful woman in the world. They're calling you that now, did you know that? I read it in your clippings just the other day. 'Is this the most beautiful woman in the world?' it said. And there was a picture of you underneath. They were inviting readers to write in and vote. I'm sure they all voted for you. I would. I'd have sent in the coupon, there and then, only it was an Italian magazine and I didn't have the right stamp."

"Lewis. It's late, and you're tired." Hélène lifted her hand to him. "Come to bed."

"I don't think I will, thank you. Not just yet. And it's kind of odd you should think I'm tired, because I don't feel tired in the least. I feel fine. I've been enjoying myself no end. A Givenchy dress. I never knew you had a Givenchy dress—before you met me."

"Lewis. I keep telling you. She made a *mistake*. . . ."

"You wore jeans a lot. And there was a blue cotton thing you used to wear that I always liked. And the coat you bought in London that time. But not a Givenchy. No—I suppose I must have forgotten that. Did he give you jewelry as well? After all, that's what he's famous for, isn't he? Jewels—giving them to women? I remember those stories. I remember one of my sisters, reading it out loud. Some gossip column. How he matched the jewels up to the women. She loved that—my sister, I mean. She thought it was the most romantic thing she ever heard. I didn't. I thought it was dumb. Why give presents like that, when you can get it for free?"

"I'm not going to listen to this anymore, Lewis. I'm going to sleep. I have to be up at six. . . ."

"You lie very well, you know. *Awfully* well. You almost took her in, that woman, Ghislaine whatever her name was. And Thad. I'll bet Thad believed you, every word. I nearly believed you, but not quite. There's a little thing you do—you ought to watch it, I'm sure you can work on it—it's very tiny, just something in the eyes. I see it because I know where to look. I've had so much practice, I suppose, night after night, day after day. It's there when I kiss you, did you know that? That little thing in the eyes, just for a minute, before you smile, they go a tiny bit dead. It's one of the things that puts me off. There are others, just a few, like the fact that you can't stand it when I touch you. Like the fact that you're so busy you can't spare me five minutes in a day. Just a few things. Nothing very serious. Nothing we can't clear up. Nothing to cry about. . . ."

He had begun to cry. Hélène could hear the tears in his voice.

He wiped them away with the back of his hand, and then he said in a quite ordinary voice, "It was a good year, 1959. I really liked it. We made the movie, and I met you. It was a very good Christmas. Do you remember the tree? We bought it on Christmas Eve, and then we decorated it, and then . . . He's Cat's father, isn't he? I suppose that does make sense? He taught you to ride and you met all his friends. He gave you a Givenchy. And he gave you Cat. You could have told me. I don't understand. I don't understand a lot of things, but especially that."

There was a long silence. Lewis was sitting on the end of the bed. He stared at the empty glass, and did not look up.

Hélène felt sick; she felt as if a band were being tightened around her chest, so she could hardly breathe. Her heart was beating terribly fast, and her mind darted away in a thousand directions at once. She looked at Lewis, and the pity and the guilt she felt were so intense it made her body ache. *I did this to him. I did it. It's my fault*—the thought went around and around in her head. When had it begun to go wrong? Why, no matter what she did, couldn't she stop it from going wrong?

After a long pause, Lewis lifted his head and looked at her. When he was drunk, it never affected his appearance; occasionally it made his eyes glazed, slightly, as if he did not quite see her, that was all. But now he was looking at her directly, with his clear hazel eyes. He looked a little puzzled.

Hélène moved. She knelt beside him. She looked at him, and he looked at her, and after another silence, she said, "Very well. It's true. I was there. But it was a long time ago, Lewis. I've never seen him again. Not since we—Lewis, please, I'm married to you. . . ."

"Is he Cat's father? Is he?"

"Lewis, no. He isn't. He isn't. . . ."

Her voice had risen; Lewis had taken hold of her arm. He looked down into her face, and then he let go of her. He said in a flat voice, "I don't believe you. Why should I? You're lying again. You lie all the time. Half lie, evade. You don't even know when you're doing it, I think. . . ."

"Lewis, I'm not lying. It's true. I wouldn't lie about that. I couldn't. Lewis, please . . ."

She had caught hold of his arm, and was pressing it tight in her hands. It suddenly seemed desperately important to convince Lewis, and for one moment she thought she had done so. His face softened, and she immediately felt an extraordinary relief. Then his face hardened again.

"Okay. Then who is?"

Hélène had begun to cry. The tears welled up out of her eyes, quite silently. They would not stop. Lewis ignored the tears; he seemed not to see them.

"Who is?" He caught her by the arm and shook her. "I think I should know. I think I have a right to know. You never think what it's like, living with her in the same house, seeing her day after day, and not knowing, wondering . . . It breaks me up, doing that. It breaks me apart. I was all right till she was born. We were all right. I felt—it's a very stupid thing, but I felt she *was* mine. I don't know why. I loved you so much, maybe. I thought she was mine, in a way. I knew she wasn't, but I felt as if she were. Until she was born, until I looked at her. And then I knew. She wasn't mine, and you weren't mine either. You think about him, whoever he was, and when you do that, I . . ."

His voice choked. Hélène said, in a quiet voice, "That's not true, Lewis. I don't. I try not to. And—" She stopped, began again. "His name was Billy. He was an American. I knew him a long time. And he's dead. He died before I even met you."

It cost her a great deal to say that. She had to make herself say the words one by one, and they fell into the silence between them like small stones tossed into water. When she had finished, she drew in her breath, and a small flat voice in her mind told her that it would be all right now. She had told Lewis the truth, and Lewis would believe her. She had done everything she could do, and now everything would be—all right.

But it wasn't. Lewis's hand tightened on her arm, his face darkened with anger and he began to shake her. He said, "You bitch. You fucking bitch. You were sixteen years old when I met you. How many of them were there, for God's sake? How many? How many?"

Then he hit her, one stinging blow with the flat of his hand, right across her face. He had cried before, and he had been angry before, many times. But this was the first time he ever hit her, and it shocked them both.

Ghislaine Belmont-Laon had asked to meet him—it was urgent, she had said—and it was Ghislaine who had suggested their meeting place, the *jardin intérieur* at the Paris Ritz. She was not to know of its associations for Edouard, but, that evening, as he sat there at the small table, they crowded in on him, images so sharply vivid that, for some time, he hardly heard what Ghislaine said.

He saw himself, approaching the table where Isobel sat in her *violette de Parme* dress; he saw her lift her face to his, and the shock of her emerald eyes, their expression first amused, and then anxious. Isobel had been dead five years; now, for an instant, and quite distinctly, he heard her voice.

He bent his head slightly, and pressed his hand across his brow; he tried to force himself to concentrate on what Ghislaine was saying, aware, dimly, that he felt very tired—a draining exhaustion and despondency, which he could not shake off. It had been with him ever since he returned from New York, and it had the effect of dissociating him from his surroundings, so that all action seemed pointless; it was even pointless to speak.

He made an effort. He looked up again and smiled at Ghislaine abstractedly. Her glass was already empty, and he ordered her another drink.

Ghislaine appeared very strung up, and she was a capable, efficient woman who had never, so far as he could remember, invented unnecessary dramas. He could not imagine why she had been so determined to see him tonight. She was dressed with particular care; Edouard, who always noted what women wore, noted that; a black suit, Saint Laurent, he would have said, severe, like all Ghislaine's clothes, emphasizing her uncompromising, slightly masculine *chic*. He complimented her on it, and on her appearance—for she looked very well—as the waiter brought her her drink. A dry martini, like Isobel. He felt, illogically, that he wished she had ordered something else.

Edouard had to return to his office; he had to see de Belfort, and talk to Richard Smythe, and he was still worrying about the takeover bid. Though he tried, politely, to disguise the fact that he was watching the time, Ghislaine, who was quick, obviously sensed his impatience. She lit a cigarette, inhaled deeply, and then, as if deciding rapidly to come to the point, began to speak.

"I know you're busy, Edouard. I know I'm taking up your time, but I felt I had to speak to you. It's rather difficult, but I'm terribly worried, and it concerns you. Well, indirectly it concerns you. I would have spoken to you sooner—but a confidence is involved. Loyalty is involved. I wasn't certain it was the right thing to do." She paused. "It's a financial matter—well, partly a financial matter. You see, I was given a tip, a stockmarket tip, and—"

"Ghislaine—I'm sorry. I never advise my friends on the market. I'm too closely involved. It's a rule I never break. . . ."

Ghislaine looked at him. Edouard was just beginning to feel impatient, when she said, "Rolfson Hotels Group."

"What did you say?"

"Rolfson Hotels Group." She leaned across the table. "Edouard, please be patient. I'm so terribly worried. You see—well, this is a little personal—but Jean-Jacques and I keep our financial affairs quite separate, and I don't have a great deal of money of my own to invest. When I was given this tip—it seemed such an opportunity. So—I bought some stock. And it rose—dramatically. It was so exciting, and then—the last couple of days. Well, you'll know, probably, it's started to fall. And I'm so frightened. I don't know what to do, whether to hang on or to sell at a loss, or what and—"

"Ghislaine. I'm very sorry." Edouard's face had become set and cold. "I cannot advise you on this. You should talk to your broker. . . ."

"I've done that. He's useless. He advised me against buying in the first place. And I would have listened to him, I always do. I'm extremely cautious, Edouard, normally. But you see—it's more complicated than that. As soon as I'd bought the stock, I realized I shouldn't have. I *knew* there was something wrong—I should have come to you right away, as soon as she told me . . ."

She paused. Her eyes were glittering, and Edouard could see that she was, quite genuinely, upset. As well she might be, he thought grimly; the Rolfson Hotels Group stock, he estimated, had a long way to fall yet.

"Ghislaine," he said more gently, "what are you talking about? Who gave you this tip?"

"That's the awful part. The really dreadful part. She told me in confidence, Edouard, and I respected that. And then, I began to see that there was something wrong, that she might have misplaced her trust. You see, unless she's sold out, she'll lose too—and much more than I will. She'd invested a great deal—not enough to do her any serious damage, but still a lot. And I'm so fond of her, so devoted to Louise. I don't want to see her hurt."

There was a long silence. Edouard's face became hard; she had never seen him look more angry, Ghislaine thought, and through her perfectly genuine anxiety about her own investment, she felt a little thrill of excitement, a touch of triumph.

"My *mother* advised you to buy this stock?" For a moment, he looked totally bewildered. "When was this?"

"Not long ago. Just over a week maybe. But Louise had been buying since February, she told me. She had cleared one hundred thousand in sterling. . . . Edouard. I blame myself. I should have spoken to you immediately, but Louise made me promise not to. Then I began to see—even before the stock dropped—how vulnerable she was. She's not young anymore, and she's always been so impetuous, and when a man is involved . . ."

He knew at once, as soon as she said that. Every strand of the pattern that had been perplexing him all week, assembled in its natural, obvious, and inevitable place.

"Who was this?" he asked, though he already knew the answer, and Ghislaine, her mind singing with gladness and triumph, told him.

When she had finished, he sat quietly for a moment. Then, to her delight, he reached across and rested his hand over hers.

"Ghislaine. I'm most terribly sorry that this should have happened. It's very serious—more serious than you realize, perhaps. I'm very grateful you did this. I understand your predicament, and I want you to know—I am in your debt." He hesitated. "I shouldn't say this, even now, but I will. You should call your broker immediately, and sell your stock. And then—please—" His tone became formal and awkward. "You will let me know the extent of any losses you have made, and I will repay them, of course."

He removed his hand, and stood up.

"I'm sorry . . . if you'll forgive me. I shall have to leave you."

Ghislaine did not leave with him. She stayed at the table, too intoxicated by the touch of his hand, the concern in his voice, to move. She felt as if she could stay there all night; she was so happy, so relieved. The money she would lose—she felt impetuously that she could lose all of it and she would not care. Edouard would make good her loss, but it was not that loss she cared about anymore. It was all the other losses, all the humiliations and dissatisfactions of her life, and the conviction she felt then, the absolute conviction, that—if she was very, very careful—Edouard would repay those too.

There was no point in trying to deny it, and Edouard noted that de Belfort did not make the attempt. He sat in Edouard's office, and listened, while Edouard spoke, point by damning point.

Never once did he show any emotion—they might have been speaking about a hypothetical case, about events from the distant past. He simply sat there, his pale heavy features immobile. He remained gazing steadily, with his pale eyes, at a point somewhere to the left of Edouard's head. When Edouard paused, the faintest of smiles crossed de Belfort's face, and for a moment Edouard had the sensation that in some obscure and perverse way, de Belfort was almost glad to have been found out. Certainly the consequences of his actions seemed to cause no alarm, or fear; in his heavy opaque way, one thing alone seemed to make him react, and that was Edouard's cold anger: that he seemed to be enjoying very much.

"You could have bought stock yourself." Edouard leaned forward, pale with the rage he was trying to control. "You could have used an intermediary. A Swiss bank, even a broker, though I can see that would have been more risky. Why use my mother?"

"Oh, I should have thought that would be obvious." Again there was a faint chilly smile. "I don't have that kind of capital, and your mother does. . . ."

And—because she is my mother, Edouard thought instinctively.

"We came to an agreement, obviously." De Belfort sounded almost bored. "A sixty-forty split on the profits. Sixty to me, forty to Louise. She wasn't inclined to haggle."

Edouard could have hit him then. The desire to step forward, grab de Belfort by the collar, and slam him back against the wall, was almost insuperable. He might have done it, too, had he not suspected de Belfort would have enjoyed it very much. Edouard had been standing; now he returned to his desk. He looked down at the papers there, then up.

"And you knew there was a strong possibility of a counterbid, I imagine, so the stock was likely to go even higher?"

"Oh, yes. I knew that. I have a friend at Matheson De Vere. They were all set to go. When we delayed, I suppose they got cold feet. The word must have spread. That's why the shares started falling."

"I see." Edouard's lips tightened. He stared at de Belfort. Even now, he found it incomprehensible, unbelievable, that any man in his position should have behaved as de Belfort had. The man's calm was incredible to him; he seemed, if anything, smug.

"You do understand what you've done?" he said at last. "You have compromised my company. You have compromised my mother, and me. You have also—irrevocably—compromised yourself. You realize that you are now unemployable—not just here, anywhere?"

"I don't quite see it like that." De Belfort regarded him with a bland obstinacy. "Not everyone shares your absolute standards. Other people in this company don't. I have my supporters, you know. Besides, I'm not the first person to do what I did. Insider trading isn't even against the law in England. . . ."

"For God's sake." Edouard pushed his papers aside in exasperation. "The whole point is that there *is* no law against this kind of exploitation. The financial world operates on trust. I don't have to explain that to you, surely? If you exploit that trust, you betray it. You undermine everything."

He stopped. De Belfort had begun to smile.

"Ah, yes. A gentleman's word is his bond—that kind of thing, you mean? Yes, well, they talk about that a lot in the City of London, just as they talk about trust. Personally, I never believe any of them. And I don't believe in trust. I never build it into *my* contracts. . . ."

"I trusted *you*." Edouard looked up at him directly. "I never liked you, as perhaps you knew. But I damn well bent over backward to help you, because I could see you were able, I could see you had promise. You've been promoted. You've been well paid. You were put in a position of considerable responsibility and influence—did it never occur to you that you owed something to this company, to the people you work with here, to me? It's beyond my imagination that someone in your position could do this."

"It probably is." Again that small smile flickered across de Belfort's face. "An honorable imagination is a severe disability. Your particular Achilles heel, I would have said."

He made the remark flatly; it stung Edouard to the quick. He looked away. An imagination limited by its inability to understand the dishonorable—yes, he could see the truth in that particular gibe. His mother, he thought, would probably say precisely the same thing.

He stared down at the columns of figures on the paper in front of him, figures which added up to fraud. And he thought, with a sense of despair, not of de Belfort, but of Hélène. He had placed his trust in her; he had placed his trust in his love for her; he saw that action, for a moment, from de Belfort's cynical point of view. An illogical, an unlikely and an obstinate trust. He saw it, just then, in the light of common day—an illusory thing, in which he had unswervingly believed.

He knew de Belfort was watching him, eager to see if his words had struck home. He did not intend to give him that satisfaction. He moved the papers across his desk, aligned them with its edge, and stood up.

"I have canceled our bid for the Rolfson Hotels Group, obviously. After this, we cannot proceed. I imagine I don't need to tell you that you're dismissed."

"You can't prosecute." De Belfort lifted his heavy-lidded eyes to Edouard's face.

"No, I can't prosecute. Unfortunately."

De Belfort sighed. "I wonder what your mother will have to say about this."

"What my mother says or does not say is no concern of yours. You will not see my mother again."

"It seems to me that's her decision. Not yours."

For the very first time, there was a flicker of anger in de Belfort's face. He shrugged. "You may enjoy ordering people around, but you can't order Louise. And you can't order me. I don't work for you anymore, remember?"

"Very well." Edouard sat down once more. He looked at de Belfort coldly. "I'll spell it out to you. You will never work in any position of seniority or trust in any reputable company—I shall personally ensure that. But if you attempt to see my mother after tonight—if you so much as communicate with her in any way—I shall go further than that." He leaned forward. "I will take you apart—do you understand that? Your financial affairs, your investments, the income you have declared to the tax authorities, and the income you have no doubt concealed, the expenses you have claimed, the cash transactions, the offshore dealings. I will have you investigated step by step, piece by piece. I shall turn you inside out, until I find whatever it takes to finish you off. However long it takes, I will do it." He paused. "I think you know me well enough to believe that. I hope for your sake that you do. Because I can assure you I will do it, and without hesitation. And you'll go where you belong. For a very long time."

There was a silence. De Belfort let out a long slow sigh. "Oh, I'm sure you would. I don't doubt it for a second. I've seen you do similar things before. No doubt you'd enjoy it, in my case, very much."

"You think so?" Edouard looked at him contemptuously. "Oddly enough, you're wrong. I might have once. Not now. And you are not a special case—you glamorize yourself too much."

De Belfort's mouth tightened; that angered him. He rose. "Very well. I shall leave the country in any case. As you say, I have no illusions about my chances here."

He turned away and moved to the door at a leisurely pace. At the door, he turned back, and looked around him with his pale heavy-lidded gaze. He looked at the furniture, the sculptures, the paintings. He looked at Edouard; no sign of hatred, no sign of resentment, no sign of any emotion at all.

"All this." He lifted one heavy hand and gestured at the room. "All these paintings. Houses. Offices. Companies. Subsidiaries. Shareholdings. All this *work*. And you have no children." He paused. "None of it will outlast you—I suppose you realize that? Don't you ever think, Edouard, what fun people will have when you're dead—picking over the spoils? No, maybe you don't." He began to smile. "Maybe that's beyond your imagination too. What a pity. I'd like to think you thought about that— just occasionally." He opened the door. "Give my regards to your mother— will you do that?"

"That godawful overpainted bitch is after you, Edouard," Christian remarked in a conversational manner. He lit a cigarette, put his feet up, and leaned back in his chair. They sat on the terrace of Louise's villa on the first day of what was supposed to be a holiday. Christian had been invited, by Edouard, at the very last moment. He was still undecided whether he was glad that he had come. There was a glass of excellent Montrachet at Christian's elbow; the sun shone; he was prepared to enjoy himself. When Edouard made no response to his sortie, Christian sighed. He knew why he had been invited, knew why he was here. He was here because Edouard was in a state of black depression, and he was to play the court jester. Sometimes this role amused him, sometimes he was resentful of it. Today he was not sure quite which.

He glanced across at his friend; Edouard gave no indication that he had even heard him. From one of the rooms beyond the terrace, Ghislaine's voice floated out to them, sharp on the still air. She was directing the moving of various heavy pieces of furniture, now here, now there. Every so often her commanding tones were interrupted by a softer voice, that of Clara Delluc, who was supervising the hanging of sixty sets of curtains.

"Even Ghislaine can't spin it out much longer," Christian went on, determined not to give up. "She could have left days ago. She's deliberately delaying. A crisis is approaching, Edouard—be warned."

"Christian—leave it, will you? I'm not interested," Edouard said. He, too, was leaning back in his chair; he was staring out at the sea.

"Well, obviously you're not interested," Christian persisted waspishly, deliberately misunderstanding him. "That won't stop her, however. She's so vain she doesn't notice, and you're so blind to your own attractions that you can't see. Honestly, Edouard, she's in a kind of *fury* of sexual excitement. Anyone but you would see it right away. It's quite terrifying. Do you think it can be her age that accounts for it? She positively *trembles* with it, Edouard, an awful black lust. I can see it burning in her eyes every time she looks at you. As if she wanted to devour you. Or possibly be saved by you. I'm not quite sure which."

"You exaggerate—as usual. And what you say is not very kind."

"Oh, for God's sake. Why should I be kind? I can't stand her, and I never could. . . ."

Christian stood up restlessly. "Look, why don't we escape for a bit? What do you say? We could drive into St. Tropez—go to Senequier's— have a marvelous boozy lunch." He paused. "Forget women—all women— for once."

"Christian, I'm sorry—I can't. My mother's arriving any moment and—I ought to be here when she arrives, that's all." He hesitated slightly, then shrugged. "Also, I have work I should do. . . ."

"This is supposed to be a holiday." Christian looked at him sternly. "I know you never have them, but you ought to learn. Lotus-eating. It grows on one, you know. . . ."

He paused, but Edouard only shook his head. Christian shrugged. The atmosphere in the house was beginning to get on his nerves, and it would only be made worse by the arrival of Louise, whom Christian had never liked. Too many bloody women, he thought; Clara would be leaving later that morning; Louise would probably give Ghislaine short shrift—then things might improve somewhat. Except for the fact that

Hélène Harte was not only in the country right now, she was close by—less than a hundred kilometers along the coast. Was that why Edouard was in this impossible mood?

He had had enough of moods, he decided; he lifted his hand in a gentle salute.

"I'll see you later then. I might watch a game of boules in the Place des Lices. Drop into the museum, perhaps. I'd like to look at their Vuillard again—and they have a quite perfect Seurat. I'll be back this afternoon. . . ." He hesitated, and then smiled wickedly. "And if Ghislaine makes a move, I want to hear all about it. Every disgusting detail—do you swear?"

"Christian—stop this, will you? If you're going, go. . . ."

"Oh, all right." Christian sighed once more. "Sometimes, Edouard," he added as he drifted away, "sometimes your probity wears me out. . . ."

Edouard watched him leave: a tall thin figure in a crumpled but elegant linen suit, a straw hat that had seen better days shading his face from the sun. The trousers were belted with his old school tie, and there was a bandanna handkerchief, of bright red silk, in his top pocket. He disappeared from view. Edouard sat alone a little longer on the terrace, looking out at the sea. One white-sailed yacht lay on the horizon, becalmed. The air smelled clean and salty.

After a while, abruptly, he rose, and took the path down to the beach. It was bordered by bushes of wild thyme, rosemary, and lavender. As he walked, he caught their scent, strong in the sun: aromatic, sharp, the fragrance of Provence.

On the deserted beach, Edouard walked back and forth for a while, kicking at the pale sand with his feet. Philippe de Belfort's parting remarks had been in his mind all week; they returned to him now. *You have no children.* It was as good as true. He had a daughter whom he could not acknowledge, a daughter who had never known him. He loved a woman who now led her own life, and would never return to him. And he had an empty obsession which he had allowed to dominate his thoughts for almost three years. He turned away, angrily, to an outcrop of rocks, and sat there looking out at the still sea.

He should marry again, perhaps. There were other reasons for marriage besides love, after all. He was thinking this when he heard footsteps crunch on the sand, and, looking up, saw that it was Clara.

He watched her approach, walking a little awkwardly on the sand, lifting her hand to shield her eyes from the sun. As she came closer, she began to smile, and Edouard stood up.

"I've come to say good-bye," she called to him when she was still a short distance away. She drew level with him, and stopped, a little out of breath.

"It's finally finished. My part of it anyway. I just wanted to see you before I left—there's a car coming for me in a minute. . . ."

"You should have let me drive you . . ."

"No—why should you? Louise is arriving any minute. It's all arranged. And besides, it's easier this way. . . ." She stopped suddenly. "Edouard—is there something wrong?"

"No. Nothing. Here, come and sit down for a while—I had an unrealistic thought, that's all. It's gone now. . . ." He spoke lightly, smiling at her, holding out his hand. Clara took it, and he drew her down beside him. They sat in silence for a while; Clara leaned back a little on her arms, so that she could look at him. He was staring out at the sea again now, as he had been when she saw him from the terrace above. There was a slight breeze from the water, and it lifted the dark hair from his forehead. He looked tired, she thought with a rush of affection for him; tired, and also bleak—and she thought for a moment of the young Edouard, back in France after finishing at Oxford, filled with such energy, and such optimism: he had captured her heart, just like that. But even then, all that time ago, he had had this ability to close himself off, gently, scrupulously, and with a regard which had pained her, allowing her to come just so near to him, and no further. He had never lied to her. He had never made her promises he knew he would not fulfill, and he had never said that he loved her.

Clara looked away. She had loved him too much to argue, too much to quarrel, and too much to leave him. She wasn't particularly proud, she thought, of the way she had accepted his terms, and she was not proud of what had happened later, when it was finally over.

She had survived; people did. But there had been five years of a hell she never wanted to experience again—a period in which she had despised herself, and felt without identity or purpose. Her work, and being successful at her work, had brought her up and out of that particular pit, and she was determined never to return there. She never wanted to fall in love again—not the way she had loved Edouard. Now she would think sometimes, when a brief affair was over: I'm lucky; I'm a free woman. Women's lives were happier without men, she had decided—even men like Edouard.

He had picked up a handful of small pebbles and began to throw them idly into the water. Quite suddenly, he said: "Are you happy, Clara?"

The question took her by surprise, and she hesitated.

"I suppose so," she said at last. "Yes. I think I am."

"I'm glad." He had turned back to look at her. He paused, and then, with something of the old simplicity, he said: "I made you unhappy. I know that. I wish I hadn't."

"Oh, Edouard—it was my choice as well, you know." She reached forward and pressed his arm gently. "No regrets. Except in my weaker moments. And I don't have those anymore."

Edouard smiled, a little wryly. He nodded, and once more turned away. Clara had seen the expression in his eyes though, he could not hide it from her; she felt it again, that rush of impotent pity and affection, and she leaned toward him impulsively.

"Oh, Edouard—what is it that's happened to you? What is it you're looking for?"

"I don't know anymore."

He stood up, suddenly and angrily, and threw the stone he was holding. It flew in a high wide arc; they both watched it rise and then fall.

"I don't know anymore," he said again. "I knew once. I think I did."

He began to walk back up the beach, and Clara followed him. She caught his hand, and Edouard stopped. Clara looked up into his face, and what she saw there frightened her.

"The world seems to me a miserable place. A formless place." He jerked out the words, then stopped, and regained his control. "I felt this before. After Isobel died . . . I'm sorry. There's no reason to burden you with this. Let me see you back to your car."

He began walking again, and Clara stood still for a moment, looking after him. She wanted to run after him, and catch up with him. She wanted to put her arms around him and shake him. She wanted to shout: *Life isn't like that; life isn't like that.* She did none of those things. She believed the words, but she knew they would sound ridiculous. A stupid defiant little cry: Edouard would not listen to it—she would not have listened to it either, a few years before, when she was in her wilderness.

She walked after him, slowly. Above them, on the terrace, Ghislaine, who had been watching them, turned away.

That night, Louise and Ghislaine, Edouard and Christian had dinner together—since Louise was present, an elaborate formal dinner, for which everyone was required to dress. The atmosphere around the table was tense; Christian, unable to understand its undercurrents, blamed Louise, who was in an ill temper, and had been from the moment of her arrival.

She came in her dark blue Bentley; behind it were two more cars, in one of which traveled her personal maid with her jewel cases, in the other the fifteen Vuitton trunks, suitcases and hatboxes Louise required for a stay of some seven days. Ghislaine joined Edouard to greet her, and that, Christian assumed, was a mistake, for from that moment on, once Louise had given them both a long cold hard look, she made it imperiously clear that Ghislaine's presence in her house was an irritant, and an insolent imposition. Ghislaine had stuck to her guns to the extent of one more night; she was leaving in the morning—and that fact had not improved her own temper either.

Louise had been taken on a tour of the completed house, and had complained mercilessly.

"Are you *sure* I approved that material, Ghislaine? I remember it quite differently. Much softer. A more subtle color altogether. Perhaps it's the way it's been hung. It looks most unattractive." She was querulous, almost tearful, in her bedroom; the other bedrooms she hardly examined at all. The billiards room was beastly; the conservatory was spoiled; the dining room was unflattering. By the time she had reached the *salon* again, she was giving her peevishness full rein.

"Well, really, Ghislaine, I suppose you must have explained it was going to be like this. But now that I see it, I'm not sure at all. There seems so very little furniture—and what there is seems so *assertive*. It creeps up on one, and crowds one in the most extraordinary way. And this pink! Did we discuss pink? Well, perhaps it's a sort of beige. It looks so dreadfully *drab*, Ghislaine, and somehow . . . somehow rather *limp*. What is it exactly?"

"It's raw silk, Louise." Ghislaine was keeping her temper with difficulty. She sounded strangled. "It's raw silk, hand woven and hand dyed. You get that particular kind of silk, Louise, only from certain silkworms, and it's very rare. I get it from a special supplier in Thailand, and it's absolutely the latest thing. Everyone is trying to get their hands on it. . . ."

"I really can't imagine why," Louise said tartly. "I've never liked Thailand anyway. I greatly preferred Burma."

She had sunk into a chair; now she rose again and gave a little cry of distress. Christian and Edouard, who had joined the grand tour, exchanged a wry glance.

"The walls, Ghislaine! What have you done to the walls? It has the most terrible effect on my lovely Cézannes. And even the Matisse Xavi loved so much. They look quite sad. Quite diminished. Edouard, Christian, don't you agree?"

Christian thought you could hang the Cézannes in a filthy attic and it would not make an atom of difference. He shrugged.

"It would be a little difficult to diminish them, Maman," Edouard said, echoing Christian's thoughts, his manner tactful. Ghislaine smiled at this; Louise glared at him furiously for such treachery.

"Perhaps if you had a brief rest, Maman. . . . You must be tired after your journey."

"I am not in the least tired. Please do not address me as if I were an invalid. Really, Edouard, you can be most astonishingly stupid sometimes. . . ."

Here she paused. She looked at Edouard; she turned and looked at Ghislaine. Her gaze traveled slowly from the top of Ghislaine's carefully arranged dark hair down to the toes of her black sling-back shoes, and up to her face once more.

"I see my mistake," she said bitingly. "I should have known better than to trust the judgment of a friend."

With that she had swept out of the room, calling for her maid. And Ghislaine and Edouard had—to Christian's enormous surprise—exchanged a look which appeared possibly guilty, and certainly conspiratorial. He could hardly believe his eyes.

And now they were at dinner. A room filled with huge vases of flowers: mimosa, jasmine, roses, orange blossom—their scent was stiflingly sweet. Four silver candelabra spaced along the length of the dining table. The Limoges dinner service. Four tight-lipped people. Louise in velvet and pinkish pearls; Ghislaine defiant in scarlet; Edouard, silent and abstracted; Christian in a green velvet smoking jacket which he wore with a canary-yellow silk bow tie. An uneasy hour passed.

Christian found it all absurd; he could hardly suppress his laughter, and became rather drunk. Then he looked down the table, saw Edouard's face, and felt remorseful. He stopped drinking immediately, but it made no difference; drunk or sober—the air was icy with suspicion and hostility.

Louise seemed to Christian to be trying out a new role: that of an imperious, impossibly demanding old woman. The only accessory she was lacking was a silver-topped cane, and Christian had an horrific vision of her, a few years from now, with just such a cane, banging it on the floor, enjoyably making everyone else's life a misery. She was now sixty-seven; her love affairs had, over the past ten years, grown more sporadic—or so Christian had heard. Presumably, she knew her charms were now inexorably fading, and this new role was the replacement for the old one of enchantress and seductress. Christian looked at her, and realized that for the first time since he had met her, she was beginning to look her age. She is old, he thought gloomily; we're all getting old. I'll be forty in two years—that's half my life gone, probably, maybe more.

He looked up at Edouard—stony-faced, saying virtually nothing—and thought: even Edouard, he is aging in front of my eyes. He looks tired, and miserable and bleak—and I remember him so well, at Oxford. When we were twenty. When we thought anything was possible. Before our choices started narrowing . . .

Christian bowed his head; he indulged his own melancholy; he began to think of graves and worms and epitaphs.

Edouard, looking at him, thought: Christian has drunk too much. He is getting maudlin. . . . Ghislaine and his mother were arguing, shrilly.

"My dear. It was Harriet Cavendish, and it was 1952. She was married to Binky at the time. I remember perfectly. . . ."

"Ghislaine. If you will forgive me. I have known Harriet since she was a child. It was 1948, and she was most certainly *not* married to Binky then, she was married to—"

"Would you excuse me?"

Edouard stood up. He looked down the table into the sudden silence that fell; into his mother's face, which was lifted to his; into the flames of the candles, which flickered and guttered. The room seemed to him to fragment, to disintegrate into crazy shards, arbitrary debris. It buckled before his gaze, then steadied. Edouard looked down the table, and he thought: this, *this*, is how we lead our lives. This malice. This pettiness. This irrelevance. How we live them, and how we end them—wasting time.

He stepped back politely from the table.

"If you will forgive me. Maman. Ghislaine. Christian. I shall have to leave you, I'm afraid. There's some urgent work I should do."

Christian had thought he would walk straight out, but he did not. He paused at his mother's chair, his face growing gentle. They looked at each other for a moment, then Louise lifted her hand to him. Edouard took it between his own, and bent over it formally. Then, abruptly, and for no apparent reason, Louise pulled her hand away.

"You are so dreadfully selfish, Edouard," she said snappishly. "I've been here only a few hours, and already you can't wait to get back to your everlasting work. Well, go—go. Leave me by myself—just as you always do. . . ."

"Hardly by yourself, Maman," Edouard began, but Louise cut him off shrilly.

"Yes, I am! Alone, and growing old. With no one caring a jot for me. . . ."

"Maman—please. You know that's not true. You know that I—"

"You? And what use are you? What use have you ever been? None. Ah . . ." She gave a little moan of distress. "It's at times like this that I most miss my beloved Jean-Paul. . . ."

She reached for a lace-edged handkerchief as she said this, and applied it to her eyes. Christian, staring at her in appalled disbelief, trying to figure out what had caused this display, saw that she was actually crying; a little.

Edouard said nothing. He had paled slightly, but otherwise betrayed no emotion. He stood stiffly by his mother's chair, looking down at her bent head. Then he wished her good night in a perfectly even tone. He gave her, as he always did, that dutiful half bow, learned in his childhood. Then he turned, and quietly left the room.

That was at ten o'clock. Some two hours later, Ghislaine stood outside her room, on the terrace overlooking the darkness which was the sea.

Edouard's departure at the end of the dinner had finished the evening. Shortly afterward, Louise had retired to bed fretfully, and Ghislaine and Christian had been left alone. Coffee was brought to them in the *salon*, and Ghislaine eyed Christian hopefully. She did not like him, but she knew he was closer to Edouard than almost anyone else, and it occurred to her that it might be helpful to question him—he had been drinking a good deal, which might make him less cautious than usual.

But Christian gave her no opportunity. With conscious rudeness, he sprawled on one of the sofas; he propped one of the new and exquisite cushions under his feet, which were clad, Ghislaine saw, in tattered and old-fashioned black velvet evening slippers.

"Ah. Time to read, how wonderful!" Christian remarked. He cocked one eye at Ghislaine, picked up a much-thumbed book, and opened it. It was Proust, and in French. Ghislaine, who had never read Proust, felt more irritated.

"Such a treat." Christian looked up at her over the top of the pages. "I reread it every summer. Well, as much of it as I can every summer. When I was younger, it was *Le Rouge et Le Noir*, and sometimes *L'Éducation Sentimentale*, and of course I still like them very much. But now I am become a man. . . ." He sighed. "And such a middle-aged man, I find it has to be Proust."

"Do you never read English novels?" Ghislaine said with a certain acidity.

"Practically never," Christian replied. "If I can help it."

He flicked the pages back and forth in an annoying manner, as if to find his place. Ghislaine observed that he had the deplorable habit of bending down their corners, and that in this particular volume, a whole host of pages had been so desecrated. She pursed her lips: she read few books, but felt obscurely that all books should be treated with more respect.

"I'm done with *Swann's Way*." Christian peered at her once more over the top of the pages. "And now I am on to Balbec. And Albertine."

"Really?"

"Proust is quite wonderful on the subject of love, don't you think?"

Again, Christian eyed her in a way Ghislaine did not quite like, and which made her uneasy. "Where was I? Ah, yes, here we are. Oh, this is a wonderful bit—I'm sure you'll remember it. Listen."

He cleared his throat, and began reading in that high-pitched drawling voice to which Ghislaine took such exception: ". . . *I had guessed long ago, in the Champs-Élysées* . . . I'll skip a bit here. . . . *That when we are in love with a woman, we simply project into her a state of our own soul, that the important thing is, therefore, not the worth of the woman, but the depth of the state. . . .*"

He paused, looked up, and smiled at her. "It goes on a lot more, of course, but there you have the nub of it, don't you agree? I often think of Edouard when I read that passage, though of course I should never say so to him."

Ghislaine gave him a cold glance. She had the distinct impression that Christian was trying to tell her something, and it was not something she wanted to hear.

"It is not very flattering to women," she said finally. "However, I suppose, Christian, that the same could be true the other way around. Women project onto men all sorts of ideas and fancies. . . ." And she thought, with a certain contempt, of Louise.

"Do they?" Christian said with a little smile on his lips. "Do they, Ghislaine? Well, you would know, of course. I've never pretended to be an expert on women."

And with that he lifted the book in front of his face, sighed happily, and was silent. Ghislaine sat there, fuming and yet not quite knowing why, feeling that she had been given a hint, and not understanding it. . . . She flicked the pages of a magazine noisily. She smoked one, then another, cigarette. And at last, when she could bear it no longer, she walked out of the room without wishing Christian good night.

She had returned to her room, but she knew she would not sleep—not after a day like this! All the events of the past hours darted back and forth in her mind: seeing Edouard, on the beach, with Clara, and the terrible swooping jealousy she had felt when she saw them. Louise's summary dismissal; her humiliating remarks—oh, how Ghislaine had longed to answer her back, and how she would have, too, if Edouard had not been there.

She felt, quite suddenly, pacing back and forth, that if she did not see Edouard tonight, before she had to go back to Paris, she would go mad. Just to be in the same room with him, just to hear him talk; that, she told herself, would be quite enough, though her imagination instantly and vividly swept her on much further than that. He was disturbed, tense, on edge, just as she was, she told herself. She could sense some crisis in him, some struggle; it was there, perceptible as electricity in the air before a thunderstorm—and she did not believe that it was entirely due to Louise, and whatever it was that had happened with Philippe de Belfort. . . .

She stopped. There it was—the perfect excuse. Surely it was not so surprising, given the circumstances, that she would want to ask Edouard about that?

I can't wait, she thought. I can't. In Paris, weeks could go by, and there would never be an opportunity like this. I have to see him. I have to talk to him.

She began to walk slowly along the terrace, in the direction of Edouard's room. As she did so, the oddest image came into her mind. She was fifteen years old again: overall, broad-shouldered, a little clumsy. She was at a garden party at St. Cloud. It was 1930, and there was Xavier de Chavigny, and on his arm was his famous wife, in a pink Chanel dress: small, delicate, ravishingly pretty—all the things Ghislaine was not and would have liked to be. She had watched them across a space of lawn: Louise said something, inaudible to Ghislaine, and tilted her face up to her husband. He smiled; then—they were not aware that anyone was watching them—he slipped his arm around her waist and moved his hand, slowly, down over his wife's hip to the top of her thigh. He let it rest there a second, then they broke apart, and moved on.

The easiness, the familiarity, of the gesture conveyed to the fifteen-year-old Ghislaine a sharp sexuality. She knew nothing, then, of course; she hardly knew the facts of life. But she knew the meaning of that gesture, her own body conveyed it to her, immediately and agonizingly. She wanted Xavier de Chavigny with all her heart and her mind and her imagination, and she had gone on with this infatuation secretly, until her first marriage, when it fell away of its own accord.

Thirty-two years ago: so why did she have this strange feeling, as she walked quietly along the terrace in her red dress, that she was keeping an appointment made then?

Edouard's room was at the other end of the house. Like her own bedroom, it had long French windows overlooking the sea. The outer shutters were open, the inner shutters closed but not latched—presumably to keep out the moths and other insects, for the curtains were not drawn, and the lights were still on.

Ghislaine stood outside, at a little distance. She did not have quite the courage yet to do anything more. She certainly didn't intend to creep around the corridors of the house and knock on his door.

She stood there perhaps ten or fifteen minutes. Edouard did not emerge. Her dress was thin silk, and she began to feel a little cold. She saw a shadow move against the louvres of the shutters, and she had just decided, almost decided, to risk it and call out to him, when she heard Edouard say something inaudible, to which Christian Glendinning replied. She did not hesitate at all then. She walked carefully and quietly toward the shuttered window, and when she was close enough, began to listen.

Inside the room, Christian was standing in the doorway, the Proust under his arm. Edouard was sitting at a table stacked with work papers, their neat piles untouched.

Christian looked from the papers to his friend. He shook his head.

"I knew you wouldn't be asleep. And I'll bet you haven't done any work. Dear God! What an evening! I thought you might need cheering up."

"You want a brandy, in other words. All right. Sit down and I'll get you one."

Christian sat; he stretched out his legs, which were very long, crossed his ankles, and folded his arms behind his head.

"God. It'll be better when the scorpion has gone, anyway. Maybe we'll be able to relax a bit then. Tonight it was a bit like dinner with the Borgias, didn't you think? Whatever's the matter with Louise?"

"A number of things." Edouard shrugged. "None of them new. You'll just have to be patient. And kind. If you could manage it."

"Oh, God. All right. I'll make an effort." Christian accepted the glass Edouard held out to him. He looked up at his friend and pulled a wry face. "You do know what's wrong, I suppose? With you, I mean. It came to me this morning. You know she's in France, that's the thing, isn't it? And not just in France, but very close—an hour's drive along the coast—less if you were doing the driving. You're here, and she's in Cannes, and that makes it worse. And it's no good looking like that, and frowning, because I'm not going to take any notice. I'm fortified with claret and Proust, and I shan't be put off."

"It isn't just that." Edouard sat down opposite Christian. "It's other things as well. Time passing perhaps. Things people say—innumerable things. I'm sorry, Christian. I know I'm not very good company."

"No. You're not," Christian agreed cheerfully. "And you know why not? Because you can't bear inertia—you never could. It's unnatural to you. You've forced yourself into it—for reasons I don't pretend to understand—and now you're sick of it. You're losing faith—Proust is terribly good on faith, by the way, you ought to reread it. Anyway—" he sat up, and leaned forward—"I think you should forget all that. Either you should just make up your mind and admit it's over, or do something positive. Get in that beastly black car of yours, drive over to Cannes, or wherever she is, and go in, and say: 'Hélène. Here I am. Are you coming with me, or are you staying?' " Christian smiled. "Don't you think that's a good scenario?"

Despite himself, Edouard smiled too.

"It has its attractions, I admit that. There's a certain recklessness and flamboyance about it which I like. . . ."

"Of course you do. Because you are reckless and flamboyant. Well, reckless anyway. When you want to be. And you want to be now—so why not?"

"Because I decided not to. That's all. It has to be her choice. And anyway. You're forgetting one or two small details."

"The husband, you mean?" Christian made a dismissive gesture. "So what for the husband?"

"Christian—stop this. I know you're trying to help—but I'd rather you didn't. Just leave it alone. I don't want to talk about it."

"Which is half the trouble."

Christian took a swallow of his brandy. He lit one of his Black Russian cigarettes, and they sat for a while in silence. Finally, Christian looked up, and in a different voice, a less flippant voice, he said, "Are you losing faith, Edouard? Or hope—or whatever it is that you've had all this time. Are you?"

Edouard stood up abruptly and turned away. He walked toward the window and then turned back.

"Sometimes," he said. "Yes. Sometimes I am. It's not very easy to go on believing in something when you have nothing to urge you on. Except memories. And obstinacy of course . . ." He smiled at Christian sadly, and then returned to his chair.

"But you don't give up?" Christian said quietly.

Edouard shook his head. "No—I don't give up. I can't perhaps. It would be like—well, it would be like giving myself up. That's all. I can't explain it better than that."

They looked at each other, and after a pause, Christian sighed.

"Oh, well," he said. "I do understand. In a way. Except—I was never very good at constancy. As you know. Such a butterfly . . ."

"You're constant in your own way," Edouard answered, and Christian, robustly, a little too quickly, because he was very English, and was becoming embarrassed, said, "Oh, balls. Well—maybe."

He stubbed out his cigarette, finished his brandy, and stood up. "Anyway. Enough of this. I've been uplifting enough for one evening. I shall go to bed." He looked at his wristwatch. "Past midnight. I should think you'll be safe from Ghislaine now, wouldn't you? She was looking quite mad after dinner, you know, the very picture of menopausal lust. It was quite frightening. But I shouldn't think nighttime visitations were quite her style, though you can never be sure, can you?"

"Christian . . ."

"Oh, and by the way—what is going on between you and her? I saw that look you exchanged, this afternoon, when Louise had swept out. You and Ghislaine. *Quite* conspiratorial. If I hadn't been certain that even your once catholic taste didn't extend to over-made-up predators *d'un certain âge*, I should have been quite suspicious. . . ."

"Christian—mind your own business, will you? I've known Ghislaine a long time, we've worked together, and as it happens she was very helpful to me recently, in a matter that relates to my mother, and not you."

"Oh, I see. That's the mystery. Well, just as long as you're aware that she has designs on you . . ."

"Christian—don't be ridiculous."

"You may find it ridiculous," Christian responded smartly. "She doesn't."

"I'm sure you're wrong. You underestimate Ghislaine. She may be many things, but she isn't stupid. You know perfectly well I've never given her the slightest reason to imagine—"

"Who needs reasons to imagine? And you, my dear Edouard, while not stupid, can be quite extraordinarily obtuse."

There was a silence. The two men looked at each other, and then Christian started to laugh. Edouard's mouth twitched slightly.

"Well, I sincerely hope you're wrong. That's all."

"I'm not wrong. I never am. I have an infallible instinct in such matters." Christian moved to the door. At the door, he paused and looked at Edouard mischievously.

"And you have to admit that whatever her reasons, Louise was right about the house—don't you think? Ghastly good taste—and don't pretend. I could see you blanching. . . ."

"All right. Ghastly," Edouard said. "And now, for God's sake, go to bed. . . ."

A door shut. Edouard sat down. He looked at the papers in front of him, and then bent his head and rested it in his hands.

Outside on the terrace, Ghislaine crept away. She wanted to be sick. She did not make a sound.

She dressed for breakfast carefully. A severe black and white linen suit. Less makeup than usual; she looked in her glass, and heard Christian's voice: *Overmade-up. Menopausal.* Horrible, twisted little queer—how she loathed him. And how she loathed Edouard de Chavigny, the ever-polite, the ever-gallant Edouard, who had not said one word in her defense that did not hurt her even more than Christian's comments; Edouard, who had laughed at her.

Breakfast was served on the terrace. Ghislaine was there first, and she stayed there, waiting. Louise would be safely in bed; she never rose before noon. Nothing was going to make Ghislaine move, until she had seen Edouard, until she had said the sentences she had been rehearsing to herself half the night. She toyed with a croissant; she drank two cups of coffee, and eventually, to her delight, she saw both Edouard and Christian come strolling across the terrace. In front of his friend, she thought—even better.

They joined her at the table. Edouard was wearing a cream linen suit; he looked tanned, handsome, much less tired than he had the night before.

"Good morning, Ghislaine. . . ."

"Such a day . . ." Christian sat down. He lifted his face to the sun. Ghislaine waited, smiling at them, the hurt and the spite rising.

She took another croissant, broke off a little piece, began to spread it with honey as Edouard spoke.

"We could go and watch a game of boules. Have lunch. Drive up into the hills . . ."

"Anything. Anything provided we don't go near a beach. I have an antipathy to beaches. . . ."

"When do you have to leave, Ghislaine? Do you have your car here?"

Edouard: being polite again, pretending concern. Ghislaine looked at him with hatred.

"I have my car—and I'll have to go in a minute. I'm driving over to see a friend, he's a property broker—buys and sells villas up and down the coast. His name's Gustav Nerval. You've come across him, perhaps?"

Of course, she thought. The idea of seeing Nerval had not actually occurred to her before, but she would do it. Yes, Nerval—who at least wasn't a hypocrite.

"The name is familiar. . . ." Edouard shook his head. "No. I don't think I've met him."

"He's a charming man—you'd like him. Oh—and I almost forgot, do you know—the most extraordinary thing . . ." She paused. "He held a little dinner a while ago, over at the Cap, for a lot of film people. I went—and do you know, I met a friend of yours there?"

"A friend of mine?" Edouard had become very still.

"You remember—Hélène? Jean-Jacques and I met her once at your place in the Loire—ages ago, 1959, was that it?"

Both men were now looking at her. Ghislaine felt a surge of triumph. She kept her voice entirely casual.

"Hélène Harte, she calls herself now. She's in films—did you know that? Quite the new face, so I hear—but then, she is so beautiful. Even lovelier than I remembered. And so nice. Much more grown-up now. I liked her enormously. . . . I was sitting next to her husband at dinner. A very good-looking young man. Very charming. It was rather touching, really—they're madly in love. At that stage when they can't take their eyes off each other. And they have a child—a lovely little girl. How time passes!"

She stopped, and gave a sudden little frown. "I reminded her that we had met, of course, and—do you know, Edouard, she couldn't remember it at all? She couldn't remember me, couldn't remember the dinner—even when I said your name, she looked quite blank for a moment. Someone else came over then, so I didn't get the chance to talk to her anymore. I expect she remembered later—she must have. It was such a lovely evening, that night in the Loire, and I always thought . . . but then, the very young are like that, aren't they? I find it a bit frightening, the way they can wipe out the past, when for us it seems so close . . ." She smiled. "Still, there you are. I thought you'd like to know I'd seen her."

She pushed aside her plate, and stood up. "Now I must rush. Doing all this work for Louise has put me behind with everything. Christian—don't read too much! Edouard, it's been so lovely to see you—and I'm sure Louise—well! We won't talk about that now."

She lifted her hand. "Good-bye. Enjoy your holiday." Then she turned and left them, filled with pride. Well done; perfectly done; she hoped her words choked him.

Gustav Nerval, she thought, as she started the engine of her smart little car. An improvement on Jean-Jacques, anyway. Not exactly a *beau idéal*, but still: Nerval—why not?

Christian and Edouard listened to the sound of her car as it disappeared into the distance. Christian said, "She's lying. Edouard—she's a stupid poisonous bitch, and she's lying."

"Why should she lie? She knows virtually nothing about it. She met Hélène once. I've never mentioned Hélène to her, ever."

"Even so. She's lying. She was enjoying herself too much. . . ."

There was a silence.

"Is she?" Edouard said finally. "She could be. On the other hand—it could be the truth. I know that. I suppose I've always known it."

He had risen to his feet when Ghislaine left. Now he sat down again. Christian opened his mouth to protest, and Edouard, with a sudden savagery that took Christian by surprise, said: "No, Christian. . . ."

Christian was silent. Edouard poured coffee. After a few minutes, unable to bear it any longer, Christian burst out: "Oh, for God's sake, Edouard. Why do you have to be like this? Why can't you—oh, I don't know—rage, talk, tell me what you're feeling, what you're thinking—go out and get drunk. What the hell, anything would be better than this. This awful silence. This closing in on yourself. . . ."

"All right."

Edouard, to Christian's astonishment, pushed back his chair and stood up.

"Very well. Let's go and get drunk. Why not? It's a long time since I did that. If I'm not capable of speech, I suppose I'm capable of getting drunk. Let's do just that, Christian."

They were flying back from Nice; the film festival was over. The limousine was large, but not air-conditioned; it was very hot. In the back sat Thad, who was humming to himself; Lewis, who was silent; and Hélène, who stared out the window.

As they approached the airport, they stopped at traffic lights, and a car came up behind them. Hélène heard its engine first, that distinctive full-throated roar; then it drew alongside, a long, low, black sports car: an Aston-Martin.

Her heart seemed to stop beating. She leaned forward, craning her neck: but it was not Edouard's car. It had different upholstery, and was driven by a stranger. The lights changed, the Aston-Martin overtook them effortlessly, and she saw, dully, that it had a Swiss, not a French, license plate.

She rested her head against the glass of the window, and shut her eyes. The shock of seeing the car had broken down all her usual defenses, and for a moment her mind was flooded with Edouard. She could hear his voice; feel his touch; smell the scent of his skin and hair. He was closer to her than at any time since she had left him, closer even than when she slipped out that night, and stood in the Rue St. Julien in Paris. The love she felt, and the longing, were acute, and acutely painful, and they left her dissociated, dazed, so that for an instant she forgot where she was, who she was with, what had just happened.

At the airport, they were delayed by photographers. *Short Cut* had just been awarded the Palme d'Or; Hélène had received the award for best actress.

The photographers jostled to get shots of Thad Angelini. They fought to get close to Hélène. Lewis hung back, pushed to one side, and unnoticed.

The photographers were yelling at Hélène in French and English and Italian: flashes of light, and flashes of sound. They became even more excited—she appeared not to hear them.

Eventually, Thad took her arm.

"They want you to smile," he said. "Listen. Can't you hear? They're trying to tell you something."

"What?" She looked at him blankly. "What? What are they saying?"

"The same thing I've always said," Thad answered. "You're a star."

And he pressed the soft skin of her arm with one of his fingernails, gently.

"You have behaved appallingly. Thoughtlessly. Selfishly. You stayed out all day, and half the night. I heard you come back—both of you. They could have heard you in St. Tropez. You were drunk. Both of you. Christian was singing."

Louise was quivering with anger. Edouard had been summoned to her room, in which there were signs of packing.

"I'm leaving. I shall return to Paris today. You may stay or go, as you please. But before you go, you will kindly explain to me exactly what has happened, and you will not fob me off with evasions and excuses. I want . . . I want to know exactly what has happened to Philippe. Where is he? Why did you dismiss him? Why can't I see him? I've been trying to telephone his house and there's no answer—no one there, not even the servants. . . . I demand to know, Edouard. I demand it. . . ." She was almost in tears.

"Maman . . ."

"I want to know, Edouard! I won't be treated like this—as if I were a child. How dare you do that! How dare you . . ."

"Very well." Edouard looked at her, saw her tremble. His head ached; his body ached; the sunlight hurt his eyes; he was unshaven, and the previous day's drinking had been pointless. It had left him feeling more bleak than before, distanced from himself, distanced from life, and above all, at this moment, distanced from his mother. He looked at her and did not even feel anger, just a cold disgust, and for that reason, perhaps, he told her what had happened, and what he had done and why, rather more baldly and directly than he would have otherwise.

Louise sat down when he began speaking. For once she did not interrupt him, but listened.

When he had finished, she sprang to her feet, and for one moment Edouard thought she was going to strike him.

"Oh, you fool! How could you have done that—how could you?

How dare you interfere! How dare you make decisions like that without even speaking to me, without even asking me. Do you know what you've done? Do you understand? No—of course you don't. Because you're too blind. Too blind and too arrogant, and too stupid . . ."

"Listen, Maman. What I did was for the best. It may be unpleasant, but you asked me to tell you, and I'm telling you. De Belfort was using my company, and he was also using you. . . ."

"Do you think I don't know that?" She rounded on him, her voice shaking with emotion. "Do you think I'm so very stupid? I suppose you do. Well, I'm not. I'm *not*, do you hear? I knew exactly what Philippe de Belfort was—I knew it the very first time I met him. And I didn't care. It didn't matter to me—what his reasons were—if he wanted my money, if he wanted my influence—so what? He wasn't the first to want those things—not by any means. It didn't matter—what mattered was that he was *there*. He bought me little gifts. Sent me flowers. Telephoned. Sent his car to meet me. When I was with him, I felt young again—and I enjoyed myself—I was *happy*. . . ."

"I would imagine, Maman, that if that is all it requires to make you happy, you will be happy again very soon. . . ."

She did strike him then; one sharp little blow across the face. She had to reach up to do it, and then she stepped back from him, the tears now falling down her face; she was trembling from head to foot with passion.

"You can't understand. You won't understand. You don't understand love, and you never will. You have no heart, and no imagination, Edouard. Jean-Paul was worth a thousand of you, for all his faults—that was why I loved him, why all women loved him. Because he was open and kind and generous, and fun—not like you—what woman would want you, except for your name and your position? No one. It would be like being married to a machine, an automaton. . . ."

Edouard took a step away from her.

"That's not true. You should not . . . It isn't true. Isobel . . ."

"Oh, Isobel!" Louise tossed her head. "Even with Isobel, you were second best. . . ."

Edouard stopped. For a moment he felt like a child again. Louise had always had this capacity, to touch him where he was most raw, and to reduce him to a state in which pain and anger were so mixed, so choking, that he could hardly speak. Louise could see that she had hurt him; triumph had come into her face, and spite. It was there for him to see quite clearly for a moment, and then Louise's mouth opened into a little jagged *O* of pain.

"He was my last chance," she said. "I'm not young anymore. Philippe was my last chance, and now you've spoiled it, the way you spoiled my life, the way you spoiled everything. . . . I hate you, Edouard, for this! I hate you. And I'll never forgive you. . . ."

Just for a moment then, her eyes bright with tears, the color staining her cheeks, she looked young again. Edouard's vision blurred; he saw her again, coming up to the nursery, smelling of roses; he heard her brittle laugh. He passed his hand across his eyes, and his vision cleared.

"Your chance was my father," he said in a cold voice. "And that chance you threw away."

He turned, and left the room. Louise had begun to laugh.

He walked out of the house, across the terrace, and down onto the beach, and there, quite suddenly, from nowhere, Hélène came to him. He felt her absolutely, and knew that she was near. He heard her voice; he felt her touch; he could smell the scent of her skin and of her hair. There was no effort of will on his part, and no struggle. One minute he was filled with blinding anger and pain, the next she was there. She wiped out Louise's words, and he felt again the old absolute conviction, and the old absolute calm.

He was afraid to investigate that conviction, afraid to analyze it in any way. He thought, quickly, as he looked out over the water: *let be*.

He half-expected that this regained calm would not last. It would be with him for a while, he told himself; then, just as before, it would depart. But this was not the case; it was as if he had reached some lowest point, from which there could be no further to fall, and then, just when he was in despair, something miraculous had happened, and he had been lifted up. Christian said, tartly, that the cure had been a good night's drinking. Edouard now thought that it might have been partly that, partly the things which had happened before, and partly the scene with Louise—her accusations had been so vicious that, in some way, he had been freed.

"I saw the other face of love—perhaps that was it," he said to Christian, and Christian sniffed. He remarked that it was that side he usually, unfortunately, saw.

Christian was perplexed by this change in Edouard; at first he welcomed it. Then, after they left St. Tropez, and the months passed, he felt less sure.

Christian was all for change; steadiness unsettled him. He liked to see a crisis resolved, yes—but he liked another crisis to take its place.

He saw Edouard, that summer, in Paris and in London; they met once, when their visits coincided, in New York. He noted his friend's regained energy and sense of purpose; he noted his curious calm. He was glad that Edouard seemed happier, but still, nothing was changed, nothing was resolved, and Edouard's apparent certitude was unfounded, he thought. He began to grow a little impatient with it; Edouard was growing complacent, he said, and when Edouard smiled and said no, that was far from the case, he revised his terms: Edouard was, he decided, becoming *fatalistic*.

"The beginning of the end," he pronounced. "Edouard, you should snap out of it."

Christian had, then, just emerged from one of his brief, turbulent love affairs. Edouard, who knew this, was patient, and stayed silent.

HÉLÈNE
AND LEWIS

LOS ANGELES, 1964

"And so, he made me lie down. Right there. It was filthy. There were cockroaches all over, and dirty dishes—no one ever washed the dishes. He made me lie down, and then he put his hand over my mouth so I couldn't scream. And then he did it to me. My own stepfather. My mother was right there, in the next room, but she was probably out cold from the drinking. I don't know. I never asked her—if she heard. I was frightened to. I never told her one thing. I was only twelve years old."

Stephani Sandrelli drew in a deep breath; she fixed Hélène with her eyes. She smoothed down her skirt, and rested her hands on her knees, folded neatly, like a well-behaved child.

"I ran away from Chicago not long after that. I'd had enough. I couldn't stand it."

Hélène frowned. She said gently, "I thought you said it was Detroit you lived in, Stephani?"

"It was Detroit first. Then Chicago. We moved. We were always moving." She stood up. "Should I go and see if they're ready for you yet? They can't be much longer. Your stand-in's been out there for hours. . . ."

"Stephani—it's all right. When they're ready, they'll—"

"It's okay. I don't mind. It's no trouble. . . ."

Stephani was outside before she could stop her, and Hélène sighed. As she opened and closed the door, a blast of hot dry air came in. Tucson, Arizona. Outside, it was ninety-five degrees, and getting hotter by the day. Inside, the air-conditioning whispered. Another state, another movie, another trailer, another character. Change of location, change of part. In the past year alone, she had filmed in Los Angeles, New York,

Massachusetts, and the Dakotas. And now the Arizona desert, for another four weeks.

Today she was waiting to die, in a hail of bullets, next to the wreck of a car, at the hands of her lover. It was three in the afternoon, they'd had technical problems, and she'd been waiting to die since she came in for makeup at six o'clock this morning. *The Runaways*, directed by Gregory Gertz, whom people were calling the next Thad Angelini, with a script originally written by a friend of Lewis's, since reworked five times by five different writers. A good script though, and a good part, but in one respect Greg Gertz did not resemble Thad; they were behind, two days at least; she thought they might go a whole week over.

On the dressing table in front of her there was a photograph of Cat, which Madeleine had sent her, taken in honor of Cat's fourth birthday. Cat was in the garden of the Los Angeles house, seated proudly on the brand-new bicycle Hélène had arranged to have sent to her. She was smiling. Hélène looked at the photograph, and felt as if she might cry. Cat looked so proud, and so pleased . . . and she herself hadn't been there. She had to fight to get time at home, and whenever she lost the fight, as she often did, in the maze of shooting schedules, script conferences, and publicity campaigns, she felt guilty, just as she did now. The bicycle was fine; but Hélène had not been there to give it to her.

Another blast of hot air; the door had opened again, and Stephani Sandrelli's face appeared around it.

"Fifteen minutes," she said, "Jack thinks fifteen minutes at most. I've asked catering to send you over some tea. I have to go now. They need me for a fitting. . . ."

"Stephani—I don't want any tea, I—"

The door had already closed again. Hélène gave a sigh of exasperation. She leaned across to the trailer windows, and watched Stephani teeter her way past the other trailers, past the generators, picking her way over equipment and cables. A group of male extras lounging outside one of the farther trailers turned to watch her as she passed; one of them pursed his lips in a whistle. Stephani's hips swung in her tight skirt; her breasts bounced up and down; and she herself seemed quite unaware of the effect this produced. When it was made evident to her, as it was now, it did not seem to please her. She glanced over her shoulder at the men, and increased her pace—as if she were running away from them. The dazzle of platinum hair disappeared from sight. Chicago, Hélène thought, or Detroit—was any of it true?

Stephani had a bit part in this movie, four lines, no more than that, but a number of crowd appearances. She had attached herself to Hélène from the first, and Hélène, irritated by her, then amused, and finally intrigued, now hadn't the heart to get rid of her. When they had been filming in the studio, Stephani had hung around the commissary, waiting for Hélène to come in. She began by running little errands, for Hélène's dresser, for wigs, for makeup. She would fetch and carry, take messages, relay phone calls: *It's no trouble*, was her constant refrain; *I don't mind. It's a pleasure.* . . .

When her services were not being utilized in this way, she would station herself somewhere from which she could watch Hélène, and would simply stare at her, wide-eyed, missing nothing, like a child on its first visit to the circus. The crew, and some of the other actors, laughed at her. Stephani was the butt of all their jokes: she was so luscious, so willing, so star-struck—and so *dumb*. Hélène felt sorry for her— that was how they first came to talk, and then, when she listened to Stephani, she became fascinated. The stammering confidences, the breathy child-like voice, so at odds with the curvaceous body. The way of talking she had, with her head drooping, shyly, looking up every so often, and fixing Hélène with that wide, startled, blue-eyed gaze. She intrigued Hélène, and Hélène watched her, wondering if she could catch that way of speaking, those characteristic gestures, wondering if she could act her.

Then, when she first arrived for the location work, Hélène began to miss things. Tiny things, unimportant things: once, a bar of soap she used; another time, a handkerchief; a day later, one of the hairbands with which she tied back her hair when she took off her makeup; the day after that, a lipstick. She thought nothing of it at first, did not even associate the missing items with Stephani's constant presence, until one day Stephani came in, and instead of the normal pale pink lipstick she wore, she had painted her lips a quite different color. Hélène recognized it; she said, "Oh, Stephani, my lipstick," before she could stop herself, and Stephani stood there, with a funny proud look on her face.

"It's true," she said. "I took them. All those things. I couldn't help it. I didn't mean any harm. I just wanted to be you."

Hélène stared at her in consternation. Then, after a little pause, she said gently, "Stephani—I don't mind, it doesn't matter. But that's silly, you know. Why should you want to be me? Why can't you be yourself?"

"Be me? Who would want to be me? I'm a nobody. I'm a joke. You're Hélène Harte. . . ."

And that was how it began, really. The conversations, in the trailer, day after hot day, the endless boredom of waiting. The tedium of filming, the endless inevitable waiting around: Stephani passed the time with her stories, and Hélène listened. The stepfather; the mother; the boyfriend; the photographer who first spotted Stephani's potential. The nude pinup that Stephani was now ashamed of. The decision to go to Hollywood. The fateful meeting, one night at a party, with the elderly agent.

"He took me to Cannes once. For the film festival. It was the year you won the prize. I've never forgotten it. It was the best year of my life, that year. He's dead now."

Hélène listened to all this with fascination. At first, she thought it was the absolute predictability of Stephani's story that absorbed her: the way in which, undeviatingly, it followed the course of all the other similiar stories she had read in a million magazines and press handouts. It was, give or take a few elements, the story of Marilyn Monroe, she supposed, on whom Stephani had clearly modeled herself, and for whom she cared, passionately.

"I saw all her movies, every one of them. And when she died, I cried. I cried every day for a week."

Hélène contrasted this with Thad's reaction to the actress's death. When he heard the news he said, "She would have died anyway. This will be good for you. This is where you stop being a star and start becoming a legend." He giggled. "You know—they're insatiable. They'll need a replacement."

But Stephani's grief seemed genuine. It was only gradually that Hélène began to notice things wrong with her stories, small discrepancies, like the one today. And this disturbed her greatly. Stephani, she began to suspect, had made herself up. Perhaps some of this lurid past was true, but other parts of it, Hélène became more and more sure, were invented. She never pointed this out too directly to Stephani, for she knew that it would hurt her. Stephani clearly believed her own tales, and it was when Hélène realized this that she knew what it was that had drawn her to the girl—she understood her own sympathy.

Had she herself not done a very similar thing? Hélène Harte, with her shadowy and vaguely glamorous European past—this Hélène Harte was every bit as much of an invention as Stephani Sandrelli.

When this first occurred to her, it made Hélène impatient, and she dismissed the thought; after all, whatever stories were spun in the newspapers by journalists desperate for copy, she did not believe them. She knew who she was. . . . And then she began to wonder: was that the case? Was she herself entirely sure, always, where truth shaded into fabrication?

Sometimes she felt very sure that she did. When she was at home in Los Angeles, with Cassie, who had been with her now three years, she felt sure of her own identity. Her first action, when she had been paid in full for her first film, had been to repay Cassie the money she owed her; they remained in touch after that, and when Cassie wrote and said that the beauty parlor was getting too much for her, and she was thinking of selling it, Hélène at once asked her to come to work for her in Los Angeles. It was a decision she had never regretted, and her reliance on Cassie had grown. Perhaps, to some extent, Cassie had taken the place of her mother: certainly, she felt free with Cassie in a way she felt with no one else. With Cassie she could talk about the past; Cassie would read out loud to her the letters she received from friends in Orangeburg, and Hélène's sense of who she was would grow strong. The South, the trailer, her mother, the feel of being poor, it all came back to her so sharply, and so vividly.

But at other times, her childhood seemed very distant, a country of the mind.

Lewis did not know the details of her previous connection with Cassie; Cassie did not know the truth of her relationship with Lewis; and there were still parts of her past that Hélène spoke of to no one.

So the truth was not a simple thing; it was layer upon layer of truths, so mixed in with lies that sometimes Hélène felt afraid, and she could not quite remember, any more than Stephani could, which truth she had told to which person, or which lie.

Sometimes, when she was with Cassie, she would think, *I am still Hélène Craig,* and she would be able to see the long chain of connections between the girl she had been and the woman she had become. But at other times, those connections were severed; she would lose all sense of who she had been, could not relate that person to the person she was now. For now, she had a public identity: she was Hélène Harte, and Hélène Harte, she felt, was a barrier between herself and other people. They did not look at her now and see Hélène Craig, who grew up on the wrong side of the tracks. They saw a famous and successful woman, apparently assured, apparently independent, born to a life not dissimilar to the one she led now. She had become famous, not just for her performances, but for other, trivial things as well. For her taste; for the clothes she wore; for a certain restraint in her manner which was interpreted as coldness; even for the fact that, unusually in Hollywood, she was never seen with a man other than her husband, and even the most energetic gossips could not drum up a breath of convincing scandal.

It was now impossible for her to enter a room without everyone in it being aware of who she was: people felt that they knew her before they met her; their opinions of her, for or against, were formed already, on the basis of films seen, or stories read. There was her reputation—a wall between her and the rest of the world—and there was Hélène, the woman she felt herself truly to be, imprisoned on the other side of it.

Thad said, when she tried to explain this to him once: "So what? You're famous. What did you think would happen?"

Not this, Hélène had wanted to reply. But she was ashamed to confess that she had been so naïve; it had never occurred to her that once she was famous, she would cease to feel free.

There was a knock on the trailer door. The location manager—they were ready for her scene now. Hélène turned to the mirror and stared at her own face. Who was she?

Well, today she was Maria, a small-town girl, a rebel, on the run with her teenage lover, caught up in a romantic elopement that went hideously wrong. Maria was about to die, just when she was about to grow up, and die suddenly, and pointlessly, as a result of a silly argument, a lovers' quarrel that went murderously off the rails.

She knew Maria; she recognized *her*, Hélène thought. She knew exactly how Maria moved and thought and hoped. She could hear Maria's voice, and she could speak with her accent. She knew everything, from the way Maria dressed and did her hair, to the little characteristic gestures she had, one of which she would use now, for the sentences Maria spoke before she died. Oh, yes, she recognized Maria, and understood her, even if she did not always understand or recognize herself.

That thought calmed her, as it always did. She felt it again, that quietness and sureness that she had first discovered in Rome, working on *Night Game*. She stood up, opened the door, and walked down the trailer steps. Stephani was back at her usual post, on the fringes, watching. As Hélène passed her, she smiled, and held up two fingers, crossed.

Hélène stood in the shade, and people fussed around her. Someone was adjusting her hair; someone was touching up her makeup. The special-effects man was making the final adjustments to the harness concealed beneath her dress. It contained tiny plastic bags of artificial blood, and a device that would burst them at precisely the right second.

Hélène was hardly aware of the people fussing and adjusting: she was in that narrow space, that limbo, between herself and Maria, waiting for the moment when the production team left her alone, and Maria would come to her.

They had finished at last; she moved forward impatiently toward her mark, and as she did so, she caught a glimpse of Stephani, just in the corner of her eye. She stopped; then moved forward again. She thought: of course—I know why I like Stephani and why I pity her. She is a mirror image of me. A distorted image, perhaps, but a reflection nonetheless. It's true: neither of us knows who we are. Is that why we both want to act?

She had reached her mark. She lifted her head and looked around her. The wrecked car; her costar, holding two shotguns; the desert stretching away into the distance; equipment; cameras; people—and where was Maria?

She lifted her hand to her eyes; the hot air shimmered.

A voice, Gregory Gertz's voice, called: "Are you okay, Hélène?"

"What? Oh, yes. I'm fine."

"Right. We're going for a take. . . ."

Sound on; camera rolling; action. She had only two lines, then she must begin to run forward. They had rehearsed it before, and now she did it. The guns were lifted; the blanks went off; the harness device worked; bright chemical blood spouted, and she died beautifully.

"Great," Greg said afterward.

He came across to her, a puzzled frown on his face. He looked at her, pressed her arm, and then turned away.

"Right. Let's get Hélène fixed up, and then do it again."

She died beautifully five times. But it was Hélène who died, not Maria. Maria had gone; she would not come back to her.

After the fifth take, Greg said: "That's it. We'll break for the day. The light's wrong, anyway." Then he came across to Hélène, and looked down at her, still with that puzzled frown on his face.

He put his arm around her waist, and said, "It's so goddamn hot. Don't worry about it. Listen—have dinner with me this evening."

It was nearly six when she returned to the trailer, half-past by the time her dresser had gone, and various production people checking the details of the next day's shoot had finally left her, and she was alone.

She felt tired, and depressed by the failure of the scene, irritated by her inability to explain it. Obviously there had been times in the past when things had gone wrong, when she had not felt satisfied with what she had done, but she had never felt that blank emptiness before, the sensation that she was outside herself, watching herself failing.

Angrily, she began to rub off her makeup. It was then, reaching for some cotton, that she noticed the photograph of Cat was missing. She looked around the dressing table in confusion: it had been here, she had been looking at it, just a few hours before. . . . She pushed aside bottles and jars; no, it was not there. She bent, and looked on the floor, to see if it had fallen—but no, it was not there either. Straightening up, she thought, *Stephani.*

Stephani herself turned up five minutes later. She put her platinum head around the door, cautiously, and Hélène turned and looked at her coldly.

"There was a photograph of my daughter, Stephani. On my dressing table. Have you seen it?"

Stephani blushed slightly under the heavy makeup she wore. She lowered her eyes, hesitated, and then came into the trailer and shut the door. She opened her purse, took out the photograph, and handed it to Hélène without a word.

"For God's sake, Stephani . . ." Hélène's temper snapped. "Stop doing this, will you? All right, if you want to borrow a lipstick or something. But not a picture of Cat. That's mine. It's private. Please don't do anything like that again."

Stephani slowly lifted her head. She looked at Hélène shyly. "I'm sorry," she said finally, in her breathy voice. "I knew I shouldn't. I knew it was wrong. It's just that—she's so pretty, isn't she? I wouldn't have kept it. I only wanted to look at it. . . ."

"Stephani. Doesn't it occur to you that I might want to look at it too? Cat's my daughter, and I miss her. I miss her very much. And I like that picture to be here. Where I can look at it."

"I won't do it again." Stephani passed her tongue across her lips. They were shiny with Hélène's lipstick. Hélène turned away in exasperation. She wiped off the last of her makeup; Stephani did not move. She watched Hélène in the mirror. After a pause, just as Hélène was about to ask her to go, she said in a small voice, "You look so lovely. Just like that. With no makeup on at all. I wish I looked like you. I wish . . . You always look so cool, so elegant. I wish I looked that way. I wish I looked beautiful, and rich."

Hélène stared at her reflection. She could think of no reply. Stephani gave an odd, sad little laugh.

"Anyway," she said. "You don't need to worry. I won't be bothering you anymore. I've only got one more scene—tomorrow. Then I'm going back to L.A."

"One more scene?" Hélène turned. "But I thought . . ."

"Yeah. So did I." Stephani shrugged. "They cut all those other scenes. Greg Gertz doesn't like me. I guess. Anyway. It's okay. I've got some work. I talked to my agent just now. He thinks he can get me in on some vampire movie—they're shooting in the studio now. But one of the girls got sick." She paused. "Six lines, he says. And a scene with Peter Cushing. That ought to be okay. I suppose."

"Stephani . . ." Hélène felt suddenly contrite.

"So. I'll come and see you before I go. And I'm sorry about the photo. Really."

She had just reached the door of the trailer. She was about to step out, when she stopped and frowned, a small puzzled slightly speculative frown.

"Hey," she said. "It's odd, you know. I never thought of it before, but it's kind of weird."

"What is, Stephani?"

"Well, you always have a picture of Cat. Right there, on your dressing table. But you never have a picture of your husband. Not there, not anywhere . . ."

"Stephani. This isn't a picture gallery. It's a dressing room, a place to work in. . . . Why should I have a picture of Lewis?"

"Oh, I don't know." Stephani gave a small dimpling smile. "He's very good-looking, isn't he?" She shrugged. "I would, but then, we're very different, I guess. . . ."

She lifted her hand in a small wave, and tripped down the steps.

"Would you like steak? Or steak?" Greg Gertz smiled at her over the top of the menu.

"Oh, steak. What a lovely idea." She smiled back at him. He turned to the waitress to give their order, and Hélène leaned back against the plastic banquette. The film star's life! She knew, from the letters she received from her fans, how most of them imagined such a life. A succession of beautiful restaurants, champagne, parties, handsome escorts and exquisite dresses. And that was part of it, sometimes. But this was part of it too. A small town eight miles from Tucson, stuck down in the middle of the desert. Gas stations; a cluster of houses; the railroad and the highway; a town in the middle of nowhere, a town that people stopped off in, and that happened to have a large motel.

The motel was their headquarters; they had taken it over for the duration of filming. It was their home, their club, their restaurant, and for one simple reason—there was no alternative.

She looked around her: walls covered in an unlikely tartan wallpaper; a line of stags' antlers; a lot of varnished wood; a bar; red banquettes. She could have been anywhere in America. It was smaller, but not very different from the Howard Johnson's where Billy took her for her fifteenth birthday.

She turned her face to the window; black plate glass, the desert beyond, but invisible. Tonight Orangeburg felt close, and she knew why that was. It was because the moment was approaching when she would go back there. She was almost prepared, almost ready, there were just a few last moves to make. . . . For a moment she saw Billy's face, and then Ned Calvert's, and realized what it was that had provoked the memory. The motel restaurant had Muzak. It was playing a medley, and the latest tune was "Blue Moon."

Greg Gertz had said something. She jumped.

"I'm sorry?"

"You're miles away, you know that? I said—how's Cat. . . ." He hesitated, just a fractional pause. "And how's Lewis?"

"Cat's fine. Very well. I missed her birthday. . . ."

"I know that." Greg Gertz was looking at her steadily.

"And Lewis—Lewis is fine. He's working on a new script. Writing, you know. It's going very well. I think." She hesitated. "I don't like to ask too much, not when he's right in the middle of it. You know what writers are like. . . ."

"Oh, sure. Don't we all?"

Greg Gertz smiled easily, but his perceptive eyes did not leave her face. Hélène felt uneasy. She hated to be asked about Lewis; she hated to have to talk about him. This was Lewis's third script. The first had gone to every producer and director in town, and was now languishing in a file at his agent's. The second had been optioned by Sphere—and that option had just run out, with no prospect of renewal or production. The third, the one Lewis was working on now, was a love story called *Endless Moments*. Lewis had announced his intention was to package and produce it himself.

Lewis, as a writer, was a failure. She knew that, Lewis knew it, and she suspected that Greg Gertz, along with the rest of Los Angeles, knew it. The shared knowledge hung between them for a moment, unspoken. Hélène looked away, quickly.

She would never admit this failure, not to Lewis's friends, not to Thad—who questioned her most of all on the subject—not to Greg Gertz; she tried very hard not to admit it to herself, and she tried especially hard to hide her knowledge of it from Lewis. She did not always succeed: Lewis could read it in her eyes, the awful painful hope that this time what he was doing was going to work, and the equally awful and painful fear that it was not. Her doubts hurt Lewis; they also made him violently angry, particularly when he had been drinking, or when he had taken some of his new pills. The pills made him wildly euphoric and confident; when they wore off they left him in the blackest despair. Lewis would not give them up; he would not give up the alcohol. He said he needed them for his writing, that they made the words flow.

"Stop interfering. Stop putting me down!" Lewis would shout. It was a constant refrain. She heard it daily. No, indeed, she did not want to talk about Lewis.

Greg Gertz, she suspected, knew this. He was a clever man, with sharp instincts, a quiet man who said little, and saw much. She had grown to like him over the weeks they had worked together; she had grown to trust him—as much as she ever trusted anyone, which was not very far. He was wary, as she was, and kept people at a distance. He was also divorced—it had been a particularly ugly divorce, with a protracted custody battle. The three children had gone to his wife. This he never discussed. She also liked him for that.

He was looking at her now, still with that slight frown, as if he were trying to figure something out. Hélène knew he wanted to ask her what had gone wrong that afternoon, and she also knew that he would wait. Meanwhile, though he had to know she would have preferred to change the subject, he persisted.

"I hadn't realized Lewis was still writing. I thought he might have decided to go back to producing for a while. He was very good at it once." He paused, realizing he had been untactful. "I don't know. Work with Thad again, perhaps?"

"I don't think so. That was another era." She forced herself to sound bright. "Lewis hasn't produced Thad's last three pictures—well, you know that. Thad handles most of that himself—he likes to coproduce now, he told me. And I suppose it's relatively straightforward, because of the tieup with Sphere. . . ."

"But they're friends still, presumably?" He put the question suddenly, and because she knew he knew the answer anyway, Hélène felt suddenly tired: why lie?

"No," she said, looking at him directly. "Not really. They hardly see each other at all. They didn't quarrel. There was no fight—nothing like that. They just drifted apart. Besides, Thad is a loner. He's close to no one. You know what he's like."

"I'm not sure I do, no." He glanced away, and then back. "I always thought he was very close to you, though. Are you saying that's not the case?"

Hélène frowned. Somewhat to her own surprise, she realized that she was not sure of the answer. "I don't think I am—close to him," she said at last. "No one is. I've worked very closely with him, obviously. And I go to his house sometimes—which no one else seems to do. He invites me over, and we have tea, and talk for an hour or so, usually about work, and then I go. That's all. . . ." She paused. "Really, I feel I know Thad no more now than I did when we first worked together. He's still as secretive—more, probably. And just as mad . . ."

She smiled then, but Greg did not smile back. He was looking at her seriously. There was a pause while the waitress delivered the steaks, french fries, and salad which had been everyone's staple diet since their day of arrival. Greg picked up his knife and fork, and then put them down again.

"So you didn't feel crowded by Thad. You didn't feel he was closing you in?"

"Thad? Closing me in? Why should I feel that?"

"I think you know why. I think that's what you felt." He paused. "Okay. You finished *Ellis*, when? A year ago. Since then you've made three films. The one with Peckinpah, the one with Huston, and this one with me. That's the longest break you've had from Thad since you started working."

"Yes—but Thad was tied up. He's been working on *Ellis*, doing the editing, the post-production. And those films came up, the parts were good. . . ."

She had spoken too fast, and she could hear the defensiveness in her own tone. Greg could hear it, too, and he smiled.

"When is *Ellis* due for release?"

"September. October perhaps. In time to qualify for the Oscars certainly. Thad wants a big première. And we're having a party—you must come. . . ."

"I'd be delighted." He was not going to be sidetracked, and Hélène could see it. He paused, and slowly began to cut up his steak.

"And then?"

"What about then?"

"We'll have finished *Runaways* by mid-July. *Ellis* won't open till the fall. What are you going to do next?"

"I'm going to take a break. Spend some time with my family. With Cat—and with Lewis. I've been promising them that for a long time. I've been promising myself. . . ."

"And then, after that? When the domestic interlude is over? What then?"

"Well, then I'll do another movie, I suppose. If the right script comes along. The right part . . ."

"I see." He put down his knife and fork, and looked her directly in the eyes. "With Thad?"

There was a little silence. Hélène looked down at her plate. "No," she said finally, "not with Thad."

"Thank you," he answered. "You've finally told me what I wanted to know."

"Cognac. Quite good cognac. Drink it. I want you to talk." They were in the sitting area of Greg Gertz's room, just down the hall from her own. Greg Gertz thrust the glass into her hand, lit a cigarette, and sat down opposite her.

Hélène looked at him: a tall man, rangily built, not handsome precisely, with a clever narrow face, brown eyes, brown hair; he usually wore brown clothes, old unmemorable clothes, clothes that were so indeterminate they were like camouflage.

"That's what I'm here to do—talk?" She smiled.

"That's right."

"What about?"

"Yourself."

"I never talk about myself."

"I know that. I've noticed it. It's one of the more interesting things about you."

Hélène supposed that was a compliment—a left-handed one. But she liked it. It made her smile.

Greg Gertz leaned forward. "But first—if it makes it any easier, there're a couple of things I'd like to say. About you. They relate to this afternoon."

"Oh, this afternoon. Listen, Greg, I . . ."

"No, you listen." He leaned forward. "Do you know the first time I saw you in a movie? Right at the beginning. Fall 1960. I'd gone to see my sister at UCLA, and she took me to see *Night Game*—it was playing a limited run at the movie theater near the campus. I didn't want to go. I'd had movies up to here, at that point. . . ." He gestured at his throat. "I'd been struggling for twelve years to get my work off the ground. Trying to get scripts together. Trying to get backing. Filling in with work I despised, because something had to pay the rent. My marriage was on the rocks, and I'd pretty well decided to throw the whole thing overboard." He stopped. "It makes me laugh now. The next Thad Angelini—you know they call me that? I'm thirty-seven years old—Thad is, what? Twenty-nine? Thirty, maybe. I don't know. All I know is that when Thad Angelini was still in film school, I'd been out there for years, fighting for a break." He leaned back in his chair. "Anyway. The point of this story is, it was 1960, and I was sick to death of Hollywood, sick to death of movies, and I got dragged to *Night Game*, which I didn't want to see, and I sat there and it was like a revelation. I came out of that movie theater so excited—well, it was like I was drunk. I thought: *that's it*. It's possible to do it, it's possible to make it work, and when you do make it work, well, it's just the best thing in the world, that's all. Better than any play. Better than any symphony. Better than any painting. A great movie." He paused, looking at her carefully. "The drive came back. I wanted to work again—and, as it happened, I started to get some breaks. Two people did that for me, and I'll never forget it. One was you, and the other was Thad."

There was a silence when he had finished. Hélène looked at him, and Greg Gertz, whose face had been animated a moment before, grew quiet. He leaned toward her.

"Did you know you were good?"

"Yes." She looked down. "I did."

"You couldn't not have known." He shrugged. "And so—I want to ask you. What went wrong after that?"

"Wrong? Nothing went wrong," Hélène answered quickly. "We made *Summer*; we made *A Life of Her Own*; we made *Short Cut*. The others did well, but *Short Cut* was a huge hit. We won the Palme d'Or, Thad got the backing to make *Ellis* . . ."

"Oh, sure. Thad could write his own ticket after *Short Cut*, but what about you? I saw you in all those movies. I saw those two he made back-to-back—what were they called? Yes, *Quickstep* and *Extra Time*. I saw you in the Peckinpah, and I've seen a rough cut of the Huston. . . ."

"And?"

"And there's no need to look so defensive." He smiled. "You were good in all of them. Very good—what did you think I was going to say, that you were bad? No—you were excellent. A little off in *Quickstep*, perhaps. I thought that was the weakest. . . ."

"Yes. So did I."

Hélène looked away. They had begun filming on *Quickstep* soon after the visit to Cannes in 1962. It had been the time when she thought most of Edouard, before she learned the trick of shutting him out of her mind. It had also been the time when Lewis had been most jealous, when he . . . but no, she didn't want to think about that.

Greg Gertz was looking at her closely. She turned back; her chin tilted.

"You're coming to a 'but,' I can hear it—what is it?"

"I'll tell you—but I'll make a bargain with you. I'll tell you what I saw if you'll tell me what you felt. Agreed?"

Hélène nodded, and he leaned forward again.

"You were good, but you were being confined. That's what I thought. After all, Thad not only directs, and now coproduces, he also writes his own movies. That's their strength and their weakness. They're *his*, through and through—they couldn't for a moment be anyone else's work. And obviously you mean a lot to Thad—he's never worked with another actress, not in a major role. A lot of European directors do that—but very few Americans. There's nothing wrong with it, in principle—except it limits you, perhaps. Thad writes your roles, he sees you in a particular way—and really, when you look at his movies closely, it's always the same way. You play different parts, the story line is different, Thad is so clever technically, and so daring, that most people don't notice. But I do."

He shrugged. "Different movie. The same woman. Always slightly mysterious, her motives never fully explained. Always ambiguous. A little dangerous perhaps. Haunting, certainly. And . . . I think you know what I'm going to say, don't you?"

"Passive?"

"Precisely that." He hesitated. "I didn't see it at first. But once I noticed it in one movie, I couldn't miss it in all the others. He wraps it all up so well. The lighting, the editing, the dialogue—it's all so brilliant that you can miss something very obvious. All the women you've played for him. They react. They never—quite—initiate any action themselves." He paused. "Lise—the part you play in *Ellis,* is that the same?"

"Yes. It is. Oh, it's so difficult to explain!" Hélène stood up, she turned, and walked away a little distance, and then swung around.

"I thought it was just me. I tried to ask Thad about it, but he said I was imagining it, making difficulties that didn't exist. 'This happens,' he said, 'and this. There's plenty of stuff going on.' He didn't know what I was talking about. And it's true—lots of things always happen in his stories."

She made a wry face. "Love affairs, intrigue, bereavements, betrayals—you can't imagine all the things that happen to Lise. But they happen *to* her. She changes, of course—you see her change, you always do in Thad's films. But she never *does* anything, she's just endlessly, mysteriously feminine. Like all the others.''

There was a little silence. Hélène's color had risen. She suddenly felt that she wished she had said none of that—it was disloyal to Thad, perhaps. She returned to her chair, and sat down again.

"You see?" She gestured at her glass. "It's the brandy—just as you said. I'm sorry . . .''

"Why should you feel the need to apologize when you say what you think? You do it rarely enough.''

He paused, watching her closely, then he said, "So—did you make a conscious decision to break away—when you did the Peckinpah film?''

"No. It wasn't conscious then. It's conscious now. I'm pleased with the work I did on *Ellis*—I'm even proud of it. But I don't want to work with Thad again—not for a while." She hesitated. "I'm not even sure how much I want to work at all. It sometimes feels very empty, and a little false. I spend so much time playing other people that I never have time to be myself.''

"It takes more than time to do that," Greg said seriously. He looked at her intently. "Is that what went wrong this afternoon?''

"Yes. It was. And I know you're right about that—I know that it isn't just a question of time.''

She bent her head and looked at her hands. Clear in her head, she heard her own voice: *When I am with you, Edouard, I don't have to be anything. I just am.*

She straightened up, and smiled at Greg brightly.

"Anyway, it's late, and I should go and get some sleep. I'll be better tomorrow. I know it was a mess this afternoon. . . .''

She rose, and Greg stood also. He seemed to hesitate for a moment, then he turned away to a chest on the far side of the room, opened a drawer, and drew out of it a large manila envelope. He handed it to her.

"What's this?''

"A script. The best script I've ever been offered. I want to film it, and I think I can get the backing. I want to do it early next year. In the spring. And I want to do it with you. If you like it." He paused. "If you feel you want to work, and I know you will. Read it. Let me know what you think." He paused again, and the intelligent brown eyes met hers. She saw the habitual wariness return to his face, and—perhaps aware that they were standing quite close—he stepped back.

"It's about a divorce. You may find . . . well, see what you think anyway.''

"All right. Thank you, Greg.''

She knew that this was the moment to go, and yet, for some reason, she hesitated. There was a peculiar tension between them now, an alertness that had not been there earlier when they were discussing films, and which had crept up on her unawares, perhaps because of his proximity.

Greg looked at her, and she looked back. He gave a sad, slightly crooked smile, lifted his hand, and touched her face.

"It wouldn't be a good idea, would it?"

"No. Probably not."

"We're both too unhappy, and that's never a good thing."

"Are we? Am I?" She raised her eyes to his.

He smiled again, and let his hand fall.

"Oh, yes. You know that. It was the other thing wrong this afternoon."

He was right, of course.

"Does it show that much?" Hélène asked bitterly.

"Sometimes," he answered. "Yes, it does. You might find it easier if you accepted it. I did. See if it helps, tomorrow. Good night, Hélène."

I n her own room, she shut the door, and leaned against it. She knew what she had wanted then, and she was ashamed that Gregory Gertz should have seen it, as she knew he had. Not even to make love necessarily, but to touch, to hold and be held—yes, she knew she had wanted that.

It was so long a time, she thought, and the body could grow starved for affection as much as the mind. She moved restlessly around the room: eighteen months—no, longer than that. Lewis had not touched her, not so much as held her hand, in that time, and neither had any other man. Lewis had, quite suddenly, closed himself off from the possibility of further sexual failures. He slept in his own room; he looked at her, sometimes, with a mixture of longing and revulsion, as if wanting her were a risk he was no longer prepared to take. More than eighteen months: how stupid she was. It was two years.

For a moment she thought she must be wrong; it was not a calculation she had wanted to make. But now that she forced herself, she knew she was correct. Two years, yes; that was when the estrangement between them had begun—in 1962, not long after they left Cannes.

The realization frightened her a little. She was always promising herself that it was temporary, this awful coldness between them. She was constantly hoping that the next time they were together, it would somehow heal—for the breach between them made her guilty. Lewis had told her so many times that it was not his doing, it was her fault.

"It isn't me that you want," he had said many times, and since in her heart she knew that was true, she never answered him.

She knew who she wanted, then, standing alone in her room. Not

Lewis. Certainly not Gregory Gertz, who had simply been there and seemed kind. She stood still, and let thoughts of Edouard enter her mind. It did not make her any happier, but it did calm her.

She looked, with longing, at the telephone. There was a certain ritual which she had come to perform when the loneliness and the unhappiness were very strong, as they were tonight. That, too, did not solve anything, but it sometimes helped her. But she had placed the call to his number once already from this telephone, just a few days before. It was too soon—and it was foolish anyway.

With no sense of achievement, she pushed the temptation aside: *no*, she thought, *not tonight*.

"I'm going now. One of the boys is giving me a lift to the airport." Stephani came tripping up the trailer steps, opening the door with a blast of hot, dry air. She was dressed in a short skin-tight skirt, shoes with four-inch stiletto heels, and a low-cut blouse. She did not appear to be wearing stockings, underpants, or a bra. Why did she invite what she also ran away from? Hélène wondered.

She looked at Stephani resignedly. This good-bye was not well timed. Hélène was about to reshoot her death scene, and the failure of the day before felt close, very close.

"I wanted to say—how grateful I am. You've been kind to me. Really kind. Not like some of the others. I'll never forget that." Stephani lowered her head, looked up again shyly. "I brought you a present. To say good-bye."

She held out a small white paper bag, eagerly. Hélène took it, and opened it. Inside was a small box containing a bottle of *Joy*.

"Oh . . ." She stared at it a moment, and then, recovering herself, eager not to hurt Stephani's feelings, she looked up with a smile.

"Stephani—how lovely. How kind of you. I love this. It—reminds me of my mother. It was the scent she always wore."

"I got it on a plane sometime." Stephani spoke a little quickly, with a certain note in her voice that Hélène had come to recognize. On a plane, Hélène thought, or from a man? At once she hated herself for being so uncharitable.

"You never use perfume. I noticed that. . . ." Stephani sounded almost accusing.

Hélène stood up. "I shall use it now. Thank you, Stephani." She held out her hand. "And good luck with the vampire movie. . . ."

Stephani clutched her hand. She held it very tight, then quickly, she reached forward, and planted a sticky kiss on Hélène's cheek.

"I wonder . . ." she was still holding on to Hélène's hand. "I wanted to ask you this, and I didn't quite dare. I mean—why should you? But . . ." She paused, and lifted the china-blue eyes to Hélène's face. "But—would you let me have your number in L.A.? I wouldn't bother you. I wouldn't give it to anyone else—but I'd like to know I could call you up sometimes, when you get back. We might get together. Have a talk. . . ."

Hélène was taken aback. As Stephani certainly knew, her number was unlisted, given to only a very few people. For a moment, she thought of giving Stephani her agent's number—but no, that was too unkind, too rude.

"All right. Here. I'll give it to you."

She found a piece of paper, scribbled the number, and handed it across. Stephani watched her do this. She took the piece of paper, folded it in careful quarters, and put it into her purse. To her consternation, Hélène saw that the wide china-blue eyes were brimming with tears.

"Gee. Thank you, Hélène. I'll never forget you, you know that?" Stephani gave a little breathy gasp and pressed Hélène's hand. "Goodbye," she called from the bottom of the steps, and began to wiggle away.

Hélène sighed. She returned to the scene ahead, and tried to concentrate, tried to force Maria to come back.

She died beautifully again. The blood spurted beautifully again. But this time it worked. Maria came back to her just in time. They did only one take, and afterward Greg Gertz came over. He pressed her hand lightly, just once.

"You see?" he said, and then he walked away.

They were having drinks in the Polo Lounge. Lewis was in the middle of the third draft of *Endless Moments*, and it was not going well. His friend, an experienced and successful screenwriter, there to give him advice, was being patient. Lewis explained the plot once. It didn't sound right, and so he explained it again; his friend, he felt, didn't seem to understand the problems he was having; he appeared unimpressed; he appeared nonchalant.

"Look, Lewis," he said finally over their second martinis. "Someone very famous once said it all. There are two plots, right? Love. And money."

Lewis looked at him anxiously. The man lit a Corona Corona, and blew the smoke in contemplative rings. He frowned.

"Who was it who said that? I think it was Balzac. On the other hand, it might have been Graham Greene."

There was a silence.

"Only two?" Lewis prompted eventually. "Ever? Like, that's it?"

"That's it."

"Jesus."

"So, just relax, Lewis. Go with the flow. The way I look at it, most motion pictures are just a love story in a journalistic setting. You think of a new setting—a railway station, postwar Vienna, the Deep South in the Civil War—it doesn't matter what the fuck it is, just make it original. Then you get two nice big bankable stars to play the leads—and there you are. Never agonize, Lewis, believe me. It doesn't pay. My main creativity goes into my tax returns."

Lewis thought about this advice all the way home. He drove fast, in his new red Porsche, with Bob Dylan playing loudly on the radio. Love. And money. It couldn't be that simple. He began to feel irritated. He began to feel sure that his friend had been putting him on.

He did not particularly like the house in the hills in which he and Hélène lived, and he never approached it happily. Ingrid Nilsson, for whom it had been built and who had lived in it before them, had been obsessed with security. For some reason, Lewis had found this catching. When he bought the house, it already had more locks than a bank vault, and the gardens were already surrounded by high walls surmounted by wire. Lewis had added to this innumerable expensive devices, all of them the latest thing. The gates were electronically operated, and could be opened only from the house, or from his or Hélène's cars. The garden itself was wired up; it was a place of electronic eyes and ears, activated by movement or body heat. The system was a nuisance, constantly being set off by birds or small animals, and now, as Lewis approached those high impenetrable gates, he wondered: was he trying to keep something out, or keep something in?

That was a stupid idea, he told himself, and it was just then, as he slowed, that he saw the man for the first time. He was standing outside Lewis's walls, looking up at them. A tall, big-boned, sandy-haired man, wearing a hat tilted on the back of his head, a cheap suit, and down-at-the-heel shoes. He was holding in his hands a map, the kind that marked movie stars' houses by name, the kind sold to tourists.

Lewis, gunning the engine of his Porsche, waiting for the remote control gates to swing back, gave the man a hard cold stare. He could see the neck of a bottle protruding from the pocket of his pants, and he thought: a lush, a bum. Lewis glared at the man, and accelerated past him in a cloud of dust. He paused to make sure the gates had shut him out, and then roared up to the house.

His irritation was growing, and he felt quite pleased that he now had a legitimate excuse to make a fuss. "There's a man hanging around the gates," he said to Cassie as soon as he could find her.

Cassie gave him one of her polite bland looks. She did not like Lewis, and Lewis did not like her. They were both usually careful to disguise this fact.

"Tall? Red-haired? Wearing a hat?"

"That's the one."

"Oh, I've seen him a couple of times. He's okay, I reckon. Some down-and-out, that's all."

"If you see him again, Cassie, you will please notify the police. He should be forced to move. That's what they're there for. After all, sometimes you and Madeleine and Cat are alone in the house." He regretted this the moment it was said.

"Jenner is usually here, Mr. Sinclair. And Mr. Hicks is in the lodge."

Jenner was the butler, Hicks, their chauffeur, and it was true, one or the other of them was almost always in the house. The person who was not was Lewis himself. Cassie, naturally, did not mention this, but the fact remained in the air between them, unspoken. Lewis turned away.

"Has Hélène phoned?" he said as an afterthought.

"Yes, Mr. Sinclair. At seven, just as she always does."

"And is Cat in bed?"

Cassie looked at her wristwatch. She hesitated. "Just about, I reckon. But she won't be asleep."

"Yes—well, it's a bit late to go up now. I don't want to get her excited. I'll see her in the morning. Oh—and Cassie. I won't be wanting dinner. I'm going out."

He had not known this until the moment he said it. Cassie merely nodded, and left.

Lewis walked through the wide hall, and into the drawing room. Hélène's room; Hélène's house; he had bought it, and she had created it, carefully, painstakingly. Lewis could see that it was beautiful, but somehow it always put him on edge.

He prowled around the room, unable to settle, unable to make up his mind what to do. He looked at the Coromandel screens, at the Chinese vases which had been a belated wedding present from his parents—his parents, who had been so appalled by his marriage but who, like everyone else, had been won over by Hélène. For a moment, he thought, sadly, of the little red room in London, with its fire, and its shabby furniture. He had been happy then; yes, he was certain. It was only later that things began to go wrong.

He poured himself a whiskey, added a little ice, and stood by the window, looking out over the garden. He could work, he supposed. He could phone Hélène—she would be home soon, anyway. The movie was almost finished; another week. He could go out; there were plenty of friends who would be glad to see him, though he had noticed that the invitations fell away a little when Hélène was not at home. There was another thing he could do, too, and he was aware of the temptation there, at the back of his mind. He pushed it aside for a while, not letting it come close. He poured himself another whiskey, and the temptation came closer. *Just a look*, it said; *just one little look.*

I'll just go into the room, Lewis told himself. I won't do any more than that. The second whiskey seemed to have disappeared, which surprised him, so he poured another, and walked through the library into a room which Hélène used as an office.

It was quite unlike all the other rooms in the house, being plainly and practically furnished. There was a desk, some bookshelves, a row of filing cabinets. Lewis leaned against them; he felt out of breath, and he had begun to sweat.

He looked at the desk. It had eight drawers, and he had, on various occasions, been through all of them. They contained stationery, notebooks full of columns of figures which seemed to relate to investments, photographs, domestic bills, things of that kind. Not the evidence for which he was searching.

He looked at the filing cabinets. They were locked, and inside the pocket of his jacket was the key. A duplicate: it had been quite easy to obtain.

He stared at the locks, felt in his pocket for the key. *What kind of woman kept love letters in a filing cabinet?* Hélène's kind, he said to himself. She must. They weren't anywhere else. He'd looked.

Exactly when he began to be obsessed with the existence of these letters, Lewis could not have said. But the obsession was there, and it grew day by day. He imagined who they might be from; he imagined what they might say; sometimes they were old love letters and sometimes they were current ones. Lewis felt he must find them, he must look at them. It didn't matter if it hurt—he knew it would hurt, but he didn't care; he wanted to *understand*.

He took one more swallow of his whiskey, put the glass down on the desk, and took the key out of his pocket. His hand was shaking; he felt a curious heady mixture of contempt for himself and pride. He opened the top drawer of the first filing cabinet, and went through it quickly and methodically. He opened the second, and the third. . . . He moved on to the next cabinet; the same thing: top drawer, middle drawer, bottom drawer.

It took him a long time, and by the end of it, Lewis was almost crying. He rummaged about desperately at the back and bottom of the drawers, but there was nothing hidden, nothing there. No love letters. No letters of a personal description at all. The files contained exactly what they looked as if they contained: all the details of Hélène's professional life. Her contracts, letters from her two agents, the one on the East Coast, the other on the West. Correspondence with various studios. Insurance policies. A note stating that her will was deposited with her lawyers; a copy of that will.

Lewis stared at it. He hadn't even known Hélène had made a will. He never had. He felt filled with a terrible self-disgust, a bitter self-hatred. He began to push files back into drawers, wildly, hardly caring that they went back in the right place. And then suddenly he realized something. By far the bulk of the files concerned Hélène's investments. He had only scanned them before, now he looked at them more carefully. He stopped, looked again.

He had known that Hélène was now rich. Obviously, she now earned a great deal of money. But this rich! He had had no idea. He stared at the listings of holdings, at the carefully documented transactions. He had introduced Hélène to her broker when they returned to America from England. James Gould, a friend of his father, whom Lewis had known since childhood.

He remembered how touched he had been; Hélène had thirty thousand dollars to invest—earned on *Night Game*—and she had been so thrilled. "I want to start that portfolio, Lewis. You remember—the one we talked about."

"Darling," he had said. "Go out and buy yourself some pretty things. Leave the portfolio till later. . . ."

But no, she'd been adamant, and Lewis hadn't had the heart to tell her that on Wall Street, her thirty thousand dollars was chicken feed. So, he'd made the appointment with James Gould III, and before Hélène set off, he warned her, "Darling, he's a very busy man. You mustn't mind if you're in and out of his office in ten minutes. All right?"

"All right, Lewis," she'd said in that funny solemn way she had, and out she'd gone. Lewis had stayed in their room at the Pierre, and waited. And waited. She came back two hours later. One and a half of them had been spent with James Gould.

Lewis had been angry. And jealous—but it had worn off. Gradually he almost forgot James Gould. He was aware, dimly, that he and various other people gave Hélène the advice and instruction which he had once given her, and he had minded that, but there were so many other things he minded more.

Now, he stared at the papers in front of him in stupefaction. Her advisors had made Hélène richer than he had ever imagined, richer than she had ever hinted to him. He looked at them; the dealings on the commodity market, the currency speculation, the property bought and sold, and as he did so, he felt the rage and indignation swell, the sense of betrayal deepen.

It wasn't evidence of a lover, but it was like a lover. It was a whole area of her life which she had shut off from him, kept secret.

Why, she had even bought property in the South of France, through that terrible shark they'd met at Cannes, Nerval. And now she was writing to Gould informing him she wished to sell it. There was other land she wanted to buy, in Alabama.

Lewis slammed the last of the files back, and hit the drawer back into place. He locked the cabinets, put the key back into his pocket, and drained the last of his whiskey in one gulp. He hated Hélène at that moment. He thought of the time when they were in London, of how he had laughingly explained to her some of the most obvious aspects of investment. How gentle he had felt then, and how sweetly and quietly she had listened to him.

And now, for years, all this had been going on. And she had virtually never mentioned it. If she had such secrets, Lewis thought in a sudden agony of despair, what others were there, and where did she hide those?

Hélène. Hélène. Hélène. Her name was beating away in his mind, and he looked around the room wildly as if somewhere, on the shelves, on the walls, he would see some thing, some little clue, which would give his wife back to him, which would help him understand.

It was at that moment that the telephone rang. It made Lewis jump. He stood staring at it blankly for a moment—the telephone on Hélène's desk, the one that was her private line. He reached across and snatched it up. He knew what he was expecting to hear: a man's voice, the lover's voice, the voice that would make everything clear.

Lewis stared at the receiver with hatred; then he said, in a firm voice, "This is Lewis Sinclair."

There was a little silence. Lewis tensed. If the man hung up now, he thought, if the bastard just hung up . . . He heard a woman's voice: soft, breathy, rather like the voice of a child.

"Oh, Mr. Sinclair," it said. "You won't remember me—though we did meet once, at Cannes. This is Stephani Sandrelli. I've just been filming with your wife, and she asked me to give you a call. When I got back to Los Angeles. She thought you might like to hear how things were going, how she is. . . ." The voice gave a little giggle. "She told me to check up on you, to tell you the truth. Make sure you were okay. Make sure you were missing her, I guess."

Lewis frowned. Even in his present state, this did not sound convincing; it was very unlike Hélène.

"I'm sorry. What did you say your name was?"

"Stephani. Stephani Sandrelli . . ."

And then he saw her; walking across the gardens of the Hotel du Cap, a blaze of platinum-blond hair, a figure that burst out of its white dress. He hesitated only a moment. He thought: *two years*, and then he said easily, his old manner coming back to him quite effortlessly, "Well, let's see. I think we should meet, don't you? I don't suppose you'd be free for dinner tonight?"

"Actually, I would," said the little breathy voice. And that was how it began.

The Runaways was completed: Hélène flew to New York and checked into the Plaza.

She was given, as always, a suite overlooking Central Park. Inside, the air-conditioning made the room chilly; outside, the city sweltered. The leaves of the trees in the park were the heavy dull green of midsummer; across the street the carriage horses that took tourists for rides shifted and sweated in the heat. Late July: New York was as hot and as humid today as Alabama. Hélène leaned against the window; across the city sirens wailed.

She was accustomed to hotel rooms, so accustomed that she hardly saw them anymore. Sometimes she felt as if she had no home, and that even the house in Los Angeles was just another impermanent base. A life of stopovers; she had been a traveler for five years.

Now she took in the details of this suite without interest. Stiff heavy silk brocade draperies at the windows, hung in elaborate loops and swags. On the bed, crisp white sheets, which crackled. Static in the air, so that every metal object touched gave her a shock. A series of pictures on the walls, placed at carefully calculated intervals—tasteful pictures, in that they were guaranteed to offend almost no one.

She unpacked methodically, hanging the expensive clothes in the closets with habitual care. A Valentino dress; shoes from Rossetti; the Saint Laurent suit she would wear, the following morning, for the meeting in James Gould's offices. *You've sold the place at Grasse? I see. Then we'd better meet to discuss this new proposal.* Gould had sounded irritable; it might not be an easy meeting.

She thought of her first meeting with Gould, in the autumn of 1960, and the memory made her smile.

She and Lewis had been staying at the Pierre; it had been hot, a day like this one, and Lewis said, "Darling. He's a very busy man. You mustn't be offended if you're in and out in ten minutes. . . ." She had smiled, and said nothing. She knew exactly what she was going to do. She had had months to think about this meeting, she had planned, scripted, and rehearsed it in her mind. It was very important to her: the first step on the road back to Alabama and Ned Calvert. She had no intention of being in and out in ten minutes, and for months she had been trying to think what she could do, what she could say. How did you make someone like James Gould III sit up and take notice, when you had just thirty thousand dollars, and he was seeing you as a favor to your husband?

When she first went into the large oak-paneled room, and was confronted with Gould, she had very nearly lost her nerve. He was tall, handsome, patrician—in his early fifties, she guessed. He had an inbred arrogance that reminded her of Lewis, though Gould was more impatient, and colder. He had also reminded her, slightly, of Mr. Foxworth. There was that same cool courtesy; the same instinctive dismissal of women. She had looked at him, and hoped that he might possess a sense of humor. There seemed no sign of it.

He was through with the polite questions about Lewis, the necessary preliminaries, very quickly. Then, just a quick, slightly impatient glance down at the papers in front of him, as if he were already regretting this favor to an old family friend.

"Let me see. Ah, yes, thirty thousand we're looking at. Well, perhaps it would be best, Mrs. Sinclair, if you were to tell me the kind of performance you were looking for? I assume you were thinking of something like gilts, perhaps? We don't have the means, unfortunately, for a very wide spread, and so I'd advise—"

"Mr. Gould."

She had interrupted him, which was possibly a mistake. She looked down at her hands, and then back up to his face. Then, since she had nothing to lose, and everything to lose, she said the sentence she had scripted, in the voice she had chosen, and felt as she did so, the same calm she felt in front of the cameras. "I want to make myself a rich woman. And I should like you to help me do that quickly. That's all."

He had been riffling through papers. He stopped doing so, and looked up at her.

"I should like," she went on, in her coolest, most English voice, "to double this money, and then double it again. For a start."

"Mrs. Sinclair. This is Wall Street. Not Las Vegas . . ."

"I know that. If I thought I had a chance of doing it at Vegas, I'd go. But I think the odds are higher here."

There was a silence, and then quite suddenly, Gould began to smile. He looked at her—really looked at her—for the first time since she had come into the room. He picked up a piece of paper in front of him, on which he had scribbled some notes, tore it carefully in half, and threw it into a wastepaper basket.

"I see," he said slowly. "Then perhaps we'd better begin again."

Hélène, looking at him, thought: he does have a sense of humor; it is going to work. And she had been right. Their friendship, and their highly successful alliance, had begun then, in that ten-minute meeting that went on for one and a half hours.

"You do understand what we would be doing?" he had said to her just before she left. "I have to be sure of that." He hesitated. "The higher the returns, the greater the risk. If we follow this course, you could make substantial gains, and they would increase, of course, as we reinvest. But it is very close to gambling, and the odds are just as bad as they would be—say—at roulette. You could make gains; the likelihood is that you will lose. Are you prepared for that?"

"I'm prepared for it, yes."

"Why are you doing this?" He looked at her closely.

"Do you need to know that?" She met his gaze levelly, and he was the first to turn away.

"No," he said with a small, slightly puzzled frown. "I suppose I don't."

She had not lost; she had won. As her earnings rose, rapidly, so she invested, and reinvested. One million; two million. It was only then that she began to feel safe, and she asked herself sometimes: was she simply making sure that she had enough to deal with Ned Calvert? Or was it something else? Was she also, step by step, ridding herself of the specter of poverty, until the point was reached when she knew beyond a shadow of a doubt that it could never lie in wait for her again? That it would never reclaim her—or Cat?

She adjusted the Saint Laurent suit on its padded silk hanger. She closed the closet door on it, and on the memories that it suddenly brought back—of her mother's pathetically cared for dresses, adjusted, unpicked, resewn, carefully pressed—all those castoffs from Mrs. Calvert.

She turned away; now, when she was incontestably rich, she sometimes felt poor, and with a bitter sense that her impoverishment was self-inflicted. She *had* more, but she felt less. She saw herself then, in the small room at the lodginghouse in Paris, hastily packing her few belongings into that cardboard suitcase, and then running down the stairs, running through the streets to the Seine. Then, when she had had nothing, she had felt as if she had everything, as if the world lay cupped in the palm of her hand.

Ah, but I was happy then, she thought, and turned away, angry with herself.

She unpacked the rest of her things, hardly conscious of what she was doing. Silk stockings; silk underwear, decorated with Brussels lace. Beside her bed, she placed her little Cartier clock, an exquisite thing of blue cloisonné enamel, with a face of rose quartz. She looked at it, and thought of the old clock on the icebox in the trailer, the old clock, and its little red stickers. Minutes ticking by; time passing.

She went into the bathroom, and unpacked her washing things, and her makeup. She held the unopened box of *Joy*, which Stephani had given her, and then, quickly and angrily, threw it away. Toothpaste. Shampoo. French soap, by Guerlain. The small mauve packet of contraceptive pills, the same brand she had been taking day after day for years. Originally prescribed by Mr. Foxworth, when they were still a novel method of contraception. She looked at them with sudden hate, and, on an impulse, opened the packet and pushed the tiny white pills out of their plastic bubble containers. One after another: Monday, Tuesday, Wednesday, Thursday . . . a whole month's worth of time, and all of it empty.

They fell into the washbasin; she turned the tap on fully, and washed them away. What was the point of them now, anyway?

She went back into the sitting room of her suite and picked up the script Gregory Gertz had given her in Arizona. She had read it once; now that *The Runaways* was completed, she had promised him she would read it again. She would read it tonight, she decided. He was in New York; they could meet briefly tomorrow to discuss it, after the meeting with Gould. And then she could catch a plane and fly home to Cat.

This thought usually calmed her, and filled her with a sense of excitement and expectation. But now, for some reason, it did not. She opened the script in front of her and began to read. But the words seemed quite meaningless; the sentences without sense. She shut the script, and looked at the delicate face of the Cartier clock. It was almost seven, almost time for her daily call to Cat.

She reached for the telephone, hesitated, and then, giving in to the temptation this time, asked to be put through to the international operator.

Her heart was beating very fast, as it always beat when she did this. How many times had she done it before, from hotel rooms across Europe, hotel rooms across America? No more than fifteen, perhaps, which was not so very much in five years. It felt like a hundred. It felt like a thousand. The first time she had done it she had been in London, in that little red room in Anne Kneale's house, sitting near the fire, waiting for Lewis, who had gone to a dance in Berkeley Square.

Her palms felt damp; her mouth was dry; she was shaking a little. She told the operator to do what she always told them to do: let the number ring three times, and then disconnect. She gave her the number in St. Cloud. The operator repeated it; she sounded bored. They always sounded bored. Perhaps they were used to such seemingly pointless requests.

"I'm connecting you now. . . ."

"Wait." Hélène swallowed. "Let it ring, will you? I'll hang up. . . ."

The operator still sounded bored. She gave a little sigh.

"Surely," she said.

Hélène sat very still, pressing the receiver tight against her ear. He would not be there. There would be no answer. George would answer, or one of the other servants. . . . What time was it in Paris, anyway? She could not think, her mind could not deal with the numbers of the differential. Ahead. Behind. Morning. Afternoon. Five years. Five hours.

She listened to the clicks, to the ringing, to the distance.

Once. Twice. Three times. This time, when she went to hang up, her hands would not move.

Edouard himself answered on the fifth ring.

"Yes?"

It was like an electric shock. A current straight to the heart. There was a silence that went on forever. When he next spoke, his voice was sharp with inquiry. He said, "Hélène?"

Then she disconnected, very quickly.

Gould was chairing the meeting, and it was drawing to a close. Unsatisfactorily. He looked down at the papers in front of him; he looked along the length of the conference table: himself, at the head of that table; ranged along it, four other men, and one woman, a woman who was about to make her first mistake in four years of quick-witted, daring, and highly successful business dealings. This fact had already been pointed out to her, by Gould himself, and by the other men in turn: a lawyer, two investment brokers, one investment manager, all of them busy men, whose advice was expensive. Hélène Harte had listened to them—she was still listening to them; or possibly she was not listening at all, it was difficult to tell. Either way, she appeared uninterested.

Gould looked at her more closely. The lawyer, a man whom he had called in, and who was meeting Hélène Harte for the first time, was rehearsing the arguments again, in the weary manner of a teacher going over the alphabet with a small child. Hélène had her face turned toward him politely. The man speaking had yet to discover that when she was this calm, and this courteous, she was adamant. Gould, who knew this already, frowned.

On her right hand, rather than her left, she was wearing a diamond ring. It was the famous ring which Lewis had bought her shortly after their marriage and which had, some years before, been the talk of Boston and New York. The lawyer speaking seemed riveted by this ring. As he went on about the cotton industry and manmade fibers, he appeared to be calculating the possible number of its carats.

Basically, what Hélène proposed to do was very simple. She was liquidating some of her assets, at a good profit, including the property bought in the South of France in 1963. These she proposed to reinvest in land. This, in itself, was perfectly acceptable. Gould himself had, over the past months, attempted to interest her in numerous excellent land investments: in England, for instance, where agricultural estates could still be bought at a low rate per acre, and where all the signs pointed to a rapid price rise. In New York itself; there was an area on the West Side, two blocks of it, and the word from City Hall was that plans to designate it a redevelopment zone were pending. The technique of buying piecemeal into such an urban site, using a number of fronting companies, and then selling at very high profit, once the area was entirely hers, had been discussed with her some months before. It had just been discussed again, at considerable length. She had merely nodded, and returned to the question of Alabama.

Using a front company called Hartland Developments, Inc., Hélène proposed to purchase some six hundred acres of cotton fields, adjacent to a small town called Orangeburg, and presently owned by a Major Edward Calvert. This plan was not acceptable. Quite simply, it was crazy.

When Gould had realized that Hélène was serious in her intentions, he had had rapid and extensive inquiries made on her behalf. The result of those inquiries now lay on the table in front of him, and they did not make happy reading.

Calvert had, for the past twelve years, invested heavily in plant and machinery; the bulk of his annual crop was no longer picked by hand, and the number of his employees had been consistently falling. He had financed his outlay on plant with bank loans, using his estate as collateral. Had his estates been better managed, had the demand for—and price of—cotton held steady, Calvert might have prospered. As it was, the estate was foundering.

The two banks to whom the estate and house were mortgaged had seen the warning lights some two years before. Since 1962, Calvert had come under increasing pressure. Interest on his loans mounted monthly; the value of his assets declined year by year. In 1963, he had suffered a bad harvest, adversely affected by weather and plant disease. He was now under threat of foreclosure, and was grasping at the possibility of selling off some of his land like a drowning man grasping at the proverbial branch. As every man around the table had been at pains to point out, he would then be operating with a smaller, depleted estate, and his chances of turnaround were virtually nil. Calvert was trying to buy time: what he was doing was winning a temporary battle that would ensure he lost the war.

James Gould's head was aching. The lawyer was still talking. Gould rubbed ineffectively at his temples. The point was, Calvert was going under, and Hélène Harte's purchase was totally pointless. The land was a bad investment; the price she seemed willing to pay was ludicrous; if it had been any other woman, or man, Gould would have thought they had taken leave of their senses. He could only assume that this was some crazy whim. Women had whims. His own divorce from his second wife had just come through, and that day Gould was not feeling well disposed toward the female sex. Only one thing held his impatience in check: the certain knowledge that Hélène Harte did not have whims. She was a clever, methodical, on occasion devious woman. Which made it all the more incomprehensible.

To his relief, just as he was about to cut the lawyer off, she did so. She adjusted the diamond ring, leaned forward, and began speaking in that low, oddly accented, husky voice. The voice was both mesmeric and succinct. Occasionally, Gould thought, he would have liked to listen to that voice when it was discussing something other than money.

"Perhaps I should make one thing clear. I did mention it earlier, but perhaps I should mention it again?"

The quiet voice cut the rebellious lawyer short. He threw up his hands and leaned back in his chair, looking irritable.

"My purchase of this land is conditional." She paused. "I will buy it, at asking price, on condition that my company is enabled to take up the existing bank loans. With the rest of the estate and the house as collateral, as before."

The silenced lawyer now gave a snort of derision.

"The banks will bless you, that's for sure. They won't be able to believe their luck. That collateral is virtually worthless, and they know it. Why do you think they're threatening foreclosure? They know they're going to get their fingers burned, they're resigned to that. Now they're mounting a salvage operation. They're trying to save the rest of their hand, and probably their arm as well."

"Excellent." Hélène smiled. "Then the deal should be simple to arrange. As you say, the banks in question will accept it."

Gould leaned forward. An idea had come to him. "Within the next year," he began slowly, keeping his eyes on Hélène's face, "probably sooner, say six months, this Major Calvert is going to default on repayments. What do you intend to do then?"

"I shall foreclose."

"He'll ask for an extension."

"I shall refuse."

"I see."

Around the table there was a little silence. The investment manager sighed and looked up at the ceiling. One of the lawyers coughed.

"How long do you intend to give him, precisely?" Gould leaned back in his seat; he tapped the table with his pencil.

Hélène frowned. She had thought: *Let him sweat, and let me watch*

him doing it. She had thought of a date, an appropriate date: July 15.
Happy anniversary, Ned.

But that date was almost a year away. Now, quite suddenly, it
seemed unbearable to wait that long. She wanted it to be over. She looked
up, and met Gould's eyes.

"Offer him six months. Until the end of next January. Give him the
impression we'll extend, but no guarantees. Will he accept that?"

"I should think he'd accept just about anything. Under the circumstances. Desperate men don't read the small print." Gould spoke dryly.
He was, he thought, beginning to understand.

"And then?" he prompted.

"Foreclosure at the end of the six months. Or as soon as he defaults.
I assume he has no other likely source of funding?"

"Not a hope in hell." The lawyer meeting Hélène for the first time
leaned forward aggressively. "No one else—with due respect—would be
crazy enough to bail him out. The upshot of this is straightforward
enough. Six months from now, seven, eight at the most, you'll be in
possession of everything he's got. A rundown estate. A rundown house.
You couldn't give it away. What's the sense in that?"

Hélène's face had become very set. She said, in a flat concise voice,
"It makes sense to me."

She bent her head slightly. She was not sure, anymore, if it really did
make sense. She ought to have felt triumph, she thought dully, and
she felt no triumph, only a sense of dragging fatigue. She stood up,
eager suddenly that the meeting should be over. She pulled on her
gloves and looked at James Gould.

"The deeds of sale, the loan transfers—how long will the documen-
tation take?"

"Not long. It's ready and waiting to go. The preliminary work has
all been done."

"Oh, good." She looked at him a little blankly. "I would like to get
it signed and sealed as soon as possible. Thank you, all of you, for your
time."

She smiled at them then, with that extraordinary smile she had,
which had the capacity to light up a room. Several of the men glanced at
one another; they all rose, and she turned away to the door. Gould
followed her. He escorted her through the outer offices as far as the
elevator, saying nothing. He pressed the button, and then, as she turned
to look at him, and began to speak, he felt suddenly that he could stay
silent no longer.

"You know him, Hélène, don't you?" he said in a quiet voice. "You
know this man Calvert, and that's the reason for all this."

She hesitated, but only fractionally. He saw something come into her eyes which he had never seen there before, and it alarmed him. Then she answered, equally quietly.

"You're right, of course. Yes. I know him."

"But Hélène, *why*? Why are you doing this?"

"Why?" She considered the question for a moment. Then she gave a small resigned smile. "He made me the woman I am," she said. "That's the reason." She paused. "Mr. Gould—you asked me that question once before—do you remember, the very first day I came to see you? Do you remember what I said then?"

"Yes. I do." Gould looked at her steadily. "You asked me if I needed to know, and I said no."

"Say no again. I'd be—very grateful."

She leaned forward as she said that, and rested her hand on his arm. Gould wanted to argue; he wanted to protest; but the touch of her hand and the expression in her eyes made him give in. He shrugged.

"Very well. No."

"Thank you," she said.

The doors opened, she turned, and stepped into the elevator. She smiled once more, and the doors closed.

Gould walked back thoughtfully to the conference room. There, the lawyer who had just experienced Hélène Harte for the first time was in full flood.

James Gould did not listen to him. He moved to the window. A long way below, across the street, a black limousine was waiting. He watched the figure of Hélène Harte cross the street and climb into the back of the car. He frowned as he watched her.

He had seen people use money as a weapon before, and it always interested him. It was legal and effective—the perfect murder weapon, he had once remarked jokingly. Today, he had seen in Hélène Harte something which surprised him, and slightly shocked him. He had seen hate.

The lawyer, carried away by his own eloquence, was now questioning not just Hélène Harte's judgments, but also her sanity. "Crazy," he said gloomily. "Just crazy."

Gould interrupted, turning around, impatient to curtail this meeting, "Hélène Harte is one of the sanest women I know. Let's leave it there, all right?"

Later he considered that statement, and silently revised it.

Was hatred ever entirely sane—any more than love was? He himself was a cool man, of moderate passions, and he doubted it.

They had been to a party at Malibu, a champagne barbecue, given on Lloyd Baker's private beach, by Lloyd Baker's wife, who was, Lewis suspected, soon to become Lloyd Baker's ex-wife. They had stayed longer than Lewis intended, and they were now on the Santa Monica Freeway, driving downtown, so that Lewis could drop Stephani off at the small apartment where she lived. It was six-thirty in the evening, and on the freeway nothing was moving, either way. Every lane, jammed solid. Lewis leaned on the horn; he swore.

"Goddammit, Stephani. I told you this was a stupid idea."

Stephani licked her lips nervously. She gave him a shy little sideways glance.

"What time does Hélène get back, Lewis?"

"I told you. Around eight. And before that, I have to get you home, get back to the house, take a shower. Jesus." He hit the horn again. "We're going to be here all night."

"It's my fault, Lewis," she said in a small voice. "I know you didn't want to take me. I know you don't want to be seen with me. . . ."

"It's not that, Stephani. You know it's not that." Lewis felt guilty and also aggrieved, since what she said was perfectly correct. "It's that I have to think of Hélène, that's all. I have . . . we should . . . well, it's a good idea to be a little discreet, that's all."

"Katie Baker won't say anything. I know her from way back. She roomed with me once. Before she met Lloyd. If I started telling people some of the things I know about *her* . . ."

"That's not the point, Stephani. We shouldn't have gone. I don't know why the hell we did. I've got a load of work to do. . . . God damn this traffic. . . ."

Lewis hit the horn again. The driver in front, in a purple Cadillac, stuck his hand out the window, and gave Lewis an unequivocal reply: one finger extended.

Lewis thumped the steering wheel in frustration. They inched forward about ten yards, and stopped once more. They were now hemmed in on all sides.

"Well. That's it. We're here for another hour."

"Lewis?" Stephani gave him another of those little sideways glances. "Don't get mad at me. I hate it when you get mad. I'm sorry, Lewis. Really I am."

She hesitated. Lewis felt slightly mollified. He shrugged.

"Give me a little kiss, Lewis. Just a little one. Please . . ."

She leaned across before he could say anything, and turned his face to hers. She looked at him solemnly with those wide baby-blue eyes, then slowly and carefully she pressed her mouth against his, and pushed her tongue between his lips. Lewis resisted; after a while, he stopped resisting, and groaned.

When he recovered himself, he observed that the purple Cadillac had moved forward another ten feet. He let the Porsche inch after it. Stephani was fumbling around on the narrow backseat.

"Where's your jacket, Lewis?"

"My jacket? It's in back. What do I want that for? It feels like about a hundred degrees. . . ."

Stephani had found the jacket. She pulled it through the gap between the seats; she wriggled a little in her seat. She said, "I like that. I like it being so warm. I like the top being down, and the sun and everything. It makes me feel . . ."

She gave him another glance, a suggestive glance. Through the heat, and the exhaust fumes, and the residue of uppers and champagne, which was making his head ache, Lewis felt a slight urgency, a shifting in his body. He forgot about the Cadillac in front.

"Keep still, now, Lewis. You're real tense, you know that? You just lean back. I'm going to make you relax, Lewis. I'm going to make you feel—just fine."

As she spoke, she slipped the jacket across his knees, and slipped her hand underneath it. She unzipped his fly. Lewis said, "Jesus. Stephani. We're on the freeway, for Godsake. . . ."

"That's right, Lewis. And I'm going to take you for a ride."

"Oh, my God . . ."

He could feel her hand easing his shorts aside. It felt warm, and slightly damp. Lewis was instantly rock-hard. Stephani grasped the shaft of his penis and began to manipulate it. After a while, turning her wide eyes to his, she said, "Do you have a Kleenex, Lewis honey? Something like that?"

From the pocket of his pants, Lewis produced an immaculately laundered white linen handkerchief. Stephani took it with a little smile. She insinuated it beneath the jacket. Lewis closed his eyes.

Stephani squeezed and stroked; the movements of her hand were fast, then slow. Lewis opened his eyes again; he looked quickly to the le.. and right; the occupants of the cars either side appeared to be paying no attention at all. He groaned, then bit his lip. He became aware that he was going to come, and come soon, and that he had better do so silently. Stephani curled her fingers tighter, she switched to a different tempo, a different technique. He reached his hand across, and felt for the weight of her breast. Through the tight white material he could feel the jut of her nipple against his palm.

Then he could no longer hold back. The restraint and the furtiveness had the effect of prolonging his orgasm; it seemed without end, and rapturous.

When it was over, Stephani zipped him up again, and withdrew her hand from under the jacket, the damp and crumpled handkerchief clutched in her palm.

Lewis looked at her; she raised the handkerchief to her face. She pressed her lips against it. She gave it a delicate little sniff. Then she smiled, and tucked it between the cleft of her large breasts. She passed her little pink tongue across her lips.

"Lewis," she said in her little girl voice. "You don't need to tell me. Now Hélène's home, you won't want to see me again. I just want you to know, I understand. And, when I'm all alone, and I'm feeling lonesome, you know what I'm going to do? I'm going to take this handkerchief, Lewis, and I'm going to think about you real hard. And then you know what I'm going to do next?"

Stephani leaned closer to him and began to whisper into his ear. Within minutes, Lewis was rock-hard again. At precisely that moment, Stephani straightened up.

"Hey, what d'you know?" she said. "We're moving."

And so they were, or the other cars were. The purple Cadillac in front was gathering speed. Lewis slammed his foot down on the accelerator.

When they reached the street where Stephani lived, he parked the car in a restricted zone, with two wheels on the pavement. He almost fell out of it in his eagerness. He propelled Stephani across the sidewalk, and up the stairs. As soon as the door was closed, they fell into bed.

They stayed there two hours, and although they had, in the past week, spent a good deal of time in this room and in this bed, it had, Lewis told himself, never been so good. A voice in his head was saying triumphantly: *You see? You see? There's nothing wrong with you. It was all Hélène's fault.*

Lewis liked that voice; he liked what it said to him. He looked at Stephani, and felt a sweet mingling of pity and lust. When they had left the Baker party, Lewis had made up his mind: he had intended to tell Stephani that now that Hélène was back home, it was all over. He could not see her again. He had to finish it.

Now, as she lay beside him, that not only seemed unnecessary, it seemed cruel; Stephani was very vulnerable. He touched her breast, and Stephani gave a little moan. Before he quite knew what was happening, Lewis found he had turned, and buried his face between her breasts. He heard himself say, "Stephani. I have to go on seeing you. I have to. I just do."

Stephani gave a little sigh. She lifted Lewis, and cradled his face, and looked into his eyes. She said, very seriously, "Lewis. I know you love her. That's all right. I love her too. I do, really. We don't have to hurt her, Lewis. She doesn't have to know." Then she did something which disconcerted Lewis very much.

She lifted her hand to her forehead, and smoothed back the waves of blond hair. She held her hair, like that, off her face, and looked at him, her blue eyes wide. "I think I look like her," she said in a little breathy whisper. "Don't you, Lewis? Just a bit?"

Lewis did not, but somehow he found he could not say so. He left her soon afterward. By the time he reached home he was over two hours late. It was nearly ten—Hélène would have been back two hours. The fact that he would have to tell a lie suddenly impressed itself on him. His mind wavered; he waited for the gates to swing back.

It was then that he caught the flicker of movement; a face, turned around to him, pale and staring, transfixed in the beams of his headlight, like an animal paralyzed by light. The man was there again.

Lewis felt angry, suddenly furiously angry. He also felt afraid—not just of the man, but of himself, of the lie he would have to tell, everything. He slammed the Porsche into gear, and accelerated past the man as if he had not seen him. The moment he was in the house, he called the Beverly Hills police; Hélène watched him, silent and ungreeted, from the far side of the room.

The squad car came immediately, but by the time they reached there, the man had gone.

"Will it be a big party, Mother?"

Cat was perched on a chair next to Hélène's desk. It was a fine, clear day, and sunlight filled the room. Cat swung her legs. She was eager to be outside.

Hélène looked down at the list on which she had been working with her secretary; on it, there were already one hundred and fifty names. She smiled at Cat.

"Yes, darling. A big party. There'll be supper, and dancing—we'll open up the ballroom. There will be music. And if you're very good, you can stay up a little, with Cassie and Madeleine, and watch the people arrive. . . ."

"I'd like that." Cat paused. Her legs stopped swinging. "Will Lewis be there?"

"Of course he will, Cat. It's his party too."

Cat frowned. "It's not his movie though, is it, Mother?"

"Well, no, not exactly, Cat. Lewis didn't work on *Ellis*, but that doesn't make any difference. It's still his party. This is Lewis's house and . . ."

She had been about to add that Lewis was her husband, but somehow the words would not be said. Cat was looking at her intently.

There was a little silence, and then Cat said, "Lewis isn't here very often. I just wondered."

"Well, he's very busy. You understand, Cat. Lewis is trying to write, he's working on his story, and he has to see a lot of people to—well, to talk about his work. That's all."

She looked away, as she said that, with a sudden feeling of hopelessness. Cat always referred to Lewis by his name; she had never, even as a very small child, referred to him as "Daddy." Hélène knew she should be used to this by now; it was impossible for her to say precisely how the practice had come about; like many other aspects of her marriage, it was a product of a cold and unspoken unease. Lewis had never said, definitely, that he preferred Cat to call him by his name; Hélène had never confessed, outright that, when speaking to Cat, she found it impossible to refer to Lewis as "Daddy," that the word stuck in her throat. The issue lay between them, and by some unspoken pact, it was never referred to by either of them. They no more spoke of that than they spoke of the separate bedrooms, or the fact that Lewis went through Hélène's desk, and knew perfectly well that she was aware of it.

They were fenced in, Hélène sometimes thought, by a cold and deteriorating politeness that threatened always to break down into outright confrontation, particularly when Lewis had been drinking. Yet even those confrontations seemed to her dishonest: Lewis rarely attacked her on the issues most central to their unhappiness. Once he had done so; now, more and more, he preferred to launch himself against minor targets—trivial targets: the time dinner was served; her choice of dress; some small imagined slight; some meaningless remark, made in passing, into which Lewis would read nuances of resentment that had never been there.

She looked sadly at Cat. One day, when Cat was older, this issue of names would have to be faced; Cat herself would come to question Lewis's role in her life. This issue, and all the others, simply lay in wait for them, Hélène felt; she saw herself and Lewis, sometimes, as erecting a careful and fragile dam, while all the time the weight of water behind it mounted dangerously.

In the meantime, all the efforts she made to keep that dam intact seemed to her more and more futile. When she had deliberately set aside this time to be at home, she had promised herself it would be different. She had imagined, as she flew back from New York, all sorts of roseate visions. She and Lewis and Cat, together, as a family. She would allow no interruptions; she would devote all her time to them. They would make expeditions together, perhaps go away for a vacation. She and Lewis would have time alone together—they would talk, they would be close again.

It had not happened, of course, any more than it had happened on other occasions, when she had also been full of resolutions and hope. In the three weeks she had now been at home, she had hardly seen Lewis at all. Either he shut himself in his study and pounded the typewriter keys, or he left the house for an endless series of meetings. Nothing she did could break through the barriers of resentment and anger Lewis erected around himself; indeed, her efforts seemed to make him more hostile.

"Please, Lewis," she had said when she had been home about two weeks. "Couldn't we go away together somewhere, just you and me and Cat? Just for a little while?"

Lewis had looked at her coldly.

"Oh, I see," he said. "I'm supposed to drop everything, just because you happen to have some time free? What I do isn't important, I suppose? Well, it may not be to you, but it is to me. I'm tied up. I've got work to do."

Hélène sighed. Cat was watching her closely, legs swinging back and forth. After a pause, she slipped down from her chair and put her arms around Hélène's neck.

"You look tired, Mother. Cassie said you looked tired, yesterday. Don't be tired. Come and play in the yard."

She hesitated, then she reached up and placed a warm kiss on her mother's cheek. Hélène hugged her. She had seen the little hesitation, the quick glance over the shoulder, and it always hurt her. She knew why Cat did that—it was because of Lewis.

Cat was an open and demonstrative child. She had always been quick to laugh, and quick to cry, and quick to show her affection. But she had learned to be wary. If Lewis saw her hug her mother, or climb on her lap, or kiss her, it always made him irritable. "You spoil her, Hélène," he would say. "She's getting far too old for that kind of thing." Or, "Cat, run along. Your mother is busy. Don't bother her now."

Hélène hated it. Cat was only four, after all. It was horrible that she should feel her affection was wrong in some way, that it was a risk to show it. Unhappiness welled up in her; she hugged Cat tightly, too tightly perhaps, as her own mother used to sometimes. And Cat, as she herself had once done, sensed the tension in her embrace, and wiggled away.

"Come on. Come swimming. I want to show you. I can swim miles and miles now. . . ."

"All right. Let's do that. It's such a lovely day."

In the pool Cat set her face. She tilted her head back, fixed her eyes on the other side of the pool, and lurched across it, arms paddling frantically, legs kicking. One foot occasionally touched the floor of the pool, to give her an extra hopping impetus. Hélène did not mention the hops.

"That was very good, darling. Very good. Try again."

She moved back into the shade of the pool house, and Cat, who was very determined, plowed her way back and forth, back and forth. Hélène watched her, and as she did so, her eyes filled suddenly with tears.

It was a pool of clear temperate water; it was surrounded by a stone terrace, and shielded by high clipped hedges of yew. The pool house, built for Ingrid Nilsson, had been fashioned in the form of a small classical temple, and a series of statues, brought from Italy, were set at intervals, among flowers.

A Hollywood pool. It did not in any way resemble a small muddy gulley surrounded by cottonwood trees. Yet Hélène could not look at it without thinking of Billy. To think of Billy, and then to look at Cat—for some reason—always made her cry. She brushed the tears away.

Cat had noticed nothing. Now she was tired of her efforts. She clambered out of the pool and sat down on the edge, swinging her legs so her feet just dangled in the water. She shook back her wet hair, and diamonds of spray glittered in the sunlight. Then, after a brief contented pause, she began to sing.

She sang a song Madeleine must have taught her, in her high clear voice:

Sur le pont d'Avignon,
L'on y danse, l'on y danse,
Sur le pont d'Avignon,
L'on y danse, tout en rond . . .

Her accent was exact; she emphasized the rhythms strongly, beating time with one small hand. Hélène stared at her. Cat's small triangular face, now smiling, was lifted to hers. Hélène looked at her black hair, made darker by the water; she looked at her dark blue eyes, and the fringe of black lashes. She had never heard Cat sing in French before.

Her mind froze; she felt her body grow cold and still. Cat was still looking up at her, her smile growing a little uncertain as she sensed something was wrong.

"Don't you like it? Did I sing it wrong?"

"No, darling. You sang it beautifully. Now sing me an American song. . . ."

Cat frowned. "I don't know any. Madeleine taught me only this one."

"Oh, well, never mind. Come and swim, Cat," Hélène said quickly.

She dived into the pool, and swam back and forth, back and forth, just the way she used to swim with Billy, until she felt exhausted, and the fear went away. When they both climbed out of the water at last, she wrapped Cat in a towel, and then held her very tight. She said to herself, silently, over and over again: Billy's baby. Billy's baby, and Cat said with a little giggle, "Don't do that. Don't do it. I can't breathe!"

When they returned to the house, finally, Lewis was waiting for them. Cat looked from his tight set face to her mother, then, without another word, she slipped past Lewis, and ran inside. He watched her go.

"Thad just called," he said in a cold voice. "He wants you to see *Ellis* on Wednesday afternoon. He's done the final cut. He says it'll take at least three hours."

"Oh. I see." Hélène hesitated. "Well—I don't have to go then. I can easily change it. If you had any plans . . ."

"Plans?"

"Plans for us, I meant." She paused. "I've been home three weeks, Lewis, and it's just that I've hardly seen you. . . ."

"Well, you won't be seeing me on Wednesday. I'm tied up the whole day. So if you want to spend the afternoon with Thad, by all means do so."

He began to walk away, and Hélène, suddenly unable to stop herself, turned after him.

"Lewis—where are you going?"

Lewis turned and gave her a cold look.

"Out," he said. "Isn't that obvious?"

Lewis had developed a new habit, a new technique, since Hélène had returned home. When he discovered how much he hated to lie, how uneasy it made him, so that he lurched constantly between the conviction that he must give Stephani up, and the equally firm conviction that it was impossible, he found a cure. He kept the cure in a small bottle in the glove compartment of the Porsche: a new brand of small red uppers. At first he had taken only one or two. Now, sometimes, he took more than that. He would take the first batch when he left home and was on the way to Stephani's. He would take the second batch when he left her to return to Hélène.

Unlike alcohol, which often made him feel depressed, and maudlin, and sometimes aggressive, the pills had the effect of calming all nerves. They gave him, until they started to wear off, an intoxicating belief in himself. With the pills inside him, Lewis knew that no matter what he did, nothing could go wrong.

When he first got up in the morning, when he was at his lowest ebb, he would feel all the old uncertainties. Then, sometimes, he would long to walk down the corridor to Hélène's room, and go in, and tell her why he had been behaving the way he had. Sometimes then, it seemed to him quite possible. He would tell her about Stephani. He would make her understand that he needed Stephani because she, Hélène, made him so unhappy. And that if only she could stop making him unhappy, he would need Stephani no more.

Sometimes, then, he would have a drink—just one drink—to give him courage. But the minute he had that, everything changed again. Then he would be glad he had not gone to Hélène. All his old grievances and anxieties would come flooding back into his mind. He would go downstairs, and when he saw Hélène, he would talk to her in the new way, the way he had discovered since the affair with Stephani began. He would be cold, and unapproachable. And he would feel within himself a new steely malice: it hurt Hélène when he behaved in this way. He could see how hard she was trying, and the more she tried, the colder and more unavailable he would become: he saw the pain it caused, and one part of his mind rejoiced, and the other part watched with a kind of helpless dismay.

Then, before the dismay could get too strong, he would leave, climb into the Porsche, and swallow the little red pills. Once they took effect, he knew he was safe in a world of unshakable certainties, which would last most of the day.

On the Wednesday when Hélène was to meet Thad, and see the completed version of *Ellis* for the first time, Lewis rose very early. He showered and dressed, went downstairs, made himself a large quantity of black coffee, shut himself in his study, and locked the door. He took out the manuscript of *Endless Moments*, now in its fourth draft, and stared at it. It was in a mess. He had rewritten it so many times that he could now no longer remember whether a particular scene was still in or had been cut. He had been looking at this draft only the previous day, and yet he found he could not remember it. The scene between the husband and the lover: that had worked once, but had he retained it? And which version of the scene worked best, the first, or the second, or the third?

Lewis stared at the pages in bewilderment. He poured some more black coffee; he thought of having a drink, and resisted. Why could he not be more like Thad? he thought with a sudden despair—Thad, who never had doubts or uncertainties or second thoughts, but saw everything plain. Thad, of course, led a life that was entirely uncluttered by emotions. He lived for his work, and in his work: he did not feel love, or jealousy, or fear, or inadequacy; Lewis had never even seen him angry, he realized, and that thought made him feel slightly better. He took another swallow of coffee; his spirits began to revive. After all, Thad the movie director might be a success, but Thad the man was a poor thing.

Two weeks before, unknown to Hélène, Lewis had been to see Thad. The memory of that meeting still smarted. He had been to Thad to humble himself, to ask if Thad would take him back, and let him produce again.

"You see, Thad," he had said awkwardly, "the writing isn't working out quite the way I hoped. I'm not giving up—I don't want you to think that. But I don't need to be doing it full-time. I could go back to producing and still write. I don't know what your plans are after *Ellis*, but we always worked so well together, and I thought . . ."

Thad had been humming, and chewing on his beard. When Lewis's voice died away, he said, "No, Lewis. I don't want you back producing. It inhibits Hélène. It won't work anymore."

Lewis stared at him. "Hélène said that?"

Thad made puffing noises. "Not in so many words. But it's what she feels. You crowd her, Lewis. Hélène needs to feel free." He paused. "If it was up to me . . . but it isn't. I have to think of her."

Lewis had hated him at that moment; he had hated Hélène even more. He hated them both now. With an angry gesture, he stood up, pushed the pages on his desk to one side, and poured himself a drink. Hélène was blocking him: he had always suspected that, and now he knew it—and Thad, who was supposed to be his friend, was letting her do it.

And yet—was that the case? Thad, after all, could have been lying. Lewis stood very still. The whiskey had hit his stomach, and he could feel its warmth, coursing. He looked out the window at the garden, in which birds sang, and the sun shone. He thought of Hélène, and for a moment felt his mind washed clean. He loved her. He trusted her. She was the fixed point in his life. Just for an instant, he felt it again, the sensation he had first had in London, that quicksilver sense of purpose, that certainty he could make it to the goal line.

He would go and talk to her. He would go and talk to her *now*. He made it as far as the door, and immediately the doubts started. He heard footsteps, outside; he heard Cat, running, and then her voice call.

If it had not been for Cat, he thought, if he did not have to live, day in, day out, with the physical reminder of Hélène's past—then he might have been all right. He turned and watched Cat. She ran across the lawn and through the trees. Who fathered her? Where? How? Did he believe the fragments of explanation Hélène had given him, or did he not? That was the heart of it, *that* was the heart of it, he thought; if he only knew that, he would know everything. He crossed to his desk, picked up the sheets of manuscript, and hurled them across the room. He ran out into the hall, and stood at the bottom of the staircase.

"Where are you, Hélène? Where are you?"

He heard himself shout the words. They seemed very loud. They reverberated in his head, they reverberated through the house. Then, the next moment, he realized he had not shouted them at all. The cry had been tremendously loud, and yet silent. A cry from the heart, a cry in the mind—to which, of course, there was no answer.

He slammed out of the house, ran around to where the Porsche was parked, and leaped in. He gunned the engine, and heard its roar; he switched on the radio and turned the volume all the way up, so the beat of the drums and the whine of the electric guitars drowned out the silence, and the emptiness. He fumbled with the glove compartment, got it open, and shook the little red pills into the palm of his hand. They were difficult to swallow, they stuck in his throat. Lewis gulped them back, released the brake, and accelerated down the drive.

The gates swung back; the road outside was empty; the man was not there, and Lewis felt a surge of relief. The man frightened him; he was no longer always sure whether he really saw him, or whether he imagined him. But—*he was not there*—that was a good omen.

Up onto the freeway; he gave the Porsche its head. He was early, Stephani would not be expecting him this soon, but it didn't matter, she would be there just the same, and when he saw her, he would feel all right. . . .

He ran the Porsche onto the sidewalk outside her house, slammed the door, dashed up the stairs. He had a key now, and he let himself in, calling her name. The living room was empty; he could see through into the bedroom, and that was empty, too, though the sheets were thrown back, and the bed unmade. . . . She wasn't out. She couldn't be out. If she was out now, Lewis knew he'd go crazy. He looked at his watch. It was ten A.M.; she had to be there; she had to. . . . He shouted her name, very loud.

And the bathroom door opened. Stephani came out. She came out shyly, slowly, her eyes fixed anxiously on his face. Lewis stared at her. There was a silence, and it seemed to him to go on forever.

Stephani was fully dressed, and fully made up. She was wearing a plain, well-cut black linen dress, which was not at all tight. She was wearing fine pale stockings on her legs, and on her feet were low-heeled, expensive black kid shoes, with small flat grosgrain bows on the fronts. She was wearing pearls around her throat—Stephani never wore pearls. The makeup was discreet, even minimal. No false eyelashes; no pink gloss on her lips. And she had done something to her hair—what had she done to her hair? Lewis stared at it. It was no longer a riot of platinum-blond waves, it was darker, more subdued, a pale gold. It was brushed back from her face, and fastened at the nape of the neck with a wide black ribbon, a ribbon of the same kind, precisely the same kind, that Hélène sometimes wore.

Lewis could not speak; he just went on staring. It was the pills, he thought confusedly; it must be the pills—he must have taken too many.

Stephani was looking at him, half anxiously, half proudly. Lewis saw that her hands were trembling a little. She suddenly gave a little nervous laugh:

"You caught me, Lewis, I wasn't expecting you. I . . ." She hesitated. "Do you see now? Do you see?" Her voice shook, it became pleading. "Tell me I'm like her, Lewis. Tell me. . . ."

"Jesus Christ. Oh, Jesus Christ . . ."

He still stared at her; he could not move; it was Hélène, and it was not Hélène; he felt as if the chemistry of his mind was altering; images and memories tangled and untangled; he was speeding forward very fast, and then backward very fast. He rubbed his hands across his eyes. He looked again, and she was still there, Hélène and not Hélène, his wife and not his wife. This wife, this Hélène, had fuller breasts, and more rounded hips; this wife, this Hélène, was looking at him in a new way, a way that made his body leap and strain in response. She was looking at him as if she wanted him—not anyone else, no figure from some past—but him, now, her husband. He could have this woman, this wife, this Hélène; have her, hold her.

He took one step forward, and he was glad she didn't speak again, because the voice, of course, was wrong. She didn't speak, because she knew she did not need to. Instead, this woman, this wife, just lifted her arms to him.

His mind fractured; he thought—she heard me call, and she answered, here she is. He fell to his knees in front of her, and buried his face between her thighs. He could smell that she wanted him. He put his hands up between her legs, and she was wearing no lacy underwear, which was wrong, but that did not matter, because she was wet and sticky the way he always wanted her to be, and she hardly ever was. He lifted his face and looked up into her eyes, waiting to see the lie and the pity. But there was no pity, and no lie: the eyes were the wrong blue, and not the right shape, but it didn't matter, the likeness was enough, it was enough. . . .

"Hélène . . ." he said. She gave a little cry.

He pulled her down beside him. Her hands were reaching for him; he could feel her urgency; he could feel his own. Such touching.

"Quickly," Hélène said, in a new breathy voice, a voice he had never heard her use before, a voice that urged him on because he could hear the need in it. "Quickly. Oh, Lewis. Quickly . . ."

The last close-up was of her face. Then the camera began to pull back, very slowly. The figure of a girl—her figure; the house behind her; the street in which she stood . . . Back and up in one long glorious and continuous movement: other streets, intersecting with the first; the network of a great city seen from the sky; its long avenues, glittering; its towers; then, slowly, still very slowly, the outline of the island on which the city had been built; a bay of water; ships; a statue with an upraised arm. The camera was moving away, faster now, and the city and the bay grew smaller and smaller. In the distance, just visible, was an outcrop of islands. One of them was Ellis Island. The music began, and the credits started to roll.

Hélène sat in silence. Thad sat in silence. After what seemed a very long time, the screen went dark. The lights in the screening room came up.

Thad glanced at her. Hélène turned her face away. It had been so good; and yet she felt uneasy.

Thad shifted a little in his seat. He crossed and uncrossed his feet. Finally he said, "Come back with me, and have some tea."

It's the best thing you've ever done. The best thing I've ever done. I knew it would be. Nothing can stop us now."

Thad sounded quite matter-of-fact. He had not asked her opinion, and Hélène doubted that he would. Her opinion did not interest him; for Thad there was only one arbiter, and it was himself. He was at the far end of his huge studio room now, filling his electric kettle, fiddling around with mugs and with tea bags: the protracted ritual of Thad's making tea.

Hélène looked at him, and then at the room in which she sat. It was on the first floor of this enormous house, in which Thad had lived for the past four years. It looked, it always looked, as if he had moved in yesterday. There was virtually no furniture, no carpets, and the long rank of windows that led out onto the balcony had no draperies. One wall was stacked with packing cases, most of them still sealed. On top of them was a pile of debris: old magazines, yellowing newspapers, bundles of scripts, some books, and a small mountain of dirty aluminum takeout dishes; it was higher than it had been; each time she came here it seemed to Hélène that it grew.

On the opposite wall was a long shelf, from which wires and cables looped. It bent under the weight of expensive and elaborate hi-fi equipment—players, tuners, tall stereo speakers, a mass of gleaming *materiel*. On this stereo, Thad claimed to listen to Wagner; he said he had a passion for Wagner. There were no records of any kind visible, however; Hélène had never heard the stereo switched on.

Behind her there was a cavernous fireplace, in which no fire was ever lit. And in front of the fireplace were two low backless seats covered in dirty graying fabric; it was on one of these that she sat, the only alternative being the floor. She folded her hands on her lap and waited. Thad was sniffing at cartons of milk; the kettle took a century to boil.

There were only two other objects in the room of any significance, and they were both television sets. As always, they were both on, tuned to different stations, the sound turned all the way down. Hélène stared at them, first one, then the other.

On the first, a quiz show was coming to its climax. A very fat woman, dressed as a chicken, had just won a car. The car was a Chevrolet; it was on a stand, and tied up like a present with huge red bows. It revolved and revolved: when the chicken-woman saw it, she went wild.

The second set was tuned to NBC. It was the evening news. President Johnson was making a speech, his skin an odd orange, because the color adjustment was wrong. After a while Johnson disappeared, and there was footage from Vietnam. Guns fired. On the other side of the Pacific, an orange village burned.

Hélène looked at the sets for a while. Then, quietly, she rose, and switched them off. She sat down again.

She had been good in *Ellis*. Watching the film, with a dispassion she had never felt before, she had been able to see exactly how she had done it. This technique; that technique; each tiny component part—she could identify each one, she could see precisely how they linked together; she could see why she had selected them, and how she had deployed them. They made absolute sense to her, and no sense at all. It was easy to be Lise, so easy that it had seemed to her, as she watched, quite without point. Lise was a figment; she lived on celluloid. She would be there forever, living her own eternal independent life, and that frightened Hélène. As she sat there in the screening room she had thought, suddenly: what about *my* life?

She had only one, and unlike Lise's life, it was finite. It grew shorter with each second that passed.

Thad came across with the tea. He said apologetically, "I'm afraid there's no milk."

Then he sat down opposite her, on the other backless seat, and beamed at her through the steam from his tea. Hélène looked at him: she had not seen Thad now for months, not seen him, not spoken to him. She had changed in that time, and for a moment she felt absolutely sure that Thad must see that. Hélène felt that her ambivalence, her dissatisfaction, must be naked in her face: but Thad seemed not to see it—or, if he noted it, he let it pass without remark. He behaved precisely as he always did; he ignored the gap of time; he continued where they had left off, as if he had last seen her not months before, but merely minutes.

True, he went through a certain number of ritual inquiries—he always did that; it amused him. He inquired after what he sometimes called her entourage: her press agent; her business manager; her three accountants; her two secretaries; her four lawyers, who, he claimed, intimidated him, though he employed equally astute lawyers himself. He inquired as to the welfare of her two agents: mainly, Hélène thought, because their names were an unending source of amusement to him: Homer on the East Coast, Milton on the West: Homer and Milton, Thad would say—now that's *really* poetic. . . .

Her answers were duller and less animated than usual, but Thad appeared not to notice. He passed on to her masseur, to Cassie, who intrigued him, and finally, last of all, to Lewis. Cat he never—ever—mentioned at all.

As he made these inquiries, the answers to which never seemed to interest him very much, Thad's small eyes winked and blinked behind his glasses. With her new detachment Hélène watched him, and wondered. She sensed some purpose behind these questions, that they were a prelude to something else, perhaps. She thought, for a moment, that it might have been Lewis, because after she had given a routine answer to Thad's routine question, Thad did seem to react.

"Oh, Lewis," he said. "I'm glad he's okay. I worry about Lewis, you know. I asked him to come back and produce with me again—did he tell you that?"

Hélène shook her head.

"Better not mention it. It's a sore point. He wouldn't—Lewis can be kind of obstinate, don't you find? And anyway, I shouldn't have asked him, really. Sphere doesn't want him. That man Scher—he's had Lewis up to *here*. Because of the drinking, I think. I don't know. Is he still drinking?"

Hélène looked at the floor. "Not excessively," she said in a flat careful voice. It was a lie, yet Thad let it go by.

He talked about *Ellis* then. He talked about the work he had done, in the post-production period. He talked about the music, and the editing. He talked about the first reactions from Sphere; about the première, which would be in September—the date was now fixed. He talked about its release, and its promotion. He outlined his strategy: this time, he said, with a little benign smile, he wanted the kudos *and* the box office. He wanted record-breaking returns, and he also wanted the Oscars.

He talked on and on, and the more he talked, the more distanced Hélène felt. She found it hard to believe, now, that she had once been so influenced by Thad. On the set, at least, she had never doubted him; off the set, she had sometimes laughed at him, and even mocked him, but she had felt, even then, a respect.

Now she wondered: was it respect she had felt, or was it dependence? She was not sure; all she knew was that it had left her, and in its place was a colder emotion. She admired him still, but she felt she did not like him very much. She could feel the force of his egocentricity, the pressure of his will, and now something within her resisted it, and resented it.

Thad does not know me. He does not understand me at all: the thought came to her, quite suddenly, the thought, and the rider that came with it. Thad not only did not know or understand her, he had no wish to do so. Who she was, and what she was, were quite unimportant to him. To Thad, she was a vehicle, or an instrument, and that was all.

She leaned forward and she interrupted him. "Thad," she said, "do you need me in your films? Do you?"

He looked a little taken aback; slightly irritated that she should have cut him off in full flow.

"Need you?" He tilted his head a little to one side. "Of course I need you. I created you."

"You created me?" She stared at him in disbelief.

Thad gave a small rusty giggle.

"Well, obviously, you have the right face. You have the right voice—or you do now. And you can act. So, yes, I suppose you could say I needed you. I just never thought of it like that."

"You always work with me." She hesitated, and the conversation with Gregory Gertz came back into her mind. "Couldn't you work with someone else?"

"No. Why? That's a dumb question. I work with *you*. I want it to be you. You're—" He paused, as if searching for the exact term, and failing to find it. He began to smile in a way Hélène disliked, craftily.

"What am I?"

Thad gave a small impatient sigh. "You're *mine*," he said, as if it were too obvious to be stated.

There was a silence. Hélène looked at him. Just for a moment, something in the way he spoke, something in his expression, made her afraid. Then the fear passed, and she realized she was angry, angrier than she had been for many years. She looked at Thad coldly, and under her gaze, he began—to her surprise—to blush. It was something she had seen him do on only one other occasion; she knew he was remembering it, just as she, then, remembered it too.

He was thinking about that room in a small house in Trastevere five

years ago, which was the only occasion when Thad had ever demon-
strated the fact that he wanted the same kind of possession as other
men. Except that it had not been the same kind of possession, it had
been an ugly desperate and distorted version of it, sex in a fairground
mirror, sex that was both pathetic, and crazed.

They had never discussed that episode. It was a taboo between
them that they both understood. Thad had never attempted a repetition
of it; Hélène, revolted, but pitying, had behaved, always, as if it had
never happened.

Now, suddenly, the memory of it lay between them again. Hélène
again heard him pant; try to speak and then stop; she felt again the slow,
the terribly slow realization that he was not just filming her anymore,
and that something was beginning to go horribly wrong. In a car accident, she had heard, people's sense of time slowed. They saw an
eighty-mile-an-hour collision very slowly, at a dreamlike pace: and it had
been like that then. The slow, extremely slow, realization of exactly
what Thad was trying to do with his hand-held camera, in which the
film still whirred.

She had kicked him then, hard, in the pit of the stomach. And he
had stopped, and then he had done precisely what he was doing now.
He had looked at her, and she had watched the blood seep up his neck
and suffuse his face. Then he had taken his glasses off, and rubbed at
his eyes. He looked defenseless without his glasses. The skin around his
eyes was flabby, and pale, unexposed to the light. He made her think of
a turtle, with its shell ripped off, and then—just when she had been
thinking that—he had, briefly, cried.

He was not crying now. But he had removed his glasses and was
rubbing his eyelids irritably, as if some speck of dust were hurting him.
Not a word was said. After a pause, Thad put his glasses back on. He
looked at her slightly uncertainly.

"I guess you know that anyway," he said.

Hélène stood up. She knew she could not bear to be in the room a
moment longer. She could not bear to sit and listen to Thad, who
wanted to own her, and who perhaps believed that he did. "I have to go
now," she said, and walked out onto the balcony.

She stood there for a moment, looking at the view. The house, like
her own, was set in the hills. In the bowl of the valley below lay Los
Angeles itself. It was six o'clock in the evening, and the air felt metallic
and hot. Over the city, in a band between buildings and sky, lay a layer
of smog. It was purplish, shaded by the softening light to a delicate rose.
It looked as if the sky were bruised.

Thad came up behind her. She turned around, and he pushed a
large and heavy envelope into her hands. It looked like the size of a script;

it was the weight of a script. Hélène felt a sense of despair. She looked up at Thad.

"What is it?"

"It's the reason I asked you to come. You didn't think I wanted to talk about Lewis, did you—or the movie? Why should I? All that's in the past."

"It's a new script?"

"I finished it last week." He stopped. "It's the second part of *Ellis*. There will be a third part, too, eventually. It's a trilogy."

Hélène stared at him. "You never told me that," she began slowly. "I thought . . ."

"You thought there was only the first part." Thad had now recovered. He giggled. "That's all right. So did everyone. Except me. I knew it was the first of three all along. I just wanted to keep it to myself for a while. A secret, you know?" He paused. "No one else knows, not yet. Not even Sphere. I'll send it to Scher next week. But you'll be the first to read it. Don't tell anyone. Don't tell Lewis even. Not yet."

Hélène drew in her breath. She thought about time. Two more films; two more parts. It would be next year at the earliest before they could begin on this project. One year. Two years. Three possibly, to complete the trilogy, even four. Four years like the last four years; four years in which, whatever else she did, she would be tied to Thad.

Thad shifted slightly on his feet; he glanced up at her. And then, immediately, she knew—why he had shown her *Ellis*, why he had asked her back here.

"You've heard about Gregory Gertz's film, haven't you?" She looked at Thad directly. "You've heard about it, and you've heard I may do it, and that's why you called. It's why you've given me this."

"No, it isn't." Thad's mouth set in an obstinate line. "You can work with Gertz if you want to. If you like making movies with a jerk like that, go ahead. He doesn't have any talent. He isn't an artist. He doesn't understand you the way I do, but why should that matter? It's work. But you have to do this script first. It's all lined up for next spring. I've worked out a shooting schedule—everything. And Sphere will give us the go-ahead. We'll be able to capitalize on the success of part one . . ."

"Next spring. I see."

Hélène turned away. She began to walk down the steps that led from the balcony to the garden. She always came into the house this way; she always left it this way. She had never seen the rest of the house. Below the large room where they always sat, there was a whole floor of other rooms, ten, maybe twelve, of them. As she went down the steps, she passed their windows: the shades, as always, were fully lowered.

She stopped for a moment at the foot of the steps. She did not even know if Thad used those rooms, she realized. Maybe he slept in one of them, maybe not. Maybe he worked in them. Maybe they were empty. She knew no more about his house, she realized, than she did about Thad himself.

She hesitated. Was Thad simply and deliberately trying to block her from working with someone else? Was that the reason he had given her this script? She had felt that a moment before; now, looking at those windows and their blank shades, she was not so sure. With Thad, there could be innumerable reasons. Even if she did not like him, she acknowledged his diversity. She turned and looked back at him: why could he not acknowledge hers?

At the foot of the steps Thad came puffing to a halt. He saw her glance; she wondered if he read her mind.

"You can take a look at the rest of the house if you like," he said. "You never have. I'd like you to see it. I do all my writing—in there."

He gestured at one of the blank windows.

"Not now, Thad. I have to get back for Cat. I like to see her before she goes to bed. . . ."

She hurried in the direction of her car. She climbed into it. Thad followed her, but he made no attempt to delay her.

He had finally realized that something was troubling her, and that something was wrong. He looked a little anxious, but Hélène knew that would not last; Thad's anxieties were always very brief.

"You will read it?" he said as she pulled away. "You will read it soon?"

"When I have time, Thad," she called, and accelerated away.

She drove home fast. Lewis was still not there, and the moment she was alone, she telephoned Gregory Gertz. Her hands were shaking a little as she placed the call, and it occurred to her that it might be better to wait, until she had time to think, until she was calmer. But she would not delay: she was already half committed to the Gertz film; it was a good script, and a good part—quite unlike any of the parts she had played before; she wanted to do it; she would not allow Thad to coerce her in this way.

To have been planning, all along, to make three films rather than one—and never to have hinted at that, never to have said one word . . . She felt angry again, and so, when Gregory Gertz answered, it was easy to say, "I've decided to do it. Yes, next spring." She paused. "If the terms are agreeable, of course."

"They'll be agreeable." She could hear the elation in his voice. "I guarantee it."

When she replaced the receiver, she sat for a while, staring straight in front of her. She did not see the room at all—she saw the future. The opening of *Ellis;* the return to Alabama; the long-planned confrontation with Ned Calvert; the film with Gregory Gertz, and the film after that, and the film after that. Lining up the work; lining up a lifetime. So much, and so little: she bent her head, and thought of Edouard.

Sometimes, when she allowed herself to do this, she had the illusion that he was very close, that he was also thinking of her. At this moment, she felt it strongly; she felt filled with the sense of him, and her heart lifted.

It was an illusion, though, and she knew that. Indulging it only made her miserable, later. She looked at the telephone, and then pushed it to one side. She had not called his number once since leaving New York; now she was not even certain whether, on that occasion, he had really said her name. That might have been an illusion too.

The envelope that Thad had given her lay on the table in front of her. She opened it and drew out the script.

It was heavy, and bound in a thick blue cover. She flicked it open and saw, to her surprise, that on the first blank page, Thad had written a dedication, in his small spidery hand.

For Hélène, it said.

Underneath it he had written a date, a date in 1959. Hélène looked at it blankly: she associated that late summer, and that year, with Edouard. It took her a moment to realize that it had other associations, also, if not for her, then obviously for Thad. The date Thad had inscribed was the date he first met her, in Paris, outside the Cinemathèque.

"And so," Stephani was saying, sitting up in bed, "I put a rinse in my hair. It was easy. It's not quite the right color yet, the bleach needs to grow out. The makeup—well, I've been practicing that. I used to watch how she did it—when we were out on location. And the clothes . . ." She gave a gentle dreamy little smile. "Hélène's are couture, of course, so I did the best I could. There's a shop about five blocks from Wilshire, well, I guess it's nearer Sunset, really. They sell copies, and designer fashions—not new ones—used ones. It's where all the stars get rid of their clothes. I know the woman who runs it. I went in there, and I was looking through the racks, and I thought, right off, as soon as I saw it—that's her, that's Hélène." She stopped; she turned to Lewis. "You were pleased? You did like it? Tell me you did, Lewis?"

"Sure," Lewis said.

He was sitting on the end of the bed, watching the color television, or rather, not really watching it, but channel-hopping. It helped to block out what Stephani was saying. He did not want to know the details. He did not want to know how it was done. That spoiled it somehow. He punched another button.

Stephani and he had been smoking a little grass; Stephani liked it afterward, and sometimes before. Lewis liked it too. It did not always combine too well with the little red pills, but today it was all right. He felt at peace; he felt dreamy. Stephani was rolling another joint now. He turned his head and watched her. Small nimble fingers; she extended a pink tip of tongue, and ran it along the edge of the paper.

"Does Hélène ever do that—sell off her old clothes? Give them to the maids, maybe? Because if she did—oh, Lewis!" She gave a little breathy sigh. "Imagine. Her very own things." She stopped and gave a sad little frown. "Except they wouldn't fit me. They'd be too tight. Way too tight . . ."

"Uh-huh." Lewis nodded. He was not listening. A baseball game; an old black and white movie; a soap; someone being interviewed; riots someplace; Lassie . . .

Lewis gave a sigh of pleasure. Lassie was saving a man who had been trapped in a mine. He loved Lassie. He had always loved Lassie, and back home in Boston, whenever she came on, the set was switched off. Lassie caught hold of the man's arm; she dragged him a few feet. She stopped and wagged her tail; she barked. Or should it be, he barked? Lewis was not sure. That struck him as funny, and he began to laugh. Then the ads came on; a pure-faced woman held up a box of detergent; Lewis punched the button again.

The soap; the riots; the interview; the movie. Lewis suddenly became very still. He punched the button again: back to the man being interviewed. He stared at the screen; he turned the sound up. Behind him Stephani crawled forward on the bed. She lay on her stomach with her chin in her hands. She, too, looked at the screen.

"Hey," she said after a while. "He's really good-looking, don't you think, Lewis?"

"Be quiet. I'm listening. . . ."

Stephani subsided for a minute or two. Then she said, "Mmmm, I like his suit too. It's like the ones you wear, Lewis. Only darker. You ought to get one like that. I like it. It's sexy."

"Will you shut up, godammit?" Lewis rounded on her, and Stephani gave him a frightened look. She bit her lip, and was silent.

Lewis stared at the screen again. He hardly heard a word that was being said; some financial matters were being discussed; it was not they which interested him. He felt quite alert now; the muzziness, the daze of a few moments before was gone. Shock had made his mind sharp as a razor.

The interview came to a close; the camera switched back to the questioner. Lewis stood up, he switched the set off. Stephani looked up at him uncertainly.

"Was that someone you know, Lewis?"

"No. I don't know him. Not exactly."

"He sounded English. . . ."

"He's not English. He's French." Lewis reached for his jacket. "I'm going home."

Stephani's eyes rounded in dismay. She knelt on the bed. "Oh, Lewis, you're mad at me. You are, aren't you? I can see it. You've turned all pale, the way you do when you get mad. . . . Oh, Lewis, what did I do?"

Lewis turned back to look at her. She was almost in tears; she looked like a woman, and also like a child. He was touched.

"You didn't do anything," he said more gently. "I'm not mad at you. Truly."

He bent and kissed her.

"I'll come tomorrow, okay?"

"Okay, Lewis." She hesitated. "Lewis, shall I . . ."

Lewis smiled. He lifted one finger and pressed it against her lips. He said: "Surprise me. . . ."

He drove home fast; just one little red pill, and he didn't really need that. He felt angry, and powerful, and free. No one at the gates. By the time he reached the house, the sky was darkening. He went into the living room. Hélène was there, alone. She was sitting, reading a book. She greeted him, and made no comment about the time, or his absence. She watched him as he walked across the room to pour himself a drink, and Lewis knew why she was doing that. She watched his eyes, and she watched his walk. She never asked, but she liked to know—how much he'd been drinking.

He lifted the heavy decanter and poured a good three inches of whisky into the glass. He held it so she could see what he was doing; let her watch; let her count them. He took a swallow of the drink, and then moved across so that he stood just in front of her, not too near, not too far, just enough. He rested his elbow on the marble mantelpiece. Hélène bent her head to her book.

Lewis knew she could feel his anger, and he was glad of it. He looked down at her bent head, at the thick pale gold hair, which she had tied back at the nape of her neck with a black silk ribbon. Should he tell her now, should he tell her what he had just seen on that television set, or should he wait? He might wait. A week. A month—as long as he wanted. He felt he would like to do that. After all, how long had he waited to find out the truth? Five years. Yes, he would wait. But still, he could feel the anger, and it was mounting. The itch to pick a quarrel was very strong. . . .

Hélène turned a page. She tried to force her mind to concentrate on the words in front of her. She could feel Lewis's anger very strongly; it was like a third person in the room; she had felt it come in with him. It could have been caused by drinking, although he did not look drunk. It could have been the pills he took. It could have been any number of things— resentment at her seeing Thad; a chance remark by a stranger.

These past weeks in particular, but also for long before that, she had grown used to these moods, and accustomed to trying to humor Lewis. Oh, so many devices. She thought of them now, all the little ways in which she tried to conciliate him. The carefulness with which she agreed with all his opinions, however contradictory; the silence she maintained, so that Lewis could talk or rage as he pleased. The efforts— the pathetic efforts—to please him. Making sure Cat was in bed early, for if she was still up when he came home, he always flew into a temper. Trying to arrange that the foods he liked would be served at the times he preferred. Wearing clothes on which he had once complimented her. Wearing jewelry that he had given her on some happy occasion in the past. Wearing her hair loose, as he preferred it. Asking him always, so considerately, about his work, his experiences, and making sure, if he bothered to ask her about hers, that the replies were brief and dismissive. Bowing to his opinions; bowing to his judgments; bowing to him. . . .

She had behaved toward Lewis, she realized then, as she sat with her face bent to her book, in exactly the same way that, years ago, when she was still a child, she had behaved to Ned Calvert. She had seen other women, women much older than herself, behave in the same way. She had seen their fixed smiles, their attempts, in public, to make light of their husband's rudeness. She had watched them, flirting a little, attempting to charm, women in their forties and older, behaving like coy little girls. She had hated their obsequiousness; now, quite suddenly, she hated her own. She thought: it is unbearable; it is humiliating; I shall never do that again. And she closed her book, and looked up at Lewis.

He was spoiling for a fight—she could see it in every line of his face, in the set of his body. On any other day in the past month, in all the months before that, she would have set out to disarm his anger, and to defuse it, no matter how she had to abase herself to do it. Now, she rebelled. She could feel the rebellion, a hard tight core of it inside her.

The instant she felt it, she knew that it had always been there, and that she had allowed it, for years, to dwindle away into a weak and self-destructive resentment. She looked at Lewis quite calmly: *not anymore.*

"Why did you never tell me about your investments?" Lewis spoke suddenly, in the calm flat voice that always presaged trouble. It was not the central issue, she knew that at once, merely a side one he would use to open the engagement.

"I would have thought you might have mentioned them to me, just once or twice, in the past four years, since I introduced you to Gould in the first place, and since they've been so successful."

"You've been through my filing cabinets then, as well as my desk?"

That surprised him, a little. He had been waiting, of course, for the placatory reply.

"Yes, I have. Why not? It's a way of checking up on you. I like to know what you do, how you spend your time. And you're not likely to tell me." His tone was still calm, not yet openly belligerent. That would come next.

Hélène looked at him coldly. "I hope you found them instructive."

"Oh, I did." He swallowed the last of the whiskey, and placed the glass, with great care, on the mantelpiece. "Instructive, and interesting. You like money, don't you? I should have realized that before." He paused. "After all, you married me for mine."

The attack was now overt. There was a long pause while they looked at each other. Then Hélène said quietly, "I didn't marry you for your money, Lewis. Not exactly."

"Not exactly?" He flushed, and his voice rose. "Not exactly? Then why did you—exactly? Because you wanted my name? Because you thought I could help your career? Or would you still have married me if I'd been poor?"

"Lewis, I was sixteen years old." Hélène sprang to her feet. "I was sixteen, and I was pregnant, and I was alone, and I was frightened. Can't you understand that? You were there, and you were kind, and I liked you very much—I don't *know* why I did it. It seemed right *then*. I was thinking of Cat, thinking of what would be best for her. I—a lot of things had happened to me the year I met you. One after another. They happened very fast, and perhaps that was part of it too. I couldn't think clearly. I didn't sit down and make a coldblooded decision. You were there. It seemed right. It seemed best. . . ."

"You married me because of Cat." His mouth twisted. "You married me because you were alone. You married me because another man had abandoned you, got you pregnant, and I was there." An expression almost of bewilderment crossed his face. "Right from the very beginning. Why was I so blind? Why was I so goddamn fucking *blind*. . . ."

"Abandoned me?" Hélène looked at him uncertainly. "I didn't say that. I said . . . I—I said I was alone."

"Don't *lie*," he said with a sudden passion. "Just don't *lie*."

He stopped for a moment, as if struggling to control himself, and through her anger Hélène thought dully, tiredly, that he was now going to say whatever it was he had meant to say from the very beginning. Some new accusation; she could not imagine what it might be—there had already been so many.

But there was no new charge. She thought he had been about to say one thing, and then stopped. Instead, he said, as he had said on many occasions before, "Did you love me? Did that enter into your calculations at all? Just once? Did it?"

Hélène looked away; then she looked back. "I thought I might come to love you," she said quietly.

Lewis's face worked. There was a silence. He said in a calm, detached voice, "Oh, I see." There was a pause; he added, as if it were an afterthought, "You bitch. You fucking bitch."

Then he hit her. It was a hard blow, to the side of the head, and it knocked her to the ground. Hélène lay there for a time, fighting to get her breathing steady, fighting not to cry. Lewis had hit her before, though never as hard, but he had not done so for some time. The fact that she had known he wanted to hit her, from the moment he first came into the room, the fact that she had been unable to prevent it—just the fact that, physically, he was the stronger of the two—all this filled her with humiliation and anger. Clear across the years, she heard her mother's voice: *He hit me once, Hélène. Just once. That was enough.*

Slowly she rose to her feet. Lewis had not moved or spoken. She waited until she was quite sure that she could speak with a steady voice.

"You shouldn't do that, Lewis," she said at last. "If you ever do that again, I'll leave you."

Lewis lifted his head and looked at her. He ran his hand through his hair, glanced around him, patted his pockets.

"Where did I put my car keys? Oh, there they are. . . ."

He picked them up from a table. He picked up the pale linen jacket he had tossed on a chair, and slung it over his shoulder. "Get a divorce then." He paused. "I've already given you grounds."

He said it quite casually, with a certain pleasure. Then he walked out of the room.

Hélène heard the engine of the Porsche. She listened to it until it faded into the distance. She sat down, and remained seated for some time, until she began to grow cold.

She did not cry: there was no point in crying. There was no point in apportioning blame, in saying, this was Lewis's fault, and this mine. They were both wrong, she thought, and they both had a measure of justification.

There it was: she looked at this thing which was her marriage, she looked at the efforts she had made to preserve it, and it seemed to her that she had fashioned and preserved a prison, both for Lewis and for herself. The expression in Lewis's eyes, when he walked out of the room, had been that of a man just granted parole. Marriage: she looked at it, and it was then, she thought later, that she first relinquished it.

After an hour or so, she stood up. It was nearly midnight, and the house was quiet. She moved around the room slowly, picking up her book, which had fallen to the floor, straightening a chair, a cushion. She did these things automatically, hardly aware of her actions. She began to switch off the lamps, one by one.

Just as she came to the last, the telephone began to ring. It startled her, the suddden ringing in the silent house. She looked at the telephone; she began to move toward it. It rang once, twice, three times. Then it stopped.

The next day, when Lewis came home—he always came home—he apologized. He was not as contrite as he used once to be, and Hélène was not as forgiving. She thought: we have both grown harder.

"I'm not sorry for what I said. I'm sorry I hit you." This distinction seemed to matter to him; Hélène let it pass.

"Did you telephone me, last night, after you left?" she asked.

"Oh, God." His face crumpled suddenly, like a child's. He sat down, and buried his face in his hands.

"I might have. I don't know. I can't remember," he said at last.

HÉLÈNE

LOS ANGELES, 1964–1965

"I can't wait. I can't wait. I can't wait."

Cat stood in the middle of the ballroom. Two bright points of color blossomed in her cheeks; her small triangular face was fierce with excitement. Hélène looked at her fondly: she had grown taller that summer, she looked suddenly older. She stood in a stream of sunlight, her hands clasped together, her face lifted. She wore her hair in a new way now, parted on one side. It was longer, and more unruly. When she was excited, as she was now, her face glowed, and her eyes lit up: in certain lights they looked almost violet. Something about her stance—the way in which she held her hands, perhaps, or lifted her head, reminded Hélène of her mother. For a moment she saw Violet quite vividly, standing in the trailer, singing the song about lilacs to an audience of one.

Cassie had seen the resemblance too; she and Madeleine stood nearby, also watching Cat, who was now practicing some wobbly pirouettes. Cassie smiled; she shook her head a little sadly.

"Poor Violet. Sometimes Cat looks so much like her. So much . . ." Cassie's remark pleased Hélène. Her heart suddenly felt light. It was a dance they were planning, after all, the party for *Ellis*—Cat was right to be excited. . . . At once she felt a new energy. She picked up her lists and notes, Cassie picked up hers, and they moved off together, thinking and planning.

It was an absurd room, really, this ballroom—a room from another era. Here, at Ingrid Nilsson's legendary parties, Valentino had once tangoed, and Swanson had waltzed. A room one hundred feet long, lit by crystal chandeliers which had been a gift from the Hungarian prince who had been, briefly, Nilsson's lover.

One side of it was ranked with tall arched windows that led out onto the terrace; at one end there was a dais for the musicians; there was a high ceiling of filigree plasterwork; tall pier glasses, reflecting the room back upon itself, and then back again. A room of ivory and gilt, pale, delicate and preposterous—a wedding cake of a room. It had not been used since they came to live here: looking at it, Hélène felt suddenly that she loved it.

"Oh, Cassie, there ought to be palms—don't you think? I'm sure there would have been. Just here, and here—and over there. And around the base of the dais—there ought to be flowers. Lots of them. Flowers with a marvelous scent—gardenias, and tuberoses—oh, and ferns. Write that down, Cassie. We ought to have ferns. . . ."

Cassie smiled. "Camellias," she said firmly. "We ought to get camellias. Violet always loved them. They'd be right. My, but wouldn't she have loved this!" She made a note, and then frowned. "You think we can get them at this time of the year? Camellias, gardenias?"

"Of course we can. This is Hollywood. We can get anything." Hélène hugged her. "Oh, Cassie. It's going to be such a wonderful party. The best party *ever*. I know it. Let's see—the musicians will be *there*. The champagne bar will be through there—shall we have some pink champagne? Cassie, Madeleine—what do you think?"

Cassie deferred to Madeleine. Madeleine was the Frenchwoman; Madeleine was the expert. She, too, was becoming caught up in the excitement; she laughed, and clapped her hands.

"But certainly. Both. The pink and the white. Like a wedding . . ." She turned and looked around the room.

"And the walls—couldn't we decorate them too? If we were to have garlands of flowers—like necklaces. You could hang them there, and there—in loops, *voyez vous*, by the mirrors—and here, between the doors. *Ça serais charmant*—white roses, perhaps. I saw that done once, when I was a little girl, for a great ball that was held at—" She broke off. "At a place near where I lived," she finished.

Her color rose slightly, but Hélène was too excited to notice. "Yes, what shall we have here?" She paused, frowning. "I know—something exotic. We should have orchids—cattleyas. Don't you remember, Cassie— someone told me. That was what Nilsson did, after she retired. She never went out. She gave no more parties. She stayed here in this house—and she grew orchids. Oh, yes . . ." She gave a little shiver. "We should have everything as she would have. Because it's still her house . . . I feel that sometimes. Do you?"

She turned; Cassie nodded. There was a little silence, then Cassie sighed. "I used to see her movies. When I was a girl. She was so beautiful. . . ."

Hélène stood still. She thought of those Nilsson films, which she, too, had seen, though much later. She thought of her own films. Images, living on. She gave herself a little shake.

"We'll do it as she would have liked," she said quietly. "For her—and all the other ghosts. . . ."

"I want to dance." Cat's voice broke in on them. "Mother, show me how to dance—please. Show me now. . . ."

Hélène and Cassie exchanged glances; Madeleine smiled. "Music," she said. "Wait, *ma petite*. We must have some music. I shall find a record. Wait." She turned and ran, out through the conservatory, and into the room beyond, leaving all the doors open. There was a pause; quietly at first, then more strongly as she turned up the volume, came the strains of a waltz. A Viennese waltz.

It was ghostly, this music, drifting through from an invisible source. For a moment, it was as if they were listening to music that came to them from the past, from all those long-dead musicians who had played here, from all those evenings of gaiety and dancing. Hélène thought that; she knew Cassie thought it too. Madeleine came back to the door to watch. Hélène crossed to Cat; she rested one hand gently around Cat's narrow waist and took her small hand in the other.

Cat looked up at her; her face filled with expectation and uncertainty.

"I'll be the man, and I'll lead. It's easy. Just follow my feet. That's it. Like this, Cat, like this . . ."

Cat stumbled at first; then, gradually, she became more confident. They began to circle to the music, slowly, and then more quickly. Hélène could feel the tautness, the suppleness of Cat's body; she looked down into Cat's face, laughingly, and Cat, laughingly, looked up. They circled, and they circled, their movements now attuned. It was a moment of simple and perfect happiness.

As the music died away, Hélène thought: I shall always remember this; always. An empty ballroom. I shall see it quite clearly, and I shall think, that day, oh, yes, that was the day when Cat and I danced. . . .

The thought made her a little sad. The happiness shaded. Cat was so very young. She might not remember. . . .

The music stopped, and Hélène took Cat's hands and pressed them tight, with a sudden urgency and passion she could not explain.

"Oh, Cat," she said. "Remember this."

"I t came this morning. I knew it would. I knew it would come. I knew Hélène wouldn't forget me!"

Stephani was holding the square of white pasteboard in her hand. The hand was trembling. With one finger she touched the engraved black letters. She turned to Lewis, her eyes shining.

"Oh, Lewis, I can hardly believe it. I'm so excited. . . ."

Lewis could not quite meet her eyes. The truth of the matter was that Stephani's invitation to Hélène's party for *Ellis* was late. All the others had been sent at least a week before. Stephani, fortunately, did not know this. Neither did she know how the invitation had come about. It was he who had engineered it. Knowing how much Stephani wanted to go, he had, quite casually, mentioned her name to Hélène, the previous morning. Hélène's hand had immediately flown to her lips. She had looked contrite.

"Oh, Lewis. How terrible. I should have asked her—I never thought. I haven't seen her since we were out on location—and I said I would. Oh, damn. Do you think it's too late? Can we send her an invitation now?"

Lewis had shrugged. "Why not?" he said. "I doubt she'll come anyway."

Yesterday. Lewis could not quite believe that particular scene had taken place. And now that he was confronted with the evidence that it had, he could not quite believe the present scene, either. To have prompted his wife into inviting his mistress to their party. To their large, grand, extremely desirable party. People were fighting all over Hollywood to obtain invitations for this party.

Why on earth had he done it? Somehow he had managed to deceive not just Hélène, but also Stephani. And—less than a week from now—he would have to face the horrendous prospect of an entire evening in which wife and mistress were together under the same roof. He sighed; *was* that prospect so terrible? At the back of his mind, somewhere, was a small creeping suspicion that it was precisely for that reason that he had done this. He wanted sometimes, he *ached* sometimes, to see them side by side, the real wife and the pretend wife, Hélène and her imitator. What would happen then, he had no idea. It was, somehow, the logical, the only conclusion to the past weeks, in which more and more, he found Hélène, the woman he loved, not in the house he shared with her, but here, in a downtown apartment, in a bed with a buttoned headboard of pale cerise velvet.

Stephani rolled a joint with her small pink nimble fingers—such nimble fingers. He took it and inhaled it.

"You're worried, Lewis," Stephani said. She put her arms around him and drew him down beside her on the bed. Lewis felt the drifting and the lifting begin in his mind. Grass sometimes made him feel as if he were high in the sky, suspended from a beautiful balloon, looking down on the world from a serene height.

From this height, it seemed to him that Stephani might come to see she could not go to the party: to attend would be a serious lapse of taste.

But no, that was ridiculous. Such a thought would never have occurred to her.

Stephani saw things with the sweet amorality of a child. In this she sometimes reminded him of Thad, and—just as with Thad—that way of looking at life relaxed him. No more rules; no more codes; good-bye Boston. Up in his balloon, Lewis giggled. Stephani liked Hélène. She loved Hélène. She almost worshipped Hélène. Apart from the one indiscretion of the beach party, they had been very careful. There had been no gossip, and it was Stephani, almost more than Lewis, who cared about this.

"We won't let her know. It's our secret. We won't ever hurt her. You're *hers* really, Lewis. I know that. . . ."

Now, gently, she began to stroke him. Slow gentle little marijuana touches. They whispered up over his thighs, over his pubic hair, over his stomach. So slow. So easy. Lewis shut his eyes.

She was wearing a petticoat of pale peach silk, which Lewis had bought for Hélène five years before, a hundred years before, in London. It was several sizes larger than the ones she usually wore because when he bought it, Hélène had been pregnant. He had found it in the back of a closet, folded away, forgotten.

Lewis's mind sighed. He turned and nuzzled his mouth against her breasts. He loved her breasts. They were heavy and milky and full. He could feel the softness of her nipple growing hard as he touched the peach silk, the peach lace; he sucked; he suckled. He could smell the scent of her skin, and moaned a little. Very faintly, too, there was the scent of lavender, and he loved that because it was the scent of his childhood. Only two women he had ever known had placed small muslin bags of lavender among all the folds of silky satiny lacy things they wore next to their skin. Only two women. Hélène and his mother. He slipped his hand between her thighs, where she felt so wonderfully, so sweetly, warm and damp. Drifting; drifting; he could open her with his fingers, like the petals of a flower.

He wanted so to be inside her, and when he was inside her, it was dark, and safe. Moving through inner space, swimming through the galaxies of her womb. The scent of lavender in his nostrils; darling Hélène. Pulsing and dreaming. He fell asleep in Hélène's arms. He slept serenely for a long time: a lifetime; a minute. Then he woke, screaming.

The man at the gates invaded his dreams; he clung to the gates, and rattled them. He cried out again and again, in the most terrifying voice: *Let me in, let me in. . . .*

Lewis clutched at Stephani; he was sweating and trembling. Stephani fetched some water and bathed his forehead. She made him stand up and walk around the room. She made him eat something, and the nightmare receded.

"You had a bad trip," she said soothingly.

Later, when Lewis had recovered, and she was sure he was all right, they watched television together. Hours of afternoon soap operas, which Stephani loved, and Lewis found soothing. In the middle of one of these programs, Stephani suddenly clasped his hand. She looked up at him, her eyes wide. "Oh, Lewis," she said. "The party. What shall I wear to the party?"

She wore a long white dress with a fishtail skirt, covered in beads and sequins. She had washed the rinse out of her hair, and returned to the normal platinum. It blazed at Lewis across the room; he felt a simultaneous relief and disappointment: she had come as Stephani Sandrelli.

He was standing on the far side of the room when she made her entrance, drinking from two glasses of champagne. First pink, then white; it amused him. Next to him was Homer, Hélène's East Coast agent, and Milton, her agent here. They were both staring at the spectacle.

"Can you believe that, Milton? I mean—can you *believe* it?"

"Homer. I cannot. I *seriously* cannot. This is 1964, right? Not 1954. Or did we just go through a time warp?"

"Some things, Milton, never change. Even in Hollywood. *Especially* in Hollywood. Some things are eternal."

"I remember Marilyn in a dress like that." Milton shook his head sadly. "Tighter, even. She couldn't go to the john. It was sewn on. Frank said—"

"Ah, but Marilyn was luminous, Milton. Luminous."

"This is true."

"Also, a truly lovely person. When she wasn't phoning at three A.M., and being a pain in the ass."

"Three A.M.? She phoned you at three A.M.? She never did that to me."

This fact seemed to distress Milton. He shook his head mournfully.

"Three. Four. Five, sometimes. Time had no meaning for Marilyn." Homer gave a sigh. "You remember her smile, Milton? You could forgive her any goddamn thing when you saw that smile. That smile registered on the Richter scale. Just like Hélène's." At precisely that moment, peering around the crowded room, Stephani saw Lewis. She, too, smiled. The two agents looked at each other.

"How would you rate that, Homer?"

"Rate it? It doesn't register at all. I would say, Milton, not the smallest tremor. How about you?"

"Short on magic, Homer. Definitely short on magic . . ."

They moved away in the direction of the bar. Lewis looked at Stephani uncertainly. Two months ago he would have said she looked like a tramp; two minutes ago he would have said she looked wonderful; now he was not sure what he thought, but he felt distanced. He felt, possibly, that she was not the woman who should be seen on his arm that evening, regardless of gossip. For a man like him, she was not, perhaps, the right accessory. He paused, gallantry and snobbishness fighting it out. Stephani had been crossing toward him, but had been waylaid. Seizing his opportunity, and despising himself as he did so, Lewis ducked behind another group of people. He skirted the room carefully, and once sure Stephani must have lost track of him, headed in the direction of his wife.

Hélène was standing near the entrance to the ballroom. He stopped a little distance away, just to look at her. She was wearing a dress that had been made for her in Paris, of a blue silk some shades darker than her eyes. When Lewis had first seen this dress being reverently unfolded from swaths of tissue paper, he had not liked it. It had seemed dull and unfeminine. But on Hélène, it was another matter; even Lewis, who did not understand women's clothes at all, and had a secret preference for soft fabrics and ruffles, could see the mastery of its cut, the perfection of its line. It was narrow, so that she appeared even taller and slenderer; it left her arms bare, and the curving neckline, stiffened and stitched like two wings, or two sprays of foliage, framed the long, perfect line of her throat.

She was standing between Thad on the one side, and Gregory Gertz on the other, but Lewis did not see them at all. The blue of her dress flared before his eyes; for a moment Lewis felt almost dizzy, as if his mind were impossibly light, filled with haze and ether. In the future, he felt, he would always see her as he saw her then. At a distance, in the blue dress, with her face turned a little away from him, her hand half lifted.

Beyond her, in the ballroom, the music began. Lewis gave himself a little shake. The hubbub of the room returned, and the press of people.

He saw that, around her throat, Hélène was wearing a narrow band of sapphires and diamonds, which he had bought her for their first wedding anniversary. He had bought it from de Chavigny in New York, because that was before they went to Cannes, before he realized how much Hélène lied. Now, he never set foot in de Chavigny: not in New York, not in Paris, not anywhere.

Still, he had bought it for her, just as he had bought, for Stephani, the necklace of brilliants she was wearing tonight. Diamonds for his wife; for his mistress, diamanté. The equation angered him; the memories angered him; there was something he might say to Hélène, tonight, when she was wearing that particular necklace. But not now.

He turned around smartly, and avoiding the Lloyd Bakers, who were bearing down upon him, he swerved away from Hélène, in the direction of a group of men. There were at least ten of them, and they clearly did not share the opinions of Homer or Milton, for in their center, much admired, was Stephani Sandrelli.

It was a successful party. Hélène looked around the room, it was crowded, but not overcrowded. In the room beyond, where supper had been served, people were just beginning to leave the groups of round tables, decorated with flowers and ribbons. In the ballroom behind her, the first couples were beginning to dance. Some of the most powerful people in Hollywood, and some of the most famous. Her eyes roved over the groups, making sure that no one was hedged in, that no one was alone, or ignored. In one corner, Joe Stein, holding court; in another a very famous female agent, surrounded by delicate young men, who occasionally let out little birdlike shrieks of delight at her latest witticism. Homer, going around introducing people to other people to whom he had already introduced them some ten minutes before. There was a certain electricity in the atmosphere of the room, which she had come to recognize, and it was that which told her the evening was a success.

Cassie had said, in her dour way, before the evening began, that in her experience most parties were a success. "Plenty to eat. Plenty to drink. Can't go wrong. No call for nerves," she had said flatly, partly because she was nervous herself.

Hélène had said nothing; she knew that was not true. Maybe it was true in Orangeburg, where parties were, on the whole, simple affairs, gatherings of friends and neighbors. Even there, she doubted it, though, for Orangeburg, too, had its social divisions, its hierarchy. Here in Hollywood, those divisions were viciously observed: the party tonight was a success partly because of its glittering guest list, but mainly because *Ellis* was a success. The reviews, with the notable exception of Susan Jerome's, had been filled with an ecstatic, and—Hélène had felt—extravagant—praise. *Ellis* was a hit: her party was a hit. It was a simple formula, and one she disliked.

Beside her, Thad and Gregory Gertz were talking. Gertz looked ill at ease; Thad was all beaming amiability. Since Thad knew that she was to make the film with Gertz in the spring—for she had told him—and since Gertz knew Thad knew, it was perhaps the amiability that was causing the unease. As well it might: Thad, in her experience, was most to be feared when he was kindly.

Occasionally, she interjected a remark, or nodded agreement at something one of them said, but she was not really listening to them. Across the room, she had seen Lewis; he started to weave his way to her through the crowd, and then, abruptly, he stopped. He stood looking at her, with an odd, dazed expression on his face. He had been drinking too much, she knew it instantly, and she looked away quickly. She had been so careful to invite, this evening, people who she thought might be of help to Lewis. A producer who had once expressed an interest in a previous screenplay; an actress who had liked the leading role in *Endless Moments;* a director with whom Lewis had once been quite friendly. Lewis, so far, had ignored all of them; if he went on drinking, he was likely to cause a scene.

She at once tensed, and then felt angry with herself. Between her and Lewis there was now an unspoken and uneasy truce; she was not going to spend the entire evening worrying about Lewis, or trying to protect him from himself. She looked back, though, a little anxiously. Lewis was now moving away; he seemed bent on talking to Stephani Sandrelli.

He shouldered his way rudely through the group of men surrounding her, took her hand, and raised it to his lips. He bent over it with exaggerated, ridiculous courtesy. Stephani looked at him uncertainly, and then laughed. Hélène flushed; she looked away. How could Lewis be so unkind? It was perfectly obvious that he was taunting Stephani, and it was cruel.

"*Long Division,*" Gregory Gertz was saying with obvious reluctance. "That's the working title, anyway."

Thad looked up at him. He hummed a little.

"*Long Division. Long Division.* Yes, well, you could always do a follow-up, I suppose. They remarry. They have children. You could call it *Multiplication.*"

"I'm not planning a follow-up," Greg replied stiffly.

"Oh, you should. You should." Thad beamed. His glasses winked and blinked. He was, Hélène thought, very angry. He paused.

"I am. To *Ellis.* I expect Hélène told you."

"No, as a matter of fact."

"Well, I am. Next year." He planted his feet a little farther apart. "Films should be longer," he pronounced. "One hour twenty, one hour forty—what's that? What can you do with that? It's child's play. I want to make longer movies. . . ."

"Yes, I noticed that in *Ellis.* . . ."

"Sequels are a way of doing it. Three hours. Four. People balk at the idea now. They won't always. They always balk at the new. The revolutionary."

"New?" Gregory Gertz's eyebrows rose slightly. "Not exactly new, surely. As I recall, a number of people have had that particular idea. Among them Erich von Stroheim. His original version of *Greed* ran to ten hours, I think. Though, of course, it was never shown. . . ." He touched Hélène's arm. "Hélène. Would you like to dance?"

There was a small tight silence. Thad looked, for a moment, like a fat pressure cooker about to explode. Then, before Hélène could move or say a word, he did an about-face of military precision, and walked out of the room.

Hélène was in no doubt that he was not only leaving the room, he was leaving the party. He looked absurd, departing at an angry trot, and Gregory Gertz laughed. Hélène rested her hand on his arm.

"I'll come and dance," she said. "But you know, you shouldn't have done that. It wasn't wise."

"I couldn't care less," Greg answered with a certain cockiness which she had never noticed in him before. "Why should I? There's nothing he can do to me." He paused. "Or you, I hope."

Hélène frowned. Damn Thad, she thought; damn him, with his megalomania, and his possessiveness. She took Gregory Gertz's arm.

"Once, perhaps," she said firmly. "Not anymore."

It was one o'clock in the morning, but people showed no signs, yet, of leaving. So many dances, so many partners; as the evening wore on, she felt more and more distanced from it. "Thank you, Hélène." Joe Stein, escorting her politely back to the side of the room, Joe Stein who, like most of her partners, had not danced with her simply because he wanted to, but because it was part of the business process. For years, he had wanted her to make a film for his company—ever since they first met in Cannes in 1962. Now, Stein had achieved his ambition. His company would produce and back *Long Division;* he glanced across at Simon Scher, who was talking to Stein's wife, Rebecca, and a slight swagger came into his walk, as if he were carrying spoils from the field of war, not escorting a woman from a dance floor. He, Joe Stein, had captured Hélène Harte from the clutches of Sphere.

Simon Scher smiled back politely, and returned to his conversation with Rebecca Stein. He was a small, neat, pleasant man, and he always smiled politely, whenever Hélène encountered him, which was not often. A businessman—but then, they were all that, men and women. And they were here to conduct an essential part of their trade—

exchanging information, and gossip, watching who was talking to whom, power-trading. . . .

Hélène evaded the next man who was pressing her to dance, and slipped away to the side of the room. There, in a lobby that led out to the bar, she was shielded from view by a pillar, and by palms. She stood there for a while, watching groups form and re-form, watching the dancers. Joe Stein now dancing with his wife, ignoring the rhythms of the music, and proceeding around the room in a stately fox-trot. Stephani Sandrelli, dancing with Randall Holt, the young man they were calling the next Lloyd Baker. The original Lloyd Baker, dancing with everyone except his wife. Lewis, performing some Bostonian gyration of his own, face fixed, eyes glazed, with a girl called Betsy, about whom Hélène knew nothing at all, except that someone had brought her, and she lived in San Francisco, and she was dressed rather as if she were a sultan's handmaiden or an Indian squaw. She had bare feet, which she stamped, and around her ankles she wore bracelets with tiny silver bells on them. She wore a long embroidered garment, like a caftan. Her flowing and beautiful auburn hair was threaded with feathers and ribbons. As Hélène watched her, she lifted her arms above her head and waved them to the beat of the music. From wrist to elbow her arms were covered with tiny bracelets of turqouise and silver. She shook her arms, and the bracelets glittered and jingled.

Gregory Gertz, now dancing with Rebecca Stein, to whom he appeared to be being assiduously polite. Hélène watched him a little anxiously: she saw him differently tonight, as perhaps less direct, less straightforward, than she had imagined. If she had not agreed to do his film, would Stein and his company have backed it? Very possibly not; was that why Gregory had been so eager that she do it—not because she was so right for the part, as he claimed, but simply because her participation, her "bankability" was useful to him? It was hardly surprising if that had been a motive—that was how things here worked. Yet he had seemed so honest, so truthful. . . .

She leaned back against the pillar. There were very few people here whom she liked, she realized, and even fewer whom she trusted.

Someone bumped into her. Someone backed into her. Her West Coast agent, Milton, tall, tanned, immaculately groomed. He was looking a little haunted.

"Homer," he said. "I'm avoiding Homer. He's had too much to drink. He's on one of his jags."

He paused, looking around him for a waiter, and checking over the room methodically. Then, recovering himself a little, he took both her hands in his, and pressed them.

"Genius," he said. "I didn't get a chance to say so before. Not a word I ever use. You never heard me use that word before. I'm using it now." He fixed her with his eyes. "Genius. By the end of that movie, Hélène, I was weeping. Tears. I cried. Elizabeth cried. Paul cried—well, nearly cried. Even that little fucker from *The New York Times* cried. We have to talk, Hélène, and we have to talk soon. Today, the phones never stopped ringing. Everyone wants you. Everyone. You shouldn't have agreed to do the Gertz picture. I warned you. It's not right for you. She's too hard, she's a bitch. People won't like that. They don't *associate* you with that. You should do the second part of *Ellis*, and then . . . I read that today, by the way. I shouldn't have read it, but I did. A pirate copy . . ." He smiled. "Hélène, it's so hot—I am telling you, it's so hot I read it and my fingers were burning. Now. Listen. Tomorrow, I want you to—"

"I'll call you tomorrow. But I won't change my mind. I've said I'll do the Gertz picture, Milton, and—"

"Said? Said? What's said? You haven't signed. There's nothing down in black and white. Now, listen, Hélène . . ."

"Tomorrow, Milton," Hélène said, and she slipped away. She moved through the lobby, past the bar, and into the conservatory. She sat down on a wicker chair, shielded by more palms, and by the cattleyas. She looked at them. She had never liked orchids, and she did not like these. Such a fluorescence of color; such fleshy petals; such predatory flowers.

From the bar behind her, voices drifted through above the music. "So, I thought, screw *you*, but I said—okay. You cut us in on the distribution deal, and—"

"Look, Homer. Cut this out, will you? The problem is, the only problem is, you will keep marrying them—"

"You want to know why, Milton? You really want to know? Because I'm a fucking romantic, that's why."

"You? A romantic?"

"That's right. That is so right. I had a terrible mother, a terrible childhood. . . ."

"I don't want to hear about your childhood, Homer. Or your mother."

"Why not?"

"Because it's old news, Homer. *Old news*."

"So. He wouldn't sign. No way. One million up front, *and* a percentage deal. I said to him, I said—"

"Thursday, Lloyd? You promise? It has to be then. The screen test's Friday, and you said . . ."

"Okay. Okay. Thursday. I'll talk to them Friday morning."

"Lloyd, you're a honey. What you want me to wear for you, baby?"

"How about a diaphragm?"

"So, I said—listen—we are talking about *art* here. Like, A-R-T, art. And he says, you know what *Short Cut* grossed in its first six weeks?

And I said—okay, so *Short Cut* was big. Well, this is going to be bigger. A helluva lot bigger. I . . ."

"Miss Harte?"

Hélène looked up. The conservatory was dimly lit, and her mind was far away. For a moment she did not recognize the man in front of her. Then she saw that it was Simon Scher. He smiled. Politely.

"Could I get you something to drink? You must be exhausted. Such a marvelous party . . ."

"No, thank you."

"May I?" He looked at her, and then sat down on a nearby chair. He pinched the crease of his pants between thumb and forefinger, and crossed his legs. Hélène wished he would go away. She wished, suddenly and passionately, that they would all go away.

". . . So I wanted to congratulate you." Scher, she realized, must have been complimenting her on *Ellis*.

"An interesting film, and a most remarkable performance. Oh, yes." He cleared his throat. "I have the script for the sequel, of course. A surprise. I had no idea there was a sequel."

"There are two," Hélène said abruptly. "*Ellis* is intended to be a trilogy."

"Oh." He looked taken aback at this. Hélène looked at him mutinously. Let Thad play his stupid secretive games; she did not intend to play them any longer.

"Yes, well, of course, Mr. Angelini always like to play his cards close to the chest. A trilogy." He paused delicately. "And, are you—that is, I gather there is a little problem . . ."

"Yes, there is. Thad wants to make the sequel in the spring. I've told him I won't do that. I'll be working on another picture then."

"Oh. I see." He frowned. "Does that mean postponing production of the sequel then? Mr. Angelini didn't mention—"

"You had better ask him, perhaps." Hélène answered him shortly. Then, regretting her rudeness slightly, and in the face of Scher's unshakable politeness, she added, more gently, "You see, I had no idea of what Thad was planning either. He sprang it on me a few weeks ago. And I haven't decided—I don't even know that I want to do the film."

"Yes. Of course. Of course. Well, no doubt, in due course . . . such an ambitious project. Fine, in principle, like all his work. But ambitious, and lengthy—" He paused. He looked at her directly. "Such a pity Mr. Angelini and your husband fell out, I've always thought. I always enjoyed working with Lewis. Marvelous enthusiasm. Oh, yes. Marvelous . . ."

Hélène looked up. "You enjoyed working with Lewis?" she said slowly. "You mean, you would like to work with him again?"

"Oh, certainly, certainly. He was very hardworking, you know, very thorough. And I always felt that he . . . well, that he helped to control some of Mr. Angelini's excesses, shall we put it like that? He could be very firm with him. Surprisingly so. In the early days"— he cleared his throat again—"when we began our partnership—"

Hélène stood up. She looked at Scher. Either he was lying, or Thad had been. She knew which of them she believed: this small polite efficient man, who was not really part of the film world at all, but a businessman transferred from his parent company, there to ensure that this oddity among Partex's more conventional products was, like the others, profitable. She held out her hand to him.

"I wish you would say that to Lewis," she said quietly. "I think it would please him very much. And I'm sure he could be persuaded to go back to producing. He misses it, you know. . . ." She took his hand. "I wonder—I ought to get back—would you excuse me?"

"Oh, but of course. Of course."

Scher turned back toward the ballroom. Hélène stood in the conservatory a few minutes longer, and then she walked out into the gardens.

The night was cool, and they were deserted. From the ballroom came the strains of a tango; shadows moved across the lighted windows. She walked across the lawns, then through the trees, and there, where the level of the ground altered, and it was quiet, she stood for a long time, looking down at the swimming pool that lay below her.

She thought of Billy, and the trip back to Alabama that was coming, week by week, inevitably closer. She thought about the future, and the life she had lined up, and then, because its emptiness made her feel cold, and lonely, she thought about the past, and Edouard.

When some time had passed, she began to walk back to the house unwillingly. She walked across the lawns again, and down onto the drive. There was a breeze blowing up; clouds scudded across the sky. As she reached the drive, the moon came out, and lit the gardens with a thin pale radiance. She crossed the curve of the drive, watching the shadows of the clouds, as the moon was now hidden, and now clear. There, she paused, and looked back down the drive, in the direction of the gates, and saw the man who was standing outside them.

It was the first time she had ever seen him, and if Cassie had not been so positive, she might almost have thought that Lewis's sightings had been imaginary. But there he was. He was standing motionless, leaning against the gates, his hands and face pressed against their rails. They were at a distance from each other, and so Hélène could not be certain if he even saw her, but she thought he did.

She stood for a moment, looking at him, separated from him by the length of moonlit gravel: a woman in a silk evening dress, and a man who was excluded.

The moon went behind a cloud, and when it sailed forth again, the man had gone. She stared down the drive in the direction of the gates. She felt no sense of fear, or threat.

From the house came a burst of laughter, louder music. She lifted her head; she associated the man with someone, she thought; it was a second or two before she realized that it was herself. Like him, she was an outsider; like him, she did not belong here. She had felt this before, but never as strongly, and it filled her with an unhappy resignation. She turned back to the house, walking slowly; then she began to quicken her pace. Something in her rebelled.

She would *not* go back to the ballroom; she would *not* go back to that party, and those people. She would go to her room, she would telephone Paris; she would telephone St. Cloud. And—this time—she would not hang up after three rings, or thirty, or three hundred. She would wait until Edouard answered, and she would speak to him.

"Oh, Lewis. It's so beautiful. I knew it would be like this. I pictured it so many times, and I knew it would be lovely. But not this lovely. Oh, Lewis, is this real silk?"

Stephani moved around Hélène's room, touching things. The long pale cream draperies at the windows, and at the head of the four-poster. She touched the delicate columns of that bed.

"Oh, Lewis. Is this old? Like, really old? Is it an antique?"

"It's Hepplewhite." Lewis glanced edgily toward the door. He felt fairly safe, but not entirely safe. "Just let me look," Stephani had begged. "I always wanted to see her house, and her room. Please, Lewis. It won't take more than a minute. . . ."

They had been in here five minutes already. Lewis was fairly sure that Hélène was fully occupied downstairs, but what if—for some reason—she came up? His own nervousness annoyed him; he chafed against it. So what if she did? They were not doing anything wrong.

He had brought a bottle of whiskey upstairs with him; in his pocket were a couple of glasses. Now, defiantly, he unscrewed the cap of the bottle. He held it up.

"You want some? It's Scotch."

"Oh, Lewis. I've had so much champagne. . . ." She giggled. "Okay—maybe a teeny drop."

Lewis poured two large measures. He swallowed his own in one gulp, and immediately felt better. Stephani was still moving around the room. She looked at the eighteenth-century engravings of landscapes. She bent and touched one of the rugs, which was of needlepoint, a piece of museum quality. She moved to the dressing table, touched the silver and lapis brushes, from Cartier, and then bent, and looked at her own reflection in the Queen Anne mirror. She straightened again, and looked around the room once more: the fireplace, the two chairs which stood near it, the bowl of white roses, the serpentine-fronted chest of drawers, which was walnut, with a fine patina, and one of the rare authenticated Chippendale pieces. A slight expression of disappointment came over her face.

"It's not quite—I thought . . ." She looked at Lewis uncertainly. "It's kind of plain, don't you think?"

"She doesn't go in for cerise velvet headboards, if that's what you mean."

Stephani flushed scarlet; her eyes rounded with reproach. Lewis at once felt ashamed of himself.

"I mean," he said more gently, "she doesn't like too much color. She likes things muted and—well, plain. You know. It's the same way she dresses. . . ."

Stephani immediately looked happier. She came over to him and took a little drink of the Scotch. She looked down at the floor, and then up at him again.

"Could I look at her dresses, Lewis? Please. Just a quick look before we go back downstairs?"

"All right. Sure. Why not?" Lewis took her arm; he was beginning to feel reckless. "They're through here."

He led her across the room and through into the dressing room beyond that. It was a large room, flanked with built-in closets from floor to ceiling. Lewis passed along them, opening their doors. Some were shallow, others like small rooms themselves. "Nightgowns. Underwear. Day dresses. Suits. Skirts. Blouses. Sweaters . . ."

"Oh. Lewis."

Stephani's face was transparent with wonder. She followed him slowly from closet to closet, occasionally reaching out a hand to touch something reverently. She lifted up a little lace camisole, and held it against her face; it was as fine and delicate as a cobweb.

"She has those made for her in France. There's some convent place, where they're famous for that lace. . . ."

Stephani laid the camisole back very carefully. She moved on. She touched the material of the dresses, one by one: wild silk, pure linen, wool barathea, tweeds woven by hand in Scotland.

"Oh," she sighed. "They're beautiful. You can feel the money." The next closet: shelf upon shelf of cashmeres, arranged carefully by colors; gray, pale blue, slate blue, Prussian blue, navy blue, black, rose, shell pink . . .

"Take a look at these." Lewis threw back another door.

And there were the evening dresses, line upon line of them. Fortuny velvet; silk moiré from Givenchy; black taffeta from Saint Laurent;

one from Hartnell with a bodice of tiny hand-stitched seed pearls. Long dresses, short dresses. Stephani passed along the racks, touching them. She looked at the labels, and her hands trembled. For a moment, Lewis thought she was going to burst into tears.

He was enjoying himself now. He felt almost brutal, though whether toward Stephani, or Hélène, he was not quite certain.

"You want to take a look at the furs? They're in here."

He opened another, heavier door, which led into the cool room, kept at a constant forty-five degrees, with controlled humidity. Stephani gave a little cry.

"Oh, I didn't know she liked furs. She never wears them. . . ."

"She doesn't. She thinks they're cruel. I bought her most of them. She wears them sometimes. When she wants to please me." Lewis shrugged.

Stephani ran forward and began touching. Red fox; Blackglama mink; lynx; a long coat of brown sables.

Stephani hesitated. She touched it. She looked back over her shoulder at Lewis, guiltily, as if she were being caught in the act of shoplifting. Then she slipped the coat off its hanger.

"Please, Lewis, please. Let me just try it on. Just for a second. I never had a fur coat. Well, I had a rabbit thing once, but that doesn't count, does it? Please, Lewis . . ."

"Go ahead. Why not? Hélène doesn't like it anyway."

They came out of the cool room, and Lewis swung the door shut.

"Put it on. Then come and show me. I'm going to get another drink."

He walked back into Hélène's bedroom, poured a large whiskey, and swallowed it. He looked around him. He had never liked this room, and now he hated it. It reminded him of his parents' home. It reminded him of nights of humiliation. Had he ever made love to Hélène successfully in this room? He was not certain. Perhaps, at the very beginning, when they first moved here, but he was not sure. He could feel the past leaping and bending in his mind, taking on a life of its own. He passed his hand dazedly across his eyes; the room would not keep quite still. It fluctuated, advanced, and then receded. An idea came to him.

On one wall there was a narrow bookcase. This bookcase, when manipulated in the correct way, swung back, and behind it was the safe. One of the safes. The safe where Hélène kept her jewelry. He knew the combination. He had been through the safe, just as he had been through her desk and her filing cabinets, because once, crazily, he had believed that maybe she kept the love letters in there.

He opened it, frowning in concentration, lifted out the boxes and the soft chamois bags, and carried them over to the bed. There, he began to tip them out, one by one, and there was his past, there was his marriage, tumbling and glittering on the bed in front of him. The diamond engagement ring; the matched pearls bought in Bond Street for Hélène's birthday; diamond earrings, bought to celebrate their second film. A Victorian belt of silver filigree; a necklace of moonstones; a long rope of amethyst beads; a diamond collar; bracelets of diamonds. Most of these things she rarely wore, and Lewis looked at them, feeling hurt and incomprehension well up inside him. Why didn't she wear them? Was there something wrong with them? Or was it because he gave them to her—was that why?

For a moment he wanted to cry. Then Stephani came back into the room, shyly, wrapped from head to mid-calf in sable.

"What do you think? Oh, Lewis. It's so soft. Do you think it suits me?"

"It suits you," Lewis said. "Come here."

She approached him slowly, and stopped just a foot away from him. She looked at him, and Lewis saw that her eyes were both dreamy and intent. She passed her tongue across her lips. He knew that expression. He knew what she wanted.

"I've been bad, Lewis. Just a little bit bad. Don't get mad now. . . ."

She lifted her hands and slowly opened the fur coat. Underneath it she was naked. Her skin looked white, almost translucent, against the fur.

"Come closer. Stand still."

Stephani advanced another step. Her nipples were hard and erect. She was trembling. Slowly and deliberately, Lewis began to pick up the jewelry from the bed. Piece by piece. "Don't move. I want you to wear it. I want you to wear it *all*. . . ."

His voice was slightly hoarse; his hands were shaking; not because he was aroused, he was hardly aroused at all, but because he felt angry and afraid. He lifted the silver belt and fastened it around her waist. He took her wrists and clipped bracelet after bracelet around them. He held out her fingers and pushed the rings onto them. Her fingers were not as narrow as Hélène's, and some of the rings would not fit. Lewis gave a cry of exasperation. He began to thread them on the long necklaces. He looped the necklaces around Stephani's throat; he fastened the dog collar of diamonds. Stephani never said a word. He removed her own earrings, and tossed them to one side. He lifted out two exquisite chandelier earrings of emeralds—he did not recognize those . . . who had given her those?—and screwed them carefully to Stephani's ears. There were still more bracelets; two he fastened around her ankles, others he looped from the belt, and from the necklaces.

"Oh, Jesus," Stephani said. "Oh Jesus."

"Wait. I haven't finished."

There was one more pair of earrings, a perfectly matched pair of solitaire diamond clips, each fifteen carats at least, maybe more. He had not given her those, either, and they were lying in a box from de Chavigny. Bitch, bitch, bitch; he felt anger flare in his mind.

"This is the important part. Keep still."

He knelt down. He pressed his face against the wiry pubic hair between Stephani's pale thighs. She peroxided it, which Lewis had never liked, but he did not care now. Very carefully, Lewis parted the lips of her sex. He licked the soft slit of flesh, and sucked the hardening point of her clitoris between his lips.

Stephani moaned, and Lewis drew back. The folds of flesh were glistening, as pink as a rose or a wound compared to the pallor of her thighs. He picked up the two earrings, and with trembling hands, fastened them to the lips of her sex, so they gripped the tight curls of hair, the two folds of flesh. He looked at them, and let out his breath in a long sigh. They looked like two stars, or two eyes above a second mouth.

That idea aroused him; he felt his body stir. He leaned forward and pressed his lips against the diamonds. He licked their flat table with his tongue. They were startlingly cold; ice cold. He lapped at Stephani's flesh, and its warmth, its musky wetness, after the coldness and hardness of the diamonds, made his mind surge. Stephani cried out.

"Jesus. Lewis. Oh, my God . . ." She arched slightly, moving against his mouth with a small erratic frantic movement. Then she stood still, and Lewis drew back. The diamonds danced before his eyes. Stephani gave a small shiver.

"Lewis—you think, maybe, we ought to—they *hurt*, Lewis . . ."

"No, they don't. They don't hurt at all. You like them. You like diamonds. You like furs. You like all that stuff. You like it when I do this to you. It makes you hot."

He stood up and gave her a little push.

"Lie down."

Stephani stared at him. Her small pink tongue passed across her lips. She reached her hand down and touched the two diamonds, delicately, with the tip of one finger; then she touched herself, one finger, with its scarlet painted nail, between the diamonds, between the folds of flesh. She withdrew it, glistening, and pressed it against Lewis's lips.

"It makes me wet." She gave a small smile, and backed away from him slowly. Holding his gaze, she lay down on the bed. Carefully, she stroked and arranged the folds of sable; still smiling, she parted her thighs. From the ballroom, Lewis could hear strains of music; they were playing a tango.

He stood at the edge of the bed, looking down at Stephani. Against the darkness of the furs, her skin was alabaster white; her breasts jutted upward through the jewels. She rested her hands across her thighs, and Lewis saw sex in colors, black as fur, white as skin, red as her painted fingernails, bright as the diamonds that glittered in the pale pubic hair like twin stars.

"Tell me you're mine. Tell me you belong to me. I own you. You sold yourself to me. Tell me the truth for once. *Tell me . . .*"

He had spoken without being conscious of doing so. The voice he hardly recognized as his own. Stephani bit her lip; through the sudden crazy anger and pain that swirled around in his mind, he could see that she was afraid, and excited, and that she did not understand. He realized that he did not want to look at her. The hair was wrong. The face was wrong. Everything was wrong.

He made a lurching movement toward the bed and lay down on top of her. He pressed his weight on her hard; he insinuated his hand between their bodies, and felt for the diamonds, felt for her. Nothing happened. His own arousal had gone. His body felt small and diminished, as still as a stone.

After a while, Stephani unzipped him. She coaxed, and stroked, and squeezed and touched. Lewis fumbled for her breasts, and sucked on them; he knelt back and stared at the diamonds, and the pale pubic hair; the fissure between the lips of her sex looked more and more like a red gash, a terrible wound. Still nothing happened, and Lewis began to cry. Stephani put her arms around him, and rocked him.

"Lewis, honey, don't do that, don't cry. It doesn't matter. You've had a lot to drink, Lewis, that's all. . . ." She hesitated. Stephani had her own kind of tact. "Maybe, you know, maybe it's because this is where you do it. With Hélène."

She gave a little shiver. Her voice became sad.

"And I don't look right tonight. It's always better when I look right. Oh, Lewis, don't cry."

Lewis lifted his head. The tears had stopped, as suddenly as they began; he started to laugh.

"That's what you think? Well, you're wrong. I hardly ever come in here. This is the first time I've been here in two years. Maybe more . . ."

Stephani's eyes grew round. She stopped stroking him, and lay very still.

"You mean," she said in a puzzled voice, after a little pause. "You mean, you don't sleep here, with Hélène?"

"Of course I don't sleep here. I sleep in my own room."

"But you don't . . . you and Hélène don't . . ."

"I've just told you. No. Not in two years, maybe longer. I can't even remember. . . ."

Lewis got up angrily from the bed. He did up his pants, straightened his shirt, adjusted his tie. Stephani lay absolutely motionless, watching him.

"Wasn't it . . . wasn't it very good? With Hélène?" she said at last, in a small voice.

"It's none of your business, but since you ask—no. It was not. At the beginning maybe, but not anymore. It was goddamn torture, if you want to know."

He crossed the room, and poured out another half glass of whiskey. His hand shook.

"For God's sake, Stephani. Get up. Take that stuff off. Get dressed."

"All right, Lewis," she answered, still in that quiet little-girl voice. She stood up, and began to take off the jewels, one by one. She put them back on the bed. She took off the sable coat, and laid it carefully next to them. She walked into the dressing room, and reemerged, some five minutes later, in the fishtail dress. She crossed to the mirror and powdered her nose thoughtfully. She took out her lipstick and painted her lips glossy pink. She picked up Hélène's silver brush and touched her hair into place. She came back to Lewis, who had slumped in a chair, and stood looking down at him. When Lewis finally looked up, he saw that she had an odd expression on her face. If it had been anyone but Stephani, he would have said it was disdain.

"You should have told me, Lewis." The words came out in a little rush. "You should have. If I'd known . . ." She stopped and lifted her chin slightly.

"You can't be right for her, that's all. I'm sure that must be it. You're just not right, and that must be horrible for her. I know how that feels. I've felt it, lots of times. Half the time, the men never notice. They can't tell the difference, or they don't care. Poor Hélène. I always thought she looked sad—you know, you'd see it in her face, when she thought you weren't looking at her. I see why now."

Lewis wanted to stand up. He managed to lean on his chair, and get to his feet. He began to shout. He could hear himself shouting, as if he were outside the room, and the voice was inside it.

"What are you saying? What are you goddamn well saying?"

The words echoed and reechoed in his head. Stephani did not answer him, and Lewis knew there was no need. He knew the answer anyway, he could read it in her face. She had wanted him because she thought he was Hélène's; now that she discovered he was not, she didn't want him anymore. The expression in her face was now pitying, and that enraged him so much that he wanted to hit her.

"I'm going home." She turned away.

Lewis clutched at her. "I'll come with you. I'll drive you. Wait. . . ."

"You're drunk, Lewis. You couldn't drive. And I don't want you to come home with me. I don't want you to come over tomorrow. If you do, I won't see you. I never want to see you again."

The room suddenly seemed to Lewis to be full of rushing noises, as if the windows were open, and a wind was blowing. It whirled around the room; it howled at him. He took a step forward, and fell over. Stephani looked at him, hesitated, and then went out and closed the door.

"Hélène . . ." Lewis cried, and there was no answer. He closed his eyes. He rested his head on his arms. He curled up in the fetal position and lay very still.

He was still there, a few minutes later, when Hélène came into the room. She had passed Stephani on the stairs, but she had been hardly aware of her. All her mind was concentrated on coming into this room, closing off the noise of the party, picking up the telephone. The band was playing a waltz; she could hear it faintly as Edouard's name danced in her mind. The certainty that, in just a few minutes, she would hear his voice, made her shake. She walked toward the telephone, seeing, for a moment, nothing else.

Then she stopped. She saw first the coat, folded across her bed, then the crumpled cover and pillows, then the little heaps of jewelry. Lewis moaned slightly; she turned and saw him. He was out cold.

The next afternoon, she came into Lewis's room. He had dragged himself back there at some point in the night, and he had slept all morning. The room was in disarray. There were leather suitcases everywhere; Lewis was packing.

Hélène sat down on a small upright chair. Lewis did not stop, or look at her once.

"Was it Stephani Sandrelli?" she said finally in a cold tired voice.

Lewis paused. He looked up. "Yes. It was. If it's of any interest to you." He thrust a shirt into a suitcase.

"Did you have to take her to my room? Take out my clothes? My jewelry?"

Lewis looked at her. Her face was pale and set. Lewis shrugged. "I didn't have to, but I did. And don't for Christ's sake ask me how long it's been going on, or something like that. Spare me that kind of farce, at least."

She stood up. "Are you leaving, Lewis?"

"Yes. I'm leaving. I was well brought up. I thought I'd save you the trouble."

"You're not to come back. Not this time. I won't live with you anymore, Lewis."

Her voice was flat. Lewis slammed the suitcase shut. "I think you're supposed to say that we're tearing each other apart—isn't that the usual line?"

"I don't know, Lewis. It's you that spends all day writing the usual lines."

Lewis stopped. He stood quite still, staring at her. The cruelty of the comeback was so unlike her; it shocked him as much as it hurt him. It shocked her too; faint color came into her face, and she turned away.

"You see?" she said. "We'll get worse. More cruel. More vicious. You and I, both of us."

Lewis hesitated. He closed the other suitcases, one by one. He carried them to the door and put them outside in the hall. He walked around his room, and carefully closed each closet door, each drawer. Hélène did not move. She seemed utterly dejected. Lewis went into his bathroom and swallowed four little red pills from the store he kept there. His eyes looked bloodshot. He smoothed his hair back into position, and looked at himself with hatred.

He walked back into the bedroom and put on the jacket of his suit, a pale gray Prince of Wales check, made for him in Savile Row, years ago, when he and Hélène were first in London.

He tried to think about that time; he tried to think about it very hard, because he felt that, if he did so, he might not say the thing he was going to say next. He waited; his mind darkened; he felt split in two, one half of him pleading against, the other urging for. The words would be spoken, they would not be held back.

He cleared his throat and heard himself say, in a perfectly casual voice, "I saw Cat's father on television a few weeks ago. I meant to tell you."

Her face lifted, as if he had hit her; her eyes widened with surprise and with pain.

"Did you miss it? Obviously you did. He was being interviewed about some merger, or some takeover—I forget which. . . ."

"Cat's father is dead." She sprang to her feet. Her face was chalk-white. "Stop this, Lewis. It's cruel. . . ."

"Oh, I know you told *me* he was dead," Lewis heard himself go on, in a reasonable voice. "But I'd have said he's very much alive. There was that interview; there was an article about him in *The Wall Street Journal*, only last week. . . ."

"You're crazy." She drew in her breath. "You drink so much, and you take those pills. You imagine things. You can't remember what happened yesterday, an hour ago. . . ."

"I can remember that, I remember it quite distinctly. Because of the shock, I suppose. You see, he looks so much like Cat, doesn't he? The hair, the eyes, everything. It's unmistakable, and I suppose it was very stupid of me not to have realized before. After all, I've seen photographs before, but they were mostly in black and white. And I've read articles, of course. The endless expansion of the de Chavigny companies—there's something about him, somewhere, most weeks. But in color, seeing him speak—well, that was different, of course. As soon as I saw that, there was no doubt."

He stopped. For a moment he thought she was going to faint, she was so drained of color. She swayed slightly, and then stood still.

She said, "Lewis. Go away. Just go away."

"All right." He started toward the door, and then stopped. A thought came to him, and he turned back.

"You know." He paused, looking now almost bewildered. "If you hadn't lied, if you'd told me right from the first, it might have been different. I might have been able to accept it then. It was not knowing, imagining, trying to understand—it, and you—that was what went wrong." He hesitated. "Hélène. Why didn't you tell me? You could have, you know. Right back at the beginning. You didn't need to lie. . . ."

"I wasn't lying. How could I tell you something that wasn't true?" She swung around to him, her voice rising in her agitation. "You've imagined this. You've made it up. Your mind plays tricks on you, Lewis. . . ."

"Yes. It does, sometimes." He looked at her intently. "I wonder. Does yours?"

The evening of the day Lewis finally left, Hélène went to her daughter's room. She read Cat a story, and Cat leaned back on the pillows, listening. When the story was over, she talked a little about what she had done that day, and Hélène wondered if she might ask about Lewis, for he had been seen to leave, by the servants, by Madeleine and Cassie, and the atmosphere of pity and embarrassment that permeated the household was intense. But Cat did not ask; Lewis was absent so often anyway. Hélène hesitated, and then decided—it would be better to break it to her gradually, and to answer the questions when, and not before, they were asked. She was not sure whether Cat would mind, or how much she would mind: she had spent so little time with Lewis.

She sat looking at her daughter, at the small fierce little face, at the hair which would stand up in spikes, and not lie down. And she saw then, that however much she loved Cat, however close they might be, her daughter was a separate person, not a baby now, but a little girl, with her own mind, her own feelings, her own memories, removed from her, and full of mysteries. Cat was old enough now to hide things from others, she no longer had that absolute transparency of the very young child. She tried to hide hurt—Hélène had seen her do it in front of Lewis. What else did she hide?

It made Hélène's heart ache a little, to acknowledge this little distance, this separation between them. She looked at Cat, and she studied her face and her hair and her eyes. It was, of course, what she had come into this room to do, what she had postponed doing all afternoon, since Lewis left. Now she looked, and was afraid to look, and had to force herself.

The hair was very dark—but her own mother's hair had been brown, and while Billy's hair hadn't been as dark as Cat's, some of his brothers and sisters had taken after their mother, who was surely as dark as Cat. And Edouard's hair was straight, whereas Cat's curled, a little. The eyes, and the straight dark brows above them: sometimes, it was true, when Cat had a certain expression on her face . . . But now she was sleepy, and they had a soft dreamy expression, not like Edouard's at all.

"What are you thinking?" Cat leaned forward.

"Of you. Of—who you look like. Nothing."

Cat frowned. She looked puzzled.

"I look like me," she said after a pause.

And at that Hélène felt relief sweep through her. Her heart lightened. She smiled, and kissed Cat gently.

"That's right. You do. You're you and there's no one else like you, and I love you very much. Now, you must lie down, and try to go to sleep. . . ."

Afterward, the doubts came back again, very often at first, but less as time passed. Hélène looked for resemblances to Billy, and found them. She collected them in her mind—this turn of the head, that way of laughing, a certain gesture of the hands—all these things she noted, and stored, and replayed, until, gradually, the force of Lewis's words diminished. What he had said could not be true; Billy was not really dead—he lived on in Cat.

Hélène spent a great deal of time alone now, and she came to like it. She began to refuse invitations. She stayed at home, often not leaving the house for days at a time, and in the evenings, when it was quiet, she would sit and fix her mind on her childhood. She would summon up the trailer park, and her mother and Ned Calvert; she would relive the things that had happened, the things that had been said: those southern days, those southern summers.

And she began to feel, more and more strongly, that what she was planning to do was not revenge—revenge was a stupid word, a word out of a melodrama—no, it was righting a wrong for her mother and for Billy that they, dead, could not right for themselves.

At night, when she went to bed, she had the most vivid dreams. In these dreams, her mother and Billy were so close, and so real to her, that sometimes, when she woke, she could still hear their voices, and feel their gentle presence in her room. She wanted them to stay, and fought against waking, against the moment when she must finally acknowledge that they had gone.

Thanksgiving came, Christmas approached, but this tangible passing of present time meant nothing to her. It seemed less real than the past, which she thought of and dreamed of.

The future seemed least real of all, a flimsy and thin construct. She was glad that she had agreed to do Gregory Gertz's film. She knew it was important to have it ahead of her, a fixed and definite point. Otherwise, she felt sometimes, she would not have been able to see beyond her return South; the trip to Orangeburg would have been a final destination.

Of Edouard she would not let herself think at all. The night she found Lewis in her room, she had not made the telephone call she had promised herself; now she would never make it. Lewis's accusations had put fortifications around that possibility: she would never consider it again.

It seemed to Hélène, during this time, that she was very well, but neither Cassie nor Madeleine shared this estimation of her physical state. They discussed it: Hélène did not eat enough, she was getting very thin, she often seemed strained.

Was it, Madeleine suggested, tentatively, once when she and Cassie were alone, was it simply because of Lewis's departure?

"If she had a grain of sense, she'd have been glad to see the back of him years ago." Cassie sniffed. "I don't think it's that. She always was a secretive girl. She doesn't want to talk, and nothing on God's earth will make her. But there's something—something on her mind."

Madeleine said nothing. She liked Hélène; she pitied her, and it would have satisfied her own nature very much if she had believed that Hélène's strange state had one obvious and spendidly romantic explanation.

One night, in their sitting room, while Cassie knitted, she suddenly decided to test this idea, even if she did so indirectly.

She drew in her breath, and counted to ten, and then she said: "Perhaps what is wrong is very simple. Maybe she is in love."

A long silence greeted this remark. Cassie's fingers stitched faster, then stopped. She looked up.

"Who with? Seems to me there's not many candidates."

Madeleine swallowed. She stared at her skirt with great concentration. "Perhaps," she said finally, "it could be someone from the past. Someone she doesn't see any longer. . . ."

Cassie pursed her lips. "What kind of talk is that? If she's in love with him, she'd still see him, wouldn't she? Talk sense."

Madeleine sighed. Sometimes, she thought, Cassie was a woman of very limited imagination.

"It could be," she said obstinately. "I think so. If you love someone very much, why should this go away, just because you do not see them? What kind of love is that?"

Cassie gave a cackle of laughter. "The best kind, I'd say. Love? The French think far too much about love. *Women* think too much about love, in my opinion. Better off without it. What does love do, that kind of love? Turns everything every which way, inside out and upside down. Causes nothing but trouble, and never lasts."

Here Madeleine felt a little outraged. She set her lips in a firm line. "This," she said, "I cannot accept."

"Makes no difference. That's the way it is."

"Weren't you ever in love, Cassie?"

"Yes. Sure, I was. When I was sixteen, seventeen, thereabouts." Cassie began to knit again, faster than ever. "And I got over it, same way I got over the chicken-pox and the measles. I never had them but once, and I never had that but once. . . ."

She stopped knitting suddenly, looked up, and caught Madeleine's eye. She began to smile a little.

"Mind though—he was a fine-looking man. A real fine-looking man. And I still remember him. Little ways he had. You know. Just sometimes."

She returned to her knitting once more, and with that, Madeleine had to be contented.

C hristmas came and went. Lewis mailed a Christmas card from San Francisco, but did not write, or telephone. At the end of December, James Gould reported from New York that Major Calvert had been late in his monthly loan repayments, had been warned, and had finally made the payment, a week late.

"I think," he said in his cool voice, "that it could be soon. Are you prepared for that?"

"I'm prepared." Hélène paused. "James—when the notice of fore-closure is served, I want to do it myself. In person."

There was a small silence on the other end of the line.

"That's not usual. It's not necessary, as I'm sure you know."

"Even so."

Gould sighed. "Very well. But don't be surprised if it's soon. I'll telephone you."

Hélène knew it would be soon—she did not need James Gould to tell her. She sensed it with every instinct she possessed. Five years, and it was very close. She would start to feel the triumph soon, she told herself. All the old passionate hatred would come back, and she would feel the way she had years before, when she sat in Cassie's living room and emptied out all the dollar bills, watching them flutter to the floor while she let the loathing loose.

Gould telephoned at the end of January, on the same day she learned she had been nominated for an Academy Award for *Ellis*.

"Calvert has defaulted," he said. "He has until midday to come up with his repayment. If he doesn't—and I think he won't—I'll set the wheels in motion. You'll have the foreclosure notice tomorrow. It has to be served within a certain number of days—I'll let you know exactly how many. . . ."

"As soon as it's here, I'll fly to Alabama."

"You're going to regret this, you know," he said mildly. "It's not a pleasant job. Which is precisely why professionals are employed to do it."

"I still want to do it."

Gould sighed. He knew that obstinate voice.

Late the next day, the notice of foreclosure arrived from New York. Hélène held the envelope in her hand, and waited again for the triumph and the hate to come back, and nothing happened.

E verything: exactly according to plan. It was all working out, Hélène told herself, precisely the way she had arranged it. The plane, on schedule. At Montgomery airport, the black Cadillac, rented, hired in the name Mrs. Sinclair.

The Cadillac, chosen for Ned Calvert's benefit, had worried her a little. Not too many single women dressed in jeans and a headscarf rented a car like this at Montgomery airport. She had expected curious looks, and she received them; the filling in of forms took, perhaps, slightly longer than was necessary. But no more than that. She altered her voice; she altered her stance; she acted, and it worked.

When she drove away ten minutes later, she knew she had not been recognized.

The route she took to Orangeburg had also been carefully planned. First, she skirted the suburbs of the city, past the Howard Johnson's where Billy had taken her for her fifteenth birthday. Then around the edge of the recent housing development where she knew Priscilla-Anne now lived—alone with her three children, according to Cassie's informants. Dale Garrett, after years of cheating on his wife, had finally traded her in for a new and fancier model.

She stopped at the end of the road where she knew Priscilla-Anne had her house. It was called Bella Vista Drive. A line of small neat red brick houses stretched into the distance, each one of them almost identical. Houses for junior executives; each had a carport and a garage; each had bright white shutters; some, in an attempt to dignify them, had had pillared porches added in imitation of a plantation mansion. The porches were out of proportion, and period; they looked pompous and absurd.

Hélène stared at them, and the green strips of lawn in front of them, intersected by short driveways, and thought of Priscilla-Anne, with her small-town blues, her ambition to move up in the world, to move here.

She wheeled the car around and headed for the Orangeburg road. There, once the strip of gas stations and used car lots had been left behind, the fields opened up, flat, on either side of the road. There were few houses, and fewer cars. The air was warm, and not yet humid, for it was still early in the year. The sky, cloudless, was the color of palest pewter. Hélène looked at the sky, and slowed, some two miles outside Orangeburg. She had decided that before she saw Ned Calvert, she would go to the cemetery.

It was a large place, serving not just Orangeburg, but also Maybury and some of the smaller towns beyond. It was bounded by a wall, and shaded in places by clumps of cottonwood trees. She parked the car, and as she climbed out, the warmth of the sun touched her skin. The cemetery was empty.

She walked along a cinder path, flanked with crosses and stones and the occasional angel. Behind her, on the road, the Montgomery bus passed, its wheels throwing up a dust cloud.

Her mother's grave had a headstone of gray marble, which Hélène had paid to have erected some years before, and had never seen. It bore a simple inscription:

Violet Jennifer Culverton. Born in England, 1919. Died in America, 1959.

Forty years. Hélène looked at the inscription doubtfully. At the time she had ordered it, it had seemed right to use her mother's family name rather than the name of the husband she so rarely spoke of, and had dismissed from her life. Now Hélène felt uncertain. Her mother had used the name Craig, after all. She might have preferred that. She might have preferred her stage name of Fortescue. She knelt down, the sun warm on the back of her neck, and pressed her hand against the short springy turf.

It took longer to find Billy's grave. It was far over at the other side of the cemetery, and in the end she found it almost by accident, when she was about to give up. The ground there rose in a hillock, and was neglected, trailing with ivy and brambles. Billy's grave was in the extreme corner, marked with a wooden cross, the letters faded by the sun and only just legible. Beside it was a more recent grave, that of his father, and beyond it, one more—that of a baby born to the Tanners the year after Billy died. Three months old; a boy, also called William.

Balanced between the graves was an empty coffee jar, and a bunch of immortelles, faded to the color of dry straw. Hélène stood looking down at the three graves. She kicked at a trail of bramble with her foot. She was filled then with a painful anger, painful because she knew it to be futile. Anger against Ned Calvert, she told herself, but she knew that was not truly the case. The anger was directed at larger and less specific targets: at a God she did not believe in; at the briefness of life; at the random and casual way in which it was extinguished.

For a moment the anger, and its accompanying sense of injustice, were so strong, that her purpose in coming here faded in her mind. She saw it from a distance, a tiny speck, a small and pointless thing, an irrelevance that had distorted her life, wrenched it out of kilter, and dominated her thinking for five years to no effect. She was no longer even sure that this action was one her mother or Billy would have wanted.

She stood, staring fixedly at Billy's grave, and then quickly turned away. She walked back to the car, stumbling a little on the rutted and uneven ground. Just outside Orangeburg, she pulled onto a patch of wasteland and changed her clothes. She made up her face with the quick skill of an actress, and arranged her hair. Then she directed the Cadillac into town.

Past the gas station and the new motel. Down Main Street. Past Cassie's old beauty parlor; past Merv Peters's drugstore and grocery; past the hardware store; past the men lounging against the shop fronts, and the groups of women shopping. Past the liquor stores on the far side of town; past the Southern Baptist church; past the Orangeburg crossing.

The world once. It looked smaller now, and shabby. Then, when she reached the point on the road, just past the trailer park, the place where Billy was shot, the hatred came back, quite suddenly. Hatred of Ned Calvert, hatred of the men in his car with him that day, hatred of the town and the people who lived in it, and the things they went on believing. Hatred of the South, and also hatred of herself, because she had been part of it once, and if she did not do this thing now, she felt she would never escape from it.

The gates to the plantation house were rusty, and hanging on their hinges. The long driveway was rutted. When the lawns in front of the white house came into view, she saw they needed cutting.

She stopped the car in front of the portico. Its paint was peeling;

from the guttering above, weeds sprouted luxuriantly. It was a large house, but not as large as she remembered.

Above the roof a patch of color drooped in the still air. As she climbed from the car, she looked up at it. The Confederate flag, still flying; Ned Calvert, still keeping faith with his ancestors.

It has to change, Hélène. It's wrong. It just has to.

She heard Billy's voice, as if he stood by her side. She felt an absolute sense of his presence.

She walked toward the house; from now on, it was going to be easy.

The butler and most of the other servants had left, some years before. She was shown into the living room by a young black woman she did not recognize, who shouted the name "Sinclair" in a singsong voice, as if the occupant of the house were deaf. She went out, and closed the door, and Hélène looked at the room.

At first, she thought it was unchanged, that it remained exactly as it had been when she sat there, a nervous child. A rank of windows, their holland blinds half lowered; heavy dark carved furniture; palms in pots; walls crowded with pictures; a grand piano, every inch of its surface dotted with photographs in silver frames. Light slanting, and motes of dust dancing: it was the same, and it was different. It was a moment before she realized that the change was in herself, and in her eyes: the room was ugly.

She thought at first that it was empty. She had imagined Ned Calvert would be sitting where he had always sat, on the couch; he would be smoking a cheroot, wearing a white linen suit, and watching her.

But the couch was empty; the chairs were empty. When she saw finally that a man—a man in a light tweed jacket—was standing by the windows, she could not believe it was Ned. She wanted to say, *You're in the wrong place, and the wrong clothes.* She stared at him as he slowly turned, and began to walk forward, hand outstretched.

"Mrs. Sinclair?"

He had stopped, and was looking at her uncertainly, screwing up his eyes, as if he were nearsighted. He hesitated, and then advanced once more, smiling.

"You're mighty punctual. You had a good flight? You were coming in from New York, I guess. . . ."

The same easy charm she remembered; the rich lazy southern voice, which she had once found so attractive. She looked at him closely: he was so little changed. From Cassie's stories, from the Orangeburg gossip about his decline, she had imagined a man much coarsened; this, she had told herself to expect. It was not the case: he was perhaps heavier than he had been, but he still maneuvered his way across the room and between the pieces of furniture with the grace of a natural athlete and fine rider.

He still looked, almost to the point of parody, the army officer, the southern gentleman; he still looked, as she had remembered, like Clark Gable in *Gone With the Wind*, more correct, perhaps, but with the same slight suggestion of raciness, the confidence of a man who knew himself to be handsome, who knew he rarely failed to charm.

His skin was tanned; his hair had grayed a little but was still thick; the military moustache was neatly clipped, and his mouth was as she had remembered it, full and red. She could not look at his mouth; she lowered her gaze to his hand, which he was extending to her. A square, well-formed hand, perfectly manicured. He had come to a halt a foot away, and was staring at her. He glanced down, his gaze taking in her clothes, and the jewelry she was wearing. As she looked up again, he frowned, as if groping for something in his memory.

Hélène, who had expected this, smiled. "How do you do?" she said in her English voice.

His mind at once made the connection. She could almost see the pieces of memory fall into place. A deep flush spread up from his neck to his cheeks; his eyes at once became wary; he let his hand fall.

"Ned. I'm so glad—you remember me, don't you? It's such a long time. Would you mind if we sat down?"

He had never been stupid, and he had certainly been cunning. She had remembered that, and planned for that, calculating what his response would be. At first, exercising all his charm, he played for time, putting the pieces together one by one: the girl he had known; the film star; the wife of a man called Lewis Sinclair; the owner of the company who had bought his land, and taken over his loans.

"Hélène Harte." He shook his head, and rolled the name in the richness of his southern drawl. "That's amazing. Just amazing. I heard of you, of course. I never saw your movies—well, I never get to the movies these days. But I must have seen pictures of you, I guess. You must take me for a fool—not knowing. And all these years, I've been thinking about you. Wondering what became of you . . ." He paused, then risked it. "Wondering what became of that lovely little girl . . ."

He lied more clumsily than she remembered. Hélène smiled.

"Oh, it doesn't matter. I've thought about you, Ned. Very often."

He shifted a little in his seat, trying to work out the next move quickly. Hélène watched him. Now that she saw him, she knew the truth was probably very simple; he had forgotten her, that was all. The moment she left Orangeburg, and with the ease of an egoist he had forgotten her. He had presumably moved on, and the next woman had wiped out all interest in the one before.

Even now he was interested neither in Hélène Craig nor in Hélène Harte. He was interested in Hartland Developments, Inc., to whom he was in debt. But the fact that this company was headed by a woman, and that woman someone he had once been able to charm, seemed, gradually, to give him encouragement.

"Your company?" He had lit a cheroot, first asking if he might smoke in her presence. He drew on it thoughtfully. "Entirely yours? Well, now, if that just doesn't beat everything. What's a beautiful woman like you doing, bothering her pretty head with business deals?"

"Oh, you know how it is . . ." She gave a vague gesture of the hand. "I have a lot of advisors."

"Sure. Sure. Well—this calls for a drink. How long is it since we met—seven years, is it?"

"Five."

"Five. I can't believe it. You were such a lovely little thing. And now look at you. A grown-up woman. A very beautiful woman." His eyes flickered away from her face, and he stood up abruptly. Hélène sensed that, for him, a drink was becoming urgent.

"What'll it be, Hélène? . . . I may call you that? A glass of sherry? A cocktail, perhaps? You won't join me in a bourbon, I take it?"

"Just some soda and ice," Hélène said.

"Surely. Surely."

He made a great play of fixing the drinks—perhaps to give himself time—and presented the glass with some ceremony. When he was seated once more, he took another pull on his cheroot. He smiled then and patted his chest.

"I've been trying to give it up. Doctor says it's bad for my heart." He paused. "Of course, I've been under a lot of strain, Hélène. I've had a lot of worries."

"I'm sorry to hear that." She paused, then put the question in her most innocent voice. "Is your wife away, Ned?"

She knew very well where Mrs. Calvert was. Cassie's letters had been full of gossip on that question. Mrs. Calvert had returned to Philadelphia for good, some nine months before; she had filed for a judicial separation. Mrs. Calvert had made it extremely plain to every tradesman in Orangeburg, and to the two banks to whom the plantation had been mortgaged, that she would take no further responsibility for her husband's debts. Hélène did not expect Ned Calvert to admit this—and he did not. What she had not expected was the reaction. He smiled, and leaned back in his seat; the smile grew wider. Clearly

he thought she asked the question because she was still attracted to
him.

"Well, now, she's away. Mrs. Calvert is away. Visiting with her
family in Philadelphia. You remember how she used to do that, Hélène,
from time to time. . . ."

His eyes met hers, lazily. It was a cue, specifically designed to
bring the question of their former relationship out into the open. He was
watching her carefully.

"I do remember that. Yes, Ned."

He hesitated, then took a large swig of bourbon, as if to fortify
himself. His confidence was growing, she felt sure, but he was still
being cautious, still feeling his way.

"I thought I'd never see you again." He managed a sigh. "I really
did. When you left—it was like all the hope went right out of my life.
It's been hard for me, Hélène, real hard, these last seven years. . . ."

"Five."

"Five, I mean five." He accepted the correction slightly irritably.
He shook his head. "Five years, and all that time I'd tell myself not to
be such a goddamn fool. You'd forgotten me. Broke clean away. Never
gave Ned Calvert a second thought. That's what I told myself. And now
you're here. Sitting opposite me, just the way you used to do. Lovelier
than ever. A married woman. Tell me, Hélène, you been married long?
You have any children?"

"I was married in 1960. I have a daughter—she'll be five next
May." She paused. "My husband and I are separated."

It gave him hope—she knew it at once. It was why she had told
him. His eyes hardened slightly, but when he spoke, his voice was heavy
with regret.

"I'm sorry to hear that, Hélène. Real sorry. A sweet girl like you.
You deserve to be happy." He paused. "I wanted to make you happy
once. Maybe I shouldn't say this now, but it's God's own truth—I cared
for you, Hélène. I cared for you a lot."

"Did you, Ned?"

"Why pretend? I'm not so young as I was. It gets important, when a
man gets older. Comes a time when he feels he just has to tell the truth,
come what may. I watched you grow up. I'm not ashamed of what I
felt. . . . I know it was wrong in some ways, but, Hélène, there are
some things a man just can't control. He tries—I tried, and my heart just
wouldn't listen. I looked at you, and it beat a little faster. . . ." He
paused. "Of course, I knew afterward. When you'd gone. I thought to
myself—Ned, you just lost the only woman that really mattered to you.
I'd look back then, and I'd wish it could have been different. I'd
wish—well, I guess I wished a lot of things. But I knew it wasn't meant
to be. I knew I had no right to feel that way, Hélène. So I bowed to

that, even when it hurt. I thought—you've got to let her go, Ned. That's just the way it's got to be. She's not for you—a lovely young girl like that, with all her life before her. Still . . ." He hesitated, glanced up at her. "I shouldn't talk about these things. Not now."

"I'm glad you did, Ned. It makes things easier, somehow."

"Yes. Still . . ." He sighed, swirling the last of his bourbon in his glass. "There're other things we have to talk about, I guess. Business affairs. After all, that's why you're here. It's no good my kidding myself you came back to see me after all this while. I'm nothing to you now. I know that. I accept that. . . . So. How come you got yourself involved in all this, Hélène? I mean, it can't be coincidence, I know that. A smart woman like you—you must have planned all this, am I right?"

The nub of the matter. He had finally brought himself to ask the question he had been burning to ask from the moment he recognized her. Hélène hesitated; she thought—*not yet.*

"You're right, of course." She paused. "I've kept in touch with people in Orangeburg. I heard you'd run into difficulties. I was looking for investment opportunities at the time, and—"

"And you thought you'd help me?" He jumped in eagerly, then stopped and shook his head sadly. "But no—I can't believe that. Why should you? Maybe you have a few feelings left for this place, maybe even for me. I'd like to think that. But I guess your advisors wouldn't let sentiment enter in—and you're too smart to let it. So, tell me, Hélène, how come you came back, after all this time, to give old Ned Calvert a helping hand?"

"Have I helped, Ned?"

"You surely have, honey!" He made an expansive gesture of the hands. "Helped? Why, last year you came near to saving me, saving this place. You didn't realize that? Those loans your company picked up on—well, I had my back to the wall then, Hélène, I won't try and deceive you. Everywhere I turned, it was the same thing. Mrs. Calvert even—well, no disrespect to my wife, Hélène—but she never did understand cotton. It makes me sad to say this, Hélène, but my wife wasn't the help and support to me that she might have been. And those goddamn banks—men I've known all my life, men I've helped in the past, men who owed me a lot . . . And what happened when I was in a tight corner? They turned their backs. That hurt. It was a betrayal. That's a strong word, maybe, but that's how it felt."

He leaned forward, warming to his theme. "They wouldn't listen to me. They wouldn't understand—the possibilities there are in this place. I can build it up again, I know I can. All I need is time. A year—maybe a year and a half. A little extra financing, yes—a small extension, just to see me through." He paused. The alert brown eyes fixed on her face. "You helped me once, Hélène. I'll never forget that as long as I live.

You came through for me, and you know what? It kind of restores my faith in human nature. And it gives me hope. After all, if you helped me once, you just might help me again."

"I see." Hélène looked down. Carefully she drew toward her the document case, and took out from it a large manila envelope. Ned Calvert's eyes focused on it at once. He had begun to sweat. He drew out a large white handkerchief and mopped his brow.

"Here. Let me freshen your drink." He stood up quickly and reached for her glass. The square tanned hand was unsteady. "You see, I don't want us to rush this, Hélène. . . ." He was moving off fast in the direction of the liquor cabinet. "The fact that you're here—that you bothered to come yourself—that means a lot to me. I feel like I can talk to you, if you'll give me the time. I can explain, go over the figures with you. Most women haven't much time for that sort of thing, of course, but you're different, I can see that. You're smart. If I could just go over them with you, I know I can make you see. . . . I lapsed on the repayments, sure, I know that. But that was just a temporary thing, a question of cash flow—you familiar with that term? I've been operating underfunded, that's the problem. With a small loan, an extension—I can get going again. It'll be a good crop this year. . . . Just the soda? You wouldn't like me to pep it up a bit?"

"No, thank you. Just as before." She paused fractionally. "I never drink alcohol when I'm doing business."

He tensed immediately, the bourbon bottle in his hand. He looked at her, then he gave an uneasy laugh. "Jesus. You are something, you know that? So cool. But you were always that way. Do you remember what I used to call you? Hélène—my little girl?" He shook his head. "You know how I thought of you, deep down? I thought of you like my daughter, the lovely little daughter I never had. . . ."

Even he knew that was too much, that the flattery and the sentiment were overdone, and there was no chance it could square with the memories they both shared. His face reddened. "Deep down," he repeated defensively. "Oh, I know I didn't always behave the way I should, and that's been on my conscience all these years. But underneath, yes, underneath, that's what I always felt."

He turned away to hide his embarrassment, the transparency of the lie. Hélène waited until he held the bourbon bottle poised over his glass. Then she said, her voice cool and detached, "That's what you felt? I see. How did you feel about my mother?"

"What's that?" She saw him tense, stand absolutely still.

"My mother. How did you feel about her?"

"I don't quite see . . ."

"Do you remember I asked you for sixty dollars once? It was for my mother. She was having a baby. Your baby. And the money was to pay for her abortion, though I didn't know that until later. The abortion went wrong, and that's how she died. She died aborting your child. Did you know that?"

Bourbon splashed over his hands. He stared down at it blankly, then put the bottle down, and slowly turned around. The color had ebbed from his face. He blinked at her, as if he couldn't understand what she had just said. One square tanned hand made a small convulsive movement.

"My child?"

"Yes."

"That's not possible."

"She went to someone in Montgomery. Sixty dollars wasn't enough, I suppose. It was too cheap. I ought to have asked you for more."

"It's not true." His mouth worked, and his voice suddenly rose. "It's a filthy goddamn lie. . . ."

He took a step toward her, his hands clenching and unclenching. Hélène turned her face away to the windows. Her voice was low and flat, and it was easier to speak if she did not look at him.

"It's ironic, I see that now. The child you never had. It might have been a boy. An heir—to all this. Except I suppose your wife would have left you then, and you wouldn't have had her money to bail you out all these years. . . ."

"Will you stop this? Will you goddamn well stop it?" He advanced toward her, his face flushed with rage. "There's not a goddamn word of truth in this. Who told you?"

"My mother."

"Then she must have been out of her mind. Crazy. She was never too stable, your mother. My God—when I think of all the things I tried to do to help her out. How Mrs. Calvert and I tried . . . I never laid a finger on your mother. Hélène—you knew her. You knew her hold on reality was never strong. Don't tell me you believed her. Don't tell me you've been thinking that all these years. Jesus, I . . ."

"I did believe her. I still do."

"Well, I'm telling you. It's a lie, start to finish. She invented the whole thing. . . ."

He came to a stop in front of her, his mouth contorted with anger. He lurched a little on his feet, then felt for a chair and sat down. He seemed to be gasping for breath. With one hand he loosened his tie, with the other he fumbled in his pockets, pulled out a brown bottle, and slipped a small white pill under his tongue. Then he leaned back in the chair. His lips were a dull bluish color.

"My heart . . ." he said at last as the color returned to his mouth. "It's my heart. I told you. I have angina. If I'm upset, I get an attack. I have to be careful—the doctor told me."

Hélène watched him as he struggled to regain his breath. The confidence, and the anger, had left his face. Looking at his small dark eyes, she could see that he was afraid. She wondered then, coldly, whether his fear was of her, or of dying. Both perhaps. All she wanted then was for it to be over. She waited until the spasm passed, and he grew calmer, then she picked up the manila envelope.

"I came here today to give you this. It's the notice of foreclosure. It became operative as of noon, yesterday. That means—"

"I know what it goddamn well means." His voice rose again. "I know what it means—and I won't accept it. You can take it away. You can tear it up. You can do anything you like. I'm going to talk to my lawyer right now. I'm not beaten yet. I'll fight you on this. You can't come in here and try and walk all over me."

"There's no point in talking to your lawyer. You know that. And it makes no difference whether you accept this or not."

"I'll fight you, I tell you." He struggled forward in his seat. "I'll fight you every goddamn inch of the way. . . ."

"You can't. It's over."

She stopped, and waited for the surge of triumph. None came.

"You planned this, didn't you?" Comprehension suddenly came into his eyes. "You set me up. You want to tell me why? You want to tell me why any sane person would deliberately set out to do this? Destroy me. Destroy this place—everything I've ever worked for. Years of history. Years of tradition." He paused, and made an effort to control himself. "Don't tell me you did it because of your mother, because I'm telling you, Hélène—I swear it to you, in God's name—if she said those things, it was a lie. Look, listen to me, will you. . . ."

Hélène stood up. His tone was half bullying, half pleading. She did not want to listen anymore.

"Yes. I planned it. I set out to do it, and it's finished. That's all. There's no point in lying, because it's done." There was a flat finality in her voice, and he obviously sensed it, because he changed tack.

"You're making one helluva mistake—you know that? Perhaps they didn't explain that to you too well—your advisors. Maybe you didn't stop to count the cost when you did all this. You serve that notice, and you know what you'll end up with? Land you can't sell. A house no one wants to buy. Maybe you ought to think a little about that."

"About money?" She turned her head. "Oh, I've thought about that. And, as it happens, you're wrong. I can sell this land. I'll get a very good price for it too."

"Oh, yes? You think I didn't go into all that? You don't have a hope in hell. So . . ." He paused, and leaned forward.

"Why not try and be reasonable about this? It's a straightforward business matter, after all. If you'll just listen to me a moment, if we talk this through. Hélène—"

"Next year . . ." She interrupted him. She sat down again. "Next year a new factory will open up this side of Orangeburg. You don't know about it yet, but I do. It's a fertilizer plant, and the planning approval for it just went through. It will employ a lot of people—two hundred, maybe more. That will mean new housing, and this plantation is the perfect site for it. When local development companies hear about that— Merv Peters's company, for instance—I think I'll have a buyer for this land, at a good price." She leaned back in her chair. "You see, my advisors are very thorough. They made a number of discreet inquiries at state government level. I was able to help a little, of course. There's a man—his name is Dale Garrett—he used to be on Governor Wallace's staff, so you may know him. They found him particularly informative about rezoning plans. And then there's . . ."

He had been listening intently. Something, quite suddenly, convinced him of what she said—the mention of Dale Garrett's name perhaps. His face flushed with anger, and his control went.

"Money. You goddamn bitch. You did this for money." He slammed his fist down on the arm of his chair. "I might have known it. You saw a chance to make a quick buck, that's why you did this. No other reason. Nothing to do with your dumb bitch of a mother. Money . . ."

"I'm not keeping the money I make from the sale." Her voice was quiet, and that seemed to enrage him further.

"Oh, you're not? I'll believe that when I see it happen. You wouldn't give a goddamn thing away, I can see that just looking at you. You always wanted money, and you'll want more. Oh, you've dragged yourself up out of the dirt, you come in here with a fortune on your back—you probably earned it on your back. But I can still see what you are. What you always were . . ."

"The bulk of the money will be given in the form of a bequest to the NAACP." She cut across his words. "For the furtherance of civil rights. Considering the history of this plantation, that seemed the right thing to do. The balance of the money, also in the form of a bequest—"

"A bequest? That sounds mighty grand, coming from a piece of white trash like you . . ."

"The balance will be used to endow a private scholarship. It will provide the college tuition for a student from this county—black or white." She paused. "It will be a form of memorial to someone I very much admired. It will be called the William Tanner Memorial Scholarship. I think Billy would have liked that."

There; it was said. It was all said. Her hands were shaking a little, and she clasped them together in her lap. There was absolute silence, and for a moment the room blurred before her eyes. She saw only the slanting rays of light, and the motes of dust, dancing. She could go now, she thought with relief. Everything had been perfectly planned, and perfectly executed, and she felt no desire to gloat. All she wanted to do now was leave, while her mind was still clear and cool, and before she had a chance to feel either anger or, worse, pity. She reached for her gloves. Across the room from her, Ned Calvert leaned back in his chair.

"The William Tanner Memorial Scholarship, well, well, well . . ." He spoke into the silence, his voice full of amusement. Then he gave a low chuckle. He levered himself to his feet, and stood looking down at her. When Hélène looked up at him, she saw he was smiling. "That has a mighty fine sound, Hélène. A mighty fine sound." He turned away, crossed the room, picked up the bourbon bottle. "I'll drink to that. I surely will."

He poured a large measure into his glass, swallowed deeply, and took his time returning to his seat. Hélène could sense his returning confidence, his new composure; she felt a tiny stabbing of unease.

"The William Tanner Memorial Scholarship." He rolled the words around his tongue, shaking his head. "In memory of someone you very much admired. That's neat. I have to say that. Real neat. You had it all worked out." He paused. "Of course—'very much admired'—that's kind of a weak way of putting it, don't you think? I'd have said it went a bit further than that, wouldn't you? I mean, sure, Billy Tanner was a dumb boy, none too bright. But you never could see that, could you? Not even that time I warned you about him. . . ."

"I didn't come here to discuss Billy with you. . . ." She reached quickly for her purse. "I came here to give you information. There's nothing to discuss."

"Oh, now, hold on there, honey. I think there's plenty to discuss." He smiled lazily. "I'm beginning to get the picture now. You had me kind of confused back there, talking about your mother and all. But now it's starting to add up. I see now. It wasn't on account of your mother you did this. It was Billy Tanner. Good ol' dumb Billy Tanner. The high-school sweetheart. The boy you loved . . ."

"I'm going." Color flared in Hélène's face. She stood up.

"Now, just you wait a minute, honey. I want to get this straight. I mean, you did love him—or am I wrong? The way I figured it, you must have loved him, going down to the pool with him the way you did, taking off all your clothes, lying down beside him, leading the poor boy on . . ."

Hélène had started to turn away. Now she stopped. Slowly she turned around and looked at him. He was smiling broadly.

"Well, I *watched* you, honey—you didn't know that? I saw it all. It was kind of touching in a way. The two of you. Both so young, naked as the day you were born, lying there under the cottonwood trees. It looked real pretty. I watched you, honey, and I said to myself, now, if that isn't the nearest thing to Adam and Eve in paradise, then I don't know what is. . . ."

"You're obscene—do you know that? I'm not going to listen to this. . . ."

"Oh, you should listen, honey." He leaned forward and fixed her with his gaze. The smile had disappeared, and his face was now hard and intent. "You listen now, and you listen well. I don't take too kindly to the way you come in here and tell me I'm lying, when all the time you're lying through your pretty little white teeth. Don't you try and pretend to me about Billy Tanner, make out you were just friends, and no more. Because I know that's not true. You're planning on funding that scholarship, then you're doing it out of *guilt*. Let's get that straight. Don't tell me you didn't figure it out, honey, a real smart girl like you. You must have known. After all, Billy Tanner died because of you."

There was sudden quiet in the room. Hélène stared at him, and for a moment, she thought she must have misheard, misunderstood. He was smiling again now, smiling broadly, and it was then, when she heard the new confidence in his voice, and when she saw him smile, that the past five years fell away; the scorn and the loathing of this man, and all he stood for, returned. She rounded on him, her voice cold with contempt.

"All right—you want to talk about it, we'll talk about it. And we won't lie. I know why Billy died, and so does everyone in Orangeburg. Billy was killed to stop him giving evidence about the riot. Evidence that would have incriminated a white man. I know that, and you know that. Things like that happen here. They happen all the time, they're still happening now. How long does it have to go on? How many more people have to die—because of people like you? Protecting yourselves—protecting your interests—protecting all this." She gestured angrily toward the window, and to the cottonfields beyond. Her breath caught, and she steadied herself. "I know who killed Billy, and why. It was either you, or one of the men with you in your car that day. And whoever it was who pulled the trigger, you were all responsible. Every one of you."

"Oh, I killed Tanner." The smile had gone, and his voice was very quiet. "I took my shotgun, and I blew him away. But not because of any evidence he might give. You think I gave a goddamn about that? You think anyone did? That evidence of his would have been thrown right out of court. Every white man in Orangeburg would've gone up on the stand and sworn blind it wasn't the way he said. Oh, no, honey. I killed Tanner, so I know. And I killed him on account of you."

"You're lying." Her voice choked in her throat. "You're filthy. How can you lie about something like that?"

"Well, now, honey, maybe I am, and maybe I'm not. I guess you'll

never be able to know for sure. Either way." He leaned back in his
chair; he crossed his legs easily; he began, once more, to smile.

"You see, honey, the trouble with you is, you want everything to be
simple, right and wrong, black and white. That's not the way it is. You
just think about what I'm telling you now, and you'll see. It makes
sense. I was wild about you, Hélène—you remember that? You just
pause a while. You think now. You remember—not the way you want it
to be, but the way it was. You liked me to touch you. You liked to see me
get all worked up. I'm not blaming you, lots of women get a kick out of
that—leading a man on, winding him up, so he's real jealous, so he's
gotten so heated up he hardly knows what he's doing anymore. I tell
you, when I went down through those trees, and I saw my lovely little
girl giving it away to that dumb boy, all the things she wouldn't give
away to me—well, I guess something just snapped in me, honey. My
control just went. Couldn't bear to see a decent white girl giving it away
to a nigger-lover like that. . . ."

He paused, watching her closely, and when she could not hide the
doubt and the sudden fear in her face, his smile grew wider.

"Mind you, I stayed there a while. Stayed till you both left. Stayed
long enough to see it didn't quite go the way you wanted it to go. Saw
Billy-boy couldn't make it. Saw you find out for yourself that Billy
wasn't quite the man you took him to be. Saw him storm the gates, so to
speak—I don't want to be indelicate now, not with a fine lady like
you—and then saw him weep when he didn't have the manpower to go
on. Wept in your arms, like a little baby. I saw that, honey—I'm not
upsetting you now? Then he got himself dressed, and you got yourself
dressed, and I came back here, and I found me my gun."

Hélène stood very still. Her skin felt as cold as ice. He had
stopped. That horrible suggestive voice had stopped, and the room was
quiet. For a moment, she did not see Ned Calvert at all. She felt the
coldness of the water on her skin, then the warmth of the air, drying it.
She felt the smooth dry ground beneath her body, and Billy's weight as
he held her in his arms. She saw the anxiousness in his blue gaze,
and—high over his head—in the gaps between the branches of the
cottonwoods, the blue of the sky. The right moment. The right thing.

"I dreamed of it too long, maybe," Billy said.

She touched his hair, which was still wet and spiky from the water.

"Don't cry, Billy," she said. "Please don't. It doesn't change anything. Next time . . ."

A bird moved in the branches. No next time, ever.

She heard herself draw in her breath; her hands moved in a shocked
incoherent movement, pressing themselves against her ears, as if she
could block out his words, but she knew she could not. There the past

was, and Ned Calvert was right: she had lied, though not in the way he thought.

"I wanted it to be *different*." She swung around to him, her voice shaking with emotion. She heard it rise, so that it sounded higher, and childish suddenly, with the simplicity of a child, and the passion of a child. "You won't understand it, it won't matter to you—but that was what I wanted. I wanted one thing—just one thing—to be simple and good and right. That's why I went to the pool with Billy that day. Not because I loved him—I didn't love him, and he knew that. Because I *cared* for him, because he cared for me. Because I wanted to give him something—something that was pure and good, not all twisted up with lies and hatred like everything else in this place. And afterward—when he was dead—I couldn't bear it. I couldn't bear to think that the very last thing for him, the last thing before he died, that it went wrong . . ."

She stopped. Tears had come to her eyes, and she brushed them angrily away. "So I did this. For Billy and my mother. Because otherwise they're dead, and there's nothing left. It's as if they never lived. No one will care how they died, or why. Just a few people will remember them, then they'll die, too, and it will be over. Wiped out. And that shouldn't happen—it's horrible. It's wrong, and it happens all the time." She stopped. Ned Calvert had not moved, and as she became conscious of his presence, and his silence, she saw that his expression had changed. The malice had gone from his face; his eyes regarded her with an odd blank dulled expression.

"That's what you thought then, that day? That's what you felt, afterward?" His voice was slow; he shook his head.

"Yes. It was." She felt a second's shame now, for her outburst, and she hesitated. She would not have wanted Ned Calvert, of all men, to see her like that. Then she looked back at him, and she realized she did not care what he had seen, or what he had thought. What she had said was the truth. She sighed. In a flat voice, she said, "I know you won't understand. Or care. I'll go now."

"I can understand. Maybe." He sounded surprised. "Yes. I reckon I can. Some of it, anyway."

He stood up and turned away from her. He moved to the windows and looked out over the gardens with that same abstracted gaze. He frowned, lifted his hand, and then let it fall again.

"My place. My father's place."

He seemed to hesitate, then he turned around slowly. "I didn't kill him." His voice was tired. "It was nothing to do with you. That was just talk. I saw you together—true enough. Then I came back here. That's all. That's the way it was." He walked past her as if he hardly saw her, and went across to the liquor cabinet. He poured himself some bourbon, and then looked down as he swirled the liquid in his glass.

"I didn't know about your mother. Or the child. Not until today. Violet never said a word. It might have been different if she had—I don't know. You see—" He paused, and lifted his head. "You see, I thought I couldn't father a child."

Hélène stared at him silently. He took a deep swallow of the bourbon. She watched his throat move. He hesitated, and then set down the glass.

"It probably would have made no difference—even if she'd said. Maybe I'd have done nothing. No guts maybe. Frightened—frightened of Mrs. Calvert, I guess. She held the pursestrings. She kept me in on a tight leash—or tried to." He shrugged. "So I didn't have me a whole lot of choice. She owned me, you see. I think, maybe, that's why—well, I talked to you about it once. Sometime. I think I did. Your mother understood, Violet understood—I reckon you thought I was shooting you a line. And I probably was. It was also true. That's the way of things, I guess. The truth's never simple."

There was another silence. He looked much older suddenly, not bitter, but fatigued. After a while, when he seemed almost to have forgotten that she was still there, Hélène said quietly, "Why are you telling me this?"

"Why not?" He gave an odd resigned smile. "Something you said got to me. Or the way you looked—just now. I don't know. There's no one else to tell, that's for sure." He looked up. "I'm not trying to change your mind, if that's what you think. I was mad at you earlier. Now I'm not. And you know, it's kind of odd, in a way, but it's almost a relief. Getting shed of it all. Getting shed of the lies. Even this place maybe." He frowned. "Never thought I'd hear myself say that. But it's what I feel. You're looking at a free man, Hélène. Yes, sir." He picked up his glass again, and lifted it; a small mocking salute. "First time in my life I ever felt that. A free man." He paused, then smiled suddenly. "You'd better go—while we're still ahead of the game, don't you reckon?"

"Maybe so."

She looked back at the manila envelope, still lying on the chair where she had left it. Then she moved to the door.

"I won medals, you know. In the war." His voice came to her suddenly, across the shadows of the room. "The Silver Star. Funny, how you can be brave in war and a coward in peace."

He was talking to himself, standing half in shadow, the slanting light falling across his body, and not striking his face. Just for an instant, then, she saw him as she had seen him that very first time, outside on the veranda, when she was five years old. A tall man in a white suit, reaching out to take her hand. "Good-bye," she said.

"Good-bye, Hélène Craig."

He chuckled. As she opened the door, and went out, he lifted his arm, and drained the last of the bourbon.

She did not drive straight back to the airport. She took the Cadillac, and parked it on the Orangeburg road. Then she walked back to the edge of the trailer park, and looked at it through the trees. She looked at it for a long time, then she turned away, and took the old route down to the pool, the route Billy had shown her. It was more overgrown now; the brambles tore her stockings, and caught on her clothes. But it was still discernible, and she knew she could have followed it blindfolded, just as she had so often followed it in the past, and in her dreams.

As she walked, her mind worked and worked. It laid out pieces of her past one by one. She saw them like a series of pictures, or stills from a film, none of them random, each interlinked. She saw herself here, with Billy, and then with Edouard in the Loire. She saw Mr. Foxworth sitting in his Harley Street consulting rooms, irritably explaining about dates. She saw Cat, her features a tiny replica of Edouard's, swinging her legs in the Hollywood pool, and singing a French song. She saw Lewis, standing in his room, his face puzzled, and suddenly intent, asking her why she should have lied to him about this.

When she reached the cottonwood trees, she took off her shoes and climbed down the bank. She looked at the still water, and at a dragonfly that whirred in the still air. All this; and one of the last things Billy had ever said to her—she remembered it now—was, *no lies*.

The jet banked over Los Angeles, and Hélène turned her face to the dark of the window. Below her, she saw a map of lights, the framework of a city; she looked at it, and saw only the framework of her past, voices and images, forming and re-forming, linking and unlinking, the geography of a city, the geography of the past.

She had not stopped to change back into her anonymous clothes, and, as she passed through the barrier at the terminal, she was recognized. A small cluster of people, staring at her, proffering pens and pieces of paper. She signed automatically, scribbling her name hastily, eager to get past. It was only when she saw the puzzled expressions that she looked down and saw she had written *Hélène Craig*.

It was dark in the hills after the glare of the freeway, and at the gates of her house, she stopped, and listened to the silence, listened to the dark. It welcomed her, she felt, and drew her on.

There was a light breeze, cool air, blowing down from the hills. She lowered the window of the car, and felt it brush against her face as if the air were substantial. The branches of a tree scratched against the high walls that protected the garden; the bushes by the side of the road bunched with shadows, but she felt no sense of threat. The gates swung back on a silent drive, and she thought, with a sense of peace and of relief: *I am coming home.*

It was late, and when she let herself into the house, it was in darkness; everyone slept. She walked slowly from room to room, switching on all the lights, until the ground floor was flooded with light, and it spilled out onto the terrace and the gardens beyond.

She walked through the rooms, touching objects as she went; it was as if she were seeing the house clearly for the first time. Each piece of furniture, each object, so beautiful, so perfect of its kind, and chosen and arranged with such care. The Coromandel screens; the deep couches covered in cream silk; the rugs, with their softly faded garlands of flowers; the chairs; the pier glasses; the tall Chinese vases filled with the armfuls of lilies. She saw now that all these things had been chosen and assembled for Edouard; she had furnished this room for him, for a man who would never see it, never stand in it.

Quietly, she sat down in a chair, and looked across the room. Such perfectionism, and all of it a substitute for joy. She let herself think then, about the past; each action, each lie, each evasion, each untruth: a secretive little girl, who had grown up into a secretive woman, deceiving others so effectively that it was comparatively easy to deceive herself. She thought of the people who had been harmed by that deceit: Edouard, above all; but also Lewis; also Cat; also herself. She thought of Billy, and the shrine of lies she had erected around his memory, and thought how much he would have hated them. She thought of her mother, and how passionately Violet had clung to the little deceptions that shored up her life; the deceptions seemed tiny beside her own. To have lied to herself about Cat's father—how could she have done such a thing? Violet, for all her wish to prevaricate, had never lied so willfully and so insanely as that.

She shut her eyes, and then opened them again. The room, elegant and restful, remained the same, but she saw it now as vacant and empty, a stage set, no more. She was free of it; she was free of the woman who had created it. She felt a queer, light-headed detachment; how ironic, she thought, that of all people, Ned Calvert should give her something she had not acknowledged she had lost: the knowledge of who she was.

She stood up, and leaving the lights on, she went upstairs to Cat's room. The shades were lowered, but there was a full moon outside, and its radiance silvered their edges and striped the floor with bands of bright light.

Cat was asleep, her eyes tight shut. One small hand clenched in a fist was curled across her pillow. Her black hair fanned out, and her breathing was soft and regular. Hélène sat down quietly at the foot of her bed, and looked at her daughter. Lovingly, her eyes traced the line of Cat's face, so like Edouard's. The features were still soft and unformed, but the resemblance was strong, even when her eyes were shut. The likeness she had shied away from; now she rejoiced in it.

She would have to tell Edouard, she thought. He must know. At that, her heart began to beat faster, and she felt a little afraid. Then she pushed the fear aside. No matter what his reaction might be, and no matter what pain it might cause her, he must know, and she must tell him.

She sat there, very still, until her agitation gradually calmed. She looked at the room, at the books on the bookshelves, the drawings pinned to the walls, the line of white rabbits that processed across the material of the shades. She looked at Cat again; her eyelids flickered slightly, and Hélène knew she dreamed. She reached out and held her hand, and after a while, quite suddenly, Cat woke.

"You're back."

She smiled up at Hélène, sleepily. Hélène moved closer to her, and Cat snuggled deeper under her covers, curling herself in a warm ball, so she rested against her mother.

"I was dreaming. A nice dream. I've forgotten it now." She gave a little yawn. "I do that sometimes. I dream, and then I wake up. I'm glad you're here."

"Do you want me to stay?" Hélène bent over her.

"Mmmm. Yes." Cat reached out one warm hand, and took hers. "Tell me a story."

"All right. What shall it be about?"

"Tell me about you. When you were little . . ." Cat's eyes flicked open, peeped up at her, then closed again. Hélène sighed. This was a request Cat had begun to make often, ever since she had been old enough to delight in the idea of her mother as a child. Hélène had always evaded the subject, or spoken vaguely of small unimportant incidents; not now.

"Very well." She paused, then began in a low voice: "Well, when I was little, I didn't sleep in a big room like this. I slept in a little room, a very tiny one. It was in a trailer—you know, you've seen them. Sometimes they have bunks, but this one was like a house, and it had beds. Two beds. One for my mother, and one for me."

"You mean you lived in it all the time?" Cat's eyes flew open again. "Not just on vacations? Not like camping?"

"No, we lived in it all the time. It wasn't very big. Just two little rooms, and there were steps down from it into a yard, with a white fence. It was painted green inside. . . ."

"How lovely. I'd like that. I'd like to live in a trailer." Cat wriggled closer, and Hélène smiled.

"It was a very old trailer," she said. "Very shabby. And it was in the South, in a place called Alabama. So, in the summer, it got very very hot, and the trailer got hot, and stuffy. When I was little, just about the age you are now—maybe a little bit older—I used to lie in bed at night, and I'd put my hands out, and touch the walls, and they were still hot, like an iron, even when it was dark outside. . . ."

"Didn't you have air-conditioning?" Cat looked puzzled.

"No, we didn't have that."

"Did you have a pool, so you could go swimming if you got hot?"

"No, we didn't have a pool. Not like the pools here. And we didn't need a pool, not really. When I wanted to go swimming, I used to go down to a little creek, and swim in the river water. I had a friend then, his name was Billy, and he taught me to swim. . . ."

"Oh, I want to know." Cat wriggled closer. "Tell me about Billy." Hélène paused, and then she began to speak, slowly at first, and then more quickly. As she spoke, she found it all came back, every tiny detail, things she had not thought of for years and years; it was all there, she could see it and smell it and feel it, where each chair stood, the colors of the plates and the cups, the sound of her mother's voice, Billy, standing in the yard in his bare feet, kicking at the dust, and smiling at her, his head a little on one side, his eyes looking slightly puzzled, as if something were happening to him, and he didn't understand it.

She talked for what seemed a long time. Sometimes Cat interjected a question, but gradually she grew drowsy, and the questions grew fewer. Her eyes closed, and her head grew heavy. She slept, falling asleep abruptly with a little sigh, as children and animals do. Hélène stroked her hair, and fell silent. She went on sitting there, feeling a great sense of release and of contentment, aware that she was getting cold, and stiff, but not caring.

At four, or perhaps five, in the morning, the light that edged the shades grew warmer, and she heard the first birds begin to sing. It was then, and with a terrifying suddenness, that the noise began. One moment the room and the house were quiet and still, the next the air vibrated with a terrible clamor.

Hélène started; her heart seemed to stop and then to pound; it was as if the noise were inside her head, it was so loud, and for a moment, in confusion and fright, she felt as if she herself had triggered the alarm. She froze for an instant, and then sprang to her feet. Beside her, Cat's eyes flew open, and she gave a cry of fear.

"Mother. What is it? What is it?"

Hélène reached for her, and held her tight.

"It's all right. It's the alarms—it's just the alarms, Cat, something's triggered them. . . ."

"I'm frightened. . . ."

"Darling, it's all right. You remember. It's happened before. It's an animal probably, or a bird—wait. . . ."

She crossed to the window and pulled up one of the shades. Behind her, Cat huddled under the bedclothes, her little face pale and scared. Hélène covered her ears with her hands and looked out over the garden.

It was lit not with the soft dawn light, but with the cold unearthly glare of halogen lamps, a light brighter than noon, that bleached the trees and grass of color. In the garden, nothing moved, there was no sign of any intruder, either innocent or sinister.

Hélène stared out across the grass. A horrible sick sense of foreboding rose in her stomach; she stared in the direction of the drive, toward the gates which, from here, were invisible. From inside the house came the sound of running footsteps, the voices of Madeleine and Cassie.

"Mother. What is it? What is it?"

Hélène turned away from the window.

"I don't know." She reached for Cat's hand. "I don't know." In the hills beyond the house, sirens began to wail.

But she did know then, when she heard the sirens—or so she thought afterward. Knew then, knew when she took the call from the station later that morning, knew when, with Cassie protesting at her side, she walked into the police morgue to make the identification.

Blue light; cold air; white tiles; the drip of sluices. One wall, banked with steel drawers, like safety deposit boxes, only larger.

Cassie caught one glimpse, and hung back. She plucked at Hélène's arm.

"You don't have to do this. There's no call. So what if it's the same man? Lewis should be doing this, not you. You should call Lewis. . . ."

"I saw him too. I'm going to do it."

"But why? This is a horrible place."

"I feel I ought to, that's all."

"Stubborn!" Cassie's chin tilted. "You was always that way. Well, if you're going in, I'm going with you."

The lieutenant in charge of the case was waiting; he held a clipboard, and looked impatient and ill at ease. He had hardly glanced at Cassie, but he stared at Hélène as if trying to convince himself that she was real. Beside him stood an attendant in a white coat. As the women advanced, the two men glanced at each other. The lieutenant shifted from foot to foot.

"Found him dead in his cell around nine. Inhalation of vomit," he said finally. "Happens all the time."

As if this were his cue, the attendant reached forward; the drawer next to them slid forward soundlessly on casters. The body was covered with heavy plastic sheet; a label like a luggage label was attached with a loop of string to one big toe.

"The bruising was caused by his fall. Those walls at your place are fifteen feet. The guy must have been crazy."

The lieutenant reached for the sheet.

"He wasn't unconscious when they brought him in. He was okay. Came as quiet as a lamb. The bruising's not as bad as it looks. We had the surgeon examine him. . . ."

He sounded aggrieved, as if the man's subsequent death were a reproach to his own efficiency. He hesitated, then tweaked the sheet aside.

"Miss Harte?" He glanced over his shoulder at Cassie. "Lady. This the same guy? Either of you recognize him?"

Hélène looked. The man's eyes were open. They were a pale bleached-out blue, and bore an expression of faint surprise, as if the fact of his own mortality had been puzzling, and unexpected. He had thin sandy hair, and the stubble of a reddish beard. A tall man, heavily boned. She hesitated.

Cassie stepped forward, looked, and stepped back. She turned away quickly.

"That's him for sure. I saw him close up. I recognize him."

"Miss Harte?"

Hélène stared at the man. Above the sheet, his chest was bare, and thickly matted with red hair. One hand was just visible. It looked too large for the thin wrist; it was square-palmed, and the fingers were callused. She thought of the night of the party, of standing on the driveway, and looking back at the gates; she thought of the odd sense of kinship she had felt then. She reached out her hand, touched the soft fuzz of hair on the man's arm, and then drew back.

"I'm not sure. It was dark when I saw him. I can't be certain."

Again the lieutenant and the attendant exchanged glances. The drawer on its smooth casters was pushed back. A sluice gurgled, and the lieutenant made a small note on his clipboard.

"Lady—you're sure?"

"I'm sure." Cassie's voice was grim. She was already walking away.

He shrugged.

"It'll be him. Once these guys get a fixation on someone, they stick with it. I'm sorry, Miss Harte. He won't be troubling you again—that's one way of looking at it. . . ."

He turned away. He was just beginning to wonder at what point it would be decent to ask for Hélène Harte's autograph—when they'd gotten the hell out of the morgue, obviously—when he realized that she wasn't following him out. He stopped. She was still standing in exactly the same place, staring at the banks of drawers, and the numbers on them.

"Do you know his name?"

She spoke quite suddenly, in that low cool voice of hers. The lieutenant jumped. He hesitated, looking down at the clipboard. Hélène did not turn her head; she did not move. The second seemed to her to lengthen, the room to grow colder and then brighter; she waited, knowing what he was about to say.

"He had a driver's license on him. No other ID. License gives his name as Craig. Gary Craig. License was issued—where is it, someplace in the South. . . ."

He was scrabbling at his notes, as if her silence and stillness unnerved him.

"Louisiana," she said.

"That's right. Louisiana." He found the entry on his clipboard. He looked up with a frown. Behind him, he was aware that the other woman had reacted. She gave an exclamation, quickly cut off, and started back to them. Hélène Harte had not moved, but the other woman had gone as white as a sheet. She was coming forward, arms outstretched, like a tigress about to defend her cub.

"Hélène, honey—wait a second now. . . ."

"It's all right, Cassie. Really. It's all right."

"What is this?" The lieutenant looked from face to face. "That name mean something to you—is that it? You knew him? There some connection here I should know about?"

She turned, and the clear gray-blue eyes met his. The other woman seemed to be trying to stop her speaking, but Hélène Harte paid her no heed. When she spoke, she did so in a quiet steady voice, and he stared at her, thinking he was hearing wrong, thinking he was going crazy. She said, "I never knew him. He was my father."

There was a silence. Then the woman beside her gave a little moan, as if it would have been better had that admission not been made. The attendant cleared his throat, and turned away, and the lieutenant, when his mind came out of deep freeze and started working again, thought: the press. Oh, Jesus.

"That's the wording I want used. Exactly that. No—I don't want it altered in any way. No—I don't intend to amplify on it. Beyond that I have no comment to make. . . ."

Hélène's voice sounded firm, and slightly weary. She was on the telephone to her press agent, Bernie Alberg, who was not taking the news well. Hélène's side of the conversation had been brief and to the point; in her hand she held a small piece of paper on which she had written out the statement she had just dictated to him. Cassie, who had been asked to stay while Hélène made the call, watched her with a frown. The statement was unequivocal, and Cassie was not sure if it was wise. Bernie Alberg thought it not merely unwise, but disastrous; Cassie could hear his voice squawking into the receiver; he was an excitable man at the best of times; now he sounded apoplectic.

Hélène held the receiver slightly away from her ear, and gave Cassie a small resigned smile. Cassie made a face. She knew Hélène could be immovable when she had decided on something, and she supposed Bernie Alberg would know it too—he was no fool. However, he clearly thought there was some possibility of changing her mind; some of the agonized squawks were now comprehensible.

"The timing's disastrous. There's your Oscar nomination to consider. They'll be voting soon. We have to keep this under wraps. There's no need for a statement. Look, listen a moment, will you? Who heard? Two guys. This isn't a problem. Just give me the lieutenant's name, will you? I'll get on to him right away. . . . None of this need come out—you hear me? None of it. Okay, so it'll cost a bit. So what else is new? There may be rumors—so we deny them. That's cool. Rumors die. Statements don't. Look, I'm coming over. I'm coming over right now. . . ."

"No, Bernie. You're not." Hélène cut him off in mid-flow. "We're not discussing this. There's nothing to discuss. Those are the facts. Any queries, and you put out that statement—"

There were some more squawks, and Hélène frowned.

"Bernie." She cut him off again. "Either you do it, or I get another press agent to do it. It's as simple as that."

There was a silence at the other end of the line. A few more remarks, inaudible to Cassie, and obviously made in a quieter tone of voice.

"Thank you, Bernie," Hélène said finally, and hung up.

She turned away to the window of a living room, and looked out at the garden. The afternoon sun struck the pale gold of her hair, and the calm oval of her face, and Cassie, looking at her, wondered at that calm. She wondered sometimes what it cost Hélène, that calm—and also what it would take to shatter it.

"He's agreed?"

"But of course."

Hélène did not look around, and Cassie's voice became gruff, as it always did when she tried to disguise her concern.

"You sure you're doing the right thing?"

"Oh, yes."

"It's just that . . ." Cassie hesitated.

She was proud of Hélène's success, and kept a scrapbook of her clippings. She was well aware that Hélène never spoke of her past in interviews; she was also aware of how journalists, facing a wall of silence, had embroidered and invented and—possibly encouraged by Bernie Alberg—had trailed hints of a background that bore no relationship to the truth.

"People think of you different," she burst out at last. "That's all. Right or wrong, that's what they think. They built up a picture of you in their minds. And Gary Craig—he don't fit into it, honey. He just don't. A father like that. A down-and-out. A lush. Maybe . . ."

"He was my father, Cassie." Hélène turned around.

"Yes, but he don't *fit*. And he wasn't like your father, not really. You never knew him even. What did he ever do for you? What did he care? Why'd he want to come around here, anyway, hanging out by those gates? He must've been crazy. . . ."

"He was looking for me, perhaps."

"Didn't bother looking for twenty years. And if he was, how come he didn't come right on in, and announce himself, straight out, same as any normal man would? He was buildin' up to it, I reckon. Biding his time. Traced you to Orangeburg, traced you here through me, that's how I see it. Then—well, who knows? Maybe he was going to sting you for a few bucks. Maybe worse. There's no telling. He could have been dangerous. . . ."

"I don't think so. I think—he just wanted to look. That's all. He was an alcoholic—a sick man—he probably didn't even know why he did it."

"Well, he's dead." Cassie's mouth set in an obstinate line. "Let sleeping dogs lie, I say. The way I see it, he never done nothing for you, so why go telling the world he's your father—a man like that?"

"Oh, Cassie. It's the truth. That's why."

"So? Bend it a little. Why not? Plenty of folks do."

"Not anymore." Hélène smiled at her gently. "I'm tired of lying, Cassie. And I'm tired of pretending. That's all."

Cassie could see the appeal in her face, and hear it in her voice. Her heart softened. She shook her head.

"Well. If you see it like that. I'd just like to save you some hurt, that's all."

"The truth oughtn't to hurt. . . ." Hélène began, and Cassie gave a derisory snort.

"*Ought* not, maybe. But it can. I seen truth cause trouble you wouldn't believe, when a little lie—now that would have eased things over real nice. Still. I won't argue. No sense in wasting my breath . . ." She paused. "You going to this funeral you're fixin'?"

She knew what the answer would be before the question was out; Hélène nodded. Cassie drew herself up.

"Well. You ain't going alone, that's for sure. I guess I'll have to come with you. You want me to do that?"

"I would like you to, yes, Cassie."

"You want me, you got me." Cassie paused, and they smiled at each other. Cassie hesitated, and then turned to the door. She looked thoughtful. In the doorway, she turned back.

"I'll wear my best black," she said decisively. "Violet would've liked that. She helped me choose it, way back. Took the skirt up for me. Yes. My best black—that'd be the thing, I reckon."

She shut the door, her expression more cheerful. Hélène smiled. She turned away then, her face growing still and thoughtful, and looked out for a while at the garden. There, Cat was playing. She had a line of dolls, with which she rarely played, but which, today, seemed to be in favor. They had been marshaled in a group, and were being plied with tea from minute china cups. A birthday tea, perhaps—another few months and it would be Cat's birthday.

She was absorbed in her task, head bent; Madeleine, Hélène saw, was taking some photographs of her. She, too, was absorbed in her task, and taking particular care with the shots. Neither of them looked up.

After a while, Hélène turned away from the window. She looked at the telephone. After the funeral; then, she thought. She did not pick it up.

The funeral of Gary Craig took place four days later at Forest Lawn. It was a brief ceremony; Hélène, and Cassie in her best black, were the only mourners at the graveside. It was a beautiful day, a day of bright sunshine with a sky the clearest of blues, and as they left the chapel, Cassie's spirits rose. It was over, she thought. Gary Craig had been laid to rest, and she now felt glad that Hélène had insisted she do the right thing by her father. He had had a good burial—that was important, Cassie considered. To her relief—and, she imagined, Bernie Alberg's—the story had not broken. No rumors, no inquiries, and so no need of a statement. Maybe Bernie had leaned on the police to keep quiet after all, in spite of Hélène's instructions. It was possible—and whether he had or not, the papers obviously hadn't gotten on to the story, which was just fine as far as she was concerned. Cassie had no time for newspapermen; skunks and vultures, she thought, every last one of them.

She and Hélène walked back, side by side, down the back pathways to where her driver, Hicks, and the long black limousine were waiting. Cassie looked out approvingly at the trees and lawns as they passed; she liked this place; it was serene, and it was tidy. Hélène's head was bent, and she was silent; Cassie was thinking, not altogether charitably, that if Gary Craig had been unlucky in life, he had been fortunate in his final resting place. Neither of them noticed the man who was standing a few feet to one side of the limo, until they reached it, and he stepped forward.

"Miss Harte?"

Hélène looked up; it was then, and only then, as he took the photograph, that Cassie realized he had a camera. Hélène stopped; she gave the man a cold stare; then, without a word, she stepped through the door Hicks was holding open for her, and into the back of the car.

Hicks and Cassie exchanged glances. Hicks, a burly man, well over six feet, who had been with Hélène three years and was devoted to her, stooped swiftly.

"You want me to get that camera, Miss Harte?"

The man was already backing away.

"Just a fan," he said nervously. "Just a fan. I only wanted one picture. . . ."

"Ain't you got no sense of decency?" Cassie rounded on him. Hicks took a step forward. Then Hélène's voice came from the car, clearly and firmly.

"Leave it," she said. "It's not important."

And it was not, she thought, later that day, when dinner was over, and Cat asleep; when she was alone. Whether the man was a fan, or from a newspaper, she was not going to hide anymore, or pretend anymore. Gary Craig was her father: she had done what she had to do. What she had to do now was much more important, and much harder.

She sat down at her desk and looked at the telephone. Much as she longed to hear Edouard's voice, she had decided against the telephone. He might not be there. He might refuse to take the call. He might not agree to meet her. Had he said her name, that evening when she telephoned from the Plaza? Had her own telephone really rung three times, the evening Lewis hit her, the evening she knew her marriage was over? She was no longer certain. She thought it possible she had imagined both things.

No, she would write. She drew out the sheets of writing paper, and looked at them. She uncapped her pen. It seemed impossible to begin. It was a letter to a stranger, after all; a man who in five years, though he must, in that time, have heard of her, had neither contacted her, nor sought her out in any way. She nearly gave up, then. An image rose in her mind—the Edouard de Chavigny of whom, sometimes, she read accounts in newspapers. A cold, self-sufficient man, who gave brusque, uninformative interviews, and who clearly did not suffer fools gladly. Not a man who would be exactly pleased to receive, after five years, a letter from an ex-mistress informing him he was the father of her child. If such a man replied at all, it would be through lawyers, informing her that such a claim, if repeated, was actionable.

And yet—the man she had known had been very different. She let the two images rest, side by side, in her mind: the public image, and the private one. Slowly, as the memories returned, the public image, the image of the newspapers, began to fade. She forgot his reputation, and thought, instead, of the man she had loved—and, because she had also trusted him, the letter, once begun, was easy to write.

She wrote for one hour. She mailed the letter herself, the next day. At noon, returning home, she knew she felt different; it was some time before she realized what the difference was. She was happy. It had been so long she had forgotten how that felt.

HÉLÈNE
AND EDOUARD

T he first warning came at the end of February, though Hélène did not perceive it as such; she interpreted it as rudeness—inexplicable rudeness. It came in the form of a telephone call, from the wife of a studio executive. Mary Lee was that familiar figure, the corporation wife—one of the most developed of that species Hélène had ever met. All the force of her considerable energy was channeled into one cause: the promotion of her husband, and, by extension, of herself. A social alpinist, who no sooner climbed one range of mountains but she set her sights upon another, Mary Lee was tanned, always; thin, always; well-groomed, always; and she had a voice that made a power drill sound harmonious. She had laid siege to Hélène for a year, and redoubled her efforts once Hélène's Oscar nomination was announced. Hélène, worn down by her persistence, finally agreed to attend one of her parties. Then, that day at the end of February, Mary Lee called to cancel.

"Hélène? Yes, it's Mary Lee. I hardly dared call—I'm just *so* embarrassed. Yes, our little dinner next week . . . I know, just when we had it all settled . . . Hélène, this is just *terrible,* but I have to call the whole thing off. And Joe Stein was coming, too, and Rebecca Stein— such darlings . . . but I simply can't risk it. Jack has this *horrible* virus—no, not flu exactly. But he has a fever, and his throat is so bad he can hardly say a word—and the doctors have been very tough. *Absolute* rest. They say he's not to do a thing, for a week at least. No work, and *no* parties! Well, you can imagine . . . so, I know it's short notice, and I feel just dreadful about this, but . . ."

Hélène said politely that she quite understood. She hoped Jack would recover soon. She hung up with a feeling of profound relief, since she had not wanted to go anyway.

She had, since her return from Alabama, made a conscious effort to pick up the threads of her social life. To serve on charity committees again; to go out to dinners and parties and luncheons again—all these things helped to distract her from the knowledge that she had written to Edouard some three weeks before, and had received no answer.

She thought no more of the canceled invitation until, only two days later, lunching with Gregory Gertz to discuss *Long Division*, she saw Mary Lee's husband, Jack, on the far side of the restaurant, apparently in perfect health. This puzzled her slightly; she was even more puzzled, a few days later, when she heard from Rebecca Stein that Mary Lee's dinner party had actually taken place, on the original date.

"We heard you had to drop out at the last moment, Hélène," Rebecca Stein said. "Such a pity. I was looking forward to seeing you."

Hélène frowned, said nothing, and thought no more about the matter. She was so busy that it was easy to forget the Mary Lees of this world: her agents were besieging her with scripts and with projects, though there was none she especially liked. She had constant meetings with Gregory Gertz, and with the rising young star, Randall Holt, who was to play the husband in *Long Division;* she had script conferences, fittings for costumes, makeup tests; there was the burgeoning round of dinners, committee meetings, and parties; and Bernie Alberg, ecstatically happy at the boost which the Academy Award nomination and the phenomenal success of *Ellis* had given to her career, filled in every spare second with yet another interview, yet another talk show appearance.

Hélène felt distanced from all this; she did not enjoy it. She would have preferred the quiet of the months at the end of the previous year, she would have preferred to spend more time with Cat. But these distractions had served her in the past, and they served her again now. It was easier to invent a thousand fertile explanations for Edouard's silence, and to believe them, if she had no time to dwell on them, but must immediately rush on somewhere else, if she could—for just a little longer, she told herself—take refuge behind her famous face, and her famous name. To be Hélène Harte was a protective device: a shield between herself and others, and also a shield between herself and her growing anxiety. For when she was alone, and when she gave herself time to think, when she was herself, the cold realization came closer and closer: *he had not written; he was not going to write.*

So, resignedly, she let the jubilant Bernie Alberg fit into her crowded schedule a photographic session for *Vogue*, a documentary being made on her work with Angelini by the BBC, a cover story in *Time* magazine. Even *Time* dug up no information about her father, and this made Bernie Alberg more jubilant still. That story was dead, he was sure of it.

Hélène looked at the story in *Time*, which concentrated on her film work, and which tipped her strongly for the Oscar. She looked at the cover photograph, and the headline beneath it, *Hélène Harte: The Face of the American Dream*. She was beginning to hate that tag, which—since *Ellis*—appeared in almost every story about her. Lise might be the face of the American Dream—whatever that really meant—but was she? She looked at the photograph, and felt she looked at a stranger.

The *Time* story came out in the first week of March, before the Academy Award voting was completed. Later the same week, she received the second warning, though, again, she did not perceive it as such. Another curious telephone call, this time from the wife of an influential newspaper publisher, a woman who was a leading light in Los Angeles society, who had persuaded Hélène, some weeks before, to serve on her prestigious charity committee. She was not a Mary Lee; she was not evasive.

"My dear," she said baldly, "I'm going to ask you to drop off the committee. I think, from everyone's point of view, that it might be wise. Don't you?"

Hélène was surprised, and mystified.

"Well, my dear," the woman went on briskly, "we are raising funds for the care of the sick and the elderly. So, I hardly think . . ." She paused. "If you'd just have your secretary send me a brief note, explaining that you're very tied up just now, and feel you haven't as much time to devote to our work as you would wish . . ."

"Why should I do that? It isn't the case."

"Possibly not, my dear. You've been very generous with your time. But I think it would be best. If you could let me have it tomorrow, before our next meeting?"

She hung up before Hélène had time to argue. Hélène angrily sent a cold note saying she was resigning from the committee at the request of its chairman. She received a one-line acknowledgment.

The third warning came later the same day, and this time it was unmistakable. Gregory Gertz telephoned her that evening. He sounded odd, and guarded. He informed her, with little preamble, that various production and technical difficulties had come up, and that filming on *Long Division* would have to be delayed. The start date could no longer be April 2. It would be two weeks after that, possibly three. Artists International, he said, would be talking to Milton first thing in the morning. He hoped this would cause no problems with her schedules. . . .

"Greg—wait a minute. I don't understand. Yesterday, when I saw you, you said—"

"Hélène, I'm sorry, I can't talk now. I have a plane to catch. I'll try to call you tomorrow. . . ."

It was then that Hélène knew there was something wrong, something that was being kept from her. Not simply because of the postponement—that was common enough, even this close to a start date—but because of Gregory Gertz's manner. She knew that tone of voice, that mingling of suppressed panic and the desire to dissemble.

Something was not just a little wrong, it was badly wrong. The next morning, at eight o'clock, Bernie Alberg called. "I'm coming around now," he said.

And, when he came, she understood.

He laid the copies of the tabloid on a table in front of her. They were still sticky, straight from the presses. He stood there looking at her, all his normal ebullience gone. He looked gray, and exhausted, as if he had been up all night. He was a plump man, and his usual manner was bouncy, punchy with adrenaline. Now he visibly sagged.

"Jesus, Hélène," he said, "I'm sorry. I'm just so sorry. Those bastards. I never had a hint, not a smell, nothing. They kept the whole damn thing under wraps, and—well, you can see—they must have been putting this together for weeks. Someone gave them a lead. Maybe the cops. Maybe that guy in the morgue. Then they went after it. They couldn't have done a story like this overnight. And now I find out that there were people who had heard, rumors, you know. And I blame myself. Blame myself? Jesus, I could shoot myself. I always thought I had my ear so close to the ground. Hélène—look—I know it isn't eight-thirty yet, but d'you think I could have a Scotch?"

He helped himself. His hands were shaking. Hélène sat down and looked at the photographs. She looked at them one by one, and the captions under them. Then she read the story: four pages of it, with a follow-up touted for the next issue.

On the first page, there was a photograph of her house, taken from the air. The caption read: *Riches—the 2-million-dollar home Hélène Harte keeps in Beverly Hills. Scene of scandal parties; once the home of legendary Ingrid Nilsson.*

Next to it was a photograph of a filthy room, possibly in some flophouse, with an inset picture of a younger Gary Craig. That caption read: *Rags: the room where the star condemned her father to die.*

On the next page there was a picture of a filthy poor white homestead. Outside it stood the wreck of a car; chickens pecked in the dirt; a tall, big-boned man, stripped to the waist, and gripping a beer can in his fist, glowered at the camera. Next to him, her face streaked with mud, was a small fair-haired toddler. It was a picture Hélène had never seen: she supposed the house was in Louisiana; she supposed the man was Gary Craig; she supposed the child was herself, for the caption told her all these things. Above it ran a banner headline: *Hélène Harte—The Nightmare Behind the Face of the American Dream.*

Was poverty the American nightmare, and riches the American dream? She looked at the headline coldly, and turned the page. There was a photograph of herself at a recent party. She remembered that photograph being taken. There had been a crush of people, and the photographer had smiled, and joked, and asked the three of them to stand closer together—herself, Lloyd Baker, and Thad. Lloyd Baker had his arm around her waist, and Hélène had just turned to smile at him. Above that, in letters an inch high, was the legend: *Super-Star Love Triangle—The Story She Did NOT Want Told.* Lower down there was a smaller photograph of Lloyd and Katie Baker, and the headline: *Lloyd Baker Love Nest—Wife Reveals All.*

She sat there, and there was a very long silence. Finally Bernie Alberg, unnerved by it, showed signs of revving up. He rose, and came across to her.

"Hélène—it won't stop there. The *National Enquirer*'s already picked up on it. They called me at home last night. This will hit the newsstands by noon, and then all hell will break loose. Once something like this starts, it snowballs. It won't just be here, it'll be everywhere. Europe—Hélène, you *know* what some of those papers are like. They're worse than the ones here. This will be syndicated worldwide. You can see—there's more to come—they're running a follow-up next week. Now, listen, we've got to do something, and we've got to do it fast. I want you on the phone to those hotshot lawyers of yours, *now*. You talk to them, I'll talk to them. I want them to come down on this like a ton of bricks. I want them to throw the book at this rag. We'll sue. We'll sue the goddamn skin off their backs. But we've got to move fast. We must. We can't let this influence the voting on the Oscars. We have to . . . Hélène?"

He stopped, looking at her closely. The animation and color that had returned to his face began to drain away.

"Judas Priest—for fuck's sake, Hélène—you're not going to put out that statement you gave me. You're not. Tell me you're not. . . ."

Hélène's face seemed to him quite expressionless. She, too, was a little pale, but otherwise betrayed no agitation at all. She simply continued to sit there, staring at the pages in front of her. She was in shock, Bernie decided—in shock.

"Look," he said more gently, "wait a minute—yes? Don't let's do anything rash now. I'll get you a drink. You need a brandy or something. . . ."

"No, thank you. I don't need a drink." She turned and looked up at him. "Bernie—you already know that some of this is true. . . ."

"Some? Some?" Bernie was trying hard to remain calm. "Hélène, one tiny fact is true, and the rest of it, the rest of it is just a tissue of lies. That's it." He seemed to find comfort in the cliché. "A tissue of lies."

"Not entirely. I don't think that picture is fake. I did live in Louisiana for a while. And the place I lived after that wasn't much better. I expect that's what they're going to run next week. A trailer park in Alabama. It's still there. They can take pictures of that too. . . ." She hesitated. "There are people there who remember me. People they can interview."

"A trailer park? Oh, sweet Jesus . . ."

"I'm afraid so." She paused. "Most of the rest is lies. My mother left my father when I was two. I lived with her until she died. I never saw my father again—I didn't even know he was alive, until the accident, until I went to identify his body." There was a silence. Bernie poured himself another drink, a small drink, just enough to loosen his thoughts up a bit; his brain felt like glue.

"Right—okay. Okay." He frowned. "Okay. We do put out the statement. We amplify it. We explain. We add a bit, maybe—like, you searched for him, years ago, like, he was a scumbag, but you forgave him, you wanted to help—you couldn't trace him. It could work. It might work. He beat your mother up, by any chance? That's the line we need. We go for the soft touch, the heartache."

"It doesn't exactly square with all the things we hinted at before, does it, Bernie?"

"I hinted. Goddamn journalists hinted. You never said a word. . . ."

"I didn't deny it, and I could have." She stood up. "Bernie, they won't buy it. And I don't want them to buy it. I'm not going to tell any more lies. Put out that statement, and that's it."

"But if we put that out—it looks as if we're admitting it. All the other stuff. How you neglected him. How you wouldn't give your dying father a buck. The guy died at your *gates*, Hélène. *No one's* going to believe you didn't know him." He paused, and looked down at the tabloid again. "And the lovers—Jesus. Not a whisper of scandal in five years, and now this. What are we going to say about the lovers?"

Hélène turned to him then, and Bernie, despite his anxiety, was impressed.

"I think," she said slowly, "I think this is so beneath contempt that it doesn't require an answer of any kind. And I don't intend to give one."

"Hélène, look, for God's sake. It won't *work* like that. Think of the Oscars . . ."

"No, Bernie." Her blue eyes blazed at him, and he realized that what he had taken for shock was anger. "I will not. And if people choose to believe this, if they pay any credence to it, they are not people I want to work with, or people I want to know. That's all. That's the end of it."

Bernie hesitated. He said quietly, "Hélène, there won't *be* an end to it. Once something like this starts, it doesn't end. It just goes on, and on."

He was right, of course. There was one quiet day of respite, and then it began. The invitations canceled, sometimes without pretense of an excuse; the calls not returned; the photographers who camped outside her gates, and followed her wherever she went; the importunate writers, who had sent scripts which they had begged her to read, who now wrote and asked for their return; the minor producers and up-and-coming directors who had once seen, in Hélène Harte, the possibility of a big break, and who, having wooed her for years, now looked straight through her when she sat at the next table in a restaurant; the fashion spreads that were apologetically postponed, and then postponed again. And the letters.

Hélène felt such disgust for the people who behaved in this way that she sometimes felt she could have put up with all their pettiness, but the letters—no. She had, of course, received some of a similar kind in the past—there was probably no actor or actress in Hollywood who had not. But these letters were far worse, and the most terrifying thing about them was their quantity. At first, there was a mere trickle of them, nine or ten a day. Once Hélène and her secretaries realized what was happening, they were burned, unread. But the process of filtering them out was not an easy one, and some of their writers went to great lengths to present them in such a way—in clean envelopes, neatly addressed, often typed—that it was difficult to distinguish them from fan mail or ordinary mail, until they were opened, and at least partially read.

Then, the tabloid which had first broken the story ran its follow-up. There was the trailer park; there was her mother, the town slut; there was Hélène, following in her mother's footsteps, when she was still a fifteen-year-old girl. There were the men who remembered how she'd been the talk of the school locker room; there was Priscilla-Anne, talking only too volubly; there was a hideous and garbled version of her relationships with Billy and with Ned Calvert—although he, clearly, had not spoken to them.

The *National Enquirer* picked up on this story too; magazines and newspapers in France, Italy, and England followed suit, spreading the story in more and more sensationalized forms. The response was immediate. The trickle of letters became a flood.

Letters which enclosed pictures of herself, either torn to shreds, scrawled with obscenities, or defaced with obscene drawings. Letters enclosing pornographic photographs, on which her own picture had been crudely superimposed. Letters in illiterate handwriting, on lined paper, and letters written with perfect spelling and careful grammar. Letters that described things she had done with their anonymous authors, or things they would have liked her to have done; letters that accused her of stealing the writer's husband, or lover; letters that told her she'd be better off dead; letters that described just how the writer intended to kill either her, or members of her family. Letters using biblical phraseology, that called her a Jezebel, or a whore of Babylon; letters from men who believed she sent them messages over the airwaves in a secret libidinous code.

They sent presents, too; a neatly wrapped parcel of feces; a small box containing clippings of pubic hair; and, once, addressed to Cat, who was prevented from opening it just in time—a small parcel containing twenty used contraceptives, wrapped in gift paper.

On that occasion, and it was the only occasion, Hélène broke down and cried. She could not believe there was such hatred in the world.

"Listen," Bernie said when he heard some of these stories. "You think they hate you. They don't. They hate themselves. Also, they're nuts. Also, they like to worship idols, and then spit on them. You know what you should do? You should go away for a while. Take Cat with you. Leave town, and take a break from all this."

"Run away, you mean." Hélène shook her head. "No. I won't do that, Bernie."

"It will get worse, you know," he said gently. "It will ease off gradually—they'll find someone else to torment. And then . . ." He shrugged. "It may get better eventually. But before it gets better, it will get worse."

And, again, he was right. At the end of March, Cassie was grabbed in a supermarket by a woman who screamed that Cassie worked for a whore. She pulled Cassie's hair, and tried to scratch her eyes out. A few days later, Cat was invited to a birthday party, and returned home in tears. The children had heard their parents talking: no one at the party would play with her.

When these things happened, Hélène was so angry she felt she wanted to leave Hollywood for good: all right, if they wanted to pillory her, but not her family, not Cassie, not Cat.

The following week, the first week of April, came her own greatest public humiliation, at the Academy Awards ceremony. Bernie Alberg had begged her not to attend; he knew she would now not win the Oscar, despite the early predictions that she was a leading contender; in such circumstances, he argued, it was better to stay away, to be as invisible as possible.

Obstinately, Hélène would not agree. She had said she would attend, and attend she did, steeling herself to deal both with those who cold-shouldered her, and with those who went out of their way to be kind. *Ellis* was given eight awards, including Best Picture, and Best Director; Hélène, as Bernie had predicted, did not win.

Thad, afterward, was studiously sympathetic, but Hélène had the impression, just the same, that he was not altogether displeased.

"You'll get it for *Ellis II*," he said confidently. "Wait and see. Don't worry."

"I'm not worried, Thad," she answered.

It was the truth. With a sense of surprise, she realized that as she said it. Thad smiled. He did not believe her, of course.

Through all this, there were some people who stood by her. All the people who worked for her were staunchly loyal. So were both Homer, and Milton; Bernie Alberg and his wife did their utmost to help. She received warm letters of support from numerous writers, directors, actors, and producers she had worked with in the past. Simon Scher wrote; Rebecca Stein not only wrote, but came to see her. James Gould sent her a crate of champagne, so she could drink, he said, to the downfall of all liars and gossipmongers. Stephani Sandrelli sent her a large bouquet of white roses, with a small note attached. "I guess you won't want to hear from me," it read, "but I wanted to send my love, and say I know it's *all lies*." Hélène was touched by this; she was touched, too, when Lewis telephoned from San Francisco. Lewis had resolutely refused to speak to a single reporter, and when he telephoned, he was sober.

"I'm sorry this has happened, Hélène," he said stiffly. "You probably won't believe me, but I am. Look, if it would help—if you'd like it—I could come back. Just for a while. Just to see you through this. It might help."

"Lewis, thank you," Hélène said gently. "But I don't want you to do that. There's no need for you to be involved. It's better like this, in the long run. I have to get through it on my own."

There was a silence, then Lewis said quietly, "I thought you might say that. You're probably right. As long as you know—if it gets to be too much—I'm here."

After that, for some reason, she found it easier. The hate mail peaked in mid-April. Then the tabloids found a new victim, in a male star with a drug habit.

Cassie said, "Honey, we're winning. You're winning. Don't let it beat you now. We're almost through the worst—I feel it in my bones."

Hélène said nothing; she was not through the worst. It was more than two months since she had mailed her letter to St. Cloud. And there had still been no answer.

In early May, Madeleine insisted that Hélène should pose with Cat for the birthday photographs which she always took religiously at this time of year. When, a couple of days later, Madeleine gave her one of the prints, Hélène looked at it with a sense of shock. Was this really herself? She looked tired, she thought, and suddenly so much older. She remarked about this to Madeleine, and Madeleine was offended. She became very fierce.

"You are wrong," she said firmly. "Quite wrong. You are beautiful in my picture. Now you do not look so much like a young girl." She paused. *"Maintenant vous êtes devenue une femme. . . ."*

A woman, and not a girl. Hélène looked at her own face in the mirror that night, and she could see what Madeleine meant. It was then, she thought afterward, as she looked at her own reflection, that she finally accepted it: Edouard would not write.

The next day, for the first time since the stories appeared, not a single hate letter was received. Hélène's spirits rose a little. She began to see that she had coped, that she had not given in, nor gone under, nor run away—and that it was this experience, perhaps, that gave her the strength to accept that the silence from Edouard would be permanent.

She began to feel—not optimism exactly—but a certain vitality and determination, and she began to be impatient to work.

Long Division had now been postponed three times. The new start date was May 19, two days after Cat's birthday. On May 18, Gregory Gertz came to see her. Hélène knew, as soon as he came into the room, that something was wrong.

It was mid-afternoon. He sat down opposite her and lit a cigarette nervously. "You may as well know straight out. I've lost the backing from A.I. They're pulling out."

Hélène stared at him.

"Now? Can they do that? At this stage?"

Gertz sighed. "They can do anything at any stage, you know that and so do I. You're never safe until the cameras are rolling, and sometimes not then. There isn't a contract in the world that their lawyers can't unravel if they set their minds to it. They'll lose their development money, of course." He gave a bitter smile. "I don't imagine that will worry them too much. Overall, they'll drop a million, not much more. I've been a fool. I should have made them really lay out up front, the way Angelini does—that way they're in so far, they can't back out. . . ."

He was having difficulty meeting her eyes. Hélène could see the tension in his body, and hear it in his voice. She paused, and then she said, "Why are they doing this? You'd better tell me. Is it because of me?"

Gertz looked at the floor. He shrugged.

"Yes. It is. Stein doesn't want you playing the wife. He's insisting I recast." He looked up. "Hélène, I told him that was unacceptable. I said, no way. I wasn't going to take that kind of thing lying down. I don't want you to think that . . ." He hesitated. He had just extinguished one cigarette, now he lit another.

"The thing is—apart from the contractual situation—this was a personal thing. I asked you to do it, way back. I really wanted you for this part. I haven't forgotten that. . . ."

He paused again, looked down at his hands, which he seemed unable to keep still, and then up again, slightly to one side of Hélène's face.

"Of course, a lot has happened since then. The script's gone through several drafts. It's changed a good deal. I'm not saying it would be impossible to recast. In some ways, I suppose you could say there are other actresses it might suit better. I mean, in your case, we always knew you'd be playing against the grain . . ." He paused. "And it did occur to me, in view of your having separated from Lewis, and all those stories in the press . . . well, that you might feel, now, that this wasn't the part for you. An unsympathetic character. A tough woman. A divorcee . . ."

He could not look at her now. He stared miserably in the direction of a painting on the wall. Hélène leaned forward.

"Greg," she said quietly, "who have you approached? Who have you been sounding out? Fonda? Remick? Someone else?"

Still looking at the floor, he told her. Hélène sighed.

"And what am I supposed to do?"

"Stein thought you might want to ask to be released from your contract."

"I see."

"Don't look like that, Hélène!" He stood up. "I said I'd put it to you, that's all. I told him he might be right. Maybe you felt you didn't want to do it anymore, but that you thought it was too late to back out. . . . I just agreed to *ask*, that's all."

He glanced down at her face, and then began to walk up and down the room.

"Try and see it my way for a moment. Think of the position I'm in. I've been working on this for a year—more. I really need this movie. If *Runaways* is a hit this summer, and then this one works—well, I'll be in a position to call the shots for once. Really do the kind of work I've always wanted to do. And besides, I have responsibilities—to the writers—to the people who helped me develop the script. Obviously—I want you for the wife. But if that means starting all over again, trying to get backing again—well then, obviously, I have to try and look at this thing unemotionally. I just don't know how easy it would be to start over, I just don't know how people are going to react when I say I want you for the wife. I mean—they could see it the same way as Stein does, and then where are we? I have to . . ."

"It's all right, Greg." Hélène stood. "You can do your movie. I'll telephone Milton today and tell him to contact A.I. and get me released. I imagine the whole thing can be arranged very quickly. I'm sure you're eager to start filming. I don't want to feel I might be holding you up."

Color ebbed and flowed in his face. He turned back to her.

"Hélène—Jesus. I don't know what to say. I mean—I can imagine how you feel. . . . If you want time to think this over—I didn't come here meaning to lean on you, I want you to know that. I can see something like this isn't an easy decision. . . ."

"Oh, you're wrong. It's extremely easy. I never work with people I don't respect."

There was a silence. Gertz flushed. "You worked with me on *Runaways*."

"Yes. I respected you then. You were very helpful to me."

"And you don't respect me now?"

"Not really. You're temporizing. You're prevaricating. . . . I'm sure you know that." She turned away coldly.

"Greg—you'd better go."

There was another silence, a longer one this time. She could sense the struggle within him. Then he said, "All right. I accept that. You're not wrong. But that's how it's got to be in this place—in most places, come to that. If you want to get anything done, if you want to work, you have to compromise."

"Oh, this is a compromise, is it?" Hélène turned around and looked him directly in the eyes. "I see. It feels like disloyalty. If you really want to know what it feels like, Greg, I'd say it feels like a kick in the teeth. However—I've had quite a few of those lately. One more doesn't make a great deal of difference—even from you."

He moved toward the door, and Hélène turned away wearily. She looked out the window, at the garden, at the clear blue sky. In the distance, over the city, a jet was banking, coming in to land.

At the door, Gregory Gertz stopped, and turned back.

"There's one thing you didn't ask."

"What's that?"

"You didn't ask why A.I.'s doing this, or Joe Stein."

"I'd have thought it was fairly obvious. Why bother to ask?"

"I would." He paused. "Don't ask me, because I can't tell you. Ask Joe Stein. Better still, ask Thad."

"Thad?" She stared at him. "What would Thad have to do with this?"

"Ask him," he said. "That's all."

She telephoned Thad as soon as Greg Gertz had left. He seemed not in the least surprised to hear from her.

"Yes, well, maybe we ought to have a talk," he said, when she'd told him why she was calling. "I was going to call anyway. I'm pretty tied up today. There's a lot going on. . . ."

"Thad—do you know something about this?"

"I might. Just a little bit. I tell you what." His voice brightened. "Come over tomorrow afternoon, and have tea."

I t was ten P.M., they had finished dinner an hour before, and now the two senators, one Republican, one Democrat, were loosening up. Across the living room of the Georgetown house Partex owned, and kept staffed for occasions such as this, Drew Johnson caught Edouard's eye, and slowly closed one of his own. Edouard glanced at his watch; behind him, Simon Scher rose quietly to his feet, and made for the door.

"I'll go check on the car. It should be here." The door closed softly behind him. Neither senator seemed to notice his departure. Drew, in a diversionary gesture, was plying them with more Chivas Regal.

The two senators were powerful men, and they had been useful. They had lent their weight where it counted most—on certain vital Senate committees—and, in the case of the Democrat, in the White House itself. Now that the controversial merger had taken place, and in precisely the way Drew Johnson and Edouard had planned it, now that Partex was only one remove from being the largest oil company in the United States, Drew was saying thank you. It was something which he did with ebullience, and obvious enjoyment: Drew never forgot his friends, just as he never forgave his enemies.

The senators, both awarded substantial stockholdings in a Partex subsidiary whose connections with its parent company were impossible to trace, were now being rewarded in simpler ways. A fine dinner. Exceptionally fine wines. Chivas Regal. Black market Cuban cigars: "Castro's privates, boys," Drew remarked with a broad smile. "Yessir! Gives me real pleasure every time I light one up. . . ."

Shortly, Edouard knew, it would be time for what Drew called "the entertainment," announced with another wink.

Edouard, who had found the dinner grandiose, and the senators tedious, who was less adept at these occasions than Drew, indeed disliked them, always left at this point. He never participated in such things, but he countenanced them nonetheless, and the fact that he was doing so now filled him with distaste.

It was not simply the question of "the entertainment"—it was far more than that. The disguises of bribery, the necessity for bribery at all, disgusted him, and filled him with self-reproach. When he had been younger, and perhaps more ruthless, he would have argued that the end could justify the means—within reason, of course. But where should the line be drawn? Edouard felt that, in the past few months, he had crossed it, in a way he had never done before. The whole long drawn-out saga of this merger had sapped his energy and, he felt suddenly, his judgment. He sat there, saying nothing, angrily aware that he had compromised his standards in achieving this deal, and he had no one to blame but himself.

"Napalm." The Democrat, one of President Johnson's key men in the Senate, was growing excitable. Throughout dinner he had kept returning to the subject of the war. "Give the Cong a taste of that and it'll be over in six months. Lyndon knows what he's doing."

The Republican senator looked pained; a tightness set in around his mouth.

"History demonstrates . . ." He paused. He had a pinched and pedantic voice, which a liberal quantity of alcohol had failed to slur. "History shows that to be a fallacious argument." He glanced in Edouard's direction. "If you take, for example, the experiences of the French in Indochina, I think you can see that conventional tactics, applied in the face of a highly organized, highly motivated—and let's not fool ourselves, in their terms, they are highly motivated—guerrilla organization—"

"Defeatist talk," the Democrat interrupted him impatiently. "I don't like to listen to talk like that. We've got boys out there in the field. Boys my son's age—younger. Dying for their country . . ."

"My own boy's draft age. You don't need to remind me of that." The Republican took a large swallow of his drink. "Strategically speaking, and I'm talking strategy now, the decision to start bombing is an unnecessary escalation. U.S. involvement should remain marginal. In Saigon—"

"In Saigon they couldn't piss in a pot unless we told them where to aim. In Saigon they wouldn't have a pot to piss *in*, if it weren't for—"

"Boys. Boys."

The Democrat held his liquor less well than the Republican; his color and his voice had risen alarmingly, and Drew was quick to intervene, as Edouard, his face taut with suppressed anger, rose to his feet.

"Boys—we going to get off the subject of politics, or what? I got guests coming aren't going to want to listen to doom and gloom. Come on, now. Break it up. Git off your high horse, fella. Have another cigar. . . ."

The Democrat shrugged. He gave a sheepish grin, reached for the cigar box, and missed. The door opened, and Simon Scher's head appeared around it; he caught Edouard's eye and nodded. "Drew. Senators. If you will forgive me . . ." Edouard was already moving toward the door.

All three men rose to their feet. Drew embraced him; the two senators shook hands without great enthusiasm. It was an embarrassing moment, in which mutual dislike was palpable, and it was saved by a diversion.

From outside came the screech of tires as a car came to a halt; doors slammed; female voices and laughter could be heard. The entertainment had arrived. The two senators exchanged quick glances; Drew grinned; Simon Scher and Edouard slipped quietly out into the hall.

They walked out of the house, and down onto the brick sidewalk. The expensive women walked by: three tall willowy figures, a drift of scent on the night air, laughter and sidelong glances from the top of the steps, then the door closed behind them.

Simon Scher was perhaps tempted; he looked back, sighed, and then turned to the waiting Lincoln. Edouard, who was not tempted, felt nonetheless a sudden aching regret, a nostalgia, a longing for female society. To be with a woman; to touch her skin; to stroke her hair—to talk about something other than the manipulations of power and money—just then he wanted that acutely. It was a long time since he had held a woman—any woman—in his arms.

He stood for a moment, looking up at the empty steps, the closed shutters; then, with a small angry gesture, he, too, climbed into the back of the Partex Lincoln. They were going straight to the airport; since late January he had been in the Middle East, in Canada, and in Japan; the merger negotiations had taken much more time than anticipated. He had been away too long.

"I'm sorry?"
They were driving alongside the Potomac; the surface of the river glittered in the moonlight; Edouard, looking out the windows of the car, became aware that Simon Scher had asked him a question.

"I said—I assume you've not had time to catch up on the developments with Sphere—and there have been a number of developments in the last couple of months."

"No, I haven't had time to catch up on Sphere." Edouard sounded annoyed. "I've hardly thought about Sphere. I saw the results of the Oscars, that's all. What's happening?"

"Well, as I say, there've been developments—quite surprising ones.

I'm not absolutely certain myself quite what's going on. We've been having a lot of problems with Angelini."

"Oh, why?"

"Well, as you know, there is the question of *Ellis II.*"

"And *Ellis III,* you said, if I remember."

"The trilogy. Yes. I was told of that possibility by Hélène Harte, not by Angelini, and when Angelini found out I knew, he was very angry indeed. The problems started then. They've been multiplying since."

"I thought it had been agreed that we would deal with the two sequels separately? There isn't even a script for the third."

"It was agreed. It was also agreed, in principle, that the filming of *Ellis II* would be postponed until later this year. Because Hélène Harte was not free to make the picture in April, which was when Angelini wanted to start. And, as it happens, I thought that was no bad thing. There were a number of aspects of *Ellis II* which were worrying us a good deal. . . ."

"You wanted a budget reworking, if I remember?"

Edouard glanced at him, and Simon Scher sighed. "Correct. We got it completed—finally—after months of stalling from Angelini. It was more than stalling, actually—I would have said he was being deliberately obstructive. He wanted virtual carte blanche, and I think he thought that if he could delay until the Academy Awards ceremony, he'd be in a better bargaining position. He wanted ten million: we got it back to six point seven million, finally, and I still think that's underestimated. There are nonreflected union increases that could take it up to seven, easily. And then there's the question of post-production expenses. Angelini's set himself a very tight schedule: an eighty-five-day shoot; six months from start date to final cut. . . ."

"He's always kept to his schedules before. . . ."

"He's never worked to a schedule like that before. Post-production on *Ellis* took the best part of a year. He sat on that film like a chicken on an egg. And *Ellis II* is longer, and on an even bigger scale. I don't believe in the budget—I still think it's made with a crystal ball—and I don't believe in the schedule either. I would have said that Angelini's Napoleonic tendencies are becoming definitely more marked. Those eight Oscars have gone to his head, for one thing. . . ."

"Simon. You almost sound as if you dislike the man. . . ."

"You know perfectly well that I can't stand him, and never could. However, he makes good films, and the box office returns on *Ellis* are phenomenal for such a serious movie. The fact that when he sits in my office and drinks tea I could cheerfully lace it with strychnine is neither here nor there. . . ." Scher paused. "No, the point is, there's something going on, something I don't like the smell of at all, and I still don't know what it is."

"Tell me."

"Well, by late January we were, in theory, all set to go. We had a budget; we had a shooting schedule; we had a start date—July first. We had everything lined up, with one exception, and Angelini started to stall again."

"What was the exception?"

"Hélène Harte's participation."

There was a silence. Scher waited. The exact reasons for Edouard's involvement with Sphere had never been explained to him, and he had been careful not to ask. But his closeness to Edouard, over a long period of time, had sharpened his instincts: the question of Hélène Harte, he suspected, was key. Which made what he had to stay next all the more difficult.

"Hélène Harte's participation is vital." Edouard's voice had become cold. "Without her, the sequel could not be made." He paused. "Before I left I was given to understand that it was more or less a matter of course."

"Angelini has insisted from the first that she will do it. He's unshakable on that point."

"You mean he's wrong?"

"I mean, we haven't had a chance to find out, because every single time we've tried to move on the Harte contract, he's warned us off. As you know," Scher hesitated, "they have a very close working relationship. And Angelini is protective of her. Very. He more or less informed me that if we took matters into our own hands and went ahead with the contract negotiations, the whole thing might fall through. He insisted it was essential that the timing be absolutely right, and that he would know when that was. In normal circumstances, I would have overruled him. But the last few months have been anything but normal."

Something in his voice made Edouard turn, and look at him closely. He said sharply, "What has happened?"

"Well, her marriage broke up, for one thing. That was his first argument for delay."

"I heard that." Edouard looked away. "That was last year. I saw some newspaper item about the separation."

"This year there have been a number of problems too."

"I saw that she did not win the Oscar. . . ." Edouard glanced at him.

"No, she didn't win." Scher's mouth tightened. He hesitated, and then slid an envelope across the seat. "I thought you probably would not have seen these, so I had a sample prepared. These are just a few of them, and not necessarily the worst examples either, I'm afraid."

Edouard opened the envelope. He switched on the reading light to his rear, and pulled the newspaper out. He looked only at the top copy, and only its front page, then he slid them back into the envelope again.

"I make it a point never to read this kind of thing."

"I know that. I wouldn't normally read them either." Scher's voice was slightly reproachful. "However, I think you should look at them, on the plane perhaps. Then you might understand why I saw Angelini's point. It did not seem a good moment to pressure Hélène Harte about her contract—indeed, to pressure her about anything at all."

"I see."

"I thought he was concerned for her welfare. I assumed that to be the case. . . ."

"And now you have reason to think otherwise?" Edouard looked at him sharply.

"Yes. I'm afraid I do." Scher hesitated. They had reached the airport. He cleared his throat. "I think he was stalling for other reasons entirely. Nothing to do with concern for Hélène Harte. Rather the reverse, in fact."

"Come to the point."

"All right. I now think that he may have—quite deliberately— sabotaged the film she was going to make in the spring. And I also think, though I could be wrong, that he's about to take the whole *Ellis* project to A.I. and Joe Stein."

"You mean—break away from Sphere?"

"Exactly that. With Hélène Harte as part of the package, needless to say."

"How do you know this?"

Scher smiled politely. He said, "I've never seen eye to eye with the husband. But I have become quite friendly with Rebecca Stein. We have a lot in common—she can't stand Angelini, and she's always liked Hélène Harte. More important, she doesn't like to see someone being used."

"And is that what is happening?"

"I'm afraid so." Scher sighed. "Yes. I think it is."

The car came to a halt. There was a silence. Edouard looked out across the lights and the building to the runway, where his plane was waiting for him. For an instant, the years telescoped, and he saw himself with Christian, back at the airport at Plymouth, leaving for Rome, thinking the search was over. He saw again Prince Raphael's library, and its Bellini bronzes. He saw the short plump figure of Thad Angelini, as Angelini explained his film, explained the woman Edouard loved, confident—supremely confident—that he, Angelini, understood and could control her.

A contest had begun then, Edouard knew. It had continued, at a distance, for the past five years, even if Angelini had no inkling of that fact. Angelini was his rival; he had sensed it then, and he felt it acutely now. Not Lewis Sinclair, nor any of the other men Hélène might or might not have been involved with: Angelini.

He had hated him on sight; now, standing on the tarmac, he hated him again. Simon Scher touched his arm. His voice was apologetic.

"Edouard. You'd better tell me what you want me to do."

Edouard looked at his watch. It was almost midnight, May 17—Cat's birthday. He hesitated.

"I have to be in Paris tomorrow. I should have been there today. Is there some way you can stall Angelini, prevent his doing anything decisive about the move to A.I. for at least twenty-four hours?"

Simon Scher smiled his small polite smile. "Well, there are his Napoleonic tendencies. There is his megalomania. . . ."

He left the sentence adrift in the air; he knew Edouard would understand and he did.

"Call him first thing in the morning, his time. Tell him, in view of the European returns on *Ellis*, we're considering revising the budget for the sequel. Upward. Tell him we'll maybe go to the ten million he wanted. Can you find out what Stein might be offering?"

"Possibly."

"Well, try. And up it by two, or three. As much as you think it'll take. But stop him doing anything for the next day—oh, and Simon. Call me as soon as I get to Paris, when I've had a chance to read these. Early afternoon, Paris time."

H e flew into the sunshine of a perfect day. The streets and the boulevards of Paris were filled with people celebrating the spring. The sidewalk cafés were crowded. The Seine glittered; there was a scent of lime blossom in the air. Edouard reached the de Chavigny headquarters shortly before two P.M., Paris time, and asked for black coffee.

Marie-Aude, his unflappable senior secretary, now married, and with her calm unimpaired by the strain of dealing with a husband and two young children in addition to her responsibilities at de Chavigny, brought him the coffee, and looked at him sternly. She was now inclined, when she dared, to be a little bossy; a certain maternalism occasionally crept into her manner. She had now worked for Edouard for eight years, and was not easily put off.

"What day is it?" she said in a firm tone of voice.

Edouard looked at her in exasperation. He relied on her totally; he was extremely fond of her, and of her family; but he did not like to be mothered, though the sparring between them, when she attempted it, amused him.

"It is May eighteenth."

"Oh, you do know . . . I thought you might have forgotten. I thought you might just possibly have lost track. Last night you were in Washington, D.C. Yesterday morning you were in Seattle. The day before that you were in Tokyo. . . ."

"I'm well aware of that. I'm now here."

"You shouldn't be here. You should be in bed. You must have jet lag."

"I do not have jet lag. I never have jet lag. I never felt better. Perhaps, some more coffee?"

His secretary poured the coffee. She passed it across the desk, folded her arms, and frowned. "I have deliberately kept the appointment book clear for this afternoon. . . ."

"Excellent." He paused. "And you may cancel any appointments made for this evening, as well."

She began to smile; a gleam of triumph appeared in her eyes. So, for once he was going to be sensible, she told herself. He would stay here an hour, two hours, just enough to make his usual routine checks, and then he would return to St. Cloud to rest. He would, this impossible man, behave like a normal man, with normal frailties, just for once. . . .

"Because," Edouard went on, seeing the gleam of triumph, "I have a great deal of work to do here. I shan't be leaving before eight. Probably later. Ah . . ." In the outer office a telephone had begun to ring.

"That will be Monsieur Scher. Put him through, would you?"

His secretary sighed. She left the room, put through the call, and then, on her other line, telephoned her mother, who could be relied on to step into the breach whenever necessary. Her mother would do the marketing for her, prepare dinner, put the two little ones to bed. . . .

"*Maman*. A little problem . . . yes, I'm afraid so. I'm not sure. At least until eight . . ."

Her mother sighed. "Nine. Let us be realistic." She paused. "So. He's back then?"

Later that afternoon, Edouard left his offices briefly, was driven to the de Chavigny showrooms, and shown straight to the vaults. There, the possible presents for Catharine were laid out for his inspection, as they were every year. This year, for the first time, he was late in making the inspection, and it was perhaps for this reason, he told himself, that the annual ritual seemed emptier than before. He found himself, for the first time, impatient with it. He was eager to return to his office; he was eager to return to the fray.

Her fifth birthday; five years. He chose the present swiftly and with less deliberation than usual: a necklace of pearls—five strands of them, one for each year. They were placed with the other gifts in the safe. Less than ten minutes had passed.

He was tempted, momentarily, to make a detour to St. Cloud, or to send a messenger to collect the small envelope which he knew would be waiting for him there, in George's safekeeping. The annual note from Madeleine; the annual photograph. He wanted to look at them; he wanted to hold them in his hands—but the need was less strong than it usually was. There was another connection now, stronger than the one which they provided him—all his instincts could sense it. For better or for worse, some crisis was approaching. He returned to his office; no messenger was sent.

At eight, being merciful, he let Marie-Aude leave. At nine, he was still at his desk, at ten, and at eleven. The last hour, between eleven and midnight, seemed to pass very slowly, and Edouard chafed, waiting for Scher's next call. He thought of the newspaper stories he had read somewhere over the Atlantic.

They had sickened him, even though he had thought that he was used, by now, to the techniques of that kind of journalism. The inter-weaving of truth and lies; the guilt by association; the use of innuendo— all those techniques had been used in stories about him in the past. But he had never had to suffer a campaign as vile, or as long-drawn-out as this one, and the fact that this should have happened to Hélène, that he had been unaware of it, that he had done nothing, made him violently angry with himself.

Nor did he understand the maneuverings of the past months, any more than Scher had the previous day. His mind went over all Scher had told him, in the course of the past hours, and it still made no sense to him. The fact that Hélène had refused to commit herself to the sequel of *Ellis* gave him hope. The next moment that hope evaporated: in the circumstances of the past months that refusal could have many explanations. Had Angelini deliberately sabotaged the film Hélène was to have made for A.I.—and if so, why? It was irrelevant to the plans for *Ellis II*: Hélène would simply have completed one film, and then gone on to work with Angelini on the other. . . .

He passed his hand tiredly across his eyes. He knew that the unnatural alertness he had felt earlier was leaving him, and that his mind was exhausted, not working as sharply as he would have liked. Tired-ness also sapped the optimism, the sense of approaching crisis he had felt earlier. He stood up, and poured himself some Armagnac; he drank that, then more black coffee. The crisis, if there was one at all, related to Hélène's work, and not to him. It was a long time since he had allowed himself to do this, but now, sitting at his desk, he looked at the future, and added up the time that had already passed, and asked himself at which point he would finally have to acknowledge that he had been wrong. In six months? A year? He knew it could not be far away, and he thought, dully, as the telephone rang: *Angelini has won.*

"It's worked." Scher sounded exhausted. "I've persuaded him to delay a decision for another twenty-four hours. And I had to go to twelve million to do it. He's playing us off now against Stein. He's seeing Hélène Harte tomorrow afternoon, and he says he'll then get an absolutely firm commitment from her. Once he's got that, he says he'll come back to me. For further discussions."

"Further discussions? You mean he thinks he can push us up from twelve million? He must be mad."

"Edouard. I've always thought he was certifiable. However, in this case it's straightforward bargaining. He probably knows we won't stick to the twelve, and he doesn't care. He'll use it as a negotiating figure with Stein, that's all."

"Stein won't go that high."

"He might."

"If Hélène Harte doesn't commit, Stein won't touch the project either."

"Obviously not. But Angelini says she will. He was quite definite on that point." Scher paused. "I know what you're going to say—and I've already done it. I'm seeing the director of the other movie tomorrow morning. Gregory Gertz. He may be able to tell us something useful, and he almost certainly won't. In which case, there isn't a great deal we can do. Once Hélène Harte commits to *Ellis II*, Angelini holds all the cards. He can take it to Stein, or he can stay with us. And I'm afraid I think she will agree. Angelini has enormous influence over her. In her present dilemma, the chance to work with someone she knows so well, playing a sympathetic character in a sequel to an established hit . . ." He paused. "I'll see if I can dig up anything, but in the meantime, I think we have to face the possibility that we're about to lose Angelini, and her."

There was silence at the other end of the line. After a long pause, Edouard said, stiffly, "Simon—you sound very tired. I'm tired. Go and get some sleep. We'll talk again in the morning. . . ."

Edouard left his office after that, and returned to St. Cloud. It was past one when he reached the house, and all the optimism he had felt earlier had now left him. Everything Simon Scher had said made sense. She would agree to make the sequel, and then the sequel to the sequel. One year; two years; possibly three. No, he knew he could not sustain his own hope and belief that long; five years was already too long to have placed such trust in the delusory. *These fragments I have shored against my being:* the line sprang into his head as he walked through the house; he heard it spoken in Hugo Glendinning's voice. In the schoolroom, when he first heard that poem, and that line, it had meant little to him; he understood it now.

In his study, as always at this time of the year, he found the first early roses; an applewood fire, the scent of which always reminded him of his childhood in the Loire; the decanter of Armagnac; the chair drawn up by the fire. In the bedroom beyond, the lamps lit, the sheets folded back, the bed prepared. In the dressing room beyond, his clothes for the morning would already be laid out. Everything was perfect, and correct, as it always was; he looked around the room, and he loathed the order, and its emptiness.

George was fussing unobtrusively, as he always did. After the ritual inquiries, and the ritual replies, after he had placed Armagnac and glass at Edouard's elbow, and made sure his chair was at the right angle to the fire, he hesitated. Edouard was wishing he would leave, but hadn't the heart to say so. He looked up; George was presenting him with a small silver tray, and on the tray was not one, but two letters. He looked at George; George's face was entirely inscrutable.

"The first arrived in early February, *Monsieur le Baron.* I observed that it bore the usual postmark, and so I kept it to one side. It was somewhat of a dilemma. I felt I should not pass it to your secretary—it is marked 'personal,' you see. And it seemed unwise to try to forward it, when you were traveling as you were. The other arrived on the usual date, just as you had told me, and I retained that, of course. But . . . I really was not sure *what* to do. I hope I did right."

George's face was now less inscrutable; Edouard could see the anxiety in it, and hear it in his voice. He felt a moment's sympathy for George, as well as affection. For George to have to confess to uncertainty, to have been unsure, for once, of the correct course, could not have been easy for him. He hated mistakes, and he was no longer young.

"You did quite the right thing, George. Thank you."

The relief was immediately apparent. George laid the tray carefully on the table, and withdrew.

Edouard looked at the two envelopes. He made himself open Madeleine's first. Two photographs this time: one of Cat, giving tea to an assembly of solemn-faced dolls; one of Cat with Hélène, in a garden. This breaking of the rules snapped his control. He let the photographs fall, and pushed the note from Madeleine to one side, unread. He picked up the other envelope; he did not recognize the writing, and it was difficult to open it, for his hands were suddenly unsteady.

There were several pages: he looked at the address at the head of the paper, and the written words blurred. Almost dropping them in his

sudden agitation, he turned to the last page, and looked at the signature—
the one word he had waited for, so long.

His hands steadied; he turned back to the first page. *Dear Edouard.*
He held the pages to the light, and bent his head. He began to read the
letter Hélène had sent, some three months before.

"The city of the angels. The citadel of dreams."
They stood on the balcony outside Thad's studio room and
looked down over the city of Los Angeles. Thad sighed.

"Come inside. I'm glad you came. I'll make some tea."

Hélène followed him into the room. It was just as before, just as it
always was. She sat down on one of the backless grayish seats; she
looked at the two television sets. On one of them, a black and white
film was playing, and after some minutes, in which she hardly saw the
flickering images at all, she recognized the film: *The Third Man.* In a
fairground in postwar Vienna, Joseph Cotten and Orson Welles were
being carried up on the huge ferris wheel. She looked away. On the
other screen, a Buddhist monk was dousing himself with gasoline. He
sat quietly, cross-legged, his saffron robes neatly tucked in. When the
flames leapt up in a corolla around his body, he did not move.

She stood up and switched the sets off. On the floor next to the sets
was a pile of newspapers and magazines. She could see her own face,
and the familiar headlines, without bending. She turned away, without
comment, and sat down again, just as Thad returned with the tea.

"Oh." He sounded irritated. "You've turned them off. That was
The Third Man. My favorite movie. One of my favorite movies." He
pushed the mug of tea into her hand with a gentle yellow-toothed smile.
"You remember how it ends?"

"I remember how it ends."

"One long take. The camera never moves. It's an incredible sequence." Thad settled himself opposite her. "Looking straight down
the drive at the cemetery. They've just buried Harry Lime. Bare trees—
lime trees, maybe. Joseph Cotten is just standing there, waiting, and
Alida Valli walks down the drive, straight toward him, straight toward
the camera. You think she's going to stop when she gets to him. But she
doesn't. She walks right on by. No one says a word. Just the zither
music. Incredible. I timed it once. He loves her, of course."

"I told you, Thad. I remember it. And I didn't come here to watch
a movie. I came here to talk."

She broke off. Having been looking at the television set in a
longing way, Thad was now looking at the pile of tabloids on the floor.
He was smiling.

"And I also wish those weren't quite so prominent," Hélène said. "Did you have to leave them out? I've seen enough of them these past months."

"Hey, Hélène. I'm sorry, I never thought . . ."

He at once stood up, picked up the bundle of newspapers, and trotted off with them to the far end of the room. He put them on top of the packing cases. He trotted back.

"Was it all true? That stuff?"

"Some of it. He was my father. Thad . . ."

"And you really grew up in that trailer?"

"Yes. Listen . . ."

"And that Major Calvert—the one that just died—he really was your first lover? You got pregnant, and had an abortion, and . . ."

"Thad. For God's sake. Leave it, will you?"

Hélène stood up angrily and turned away. Ned Calvert had died two days after the story came out. At the wheel of his car, on the Orangeburg road, just near where he used to pick her up after school. A coronary. She shut her eyes. Had he known he was going to die soon? Had the story contributed to it? Or had she? She turned back and looked at Thad carefully. She herself had only just heard of his death in a letter sent from Orangeburg to Cassie.

"How did you know he'd died, Thad?"

"I saw an item somewhere this morning. Quite small. I just happened to notice it."

"You must have been paying a great deal of attention then. I didn't know you even read papers like that."

He looked up. "Oh, I read everything about you," he said with a little smile. "I was concerned. Naturally."

"Oh, naturally." She returned to her seat. "So concerned, that when all that was going on, I never heard from you once. Not so much as a telephone call. However . . . I didn't come here to talk about that either. I came here to talk about *Long Division*. You know something about that. . . ."

"Oh, I know all about it."

"Fine. Then you can tell me what you know."

"All right," he said with a surprising meekness. "Not that there's much to tell. You've probably guessed. Or Gertz told you. Stein didn't like all the publicity you were getting. He thought the part of the wife was wrong for you now. It's too hard. It's too unsympathetic. Stein thinks you've got image problems, and he's quite right. Stein thinks you need building up again. And the Gertz movie would have made it worse, not better. So he leaned on Gertz, which is like leaning on a sandcastle, and Gertz collapsed. That's all."

"I see." Hélène looked at him coldly. "You seem very friendly with Joe Stein suddenly. Why's that?"

"Ah, well. Now, that's the interesting part." Thad began to smile. "I'm leaving Sphere. I'm going over to Stein. And I'm taking both the sequels to *Ellis* with me."

"You're what?"

Thad began to look impatient. "I'm going over to Stein. It's simple. I've had enough of Sphere. I've made that company a fortune, and all they do is quibble. They wouldn't accept my budget for *Ellis II;* they wanted to cut me back to six point seven million dollars, which is way too low. And I don't like that man Scher. I don't trust him. He sits there being polite, and thinking he can order me around. Well, he can't, that's all. I needed Sphere once. I don't need them now. And Stein has been trying to get us for years—"

"Did you just say 'us,' Thad?"

"Yes, us. Of course I said us. I can't do *Ellis* without you, can I?"

"I wouldn't have thought so, no."

"Well, I can't. However—that's beside the point. The point is, the minute Sphere found out about Stein, they backed down *quite* a lot. Oh, yes." He rubbed at his beard, and beamed at her. "You know how many times that little prick Scher called me yesterday? Twelve times. I've really got them on the run. They've upped the budget figures to twelve million. Just in the last twenty-four hours."

"Twelve?" Hélène stared at him. "So—are you telling me that you're going to stick with Sphere?"

Thad giggled. "No. I'm not. But they don't know that yet. It's pushed Stein up too. He's gone to thirteen and a half million, and that's more than enough. I'll go with Stein."

"I see." Hélène looked down at her hands. She did begin to see. She saw very clearly. "And Stein wants someone else to play Lise, presumably?"

She knew that would draw him, and it did.

"Someone else?" He blinked. "Don't be stupid. He wants you."

"I thought there was a problem with my image?"

"For *Long Division*, I said. Not for *Ellis*. That's a totally different thing. Lise is a sympathetic character. People associate you with Lise. By the time they see you in the sequel—well, it will just wipe out all this stuff in the papers, that's all. And then, they'll think about you in the old way. Your problems will be over." His smile grew broader. "*Ellis* can do that for you. I can do it for you. No one else can."

Hélène put the mug of tea down on the floor. She said carefully, "Well, it's very good of you, Thad. And I'm sure I ought to feel grateful. But do you know, the odd things is, I don't actually care about my image anymore. And I don't care about what all those people out there think about me, either—"

"That's not true. You have to care," Thad interrupted her. "They made you what you are. You need them. . . ."

"No, I don't. And I don't intend to let them determine who I am, and what I do. Not anymore. Not them, and not you, Thad, either."

She paused. There was a little silence. Thad was watching her intently. She would ask one more question, she thought, although she already knew the answer.

"The sequel," she said. "*Ellis II*. When are you planning on doing it? Is it still July?"

He at once looked relieved.

"Well, we could wait till then, of course. Sure." He leaned forward. "But I thought—we're all ready to go. We can tie up the formalities very fast. You're not doing the Gertz picture now—you're free. So I think we could start filming—oh—at the latest by the middle of June . . . provided we don't have any hitches, of course."

"You will have a hitch." Hélène stood up. "I'm not doing it."

"What?"

"You set it up, didn't you?" She looked down at him coldly. "You set up the whole thing with Joe Stein. You said you'd go over to him and to A.I. on two conditions . . ."

"One condition. More money. That's all. It was a question of getting the budget the movie needed, that's as far as it went. . . ."

"Two conditions. More money, and that I didn't make *Long Division* with Gregory Gertz. That was it, wasn't it, Thad?"

"No, it wasn't. I had nothing to do with that. That's a crazy idea. It was a question of timing, a question of image, I already told you. . . ."

"Yes. You already told me, and I don't believe you. I know you too well, Thad. I've begun to see how you operate. Although why, in God's name, it should matter to you that I was doing that film, I don't know. . . ."

"I wanted you to do *Ellis II*. I wrote it for you. . . ." His voice had become sulky. He was now standing, shifting from foot to foot.

"Thad—can't you see that doesn't make any difference? By the time you gave me that script I had already more than half decided to do the other movie. . . ."

"You'd already made one film with him. Why did you need to make another?" He hesitated. "Anyway. I don't like Gertz. I despise him. I made you a star, and now he's trying to exploit that. He was stealing you, that's all."

"I won't have you do this, Thad. I will not have you trying to run my life. . . ."

Hélène turned angrily away. She crossed to the balcony doors, and Thad hastened after her.

"What are you doing?"

"Thad, I'm going."

"No, wait . . ." He reached up and touched her arm. Hélène hated him to touch her, and she flinched. Thad immediately dropped his hand.

"Don't go. Stay just a moment. There's something I have to show you. Please, Hélène. Stay awhile. And I'll tell you. I swear I will. I'll tell you everything."

Hélène hesitated. To her surprise, Thad hurried across the room and opened a door on the far side. Through it, she could glimpse a landing, and a flight of stairs leading down.

"Please. Come with me. It won't take long."

"Thad—I should get back, anyway. I promised Cat I wouldn't be long. . . ."

"Five minutes. Really."

He went out onto the landing, and after a pause, Hélène followed him. She felt reluctant, and also, she realized, a little fearful—which was why she had mentioned Cat. The excuse was untrue; Cat was out all afternoon, with Cassie.

She stopped at the top of the stairs. Thad was already halfway down them. He looked up at her.

"Please," he said again. "It's not much to ask, is it? I want you to understand. I want to explain."

Hélène began to go down the stairs, and Thad smiled. He hurried on ahead of her, and Hélène, despite her uneasiness, looked around her curiously.

There was little to see. The stairs were uncarpeted; their rails, and the walls, were painted white. At the foot of the stairs there was a long corridor, flanked with closed doors, and lit by a window at each end. On both the windows were white shades, fully lowered. The corridor smelled of disinfectant and damp.

"Through here."

Thad padded along the corridor to the third door. He stopped, and again waited for Hélène to catch up with him. He smoothed down the lapels of his black suit, and glanced up at her, his head a little on one side, a small smile on his lips.

"This is my room. Where I work. I think you'll like it. You ought to."

He reached for the key, turned it, and pushed the door back with a flourish. Then he stepped back to allow Hélène to enter. She took a step forward, faltered, and came to a halt. She stared at the room in silence. Behind her, Thad gave a high nervous giggle.

The room was not large, and it resembled a cell. There was one window, to which the white shade was nailed, and then sealed with tape. There was one narrow single bed, neatly made; one desk, its surface completely bare, and one chair. Apart from that, the room was empty, except for the photographs, and they were everywhere.

They covered the ceiling, all four walls, and the floor; there were thousands of them. Some had been cut from newspapers or magazines, other were publicity stills from the films she had made with Thad. Thousands of images of herself, some large, some small; some in color, some in black and white. In every picture she was alone, and any other person with her had been neatly cut out. It had been carefully and painstakingly assembled, this whole crazy collage; each picture exactly joined the one next to it, and the finished surfaces had been varnished over, so they shone. In the center of the floor, almost beneath her feet, was the poster of her they had used for *Short Cut;* a girl in a white dress, *herself* in a white dress, carefully pasted to the floor. It was a little dusty. Thad bent and brushed at it fussily. Then he straightened up and smiled proudly.

"I've started on the room next door now," he said. "I do the ceiling first, then the walls, then the floor."

"Thad, *why?*"

Hélène swung around to him, her eyes wide with disbelief and shock. There was a silence. Thad sighed.

"Don't you like it? I thought you would."

"Thad, it's not that . . ." Hélène felt a terrible ache of pity tighten around her heart. All her anger had gone. She tried to find some words that would not hurt him, but nothing seemed right, nothing seemed possible.

"Maybe you see now." Thad drew in a small shuddery breath. "I couldn't let you do the Gertz movie. It wasn't right for you. You shouldn't be working with Gertz. You should be working with me. So, yes—it's true. I went to Joe Stein, and I offered him a deal. He bought it right away. I knew he would. Directors like Gertz are nothing. Hollywood is full of men like Gregory Gertz. A little talent; some energy; some brains. But he's not an *artist,* Hélène. He's not like me."

He stopped for a moment, breathing quickly, his eyes intent on hers.

"I thought you'd know, when you saw the dedication in the script I gave you. I wrote the date, and everything. The date we met."

"I know you did, Thad. But . . ."

"I just couldn't understand then. How you could see that, and read the script, and then not do it. It didn't make any sense. It hurt me. It was like—it was like you didn't love me."

"Thad—look. We're friends, and we've worked together, but . . ."

"We're not friends. You shouldn't say that. You know it's not true."
He moved slightly, so that he was blocking the door. "I don't want to
use the word *love*. It's a dumb word. People say *love*, and they mean *sex*.
I don't mean that. I'm not interested in that. I don't want to kiss you. I
don't want to touch you—" He broke off and gave a small giggle. "I
touch your pictures, at night sometimes. That's different. And I'd like
to film you—you know, if we were on our own. . . ." He gave a sudden
shiver, and twisted away from her. "I'd like to film you now. I wish . . .
Hélène, let me get my camera. Please, let me . . ."

"Thad—no."

He stopped. He turned around again and tilted his head on one
side, looking up at her.

"Tell me you understand. I know you do. I know you always have.
But I'd like to hear you say it, just once."

"Say what, Thad?"

"Well, we're bound together, you and I. I knew it the first time I
saw you. We're united. We always have been, and we always will be.
Even when we're dead—long after we're dead—people will look at the
movies we made together, and they'll *know*. It's just like being married—
only better than that. Don't you see?"

There was a silence, while they looked at each other. Hélène was
beginning to feel afraid, and she hoped Thad could not see that. After a
while, when he said nothing more, and did not move, she drew in her
breath to steady herself.

"Thad, that isn't true, you know," she said gently. "I can see that
you believe what you say, but you have to understand. I don't feel that,
and I never realized that you felt it either. I respect your work. But I
don't love you, Thad. I don't feel bound to you. And . . ." She hesitated. "And you shouldn't have done what you did, Thad, whatever the
reason. Even loving someone doesn't give you the right to try and
control another person's life."

He was silent for a moment, looking at her. In the dim light of the
room, his glasses obscured the expression in his eyes, and his face
showed no emotion. He nodded once or twice, that was all, then he
reached across and opened one of the drawers of his desk. He took
out a large pair of scissors, pushed the drawer shut, and then flexed the
scissors, open and shut, in the air. He said: "Do you like my suit?"

Hélène's throat felt dry and tight. She tried not to look at the
scissors. She said, in a quiet voice, "It's the same as all your other suits,
Thad."

"Yes. The same. I copied the idea from someone I met once. It
seemed like a good idea." He took a step forward. "Don't move."

Hélène had backed away slightly. The wall and the window were
behind her; the bed was to her right, hemming her in; Thad was still

blocking the path to the door. In a moment, she told herself, in a moment, Thad would stop smiling, and he would put down those scissors, and then they would both leave this horrible insane room, and everything would be all right. . . .

He was in front of her now. He lifted the scissors and stroked them against her face. Hélène forced herself to keep still.

"Thad," she said carefully. "Put those down."

"In a minute. Keep still."

He lifted his free hand, and with a surprising delicacy, traced the outline of her face. His hand trembled a little. He raised it higher, and stroked her hair, just once. "You're afraid," he said. "Don't be. You're beautiful. You're the most beautiful thing I've ever seen. You have beautiful eyes, and beautiful hair. . . ."

The scissors were pointing at her eyes. On Thad's face there was an expression of absolute concentration. Hélène wanted to scream, and was afraid to scream. She shut her eyes and twisted her face away. She felt the cold metal of the scissors glance against her throat. Then she felt Thad hold her neck, and the scissors cut.

She opened her eyes. In his hands, Thad held one long pale lock of her hair. He looked at it. He wound it around his finger. He expelled his breath in an unsteady sigh. Then he looked up at her once more, and began to smile, his ordinary, his amiable smile.

"I'll keep this. Thank you."

He trotted across to the desk and put the scissors and the hair in one of the drawers.

"It's all right. I'm sorry if I frightened you. I just felt I'd like to keep this. I do understand—what you said. And that's all right. You're not ready. You haven't realized it yet—that we belong together. You will one day." He began to make humming noises; he began to chew on his beard.

"I might do some work now. So if you still want to go . . ."

Hélène moved quickly to the door. Thad had opened another drawer and was rummaging around among some papers, his manner exactly as always. Just as she reached the door, he looked up and said, "You won't do *Ellis*—you won't change your mind?"

"Is that why you brought me down here—to change my mind?"

"I thought it might help."

"No, Thad."

She waited for the arguments, the renewed pleas. None came.

"Oh, well. That's all right." He sounded unconcerned. "You're angry with me now. It's not the moment. It will keep. Everything will keep. . . ."

"Thad—I'm not going to change my mind about this, now more than ever."

"Aren't you?" He smiled. "God makes movies, you know. They're full of patterns, just like mine. A beautiful dance, with intricate steps. You can't predict the end of my movies. And you can't predict the future. How do you know you won't change your mind—a year from now? Two years? Ten?"

Hélène stared at him. "Thad—you don't even believe in God. And I can't believe you'd wait ten years to make *Ellis* with me. . . ."

"Oh, I might. I'm very patient. Not ten maybe. We'll see." He looked down at his watch. "Maybe I won't work now. Maybe I'll catch the end of *The Third Man*. I'll come up with you."

The moment they were back in the studio, Thad settled himself on one of the grayish seats. A television set flickered into life. Hélène crossed to the balcony doors. Thad did not even look up.

On the screen, the sequence Thad had described earlier was just beginning. Hélène wondered then, suspiciously, if he had purposely timed it like that: it was possible—Thad was capable of anything. Had he meant any of the things he had said? At the time, she had not doubted him for a second, but now she was not so sure: it could just as easily have been a device on Thad's part, one more way of persuading her.

She turned back to watch the screen. Alida Valli was about to begin that long final walk: walking out of the frame, walking out of someone's life. Hélène felt the most extraordinary sense of exhilaration grip her: she could not wait to leave this house; she could not wait to leave Thad.

"Good-bye, Thad," she said.

Thad lifted one pink hand in a vague wave. He did not turn around.

Hélène stepped out onto the balcony; she took a deep breath of the air; she looked out over the bowl of the valley and the city below, and she thought: *I'm free. I don't have to stay here. I don't have to do a film. I don't have to go home to a man I should never have married. I can go anywhere, and do anything I like.* There was the future, open and empty, for the first time in five years. She walked quickly to the top of the steps. There, one last time, she looked back. Alida Valli was walking down the cemetery road; Joseph Cotten was waiting in vain, and Thad, hunched over his watch, was timing the take.

W alking out of the frame; walking out of someone's life. She stopped by her car, which was parked at the top of Thad's long snaking driveway. It was a black Mulliner Bentley Continental, with pale beige upholstery of hide; a rare car, and one unique in Hollywood. It had been chosen, like so many of the things she owned, because it reminded her of Edouard; not simply because it was beautiful in itself, or because she loved to drive it—but because, when she drove it, Edouard felt close.

She climbed into the car, impatient with herself at the thought, and accelerated down the driveway. As she started to pull out onto the narrow road that wound down the canyon through the hills, she stopped. Parked to one side of the road was a Ford; standing by the Ford, camera poised, was a thin, seedy-looking man, with a narrow ferret's face; the man who had taken her photograph at Forest Lawn; the man who had, these past months, followed her most persistently. She heard his camera click; she wrenched on the handbrake, and climbed out. The thin man was already backing away in the direction of the Ford; Hélène advanced on him, and he stopped. She was a head taller than he; he squinted up at her nervously. She held out her hand.

"Give me that camera."

He backed off until he was half-pinned against the rear of the Ford.

"Don't start anything. I didn't mean any trouble. This is my job. I . . ."

"I said, give me that camera."

He clutched it more tightly. His voice rose in a whine. "Listen. Just don't cause trouble. You can't do this. There's no law against . . ."

Hélène reached out suddenly, taking him by surprise. She wrenched the camera out of his grasp, and stepped back, so she stood by the edge of the road. To her left, there was a sheer drop of several hundred feet. The thin man came after her, hesitated, and stopped. Hélène opened the camera, and pulled out the film. She held it up to the light, and then tossed it over the edge, and into the undergrowth. Then she handed him the camera, turned, and without another word, climbed back into the Bentley, and accelerated away. The thin man just stood there, sweating and trembling, staring after her.

She drove fast then, and recklessly, taking the winding road at high speed. Half a mile from her own house, she slammed on the brakes; the car skidded to a halt.

She sat there, her breath coming quickly, on the narrow empty road, under an unreal Technicolor-blue sky. Then, lifting her hand, she looked at the engagement ring she still wore, the famous diamond. She took it off. She took her wedding ring off. She held them both for a moment, glinting between her fingers, and then, reaching back her arm, she hurled them away from her with all her force. They spun up, glittering, and then tumbled out of sight in the undergrowth of the hillside.

Without a second look, she pulled away again, and drove the rest of the way more slowly.

The house, when she reached it, was quiet. She hurried inside, calling to Cat, and then stopped, remembering. Of course, Cat was not there, nor Cassie; they would not be back for a while. She stopped in the middle of the hall, feeling, through the succession of contrary emotions, a sudden and acute loneliness. Wave after wave of it eddied through her body, and because she would not give in to it, she did as she had done as a child—she stood still, fighting it, bleakly willing it to go away.

When she was sure she was in control of herself once more, she crossed to the door of the living room. The heels of her shoes tapped and echoed on the old tile floor. She turned the handle, and pushed the door back, thinking, as she did so, that she and Cat would leave this house, live somewhere else: it was too full of ghosts now, not only Ingrid Nilsson's, but also her own.

Across the room, directly facing her, a man was sitting in a chair. He must have heard her footsteps, because his attitude was listening and intent. He was leaning forward, his hands gripping the arms of the chair, his face lifted toward the door. Hélène stopped. Across the room, Edouard rose silently to his feet.

They both stood still, looking at each other. The shock was so acute that Hélène could not have moved, or spoken. She stared at him, and the silence seemed to her clamorous, full of energy. Edouard lifted his hand, and then let it fall.

A tall, dark-haired man, in a black suit; the hand he had lifted was not steady. With the clarity of shock, she saw him for a moment distantly and with great precision, someone she had always known, someone she had never met before. She noted the features of his face as she might have done a stranger's: the hair, so; the planes of nose and cheek, so; the line of the mouth, so.

Words, phrases and sentences moved into her mind, and out of it, leaving a vacancy. The room blurred, and then came sharply into focus, and as it did so she felt an absolute joy, more powerful than any words. It made her thoughts grow still; it made the room grow still. She felt it arc across the space that divided them, and touch him, a current of astonishing force. It was so powerful, this irresistible, this crazy and idiotic joy which she felt, that she began to smile—she had to smile— and it seemed to affect him in the same way also, because at the same instant his eyes lit, and he smiled back at her.

He took one step forward, and then stopped, his face growing still once more. The directness, the reticence, the desire to disguise strong emotion, and the negligent ease of manner he adopted to do so—she saw all those qualities which she had loved, and recognized them, at that instant.

Edouard's face was not calm, but when he spoke, his voice was perfectly level.

"I told myself that you would write, one day. Or that I would pick up a telephone and hear your voice. Or walk into a room and find you waiting for me. I told myself that, every day, for five years. . . ."

"But I wrote. Edouard—I did write. . . ." She started toward him, and then stopped.

"I know you did. And as soon as I received the letter, I came. You must have known that I would. You can't have doubted that—not for one second." He stopped. "Tell me you knew that—tell me. . . ."

"Oh, I knew. I always knew." She lifted her eyes to his, though she could hardly see him for a sudden dazzle and blindness. "I knew—and then I thought . . ."

"I know about the thoughts," he said, and a note of self-mockery entered his voice, quite at odds with the expression in his eyes. "And they don't count. They don't matter." He stopped. "Do you think you could come a little closer?" Hélène moved.

"Closer still?"

She took one more step. They stood very close, looking at each other. Time stopped; the world stopped; then he put his arms around her, and held her, tightly, against the beating of his heart.

"Did you know that I searched for you? Did you know that?"

It was later, much later, and Edouard, who had spent the long flight from Paris planning all the things he would say, and in what order, now found that he could remember none of them. They flew into his mind with feverish speed, and then out again, and he knew that what he was saying, all the things he was trying to tell her, were coming out in all the wrong way, backward, and were probably bewildering her—but he did not care in the least. One moment he was talking about last week, the next about last year. He had told her about Madeleine, and Anne Kneale—yes, he had—but he had not yet told her about the photographs of Cat, or the presents he had stored away for the day when Hélène and his daughter came back; and he had not told her about the times when he had returned to the little church of St. Julien le Pauvre; or the time at St. Tropez, when he had stood there on the beach, looking out to sea, so close to losing all hope, and then had felt it come back to him. They had been sitting side by side; then he had leapt to his feet, and begun pacing back and forth, the words tumbling out confusingly and passionately. Now, because he found it impossible, intolerable, not to be close to her, he came back again, and sat down again, and took her hands in his.

Hélène was looking at him, her eyes alight with happiness. She, too, had been trying to speak, and to explain—and her account was no more ordered than his own: they both began, broke off, began again, and—

realizing this at the same moment—they both smiled. Hélène pressed her hands over her ears.

"Oh, Edouard, you go too fast. I can't think. It's so much time, and now it feels like no time at all. I feel as if you were here always. . . ."

"I was here always, in a sense. . . ."

"I feel as if I left the Loire yesterday." She sighed, and reached for his hand. "Edouard—I went creeping out of your house, and it was hateful. I wanted to stop. I wanted to write you a note. I wanted to explain, and I was too frightened to explain. . . ."

"My darling. I wish you hadn't felt that. Even if it had not been my child—what did you think I would have done if you'd told me?"

"I don't know." She shook her head. "Edouard—I don't know. I thought you would stop loving me, I suppose."

"Never think that." He drew her into his arms. "It wasn't possible then. It never will be . . ." He paused, and tilted her face gently to his. "You didn't know that I looked for you—then?"

Her eyes widened.

"You looked for me? Then, when I left the Loire? But . . ."

Taking her hands, Edouard explained. He told her how he had traced her, how he had traveled to Rome. He told her about the conversation with Thad.

She listened quietly, her face growing still. When he had finished, the color rushed into her face, and she sprang to her feet.

"I *hate* Thad," she cried with sudden agitation. "I hate him. He's evil. He never once told me that. He tries to manipulate people—he tries to make up their lives for them, as if they were part of one of his films. . . ."

She stopped, and looked at Edouard, and her face grew calmer. She turned back to him, and sat down again, and reached for his hand.

"Thad is a fool," she said simply. "All those things he said to you—he was so wrong. You see—Thad's right about all the little things of life, and wrong about all the large ones. I realized that in the end. You can see it in his work, it's there, in his films."

Edouard looked at her steadily.

"Was he wrong—about you?"

"He was wrong. I promise you he was wrong." She hesitated. "Do you remember the first night you took me back with you to St. Cloud?"

"I think I recall it, yes." Edouard smiled.

"I was very earnest, I know. But do you remember—I said I would have stayed with you right away, the moment we met?"

"I remember."

"Well, that was *always* true." She leaned toward him. "If you had found me in Rome, and asked me to come back—if you had come to me at any time in the past five years, and had asked me—I would have come. I couldn't have refused you—not if I'd known you wanted me. There it is." She hesitated.

"Edouard—I tried not to love you. I tried very hard. I was trying to be Lewis's wife, and it seemed so wrong and so treacherous to go on thinking of you." She shook her head sadly. "I used to set myself stupid goals. I would say—I will not think of Edouard for a whole day. For two days . . ."

"And did you succeed?" Edouard asked gently.

"No. I didn't succeed. I thought I wanted to, because I could see Lewis knew, and I could see it made him unhappy. But the truth of it was—even when I tried to drive it out, like an exorcism, it wouldn't go. Because I didn't want it to go, not really. I wanted it there. I felt that if—if I killed that love off, I would have killed myself off too—" She broke off, and with a little cry, clasped his hand more tightly.

"Oh, Edouard—why didn't you come to me? Why didn't you write, or telephone, or—"

"I wanted to do that more than anything in the world, Hélène, I promise you. But I thought . . . I must wait. You see, sometimes I was so certain that you couldn't forget. And I thought then, that if I left you free, if you achieved all the things you seemed to want to achieve, then—one day—as a free choice, you would come to me, or write to me. . . ." He paused. "Those were the better times. When I believed that."

"And the other times—what about those?"

"Ah, those. I'd prefer to forget those. There were so many reasons—it could all have been a delusion. I knew that. You were married to someone else—you might have been perfectly happy. I was even told once, by someone who met you both, that you were. I couldn't understand about Cat—how you could do that. Unless you wanted to turn your back on me, unless it had been just a trivial thing, an episode you'd forgotten." He paused. "Unless you were not you, but a quite different woman. And whenever I was about to convince myself of that, with a thousand arguments, all of them very sensible, very rational—I would stop. Because I could not believe . . . I *knew* I had not been wrong." He stopped.

Hélène, who had seen the pain in his eyes, had bent her head. He lifted her face to his.

"You telephoned me, didn't you?" he said gently. "I knew that it was you. Three rings and then silence. Only—once, you did not hang up. Did you hear me say your name?"

"Yes."

"And did you know that I once did the same thing?"

"Oh, Edouard. I knew. And then I persuaded myself I was wrong. . . ."

"And when you were in Paris—did you ever go back, to the place where we met?"

"Yes, once. I could feel you there."

"I felt you there too. Many times."

They looked at each other. Edouard lifted his hand, and gently traced the lines of her face. With a sudden swift gesture, Hélène caught his hand, and pressed her lips against it.

"All that time. Five whole years." She hesitated, and then looked up at him with a quick vehemence. "Edouard—I was such a *child*. Younger than I had told you. There was such a gap of experience between us then—not age, that doesn't matter—but experience. Think of all the things you had done, all the things you had been. And I—I hardly knew who I was. I hadn't the courage to be myself then. I told lies—I lied to you. It *hurts* me to think how I lied. . . ."

"My darling, I understand the reasons for that."

"No, listen. Look, Edouard, I'm different now. You can even see it in my face. See—I have lines. Here, and here, and here." She touched her face, her expression very serious, and Edouard, who remembered these moments of grave and impassioned earnestness, and who loved her for them, bent forward, and gently kissed the lines.

"I'm proud of those lines, Edouard. I'm *glad* they're there. Because now—I'm not a child anymore. I'm closer to you. I feel closer to you. . . ."

She broke off, and Edouard took her two hands between his. He began speaking very carefully.

"In two day's time—listen—the SS *France* sails from New York. I've made reservations for you, for me, for Cat and for Madeleine, and also for Cassie, if she would like to come."

"Edouard . . ."

"They were made as soon as I read your letter. Well, as soon as the shipping office opened the next day . . ." He smiled. "If you don't want to come back to France, we'll go somewhere else. I don't care where. Anywhere. But I will not live without you again. I cannot live without you again. And—" He paused.

"You cannot remain married to Lewis."

"I never was married to Lewis. I couldn't be." She looked away. "Edouard . . ."

"You are not going to argue. You are going to choose. Hélène . . ." He broke off, his calm deserting him. "We have this one life. We've lost five years of it."

"I've already chosen." She spoke so quietly, her head bent, that for an instant Edouard did not catch her words. Then she looked up, and he saw the affirmation in her eyes.

"Yes?"

"Yes. I love you, Edouard. Oh, I love you so much. . . ."

She put her arms around his neck, with that quick impulsiveness which he had always loved. Edouard bent his head and kissed her.

It was only later, when her mind was filled with a thousand things she wanted to say to him, that she suddenly remembered one that was less pleasant to recall. She stood up, opened a drawer, and took out from it a bundle of newspaper clippings.

"I had forgotten. You've been away. You won't have seen these. You have to see them. Oh, Edouard—I want you to know that I wrote to you before this happened, before any of it began. But I can't let you decide now, not without looking at these."

"Give them to me."

He stood up and held out his hand. Hélène passed the newspapers to him. Edouard did not look at them.

"I've already seen them—some of them. I know precisely how little is true. I know when you wrote, and I know when this began. Hélène, stop this." He turned and threw the newspapers into the fireplace, then bent and set a match to them. He straightened up, and looked at her, a smile beginning on his lips.

"I'm perfectly used to scandal. And no doubt when we sail together from New York, we shall create a great deal more."

"Edouard . . ."

"Forget all that. None of it is important. Here."

She had moved toward him. Now he reached into his pocket and drew something out.

"You forgot this once."

He opened his hand; lying in his palm was a square-cut diamond ring, the ring he had once given her.

Hélène looked at it silently.

Edouard took her hand.

"Put it on."

She hesitated only for a moment, then she picked up the ring and slid it on her finger.

Edouard took her hand in his. Their eyes met.

"I knew," she said just as she had said to him once before.

"*We* knew," he corrected her.

Hélène lifted her hand, and the diamond struck the light. She began to say something, stopped because there was no need for words, stopped for the quick bright certainty in her mind, and stopped because Edouard, impatient with words, had caught her to him.

Edouard met his daughter for the first time, later that day. The little girl of the photographs, whose face was a tiny mirror-image of his own.

She burst into the room in which they were sitting, full of excitement about her expedition that afternoon.

She came to a halt when she saw the stranger; Edouard got to his feet gravely and courteously. An introduction was performed. Cat shook hands; she retreated to a chair, sat down quietly, and for some while said nothing. She swung her legs back and forth, occasionally glancing across at her mother, then turning back to look at the man again with that still careful gaze.

Edouard was reminded of Grégoire; he felt that he was being judged, which made him tense, and Hélène, who could sense this, watched him with admiration—no one else would have known. He talked to Cat seriously, as he might have to another grown-up, as he had to Grégoire. She listened; she answered him, hesitantly at first, then more spontaneously. Then, suddenly, as children do, she decided to accept him. She stood up and looked at him.

"Have you seen the garden? Would you like to see the garden? I'll show you if you like. And then, I'll show you my room. I have a French book in my room. Madeleine gave it to me."

"I should like that very much."

Edouard rose; he and Hélène followed her. They toured the garden exhaustively; they followed Cat up the stairs to her room. There, Edouard sat down on the small bed. He was shown the French book, and all the English books. Hélène stood a little way off, and watched them quietly, two dark heads, bent over the pages.

"I know some French words." Cat looked up. "Madeleine taught me them. And how to say a French *r*, like a growl. I can do that sometimes." She paused, looking at him. "Do you know Madeleine too, or just my mother?"

"Yes. I do. I knew Madeleine—oh, a long time ago. Before she was grown up. And I knew her family."

This seemed to please Cat. She smiled, as if quite sure now that Edouard's credentials were in order.

"And do you live in France all the time, when you're not traveling?"

"I have a house near Paris. And one in the country, near where Madeleine used to live. And one by the sea." He paused. "If you liked, you could come and visit them."

"Could I?" Two round patches of pink appeared in her cheeks. "With my mother?"

"But of course. And Madeleine and Cassie if you liked."

On the rare occasions when Cat had joined Hélène on location, or had gone away with Hélène and Lewis for a vacation, she had conceived a passion for airplanes. Now her eyes widened.

"Could we fly?"

"We could. Or perhaps we could go on a ship. A very big ship. You'd have your own room on it. . . ." Edouard, who was eager to make this alternative tempting, felt his inspiration failing. "With—with round windows. They're called portholes."

"And bunks," Hélène said quickly.

Cat's color became hectic. "Bunks? Like you have in trailers? Oh, *yes!*"

"That's decided then. We shall do it. We shall go in my airplane to New York, and then take a ship."

"When? When? Tomorrow?"

"The day after tomorrow." Seeing a trace of his own impatience in his daughter's face, he began to smile. He observed that she did not mention Lewis Sinclair, and that the possibility of his joining this expedition did not seem to occur to her. This increased his sense of optimism. When Cat had disappeared to bed, and Hélène cried, he pressed her hand. It would be all right, he told her. It would all work out—gently, gradually. They had time, after all; so much time.

E douard returned to the house the next morning; he was introduced to Cassie. Cassie, clearly, already knew something of the story, perhaps from Hélène, perhaps from Madeleine. Edouard had the impression that, as she surveyed him, she was now filling in the rest of the details for herself. Edouard, amused by her stern and searching glance, attempted to explain about the *France*.

"Where Hélène goes, I go. Where she stays, I stay." Cassie drew herself up to her full height, as if daring him to challenge this statement. "You got her, you got me, I reckon."

Edouard professed himself delighted. He looked forward to the confrontation between George and this plainspoken woman; Cassie, for her part, was impressed, and also charmed. She had no intention of letting Edouard see that yet, however. *Early days,* she said to herself; *early days.*

"And no French," she said, fixing him with a gimlet glance. "Can't twist my tongue 'round it, never could. Too old to start now. And what's more—you've hardly left us any time for proper packing."

She swept off, arms full of swathes of tissue paper. Edouard, unused to a household in which women were packing in earnest, retreated, a little bemused. He entertained Cat, with stories and books. She showed him her paintings. Then, that afternoon, when she was whisked away, full of protests, by Madeleine, he spent two idyllic hours with Hélène, who was—at one and the same time—exhibiting the symptoms of a woman in love, and a woman who was frantically and distractedly trying to organize her departure. Edouard enjoyed all this. He lounged in a chair, surrounded by boxes and suitcases, and marveled whenever she blushed. He found it charming when she could not decide between one dress and another, when she leaned back on her heels and sighed, as if all decisions were beyond her.

"My darling," he said, his eyes resting lazily upon her, "take them all. Or leave them all behind and I'll buy you new ones. It doesn't matter. . . ."

Their eyes met. They were in her bedroom, and a certain tense awareness of that became apparent to them both.

"Not here. Not now . . ." Edouard said reluctantly, his lips against her hair. Moments later the tension was forgotten, and it was simply delightful to be a man, surrounded by femininity—by lace and petticoats and gloves and hats—by seriousness one moment, and by the most charming frivolity the next.

Hélène found herself in a state of ecstasy and terror. Everything was happening too fast, and not fast enough. On the one hand, she felt a perplexing desire to do nothing at all; simply to look at Edouard, or to hear his voice, or to touch his hand, seemed fulfillment enough. It had been a very long time since she had experienced that particular havoc of the senses, and that particular state of dazed bliss. She was inclined to indulge it; she was not entirely capable of controlling it; when she recognized that something similarly irrational was happening to Edouard, apparently the most controlled and rational of men, and that she could provoke it with a word or a glance, she found she wanted to provoke it, wanted it very much. The swiftness of his reaction, and the reassurance that it gave her—this was tempting. She did not give packing her undivided attention; she was inclined to flirt.

On the other hand, breaking through the delightful daze of mind and senses, there were other, less seductive imperatives. She could not, she said, simply depart. . . . There were people who must be informed. Here Edouard was no help at all. He saw no reason why not. He was by then in a state of such exaltation and impatience that he was finding it difficult to believe that such a person as Lewis Sinclair existed—and as for agents, lawyers, secretaries, accountants, they had vanished from the face of the earth, and they had, he noted with particular pleasure, taken Thaddeus Angelini with them.

Hélène, fighting the pleasurable daze, was adamant.

"Inform them then . . ." Edouard said with an amused and magisterial wave of the hand. He frowned. "Perhaps I should go?" This possibility appalled him. Luckily, it seemed to appall Hélène too. No, she said; he must stay. She would do it quickly, quickly.

And so she made a chain of telephone calls, sitting at the desk in her office, and Edouard dutifully sat opposite her, in an upright chair, and piled paper clips into a mountain, knocked it over, and then piled it up again. He looked at the ledgers and the files and the evidence of Hélène's business life; he listened to her voice as it managed to give the minimum information necessary with the maximum calm; he looked at the way the light shone on her hair, and the way her fingers twisted and untwisted the cord of the telephone.

The call to Thad Angelini was particularly brief—Angelini showed no interest in Hélène's plans. This surprised Edouard somewhat, but he was in no frame of mind to consider it further. Only the call to Lewis took any length of time, and that was because he was obviously having difficulty understanding what Hélène was saying. She had to repeat the simplest phrases, and when she eventually replaced the receiver, Edouard could see her distress.

"He'd taken something. Some pills, perhaps. I don't know." She gave a little helpless gesture of the hand. "He wasn't really listening."

Edouard at once sobered; his mind sharpened. At that moment, when he admitted to himself for the first time exactly how jealous he had been of this man, the jealousy suddenly departed. Lewis Sinclair had loved Hélène, after all; and for an instant Edouard felt a kinship with him, and an understanding of him, which he had never had before.

He felt a little ashamed, then, of his earlier and carefree happiness. It reminded him that he must be careful: the past could not simply be undone, without regard for its complexities. A marriage was involved, and though it hurt him to realize that that marriage had secrets and convolutions and loyalties to which he was not party, he knew he must accept that.

That evening they left Los Angeles in Edouard's plane, so that they would be in New York in time for the sailing the next day. It was only when they were airborne that Edouard suddenly realized something which appalled him.

Hélène still did not know of his own involvement with Partex and with Sphere; in the confusion, and the happiness, the rush of explanations, that one central fact had been omitted.

Edouard sat very still. He looked across at Hélène, who was sitting opposite him. Cat was looking out the window excitedly, thrilled to be in a plane that had no other passengers; Hélène was pointing out landmarks still visible below. The plane was climbing, and, as they entered the cloud line, Cat cried out with pleasure.

Edouard hesitated. His first instinct was to tell Hélène as soon as they were alone. Then he remembered all the things she had said about Thad Angelini, and the ways in which he had tried to control her life. He remembered how angry Angelini had made her, and he felt a certain fear.

If he told her now, it would look as if he had deliberately concealed the information until they left. It might seem, to Hélène, that he had acted wrongly. To some extent, he knew, both Angelini and she owed their success to him. Sphere had given them opportunities they might have spent years fighting for in the Hollywood marketplace, opportunities that might otherwise have been denied them both. For all her willingness to leave Los Angeles, Hélène was proud of her work, proud of her achievements: how would she regard them if she knew the truth, and how would she then regard him?

He had done these things because he loved her—but Angelini might have claimed the same thing. Edouard looked at Hélène's face, bent toward Cat, and then looked away.

He did not want to deceive her; he hated the thought that anything so important should be kept back, but to tell her now . . .

The plane leveled at cruising height; Edouard looked back at Hélène once more. He looked at the curve of her cheek, at the brightness in her eyes, the beauty of her face, and he decided.

He would Telex Simon Scher from the ship; he would instruct him to wind down Sphere's operations, and then to sell it off, and to keep his own name out of all dealings, as before. He would not tell Hélène, now or in the future; his connection with the company, that role he had played in her life, would be relegated to the past.

Hélène looked up from Cat at that moment, and smiled at him happily.

Edouard smiled back, with sudden relief. It was not such a terrible thing, after all, he told himself, and besides—it was the only secret he would keep.

Cat had a cabin with a bunk and a porthole; Cassie and Madeleine had cabins that were larger, but similar, on either side of her. Cat was in transports of delight. Even before they sailed, she had explored the whole ship. She had seen the swimming pool, and the movie theater, the library and the ballroom. She had peeped into the various restaurants, and examined the lifeboats.

She stood between Edouard and Hélène when the great ship finally eased away from the quay; she leaned on the rail and waved to all the people who were so unlucky as to be staying on shore. She counted the tugboats; she gazed at the Statue of Liberty, and at the outline of Ellis Island in the distance, when Hélène pointed it out.

"Thank you," Cat said to Edouard. "Oh, thank you. It's *much* better than an airplane." She stopped, and then realizing she might have been untactful, added, "Even *your* airplane, which was very nice."

She found fault with only one thing. When she came up to the higher deck, where Edouard and Hélène had separate but adjoining staterooms, she looked around Hélène's in consternation. It was large, and filled with flowers. It was very pretty . . . but it had a bed.

"Oh, Mother, what a shame. You don't have a bunk. . . ." She looked up at Edouard. "Do you have a bunk, Edouard?"

Edouard smiled; he and her mother exchanged a mystifying glance.

"Well, no. I have a bed, too, I'm afraid. You can come and bounce on it if you like. They're both very comfortable."

Cat stood and stared at the ground. Her face became very red. After a pause, she said, in the small voice of one prepared to make the supreme sacrifice, "I bet Mother would rather have a bunk. I'll change places with her. If she wants to."

Edouard coughed. He turned away and coughed some more. Hélène crouched down to Cat, and, to her daughter's great relief, said, "Darling, it's very kind of you. But really, I'm quite happy here. . . ."

"All right then," Cat said nonchalantly. "Maybe I'll go and play with those ring things. . . . Madeleine's going to show me. I'm going to beat her, and Cassie. . . ."

She made a speedy retreat, in case her mother should change her mind.

"My mother has a bed, not a bunk," she said to Cassie and Madeleine when they began their game of quoits. "So does Edouard. I said Mother could have my bunk if she'd rather, but she said no."

It was very odd, because this seemed to make Cassie cough. She went quite red in the face, as if she were laughing. Only Madeleine took the news in her stride.

"*Attention, ma petite.* Concentrate now. It is very difficult this game, we have to master it before we reach France, and we only have five days. . . ."

"Perhaps Edouard will play."

"Maybe. Maybe. But you mustn't bother them, Cat, they may be a little busy. . . ."

Cat gave a resigned sigh. She didn't mind. There were so many things to do, so many places to explore. How stupid grown-ups were, she thought, to be busy in such a wonderful playground as this.

O n their first night at sea, long after dinner, Edouard and Hélène walked on the deck, and then stood, at the stern of the ship, looking down at the water. They were quite alone. Behind them, the ship was lit up. In the saloons, people were drinking and talking and playing bridge; in the ship's ballroom, they were dancing, and they could just hear the music above the thrum of the huge engines.

It was cold on deck, and the Atlantic was dark and unmoving, almost without waves except those caused by the wake of the ship. Hélène shivered a little, and Edouard drew her closer to him. They stood for some time, silently and contentedly. "We are between two continents," Hélène said at last.

Edouard pressed her hand. And two lives, he thought, knowing it was what she had meant. He turned to look at her, her profile pale and clear-cut in the dark air, the wind lifting the fair hair from her forehead.

"Will you miss it?" he said finally. "All these things and places that I'm asking you to leave behind?"

"No." Hélène looked up at him quickly. "I had left them behind already, before you asked me to come away with you. There is nothing I shall miss. I feel as if I'm coming home." She hesitated. "Everything, and everyone, that most matters to me, is with me on this ship now. None of the other things matter. I've done them, and now I'm glad just to leave them behind."

Edouard pressed her closer to him, and they stood there a while longer. Then, with one accord, and without a word's being spoken between them, they turned and walked slowly back to their cabins.

They went into Hélène's, and she did not turn on the light. As Edouard shut the door and moved forward, she lifted her arms to him. The coat she had draped around her shoulders fell to the floor, and Edouard felt the glance of her bare arms against his throat. They had both been a little afraid of this moment, Hélène thought. But now that it was here, she felt only peace, and a sweet relaxing. The past five years were gone, as soon as she touched him.

Afterward, they lay for a long time in each other's arms; Hélène felt as if they floated, just above the water, just above the distant hum of the engines, calmly and serenely upon an ocean of contentment. They talked, slept, touched, talked, slept once more.

Since they rarely left this cabin, the voyage felt like five days of dreaming, and five days which obliterated five years.

"I never left you," she said one night.

"You couldn't leave. I couldn't let you," he answered.

On the fifth day, they reached France.

When they docked, Christian was there to meet them.

"You may not yet know this," he said to Hélène, "but I played a most significant role in this drama. I have no intention of ever letting either of you forget it. Now, hurry up, the car's waiting—you shall come straight to my apartment and drink champagne. Oh—and this is the little Cat."

He turned to Cat, who was staring at him wide-eyed, taking in the battered panama, the wine-red floppy bow tie, and the ancient pair of white flannel trousers.

Christian held out his hand, and shook Cat's. "We can't call you Cat, you know," he said. "You haven't grown enough yet. I shall introduce you to my Siamese, and I shall address you as Kitten. Now, come along . . ."

He ushered them toward the customs sheds; beyond, in the parking area, a black Rolls-Royce was waiting.

At the last moment, with one accord, both Hélène and Edouard looked back. They looked up at the ship, and at the passengers, so small from here, still lining the decks; they looked at each other, and smiled, and followed Christian.

On board, on one of the upper decks, one man watched their progress with particular interest. From here he had a clear view. He watched them enter customs—the man, the film star, the child, two other women, and the man wearing a ridiculous hat. Philippe de Belfort leaned on the rail, his pale heavy face expressionless. He watched them enter the sheds, and emerge on the other side. He watched them separate into two cars, and a third pull alongside for the luggage: little changed, he thought, Edouard de Chavigny still traveled, as he lived, with style.

It had occurred to him that Edouard might have seen his name on the passenger list, might even have sought him out to demand to know why he was returning to France. De Belfort felt a passing regret that he had not done so: he might have enjoyed the confrontation, he felt. But presumably he had not seen the name; perhaps, de Belfort thought, with a small smile, perhaps he was too occupied to scan passenger lists, or even to pay attention to those who sat, not many tables distant, in the first-class dining room.

He watched the procession of cars disappear into the distance, and then walked slowly to the gangplank. It was pleasant to be returning to France after such a long absence. The dust had settled now, and there were people who would welcome him back, though, obviously, he would have to be careful.

He passed through customs and immigration swiftly, and saw, with a certain satisfaction, that the Mercedes he had expected was waiting for him. He climbed into it, and waited patiently for his luggage to be loaded. Then he leaned back, and gave the driver directions. He smoothed down the folds of his vicuña overcoat, noted the fittings of the Mercedes with approval.

The intervening years had been kind to him, and he had prospered.

They spent a week at St. Cloud, several weeks by the sea in Normandy, and the rest of the summer at the château in the Loire. Edouard would fly to Paris, and then fly back, hating to leave, impatient to return. In the Loire, he taught Cat to ride, and with her and Hélène, he rode the same routes he had once ridden with Grégoire. The months passed: Christian came to stay, and so—for a while—did Anne Kneale: it was a time of great happiness.

Newspapers and magazines, of course, speculated at some length on this new liaison. And, elsewhere, other lives continued. Lewis Sinclair sold Ingrid Nilsson's house in the hills to a rock star, and moved into a house in San Francisco close to the junction of Haight Street and Ashbury. He shared it with Betsy, whom he had met for the first time at the *Ellis* party, and in whom he had quickly found a substitute for Stephani Sandrelli.

There were riots, that summer, in the Watts district of Los Angeles, and Thad Angelini watched them on his silent television, occasionally averting his eyes to look at the quiz show, or soap opera, or old movie, which played on the other.

He was making a new film, for A.I. and Joe Stein: it was still in its early stages, and he never spoke of the *Ellis* sequels to anyone.

In the small town of Orangeburg, Alabama, the Calvert house was demolished, and the earth movers of Merv Peters's new construction company dug up the fields of the Calvert plantation.

In Bella Vista Drive, an overweight housewife, who had reverted to her maiden name of Priscilla-Anne Peters, decided that, when her father's new estate was built, she might move back to Orangeburg. She spent her afternoons reading magazines, and planning her decor, drinking vodka, while the kids screamed in the yard. Occasionally she came across articles on Hélène Harte, who seemed to have landed on her feet again, according to the gossip columns, anyway. These items of information about her childhood friend always made her especially ill-tempered: life, she told herself, was unfair—to be her age, and still to get small-town blues. . . .

But these things, all these things, happened somewhere else. Hélène and Edouard knew of some of them, but they seemed distant, and part of another reality. Sometimes, standing at the windows of the château, and looking out across its park, over a view that excluded the twentieth century, Hélène would feel that she had never left this place, and that all the events of the past five years had happened to someone else. But at other times, she knew that was not the case. She looked at her room, she looked at the furniture of Adeline de Chavigny, and her portrait which still hung above the fireplace, and she no longer felt like an intruder. She felt that she had, now, a right to be here, and that this place now accepted her.

After the wine-harvest, and the annual supper that followed, they returned to Paris for the fall. Then, in December, they went back to the Loire to celebrate Edouard's fortieth birthday. They dined alone and drank a bottle of the claret Xavier de Chavigny had laid down in 1925, the year of Edouard's birth. A prewar wine: Edouard looked down the table at Hélène, and smiled; he thought of all those prewar summers of his childhood, and of all the summers to come. When he looked to the future, he realized, he saw no very precise images, just himself, and Hélène, as they were now, and—from outside—the cries and shouts of the children they would have, who would be in the gardens, playing.

After dinner, they wrapped themselves in coats, and pulled on boots and scarves, and walked, down across the park, and toward the water meadows.

It was a cold night, with a clear sky, and a high thin sickle of a moon. They walked through the chestnut woods, and came to a halt on a bluff of land that looked over the Loire. The river was wide at this point, and its shores wooded; the water was calm, gray rippled with silver.

There, they stood still, looking out over the river. It was to this precise place, where he had often walked as a child, that Edouard had once dreamed of bringing Célestine. When he had been sixteen years old, and planning that impossible future, it was here that he had envisaged himself, with the woman he loved.

He had brought Isobel here, often. He had come here, years before, with Hélène, when they first came to the Loire, and he was teaching her to ride. He had come to this place, alone, on many occasions afterward, during the years they were apart, and had stood here, on this exact spot, thinking of her. Now the night was quiet; the wind lifted the bare branches of the chestnut trees, and then was still; the moon cast a band of light across the water. He was thinking of the past, and out of the past, an image came to him, suddenly, and—as it always did—without warning. For an instant, he saw not the river, but a wall of debris; he saw a sunlit square in which the silence after the explosion was deafeningly loud, and the dust was settling.

The image was there, and then was gone. Hélène moved slightly, and lifted her face to him; Edouard moved close to her. The image had come to him, he thought, for the last time; and with that thought came a sense of great release, of hope. Trying to shape a conviction which was fierce in his mind, but unformed, he told himself that—this time—there would be no tricks of fate, no twists, no pain, no darkness, no abyss.

He took Hélène's hand, and they turned to walk back toward the house. Halfway across the park, laughing because it was so cold, laughing because they were happy, they broke into a run.

As they reached the house, a clock was chiming midnight.

EDOUARD AND HÉLÈNE

1967—1975

"A clean sweep," Christian said. "Have done with the past. I'd absolutely made up my mind." He paused, looking around him, an expression of almost clownish despair on his features. "But now that I actually look at it all, it doesn't seem so simple. Edouard—what do you think? Shall I try to find a bottle of wine? Do you think a drink might help?" He made a plaintive face. "The dismals are coming upon me."

"Some wine, definitely. Then you'll feel better. You can't expect it to be easy."

"I'd better try the cellar. There might be some cooking sherry in the kitchen, though I doubt it. There won't be anything else up here. Ma never touched the stuff. My father did, of course. Two pink gins before luncheon. One whisky and water before dinner, and one afterward. It never varied." Christian stopped. "Isn't it extraordinary? I'd quite forgotten that until this moment. He's been dead ten years. Why pink gins, I wonder? He was an army man, not navy. How odd."

"Army?" Edouard looked blank.

"Gin. It's a naval drink. When the sun sets over the yardarm, or possibly the Empire, British naval officers have a drink, and for some reason it's supposed to be gin. But my father never set foot on a ship in his life if he could avoid it. He was a cavalry officer, and he thought you could date the decline of this country from the introduction of the tank. So—it's odd, that's all. Now I wished I'd asked him." He attempted a wan smile. "Never mind. I'll go and raid the cellar before I feel any worse. You wait here—I shan't be a moment."

He opened the drawing room door, and went out into the hall. Edouard listened to the sound of his footsteps, loud on the old flagged stone floors, disappearing in the direction of the kitchen regions. He looked around him. The house seemed unnaturally silent, and very still; Edouard had, for a moment, the sensation that it was waiting for something.

He stood, listening to the quality of the silence. Quaires Manor: Christian's childhood home, close to the borders of Berkshire and Oxfordshire, looking across country to the Berkshire downs. In the last few years Edouard had visited it rarely, usually to provide moral support for Christian when he came to visit his mother. But twenty years before, when he and Christian were at Oxford, this house had been like a second home to him. Which meant he must have stayed here in the winter—he knew he had done so—yet when he thought of this house, he realized, he associated it always with summer.

One of those tricks of the mind, by which certain passages of the past are erased, and others heightened: in his mind's eye, Edouard saw this house, and this garden, in the first flush of May and June, bathed in a particular light, the thick dusty gold of late afternoon, that space at the end of the day when evening approaches very slowly, its progress measured in the shadows across the lawn.

It was June now, and late morning. The sun was moving around to the south façade of the house, and beginning to slant in through the tall sash windows. Nothing had changed in twenty years, the house was scarcely altered—but then, that was not surprising: it had altered very little in the previous two hundred.

It was a very English house, and a very English room. Compared to a French house of similar grandeur, it was informal; it made no acknowledgment to fashion. Pale, much-washed chintzes, garlanded with flowers, hung at the windows, and covered the deep chairs and sofas. The furniture, much of which was very fine, was disposed about the room with a settled air, as if each piece had stood there always, and could stand nowhere else. It smelled of beeswax, and, muskily, of the pot-pourri Christian's mother made each year, and which lay in a Worcester bowl on the Pembroke table next to him. Edouard touched the dried petals with his fingers, and the scent of the past, of last summer, and summers twenty years before, rose up to him.

On the walls hung that idiosyncratic mixture of paintings which so infuriated Christian, in which eighteenth-century family portraits of an excellence even Christian could not deny rested next to an assortment of Victorian watercolors, fading images of Swiss lakes, and Indian vistas, many of them the handiwork of long-dead cousins and aunts. Edouard liked their juxtaposition; he liked this room; he liked this house.

In the fireplace, as always in summer, the iron basket was piled high with pine cones collected from the garden. Next to it, by the chair in which Christian's mother had always sat, was the rug sacred to her succession of pugs; the work basket containing her tapestry wools and silks; a table piled high with copies of *The Field,* and Royal Horticultural Society journals, and—on top of the pile—the last books mailed to her, as a country member, by the London Library. Her spectacles, round, tortoiseshell-framed, uncompromising as she had been, still lay on top of the books.

She had died three weeks before, quietly, as she had lived.

Edouard looked at that pile of books. He picked up the one on top and saw that it was an account of the plant-gathering expeditions of Ernest Wilson, in China. As he picked it up, a small piece of paper fluttered out, and Edouard saw that it was a note Christian's mother had written to herself. It read: *Delphiniums in South Border must come out. They are too big, and too bogus. Rosa turkestanica—in the rondel? Good against the yew—like a harlequin.*

When had she written that? Edouard gently placed the note to one side, where it would not be lost. He moved toward the windows, frowning thoughtfully, and looked out across the famous garden. He could see Christian's mother now, bending to smell a rose here; stooping to pull out an offending weed there; pausing to look down her celebrated herbaceous borders, and then pulling out a small notebook, and scribbling something.

"You're not going to change the plantings, surely?" he had said to her once when she did this. He had been twenty, and Christian's mother forty-five, perhaps fifty. He had been in awe of her.

"They're perfect," he had added, and Christian's mother had smiled. She had looked at him with her sharp blue eyes, which so resembled Christian's. Her face was shaded by an ancient straw hat which she wore always when gardening in the summer.

"Edouard. Gardens are *never* perfect. That is why I like them."

Edouard stood now, looking across the lawn to the high brick wall which enclosed this first part of the garden. The roses which were trained against it in such carefully contrived, apparently natural abundance, were now in flower. *Aimée Vibert, Madame Isaac Pereire, Celestial,* with its soft gray foliage; *Zepherine Drouhin, Lady Hillingdon, Gloire de Dijon,* fading now, its beautiful buff-colored flowers smelling fragrantly of tea. Edouard heard their names, spoken in Christian's mother's voice.

He opened the window and stepped out onto the terrace. It had rained earlier, and now the sun was drawing moisture from the grass: its scent was intensely strong—the scent of summer.

For a moment Edouard saw the lawn peopled: young men in white flannels; a game of croquet, at which Christian fiendishly excelled; a covey of young women in the distance. He heard and saw the past vividly: the click of balls against mallets; laughter at some remove. He looked away, looked back, and it was gone.

The house was quiet once more; the garden was quiet once more. He turned back into the drawing room, just as Christian reappeared.

"So. There we are."

Christian tilted his panama hat over his eyes, and leaned back against the wooden bench on which he was sitting; they were outside on the terrace, half in sun, half in shadow. The bottle of Montrachet was half empty: Christian had immersed it in a watering can into which he had tipped as much ice as the elderly refrigerator could provide.

He lit one of his Black Russian cigarettes, and Edouard saw, to his surprise, that Christian was truly upset. His hand was shaking slightly.

"It's the *past*," Christian said, with sudden vehemence. "It was stupid of me, but somehow I didn't expect it to come rushing back like this. I thought I'd done with this place, and all the memories, years ago. I didn't think it would affect me at all." He made a wry face. "*Temps perdu:* and I thought it *was* lost. Now I find it isn't."

"The past never is," Edouard said gently. "It's always there, just below the surface. You shouldn't fight it, Christian, you ought to be glad it's there." He paused. "We *are* our past, after all. Everything we've done, everything that has happened to us—that's what we are."

"That's all very well for you to say." Christian reached across and poured the remaining wine for them. "You've come to terms with your past. You were always better at that than I was, anyway. You've always had the ability to use the past to shape the future. Even when we were at Oxford, even then. You wanted to build on your father's work, take what he had done a step further, and a step further after that. I was terribly impressed. I knew you'd do it, and you did. It was the same with Hélène. You were determined you would have a future together, and now you have." He sighed.

"And I'm glad of that. You're happy, and Hélène is happy, and that makes me happy. Also—well, it's reassuring, I suppose. It restores one's faith in the power of the will. There you are—author of your own fate. Oh, hell." He took a large swallow of his wine. "I'm not sure it does make me feel better. Maybe it makes me feel worse."

"I don't know that I agree with you." Edouard paused. "Sometimes I think as you do—I think I see a clear pattern of cause and effect: because I did this, and Hélène did that—sometimes I feel we chose. At other times . . . I'm not so sure. After all, so much is chance. If my father had not died when he did, if Jean-Paul had lived, if Hélène had walked in a different direction on the day I met her—do you see?"

"Oh, God. You're going to be determinist and French." Christian shrugged. "Well, I don't believe any of that. I take an extremely sanguine and English view of the matter. The fault, dear Edouard, lies not in our stars, but in ourselves, and all that . . ."

"All right." Edouard could hear the exaggeration and affectation coming into Christian's voice, and knew it was there to disguise the emotion he felt. "But in that case, I see no reason for you to reproach yourself. You always knew what you wanted to do—every bit as much as I did. And you've done it, with great success. You wanted to open your gallery, you wanted to introduce the work of new painters to this country, you wanted—"

"I wanted to break away from my past. All this." Christian waved his hand in a wide gesture that took in the house and garden and the countryside beyond. "*That's* the difference between us. You were always close to your past—you were loyal to it. And I couldn't wait to kill mine off. Christian Glendinning, the self-invented man. Nothing to do with England—not this England, anyway. I tried awfully hard, Edouard. I read the wrong books, and wore the wrong clothes, and said the wrong things. I voted for the wrong party—when I bothered to vote at all. And of course, I went to bed with persons of the wrong sex." He paused. "Do you know I once told my mother I was homosexual? I actually said the words. I was so bloody sick and tired of the fact that nobody took the least bit of notice—though they all knew perfectly well—that one day I actually told her. We were sitting in there." He jerked his thumb in the direction of the drawing room. "Mother was sewing. Petitpoint. And I said: 'Of course, you do know, don't you, Ma? I'm homosexual. A pansy. A queer. A nancy-boy—one of them.' And do you know what my mother said?"

"No."

"She looked up from her sewing, over the top of her spectacles, and said, 'Well, Christian, if it makes you happy. But it might be better not to say so in front of your father. Certainly not before dinner, anyway.' That was it. I couldn't believe it. Then she started talking about planting hostas in the north border."

Edouard repressed a smile.

"I was so angry, I walked out. I couldn't bear it, you see. I wanted them all to see that I was different from them. That I didn't belong—anymore than Hugo ever belonged. But they would never acknowledge that. No matter what I did, they accommodated it. That's what the British do, you know. They accommodate, and then they assimilate. It's very effective. It's their way of disarming the opposition, and it works. It's why we've never had a revolution, and never will. If Robespierre or Danton had been English, you know where they'd have ended up? I do. They'd have been justices of the peace. They'd have been given seats in the House of Lords. They'd have died an ornament of committees. Just like me. Do you know I sit on committees now? I do. Isn't that terrible?"

"There are worse fates, perhaps," Edouard said mildly.

Christian gave him a waspish glance. "Possibly. I shouldn't have said so when I was twenty." He paused. "Anyway, the point of all this is—they were right, and I was wrong. I've just discovered that. I never escaped from all this. I just thought I had. But here it was—all this. Waiting for me. Waiting to claim me as its own." He gave a tragic sigh.

"Do you feel that?" Edouard looked at him intently.

Christian shrugged. When he next spoke, his voice was less histrionic. "Yes, I do. Look at this place. Eight hundred acres of farmland; a home farm; nearly ten acres of gardens. This house—this undeniably beautiful house, where generations of harmless, deeply conservative Glendinnings have lived since God knows when. My father bought it from a cousin in 1919, and it was in a mess. None of the garden was here—my mother created that. I was born here. My sisters were born here. And now it's mine. None of my sisters wants it—they all have huge places of their own. So—what am I to do with it?"

"You could live in it when you're in this country."

"Live in it? Edouard, don't be absurd. It has something like fifteen bedrooms. It's not a house for a bachelor. Besides, I like the way I live now. A very pleasant little box in London, a slightly bigger box in Paris, and a slightly smaller one in New York. And look at all this . . ." He gestured back toward the house. "All that furniture, all those paintings. Accretions. What's the point? I've no one to leave them to. Oh, God. It makes me feel ill just thinking about it."

"Well, if you don't want it, and your sisters don't want it—you'll have to sell it, I suppose?"

"That's the trouble." Christian leaned forward and lit another cigarette. "I'd already decided on that. I'd quite made up my mind. The sisters can have what they want, and the rest can go to Sotheby's or Christie's, and I'll sell the house. It seemed perfectly simple. Until today."

"And now?"

"Now I *mind*." Christian looked away. "I find I actually *mind*. I keep imagining, you see, the sort of person who'll buy it. Some frightful businessman from the City—sorry, Edouard—who's just made a killing on the market. He'll have the garden dug up and laid to lawn for ease of maintenance. He'll put some perfectly ghastly bright blue swimming pool where the rose garden is. His wife—oh, God, I can just see his wife. She'll fill the kitchen with gleaming units and then never set foot in it. And then she'll call in someone like Ghislaine Belmont-Laon to give it the English country house look." He looked at Edouard piteously.

"They'll kill it off, do you see? All the things I used to think I wanted killed off. And I shall mind. Most dreadfully." He paused. "Do you know they're all still there, in the cellar—my father's wines? I found them when I went down just now. Not touched since the day he died. His wine book's there as well. Meticulously filled in. Dates.

Comments. Quantities. He was rather good on wine, which was odd, because he was a terrible English puritan about food. His favorite meal was fish pie with runner beans, and treacle tart for pudding. And he liked greengages very much. He always insisted on picking them himself. Oh, hell and damnation—I'm sorry about this, Edouard."

Tears had come to his eyes. He rose irritably and turned away. Edouard half-stood, and Christian waved a hand at him angrily. "It's all right. I'll be fine in a minute." He turned and stared fixedly at a shrub border.

After a pause, Edouard rose also. "I'll go and make some coffee. Would you like some brandy—something like that? There's a flask of Armagnac in my car."

"Actually that might be quite a good idea."

Christian did not turn around, and Edouard quietly left him. He fetched the Armagnac from the car, went down the long flagged passageway to the old-fashioned kitchen, and made coffee.

Tucked between the coffee tins and the tins of Earl Grey, Lapsang, and Ceylon, were packets of seeds, with dates written on them. On the kitchen table was a shopping list: one lamb cutlet; one packet of oat cakes; half a pound of butter; a quarter of cheese. A widow's shopping list. Edouard looked at it, and felt his heart move with pity. Christian's mother had lived here alone for ten years: he felt guilty then, remembering how rarely either of them had come to see her. Even now he found it difficult to imagine the house as it must have been for her: he still saw it as it had been twenty years before, always crowded with people. He imagined it all being sold off, auctioned and altered, and like Christian, he found he hated the idea that something so loved and so preserved should be changed; for a moment he heard Philippe de Belfort's voice: *Don't you ever imagine them, Edouard, when you're dead, picking over the spoils?*

He took the coffee and the Armagnac back to the garden. Christian was now sitting down again, smoking another cigarette, and looking more in control of himself.

Edouard poured him a glass of brandy and some coffee. He sat down, hesitating to speak.

"You're sure," he said finally, "quite sure—that you don't want to live here yourself? That none of your sisters does?"

"No, I've told you. Absolutely not. We had a family conference, after the funeral. We agreed then. Lock, stock, and barrel. Well, nearly. No sentiment."

"Would you let me buy it?"

"What?" Christian stopped, the glass halfway to his lips.

"Would you let me buy it?"

There was a small silence. Christian's narrow face flushed.

"Oh—for God's sake, Edouard. You don't have to take friendship that far, you know. I didn't intend—"

"I know you didn't. And I'm not asking out of friendship. Well, not exactly."

"Then why *are* you asking?"

Edouard looked down at the table, and Christian, looking at him suspiciously, saw that he was trying hard to keep his face calm, and was not quite succeeding. Happiness was breaking through.

"Hélène and I—that is, all the formalities have finally been sorted out. Her divorce is final now, so we can be married. And . . ."

"Oh, my God. Oh, my *God.*" Christian lifted his head and gave the most extraordinary war whoop. "When? When? Damn you, Edouard, you never said one word . . ."

"Next week."

"Next week? Next week? I can't believe it. This is wonderful. This is absolutely wonderful. . . ."

Christian leapt to his feet. He gave Edouard an extravagant embrace, nearly knocking the table flying as he did so.

"Where? How? I'm going to be the best man, I hope? If I'm not best man, I shall never speak to you again. I *adore* weddings. Are you going to have a madly grand one, or one of those delicious furtive ones where you just nip away somewhere and—"

"Christian—" Edouard attempted to cut through the tumbling words, but he could not help smiling. "Christian. I'm trying to make you a business proposition."

"A business proposition, at a time like this? You're mad. You're inhuman. You're . . . what?"

"If you would really like to sell this house, I should very much like to buy it. That's all."

Christian stopped hopping about. He sat down. He looked at Edouard.

"But why?" he said at last. "I don't understand. Is there some connection between these two extraordinary statements?"

"Yes. There is. I want to give Hélène a wedding present. And I thought—if you liked the idea"—Edouard smiled—"I might give her an English house. And an English garden."

"W̶hen she was a child . . ." They were driving back to London; Edouard glanced in his sideview mirror, pulled the Aston-Martin out, and overtook three cars and one tractor. Christian shut his eyes.

"When she was a child—I wouldn't tell anyone else this, but I know Hélène has talked to you about it a little—she lived in that trailer park in Alabama, you remember?"

"I remember. She described it to me once."

"She lived there with her mother, and her mother used to talk to her about England and the house where she grew up." He paused. "You remember that house—in Devon?"

"Who could forget it?"

"Her mother used to talk about that place, and its garden. Especially its garden. She conjured something up—something Hélène never forgot. An image of a beautiful, tranquil, perfect place. When Hélène was small, her mother used to leave her alone for quite long periods, and do you know what Hélène used to try to do sometimes? She would make a garden. An English garden. She used to gather up pebbles, and wild flowers and weeds, and then scratch about in the earth, and plant them, so that when her mother came home, she could give her an English garden. Only, of course, it was very hot, and the soil was very dry, and often her mother was late, and by the time she came back, all the plants had withered and died. She told me that once. I've never forgotten it." He paused, his eyes on the road ahead.

"Then, when she finally came back to England, to her aunt's, and she saw that dismal place, it was a terrible shock to her. She'd just lost her mother, and her only friend—she came to England, and she saw that place. She finds it difficult to talk about, even now. You see, it was the moment when she saw, with her own eyes, exactly how much of a fantasist her mother was. She knew already, in some ways—she could see that her mother deluded herself. But I think Hélène had always believed in that perfect garden. And then she found it didn't exist. That was just a delusion too. And it was Hélène's delusion as well. She'd inherited it from her mother."

"Oh, God, that's sad. I never knew about that." Christian sighed. "The things we inherit."

"So." Edouard glanced in his mirror again, and seeing the road clear before and behind, accelerated. "So. I had been trying to think. I wanted to give her something special, something that would have a particular meaning for her. And when I was standing in your house this morning, I thought of it then. It's the most English house I know. And the most perfect of English gardens." He smiled. "And I promise you, we wouldn't put a swimming pool in the rose garden."

"There you are then." Christian gave Edouard a sly glance. "And I do take it that I can rely on you *not* to bring in Ghislaine? I don't think I'd like to see the scorpion get her pincers on it. . . ."

"You may certainly rely on that. Ghislaine's only worked on my showrooms, never my houses—and that was a long time ago."

"What happened to her? She did marry that man Nerval, didn't she?"

"Indeed she did. She divorced Jean-Jacques, rather scandalously. Then she married Nerval. But I haven't seen her for several years. There was a little problem with the tax authorities, I think—some rather shady company in the Cayman Islands. Anyway, she and Nerval left France. I hear they're now carving up what's left of Marbella—very successfully, I believe."

"Marbella. Well, well, well."

"Hélène met Nerval once or twice. She bought and sold a house through him. He quite amused her, I think. She said he was so transparently a rogue. A smiling villain. Totally unscrupulous, of course."

"Oh, I'm so *glad*." Christian smiled. "The scorpion has been given her just deserts then."

"As a matter of fact, I hear they're very happy. They suit each other perhaps." Edouard glanced across at him. "Just never mention her name in front of my mother. Ghislaine is now her *bête noire*—has been ever since we were at St. Tropez that time, you remember?" He paused. "She regards Ghislaine as her enemy. And me as well, perhaps."

His tone had become less casual, and Christian looked at him curiously.

"You won't say why, I suppose?"

"There's no point really. It's a long, complicated story. I did something which I thought was in my mother's best interests, and my mother has never forgotten it, nor forgiven it, that's all." He shrugged. "She's changed a great deal, Christian. You'd hardly recognize her now. She dresses quite differently. She's become very religious. . . ."

"Religious, Louise? I don't believe it."

"Oh, it's true." Edouard smiled. "The whole house is redolent of priests. Every time I go there I can hear the swish of soutanes." He paused, and then, thinking of Christian's mother, thinking that Louise, however exasperating, might also be lonely, he added, "You should come to see her when you're next in Paris, Christian. You'll see what I mean."

"I shouldn't think I'd be madly welcome. Louise could never stand me."

Christian lit a cigarette, leaned back in his seat, and let Edouard concentrate on his driving for a while. He turned his head and looked out the window. They had covered the distance fast, and were now approaching the outskirts of London. As the traffic became heavier, and Edouard was forced to slow down, Christian could look at his surroundings properly. The fields were giving way to roads, to line after line of semi-detached mock-Tudor houses, and uninviting pubs. Away to his right, great yellow scars cut through the land; huge earth movers crawled, and dug. They were constructing the new London-Oxford motorway. When it was finished, this trip, which had been so slow and tortuous during his university days, would be reduced to well under an hour— forty minutes, he thought, with Edouard's driving. And he could re- member bowling along this road in an old Morris Minor, his very first car: London to Magdalen College in under two hours! It had seemed an achievement, then.

"God, how everything changes." He turned to look at Edouard. "We're both over forty now. Do you know I used to think that would be quite ghastly? And now it's come upon me, I find I rather enjoy it. The perspective alters. I like that. People come and go—they drift into one's life, and then out of it again. One hears stories about them—little snippets of information, like Ghislaine's marrying Nerval, and zipping off to Marbella—some go up, and others go down. Some alter in the most unexpected ways, and others remain precisely the same. It's so *interesting*. Like reading a marvelous novel. Heigh-ho. I wonder how we'll be in another twenty years—when we're sixty."

"We'll still be friends." Edouard glanced across at him with a smile.

"Oh, yes." Christian smiled back. "I've no doubts on that score. That's one of the better things. And I know just how we'll be, actually, now that I come to think of it. You'll be even more powerful and distinguished—you'll serve on a *million* committees. You'll be a paterfa- milias. God, Cat will probably be married, you'll be a grandfather by then. And I—I shall be an aging enfant terrible. People will be rather rude about me, and say I'm old hat. And then, when I get to seventy, they'll all discover me again, and turn me into a national monument. The Cecil Beaton of the gallery world. That's the thing—to hang on until you're seventy. You can't go wrong then. You become a sage, and everyone says what perfectly marvelous *style* you have. Then we sell our memoirs to the Sunday newspapers, and all our friends publish their diaries and letters, and we become an industry—like the Bloomsbury Group. I can't wait. That's when the past *really* begins to pay off." He gave Edouard a provocative glance.

"So—I hope you're keeping a record of everything. Otherwise all those academics and research students are going to be awfully disap- pointed. Diaries. Letters. Notebooks . . ."

"Absolutely not." Edouard saw a small space in the flow of traffic, eased through it, and accelerated. "I hate that kind of thing. As you know perfectly well. I rarely even keep photographs."

"No, you don't, do you?" Christian frowned. "I remember. When we were looking for Hélène—you didn't even have a photograph of her—just that one your groom brought. Why is that?"

"I don't know, really. I prefer not to document my past, that's all. I prefer just to think about it. Letters, photographs—I don't know. I think they distort."

"Doesn't memory?" Christian glanced at him sharply.

"Perhaps."

"After all, everyone remembers the past differently. It isn't a fixed thing. Even one's own perceptions of it change all the time."

"It doesn't stay still, you mean?"

"God, no. My past is constantly popping up. It manifests itself in the most surprising ways."

"That's because you have an extremely disreputable past."

"Oh, I *know*." Christian gave a smile of self-satisfaction. "And so do you, I might point out."

"That—all that—is over," Edouard said firmly.

"I wouldn't count on it. You never can. You can't even count on the present. Just when you think it's marvelously calm and placid, there's something else going on, just out of your field of vision. Down the street, 'round the corner, in another country: you're perfectly happy, and meanwhile . . ."

"I know that. I learned that lesson the night of my sixteenth birthday." Edouard spoke rather abruptly. Then, regretting that, for he enjoyed Christian when he was in a talkative mood, he turned back with a smile.

"You know Hélène's in London? And Cat. We're staying at Eaton Square overnight—why don't you come back and have dinner?"

"Marvelous. I'd like that."

"If you want to, we could go and see my solicitors in the morning. Then we could make all the arrangements about the house—unless you want to think it over?"

"Absolutely not. And I'd love to visit your solicitors. Smith-Kemp, isn't it? My father used them. Do they still have those deliciously Dickensian offices?"

"Oh, yes."

"And a glass of sherry, when you've come to the end of the meeting?"

"Invariably."

"Too wonderful. I shall certainly come. It's pleasant to know some things don't change."

"And not a word to Hélène about the house. You promise? I want it to be a surprise."

"Edouard—would I?" Christian sounded wounded. "You know I adore secrets. I shall be as silent as the grave."

"Don't promise the impossible. If you could just refrain from your usual little *hints* . . ."

"Hints? Hints? You do me an injustice there, Edouard."

"Do I?" said Edouard dryly, and accelerated into the city.

A secret. A surprise. Hélène loved surprises, and she loved to give presents, especially to Edouard. This present, which was still a secret, and would be a surprise, her wedding present to him, filled her with great excitement. She felt as if she were walking on air. She still felt that—although she had been walking a long way. All the way up Bond Street where she had been shopping; across Oxford Street; through the narrow winding Marylebone Lane; into the High Street, parallel with Harley Street, where Mr. Foxworth still had his consulting rooms; north past the church where Robert Browning had married Elizabeth Barrett, and north again, heading for St. John's Wood, where Anne Kneale now had her studio, across Regents Park.

She could have picked up a taxi at any point along the way, but today she felt she could not bear to be confined in a car: she wanted to walk, she felt borne along on happiness. In just over a week, she would be married to Edouard; she increased her pace as she came into the park; she felt she wanted to dance rather than walk. Such a long time—two years of lawyers, and then more lawyers, two years in which progress had been so terribly slow, not because Lewis was opposing the divorce, but simply because, these days, he never answered letters, and it took weeks for his lawyers to prise so much as a signature from him.

She paused, and then turned off, making a small detour toward the boating lake, and the brightly painted bandstand. In that time, she had sometimes despaired, though Edouard never did. This unlocking, this disentangling of a marriage, of the past—it had seemed to her so sad that it had to be done in this dry and official way, even when both parties were perfectly amicable, and the arrangements to be made—for she wanted nothing from Lewis—were straightforward. Signatures; documents; letters from one lawyer to another—she had hated it all.

She still felt guilty toward Lewis, she still felt that she had played a part in his decline—and the decline had been so sharp, so accelerated, since she left America.

She stopped near the lake, in the sunlight, and thought of the letters which Lewis had sent her. Long, rambling, confused letters, pages of them, in which he hardly seemed to be aware of what time of year it was, let alone what was happening. She had spoken to him on the telephone, too, several times, in the first year she was in France, and the conversations had been impossible. She could hear the pills in his voice: the bursts of frantic confidence, or—on another occasion—the slow, disoriented groping after a reality which clearly pained him.

This year, she had hardly spoken to him at all, and he had answered none of her letters. Whenever she telephoned him now, either Betsy, or one of the other, ever-changing cast of people who seemed to stay in the house, would answer. And they might make an excuse. *Sorry,*

Lewis is asleep. Lewis is a bit spaced-out just now. Or sometimes they wouldn't even bother to do that: they might just laugh, and say, *Lewis? Who's he?*

It alarmed her, sometimes. Once, in desperation, she wrote to Thad, asking if he would go to see Lewis, and make sure he was all right. On another occasion, she even wrote to his mother. Thad never answered. Emily Sinclair sent a small frosty note: Lewis's family were perfectly well aware of Lewis's situation. In a few lines, she managed to suggest both that Hélène's concern was unnecessary, and that it came too late. Hélène had not tried to write again, and when she had told Edouard her worries, he had been firm: "My darling. Lewis is an adult, not a child. Look, you see, he's answered the last letter from my lawyers now—he's signed the documents. Hélène. You can't worry now about trying to prop Lewis up."

He had even shown her Lewis's signature on the legal papers, and Hélène had looked at it in silence. He had used the familiar broad-nibbed Mont Blanc pen; the signature he had scrawled, which ended his marriage, was large, flowingly inscribed, the individual letters cramped, the up-and-down strokes exaggerated. The writing she remembered; the person she remembered. She could see all Lewis's paradoxes, the flamboyance and the insecurity, just in those two words. She thought then of those letters he had sent her from Paris, with their wild affirmations of love, their boyish optimism, and she felt very sad. She had loved Lewis, she thought, though he could never see that, and she had, in any case, loved him in the wrong way, the way he could never accept, as a mother might love a child.

Protectiveness. She stood still, looking across the lake. Several couples and some children were rowing back and forth in the sunshine. Around her, on the lawns surrounding the little bandstand, people sat in deck chairs, and read, or slept, or simply lay lifting their faces to the sun. Edouard was right, she thought suddenly; he was right—but it was not easy.

She turned away from the bandstand and the water. She began to walk, more quickly, toward the northern boundary of the park. At once, irrepressibly, her spirits rose again. She could not be unhappy on such a day; she could not; it was impossible.

They were to be married in the Loire, in a small country town some ten kilometers from the château: a civil wedding, of course; as a divorced woman she had no alternative. A quiet marriage, a simple marriage: it was what they both wanted. No fuss. No publicity. Just a very few friends. Christian would be there, of course, Edouard was to ask him today; and Anne Kneale; Madeleine, who would be marrying shortly herself; Cassie, who had a new outfit for the occasion, of which she was inordinately proud; and Cat—who did not comprehend any of the complications attendant on this wedding; Cat, who seemed to have forgotten she ever knew someone called Lewis Sinclair; Cat, aged seven, who adored Edouard, and who regarded this marriage as the happiest, most exciting, and most inevitable thing in the world.

Hélène smiled to herself, and quickened her pace. North again toward the leafy streets and quiet backwaters of St. John's Wood. Past the grand and rather vulgar houses of Avenue Road, which always reminded her of Hollywood, and into a network of smaller streets, and leafy gardens. The lilac was in bloom: huge heavy trusses of vanilla-white flowers hung over the sidewalk; she stopped to smell them as she passed.

She loved London now, she thought with a sudden passion. She loved it as she loved Paris, and the village of the Loire, because these places she associated with Edouard, and with their love for each other. They came to London often, and now, when she walked as she did today, she constantly passed places which brought back memories. Here they had driven; there they once discovered a little restaurant; there they once went to a party, and then, very late, when the streets were deserted, just walked together, hand in hand, and talking, taking no particular direction, just letting their footsteps guide them. In so many places—in Paris, when she looked across the Seine to the Île de la Cité; in the Loire, at the neighboring market, perhaps, which they sometimes visited, for they both loved markets; here, by the slopes of Primrose Hill, where they had once walked at night, and stopped at the summit to look across the city; or even in crowded places—Piccadilly Circus, the Bayswater Road, one particular corner in Knightsbridge—all these places were alive with Edouard. These places were their places, and the fact that other men and women, other lovers, before and after them, might pass the same way, and feel the same sense of claim, only strengthened the intensity of her feelings.

She stood quietly, just near the lilac tree: for a moment their love seemed to her very large, a great thing, so powerful it made the city silent. The next it was small but vital, part of a long continuum. Lovers and a city; she quickened her pace once more, and as she did so felt a great serenity and contentment: she and Edouard, she felt, were now part of London's past; they were part of the spirit of the place.

Anne Kneale's studio was now in the garden of a gabled, rambling white-painted house, where, it was rumored, Edward VII once entertained Lily Langtry. Inside, it was very similar to her old Chelsea studio, which she had abandoned promptly when the waves of fashion threatened to engulf it.

"My greengrocer is now a clothes shop," she had said gruffly. "They don't call it a clothes shop, or even a dress shop. They call it a boutique. And I can't buy a cauliflower the length of the King's Road. I'm moving."

She had moved, and taken her ambience with her. In the sitting room of the new house, there were still faded kelim rugs, still two fat red velvet chairs, still a line of pebbles, and a vase of bird's feathers on the mantelpiece. And her studio was every bit as disorderly as the old one had been.

Today, Hélène entered it apprehensively, for Anne had been painting a portrait of Cat—the wedding present. The surprise! And she herself was to see it today, for the first time. When she came in, the session was clearly over, and she thought Anne was pleased: she was being extremely truculent, and—just as with Cassie—that was usually a good sign. Cat was sitting perched on the edge of a table, eating an orange with a fine unconcern for the mess she was making. The juice ran down her bare brown arm, and she licked at it, and then gave Hélène an orangy kiss.

"Like painting an eel," Anne was saying in her most churlish voice. "I bribed her. I threatened her. None of it the least bit of good. She can't keep still for more than five seconds. I shall never, under any circumstances, paint a child that age again. . . ."

Cat made a small rebellious face, and Anne, seeing her, repressed a smile. She turned back to Hélène.

"However. You may look at it now. I suppose."

She led Hélène around to the far side of the easel, folded her arms, and scowled at her own handiwork. But Hélène was not deceived either by the tone, or the expression of dissatisfaction. She looked at the painting quietly.

In it, Cat was sitting much as she was now, perched on the edge of the table, poised to move—as she always was. Behind her, through the long studio window, were glimpses of Anne's wild, untamed garden. The garden was like Cat: abundant, generous, undisciplined, and also beautiful. There was her daughter—a little girl still, but with an unconscious grace in the disposition of her limbs, caught with an expression on her face, startled, alert, about to break into laughter, an expression that was very characteristic of her, and at the same time—Hélène saw it now—curiously adult.

She looked at the painting for a long time, greatly moved. She turned to Anne, and embraced her warmly.

"Oh, Anne. It's beautiful. You've shown me my daughter—and you've shown me the woman she will become. . . ."

Anne permitted herself a smile. She glanced across at Cat, who was not listening, and who had retreated to the far end of the studio.

"I hope so. I thought that—" Anne hesitated. She lowered her voice. "I showed it to her, Hélène. She could see the resemblance to Edouard straightaway. She remarked on it—it was the first thing she said." Anne paused; she pressed Hélène's arm. "You should tell her," she said. "I know you both wanted to wait for the right moment. Well, it's come."

They stayed to have tea with Anne, served in the old blue Spode cups that Hélène remembered. Then, in the early evening, they found a taxi and opened all the windows, and settled back for the long journey to Eaton Square.

"Will Edouard bring Christian back, do you think?" Cat said.

"Oh, I expect so. It can't have been very pleasant for him, going back to his old home. I imagine he'll be sad, and we'll need to cheer him up."

"I'll cheer him up. I'll show him some of my card tricks. Cassie just taught me a new one. . . ."

Cat was sitting on the jump seat, as she always did, leaning with the sway of the cab. Her long thin legs were stretched out; her hair, as ever, stuck up in disorderly waves and tufts. Her face, usually so animated, wore a slightly dreamy and abstracted expression.

Hélène sat opposite her, watching her, thinking of what Anne had said. She knew she was right. Cat was seven now—they could not delay much longer. She tried now, as she had often tried in the past, to frame the correct sentences in her mind, so they were clear and comprehensible to a child, so that Cat was left, as much as was possible, without doubts or worries. But Hélène could think of so many causes for doubt herself that, in the end, as in the past, the sentences would not be spoken, and she was silent.

They crossed Hyde Park; Cat lolled against the window, watching the people, the dogs, the children playing. She pointed to the Serpentine, and the boats on it, and then, as they reached the gates on the south side of the park, she looked back at Hélène.

"You know I went to play with Lucy Cavendish the other day?"

"Yes, darling."

"Well, Lucy says her daddy isn't her daddy. He's her—" she paused, frowning. "Her stepfather. Her real daddy used to be married to her mummy, but he isn't anymore. She's married to someone else, and he's married to someone else. . . ."

"Yes?" Hélène said cautiously. Her heart had begun to beat very fast.

"Lucy says it's nice. Having two. Daddys I mean." She paused;

they were halfway down Exhibition Road. "Lewis wasn't my daddy, was he? I mean—not my real daddy?" It was the first time Hélène had heard her mention Lewis's name in the past year. Her eyes were now fixed on Hélène's face.

"No, Cat, he wasn't. Lewis was . . . was more like a stepfather in a way. When I was married to him. But I'm not married to him anymore. . . ."

"Oh, I know." Cat sounded offhand. "You're going to marry Edouard. Which is *much* better." She hesitated. "I liked Lewis. Sometimes I did. But he wasn't there very often." Her brow wrinkled. "I don't think I remember him very well. A little bit. I remember the house, and my room—with the rabbits on the blind, and the garden. . . ."

She stopped. There was a pause; they had reached Chelsea, they were turning in the direction of Eaton Square. Hélène reached in her bag for her purse, her mind full of a thousand sentences now, all jumbled, all flurried.

"I look like Edouard. *Just* like Edouard. I could see it when I looked at Anne's painting. I never noticed before."

Hélène leaned forward.

"Of *course* you look like Edouard, Cat. You're his daughter."

There was a small silence. The cab drew up to a halt outside their house. Cat opened the door, bounded out, and then held it back politely for Hélène. Hélène paid the driver. As the cab began to pull away, and they stood on the sidewalk together, Cat gave a small skip and a jump.

"Edouard's my real daddy? He is? He is?"

"Darling, yes—and we would have lived with Edouard before, always, right from the day you were born, but—"

Cat was not interested in such ramifications. She clapped her hands.

"I knew it! I knew it! Oh, I'm so glad." She stopped. "Does Cassie know? And Madeleine?"

"Yes, darling."

"And Christian?"

"Yes."

"How stupid of me. Lucy Cavendish said he was, and I said yes, and then I wasn't sure. I felt a bit muddled."

"But you don't feel muddled now?"

"Now?" Cat gave her a scornful look. "Oh, not now, of course not." She paused. "It's a pity we didn't always live with him, I think. But that was such a long time ago. And I was very little. . . ." She tilted her face up to Hélène. "We'll always live with him now, won't we?"

"Of course, darling, always."

"Oh, I'm so *glad*." Cat gave another skip and a jump. "I'll talk to him all about it tonight," she said with a decisive air, and then she ran into the house.

"And your card was . . ."

Cat held the deck in her slender hands. Christian, stretched out in a chair, long legs crossed, arms behind his head, surveyed her quizzically.

"The king of diamonds! *Le voilà!*" With some dexterity, Cat extracted the card, and held it aloft. Christian obligingly looked stupefied.

"Astonishing. Quite astonishing. Cat—I can't believe it. Was it magic, or was it a trick?"

"Magic," Cat said firmly.

Christian shook his head and took a swallow of his whisky. "If I had not just witnessed it, with my own eyes—I should never have believed it. Will you do it for me again sometime? You're a wizard. Or a witch. What else can you do? Can you tell fortunes?"

Cat glanced at Cassie, who was standing magisterially by the door, arms folded, in an attitude that said: *bed.*

"Not yet." She began to move obediently and reluctantly to the door. "I might learn though. Madeleine says she knows how to do it. And Cassie can read tea leaves in the bottom of a cup. Her grandmama showed her. You look at the patterns the leaves make, and—"

"Cassie. You have hidden depths." Christian's eyes turned to her lazily; he smiled. "I took you for many things, but never a sibyl. . . ."

Cat was giving beseeching glances toward Edouard and Hélène, who were watching this scene from the far end of the room. Hélène inclined her head very slightly, and Cat's face at once brightened. Cassie gave both Cat and Christian a stern look.

"I can see into the future all right," she said crisply. "And I can see when someone's playing for time. I can see it's seven o'clock now, and someone's not going to be in bed until nearly eight at this rate. And I can see—"

"No, you can't, Cassie," Cat said in a meek tone of voice. "I'm coming now. And tonight I'll be *especially* quick. . . ."

She went around the drawing room to say her formal good nights. Christian, who found her very droll, stood up, kissed her hand, clicked his heels, and smacked her bottom. Hélène hugged her, and then, as Edouard went to kiss her, said quickly, "Maybe Edouard will come up and say good night, Cat. If you're very quick. Not too long in the bath now . . ."

Edouard smiled, and promised, and Cat scampered away. Hélène crossed to Christian, and sat down next to him. "Now," she said. "Tell me all about it, Christian. Was it very hard? Were you glad Edouard went with you?"

"Oh, awfully glad. For all sorts of reasons," Christian began.

Edouard gave him a sharp warning look, and Christian, who enjoyed teasing him, settled back into a careful and innocuous account of their day. Edouard watched them both, half-listening for a while; he moved to the long windows, and the balcony that overlooked the square gardens. After a while he replenished their drinks, and then, at a sign from Hélène, left them to say good night to Cat.

He climbed the stairs slowly. Today, for some reason, perhaps because of his conversation with Christian, and the visit to his parents' house, the past seemed very close. Just then, in the drawing room, when Cat produced that card—*The king of diamonds, le voilà!*—he had both seen and heard Pauline Simonescu: *The cards first, Monsieur le Baron. Then you can begin your future.*

It was 1967 now: he had not seen Pauline Simonescu since 1959, on that occasion when, not long before he met Hélène, he had decided to leave her house in Paris and never return there. She had left Paris—or so he had heard; he did not know now whether she was alive or dead. He had hardly thought of her for years, and yet tonight, when Cat produced that particular card, he had seen her vividly. For a moment it had been as if she had reached out, and laid her hand, with its ruby ring, on his arm, and he had felt again that tension, that sensation of curious force.

He stopped on the first landing, where he and Hélène had their rooms—rooms which had once, during the war, been his mother's, and which were almost unrecognizable now. He thought of the occasions, then, when he had bounded up these stairs, two at a time, hastening to the security of his room, where, on his chart, he would enter the references to the progress of the war in blue ink, and the coded references to Célestine in red. He saw Célestine, with her red-gold hair piled on top of her head, her dressing gown falling open a little. He saw Célestine as he had seen her at the end, last year when she was dying, lying propped up against the pillows in a room in a nursing home in St. John's Wood, where her bills had, for years, been quietly settled through the offices of the eternally efficient, eternally discreet Smith-Kemp.

"I should like champagne," she had said once. It was almost the only thing she did say as she drifted back to consciousness, and then drifted away again.

He stopped on the second landing. He was glad, now, that he had always kept the lease on this house; glad he and Hélène now used it so often. It was pleasant to feel the past so close. He leaned against the banisters, and thought of dancing, downstairs, with Isobel, slowly circling a room, while a scratchy dance tune played on a wind-up gramophone. Tonight the house was very quiet; he listened for a moment, almost expecting to hear the sound of that scratchy gramophone record, with its wartime gaiety: but there was only silence. Then, as he turned toward the room in which Cat now slept, and which once had been his room, he heard, quite distinctly, Jean-Paul's voice. He heard him laugh, felt the weight of his arm around his shoulders: "What a dance they like to lead us, women—eh, little brother?"

He felt a moment's sharp regret, a piercing nostalgia; all the old, intense, and increasingly hopeless affection for his brother came back to him, and he remembered Jean-Paul, then, not as he had been toward the end, but as he had been in the war years, in the time when Edouard would have forgiven him anything.

He gave a little shrug, and went into Cat's room. She was sitting up in bed, with a book in front of her, though she did not appear to be reading it.

Edouard smiled at her, and she smiled back; he at once felt the past slip away in the quiet of the room: Cat's room—not his anymore. That past had no reality for Cat: as all children do, she lived for the present.

He moved quietly around the room, looking at her books, and at the pictures which she had painted, of which she was very proud. He looked out the small high window: there, across the square, he had once been able to see the blackened gap where a house had been bombed: a direct hit. There was no trace now, of course. Looking at the view, he was no longer certain which house it had been.

Cat was watching him expectantly. With an apologetic smile he turned back to her, and sat down on her bed. He took her small hand, and let it rest between his own.

"I keep thinking about the past today. I'm sorry, Cat. It feels very close for some reason. This used to be my room once."

"I know. In the war. When you lived here." She hesitated a moment. Two bright points of color stood out on her cheeks. "Did you know mother then?"

"Goodness, no. I was only a boy—fifteen, sixteen years old." Edouard pressed her hand gently. "I didn't meet her until much later. Years after the war ended."

"Did you meet her in London?"

"No. In Paris." Edouard hesitated, and then, because he, too, like Hélène, had worried about Cat, and how much she knew or could understand, he did not stop there as he might have on another occasion, but went on.

"I met her in Paris. Standing outside a church. It's called St. Julien le Pauvre, and there's a small park—like a little square—just near it. I took you there once—you probably don't remember. . . ."

"I think I do." Cat frowned. "Did you think she was beautiful?"

"I thought she was very beautiful." Edouard smiled gently. "I fell in love with her instantly. Just like that! *Un coup de foudre*—that's what we say, in France. Like a thunderclap . . ." Cat giggled.

"It's true. It can happen. I never thought so before. . . ." He paused. "I remember my father telling me that. When he met my mother, Louise—it was a very long time ago, at the beginning of the First War, not the second one. He saw her dancing . . . and he fell in love with her. Just like that."

"But you didn't marry her then. You're going to marry her now, instead. . . ."

Cat's expression had become a little anxious. She was leading up to something, Edouard could see that, and it seemed to make her both excited and a little fearful.

"No. I wanted to. But all sorts of things happened—complicated things—I'll explain them to you one day." He paused. Cat's gaze was fixed on his face. "The important thing to remember, always, is that your mother and I always loved each other very much. We did things in the wrong order perhaps—grown-ups do that sometimes, for all sorts of reasons. But we've straightened them all out now, and that's why we have this wedding to look forward to. You are looking forward to it, aren't you, Cat?"

"Oh, yes!" Her eyes lit. "Very much. Cassie has a new hat, with a feather. And I have a new dress. . . ." She paused. "I'm not supposed to tell you about the dress, because it's a surprise. But it's blue. Like cornflowers. I like blue. It's my favorite color, and this dress is very pretty." She stopped. "I know you're my real daddy now. I thought you were, but I was a little muddled, so today I asked Mother, and she told me."

He could feel her excitement and agitation. Her small fingers tightened and then relaxed against his. Edouard's heart welled with love for her; he was very moved, and tears came to his eyes. He looked quickly away, afraid she might misinterpret them, and then back at her.

"But of course. My daughter. My only child." He managed to control his voice. "And we look like each other a little bit, don't you think?"

"Oh, yes. I could see it when—" Cat suddenly broke off mysteriously. "I noticed," she added, and at once became sternly practical. "And so I have to decide. I've been thinking about it. I have to think what to call you. I could still call you Edouard, or I could call you Papa, or Daddy. Which do you think?" She looked at him earnestly.

"I think any of them will do. All of them. You could even take turns. I could be Papa when I was stern, and Daddy when I was indulgent, and—"

"You're never stern!" Cat laughed.

"Ah, that's because you've never been truly naughty. Just you wait. I can be very stern indeed. I can be quite terrifying. Look." Edouard composed his features into the most cold and intimidating look he could manage.

Cat was unimpressed. She laughed again. Her hand tightened its grip. "I like you," she said simply.

"That's fortunate." Edouard looked at her solemnly. "I like you too. I've liked you since the day you were born."

"Truly?"

"Oh, yes. Someone once said to me—" Edouard glanced away. "They said they'd much rather be liked than loved. What do you think?"

Cat frowned. She gave the question serious consideration. "Both," she said finally.

"That's good. Because I like you very much, and I love you very much. And I'm also very proud of you." He bent forward and kissed her. Cat put her arms tight around his neck, and planted a loud wet kiss somewhere in the region of his nose.

"And now you must lie down and go straight to sleep. And no reading after lights out—promise?"

"I promise."

She wriggled farther down under the bedclothes, turned on her side, rested her hand under her cheek, and closed her eyes. Edouard switched off the small lamp by her bed and moved quietly to the door. There he stood for a moment, watching her; her eyes flickered open once more, and then closed. She let out a little sigh; her breathing quietened, and became regular. Edouard watched her for a while, happiness fierce in his heart, and then, seeing that, with the ease of a child, she was almost asleep, he left the room quietly, leaving the door ajar, as she liked it.

As he came into the drawing room, Hélène was saying, "So what will you do, Christian? It would be very hard for you to sell it, surely?"

And Christian, loyally, was saying, "Oh, God, I don't know. A solution will come to me, I expect."

They broke off as Edouard came in.

Hélène knew at once, from Edouard's face, what Cat had spoken to him about. She sprang up, and went to him. Edouard put his arm around her, rested his head for a moment against hers. It was the briefest of gestures; Christian, watching them from across the room, could see in it, brief as it was, an intimacy, and a certainty of affection; they were, for an instant, so strong, that they were like a presence in the room. He was excluded, he was aware of that, but he did not mind. Happiness was infectious, he thought: he could see it transfigure Hélène's face, Edouard's face; he felt it transfigure him.

What had happened was explained, and Christian was delighted.

"Ah, well, then," he said in the drawl he used to disguise extreme exuberance. "This is splendid. I feel rather avuncular. I feel benign— and we haven't even had dinner yet, and Hélène says there's salmon, which I *particularly* like, and strawberries, which make me dreadfully greedy, and then we can all sit and talk—really, it's turned into a splendid day, memorable for all sorts of reasons. . . ."

Edouard gave him a warning glance, and Christian smiled with a certain glint in his eye. He lifted his glass.

"We should have a toast. I know—the old Oxford one, Edouard. Do you remember? Champagne and punts, and the appalling spectacle of the dawn coming up over Christ Church meadows, after a Commem. Ball?"

He stood, lifted his glass a little higher, and waved it about, so the whisky slopped dangerously.

"Edouard. Hélène. Happy days . . ."

The marriage took place on the twenty-third of June. On that day, a Friday, Lewis Sinclair was sitting alone in the room he shared with Betsy, high up on the attic floor of the tall house near the junction of Haight and Ashbury. From the outside, it was a San Francisco house, a gingerbread house, with gables and dormers, and elaborately carved clapboarding; inside, it was not like being in San Francisco at all. It was a little like being in India, Lewis imagined, though he had never been to that country, or possibly in Turkey, or possibly nowhere at all, in a room that was outside space, and outside time.

Lewis lay on a rug on the floor, a kelim rug. Behind his back was a pile of cushions, embroidered in brilliant peacock colors, and decorated with fragments of mirror glass. It was a quiet room, high above the traffic, and through the small window he could see only the sky. Sound was muffled further by the rugs and hangings which entirely covered the walls. Above the door, Betsy had painted the words *Peace and Love*, in Day-Glo orange. Lewis looked at the words: through the floorboards, beneath the layers of rugs, he thought he could hear voices—Betsy's voice, Kay's voice; the Shaman's voice.

Sometimes he thought he heard Hélène's voice, too, but he knew that was an illusion. Hélène was not in the room underneath, she was in the past. He frowned, and her voice went away. He looked down: propped against his knees there was a calendar.

It was a very long time since Lewis had used or looked at such a thing. He thought that it was today that Hélène was marrying Edouard de Chavigny, but he was not entirely sure. Of late, time seemed to him to have its own rhythms. He had known long before that time did not proceed in an orderly manner, as other people seemed to think that it did. Even when he had been living with Hélène, he had found that. But now it did not just bend back upon itself, and loop, as it used to do, so that he was not quite sure whether he had done or said something, but merely imagined it—now, time had a life of its own, and it took Lewis with it, it bore him up, like a feather on the wind. Sometimes it rushed forward, sometimes it sped back; sometimes two, three, or four apparently separate things seemed to happen at once, and the barriers of years between them were simply not there at all.

He stared at the calendar fixedly. Obviously, dates existed; they had some kind of reality, and he felt that he would have liked to be sure whether it was today that Hélène was marrying, or next week, or last year.

Lewis stared at the small numbered squares. They made him think of those horrible math problems he had been assigned at school. During vacations, his father used to go over them with him, trying to keep his voice patient. *Lewis, if you will concentrate. Now. Let us suppose that five men take three hours to plow a field of three acres. That means, if seven men plowed the same field . . .*

He shut his eyes. He let the calendar fall to the floor. Today, last week, next year. It was all meaningless.

Sometimes, when he shut his eyes, he felt weightless; he floated. He felt this now, as if his body rose from the floor, and moved gracefully above the cushions and rugs and little incense holders, and Tiffany lamps, occasionally bumping pleasantly against the ceiling, like a cork carried by a wave.

He rather wished, as he floated, that Betsy might come up. He considered the possibility of his going down to her, but it seemed such a long way to the door, and besides, Betsy wouldn't be alone. She was never alone. This house was too full, Lewis thought: it was too full of people who came and went, and he was not sure which of them were real. Had his mother been here, for instance? He thought she might have been, because once, lying here, floating here, he had smelled not joss sticks but lavender. And Stephani—had she been here? He thought she might have been, because he had seen the fur against her white skin, and the diamonds like stars between her thighs. But that would not have been Stephani, of course: that would have been Hélène. When Stephani came she wore a fishtail dress, with sequins like iridescent scales, so she looked like a mermaid.

Betsy came: of that he was certain. He bobbed against the ceiling, and thought about Betsy, whose body was tiny and fragile, whose wrists he could circle, easily, with finger and thumb. Betsy covered him with that long thick curtain of auburn hair, and she wound her legs around his waist, and at the moment of climax, her small hands beat a tattoo against his spine. He could hear this sound now, like the falling of raindrops on leaves, and then the tintinnabulation of her bracelets, jingling in his ears like distant bells.

Now, or yesterday, or last year, or tomorrow. When had he last heard those bells? Again he was not certain. He opened his eyes and then shut them again. The ceiling was beginning to feel soft, and this relaxed him. He dreamed. In this dream, Thad came to visit him, and sat down cross-legged in his black suit, and nodded like a Buddha, just as he always used to do.

In this dream, Thad asked Lewis questions. So many foolish questions. All about some past which he seemed not to realize was very, very distant. He wanted to know about Sphere, and Partex Petrochemicals, and about people called Drew Johnson and Simon Scher. In particular, he wanted to know who made the decisions at Sphere—who, as he put it, called the tune.

"I only met Scher. I was never interested in all that," he kept saying. "But you were, Lewis. You met Scher a lot. You met Drew Johnson in Paris. You went out to his plane—remember, you told me, Lewis?"

In his dream, Lewis stared at Thad. The names he was using were familiar; Lewis thought he might have read them in a story, heard them used in some film. He didn't answer Thad, because of course he knew it was a dream, so there was no point. Thad seemed not to realize this. He stood up. He shook Lewis. He gave his arm a sharp pinch.

"Lewis, will you *listen*? I met someone. A girl—never mind what girl. She used to work for Simon Scher as a secretary. Now she works at Fox. She told me something interesting, Lewis. Really interesting. All the decisions, the budgeting, when we made our movies—we thought it was Scher who gave the final okay, yes? Well, she said it wasn't. She said he never made a move, not one move, until he'd checked first with—"

In the dream, Thad stopped at this point. He took off his glasses, and panted on them and rubbed them on his sleeve, and Lewis said, "Thad, she would have introduced us to Fellini. She said so." Thad stared at him again. His mouth pursed up small and tight. "Can you hear me, Lewis?" he said. "Is one single word getting through to you?"

Then Lewis began to laugh. It seemed so funny that Thad, who knew everything, who was always so certain, didn't realize that this was a dream, and that none of it was happening at all. Once he began to laugh, he could not stop. But that was not because of Thad, that was because of the pill Betsy had given him, which the new candyman had brought. These pills made your stomach ache, as if you'd pulled a muscle in a football game, and then they made you laugh.

In the dream, this laughter made Thad very angry. He stood up. He said, "Jesus, Lewis, you are *sick*. You *smell*. You're pathetic. No wonder Hélène walked out." He knelt down, and put his face very close. "She never wanted you. I never wanted you. You had money, that's all, Lewis. Money. Did you realize that?"

Lewis stopped laughing then, and began to cry. Thad seemed pleased, and not long afterward, he left.

Lewis opened his eyes. He watched the words *Peace and Love* grow large, then small, bright then obscure, until he was sure the dream was over. He had this dream quite often, and it had different endings. Sometimes he stayed here, floating and weeping, and sometimes he stood up, and ran after Thad, and Thad waited for him. Then they went off down the street together, arm in arm, and Lewis knew Thad had not said any of those things, and they were friends again. "We'll go see *The Seventh Seal*, Lewis, it's a great movie. I've seen it thirty-five times. . . ."

Lewis sat up. Suddenly he felt extremely nervous, so that his hands shook. He had to know, he thought. He had to know about Thad, and whether it was really a dream. He had to know what the date was. He had to know now.

He pushed himself to his feet and made his feet walk. One in front of the other, across the room, out the door, down the stairs. He struggled with the door of the room below, and when he opened it, the wail of the music hit him so hard that he staggered.

The beat of drums, the whine of a bass guitar. He looked around the room, expecting to see Hélène, because he had heard her voice, quite distinctly, from the stairs. But Hélène wasn't there: just Betsy, and Kay, and the Shaman. The Shaman was six feet six inches tall, his head shaved and gleaming. The Shaman was dancing.

"Thad," Lewis said. He said it very clearly, so there could be no mistake. "Thad. Was he here just now? Was I talking to him?"

"It's Lewis. What d'you know? He can walk."

Kay looked up at him from the floor where she lay. Betsy, who was sitting beside her, stood up and came across to him. A drift of hair; leaves the color of maples in the fall.

"Lewis? Are you all right?" She looked up at him. "That was three weeks ago, Lewis. I told you before, remember? Three weeks. Maybe four. He didn't stay long."

The Shaman paused in his dancing. He smiled. He said, "Angeliiiini, Angeliiiini . . ." And then he began to spin, around and around, very gracefully, chanting the name like an invocation.

Lewis watched him. The Shaman's hips swayed; he lifted his arms above his head, and described circles and spirals through the air. Betsy pulled at Lewis's arm. She was trying to make him sit down.

"I don't want to sit down," Lewis said as he sat. "I want to watch the ballet."

"The ballet. Jesus."

Kay stood up. She came across and moved so that she was blocking Lewis's view. Then she knelt down and put her face very close to Lewis. Too close. Lewis blinked at her. Her eyes looked small and red and hot and full of hatred. He could smell that hatred, it was as sharp as the smell of sweat, and it frightened him. He couldn't understand why Kay felt like this. He couldn't understand why Betsy let her live here, why she didn't make her go away.

"I've got something for you, Lewis. Something special. I've been keeping it."

She was wearing jeans. She always wore jeans. Men's jeans, and a man's shirt, and with her hair cut short like a man too. Now she put her hand into the pocket of the jeans, and pulled out a scrap of paper. Inside the paper was something small and round and white. Lewis looked at it.

"Kay. Don't give him that stuff—not now." Betsy made a little rush forward, and Kay reached up, and put an arm around her waist.

"Why not? It's all right. He'll like it. He wants it—you do, don't you, Lewis? You like pretty things, I know you do. Pretty cars, and pretty houses, and pretty clothes and pretty girls. You take this, Lewis, and you just won't believe how pretty life is. Beautiful colors. Beautiful shapes. Beautiful sounds. You want the sun and the moon to play with, Lewis? You'll have them—right there in the palm of your hand. Oh, Lewis, you'll see the moon so close you wouldn't believe—"

"Kay . . ."

"It's okay, Betsy. It's okay." She leaned forward, and kissed Betsy on the lips. Lewis watched. He could feel something, and he thought it was anger, but it was so far away, so buried. . . . He was still groping for it, when Kay turned back to him.

"Come on now, Lewis," she crooned, her voice very sweet. "Open wide, now. That's a good boy. Now, swallow it, Lewis. That's it. Down the little red lane . . ."

Lewis swallowed, and Kay began to laugh.

After that, she left him alone, so Lewis felt glad he'd done as she said. She went back and lay down on the cushions, and then Betsy went, and lay down next to her. They were smoking, and the Shaman was dancing, and the music was playing. Lewis watched the Shaman's muscles ripple across his bare back. He watched Kay, who was stroking Betsy's hair; she was kind to Betsy; Lewis closed his eyes.

He looked at the blackness, and watched time begin to dance. There was a rocking horse he had had as a child, with a thick mane, and black and white spots on his haunches. There was the crowd at the Harvard-Yale game, their applause like the buzzing of a million flies, like the music of the sea in a shell. There was his father, and the gates of the Beacon Hill house were barred against him; he rattled them gently, and they mixed with the sound of Betsy's bracelets. There was his mother, and the scent of lavender, as she bent over his bed to kiss him good night. And there was Hélène, cradling him in her arms, while behind her there was a flight board, and its numbers were spinning.

They spun slowly at first, then gradually faster, so fast that Lewis opened his eyes.

What he saw then was so lovely that he cried out in wonder at it. Colors so emblazoned in the air that he could smell them; shapes so fluid and so composed that he could hear them; music whose blue he could taste on his tongue. A universe of light; a room in heaven.

He lifted his hand, and raised it slowly in front of his face. He saw the fingers and the palm, the knuckles and the wrist. He saw into the texture of the skin, and beyond, to the tiny capillary veins of blood. He saw into the river of the artery, and saw the sweet sure pumping of his heart. There was the structure of tissue: he saw and understood the beautiful mechanism of muscle and nerve. He bent his head, looking closer, and saw God.

So close. Inside him. Not far away, or insubstantial, but there, inside the tissue, inside the muscle, inside the bone. A God in each particle, in each gene: a God, there, in the flexing of his finger. Lewis lifted his eyes from his hand, and there in the blazing brightness of the room, the stars moved and the planets danced.

Lewis heard the salt of his tears falling. He saw the words that he spoke. He watched them curl from his lips, and spiral gently across the room, a curl of words, a helix as delicate as butterflies. They glanced and flickered against the white and the red and the sapphire and the green. They touched and flowered against the blackness of Kay's hair, and the crescent moons of her closed eyes. They fluttered against Betsy's white neck, and brushed the long curve of her bare spine. Shadows and valleys; air mauve as woodsmoke; and the Shaman, who could make magic, rising and falling, rhythmic as an ax, into Betsy's body and out of it; ivory and ebony. A man and a woman: God in each gleaming stroke. Lewis watched with a still heart: he had never seen anything more lovely.

"Hélène."

He touched the word, and felt it humming.

"Hélène," he said again. "Hélène. Hélène."

And then, out of the quiet of the color, Kay uncoiled. She said, "Betsy. He's watching you. Lewis is watching you fucking."

The words came at him like a great and malevolent hissing. All the peace and the color in the room fractured and distorted. Lewis stared at the universe, and saw it bend and bulge: it flew apart into a million fragments. The air was gray with its debris.

He stood up. He said, "You don't understand. You can't *see.*"

No one spoke; no one seemed to hear him, though he thought he shouted the words into the debris very loudly.

He knew he must move. He dreamed his passage to the door, dreamed it again and again, so the four steps became forty. He dreamed the stairs, and the door of his attic room; he dreamed locking the door to keep the debris out; he dreamed the sound of the debris outside, knocking.

He stood very still in the quiet of the room, and let God come back to him. When he felt God's breath and pulse, he grew calmer, and the darkness of the room began to glow for him. He moved to the window and looked out at the touchable stars, at the moon which he could pluck as easily as an orange. He thought of flying.

He knew he could fly. He had flown once before, somewhere— down through the eye of the storm, where the air spun him gently. It seemed important to know when and where, and—as he climbed up onto the windowsill—the memory came to him like a vision.

Standing at the top of the stairs, looking down into a ballroom, that was when it began. Outside, Berkeley Square glittered with snow, and the trees were frosted silver. But inside, the house was warm and fragrant. He saw the men and women circling; he saw the swirl of dresses. . . . In the cool night air high above the streets of San Francisco, a sound began, faintly at first, then more strongly. Music; sweet music; the sound the stars and the planets made, waltzing. Perfect time: perfect love. He heard the woman calling to him, with a voice like starlight. His mother. His wife. Pale as moonshine, dark as night, eyes like diamonds, calling.

"I'm coming," Lewis cried.

He stood a moment, poised. Outside the door, the debris knocked.

When he dived into the dark and flew downward, the air was singing.

After their marriage, Hélène and Edouard went away together for three weeks. They went to Istanbul, and stayed at a *yali*, once the summer residence of a Romanian nobleman, which Xavier de Chavigny had bought in the twenties. It was on the eastern shore of Turkey, and it overlooked the waters of the Bosporus.

The house, unchanged since the turn of the century, and rarely visited, was cool and quiet. From the wide, brass-postered bed, with its white canopy, Edouard and Hélène could look out the tall windows opposite, to the water which lapped to within a few feet of the glass. The outside of the windows was barred with a delicate fretwork of iron. It was fashioned in intricate patterns, and when the sun moved around to shine on this side of the house, it cast a filigree of shadows on the floor of the room: Ottoman lace, a carpet of monochrome.

Beyond the window, light danced on the water, and they both grew fascinated by this endless movement and refraction. They were reluctant to leave that room, or each other. They took breakfast there—strong coffee, bread, and rose-petal jam. They watched the boats that plied back and forth between the two shores, between the Western world and the Eastern. Across the water, shimmering in a miasma of light, they could see the city of Istanbul, the domes and minarets of its palaces and mosques. Sometimes they took dinner in this room, too, and sat quietly together afterward, watching the moon rise, and watching the patterns it cast upon the water.

Their second child was conceived in this room, conceived one night when few words were spoken, conceived—Hélène sometimes felt afterward—out of the shadows and the silver, out of touches that were as slow and rhythmic as the movement of the water.

They both knew a new life had begun: locked together, they had an absolute sense of its conception. Edouard lifted himself a little, and looked down into her eyes. Hélène felt she moved in the depths of his gaze: she lifted her arms, braceleted with silver light, and wrapped them around his neck. The warmth of his skin, and its dampness, delighted her.

White light in her mind. Time out of time. She pressed her lips against his hair; she said his name, and other things, with a sudden feverish need, as if words could hold this moment, and fix it. Then she stopped speaking: the words were too small.

Edouard took her hand and pressed it against his lips. He held her, and they lay quietly together, listening to the lapping of the water.

T he next day, they flew back from Istanbul in Edouard's plane. Hélène could sense some excitement in Edouard, which she could see he was at pains to conceal, and which puzzled her. She was more puzzled still when she saw their flight plan, and discovered they were flying, not to Paris, but to Heathrow.

"Are we going to London, then? But Edouard, I thought . . ."

"Not London. London is just en route. Wait and see. . . "

She could persuade him to say nothing more.

At Heathrow, the black Rolls-Royce Phantom was waiting for them. They settled themselves in the back, and still Edouard could not be persuaded to explain.

Hélène felt a tiny sense of disappointment, but she concealed it. She had been looking forward to seeing Cat, and Cassie and Madeleine. She had been looking forward to taking Edouard into his study, and showing him the portrait of Cat, which she had been saving for this moment. But this would wait, she told herself. She glanced at Edouard. His face was composed and still, and told her nothing. She watched the road signs: they seemed to be driving in the direction of Oxford, and—as they cleared the outer suburbs of London—she found that Edouard's suppressed excitement was catching. She forgot about Paris; she became more and more intrigued.

After some time they turned off the main Oxford road, onto a smaller road, and then one smaller still. They began to climb: it was late afternoon, and, as the hills and valleys of the Downs opened before them, Hélène gave an involuntary cry of pleasure.

"Oh, Edouard—it's so beautiful. Where are you taking me?"

"Wait and see," Edouard answered infuriatingly.

Five minutes later, they came to a small lodge house, and a pair of tall iron gates between stone pillars. They entered a long winding drive lined with tall beech trees and bordered with paddocks on either side. Then the drive curved around a bend, and Quaires Manor and its gardens came into view. A long brick house, with sash windows, and a steep roof; Hélène looked from the house to the garden, and gave a cry of delight. As if her exclamation were a cue, Edouard's driver halted the car, Edouard opened the door, and helped her out. He placed one finger against her lips, and then, taking her hand, he led her along a gravel walk, and through into the gardens.

The gardens were empty and quiet, except for birdsong. They passed through an archway of clipped yew, along a path that led past a small octagonal gazebo, and toward a central rondel, fragrant with roses in the still, cooling air. There they stopped, and looked back up toward the house, and there Edouard explained.

"For you," he finished gently, "and also for your mother, whom I never knew. And for Christian's mother, who would have liked you, and who would have liked to know—" He paused. "Well, that all this would be taken care of, perhaps. For Cat, and for all the other children that I hope we shall have." He broke off, and seeing the expression on her face, held her close, until she was calmer.

Hélène clasped his hand. She closed her eyes and let the past come back: the child in Alabama, the woman here. Edouard made sense of her life, she thought confusedly, and when she tried, in a rush of words, to explain this to him, she knew that he understood.

He lifted her face to his, and looked down into her eyes, his gaze growing still and intent.

"Loving you and being with you gives meaning to every moment of each day," he said. "It will always be so. Hélène, come back to the house."

They walked slowly across the lawns, and then, just as Hélène was about to say, impulsively, that she wished Cat were there, a door burst open, and Cat, unable to bear the suspense any longer, rushed out to greet them, and Cassie, Madeleine, and Christian came out from hiding, too, so that the lawns, quiet and empty a moment before, were suddenly peopled.

"Champagne, champagne," Christian was shouting.

Cat was tugging at Edouard's hand. "There's a surprise for you, there's a surprise for you too. Daddy, come quickly, come quickly. . . ."

And she pulled Edouard into the drawing room, where, carefully and artfully hung by Christian, Anne Kneale's portrait of Cat was waiting for his inspection.

Edouard looked at it for a long time, one arm around Cat, one arm around Hélène. Cat peeped up at him anxiously, watching the play of emotions on his face—the surprise, the pleasure, the pride, then a gentleness which became almost sad.

Hélène, also watching this, understood. But Cat was too young. She pulled at Edouard's sleeve.

"Do you like it, Daddy? Do you?"

"I like it very very much. It makes me very happy."

"But you don't look happy—Daddy, you look sad."

Edouard bent and lifted her in his arms. "That's because I'm older than you, Cat. When grown-ups are most happy, they sometimes feel a little sad, just at the same time. You'll understand when you're older." He hesitated, and glanced at Hélène.

"We think of time passing, Cat," Hélène said quickly. "That's all."

Cat glanced from one to the other. Edouard kissed her. When she was quite certain that he truly liked the painting, she wriggled free of his embrace, with her characteristic quick impatience. Grown-ups, she thought, could make things so complicated when they were really very simple. She was about to break away, and run out again, when something in the quietness of the room, something in the looks her father and mother exchanged, made her pause. Here was a mystery; an adult mystery. For a second, she felt it touch her, and it made her want to shiver, like the touch of a shadow after the sun on her skin. She shifted from foot to foot, looking up at them uncertainly.

"Like I feel, sometimes? At the end of a nice day? When it's been so nice you don't want it to end—you don't want to go to bed?"

Edouard smiled. "A little like that, yes."

Cat's face cleared. "Oh, that's all right then. When I feel like that, I know it's silly really. Because it will be just as nice tomorrow. . . ."

She smiled at them blithely, eager to reassure them both, and when she saw them smile, she was content. She ran out to the garden, where Christian allowed her to help open the champagne. He poured her a glass, very solemnly—the first champagne she had ever tasted—and afterward, Cat always remembered that evening with a special precision.

She would tell herself that it was because of the surprise, or because of the champagne, and because drinking it made her feel grown-up. But she knew that was not truly the case. It was because of the way her parents had looked at each other in that still room.

"Why are grown-ups a little sad when they're most happy, Christian?" she said later, when she and Christian were alone in the garden, and the shadows were lengthening.

Christian could always be relied upon to give an answer, and he gave her one now. He frowned a little, looking toward the roses that grew against the walls, and Cat was not to know that he could not look at them without seeing, and hearing, his mother. "Because they know the best things, even the really good things, never last," he said quietly. "That's all, little Kitten."

"Why not? Why don't they last?" Cat turned to him fiercely.

"Oh, we get older, I suppose. People die, Cat. That's why." And he stood, and left her, with an odd abruptness.

Cat, who was used to Christian's sometimes sudden changes of mood, watched him go. Then she sat quietly, hugging her knees, looking out across the garden.

She tried to figure out what he meant. She tried to think about death, but she had never seen a dead person, or even a dead animal; it was something out of books, and not real to her. "Death," she said to herself under her breath, trying out the word. "Death."

An owl flew over. She sat very still and watched the pale shape quarter the lawn with a slow deep beat of white wings. In the undergrowth beneath the boundary hedges, a small animal squeaked, and the owl flew on, into the fields and out of sight. She stayed very still, breathing quietly; she watched a soft fuzzy moon as the branches of the trees first obscured, and then revealed it. She felt quiet and still and secret, as if she were invisible, and she liked that; she hugged the feeling to her. Then, from inside the house, her mother called, and she realized she was cold.

She jumped up and ran quickly into the warmth and the light. She hugged her mother, her father, Christian, everyone, with a sudden quick fervor which she did not understand, and they said she might stay up, just this once, for supper with them. And that was so grand, so unprecedented, so exciting, that while it lasted, she forgot what Christian had said, she forgot how she had felt when she sat in the garden.

It came back to her when she went to bed, and lay in the quiet of an unfamiliar room. She could hear the voices downstairs. She heard the owl hoot. She felt, for a moment, as if she were on the brink of some huge discovery, which excited her, but of which she was also a little afraid. She tried to unwind it, this thought, this feeling, which was tangled away somewhere in her mind. But she was tired, and the thought would not unravel: she fell asleep.

She thought of the feeling again though, one week later, when they returned to Paris. She was in the room with Edouard and Hélène, when Hélène opened the letter.

She saw her mother go pale, and give an odd kind of gasp. She saw Edouard go to her quickly, and take the letter from her hand. She knew something had happened then, something that somehow connected, and she couldn't think what it could be, until—much later—Edouard came up to her room and explained, quietly and gently, that there had been an accident, and Lewis Sinclair was dead.

She cried then—because she was shocked, and suddenly afraid. Edouard held her in his arms, and talked to her, and soothed her until the tears stopped. And Cat clung to him, very tightly. She was not quite sure why she cried, and afterward, much later, when Edouard left her, she felt a little guilty. She tried to think of Lewis, she tried to remember him, but she knew the memories were vague and imprecise. *I ought to remember better*, she said to herself.

Then she cried again, fiercely and bitterly. But she knew, in her heart, that she was not crying for Lewis—not exactly. A little bit for him, because it was horrible not to be alive anymore: but also for her father and her mother, and a look that had passed between them; also for Christian, and also for herself: sitting in a garden, alone, and watching an owl fly over.

"This is my fault," Hélène said to Edouard that night, with a sudden bitter intensity. She picked up Emily Sinclair's letter, and then laid it down. The color rushed into her face and then ebbed away. She stood up, her eyes glittering with agitation.

"Edouard—I did this to him. I began it. I made him marry me. I made him miserable. I knew it was wrong, and I still did it."

"That isn't true." Edouard gripped her by the arms. "Nothing is that simple, Hélène. Nothing."

Hélène looked up at him, and then turned her face away.

"Nothing," Edouard said again. He felt suddenly the most angry and passionate conviction. "Hundreds of factors," he said sharply. "Thousands of incidents. They all contribute to something like this. Chance contributes to it. You can't just impose one shape, and say—it was because of that, and only that. Blaming yourself is futile. . . ." He paused, and his face hardened. "It's also selfish. I know, because I've done it."

Hélène's face grew still. Edouard knew that some of his words, at least, had reached her.

"Do you believe that?" she said, more quietly.

"Yes. I do."

He said no more then, but let Hélène cry. Her grief, he knew, would not be like Cat's. Cat was a child, and could not grieve for long. The process, for Hélène, was much more difficult, and more drawn out. He waited, patiently, comforting her when she needed to be comforted, listening when she needed to talk, and remaining quiet when she needed to be silent. It touched him that someone so capable of giving should feel that she had been destructive, and that she should blame herself, and never Lewis, for what had happened.

Time would alter that view, he hoped. He felt compassion for Lewis Sinclair, and it was not for him, he thought, to point out that Lewis's self-destructiveness had always been there; Hélène would come to see that in the end.

A month after they returned from Istanbul, her pregnancy was confirmed, and when Edouard saw the happiness in her face as she told him, he knew that she would come through this, as she had come through grief in the past, in her own way, and at her own pace. He watched her anxiously, watched the silences grow less frequent. He watched the irrepressible contentment break through, and was glad.

"One cannot mourn forever," his mother, Louise, remarked, one day, when they called to visit her. She sighed, and pressed her hand against her heart. She was not referring to Hélène, of course: Hélène's experiences did not pierce the shell of Louise's egotism. She was referring to herself, merely harking back to a refrain that had always been one of her favorites.

Edouard, who could never hear her say this without remembering precisely how brief a time she had mourned his father, looked away impatiently. Hélène met his eyes.

"I know," she said quietly.

There was a moment's unspoken understanding between them, which Louise sensed, and which made her irritable. She brushed at the skirts of the pale lavender dress she was wearing, and changed the subject. Edouard at once became impatient to leave. The recent atmosphere of his mother's house, its air of quiet and bogus religiosity, he found suffocating. Now Louise chose to have her blinds always half lowered. She sat in a dim light, and fingered the crucifix she had taken to wearing around her neck. She had dressed for the past two or three years, not in the chic highly fashionable clothes she had once favored, but in loose gowns that were an echo of her youth, that were modest, and flowing, and always in the subdued colors of semi-mourning—dove-gray, a muted blue, occasionally, if she were feeling very assertive of her new role, deep black.

She devoted herself now to good works: her constant companions were either the priests, or other widows of impeccable mournfulness, who spoke to her of their mutual good works. Once, making one of his routine brief visits, Edouard had come across one such gathering. Louise had sat there, listening to the talk of starving orphans in Africa, and her eyes had sparkled with an unmistakable rage and malice. The new role was a replacement for the old one, that was all: it was Louise's way of acknowledging that, alas, she could no longer fascinate as she had once done; she could no longer attract lovers.

Her hypocrisy and her fretfulness irked him now more than it used to. He could not enter her house without being eager to leave, and Louise, sensing this, would look at him with a cold measured dislike, occasionally risking—if Hélène were present—the overtly reproachful.

"It's all a sham," he said angrily on that particular occasion, when they finally left. He took Hélène's arm. "My mother has never in her life grieved for anything except herself."

"Oh, I expect she has, in her way," Hélène said. She stopped suddenly on the sidewalk. She stood very still, and then turned to him with a quick impulsiveness.

"Anyway, what she said was true. Right or wrong, I feel happy, Edouard. I can't help it. Here. Feel." She took his hand and pressed it against the swell of her stomach. All around them, people moved, cars roared down the Faubourg. But Edouard was conscious of none of them. Beneath his hand, he felt his child move for the first time. A slow, hesitant, rolling bumpy motion.

Hélène frowned, and then laughed. Edouard gathered her in his arms and, oblivious to Paris, kissed her.

"It's a boy," Hélène said happily. "Edouard, I know it's a boy—I'm quite certain."

She was right. It was a boy. He was born in April 1968, and they called him Lucien. The year of his birth was a violent one, memorable for assassinations, for invasion, and for riots, which, in Paris, tore a city apart, divided families and generations, and caused Louise de Chavigny, in her view, not only spiritual agony, but also a great deal of inconvenience.

"In America perhaps," she said acidly, one summer's afternoon when she had been persuaded by Hélène to come out to St. Cloud to have tea, and to see Lucien, on whom, to Edouard's surprise, she doted. "America has always been a violent country. But here—in Paris. To find streets closed off. To hear them shouting slogans, and see them marching, building barricades . . ." She gave a small shudder, as if the demonstrators had been encamped outside her own house. "I simply cannot understand what they're protesting about. It's the work of foreign agitators. In my view, they should all be deported. . . ."

She spoke with some spirit. She was, Edouard noted, in an excellent humor, in spite of her complaining, and he assumed this must be the events of the past month, which had enlivened what she now referred to as her "drab" existence. Her animation was apparent not just in her voice, but also in her appearance: for the first time in three years she had cast aside the somber and unflattering dresses: she was wearing, today, one of pink silk. Her pearls, not the crucifix, were around her throat. She had altered her hairstyle, and was even wearing discreet makeup once more. She looked much younger, and still lovely: it was perhaps the knowledge of this, as well as the stimulus of outrage, Edouard thought, which made her so animated.

He was hardly listening to what she was saying, in any case. Louise's political opinions were of no interest to him, and he had long ago learned to block them out. He was looking with affection at Cat, who lolled against her mother's chair, and at Lucien, who sat on Hélène's lap, and occasionally, almost regally, waved his silver rattle.

Lucien had clear blue eyes, of a lighter shade than Edouard's or Cat's. He had a cap of profuse reddish-gold curls, the face of an angel, and the temper of a devil. Cassie called him a little tyrant, fondly; even George could not look at that small, oddly imperious little face without breaking into a smile.

"Such a little darling. So handsome." Louise, having disposed of the riots to her own satisfaction, leaned across and cooed at Lucien. He regarded her levelly, with his wide blue eyes. Louise looked at him closely, and then looked up at Edouard. She smiled her sweetest and most maternal smile, and Edouard at once tensed.

"Of course, you know who it is that he resembles?" Louise's eyes were now fixed on Edouard's face. "*I* noticed it at once."

"Both of us, I suppose . . ." Edouard shrugged.

Louise's smile widened.

"Edouard, how absurd you are. Men are so blind. It's perfectly obvious. He's precisely like, exactly like, my darling Jean-Paul."

Quite how, or when, Hélène first began to play a part in Edouard's business activities, neither of them could afterward say: the process was gradual, and to begin with almost imperceptible. "It crept up upon me," Edouard would later say with a smile.

Hélène had, from the first, taken an interest in his work, and

Edouard had, from the first, seen that she possessed a quick understanding and an instinct for financial affairs which he had always believed to be rare in women. Before and after their marriage, she continued to manage her private portfolio of investments, still through the offices of James Gould in New York, and also through brokers in Paris and in London. She did not bother Edouard with the details of these investments, but they were, on occasion, discussed; Edouard noted then her shrewdness, was impressed, but thought no more about it. Hélène noticed this, and was amused by it, but said nothing: Edouard's attitude to women was chivalric, conditioned by his generation and his upbringing. Hélène knew perfectly well that deep down Edouard held very simple beliefs: he believed in marriage, he believed in the family; if he had been called upon to define his own role in that union, he would probably have said that he saw himself as a provider, and as a protector, though his natural reticence on such matters might have inclined him not to define at all.

Clara Delluc, with whom Hélène gradually, in Paris, became friends, once said with a smile, "Edouard is full of paradoxes. He admires independence, in men and in women. When I was beginning my work, trying to build a career, Edouard helped me more than anyone."

She seemed about to go on, and then hesitated. Hélène smiled. "But?" she prompted.

Clara laughed. "But I think he still believes it's a little unnatural. He can't quite believe that a woman—any woman—can be truly happy unless she is married and has children. Though, of course, he would say the same of a man." Clara paused; she had not married, and she had never had children.

"And who knows?" She gave a wry smile. "He may not be entirely wrong. Perhaps women need both. Though I would never admit that to Edouard . . ."

Shortly after the birth of Lucien, Edouard began to explain his business concerns to Hélène in more detail. Hélène saw that, although the ramifications of the company were extensive and complex, its central organization was very simple. It remained a private company; within that company, Edouard held ninety percent of the voting stock, and his mother ten. Louise's holding, which had come to her through Xavier, and would pass to Edouard on her death, entitled her to a seat on the board. In thirty years, she had never attended a board meeting.

Edouard explained, hesitantly, as if expecting possible opposition from Hélène, that this division of stock needed review: he wanted to transfer a fifteen-percent holding to Hélène direct; he wanted her to join the board of the company.

Hélène knew quite well why he had done this: with the birth of Lucien, he had had to alter his will, and Edouard, cautious and methodical in all such things, was ensuring that, should anything happen to him, Hélène, who would hold Cat's and Lucien's interests in trust for them until they came of age, would feel familiar with the workings of the company.

She accepted, gladly: she attended her first de Chavigny board meeting in the spring of 1969: she was, as she had known she would be, the only woman present.

The other board members, all much older than she, were precisely as she expected. They were able, they were astute, and to her they were deferential. They welcomed her charmingly—and then they proceeded to ignore her completely. Very occasionally, when one of the men present feared the discussions might have become a little too technical for her, he would call a gentle halt to the proceedings in order that they might be explained to Hélène in words of one syllable.

Hélène accepted this gracious patronage quietly. For the first four or five board meetings she attended, she said very little. She bided her time, watching the men around the table, listening to their arguments and their counterarguments, deciding in her own mind which of the men present had most to contribute, and which least. She watched them, and she weighed them, noting with interest their various alliances and rivalries, and—she was pleased to note—her relative silence was effective. After the first two or three meetings, they seemed almost to forget that she was there: their behavior was then the more revealing.

Edouard did not underestimate her, and occasionally she would catch a gleam of amusement in his eyes when one of his colleagues patiently and laboriously explained some terms or practices with which, Edouard knew perfectly well, Hélène was already familiar. But he never said anything, either during the meetings, or afterward when they were alone. He was waiting, Hélène knew, and it amused him to wait.

So, possibly, Hélène's involvement began then, when she was appointed to the board. Hélène knew Edouard would not have pressed her: had she been content to remain simply a silent ornament to the board table, Edouard might have been disappointed, but he would have accepted it as her choice. She herself felt, however, that her involvement dated from a point later in 1969, when she first discussed with him openly the other board members, and the agenda of the meeting she had just attended.

"Shall I list the factions for you?" she said with a smile, when they were at dinner together that night.

"Please do."

Edouard leaned back in his chair. Hélène dealt swiftly, and accurately, with the factions. When she had finished, Edouard's smile had grown broader.

"So—you think all those weighty and carefully researched arguments Temple was putting forward against the further expansion of the hotel division—you think they were biased?"

"I'm certain they were." Edouard noted with amusement that Hélène's pretense of detachment was slipping away: her color had risen, and she spoke rapidly, and with animation. "I'm quite sure. Temple can't bear Bloch—they're equally influential at the moment, but if Bloch's plans for the hotel division were implemented, it would divert assets Temple wants earmarked for the Sardinian villa development. It would give Bloch more influence and more power, and Temple doesn't want that to happen. Besides, I thought his arguments were wrong. The hotel division has been virtually static for the past three years, you've consolidated your existing holdings—it looks like the moment to expand."

"I see."

Edouard made a small pyramid with his fingers. This was precisely what he himself thought. He looked at Hélène thoughtfully. "It's interesting," he said slowly. "I knew you were watching them. You see it like a play."

"In some ways, yes." Hélène leaned forward. "On the one hand there're the arguments they put forward, but you can't judge those on purely commercial grounds. You have to understand the men who make them, and their interrelationships—because that affects their proposals. It's the politics of it, if you like. That interests me."

"And what else did you think while you were watching them so carefully and unobtrusively—on general grounds?"

"Generally?" Hélène paused. "Well, generally, I was impressed. They're able, and they speak their minds on most issues, with one possible exception, I thought."

"And that was?"

"The jewelry division. There's still some opposition to the Wyspianski collections, isn't there? I could sense it. But they're for the most part afraid to cross you on that, so they defer." She hesitated. "And they're all men, Edouard. It just struck me that might be one of the problems. They don't have your interest in Floryan's work, I don't think they understand it. And the jewelry division is the only one whose products are aimed primarily at a female market. I think those two facts might be connected." She paused. "I could see—they're quite at ease when they're dealing with hotels, or property, or wine—but when it comes to the jewelry division, they all become a little impatient."

"Are they wrong?"

"You know they're wrong." She leaned forward. "Floryan is an artist. His work is the finest in the world. It's unique, and it's part of a long company tradition. The identity of de Chavigny is bound up with that tradition, you can't separate the two. All the prestige associated with the name, it flows from the one central activity. You can't classify what Floryan does for the company purely in terms of profit and loss. If they had their way, if the jewelry division were sold off—and I think that's what some of them would like to see—de Chavigny would be just another faceless multinational corporation. They should understand that."

Edouard frowned. He thought of Philippe de Belfort, and of the arguments he had once propounded. It angered him that they should still linger on, as if, though de Belfort had left de Chavigny, his influence remained, a ghostly legacy. Sometimes Edouard felt that influence had grown stronger this past year; many times, in the past few months, he had recognized de Belfort's arguments in other men's mouths, phrased in almost the same way. It disturbed him; and it consoled him, now, to hear Hélène taking the opposite stance.

He looked up at her with a dry smile. "Anything else?"

"One other thing. It concerns you."

"Oh, I see. I might have known I wasn't immune. Tell me."

"You should deputize more." Hélène paused. "I understand why you haven't. Partly because of the hours you used to work, partly because, among the men I've met, there's really no obvious candidate. But you need someone, Edouard. Someone you can trust absolutely. Someone to cover for you. And perhaps—someone to watch your back."

"You think that?" Edouard looked up quickly.

Hélène hesitated. "I do think that," she said finally, with some reluctance. "Any man in your position has to consider that, and you, perhaps, more than most."

"Why is that?" Edouard looked at her steadily.

Hélène sighed. "Oh, Edouard. Because you excite envy, I think, that's why."

Edouard looked away when she said that. He seemed surprised, as if the idea, so obvious to her, had not occurred to him before, and made him uncomfortable.

Shortly afterward, they left the dinner table, and the conversation changed to more personal concerns. It was not referred to again for some weeks. Hélène continued to attend board meetings, and began, gradually—to the severe shock of the men present—to voice her opinions, quietly and incisively. Now, when Edouard brought work home, he discussed it with her: they looked at his papers together, and slowly Hélène began to piece together a much more detailed understanding of de Chavigny, its many interests, and how, within the executive divisions of the company, they were structured. She met an increasing number of the de Chavigny senior personnel—and to her amusement, as her influence on board meetings became gently and then more strongly apparent, the very men who had so courteously patronized her before, now began to seek her out. Deftly, and delicately, they sought to involve her in their power games and their maneuverings: initially, perhaps, because they thought she had Edouard's ear, but—more gradually—because they realized that if her viewpoints held sway, it was because they were rational.

"You think like a man, Madame," said Monsieur Bloch graciously one evening, at a party of his that she and Edouard attended.

He clearly saw this as a compliment: Hélène let it pass.

She assumed that her suggestion to Edouard regarding his need for a lieutenant or deputy had been forgotten, for Edouard did not refer to it again; but in this supposition, she was wrong.

At the beginning of 1970, Hélène looked up one morning from the pages of the *Financial Times*, which she read each day at breakfast, and passed it across to Edouard.

She was flanked, on one side, by Cat, in her convent school uniform, who was as usual late, in a cross mood, and bolting her breakfast at high speed; and on the other hand by Lucien, trapped in a highchair he detested, who was attempting to eat a soft-boiled egg, unaided. Hélène, who liked breakfasts *en famille*, was unflurried. She dealt with Lucien and the problems of his egg; she turned to Cat and persuaded her to finish eating, and also—which was more difficult—to tidy her unruly hair before she left for her classes.

The spectacle of Hélène, with her hair loose, *en déshabille*, dressed in a simple blue cotton dressing gown the color of her eyes, made Edouard inclined to delay. When Cat kissed them both and rushed off to school, and Lucien was claimed for the nursery by his new English nanny, Edouard was considering whether, just this once, he might not delay his arrival at the office by at least one hour.

He stood up, without looking at the article Hélène had indicated, and let the *Financial Times* fall. He walked around the table to Hélène, and rested his hand gently on the nape of her neck, lifting her hair, and letting it brush through his fingers.

Hélène bent her head back and looked up at him: he saw the answering response in her eyes, the stilling of her face. He bent, and kissed her on the lips; he slipped his hand down over her throat, and under the soft blue cotton; Hélène sighed. She stood up and rested against him, in his arms.

"You'll be late. . . ."

"I know I'll be late. I don't give a damn."

She was about to protest further, though without great conviction. Edouard, who could feel the warmth, and the sudden lassitude in her body, stopped her from further words.

He was one and a half hours late, but before he left, as they came back downstairs, Hélène, with a smile, retrieved the copy of the *Financial Times* from the dining room and pushed it into his hands.

"You should read that." She attempted to look at him sternly. "I won't be put off. You were going to bid once for the Rolfson Hotels Group, weren't you? I remember your saying. Well, you should bid again now."

Edouard groaned. "So that's the kind of woman you are. That's what you were thinking about just then, when I . . ."

Hélène kissed him. Her eyes danced.

"No. Not then. As you know very well. But I am now. And so should you."

The bid was made, in the summer of 1970, and was successful. It had two direct repercussions. Edouard, tied down by the negotiations for weeks, finally admitted to himself that when Hélène had said he needed a deputy, she was right. As soon as he acknowledged that to himself, he placed a call to the only man he was certain had all the qualifications he needed: Simon Scher.

He put his proposals clearly and concisely, without preamble. From Texas, all the way across the Atlantic, he could hear the smile, and the surge of elation in Scher's voice.

"Well, now, Edouard. It's been a long transfer. I guess Drew might be persuaded to let me go. And you do get very tired of grilled steer. . . ." He paused. "When might you want me?"

Edouard also smiled. He knew perfectly well that the negotiations would hardly be straightforward, and Drew Johnson might well oppose the move.

"Tomorrow," he said carefully.

There was a small silence, then Scher laughed.

"I don't believe it," he said. "It must be marriage. You've become a patient man."

Scher finally returned to de Chavigny at the end of 1970, in the same month that Edouard and Hélène celebrated the birth of their third child, another boy, whom they named Alexandre.

"He ought perhaps to have had Rolfson among his names," Edouard said as he cradled the baby in his arms. He looked at Hélène dryly. "Considering the time and place and circumstances when he was conceived."

"What nonsense," she said. "Considering the circumstances, you can't possibly be certain."

"Oh, yes, I can." Edouard lifted Alexandre in his arms and looked at him solemnly. "You came into this world because of the *Financial Times*. There now. What do you think of that?"

Alexandre gurgled obligingly, and they both laughed.

There was one third repercussion, but it was very small, and in the elation surrounding the successful bid, the arrival of Simon Scher, and the birth of his second son, Edouard hardly noted it at all. It puzzled him for the space of a few hours—then, dismissing it, he allowed it to slip from his mind. It came in the form of a telegram, delivered to his offices on the day the Rolfson Hotels Group takeover was completed.

It read: *Congratulations on the bid—belatedly.* It had been sent from Portugal, and it was unsigned.

In the spring of the next year, shortly before Cat's eleventh birth-day, Thaddeus Angelini came back into their lives. He did so without warning. There was no letter, no telephone call, there was merely an invitation, sent not by Thad himself, but by the public relations com-pany that was organizing the première of his latest film, an epic about the American Civil War, which was called *Gettysburg*.

Hélène looked at the invitation, and at first assumed that she and Edouard had been invited because the première was in aid of a charity for which they had both worked in the past. Then she wondered: was that the reason—or had the invitation been made at the request of Thad?

She glanced down at the date: May 19, two days after Cat's birth-day, and also precisely six years since she had last seen Thad. Could that be right? It seemed to her very much longer, and the days when she had worked in Hollywood very remote. But no: she calculated the years, and saw that she was correct. Six years ago to that day, she had visited Thad's house, and he had taken her down to that room with its insane collection of photographs. Once she was sure of the coincidence, she was also sure that Thad had arranged the invitation, and her first instinct was to refuse it; but she hesitated, and eventually changed her mind.

Partly, and she knew this, it was curiosity. In the six years that had passed, Thad had never contacted her once. Even when Lewis died, there had been no call, and no letter. What Hélène knew of him she learned from newspapers, and it was not a great deal. He had made a string of films, first for Joe Stein at Artists International, and then for a succession of other studios: two of them had been modest successes with the critics, but none had succeeded at the box office. In interviews, Thad blamed the studio system for this. With Sphere, he had enjoyed a measure of independence. Now, he claimed, his work was thwarted from first to last by constant and philistine interference.

His reputation as a director had declined, Hélène was aware of that. He had recently been compared, unfavorably, with other directors, including Gregory Gertz, and a whole generation of new names, who were being called the coming men. The two films she had seen had only served to confirm the reactions of the critics: she had liked neither, and had been surprised that Thad, whose work had always been so precise and assured, should demonstrate such uncertainty of touch.

Some of the younger European critics, she had noted with a smile, had begun to date the decline in Thad's work from the ending of her own partnership with him, and one particularly excitable French critic had proclaimed that, in losing Hélène, Angelini had lost his muse. This she did not take seriously, though she noticed once or twice that, when the idea was put to Thad in interviews, he responded very irritably.

The truth of the matter was, she thought, as she looked at the square of pasteboard, she had almost forgotten Thad. She was so occupied with her family, and with her work at de Chavigny, that all memories of Thad had receded. Like Hollywood, he had been relegated to the past.

But still, she was a little curious, and she also felt a certain lingering loyalty to Thad. It gave her no satisfaction to see critics who had once fawned over him now turn on the attack, often dismissing, in the process, earlier work they had once praised. *Gettysburg*, she had noted, with pleasure, seemed to have been a major success in America, reversing the tide of Thad's critical fortunes. It was breaking box office records; it had been acclaimed by Susan Jerome—yes, Hélène thought, she owed it to Thad at least to go to the première.

When she put the idea to Edouard, he agreed, but unwillingly. Hélène assumed that the reluctance was due to Edouard's dislike of Thad, but this was not entirely the case.

When she showed him the invitation, Edouard looked at it, then tossed it back. He stood up. "Very well," he said shortly. "You're probably right. We'll go."

He turned away—angrily, Hélène thought—and Edouard was angry, but not with her. He was angry with himself. Simon Scher had now been working with him for over six months: Edouard was perfectly well aware of the fact that Scher's arrival had been the moment, if ever there was one, to tell Hélène of his own previous involvement with Partex, and with Sphere. He had, in fact, decided to do so, resolved to do so: he had had the necessary sentences framed in his mind. But whenever he came to say them, he deferred.

He had—and this was in some ways worse—told her part of the truth. He had told her that Simon Scher had a previous association with his own companies, going back many years. He had even told her that both he and his mother held stock in Partex Petrochemicals. And there, abruptly, he had stopped, finding himself quite unable to go on. On the first occasion he had tried to tell her, Hélène had been nursing Alexandre. She had lifted her face, and looked up at him, quite obviously unsuspecting, and delighted by the news of Scher's appointment.

"I had no idea you even knew him. And you're sure he's the right man? Oh, Edouard, I'm so glad."

Edouard had been dismayed. He kept hoping that Hélène would question him further, because he knew that though he might lie to her by evasion and omission, he could never lie to her directly. If only she had asked him—But Edouard, did you never know he was working with Sphere?—then, he knew, he would have told her. But she never asked, never cross-examined him. This complete trust was, more than anything else, the one thing which made him unable to speak. To have kept silent on the question in the first place was one thing, but to have kept silent for six years—what would Hélène's reaction be once she knew that?

Edouard felt it would undermine their shared past, undermine her trust in him. Try as he would, time and time again, he could not bring himself to speak. When the moment of Hélène's first meeting with Simon Scher in Paris came and went, and still no questions arose, Edouard knew himself to be trapped. Scher was inclined to dismiss the matter.

"Edouard, it's ancient history now. Forget it," he said. But Edouard could not forget it. The lie diminished him in his own eyes: he could not believe that it would not diminish him in Hélène's.

He was not familiar with the guilt that comes from deceit, and so, when he experienced it, it made him angry. He found himself constantly on edge, whenever Simon Scher and Hélène met, which they did with increasing frequency; whenever some article about Partex appeared in the newspapers; whenever the question of his or Louise's continuing investment in that company came up—as it did, on various occasions when, in front of Hélène, Louise might take it into her head to discuss the management of her portfolio, over which she had, in the past year, become increasingly fretful.

At the same time he was worried about Partex itself, and the aggressive policy of expansion Drew Johnson was set on. Those doubts, which had begun at the time of the last Partex merger, had multiplied since, and multiplied still more, once Simon Scher returned to Paris. Scher's presence, and Edouard's influence, had, in the past, acted as a brake to Drew Johnson's impetuosity; within six months of Scher's return, it was becoming clear that the brakes were off. Johnson embarked on a program of heavy borrowing, and when Edouard and Simon Scher looked at those borrowing figures, they were both alarmed.

When, not long before the première of *Gettysburg*, Drew Johnson began to throw out hints that he was interested in strengthening his own stockholdings in Partex, Edouard therefore felt a certain relief. At another time, he might have hesitated, but now he did not. To Johnson's transparent delight, he agreed to sell.

"You think you can persuade your mother to transfer her stock?" Drew asked.

It was almost his only question, and Edouard felt a mixture of distaste, regret, and relief, at such an end to what he had once regarded as a partnership.

The sale of his own shares was organized very swiftly. Edouard anticipated problems in persuading Louise, however, and arranged to see her, finally, on the afternoon of May 19, before the première of *Gettysburg*.

He went to his mother's house, expecting fretful inquiries and time-wasting arguments, and armed with the evidence of Partex's latest borrowing figures.

To his surprise, Louise did not argue at all. She seemed almost pleased at the suggestion.

"I did tell you, Edouard," she said with a little smile. "I've been wanting to liquidate some of my assets for some while. . . ."

"I know that, Maman," Edouard said patiently. "But this sale isn't a small matter. These are sizable holdings. You will realize a lot of money. . . ."

"Shall I?" Louise tilted her head to one side coquettishly. "Such fun . . ."

Edouard frowned. His mother was looking, that day, particularly well. She seemed relaxed and happy; there had, for once, been no complaints about her health. But her behavior worried Edouard nonetheless. Louise was now seventy-six, though this was a closely guarded secret. She had become, in the past year or so, even more unpredictable. Sometimes, as today, she dressed like her old self, and would seem gay and lively; at other times, for no apparent reason, she would revert for weeks to her previous gloom, to the gray dresses, the lowered blinds, the priests. Her temper, always uncertain, was now very volatile, and she had become very ticklish over the most minor matters. Now she disliked Edouard to visit, as he had used to sometimes, either with no advance warning, or after a casual telephone call made as he was leaving his office.

"It fusses me so, Edouard," she would say. "I like to *plan* my days. I'm not young now. I don't *like* unexpected visits—it's so inconsiderate."

This meeting had been carefully and politely arranged three days in advance. And now, as he sat looking at her, Edouard wondered whether Louise's grip was slipping, whether she had any idea of the seriousness of the moves they were discussing. Privately, he resolved to have a word with her doctors; there and then, ignoring the odd quality of her smile, he attempted to explain that if she sold this stock, they were talking, not in hundreds of thousands, but in millions of dollars.

Louise cut him off. "I *understand,* Edouard," she said pettishly. "You've explained once. You don't have to do so again."

"I'm just trying to make you see, Maman, that it's not just a question of selling the stock. I can arrange that for you very simply."

"Please do."

"But you then have to decide where you want to reinvest, and I thought . . ."

Louise stood up. She glanced at her wristwatch, which she still always wore fastened to her wrist by a black velvet ribbon.

"Edouard, if I need your advice, I shall ask for it. As it happens . . ." She gave another little smile. "I have some ideas of my own. I do have them, you know, and it is my money. . . ." Edouard also rose. It was growing late; he had to return to St. Cloud to change for the première; Louise's attitude was annoying him.

He was inclined, then, simply to walk out, and let her have her way. He began to move to the door, and then he had second thoughts: Louise was not young anymore. However angry she made him, he still had responsibilities to her. . . . He turned back.

"Perhaps if you'd just tell me your ideas, Maman. Then, perhaps, I might be able to assist you—"

Louise did not give him time to complete the sentence.

"I'm going to invest in *property,* Edouard. I've always liked that. I understand it. Houses, not silly little pieces of paper. I shall buy property, and I shan't need your advice, Edouard, and I'm sure that will be a relief to you—after all, you're so tied up with your family now, it must be a great burden to you, having to concern yourself with all my little affairs. . . ."

"Property where, Maman?" Edouard said tiredly.

Louise smiled. "Portugal," she said sweetly.

Edouard hesitated, then, abruptly, his patience snapped.

"As you wish," he said coldly, and left.

Gettysburg began on a battlefield: Thad had always photographed death beautifully, Hélène thought, and he did so now. One long slow tracking shot in on a field still covered with thin morning mist; it was only as the camera moved in closer that the carnage became apparent: not hummocks, or tussocks of grass, as they appeared from a distance, but bodies. The battle had long been over, and in the field nothing moved.

Men with arms outflung, backs arched, legs sprawled; men lying two, three, four deep, their attitudes a parody of an embrace. It was as formally, as confidently and as beautifully composed as a painting by

Delacroix. Too beautifully composed: Hélène looked, and then looked away.

She was already regretting that she had decided to come, and wishing that it were possible to leave. Beside her, Edouard sat stiffly, his face turned to the screen, his expression cold. He had been angry when he returned, late, from his visit to Louise, and his temper had not been improved by his arriving home in the middle of an impassioned quarrel between Lucien and Cat, into which, by the time he arrived, Hélène, too, had been drawn.

It was the first such quarrel Edouard had witnessed; Hélène, who had watched their growing frequency these past months with a sense of sadness and confusion, had tried to keep them from him, telling herself that it was simply a phase. Both Cat and Lucien were at difficult ages, and occasional jealousy between them was inevitable. But the quarrels had continued, with no sign of abating, and today, as always, the squabble flared up suddenly, the result of one small incident.

Today, it had been a drawing, on which Cat had been working for days. She loved to draw, and to paint, and took painstaking care over her work. This drawing, of the garden at Quaires, had just been completed. Somehow Lucien, while Cat was at school, had managed to give his nanny the slip, and had found his way into Cat's room. When she came home, she found the drawing had been scribbled on, her work almost hidden under Lucien's red crayon marks. By the time the shouts and screams of temper reached Hélène, and she had run up to the nursery with Cassie, the damage had been done. Lucien was scarlet with rage; Cat was shaking; the drawing was lying on the floor torn in pieces, and on Lucien's arm there was a bright red mark where Cat had slapped him.

"He did it on purpose. He did! I know he did. . . ." Cat was almost sobbing with outrage. "I showed it to him yesterday. He knew it was special. . . ."

"Stupid drawing . . ." Lucien kicked the torn pieces of paper with his foot.

Cat sprang at him again, and might well have slapped him again had not Hélène managed to stop her. In the room beyond, confined to his crib, Alexandre joined in the mêlée: he began to wail.

"Cat. Control yourself. You mustn't lose your temper like this. Lucien's only three. Of course he didn't do it intentionally. . . ."

"That's right—take his side! You always take his side. Always. Always . . ."

Cat's voice had risen uncontrollably; her eyes were vivid with tears. Lucien was standing stock still, holding his ground; as Hélène turned to look at him, he gave her one of his still, measuring looks, which Hélène found unnerving in a child so young. There was a curious element of defiance in them, as if Lucien were waiting for the opportunity to test his will against hers. She was just thinking this, and at the same moment telling herself not to be absurd, when Edouard walked into the room, his face pale with anger.

"Exactly what is going on?"

His voice cut through the noise, and there was a silence. Then everyone began to speak at once, Cat and Lucien most stridently, claim and counterclaim.

"He spoiled my drawing—he did it on purpose!"

"Cat smacked me. She smacked me on my arm. . . ."

The expression on Edouard's face eventually silenced them. He said, in a cold voice, "Lucien. You will not go into Cat's room again. And you will not touch her things again. If you do, you will be punished—do you understand? And Cat, you will not bully Lucien. You will learn to control your temper. How dare you slap a three-year-old child?"

Cat swallowed. Her mouth was trembling, and Hélène could see that she was about to burst into tears. She looked at Edouard, then down at the drawing, then back at Edouard. Then she burst out, "It wasn't a hard smack. I lost my temper, that's all. I worked on that drawing all week. I—"

"Go to your room."

Edouard cut across the rising torrent of words, and Cat stopped. She stared at Edouard, still shaking with the emotion she felt, and then, without a word, she turned and ran out of the room.

Lucien watched her go, his small face quite expressionless. Edouard looked down at him.

"And you, Lucien. You will apologize to Cat in the morning. You will never do anything like this again. Do you understand?"

Lucien lifted his blue eyes to his father's face, and gave him an angelic smile. "No, Papa," he said quietly.

Edouard looked at him for a moment, then turned, and abruptly walked out of the room.

Now, in the theater, Hélène glanced again at Edouard's averted face. She could see that he was still angry, and she wondered if he, too, was thinking of this scene, as she was, or if he had had a quarrel with Louise. She tried to force her attention back to the screen, but she could not concentrate. She kept thinking about Cat, suddenly seeing a connection between a whole series of small incidents which she had dismissed at the time; these were not simply the quarrels between brother and sister, but other occasions over the past year, when Cat had seemed unhappy, or uncommunicative, or withdrawn. She had explained these to herself in so many ways: it was Cat's age—she was approaching puberty; it was a process of adjusting to the presence of a new baby; it was, perhaps, her school, which Cat had once liked passionately but now claimed to hate. She thought suddenly: we are not as close as we were; Cat does not turn to me as she once did. And the conviction that this was true, that it was also perhaps inevitable, a part of Cat's growing-up, made her both guilty and miserable.

Oh, why had they come? She longed, then, to be able to talk to Edouard, who, in the car coming here, had scarcely uttered one word. Unhappily, she forced her eyes back to the screen and made herself concentrate. She had missed half the plot; she stared at the actors with a sense of confusion: they were somewhere in the South; there was a young girl, and a much older man, a major in the Confederate army. . . . She tensed, she watched more closely, and then, with a growing sense of shame and of anger, she realized what Thad had done.

The film lasted two hours. When the lights came up, Edouard's face was grim. He leaned across and took Hélène's arm, but although he gripped it tightly, his voice was gentle.

"We're not staying for the reception. Come on. We're leaving."

"No. I won't do that." Hélène stood up. "I'm staying. And I'm going to speak to Thad. I want to know why he did that."

"It will only upset you, Hélène. It's better just to leave it."

"No. I won't."

"Then let me speak to him."

"No, Edouard. I shall."

She saw him hesitate; his reluctance was obvious—but he gave in. They went to the reception, and for forty-five minutes, Thad managed to avoid her. Hélène watched him coldly from across the room, hemmed in on all sides by journalists and well-wishers. She could sense the excitement in the room, that odd vicarious excitement she remembered from Hollywood, which told her the film would be a success here, just as it had been in America. She waited. Then, seizing the moment when Edouard was drawn away from her side for the first time, and there was at the same instant a gap in the people surrounding Thad, she crossed quickly to his side, and looked down at him.

He appeared unchanged; he showed no signs of pleasure, or surprise, or embarrassment; he behaved just as he always behaved, as if the last six years had never been. The small dark eyes glinted up at her behind the tinted glasses; he was sweating slightly, but then, the room was hot.

The other people melted away. Thad nodded, and then smiled. He said, "Hélène."

"Why did you do that, Thad?"

"Do what?" He lifted his face to hers, and blinked.

"I thought this was supposed to be a film about the Civil War?"

"So it is."

"It's also the story of my life. Part of my life. You've changed the period and the names, that's all. I suppose I should be grateful for that."

"It's an original story." Thad shifted from foot to foot. "I should know. I wrote it."

"It's unforgivable. It's cheap."

Thad sighed. "It would have been better if you'd been in it, I admit that. That girl's all right. But she's not special. It's a good film though. It's the best thing I've done since *Ellis*."

Hélène looked at him. He appeared quite unconcerned: the same old rocklike certainty, not the smallest flicker of doubt.

"The daughter, Thad," she said in a cold voice. "Why did you kill off the daughter?"

"How d'you mean?" Thad tilted his head to one side and looked up at her owlishly.

"You know exactly what I mean. You have a character based on me, and that character has a daughter. At the end of the film, the daughter is killed. You do remember that, I suppose?"

"Oh, *that*." Thad shrugged. "I don't know why I wrote it that way. It was just right."

"You did it to hurt me."

"Does it hurt you?" He looked slightly interested.

"Yes. It does. The whole film does."

"I didn't think it would. I really didn't. I never thought of that once." Thad shook his head. He appeared genuinely surprised, even contrite. "I'm sorry, Hélène. You ought to know I wouldn't want to hurt you. Why should I? I want to work with you again. I still do. I want you to come back. . . ." He glanced across the room, hesitated, and then began to speak more rapidly. "I'm going to start a new script. When it's finished, I want you to read it. That's why I wanted you to come tonight. So I could tell you. I didn't want to just send it. It will be a good script: a great part. We could shoot it in six weeks. It's a love story—well, a kind of love story. It's set in Paris and London, and—"

"I'll never work with you again." Hélène interrupted him. "If you send me any scripts, I'll tear them up." She stopped. "Paris and London?"

"Yes." Thad looked impatient. "And I wouldn't even need you for the whole six weeks. I could work on the schedules, dovetail your scenes, get it down to a month. You could spare a month, couldn't you? You must want to work again. You must be bored with all this." He gestured at the room. "You know what you're doing? You're frittering away your life. You . . ." He did not complete the sentence, for Edouard had joined them. Through her own indignation and anger, Hélène could immediately sense the tension. The two men looked at each other. Thad rocked a little, back and forth on his heels. The light twinkled against his spectacles. He smiled. "Did you like the film?"

He attempted to keep the challenge out of his voice, but he did not entirely succeed.

Edouard looked at him levelly. He appeared to give the question serious consideration.

"No," he said calmly, after a pause. "I found it rather third rate."

Thad had perhaps not been expecting direct rudeness, and was in any case unfamiliar with Edouard's ability to insult with deadly politeness. For a moment, the smile remained fixed on Thad's face; when he realized, belatedly, that it was inappropriate, it disappeared.

"Hélène. Shall we go?"

Edouard took her arm and led Hélène from the room. It was a deliberately leisurely departure, Edouard stopping, here and there, to speak to acquaintances and friends. Neither he nor Hélène looked back, and Thad remained in the same position, for some time, watching them until they finally left the room.

When they reached home, and were alone, Hélène said, "Was it third rate, Edouard? Did you really think that?"

Edouard did not reply at once. He was standing, his face slightly averted from her, looking out the windows of his study toward the gardens, and the city beyond. Now that the anger he had felt as he watched the film had abated, he realized that he felt very tired, and the tiredness was connected with the continuing deception about Sphere. To lie was curiously debilitating, he thought, and decided, at that moment, that he would tell Hélène the truth tonight. But not yet: in a little while, when she was calmer. He turned back.

"No," he said quietly. "It has the faults of all his work, and I could hardly look at it objectively. But it wasn't third rate. It was good."

"I'm glad you felt that," Hélène said simply. "I'm not sorry you said that to Thad—he deserved it. But I'm glad it's not what you really felt."

"My darling, why?"

"Because it *was* good. There's no point in pretending to oneself that it wasn't. Thad is an artist—I always knew that. It's because he's an artist that he uses people as he does. Their lives mean nothing to him, they're simply material for his work. Happiness, suffering, love, hatred—they're all one to Thad. They interest him. He observes them. He watches all the little ways they manifest themselves, and then he uses them. Mine, or anyone else's. He feels no direct concern, and certainly no compassion." She sighed. "And I'm sure, if you told him that, it would puzzle him very much. He wouldn't know what you were talking about. If he said anything at all, which he probably wouldn't, he'd say all artists were like that. And that they had to be. Perfectly detached. And perfectly amoral."

Edouard looked at her silently. She was frowning slightly, and she spoke quietly, without emotion, as if it were necessary for her to define this to herself. She looked away, and then back at him. Her hands moved, in a sudden, quick, flurried gesture, and she began to speak again, more rapidly.

"I tried to explain that to him once. That there were things that were more important to me than my work. Just living. Just perfectly ordinary everyday things, like being here with you now, or being with Cat. Little things. The stuff of life . . . But he could never understand that, of course. Those things don't last, so they're unimportant to him. Just incidents that he might be able to use, or might decide to cut. Whereas his films will always be there. Forever and ever. Long after he's dead, or I'm dead." She broke off. "He said that to me once."

"Hélène . . ." Edouard was moved by her sudden distress. He turned toward her.

"He took part of my life." Hélène raised her face to his. "A part I hated, a part I was ashamed of for a long time, and a part I was proud of, too, in some ways. Things that were unclear and confused—he took all those things, and he shaped them, and made sense of them. He made them into his film. He made them into *art*. . . ." She paused, and her voice grew steadier. "And I minded—then, when I was watching."

"And now?"

"Now I don't mind. Isn't that curious? Quite suddenly, I don't. Because I see—it wasn't *like* that. He made it more—and he also made it less. Both at the same time. Do you understand?"

"I understand."

Edouard put his arms around her and held her close against his heart. They stood quietly together, and after the anxiety of the day's events, Edouard felt himself grow still and calm. He felt at peace. He thought: I shall tell her now, and was about to speak, when abruptly, and with a sudden restlessness, Hélène withdrew from his embrace.

"I just wish he hadn't made the daughter die, Edouard," she said with a sudden new agitation. "I wish he hadn't done that. His films are uncanny sometimes—they predict the future. He's done it before, I see that now. My marriage to Lewis, the things that went wrong—he put those in his films, too, they're there—in *Extra Time*, in *Short Cut*. He wrote things *before* they happened. It's as if he can see ahead. . . ."

"My darling, don't be foolish. He was constructing a story, that's all. It doesn't mean—"

"Oh, Edouard, I'm so worried about Cat." Hélène turned back to him. "That quarrel today. Other things, just little things—I was thinking about them tonight. I wanted to talk to you about them. . . ."

Edouard sat down and drew her down beside him.

"Then tell me," he said gently.

And Hélène began to do so. Edouard listened, and spoke, and they talked for a long time. But as he did so, Edouard felt a slight detachment, a passing regret. This was not what he had meant to discuss, not what he had meant to say.

The conversation could not be turned. Hélène's worries were of more immediate importance, he told himself, later, when he went to bed. But still, he was angry with himself: an opportunity, the right opportunity, had been lost.

At the convent school, there was one girl in particular whom Cat had always loathed. Her name was Marie-Thérèse, and she had come to the school late, some time after Cat, and not long before the birth of Cat's younger brother, Alexandre, in 1970, the year Cat was ten.

The convent they both attended was an exclusive one, its intake of pupils coming, in the main, from old, distinguished, conservative French families. The criteria for the selection of pupils were primarily social, but there were certain exceptions. There were girls at the school whose places had been achieved on scholastic merit; there were some who were the daughters of newly rich businessmen of sufficient influence to obtain them entrance; there were one or two girls in each year who were taken on out of charity, because their mothers were widowed, perhaps, and whose fees were paid on a scholarship basis. But Marie-Thérèse came into none of these categories, and her presence in the school was, from the first, something of a mystery. Her parents were known to be pious, and reasonably well-off, though they were by no means rich by the standards of the school. They were neither influential, nor well-connected; her father was rumored to have something to do with the sale of automobile tires, and some of Cat's friends, with a certain snobbish glee, would make jokes about this. According to them, Marie-Thérèse's mother had obtained her place on the strength of her church connections.

Marie-Thérèse had long blond hair, which she wore neatly, in regulation braids. Physically, she was well-developed for her age, and inclined to plumpness; she became the first girl in Cat's class to acquire perceptible breasts, and this, combined with a habitual sweetness of expression, earned her some status, and some liking, for a while. The more snobbish girls disdained her from the first, and were not to be won over by her somewhat simpering attempts at friendship.

Cat, seeing this, had at first felt sorry for her, and had even tried to initiate certain casual overtures. These were a mistake. Cat was aware that she was not being sincere: she disliked Marie-Thérèse instinctively.

It took her some weeks to realize that Marie-Thérèse disliked her right back, and that Cat's attempts to be polite to her had deepened the dislike into something closer to hate. Perhaps she found Cat's overtures patronizing—for she was a prickly girl, who quickly took offense. Perhaps she merely hated Cat for her cleverness, or her appearance—though this did not occur to Cat. Whatever the reason, she hated her, and once Cat's approaches had met with no response, she gave up the effort, and resigned herself to hostility; it was honest, at least. But she had never encountered hostility of this kind before, and as time passed, Cat began to believe that all the things that suddenly began to go wrong in her life had one root cause. Marie-Thérèse. *I was happy until I met her,* Cat sometimes thought; the girl's advent became a demarcation point in her life.

Before the arrival of Marie-Thérèse, Cat's career at school had been a sunny one. She was naturally quick at her lessons. She made friends easily, and the nuns, though they sometimes shook their heads at her impetuosity, or her tendency to immodesty—such as hitching up her skirts and tucking them in her panties when they skipped in the playground—they were willing to forgive. They reprimanded, but they were, on the whole, won over by her openness of nature, her goodwill, her transparent honesty.

Once Marie-Thérèse arrived, this began to change. Marie-Thérèse quickly discovered Cat's temper, and the surest ways of provoking it. It was so easy to make the arrogant, stuck-up Catharine de Chavigny fly into a rage: she could tattle on one of Catharine's friends; she could hide Catharine's schoolbooks, spill ink on her drawings; poke fun at her figure, which was slender to the point of boyishness. She could snigger, and remark that Cat looked more like a boy than a girl. She could throw stones at the pigeons in the convent grounds—even when she missed, as she usually did, Cat would leap at her furiously, and could then usually be further provoked into a stinging slap. Then, when trouble ensued, and an investigation was launched, Cat would be punished, and—best of all—the stupid girl could even be relied on to remain unshakably silent, and never to accuse Marie-Thérèse.

This campaign Marie-Thérèse pursued with zest throughout their eleventh year, and she noted, with spiteful delight, that in that year, the nuns became less indulgent to Cat, and more stern. On one occasion her parents were even called in to see the Mother Superior, and Marie-Thérèse quaked. But the truth did not come out, even then. Cat's hateful parents, who swanked up to the school in their hateful Rolls-Royce, were informed Cat was becoming a problem; she was seriously undisciplined. When this news leaked back to Marie-Thérèse, she was in a fine humor for the rest of the week.

Cat viewed this change in her own fortunes with bewilderment. She knew she associated it with all sorts of other things which also made her unhappy and uneasy. She hated that year. At home, there was not just Lucien, but also another baby boy. Her beloved Madeleine had left, to be married and have children of her own, and though Cat still sometimes saw her, she missed her very much. She resented Lucien, she knew she did, and the resentment made her squirm with guilt: he was only little, he was her brother, she knew she ought to love him. And she did love him, and Alexandre, sometimes, but at other times she wished they had never been born, she wished things had stayed as they were in the days when there were not three children clamoring for attention.

This was wicked; she knew it was wicked. For a period, she became passionately and intensely religious, spending hours on her knees, fervently praying God to make her a better and more natural daughter and sister. But the prayers did not work, and after a while Cat abandoned them. She began to regard piety with scorn: she began to resent the constant prayers, the constant services, the constant insistence on religion at school. She refused, abruptly, to attend confession—and this created a storm.

Her body was changing, too, everything was changing: she was almost twelve, and suddenly she felt the world was falling apart, nothing was stable. She would take off her clothes, sometimes, in the secrecy of her own room, and stare at herself in the mirror. The beginnings of fine hair between her thighs and under her arms; the first slight swell of her breasts. Sometimes she hated these signs of approaching womanhood, and hated them passionately. She would squash the breasts down, pretend they were not there, tell herself that she had never wanted to be a girl anyway, that she wished she had been born a boy. At other times she would stare at her own figure, and hate it for the slowness of its development: then she would wish that her breasts would grow faster, and the pubic hair be more discernible. When her periods began, she felt joyful and hopeless, freed and trapped, both at once, and, not long afterward, in a sudden frenzy of resentment at her own gender and at her incapacity to remain a child or to become a woman, she cut off her hair.

She had worn her hair, at school, in unruly braids. She cut it one night, alone in her room, with a huge pair of Cassie's dressmaking scissors. Snip—just like that—just below the ear, some sawing and tugging, and it was done. The two braids, like sad dead animals, lay in the palm of her hand. She came down to breakfast the next morning, and there was a terrible scene.

She had expected the fiercest reaction to come from her mother, for her mother fussed about the way Cat looked and dressed in a way she had come to hate. But it did not: it came from her father, who was coldly furious.

"It's my hair. I suppose I have a right to cut it off." Cat had tilted her chin defiantly; she was the ruder because his reaction shocked her, and she was close to tears.

"It looks ugly," he said coldly, and then, perhaps because he was trying to contain his anger, he walked out of the room.

Cat was terribly hurt. It was the worst moment of her life. She felt as if she wanted to die. She prayed for the ground to swallow her up. She ran back upstairs and stared at her face in the mirror, and her father was right. It did look ugly; it looked worse than that—it looked grotesque.

She wept then bitterly. She had a confused sense that she had done something irrevocable. Edouard cared for beautiful things—she knew that; he had taught her to care for them also. Hundreds of different kinds of things: it might have been a piece of jewelry or a perfectly tended vine; a Limoges plate, hand-painted in the eighteenth century; or the color of a wild flower growing in a hedgerow. He insisted on beauty; he insisted on excellence, whether the object in question was something very valuable or something very simple. He insisted on the same things in people. Cat had watched him, and she knew—he loathed, not ugliness of appearance, though that certainly did not draw him, but ugliness of nature or character or behavior or manners. Hypocrisy; insincerity; malice; obsequiousness; snobbishness; injustice—he hated all these things, and Cat hated them too.

As she lay on her bed and wept, she felt as if she had destroyed herself in her father's eyes: he saw her as she was, she thought, he saw all her jealousy, and her resentment, and her meanness, it was they he found ugly, not simply her hair.

And he was right: she was detestable; loathsome. She hated herself for her temper and her pride and her arrogance; she hated herself for loving her father so much, and then being rude to him. She despised herself, and it seemed perfectly clear to her that her father must despise her as well.

"Edouard. You must try to understand. It's difficult for Cat just now. I remember how it felt, being half a child and half a woman, not sure if you want to be either. And also—she has brothers now. That makes it harder. . . ."

It was the same evening, and Cat, who had come creeping downstairs to the drawing room, intending to apologize to Edouard, who had just returned from his office, froze outside the door. She couldn't bear to go in, or to turn away: she eavesdropped, with a lurching sense of shame.

"Why does it make it harder?" Her father sounded impatient.

"Well, I don't know how much she understands . . ." Her mother paused. "All the resentment of Lucien. He's not just your son, Edouard, he's also your heir. She senses that, even if she doesn't fully understand it. Perhaps she feels you always wanted a son."

"I did always want a son. That doesn't affect my feelings toward Cat."

"It may not to you, Edouard—but it could seem so to Cat, can't you see that? Why do you think she chose to cut off her hair? Because she's frightened to look like a woman yet, and because—maybe unconsciously—she thinks we would love her more, value her more, if she were a boy."

There was a silence. In the room, Edouard looked at Hélène with sudden consternation. Hélène saw comprehension, and then both regret and tenderness come into his face. But Cat, of course, saw none of this. She heard only what he said.

"Not 'we.' You mean I would feel that," he said quietly, and outside, miserably, Cat crept away.

Edouard talked to Hélène a little while longer, blaming himself, and then went up to Cat's room to try to talk to her. Cat longed to throw herself in his arms; her throat felt tight and choked with the love and the pain she felt. But somehow she could not do it. Her face scarlet with repressed emotions, she answered Edouard shortly and proudly, and when he tried to put his arm around her, and be gentle, she pushed him away. When, finally, he left her, his face bewildered and sad, she sat alone, hating herself even more. *If I had been a boy. If I had been a boy—a son . . .* The words went around and around in her head: they would not go away. Sometimes she could hear a little voice crying out, somewhere in her head—but he loves you, you know he does. But she would not listen to that voice; it was a lying voice. Yes; her father loved her, but not the way he loved Lucien and Alexandre: not as much.

After that, things became worse. She felt ugly and awkward and stupid. She constantly knocked things over; she seemed unable to frame sentences anymore without, in the very middle of them, becoming aware that what she was saying was foolish and inept. At home, she withdrew from her family, and spent hours in her room, reading novels about women who were impossibly beautiful and impossibly clever, for whom men were consumed with passion. She would have liked to resemble those heroines: once or twice, at parties given by school friends, she tried out some of their attitudes on the young brothers who were present, and discovered, with a precarious sense of triumph, that they were a success.

She tried them out again, more flagrantly, that summer, the summer of 1972, during the weeks she spent in the Loire with her family. She was caught kissing the son of one of the estate managers, in the vineyards, by Edouard. The kiss itself had been a disappointment—Cat did not even like the boy very much—but Edouard's subsequent anger was frightening.

"Why shouldn't I kiss him? He wanted to kiss me."

"I'm sure he did. He's sixteen years old. I . . . Cat, his father works for me. It might have gone further. Apart from anything else, you're too young."

"He didn't think so."

"Go to your room."

They left the Loire shortly after that, and went to England, and to Quaires for the rest of her summer holidays. There, Cat knew, she was carefully watched over. She began to feel resentment, she began to feel a certain heady sense of rebellion. But when she returned to school for the fall term, things steadily became worse.

Marie-Thérèse had found a new way of tormenting her. Her mother—despite her vaunted piety—was an avid reader of gossip columns and women's magazines, and so, from conversations overheard at home, Marie-Thérèse was supplied with a rich fund of new material. She saw at once that these new weapons struck home.

"Your father's a stinking Jew," she said one day, sidling up to Cat in the playground.

Cat, that morning filled with a sense of martyred rebellion against both her mother and her father, was immediately stung. Rebellion translated itself into loyalty in a second.

"My father is one quarter Jewish, and you're four quarters contemptible," she said fiercely, with a toss of her head.

But Marie-Thérèse had seen the flush, the moment of blank pain in her eyes: she resolved to try harder.

"Your father used to keep mistresses. He probably still does," she said the next day. This was very daring. No pupil was supposed to discuss anything so impure. It earned her a stinging slap.

The best thing of all, Marie-Thérèse kept to herself, awaiting the perfect moment, the moment when she dared to say the terrible words, which her mother had only uttered in shaken tones, with a lowered voice. Marie-Thérèse kept this piece of information to herself. She nursed it for weeks, for months. Then, one winter's day, the following February, when she had been particularly stung by one of Cat's slighting remarks, she decided: now, when Cat was in the playground, surrounded by a group of her stuck-up friends. She approached them.

"I know something about you, Catharine de Chavigny. You think you're so pretty. You think you're so clever. I bet your friends don't know what I know."

"So, tell us." Cat shrugged. "Then we'll see."

Her arrogance, her casualness, were unbearable. Red in the face, stammering with pent-up dislike, Marie-Thérèse finally came out with the word.

"You're—you're a bastard."

Catharine went white. Marie-Thérèse felt a surge of triumph.

"You are! You are! My mother read it in a paper. You were seven years old before your father married your mother. She was married to someone else. She made horrible films, and took off all her clothes. She's immoral, my mother said so. You might not even be Catharine de Chavigny. You might be Catharine Anybody. . . ."

"That's a filthy lie!"

Cat had been sitting on a wall. Now she leapt down, fists bunched. Marie-Thérèse was scared, but she held her ground.

"Your mother's divorced—"

"So what, you little bourgeoise?"

"Your mother's divorced, and your father's a playboy, and you're a bastard, so there, Catharine de Chavigny. . . ."

Cat sprang at her. She knocked Marie-Thérèse to the ground. They rolled over and over, screaming and kicking and punching until they rolled against the long black skirt of a nun's habit. After that, the end was swift.

The two of them stood in front of the Reverend Mother, Marie-Thérèse with her head bent, Catharine staring defiantly at the wall.

"Catharine. I should like an explanation."

Cat continued to stare at the wall. She said nothing.

"Marie-Thérèse. Perhaps you would give me one."

Marie-Thérèse did. She had plenty to say, and all of it exonerated her. The Reverend Mother heard her out, and then, alone with Cat, made one last attempt to secure an explanation. When Cat obstinately refused to give her one, the Reverend Mother sighed. She explained, quietly, that this kind of insubordination left her with no choice. She was not necessarily prepared to accept Marie-Thérèse's account, but when she asked for an explanation from Cat, in a matter as serious as this, she expected obedience; she expected a reply.

She did not receive one; neither did Edouard or Hélène. Later the same day, after a flurry of meetings, Cat was expelled.

She was tutored at home for the remainder of the school year, and then it was explained to her, gently and carefully by Hélène and by Edouard, that they had decided to send her to boarding school in England. She would go to a very famous school next September. Meanwhile, the summer would be spent in England, at Quaires.

Cat listened to all this in silence. She could not bear to look at her father for the pain and love and indignation she felt. She almost told them then; she longed to tell them, but she knew the words would hurt them as much as they had hurt her when Marie-Thérèse spoke them. So she said nothing.

"You do understand, Cat?" Hélène said gently. "We felt it would be best for you to begin again, somewhere else." She paused, and Cat, who could see how hard she was trying, felt worse.

"We'll go to Quaires," Edouard said. "We'll spend the summer there. It will be a marvelous summer. And then you can put all this behind you, Cat. It will be in the past."

It would never be in the past, Cat knew that, but she did not say so.

"I understand," she answered stiffly.

And she did, she thought. One summer at Quaires, and then banishment. They left for England in the middle of July.

The croquet lawn at Quaires lay to the southeast of the house, and was bathed by the morning sun. It was almost eleven o'clock, a perfect summer's day. Christian, standing in the center of the lawn, in a crumpled white linen suit, swung his mallet back and forth meditatively, and surveyed the disposition of the croquet balls. Hélène, whom he had taught, watched him carefully; she had just played, she felt, an extremely crafty shot. From the terrace behind them, Edouard sat watching them contentedly, stretched out in the sun, the morning's newspapers tossed to one side.

Christian frowned. Though he was capable of gallantry, it did not extend to the strategy of games, which he liked to win. He gave Hélène an amiable smile; he lined up his shot. There was a sharp click as mallet connected with ball. Christian ambled across to look at the damage done. He squatted down on his heels, and then, as Hélène approached, looked up with a lazy grin.

"I rather think that's done for you. I rather think I've won."

"Damn you, Christian." Hélène looked down at her ball, which had been knocked smartly to one side, and at Christian's, which had traveled smartly through the final hoop. Hers was now virtually unplayable. She sighed.

"Oh, all right. I concede. You're a fiend at this game, Christian. I'm never going to beat you. . . ."

Christian laughed, and put an arm around her shoulders. Together they strolled back across the grass to Edouard.

"Darling, you never had a prayer. He was determined to finish you off, and I know why. It's time for the cricket to begin at Lords. You want to listen to the test match—admit it, Christian."

"I confess." Christian threw himself down in a chair.

"You could watch it on the television, if you'd prefer, Christian," Hélène began.

"Watch it? Watch it? Certainly not. That wouldn't be the right way to go about it at all. Far too modern. Quite un-English. No, I shall sit here, if I may, and listen to it on the wireless. I shall be entirely occupied until this evening. And if Edouard had any sense, he would do the same. Going up to London, on a day like this. You're insane, Edouard. . . ."

"What he means is, he'll listen with great attention for half an hour, and then he'll fall asleep. . . ." Edouard stood up with a smile, and a glance at Hélène. "And I don't want to go to London either, but it won't take long." He glanced at his watch. "An hour with Smith-Kemp at most, then I want to stop in at Eaton Square to pick up some gardening books. . . . If the traffic's not too bad, I should be back by three. Round about the time Australia bowls England out, I should imagine . . ."

Christian picked up a cushion and threw it at him. Edouard caught it.

"Absolute rubbish. I anticipate an heroic stand." Christian yawned. "Give Charles Smith-Kemp my regards. Tell him not to forget the regulation glass of sherry. He ought to be in an Agatha Christie novel— have you ever told him that? The absolute model of the family solicitor, who might—just possibly—have been the very man who did the wicked deed in the late colonel's library . . ."

"Not anymore." Edouard smiled. "Charles has a new passion. He's fallen in love with the modern world—high technology. Well, technology anyway. They've moved offices. Plate glass and rubber plants and the very latest thing in what he still calls typing machines. I'm to be given a tour of inspection. . . ."

"Oh, God. Is nothing sacred?" Christian opened one eye. "What's happened to the old offices?"

"They're being pulled down. An insurance company is going to build a tower block on the site. Sorry about that, Christian—I don't like it either."

"Well, at least nothing changes *here*," Christian said in a disgruntled voice. He lifted his hand in a lazy salute. "See you later."

He reached across and switched on his transistor radio, one of his few concessions to modernity. As Hélène and Edouard turned back into the cool rooms of the house, the soothing tones of the cricket commentary drifted in the air behind them.

Edouard put his arm around Hélène's waist; she rested her head against his shoulder.

"Will it be all right, Edouard?"

"Perfectly all right, I promise you. If necessary, we'll take out an injunction, but I don't think it will even come to that. Don't worry about it, darling. I'm not worrying, and neither is Smith-Kemp. He says it's open and shut: that film will never be made." He bent his head, and kissed her. "Now—tell me—what are you going to do? You don't want to change your mind and come with me?"

"Oh, Edouard—I'd like to. But I'd better not. I promised Floryan

I'd finish going over the new designs—I need to look at those provisional figures. If I start now, I'll be finished by the time you're back. . . ."

Edouard smiled. "You work too hard."

This was a a customary joke between them, and Hélène gave him a little push. The push turned into an embrace.

"And the children?" Edouard said eventually.

"They'll be well occupied. Lucien and Alexandre are going to have a picnic lunch in the treehouse—to which I'm invited." She smiled. "And Cat said she might go riding. If I finish in time, I'll go with her."

"Well, just don't let her go near Khan, that's all. I know she's longing to ride him, and she mustn't. It's not safe."

"Edouard, she won't. Cat's very sensible about things like that. Stop worrying. You must go—you'll be late. . . ."

"Oh damn—having to do this on such a perfect day. Damn Angelini . . ." He paused, and his arms tightened around her waist. "We did do the right thing to come here for the summer, didn't we?"

"Absolutely the right thing. I knew it would work—there's something about this place. A curious magic. It makes people restful, and calm. It makes them happy. Even Cat. She's much better, Edouard, you can see that. I think she's beginning to accept the school thing. This last week, she's almost been like her old self. She loves it here. . . ." She lifted her face to his. "Don't you feel that?"

"Yes. I do. I'm certain of it. It was just a phase, perhaps, as you said. . . ." He glanced down at his watch. "God, you're right. I must go. Don't forget Christian's wine—he likes the Montrachet. There's some in the fridge. Oh, and if you could persuade Cassie *not* to iron my shirts. George regards that as his province, he mentioned it again this morning. . . ."

"They like squabbling. They both enjoy it very much." Hélène smiled. They crossed out from the house onto the gravel sweep at the front, and Edouard opened the door of the black Aston-Martin.

"I know they do." He paused. "Unlike us."

"Unlike us."

Their eyes met; Hélène rested her hand in his.

"I love you," Edouard said. He kissed her palm, and then folded her fingers over it, as if they could enclose the imprint of his lips.

He climbed into his car; the engine roared; he lifted his hand in a wave, and Hélène watched the car until it disappeared around the bend in the drive.

She lifted her face happily to the sun, and drew in a deep breath of the still, sweet air. In the trees that framed the drive there was a covey of wood pigeons. She listened for a moment to their soft murmuring, then she turned back into the cool shade of the house.

Cat came clattering down the stairs at full tilt as Hélène walked into the hall. She was dressed for riding, in jodhpurs and a white open-necked shirt; her riding hat swung from her arm.

"Isn't it the most perfect day?" She crossed to Hélène, and gave her an impulsive kiss. "I thought I'd go for my ride now—before it gets too hot. May I?"

"I can't come with you now, Cat. . . ."

"Oh, that's all right. I'm not going far. We could all go out again this evening anyway, with Daddy. I'll be back in time for lunch—and I'll be starving. Please . . ."

"Oh, all right. But don't go too far." Hélène smiled. "Oh, and you won't go near Khan, will you, Cat? Your father mentioned it specially. . . ."

"Lord, no. I'll take Hermione, I think. Poor old thing. She needs some exercise; she's getting fat. I haven't taken her out for days. Where did I leave my crop?"

"Where you always leave it. On the floor. Cassie put it with the coats and boots, I think. . . ."

"Got it."

Cat stopped and turned back with a smile. She tilted her head with a quick impatient movement which was very characteristic of her, and Hélène, looking at her tall slender figure, at her tanned eager face, and at the hair, which had now grown back after its savage cutting and once again curled and waved to her shoulders, thought, suddenly: how beautiful she is, my daughter.

Cat turned and ran out of the house, in the direction of the stables, and Hélène watched her, the love she felt for her suddenly painfully intense.

When she had disappeared from view, Hélène fetched some wine for Christian, who had, indeed, fallen asleep, and then walked through the quiet house to the room she used as a study.

It looked out to the west; in the distance she could just see the small figures of Lucien and Alexandre, hastening across the lawn with Cassie and their nanny. They seemed to be carrying an immense amount of equipment for this picnic. Baskets, and rugs, and cushions, and a cricket bat . . . She smiled, and began to lay out on her desk the designs for Wyspianski's new collection, together with its provisional marketing details.

She worked on them, quietly and pleasurably, for almost an hour. Then, just after twelve, the telephone rang.

She picked it up herself, thinking it might be Edouard, who would have reached London by now. But it was not Edouard: the line buzzed; there was a breathy pause. Then, without explanation or preamble, Thad began to speak. He was calling from Heathrow Airport.

For a moment, Hélène was so surprised that she could hardly speak; she could not even take in what Thad was saying.

"So, I'm coming down now. I have a car waiting. I can be there in less than an hour. Is your husband there?"

"No, Thad, he's not. How did you get this number?"

"Someone gave it to me, I guess. And the address. Look, I have to see you, and I have to talk."

"Thad, if you want to talk to me, you can do it through my lawyer."

"I can't. I don't like lawyers. They fuck things up. I need to see you. Not just about this. There's something else. It's important."

"Thad. Wait a minute . . ."

"You can always shut the door in my face."

He giggled. Hélène heard the familiar rusty sound, on its rising note; then the dial tone droned in her ear. He had hung up. Annoyed, she replaced the receiver and opened her desk drawer. There lay the copy of the script Thad had sent; one copy—the other was with Charles Smith-Kemp. Paris and London, a love story of a sort: another reworking, by Thad, of episodes from her life. This time, though, she was determined the film would not be made. She pushed the drawer closed and returned to her work.

Once, Thad's interference would have affected her so much that she would have found it impossible to concentrate on anything else. But not now. Now Edouard had made her responsible for this collection, and for the development of the whole jewelry division of de Chavigny. That mattered to her; she would not allow even Thad to intrude. She bent her head, and after fifteen minutes or so, almost forgot him.

Once, in the distance, out of sight from this side of the house, she heard the sound of hooves. Cat was leaving for her ride; she looked up, and smiled, then bent again to Wyspianski's designs.

Just when she made the decision, Cat was not sure. Was it before she even left the house? Was it when she came to the stables, and looked at sweet-tempered Hermione, who was such a dull ride? Or was it when, hesitating between the other horses, she approached the stall where Khan was stabled, and he whinnied as she lifted her hand? She stroked him then, tentatively, for she knew he was unpredictable, and Khan blew gently down his nose, and nudged her with his velvety muzzle—Khan, sixteen hands high, the most beautiful black stallion she had ever seen—whom she had expressly been forbidden to ride.

She was not conscious of making any decision even then. One moment she was in the yard, the next she had fetched the saddle and tack. He stood docilely while she fixed them in place; when she led him out, he came as obediently as a lamb. Cat looked at him doubtfully; it was still not too late to change her mind. But it was such a beautiful day, and he was so beautiful, and she knew she rode well. She imagined the scene, later that afternoon.

"Oh, by the way, Daddy. I rode Khan. . . ."

Edouard might be angry, but he would also be impressed. Suddenly the temptation was too strong to resist. She mounted him, and Khan let her mount without any sign of nerves. The moment she was on his back, Cat felt a winging confidence. She pressed her knees against his flanks, and urged him on; Khan obediently walked out of the yard, down the back drive, along the lane, up onto the bridle path that went on for miles over the Downs.

There was not one other person in sight. The sky was a cloudless blue; the sun warmed her arms; Khan had a mouth like silk, responsive to the slightest touch. With a feeling of elation, she urged him into a trot, and—as always when she was on horseback—all Cat's anxieties fell away. Nothing seemed terrible anymore, not even the things Marie-Thérèse had said. They were distanced now, by the weeks in this place she loved. What did she care for Marie-Thérèse? She was petty. The things she said were petty, and in any case, Cat would never see her again.

A lark rose ahead of them, soaring into the sky, and Cat reached forward to stroke Khan's powerful neck. She began to chant to him softly, the poem which had given him his name:

In Xanadu did Kubla Khan
A stately pleasure-dome decree;
Where Alph, the sacred river, ran
Through caverns measureless to man
Down to a sunless sea . . .

She loved the words, and Khan seemed to like them too. His ears pricked; he moved gracefully from a trot to a canter. It was so exhilarating that Cat wanted to shout aloud. She leaned with him, moving with the rise and fall of his body; Khan increased his stride.

If only her father were here to see her now. The thought came into her mind, and then went out of it again; for the first time since she had mounted she felt a dart of fear. Khan had begun to gallop; faster and then faster—she had never ridden so fast. She gave him his head for a while, then, when she felt herself tiring, she tried to rein him back. Nothing happened; the reverse happened. The more she pulled on the reins, the faster he galloped. It was then that she began to feel very afraid, and terribly alone. The horse sensed her fear; they always did.

She saw his eyes roll, his ears flatten; she felt a shudder pass through his body, and braced herself; then, again, his stride lengthened. They were already at least three miles from home.

"Amazing," Charles Smith-Kemp said with languid enthusiasm. "Amazing, what some of these newfangled typing machines can do."

He leaned over his secretary's desk, and peered down into the workings of her typewriter, rather in the manner of a seer consulting the prophetic entrails of some bird. He straightened up, and the young woman gave him a bright smile.

"Coffee, Mr. Smith-Kemp?"

"In about twenty minutes, Camilla." He paused, and glanced at Edouard. "Unless you'd like a glass of sherry?"

"Neither, thank you. I'm eager to get back. . . ."

Edouard repressed a smile. Clearly the glasses of sherry had been dispensed with, along with the old shabby paneled offices, the worn leather chairs, the atmosphere of a gentleman's club. Perhaps coffee went with plate glass and rubber plants, gleaming chrome and dividing panels, he thought inconsequentially.

He followed Smith-Kemp into his inner office, from where there was an excellent view of the depradations being practiced upon the City by a new generation of architects. He settled himself in an uncomfortable chair on one side of the desk; Smith-Kemp settled himself on the other. He, too, had a new chair; it was covered in black matte leather, and it rotated. Smith-Kemp seemed to enjoy this novelty, for he swiveled it back and forth a few times, like a child with a new toy, before he got down to business. Smith-Kemp had been educated at Winchester, and he had an arrogance of mind familiar in products of that school, carefully disguised, in his case, by an habitually languid manner. His expression was usually that of a man about to fall asleep; now he propped himself against his desk as if only that support prevented somnolence. When he spoke, however, what he said was always incisive and sharp. This morning, he permitted himself a small smile.

"We've won," he said without preamble. "Basically, we've won. I have the letter here from Angelini's production company. It arrived via their solicitors this morning, by hand." He fingered the letterhead of the lawyers in question. "Not an *awfully* impressive firm."

He passed the letter across the desk. Edouard read it quickly.

"They're going to back down," he said. "I've read letters like that before."

"Oh, indubitably." Smith-Kemp swallowed what might have been a yawn. "He had trouble raising the backing, in any case, or so I gather. He's been hawking this particular property all over London, and he wouldn't have done that if he could have raised backing in the States. This production company aren't committed—and they won't commit now. I knew they'd back down at the first hint of litigation. All that remains now is to get all copies of the script withdrawn, and that should be straightforward enough. It constitutes a gross act of libel—counsel had no doubts on that score, and neither had I." He paused. "The man really does have the most extraordinary nerve. To write it is bad enough, but to assume he could actually persuade Hélène to take part in it—he must be mad."

"I would not call him a balanced man."

"So, you can tell Hélène not to concern herself. This film will not be made."

"You're sure there are no possible loopholes?"

"Loopholes? My dear Edouard. Certainly not."

"That's good to know." Edouard leaned forward; he glanced at his watch. "Now, you said there were one or two other matters . . ."

"Only minor ones, Edouard. Signatures, really . . ."

Smith-Kemp began to speak again, and Edouard listened, but with only half his attention. His mind drifted away to the past, to those old, oak-paneled offices, and to the day, so many years before, when he had sat in them, trying to explain to Charles Smith-Kemp's father exactly what he wished done regarding Madame Célestine Bianchon, and the house in which she lived in Maida Vale.

He had stammered and blushed; he had tried to sound nonchalant; he had tried to sound like Jean-Paul. And Henry Smith-Kemp, presumably primed by Jean-Paul, had been reassurance itself. . . .

"If you would be good enough to confirm that I have the correct spelling of the name. Bianchon. Célestine. Charming, charming. Three or four weeks I should anticipate. If you would remind Jean-Paul that I shall be needing his signature . . ."

Edouard shut his eyes. From outside the plate-glass windows came the steady hum of the City traffic. For a moment the past felt close: he could reach out—he could touch it.

He opened his eyes again. Charles Smith-Kemp had passed some documents across his desk. Edouard read them quickly, took out his platinum pen, and signed. He glanced at his watch. It was half-past twelve.

"You mentioned one other matter—concerning my brother?"

"Ah, yes. Yes indeed."

To Edouard's surprise, Smith-Kemp's manner became less languid. He came as near as he ever did to looking embarrassed. He turned, opened a cupboard behind him, and drew out an old-fashioned black metal deed box. He placed it in front of him on the desk. Across the front, painted in perfect copper-plate writing, were the words: BARON DE CHAVIGNY.

"It was discovered during the course of the move." Charles Smith-Kemp sighed. "It's occurrences like this that make me realize we should have moved years ago. Those old offices were quite impossible. No room for storage. The most disorderly system—we relied on the older clerks, and when they retired, one by one, I'm afraid things were misplaced. Lost." He paused. "This should have been handed over to you at the time of your late brother's death, with all his other papers. It's a bad oversight on our part. I apologize, Edouard."

Edouard looked at the box. It had a squat and malignant appearance.

"Is it important?"

"I haven't opened it, of course." Smith-Kemp looked offended at the very suggestion. "It is marked, you see, on the rear."

He turned the box around. On the other side, also in neat copper-plate, it was inscribed: PRIVATE AND CONFIDENTIAL.

Edouard smiled. "Goodness knows when I last saw one of those. I thought they were extinct."

"They served a purpose, I suppose." Smith-Kemp looked at the box with distaste. "We don't use them now, of course. Quite soon, I intend all our material to be computerized. Then we shan't even need files." His eyes lit. "Microfilm, Edouard. Tapes. Efficient—and remarkably discreet. I was looking into it only the other day. It seems you can use coding systems, quite ingenious. Of course, the initial outlay is very high, and—"

"Do you have the key?" Edouard, who did not want a further lecture on the advances of technology, cut him off.

Smith-Kemp looked faintly wounded. "Oh, yes. It was filed in the appropriate place. Once we had discovered the box, the key was simplicity itself."

He passed the key across the desk. Edouard stood up.

"It's not likely to be of any consequence anyway," he said. "Don't worry about it. If it were anything of importance, I should have known it was missing years ago."

"Do you want to take it with you?" Smith-Kemp looked at the box with dislike.

"Why not? Since I'm here, I may as well. . . ."

Smith-Kemp escorted him as far as the elevator. Outside, Edouard walked the few blocks to his car, swinging the case by its metal handle. The sun was strong, and his spirits lifted: down Bury Court, into St. Mary Axe, along Houndsditch: he liked the names of streets in the City.

He looked at his watch, debated whether to go back to Eaton

Square for the gardening books, which could easily be sent on, and finally decided that he would. It was not far out of his way.

He drove across London impatiently. The traffic was bad, and no matter which route he took, he seemed unable to escape it. Once or twice, he glanced down at the box on the seat beside him, feeling that he might have preferred it to remain unfound. It made him think of Jean-Paul; it made him think of Algeria.

He slotted a tape into the car stereo. The Beethoven piano pieces, Seven Bagatelles. This music, which he had played so often before, when he was less happy than he was now, soothed him, as always. He forgot the box, and listened to the tumbling notes, the ease of transition to the cadence.

He was approaching the end of the Mall, and turning into Constitution Hill with Green Park on his right, when he saw her. There was no car close behind him, and he slammed on the brakes, skidding to a halt, staring after the small dark figure on the far side of the road: a woman—she was just turning into the park.

Pauline Simonescu: he was almost certain of it. The woman had been tiny, old, wearing black, and something about her walk, a certain imperiousness in the angle of the head . . . He leapt out of the car, and ran across the street, dodging the passing traffic. It couldn't be possible, surely? And yet—why not? She had left Paris, she might be here, she might still be alive—he had no reason to believe she was dead.

He ran across to the entrance of the park, looking for the small figure eagerly. He would like to tell her, he thought, what had happened to him, how the future she had claimed to see had turned out. He would like to see her; like to assure himself that she was alive, was well. . . .

He came to a stop at the entrance to the park. Here, one path proceeded a short way, and then divided. She was not in sight.

He ran to the place where the path forked; he looked to the left, and then to the right. From here, at the intersection, he had a clear view into the distance. The figure of the old woman—whether Pauline Simonescu or some other—was nowhere to be seen.

He stood, frowning and perplexed, unable to understand how he could have lost sight of her. Then, with a shrug of disappointment, he turned back. When he was crossing the street, he thought—then—he must have missed her.

At the exit from the park he paused, looking back one last time. The sun beat down on his head; the leaves of the trees whispered and shifted; for a moment the traffic of the City seemed to lull, and the air, heavy with exhaust fumes, was silent.

He returned to Eaton Square and collected the gardening books. Then, just as he was about to leave, he turned back. He looked at the deed box, which he had left carelessly on his desk. He felt the small key in his pocket.

On impulse, he closed the door, went back to the desk, lifted the box, and opened it. Inside was one bulky envelope, which felt as if it contained a folder. It was tied with string, and sealed with red wax. On the outside of the envelope, again in perfect copperplate, the ink brown and faded, were the words: MRS. VIOLET CRAIG, FORMERLY FORTESCUE.

Underneath the file there was a photograph, the only other object in the box. A studio portrait. From it stared back at him the face of a young woman, a face he had forgotten until now, a face he had neither seen nor thought of for over thirty years. The face of a born victim. She was wearing a chic little hat: she was smiling.

"It's impossible to hide things. In the end they always come out."

Thad seemed to find this fact satisfying. He leaned back against flowered chintz, and smiled. He waited, watching Hélène.

"He didn't tell you, did he?" he said quietly. "He didn't tell you about Partex and Sphere, or the money that backed our movies, or Simon Scher. Nothing. I knew he hadn't."

Hélène hesitated. She was very tempted to lie, to say that of course Edouard had told her, she had known for years. But it was not something she could brazen out, and Thad would know at once that she was not telling the truth. She looked away.

"No," she said finally. "No. Edouard didn't tell me."

Thad said nothing. He continued to look at her, as if he judged that at this particular moment her own thoughts could do Edouard more harm than any words of his. Hélène could feel his satisfaction, and his triumph, and also the manipulation of his will. It sucked at her, across the space that divided them, winding her into some space where Thad was in control. She needed strength to resist that pull, and just then she felt weak, for what he had said had come as a great shock to her. All these years—and Edouard had said nothing. His silence was inexplicable to her; to have kept something so central a secret from her for so long. Did he not trust her? How could he have lied?

She had had such an absolute faith in Edouard, such certainty that there was no deceit between them, that this revelation hurt her very much. It also frightened her. As her mind darted back and forth, trying to account for it, trying to understand it, she felt a hundred little doors at once open up on other suspicions: if he had deceived her over this, in what other ways might he have lied?

Forcing her mind away from such thoughts, and despising herself for entertaining them, she turned slowly back to Thad and looked at him levelly. She had no reason to trust him, after all.

"How did you find out?" she said coldly.

"Oh, it was easy." He smiled, and she heard the conceit creep back into his voice. "I first heard about it a long time ago. I met a girl who used to be Simon Scher's secretary. He fired her, so she wasn't exactly well-disposed toward him. She told me. But she was dumb—neurotic. She might have been making it up. I tried to check with Lewis, though I don't think he knew. It was just about a month before he died. That was hopeless. I mean, really hopeless. Lewis couldn't remember the days of the week." He paused. There was not a shadow of regret in his voice, nor of pity. He spoke of Lewis as if they both hardly knew him.

"I forgot about it for a while after that. I was busy. Then—I met you in Paris, after *Gettysburg*, you remember? I watched him then—your husband. He looked like he thought he owned you. I didn't like that. I didn't like what he said about my movie. It wasn't true. So—I decided to find out. I knew it was no good trying to get Scher to talk; he'd gone back to Paris by then anyway. So, I went to the top. I saw that guy at Partex. Johnson. He told me."

"You saw Drew Johnson?"

"Sure." Thad gave a little giggle. "It wasn't difficult. I'm famous. Your husband had just pulled out of Partex, Johnson bought his stock, and it took a big dive. Partex had a lot of problems right then. They're okay now. Anyway, I asked, and he told me. Johnson didn't know why he'd done it, of course. But I did."

Hélène turned away to the window. Her mind was beginning to function again; two years ago—that had all happened more than two years ago. Why had Thad waited until now to give her this piece of information? She knew the answer to that, of course. It was lying inside a blue binder in the drawer of her desk.

She at once felt calmer. Through the window, across the lawns, she could see Lucien and Alexandre climbing the rope ladder to their tree house; Cassie was handing up the picnic things. Hélène touched the diamond ring on her finger; she thought of Edouard's many gifts, the most important of which was his love. She knew why he had done this, she thought, and her heart lifted.

Thad made a small contemplative humming noise. He said, "He did it to thwart me. He hates me. It was a way of destroying Lewis, too, indirectly—giving him enough rope to hang himself. But that wasn't the main reason. The main reason was me."

Hélène turned around. "It seems an odd way of thwarting you, Thad. That financing enabled you to make your best films."

"I haven't made my best films, not yet." Thad glanced up irritably. "He wanted to own me, that's all. Buy me up. Let me think I was free, and all the time he was pulling the strings. Manipulating me. It was a power game. I had the vision. I had the genius. And he had the money. He was *playing* with me, all that time. He let me make the first part of *Ellis*, and then, when it came to the second part, when he saw how good it was, he canceled, he pulled out. . . ."

His voice had risen. He stood up in sudden agitation, shifting from foot to foot.

"I hate those movies we made now. I can't look at them. He's spoiled them. . . ."

"Thad, none of that is true." Hélène looked at him coldly. "If you remember, you took *Ellis II* to Joe Stein at A.I. For more money."

"He took you away . . ." Thad appeared not to have heard her; his face was now tight and intent, and he was speaking rapidly. "He came back, and he took you away. He did it deliberately, so I couldn't finish the trilogy. He wanted to destroy my work—he knew I needed you. So he bought you up. He took you back to France and buried you with money and houses and children. I know what he thought—he thought if he did that, you'd never break free. . . ."

"Thad—stop this." Hélène turned on him angrily. "Your egotism is monstrous—do you know that? I won't have you stand there and say those things. I told you not to come. I don't want you here. I'd like you to go, now."

"We haven't talked about the script. I have to talk about the script. Now that you know all this, now that you see what he's like, how he lies, how he manipulated you as well as me—well, you must see things differently, that's all. . . "

He had become very agitated. His small pink hands described circles in the air. Flecks of spittle flew as he spoke, and lodged in his beard. He wiped at them absentmindedly, his eyes glinting and winking behind their glasses, never leaving her face.

"I can't wait any longer. You're getting too old. You're thirty." He took a step forward. "But if we did this film, this year, we could do *Ellis* next year. I'd have to be very careful how I shot it, but I could manage it, Hélène, I know I could." He peered nearsightedly at her face. "There are some lines, but I'll never let them show, Hélène, you don't need to worry. And then, for the third part, Lise is older then, so it'll be all right. And after that . . . Five years, we've got five at least, maybe a bit more. With the right lighting, the right makeup—maybe a little plastic surgery, not much. We could still be filming ten years from now—when you're forty. Think of that, Hélène . . ."

There was a silence. She looked at Thad, sublimely unaware of how mad he sounded. Then, with a quick decisive gesture, she turned away, opened the drawer of her desk, and took out his script. "Thad. Go away, and take this with you." She thrust it into his hands. "I'm not making this film, or *Ellis*, or any other film. I will never work with you again."

There was a silence. Thad looked down at the script in his hands, and then back up to her face.

"I wrote this for you. . . ."

"You should not have written it at all. You had no right."

"I wrote it for you. I sent it to you. And you didn't even reply. You just went to your lawyer. Or *he* did." His voice shook slightly. "Are you going to drop that action?"

"No, I'm not. You're going to drop that film. You're going to stop writing scripts about me and my life. You've done it once, and I'm not going to let you do it again. That's all. And if you thought you'd change my mind by coming here and telling me about Edouard and Sphere, you were wrong. It makes no difference at all. Now, will you please go?"

Thad did not move. He stood absolutely still, his feet planted slightly apart, breathing quickly. As Hélène looked at him, she saw the color begin to seep up over his neck, and into his face, a dull, livid flush.

"I need you." He said it flatly and obstinately. "I need you for my work. You don't mean this. You can't mean it. You have to come back. I've always known you'd come back." He stopped, began again. "I've finished nearly all the rooms now, do you know that? There's only one left." He swallowed. "If you were there, all the time, I think I could stop doing that. I wouldn't need the photographs anymore. Maybe."

"Thad. You don't need them now. And you don't need me."

"Yes, I do."

"No. You need your idea of me, that's all. That was always the case." Her voice had grown quieter. "It was the same with Lewis. I understand that now."

She turned away to the door, and opened it. For a moment, Thad did not move. Then, slowly, he came after her. The comparison with Lewis had angered him, she knew that at once. She could feel his anger, though his face remained expressionless and still. He came to a halt very close to her, and looked her in the face.

"You've changed."

He made it sound like an accusation, as if she had committed an unpardonable fault.

"You've changed—or he's changed you." He gave an odd little gesture of the hand. "I made you into something once. I made you into a woman. The kind of woman men dream about. I did that—not you. You were nothing when I met you. Just a teenaged girl, no different from a thousand other girls. Photogenic, that was all. I gave you a look. I gave you a voice. I gave you an identity. I even gave you Lewis. And you've thrown it all away. For this."

He gestured at the room, and looked at her again, a note of appeal creeping into his voice. "How could you do that? How could you be so dumb? What do you want with all this—this stuff?"

"Thad—this is my home. . . ."

"*One* of your homes. How many do you need? It's obscene. All these things . . ."

"Thad. I care for this house. I love my husband. I love my children. I'm *happy*—is that so difficult to understand?"

"Yes, it is." Thad sounded combative once more. "Because it doesn't last. Marriages don't last. What people call love doesn't last. You can't be sure of something like that. Your husband—does he love you?"

"Thad—stop this. . . ."

"Does he? Or does he lie about that, too, the same way Lewis did? Lewis was always going on about how much he loved you. That didn't stop him screwing half of Hollywood. That didn't stop him hitting you—did it?" He paused, and gave a little giggle. "Where's your husband now?"

"He's in London. Thad, this is none of your business. . . ."

"Is he? Where in London? Who with?" He looked at her intently. "You think you know, but you might be wrong. How long did he lie to you about Sphere? How many years? What else do you think he lies about, Hélène? He could be with another woman right now—you wouldn't know. He had lots of women once, I read about that. He probably screws around. Most men do. Sex with the same woman gets boring, they all say that. And Lewis always said you were a lousy lay. I didn't believe him, of course. Lewis couldn't get it up, that's all. But that's what he said. . . ."

Quite suddenly, the malice and the anger had become desperate. Just for a moment, when he began to speak, Hélène had felt the doubts begin to snake into her mind. She hated herself for them, and she despised herself for them. Then, somehow, he went too far, he pushed too hard, and she knew she did not believe him. She almost pitied him, and the doubts died.

It was always a mistake to show Thad sympathy, however, for he capitalized upon it instantly, so she kept her voice cold.

"Thad. You don't understand love. And you don't understand trust. It's one of the things that's wrong with your films. I'm not going to argue with you, and I'd prefer not to remember you like this. Please go . . ."

"You're boring." Thad's eyes were now intent on her face. He gave a sudden whistling little sigh, and rubbed at his beard reflectively. "How come I didn't see that before? You know what you are now? You're ordinary—just like anyone else. A married woman. A mother. A nothing. He did this to you, and you let him. I wouldn't want to work with you now anyway. Not now that I really look at you. Here." He thrust the script back into her hands. "If you really don't want to do this, you can throw it away."

"Throw it away?"

"Why not? I don't want it."

A smug little smile moved his lips. He still did not believe her, even now. Hélène's mouth set. She took the script, crossed the room to her desk, and threw it into the wastepaper basket. Thad watched her do it. He made no sound. As the script fell, he lifted his two pink hands in a quick involuntary gesture—perhaps of protest, perhaps of supplication. Then he let them fall.

For a moment, Hélène thought he was going to cry. He removed his glasses, and rubbed his eyes. Then he put the glasses on again and turned to the door. He bustled out into the hall, as if nothing had happened, his manner composed and benign once again. Hélène followed him, a little uncertainly, aware that she had been made to feel cruel and unjust, which was one of Thad's specialities.

On the steps outside, he turned to her, and to her considerable surprise, shook her hand. He held it tight between his small plump palms, glancing over his shoulder in the direction of his Mercedes. It was chauffeur-driven; the engine fired.

"Oh, well. I'll find someone else, I guess. Someone special, the way you were once." He smiled his gentle wolfish yellow-toothed smile. "I saw your daughter as I came up the drive. I guess it was your daughter. Dark hair, a white shirt. She was riding. A big black horse . . ."

"Yes, that would be Cat. . . ."

Hélène was only half-listening. She was eager for him to be gone. From the garden beyond she could hear Lucien and Cassie calling her.

"She's got a very striking face, your daughter." He giggled. "Someone should put her in the movies, you know that?"

He saw the immediate uneasiness in her face, and he smiled again, the same old gentle smile. "Just a joke, Hélène. Just a joke . . ."

He climbed into the car without another word, and it pulled away. The moment it was out of sight, Hélène felt a surge of release. If she could manage it, she thought, she would never see Thad again. And Cat would never meet him.

She turned back into the house, wishing impatiently that Edouard would return soon. She would tell him about Thad's visit at once. She would tell him she knew about Sphere. . . .

She stopped. Why had Edouard never told her? Could he possibly have feared that it would come between them? At once she felt certain that she was right: she knew, after all, how it was to be trapped by an evasion. Oh, if only Edouard would hurry back soon. Then she would tell him just how absurd that was, how little it mattered now, and how much she loved him.

He did this for me, she thought as she came out onto the terrace on the far side of the house: all those years, and saying nothing. She felt a great intensity of love for Edouard then, and a longing to be with him. She looked out across the garden, to the rondel of yew. In the distance, the small figures of Alexandre and Lucien were waving. In his chair on the terrace, Christian was just stirring. The cricket commentator was going over the details of that morning's play: England had been bowled out by Australia, just as Edouard had predicted, though rather sooner.

A black horse. Thad's sentence, to which she had paid so little attention at the time, suddenly floated into her mind again, through the surge of happiness. The scene before her froze; her body tensed. A black horse. There was only one black horse among the many in the stables, and it was not the horse Cat had said she would be riding.

For a moment she stood absolutely still, telling herself that Thad must have made a mistake. Then, with a small indistinct cry of fear, she began to run across the lawns, along the rear drive toward the stables.

The horses whinnied at her approach, and she ran frantically along the line of box stalls. Hermione was there; all the horses were there— except Khan.

He had burnt the papers. He had burnt the file, the envelope, and the photograph, one by one, in the fireplace of the Eaton Square study, carefully and methodically.

The letters between Jean-Paul and Gary Craig's commanding officer. Jean-Paul's careless note to Henry Smith-Kemp: "He tells me Craig will do it for five thousand dollars. That seems fair enough, and best for all concerned. Please make all the necessary arrangements, in your firm's name, naturally. Craig has no bank account, I gather, so it will have to be in cash. And please make it absolutely clear to Miss Fortescue that I am acting merely as a friend. There must be no acknowledgment of paternity in writing. I have no doubts myself, but fortunately there is nothing that could stand up in a court of law, provided the whole matter is handled with your usual discretion. . . ."

He had seen the receipted bills for the delivery and the hospital expenses. He had seen the one letter from Violet herself, written from the hospital, to Henry Smith-Kemp: "Please inform M. Jean-Paul de Chavigny that his daughter is very beautiful and in good health. I should like him to know that I have called her Hélène; I felt she should have a French name. He need have no further anxieties. Please assure him that

I shall not contact him again, nor make further calls on his already considerable generosity. . . ."

A proud letter. She had clearly kept her promise. There were only two other items in the file: a receipted bill from a Mayfair florist, for bouquets sent to Mrs. Craig on her departure for America; and a brief note, from Jean-Paul, hastily scribbled in Paris. The file on Mrs. Craig could be closed; he thanked Mr. Smith-Kemp for his efficiency and discretion in such a delicate matter.

One match, carefully applied, and they all burned, one by one. Money as a way of buying off guilt; money as a way of avoiding responsibility. As Edouard watched the papers burn, he felt shame for Jean-Paul, but no censure. How could he? While these arrangements were being made, was not the accommodating Mr. Smith-Kemp also engaged on Edouard's behalf, giving money, when he had once meant to give love?

When the last paper was burned, Edouard, who had been kneeling, stood up and walked to the window. Below was the balcony where, as a boy, he had dreamed of firing at a phantom enemy. Across the street were the square gardens, where the air raid warden had once had his station: now, children played on the grass in the sun, while their uniformed nannies sat on benches and gossiped. No blackened gap beyond the terraces now; nothing left of the past; just peace, and prosperity, the closeness of a city summer.

The turmoil was all in himself; the war was in his mind and his heart. For a moment, standing quite still, it was as if the two images were superimposed, the one upon the other: he saw them both. The sunlit square was light and dark; he heard the drone of the planes' engines, and it mixed with the murmur of the traffic below. Peace, and yet he saw the bombs fall from the sky, silver in the searchlights; they fell with a hallucinatory slowness, aimed and randomly scattered; destruction from a distance. There was a long quiet time before their explosion, and when it came, the explosion was silent. A long, slow time; he thought: a lifetime.

His brother's daughter. He thought of Hélène, and of their children. His mind functioned with the hateful clarity of shock; it was ice cold, precise, and implacable: a series of images; a sequence of information; this and then that. It was quite clear to this machine of a mind that there was one course of action open to him, and one only. To destroy the evidence. To remain silent. He thought: Hélène must never know; our children must never know.

There was a small box on the table next to him; he picked it up blindly, and blindly laid it down again. He thought: they will never know, and I shall never forget. Then he turned, and walked out into an altered world.

He was in the Aston-Martin, the engine had fired, he was already driving, when, rebelling against the dictates of his mind, the pain struck him with the force of a physical blow. It fractured in his heart; it stabbed at his mind. He saw a future distorted by a necessary silence. Nothing happened: his hands on the steering wheel remained steady; the revolutions of the car's engine remained regular; in a dark world, the sun still shone.

He had stopped, he realized, at a crossing. In front of him, a young woman passed, with a small child in a blue and white striped stroller. The child was wearing yellow, the woman green. The child was pointing, the woman hurrying. He saw them with great exactness, these strangers.

He thought: *We can have no more children*, and as the full implications of that were understood, the pain was suddenly so loud that he expected them to hear it, this woman, and this child. He expected them to look up, to stare at him.

But they did not, of course. They crossed without a glance, they in their world, he in his. It was then, perhaps, that he decided. When they reached the sidewalk on the far side, he let in the clutch, changed gear, and accelerated. Up onto the overpass west; out of the city.

Between London to the east, and Oxford to the west, there was now a stretch of fast open motorway, with few cars. There, some ten miles from Oxford, he gave the black Aston-Martin its head. Music and speed: he pushed a button, and the air became Beethoven. Seven Bagatelles, Opus 33, recorded by Schnabel in November 1938. Out of the past, the vision of the music sang to him. Gaiety and desolation; stress and resolution. *Andante grazioso; quasi allegretto; scherzo:* he drove faster. It was three o'clock. He was eager to be . . . at home.

He saw the space, clearly, a second or two before he reached it, just at the edge of the perfect bend. A space, very bright, and very lovely, arching open to him out of the music. He saw it and recognized it, with a faint passing sense of surprise that he should see so late, and only now, this place which had been there all along, which had been waiting for him to come and claim it. Such light and such silence, he thought, at the heart of the music. Not a way out, but a way through. He touched the wheel very lightly.

He felt no fear; the entrance was there; he had seen it or dreamed it many times, and its familiarity was reassuring to him. Peace, one pulse-beat away; the only impediment, pain. A quicker pain this, though, than its alternatives, for himself, and for Hélène.

Allegretto: the music skidded, and the world turned. After the crash, it was dark, and very quiet. There was blood in his eyes, and he thought for a moment that he had lost his vision. Then he realized that he was not blinded; he had only to turn his head, very slightly. He did so, and the bright place winged its way to him. One last small tussle of breath, then the letting go was easy.

I t was past four o'clock, and Hélène was standing, with Cat, outside the stables, when she heard the car come up the drive.

Cat was still holding Khan by his bridle; his flanks and withers were shiny with sweat; Cat was shaking. She, too, heard the car, and she looked at Hélène pleadingly.

"It will be Daddy. Don't tell him yet. Please. Let me deal with Khan. I'll rub him down, and then I'll come back to the house, and I'll tell him. I want him to understand. I wanted to show him, that I could ride Khan, that I could do it, and I did do it. I did!"

Hélène looked at her silently. "Very well," she said finally, and turned away.

Cat had no idea of the anxiety she had felt, and no idea of the relief she felt now. It was so intense that she did not trust herself to speak. Instead, leaving Cat where she was, she began to walk, and then to run, in the direction of the house. The sun was in her eyes, and she lifted her hand to shield them, searching eagerly for the first glimpse of Edouard's car. As she rounded a corner, and the gravel sweep in front of the house came into view, she stared in confusion. It was not a black car, it was a white one, and two uniformed police officers, one a man the other a woman, were just climbing out of it.

T hey wanted her to go into the house, but Hélène would not, so in the end, they told her in the garden, in a small private space, enclosed by yew hedges, where she and Edouard often sat together in the evenings.

Her mind had been filled with Cat; she had had no presentiment, and she listened to this uniformed man and woman, who were speaking gravely about times and bends and speeds, and ambulances and hospitals. She found it difficult to understand what they were saying.

"But he's not dead?" She interrupted them, turned to them eagerly. "He can't be dead. Is he hurt? How badly is he hurt? You have to tell me. I must go to him."

The uniformed man and woman looked at each other. They tried to persuade her to sit down, and when she would not do so, they began to explain, again and again. The woman was speaking when, from Hélène's face, they both knew that she had finally understood. The woman's voice faltered then. She said, "It would have been very quick."

"Instantaneous," the man added.

Hélène looked at them, though she did not see them. She said, "Is there another kind of death?"

Later, they drove her to some place. A cool quiet hospital place, on the outskirts of Oxford. It was where Edouard had been taken, though they must have known it was too late. They drove her there, and escorted her in, and stood in the doorway, until she rounded on them, her eyes flaring with anger, her face white.

"I want to be alone with him."

They looked at each other; they retreated before the expression in her eyes; they left.

When she was alone with him, and the door was shut, Hélène took Edouard's hand, which felt cool and dry to her touch. She bent her head, and rested her face against his. She could feel that he was broken; she could see that he had gone. She pressed her lips against his hair; silently, willing the impossible with all her strength, she begged him to listen, she begged him to speak. Not a great many words: two; one; just her name. Let him hear me. Let him know. Please God. She thought the phrases, and they sounded to her immensely loud in the silence. Edouard's hand lay still in hers; there was no answering pressure from his fingers. Someone had closed his eyes. Not her. She felt her heart break.

They had placed his body on a bed. After a while, she sat, and then lay, beside him. She pressed her face gently against his chest, lying as she had lain so often, listening to the beat of his heart. After a while, quietly, she began to talk to him. She talked about things that had happened in the past, things he had said and things he had done, and how much they had meant to her. She told him, in a low voice, which broke off, and then began again, what had happened, how they had told her, what she had felt. The words choked her; she felt a terrible urgency. They would take him away. They would not let her see him again.

She fussed over him then, with small fluttering hopeless movements. Resting his hands, stroking his hair. And then she stopped, and grew still, and just stayed there, in the quiet, with him. Finally, she rose. She turned away. She turned back. She kissed him for the last time, bending over him. It seemed wrong to kiss him on the lips, so she kissed his cheek, and then his closed eyes. Then she left him. They drove her back to Quaires, and carefully, as gently as she could, she told

Lucien and Alexandre and Cat. Christian, who was distraught, offered to help, and to come with her when she did this. But Hélène, who was calm and still, refused him gently.

"No, Christian. I must do it," she said. This calm would not leave her, it would not break. It remained with her, so that she felt as if she moved in slow motion through a dream, when she told the children, when Cassie embraced her and wept, when Christian broke down.

It would not go away. At night it was with her when she could not sleep; in the morning it waited for her to open her eyes. Nothing seemed able to pierce it: she could not weep. It was with her when Christian fetched Edouard's belongings from the hospital. A watch; a platinum pen; a wallet. Just three things. In the wallet, there was a little money—Edouard rarely carried much money—and a driver's license. No photographs. No item of any kind that could give her one last message after death. She laid them out on the table in front of her, and touched them, thinking: I shall cry now. I shall be able to cry now. But she could not.

The calm was like a shield, and it protected her. It took her through the arrival of Louise, the arrival of a white-faced Simon Scher. It took her through the headlines in the newspapers, and the renewed, and often sensational, coverage of Edouard's life. It took her, unscathed, through the inquest, through the letters which began to arrive from all over the world, and which she answered, methodically and carefully and promptly, each afternoon. It remained with her when she made the arrangements for the funeral, which would be in the Loire, and when the endless meetings with the lawyers began.

All this was real, and it was not real. She looked at these people and these events from behind the glassy shield of her calm, and she cut their condolences short, however sincere they were. She knew that behind that shield her mind, her whole body, ached with the pain of her loss, but she did not want anyone to glimpse it: it belonged to Edouard, and she was too proud.

Edouard's body was flown back to the Loire in his private plane, and Hélène flew with it, alone. It was to lie, the night before the funeral, in the chapel of the château, near the memorials to Edouard's father, to Jean-Paul, to Isobel, and to Grégoire. Hélène stayed there, sitting upright, her hands folded, for many hours, until it had grown dark, and her body was stiff with cold. When, finally, she went back to the house, Christian, who was staying there with her, pressed a small package into her hands, when he wished her good night.

"It's the Beethoven tape," he said quietly. "The one Edouard had in his car. I know he would have been playing it. I thought you might want to listen to it."

"The Beethoven?"

"When my mother died, I went all over the house—looking for something, I don't quite know what. Some letter. Some message. There was nothing, of course. I thought you might have felt that. I thought you might be glad to have this."

Hélène looked down at the small cassette, her face blank.

"This tape? You mean this is the tape from Edouard's car?"

Christian's face grew gentle.

"No, Hélène. The same recording, not the same tape. The tape in the car—well, that was broken. . . ."

"Oh, yes. Of course. Thank you, Christian."

She went upstairs to her room and played the tape. She had listened to it many times before, when she drove with Edouard, and when she heard it now, quite suddenly, the music broke through the defenses she had erected. *Andante grazioso; quasi allegretto:* then she wept.

The next day, when she needed the calm again, it came back. She put it on, with her black clothes, like a cloak. It protected her, through the service itself, through the burial, which took place in the de Chavigny burial ground, close by the chapel. It was set on rising ground, overlooking the vineyards and the water meadows beyond, with their groves of chestnut trees; its boundaries were marked by a line of thin dark cypress trees, planted in the lifetime of Edouard's great grandfather.

In the fields below, nothing moved; the air was cool and the sky milky, lit by a thin sun and diffused by banked pale clouds. There was already an autumnal scent in the air, though it was still summer, and the grapes were not yet harvested. The leaves of the chestnut trees in the distance had just begun to turn; there were touches of yellow among their leaves, and in the air there was the scent of rain, and of woodsmoke.

Hélène stood and listened to the words she had known she would hear, among the faces she had known she would see. This crowd of people in black: Edouard's best friend on one side of her, his closest associate on the other. She looked across to the still pale faces of Lucien, Alexandre, and Cat; Alexandre too young to understand; Lucien defiant and fearful; Cat's face twisted and pinched with grief.

Beyond them, other faces; so many faces. Louise, in deep mourning, her face veiled; several members of the Cavendish family, from England; Alphonse de Varenges, who had once been so kind to her in the Loire, and who had talked to her about trout fishing, standing very upright, like the old soldier he was; beside him stood his wife, Jacqueline, frowning, perhaps in an attempt to keep back the tears which she would certainly have scorned to shed in a public place. Jean-Jacques Belmont-Laon, head bent, with his new wife; Drew Johnson, who had flown from Texas; Clara Delluc, whose eyes were puffy and red from weeping. Cassie, standing very upright, with Madeleine, her husband, and her two children. George, standing toward the back, looking suddenly aged, head bowed. Floryan Wyspianski, lifting his great bearlike head to the sky, his gentle face a mask of bewilderment. Representatives from the de Chavigny companies—she saw Monsieur Bloch, and his rival, Temple. Faces from the recent past, faces from further back: Isobel's brother, William, whom Hélène had never met; a group of men who had been at Magdalen with Edouard. Representatives of various government departments; politicians; senior colleagues from other companies and from the Paris Bourse; friends from London, from Paris, from New York. She saw them, and she did not see them; she heard, and did not hear, the priest's words.

Toward the end of the ceremony, it began to rain, lightly at first, then more heavily. One or two people glanced up in sudden consternation; Louise gave a moan. Someone handed Hélène a little trowel, a ridiculous thing, containing a handful of earth. The rich, crumbly soil of the Loire. Hélène took it, and leaned forward. Drops of rain fell on her head, on the polished surface of Edouard's coffin, on the silver plate on which they had engraved his name. She tipped the earth from the trowel into her bare hand, felt its coolness and weight for an instant, and then scattered it, steadily, not letting her hand shake, for Edouard's sake.

It was over, and as some of the people began to move away, she could sense their embarrassment, she could almost smell it. Death made people awkward, she thought. Christian took her arm; he and Simon Scher began to lead her away.

She stopped once, and looked back. With a conscious effort, straining all the resources of her body and her mind, she willed her love to Edouard, as she had done before, on other occasions, across other distances. The narrow columns of the cypress bent with the wind, then straightened; a cloud moved across the face of the sun, and then passed. For a moment the sky was lit with a watery radiance; she turned away.

The calm was there, waiting for her. It protected her, as she shook hands with so many people, heard so many brief words of condolence, as those who were not returning to the house grouped, regrouped, and then left.

The last of all was a tall, stout man, with a pale complexion and heavily lidded eyes; he was dressed in the most correct mourning. He had been standing, hatless, apparently unaffected by, or unaware of, the rain, a little to one side, toward the back, when they stood by the graveside. Afterward, she had seen him speak to Louise, but Louise had departed indoors, weeping, at the first sign of rain.

Now the man came forward; he halted; he bent, with great formality, over her hand.

She did not recognize him; she looked at him from behind her calm, hardly seeing him.

"My sincere condolences, Madame." He straightened up. "Your late husband and I once worked together. Many years ago now." Seeing the blankness in her face, he inclined his head.

"Philippe de Belfort," he said, backed off a few respectful paces, and then turned away.

Hélène watched him walk away, down the narrow road, in the direction of the gates, where a large black Mercedes was waiting.

When he was a decent distance, and perhaps when he thought he was unobserved, for he glanced over his shoulder first, he unfurled the umbrella he was holding, shook it once or twice, fussily, opened it, and then raised it above his head. Thus protected, he hastened the remaining distance to his car, and climbed in, without looking back.

After that, she lived, and she did not live. The glassy calm rarely left her; she functioned, looking at the world with a detachment which left her only when she was at home, or when she was alone.

Time inched forward, day after slow day. Yesterday; today; tomorrow. Fall became winter, and winter, spring. She watched this alteration of the seasons, and resented the predictability and the punctuality of their change. Once in the early morning, when they were staying at Quaires for Christmas, she walked for a long way out of the grounds, and up a bridle path onto the Downs, where the hills sloped westward. It had snowed during the night, and she was the first person to walk that way that day, her feet cutting into the crisp new snow. It was very cold, and when she eventually stopped, on high ground, she looked out at a landscape made scarcely recognizable by the snow. The land was white; the trees of the woods were bare and black against a sky of unrelieved pallor, heavy with the threat of further snow. She thought, then, of the morning she had stood in the small cold bedroom in London, looking out at the snowy street, and feeling, for the first time, her child quicken inside her.

She turned back to the house sadly; feeling, as she had felt for months, that something within her was broken, destroyed, and it would never stir again. She stopped, and then walked on again, taking a path that led back through the gardens. In the rondel of yew, she stopped again, and thought of Edouard, and then let her mind travel back, and further back, over the years: Edouard, Lewis, Billy. Three deaths, three fatalities. She broke off a small icicle from the hedge, took off her glove, and let it lie in her palm, bright as the diamond she wore on her finger.

After a while, the warmth of her skin melted it, and she turned and walked back to the house, and the other memories which waited for her.

Other people adjusted—that was the term, she knew. She could see them, watching her, taking their cue from her, waiting for the moment when it would be possible to behave as they had before all this happened. Life went on, people forgot, and she did not resent this; she tried very hard to behave in the same way that she always had. It was perhaps a success; those who did not know her well seemed to think so, but Hélène herself felt only half alive.

She watched her children, inevitably, come to terms with their loss. Lucien, the most robust, recovered the most quickly. With Alexandre, it was difficult to tell, for he was so young. To begin with, he kept asking for his father, and demanding to know where he was; but as the months passed, these questions became less frequent, and one spring evening, in Paris, when Hélène came up to him to say good night, he took her hand, and said, "Papa won't come again, will he?"

"No, Alexandre."

His small face looked up at her anxiously. He paused, and then said, "I should like to see him."

His tone was wistful, but accepting; he settled down to sleep. Hélène bent and kissed him: she loved Alexandre very much, painfully, and protectively. She loved him for his gentleness, for his slowness, for the fact that he had been late to walk, and late to speak, for the fact that he looked so exactly like Edouard. She thought, as she straightened up, and he closed his eyes: our last child. Tears came to her eyes; she knew she would have no more children.

Cat grieved more angrily, more fiercely, than the younger children: she was old enough to understand her loss. This shared sense of loss brought them very close to each other again; but Cat, too, had her own life. She had insisted on going to her boarding school in England, because her father had chosen it. She began to settle in and make friends there; Hélène was frightened to burden her with a past she herself could not shake off, and so she made a conscious effort to steer Cat away from such thoughts and memories, and toward her future.

Meanwhile, she continued her life. She continued her work, but its meaninglessness without Edouard repelled her, and made her lose patience with it. For a while, in the first year after Edouard's death, she continued to supervise the arrangements for the new Wyspianski collection, and she continued to attend board meetings at de Chavigny headquarters. She sat now in Edouard's chair, at the head of the table.

Once, those meetings had amused and absorbed her. But now, with her new detachment, she viewed them with increasing distaste. The politics, the maneuverings—these all seemed so petty now. Even the decisions reached seemed without point; how much difference would it have made, she felt, if they had elected, not this course, but its very opposite?

In the fall of 1974, she ceased to attend the meetings. When Simon Scher came to her with decisions so major they required her consent, she would listen to him listlessly, hardly taking in his arguments; usually she would simply ask him which course had the support of the majority of the board, and then she would authorize it.

Even when he told her that, for a number of reasons—all cogent, for he listed them—it was felt that the plans for the next Wyspianski collection should be postponed, she agreed. Scher, who had opposed this move, looked at her intently.

"You can overrule them on this, you know, Hélène," he said quietly. "I didn't expect you to give in. Not on this."

She turned away irritably, because she could hear the reproach in his voice.

"Hélène. Apart from your personal holding, you also have your children's share in the company, in trust. Technically, until they come of age, the company is in your hands, just as it was in Edouard's. I can only argue with the board. You can do much more than that."

"It's only a postponement."

"For the moment. Yes."

"Then I agree to a postponement. That's all."

"Won't you come to the next meeting—Hélène?"

"I would prefer not to."

He left her then, without further argument. Three days later, Wyspianski came to see her, to ask her to intercede. When she refused, he looked at her in bewilderment; for a moment, she thought he was going to burst out into angry reproach, but he did not. His face grew sad, and then he shook his head.

"Edouard believed in my work. He fought for it, he fought for me. I always thought that you—" He broke off, and seeing the expression on her face, apologized.

"I am sorry," he said stiffly. "I understand. I should not have troubled you with this."

It was not the last reproach she received. She received a rebuke from Cassie, who turned on her suddenly one day, when Hélène had just agreed, without interest, to some domestic arrangement on which she had been consulted.

"When you going to snap out of this?" Cassie's face had become quite red. "You're going about like you was walking in your sleep. You think that's what he'd have wanted? Well, I'm telling you, he wouldn't."

That stung her; when she was alone, it made her weep, hopelessly and angrily. But the next day, the calm came back again, and she began to avoid Cassie, fearing another attack.

But the fiercest rebuke of all came from Cat, when she returned to France for the summer holidays, and discovered that the Wyspianski collection had been postponed again. She went to have tea with Floryan, at his atelier, as she often did, and when she returned, she came storming into Hélène's room.

"Floryan says the collection's been postponed again. I know he thinks it will never be made—he didn't say that, but I know it's what he thinks. What are you doing, Mother? Why are you letting it happen like this?"

"It's the board's decision. They felt it was wise. . . ."

"Who cares what they thought! If Daddy had been alive, this would never have happened. He wouldn't have let it happen. He *cared* about Floryan's work. I thought you cared. And you just sit there, and do nothing. It's so awful. It's so cowardly. . . ." Her voice rose. "Please, Mother, don't do this. . . ."

"Cat, you don't understand. . . ."

"I do! I understand!" Cat lifted her flushed face, her eyes bright with anger and frustration. "I understand only too well. Daddy's dead. And you've given up."

She ran out of the room and banged the door behind her. Hélène stood alone, quietly, thinking. The next day, she sent for Simon Scher, and also for Christian.

"There are a number of factors." Simon Scher sat opposite her in the drawing room at St. Cloud. Christian lounged on her right, listening carefully, smoking a chain of Black Russian cigarettes. "In the first place, there are a number of people within the company, and they're jockeying for power—chiefly Temple, and Bloch, but there are also others. I expected that, and it can be contained, just as it was contained when Edouard was alive. Both Temple and Bloch are valuable to the company—they just need to have it made very clear to them exactly how far they can go. Once they see that, and they accept it, I don't think they'll cause further trouble."

Scher paused, and looked at Hélène carefully. "However, there's another problem, and it's a more serious one. Has your mother-in-law spoken to you about her shareholding?"

"Louise? No."

"She holds ten percent of the de Chavigny stock. It entitles her to a seat on the board. . . ."

"I'll bet she never uses it," Christian put in, and Scher gave a tight smile.

"No. She doesn't. In any case, that's irrelevant now. She wants to transfer her stock, and her seat on the board, to someone else. A friend of hers, who's apparently had great success with property speculation in Spain and Portugal. His name is Philippe de Belfort." He glanced at Hélène. "Apparently, your mother-in-law invested heavily in his Portuguese developments, and she's done very well out of it. He has a tie-up with a man called Nerval. Gustav Nerval."

"I don't believe it." Christian sat up. "The scorpion's husband."

"Nerval?" Hélène frowned. "But I thought—there was some scandal. He's a shark, he always was. It can't be a very reputable company. . . ."

"Oh, extremely disreputable, I should imagine," Scher said dryly. "Successful though, for the moment."

"But Louise can't do this." Hélène stood up angrily, "Legally, she can't do it. She can't assign her holdings to this man or anyone else. They're entailed. Now that Edouard is dead, they pass from her directly to the children."

"Oh, I'm sure she knows that. It's just a ploy. She wants de Belfort on the board of de Chavigny, and she's determined to get him there. This is her first move. She will make others. She's been holding a little series of dinners—I suppose you hadn't heard that? For Temple. For Bloch. To introduce them to de Belfort again . . ."

"Again? Who is this man?"

Scher heard the imperious note come back into Hélène's voice, and he smiled to himself. Carefully, and precisely, he told her. When he had finished, he leaned back in his chair with an air of satisfaction.

"It happened at the time of Edouard's first bid for the Rolfson Hotels Group. I was in America then, but of course, it was common knowledge in Paris, and in London. I've been through all the files, Edouard was very thorough; it's all precisely documented. De Belfort went to South America for a period, and then he came back, about ten years ago. He's been in Spain and Portugal ever since. And I gather he's been in contact with Louise, though I'm sure Edouard knew nothing of that."

"De Belfort! The company Cassius. I remember now." Christian sat forward excitedly. "Of course. Edouard always said—"

"He was at the funeral." Hélène interrupted him. "Don't you remember? It was raining, and he was the last man to come up."

"He's back in France now—more or less permanently. Wooing people within the company, people like Temple, who aren't sure which way to jump. There was always a certain amount of opposition to the Wyspianski collections, but I think you'll find that a great deal of the recent opposition stems from him. He was always against that side of the company; he's intelligent; he can be a very persuasive man. Of course . . ." He looked down at his hands modestly, and spread his fingers. "Of course, it would be possible to make things quite uncomfortable for him in this country. Really quite uncomfortable. There's a great deal of information on him in Edouard's files which would interest the tax authorities very much. And of course, if Hélène were to make it clear, absolutely clear, to the entire board, that de Belfort was never getting so much as a toe in the door . . . If we were to reverse our decision to postpone the Wyspianski collection, and set a new date. If we were to make a stand on that, and on various other matters . . ."

He allowed his voice to trail away. He continued to look at the back of his hands with great concentration for a few minutes longer, and then he looked up at Hélène directly. He smiled, politely; and Hélène, with amusement, with a surge of energy she had never expected to feel, recognized that smile, and remembered it.

"A showdown!" Christian sprang to his feet. "A showdown. I love them. Edouard loved them. If this man has anything to do with the scorpion, or Louise, he's bound to be perfectly frightful. We have to go onto the attack. Hélène—you have to go onto the attack. . . ."

He stopped. Hélène was not listening. Her face had become suddenly animated.

"I've wasted time," she said slowly. "I see that now. I've behaved in a way Edouard would have hated." She stood up.

"Simon. Christian—I'm sorry."

She paused, and Christian, watching her, saw her expression change. There was a certain set to her lips, a certain angle at which she held her head, a certain glint of determination in the eyes. He recognized Edouard in her, at that moment, as if she were a de Chavigny by birth, and not just by marriage. She turned to Simon Scher.

"Simon, when is the next board meeting?"

"Not for another three weeks. You could, of course, call one whenever you wished."

"And how long to see off de Belfort?"

"Oh, well, if we were to see him, mention certain things, make it clear he'll never make it to the front lobby, let alone the boardroom—not long."

"A week?"

"More than adequate, I should have said. The man has a good instinct for self-preservation."

"We'll see him a week from now. The board meeting in ten days' time. And I want some plans drawn up to have the Wyspianski collection rescheduled."

"Oh, good. Oh, good," Christian said. "I can't wait to hear what happens. Hélène—the moment you and Simon have seen him, I'm coming to dinner. I'll fly over from London if necessary. I want to hear it all, every appalling detail. . . ."

Christian loved drama, of course. He was perhaps envisaging some splendid and impassioned confrontation. In which case, he was going to be disappointed: Hélène sensed that, as soon as she met de Belfort.

The interview was conducted in Edouard's office at the de Chavigny headquarters. It had remained unchanged since his death, and as de Belfort came into the room, with his heavy deliberate tread, Hélène saw him glance around him, and note that. He looked at the bronzes, at the black desk, at the Jackson Pollock. Then he drew up a chair on the far side of the desk, facing Hélène and Simon Scher, who sat a little to one side.

He looked at them, with his pale heavy-lidded eyes, while first Scher, and then Hélène, spoke. His face never betrayed the least emotion; he looked, if anything, almost bored.

When they had both finished, he gave a faint smile. He rested his large pale hands on the surface of the desk, and flicked at its surface with one well-manicured finger.

"Oh, well. I shall return to Portugal then, and Spain. You can hardly interfere with my activities there. All that was in the files? Really? You know, Edouard would have done awfully well working for a police state. . . ."

He saw Hélène's flush of anger, and it seemed to please him, momentarily. Some slight animation appeared in his pale heavy face; it flickered in his eyes, and then was gone. He gave a small shrug.

"I'm not too disappointed. Louise was very optimistic about my chances here—but then, Louise is a stupid woman. There was a time when I thought she might be correct, when I thought I might be able to fill the vacuum, so to speak. Now—" He paused. "Well, the zest has gone out of it somehow, in any case. It was rather more amusing to operate from the sidelines, to slip in and out of France, to advise Louise—when Edouard was still alive. Besides, we're doing extremely well, Nerval and I. To return here now—it might cramp my style a little, I think. . . ."

Hélène leaned forward. "Before you go," she said, "there's one thing that interests me. Why did you always oppose the Wyspianski collections? Why did you oppose that part of the company's work? You're not stupid. I can't believe you were unable to see how important it was."

De Belfort smiled faintly; he looked at her with slightly more interest than he had before.

"Why? I'm sure you know the answer. Because it mattered so much to Edouard, of course."

"But the work was good. The collections were always very fine. And simply from a commercial point of view, they were a success from the first. Do you mean to say that you disliked Edouard so much that you could not make an objective business decision?"

"Is there such a thing?" De Belfort stood up. "Are you making an objective decision now? Is Mr. Scher?"

"It's objective in my case." Simon Scher leaned forward. "I don't even know you. But I do know your record, and that's enough to make me sure we have no place for you here."

De Belfort turned a cold haughty gaze upon him. There was a pause, then de Belfort looked away, his lips pursed with a kind of patrician disdain. He regarded Hélène levelly, then, slowly he swiveled around in his chair, and looked about the room, his expression close to regret.

"I always said this would never outlast Edouard. I told him that once—did he ever mention it to you?"

"He never mentioned your name," Hélène said coldly. "And if that was what you predicted, you were wrong."

"I wonder." Again de Belfort smiled, that slow glacial smile. "Not that I doubt your energies for one moment, Madame, I hope you understand. I hear that—for a woman—you are very able. No, no—but in the long term? How many children is it? Three? A girl and two boys, I believe. Very difficult. One of them might take after Edouard, of course, but it's hardly likely they both will. Louise tells me the elder boy—Lucien, isn't it?—so much resembles her son Jean-Paul, and Jean-Paul, or so I've always heard, would have finished this company within three years, had it not been for Edouard. So I doubt the future is as assured as all that. One of the weaknesses of a private company—too few children, and there's no one suitable to carry on; too many, or the wrong kind, and they squabble so viciously that—"

"None of this is your concern. You were not invited here to speculate on the future of this company. You might do better to concern yourself with your own."

Simon Scher had spoken, tersely, rising as he did so. Hélène said nothing, and de Belfort noted that. He looked at her intently, then got to his feet with a smile. He took his time, looking around the austere room, from painting to painting, object to object. Then, just before he left, he turned back to Hélène.

"You know, it's quite odd," he remarked in an easy conversational tone. "I did dislike your husband very much—just as you suggested. *Disliked* is possibly the wrong term. I hated him. Such an arrogant man. Living in the wrong era, I always felt, despite his success. Not a part of the modern world at all. And yet—the odd thing is, the unaccountable thing is—now that he's dead, I rather miss him. He leaves a gap in my life—which would no doubt have amused him very much. Now, who would have predicted that?"

He gave a small puzzled frown; then, ponderously, in a leisurely way, he left the room. Hélène watched him leave, thoughtfully; from the first moment he came in, he had reminded her of someone, but she had been unable to place who it was. When he made those last few remarks, and then turned to go, it suddenly came to her. Physically, of course, they were nothing alike; it was perhaps what had confused her. But she had sensed his hate, and his antagonism, before he spoke of it—and that she had recognized. He reminded her of Thad.

She tried to explain this, that night, to Christian, and he, after the first burst of elation at what he regarded as clear-cut victory, listened quietly.

"They both needed him, in a way—do you understand, Christian? They needed the rivalry. Maybe they even needed the hate. I don't know. Perhaps people do need that, just as people need love."

"He enjoyed the contest, you mean?" Christian looked thoughtful. "Yes. I can see that." He paused. "Men like Edouard attract hate— though he could never understand that. Also love, of course."

Hélène heard the affectation leave his voice; she heard the catch of regret in it. She leaned across the dining table, and rested her hand on his.

"Oh, Christian," she said sadly. "I know."

"I loved him very much," he said jerkily. "He could be arrogant, and obstinate and impossible. He made me laugh. He made me think. He was also the kindest man I ever met. Hugo thought—my cousin Hugo said . . . Oh, hell. I'm sorry about this, Hélène."

"Don't be," she said simply as he turned his face away. She waited awhile, and then got Christian a brandy. She sat down again and rested her arms on the table, her face in her hands.

"Tell me about him, Christian. I wish you would. Tell me what he was like—when you first met him, before I knew him."

Christian looked up. "It won't hurt you?"

"No. Not now. I want you to."

"I understand that. To begin with, you can't bear to say or hear anything at all, and then, after that—" He paused. "I'll tell you how I first met him. I'd heard of him before, through Hugo. But this was the first day we met. It was in London, in Eaton Square, about a month before we were both going up to Oxford. Hugo said . . ."

He began to speak more rapidly, with his usual animation, his hands gesturing wildly in the air.

Hélène listened. She saw the street, and the house, and Christian's eighteen-year-old friend. And after a while, as he spoke, she felt that icy calm, which had already begun to desert her, slip further away, and further, and with a sense of release she let it go.

Christian talked on; the candles on the table burned lower. His Edouard; her Edouard.

That night, when she went to bed, she reached out her hand as she did every night, to touch the cool space on the sheets beside her. She let it rest there, and closed her eyes, knowing that tonight she would sleep. Now that the calm had gone, and the inertia had gone, Edouard was very close to her.

I shall take the children to Quaires, she thought, for the summer.

That summer Hélène arranged for a certain box to be sent from Paris to England, and, one evening, kneeling on the floor of the drawing room at Quaires, Cat opened it.

It was an antique box, the size of a small trunk, with a domed lid, covered in fine leather, which had faded to a soft mossy green; on its lid was the de Chavigny crest, and Cat's initials. Cat's hands trembled a little as she opened it: she did not know what it contained, but she knew that it was important, that it related in some way to her father, the second anniversary of whose death had just passed. Inside the box were two trays, with compartments, which lifted out, and inside the trays were a series of other exquisitely made leather boxes. Jewelry cases. She knelt back on her heels, afraid to open them.

The room was still and quiet; outside, the light was fading from the thick dusty gold of late afternoon, to the blue of twilight; shadows sloped across the lawn. After a while, Hélène crossed to her, and knelt down beside her.

"Cat, I wanted you to see them; I wanted you to know," she said gently. "It was too soon before, but I thought, now—"

She hesitated, and lightly touched one of the small boxes in front of them.

"Before we came back to Edouard, the years when we were in America—every year, Edouard remembered your birthday. He chose a present for you, and it was put in the safes in Paris. To wait for you. To wait for when you came back." She paused. "There's one to mark your birth—this one here. And then one for each year after that. They're each dated—you'll see."

"Every year? Before he even knew me?" Cat lifted her eyes to Hélène's face.

"Every year. And after we came back, he continued, just the same. And I continued, after he died. Oh, Cat, I wanted you to see them. He loved you so much." She touched Cat's hand. "Open them, darling. Open them, please. . . ."

Very carefully, Cat began to do so. *For Catharine, with my love, 1960.* A necklace of pearls, rose, and briolette-cut diamonds, an exquisite delicate thing, like a circlet of flowers, which she knew at once could have been designed only by Wyspianski. *For Catharine, with my love, 1961.* A Cartier tiara, of black onyx surmounted with pearls; *1962:* a Chinese necklace of carved coral, with tiny carved flowers spilling little clusters of onyx and diamonds. Year after year; box after box: a necklace with five strands of perfectly matched pearls for her fifth birthday. Two matching bracelets, so cunningly mounted they appeared to have been carved from sapphires. Lapis and gold; every stone except emeralds; *1973,* the year of his death, a cabochon ruby ring, which fit her finger exactly.

Cat looked at them in wonder and bewilderment. Tears came to her eyes; a tiara—would she ever wear a tiara? It touched her heart that her father should have chosen something so much a part of his era, and taking it from its box, she pressed it against her face, thinking that yes, if she wore one, ever, it would be this one.

She held it away from her face, looking at it, tracing its outline with her fingers. Her face grew fierce and tight, and then abruptly, with a little cry, she set it down again, and rose to her feet.

"I want to show you something—Mother, wait. Wait there." She ran from the room and returned, a few minutes later, clutching a folder under her arm. She knelt down beside Hélène, her hands shaking, and opened it carefully. It was a portfolio of designs, jewelry designs; page after page of them, each signed and dated, and drawn, as Cat always drew, meticulously.

"I've been working on these for a year. When I'm in Paris, I show them to Floryan and he helps me. He tells me what is technically possible, and what impossible. This one—you see. I had to revise it. It couldn't have been made, not the way I first drew it. And this one—oh, I like this one. I think this is one of the best. Mother, I know they're not very good yet, but they'll get better—as I learn, as I work on them. . . ."

She lifted her face eagerly to Hélène's, and Hélène drew the folder toward her. She bent over them intently. She had had no idea that Cat was working on these, and they were good; they were imaginative. She turned the pages slowly, scrutinizing each drawing, and the small technical notes Cat had made in the margins. "But Cat—these are beautiful. They're very fine. . . ."

"I didn't want to show you before. Not until I had enough. Not until I felt satisfied with them . . ." Cat paused. She gestured shakily to the little boxes in front of her, and then back to the drawings.

"I wanted you to know—I wanted Daddy to know. That I shall carry it all on. All this. The jewelry. The company. Oh, I know I have so much to learn, but I will learn, if you'll teach me." She hesitated. "I know how much you've done. Floryan says you've saved the collection, saved the company. I asked Christian, and he said—it will go from strength to strength. And I wanted you to see—that it won't stop there." She broke off, and her flushed face grew still. "I understand about Lucien. And Alexandre. I know Lucien will take priority over me. I accept that. But I wanted you to know—whatever Lucien does, whatever Alexandre does—I shall be there. To carry on."

She stopped again, and bent her head. Hélène, touched by the fierceness and impetuosity with which she spoke, looked at her tenderly. There was a little silence: Cat did not accept Lucien's precedence as easily as she said, Hélène thought, but she did not for a second doubt her determination. After a pause, she reached across and took Cat's hand. Cat pressed hers tightly. She lifted her face and turned to Hélène, her eyes shining, and suddenly wide with uncertainty, and appeal.

"Can I do that? Oh, Mother—can I? Sometimes I feel so sure that I can. I know it. And at other times, I feel afraid. I think how difficult it is, how big it is—and then I think it's just a stupid boast. A fantasy . . ."

Hélène hesitated. She leaned forward and put her arm around Cat's shoulders. She could feel that her daughter was almost quivering with the emotion and the tension she felt.

"Oh, Cat. When I was your age—do you know what I believed then?"

"Tell me."

"I believed that anything was possible. *Anything.* If you willed it enough. If you were determined enough." She paused. "I was quite certain of that—then."

She spoke carefully, but Cat heard the note of regret in her voice, the shading of sadness.

At once she twisted away from her mother's embrace. "You thought it then? Weren't you right? I'm sure you were right. I feel that now—it's just what I feel. . . ."

"Perhaps I was right." Hélène looked away. "I think that kind of certainty—that kind of determination—can carry you a very long way. There will always be some things, some things you can't control. . . ."

The sentence died away; she was thinking of Edouard, whom no willpower in the world could bring back. But Cat, fifteen years old, filled with the certainty of her youth, did not, perhaps, follow the line of her thoughts, or had perhaps simply ceased to listen.

She knelt upright, those two patches of color hectic in her cheeks, her mouth set in a line that reminded Hélène of Edouard. "I don't believe in limitations. I never shall. Daddy never did. I shall do this, Mother. I swear to you I shall. I swear it now. . . ." She lifted her hand,

and rested it for a moment on the lid of the box in front of her, and Hélène, who understood that she needed this belief now, and perhaps needed the solemnity of an oath, said nothing, but just watched her quietly.

Cat stayed in the same position, kneeling upright, hand extended in a queer stiff gesture, her face lifted toward the windows and the gardens; then, abruptly, as if she had suddenly become self-conscious, she stood up.

"How quiet it is, this evening!"

She turned back, and as Hélène also rose, Cat put her arms around her, and gave her one of her quick impulsive hugs. "I want to go outside. Just for a while. On my own. I want to think—you don't mind?"

"Of course I don't mind. You go. I'll call you when supper's ready. . . ."

At the windows, Cat paused, and looked back. She frowned slightly. "When you were my age . . . I never thought of that before. That you were my age, once. . . ."

She hesitated, and Hélène smiled. Cat turned, and ran out into the garden.

W hen she had gone, Hélène sat for a while in the cool of the room. From other regions of the house came distant noises: the sound of Cassie, singing to herself, and clattering pans as she prepared supper. From upstairs, the noise of running feet as the seven-year-old Baron de Chavigny and his four-year-old brother were hustled to bed. From outside, the murmuring of wood pigeons, and the sound of birdsong. A still evening.

She had been touched by Cat's words, and by the passionate intensity with which they had been spoken. They brought the past rushing back to her: she thought of Edouard, as Christian had described him, up in arms against the world, if need be, on behalf of his dead father. She thought of herself, sitting on the steps in the trailer park, looking up at the night sky, and the southern stars, and believing that anything—anything—was possible.

It was important to believe that, she thought suddenly, almost angrily. If you didn't believe it when you were fifteen years old—when would you believe it?

She feared for Cat, though. It hurt her to think of that brightness of spirit becoming tarnished with time, and experience. She stood up. Time passing, and the sadness of its passing—at once, as often happened, she ached for Edouard. She stood still, and waited, as she had learned, for the first acuteness, the first edge of the pain to pass. She moved around the room, restlessly: there, on the walls, were Anne Kneale's two portraits, the one of Cat as a child, the one of herself, only a little older than Cat was now. She looked at it curiously, hardly able to believe that it was herself, and then turned away.

Edouard's chair. The table at which he sometimes wrote letters. Edouard's tapes and records. Edouard's books.

She touched each of these objects as she passed them—the chair, the surface of the table, the worn spines of the books. Some of these dated from his boyhood; she had had them brought down here when the house in Eaton Square was sold. She touched them, not looking at their titles, and then drew one out at random. She did as she always did with Edouard's books—held it loosely in her hand, to see if it would fall open at some particular place, which he had marked by constant reference.

This was a collection of poems, and it fell open at once, near the beginning of the book, where a piece of paper was folded between the pages. She took the paper, and smoothed it out; there, in a boyish version of Edouard's handwriting, a poem from the book had been carefully and neatly copied out. John Donne: *The Anniversarie.* Underneath it was a date: *August 22nd 1941.* She did not know the poem, and she read it carefully, line by line of affirmation, the unfamiliar words sounding in her ears with Edouard's voice. She listened to the music of its certainty, and of its promise, clear across three hundred years, clear across thirty.

This, no tomorrow hath, nor yesterday. She closed the book, and held the piece of paper tight in her hand. Why had Edouard copied it? She would never know; but she felt sure she had been meant to find it.

The pain ebbed; her heart was as still and as sure as if Edouard were there in the room with her. She felt a strong yet confused sense that it was *this* which was important, this love which animated her, which had not been altered or diminished in any way by his death. For Edouard, as much as for herself, she crossed to the stereo, and inserted the Beethoven tape. The music began, tumbling into the evening air; she moved to the window, and looked out at the garden, and the figure of Cat, in the distance. The music mingled with the shadows, and with the scent of the damp grass. Across the lawns, she saw Cat stand still, a pale shape against the darkness of the yew hedges behind her. She lifted her face, listening to the music. Hélène thought she smiled; then Cat lifted her bare arms; slowly she began to dance.

She turned, and turned again, moving slowly and gracefully in the gray and mauve of the evening air, rejoicing in the coolness of the grass against her feet, and the patterns of light upon her skin. Her mother had been watching her, and Cat thought she had smiled. But now she had left the open window, and Cat, unwatched, was alone in the garden, alone in the evening, alone with the music.

She stopped dancing, and stood quite still, letting her arms fall by her side. She lifted her face to the sky, in which the stars were still invisible. A pale fuzzy moon was just rising, its edges softened and blurred; it hung there in the sky, giving only a little veiled light.

In the distance, she heard an owl hoot. A long wavering cry. Cat kept very still, as she had once before in this garden, on a night very like this. She looked toward the woods, straining her eyes, and then she glimpsed it: a white shape; the measured beat of its wings. It dipped low across the lawn, making no sound, quartered the fields beyond, and then was gone.

She stayed there, hoping it might come back, but it did not. Color faded from the air; the music from the house grew plaintive, and then assertive once more. She was growing cold, but she felt reluctant to leave: the garden, and the moon, and the owl all felt powerful to her. She felt powerful herself, the way she had felt two years ago, up on the hillside, when the fear left her, and she realized she could ride Khan. She felt charged—by the accident of circumstance, the clash and resolution of the music, the stillness of the night.

She held the feeling to her, nursed it. She said her father's name to herself, once, twice, three times, like a charm, for it was an evening when magic could be made, and when anything was possible.

She felt him there then, for an instant, as real as if he had reached out and touched her hand, and to her own surprise, she realized that she had tears on her cheeks, yet she did not feel sad.

The music was filled with gaiety now. She slipped off her shoes, and curled her toes in the cool grass. Then, lifting her arms high, she began to dance once more, turning and turning. She danced for her father, and for her mother; for the cool of the evening, for the beauty of the music, and for herself. And as she danced, she thought: *I shall do such things, such things . . .*

No one had ever felt so certain before—she was sure of it. The feeling was heady; it buoyed her up. She knew a sense of lightness, of great contentment. The garden was still and dark; the sky was shining; and from the house, her mother was calling.

She stopped dancing, and stood still. Then, with a small shiver, which might have been excitement, and might have been fear—so much was beginning—she turned, and ran back from the garden, and into the house.

AUTHOR'S NOTE

The film that actually won the Palme d'Or at Cannes in 1962 was the Brazilian *O Pagador de Promessas*.

In 1965, the Academy Award for Best Picture went to *The Sound of Music;* the Best Actress award went to Julie Christie, for *Darling;* and the award for Best Director went to Robert Wise, for *The Sound of Music.*